SONIC

SONIC THE HEDGEHOG™

BOOK 3

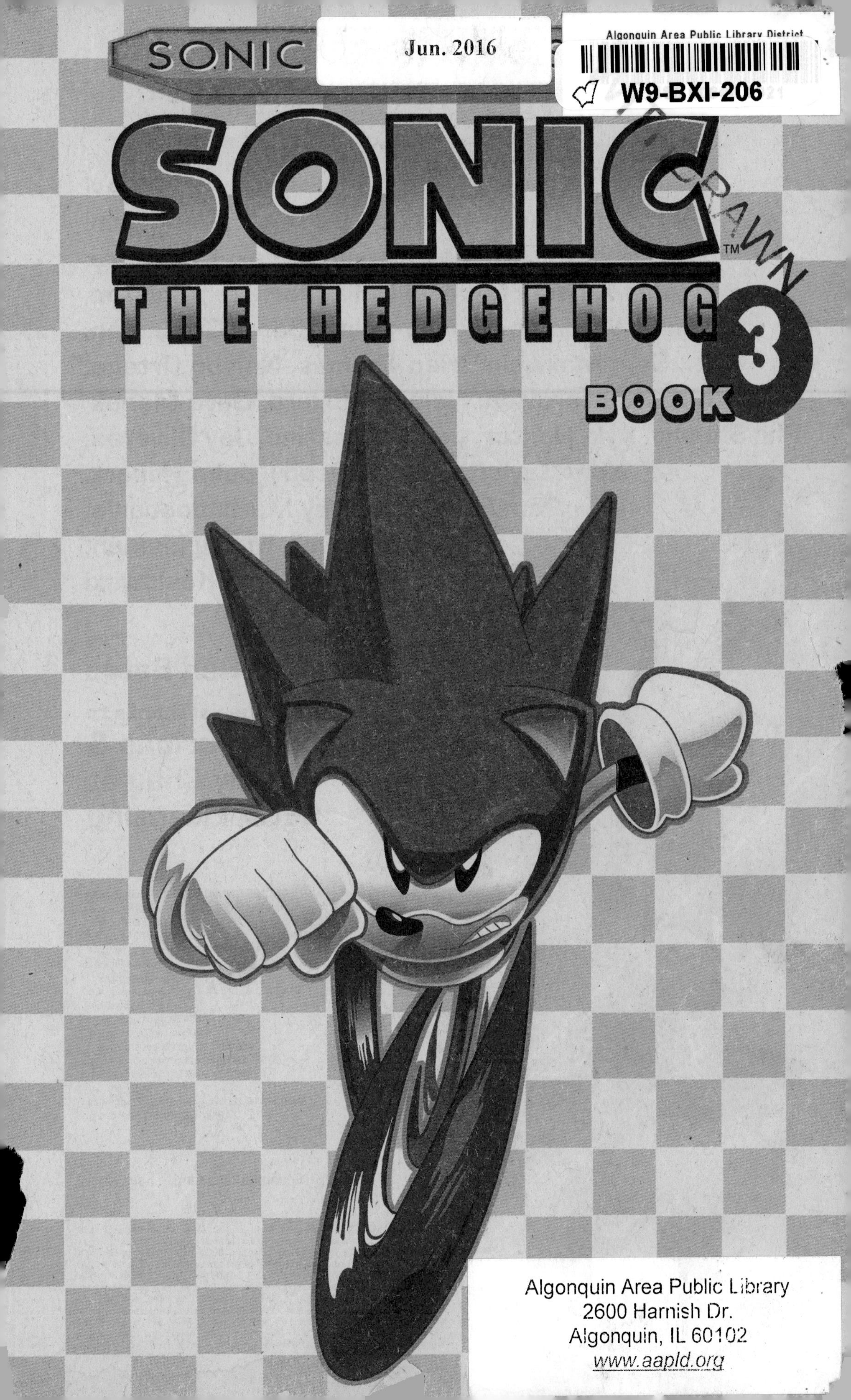

SONIC LEGACY SERIES

Featuring the talents of

Ken Penders, Patrick Spaziante, Ian Flynn, Karl Bollers, Art Mawhinney, Angelo DeCesare, Jim Amash, Michael Gallagher, Tom Rolston, Vickie Williams, Manny Galan, Barry Grossman, Sam Maxwell, Brian Thomas, Nelson Ortega, Mike Kanterovich, Nelson Ribiiero, Dave Manak, Phil Sheehy, Kyle Hunter, Jon D'Agostino, Jay Oliveras, Kent Taylor, Andrew Pepoy, John Hebert, Pam Eklund, Harvey Mercadoocasio, Jeff Powell, Mindy Eisman, Rich Koslowski

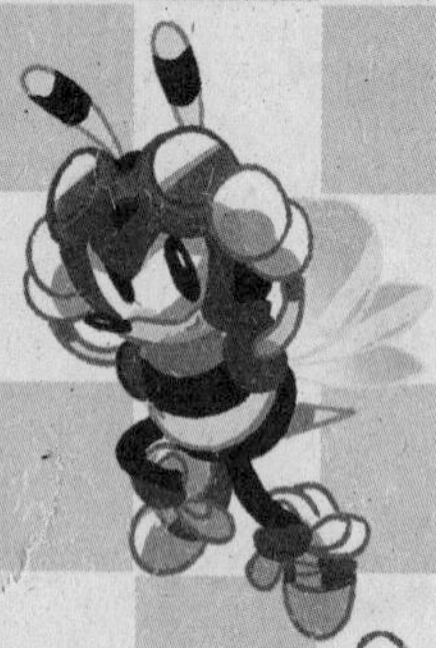

Cover by

Ben Bates

Special thanks to

Anthony Gaccione & Cindy Chau at SEGA Licensing

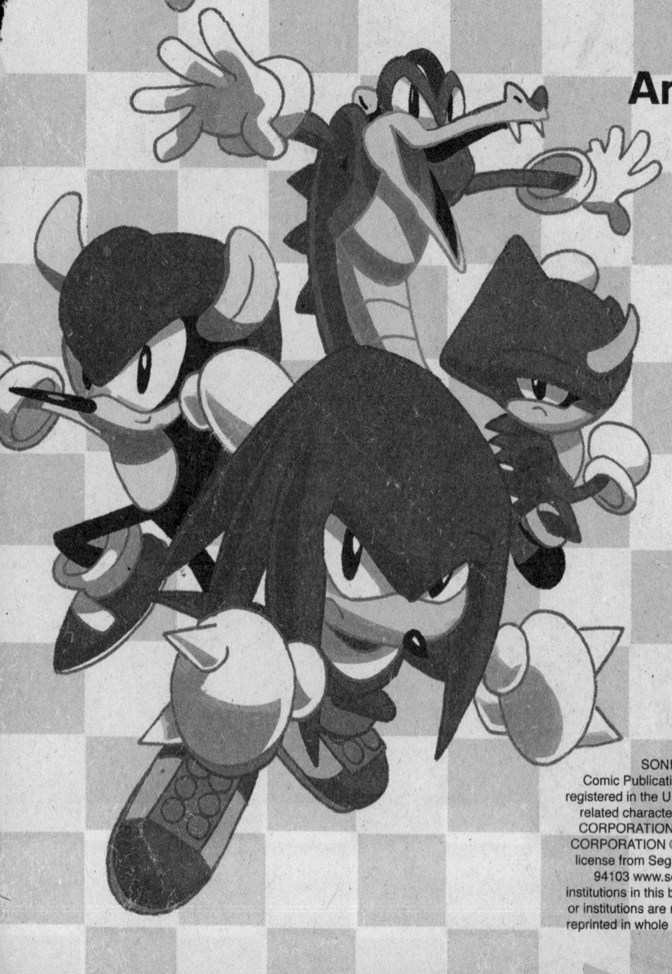

ARCHIE COMIC PUBLICATIONS, INC.
JONATHAN GOLDWATER, publisher/co-ceo
NANCY SILBERKLEIT, co-ceo
MIKE PELLERITO, president
VICTOR GORELICK, co-president, e-i-c
JIM SOKOLOWSKI, senior vice president of sales and business development
HAROLD BUCHHOLZ, senior vice president of publishing and operations
PAUL KAMINSKI, exec. director of editorial/compliation editor
VINCENT LOVALLO, assistant editor
STEPHEN OSWALD, production manager
STEVEN SCOTT, director of publicity and marketing
CARLY INGLIS, editorial assistant/proofreader
ELIZABETH BORGATTI, book design

ArchieComics.com Sega.com

ISBN: 978-1-936975-75-4

TABLE OF CONTENTS

5 "THE DAY ROBOTROPOLIS FELL"

22 "BUNNIE'S WORST NIGHTMARE"

31 "THE RISE OF ROBOTROPOLIS...

   THE FALL OF SONIC"

48 "BEDTIME TAILS"

57 "RAGE AGAINST THE MACHINE"

83 "COURT MARTIAL"

108 "AND ONE SHALL SAVE HIM"

132 "IN EVERY KINGDOM THERE MUST

   EXIST A LITTLE CHAOS"

148 "KNUCKLES QUEST"

158 "THE DREAM ZONE"

185 "BLACK AND BLUE AND

   RED ALL OVER"

209 "GUERILLA THRILLER"

224 "KNUCKLES QUEST III"

233 "COUNTDOWN TO ARMAGEDDON"

249 "KNUCKLES QUEST IV"

259 "ENDGAME - PART 1"

283 "ENDGAME - PART 2"

307 "ENDGAME - PART 3"

332 "ENDGAME - PART 4"

373 "DOWN AND OUT

   IN DOWNUNDA"

390 "TOTAL RE-GENESIS"

408 "REALITY BYTES"

433 "THE DISCOVERY ZONE"

451 "FIRST CONTACT"

458 "UNFINISHED BUSINESS"

464 "SOUNDS OF SILENCE"

483 "RUNNING TO STAND STILL"

505 SPECIAL FEATURES

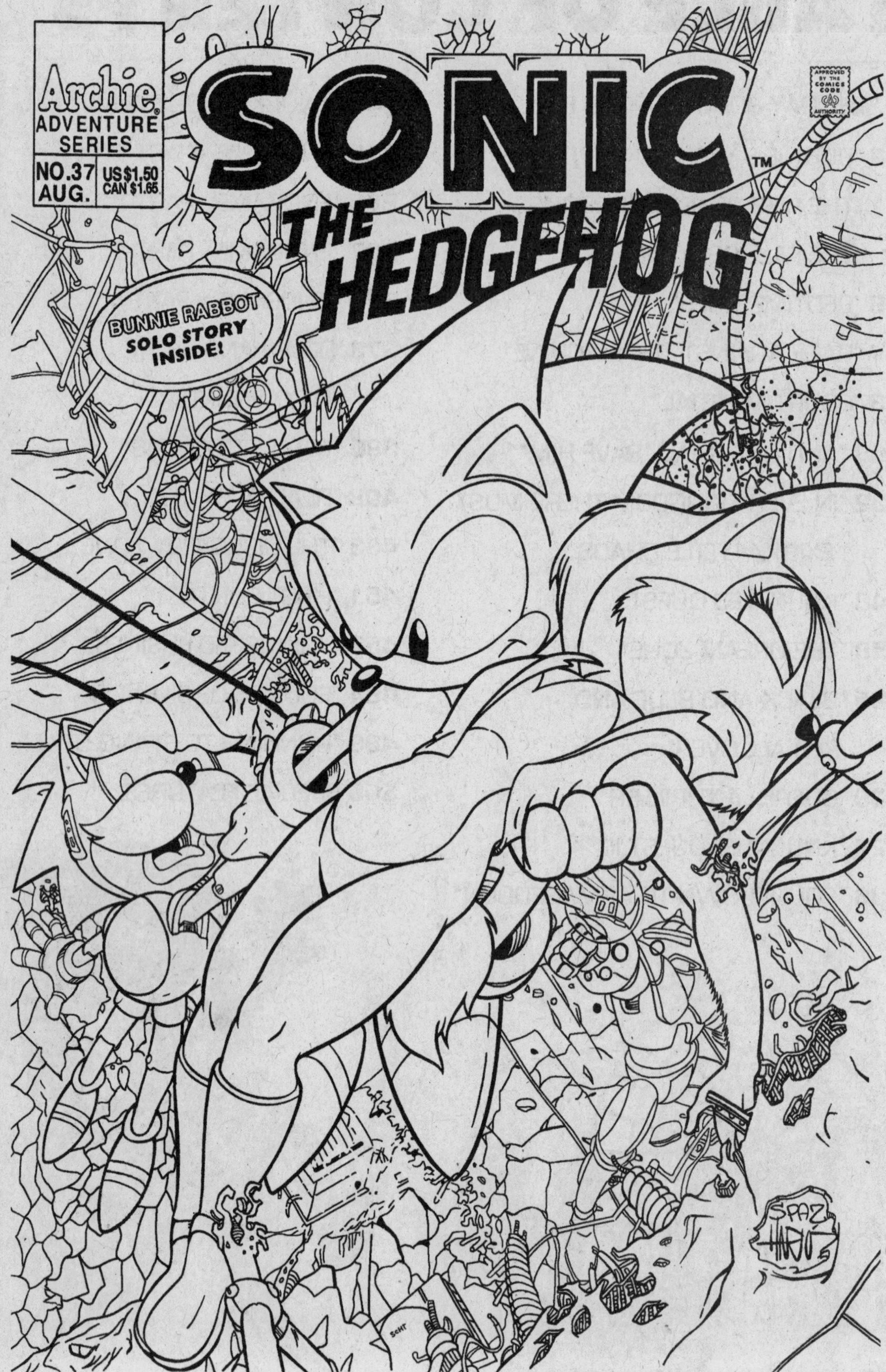
Archie
ADVENTURE SERIES
NO.37 AUG.
US$1.50 CAN $1.65
SONIC™
THE HEDGEHOG
BUNNIE RABBOT SOLO STORY INSIDE!

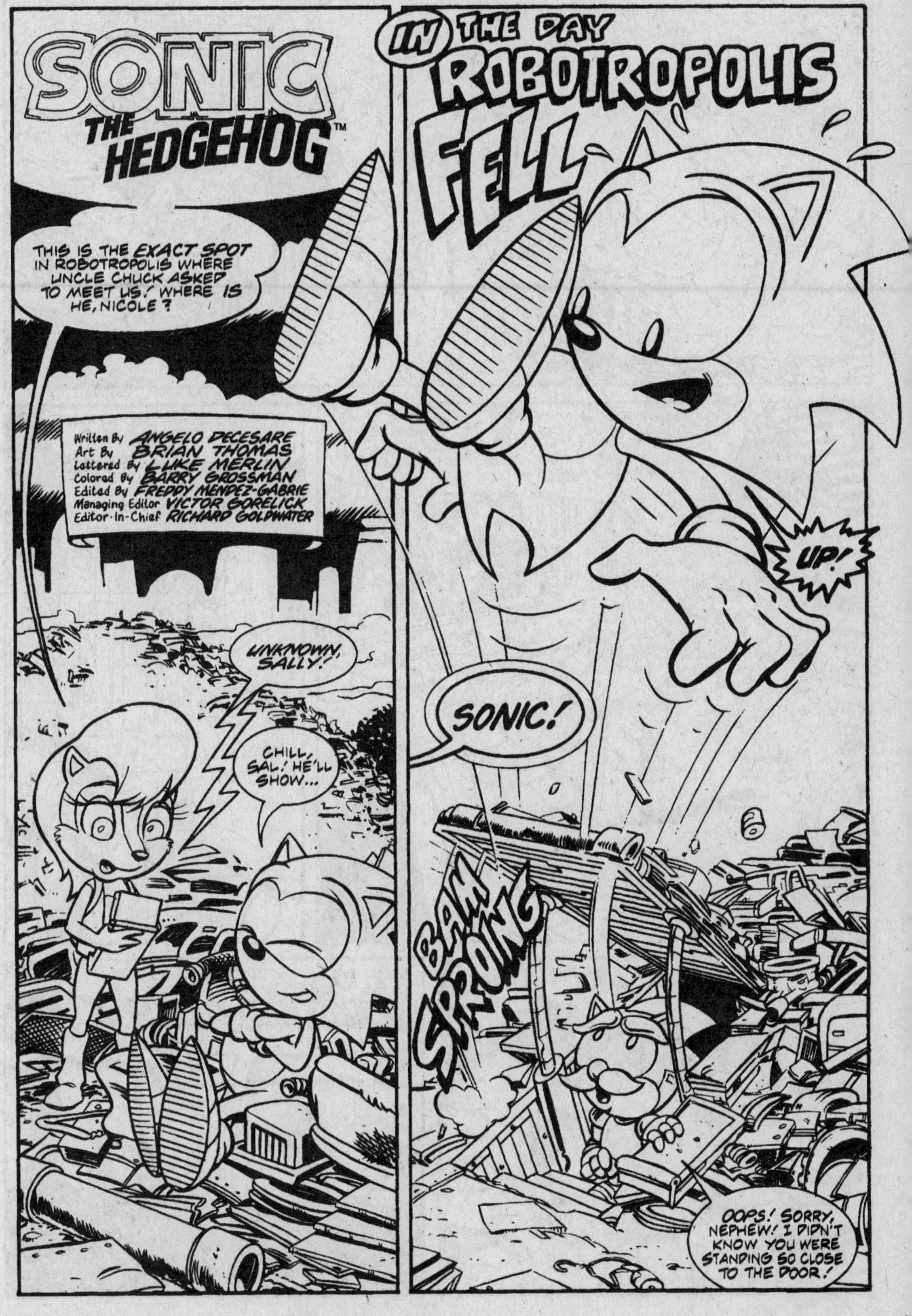
SONIC THE HEDGEHOG™
IN THE DAY ROBOTROPOLIS FELL
THIS IS THE EXACT SPOT IN ROBOTROPOLIS WHERE UNCLE CHUCK ASKED TO MEET US! WHERE IS HE, NICOLE?
Written By ANGELO DECESARE
Art By BRIAN THOMAS
Lettered By LUKE MERLIN
Colored By BARRY GROSSMAN
Edited By FREDDY MENDEZ-GABRIE
Managing Editor VICTOR GORELICK
Editor-In-Chief RICHARD GOLDWATER
UNKNOWN, SALLY!
CHILL, SAL! HE'LL SHOW...
SONIC!
UP!
BAM
SPRONG
OOPS! SORRY, NEPHEW! I DIDN'T KNOW YOU WERE STANDING SO CLOSE TO THE DOOR!

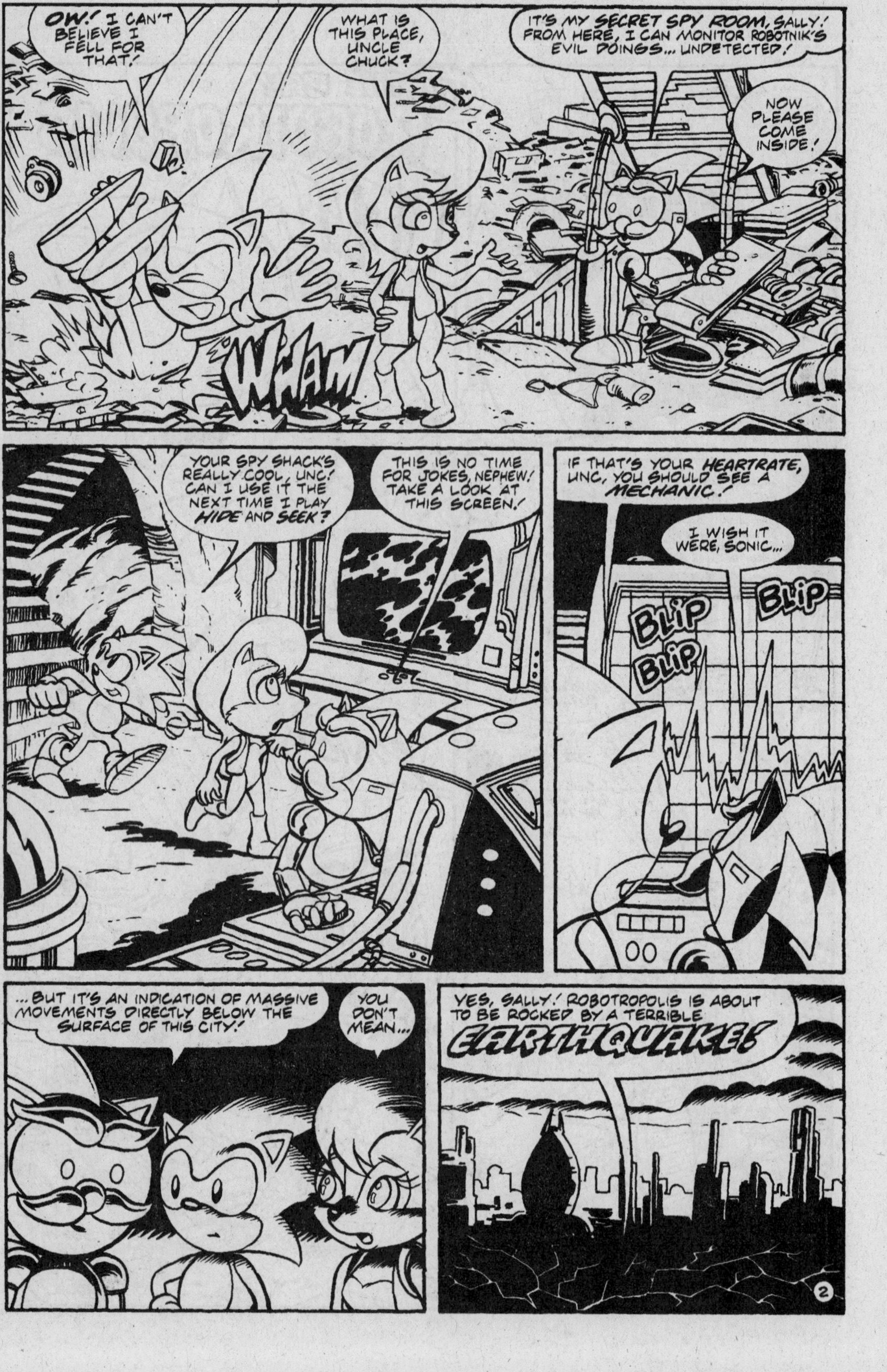
OW! I CAN'T BELIEVE I FELL FOR THAT!
WHAT IS THIS PLACE, UNCLE CHUCK?
IT'S MY SECRET SPY ROOM, SALLY! FROM HERE, I CAN MONITOR ROBOTNIK'S EVIL DOINGS... UNDETECTED!
NOW PLEASE COME INSIDE!
WHAM
YOUR SPY SHACK'S REALLY COOL, UNC! CAN I USE IT THE NEXT TIME I PLAY HIDE AND SEEK?
THIS IS NO TIME FOR JOKES, NEPHEW! TAKE A LOOK AT THIS SCREEN!
IF THAT'S YOUR HEARTRATE, UNC, YOU SHOULD SEE A MECHANIC!
I WISH IT WERE, SONIC...
BLIP
BLIP
BLIP
...BUT IT'S AN INDICATION OF MASSIVE MOVEMENTS DIRECTLY BELOW THE SURFACE OF THIS CITY!
YOU DON'T MEAN...
YES, SALLY! ROBOTROPOLIS IS ABOUT TO BE ROCKED BY A TERRIBLE
EARTHQUAKE!
2

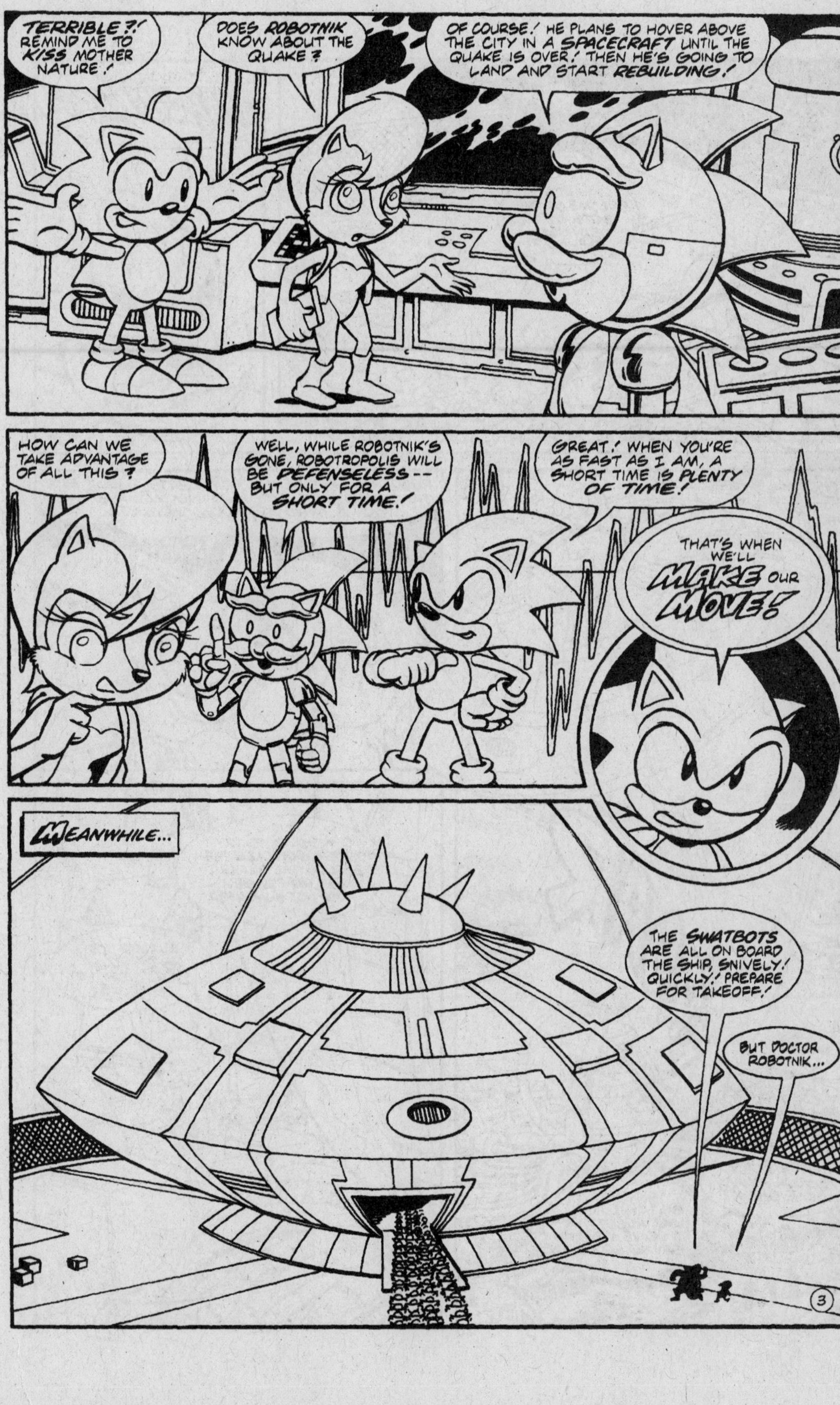
TERRIBLE?! REMIND ME TO KISS MOTHER NATURE!
DOES ROBOTNIK KNOW ABOUT THE QUAKE?
OF COURSE! HE PLANS TO HOVER ABOVE THE CITY IN A SPACECRAFT UNTIL THE QUAKE IS OVER! THEN HE'S GOING TO LAND AND START REBUILDING!
HOW CAN WE TAKE ADVANTAGE OF ALL THIS?
WELL, WHILE ROBOTNIK'S GONE, ROBOTROPOLIS WILL BE DEFENSELESS-- BUT ONLY FOR A SHORT TIME!
GREAT! WHEN YOU'RE AS FAST AS I AM, A SHORT TIME IS PLENTY OF TIME!
THAT'S WHEN WE'LL MAKE OUR MOVE!
MEANWHILE...
THE SWATBOTS ARE ALL ON BOARD THE SHIP, SNIVELY! QUICKLY! PREPARE FOR TAKEOFF!
BUT DOCTOR ROBOTNIK...
3

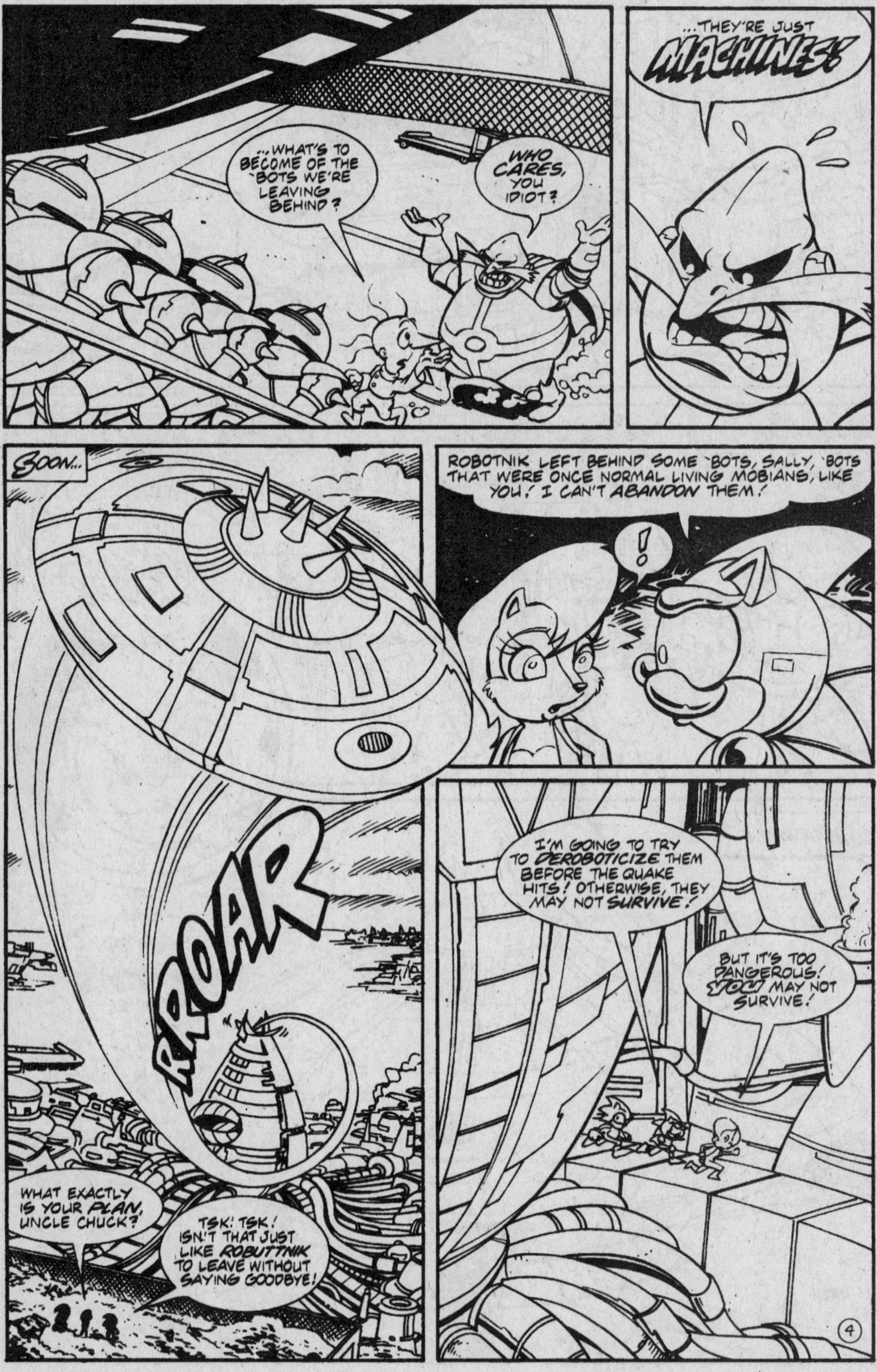
...WHAT'S TO BECOME OF THE `BOTS WE'RE LEAVING BEHIND?
WHO CARES, YOU IDIOT?
...THEY'RE JUST MACHINES!
SOON...
ROBOTNIK LEFT BEHIND SOME `BOTS, SALLY, `BOTS THAT WERE ONCE NORMAL LIVING MOBIANS, LIKE YOU! I CAN'T ABANDON THEM!
!
RROAR
I'M GOING TO TRY TO DEROBOTICIZE THEM BEFORE THE QUAKE HITS! OTHERWISE, THEY MAY NOT SURVIVE!
BUT IT'S TOO DANGEROUS! YOU MAY NOT SURVIVE!
WHAT EXACTLY IS YOUR PLAN, UNCLE CHUCK?
TSK! TSK! ISN'T THAT JUST LIKE ROBUTTNIK TO LEAVE WITHOUT SAYING GOODBYE!
4

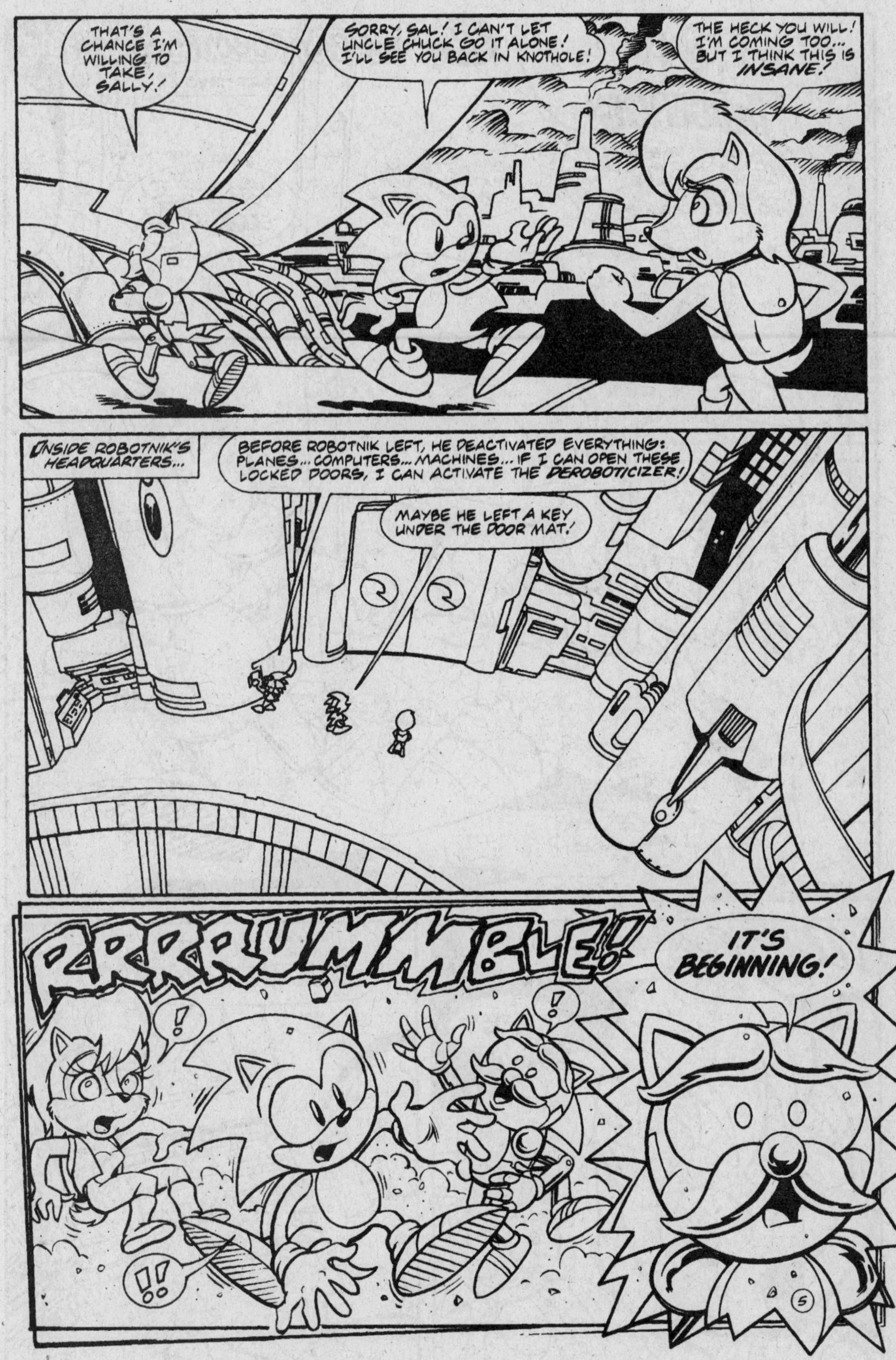
THAT'S A CHANCE I'M WILLING TO TAKE, SALLY!
SORRY, SAL! I CAN'T LET UNCLE CHUCK GO IT ALONE! I'LL SEE YOU BACK IN KNOTHOLE!
THE HECK YOU WILL! I'M COMING TOO... BUT I THINK THIS IS INSANE!
INSIDE ROBOTNIK'S HEADQUARTERS...
BEFORE ROBOTNIK LEFT, HE DEACTIVATED EVERYTHING: PLANES... COMPUTERS... MACHINES... IF I CAN OPEN THESE LOCKED DOORS, I CAN ACTIVATE THE DEROBOTICIZER!
MAYBE HE LEFT A KEY UNDER THE DOOR MAT!
RRRRUMMBLE!
IT'S BEGINNING!
!
!
!!
5

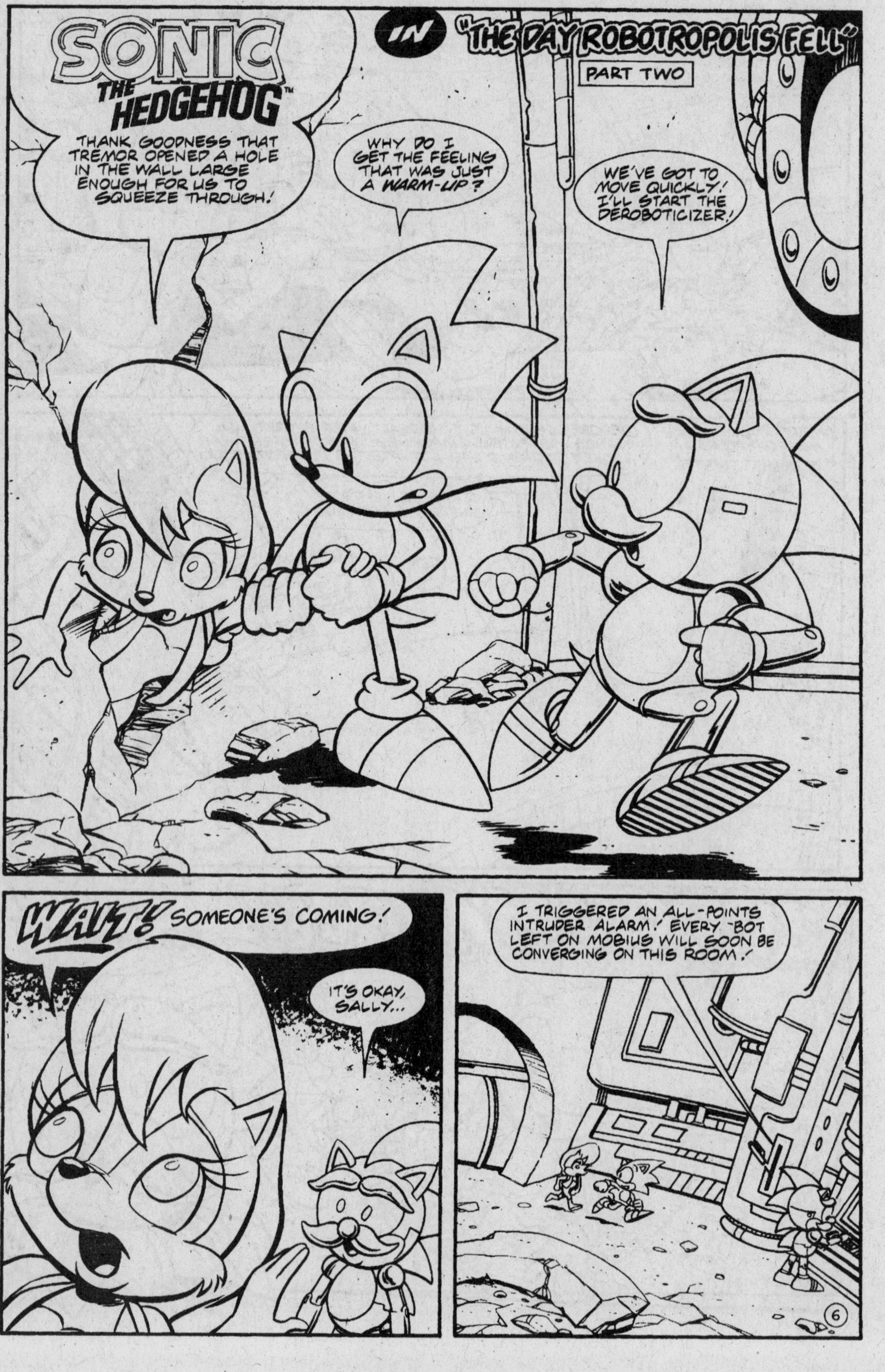
SONIC THE HEDGEHOG™
IN "THE DAY ROBOTROPOLIS FELL"
PART TWO
THANK GOODNESS THAT TREMOR OPENED A HOLE IN THE WALL LARGE ENOUGH FOR US TO SQUEEZE THROUGH!
WHY DO I GET THE FEELING THAT WAS JUST A WARM-UP?
WE'VE GOT TO MOVE QUICKLY! I'LL START THE DEROBOTICIZER!
WAIT! SOMEONE'S COMING!
IT'S OKAY, SALLY...
I TRIGGERED AN ALL-POINTS INTRUDER ALARM! EVERY 'BOT LEFT ON MOBIUS WILL SOON BE CONVERGING ON THIS ROOM!
6

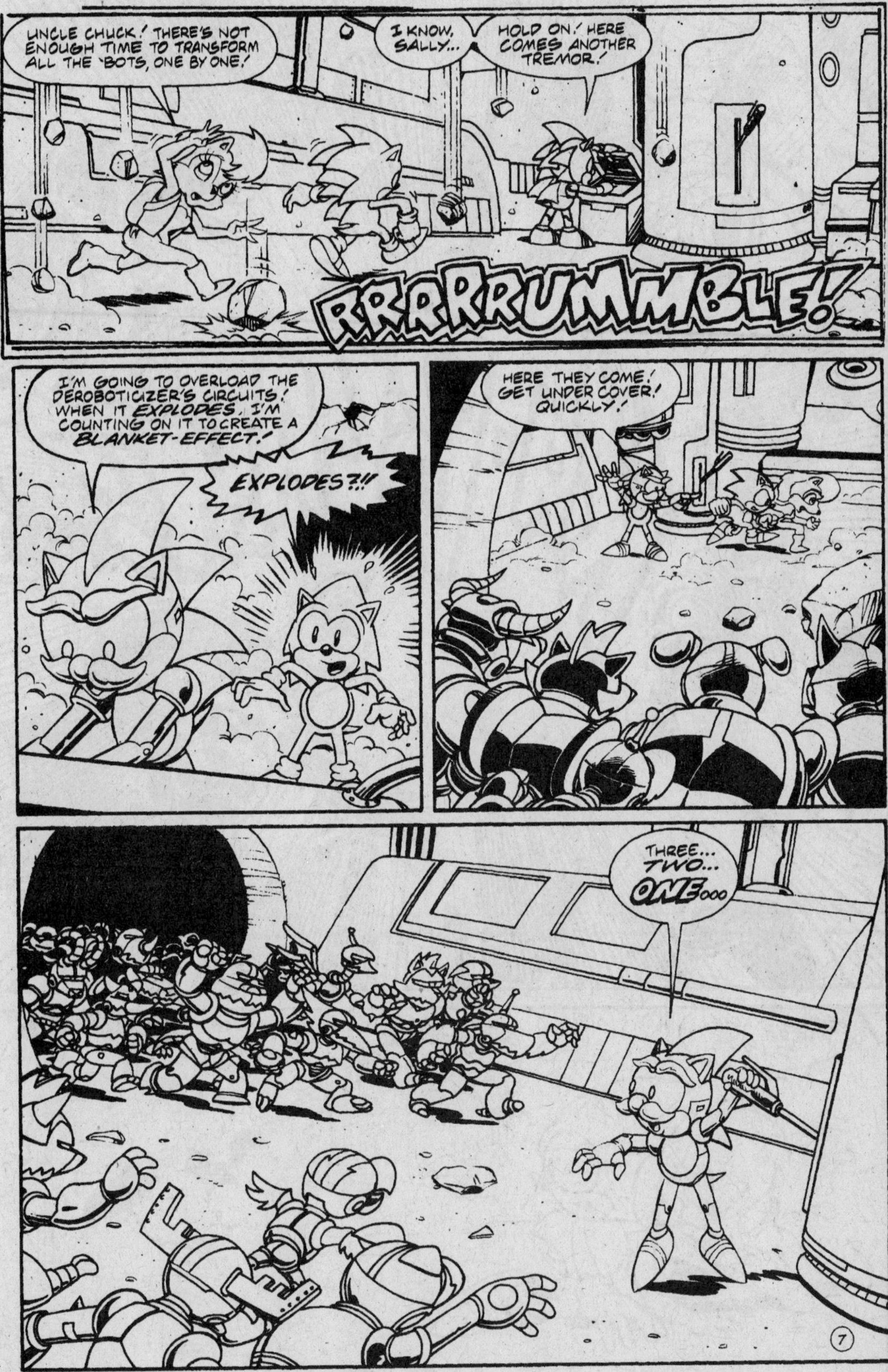
UNCLE CHUCK! THERE'S NOT ENOUGH TIME TO TRANSFORM ALL THE 'BOTS, ONE BY ONE!
I KNOW, SALLY...
HOLD ON! HERE COMES ANOTHER TREMOR!
RRRRRUMMBLE!
I'M GOING TO OVERLOAD THE DEROBOTICIZER'S CIRCUITS! WHEN IT EXPLODES, I'M COUNTING ON IT TO CREATE A BLANKET-EFFECT!
EXPLODES?!!
HERE THEY COME! GET UNDER COVER! QUICKLY!
THREE... TWO... ONE...
7

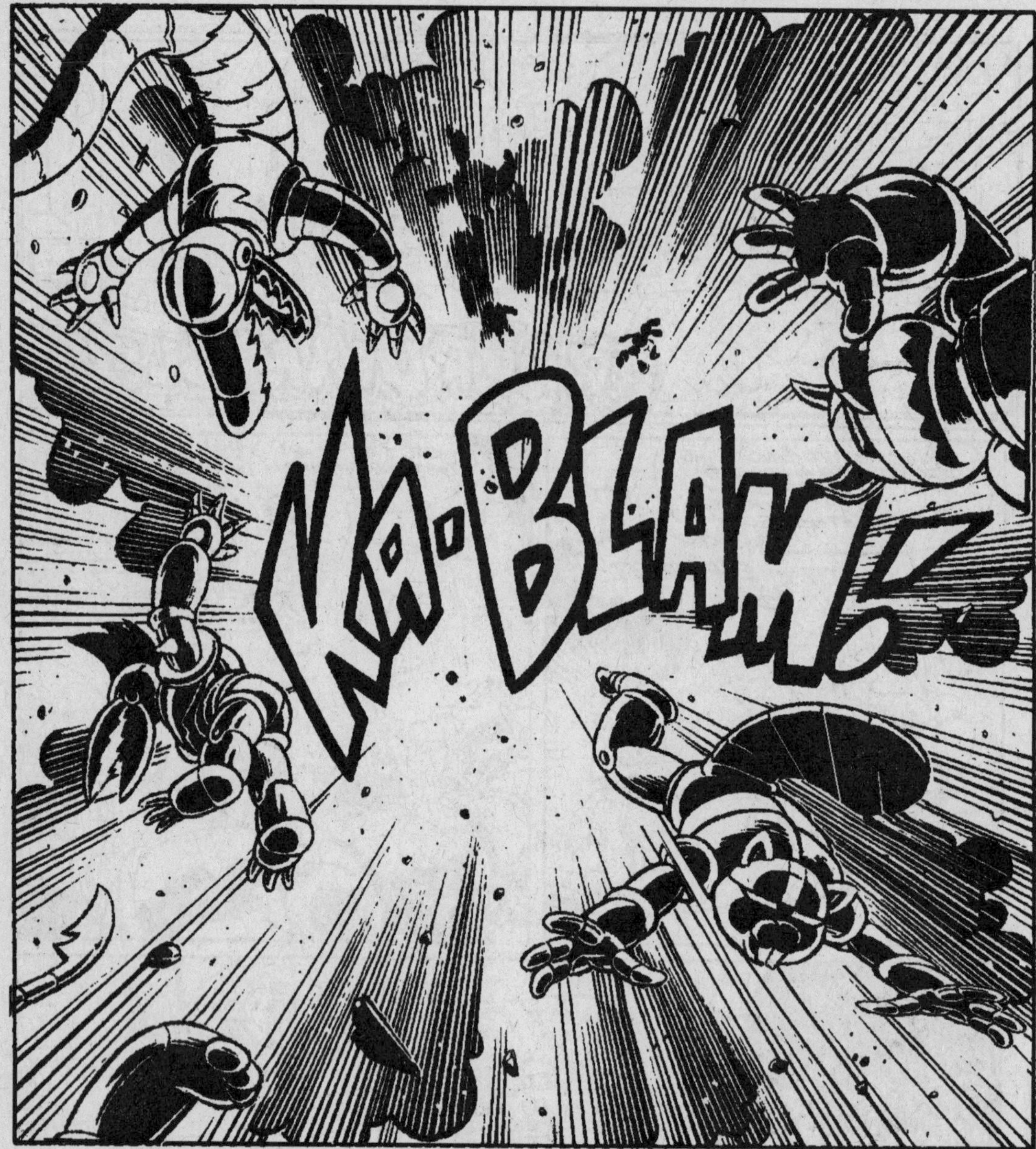
KA-BLAM!

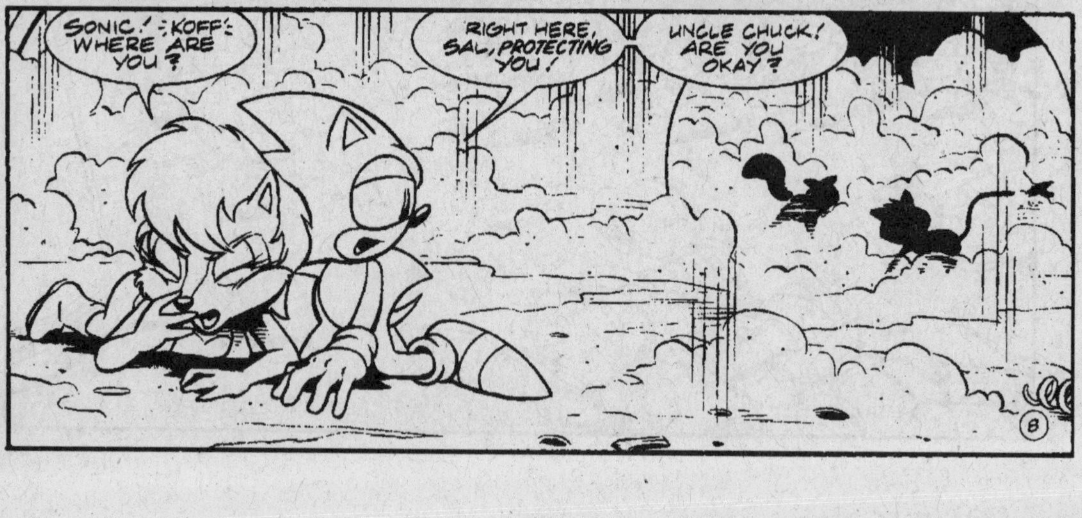
SONIC! :KOFF: WHERE ARE YOU?
RIGHT HERE, SAL, PROTECTING YOU!
UNCLE CHUCK! ARE YOU OKAY?
8

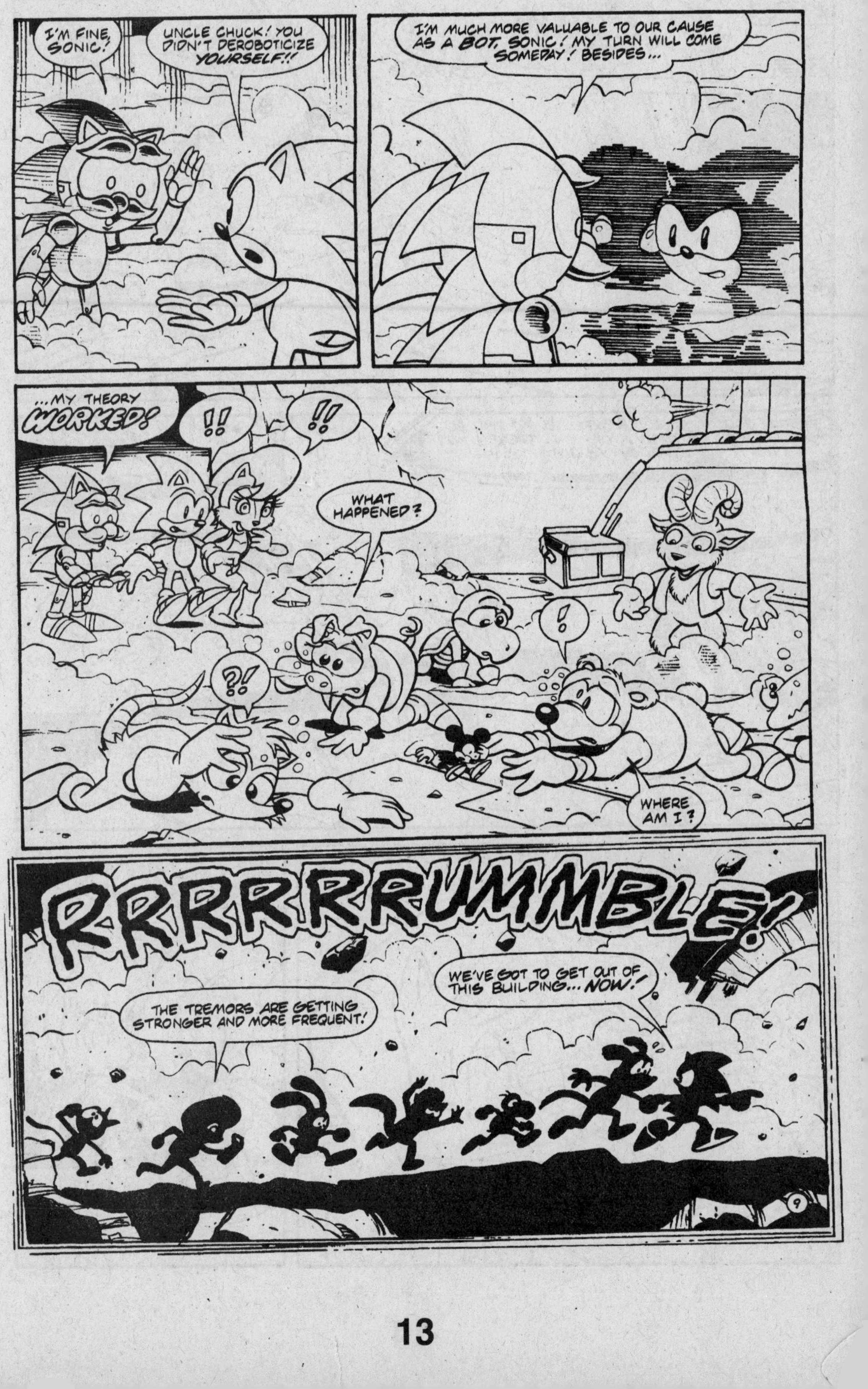
I'M FINE, SONIC.
UNCLE CHUCK! YOU DIDN'T DEROBOTICIZE YOURSELF!!
I'M MUCH MORE VALUABLE TO OUR CAUSE AS A BOT, SONIC! MY TURN WILL COME SOMEDAY! BESIDES...
...MY THEORY WORKED!
!!
!!
WHAT HAPPENED?
!
?!
WHERE AM I?
RRRRRRUMMBLE!
THE TREMORS ARE GETTING STRONGER AND MORE FREQUENT!
WE'VE GOT TO GET OUT OF THIS BUILDING... NOW!
9

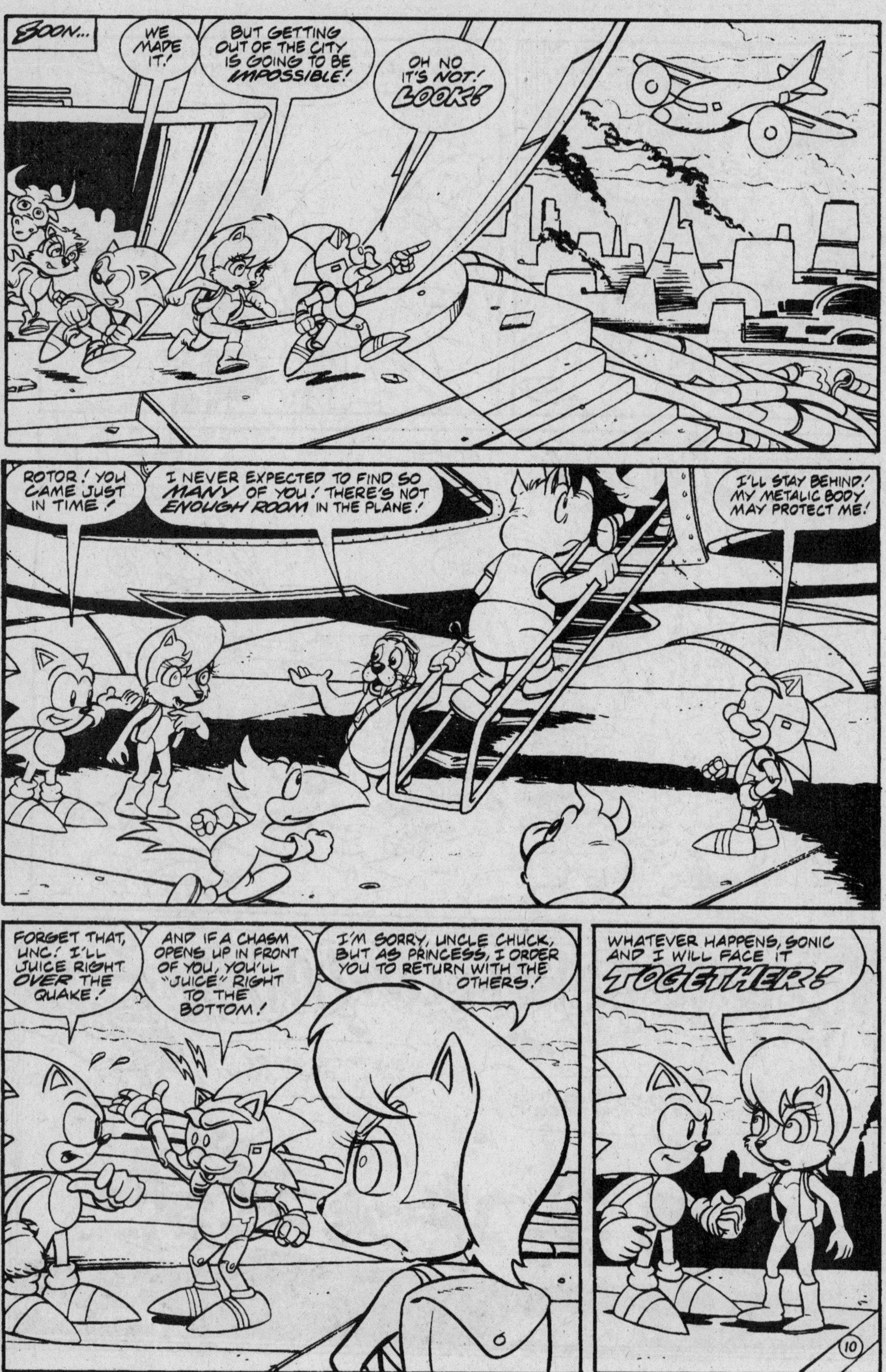
SOON...
WE MADE IT!
BUT GETTING OUT OF THE CITY IS GOING TO BE IMPOSSIBLE!
OH NO IT'S NOT! LOOK!
ROTOR! YOU CAME JUST IN TIME!
I NEVER EXPECTED TO FIND SO MANY OF YOU! THERE'S NOT ENOUGH ROOM IN THE PLANE!
I'LL STAY BEHIND! MY METALIC BODY MAY PROTECT ME!
FORGET THAT, UNC! I'LL JUICE RIGHT OVER THE QUAKE!
AND IF A CHASM OPENS UP IN FRONT OF YOU, YOU'LL "JUICE" RIGHT TO THE BOTTOM!
I'M SORRY, UNCLE CHUCK, BUT AS PRINCESS, I ORDER YOU TO RETURN WITH THE OTHERS!
WHATEVER HAPPENS, SONIC AND I WILL FACE IT TOGETHER!
10

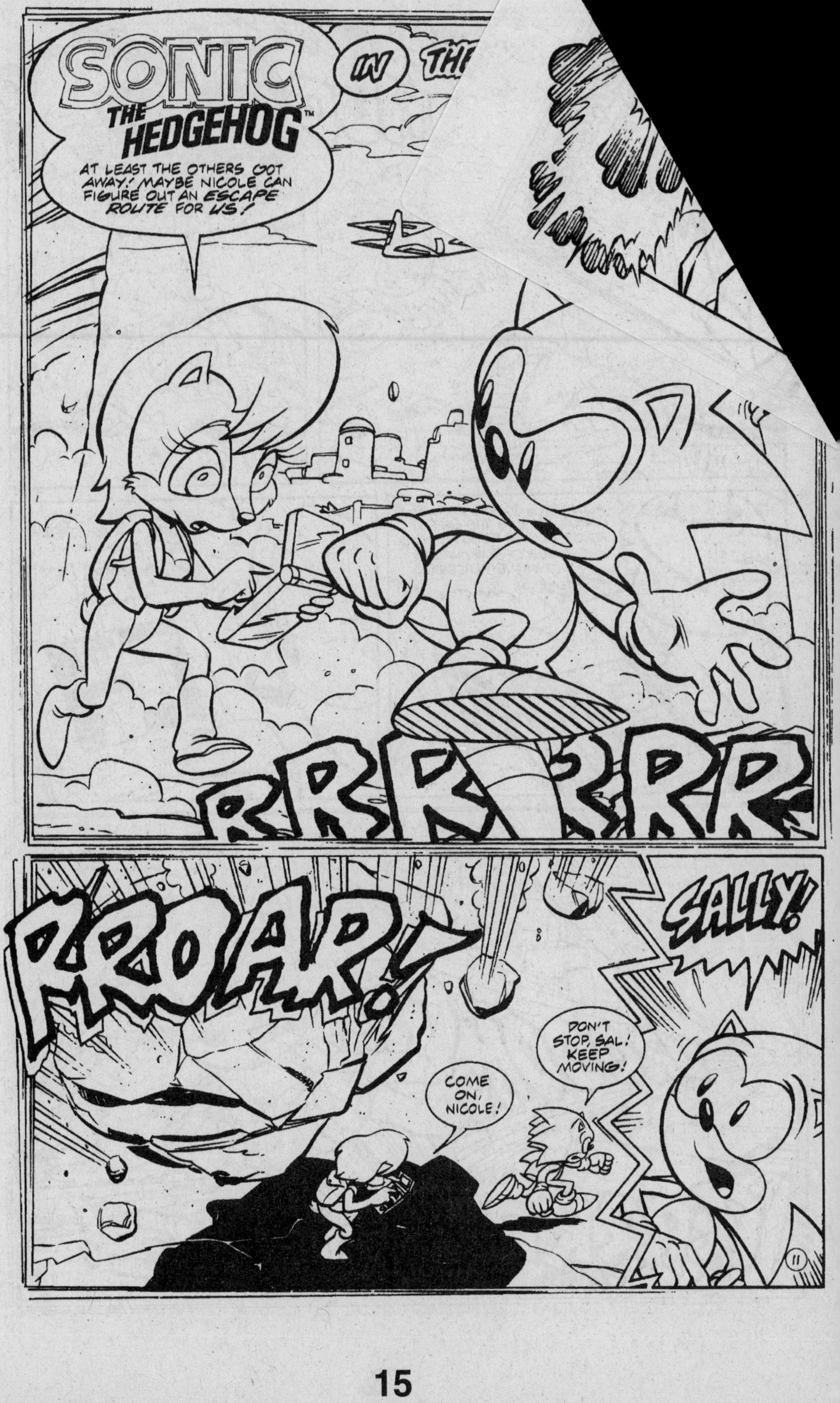

SONIC THE HEDGEHOG™
IN THE
AT LEAST THE OTHERS GOT AWAY! MAYBE NICOLE CAN FIGURE OUT AN ESCAPE ROUTE FOR US!
RRRRRR
RROAR!
SALLY!
DON'T STOP, SAL! KEEP MOVING!
COME ON, NICOLE!

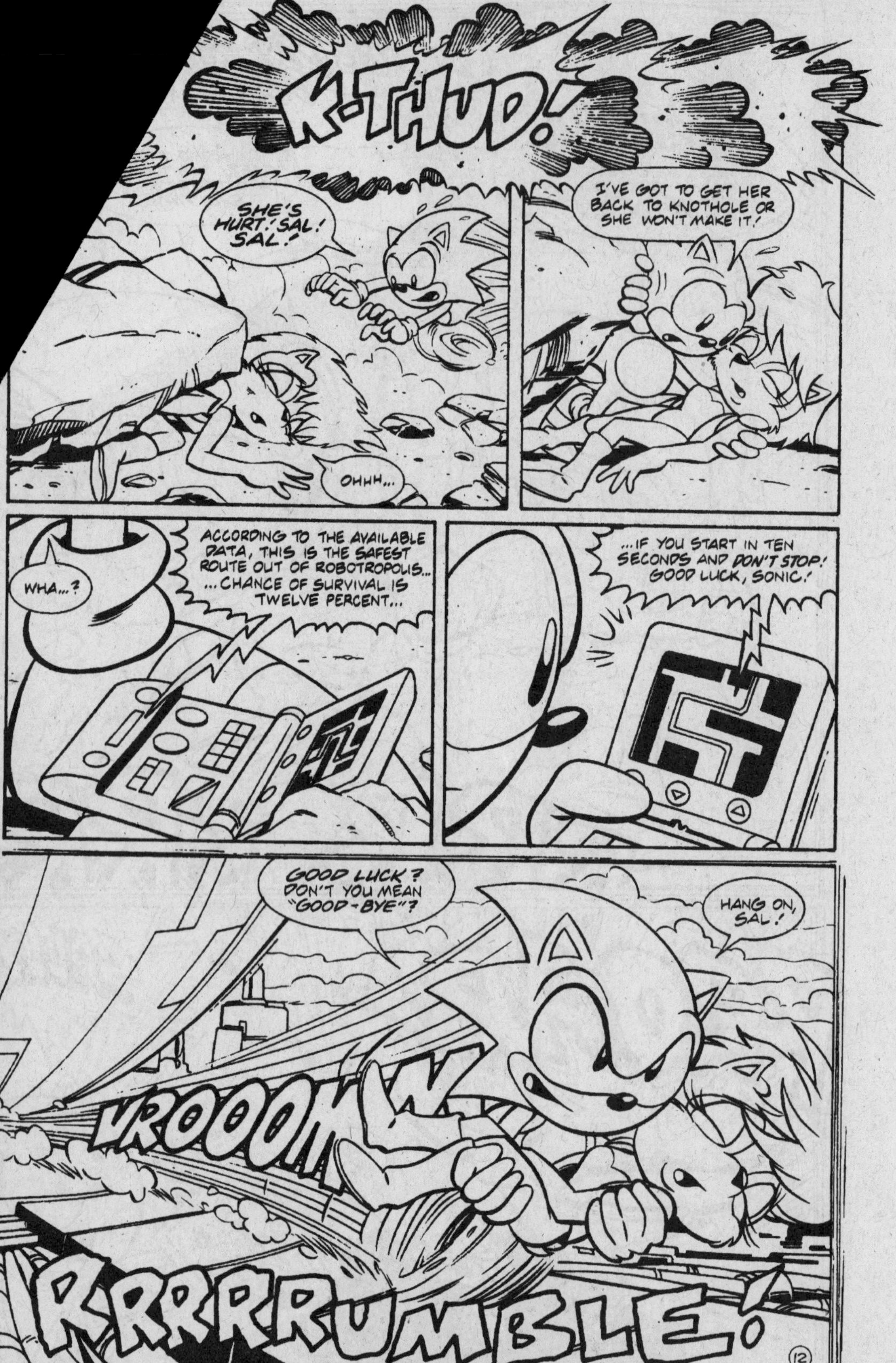
K-THUD!
SHE'S HURT! SAL! SAL!
OHHH...
I'VE GOT TO GET HER BACK TO KNOTHOLE OR SHE WON'T MAKE IT!
WHA...?
ACCORDING TO THE AVAILABLE DATA, THIS IS THE SAFEST ROUTE OUT OF ROBOTROPOLIS... ...CHANCE OF SURVIVAL IS TWELVE PERCENT...
...IF YOU START IN TEN SECONDS AND DON'T STOP! GOOD LUCK, SONIC!
GOOD LUCK? DON'T YOU MEAN "GOOD-BYE"?
HANG ON, SAL!
VROOOOM
RRRRRUMBLE!
12

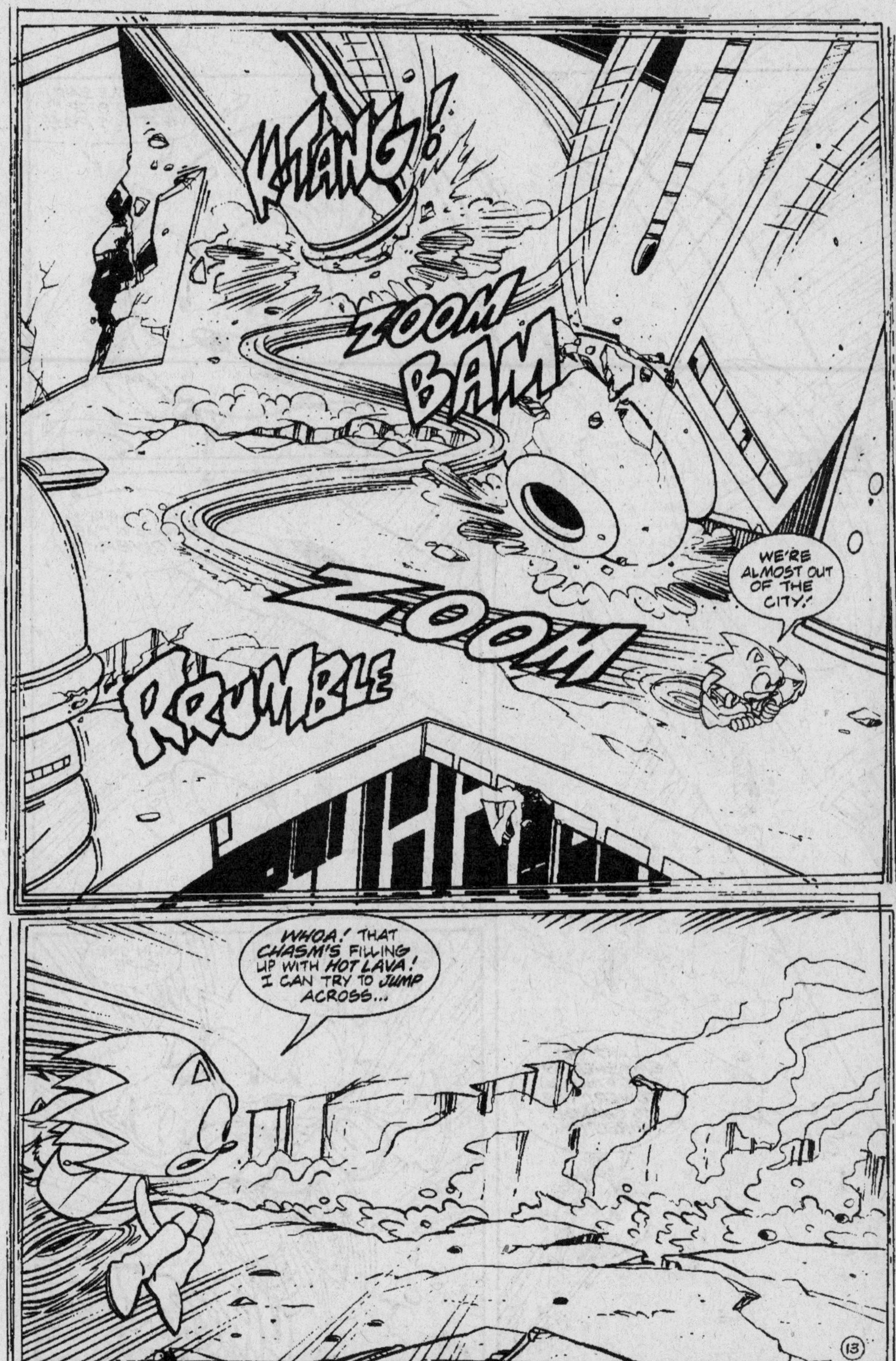
K-TANG!
ZOOM
BAM
WE'RE ALMOST OUT OF THE CITY!
ZOOM
RRUMBLE
WHOA! THAT CHASM'S FILLING UP WITH HOT LAVA! I CAN TRY TO JUMP ACROSS...
13

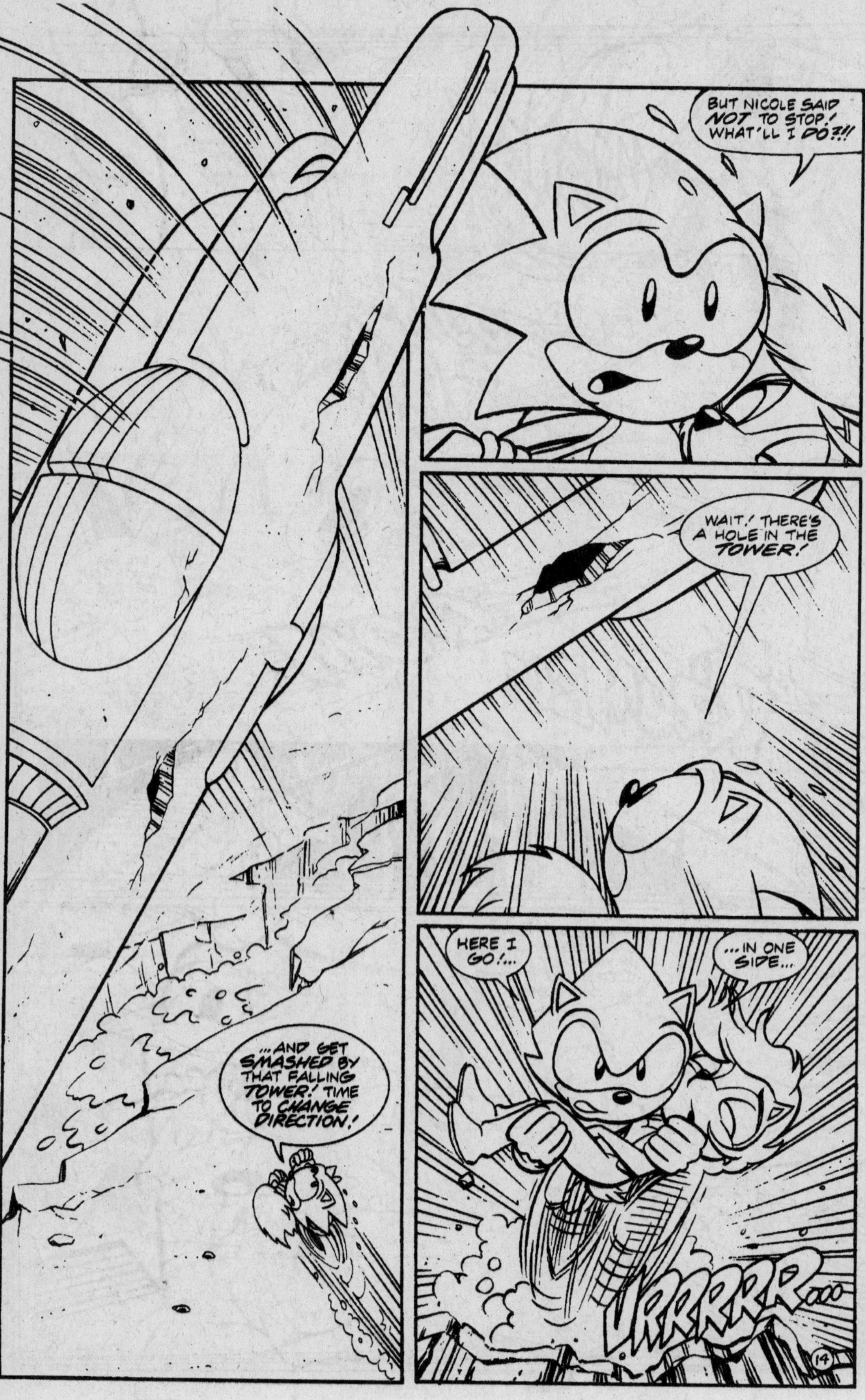
...AND GET SMASHED BY THAT FALLING TOWER! TIME TO CHANGE DIRECTION!
BUT NICOLE SAID NOT TO STOP! WHAT'LL I DO?!!
WAIT! THERE'S A HOLE IN THE TOWER!
HERE I GO!...
...IN ONE SIDE...
VRRRRRRooo
14

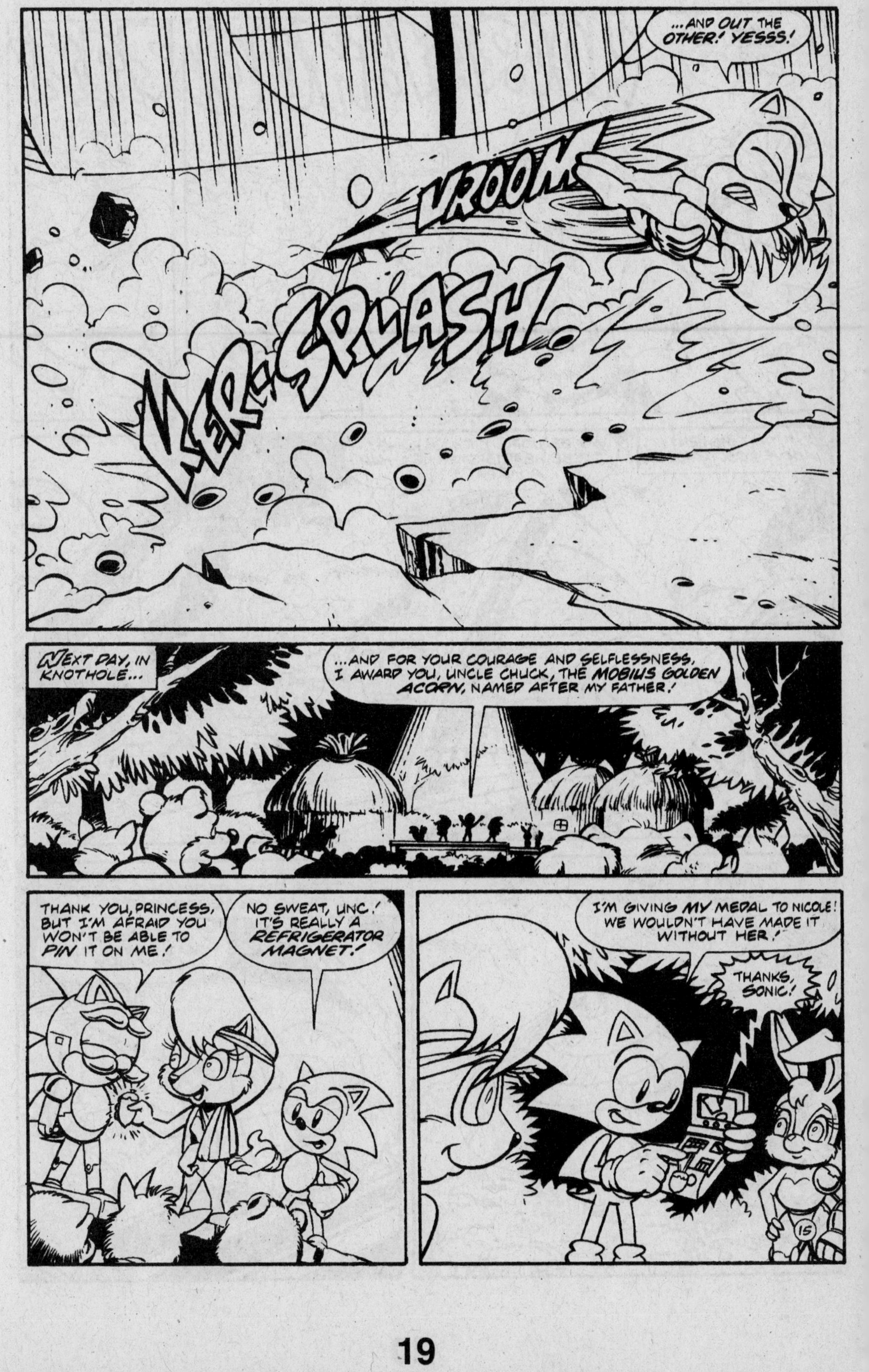
...AND OUT THE OTHER! YESSS!
VROOM
KER-SPLASH
NEXT DAY, IN KNOTHOLE...
...AND FOR YOUR COURAGE AND SELFLESSNESS, I AWARD YOU, UNCLE CHUCK, THE MOBIUS GOLDEN ACORN, NAMED AFTER MY FATHER!
THANK YOU, PRINCESS, BUT I'M AFRAID YOU WON'T BE ABLE TO PIN IT ON ME!
NO SWEAT, UNC.! IT'S REALLY A REFRIGERATOR MAGNET!
I'M GIVING MY MEDAL TO NICOLE! WE WOULDN'T HAVE MADE IT WITHOUT HER!
THANKS, SONIC!
15

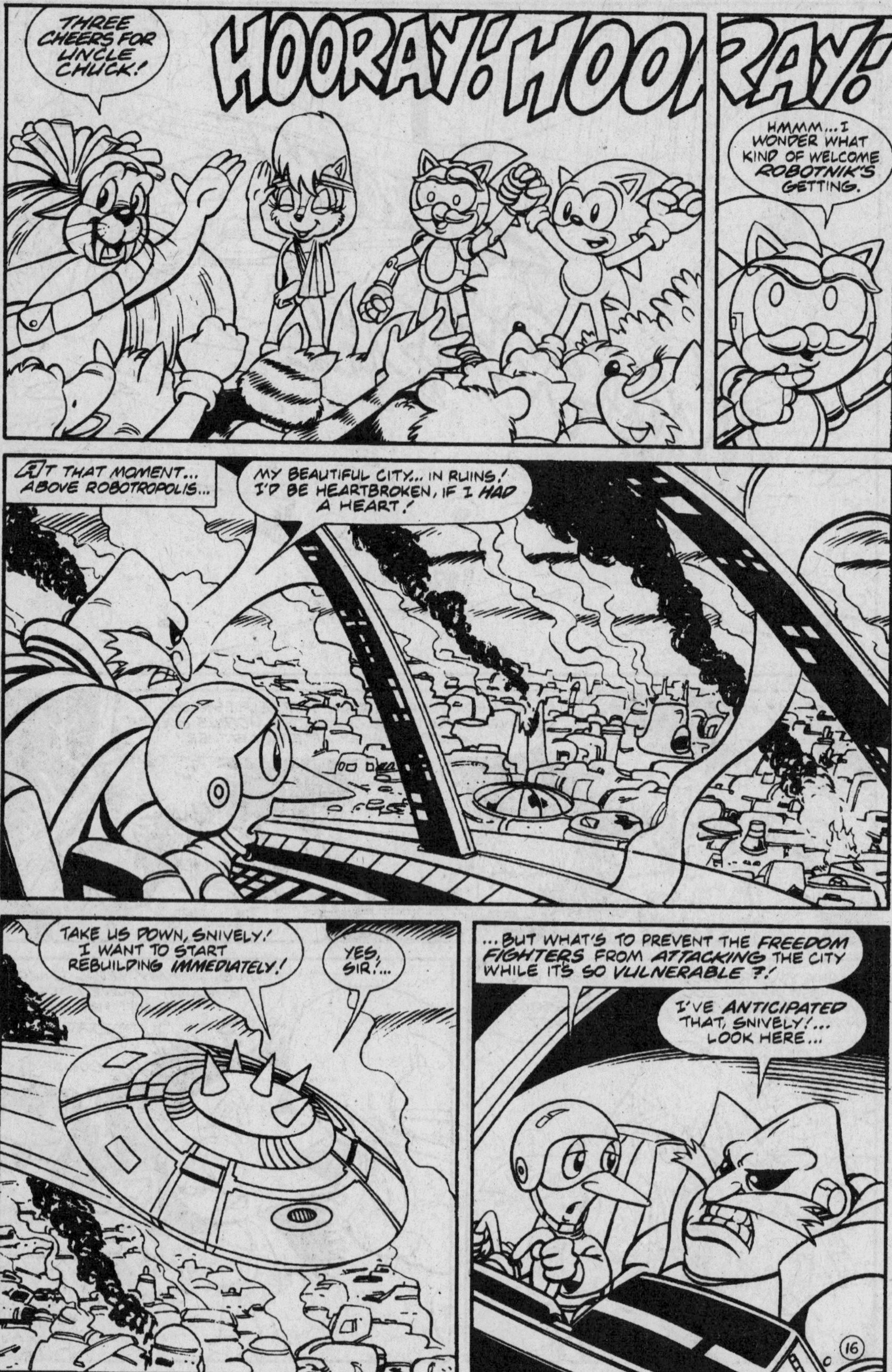
THREE CHEERS FOR UNCLE CHUCK!
HOORAY! HOORAY!
HMMM... I WONDER WHAT KIND OF WELCOME ROBOTNIK'S GETTING.
AT THAT MOMENT... ABOVE ROBOTROPOLIS...
MY BEAUTIFUL CITY... IN RUINS! I'D BE HEARTBROKEN, IF I HAD A HEART!
TAKE US DOWN, SNIVELY! I WANT TO START REBUILDING IMMEDIATELY!
YES, SIR!...
...BUT WHAT'S TO PREVENT THE FREEDOM FIGHTERS FROM ATTACKING THE CITY WHILE IT'S SO VULNERABLE ?!
I'VE ANTICIPATED THAT, SNIVELY!... LOOK HERE...
16

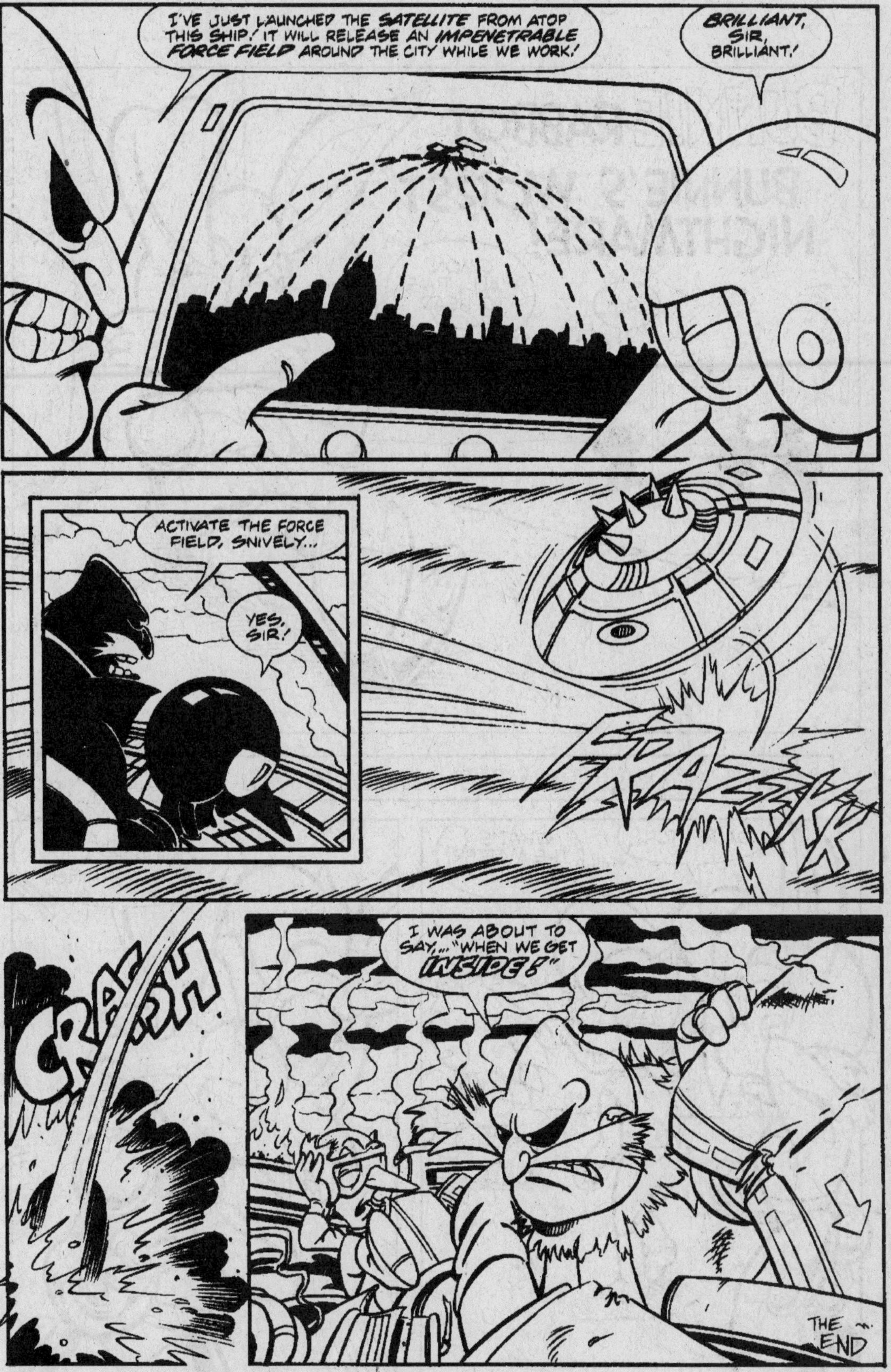
I'VE JUST LAUNCHED THE SATELLITE FROM ATOP THIS SHIP! IT WILL RELEASE AN IMPENETRABLE FORCE FIELD AROUND THE CITY WHILE WE WORK!
BRILLIANT, SIR, BRILLIANT!
ACTIVATE THE FORCE FIELD, SNIVELY...
YES, SIR!
FZASSKK
CRASH
I WAS ABOUT TO SAY... "WHEN WE GET INSIDE!"
THE END

BUNNIE RABBOT IN BUNNIE'S WORST NIGHTMARE!

YAH!

C'MON, Y'ALL, TIME TO HEAD BACK!

STORY & ART: RICH KOSLOWSKI LETTERING: MINDY EISMAN

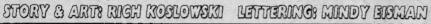

DANG ITCH!

WHAT'S THE MATTER, BUNNIE?

MUST'VE LAID IN SOME POISON IVY OR SOMETHING!

SCRATCH!

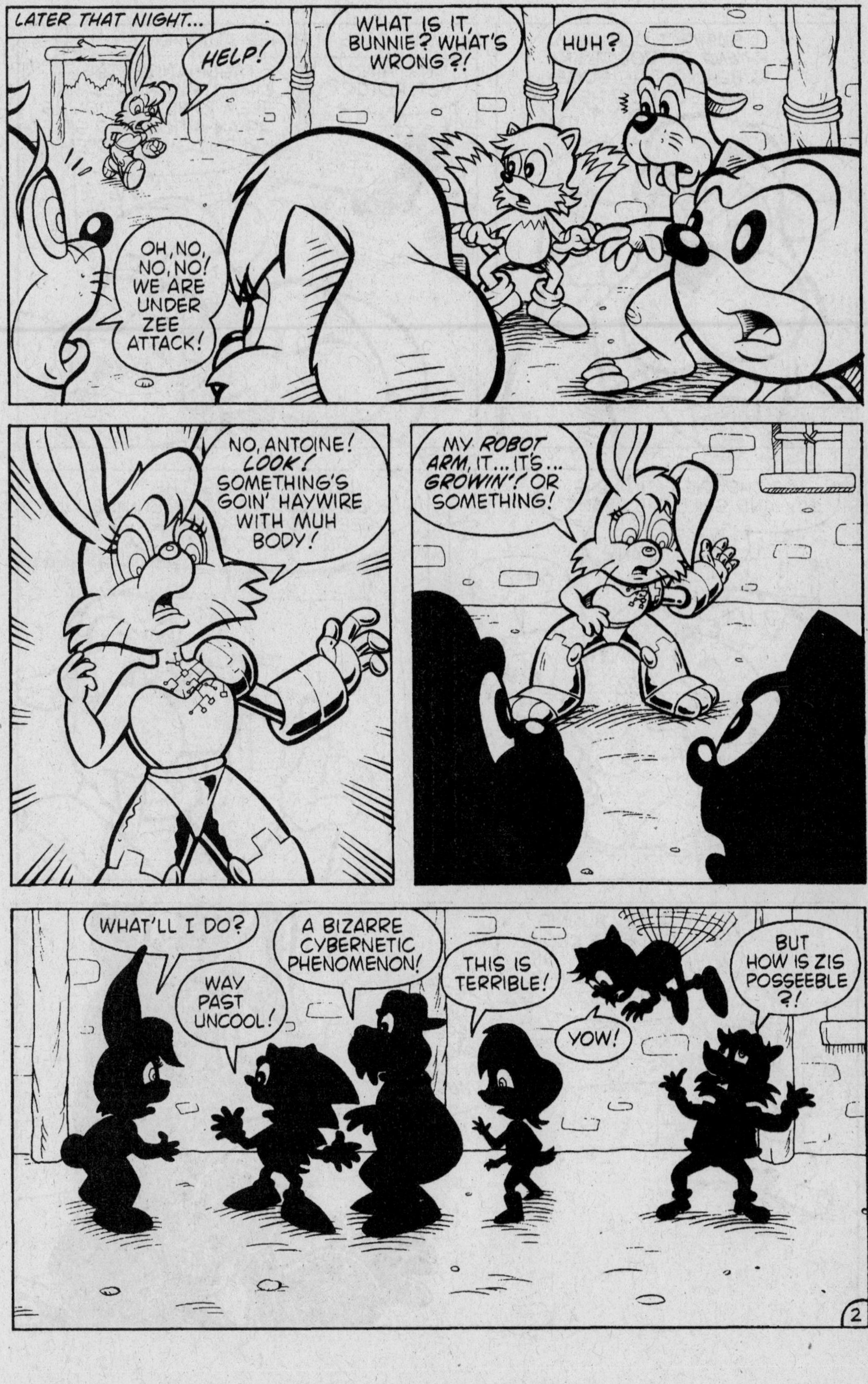
LATER THAT NIGHT...
HELP!
WHAT IS IT, BUNNIE? WHAT'S WRONG?!
HUH?
OH, NO, NO, NO! WE ARE UNDER ZEE ATTACK!
NO, ANTOINE! LOOK! SOMETHING'S GOIN' HAYWIRE WITH MUH BODY!
MY ROBOT ARM, IT... IT'S... GROWIN'! OR SOMETHING!
WHAT'LL I DO?
WAY PAST UNCOOL!
A BIZARRE CYBERNETIC PHENOMENON!
THIS IS TERRIBLE!
YOW!
BUT HOW IS ZIS POSSEEBLE?!
2

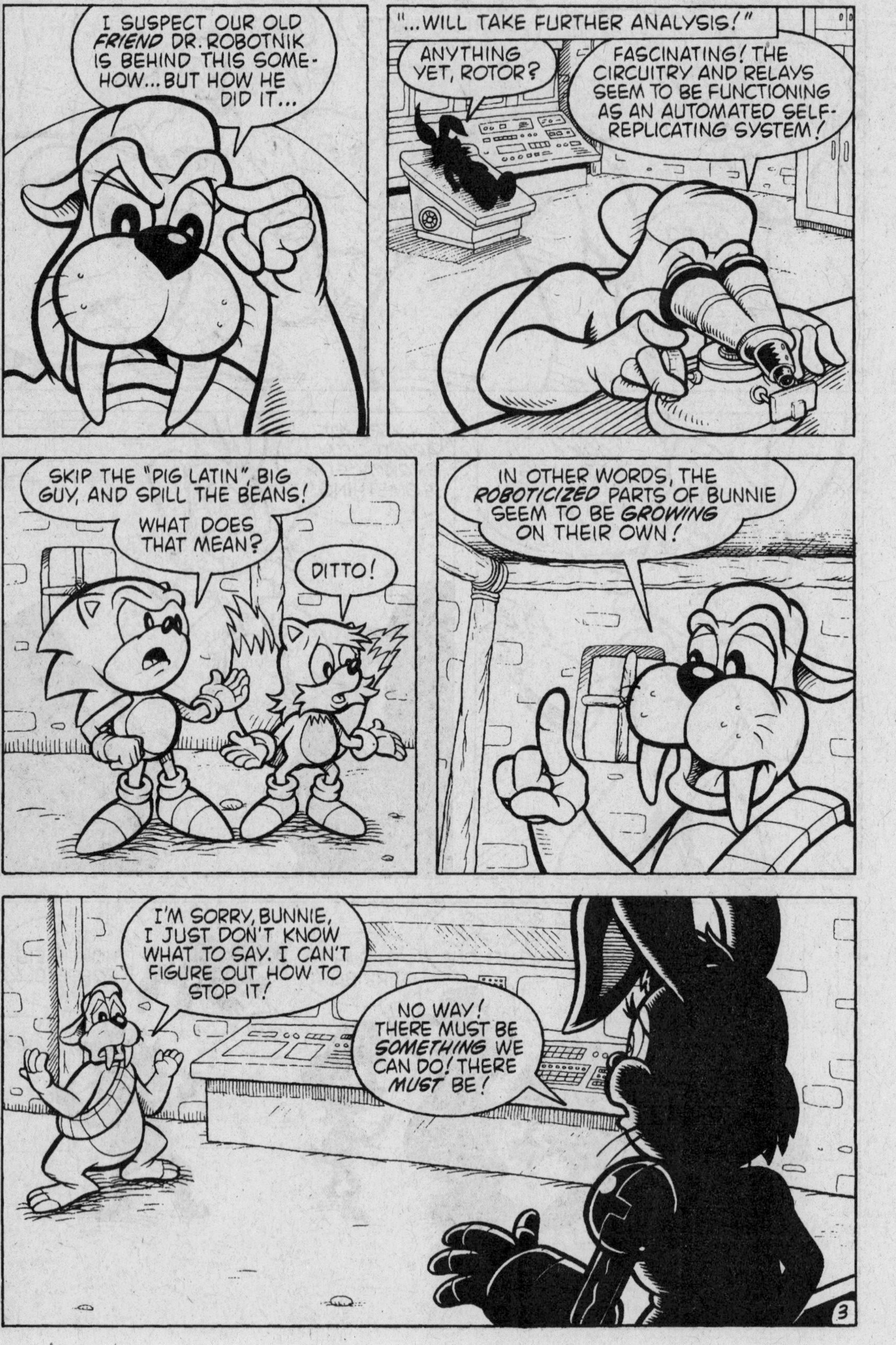
I SUSPECT OUR OLD FRIEND DR. ROBOTNIK IS BEHIND THIS SOME-HOW... BUT HOW HE DID IT...
"...WILL TAKE FURTHER ANALYSIS!"
ANYTHING YET, ROTOR?
FASCINATING! THE CIRCUITRY AND RELAYS SEEM TO BE FUNCTIONING AS AN AUTOMATED SELF-REPLICATING SYSTEM!
SKIP THE "PIG LATIN", BIG GUY, AND SPILL THE BEANS!
WHAT DOES THAT MEAN?
DITTO!
IN OTHER WORDS, THE ROBOTICIZED PARTS OF BUNNIE SEEM TO BE GROWING ON THEIR OWN!
I'M SORRY, BUNNIE, I JUST DON'T KNOW WHAT TO SAY. I CAN'T FIGURE OUT HOW TO STOP IT!
NO WAY! THERE MUST BE SOMETHING WE CAN DO! THERE MUST BE!
3

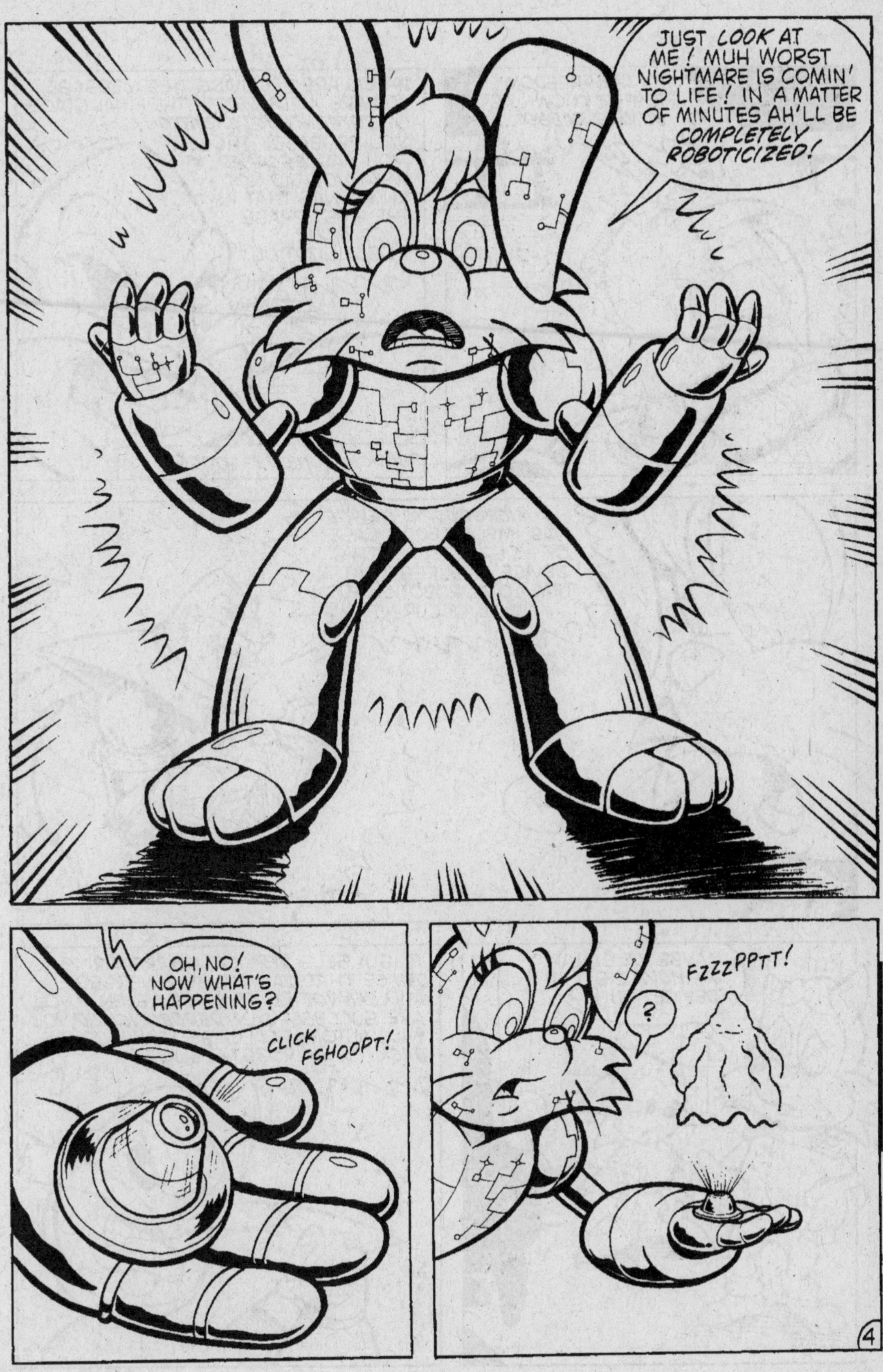
JUST LOOK AT ME! MUH WORST NIGHTMARE IS COMIN' TO LIFE! IN A MATTER OF MINUTES AH'LL BE COMPLETELY ROBOTICIZED!
OH, NO! NOW WHAT'S HAPPENING?
CLICK
FSHOOPT!
?
FZZZPPTT!
4

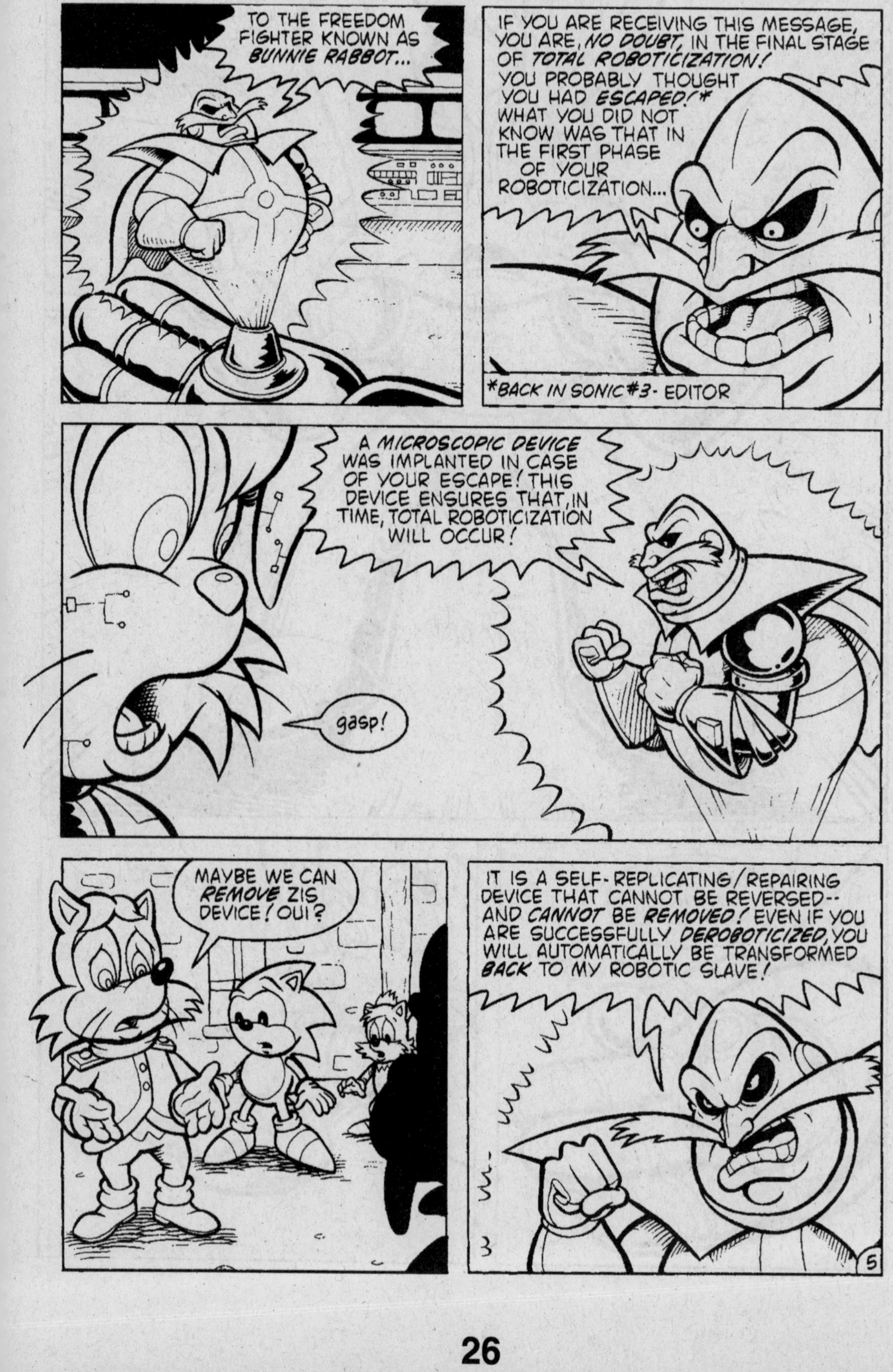

TO THE FREEDOM FIGHTER KNOWN AS BUNNIE RABBOT...
IF YOU ARE RECEIVING THIS MESSAGE, YOU ARE, NO DOUBT, IN THE FINAL STAGE OF TOTAL ROBOTICIZATION! YOU PROBABLY THOUGHT YOU HAD ESCAPED!* WHAT YOU DID NOT KNOW WAS THAT IN THE FIRST PHASE OF YOUR ROBOTICIZATION...
*BACK IN SONIC #3 - EDITOR
A MICROSCOPIC DEVICE WAS IMPLANTED IN CASE OF YOUR ESCAPE! THIS DEVICE ENSURES THAT, IN TIME, TOTAL ROBOTICIZATION WILL OCCUR!
gasp!
MAYBE WE CAN REMOVE ZIS DEVICE! OUI?
IT IS A SELF-REPLICATING/REPAIRING DEVICE THAT CANNOT BE REVERSED-- AND CANNOT BE REMOVED! EVEN IF YOU ARE SUCCESSFULLY DEROBOTICIZED, YOU WILL AUTOMATICALLY BE TRANSFORMED BACK TO MY ROBOTIC SLAVE!
5

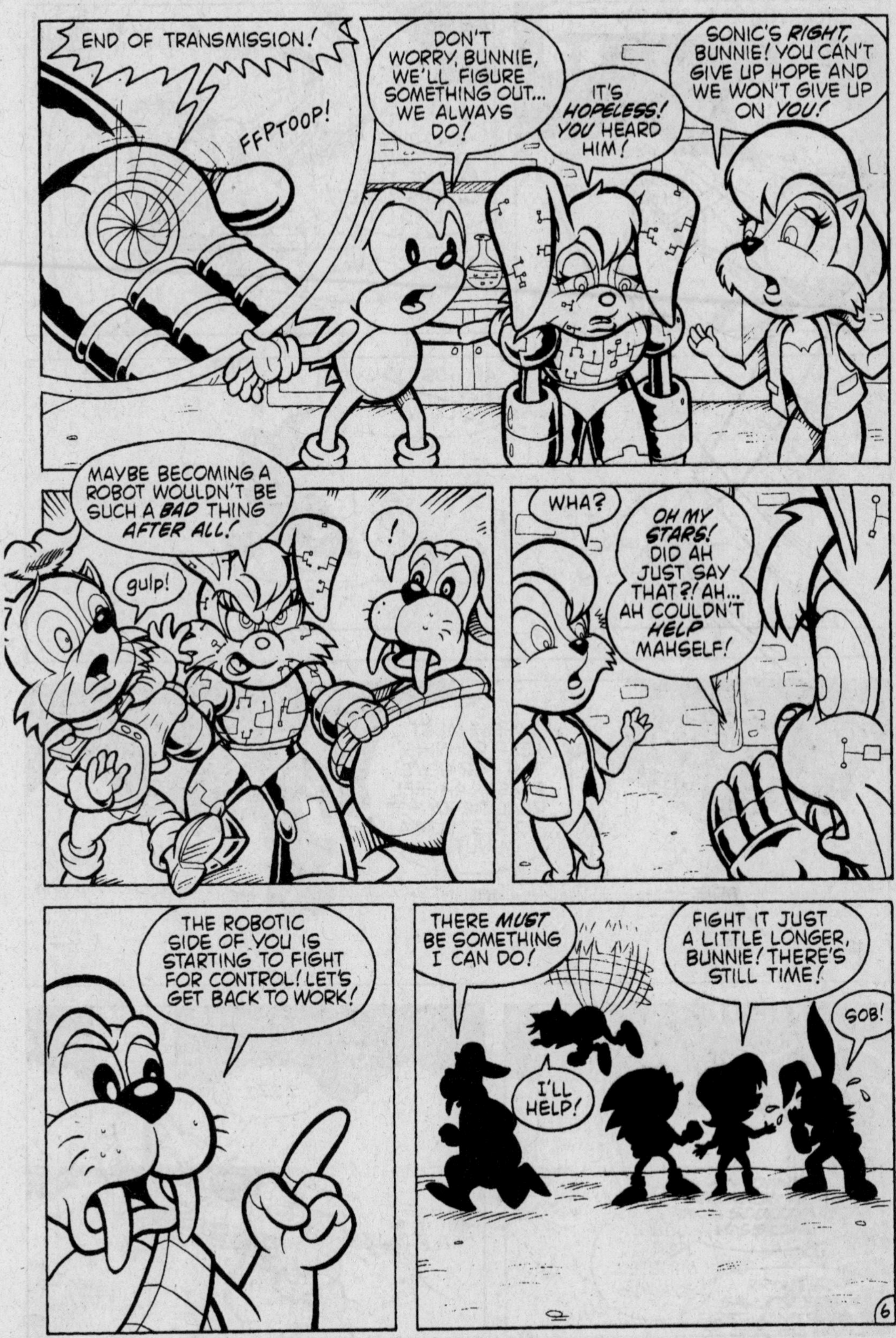
END OF TRANSMISSION!
FFPTOOP!
DON'T WORRY, BUNNIE, WE'LL FIGURE SOMETHING OUT... WE ALWAYS DO!
IT'S HOPELESS! YOU HEARD HIM!
SONIC'S RIGHT, BUNNIE! YOU CAN'T GIVE UP HOPE AND WE WON'T GIVE UP ON YOU!
MAYBE BECOMING A ROBOT WOULDN'T BE SUCH A BAD THING AFTER ALL!
gulp!
!
WHA?
OH MY STARS! DID AH JUST SAY THAT?! AH... AH COULDN'T HELP MAHSELF!
THE ROBOTIC SIDE OF YOU IS STARTING TO FIGHT FOR CONTROL! LET'S GET BACK TO WORK!
THERE MUST BE SOMETHING I CAN DO!
I'LL HELP!
FIGHT IT JUST A LITTLE LONGER, BUNNIE! THERE'S STILL TIME!
SOB!
6

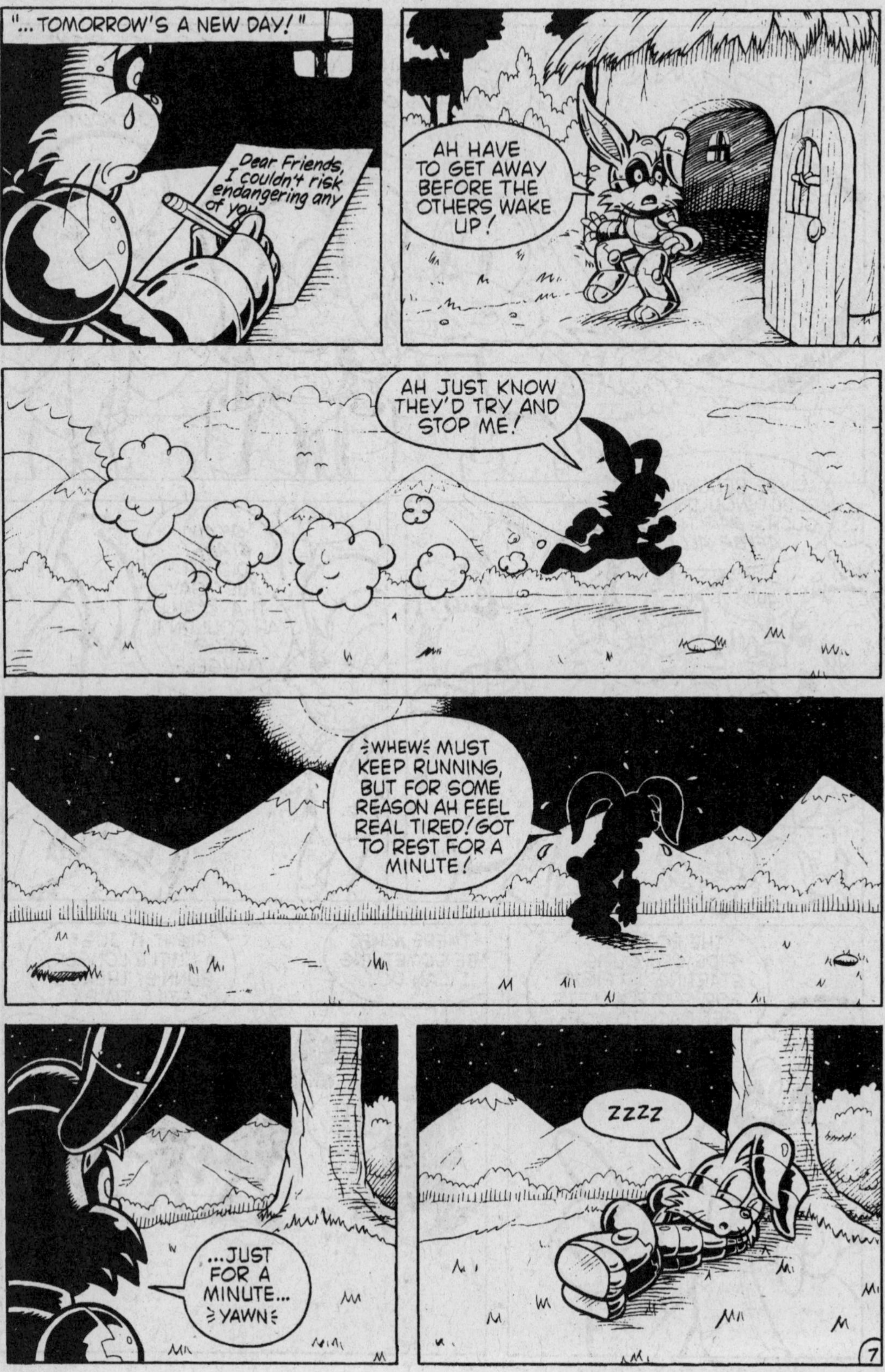
"...TOMORROW'S A NEW DAY!"
Dear Friends, I couldn't risk endangering any of you
AH HAVE TO GET AWAY BEFORE THE OTHERS WAKE UP!
AH JUST KNOW THEY'D TRY AND STOP ME!
WHEW MUST KEEP RUNNING, BUT FOR SOME REASON AH FEEL REAL TIRED! GOT TO REST FOR A MINUTE!
...JUST FOR A MINUTE... YAWN
ZZZZ
7

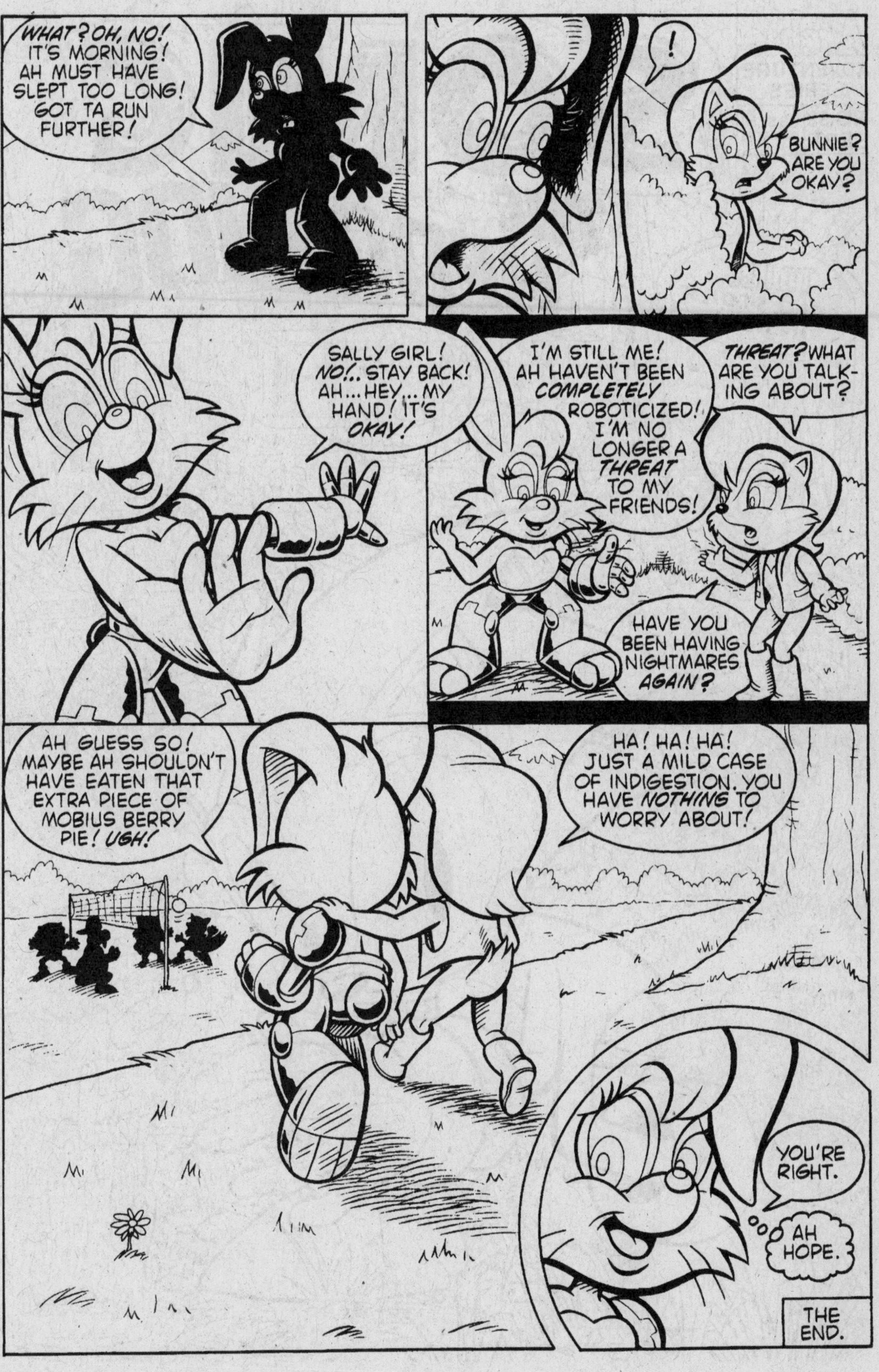
WHAT? OH, NO! IT'S MORNING! AH MUST HAVE SLEPT TOO LONG! GOT TA RUN FURTHER!
!
BUNNIE? ARE YOU OKAY?
SALLY GIRL! NO!.. STAY BACK! AH... HEY... MY HAND! IT'S OKAY!
I'M STILL ME! AH HAVEN'T BEEN COMPLETELY ROBOTICIZED! I'M NO LONGER A THREAT TO MY FRIENDS!
THREAT? WHAT ARE YOU TALKING ABOUT?
HAVE YOU BEEN HAVING NIGHTMARES AGAIN?
AH GUESS SO! MAYBE AH SHOULDN'T HAVE EATEN THAT EXTRA PIECE OF MOBIUS BERRY PIE! UGH!
HA! HA! HA! JUST A MILD CASE OF INDIGESTION. YOU HAVE NOTHING TO WORRY ABOUT!
YOU'RE RIGHT.
AH HOPE.
THE END.

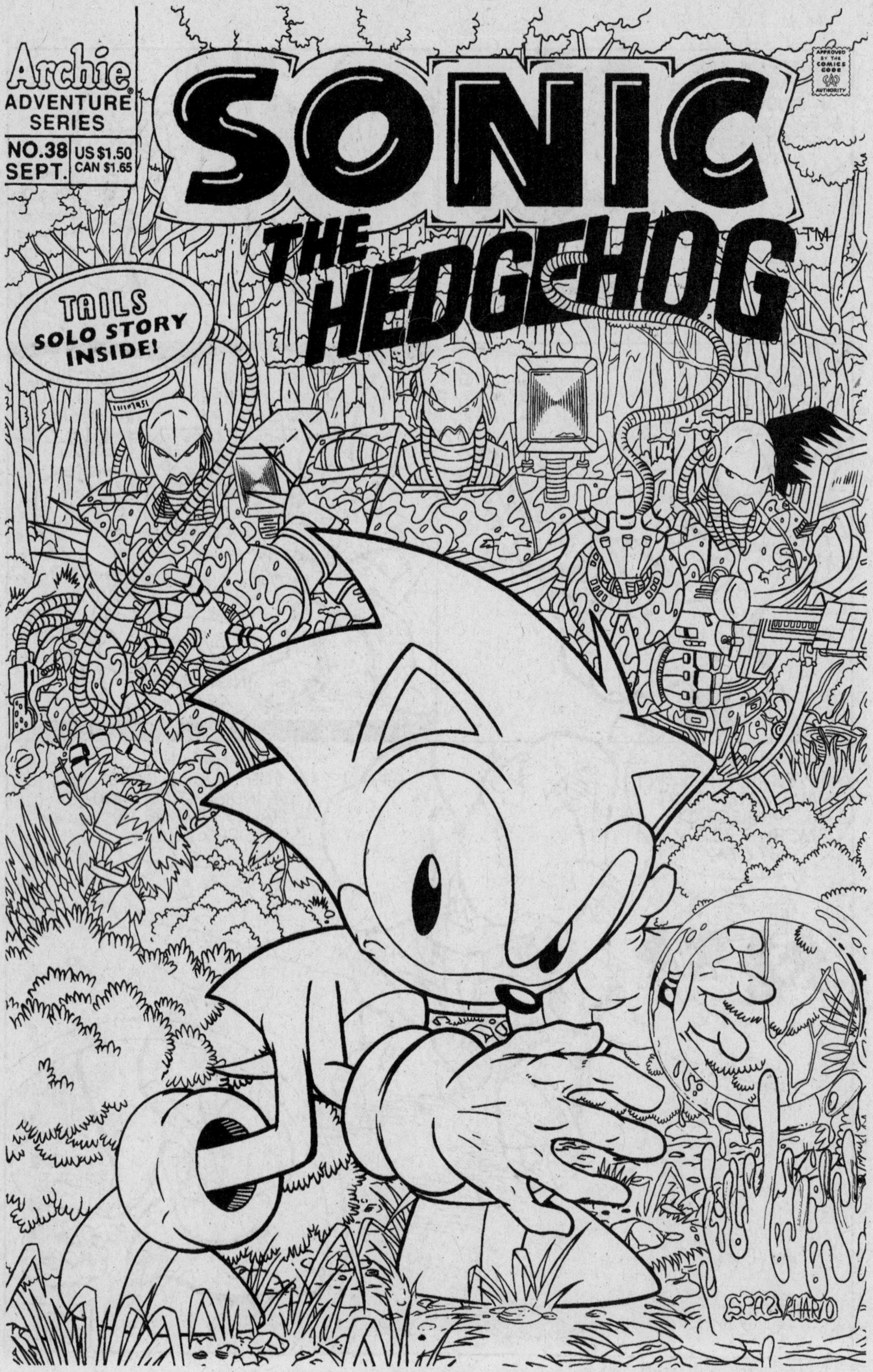
Archie
ADVENTURE SERIES
NO.38 SEPT.
US $1.50
CAN $1.65
SONIC THE HEDGEHOG™
APPROVED BY THE COMICS CODE AUTHORITY
TAILS SOLO STORY INSIDE!
SPAZ

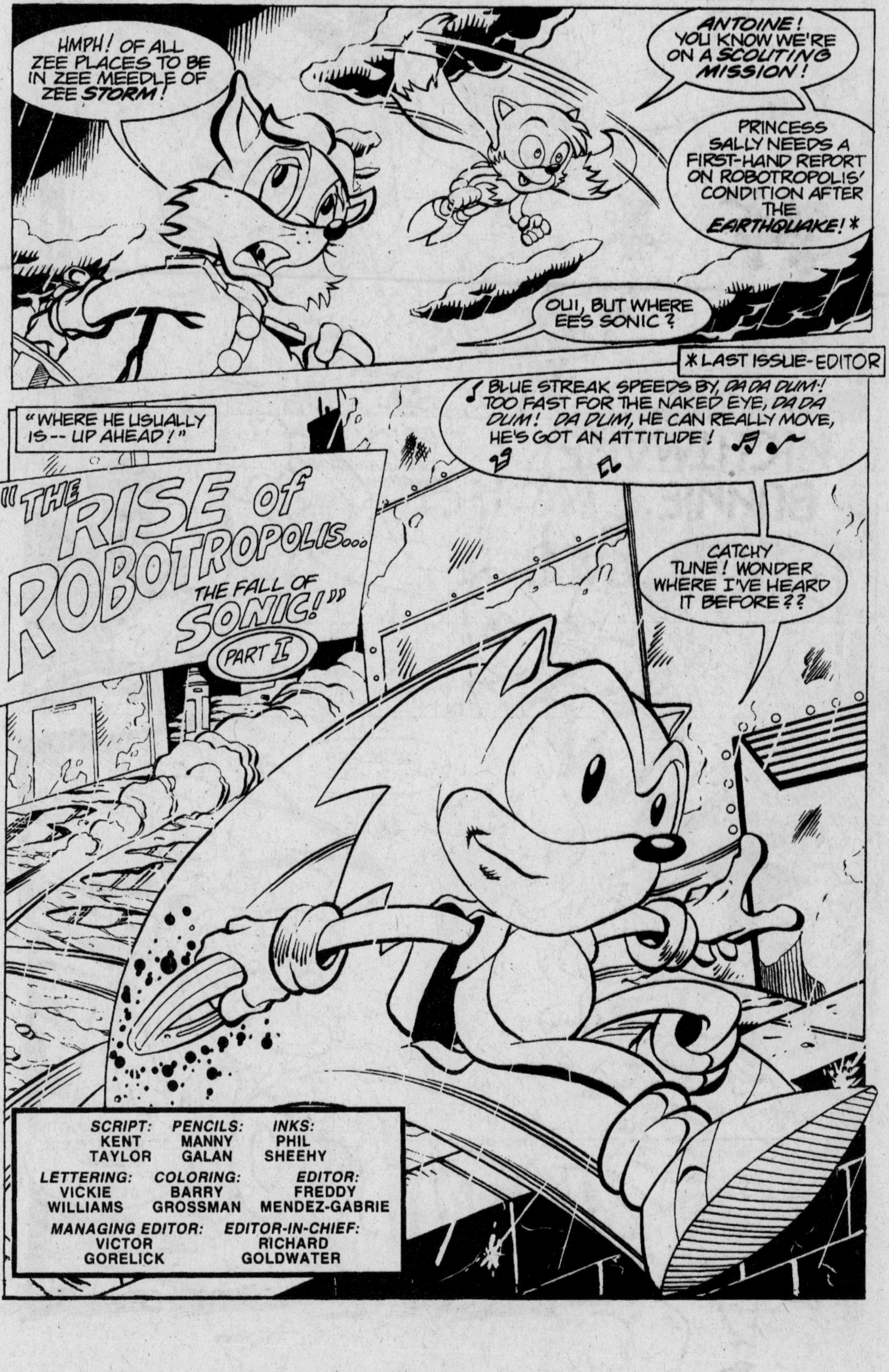

HMPH! OF ALL ZEE PLACES TO BE IN ZEE MEEDLE OF ZEE STORM!
ANTOINE! YOU KNOW WE'RE ON A SCOUTING MISSION!
PRINCESS SALLY NEEDS A FIRST-HAND REPORT ON ROBOTROPOLIS' CONDITION AFTER THE EARTHQUAKE! *
OUI, BUT WHERE EES SONIC?
* LAST ISSUE-EDITOR
"WHERE HE USUALLY IS -- UP AHEAD!"
BLUE STREAK SPEEDS BY, DA DA DUM! TOO FAST FOR THE NAKED EYE, DA DA DUM! DA DUM, HE CAN REALLY MOVE, HE'S GOT AN ATTITUDE!
"THE RISE of ROBOTROPOLIS... THE FALL OF SONIC!"
PART I
CATCHY TUNE! WONDER WHERE I'VE HEARD IT BEFORE??
SCRIPT: KENT TAYLOR
PENCILS: MANNY GALAN
INKS: PHIL SHEEHY
LETTERING: VICKIE WILLIAMS
COLORING: BARRY GROSSMAN
EDITOR: FREDDY MENDEZ-GABRIE
MANAGING EDITOR: VICTOR GORELICK
EDITOR-IN-CHIEF: RICHARD GOLDWATER

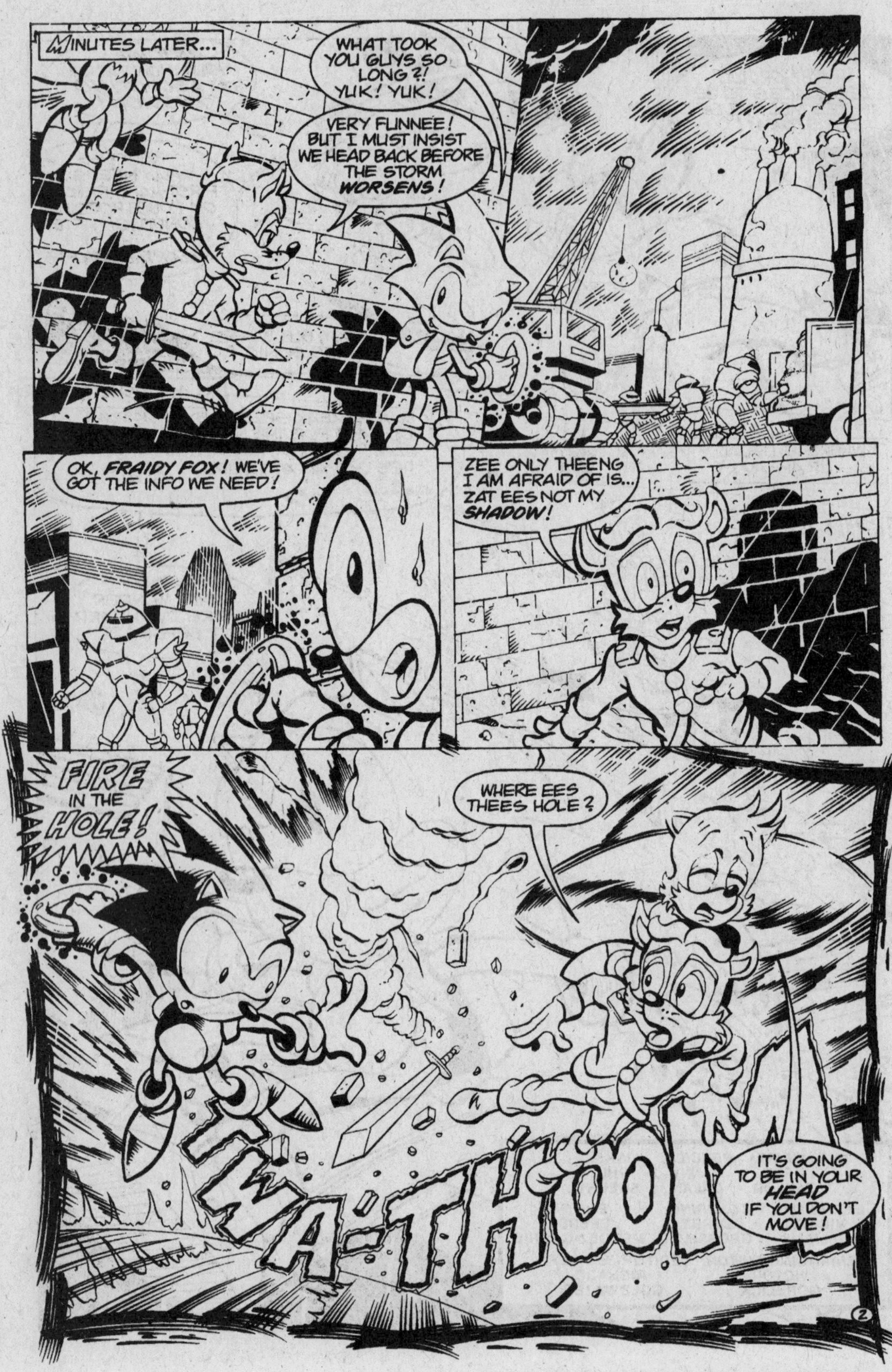
MINUTES LATER...
WHAT TOOK YOU GUYS SO LONG ?! YUK! YUK!
VERY FUNNEE! BUT I MUST INSIST WE HEAD BACK BEFORE THE STORM WORSENS!
OK, FRAIDY FOX! WE'VE GOT THE INFO WE NEED!
ZEE ONLY THEENG I AM AFRAID OF IS... ZAT EES NOT MY SHADOW!
FIRE IN THE HOLE!
WHERE EES THEES HOLE ?
WA-THOOM
IT'S GOING TO BE IN YOUR HEAD IF YOU DON'T MOVE!
2

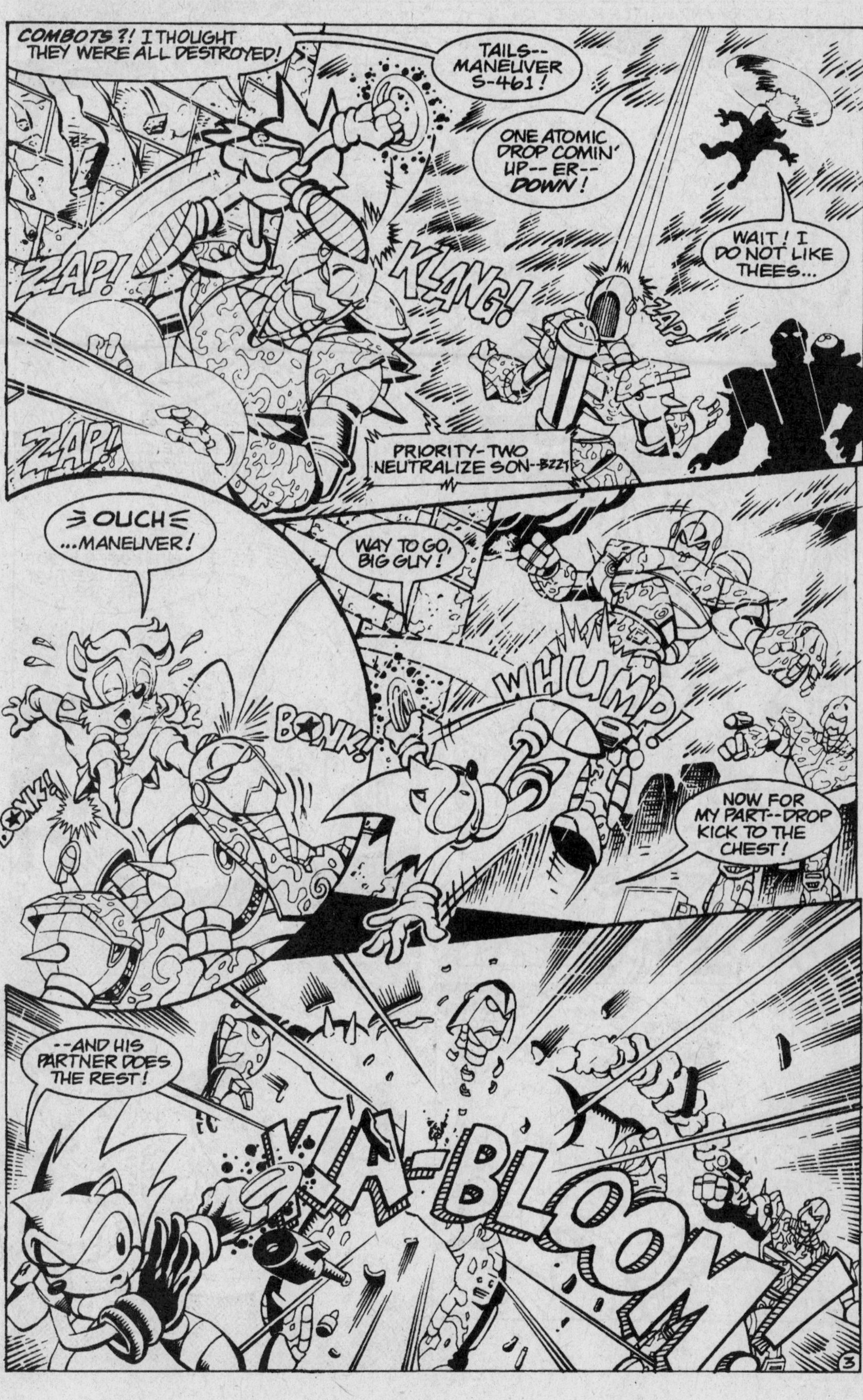
COMBOTS?! I THOUGHT THEY WERE ALL DESTROYED!
TAILS-- MANEUVER S-461!
ONE ATOMIC DROP COMIN' UP-- ER-- DOWN!
WAIT! I DO NOT LIKE THEES...
ZAP!
KLANG!
ZAP!
ZAP!
PRIORITY-TWO NEUTRALIZE SON--BZZT
OUCH ...MANEUVER!
WAY TO GO, BIG GUY!
WHUMP!
BONK!
BONK!
NOW FOR MY PART--DROP KICK TO THE CHEST!
--AND HIS PARTNER DOES THE REST!
KA-BLOOM!
3

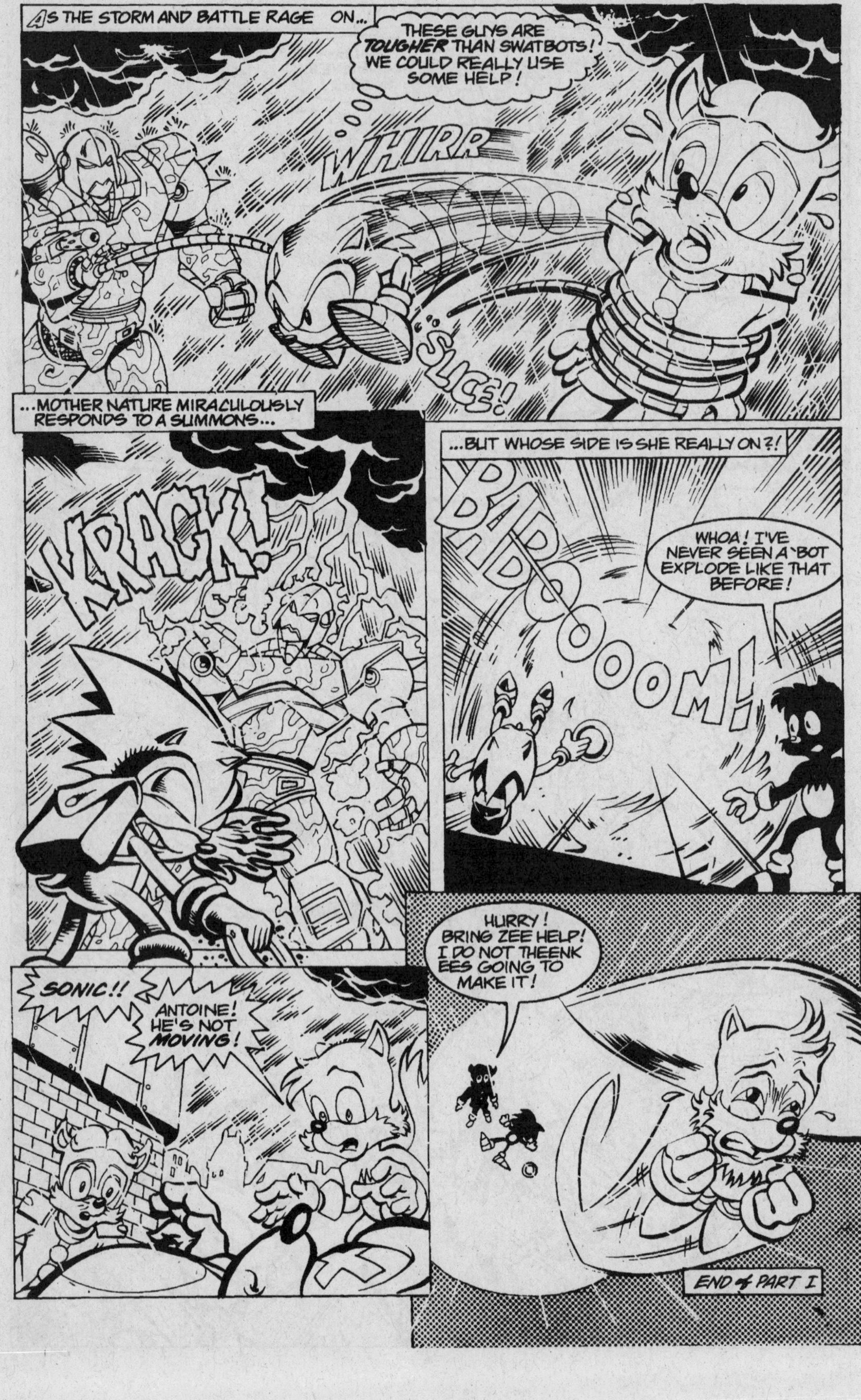
AS THE STORM AND BATTLE RAGE ON...
THESE GUYS ARE TOUGHER THAN SWATBOTS! WE COULD REALLY USE SOME HELP!
WHIRR
SLICE!
...MOTHER NATURE MIRACULOUSLY RESPONDS TO A SUMMONS...
KRACK!
...BUT WHOSE SIDE IS SHE REALLY ON?!
BADOOOOOM!
WHOA! I'VE NEVER SEEN A 'BOT EXPLODE LIKE THAT BEFORE!
SONIC!!
ANTOINE! HE'S NOT MOVING!
HURRY! BRING ZEE HELP! I DO NOT THEENK EES GOING TO MAKE IT!
END of PART I

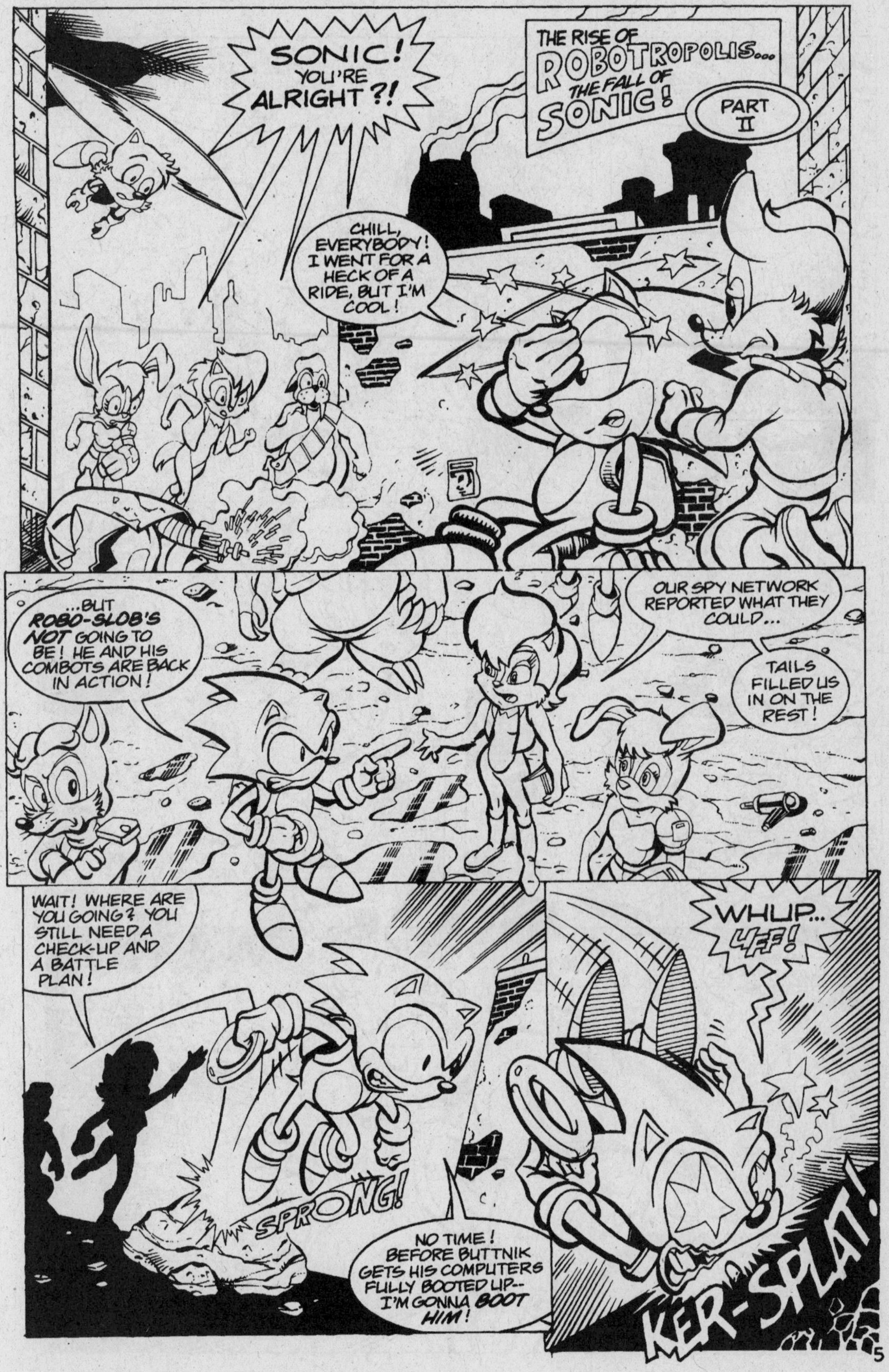
SONIC! YOU'RE ALRIGHT ?!
THE RISE OF ROBOTROPOLIS... THE FALL OF SONIC!
PART II
CHILL, EVERYBODY! I WENT FOR A HECK OF A RIDE, BUT I'M COOL!
...BUT ROBO-SLOB'S NOT GOING TO BE! HE AND HIS COMBOTS ARE BACK IN ACTION!
OUR SPY NETWORK REPORTED WHAT THEY COULD...
TAILS FILLED US IN ON THE REST!
WAIT! WHERE ARE YOU GOING? YOU STILL NEED A CHECK-UP AND A BATTLE PLAN!
SPRONG!
NO TIME! BEFORE BUTTNIK GETS HIS COMPUTERS FULLY BOOTED UP-- I'M GONNA BOOT HIM!
WHUP... UFF!
KER-SPLAT!
5

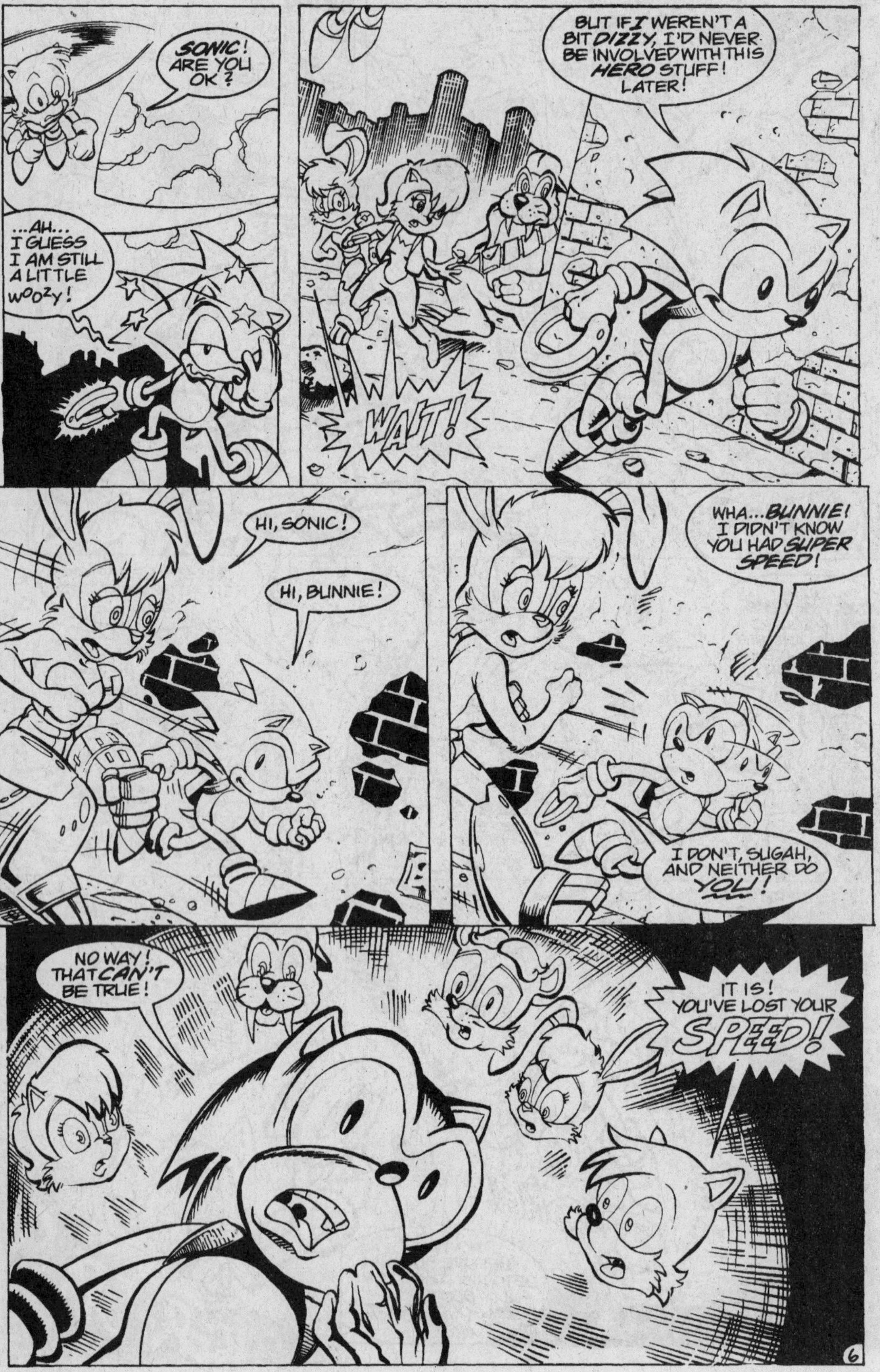
SONIC! ARE YOU OK?
...AH... I GUESS I AM STILL A LITTLE WOOZY!
BUT IF I WEREN'T A BIT DIZZY, I'D NEVER BE INVOLVED WITH THIS HERO STUFF! LATER!
WAIT!
HI, SONIC!
HI, BUNNIE!
WHA...BUNNIE! I DIDN'T KNOW YOU HAD SUPER SPEED!
I DON'T, SUGAH, AND NEITHER DO YOU!
NO WAY! THAT CAN'T BE TRUE!
IT IS! YOU'VE LOST YOUR SPEED!
6

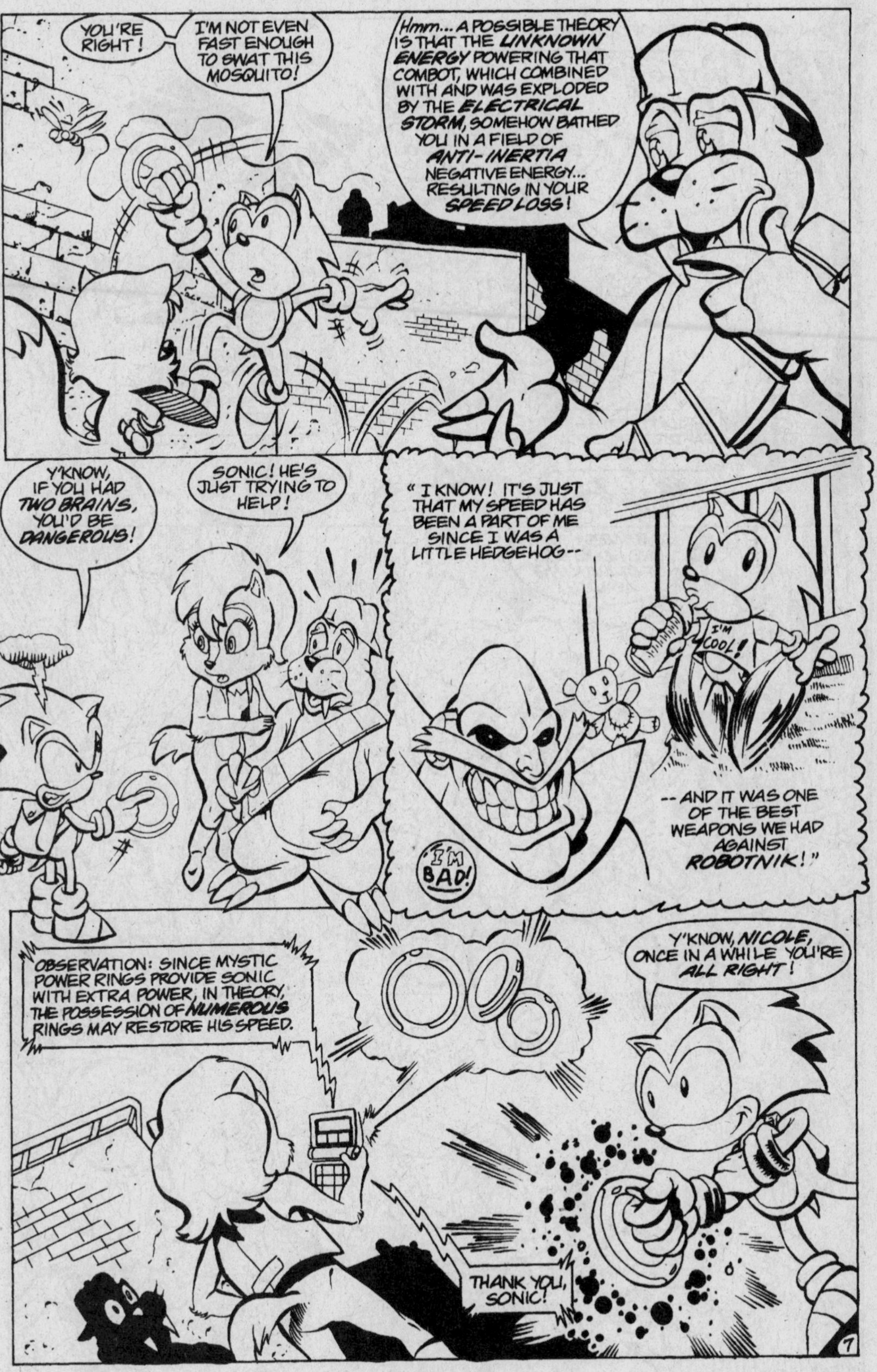
YOU'RE RIGHT!
I'M NOT EVEN FAST ENOUGH TO SWAT THIS MOSQUITO!
Hmm... A POSSIBLE THEORY IS THAT THE UNKNOWN ENERGY POWERING THAT COMBOT, WHICH COMBINED WITH AND WAS EXPLODED BY THE ELECTRICAL STORM, SOMEHOW BATHED YOU IN A FIELD OF ANTI-INERTIA NEGATIVE ENERGY... RESULTING IN YOUR SPEED LOSS!
Y'KNOW, IF YOU HAD TWO BRAINS, YOU'D BE DANGEROUS!
SONIC! HE'S JUST TRYING TO HELP!
"I KNOW! IT'S JUST THAT MY SPEED HAS BEEN A PART OF ME SINCE I WAS A LITTLE HEDGEHOG--
I'M COOL!
I'M BAD!
--AND IT WAS ONE OF THE BEST WEAPONS WE HAD AGAINST ROBOTNIK!"
OBSERVATION: SINCE MYSTIC POWER RINGS PROVIDE SONIC WITH EXTRA POWER, IN THEORY, THE POSSESSION OF NUMEROUS RINGS MAY RESTORE HIS SPEED.
Y'KNOW, NICOLE, ONCE IN A WHILE YOU'RE ALL RIGHT!
THANK YOU, SONIC!
7

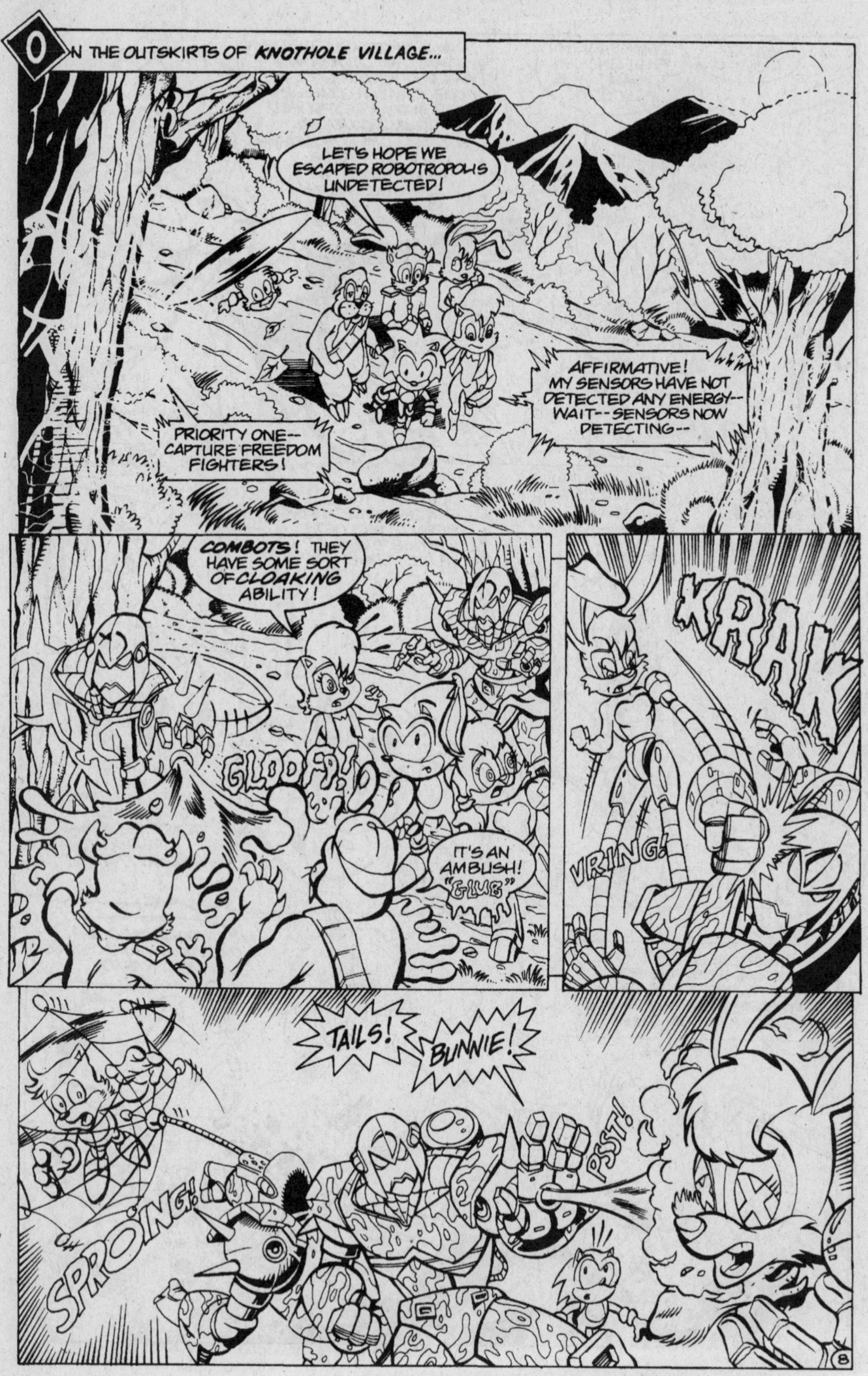
ON THE OUTSKIRTS OF KNOTHOLE VILLAGE...
LET'S HOPE WE ESCAPED ROBOTROPOLIS UNDETECTED!
AFFIRMATIVE! MY SENSORS HAVE NOT DETECTED ANY ENERGY-- WAIT--SENSORS NOW DETECTING--
PRIORITY ONE-- CAPTURE FREEDOM FIGHTERS!
COMBOTS! THEY HAVE SOME SORT OF CLOAKING ABILITY!
GLOOF!
IT'S AN AMBUSH! "GLUB"
KRAK
VRING!
TAILS!
BUNNIE!
SPROING!
PSST!
8

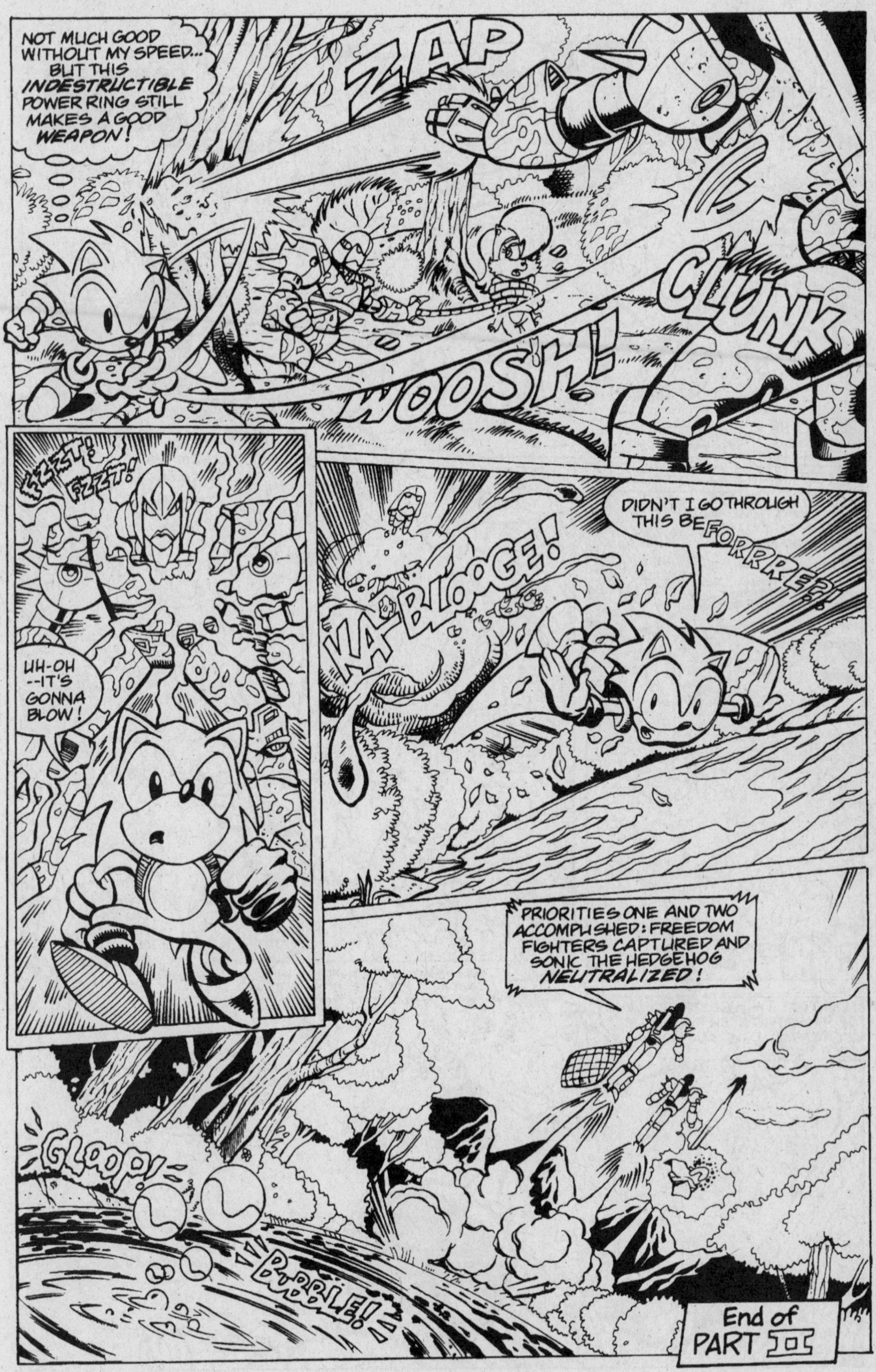
NOT MUCH GOOD WITHOUT MY SPEED... BUT THIS INDESTRUCTIBLE POWER RING STILL MAKES A GOOD WEAPON!
ZAP
CLUNK
WOOSH!
FZZZT! FZZZT!
UH-OH --IT'S GONNA BLOW!
KA-BLOOGE!
DIDN'T I GO THROUGH THIS BEFORRRRE?
PRIORITIES ONE AND TWO ACCOMPLISHED: FREEDOM FIGHTERS CAPTURED AND SONIC THE HEDGEHOG NEUTRALIZED!
GLOOP!
BUBBLE!
End of PART II

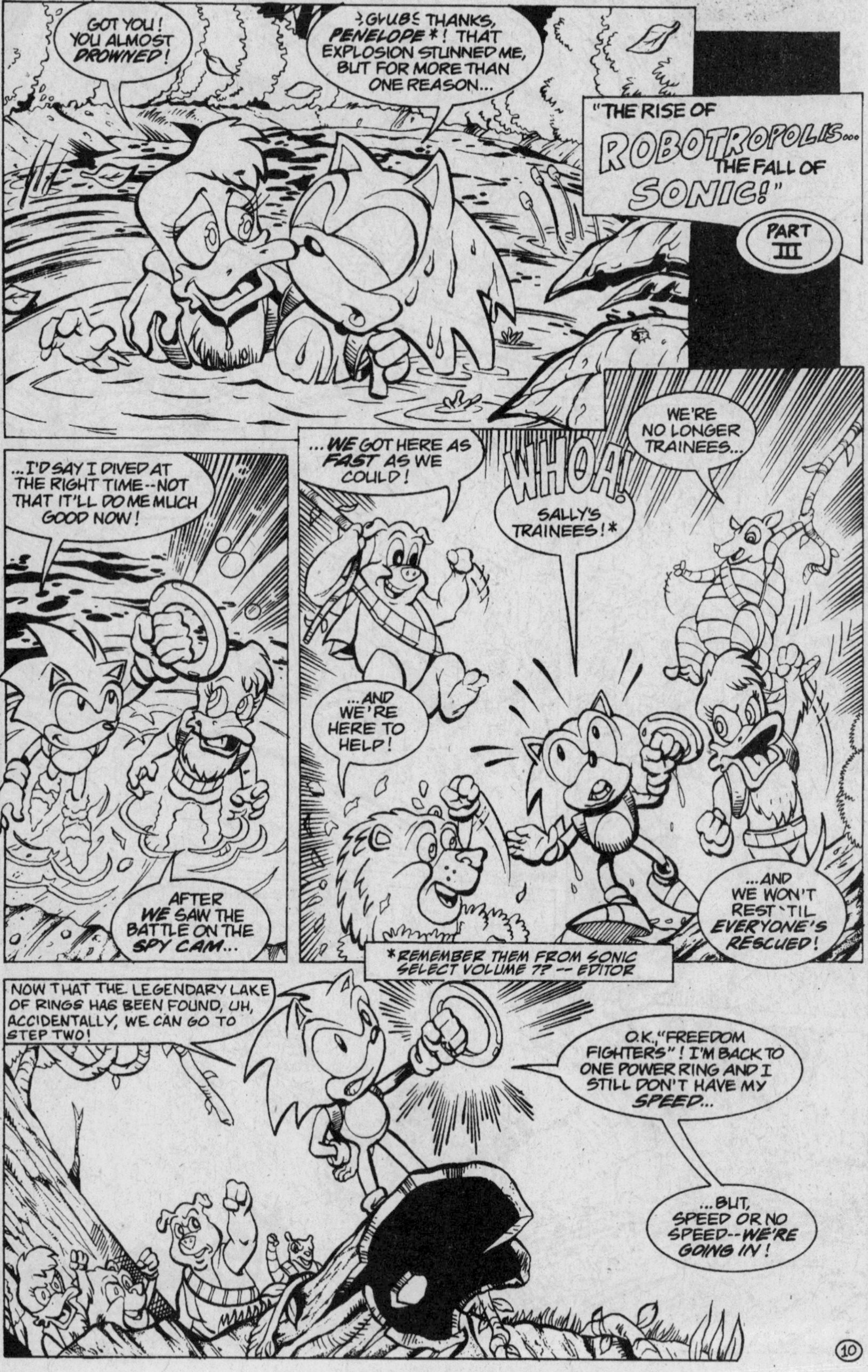
GOT YOU! YOU ALMOST DROWNED!
GLUB THANKS, PENELOPE*! THAT EXPLOSION STUNNED ME, BUT FOR MORE THAN ONE REASON...
"THE RISE OF ROBOTROPOLIS... THE FALL OF SONIC!"
PART III
...I'D SAY I DIVED AT THE RIGHT TIME--NOT THAT IT'LL DO ME MUCH GOOD NOW!
AFTER WE SAW THE BATTLE ON THE SPY CAM...
...WE GOT HERE AS FAST AS WE COULD!
WHOA!
SALLY'S TRAINEES!*
WE'RE NO LONGER TRAINEES...
...AND WE'RE HERE TO HELP!
...AND WE WON'T REST 'TIL EVERYONE'S RESCUED!
*REMEMBER THEM FROM SONIC SELECT VOLUME 7? -- EDITOR
NOW THAT THE LEGENDARY LAKE OF RINGS HAS BEEN FOUND, UH, ACCIDENTALLY, WE CAN GO TO STEP TWO!
O.K., "FREEDOM FIGHTERS"! I'M BACK TO ONE POWER RING AND I STILL DON'T HAVE MY SPEED...
...BUT, SPEED OR NO SPEED--WE'RE GOING IN!
10

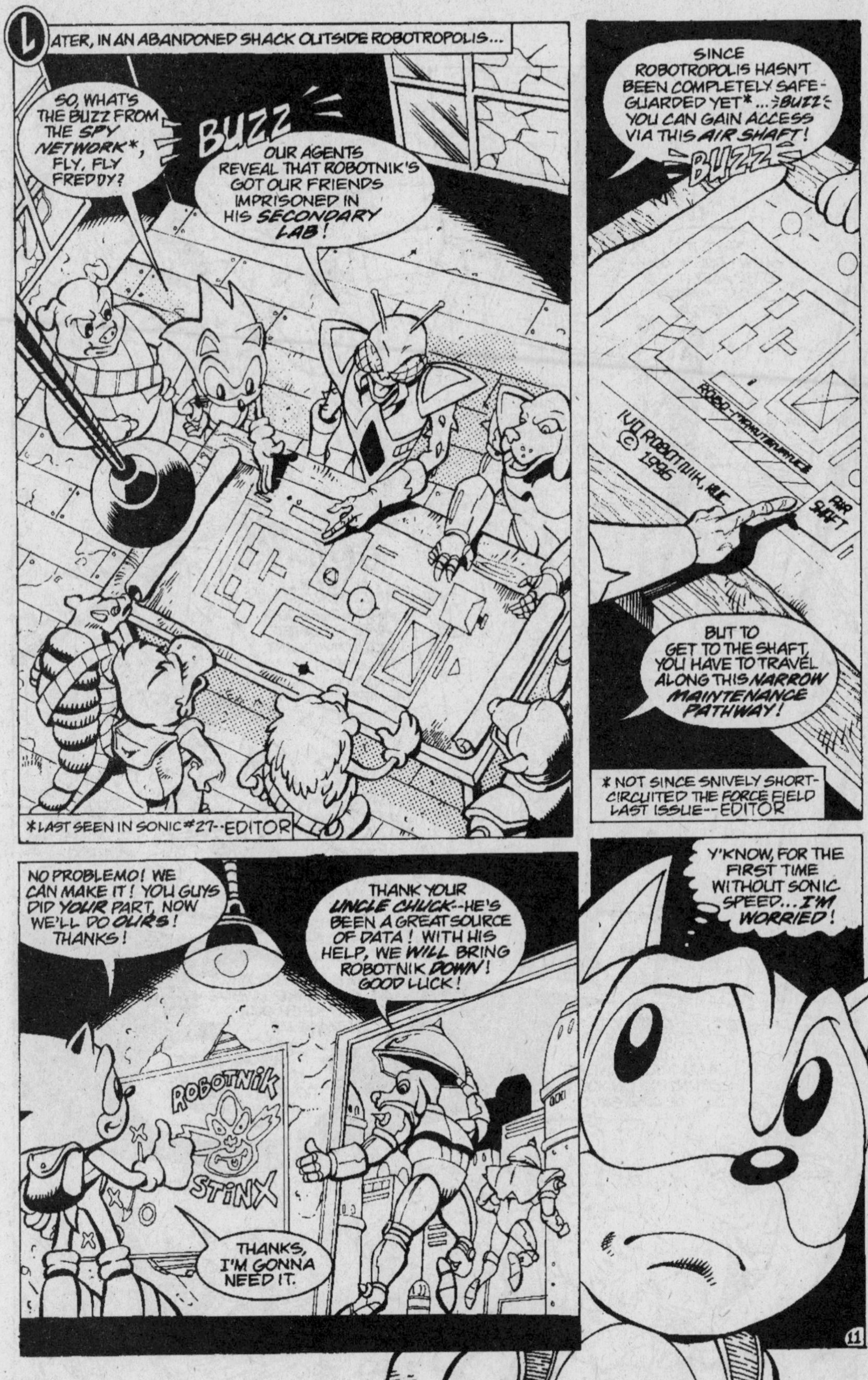
LATER, IN AN ABANDONED SHACK OUTSIDE ROBOTROPOLIS...
SO, WHAT'S THE BUZZ FROM THE SPY NETWORK*, FLY, FLY FREDDY?
BUZZ
OUR AGENTS REVEAL THAT ROBOTNIK'S GOT OUR FRIENDS IMPRISONED IN HIS SECONDARY LAB!
*LAST SEEN IN SONIC #27--EDITOR
SINCE ROBOTROPOLIS HASN'T BEEN COMPLETELY SAFE-GUARDED YET*...BUZZ YOU CAN GAIN ACCESS VIA THIS AIR SHAFT!
BUZZ
IVO ROBOTNIK, INC. © 1996
AIR SHAFT
BUT TO GET TO THE SHAFT, YOU HAVE TO TRAVEL ALONG THIS NARROW MAINTENANCE PATHWAY!
* NOT SINCE SNIVELY SHORT-CIRCUITED THE FORCE FIELD LAST ISSUE--EDITOR
NO PROBLEMO! WE CAN MAKE IT! YOU GUYS DID YOUR PART, NOW WE'LL DO OURS! THANKS!
THANK YOUR UNCLE CHUCK--HE'S BEEN A GREAT SOURCE OF DATA! WITH HIS HELP, WE WILL BRING ROBOTNIK DOWN! GOOD LUCK!
ROBOTNIK STINX
THANKS, I'M GONNA NEED IT.
Y'KNOW, FOR THE FIRST TIME WITHOUT SONIC SPEED... I'M WORRIED!
11

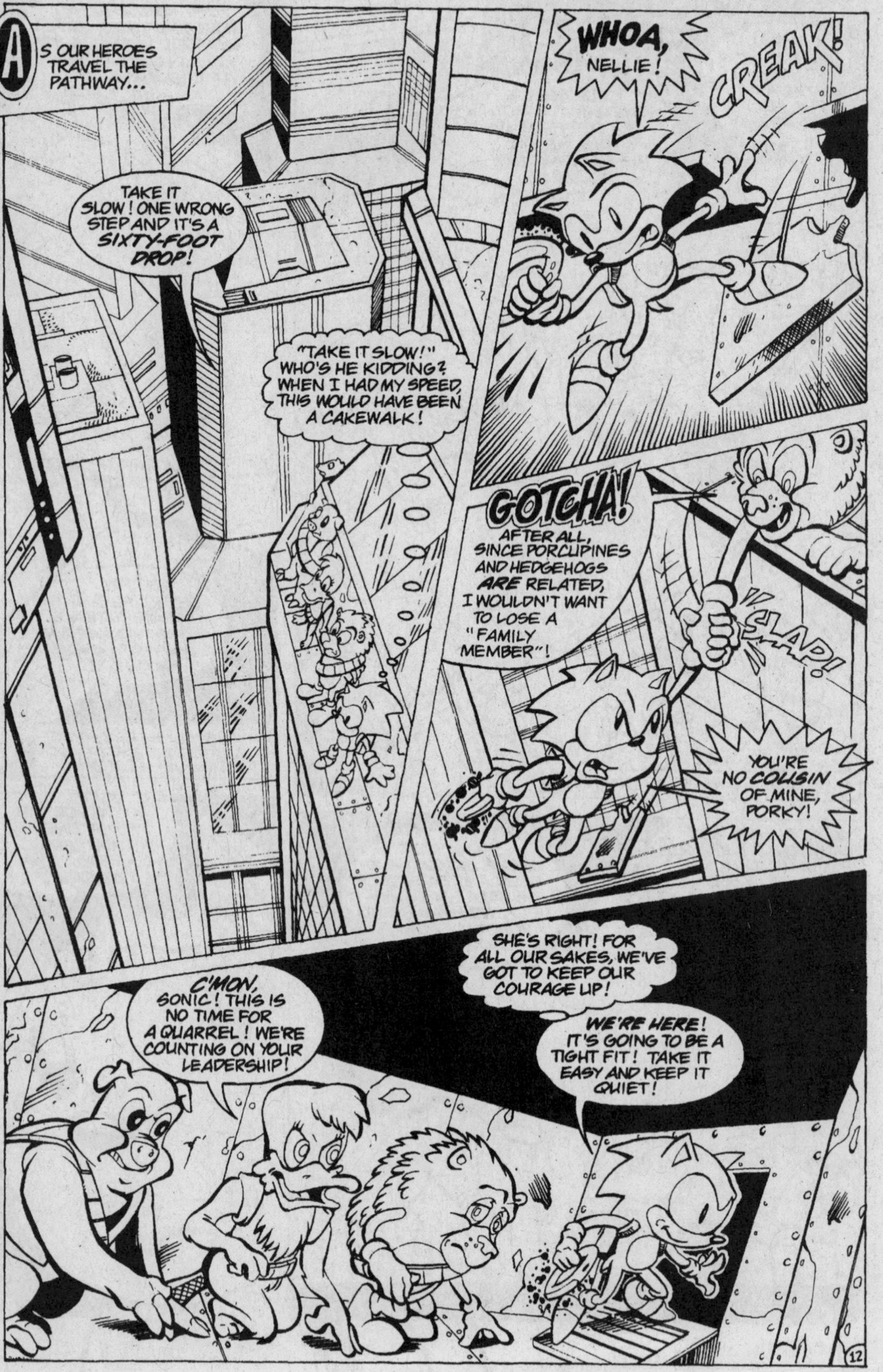
AS OUR HEROES TRAVEL THE PATHWAY...
TAKE IT SLOW! ONE WRONG STEP AND IT'S A SIXTY-FOOT DROP!
"TAKE IT SLOW!" WHO'S HE KIDDING? WHEN I HAD MY SPEED, THIS WOULD HAVE BEEN A CAKEWALK!
WHOA, NELLIE!
CREAK!
GOTCHA! AFTER ALL, SINCE PORCUPINES AND HEDGEHOGS ARE RELATED, I WOULDN'T WANT TO LOSE A "FAMILY MEMBER"!
SLAP!
YOU'RE NO COUSIN OF MINE, PORKY!
C'MON, SONIC! THIS IS NO TIME FOR A QUARREL! WE'RE COUNTING ON YOUR LEADERSHIP!
SHE'S RIGHT! FOR ALL OUR SAKES, WE'VE GOT TO KEEP OUR COURAGE UP!
WE'RE HERE! IT'S GOING TO BE A TIGHT FIT! TAKE IT EASY AND KEEP IT QUIET!
12

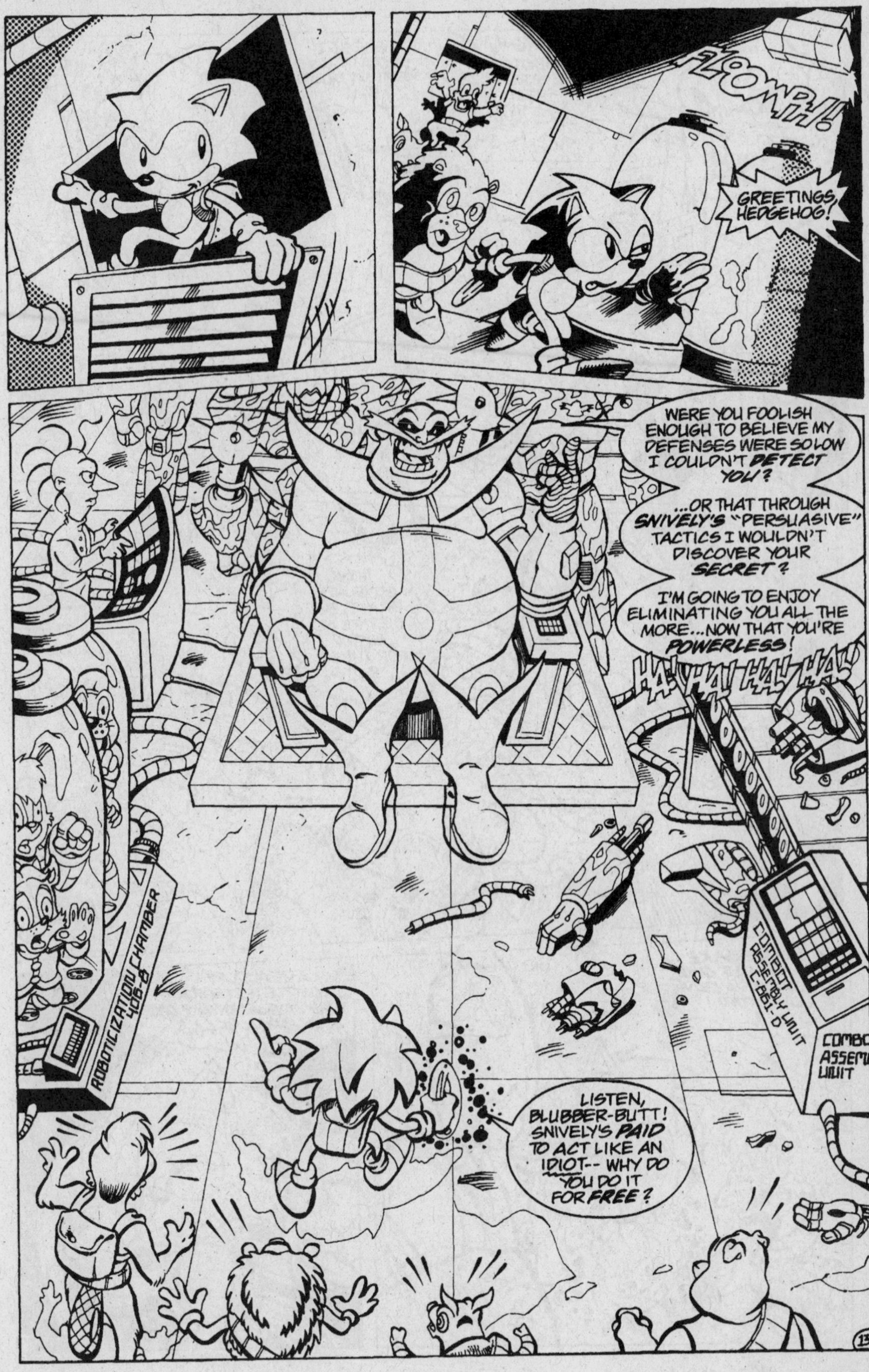
FLOOMP!!
GREETINGS, HEDGEHOG!
WERE YOU FOOLISH ENOUGH TO BELIEVE MY DEFENSES WERE SO LOW I COULDN'T DETECT YOU?
...OR THAT THROUGH SNIVELY'S "PERSUASIVE" TACTICS I WOULDN'T DISCOVER YOUR SECRET?
I'M GOING TO ENJOY ELIMINATING YOU ALL THE MORE...NOW THAT YOU'RE POWERLESS!
HA! HA! HA! HA!
ROBOTICIZATION CHAMBER 406-B
COMBOT ASSEMBLY UNIT C-861-D
COMBO ASSEM UNIT
LISTEN, BLUBBER-BUTT! SNIVELY'S PAID TO ACT LIKE AN IDIOT-- WHY DO YOU DO IT FOR FREE?
13

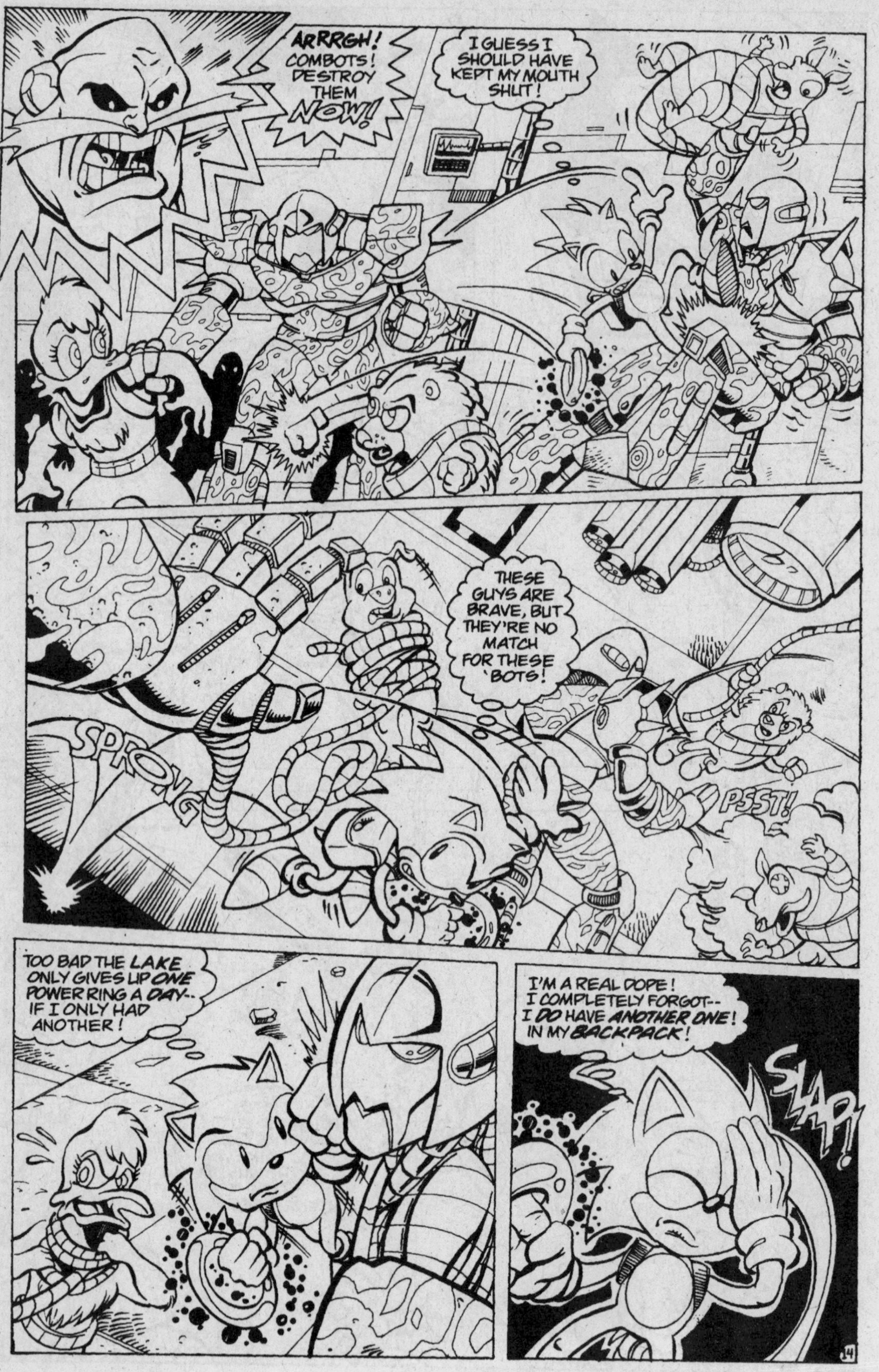
ARRRGH! COMBOTS! DESTROY THEM NOW!
I GUESS I SHOULD HAVE KEPT MY MOUTH SHUT!
THESE GUYS ARE BRAVE, BUT THEY'RE NO MATCH FOR THESE 'BOTS!
SPROING
PSST!
TOO BAD THE LAKE ONLY GIVES UP ONE POWER RING A DAY.. IF I ONLY HAD ANOTHER!
I'M A REAL DOPE! I COMPLETELY FORGOT-- I DO HAVE ANOTHER ONE! IN MY BACKPACK!
SLAP!
14

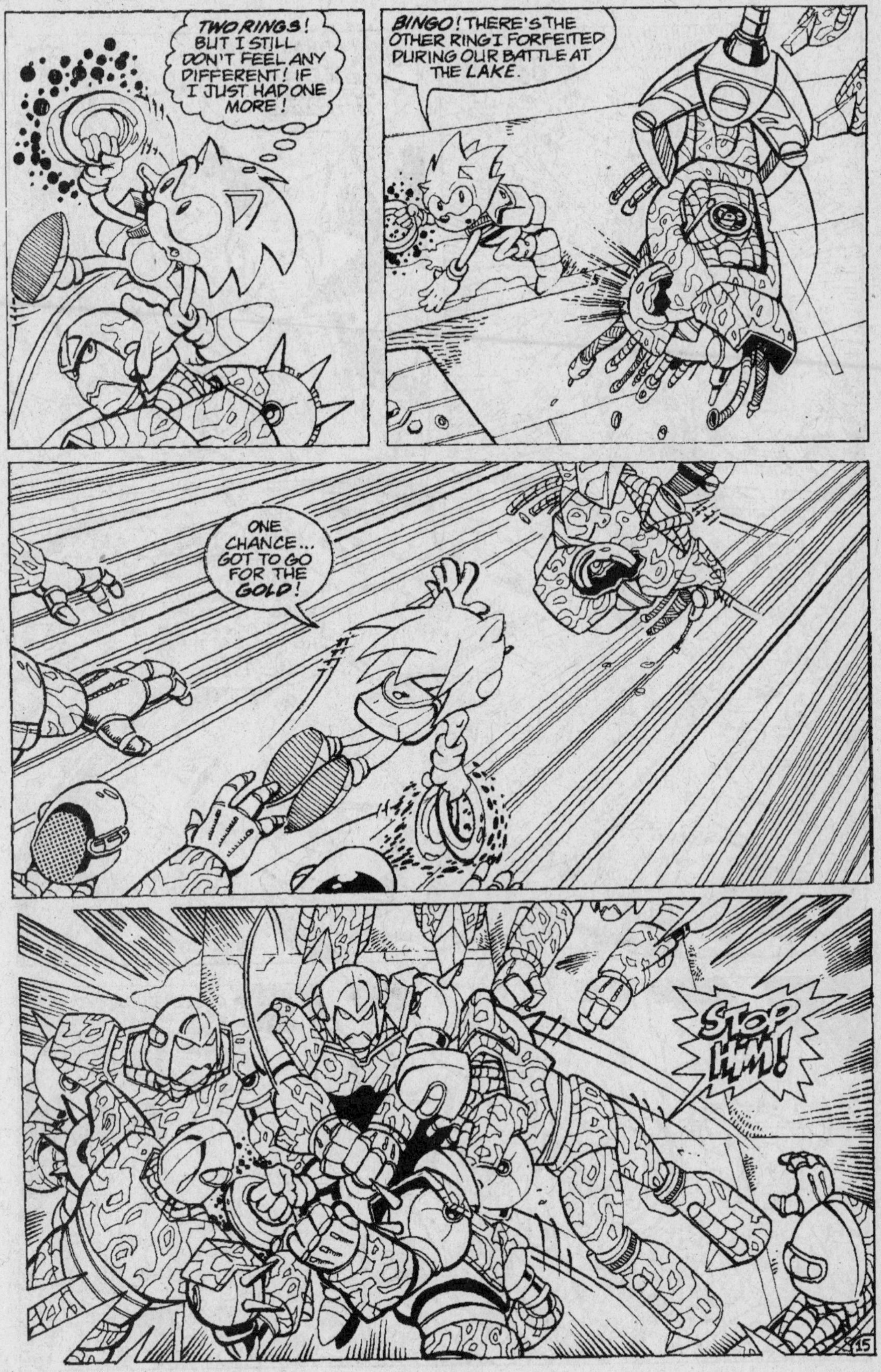
TWO RINGS! BUT I STILL DON'T FEEL ANY DIFFERENT! IF I JUST HAD ONE MORE!
BINGO! THERE'S THE OTHER RING I FORFEITED DURING OUR BATTLE AT THE LAKE.
ONE CHANCE... GOT TO GO FOR THE GOLD!
STOP HIM!
15

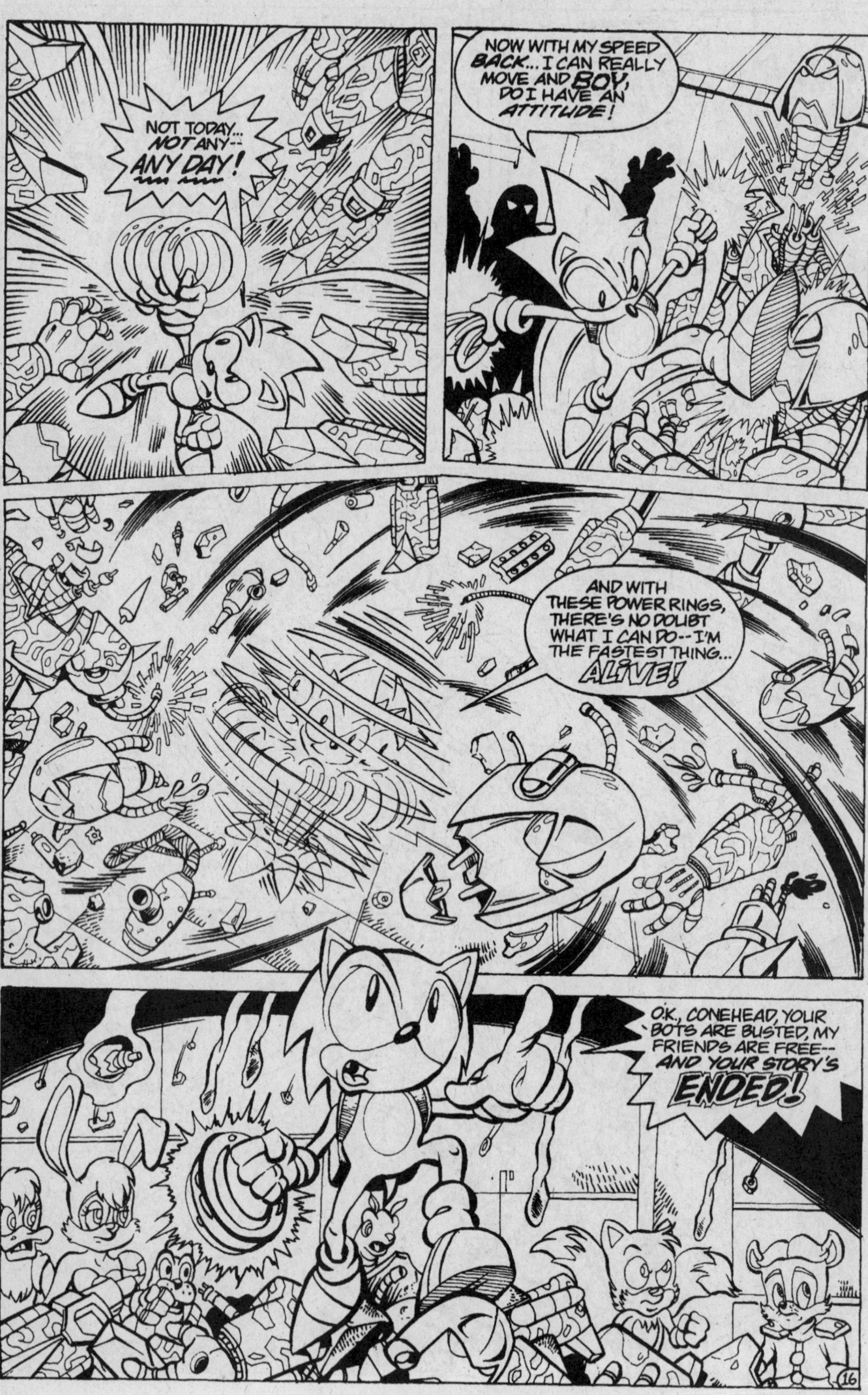
NOT TODAY... NOT ANY-- ANY DAY!
NOW WITH MY SPEED BACK... I CAN REALLY MOVE AND BOY, DO I HAVE AN ATTITUDE!
AND WITH THESE POWER RINGS, THERE'S NO DOUBT WHAT I CAN DO--I'M THE FASTEST THING... ALIVE!
O.K., CONEHEAD, YOUR BOTS ARE BUSTED, MY FRIENDS ARE FREE-- AND YOUR STORY'S ENDED!
16

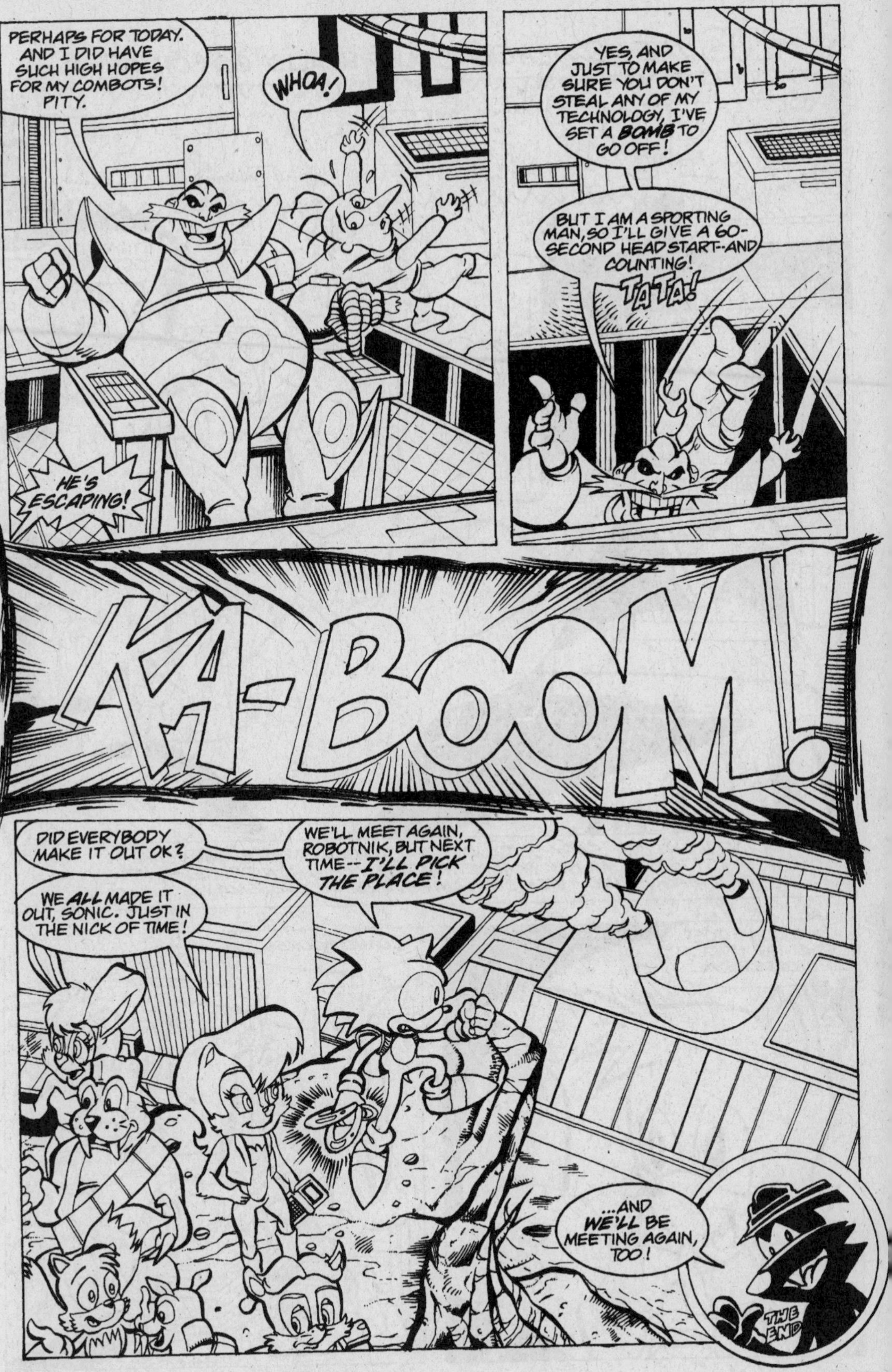
PERHAPS FOR TODAY. AND I DID HAVE SUCH HIGH HOPES FOR MY COMBOTS! PITY.
WHOA!
HE'S ESCAPING!
YES, AND JUST TO MAKE SURE YOU DON'T STEAL ANY OF MY TECHNOLOGY, I'VE SET A BOMB TO GO OFF!
BUT I AM A SPORTING MAN, SO I'LL GIVE A 60-SECOND HEAD START--AND COUNTING!
TA TA!
KA-BOOM!
DID EVERYBODY MAKE IT OUT OK?
WE ALL MADE IT OUT, SONIC. JUST IN THE NICK OF TIME!
WE'LL MEET AGAIN, ROBOTNIK, BUT NEXT TIME-- I'LL PICK THE PLACE!
...AND WE'LL BE MEETING AGAIN, TOO!
THE END

SONIC THE HEDGEHOG COULD REALLY GO FOR A FEW...

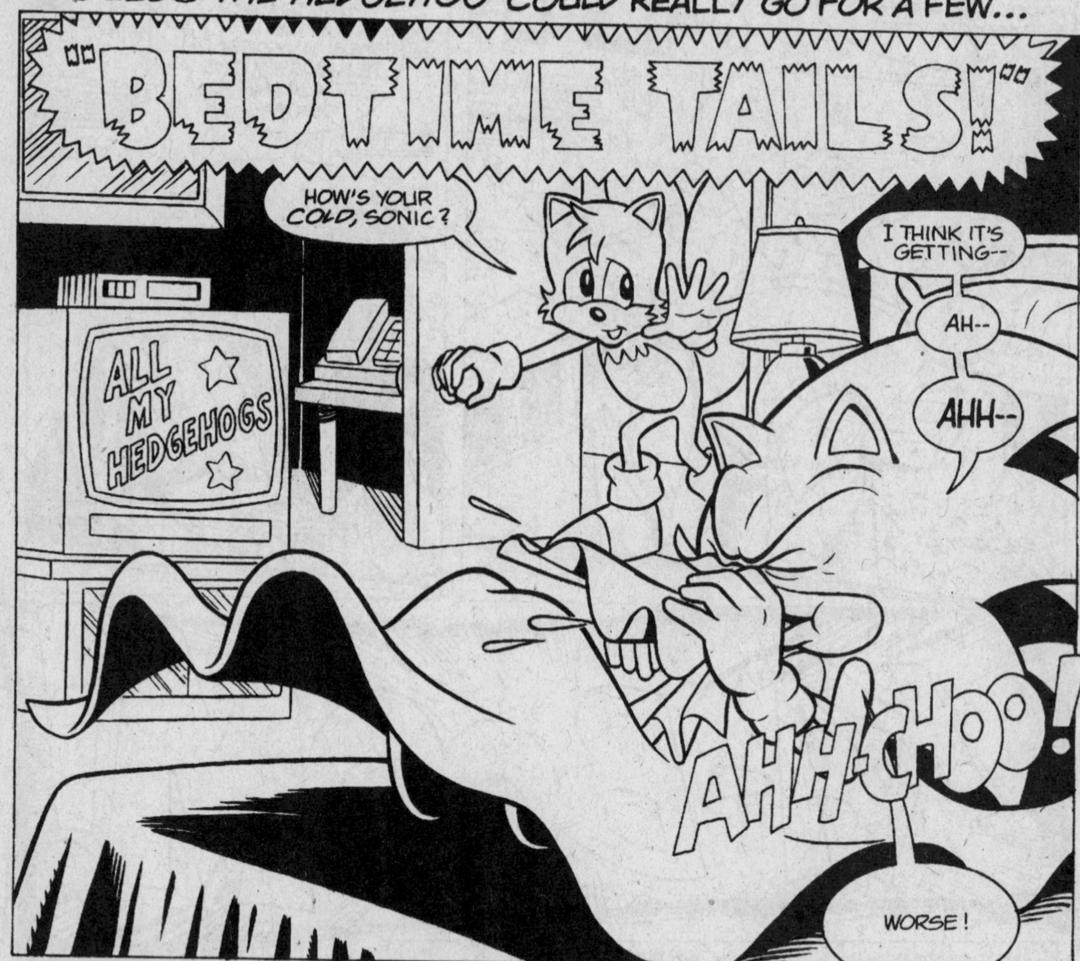
"BEDTIME TAILS!"
HOW'S YOUR COLD, SONIC?
ALL MY HEDGEHOGS
I THINK IT'S GETTING--
AH--
AHH--
AHH-CHOO!
WORSE!

A SCINTILLATING SAGA OF TRIUMPH AND TRAGEDY CRAFTED WITH CARE IN THE MIGHTY MOBIUS MANNER BY MIKE KANTEROVICH & KEN PENDERS, WITH JON D'AGOSTINO, VICKIE WILLIAMS, & BARRY GROSSMAN.

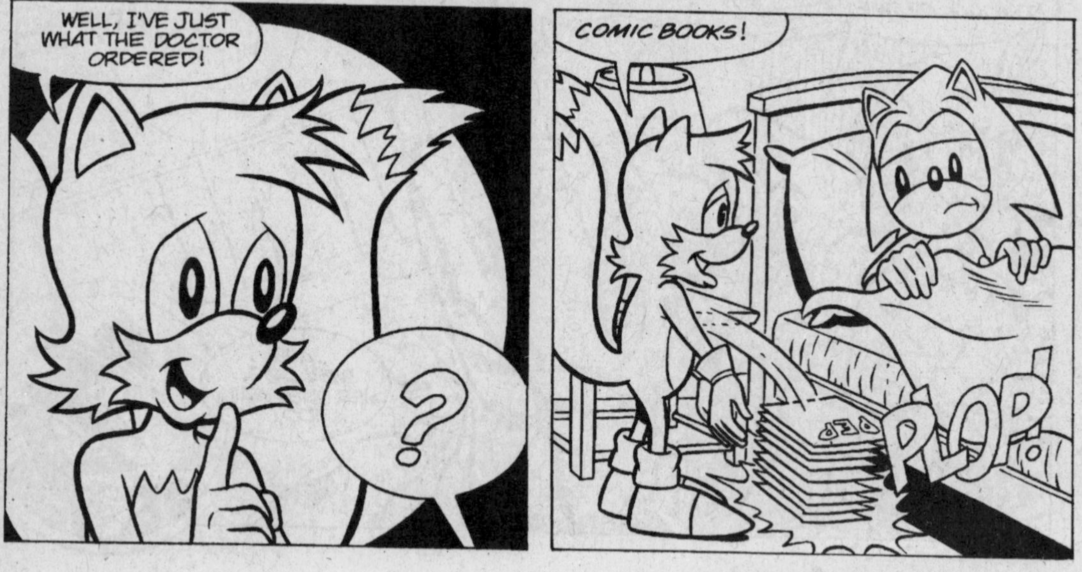
WELL, I'VE JUST WHAT THE DOCTOR ORDERED!
?
COMIC BOOKS!
PLOP!

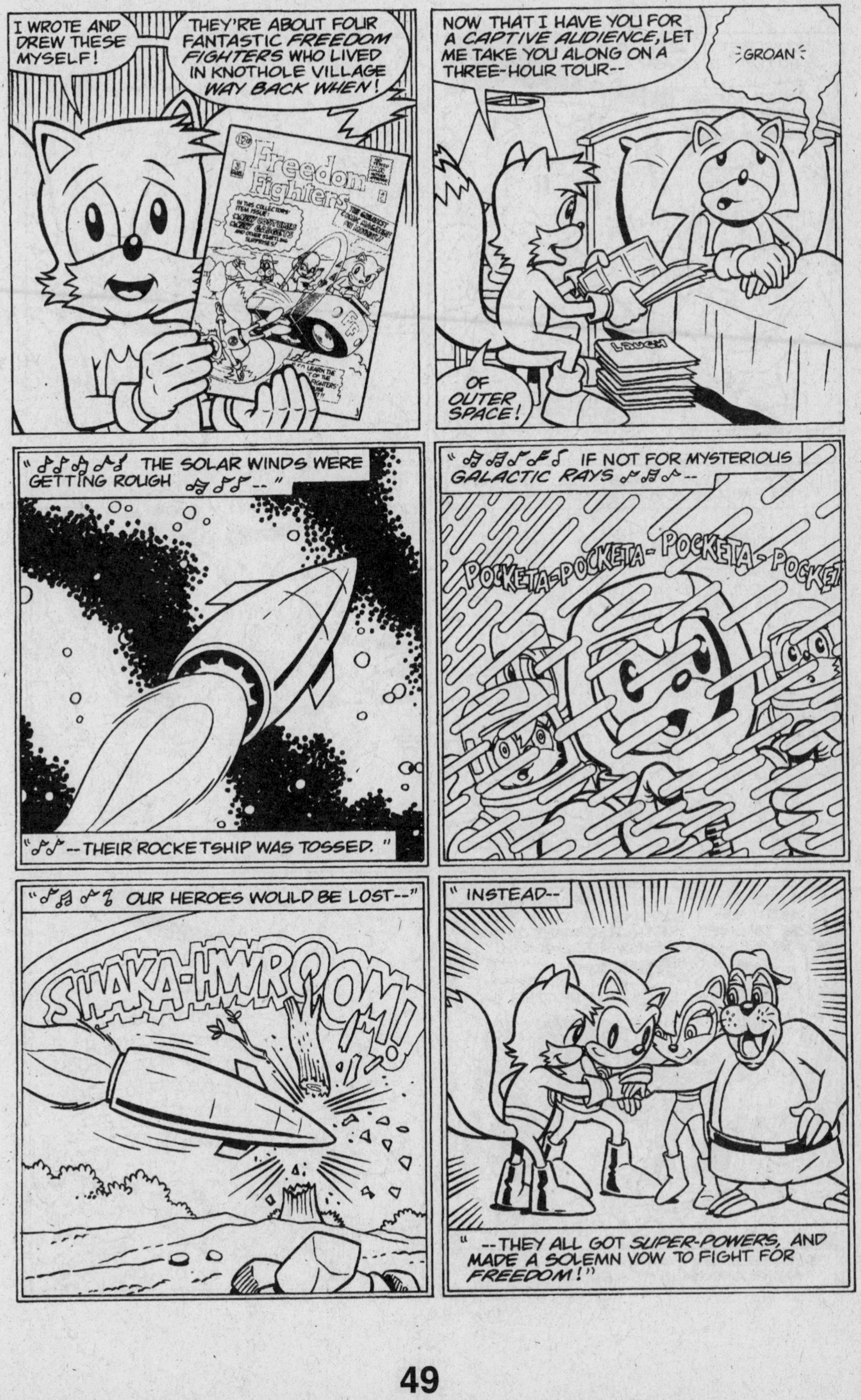
I WROTE AND DREW THESE MYSELF!
THEY'RE ABOUT FOUR FANTASTIC *FREEDOM FIGHTERS* WHO LIVED IN KNOTHOLE VILLAGE *WAY BACK WHEN*!
Freedom Fighters
NOW THAT I HAVE YOU FOR A *CAPTIVE AUDIENCE*, LET ME TAKE YOU ALONG ON A THREE-HOUR TOUR--
GROAN
OF OUTER SPACE!
"♪♫♪♫ THE SOLAR WINDS WERE GETTING ROUGH ♪♫♪--"
"♪♪ --THEIR ROCKETSHIP WAS TOSSED."
"♪♫♪♫ IF NOT FOR MYSTERIOUS *GALACTIC RAYS* ♪♫♪--
POCKETA-POCKETA-POCKETA-POCKET
"♪♫♪♪ OUR HEROES WOULD BE LOST--"
SHAKA-HWROOM!
"INSTEAD--
"--THEY ALL GOT *SUPER-POWERS*, AND MADE A SOLEMN VOW TO FIGHT FOR *FREEDOM*!"

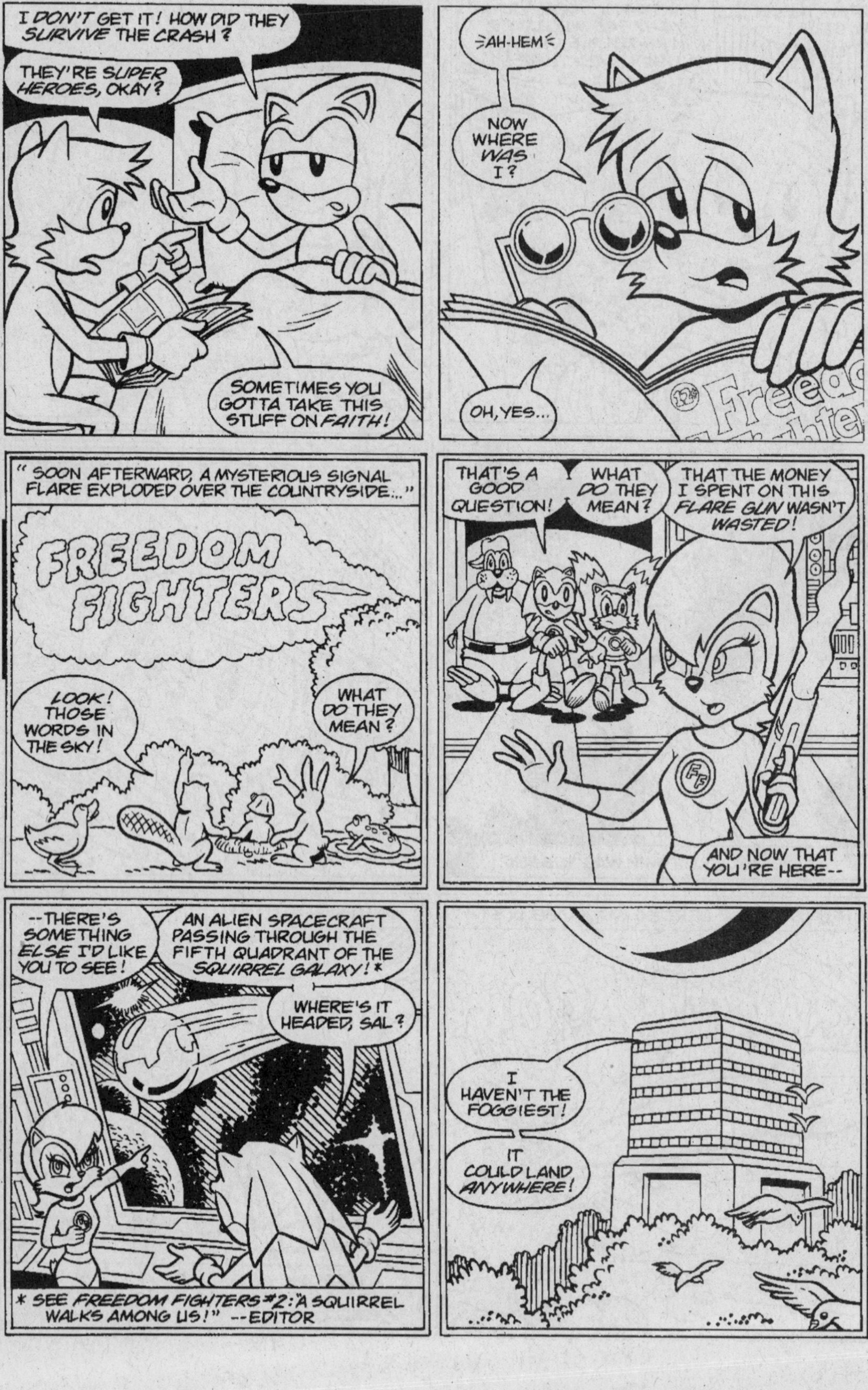
I DON'T GET IT! HOW DID THEY SURVIVE THE CRASH?
THEY'RE SUPER HEROES, OKAY?
SOMETIMES YOU GOTTA TAKE THIS STUFF ON FAITH!
AH-HEM
NOW WHERE WAS I?
OH, YES...
"SOON AFTERWARD, A MYSTERIOUS SIGNAL FLARE EXPLODED OVER THE COUNTRYSIDE..."
FREEDOM FIGHTERS
LOOK! THOSE WORDS IN THE SKY!
WHAT DO THEY MEAN?
THAT'S A GOOD QUESTION!
WHAT DO THEY MEAN?
THAT THE MONEY I SPENT ON THIS FLARE GUN WASN'T WASTED!
AND NOW THAT YOU'RE HERE--
--THERE'S SOMETHING ELSE I'D LIKE YOU TO SEE!
AN ALIEN SPACECRAFT PASSING THROUGH THE FIFTH QUADRANT OF THE SQUIRREL GALAXY!*
WHERE'S IT HEADED, SAL?
* SEE FREEDOM FIGHTERS #2: "A SQUIRREL WALKS AMONG US!" --EDITOR
I HAVEN'T THE FOGGIEST!
IT COULD LAND ANYWHERE!

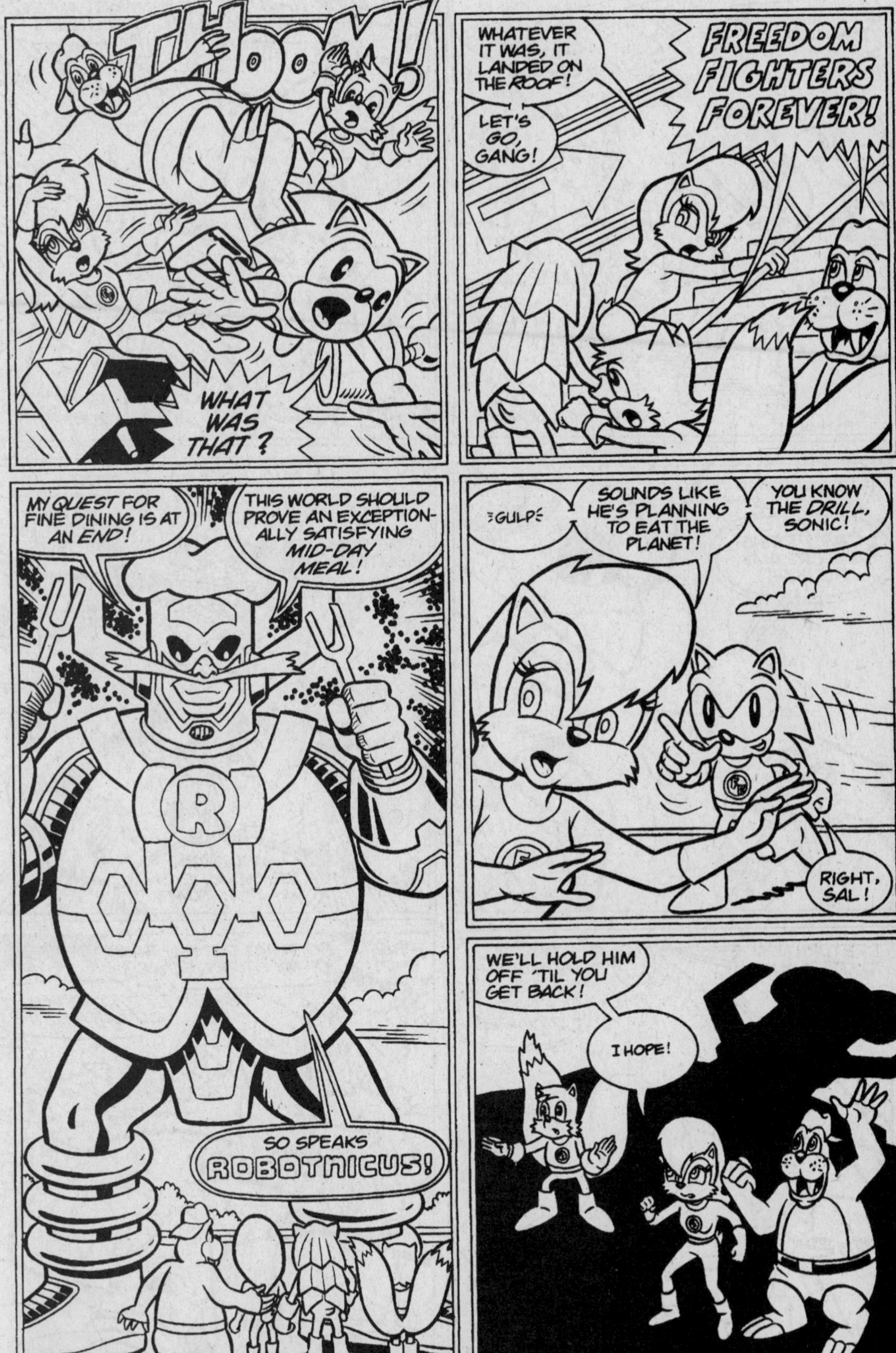
THOOM!
WHAT WAS THAT?
WHATEVER IT WAS, IT LANDED ON THE ROOF!
LET'S GO, GANG!
FREEDOM FIGHTERS FOREVER!
MY QUEST FOR FINE DINING IS AT AN END!
THIS WORLD SHOULD PROVE AN EXCEPTIONALLY SATISFYING MID-DAY MEAL!
SO SPEAKS ROBOTNICUS!
GULP
SOUNDS LIKE HE'S PLANNING TO EAT THE PLANET!
YOU KNOW THE DRILL, SONIC!
RIGHT, SAL!
WE'LL HOLD HIM OFF 'TIL YOU GET BACK!
I HOPE!

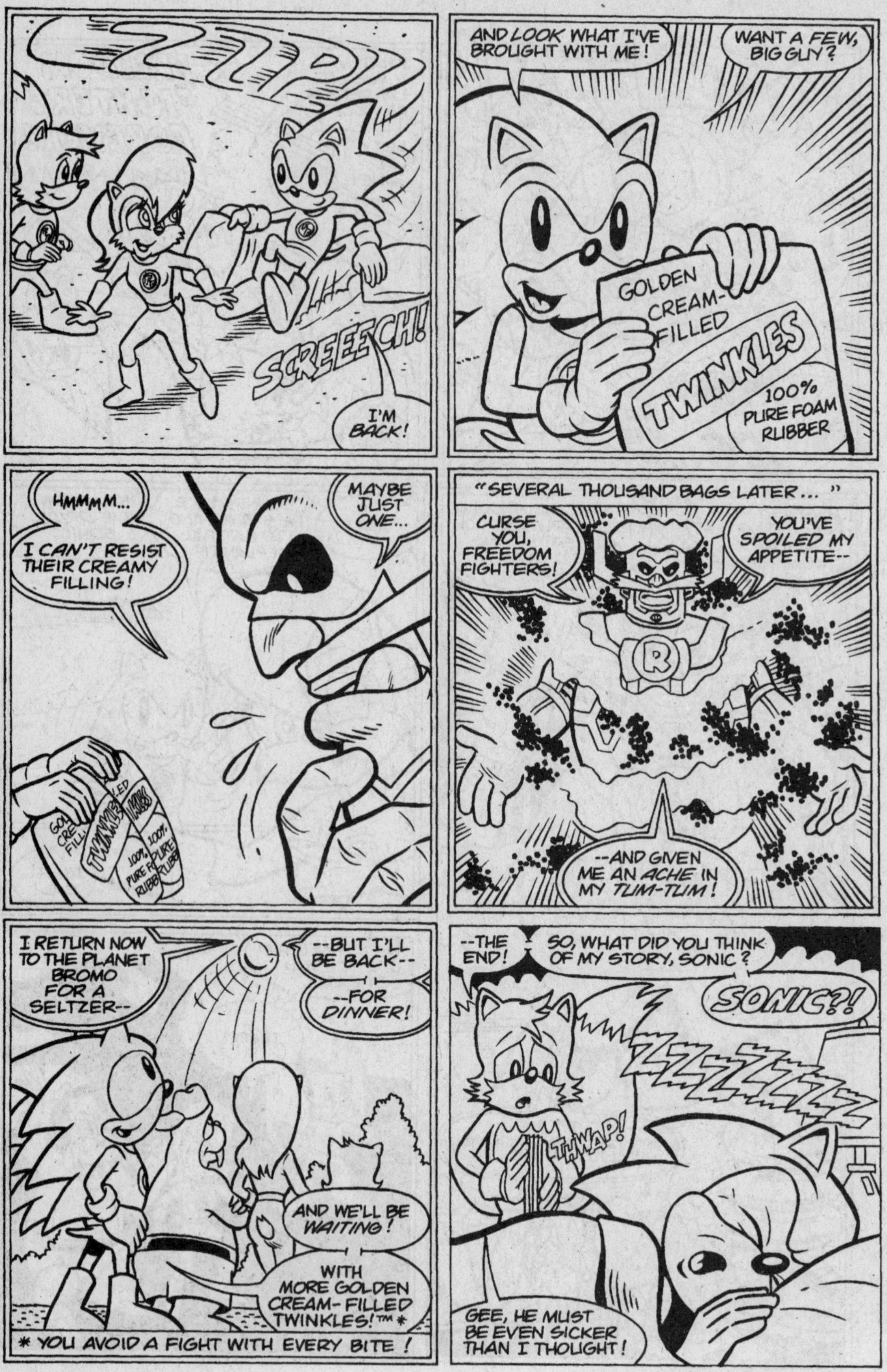
ZZIP!
SCREEEECH!
I'M BACK!
AND LOOK WHAT I'VE BROUGHT WITH ME!
WANT A FEW, BIG GUY?
GOLDEN CREAM-FILLED
TWINKLES
100% PURE FOAM RUBBER
HMMMM...
I CAN'T RESIST THEIR CREAMY FILLING!
MAYBE JUST ONE...
"SEVERAL THOUSAND BAGS LATER..."
CURSE YOU, FREEDOM FIGHTERS!
YOU'VE SPOILED MY APPETITE--
--AND GIVEN ME AN ACHE IN MY TUM-TUM!
I RETURN NOW TO THE PLANET BROMO FOR A SELTZER--
--BUT I'LL BE BACK--
--FOR DINNER!
AND WE'LL BE WAITING!
WITH MORE GOLDEN CREAM-FILLED TWINKLES!™ *
* YOU AVOID A FIGHT WITH EVERY BITE!
--THE END!
SO, WHAT DID YOU THINK OF MY STORY, SONIC?
SONIC?!
ZZZZZZZ
THWAP!
GEE, HE MUST BE EVEN SICKER THAN I THOUGHT!

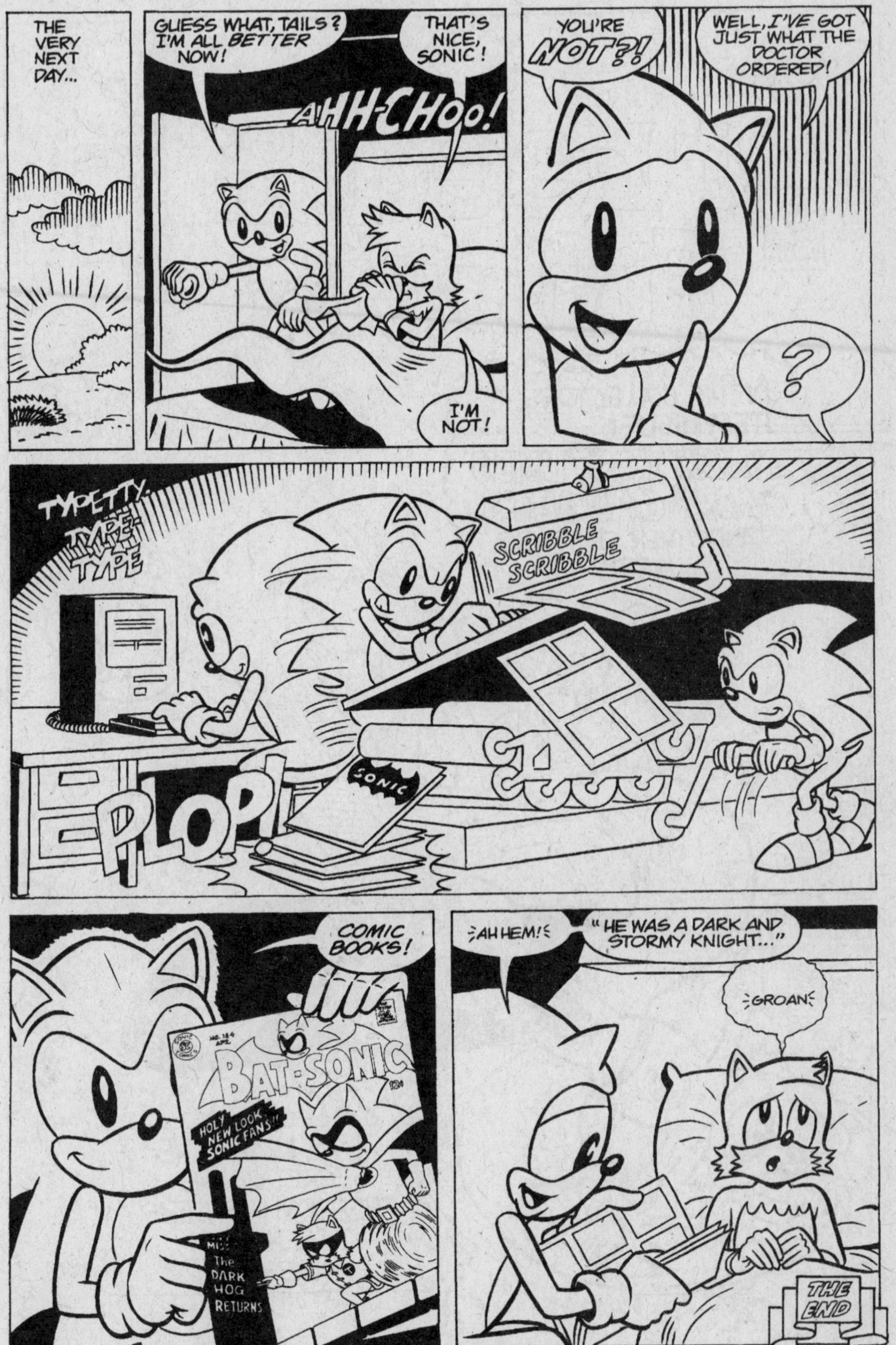
THE VERY NEXT DAY...
GUESS WHAT, TAILS? I'M ALL BETTER NOW!
THAT'S NICE, SONIC!
AHH-CHOO!
I'M NOT!
YOU'RE NOT?!
WELL, I'VE GOT JUST WHAT THE DOCTOR ORDERED!
?
TYPETTY-TYPE-TYPE
SCRIBBLE SCRIBBLE
SONIC
PLOP!
COMIC BOOKS!
BAT-SONIC
HOLY NEW LOOK SONIC FANS!!
The DARK HOG RETURNS
AHHEM!
"HE WAS A DARK AND STORMY KNIGHT..."
GROAN
THE END

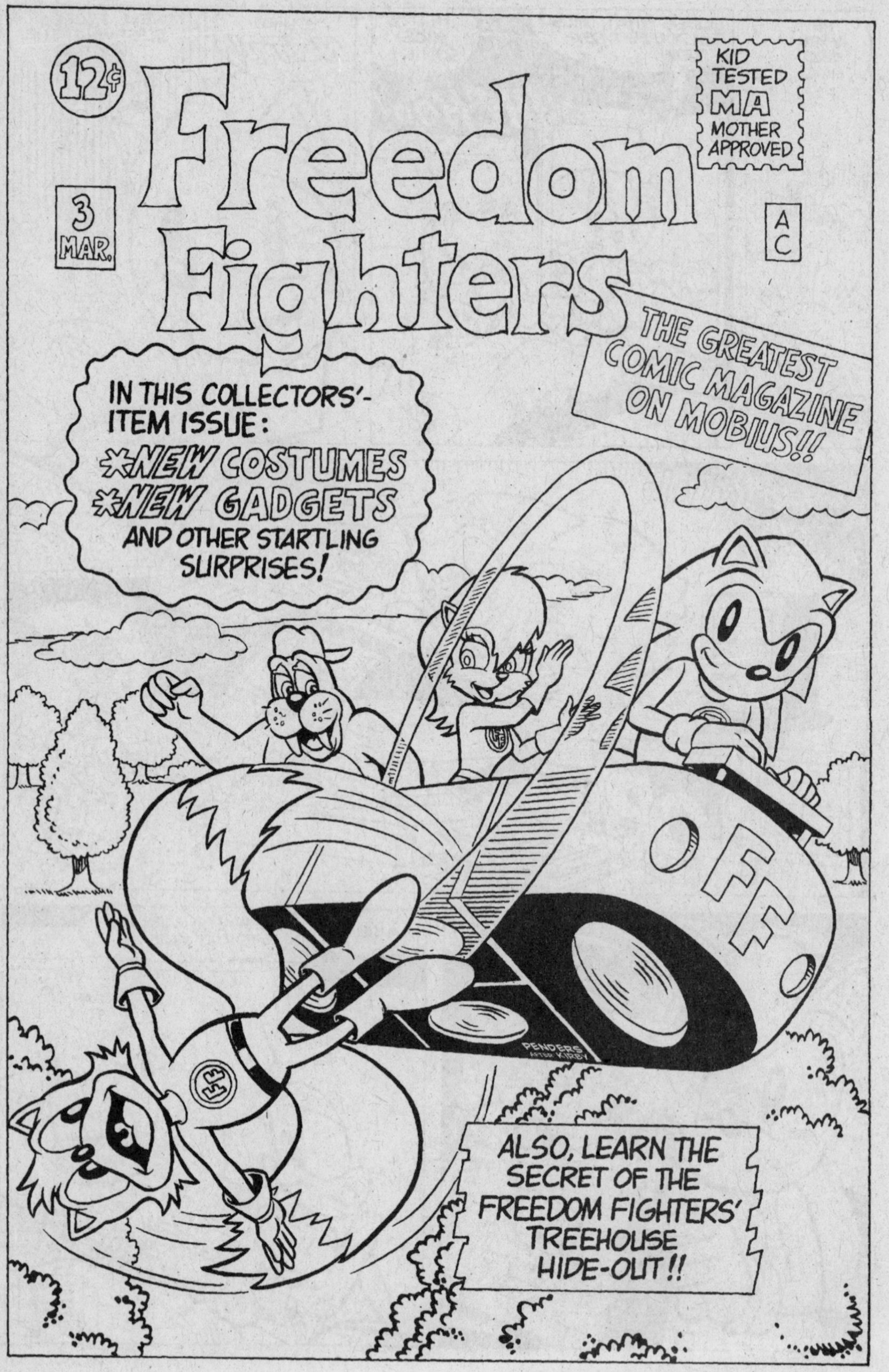
12¢
Freedom Fighters
KID TESTED MA MOTHER APPROVED
3 MAR.
A C
THE GREATEST COMIC MAGAZINE ON MOBIUS!!
IN THIS COLLECTORS'-ITEM ISSUE:
*NEW COSTUMES
*NEW GADGETS
AND OTHER STARTLING SURPRISES!
FF
PENDERS AFTER KIRBY
ALSO, LEARN THE SECRET OF THE FREEDOM FIGHTERS' TREEHOUSE HIDE-OUT!!

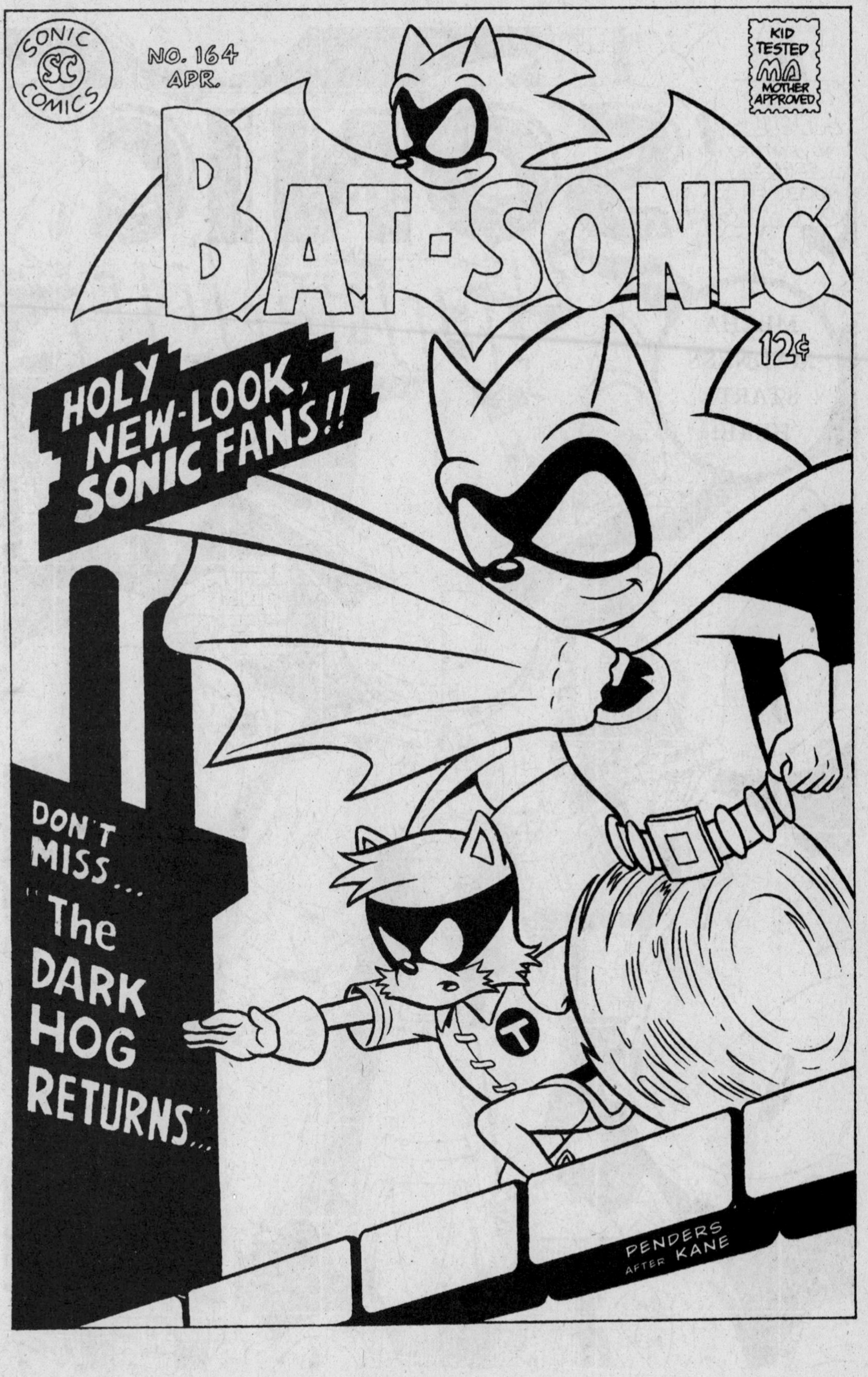
SONIC SC COMICS
NO. 164
APR.
KID TESTED
MA
MOTHER APPROVED
BAT-SONIC
12¢
HOLY NEW-LOOK, SONIC FANS!!
DON'T MISS... "The DARK HOG RETURNS"...
PENDERS AFTER KANE

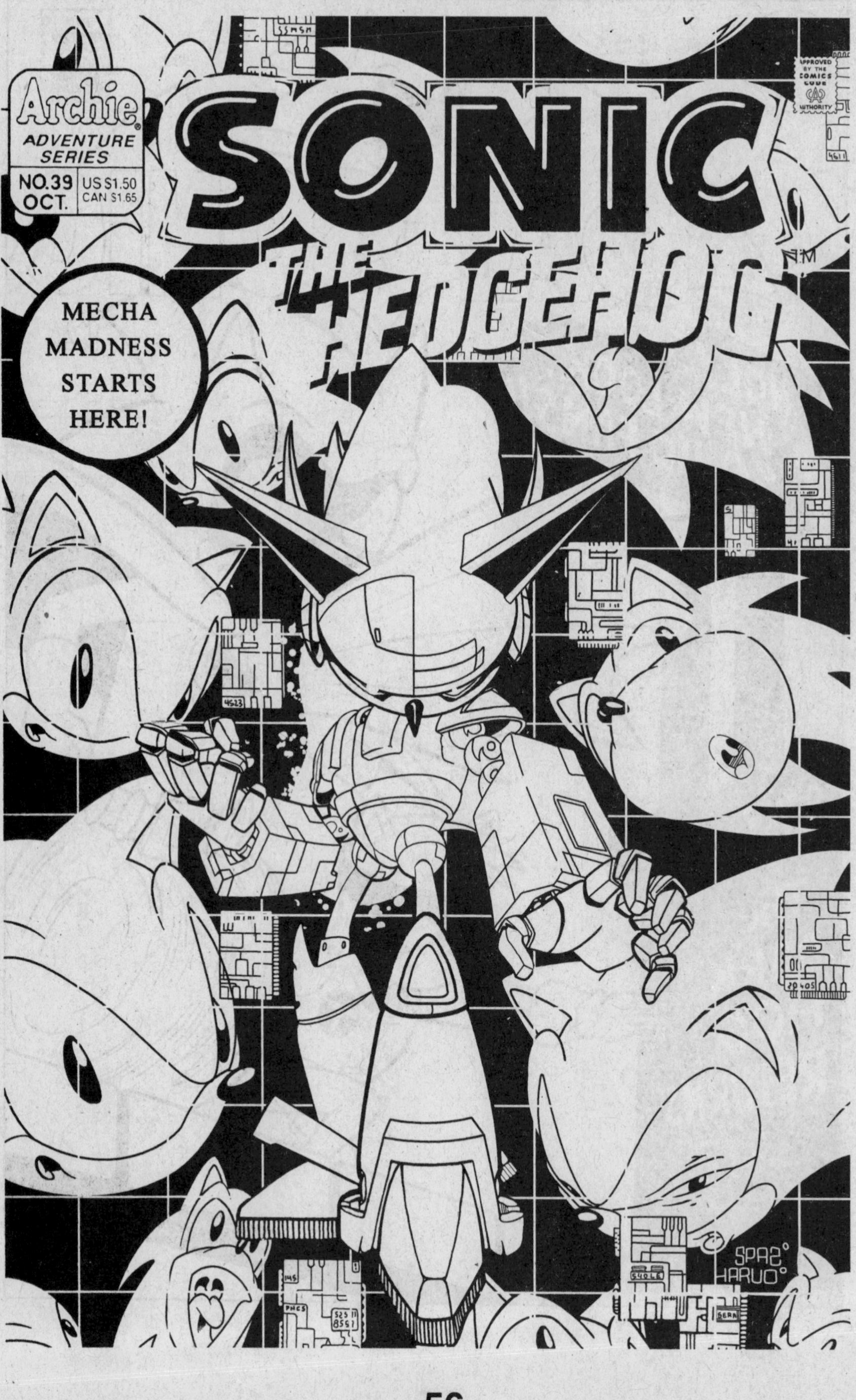
Archie
ADVENTURE SERIES
NO.39 OCT.
US $1.50
CAN $1.65
APPROVED BY THE COMICS CODE AUTHORITY
SONIC THE HEDGEHOG
TM
MECHA MADNESS STARTS HERE!
SPAZ
HARUO

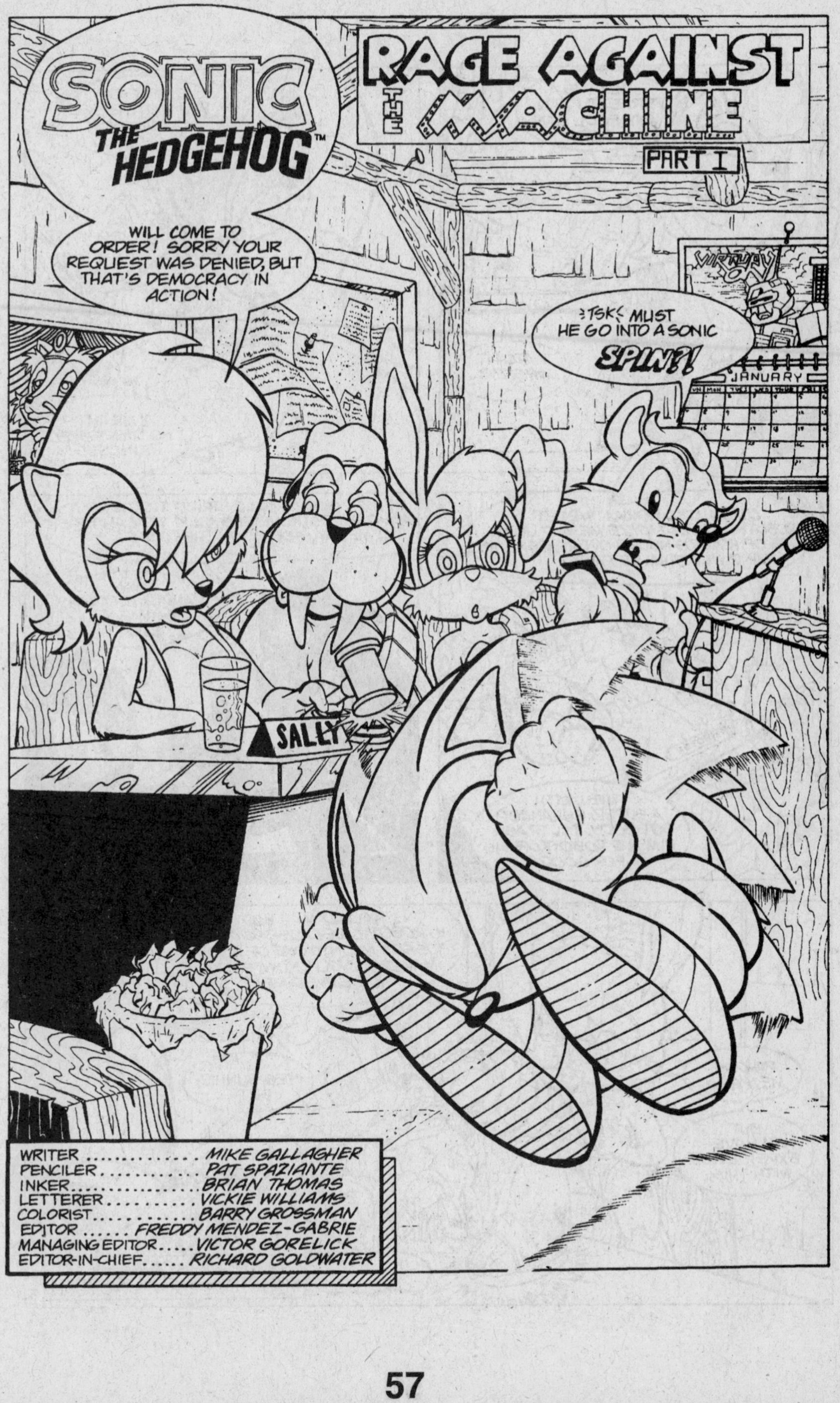
SONIC THE HEDGEHOG™
WILL COME TO ORDER! SORRY YOUR REQUEST WAS DENIED, BUT THAT'S DEMOCRACY IN ACTION!
RAGE AGAINST THE MACHINE
PART I
TSK MUST HE GO INTO A SONIC SPIN?!
JANUARY
SALLY
WRITER............MIKE GALLAGHER
PENCILER............PAT SPAZIANTE
INKER............BRIAN THOMAS
LETTERER............VICKIE WILLIAMS
COLORIST............BARRY GROSSMAN
EDITOR......FREDDY MENDEZ-GABRIE
MANAGING EDITOR.....VICTOR GORELICK
EDITOR-IN-CHIEF......RICHARD GOLDWATER

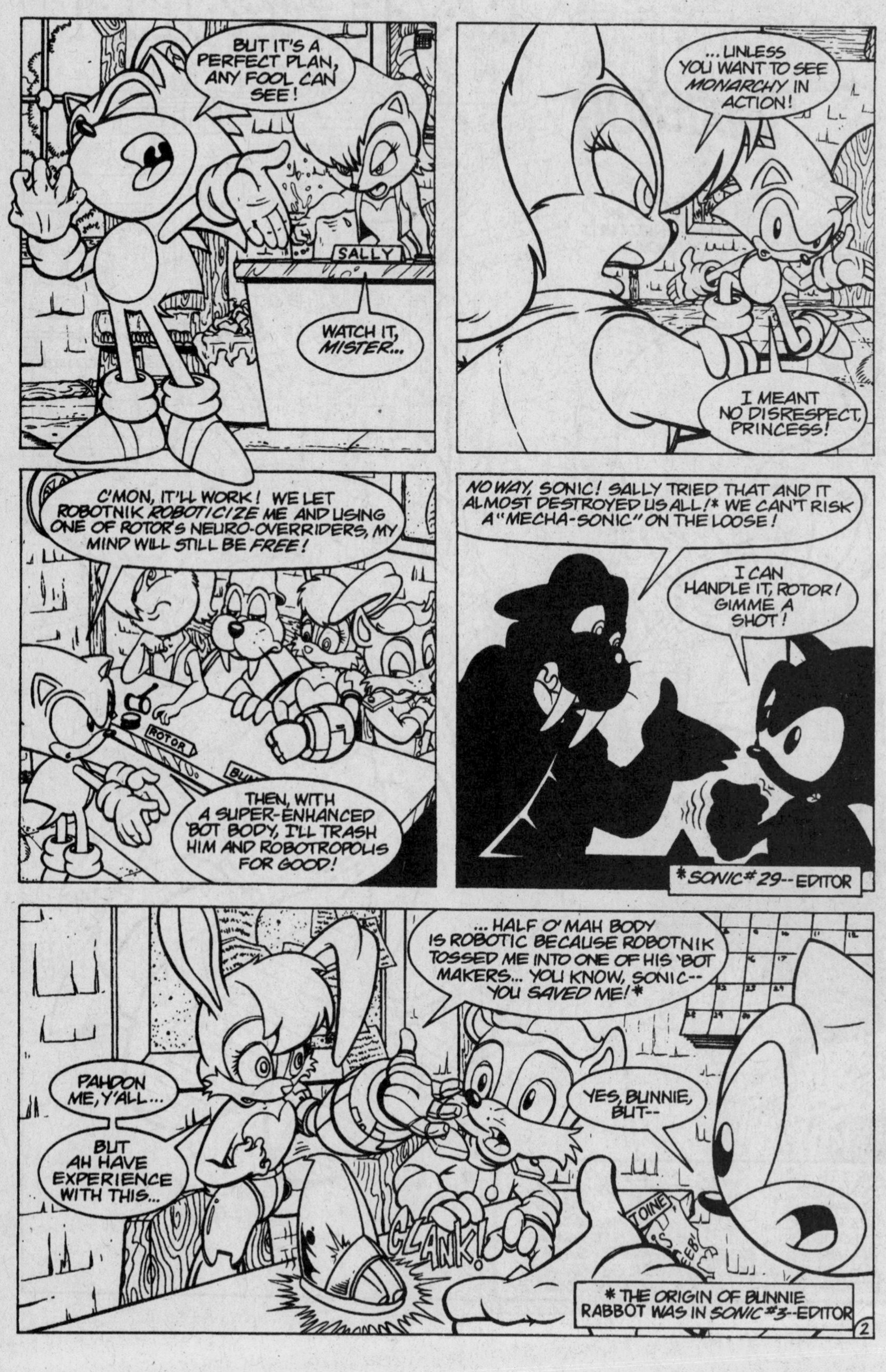
BUT IT'S A PERFECT PLAN, ANY FOOL CAN SEE!
SALLY
WATCH IT, MISTER...
...UNLESS YOU WANT TO SEE MONARCHY IN ACTION!
I MEANT NO DISRESPECT, PRINCESS!
C'MON, IT'LL WORK! WE LET ROBOTNIK ROBOTICIZE ME AND USING ONE OF ROTOR'S NEURO-OVERRIDERS, MY MIND WILL STILL BE FREE!
ROTOR
THEN, WITH A SUPER-ENHANCED 'BOT BODY, I'LL TRASH HIM AND ROBOTROPOLIS FOR GOOD!
NO WAY, SONIC! SALLY TRIED THAT AND IT ALMOST DESTROYED US ALL!* WE CAN'T RISK A "MECHA-SONIC" ON THE LOOSE!
I CAN HANDLE IT, ROTOR! GIMME A SHOT!
*SONIC #29--EDITOR
PAHDON ME, Y'ALL...
BUT AH HAVE EXPERIENCE WITH THIS...
...HALF O' MAH BODY IS ROBOTIC BECAUSE ROBOTNIK TOSSED ME INTO ONE OF HIS 'BOT MAKERS... YOU KNOW, SONIC-- YOU SAVED ME!*
YES, BUNNIE, BUT--
CLANK!
* THE ORIGIN OF BUNNIE RABBOT WAS IN SONIC #3--EDITOR
2

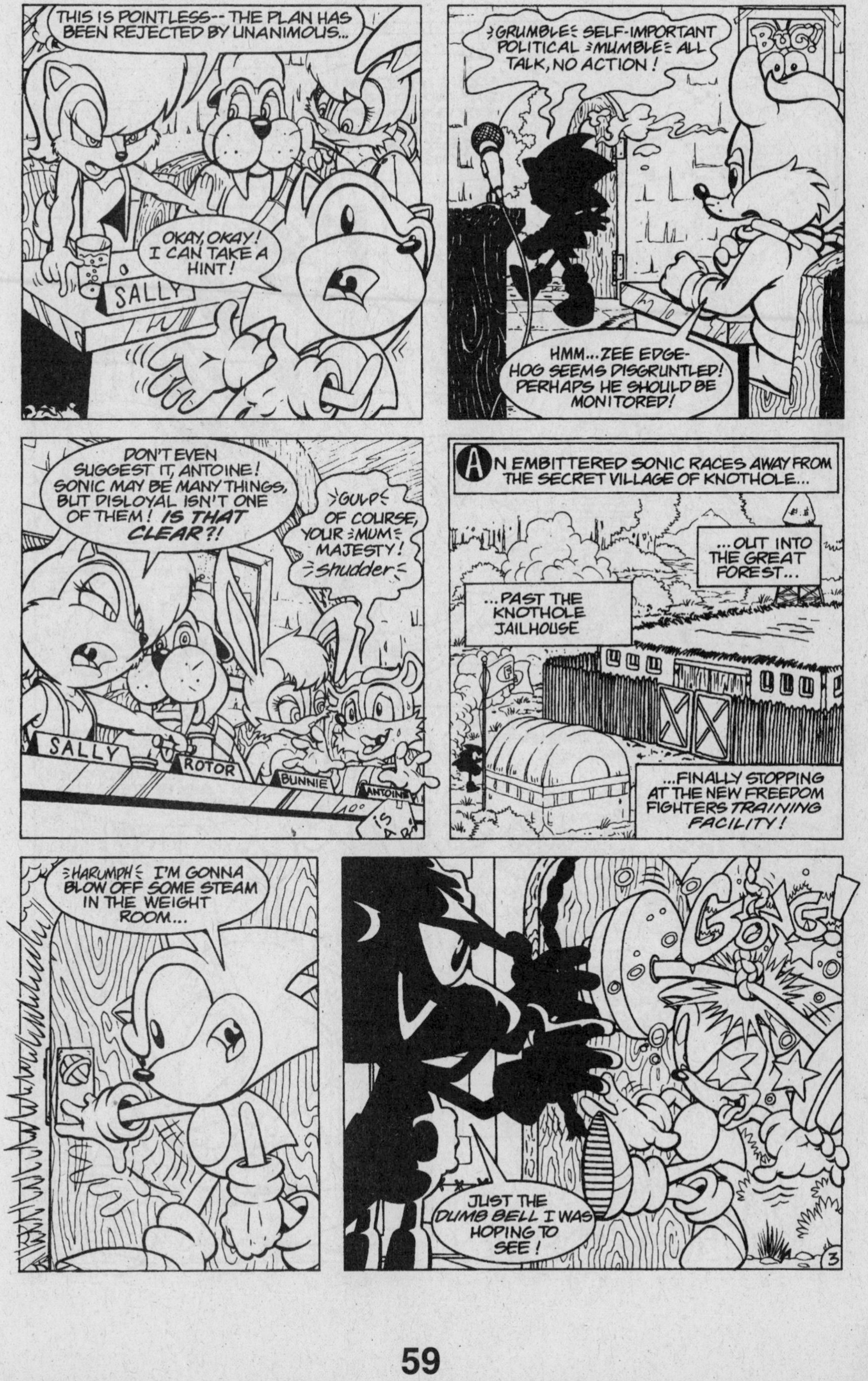

THIS IS POINTLESS-- THE PLAN HAS BEEN REJECTED BY UNANIMOUS...
OKAY, OKAY! I CAN TAKE A HINT!
SALLY
GRUMBLE SELF-IMPORTANT POLITICAL MUMBLE ALL TALK, NO ACTION!
HMM... ZEE EDGE-HOG SEEMS DISGRUNTLED! PERHAPS HE SHOULD BE MONITORED!
DON'T EVEN SUGGEST IT, ANTOINE! SONIC MAY BE MANY THINGS, BUT DISLOYAL ISN'T ONE OF THEM! IS THAT CLEAR?!
GULP OF COURSE, YOUR MUM MAJESTY! Shudder
SALLY
ROTOR
BUNNIE
ANTOINE
AN EMBITTERED SONIC RACES AWAY FROM THE SECRET VILLAGE OF KNOTHOLE...
...OUT INTO THE GREAT FOREST...
...PAST THE KNOTHOLE JAILHOUSE
...FINALLY STOPPING AT THE NEW FREEDOM FIGHTERS TRAINING FACILITY!
HARUMPH I'M GONNA BLOW OFF SOME STEAM IN THE WEIGHT ROOM...
GONG!
JUST THE DUMB BELL I WAS HOPING TO SEE!
3

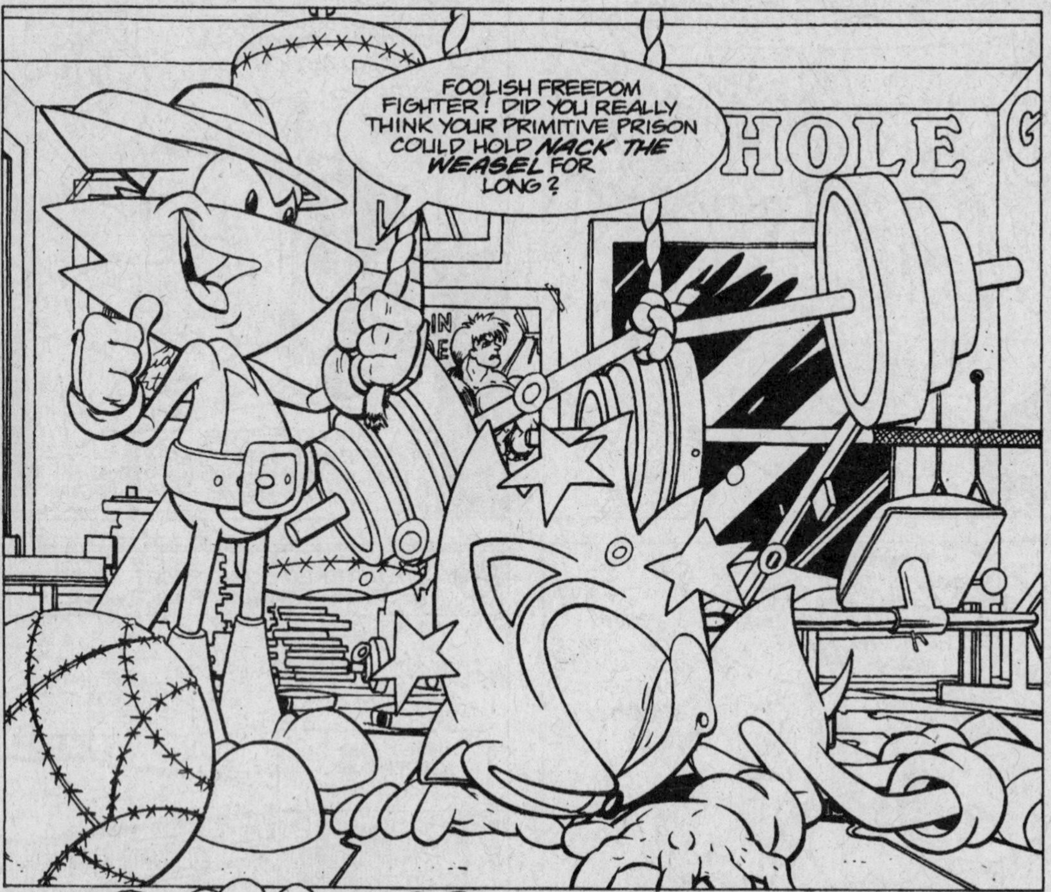
FOOLISH FREEDOM FIGHTER! DID YOU REALLY THINK YOUR PRIMITIVE PRISON COULD HOLD NACK THE WEASEL FOR LONG?
HOLE

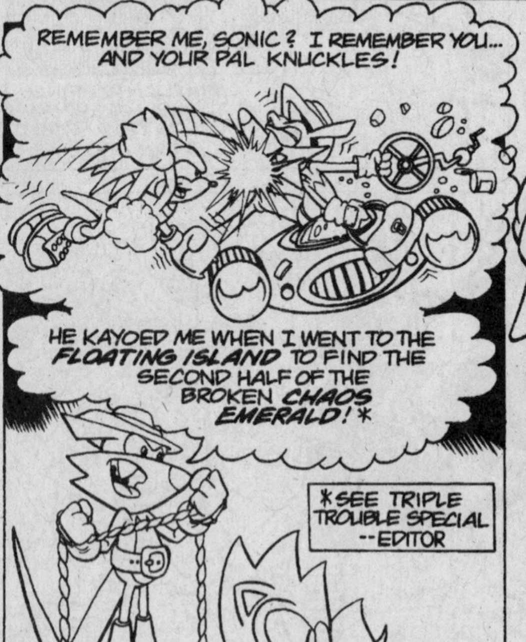
REMEMBER ME, SONIC? I REMEMBER YOU... AND YOUR PAL KNUCKLES!
HE KAYOED ME WHEN I WENT TO THE FLOATING ISLAND TO FIND THE SECOND HALF OF THE BROKEN CHAOS EMERALD! *
* SEE TRIPLE TROUBLE SPECIAL --EDITOR

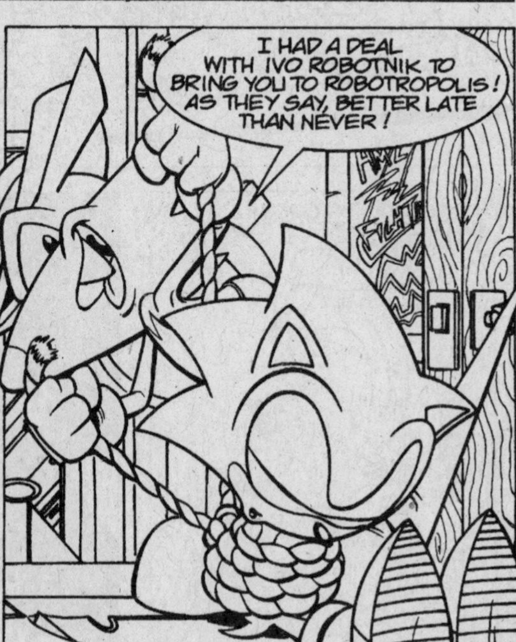
I HAD A DEAL WITH IVO ROBOTNIK TO BRING YOU TO ROBOTROPOLIS! AS THEY SAY, BETTER LATE THAN NEVER!

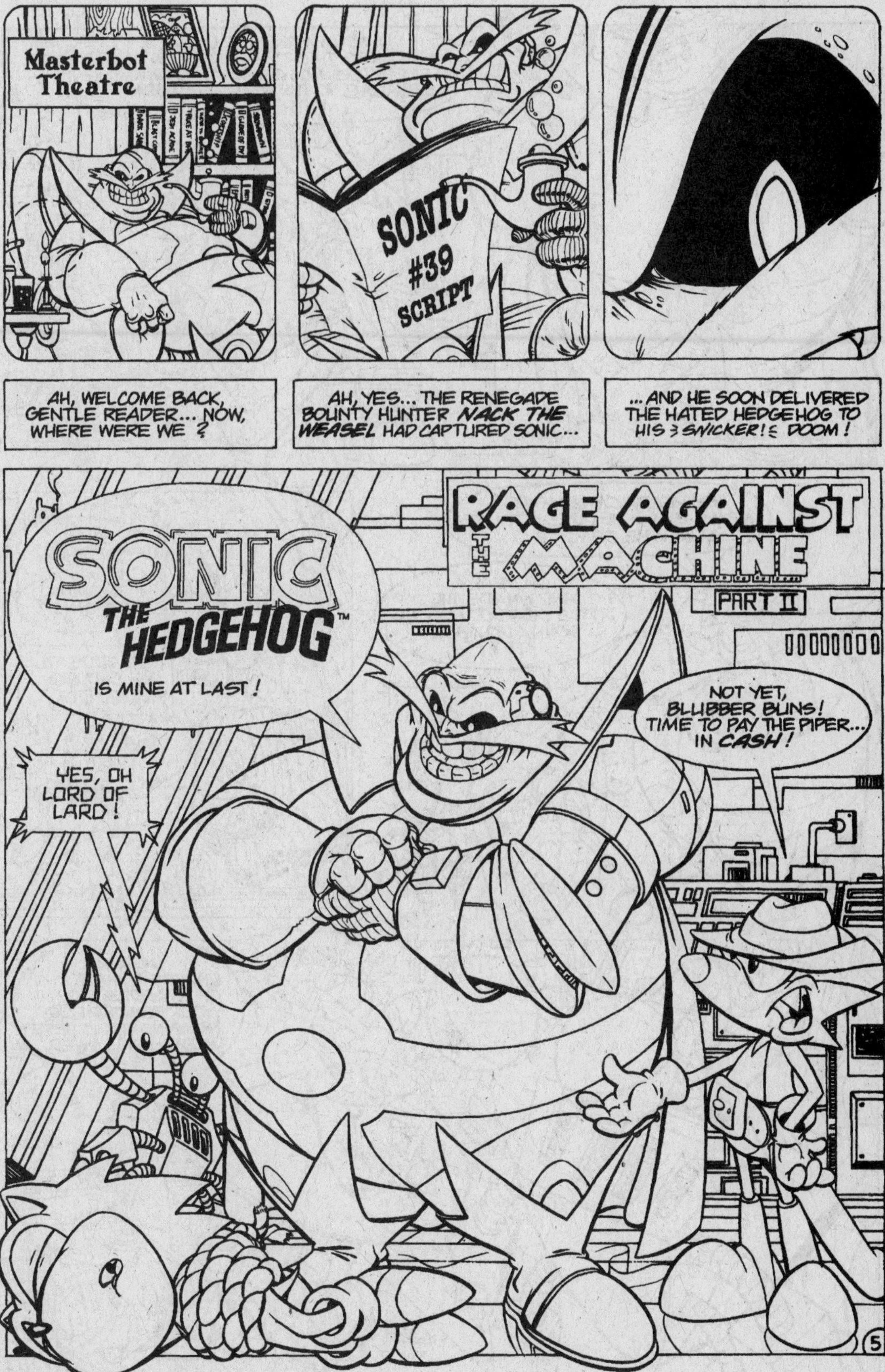
Masterbot Theatre
SONIC #39 SCRIPT
AH, WELCOME BACK, GENTLE READER... NOW, WHERE WERE WE ?
AH, YES... THE RENEGADE BOUNTY HUNTER NACK THE WEASEL HAD CAPTURED SONIC...
...AND HE SOON DELIVERED THE HATED HEDGEHOG TO HIS ≷SNICKER!≶ DOOM!
RAGE AGAINST THE MACHINE
PART II
SONIC THE HEDGEHOG™ IS MINE AT LAST!
NOT YET, BLUBBER BUNS! TIME TO PAY THE PIPER... IN CASH!
YES, OH LORD OF LARD!
5

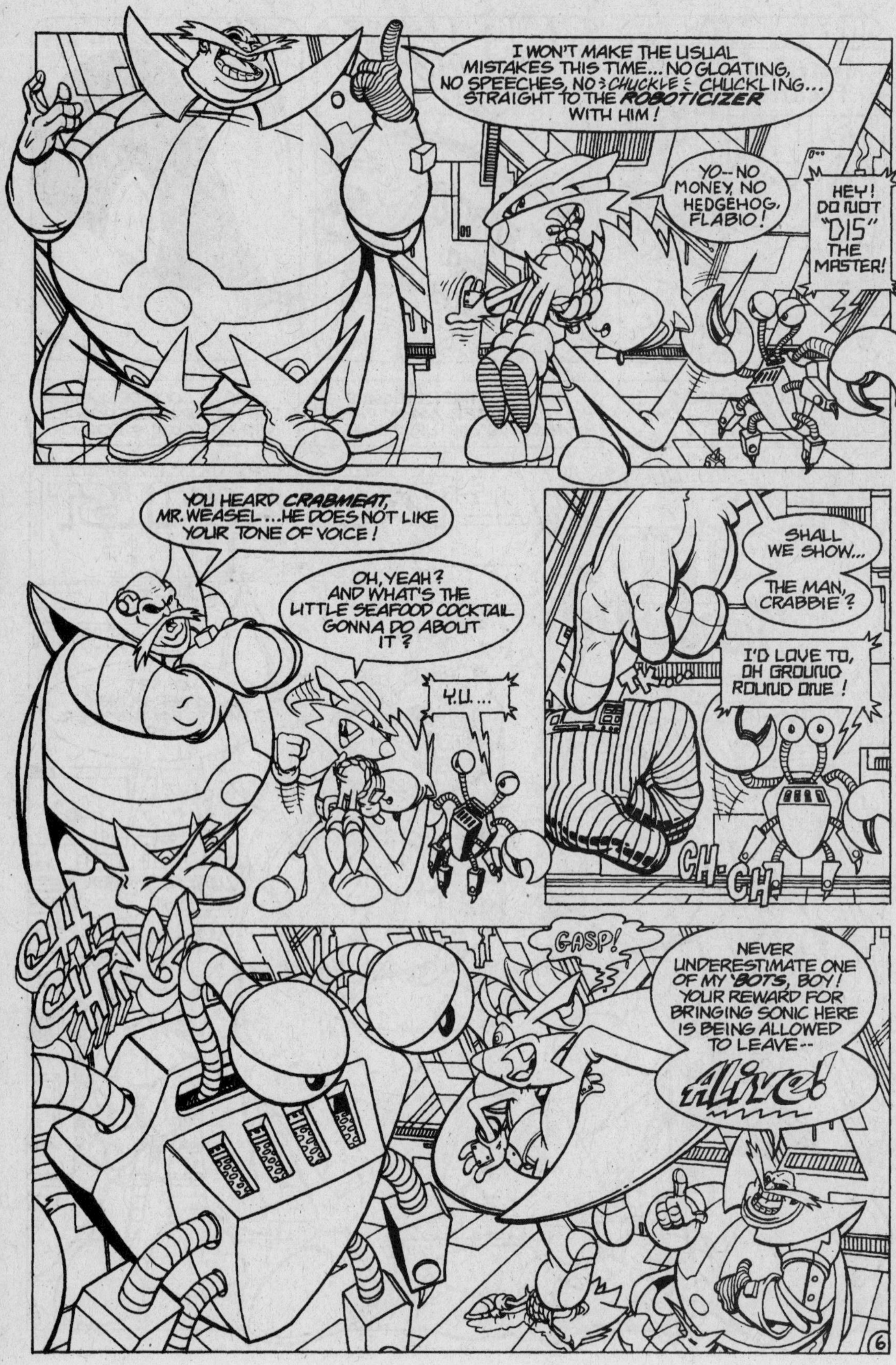
I WON'T MAKE THE USUAL MISTAKES THIS TIME... NO GLOATING, NO SPEECHES, NO CHUCKLE CHUCKLING... STRAIGHT TO THE ROBOTICIZER WITH HIM!
YO-- NO MONEY, NO HEDGEHOG, FLABIO!
HEY! DO NOT "DIS" THE MASTER!
YOU HEARD CRABMEAT, MR. WEASEL... HE DOES NOT LIKE YOUR TONE OF VOICE!
OH, YEAH? AND WHAT'S THE LITTLE SEAFOOD COCKTAIL GONNA DO ABOUT IT?
Y.U. ...
SHALL WE SHOW...
THE MAN, CRABBIE?
I'D LOVE TO, OH GROUND ROUND ONE!
TK...
CH-CH
GASP!
NEVER UNDERESTIMATE ONE OF MY 'BOTS, BOY! YOUR REWARD FOR BRINGING SONIC HERE IS BEING ALLOWED TO LEAVE--
Alive!
6

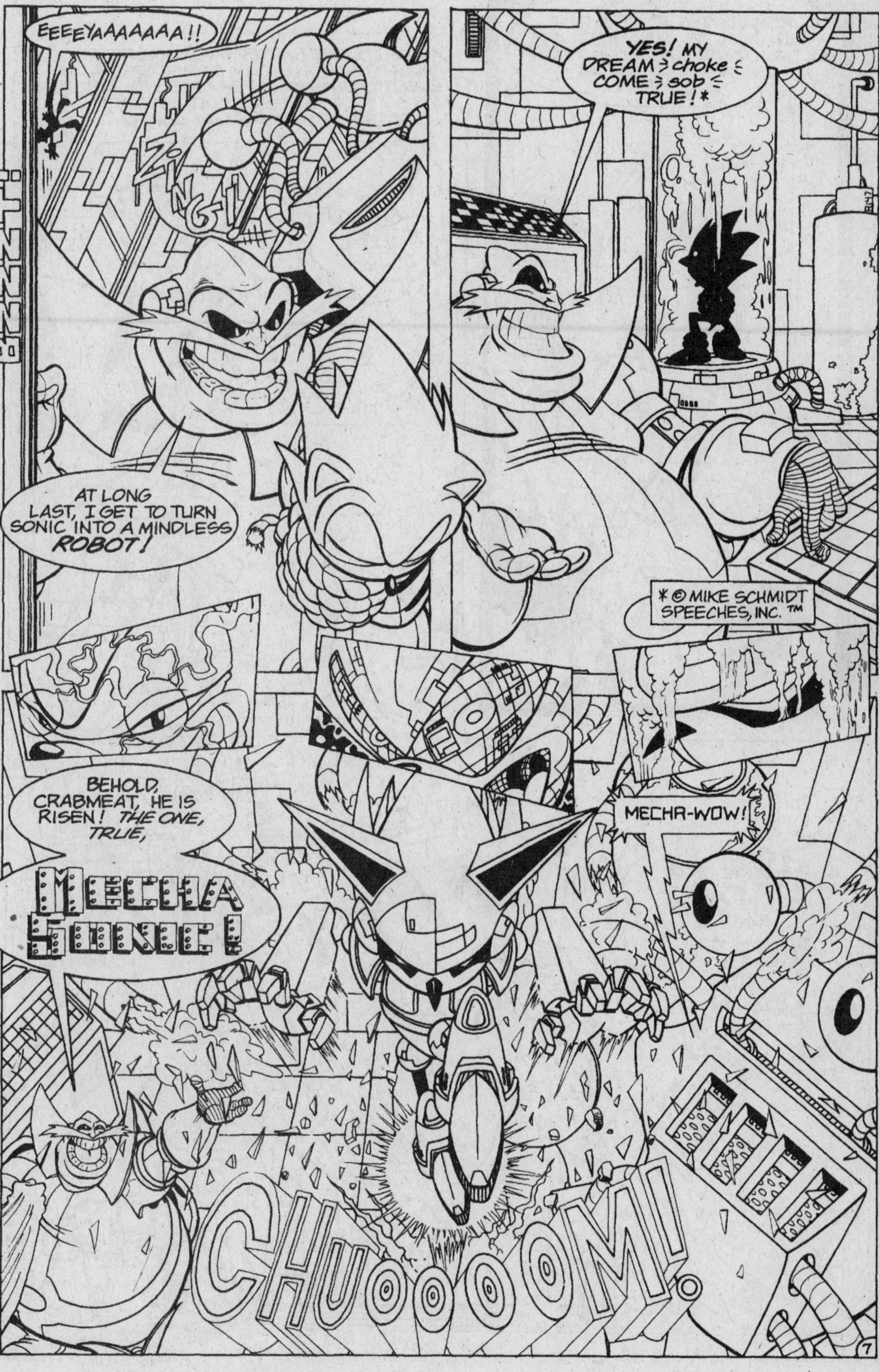
EEEEYAAAAAAA!!
BZZZZT!
ZING!
YES! MY DREAM ≶choke≶ COME ≶sob≶ TRUE! *
AT LONG LAST, I GET TO TURN SONIC INTO A MINDLESS ROBOT!
* © MIKE SCHMIDT SPEECHES, INC. ™
BEHOLD, CRABMEAT, HE IS RISEN! THE ONE, TRUE,
MECHA SONIC!
MECHA-WOW!
CHUOOOOM!
7

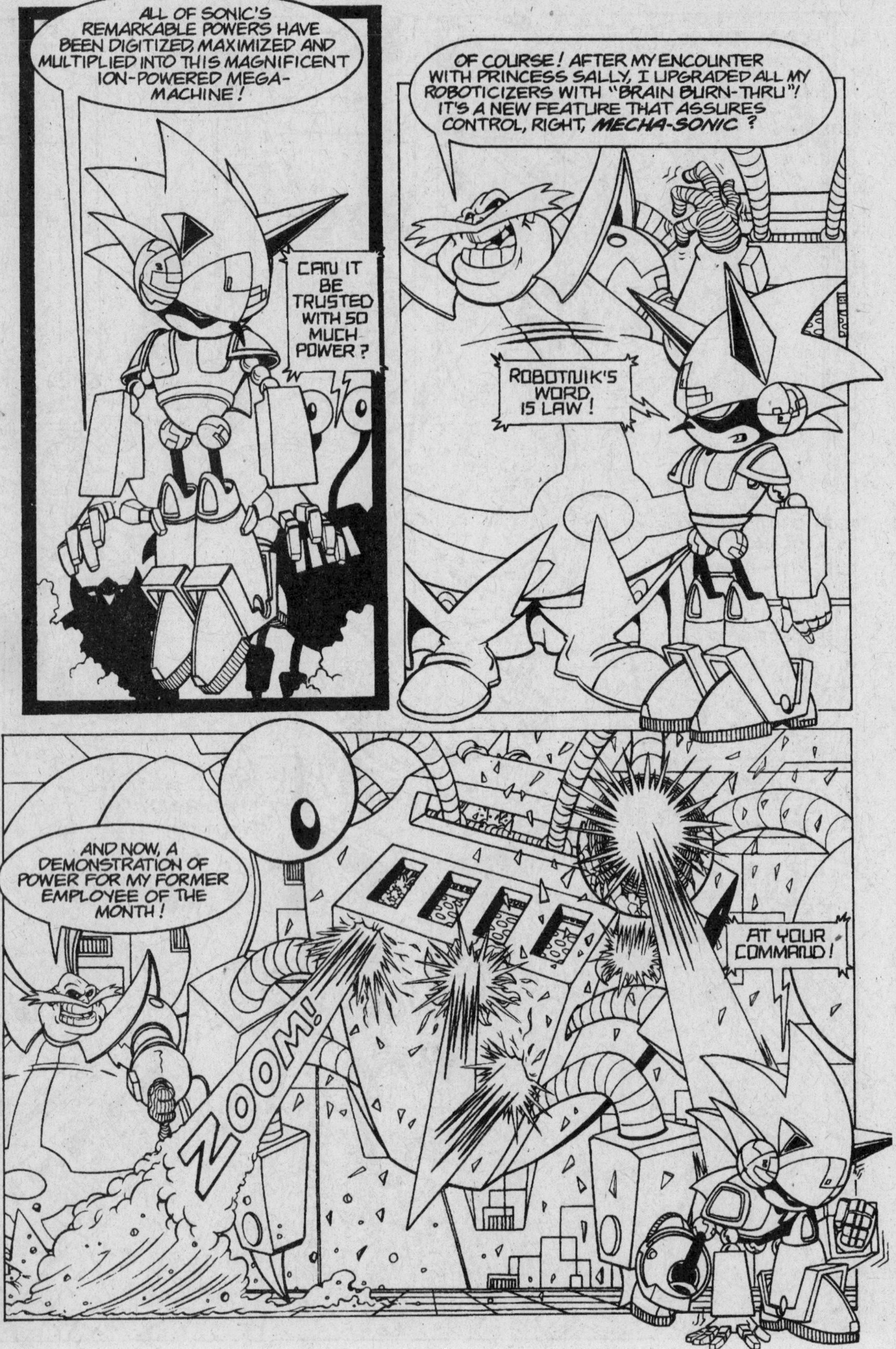
ALL OF SONIC'S REMARKABLE POWERS HAVE BEEN DIGITIZED, MAXIMIZED AND MULTIPLIED INTO THIS MAGNIFICENT ION-POWERED MEGA-MACHINE!
CAN IT BE TRUSTED WITH SO MUCH POWER?
OF COURSE! AFTER MY ENCOUNTER WITH PRINCESS SALLY, I UPGRADED ALL MY ROBOTICIZERS WITH "BRAIN BURN-THRU"! IT'S A NEW FEATURE THAT ASSURES CONTROL, RIGHT, MECHA-SONIC?
ROBOTNIK'S WORD IS LAW!
AND NOW, A DEMONSTRATION OF POWER FOR MY FORMER EMPLOYEE OF THE MONTH!
AT YOUR COMMAND!
ZOOM!

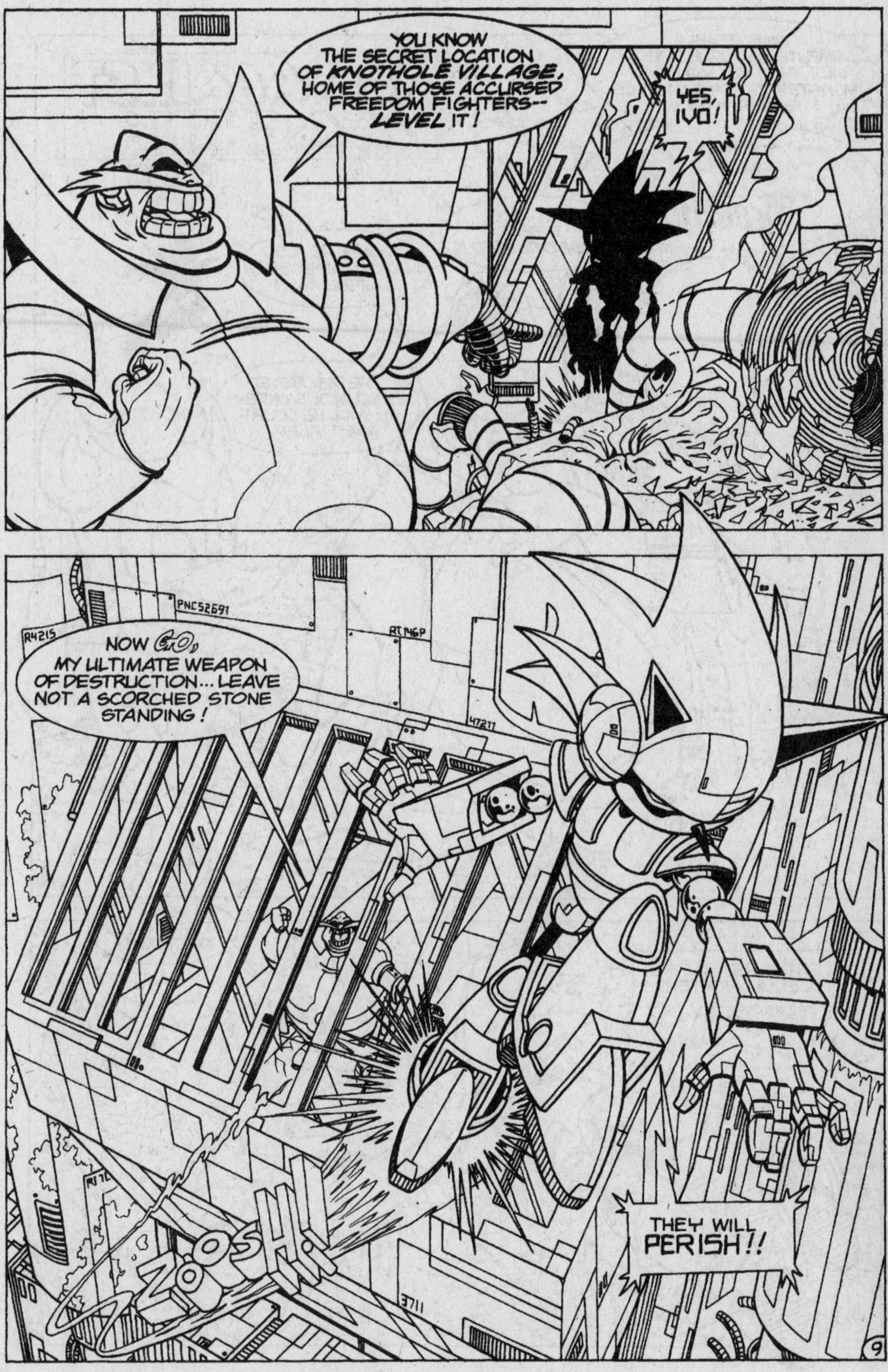
YOU KNOW THE SECRET LOCATION OF KNOTHOLE VILLAGE, HOME OF THOSE ACCURSED FREEDOM FIGHTERS-- LEVEL IT!
YES, IVO!
NOW GO, MY ULTIMATE WEAPON OF DESTRUCTION... LEAVE NOT A SCORCHED STONE STANDING!
ZOOOSH!
THEY WILL PERISH!!
9

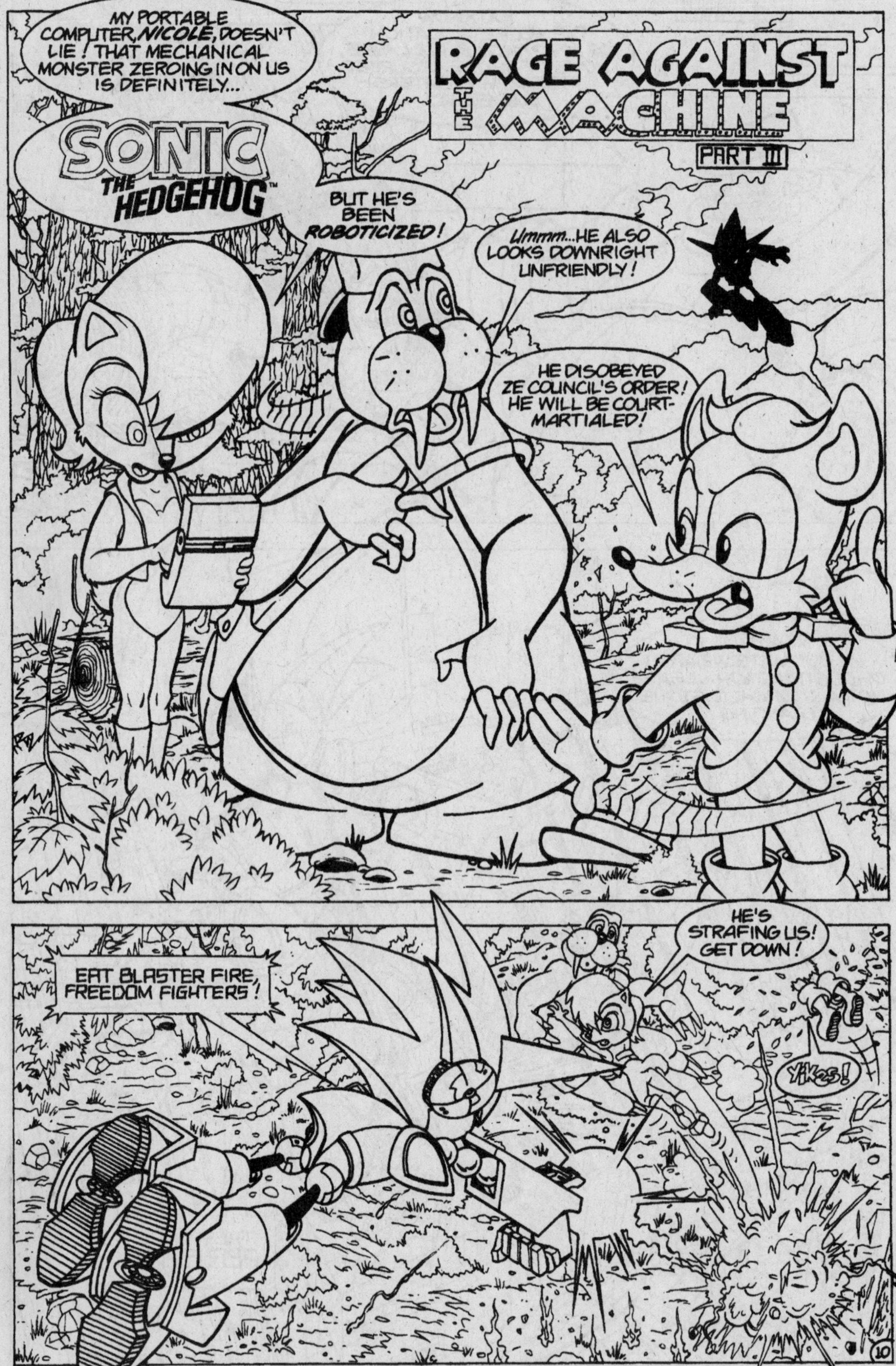
MY PORTABLE COMPUTER, NICOLE, DOESN'T LIE! THAT MECHANICAL MONSTER ZEROING IN ON US IS DEFINITELY...
SONIC THE HEDGEHOG™
RAGE AGAINST THE MACHINE
PART III
BUT HE'S BEEN ROBOTICIZED!
Ummm...HE ALSO LOOKS DOWNRIGHT UNFRIENDLY!
HE DISOBEYED ZE COUNCIL'S ORDER! HE WILL BE COURT-MARTIALED!
EAT BLASTER FIRE, FREEDOM FIGHTERS!
HE'S STRAFING US! GET DOWN!
YIKES!
10

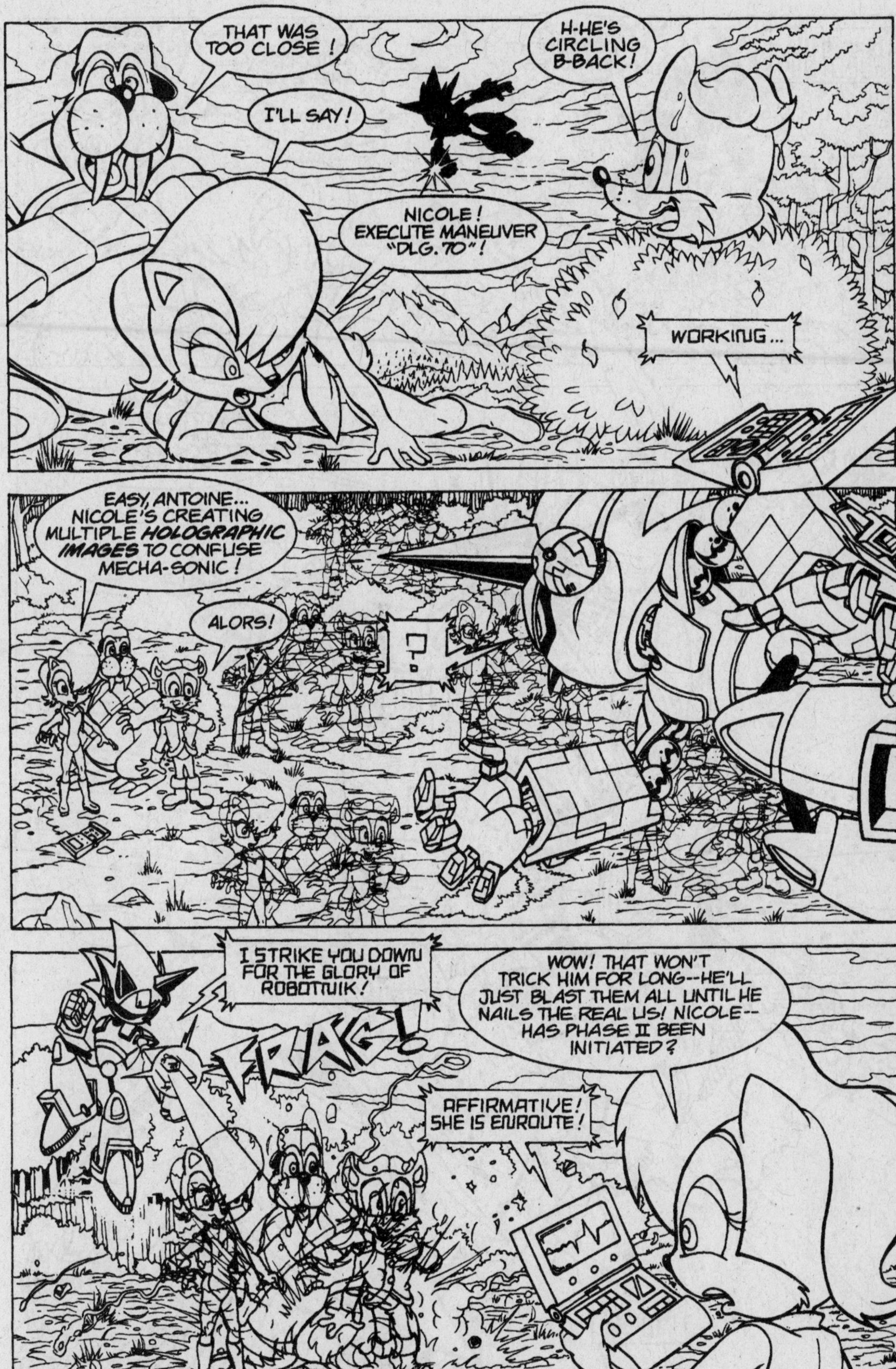
THAT WAS TOO CLOSE!
I'LL SAY!
H-HE'S CIRCLING B-BACK!
NICOLE! EXECUTE MANEUVER "DLG. 70"!
WORKING...
EASY, ANTOINE... NICOLE'S CREATING MULTIPLE HOLOGRAPHIC IMAGES TO CONFUSE MECHA-SONIC!
ALORS!
?
I STRIKE YOU DOWN FOR THE GLORY OF ROBOTNIK!
FRAG!
WOW! THAT WON'T TRICK HIM FOR LONG--HE'LL JUST BLAST THEM ALL UNTIL HE NAILS THE REAL US! NICOLE-- HAS PHASE II BEEN INITIATED?
AFFIRMATIVE! SHE IS ENROUTE!
11

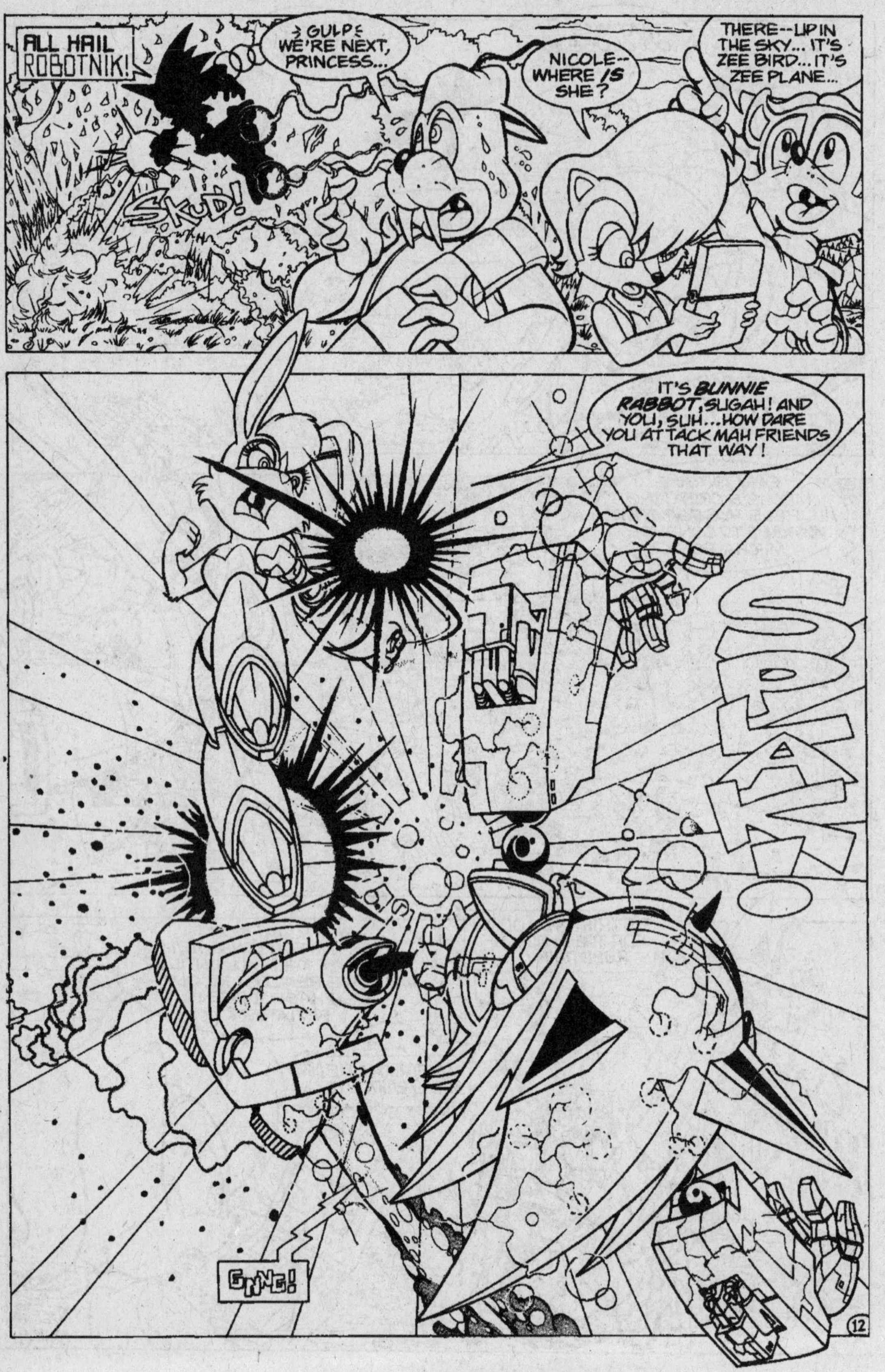
ALL HAIL ROBOTNIK!
SKUD!
GULP WE'RE NEXT, PRINCESS...
NICOLE-- WHERE IS SHE?
THERE--UP IN THE SKY... IT'S ZEE BIRD... IT'S ZEE PLANE...
IT'S BUNNIE RABBOT, SUGAH! AND YOU, SUH...HOW DARE YOU ATTACK MAH FRIENDS THAT WAY!
SPLAK!
GNNG!
12

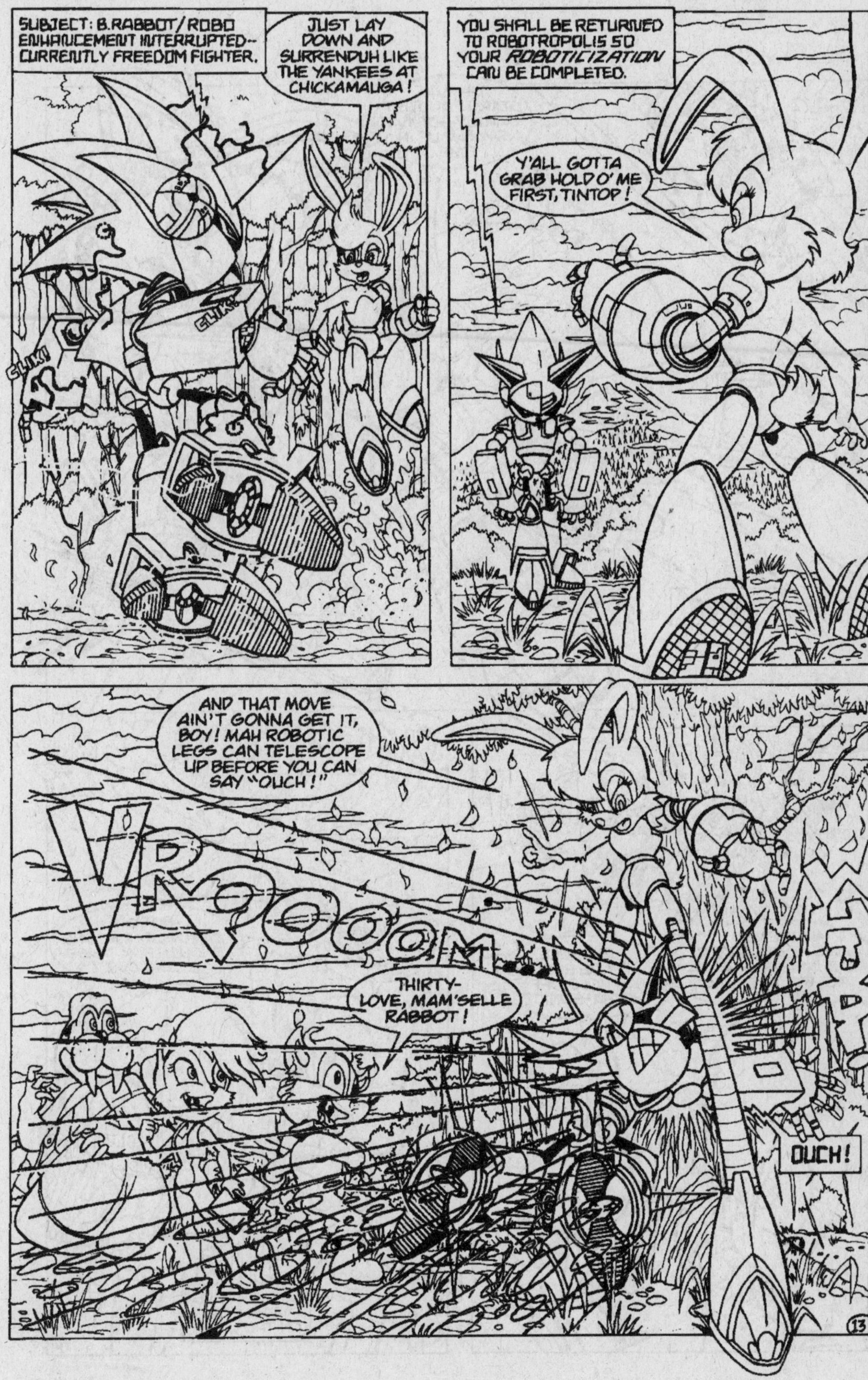
SUBJECT: B.RABBOT/ROBO ENHANCEMENT INTERRUPTED-- CURRENTLY FREEDOM FIGHTER.
JUST LAY DOWN AND SURRENDUH LIKE THE YANKEES AT CHICKAMAUGA!
CLIK!
CLIK!
YOU SHALL BE RETURNED TO ROBOTROPOLIS SO YOUR *ROBOTICIZATION* CAN BE COMPLETED.
Y'ALL GOTTA GRAB HOLD O' ME FIRST, TINTOP!
AND THAT MOVE AIN'T GONNA GET IT, BOY! MAH ROBOTIC LEGS CAN TELESCOPE UP BEFORE YOU CAN SAY "OUCH!"
VROOOOOM
THIRTY-LOVE, MAM'SELLE RABBOT!
OUCH!
13

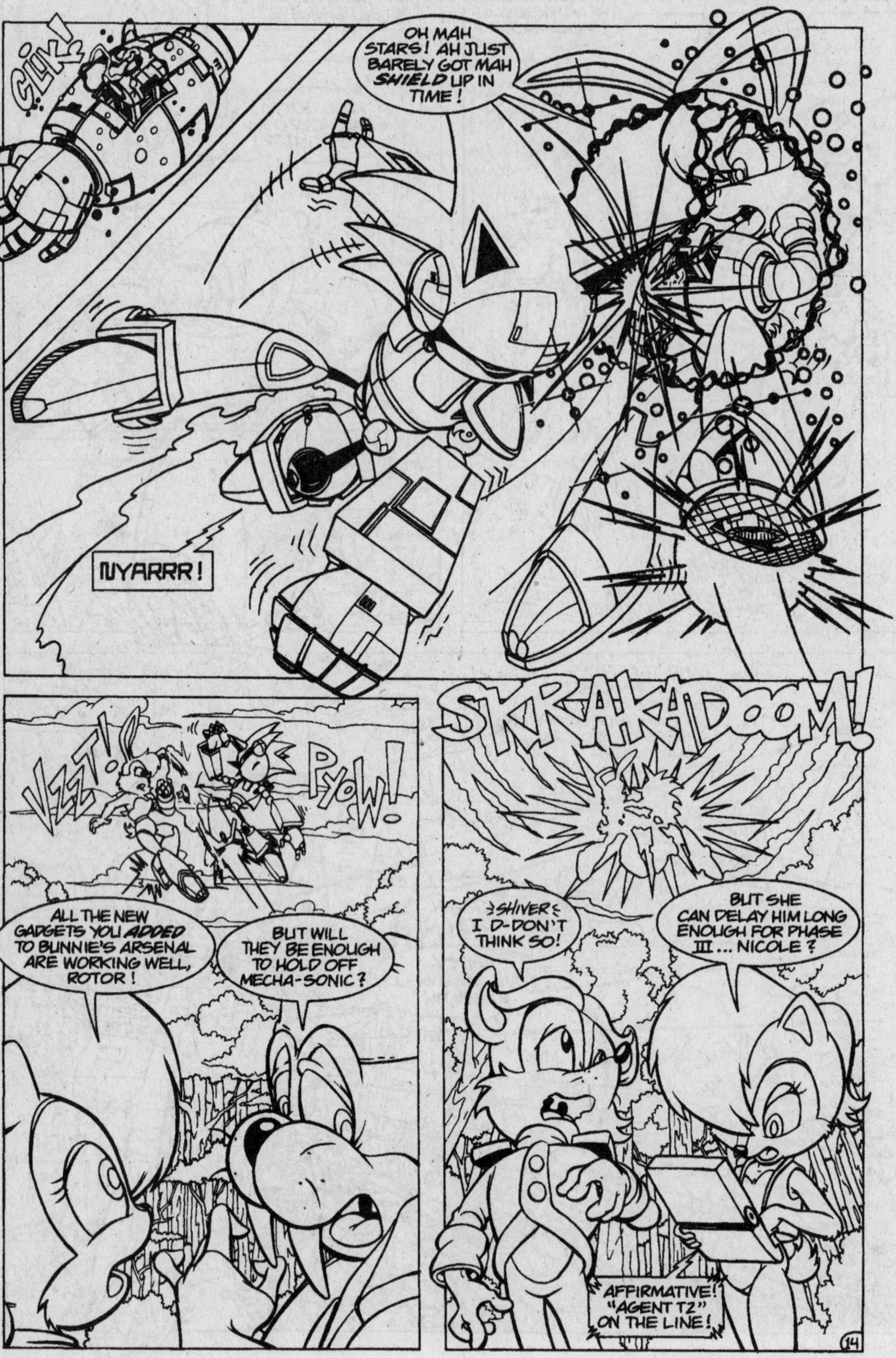
CLIK!
OH MAH STARS! AH JUST BARELY GOT MAH SHIELD UP IN TIME!
NYARRR!
VZZZT!
PYOW!
ALL THE NEW GADGETS YOU ADDED TO BUNNIE'S ARSENAL ARE WORKING WELL, ROTOR!
BUT WILL THEY BE ENOUGH TO HOLD OFF MECHA-SONIC?
SKRAKADOOM!
SHIVER I D-DON'T THINK SO!
BUT SHE CAN DELAY HIM LONG ENOUGH FOR PHASE III ... NICOLE?
AFFIRMATIVE! "AGENT T2" ON THE LINE!
14

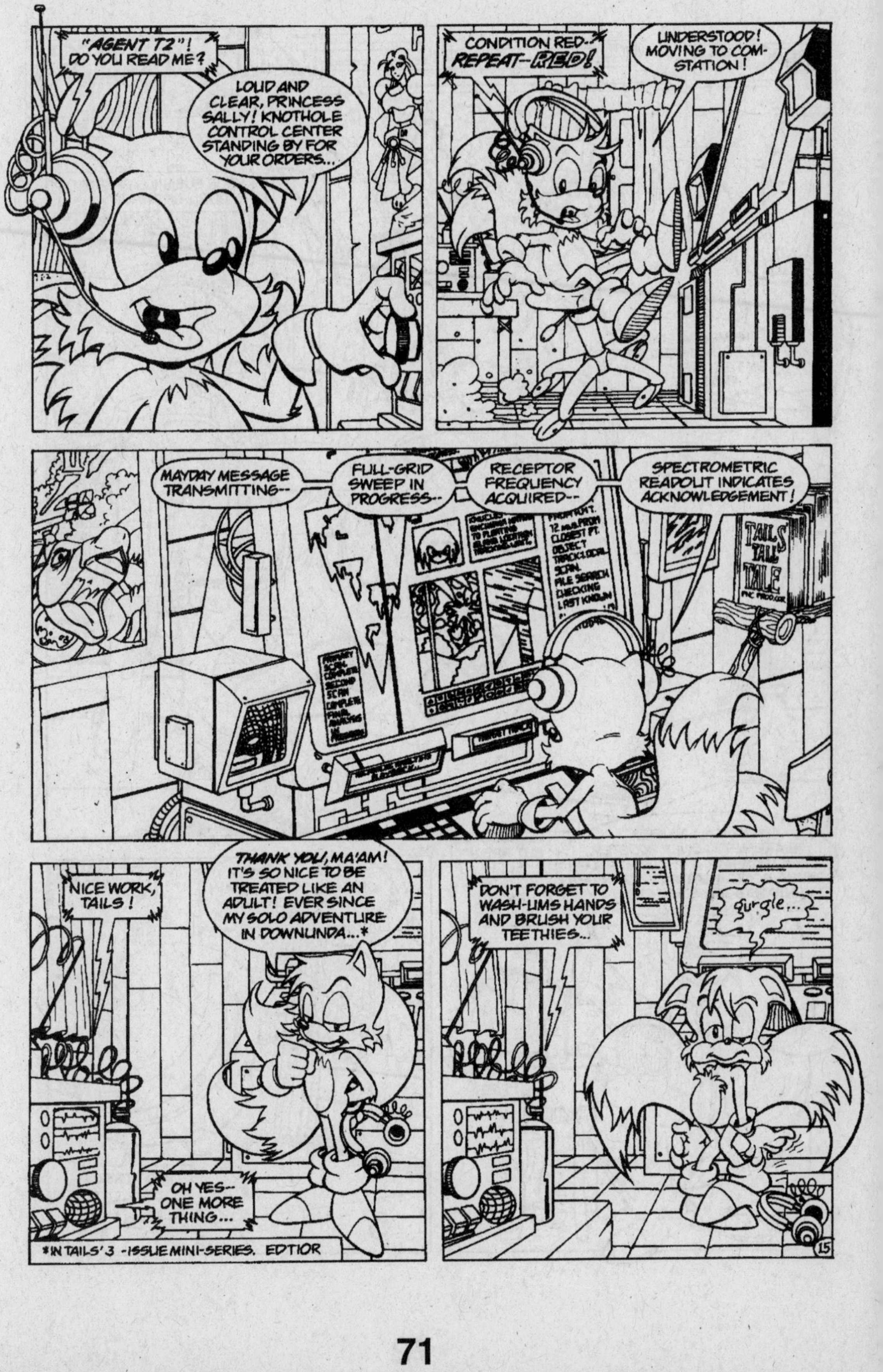
"AGENT T2"! DO YOU READ ME?
LOUD AND CLEAR, PRINCESS SALLY! KNOTHOLE CONTROL CENTER STANDING BY FOR YOUR ORDERS...
CONDITION RED-- REPEAT--RED!
UNDERSTOOD! MOVING TO COM-STATION!
MAYDAY MESSAGE TRANSMITTING--
FULL-GRID SWEEP IN PROGRESS--
RECEPTOR FREQUENCY ACQUIRED--
SPECTROMETRIC READOUT INDICATES ACKNOWLEDGEMENT!
NICE WORK, TAILS!
THANK YOU, MA'AM! IT'S SO NICE TO BE TREATED LIKE AN ADULT! EVER SINCE MY SOLO ADVENTURE IN DOWNUNDA...*
OH YES-- ONE MORE THING...
DON'T FORGET TO WASH-UMS HANDS AND BRUSH YOUR TEETHIES...
gurgle...
*IN TAILS' 3 -ISSUE MINI-SERIES. EDTIOR
15

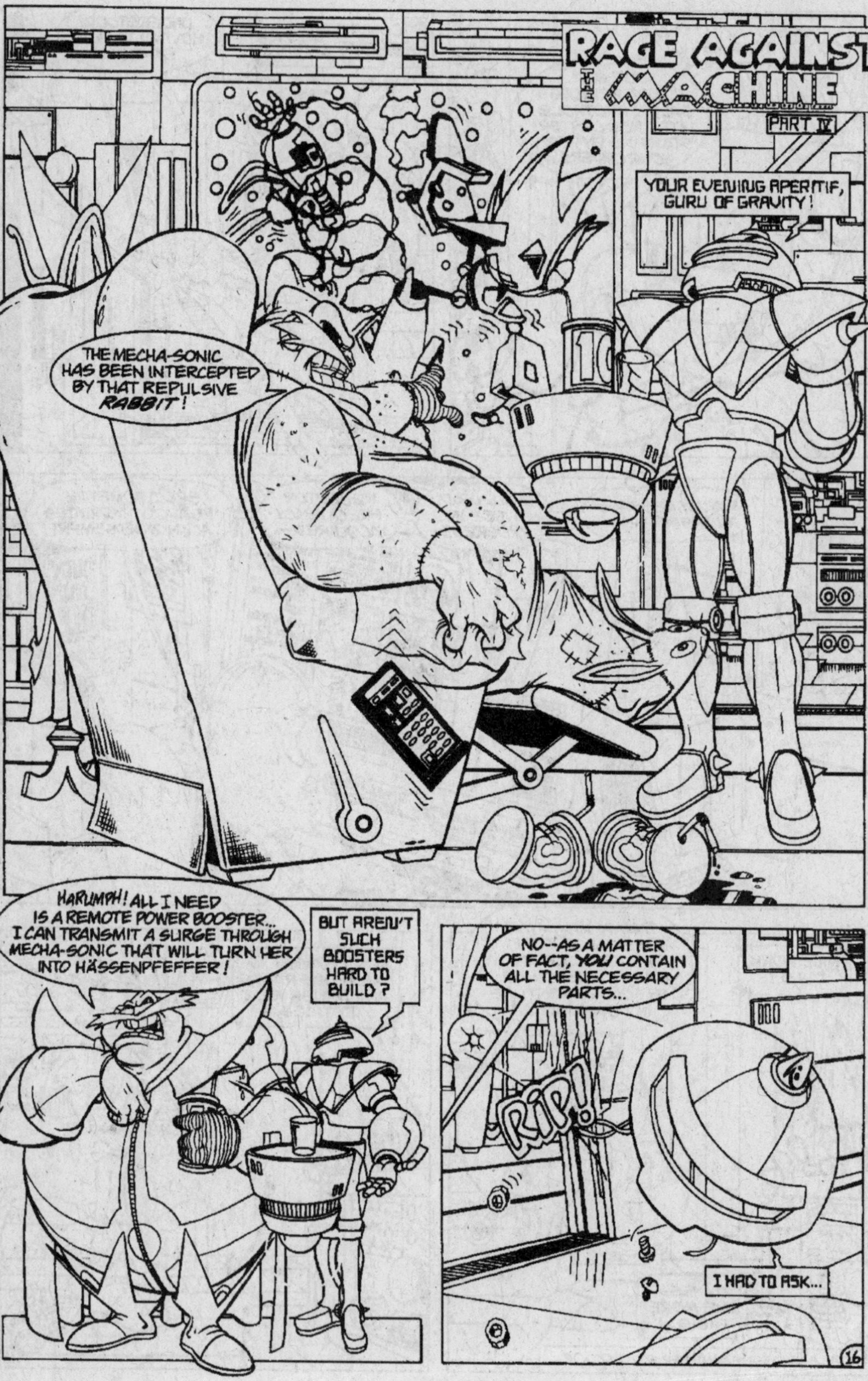
RAGE AGAINST THE MACHINE
PART IV
YOUR EVENING APERITIF, GURU OF GRAVITY!
THE MECHA-SONIC HAS BEEN INTERCEPTED BY THAT REPULSIVE RABBIT!
HARUMPH! ALL I NEED IS A REMOTE POWER BOOSTER... I CAN TRANSMIT A SURGE THROUGH MECHA-SONIC THAT WILL TURN HER INTO HÄSSENPFEFFER!
BUT AREN'T SUCH BOOSTERS HARD TO BUILD?
NO--AS A MATTER OF FACT, YOU CONTAIN ALL THE NECESSARY PARTS...
RIP!
I HAD TO ASK...
16

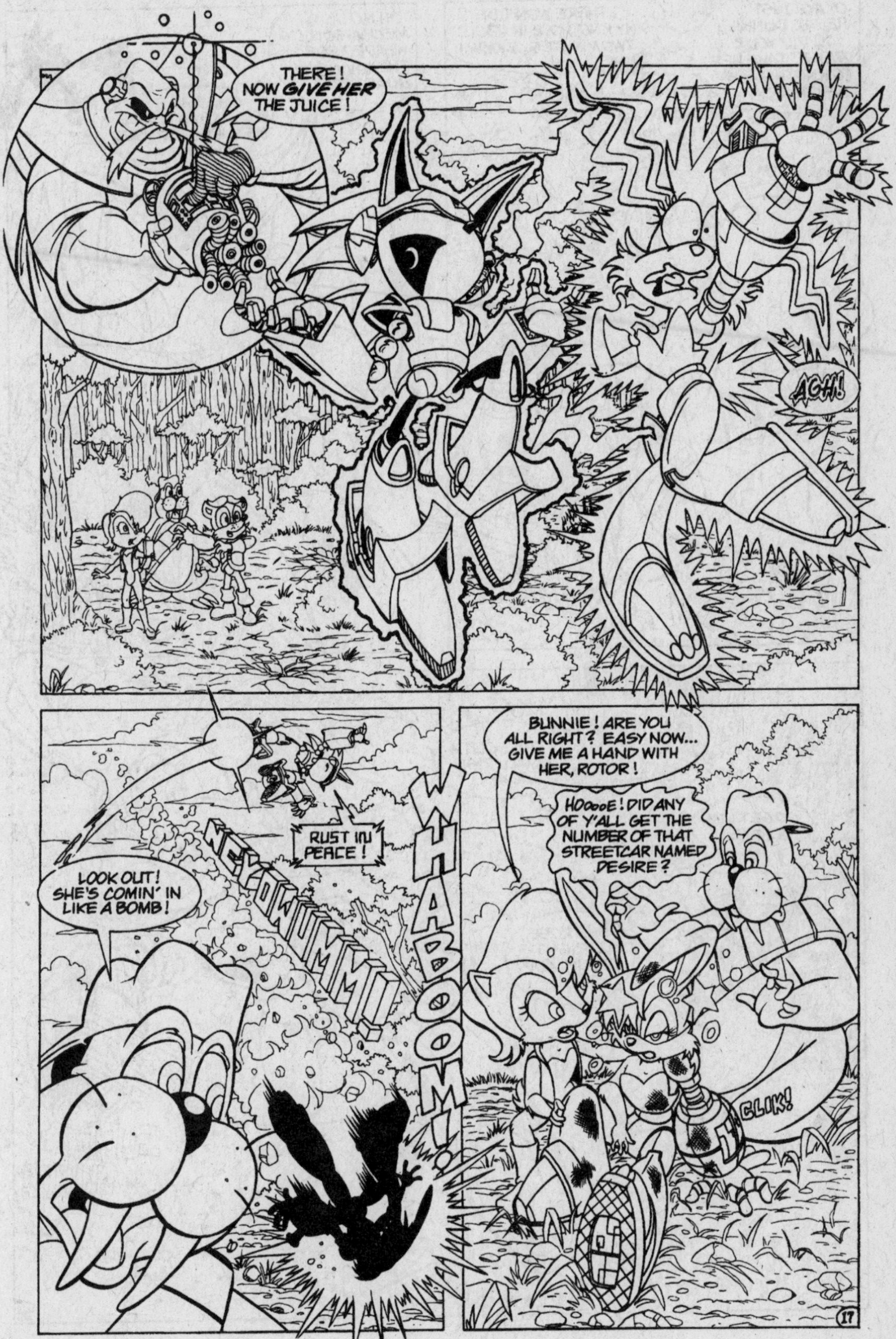
THERE! NOW GIVE HER THE JUICE!
AGH!
RUST IN PEACE!
NEYOWMMM!
WHABOOOM!
LOOK OUT! SHE'S COMIN' IN LIKE A BOMB!
BUNNIE! ARE YOU ALL RIGHT? EASY NOW... GIVE ME A HAND WITH HER, ROTOR!
HOOooE! DID ANY OF Y'ALL GET THE NUMBER OF THAT STREETCAR NAMED DESIRE?
CLIK!
17

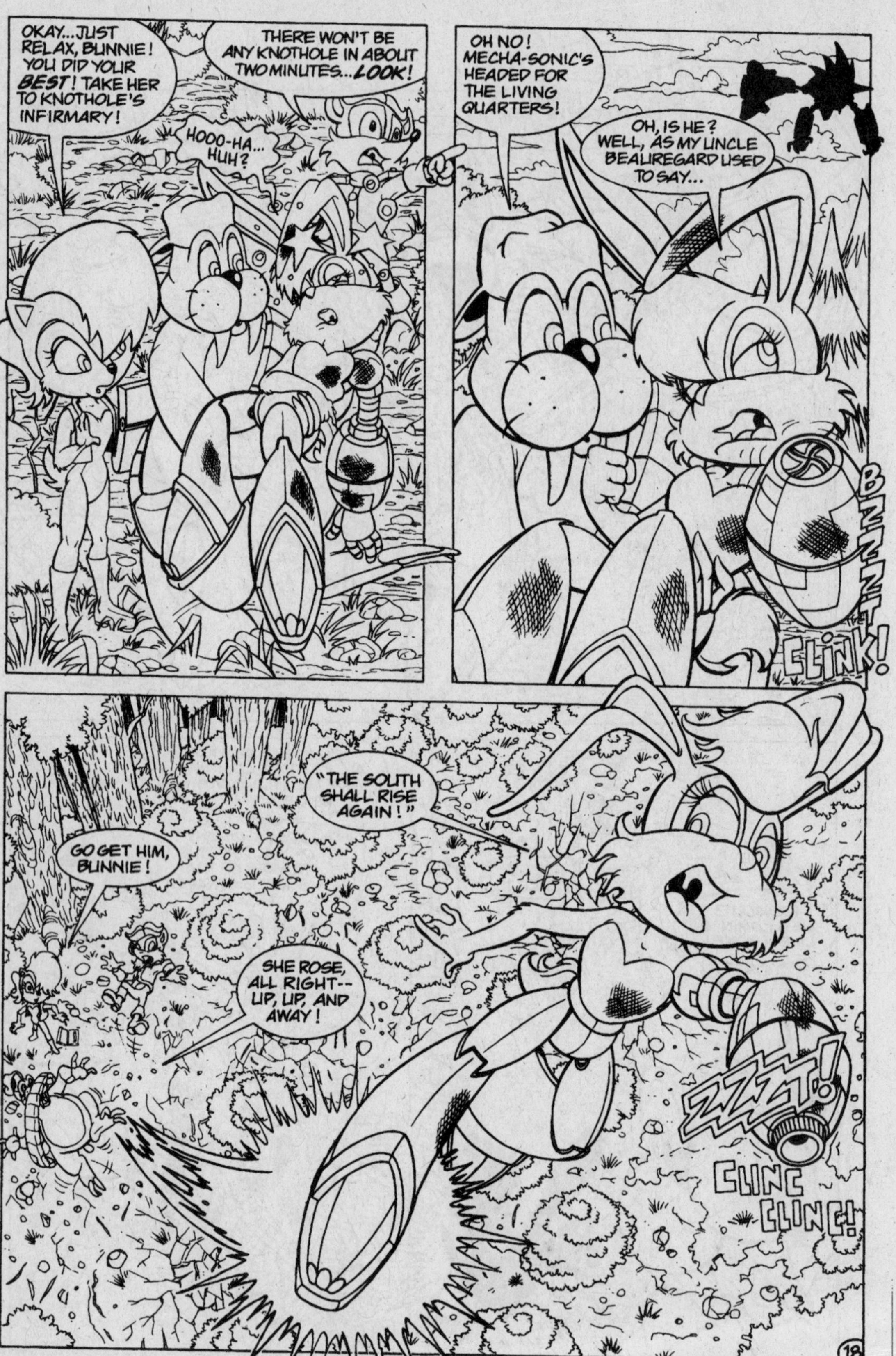
OKAY...JUST RELAX, BUNNIE! YOU DID YOUR BEST! TAKE HER TO KNOTHOLE'S INFIRMARY!
THERE WON'T BE ANY KNOTHOLE IN ABOUT TWO MINUTES...LOOK!
HOOO-HA... HUH?
OH NO! MECHA-SONIC'S HEADED FOR THE LIVING QUARTERS!
OH, IS HE? WELL, AS MY UNCLE BEAUREGARD USED TO SAY...
BZZZZT
CLINK!
"THE SOUTH SHALL RISE AGAIN!"
GO GET HIM, BUNNIE!
SHE ROSE, ALL RIGHT-- UP, UP, AND AWAY!
ZZZT!
CLINC CLINC!
18

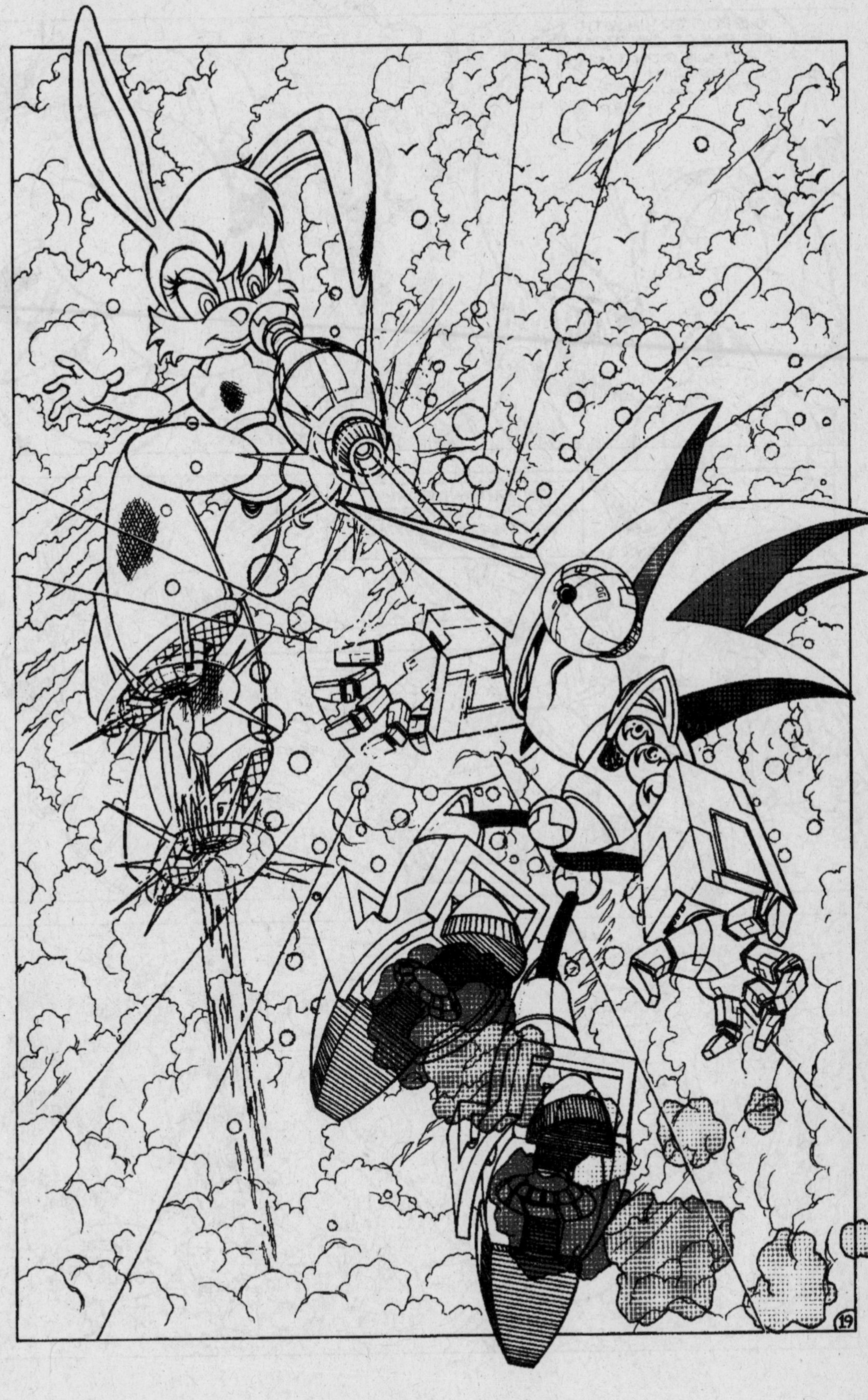
19

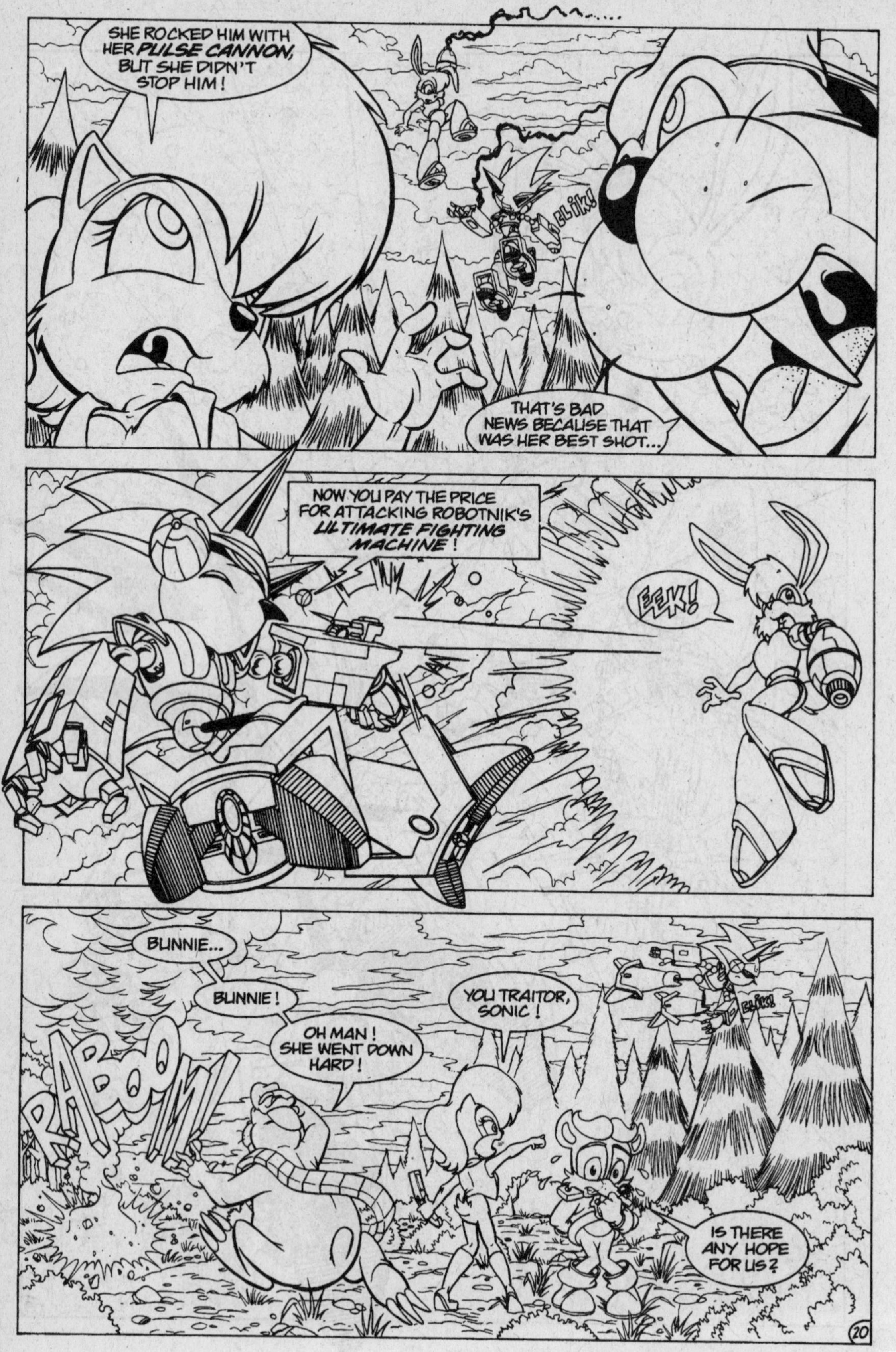
ARRA.....
SHE ROCKED HIM WITH HER PULSE CANNON, BUT SHE DIDN'T STOP HIM!
ELIK!
THAT'S BAD NEWS BECAUSE THAT WAS HER BEST SHOT...
NOW YOU PAY THE PRICE FOR ATTACKING ROBOTNIK'S ULTIMATE FIGHTING MACHINE!
EEK!
BUNNIE...
BUNNIE!
RABOOM!
OH MAN! SHE WENT DOWN HARD!
YOU TRAITOR, SONIC!
ELIK!
IS THERE ANY HOPE FOR US?
20

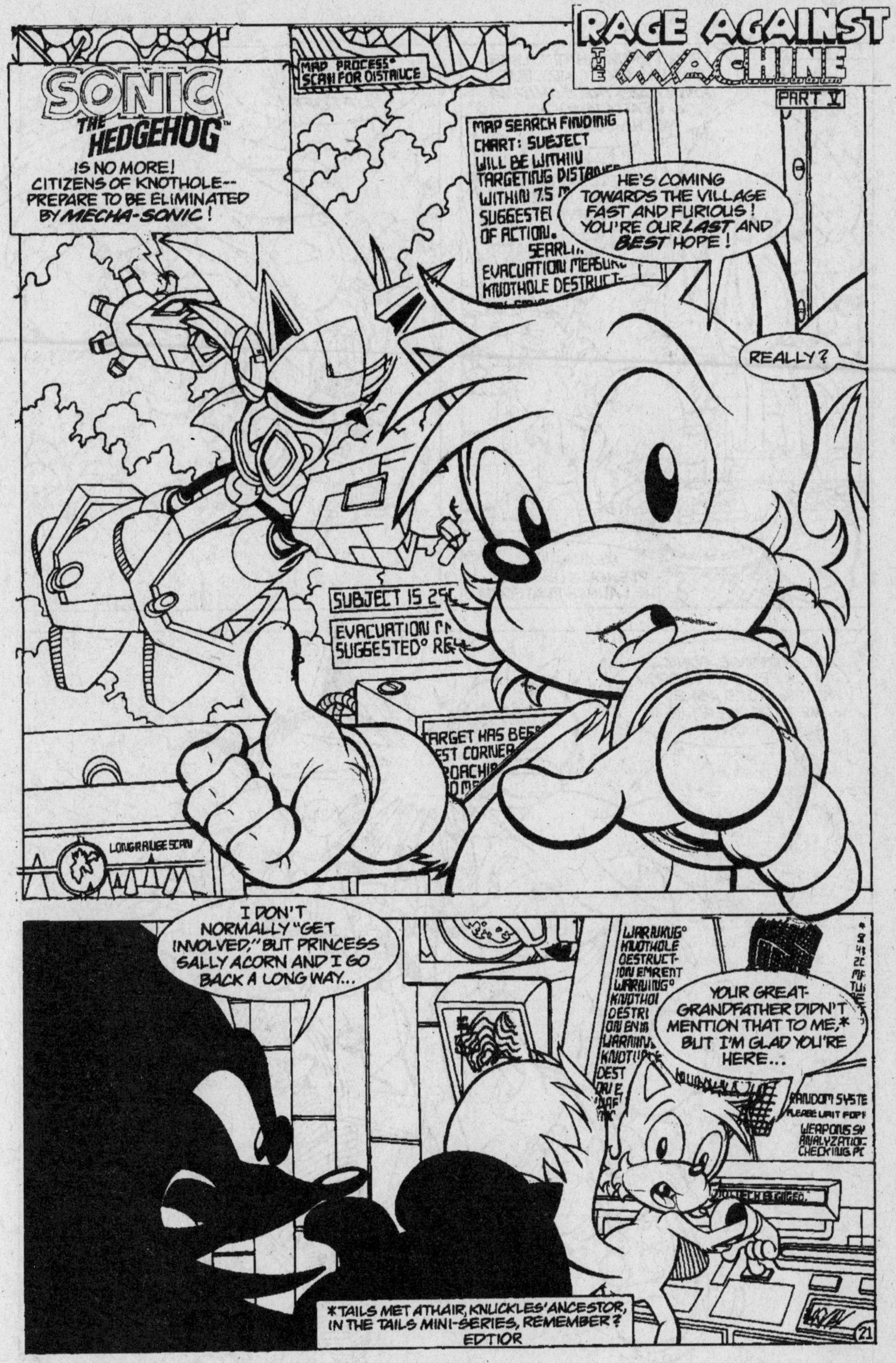

RAGE AGAINST THE MACHINE
PART V
SONIC THE HEDGEHOG IS NO MORE! CITIZENS OF KNOTHOLE-- PREPARE TO BE ELIMINATED BY MECHA-SONIC!
HE'S COMING TOWARDS THE VILLAGE FAST AND FURIOUS! YOU'RE OUR LAST AND BEST HOPE!
REALLY?
I DON'T NORMALLY "GET INVOLVED," BUT PRINCESS SALLY ACORN AND I GO BACK A LONG WAY...
YOUR GREAT-GRANDFATHER DIDN'T MENTION THAT TO ME,* BUT I'M GLAD YOU'RE HERE...
*TAILS MET ATHAIR, KNUCKLES' ANCESTOR, IN THE TAILS MINI-SERIES, REMEMBER? EDTIOR
21

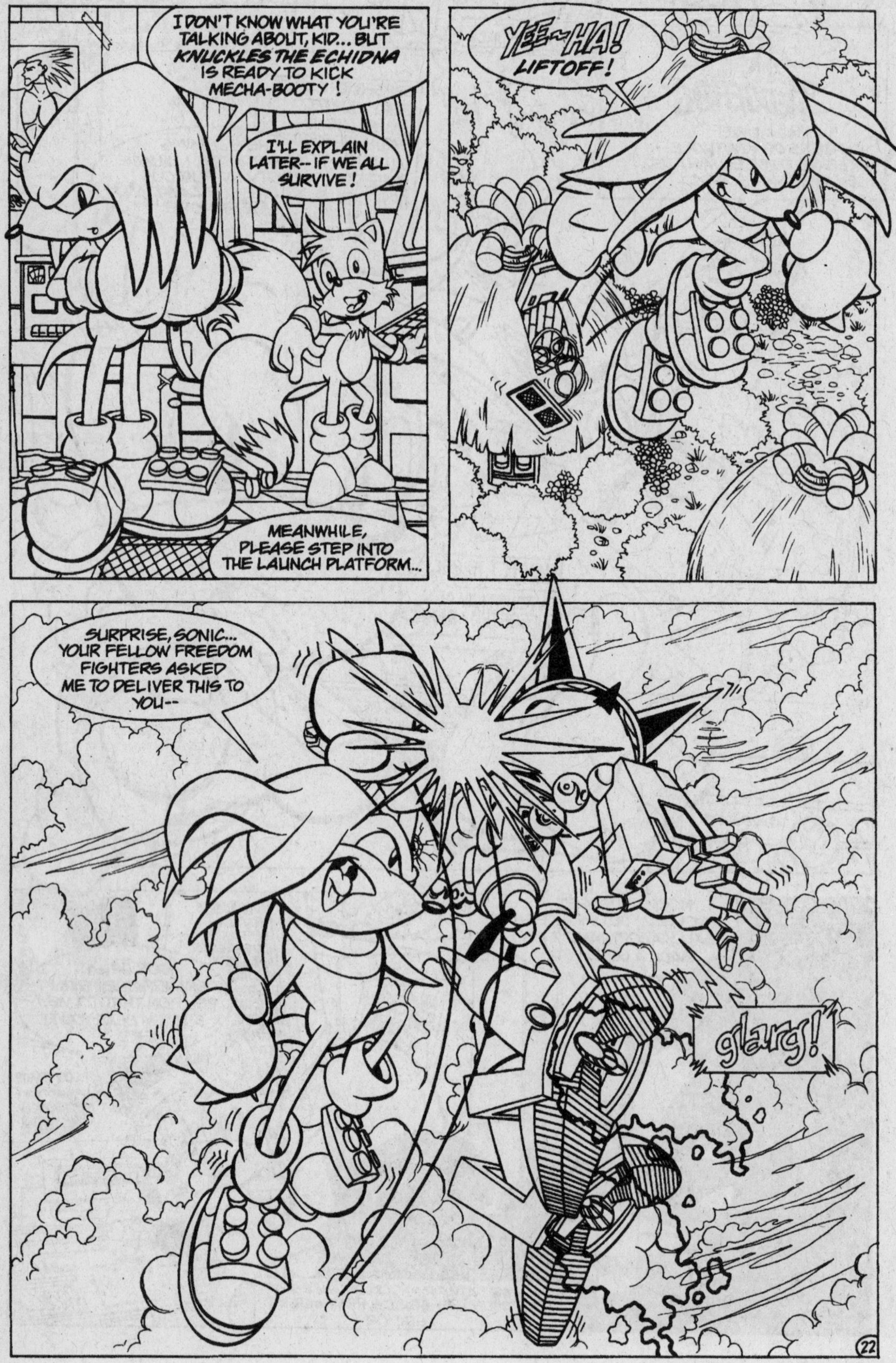
I DON'T KNOW WHAT YOU'RE TALKING ABOUT, KID... BUT KNUCKLES THE ECHIDNA IS READY TO KICK MECHA-BOOTY!
I'LL EXPLAIN LATER-- IF WE ALL SURVIVE!
MEANWHILE, PLEASE STEP INTO THE LAUNCH PLATFORM...
YEE-HA! LIFTOFF!
SURPRISE, SONIC... YOUR FELLOW FREEDOM FIGHTERS ASKED ME TO DELIVER THIS TO YOU--
glarg!
22

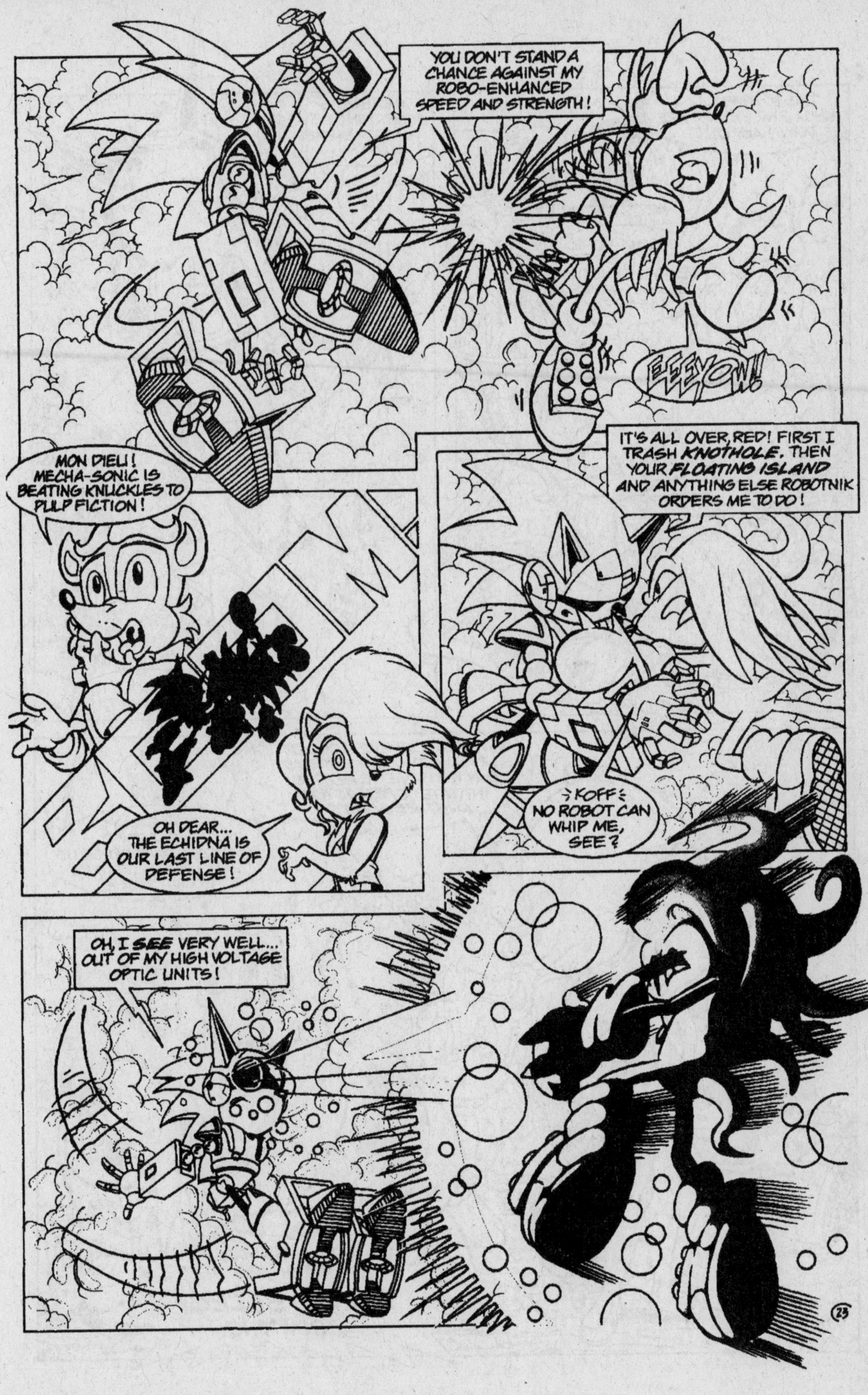
YOU DON'T STAND A CHANCE AGAINST MY ROBO-ENHANCED SPEED AND STRENGTH!
EEEYOW!!
MON DIEU! MECHA-SONIC IS BEATING KNUCKLES TO PULP FICTION!
OH DEAR... THE ECHIDNA IS OUR LAST LINE OF DEFENSE!
IT'S ALL OVER, RED! FIRST I TRASH KNOTHOLE. THEN YOUR FLOATING ISLAND AND ANYTHING ELSE ROBOTNIK ORDERS ME TO DO!
KOFF NO ROBOT CAN WHIP ME, SEE?
OH, I SEE VERY WELL... OUT OF MY HIGH VOLTAGE OPTIC UNITS!
23

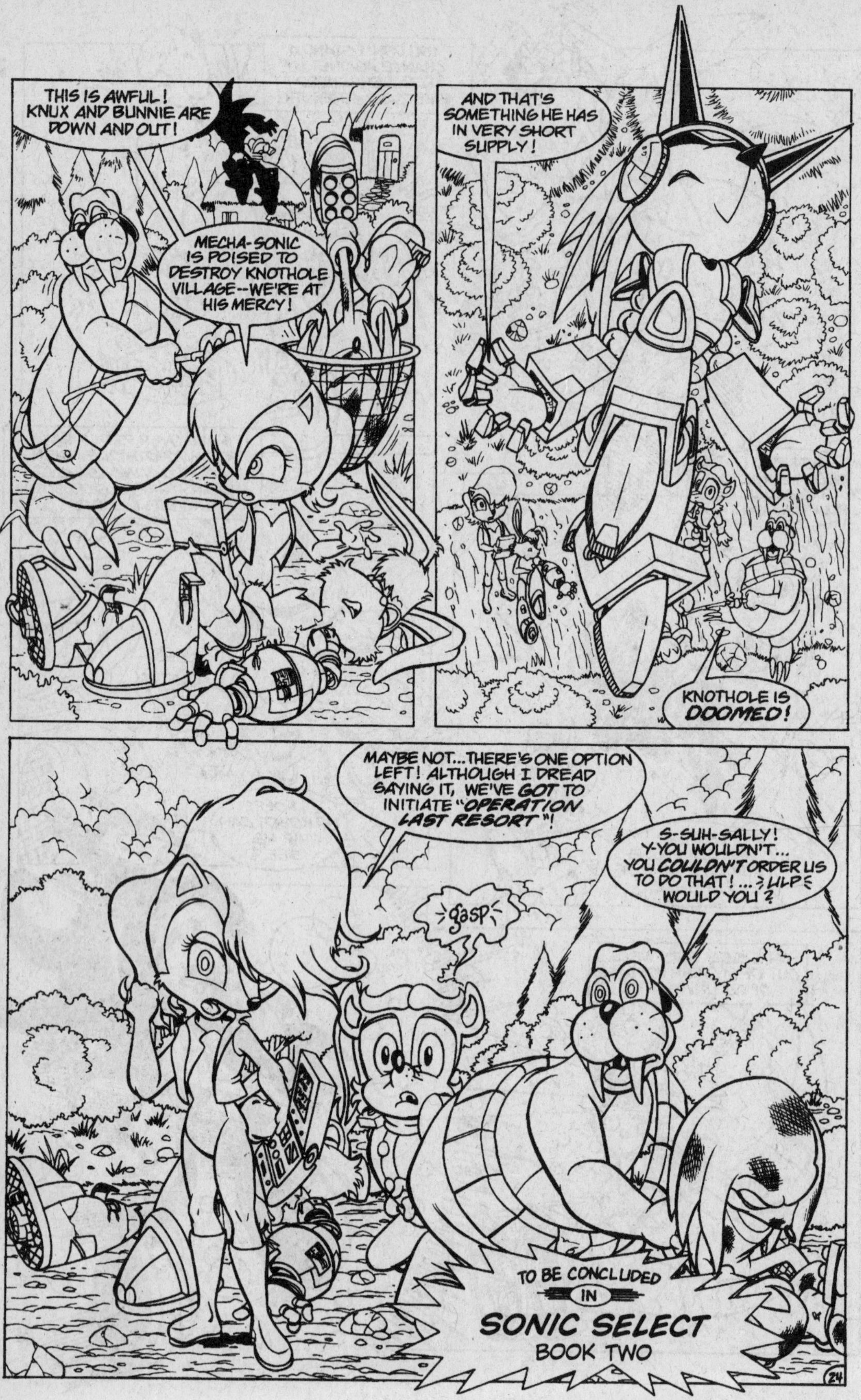
THIS IS AWFUL! KNUX AND BUNNIE ARE DOWN AND OUT!
MECHA-SONIC IS POISED TO DESTROY KNOTHOLE VILLAGE--WE'RE AT HIS MERCY!
AND THAT'S SOMETHING HE HAS IN VERY SHORT SUPPLY!
KNOTHOLE IS DOOMED!
MAYBE NOT...THERE'S ONE OPTION LEFT! ALTHOUGH I DREAD SAYING IT, WE'VE GOT TO INITIATE "OPERATION LAST RESORT"!
gasp
S-SUH-SALLY! Y-YOU WOULDN'T... YOU COULDN'T ORDER US TO DO THAT! ... ULP WOULD YOU?
TO BE CONCLUDED IN SONIC SELECT BOOK TWO
24

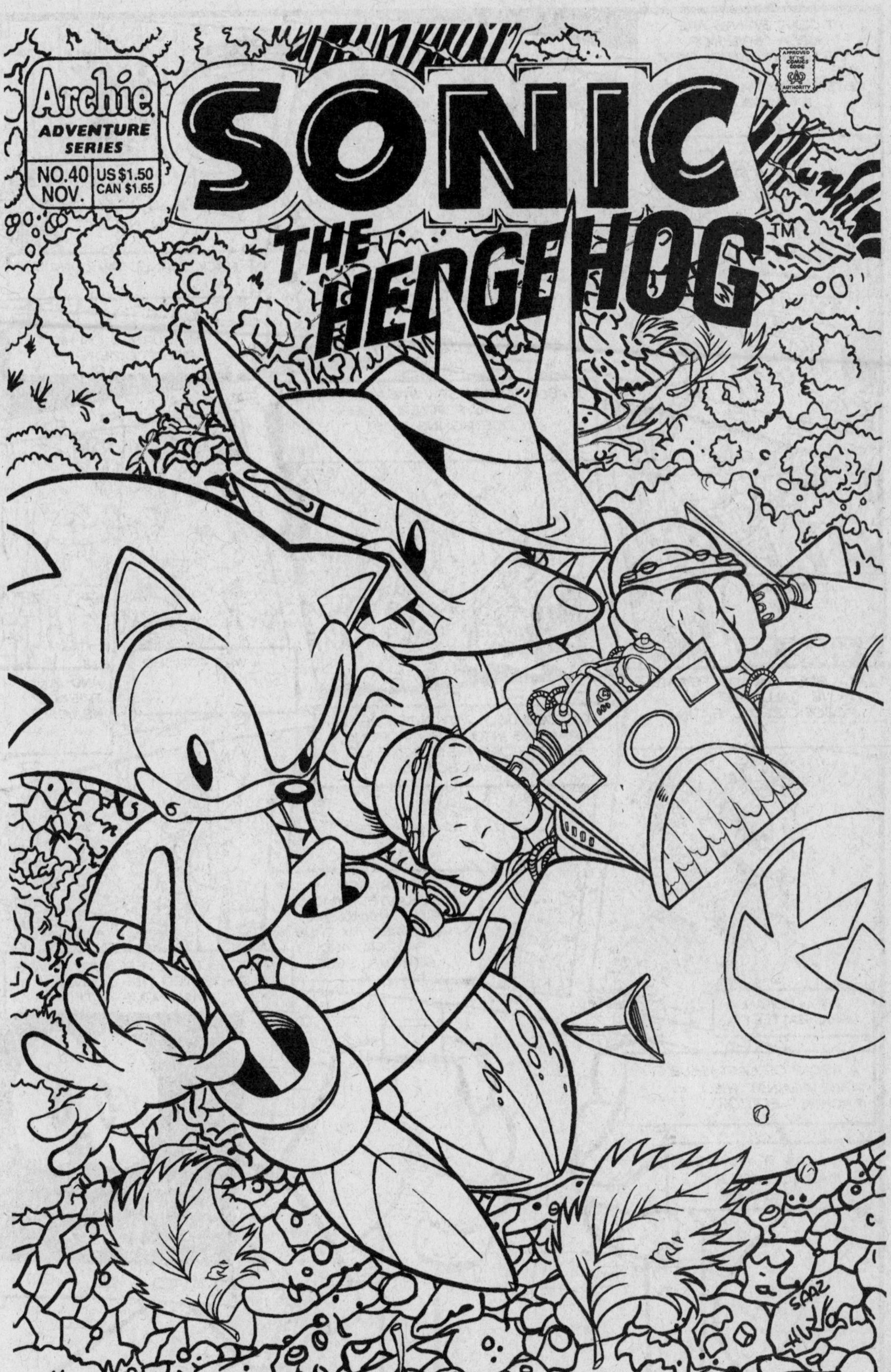

Archie
ADVENTURE SERIES
NO.40
NOV.
US $1.50
CAN $1.65
SONIC THE HEDGEHOG™

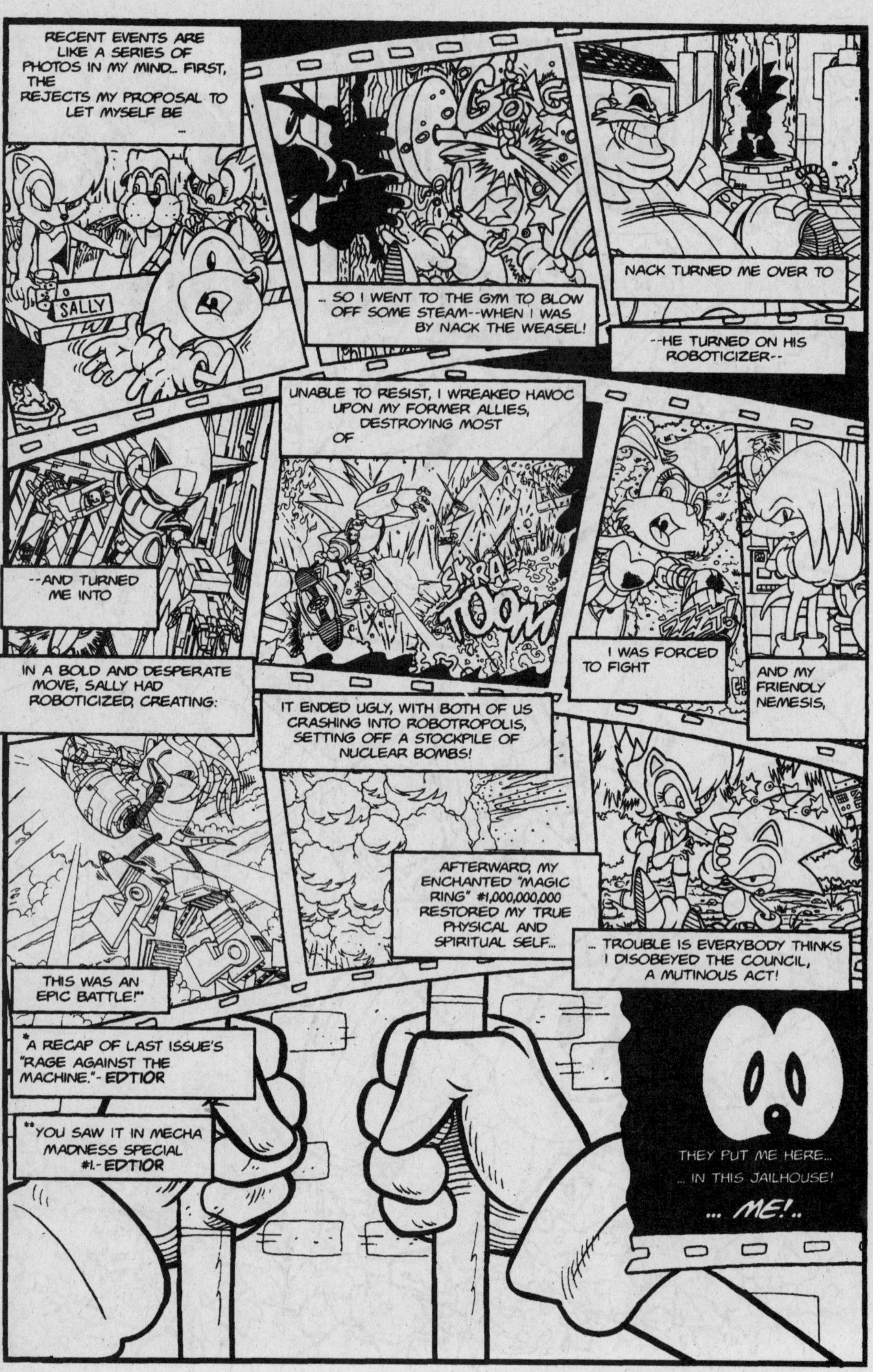
RECENT EVENTS ARE LIKE A SERIES OF PHOTOS IN MY MIND... FIRST, THE REJECTS MY PROPOSAL TO LET MYSELF BE ...
SALLY
... SO I WENT TO THE GYM TO BLOW OFF SOME STEAM--WHEN I WAS BY NACK THE WEASEL!
NACK TURNED ME OVER TO
--HE TURNED ON HIS ROBOTICIZER--
--AND TURNED ME INTO
UNABLE TO RESIST, I WREAKED HAVOC UPON MY FORMER ALLIES, DESTROYING MOST OF
SKRA-TOOM
I WAS FORCED TO FIGHT
AND MY FRIENDLY NEMESIS,
IN A BOLD AND DESPERATE MOVE, SALLY HAD ROBOTICIZED, CREATING:
IT ENDED UGLY, WITH BOTH OF US CRASHING INTO ROBOTROPOLIS, SETTING OFF A STOCKPILE OF NUCLEAR BOMBS!
THIS WAS AN EPIC BATTLE!**
AFTERWARD, MY ENCHANTED "MAGIC RING" #1,000,000,000 RESTORED MY TRUE PHYSICAL AND SPIRITUAL SELF...
... TROUBLE IS EVERYBODY THINKS I DISOBEYED THE COUNCIL, A MUTINOUS ACT!
*A RECAP OF LAST ISSUE'S "RAGE AGAINST THE MACHINE."- EDTIOR
**YOU SAW IT IN MECHA MADNESS SPECIAL #1.- EDTIOR
THEY PUT ME HERE...
... IN THIS JAILHOUSE!
... ME!..

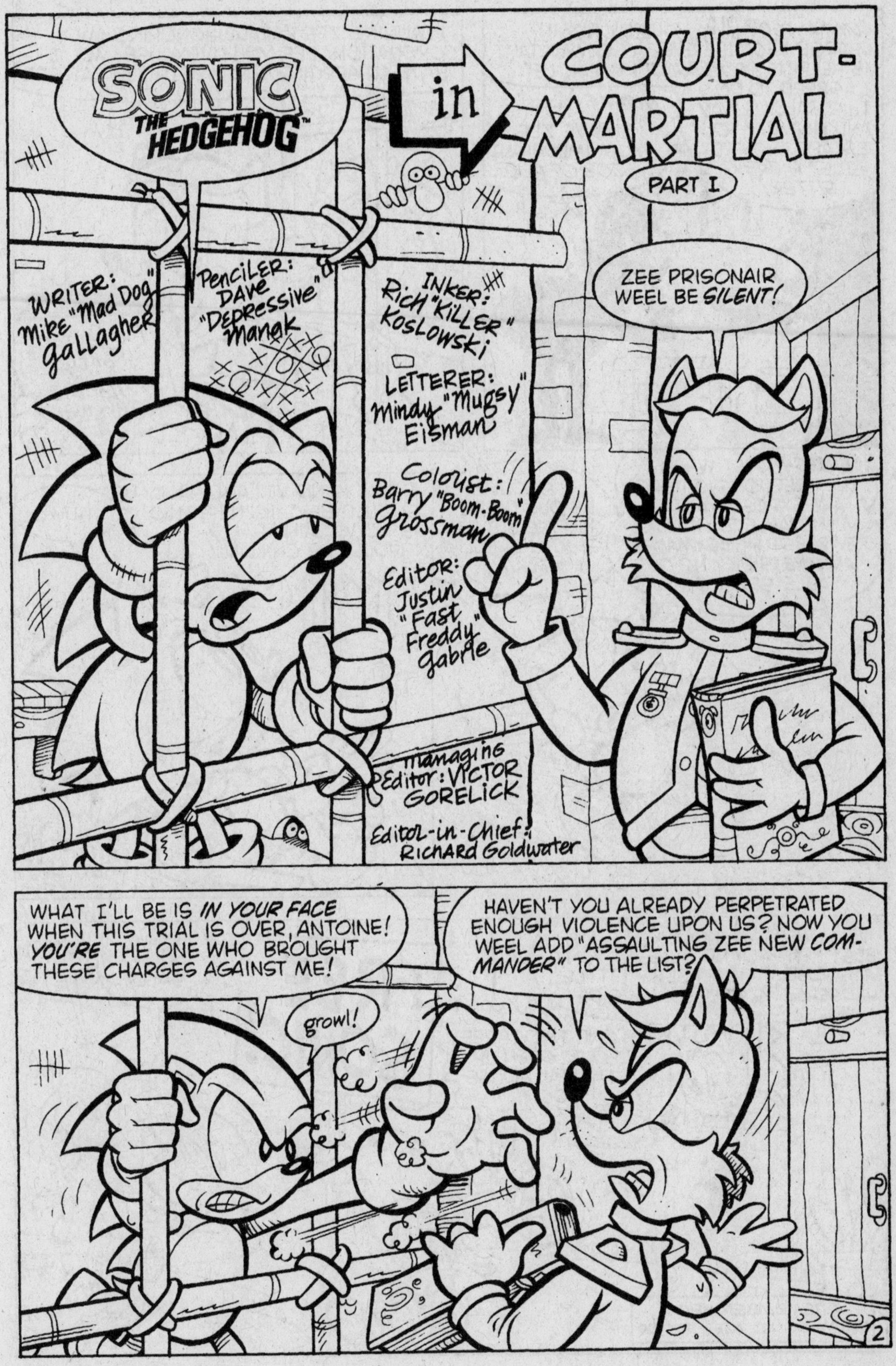
SONIC THE HEDGEHOG
in
COURT-MARTIAL
PART I
WRITER: Mike "Mad Dog" Gallagher
PENCILER: Dave "Depressive" Manak
INKER: Rich "Killer" Koslowski
LETTERER: Mindy "Mugsy" Eisman
Colorist: Barry "Boom-Boom" Grossman
Editor: Justin "Fast Freddy" Gabrie
Managing Editor: VICTOR GORELICK
Editor-in-Chief: RICHARD Goldwater
ZEE PRISONAIR WEEL BE SILENT!
WHAT I'LL BE IS IN YOUR FACE WHEN THIS TRIAL IS OVER, ANTOINE! YOU'RE THE ONE WHO BROUGHT THESE CHARGES AGAINST ME!
growl!
HAVEN'T YOU ALREADY PERPETRATED ENOUGH VIOLENCE UPON US? NOW YOU WEEL ADD "ASSAULTING ZEE NEW COMMANDER" TO THE LIST?
2

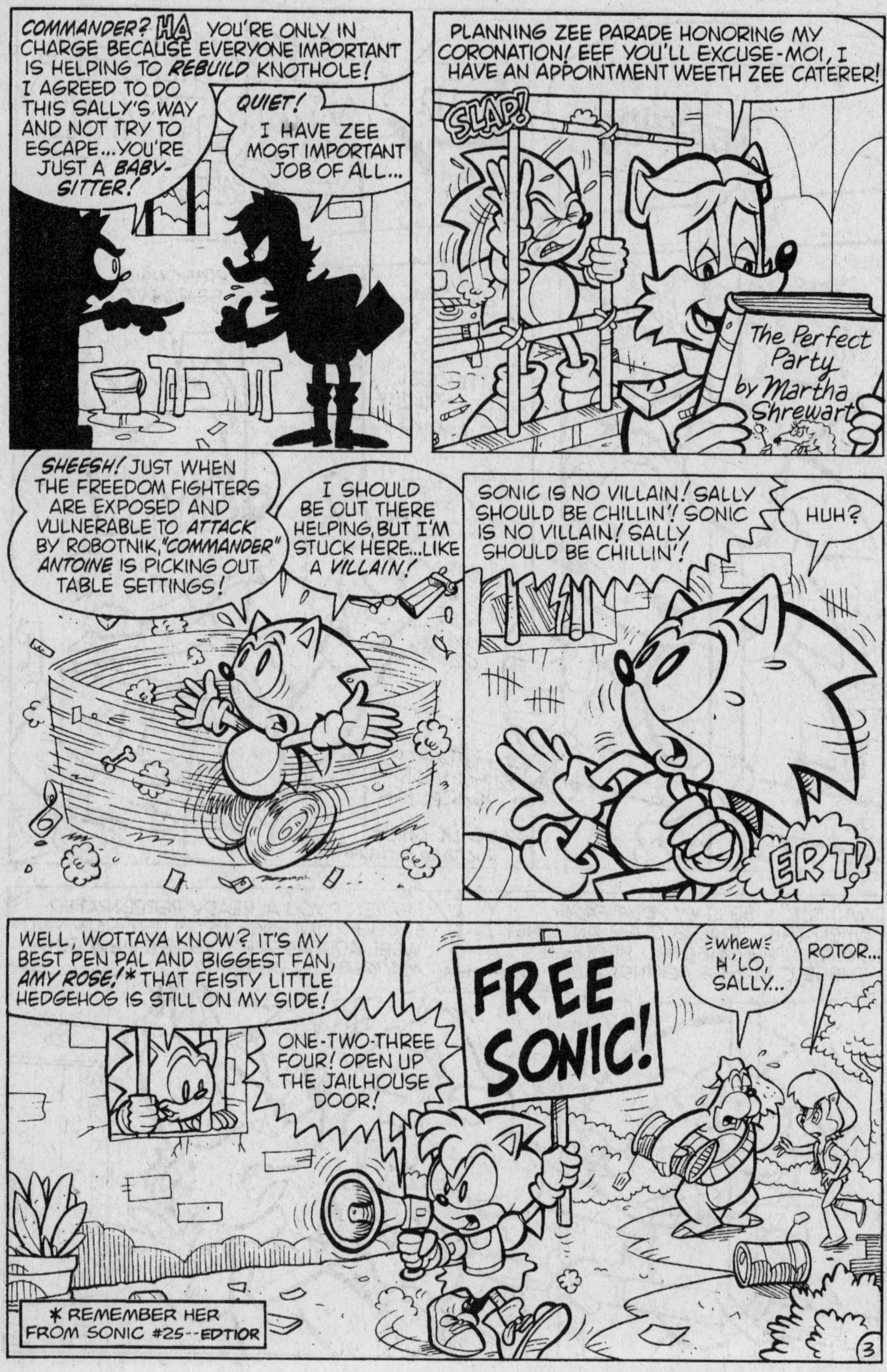
COMMANDER? HA YOU'RE ONLY IN CHARGE BECAUSE EVERYONE IMPORTANT IS HELPING TO REBUILD KNOTHOLE!
I AGREED TO DO THIS SALLY'S WAY AND NOT TRY TO ESCAPE...YOU'RE JUST A BABY-SITTER!
QUIET! I HAVE ZEE MOST IMPORTANT JOB OF ALL...
PLANNING ZEE PARADE HONORING MY CORONATION! EEF YOU'LL EXCUSE-MOI, I HAVE AN APPOINTMENT WEETH ZEE CATERER!
SLAP!
The Perfect Party by Martha Shrewart
SHEESH! JUST WHEN THE FREEDOM FIGHTERS ARE EXPOSED AND VULNERABLE TO ATTACK BY ROBOTNIK, "COMMANDER" ANTOINE IS PICKING OUT TABLE SETTINGS!
I SHOULD BE OUT THERE HELPING, BUT I'M STUCK HERE...LIKE A VILLAIN!
SONIC IS NO VILLAIN! SALLY SHOULD BE CHILLIN'! SONIC IS NO VILLAIN! SALLY SHOULD BE CHILLIN'!
HUH?
ERT!
WELL, WOTTAYA KNOW? IT'S MY BEST PEN PAL AND BIGGEST FAN, AMY ROSE!* THAT FEISTY LITTLE HEDGEHOG IS STILL ON MY SIDE!
FREE SONIC!
ONE-TWO-THREE FOUR! OPEN UP THE JAILHOUSE DOOR!
whew H'LO, SALLY...
ROTOR...
* REMEMBER HER FROM SONIC #25--EDTIOR
3

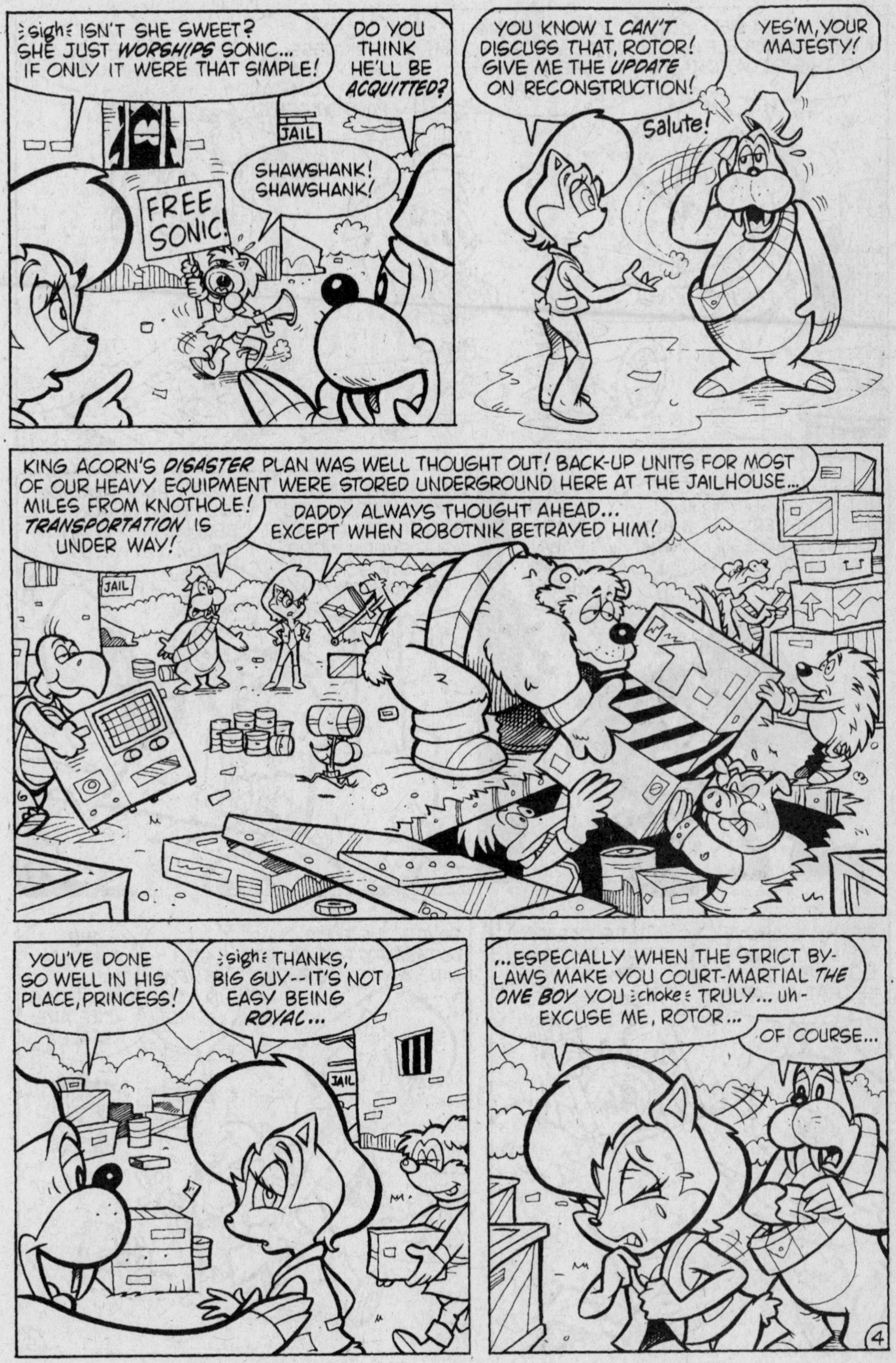
⁝sigh⁝ ISN'T SHE SWEET? SHE JUST WORSHIPS SONIC... IF ONLY IT WERE THAT SIMPLE!
DO YOU THINK HE'LL BE ACQUITTED?
JAIL
SHAWSHANK! SHAWSHANK!
FREE SONIC!
YOU KNOW I CAN'T DISCUSS THAT, ROTOR! GIVE ME THE UPDATE ON RECONSTRUCTION!
YES'M, YOUR MAJESTY!
Salute!
KING ACORN'S DISASTER PLAN WAS WELL THOUGHT OUT! BACK-UP UNITS FOR MOST OF OUR HEAVY EQUIPMENT WERE STORED UNDERGROUND HERE AT THE JAILHOUSE... MILES FROM KNOTHOLE! TRANSPORTATION IS UNDER WAY!
DADDY ALWAYS THOUGHT AHEAD... EXCEPT WHEN ROBOTNIK BETRAYED HIM!
JAIL
YOU'VE DONE SO WELL IN HIS PLACE, PRINCESS!
⁝sigh⁝ THANKS, BIG GUY--IT'S NOT EASY BEING ROYAL...
JAIL
...ESPECIALLY WHEN THE STRICT BY-LAWS MAKE YOU COURT-MARTIAL THE ONE BOY YOU ⁝choke⁝ TRULY... uh- EXCUSE ME, ROTOR...
OF COURSE...
4

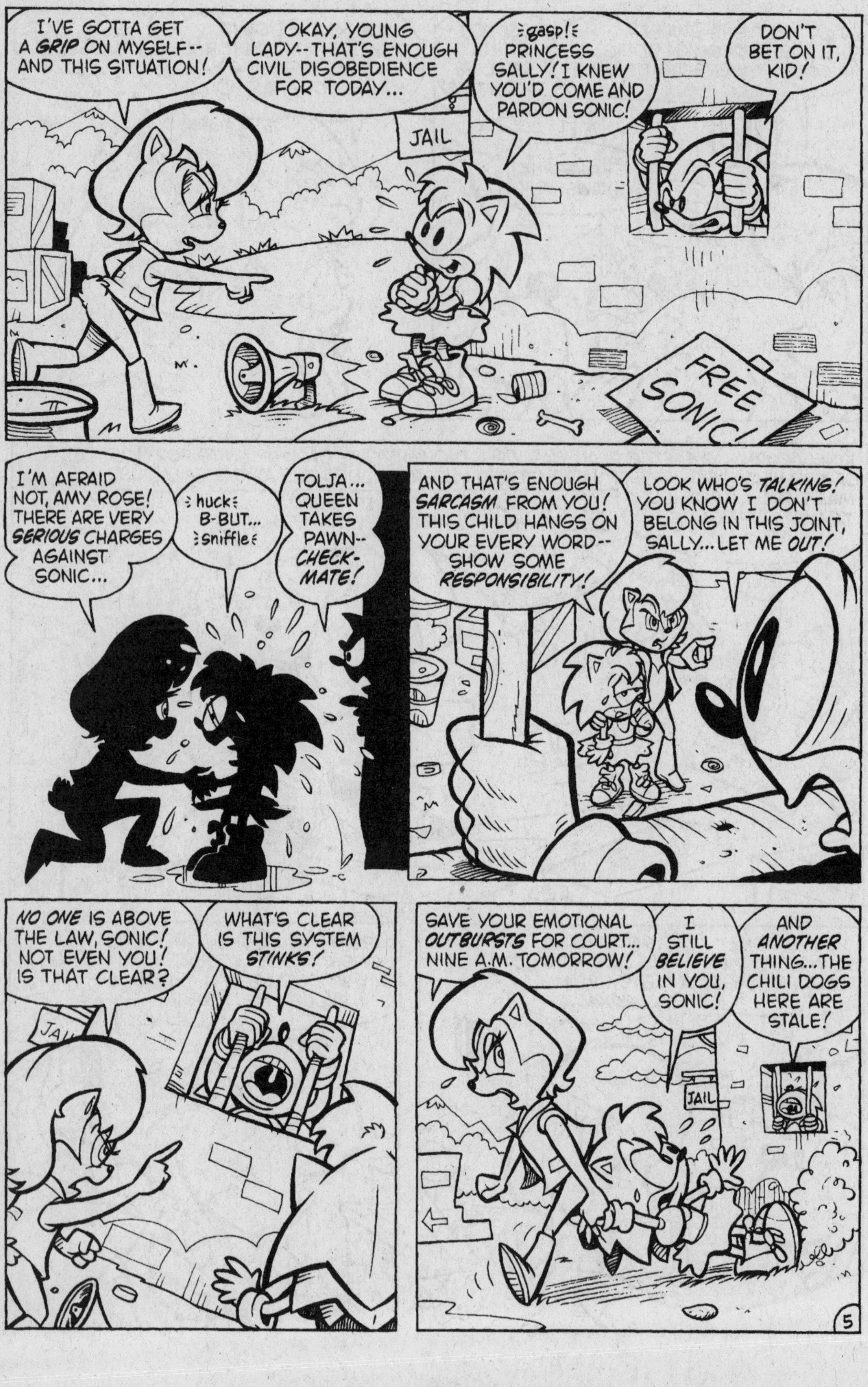
I'VE GOTTA GET A GRIP ON MYSELF-- AND THIS SITUATION!
OKAY, YOUNG LADY--THAT'S ENOUGH CIVIL DISOBEDIENCE FOR TODAY...
gasp! PRINCESS SALLY! I KNEW YOU'D COME AND PARDON SONIC!
DON'T BET ON IT, KID!
JAIL
FREE SONIC!
I'M AFRAID NOT, AMY ROSE! THERE ARE VERY SERIOUS CHARGES AGAINST SONIC...
huck B-BUT... sniffle
TOLJA... QUEEN TAKES PAWN-- CHECK-MATE!
AND THAT'S ENOUGH SARCASM FROM YOU! THIS CHILD HANGS ON YOUR EVERY WORD-- SHOW SOME RESPONSIBILITY!
LOOK WHO'S TALKING! YOU KNOW I DON'T BELONG IN THIS JOINT, SALLY... LET ME OUT!
NO ONE IS ABOVE THE LAW, SONIC! NOT EVEN YOU! IS THAT CLEAR?
WHAT'S CLEAR IS THIS SYSTEM STINKS!
SAVE YOUR EMOTIONAL OUTBURSTS FOR COURT... NINE A.M. TOMORROW!
I STILL BELIEVE IN YOU, SONIC!
AND ANOTHER THING... THE CHILI DOGS HERE ARE STALE!
JAIL
5

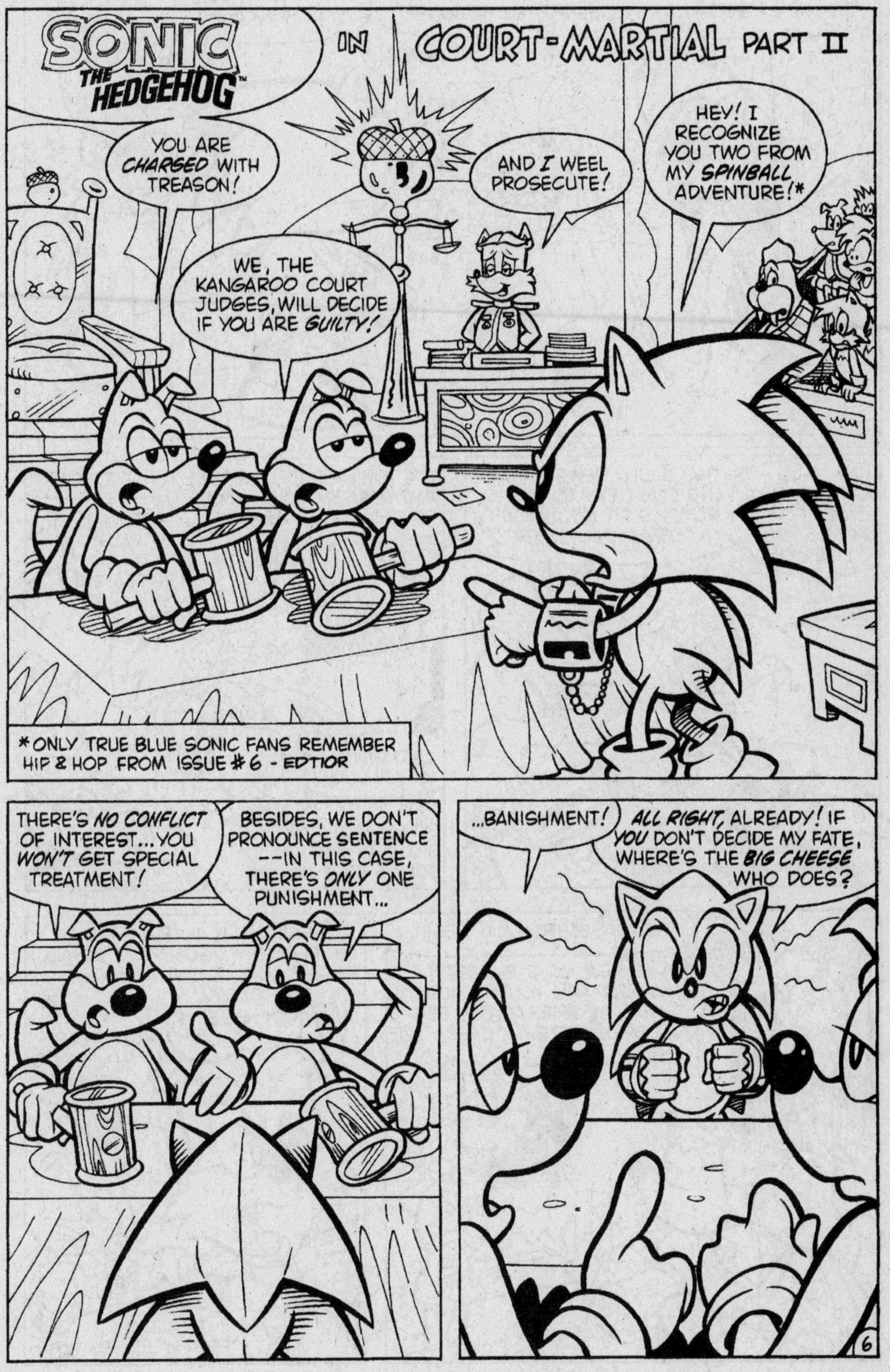
SONIC THE HEDGEHOG™
IN
COURT-MARTIAL PART II
YOU ARE CHARGED WITH TREASON!
WE, THE KANGAROO COURT JUDGES, WILL DECIDE IF YOU ARE GUILTY!
AND I WEEL PROSECUTE!
HEY! I RECOGNIZE YOU TWO FROM MY SPINBALL ADVENTURE!*
*ONLY TRUE BLUE SONIC FANS REMEMBER HIP & HOP FROM ISSUE #6 - EDTIOR
THERE'S NO CONFLICT OF INTEREST...YOU WON'T GET SPECIAL TREATMENT!
BESIDES, WE DON'T PRONOUNCE SENTENCE --IN THIS CASE, THERE'S ONLY ONE PUNISHMENT...
...BANISHMENT!
ALL RIGHT, ALREADY! IF YOU DON'T DECIDE MY FATE, WHERE'S THE BIG CHEESE WHO DOES?
6

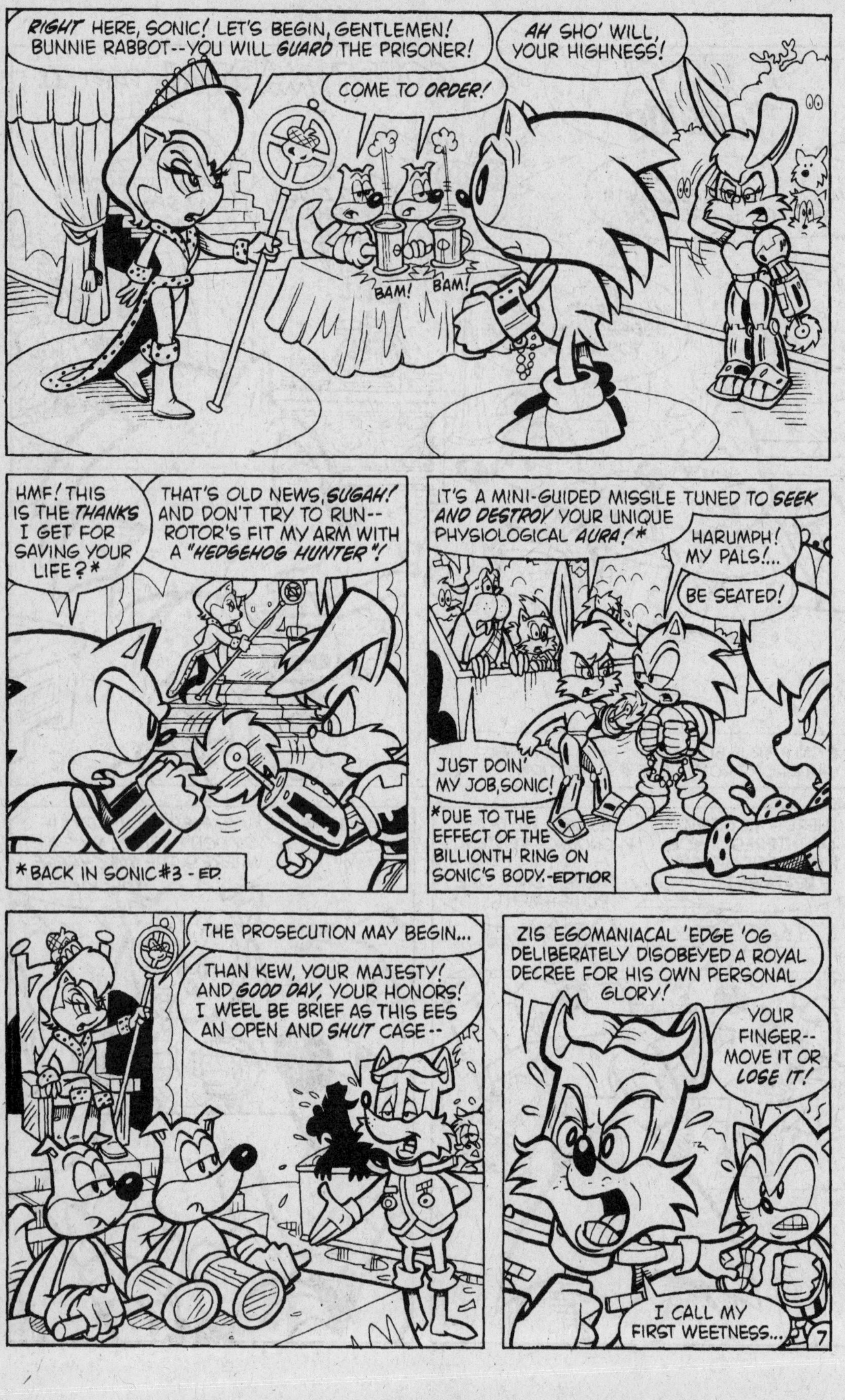
RIGHT HERE, SONIC! LET'S BEGIN, GENTLEMEN! BUNNIE RABBOT--YOU WILL GUARD THE PRISONER!
AH SHO' WILL, YOUR HIGHNESS!
COME TO ORDER!
BAM! BAM!
HMF! THIS IS THE THANKS I GET FOR SAVING YOUR LIFE?*
THAT'S OLD NEWS, SUGAH! AND DON'T TRY TO RUN-- ROTOR'S FIT MY ARM WITH A "HEDGEHOG HUNTER"!
*BACK IN SONIC #3 - ED.
IT'S A MINI-GUIDED MISSILE TUNED TO SEEK AND DESTROY YOUR UNIQUE PHYSIOLOGICAL AURA!*
HARUMPH! MY PALS!...
BE SEATED!
JUST DOIN' MY JOB, SONIC!
*DUE TO THE EFFECT OF THE BILLIONTH RING ON SONIC'S BODY.-EDTIOR
THE PROSECUTION MAY BEGIN...
THAN KEW, YOUR MAJESTY! AND GOOD DAY, YOUR HONORS! I WEEL BE BRIEF AS THIS EES AN OPEN AND SHUT CASE--
ZIS EGOMANIACAL 'EDGE 'OG DELIBERATELY DISOBEYED A ROYAL DECREE FOR HIS OWN PERSONAL GLORY!
YOUR FINGER-- MOVE IT OR LOSE IT!
I CALL MY FIRST WEETNESS...
7

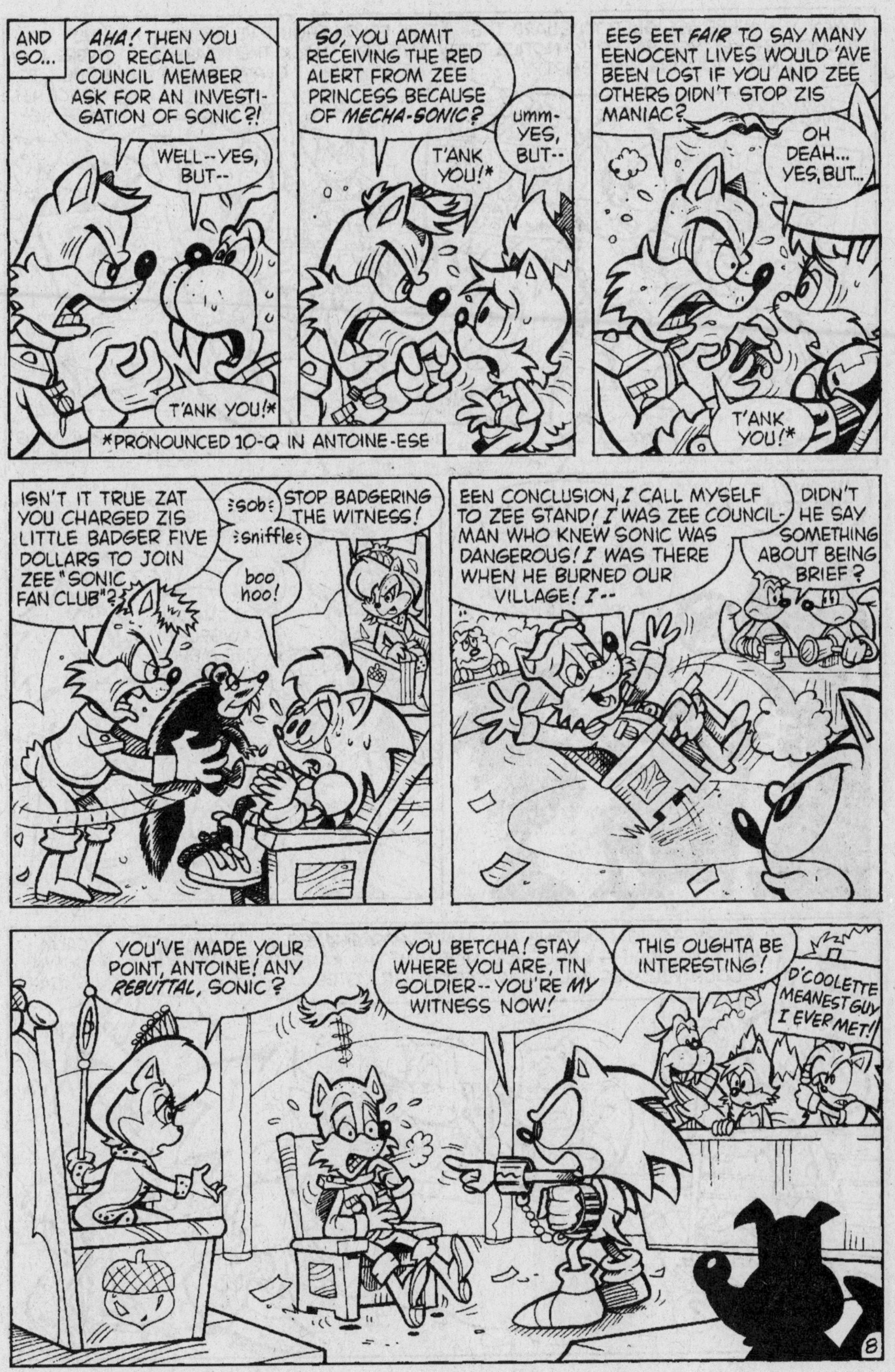
AND SO...
AHA! THEN YOU DO RECALL A COUNCIL MEMBER ASK FOR AN INVESTIGATION OF SONIC?!
WELL--YES, BUT--
T'ANK YOU!*
SO, YOU ADMIT RECEIVING THE RED ALERT FROM ZEE PRINCESS BECAUSE OF MECHA-SONIC?
umm-YES, BUT--
T'ANK YOU!*
EES EET FAIR TO SAY MANY EENOCENT LIVES WOULD 'AVE BEEN LOST IF YOU AND ZEE OTHERS DIDN'T STOP ZIS MANIAC?
OH DEAH... YES, BUT...
T'ANK YOU!*
*PRONOUNCED 10-Q IN ANTOINE-ESE
ISN'T IT TRUE ZAT YOU CHARGED ZIS LITTLE BADGER FIVE DOLLARS TO JOIN ZEE "SONIC FAN CLUB"?
sob
sniffle
boo hoo!
STOP BADGERING THE WITNESS!
EEN CONCLUSION, I CALL MYSELF TO ZEE STAND! I WAS ZEE COUNCILMAN WHO KNEW SONIC WAS DANGEROUS! I WAS THERE WHEN HE BURNED OUR VILLAGE! I--
DIDN'T HE SAY SOMETHING ABOUT BEING BRIEF?
YOU'VE MADE YOUR POINT, ANTOINE! ANY REBUTTAL, SONIC?
YOU BETCHA! STAY WHERE YOU ARE, TIN SOLDIER--YOU'RE MY WITNESS NOW!
THIS OUGHTA BE INTERESTING!
D'COOLETTE MEANEST GUY I EVER MET!
8

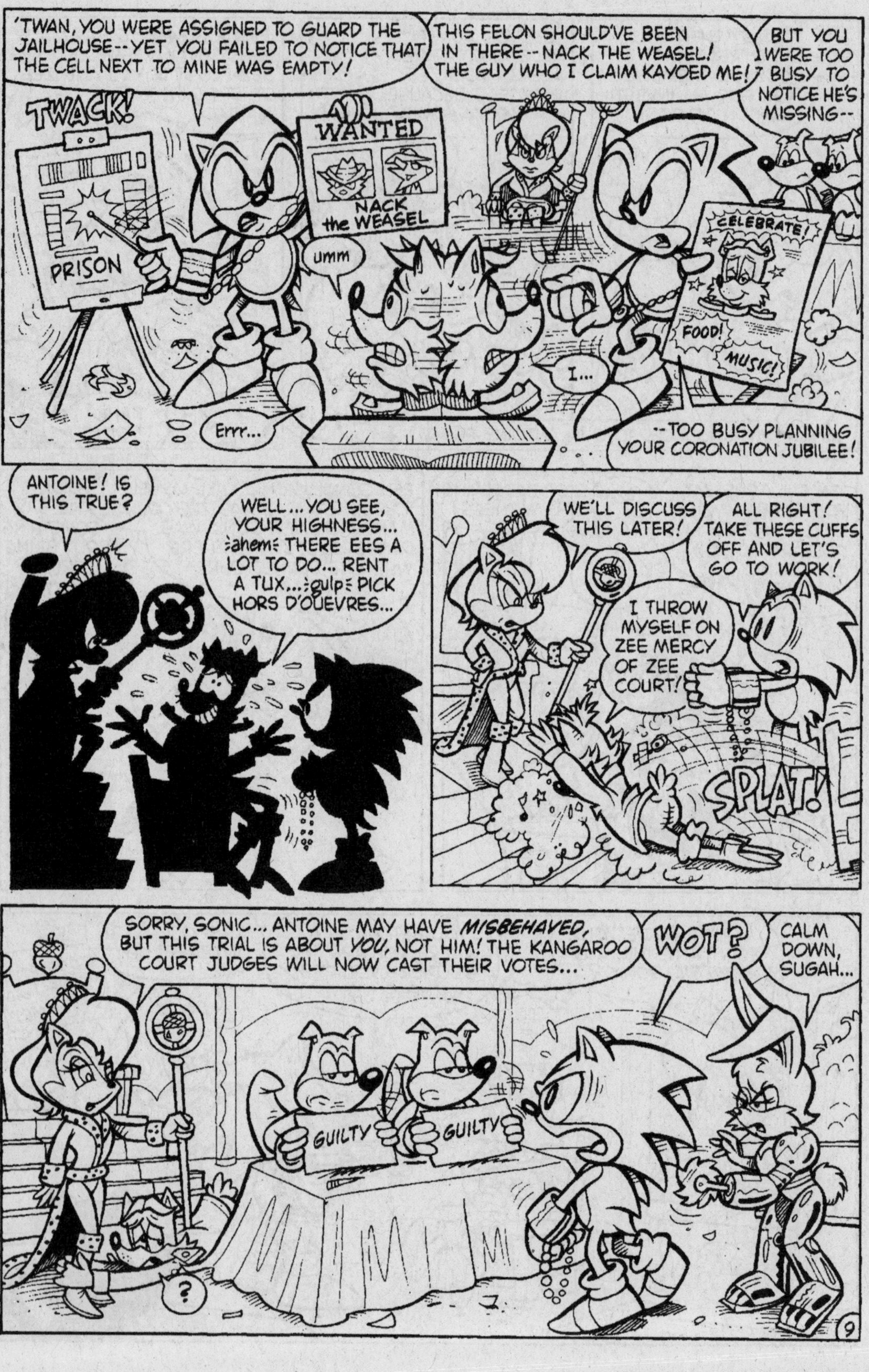
'TWAN, YOU WERE ASSIGNED TO GUARD THE JAILHOUSE--YET YOU FAILED TO NOTICE THAT THE CELL NEXT TO MINE WAS EMPTY!
TWACK!
PRISON
WANTED
NACK the WEASEL
umm
Errr...
THIS FELON SHOULD'VE BEEN IN THERE--NACK THE WEASEL! THE GUY WHO I CLAIM KAYOED ME!
BUT YOU WERE TOO BUSY TO NOTICE HE'S MISSING--
CELEBRATE!
FOOD!
MUSIC!
I...
--TOO BUSY PLANNING YOUR CORONATION JUBILEE!
ANTOINE! IS THIS TRUE?
WELL... YOU SEE, YOUR HIGHNESS... ahem THERE EES A LOT TO DO... RENT A TUX... gulp PICK HORS D'OUEVRES...
WE'LL DISCUSS THIS LATER!
ALL RIGHT! TAKE THESE CUFFS OFF AND LET'S GO TO WORK!
I THROW MYSELF ON ZEE MERCY OF ZEE COURT!
SPLAT!
SORRY, SONIC... ANTOINE MAY HAVE MISBEHAVED, BUT THIS TRIAL IS ABOUT YOU, NOT HIM! THE KANGAROO COURT JUDGES WILL NOW CAST THEIR VOTES...
WOT?
CALM DOWN, SUGAH...
GUILTY
GUILTY
?
9

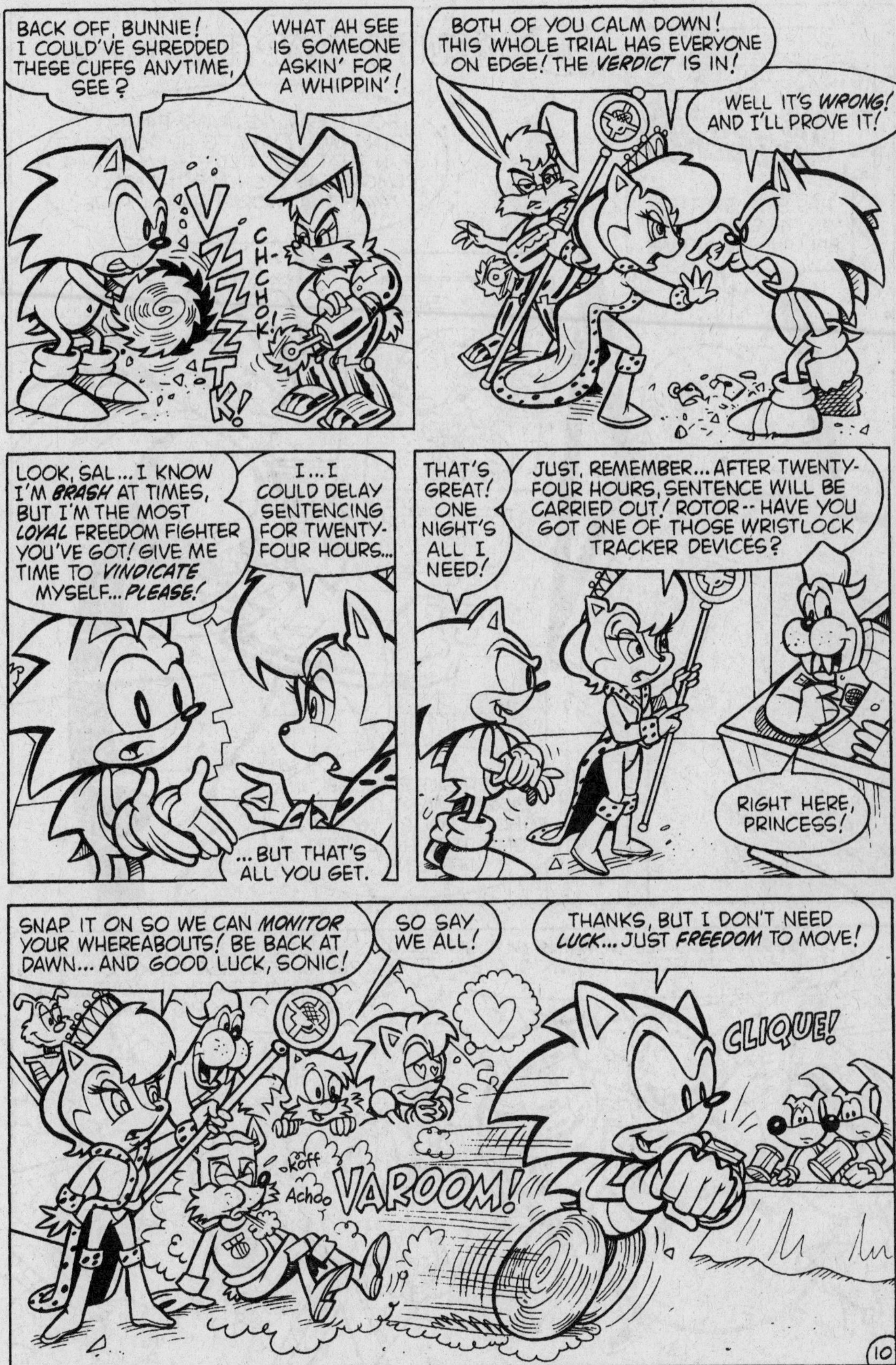
BACK OFF, BUNNIE! I COULD'VE SHREDDED THESE CUFFS ANYTIME, SEE?
WHAT AH SEE IS SOMEONE ASKIN' FOR A WHIPPIN'!
VZZZZTK!
CH-CHCHOK!
BOTH OF YOU CALM DOWN! THIS WHOLE TRIAL HAS EVERYONE ON EDGE! THE VERDICT IS IN!
WELL IT'S WRONG! AND I'LL PROVE IT!
LOOK, SAL... I KNOW I'M BRASH AT TIMES, BUT I'M THE MOST LOYAL FREEDOM FIGHTER YOU'VE GOT! GIVE ME TIME TO VINDICATE MYSELF... PLEASE!
I... I COULD DELAY SENTENCING FOR TWENTY-FOUR HOURS...
...BUT THAT'S ALL YOU GET.
THAT'S GREAT! ONE NIGHT'S ALL I NEED!
JUST, REMEMBER... AFTER TWENTY-FOUR HOURS, SENTENCE WILL BE CARRIED OUT! ROTOR -- HAVE YOU GOT ONE OF THOSE WRISTLOCK TRACKER DEVICES?
RIGHT HERE, PRINCESS!
SNAP IT ON SO WE CAN MONITOR YOUR WHEREABOUTS! BE BACK AT DAWN... AND GOOD LUCK, SONIC!
SO SAY WE ALL!
THANKS, BUT I DON'T NEED LUCK... JUST FREEDOM TO MOVE!
CLIQUE!
koff
Achoo
VAROOM!
10

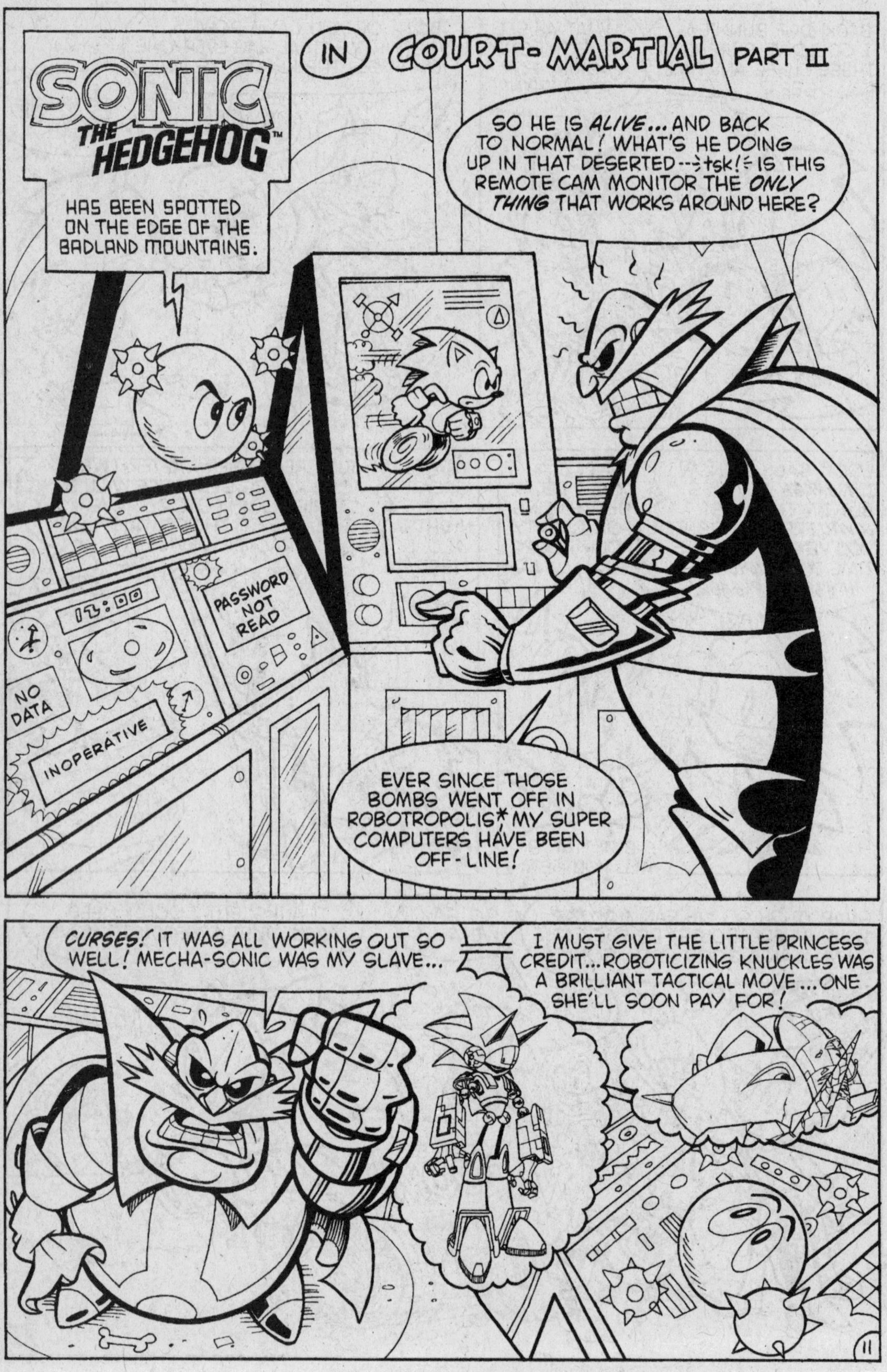
SONIC THE HEDGEHOG™
IN COURT-MARTIAL PART III
HAS BEEN SPOTTED ON THE EDGE OF THE BADLAND MOUNTAINS.
SO HE IS ALIVE... AND BACK TO NORMAL! WHAT'S HE DOING UP IN THAT DESERTED--tsk!--IS THIS REMOTE CAM MONITOR THE ONLY THING THAT WORKS AROUND HERE?
PASSWORD NOT READ
NO DATA
INOPERATIVE
EVER SINCE THOSE BOMBS WENT OFF IN ROBOTROPOLIS* MY SUPER COMPUTERS HAVE BEEN OFF-LINE!
CURSES! IT WAS ALL WORKING OUT SO WELL! MECHA-SONIC WAS MY SLAVE...
I MUST GIVE THE LITTLE PRINCESS CREDIT... ROBOTICIZING KNUCKLES WAS A BRILLIANT TACTICAL MOVE... ONE SHE'LL SOON PAY FOR!
11

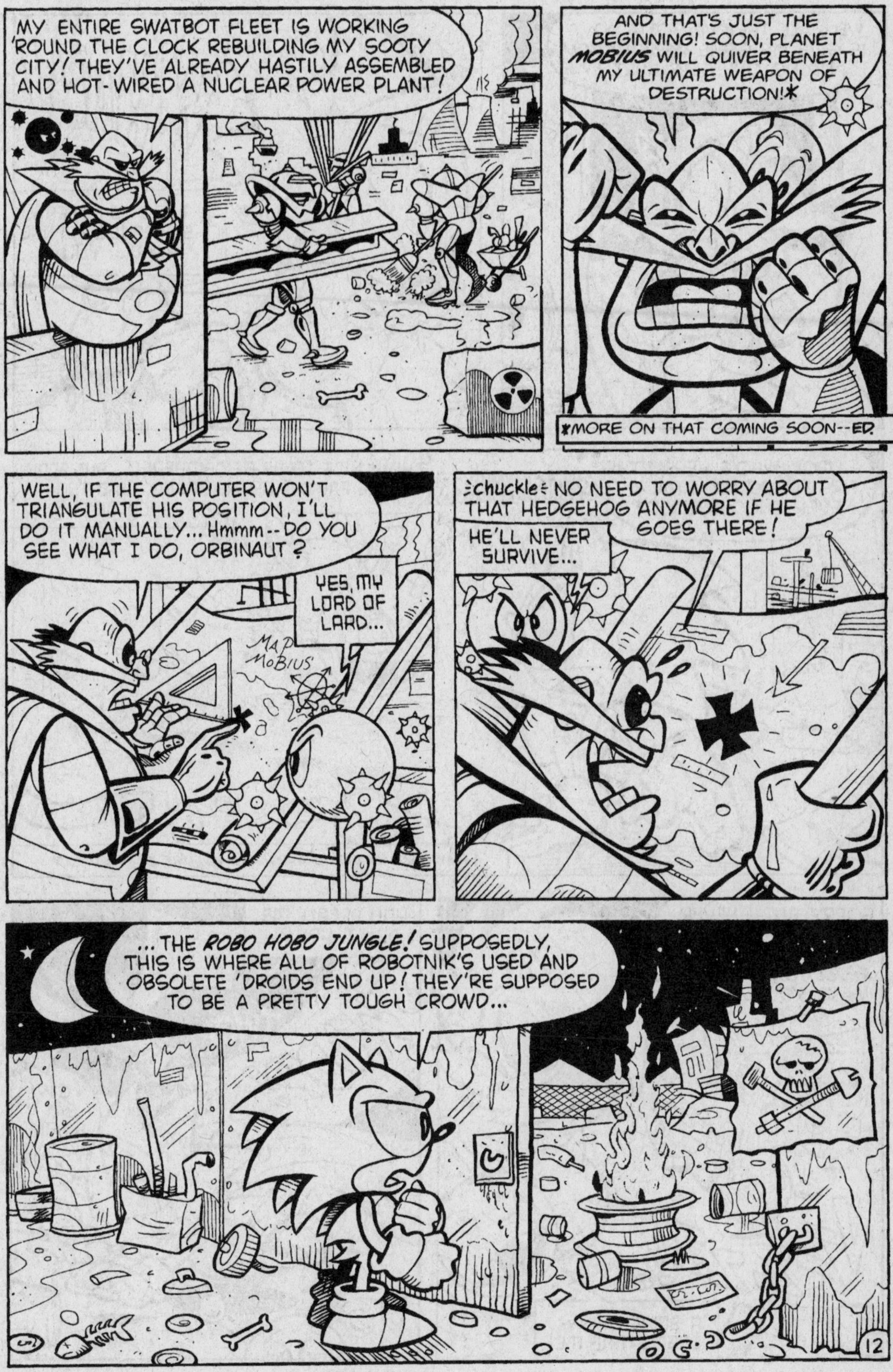
MY ENTIRE SWATBOT FLEET IS WORKING 'ROUND THE CLOCK REBUILDING MY SOOTY CITY! THEY'VE ALREADY HASTILY ASSEMBLED AND HOT-WIRED A NUCLEAR POWER PLANT!
AND THAT'S JUST THE BEGINNING! SOON, PLANET MOBIUS WILL QUIVER BENEATH MY ULTIMATE WEAPON OF DESTRUCTION!*
*MORE ON THAT COMING SOON--ED.
WELL, IF THE COMPUTER WON'T TRIANGULATE HIS POSITION, I'LL DO IT MANUALLY... Hmmm--DO YOU SEE WHAT I DO, ORBINAUT?
YES, MY LORD OF LARD...
MAP MOBIUS
≡chuckle≡ NO NEED TO WORRY ABOUT THAT HEDGEHOG ANYMORE IF HE GOES THERE!
HE'LL NEVER SURVIVE...
...THE ROBO HOBO JUNGLE! SUPPOSEDLY, THIS IS WHERE ALL OF ROBOTNIK'S USED AND OBSOLETE 'DROIDS END UP! THEY'RE SUPPOSED TO BE A PRETTY TOUGH CROWD...
12

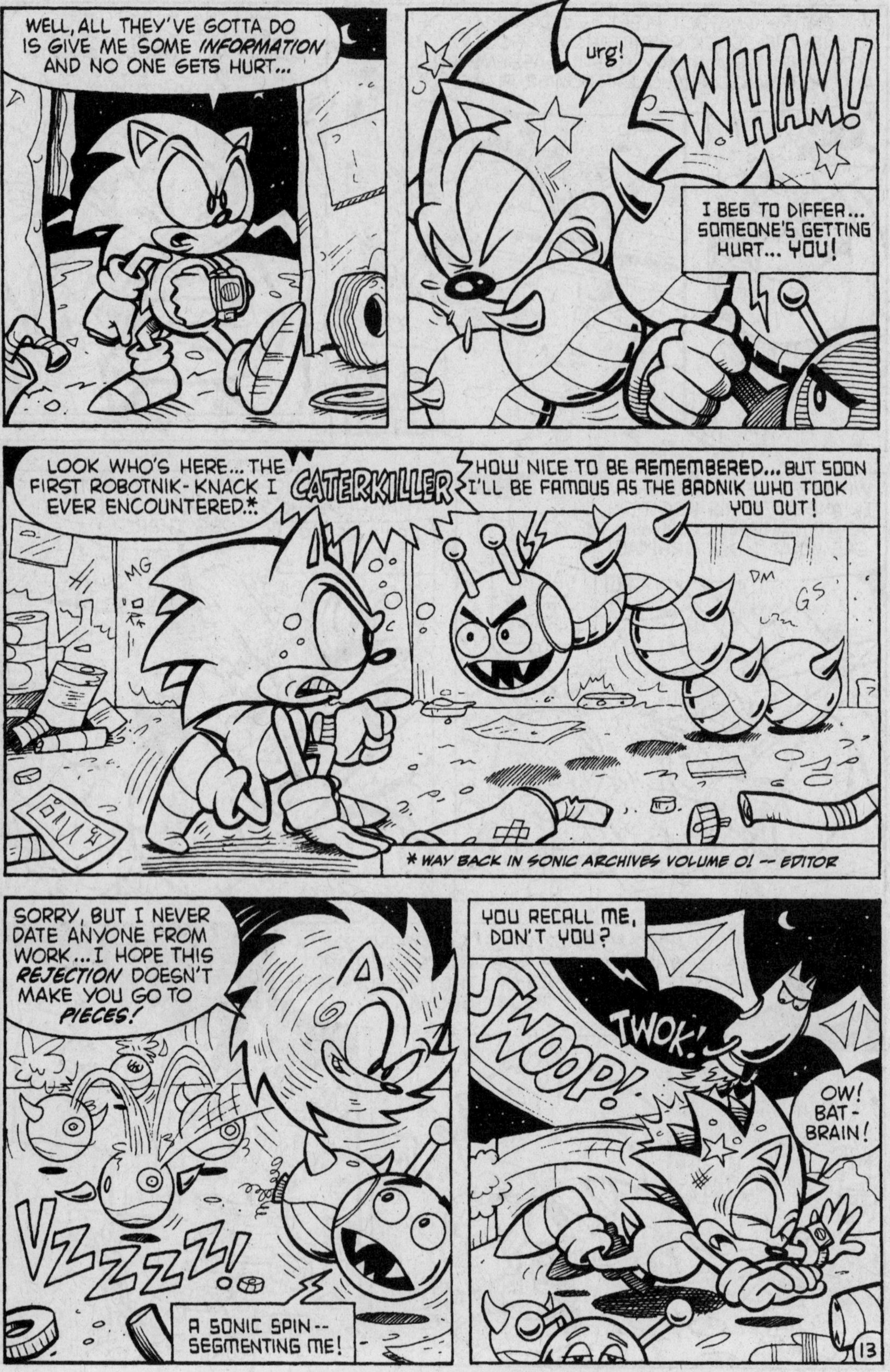
WELL, ALL THEY'VE GOTTA DO IS GIVE ME SOME INFORMATION AND NO ONE GETS HURT...
urg!
WHAM!
I BEG TO DIFFER... SOMEONE'S GETTING HURT... YOU!
LOOK WHO'S HERE... THE FIRST ROBOTNIK-KNACK I EVER ENCOUNTERED.*
CATERKILLER
HOW NICE TO BE REMEMBERED... BUT SOON I'LL BE FAMOUS AS THE BADNIK WHO TOOK YOU OUT!
* WAY BACK IN SONIC ARCHIVES VOLUME 0! -- EDITOR
SORRY, BUT I NEVER DATE ANYONE FROM WORK... I HOPE THIS REJECTION DOESN'T MAKE YOU GO TO PIECES!
VZZZZZ!
A SONIC SPIN-- SEGMENTING ME!
YOU RECALL ME, DON'T YOU?
SWOOP!
TWOK!
OW! BAT-BRAIN!
13

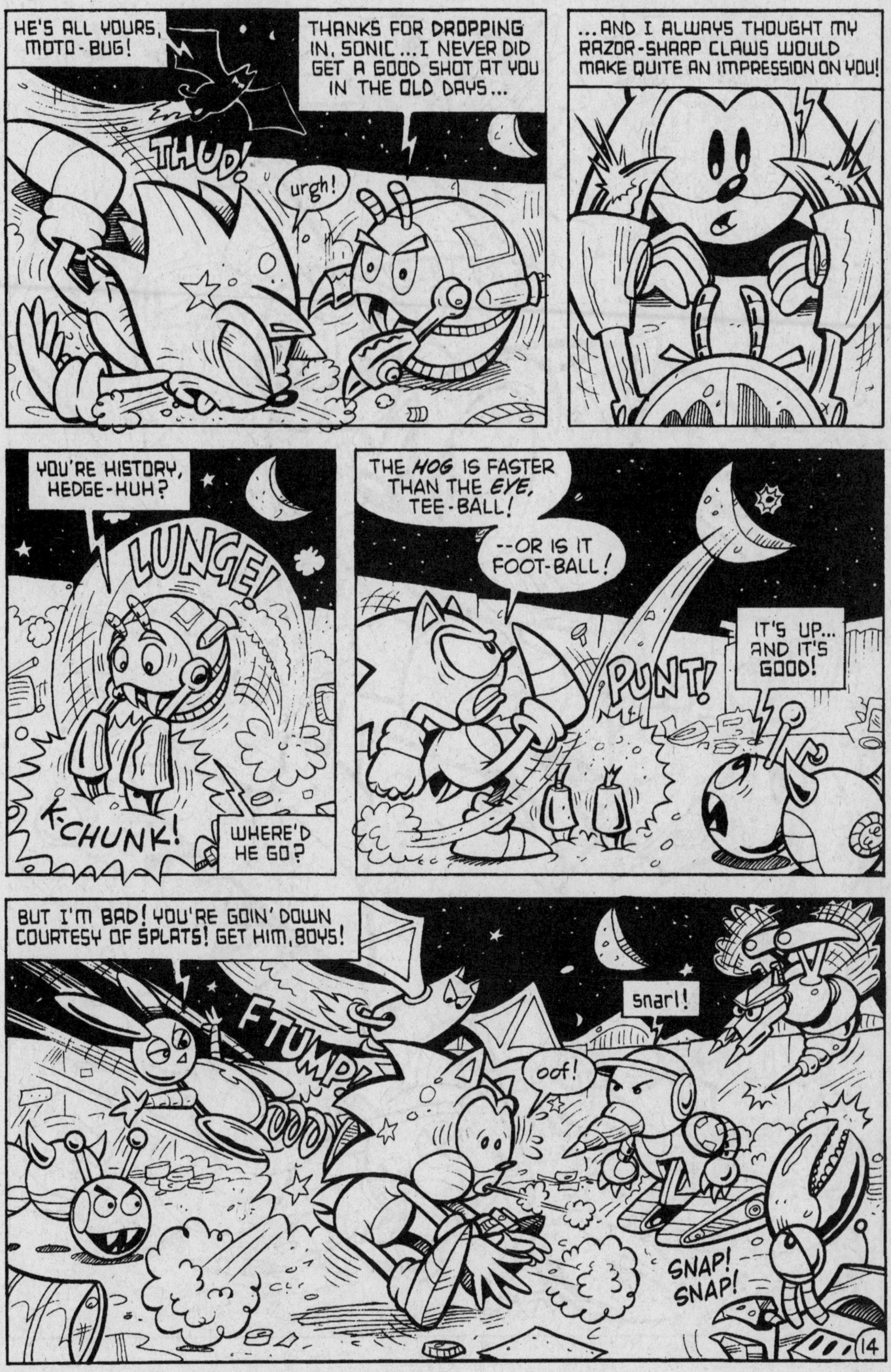
HE'S ALL YOURS, MOTO-BUG!
THUD!
THANKS FOR DROPPING IN, SONIC ... I NEVER DID GET A GOOD SHOT AT YOU IN THE OLD DAYS ...
urgh!
... AND I ALWAYS THOUGHT MY RAZOR-SHARP CLAWS WOULD MAKE QUITE AN IMPRESSION ON YOU!
YOU'RE HISTORY, HEDGE-HUH?
LUNGE!
K-CHUNK!
WHERE'D HE GO?
THE HOG IS FASTER THAN THE EYE, TEE-BALL!
--OR IS IT FOOT-BALL!
PUNT!
IT'S UP... AND IT'S GOOD!
BUT I'M BAD! YOU'RE GOIN' DOWN COURTESY OF SPLATS! GET HIM, BOYS!
FTUMP!
oof!
snarl!
SNAP! SNAP!
14

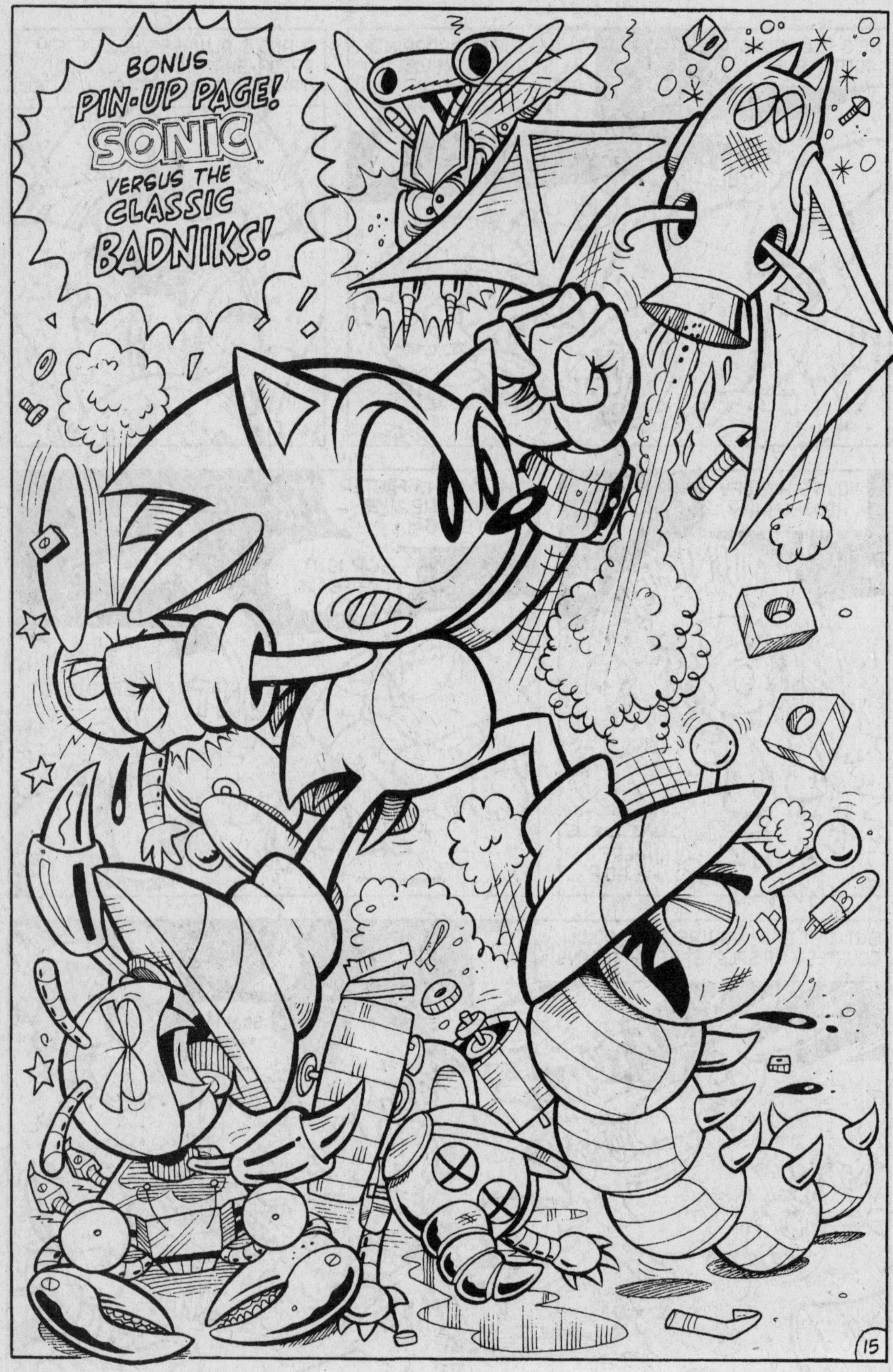
BONUS
PIN-UP PAGE!
SONIC™
VERSUS THE
CLASSIC
BADNIKS!
15

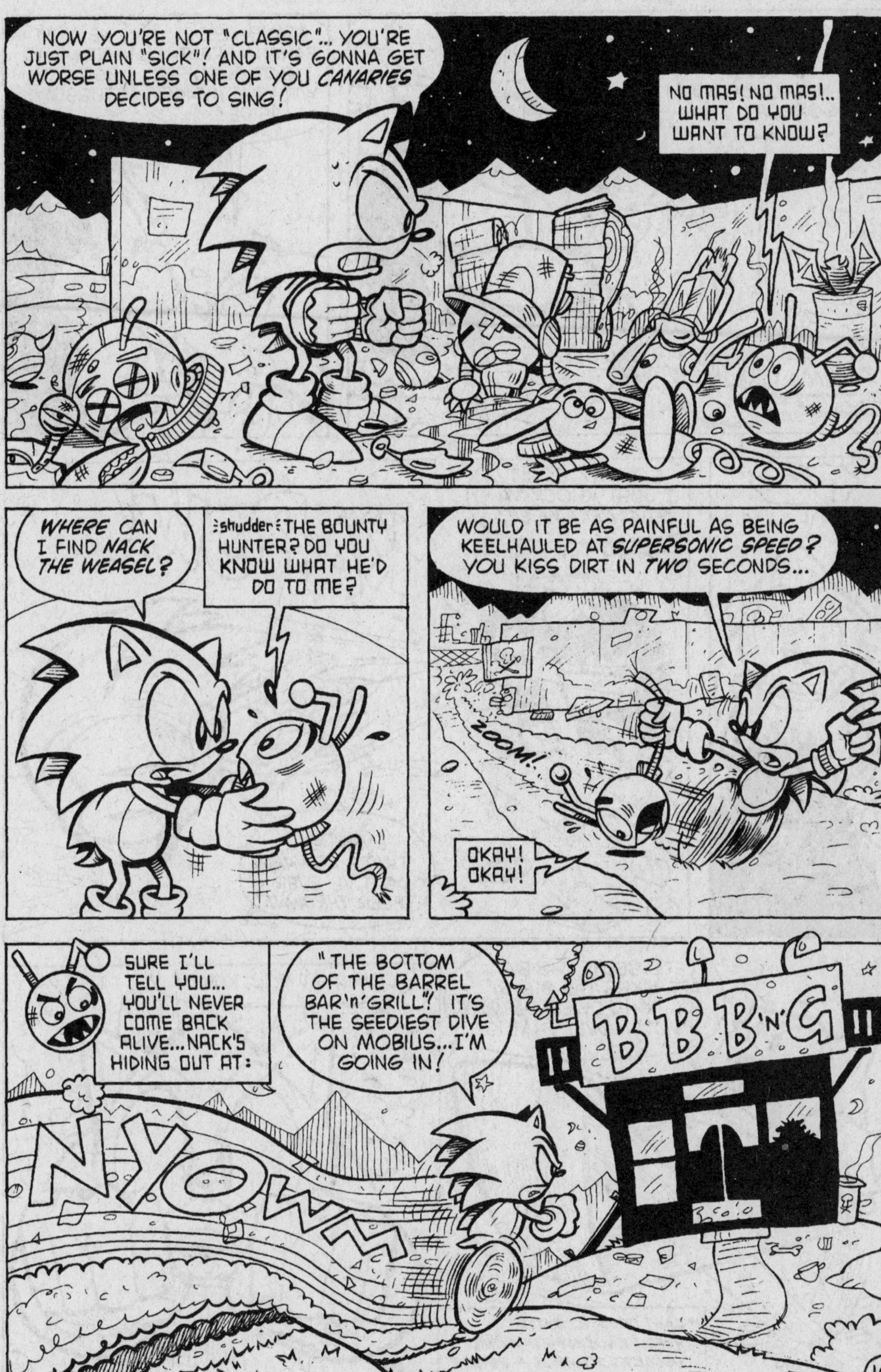
NOW YOU'RE NOT "CLASSIC".. YOU'RE JUST PLAIN "SICK"! AND IT'S GONNA GET WORSE UNLESS ONE OF YOU *CANARIES* DECIDES TO SING!
NO MAS! NO MAS!.. WHAT DO YOU WANT TO KNOW?
WHERE CAN I FIND *NACK THE WEASEL*?
:shudder: THE BOUNTY HUNTER? DO YOU KNOW WHAT HE'D DO TO ME?
WOULD IT BE AS PAINFUL AS BEING KEELHAULED AT *SUPERSONIC SPEED*? YOU KISS DIRT IN *TWO* SECONDS...
ZOOM!
OKAY! OKAY!
SURE I'LL TELL YOU... YOU'LL NEVER COME BACK ALIVE...NACK'S HIDING OUT AT:
"THE BOTTOM OF THE BARREL BAR'n'GRILL"! IT'S THE SEEDIEST DIVE ON MOBIUS...I'M GOING IN!
BBB'N'G
NYOWM
16

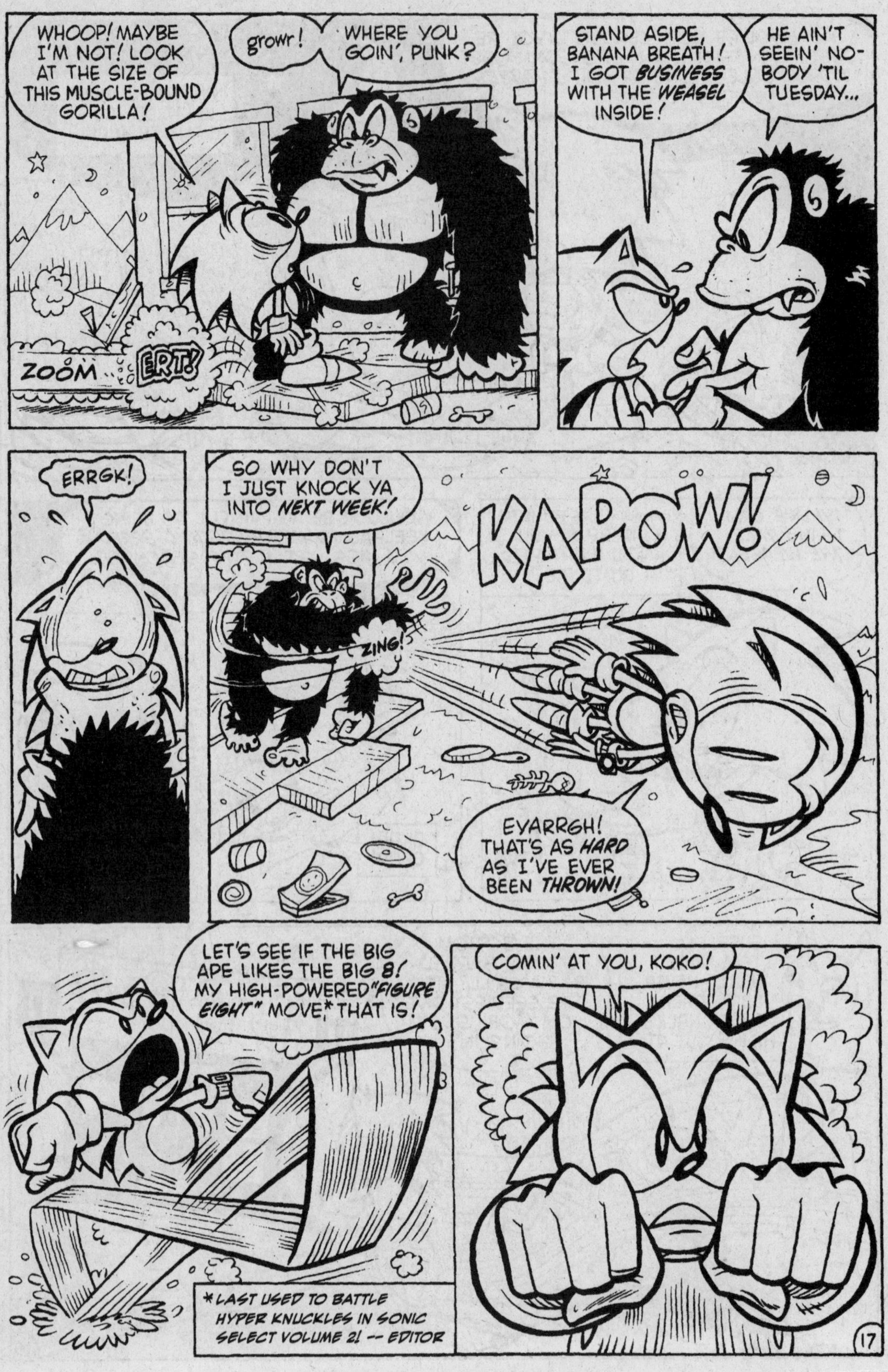
WHOOP! MAYBE I'M NOT! LOOK AT THE SIZE OF THIS MUSCLE-BOUND GORILLA!
growr!
WHERE YOU GOIN', PUNK?
ZOOM
ERT!
STAND ASIDE, BANANA BREATH! I GOT BUSINESS WITH THE WEASEL INSIDE!
HE AIN'T SEEIN' NO-BODY 'TIL TUESDAY...
ERRGK!
SO WHY DON'T I JUST KNOCK YA INTO NEXT WEEK!
KAPOW!
ZING!
EYARRGH! THAT'S AS HARD AS I'VE EVER BEEN THROWN!
LET'S SEE IF THE BIG APE LIKES THE BIG 8! MY HIGH-POWERED "FIGURE EIGHT" MOVE,* THAT IS!
*LAST USED TO BATTLE HYPER KNUCKLES IN SONIC SELECT VOLUME 2! -- EDITOR
COMIN' AT YOU, KOKO!
17

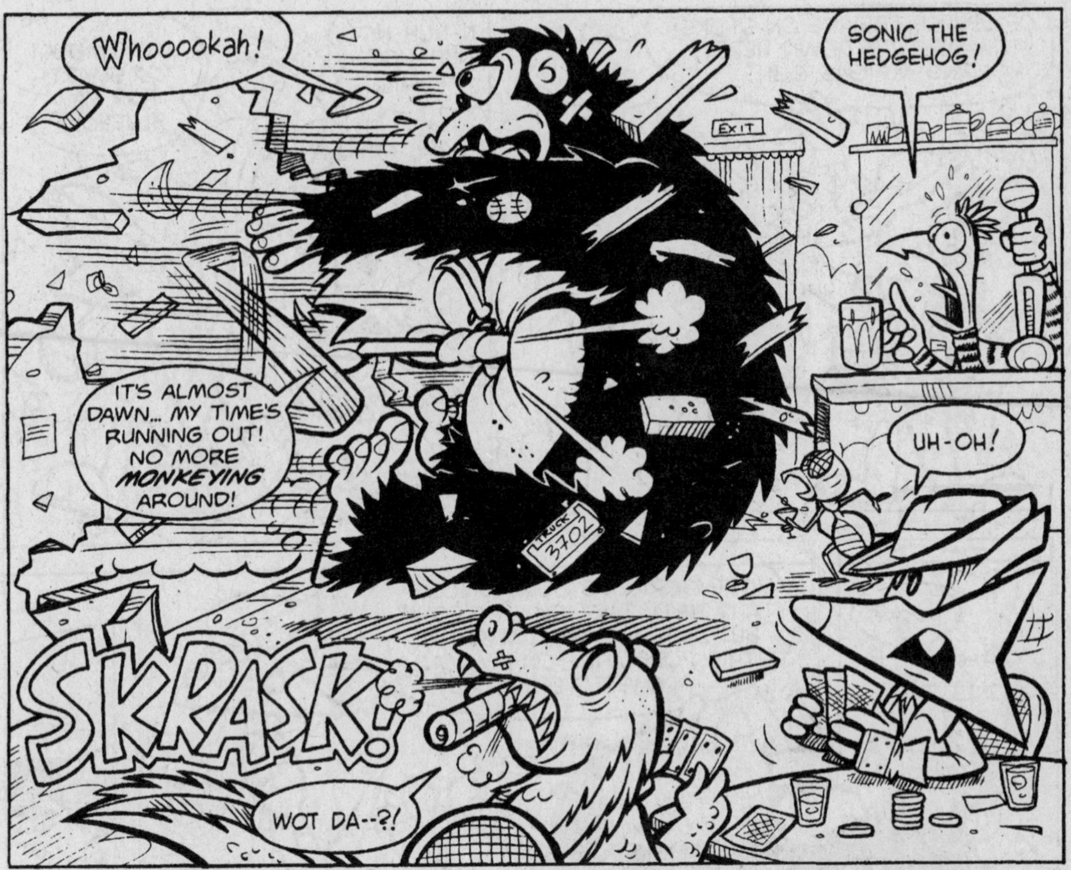
Whoooookah!
SONIC THE HEDGEHOG!
EXIT
IT'S ALMOST DAWN... MY TIME'S RUNNING OUT! NO MORE *MONKEYING* AROUND!
UH-OH!
TRUCK 3702
SKRASK!
WOT DA--?!

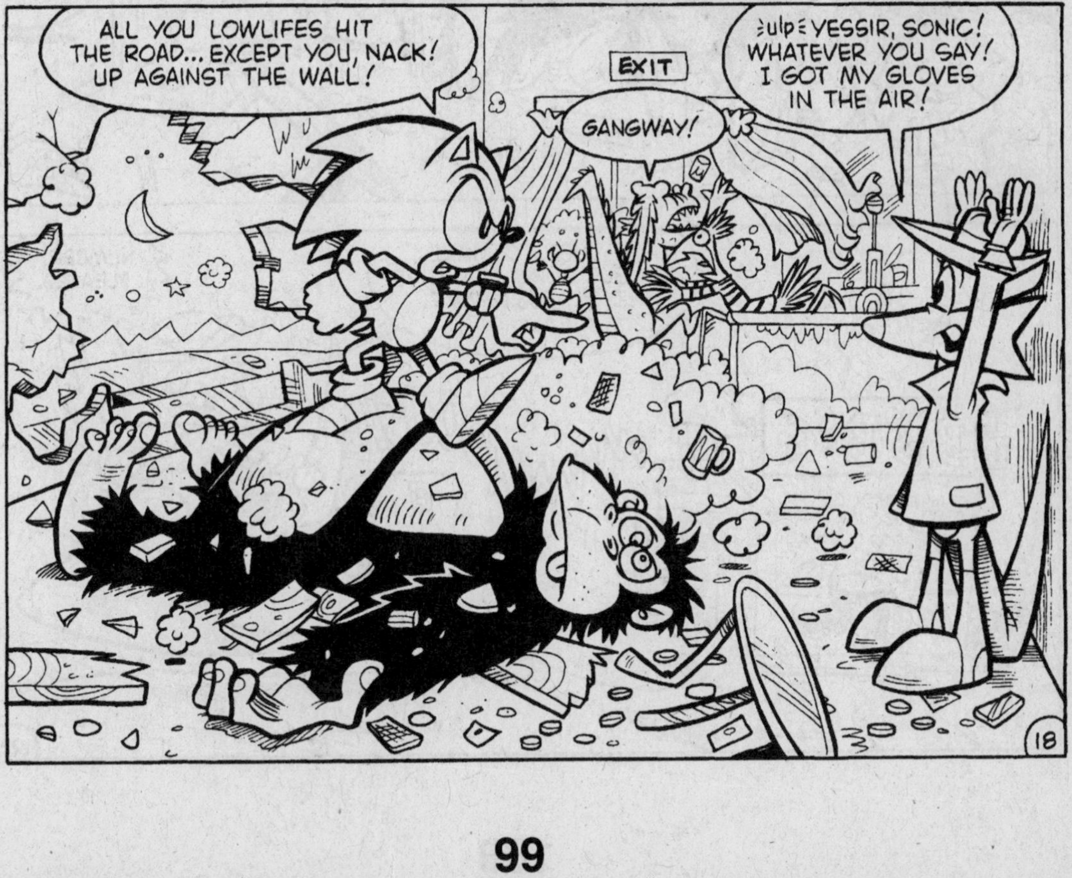
ALL YOU LOWLIFES HIT THE ROAD... EXCEPT YOU, NACK! UP AGAINST THE WALL!
EXIT
GANGWAY!
=ulp= YESSIR, SONIC! WHATEVER YOU SAY! I GOT MY GLOVES IN THE AIR!
18

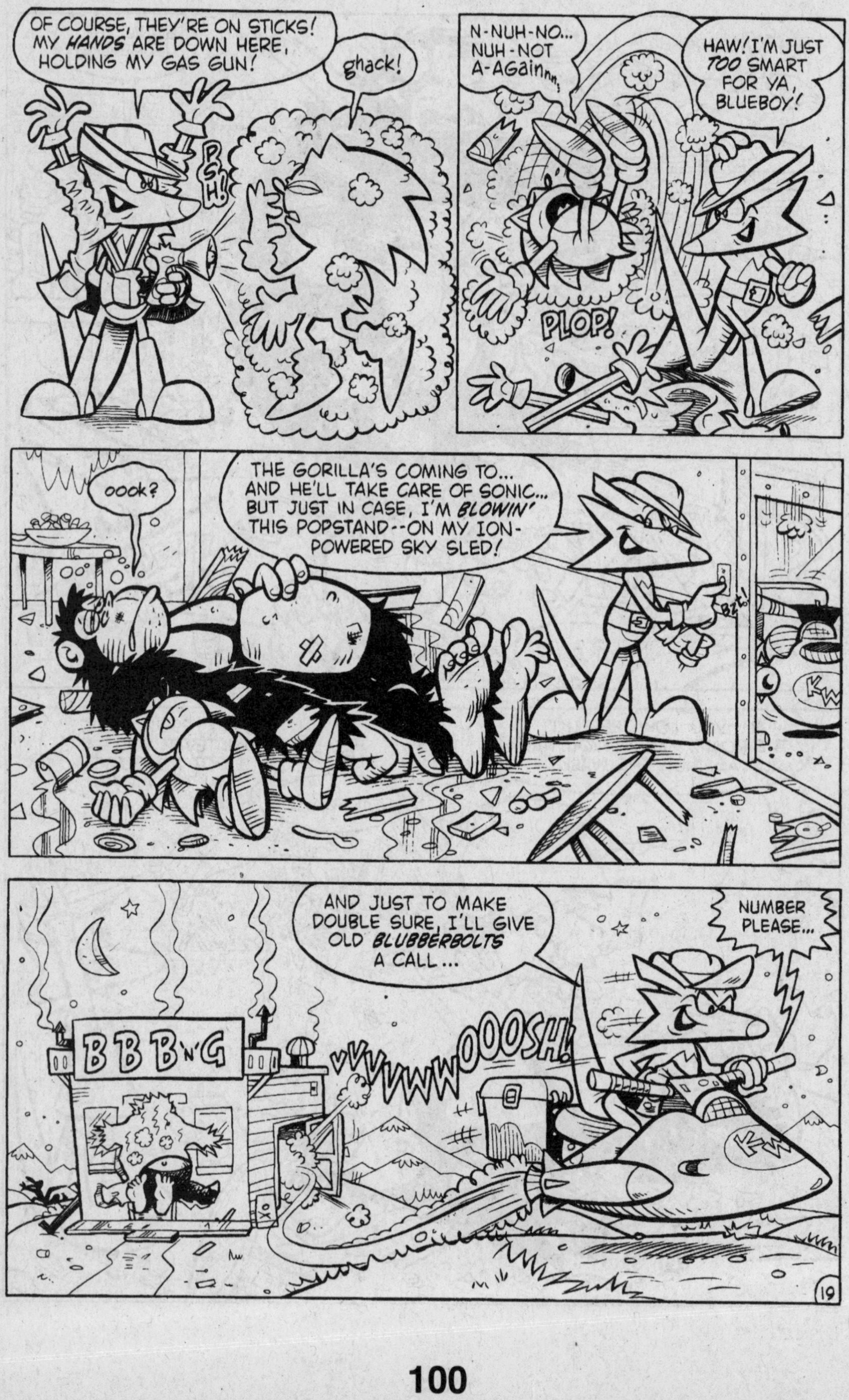
OF COURSE, THEY'RE ON STICKS! MY HANDS ARE DOWN HERE, HOLDING MY GAS GUN!
ghack!
PSH!
N-NUH-NO... NUH-NOT A-Againnn...
HAW! I'M JUST TOO SMART FOR YA, BLUEBOY!
PLOP!
oook?
THE GORILLA'S COMING TO... AND HE'LL TAKE CARE OF SONIC... BUT JUST IN CASE, I'M BLOWIN' THIS POPSTAND--ON MY ION-POWERED SKY SLED!
AND JUST TO MAKE DOUBLE SURE, I'LL GIVE OLD BLUBBERBOLTS A CALL...
NUMBER PLEASE...
BBB'N'G
VVVVWWOOOSH!
19

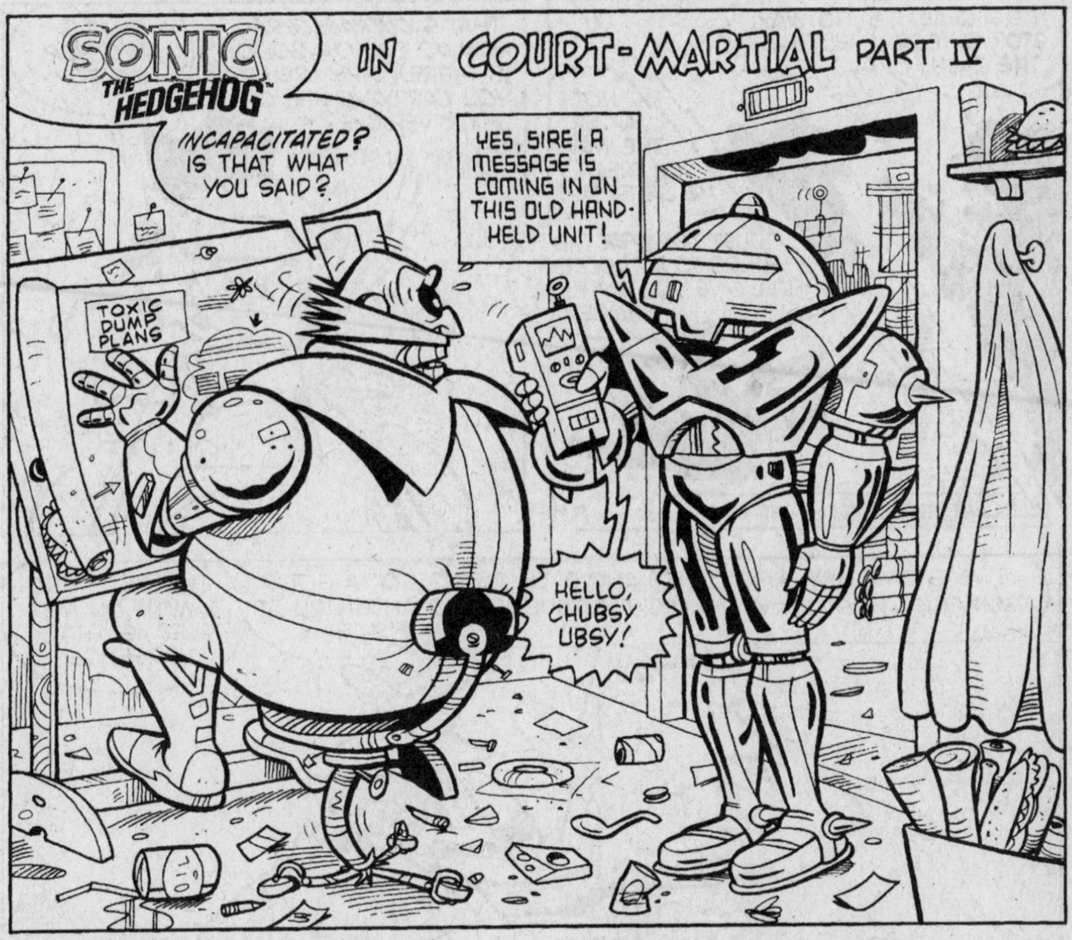
SONIC THE HEDGEHOG™ IN COURT-MARTIAL PART IV
INCAPACITATED? IS THAT WHAT YOU SAID?
YES, SIRE! A MESSAGE IS COMING IN ON THIS OLD HAND-HELD UNIT!
TOXIC DUMP PLANS
HELLO, CHUBSY UBSY!

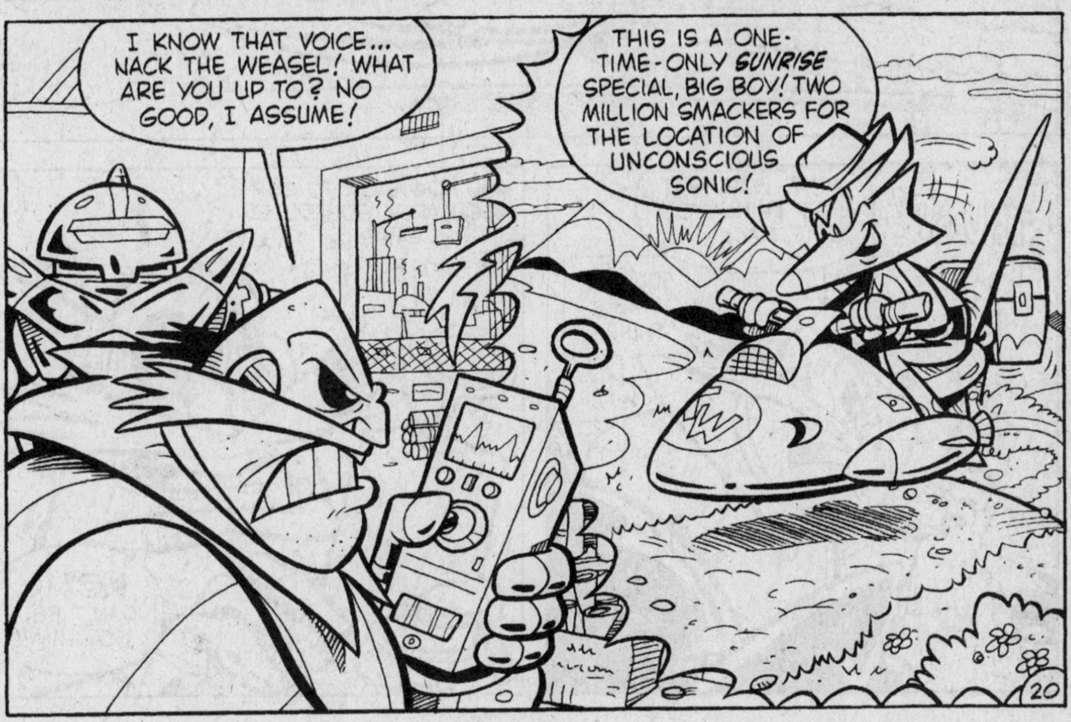
I KNOW THAT VOICE... NACK THE WEASEL! WHAT ARE YOU UP TO? NO GOOD, I ASSUME!
THIS IS A ONE-TIME-ONLY SUNRISE SPECIAL, BIG BOY! TWO MILLION SMACKERS FOR THE LOCATION OF UNCONSCIOUS SONIC!
20

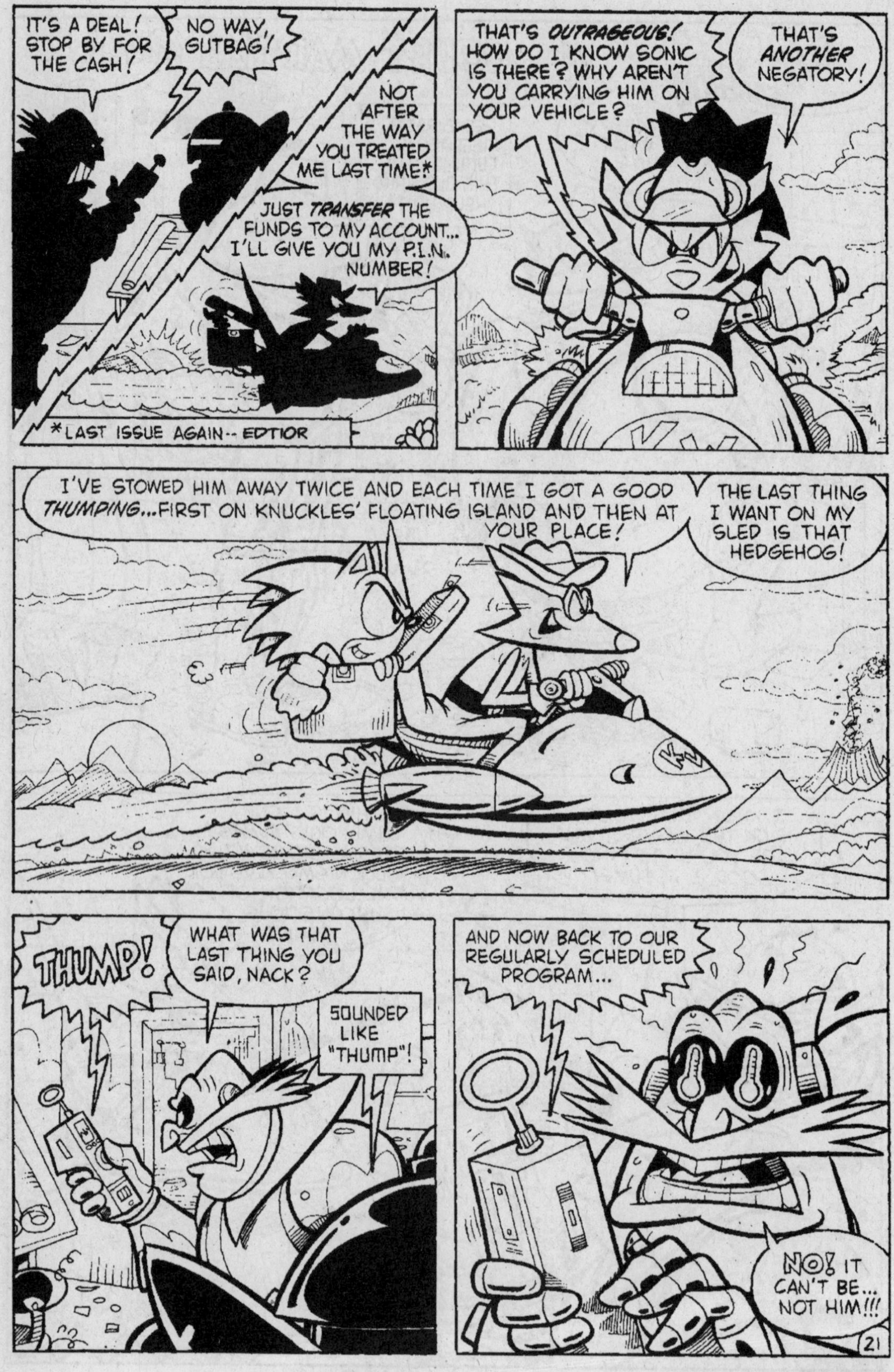
IT'S A DEAL! STOP BY FOR THE CASH!
NO WAY, GUTBAG!
NOT AFTER THE WAY YOU TREATED ME LAST TIME!*
JUST TRANSFER THE FUNDS TO MY ACCOUNT... I'LL GIVE YOU MY P.I.N. NUMBER!
*LAST ISSUE AGAIN-- EDTIOR
THAT'S OUTRAGEOUS! HOW DO I KNOW SONIC IS THERE? WHY AREN'T YOU CARRYING HIM ON YOUR VEHICLE?
THAT'S ANOTHER NEGATORY!
I'VE STOWED HIM AWAY TWICE AND EACH TIME I GOT A GOOD THUMPING...FIRST ON KNUCKLES' FLOATING ISLAND AND THEN AT YOUR PLACE!
THE LAST THING I WANT ON MY SLED IS THAT HEDGEHOG!
THUMP!
WHAT WAS THAT LAST THING YOU SAID, NACK?
SOUNDED LIKE "THUMP"!
AND NOW BACK TO OUR REGULARLY SCHEDULED PROGRAM...
NO! IT CAN'T BE... NOT HIM!!!
21

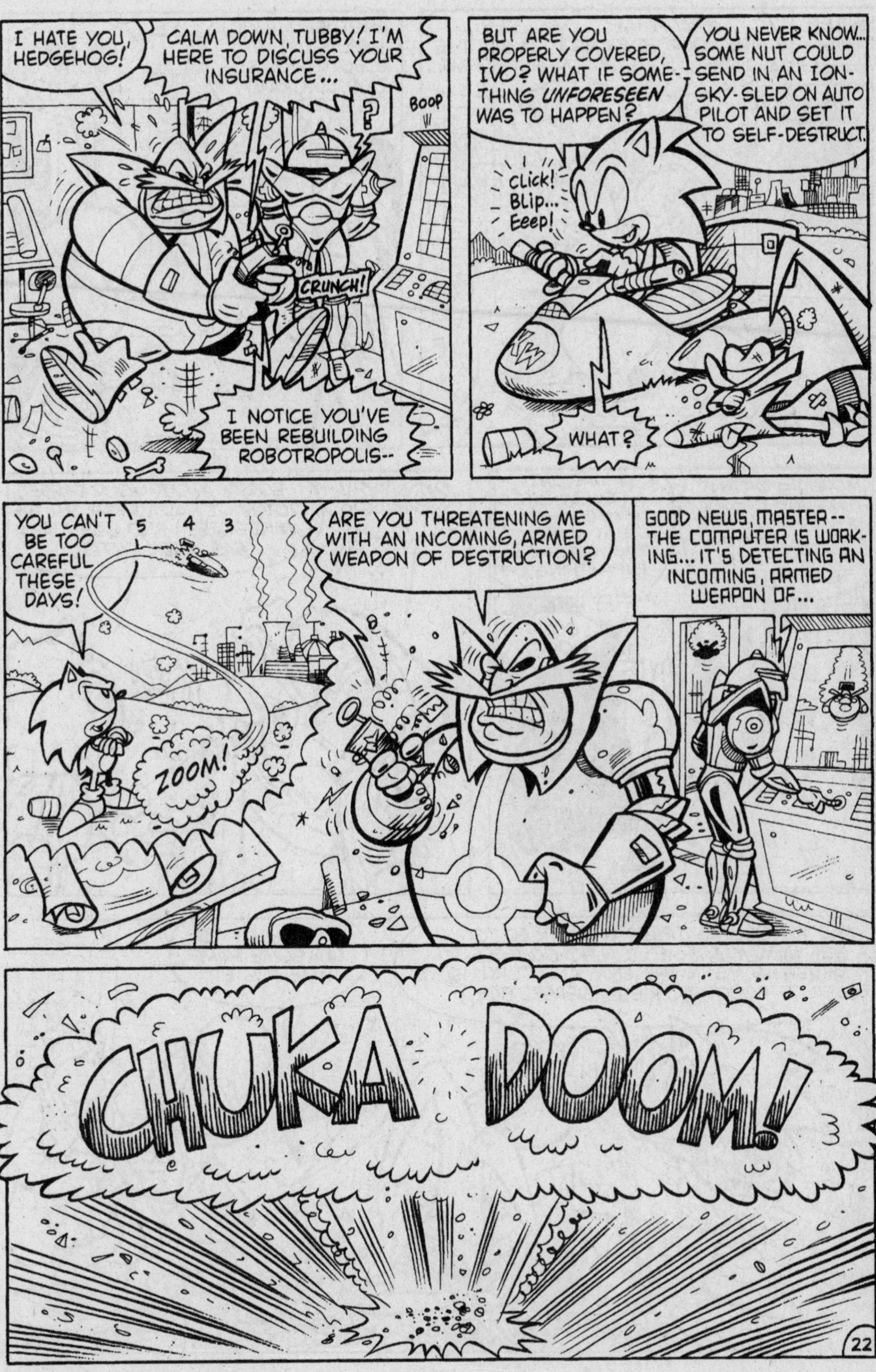
I HATE YOU, HEDGEHOG!
CALM DOWN, TUBBY! I'M HERE TO DISCUSS YOUR INSURANCE...
?
BOOP
CRUNCH!
I NOTICE YOU'VE BEEN REBUILDING ROBOTROPOLIS--
BUT ARE YOU PROPERLY COVERED, IVO? WHAT IF SOMETHING UNFORESEEN WAS TO HAPPEN?
YOU NEVER KNOW... SOME NUT COULD SEND IN AN ION-SKY-SLED ON AUTO PILOT AND SET IT TO SELF-DESTRUCT.
Click! Blip... Eeeep!
WHAT?
YOU CAN'T BE TOO CAREFUL THESE DAYS!
5 4 3
ZOOM!
ARE YOU THREATENING ME WITH AN INCOMING, ARMED WEAPON OF DESTRUCTION?
GOOD NEWS, MASTER -- THE COMPUTER IS WORKING... IT'S DETECTING AN INCOMING, ARMED WEAPON OF...
CHUKA DOOM!
22

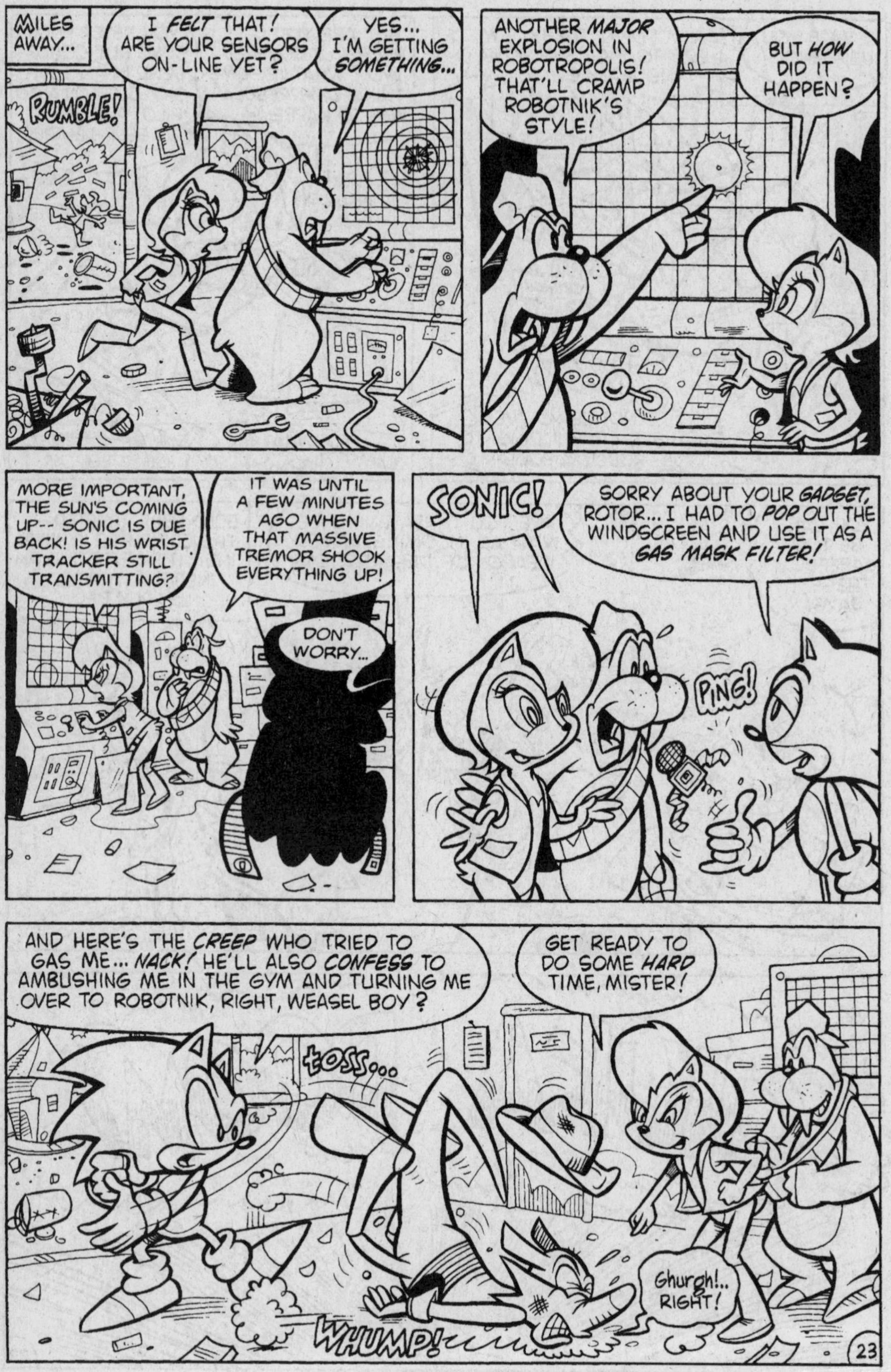

MILES AWAY...
I FELT THAT! ARE YOUR SENSORS ON-LINE YET?
YES... I'M GETTING SOMETHING...
RUMBLE!
ANOTHER MAJOR EXPLOSION IN ROBOTROPOLIS! THAT'LL CRAMP ROBOTNIK'S STYLE!
BUT HOW DID IT HAPPEN?
MORE IMPORTANT, THE SUN'S COMING UP-- SONIC IS DUE BACK! IS HIS WRIST TRACKER STILL TRANSMITTING?
IT WAS UNTIL A FEW MINUTES AGO WHEN THAT MASSIVE TREMOR SHOOK EVERYTHING UP!
DON'T WORRY...
SONIC!
SORRY ABOUT YOUR GADGET, ROTOR... I HAD TO POP OUT THE WINDSCREEN AND USE IT AS A GAS MASK FILTER!
PING!
AND HERE'S THE CREEP WHO TRIED TO GAS ME... NACK! HE'LL ALSO CONFESS TO AMBUSHING ME IN THE GYM AND TURNING ME OVER TO ROBOTNIK, RIGHT, WEASEL BOY?
GET READY TO DO SOME HARD TIME, MISTER!
TOSS...
Ghurgh!.. RIGHT!
WHUMP!
23

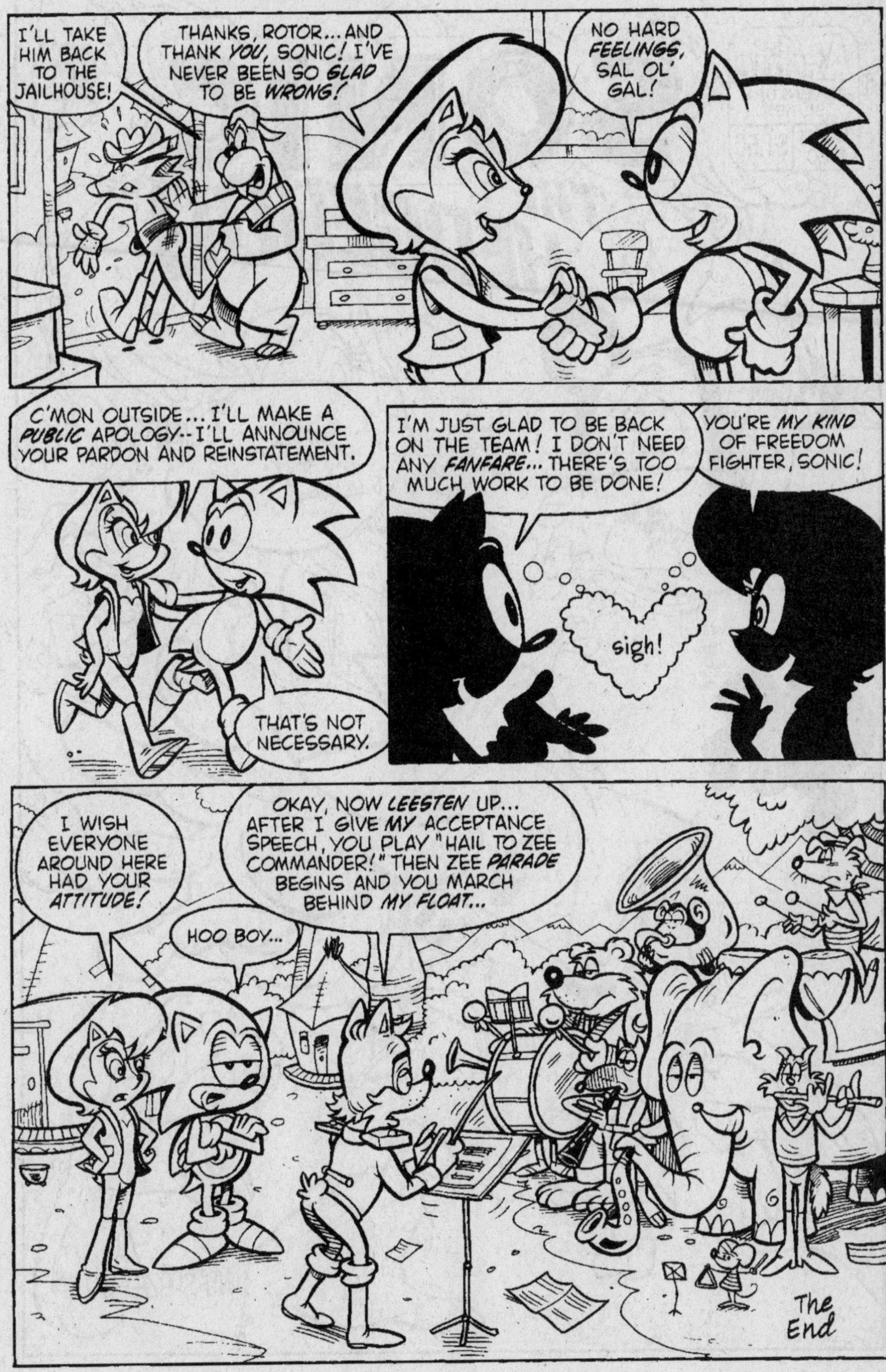
I'LL TAKE HIM BACK TO THE JAILHOUSE!
THANKS, ROTOR... AND THANK YOU, SONIC! I'VE NEVER BEEN SO GLAD TO BE WRONG!
NO HARD FEELINGS, SAL OL' GAL!
C'MON OUTSIDE... I'LL MAKE A PUBLIC APOLOGY--I'LL ANNOUNCE YOUR PARDON AND REINSTATEMENT.
THAT'S NOT NECESSARY.
I'M JUST GLAD TO BE BACK ON THE TEAM! I DON'T NEED ANY FANFARE... THERE'S TOO MUCH WORK TO BE DONE!
YOU'RE MY KIND OF FREEDOM FIGHTER, SONIC!
sigh!
I WISH EVERYONE AROUND HERE HAD YOUR ATTITUDE!
HOO BOY...
OKAY, NOW LEESTEN UP... AFTER I GIVE MY ACCEPTANCE SPEECH, YOU PLAY "HAIL TO ZEE COMMANDER!" THEN ZEE PARADE BEGINS AND YOU MARCH BEHIND MY FLOAT...
The End

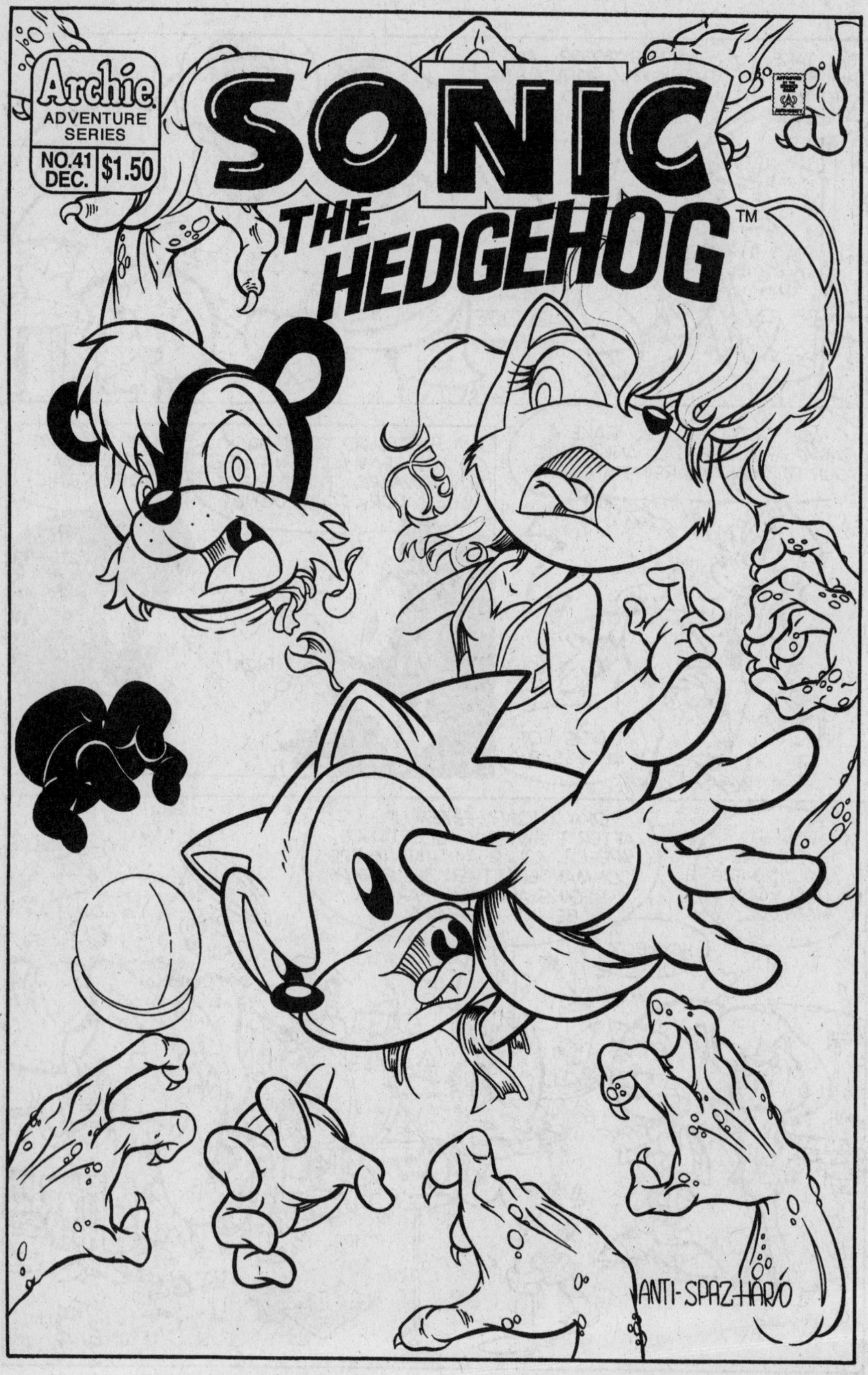
Archie
ADVENTURE SERIES
NO.41 DEC.
$1.50
SONIC THE HEDGEHOG™
ANTI-SPAZ-HARO

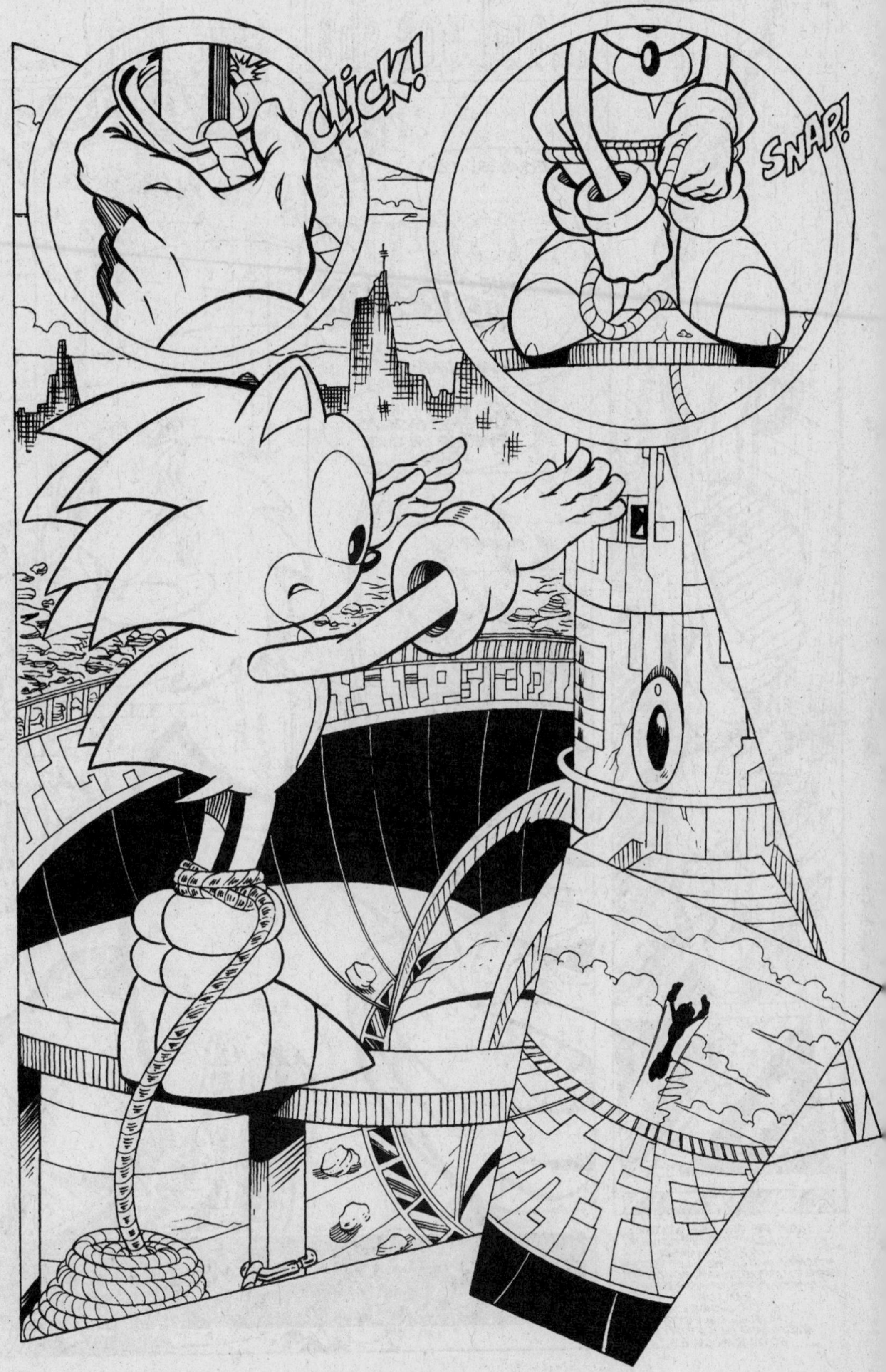
CLICK!
SNAP!

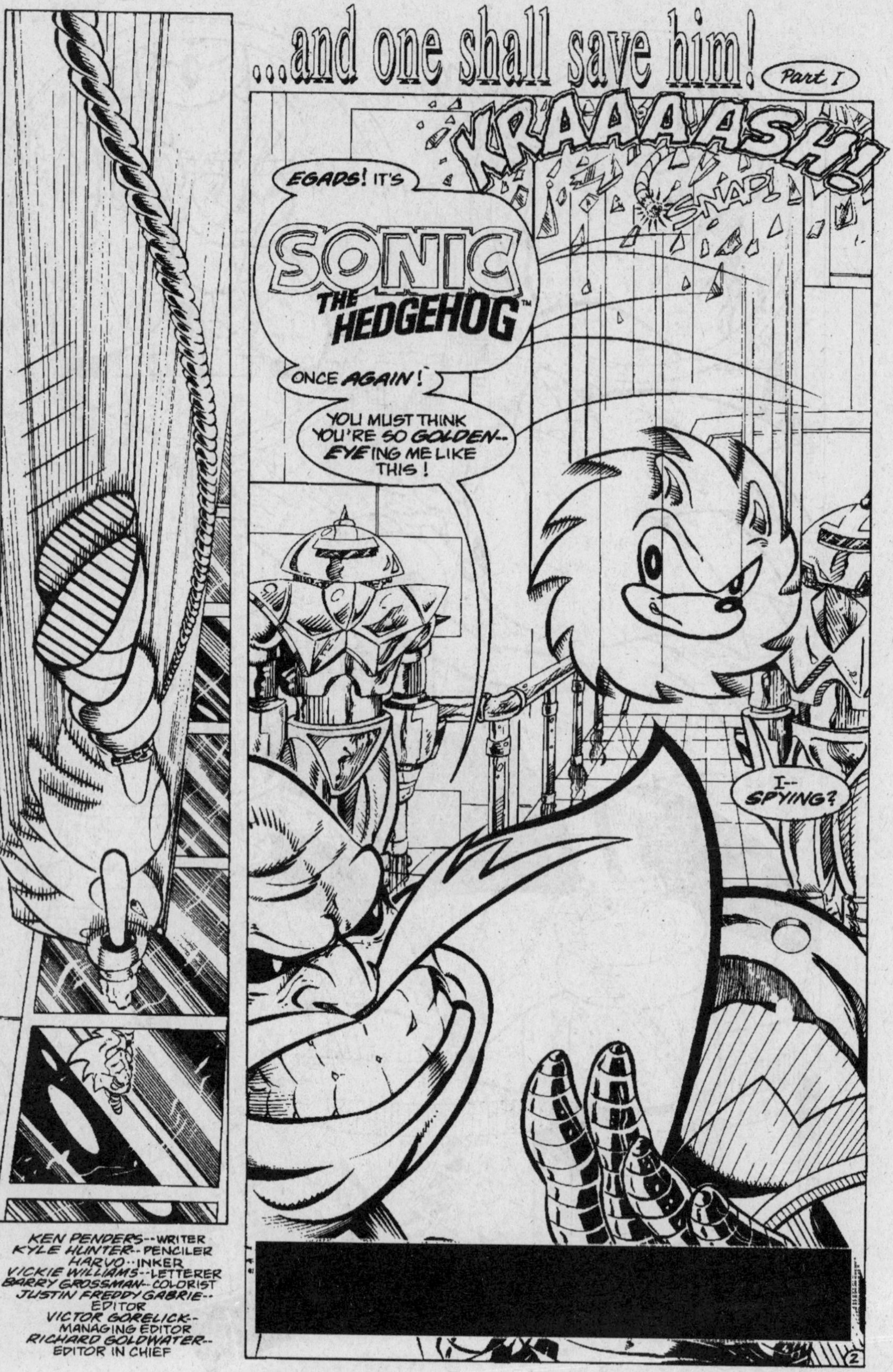
...and one shall save him!
Part I
KRAAAASH!
SNAP!
EGADS! IT'S
SONIC THE HEDGEHOG™
ONCE AGAIN!
YOU MUST THINK YOU'RE SO GOLDEN-- EYEING ME LIKE THIS!
I-- SPYING?
KEN PENDERS--WRITER
KYLE HUNTER--PENCILER
HARVO--INKER
VICKIE WILLIAMS--LETTERER
BARRY GROSSMAN--COLORIST
JUSTIN FREDDY GABRIE--EDITOR
VICTOR GORELICK--MANAGING EDITOR
RICHARD GOLDWATER--EDITOR IN CHIEF
[redacted]

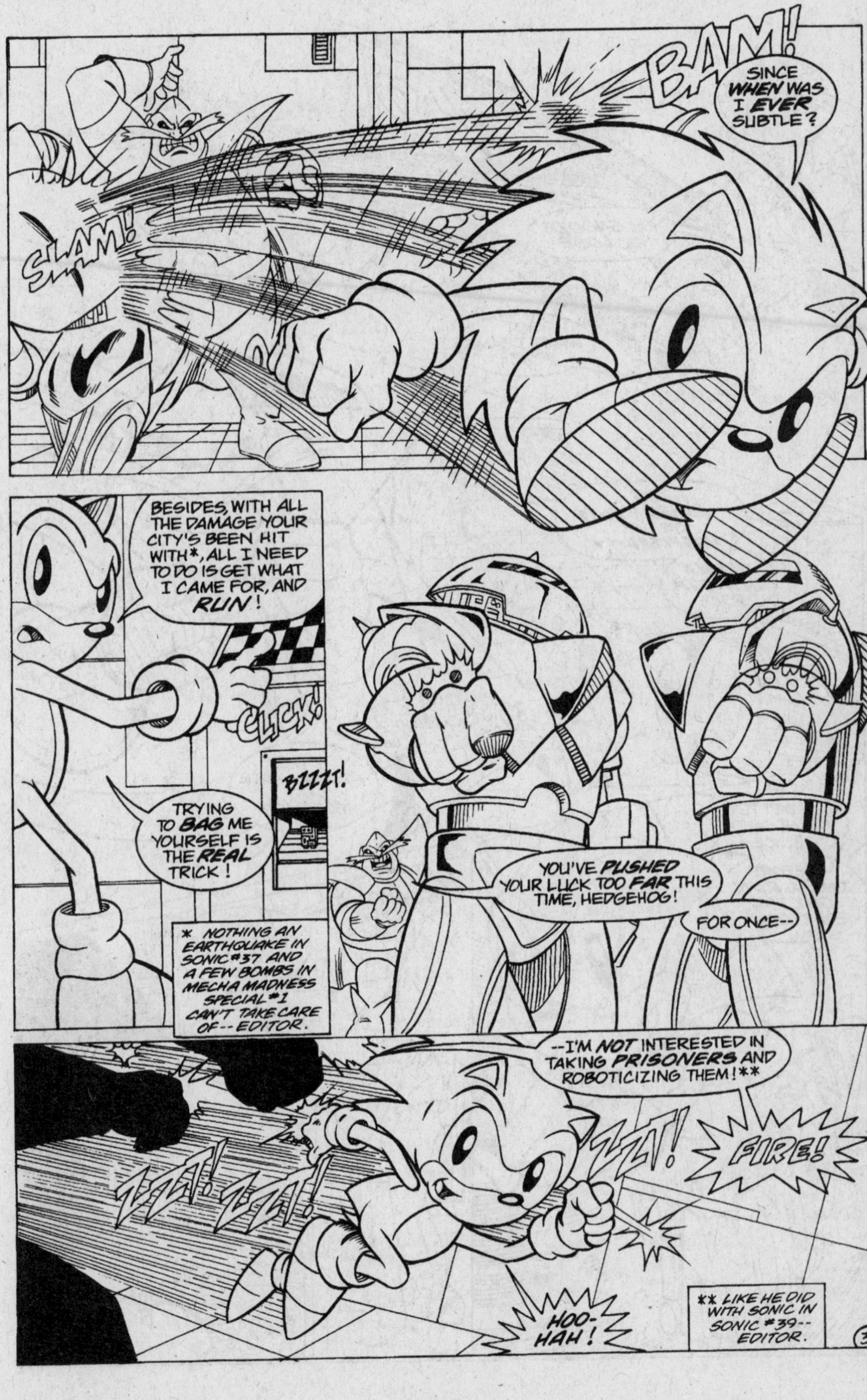
BAM!
SINCE WHEN WAS I EVER SUBTLE?
SLAM!
BESIDES, WITH ALL THE DAMAGE YOUR CITY'S BEEN HIT WITH*, ALL I NEED TO DO IS GET WHAT I CAME FOR, AND RUN!
CLICK!
BZZZT!
TRYING TO BAG ME YOURSELF IS THE REAL TRICK!
* NOTHING AN EARTHQUAKE IN SONIC #37 AND A FEW BOMBS IN MECHA MADNESS SPECIAL #1 CAN'T TAKE CARE OF-- EDITOR.
YOU'VE PUSHED YOUR LUCK TOO FAR THIS TIME, HEDGEHOG!
FOR ONCE--
--I'M NOT INTERESTED IN TAKING PRISONERS AND ROBOTICIZING THEM!**
ZZZAT! ZZZAT! ZZZAT!
FIRE!
HOO-HAH!
** LIKE HE DID WITH SONIC IN SONIC #39-- EDITOR.
3

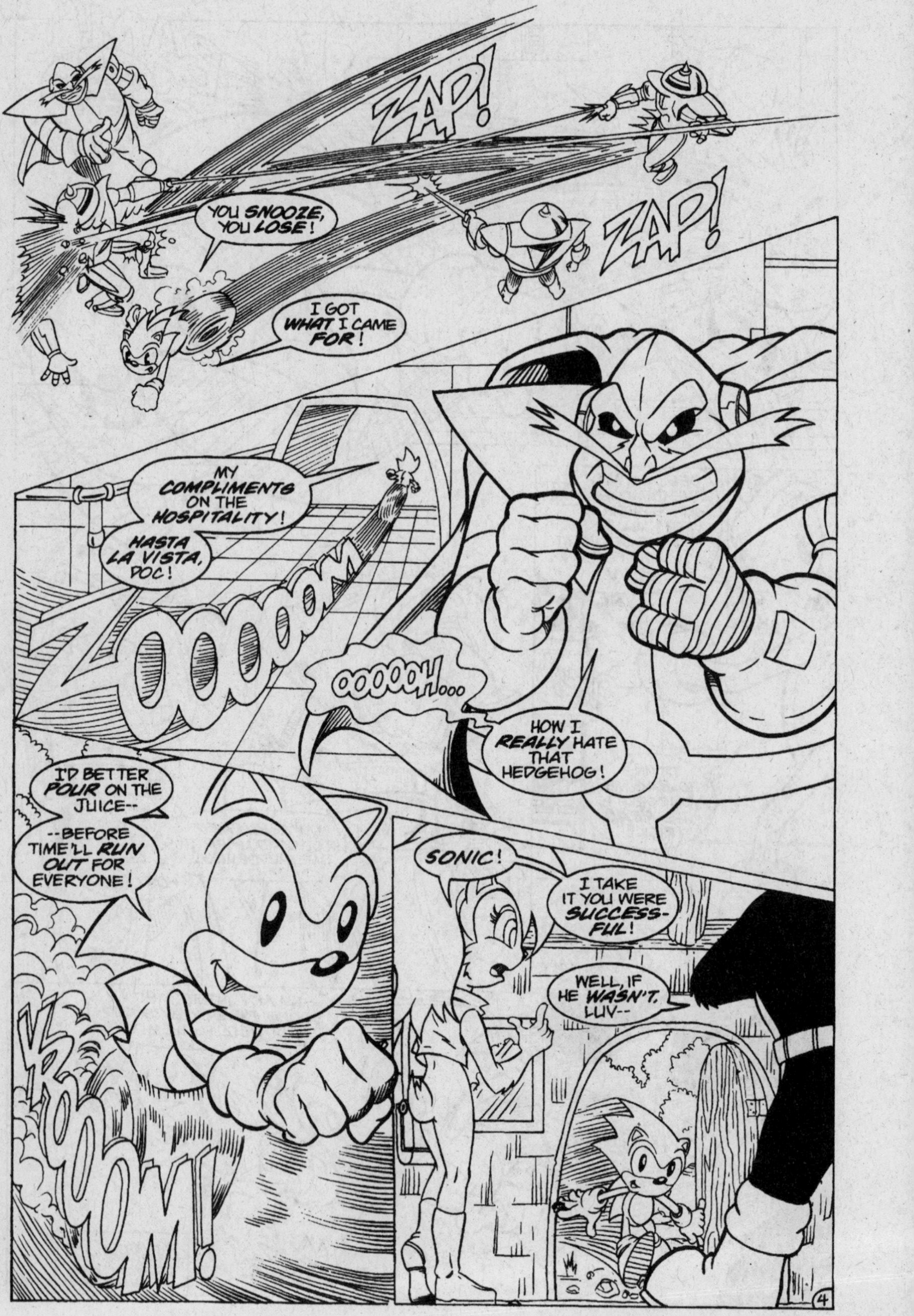
ZAP!
ZAP!
YOU SNOOZE, YOU LOSE!
I GOT WHAT I CAME FOR!
MY COMPLIMENTS ON THE HOSPITALITY!
HASTA LA VISTA, DOC!
ZOOOOOOM
OOOOOH...
HOW I REALLY HATE THAT HEDGEHOG!
I'D BETTER POUR ON THE JUICE--
--BEFORE TIME'LL RUN OUT FOR EVERYONE!
KROOOM!
SONIC!
I TAKE IT YOU WERE SUCCESS-FUL!
WELL, IF HE WASN'T, LUV--
4

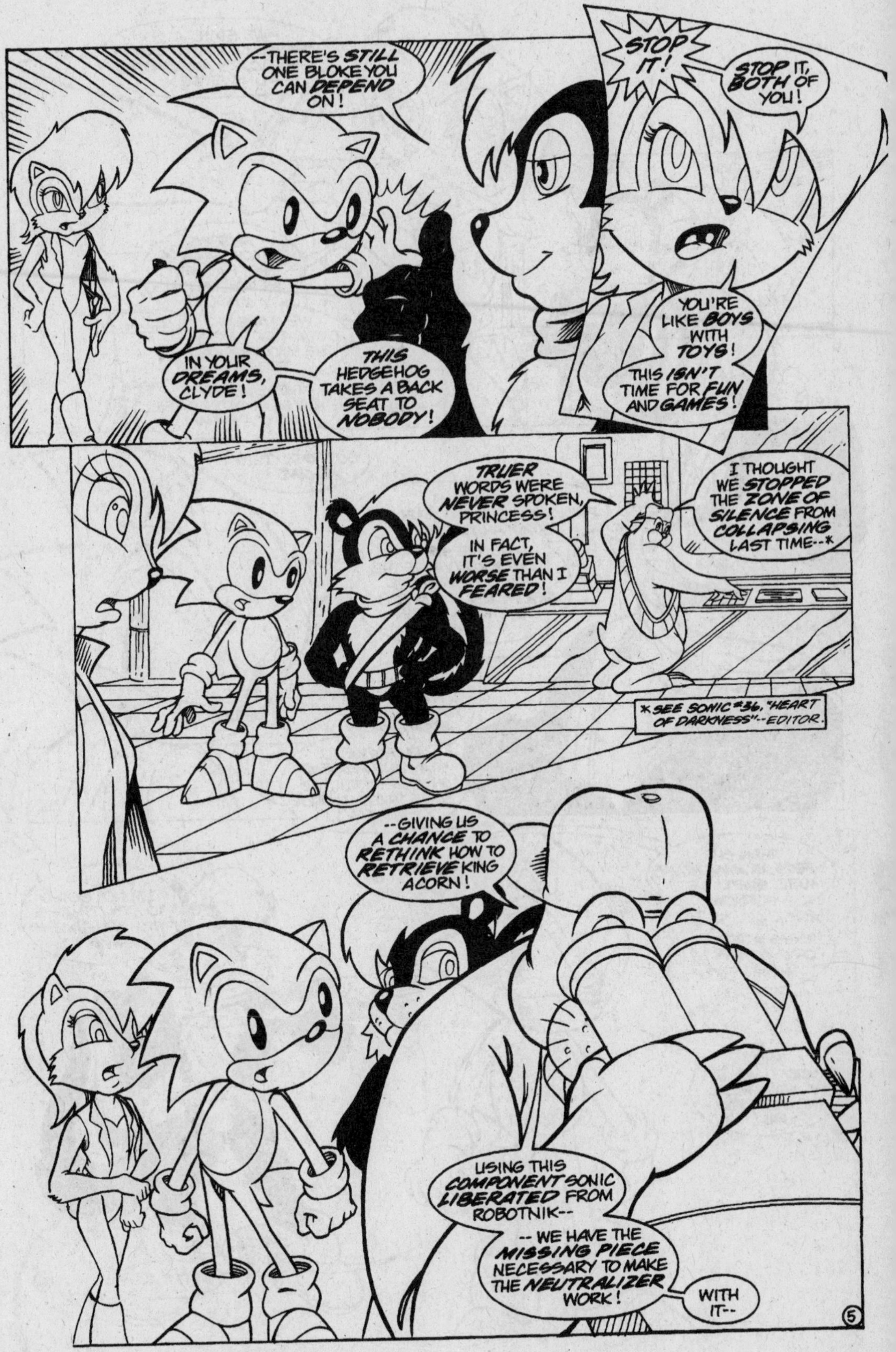
--THERE'S STILL ONE BLOKE YOU CAN DEPEND ON!
IN YOUR DREAMS, CLYDE!
THIS HEDGEHOG TAKES A BACK SEAT TO NOBODY!
STOP IT!
STOP IT, BOTH OF YOU!
YOU'RE LIKE BOYS WITH TOYS!
THIS ISN'T TIME FOR FUN AND GAMES!
TRUER WORDS WERE NEVER SPOKEN, PRINCESS!
IN FACT, IT'S EVEN WORSE THAN I FEARED!
I THOUGHT WE STOPPED THE ZONE OF SILENCE FROM COLLAPSING LAST TIME--*
*SEE SONIC #36, "HEART OF DARKNESS"--EDITOR.
--GIVING US A CHANCE TO RETHINK HOW TO RETRIEVE KING ACORN!
USING THIS COMPONENT SONIC LIBERATED FROM ROBOTNIK--
--WE HAVE THE MISSING PIECE NECESSARY TO MAKE THE NEUTRALIZER WORK!
WITH IT--
5

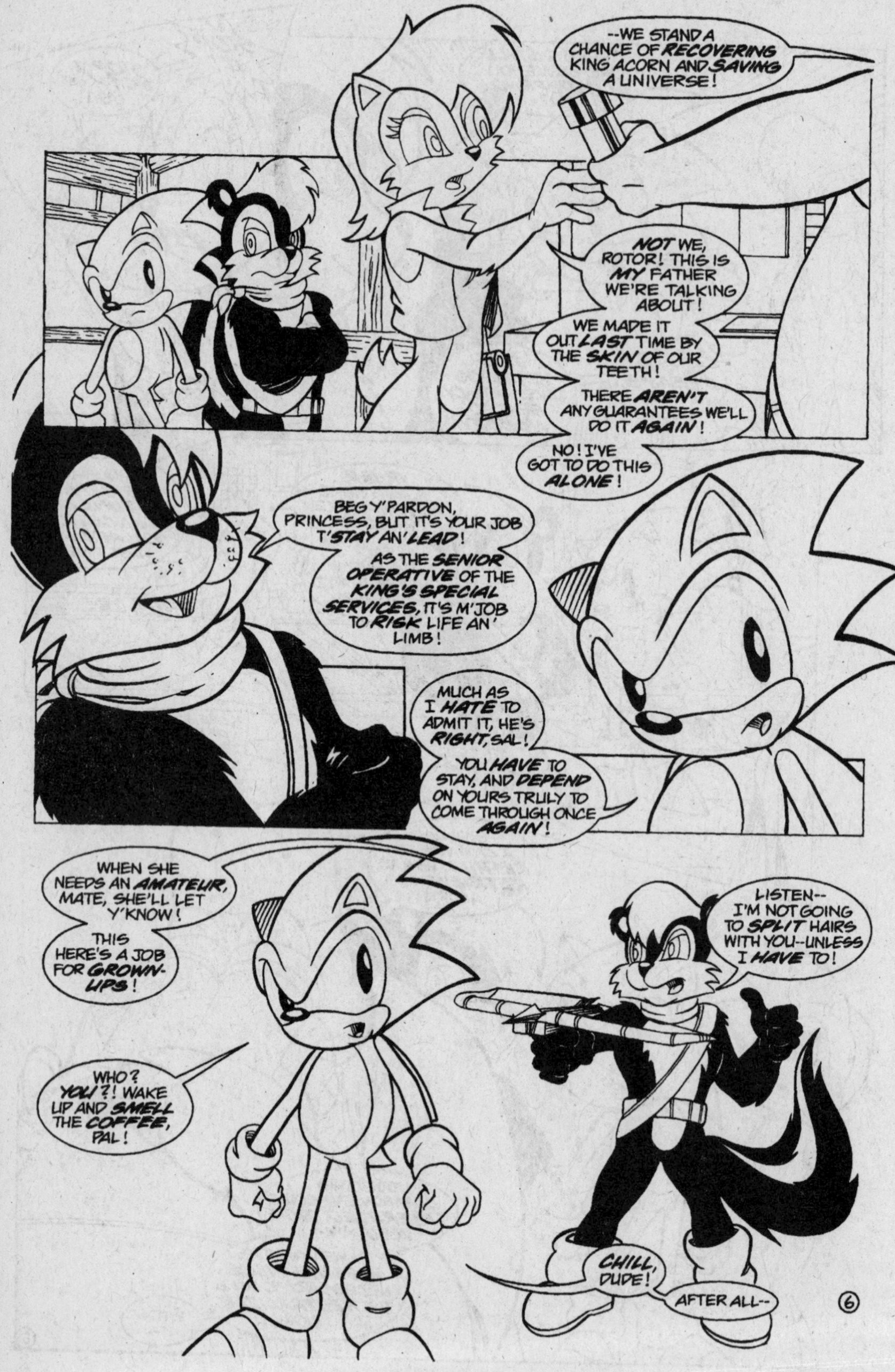

--WE STAND A CHANCE OF RECOVERING KING ACORN AND SAVING A UNIVERSE!
NOT WE, ROTOR! THIS IS MY FATHER WE'RE TALKING ABOUT!
WE MADE IT OUT LAST TIME BY THE SKIN OF OUR TEETH!
THERE AREN'T ANY GUARANTEES WE'LL DO IT AGAIN!
NO! I'VE GOT TO DO THIS ALONE!
BEG Y'PARDON, PRINCESS, BUT IT'S YOUR JOB T'STAY AN' LEAD!
AS THE SENIOR OPERATIVE OF THE KING'S SPECIAL SERVICES, IT'S M'JOB TO RISK LIFE AN' LIMB!
MUCH AS I HATE TO ADMIT IT, HE'S RIGHT, SAL!
YOU HAVE TO STAY, AND DEPEND ON YOURS TRULY TO COME THROUGH ONCE AGAIN!
WHEN SHE NEEDS AN AMATEUR, MATE, SHE'LL LET Y'KNOW!
THIS HERE'S A JOB FOR GROWN-UPS!
WHO? YOU?! WAKE UP AND SMELL THE COFFEE, PAL!
LISTEN-- I'M NOT GOING TO SPLIT HAIRS WITH YOU--UNLESS I HAVE TO!
CHILL, DUDE!
AFTER ALL--
6

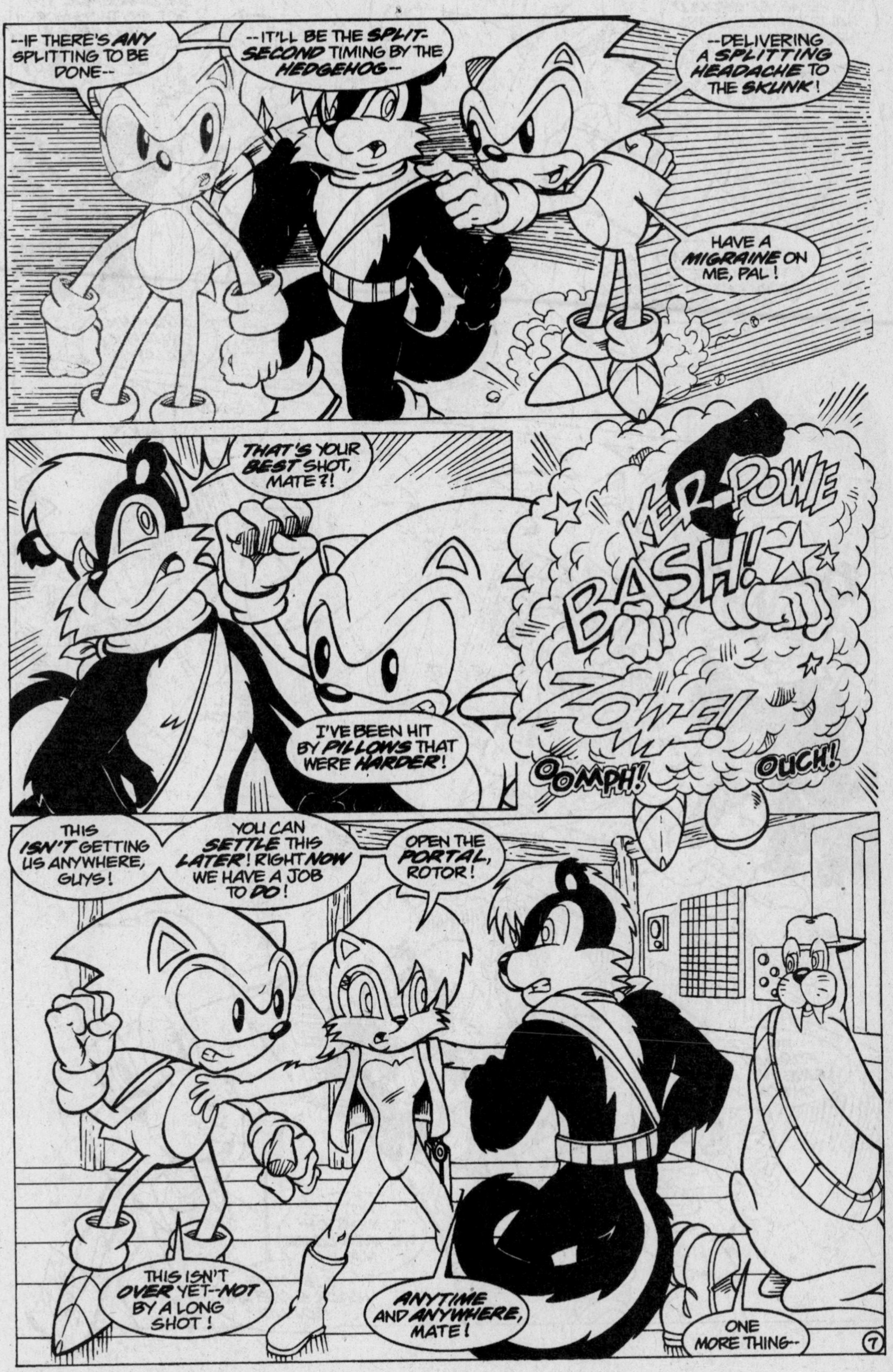
--IF THERE'S ANY SPLITTING TO BE DONE--
--IT'LL BE THE SPLIT-SECOND TIMING BY THE HEDGEHOG--
--DELIVERING A SPLITTING HEADACHE TO THE SKUNK!
HAVE A MIGRAINE ON ME, PAL!
THAT'S YOUR BEST SHOT, MATE?!
I'VE BEEN HIT BY PILLOWS THAT WERE HARDER!
KER-POWIE
BASH!
ZOWIE!
OOMPH!
OUCH!
THIS ISN'T GETTING US ANYWHERE, GUYS!
YOU CAN SETTLE THIS LATER! RIGHT NOW WE HAVE A JOB TO DO!
OPEN THE PORTAL, ROTOR!
THIS ISN'T OVER YET--NOT BY A LONG SHOT!
ANYTIME AND ANYWHERE, MATE!
ONE MORE THING--
7

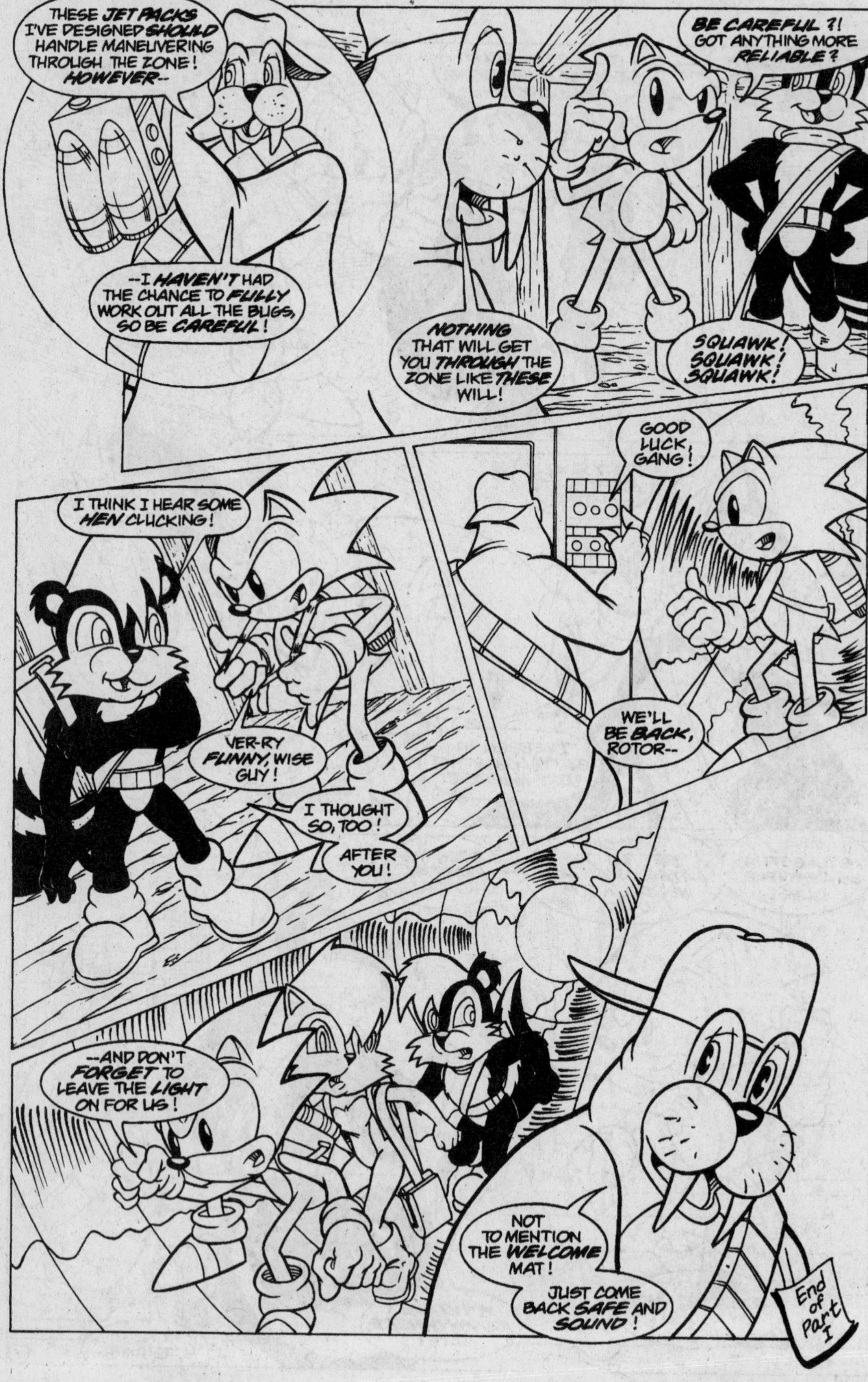
THESE JET PACKS I'VE DESIGNED SHOULD HANDLE MANEUVERING THROUGH THE ZONE! HOWEVER--
--I HAVEN'T HAD THE CHANCE TO FULLY WORK OUT ALL THE BUGS, SO BE CAREFUL!
BE CAREFUL ?! GOT ANYTHING MORE RELIABLE?
NOTHING THAT WILL GET YOU THROUGH THE ZONE LIKE THESE WILL!
SQUAWK! SQUAWK! SQUAWK!
I THINK I HEAR SOME HEN CLUCKING!
VER-RY FUNNY, WISE GUY!
I THOUGHT SO, TOO!
AFTER YOU!
GOOD LUCK, GANG!
WE'LL BE BACK, ROTOR--
--AND DON'T FORGET TO LEAVE THE LIGHT ON FOR US!
NOT TO MENTION THE WELCOME MAT!
JUST COME BACK SAFE AND SOUND!
End of Part I

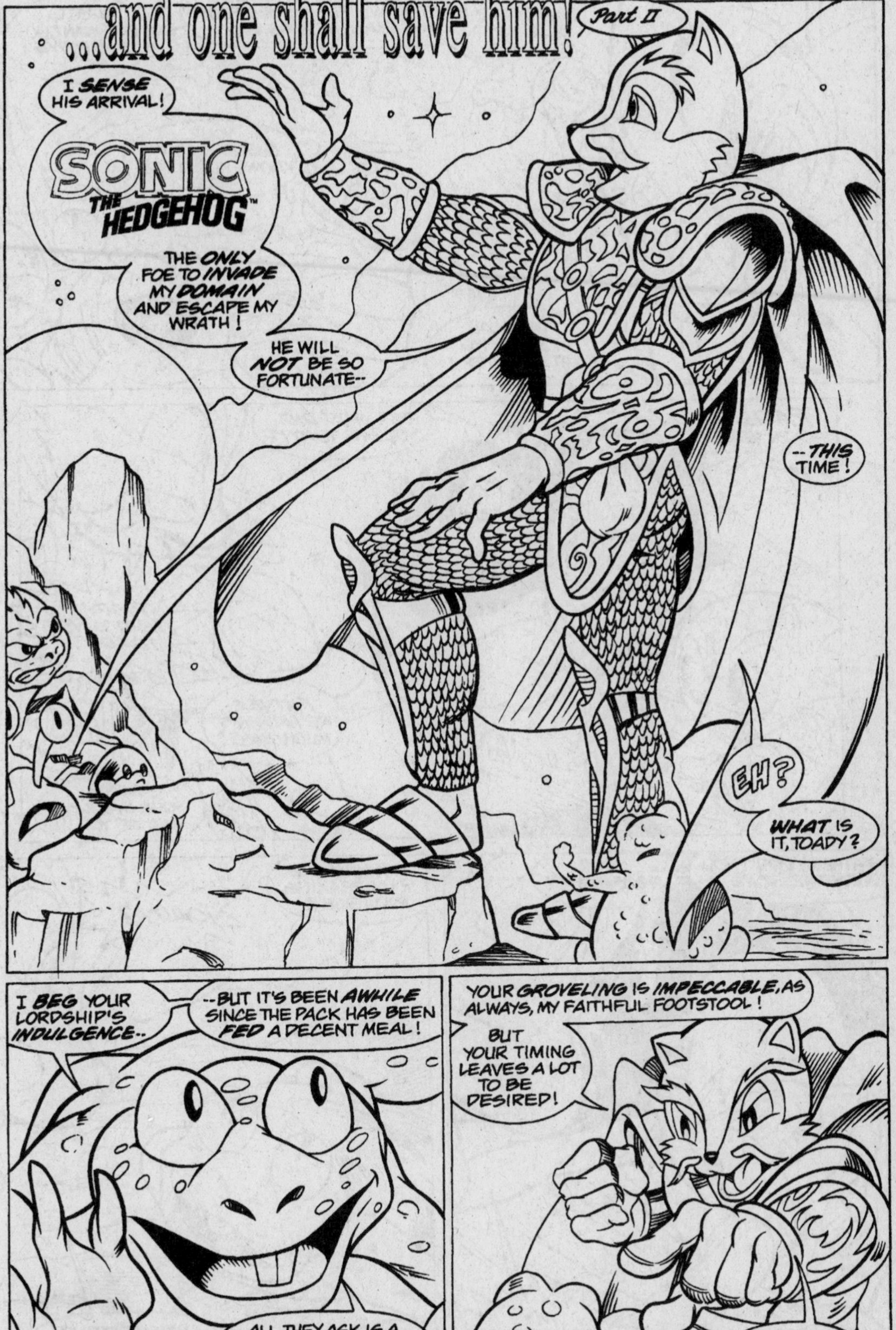
...and one shall save him!
Part II
I SENSE HIS ARRIVAL!
SONIC THE HEDGEHOG™
THE ONLY FOE TO INVADE MY DOMAIN AND ESCAPE MY WRATH!
HE WILL NOT BE SO FORTUNATE--
--THIS TIME!
EH?
WHAT IS IT, TOADY?
I BEG YOUR LORDSHIP'S INDULGENCE..
--BUT IT'S BEEN AWHILE SINCE THE PACK HAS BEEN FED A DECENT MEAL!
ALL THEY ASK IS A CRUMB OR TWO, SIRE!
YOUR GROVELING IS IMPECCABLE, AS ALWAYS, MY FAITHFUL FOOTSTOOL!
BUT YOUR TIMING LEAVES A LOT TO BE DESIRED!
HOWEVER--
9

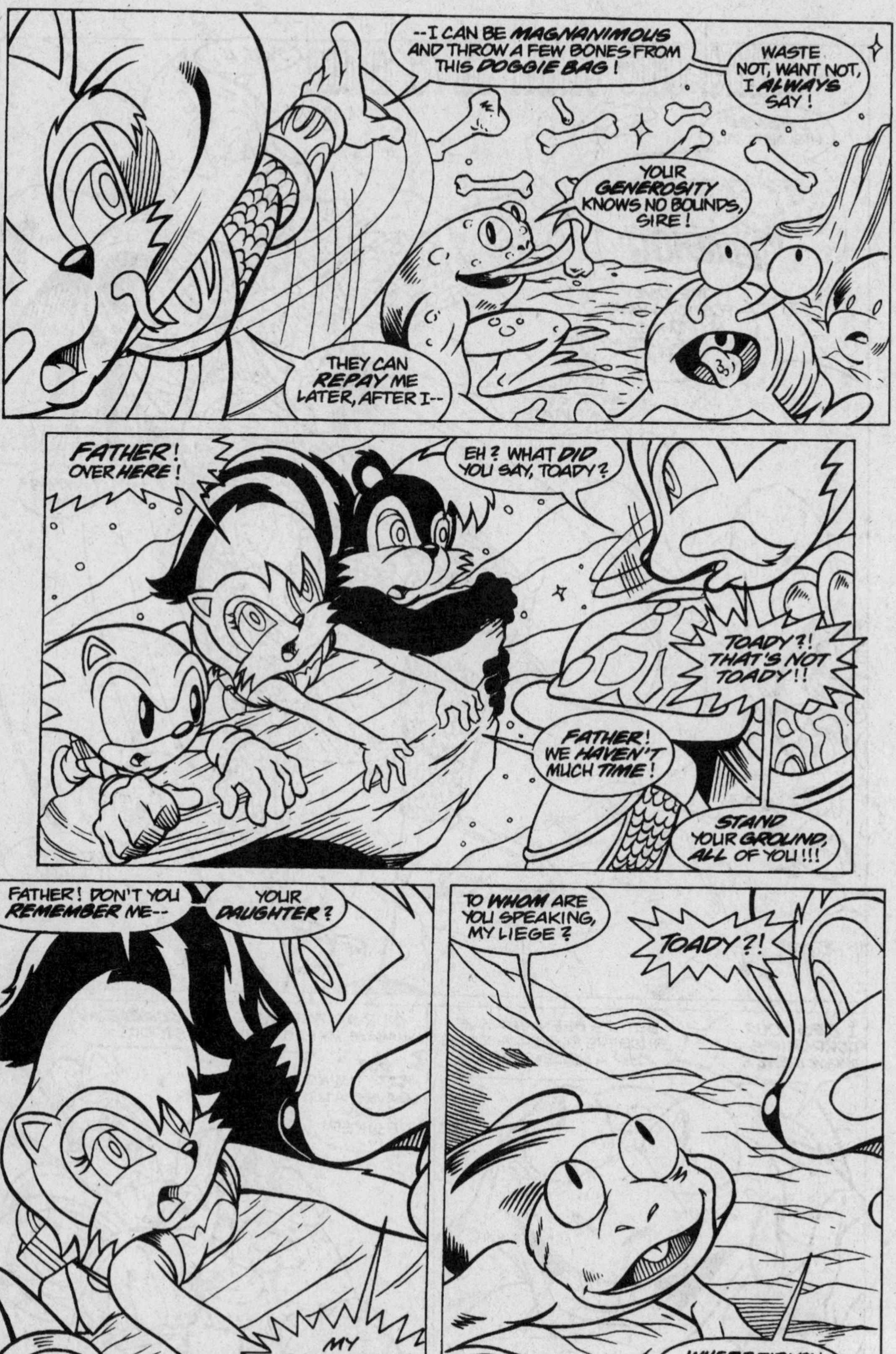
--I CAN BE MAGNANIMOUS AND THROW A FEW BONES FROM THIS DOGGIE BAG!
WASTE NOT, WANT NOT, I ALWAYS SAY!
YOUR GENEROSITY KNOWS NO BOUNDS, SIRE!
THEY CAN REPAY ME LATER, AFTER I--
FATHER! OVER HERE!
EH? WHAT DID YOU SAY, TOADY?
TOADY?! THAT'S NOT TOADY!!
FATHER! WE HAVEN'T MUCH TIME!
STAND YOUR GROUND, ALL OF YOU!!!
FATHER! DON'T YOU REMEMBER ME--
YOUR DAUGHTER?
MY DAUGHTER?!
TO WHOM ARE YOU SPEAKING, MY LIEGE?
TOADY?!
WHERE DID YOU DISAPPEAR TO?
10

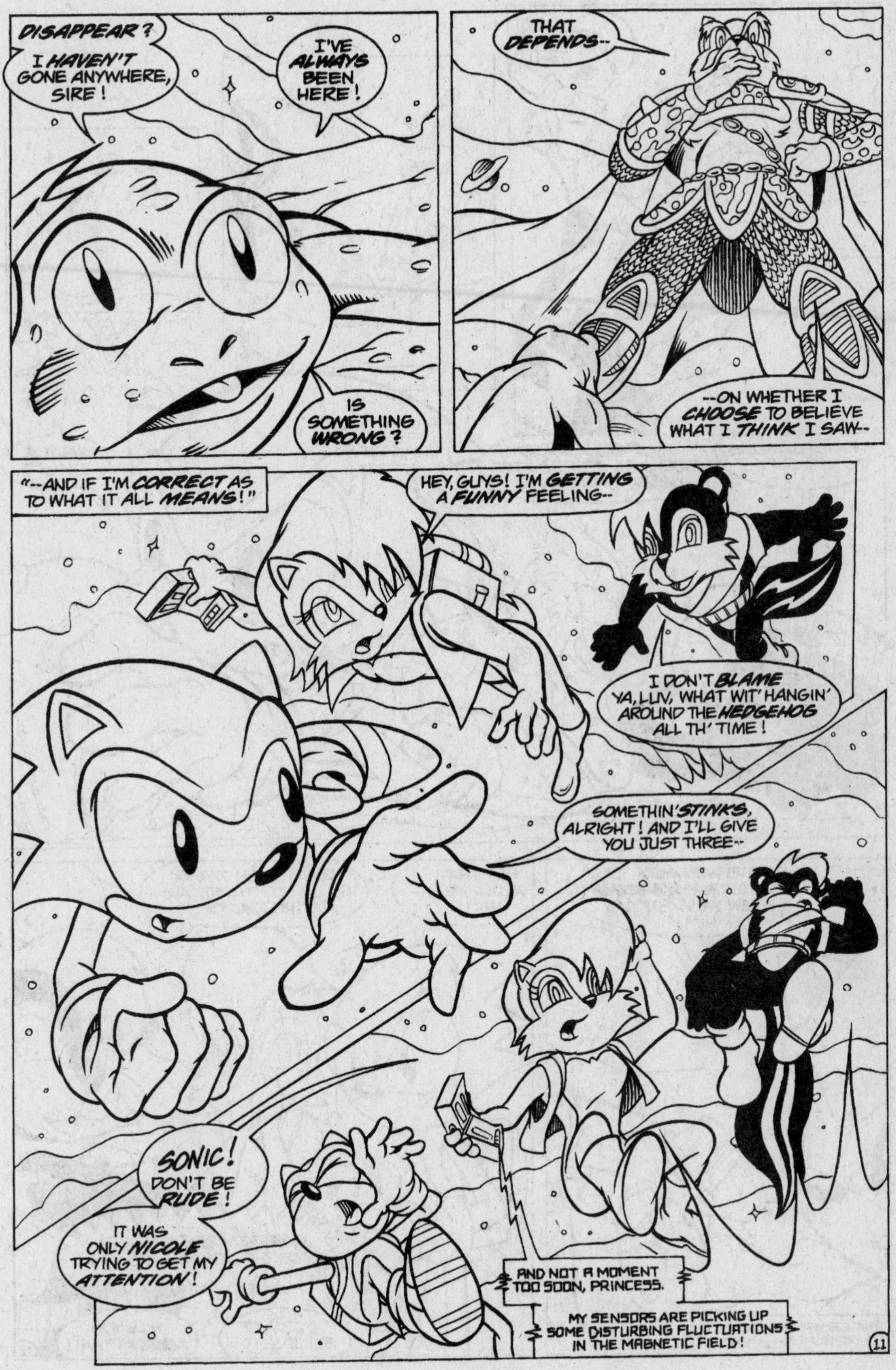
DISAPPEAR?
I HAVEN'T GONE ANYWHERE, SIRE!
I'VE ALWAYS BEEN HERE!
IS SOMETHING WRONG?
THAT DEPENDS--
--ON WHETHER I CHOOSE TO BELIEVE WHAT I THINK I SAW--
"--AND IF I'M CORRECT AS TO WHAT IT ALL MEANS!"
HEY, GUYS! I'M GETTING A FUNNY FEELING--
I DON'T BLAME YA, LUV, WHAT WIT' HANGIN' AROUND THE HEDGEHOG ALL TH' TIME!
SOMETHIN' STINKS, ALRIGHT! AND I'LL GIVE YOU JUST THREE--
SONIC! DON'T BE RUDE!
IT WAS ONLY NICOLE TRYING TO GET MY ATTENTION!
AND NOT A MOMENT TOO SOON, PRINCESS.
MY SENSORS ARE PICKING UP SOME DISTURBING FLUCTUATIONS IN THE MAGNETIC FIELD!
11

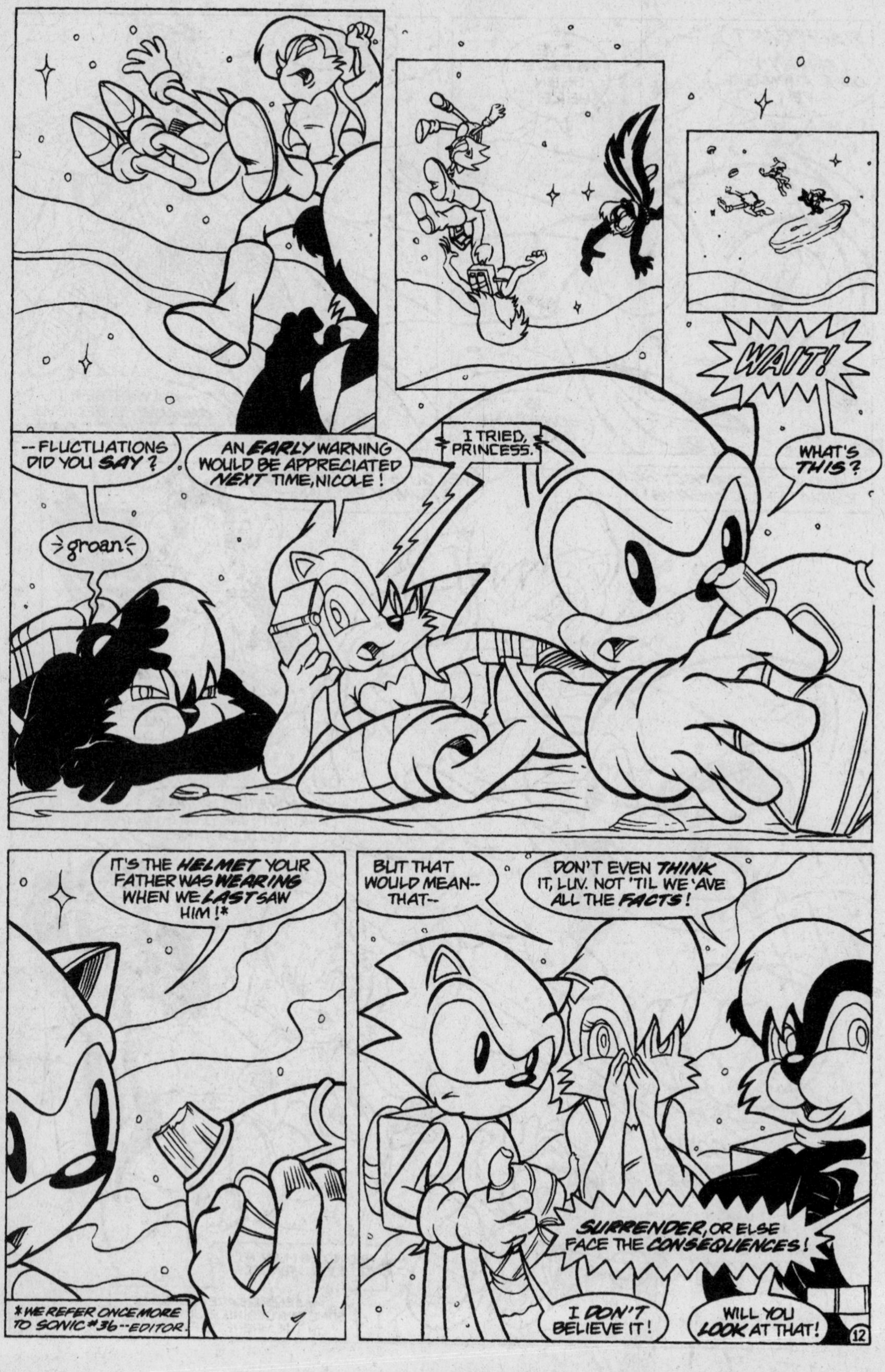
WAIT!
--FLUCTUATIONS DID YOU SAY?
AN EARLY WARNING WOULD BE APPRECIATED NEXT TIME, NICOLE!
I TRIED, PRINCESS.
WHAT'S THIS?
groan
IT'S THE HELMET YOUR FATHER WAS WEARING WHEN WE LAST SAW HIM!*
*WE REFER ONCE MORE TO SONIC #36--EDITOR
BUT THAT WOULD MEAN-- THAT--
DON'T EVEN THINK IT, LUV. NOT 'TIL WE 'AVE ALL THE FACTS!
SURRENDER, OR ELSE FACE THE CONSEQUENCES!
I DON'T BELIEVE IT!
WILL YOU LOOK AT THAT!
12

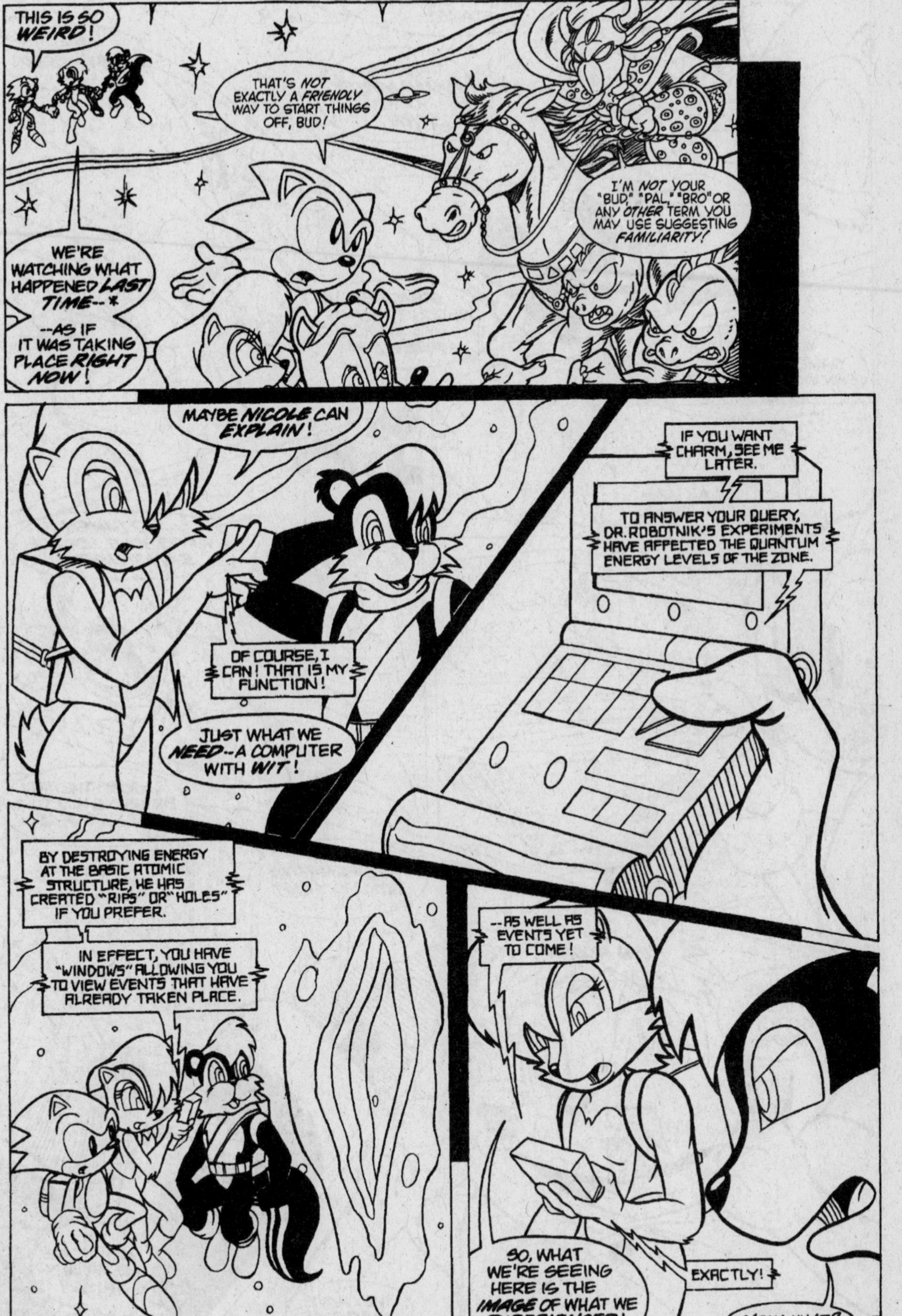
THIS IS SO WEIRD!
THAT'S NOT EXACTLY A FRIENDLY WAY TO START THINGS OFF, BUD!
I'M NOT YOUR "BUD," "PAL," "BRO" OR ANY OTHER TERM YOU MAY USE SUGGESTING FAMILIARITY!
WE'RE WATCHING WHAT HAPPENED LAST TIME--*
--AS IF IT WAS TAKING PLACE RIGHT NOW!
MAYBE NICOLE CAN EXPLAIN!
OF COURSE, I CAN! THAT IS MY FUNCTION!
JUST WHAT WE NEED--A COMPUTER WITH WIT!
IF YOU WANT CHARM, SEE ME LATER.
TO ANSWER YOUR QUERY, DR. ROBOTNIK'S EXPERIMENTS HAVE AFFECTED THE QUANTUM ENERGY LEVELS OF THE ZONE.
BY DESTROYING ENERGY AT THE BASIC ATOMIC STRUCTURE, HE HAS CREATED "RIPS" OR "HOLES" IF YOU PREFER.
IN EFFECT, YOU HAVE "WINDOWS" ALLOWING YOU TO VIEW EVENTS THAT HAVE ALREADY TAKEN PLACE.
--AS WELL AS EVENTS YET TO COME!
SO, WHAT WE'RE SEEING HERE IS THE IMAGE OF WHAT WE EXPERIENCED!
EXACTLY!
NOW WHAT?
13

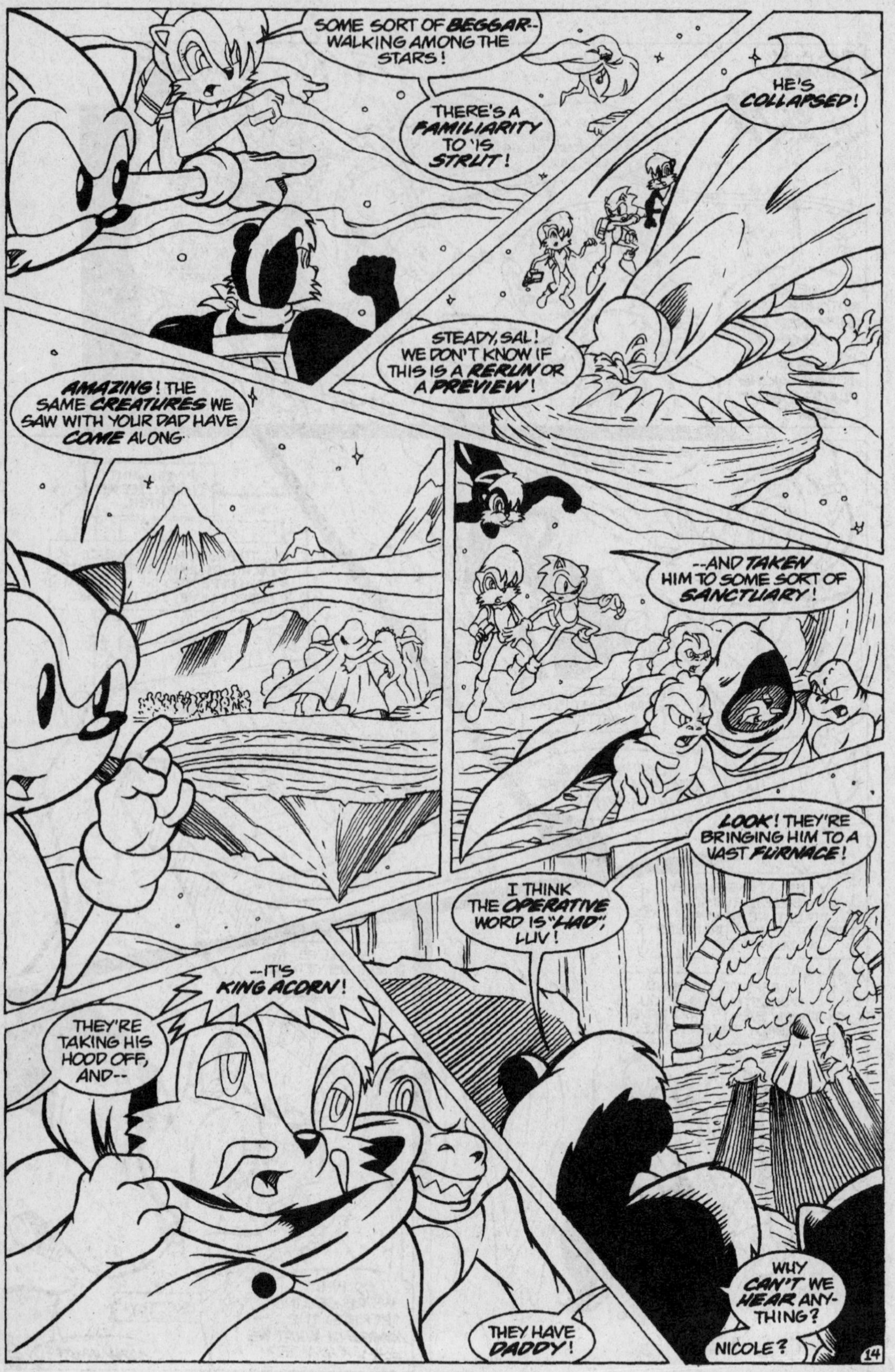
SOME SORT OF BEGGAR--WALKING AMONG THE STARS!
THERE'S A FAMILIARITY TO 'IS STRUT!
HE'S COLLAPSED!
STEADY, SAL! WE DON'T KNOW IF THIS IS A RERUN OR A PREVIEW!
AMAZING! THE SAME CREATURES WE SAW WITH YOUR DAD HAVE COME ALONG
--AND TAKEN HIM TO SOME SORT OF SANCTUARY!
LOOK! THEY'RE BRINGING HIM TO A VAST FURNACE!
I THINK THE OPERATIVE WORD IS "HAD", LUV!
THEY'RE TAKING HIS HOOD OFF, AND--
--IT'S KING ACORN!
THEY HAVE DADDY!
WHY CAN'T WE HEAR ANYTHING?
NICOLE?
14

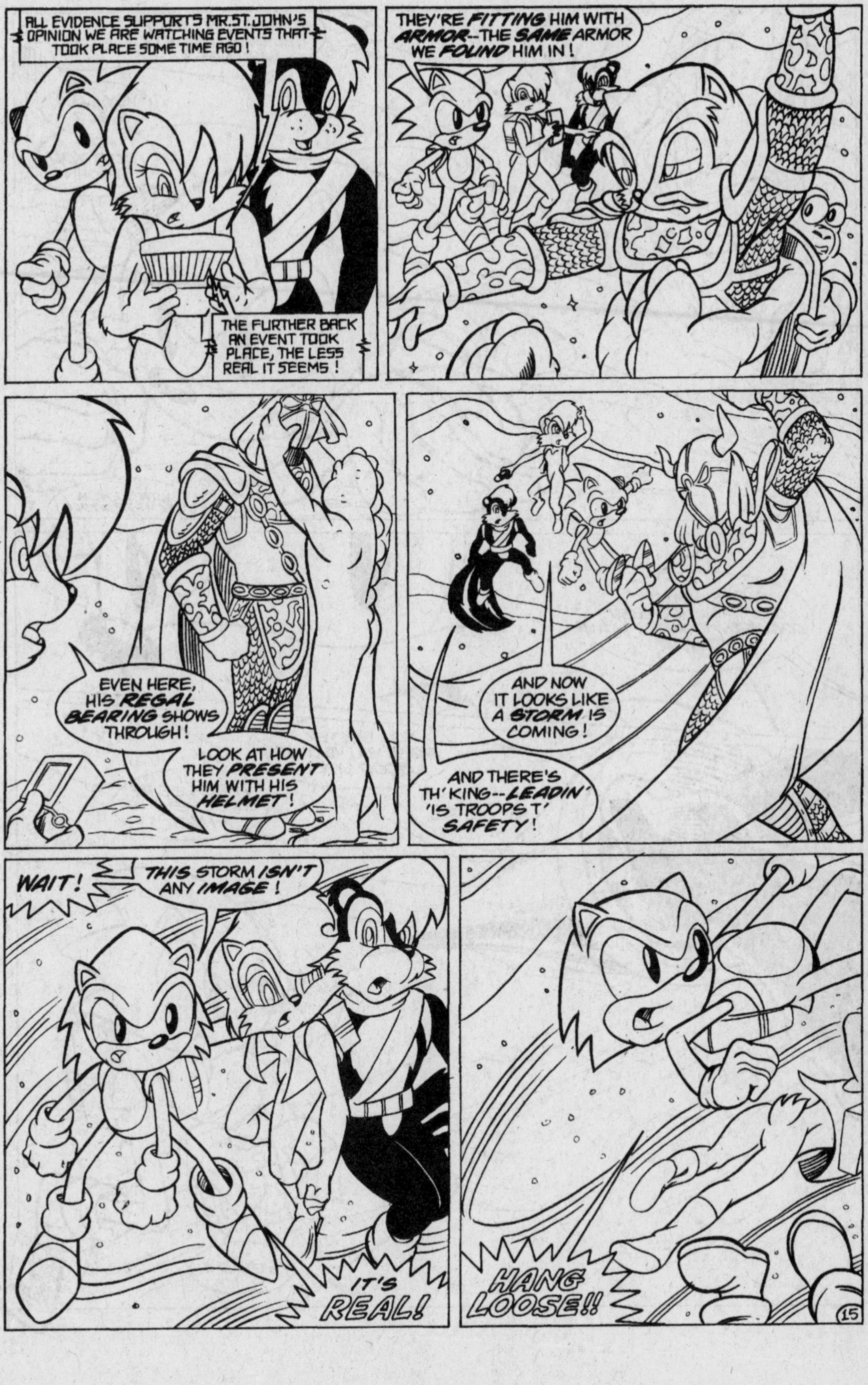
ALL EVIDENCE SUPPORTS MR. ST. JOHN'S OPINION WE ARE WATCHING EVENTS THAT TOOK PLACE SOME TIME AGO!
THE FURTHER BACK AN EVENT TOOK PLACE, THE LESS REAL IT SEEMS!
THEY'RE FITTING HIM WITH ARMOR--THE SAME ARMOR WE FOUND HIM IN!
EVEN HERE, HIS REGAL BEARING SHOWS THROUGH!
LOOK AT HOW THEY PRESENT HIM WITH HIS HELMET!
AND NOW IT LOOKS LIKE A STORM IS COMING!
AND THERE'S TH' KING--LEADIN' 'IS TROOPS T' SAFETY!
WAIT!
THIS STORM ISN'T ANY IMAGE!
IT'S REAL!
HANG LOOSE!!
15

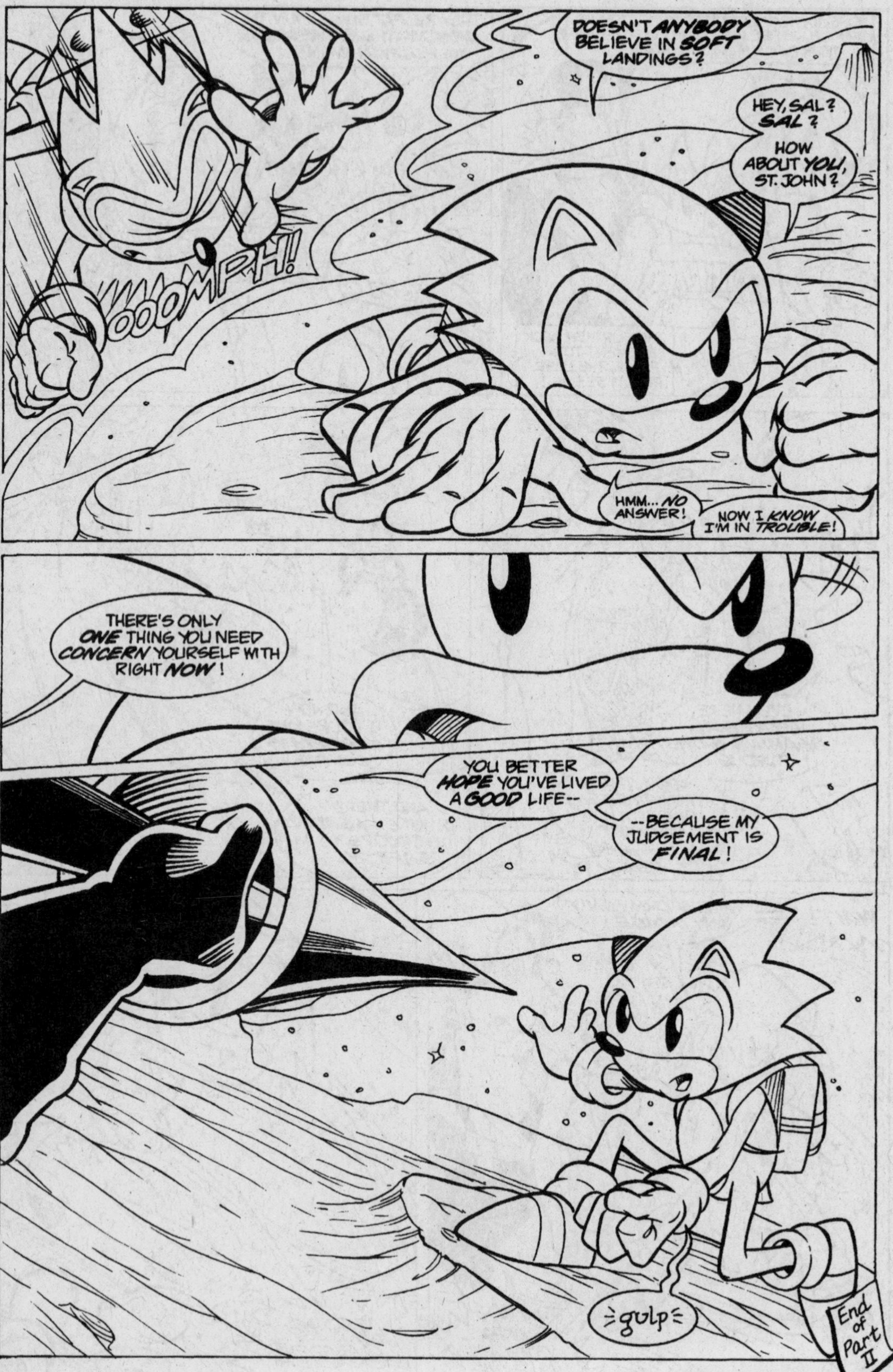

DOESN'T ANYBODY BELIEVE IN SOFT LANDINGS?
WHOOOMPH!
HEY, SAL? SAL?
HOW ABOUT YOU, ST. JOHN?
HMM... NO ANSWER!
NOW I KNOW I'M IN TROUBLE!
THERE'S ONLY ONE THING YOU NEED CONCERN YOURSELF WITH RIGHT NOW!
YOU BETTER HOPE YOU'VE LIVED A GOOD LIFE--
--BECAUSE MY JUDGEMENT IS FINAL!
gulp
End of Part II

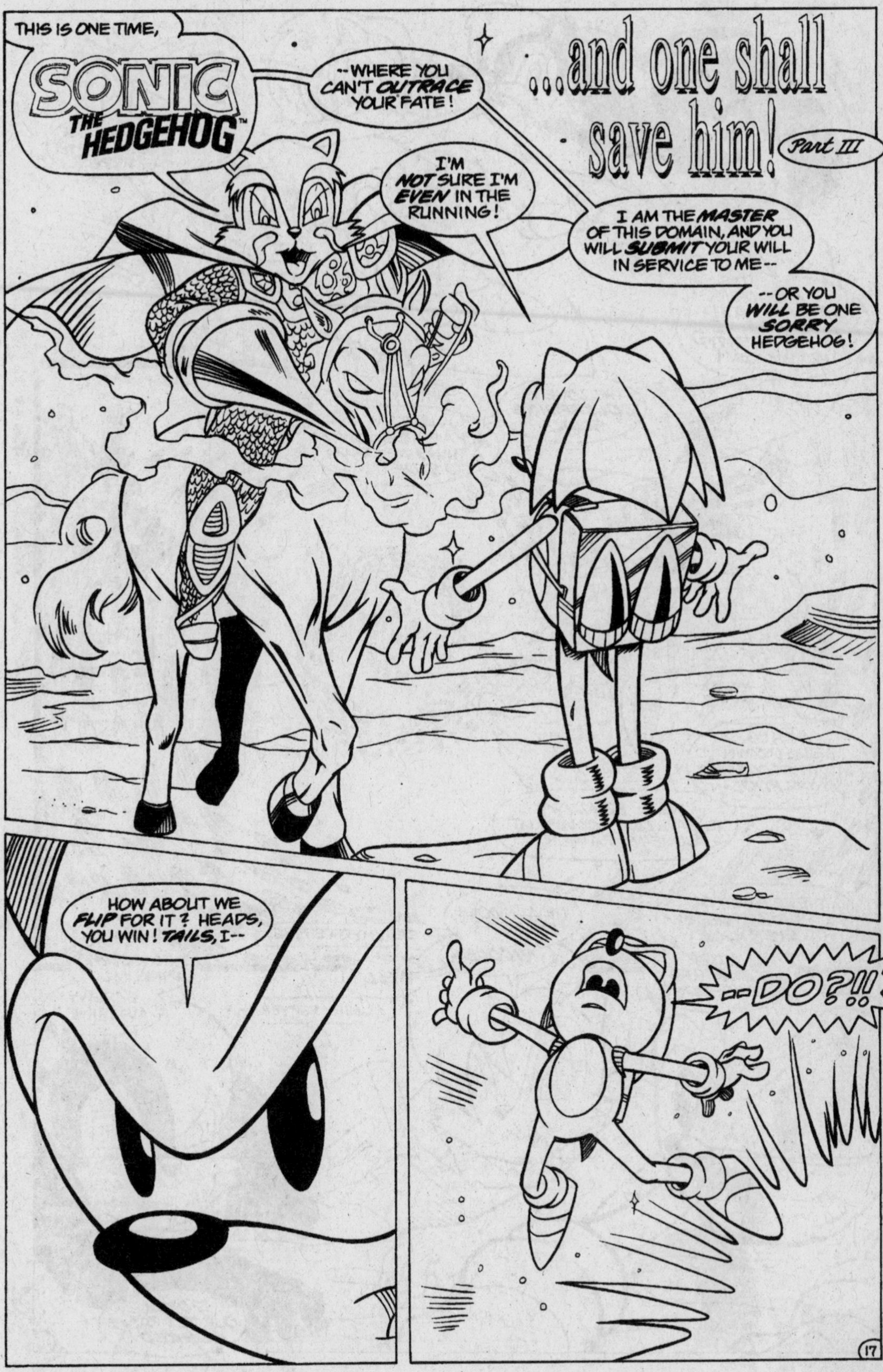
THIS IS ONE TIME,
SONIC THE HEDGEHOG™
--WHERE YOU CAN'T OUTRACE YOUR FATE!
...and one shall save him! Part III
I'M NOT SURE I'M EVEN IN THE RUNNING!
I AM THE MASTER OF THIS DOMAIN, AND YOU WILL SUBMIT YOUR WILL IN SERVICE TO ME--
--OR YOU WILL BE ONE SORRY HEDGEHOG!
HOW ABOUT WE FLIP FOR IT? HEADS, YOU WIN! TAILS, I--
--DO?!!
17

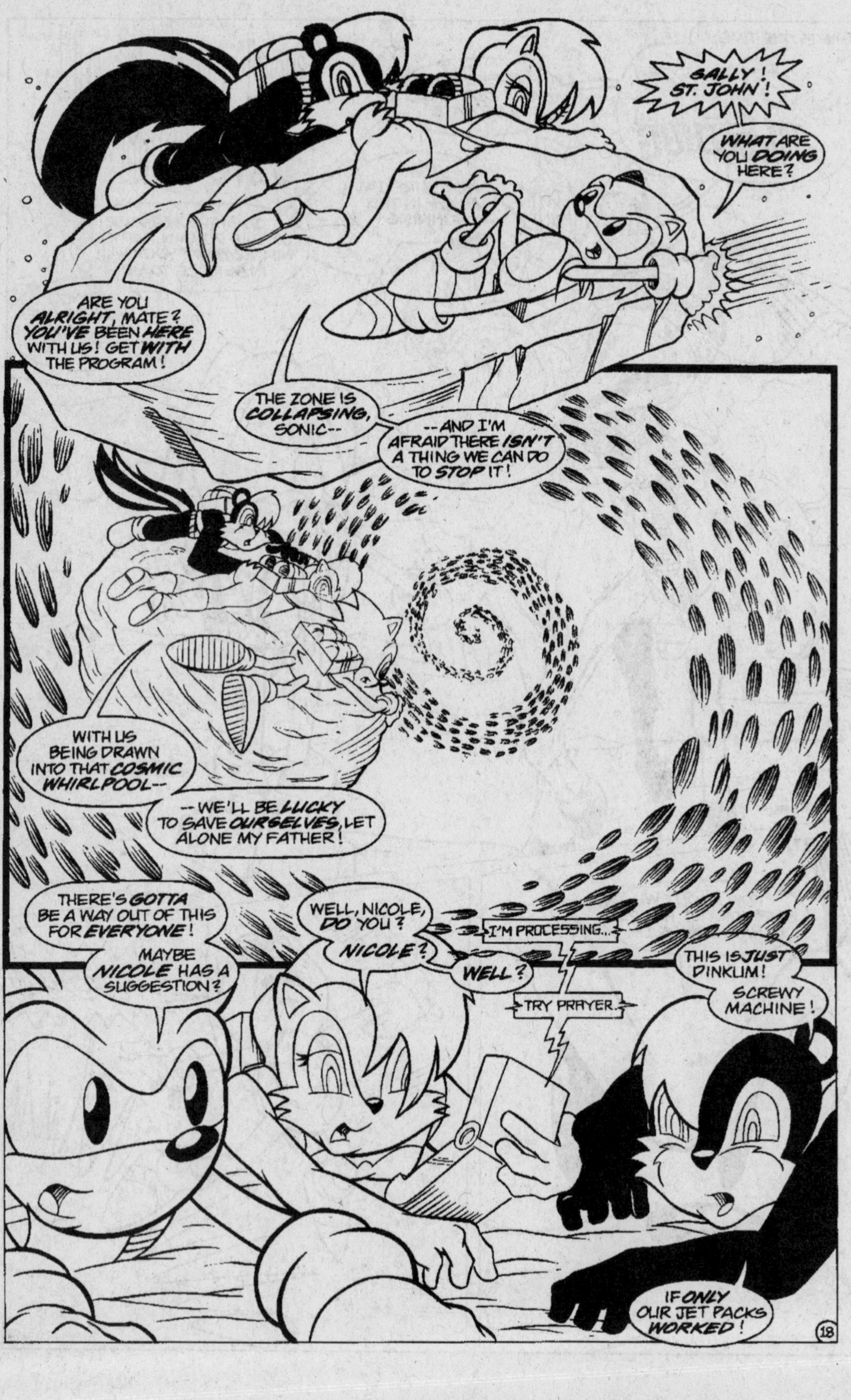
SALLY! ST. JOHN!
WHAT ARE YOU DOING HERE?
ARE YOU ALRIGHT, MATE? YOU'VE BEEN HERE WITH US! GET WITH THE PROGRAM!
THE ZONE IS COLLAPSING, SONIC--
--AND I'M AFRAID THERE ISN'T A THING WE CAN DO TO STOP IT!
WITH US BEING DRAWN INTO THAT COSMIC WHIRLPOOL--
--WE'LL BE LUCKY TO SAVE OURSELVES, LET ALONE MY FATHER!
THERE'S GOTTA BE A WAY OUT OF THIS FOR EVERYONE!
MAYBE NICOLE HAS A SUGGESTION?
WELL, NICOLE, DO YOU?
NICOLE?
I'M PROCESSING...
WELL?
TRY PRAYER.
THIS IS JUST DINKUM!
SCREWY MACHINE!
IF ONLY OUR JET PACKS WORKED!
18

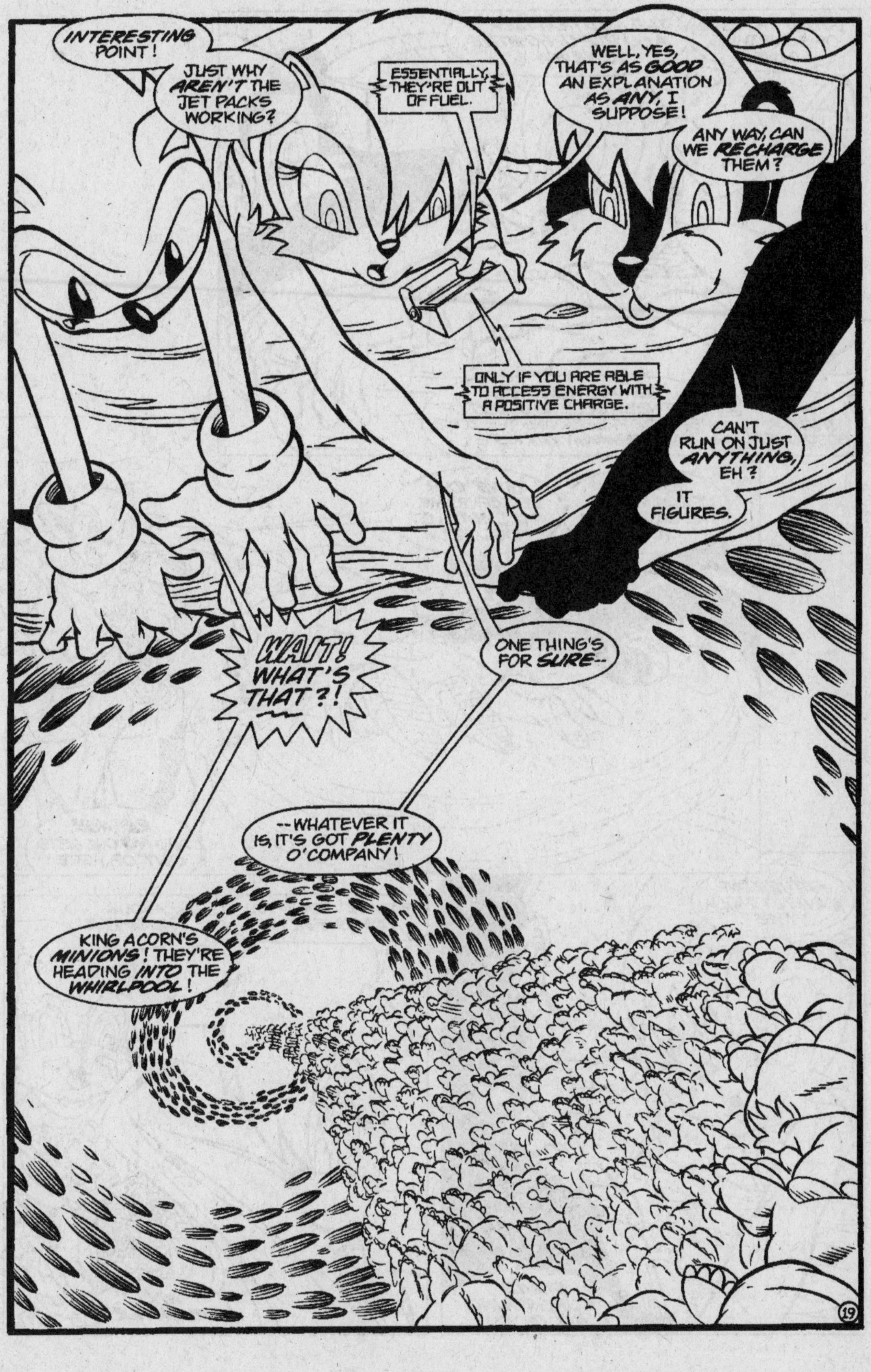
INTERESTING POINT!
JUST WHY AREN'T THE JET PACKS WORKING?
ESSENTIALLY, THEY'RE OUT OF FUEL.
WELL, YES, THAT'S AS GOOD AN EXPLANATION AS ANY, I SUPPOSE!
ANY WAY, CAN WE RECHARGE THEM?
ONLY IF YOU ARE ABLE TO ACCESS ENERGY WITH A POSITIVE CHARGE.
CAN'T RUN ON JUST ANYTHING, EH?
IT FIGURES.
WAIT! WHAT'S THAT?!
ONE THING'S FOR SURE--
--WHATEVER IT IS, IT'S GOT PLENTY O'COMPANY!
KING ACORN'S MINIONS! THEY'RE HEADING INTO THE WHIRLPOOL!
19

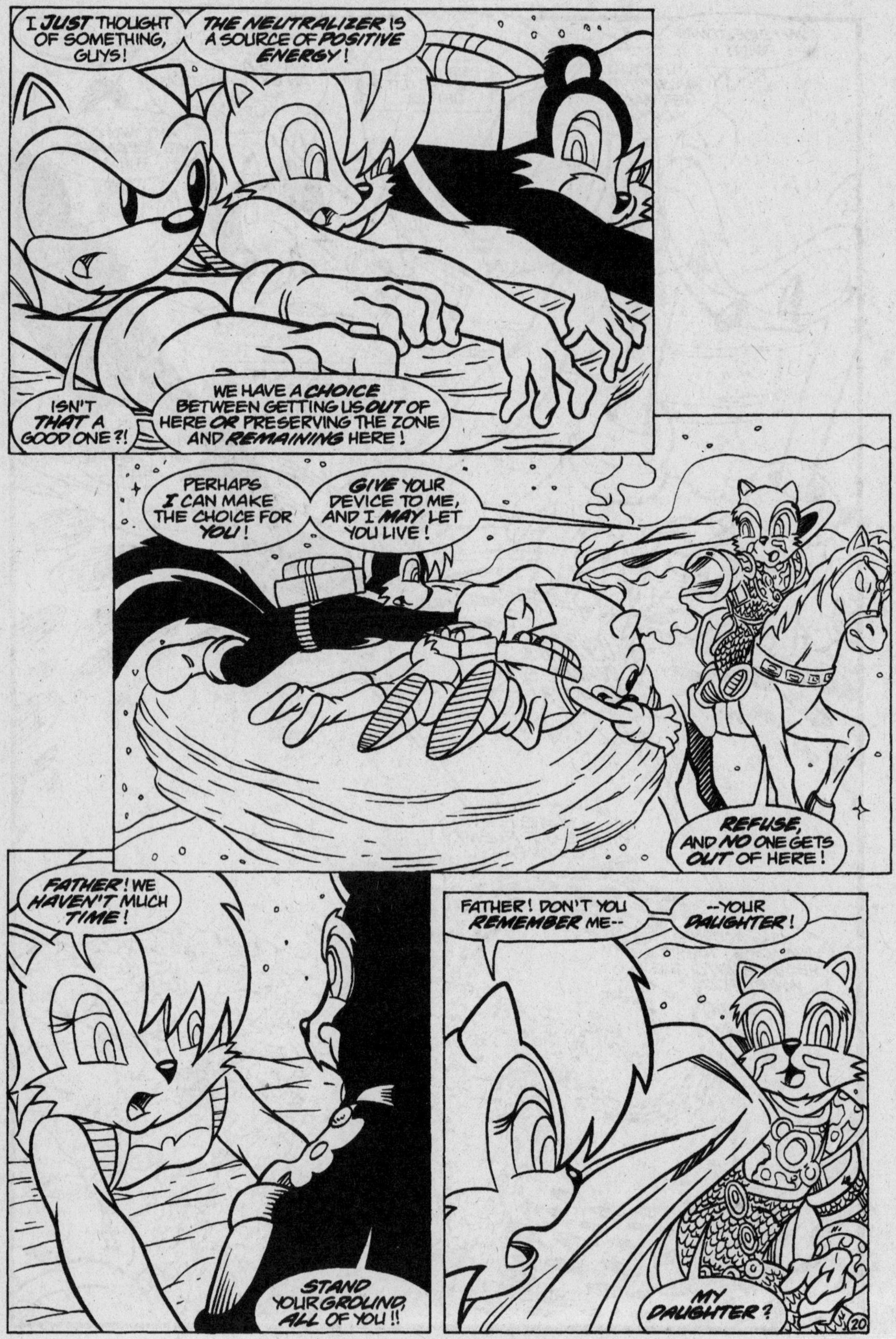
I JUST THOUGHT OF SOMETHING, GUYS!
THE NEUTRALIZER IS A SOURCE OF POSITIVE ENERGY!
ISN'T THAT A GOOD ONE?!
WE HAVE A CHOICE BETWEEN GETTING US OUT OF HERE OR PRESERVING THE ZONE AND REMAINING HERE!
PERHAPS I CAN MAKE THE CHOICE FOR YOU!
GIVE YOUR DEVICE TO ME, AND I MAY LET YOU LIVE!
REFUSE, AND NO ONE GETS OUT OF HERE!
FATHER! WE HAVEN'T MUCH TIME!
STAND YOUR GROUND, ALL OF YOU!!
FATHER! DON'T YOU REMEMBER ME--
--YOUR DAUGHTER!
MY DAUGHTER?
20

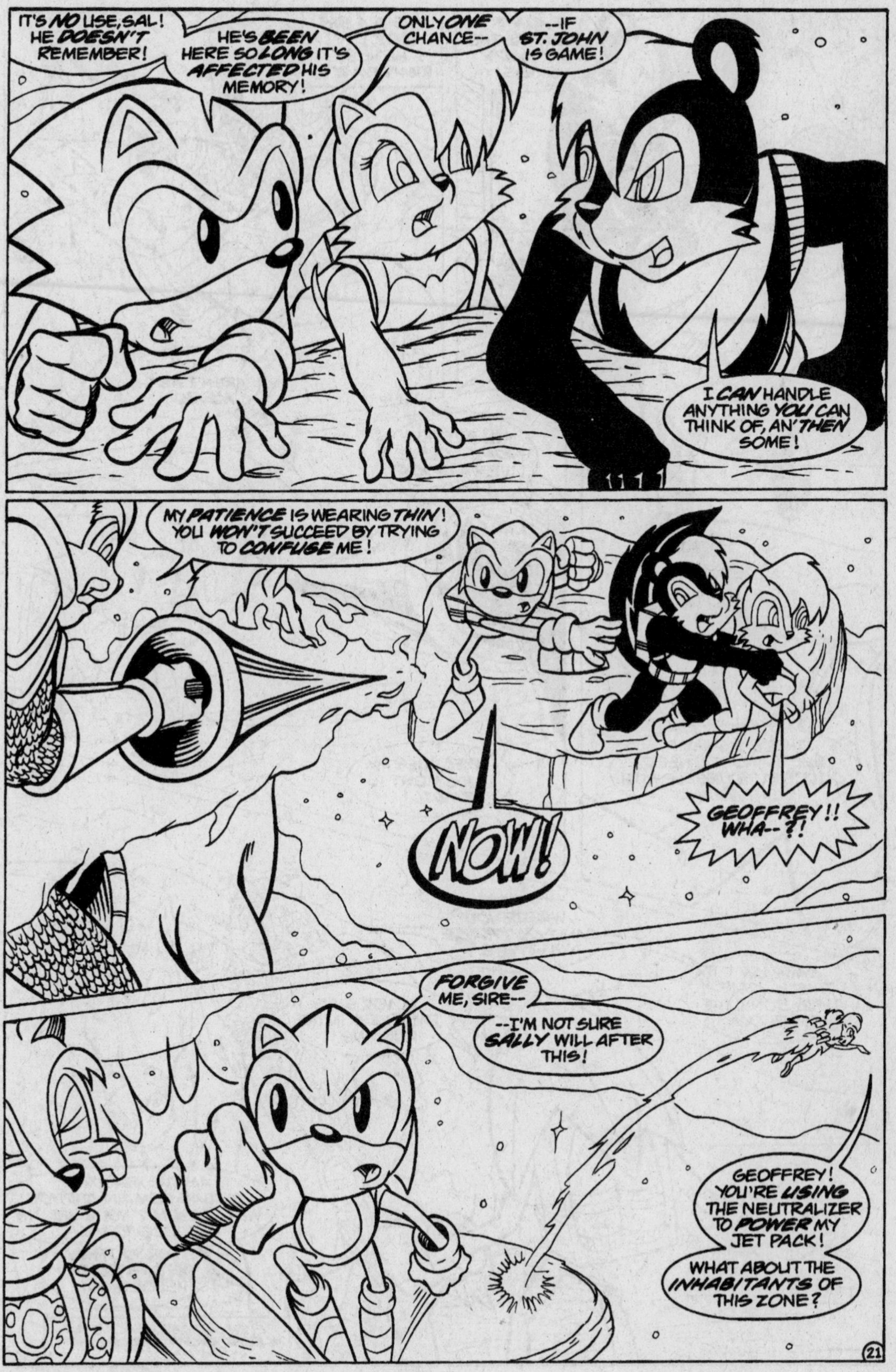
IT'S NO USE, SAL! HE DOESN'T REMEMBER!
HE'S BEEN HERE SO LONG IT'S AFFECTED HIS MEMORY!
ONLY ONE CHANCE--
--IF ST. JOHN IS GAME!
I CAN HANDLE ANYTHING YOU CAN THINK OF, AN' THEN SOME!
MY PATIENCE IS WEARING THIN! YOU WON'T SUCCEED BY TRYING TO CONFUSE ME!
NOW!
GEOFFREY!! WHA--?!
FORGIVE ME, SIRE--
--I'M NOT SURE SALLY WILL AFTER THIS!
GEOFFREY! YOU'RE USING THE NEUTRALIZER TO POWER MY JET PACK!
WHAT ABOUT THE INHABITANTS OF THIS ZONE?
21

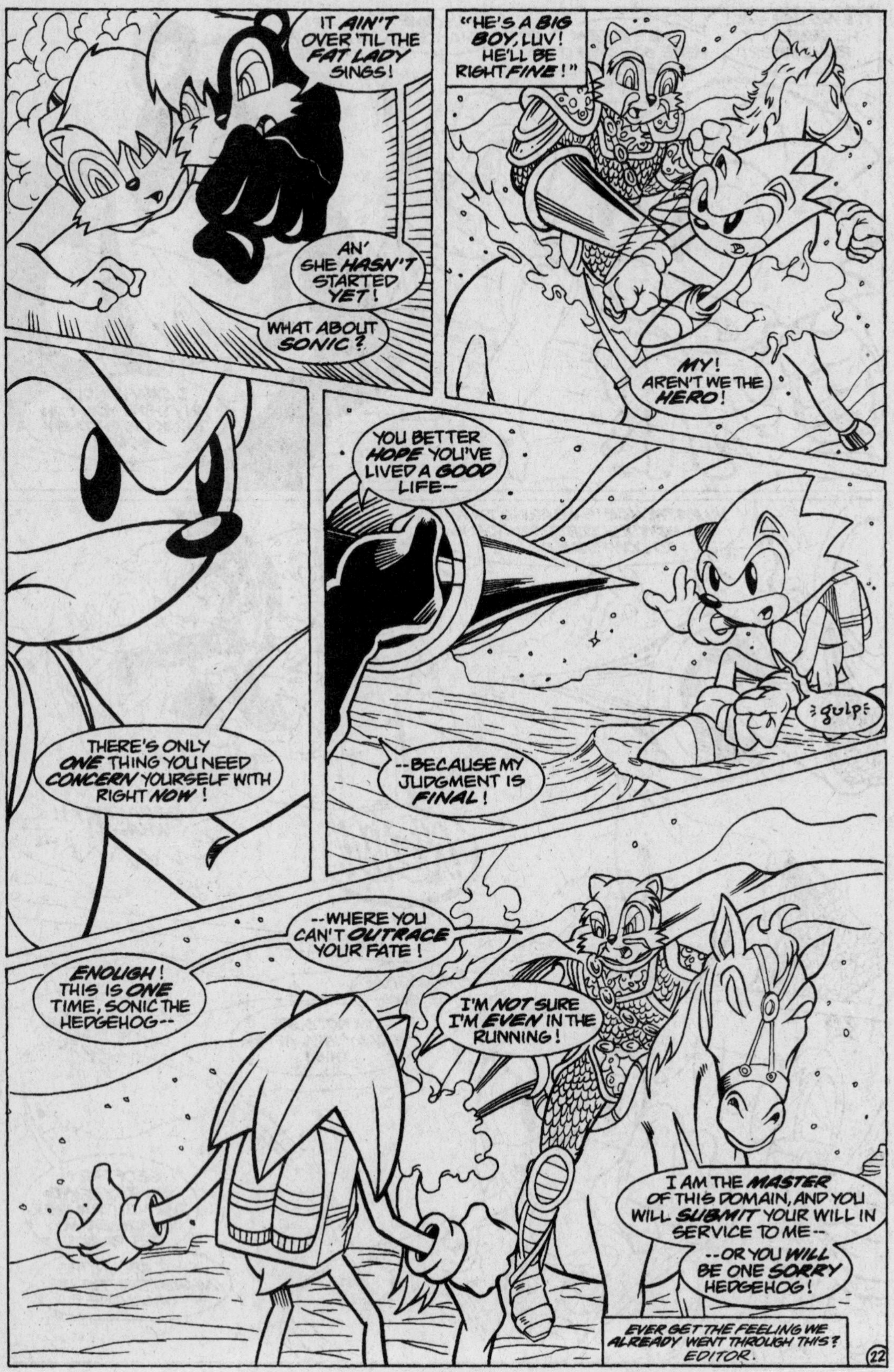
IT AIN'T OVER 'TIL THE FAT LADY SINGS!
AN' SHE HASN'T STARTED YET!
WHAT ABOUT SONIC?
"HE'S A BIG BOY, LUV! HE'LL BE RIGHT FINE!"
MY! AREN'T WE THE HERO!
THERE'S ONLY ONE THING YOU NEED CONCERN YOURSELF WITH RIGHT NOW!
YOU BETTER HOPE YOU'VE LIVED A GOOD LIFE--
gulp
--BECAUSE MY JUDGMENT IS FINAL!
ENOUGH! THIS IS ONE TIME, SONIC THE HEDGEHOG--
--WHERE YOU CAN'T OUTRACE YOUR FATE!
I'M NOT SURE I'M EVEN IN THE RUNNING!
I AM THE MASTER OF THIS DOMAIN, AND YOU WILL SUBMIT YOUR WILL IN SERVICE TO ME--
--OR YOU WILL BE ONE SORRY HEDGEHOG!
EVER GET THE FEELING WE ALREADY WENT THROUGH THIS? EDITOR.
22

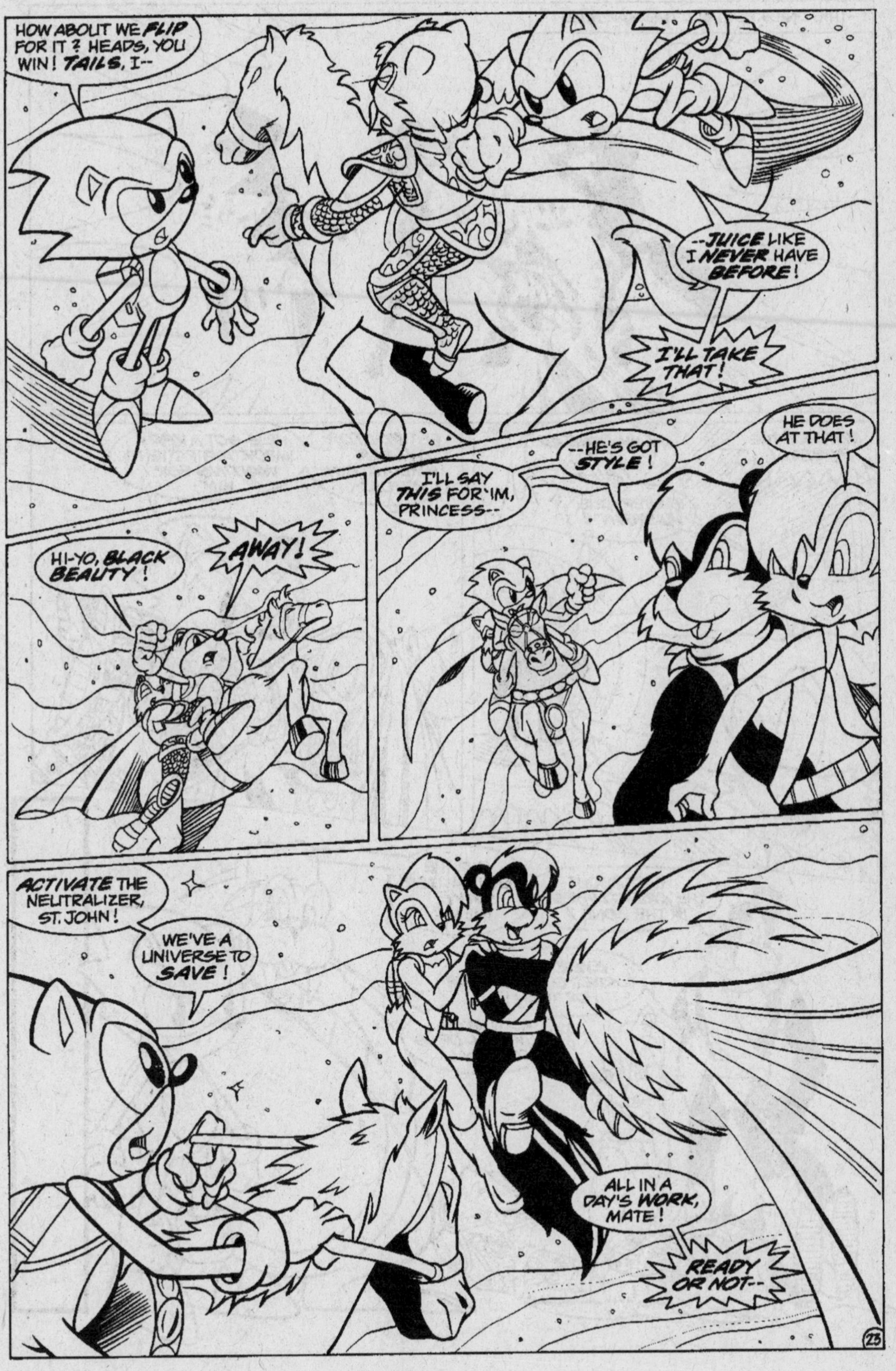

HOW ABOUT WE FLIP FOR IT? HEADS, YOU WIN! TAILS, I--
--JUICE LIKE I NEVER HAVE BEFORE!
I'LL TAKE THAT!
HI-YO, BLACK BEAUTY!
AWAY!
I'LL SAY THIS FOR 'IM, PRINCESS--
--HE'S GOT STYLE!
HE DOES AT THAT!
ACTIVATE THE NEUTRALIZER, ST. JOHN!
WE'VE A UNIVERSE TO SAVE!
ALL IN A DAY'S WORK, MATE!
READY OR NOT--
23

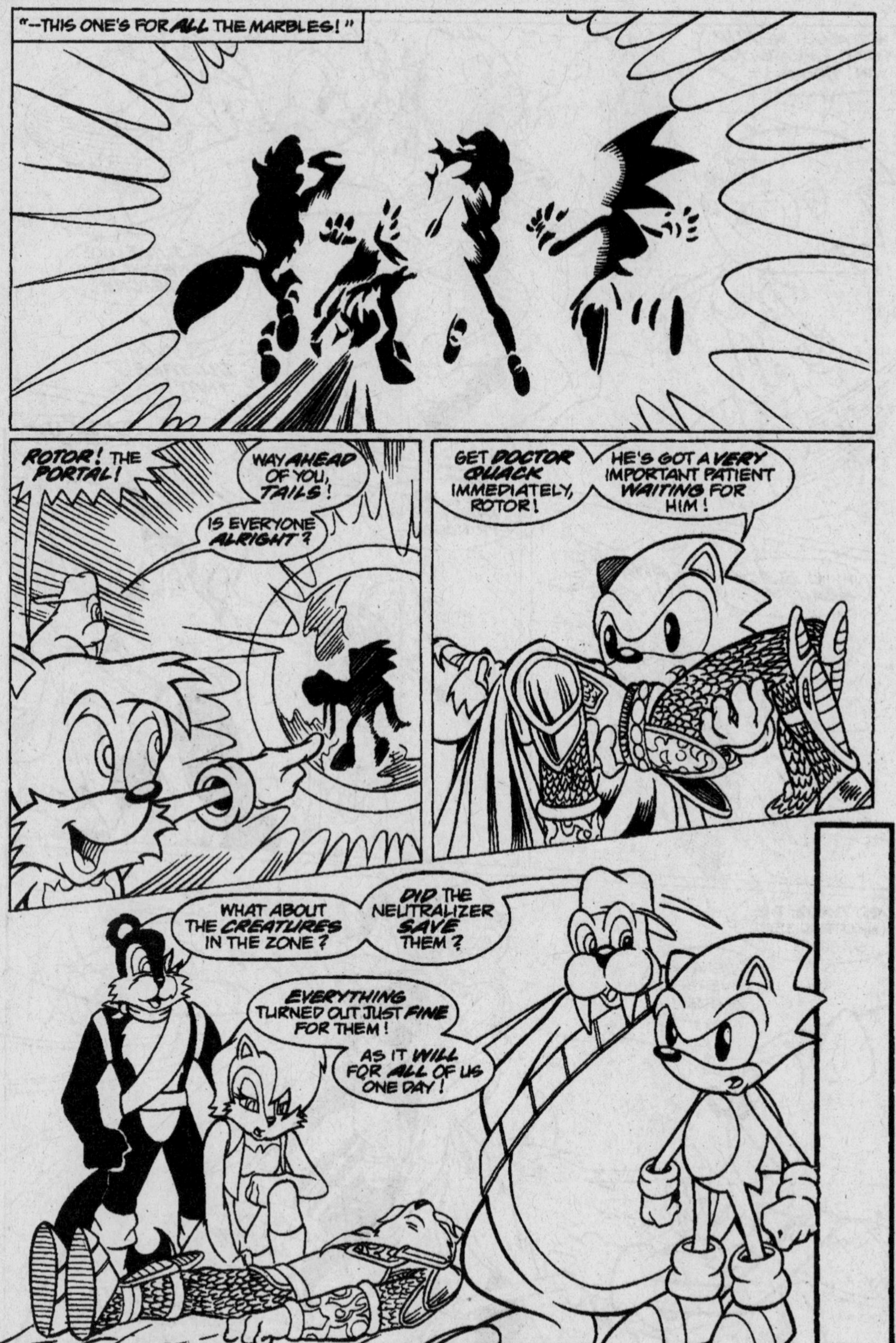
"--THIS ONE'S FOR ALL THE MARBLES!"
ROTOR! THE PORTAL!
WAY AHEAD OF YOU, TAILS!
IS EVERYONE ALRIGHT?
GET DOCTOR QUACK IMMEDIATELY, ROTOR!
HE'S GOT A VERY IMPORTANT PATIENT WAITING FOR HIM!
WHAT ABOUT THE CREATURES IN THE ZONE?
DID THE NEUTRALIZER SAVE THEM?
EVERYTHING TURNED OUT JUST FINE FOR THEM!
AS IT WILL FOR ALL OF US ONE DAY!

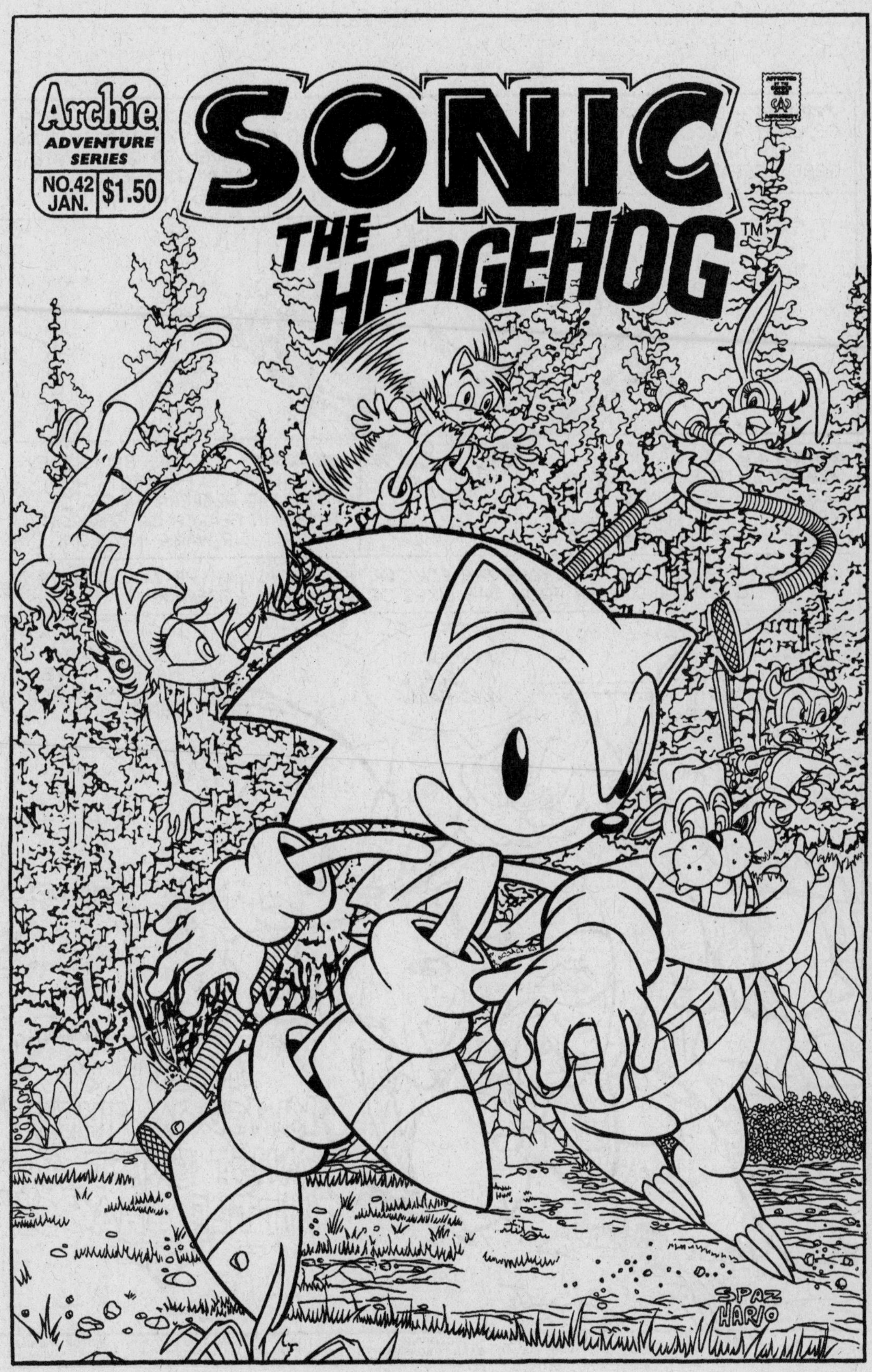
Archie
ADVENTURE SERIES
NO.42 JAN.
$1.50
SONIC THE HEDGEHOG™
SPAZ HARJO

TYRANNY-- LIKE A DARK CLOUD IT SHADOWS A LAND, CAUSING THE VALIANT TO REBEL, CREATING WAR...

WAR-- ITS SOLDIERS ARE OFTEN CALLED *FREEDOM FIGHTERS*, WHO ARE SOMETIMES DRIVEN TO DESPERATE ACTS, EVEN AGAINST THOSE WHO HAVE ATTEMPTED NEUTRALITY...

NEUTRALITY-- A POSITION IN WAR THE FABLED *FLOATING ISLAND* HAS BEEN UNABLE TO MAINTAIN AS ITS NATIVES LOOK FOR HOPE FROM ITS GUARDIAN...

GUARDIAN-- THE ONE BEING THEY DEPEND ON TO PROTECT THEM FROM THE DESPERATE ACTS OF THOSE IN SEARCH OF *FREEDOM* AND THEIR WAR'S INVASION...

INVASION-- SOMETHING *KNUCKLES THE ECHIDNA* NEVER THOUGHT HE WOULD HAVE TO CONTEND WITH FROM THE LIKES OF *SONIC THE HEDGEHOG!*

ARE YOU CRAZY-- BARGING IN HERE AND DEMANDING I FORK OVER MY *CHAOS EMERALD?!*

WITHOUT IT, MY *ISLAND* WILL FALL!

I'VE GOTTA HAVE IT -- THE FATE OF *MOBIUS* DEPENDS ON IT!

"IN EVERY KINGDOM THERE MUST EXIST A LITTLE CHAOS!"
PART 1

SCRIPT: KENT TAYLOR   ART: ART MAWHINNEY   INKER: PHIL SHEEHY   LETTERING: MINDY EISMAN   COLORING: BARRY GROSSMAN   EDITOR: J. FREDDY GABRIE   MANAGING EDITOR: VICTOR GORELICK   EDITOR-IN-CHIEF: RICHARD GOLDWATER

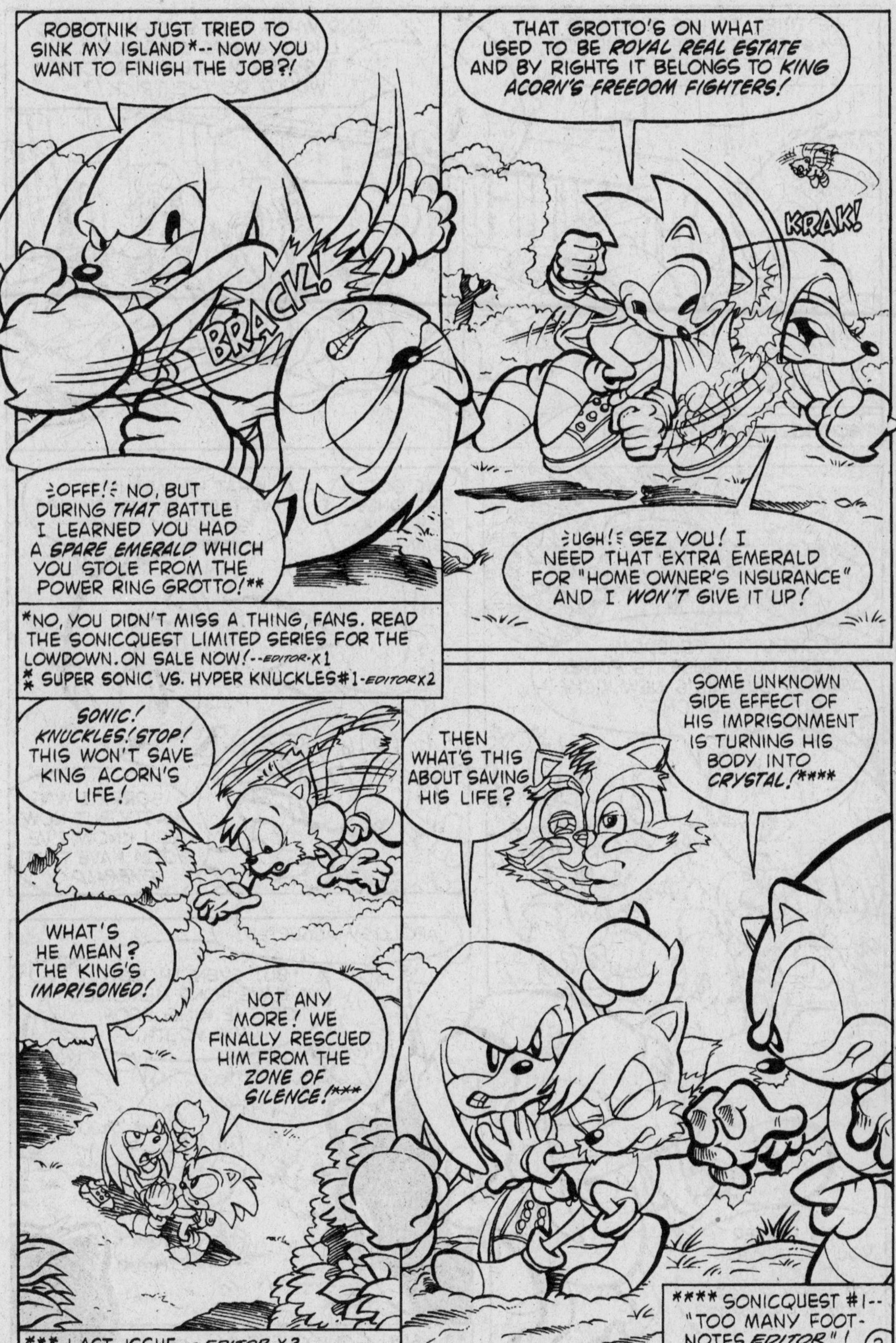
ROBOTNIK JUST TRIED TO SINK MY ISLAND*-- NOW YOU WANT TO FINISH THE JOB?!
BRACK!
OFFF! NO, BUT DURING THAT BATTLE I LEARNED YOU HAD A SPARE EMERALD WHICH YOU STOLE FROM THE POWER RING GROTTO!**
*NO, YOU DIDN'T MISS A THING, FANS. READ THE SONICQUEST LIMITED SERIES FOR THE LOWDOWN. ON SALE NOW! --EDITOR X1
** SUPER SONIC VS. HYPER KNUCKLES #1 -EDITOR X2
THAT GROTTO'S ON WHAT USED TO BE ROYAL REAL ESTATE AND BY RIGHTS IT BELONGS TO KING ACORN'S FREEDOM FIGHTERS!
KRAK!
UGH! SEZ YOU! I NEED THAT EXTRA EMERALD FOR "HOME OWNER'S INSURANCE" AND I WON'T GIVE IT UP!
SONIC! KNUCKLES! STOP! THIS WON'T SAVE KING ACORN'S LIFE!
WHAT'S HE MEAN? THE KING'S IMPRISONED!
NOT ANY MORE! WE FINALLY RESCUED HIM FROM THE ZONE OF SILENCE!***
*** LAST ISSUE -- EDITOR X3
THEN WHAT'S THIS ABOUT SAVING HIS LIFE?
SOME UNKNOWN SIDE EFFECT OF HIS IMPRISONMENT IS TURNING HIS BODY INTO CRYSTAL!****
**** SONICQUEST #1-- "TOO MANY FOOT-NOTES EDITOR"!
2

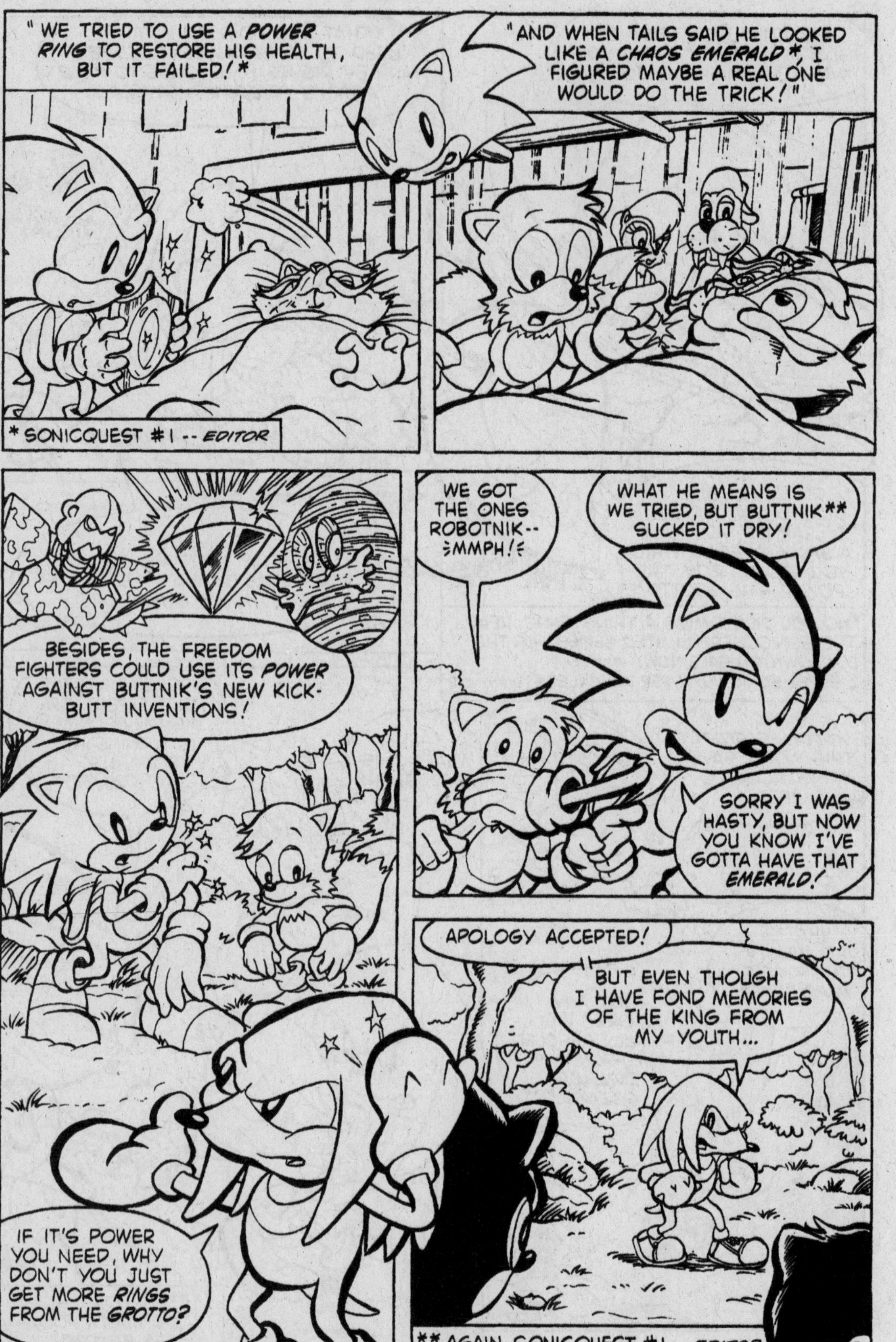
"WE TRIED TO USE A POWER RING TO RESTORE HIS HEALTH, BUT IT FAILED!*
* SONICQUEST #1 -- EDITOR
"AND WHEN TAILS SAID HE LOOKED LIKE A CHAOS EMERALD*, I FIGURED MAYBE A REAL ONE WOULD DO THE TRICK!"
BESIDES, THE FREEDOM FIGHTERS COULD USE ITS POWER AGAINST BUTTNIK'S NEW KICK-BUTT INVENTIONS!
IF IT'S POWER YOU NEED, WHY DON'T YOU JUST GET MORE RINGS FROM THE GROTTO?
WE GOT THE ONES ROBOTNIK-- MMPH!
WHAT HE MEANS IS WE TRIED, BUT BUTTNIK** SUCKED IT DRY!
SORRY I WAS HASTY, BUT NOW YOU KNOW I'VE GOTTA HAVE THAT EMERALD!
APOLOGY ACCEPTED!
BUT EVEN THOUGH I HAVE FOND MEMORIES OF THE KING FROM MY YOUTH...
** AGAIN, SONICQUEST #1 -- EDITOR
3

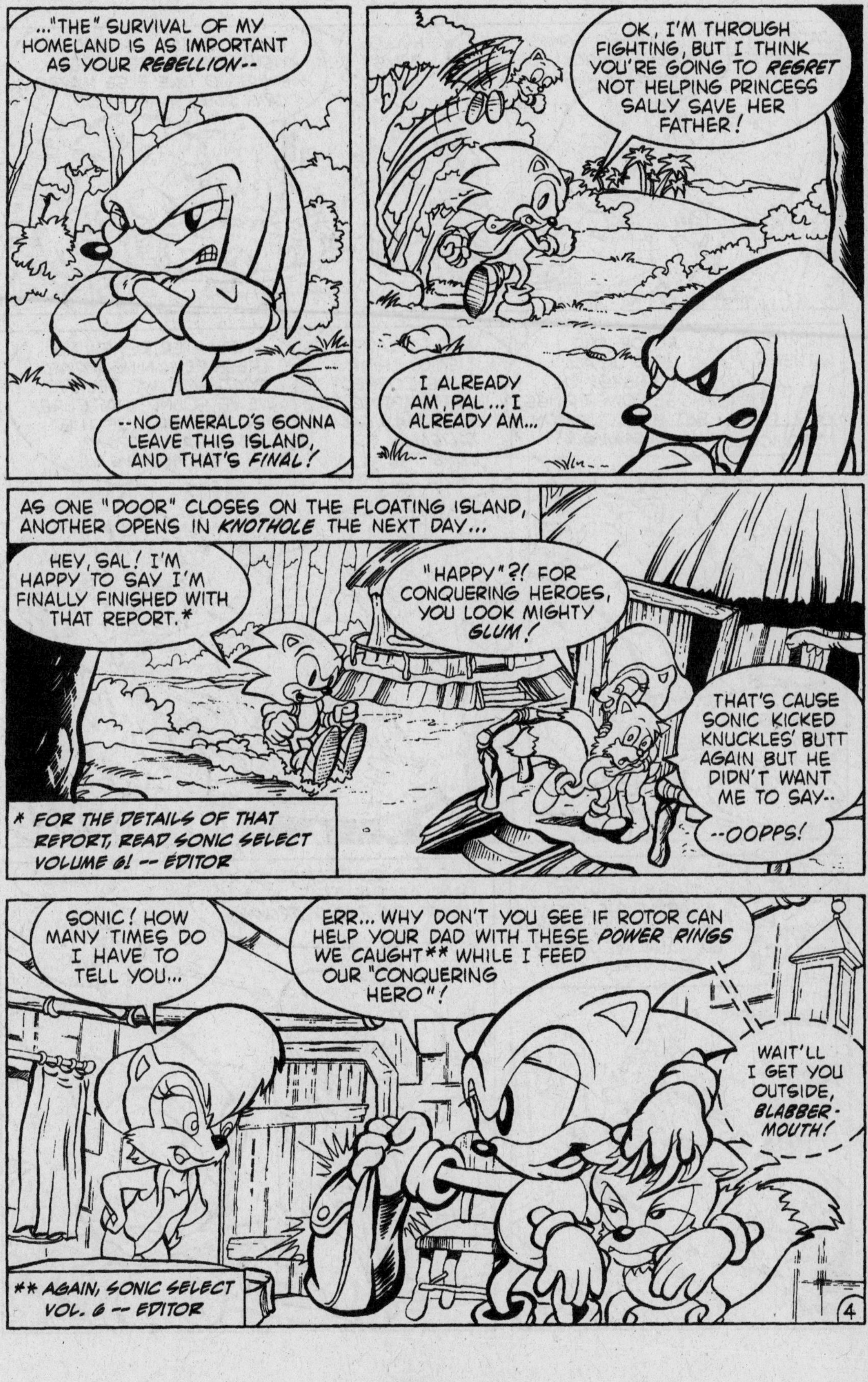

..."THE" SURVIVAL OF MY HOMELAND IS AS IMPORTANT AS YOUR REBELLION--
--NO EMERALD'S GONNA LEAVE THIS ISLAND, AND THAT'S FINAL!
OK, I'M THROUGH FIGHTING, BUT I THINK YOU'RE GOING TO REGRET NOT HELPING PRINCESS SALLY SAVE HER FATHER!
I ALREADY AM, PAL... I ALREADY AM...
AS ONE "DOOR" CLOSES ON THE FLOATING ISLAND, ANOTHER OPENS IN KNOTHOLE THE NEXT DAY...
HEY, SAL! I'M HAPPY TO SAY I'M FINALLY FINISHED WITH THAT REPORT.*
"HAPPY"?! FOR CONQUERING HEROES, YOU LOOK MIGHTY GLUM!
THAT'S CAUSE SONIC KICKED KNUCKLES' BUTT AGAIN BUT HE DIDN'T WANT ME TO SAY..
--OOPPS!
* FOR THE DETAILS OF THAT REPORT, READ SONIC SELECT VOLUME 6! -- EDITOR
SONIC! HOW MANY TIMES DO I HAVE TO TELL YOU...
ERR... WHY DON'T YOU SEE IF ROTOR CAN HELP YOUR DAD WITH THESE POWER RINGS WE CAUGHT** WHILE I FEED OUR "CONQUERING HERO"!
WAIT'LL I GET YOU OUTSIDE, BLABBER-MOUTH!
** AGAIN, SONIC SELECT VOL. 6 -- EDITOR
4

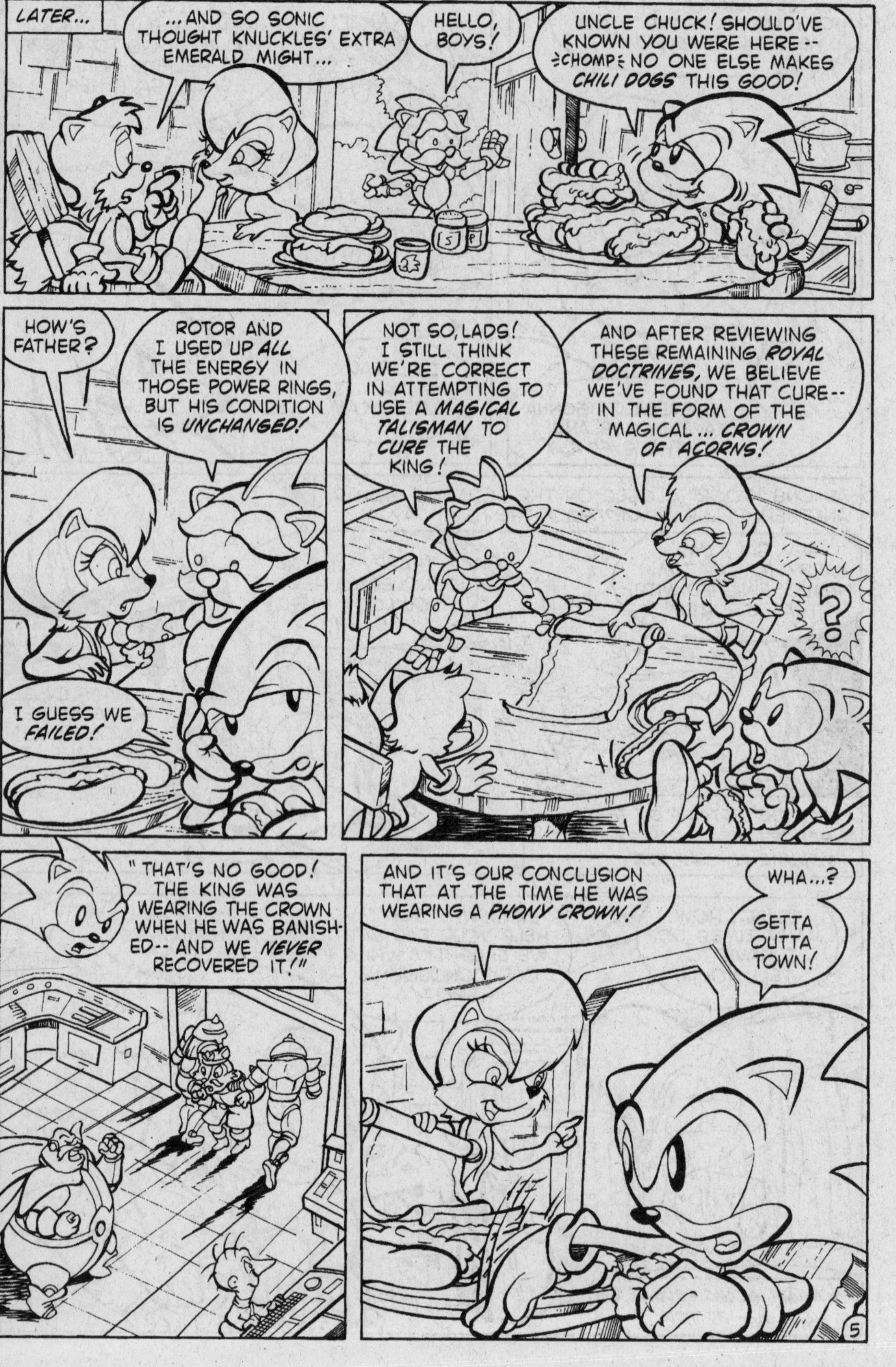
LATER...
...AND SO SONIC THOUGHT KNUCKLES' EXTRA EMERALD MIGHT...
HELLO, BOYS!
UNCLE CHUCK! SHOULD'VE KNOWN YOU WERE HERE-- CHOMP NO ONE ELSE MAKES CHILI DOGS THIS GOOD!
HOW'S FATHER?
ROTOR AND I USED UP ALL THE ENERGY IN THOSE POWER RINGS, BUT HIS CONDITION IS UNCHANGED!
I GUESS WE FAILED!
NOT SO, LADS! I STILL THINK WE'RE CORRECT IN ATTEMPTING TO USE A MAGICAL TALISMAN TO CURE THE KING!
AND AFTER REVIEWING THESE REMAINING ROYAL DOCTRINES, WE BELIEVE WE'VE FOUND THAT CURE-- IN THE FORM OF THE MAGICAL... CROWN OF ACORNS!
?
"THAT'S NO GOOD! THE KING WAS WEARING THE CROWN WHEN HE WAS BANISHED-- AND WE NEVER RECOVERED IT!"
AND IT'S OUR CONCLUSION THAT AT THE TIME HE WAS WEARING A PHONY CROWN!
WHA...?
GETTA OUTTA TOWN!
5

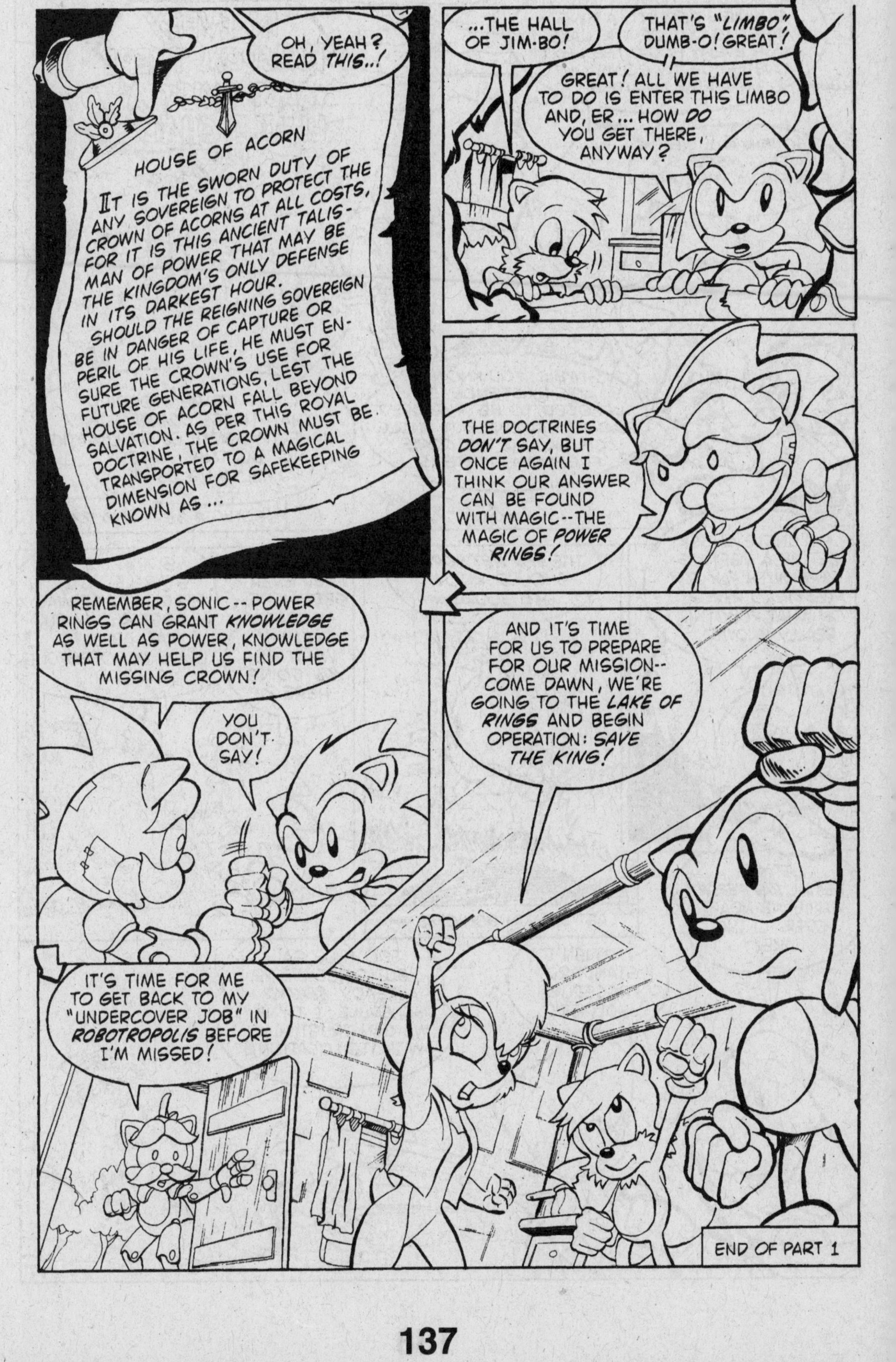
OH, YEAH? READ THIS..!
HOUSE OF ACORN
IT IS THE SWORN DUTY OF ANY SOVEREIGN TO PROTECT THE CROWN OF ACORNS AT ALL COSTS, FOR IT IS THIS ANCIENT TALIS-MAN OF POWER THAT MAY BE THE KINGDOM'S ONLY DEFENSE IN ITS DARKEST HOUR. SHOULD THE REIGNING SOVEREIGN BE IN DANGER OF CAPTURE OR PERIL OF HIS LIFE, HE MUST EN-SURE THE CROWN'S USE FOR FUTURE GENERATIONS, LEST THE HOUSE OF ACORN FALL BEYOND SALVATION. AS PER THIS ROYAL DOCTRINE, THE CROWN MUST BE TRANSPORTED TO A MAGICAL DIMENSION FOR SAFEKEEPING KNOWN AS ...
...THE HALL OF JIM-BO!
THAT'S "LIMBO", DUMB-O! GREAT!
GREAT! ALL WE HAVE TO DO IS ENTER THIS LIMBO AND, ER ... HOW DO YOU GET THERE, ANYWAY?
THE DOCTRINES DON'T SAY, BUT ONCE AGAIN I THINK OUR ANSWER CAN BE FOUND WITH MAGIC--THE MAGIC OF POWER RINGS!
REMEMBER, SONIC--POWER RINGS CAN GRANT KNOWLEDGE AS WELL AS POWER, KNOWLEDGE THAT MAY HELP US FIND THE MISSING CROWN!
YOU DON'T SAY!
AND IT'S TIME FOR US TO PREPARE FOR OUR MISSION--COME DAWN, WE'RE GOING TO THE LAKE OF RINGS AND BEGIN OPERATION: SAVE THE KING!
IT'S TIME FOR ME TO GET BACK TO MY "UNDERCOVER JOB" IN ROBOTROPOLIS BEFORE I'M MISSED!
END OF PART 1

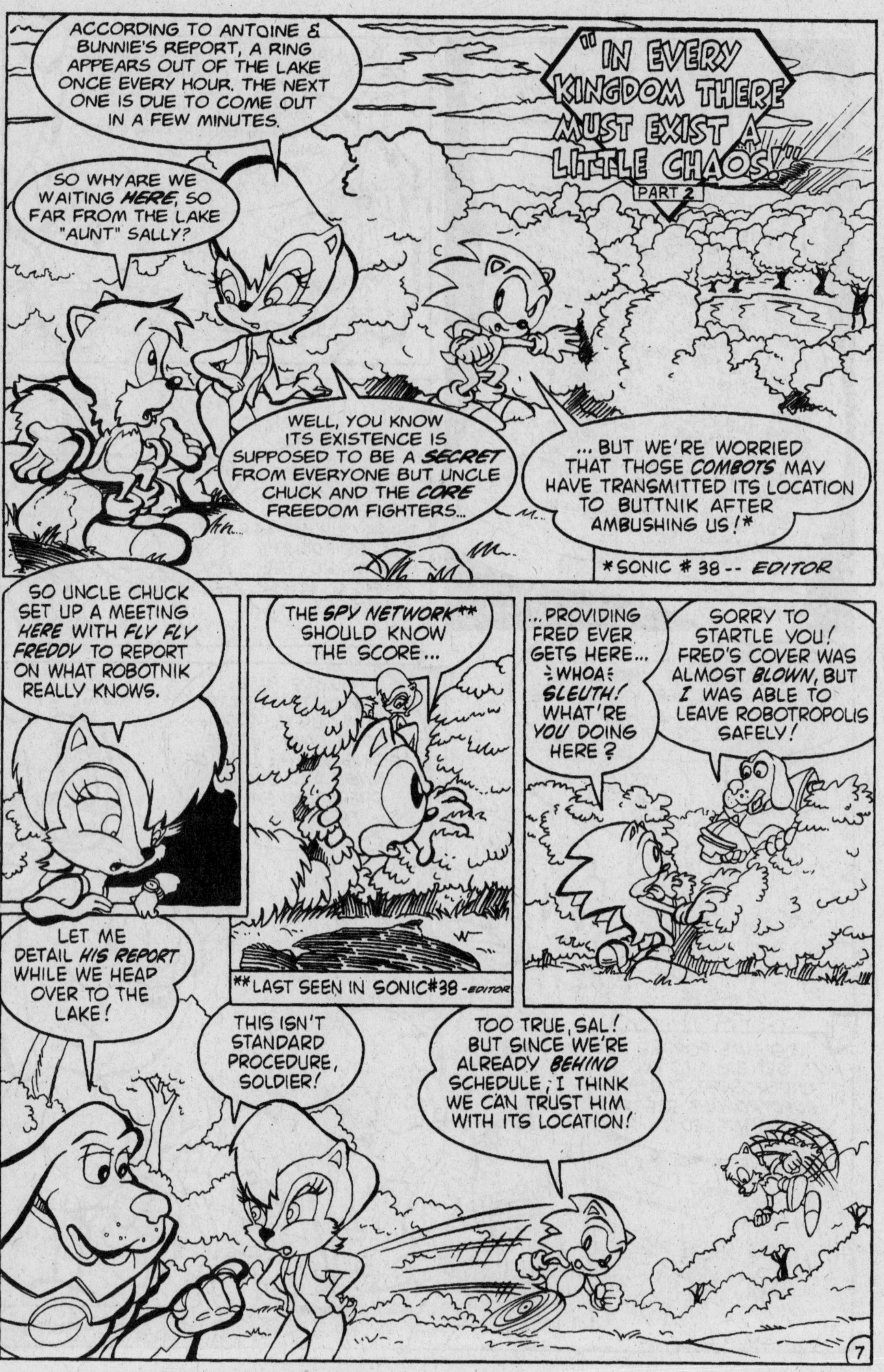
ACCORDING TO ANTOINE & BUNNIE'S REPORT, A RING APPEARS OUT OF THE LAKE ONCE EVERY HOUR. THE NEXT ONE IS DUE TO COME OUT IN A FEW MINUTES.
"IN EVERY KINGDOM THERE MUST EXIST A LITTLE CHAOS!"
PART 2
SO WHYARE WE WAITING HERE, SO FAR FROM THE LAKE "AUNT" SALLY?
WELL, YOU KNOW ITS EXISTENCE IS SUPPOSED TO BE A SECRET FROM EVERYONE BUT UNCLE CHUCK AND THE CORE FREEDOM FIGHTERS...
... BUT WE'RE WORRIED THAT THOSE COMBOTS MAY HAVE TRANSMITTED ITS LOCATION TO BUTTNIK AFTER AMBUSHING US!*
*SONIC # 38 -- EDITOR
SO UNCLE CHUCK SET UP A MEETING HERE WITH FLY FLY FREDDY TO REPORT ON WHAT ROBOTNIK REALLY KNOWS.
THE SPY NETWORK** SHOULD KNOW THE SCORE...
**LAST SEEN IN SONIC#38 -EDITOR
...PROVIDING FRED EVER GETS HERE... WHOA! SLEUTH! WHAT'RE YOU DOING HERE?
SORRY TO STARTLE YOU! FRED'S COVER WAS ALMOST BLOWN, BUT I WAS ABLE TO LEAVE ROBOTROPOLIS SAFELY!
LET ME DETAIL HIS REPORT WHILE WE HEAD OVER TO THE LAKE!
THIS ISN'T STANDARD PROCEDURE, SOLDIER!
TOO TRUE, SAL! BUT SINCE WE'RE ALREADY BEHIND SCHEDULE, I THINK WE CAN TRUST HIM WITH ITS LOCATION!
7

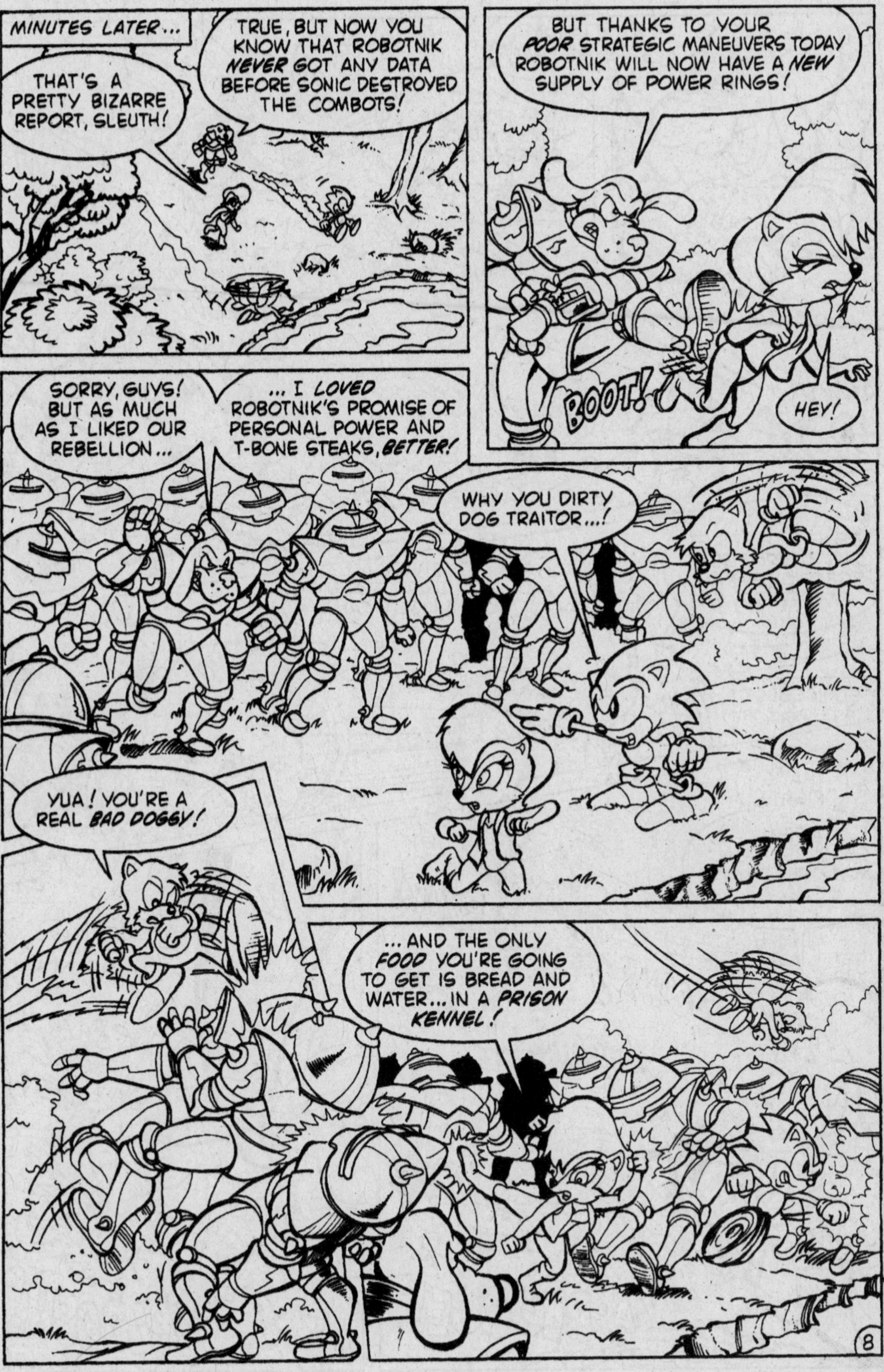
MINUTES LATER...
THAT'S A PRETTY BIZARRE REPORT, SLEUTH!
TRUE, BUT NOW YOU KNOW THAT ROBOTNIK NEVER GOT ANY DATA BEFORE SONIC DESTROYED THE COMBOTS!
BUT THANKS TO YOUR POOR STRATEGIC MANEUVERS TODAY ROBOTNIK WILL NOW HAVE A NEW SUPPLY OF POWER RINGS!
BOOT!
HEY!
SORRY, GUYS! BUT AS MUCH AS I LIKED OUR REBELLION...
... I LOVED ROBOTNIK'S PROMISE OF PERSONAL POWER AND T-BONE STEAKS, BETTER!
WHY YOU DIRTY DOG TRAITOR...!
YUA! YOU'RE A REAL BAD DOGGY!
... AND THE ONLY FOOD YOU'RE GOING TO GET IS BREAD AND WATER... IN A PRISON KENNEL!
8

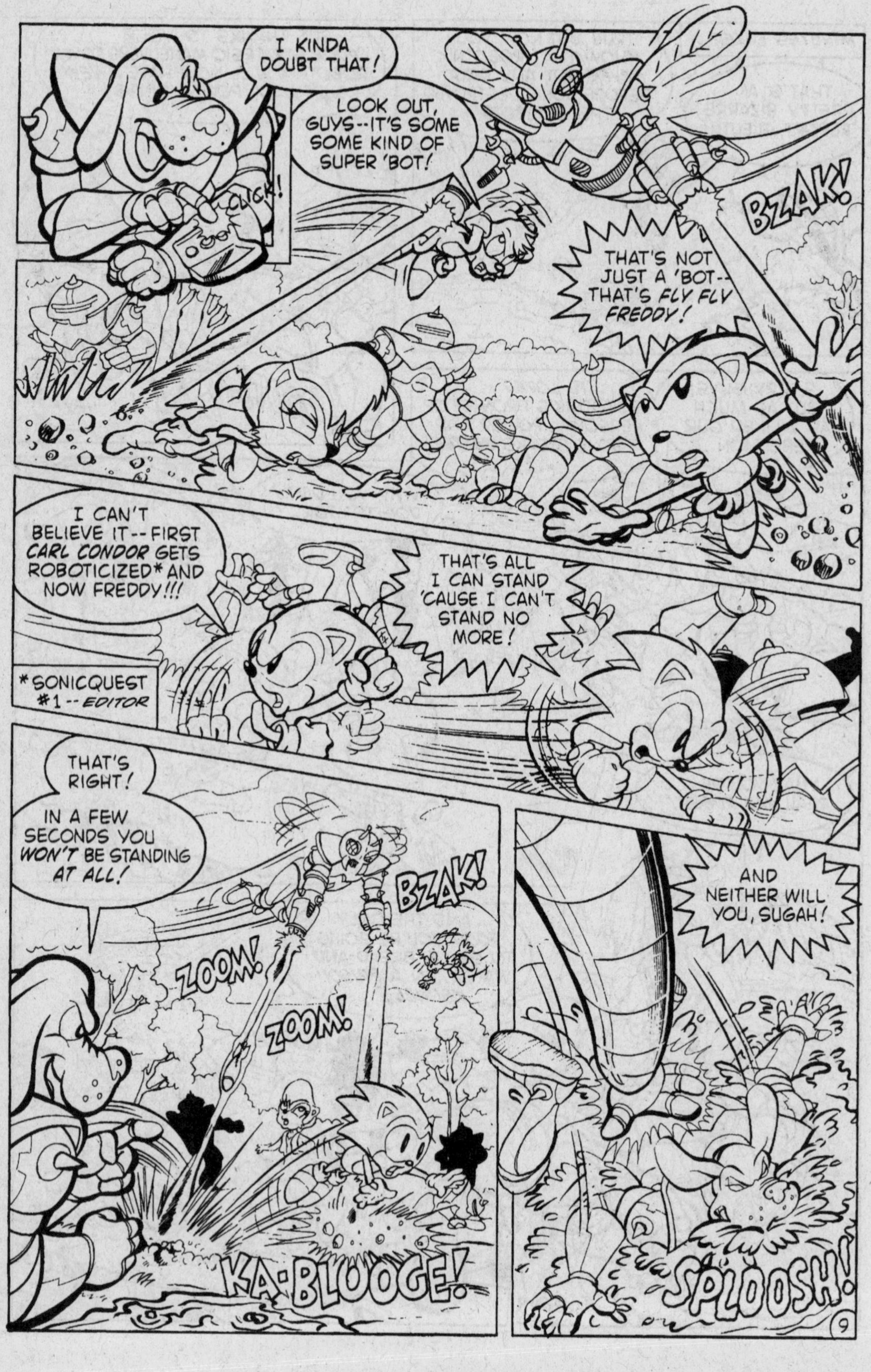
I KINDA DOUBT THAT!
CLICK!
LOOK OUT, GUYS--IT'S SOME SOME KIND OF SUPER 'BOT!
BZAK!
THAT'S NOT JUST A 'BOT--THAT'S FLY FLY FREDDY!
I CAN'T BELIEVE IT--FIRST CARL CONDOR GETS ROBOTICIZED* AND NOW FREDDY!!!
THAT'S ALL I CAN STAND 'CAUSE I CAN'T STAND NO MORE!
*SONICQUEST #1 --EDITOR
THAT'S RIGHT!
IN A FEW SECONDS YOU WON'T BE STANDING AT ALL!
BZAK!
ZOOM!
ZOOM!
KA-BLOOGE!
AND NEITHER WILL YOU, SUGAH!
SPLOOSH!
9

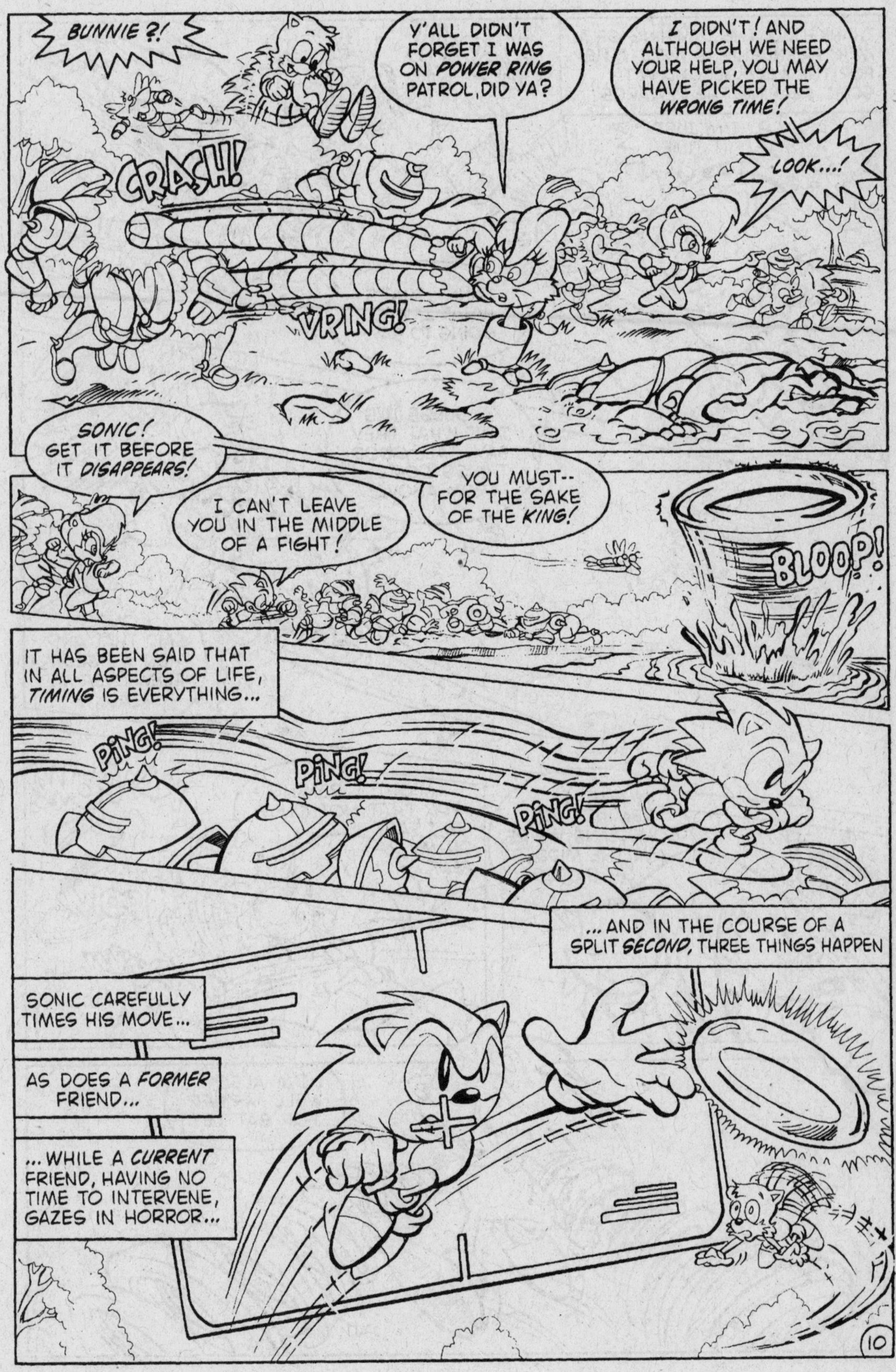
BUNNIE ?!
Y'ALL DIDN'T FORGET I WAS ON POWER RING PATROL, DID YA?
I DIDN'T! AND ALTHOUGH WE NEED YOUR HELP, YOU MAY HAVE PICKED THE WRONG TIME!
LOOK...!
CRASH!
VRING!
SONIC! GET IT BEFORE IT DISAPPEARS!
I CAN'T LEAVE YOU IN THE MIDDLE OF A FIGHT!
YOU MUST-- FOR THE SAKE OF THE KING!
BLOOP!
IT HAS BEEN SAID THAT IN ALL ASPECTS OF LIFE, TIMING IS EVERYTHING...
PING!
PING!
PING!
...AND IN THE COURSE OF A SPLIT SECOND, THREE THINGS HAPPEN
SONIC CAREFULLY TIMES HIS MOVE...
AS DOES A FORMER FRIEND...
...WHILE A CURRENT FRIEND, HAVING NO TIME TO INTERVENE, GAZES IN HORROR...
10

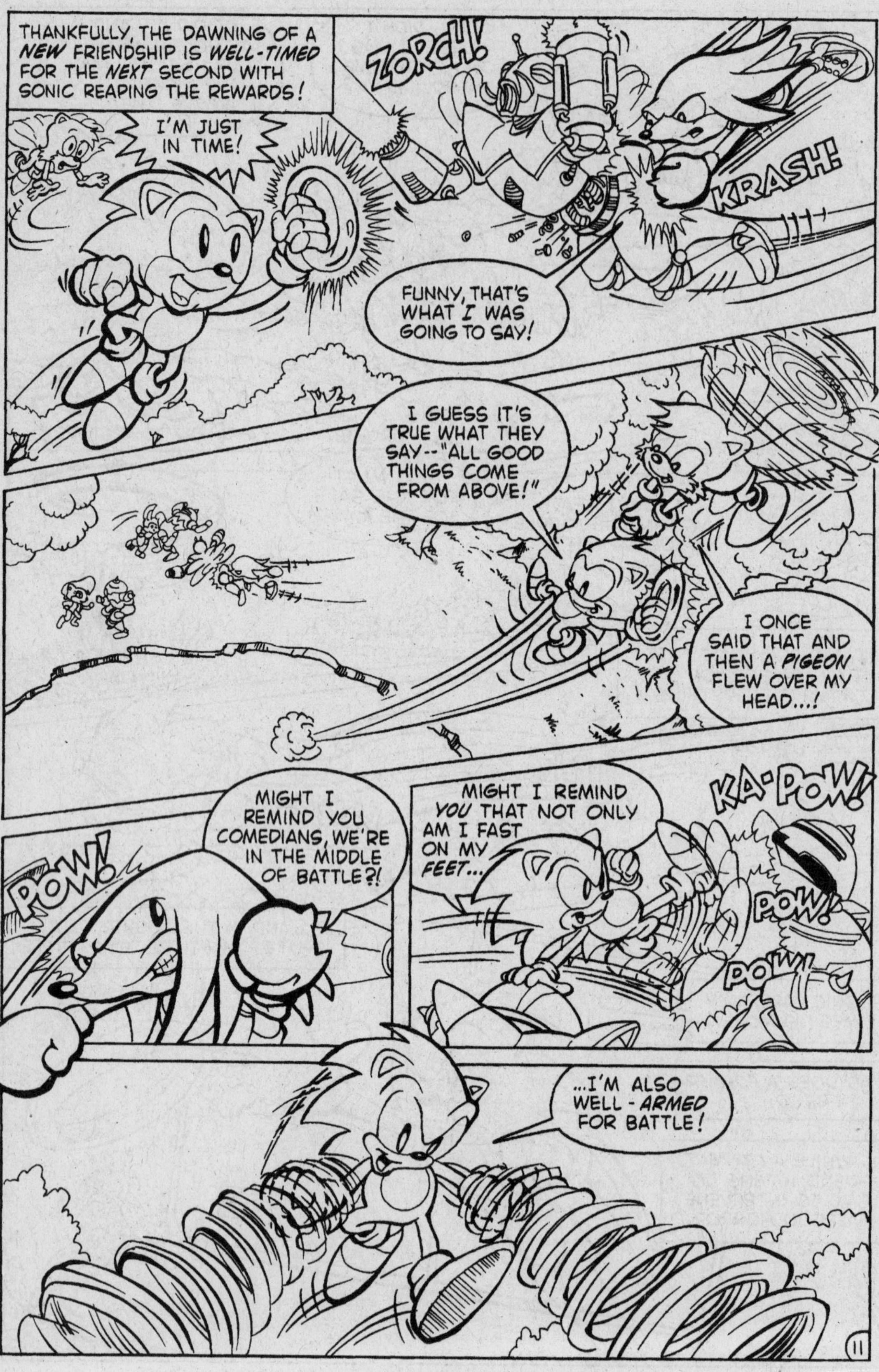
THANKFULLY, THE DAWNING OF A NEW FRIENDSHIP IS WELL-TIMED FOR THE NEXT SECOND WITH SONIC REAPING THE REWARDS!
ZORCH!
I'M JUST IN TIME!
KRASH!
FUNNY, THAT'S WHAT I WAS GOING TO SAY!
I GUESS IT'S TRUE WHAT THEY SAY--"ALL GOOD THINGS COME FROM ABOVE!"
I ONCE SAID THAT AND THEN A PIGEON FLEW OVER MY HEAD...!
POW!
MIGHT I REMIND YOU COMEDIANS, WE'RE IN THE MIDDLE OF BATTLE?!
MIGHT I REMIND YOU THAT NOT ONLY AM I FAST ON MY FEET...
KA-POW!
POW!
POW!
...I'M ALSO WELL-ARMED FOR BATTLE!
11

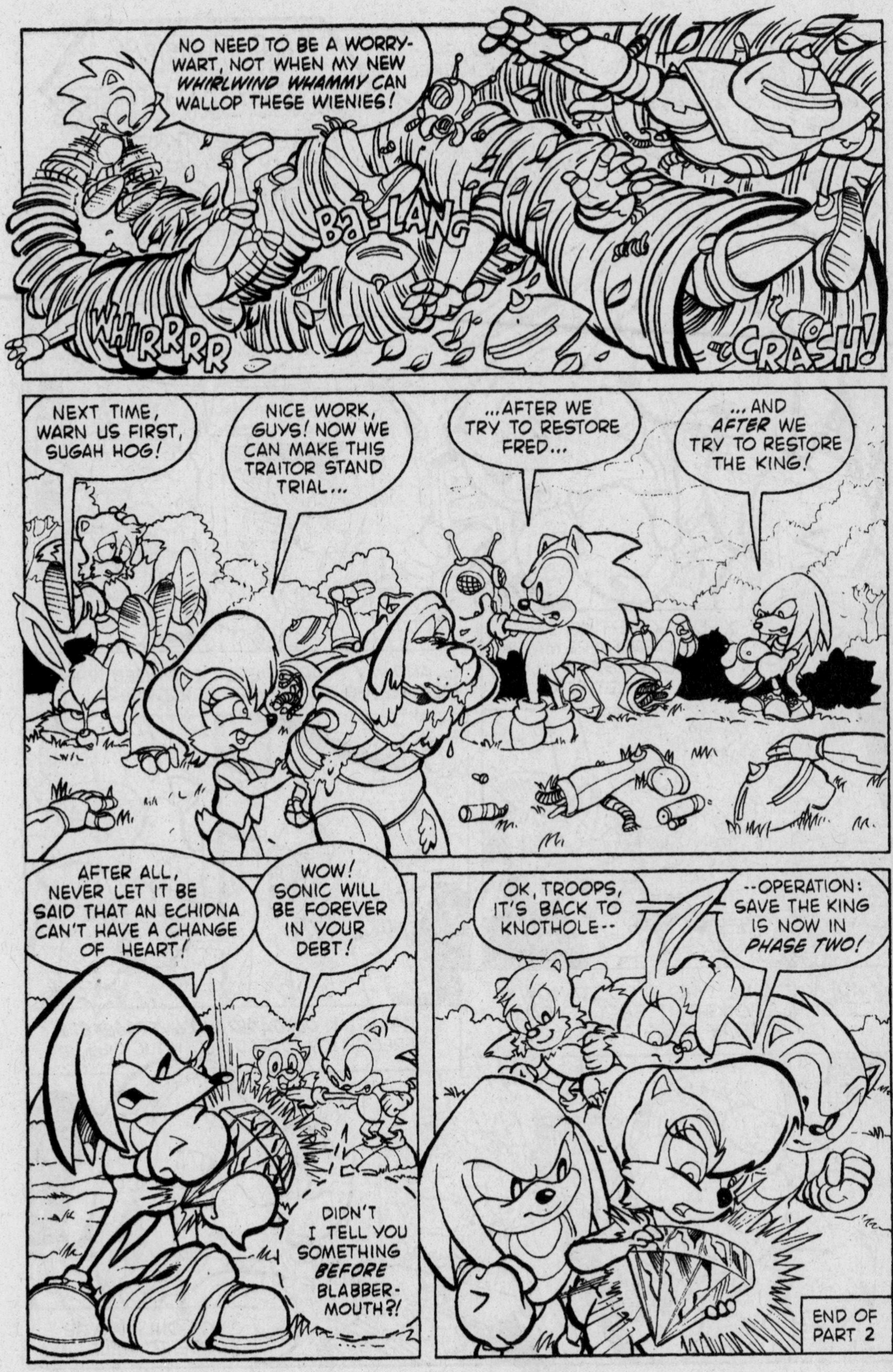
NO NEED TO BE A WORRY-WART, NOT WHEN MY NEW WHIRLWIND WHAMMY CAN WALLOP THESE WIENIES!
BA-LANG
WHIRRRR
CRASH!
NEXT TIME, WARN US FIRST, SUGAH HOG!
NICE WORK, GUYS! NOW WE CAN MAKE THIS TRAITOR STAND TRIAL...
...AFTER WE TRY TO RESTORE FRED...
...AND AFTER WE TRY TO RESTORE THE KING!
AFTER ALL, NEVER LET IT BE SAID THAT AN ECHIDNA CAN'T HAVE A CHANGE OF HEART!
WOW! SONIC WILL BE FOREVER IN YOUR DEBT!
DIDN'T I TELL YOU SOMETHING BEFORE BLABBER-MOUTH?!
OK, TROOPS, IT'S BACK TO KNOTHOLE--
--OPERATION: SAVE THE KING IS NOW IN PHASE TWO!
END OF PART 2

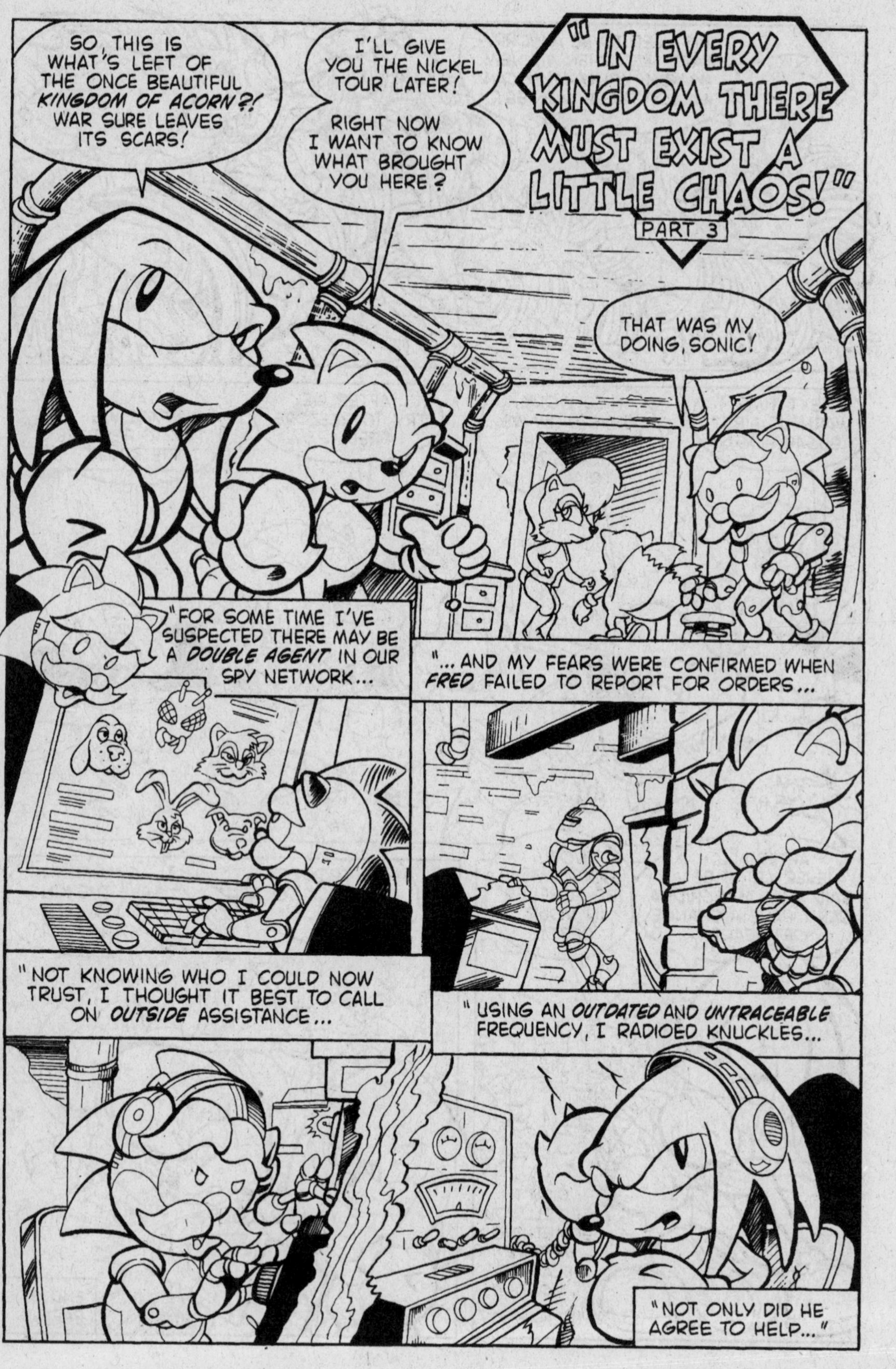

SO, THIS IS WHAT'S LEFT OF THE ONCE BEAUTIFUL *KINGDOM OF ACORN*?! WAR SURE LEAVES ITS SCARS!
I'LL GIVE YOU THE NICKEL TOUR LATER!
RIGHT NOW I WANT TO KNOW WHAT BROUGHT YOU HERE?
"IN EVERY KINGDOM THERE MUST EXIST A LITTLE CHAOS!"
PART 3
THAT WAS MY DOING, SONIC!
"FOR SOME TIME I'VE SUSPECTED THERE MAY BE A *DOUBLE AGENT* IN OUR SPY NETWORK...
"...AND MY FEARS WERE CONFIRMED WHEN *FRED* FAILED TO REPORT FOR ORDERS...
"NOT KNOWING WHO I COULD NOW TRUST, I THOUGHT IT BEST TO CALL ON *OUTSIDE* ASSISTANCE...
"USING AN *OUTDATED* AND *UNTRACEABLE* FREQUENCY, I RADIOED KNUCKLES...
"NOT ONLY DID HE AGREE TO HELP..."

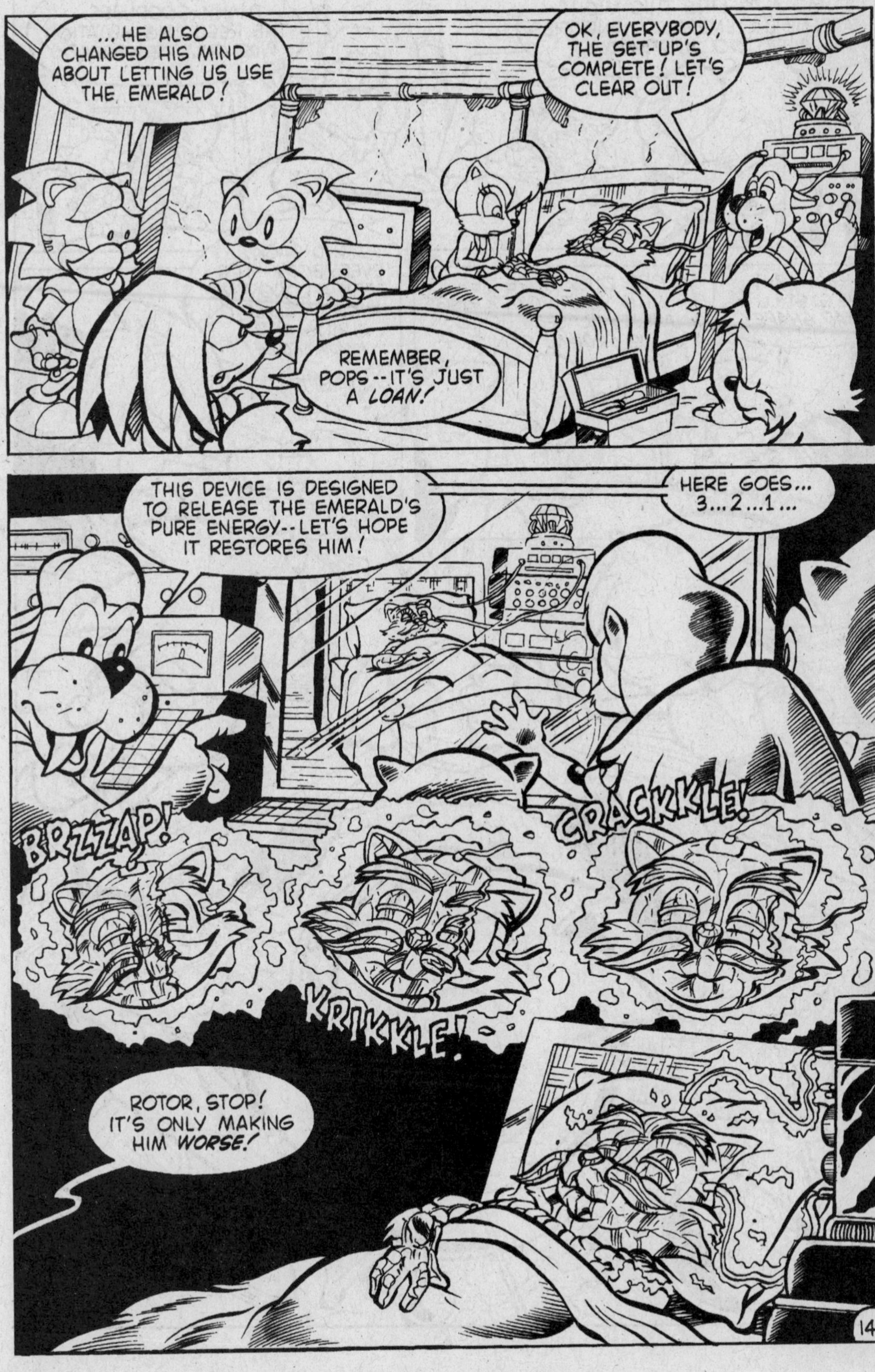
...HE ALSO CHANGED HIS MIND ABOUT LETTING US USE THE EMERALD!
OK, EVERYBODY, THE SET-UP'S COMPLETE! LET'S CLEAR OUT!
REMEMBER, POPS--IT'S JUST A *LOAN!*
THIS DEVICE IS DESIGNED TO RELEASE THE EMERALD'S PURE ENERGY--LET'S HOPE IT RESTORES HIM!
HERE GOES... 3...2...1...
BRZZZAP!
CRACKKLE!
KRIKKLE!
ROTOR, STOP! IT'S ONLY MAKING HIM *WORSE!*
14

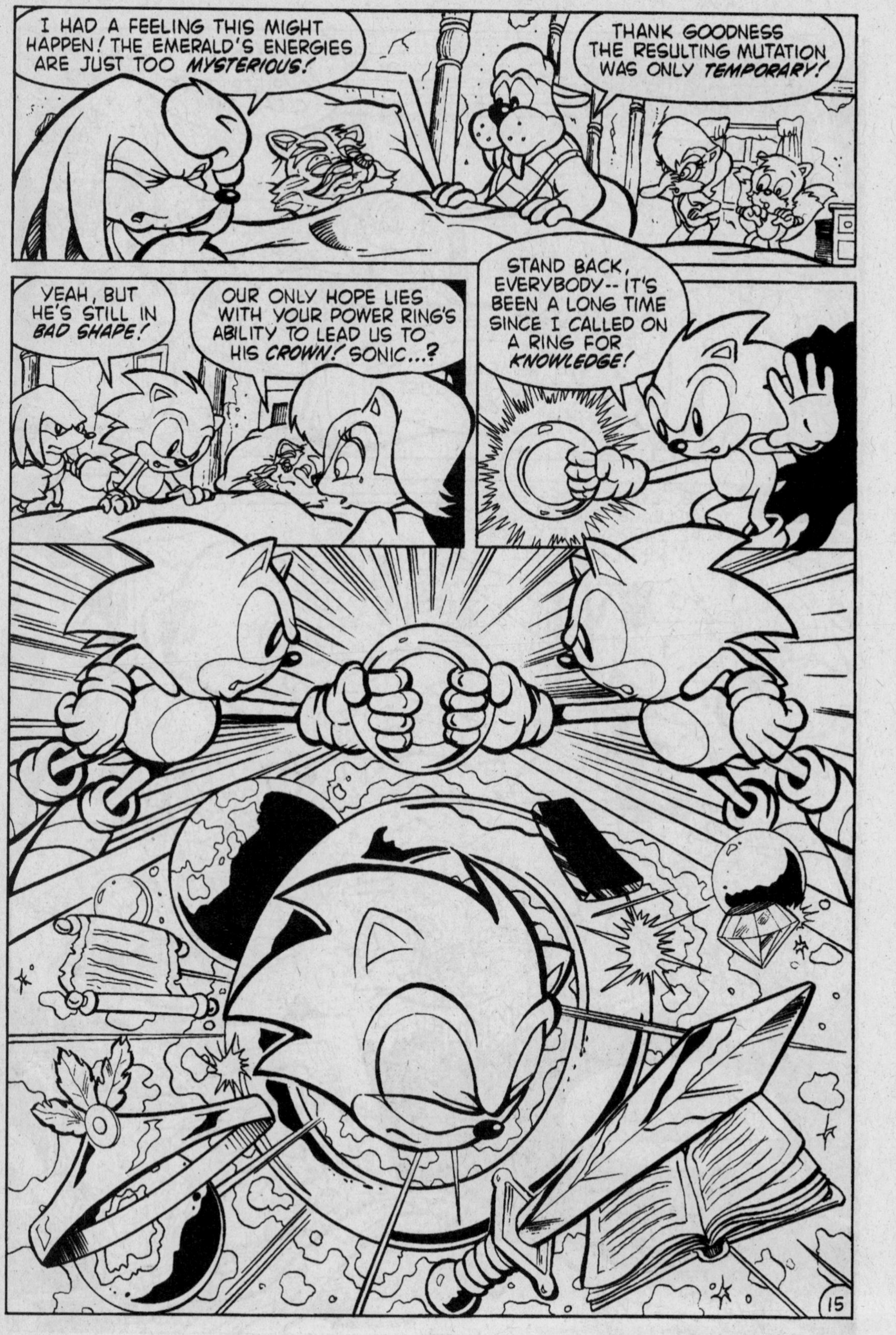

I HAD A FEELING THIS MIGHT HAPPEN! THE EMERALD'S ENERGIES ARE JUST TOO MYSTERIOUS!
THANK GOODNESS THE RESULTING MUTATION WAS ONLY TEMPORARY!
YEAH, BUT HE'S STILL IN BAD SHAPE!
OUR ONLY HOPE LIES WITH YOUR POWER RING'S ABILITY TO LEAD US TO HIS CROWN! SONIC...?
STAND BACK, EVERYBODY-- IT'S BEEN A LONG TIME SINCE I CALLED ON A RING FOR KNOWLEDGE!
15

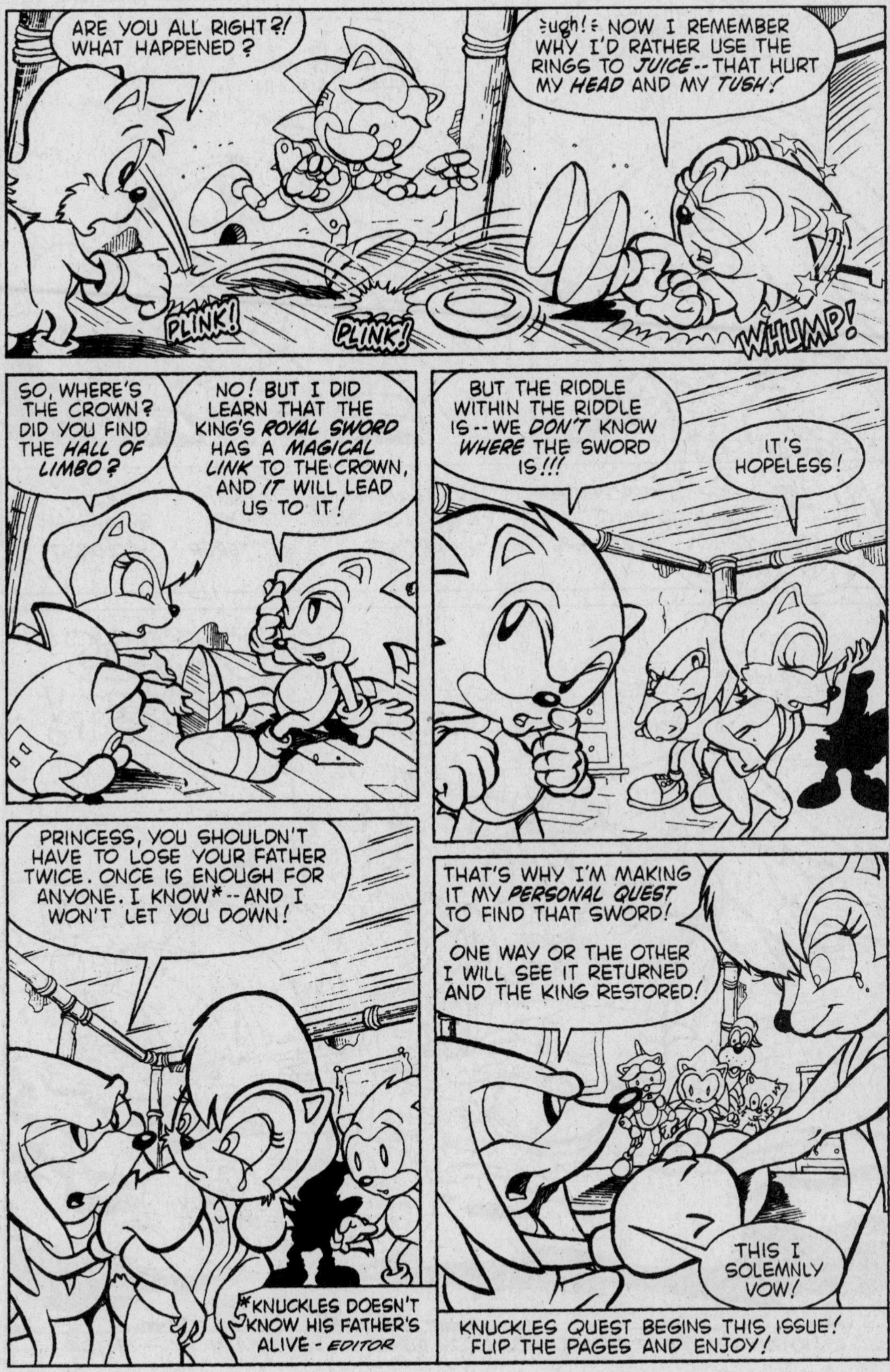
ARE YOU ALL RIGHT?! WHAT HAPPENED?
UGH! NOW I REMEMBER WHY I'D RATHER USE THE RINGS TO JUICE--THAT HURT MY HEAD AND MY TUSH!
PLINK!
PLINK!
WHUMP!
SO, WHERE'S THE CROWN? DID YOU FIND THE HALL OF LIMBO?
NO! BUT I DID LEARN THAT THE KING'S ROYAL SWORD HAS A MAGICAL LINK TO THE CROWN, AND IT WILL LEAD US TO IT!
BUT THE RIDDLE WITHIN THE RIDDLE IS--WE DON'T KNOW WHERE THE SWORD IS!!!
IT'S HOPELESS!
PRINCESS, YOU SHOULDN'T HAVE TO LOSE YOUR FATHER TWICE. ONCE IS ENOUGH FOR ANYONE. I KNOW*--AND I WON'T LET YOU DOWN!
*KNUCKLES DOESN'T KNOW HIS FATHER'S ALIVE - EDITOR
THAT'S WHY I'M MAKING IT MY PERSONAL QUEST TO FIND THAT SWORD!
ONE WAY OR THE OTHER I WILL SEE IT RETURNED AND THE KING RESTORED!
THIS I SOLEMNLY VOW!
KNUCKLES QUEST BEGINS THIS ISSUE! FLIP THE PAGES AND ENJOY!

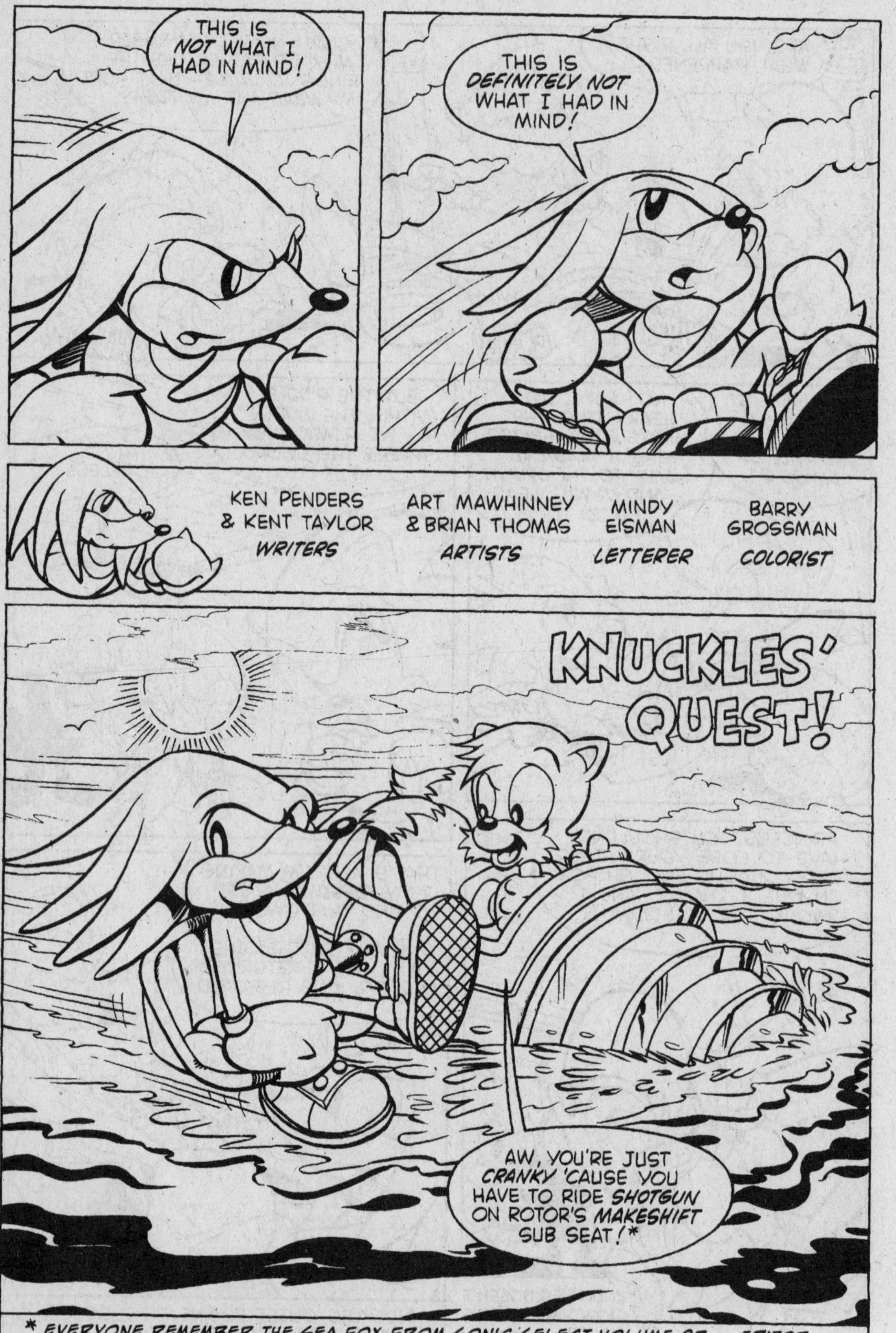
THIS IS NOT WHAT I HAD IN MIND!
THIS IS DEFINITELY NOT WHAT I HAD IN MIND!
KEN PENDERS & KENT TAYLOR WRITERS
ART MAWHINNEY & BRIAN THOMAS ARTISTS
MINDY EISMAN LETTERER
BARRY GROSSMAN COLORIST
KNUCKLES' QUEST!
AW, YOU'RE JUST CRANKY 'CAUSE YOU HAVE TO RIDE SHOTGUN ON ROTOR'S MAKESHIFT SUB SEAT!*
* EVERYONE REMEMBER THE SEA FOX FROM SONIC SELECT VOLUME 8? -- EDITOR

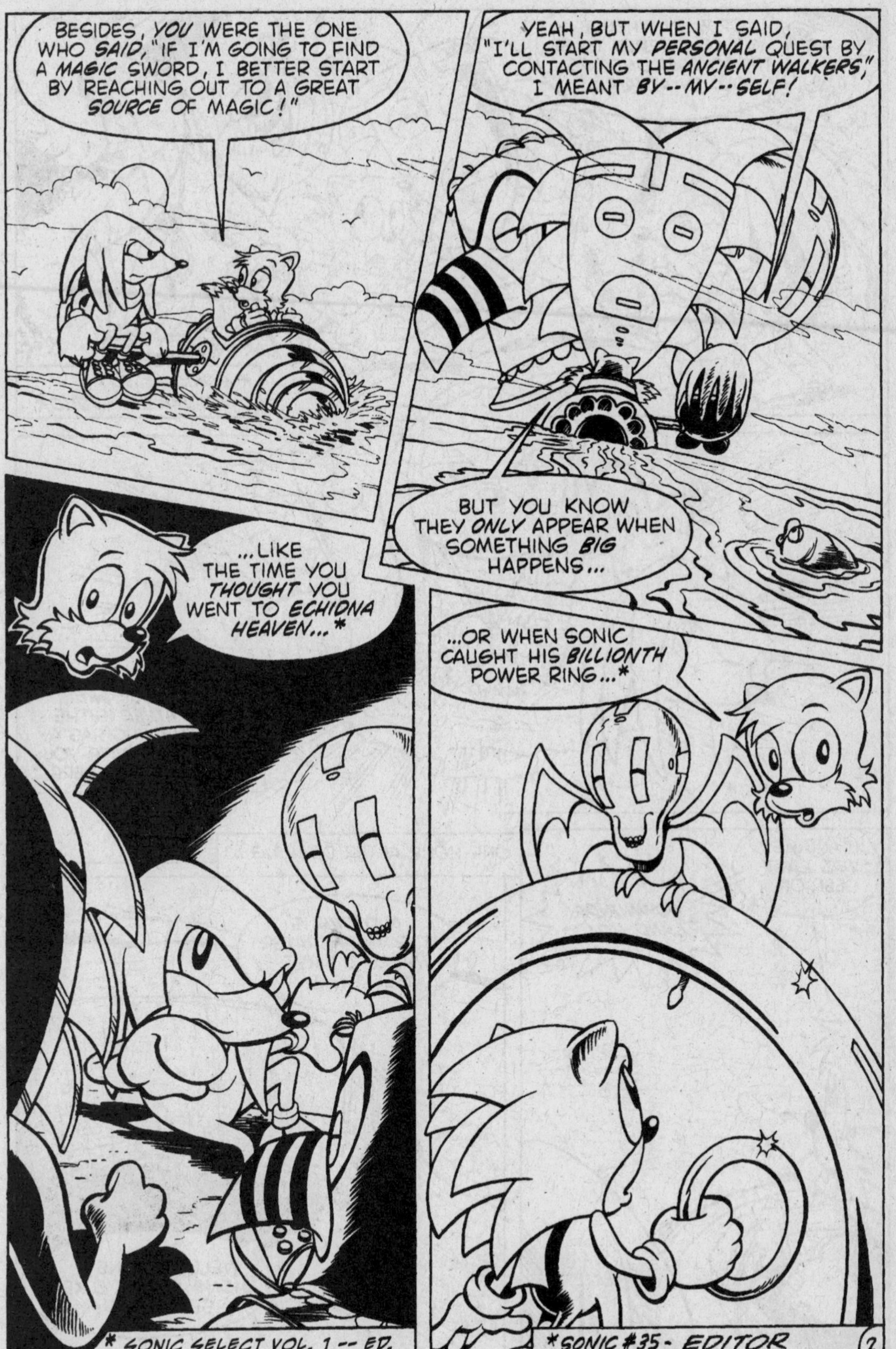
BESIDES, YOU WERE THE ONE WHO SAID, "IF I'M GOING TO FIND A MAGIC SWORD, I BETTER START BY REACHING OUT TO A GREAT SOURCE OF MAGIC!"
YEAH, BUT WHEN I SAID, "I'LL START MY PERSONAL QUEST BY CONTACTING THE ANCIENT WALKERS," I MEANT BY--MY--SELF!
BUT YOU KNOW THEY ONLY APPEAR WHEN SOMETHING BIG HAPPENS...
...LIKE THE TIME YOU THOUGHT YOU WENT TO ECHIDNA HEAVEN...*
...OR WHEN SONIC CAUGHT HIS BILLIONTH POWER RING...*
* SONIC SELECT VOL. 1 -- ED.
*SONIC #35 - EDITOR
2

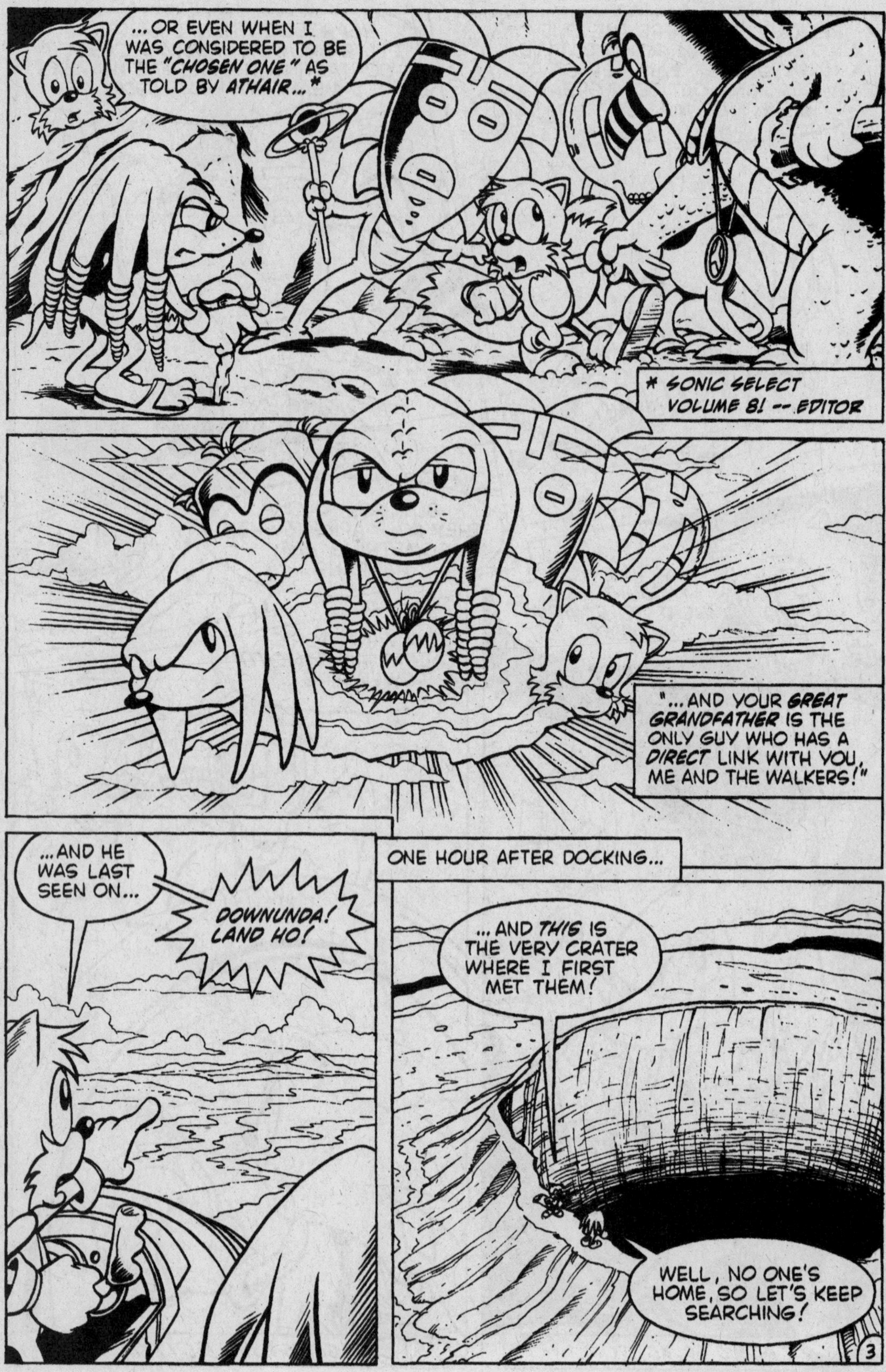
...OR EVEN WHEN I WAS CONSIDERED TO BE THE "CHOSEN ONE" AS TOLD BY ATHAIR...*
* SONIC SELECT VOLUME 8! -- EDITOR
"...AND YOUR GREAT GRANDFATHER IS THE ONLY GUY WHO HAS A DIRECT LINK WITH YOU, ME AND THE WALKERS!"
...AND HE WAS LAST SEEN ON...
DOWNUNDA! LAND HO!
ONE HOUR AFTER DOCKING...
...AND THIS IS THE VERY CRATER WHERE I FIRST MET THEM!
WELL, NO ONE'S HOME, SO LET'S KEEP SEARCHING!
3

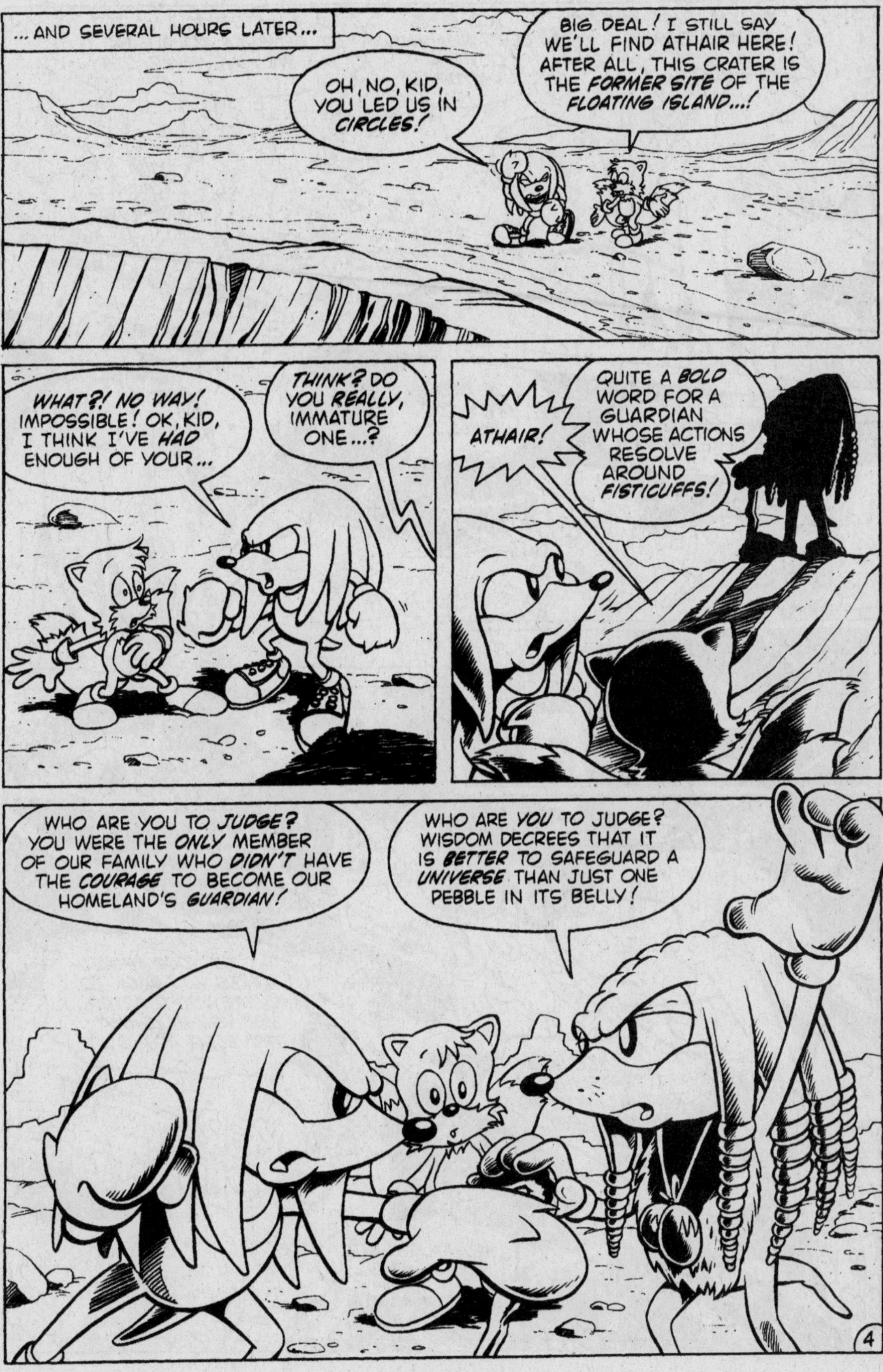

...AND SEVERAL HOURS LATER...
OH, NO, KID, YOU LED US IN CIRCLES!
BIG DEAL! I STILL SAY WE'LL FIND ATHAIR HERE! AFTER ALL, THIS CRATER IS THE FORMER SITE OF THE FLOATING ISLAND...!
WHAT?! NO WAY! IMPOSSIBLE! OK, KID, I THINK I'VE HAD ENOUGH OF YOUR...
THINK? DO YOU REALLY, IMMATURE ONE...?
ATHAIR!
QUITE A BOLD WORD FOR A GUARDIAN WHOSE ACTIONS RESOLVE AROUND FISTICUFFS!
WHO ARE YOU TO JUDGE? YOU WERE THE ONLY MEMBER OF OUR FAMILY WHO DIDN'T HAVE THE COURAGE TO BECOME OUR HOMELAND'S GUARDIAN!
WHO ARE YOU TO JUDGE? WISDOM DECREES THAT IT IS BETTER TO SAFEGUARD A UNIVERSE THAN JUST ONE PEBBLE IN ITS BELLY!
4

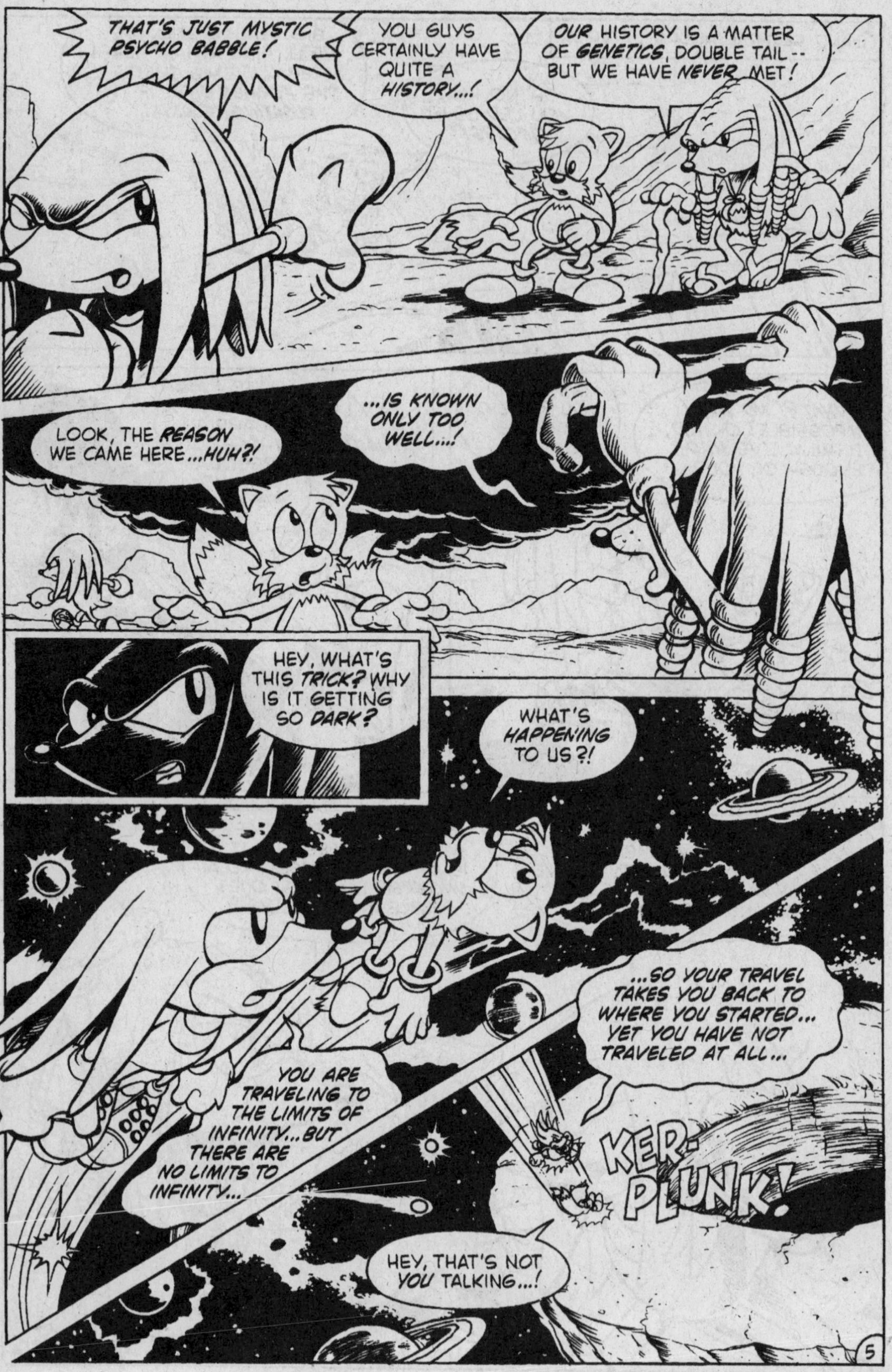
THAT'S JUST MYSTIC PSYCHO BABBLE!
YOU GUYS CERTAINLY HAVE QUITE A HISTORY...!
OUR HISTORY IS A MATTER OF GENETICS, DOUBLE TAIL -- BUT WE HAVE NEVER MET!
LOOK, THE REASON WE CAME HERE...HUH?!
...IS KNOWN ONLY TOO WELL...!
HEY, WHAT'S THIS TRICK? WHY IS IT GETTING SO DARK?
WHAT'S HAPPENING TO US?!
YOU ARE TRAVELING TO THE LIMITS OF INFINITY...BUT THERE ARE NO LIMITS TO INFINITY...
...SO YOUR TRAVEL TAKES YOU BACK TO WHERE YOU STARTED... YET YOU HAVE NOT TRAVELED AT ALL...
KER-PLUNK!
HEY, THAT'S NOT YOU TALKING...!
5

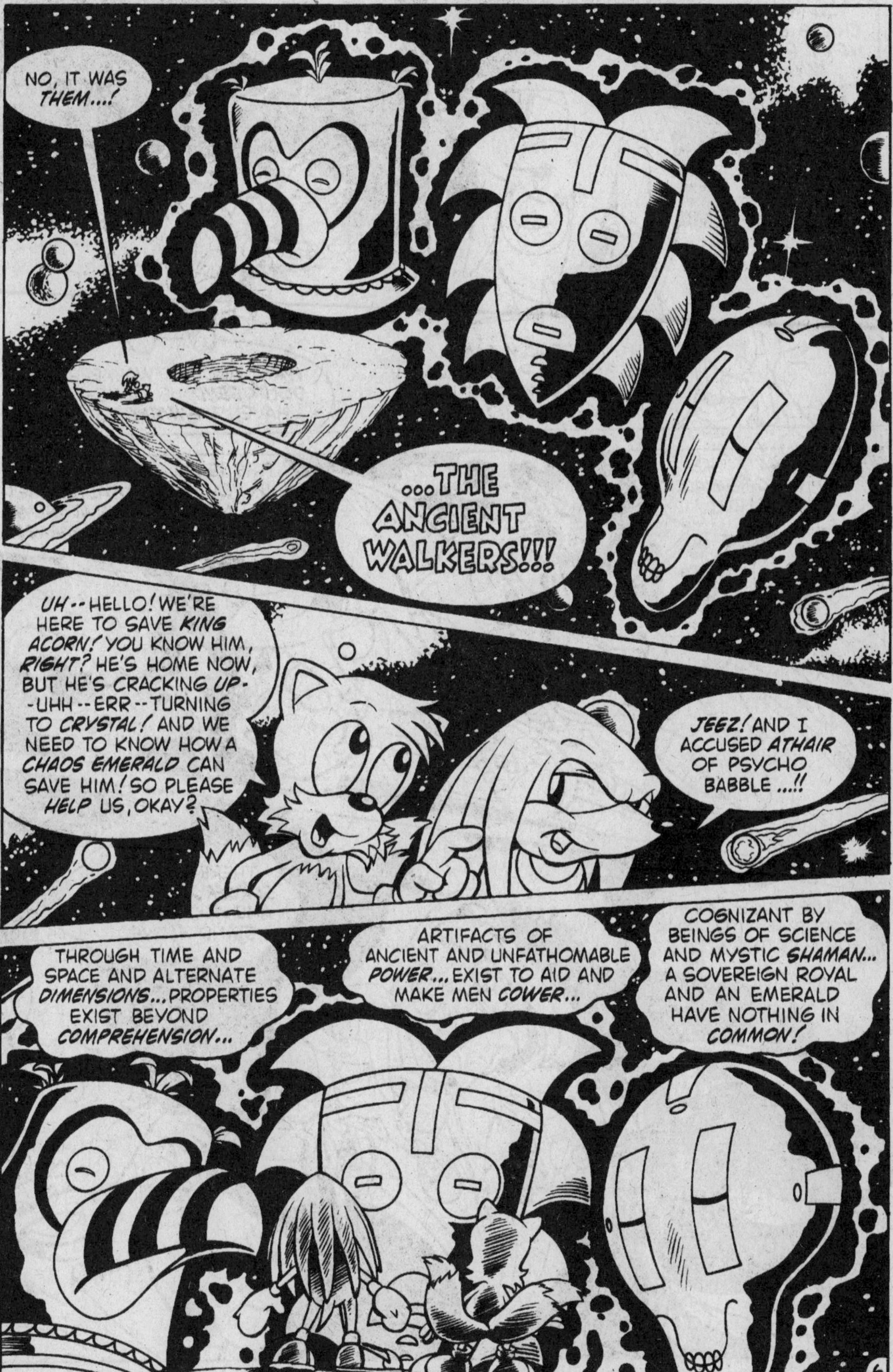
NO, IT WAS THEM...!
...THE ANCIENT WALKERS!!!
UH--HELLO! WE'RE HERE TO SAVE KING ACORN! YOU KNOW HIM, RIGHT? HE'S HOME NOW, BUT HE'S CRACKING UP--UHH--ERR--TURNING TO CRYSTAL! AND WE NEED TO KNOW HOW A CHAOS EMERALD CAN SAVE HIM! SO PLEASE HELP US, OKAY?
JEEZ! AND I ACCUSED ATHAIR OF PSYCHO BABBLE...!!
THROUGH TIME AND SPACE AND ALTERNATE DIMENSIONS... PROPERTIES EXIST BEYOND COMPREHENSION...
ARTIFACTS OF ANCIENT AND UNFATHOMABLE POWER... EXIST TO AID AND MAKE MEN COWER...
COGNIZANT BY BEINGS OF SCIENCE AND MYSTIC SHAMAN... A SOVEREIGN ROYAL AND AN EMERALD HAVE NOTHING IN COMMON!
6

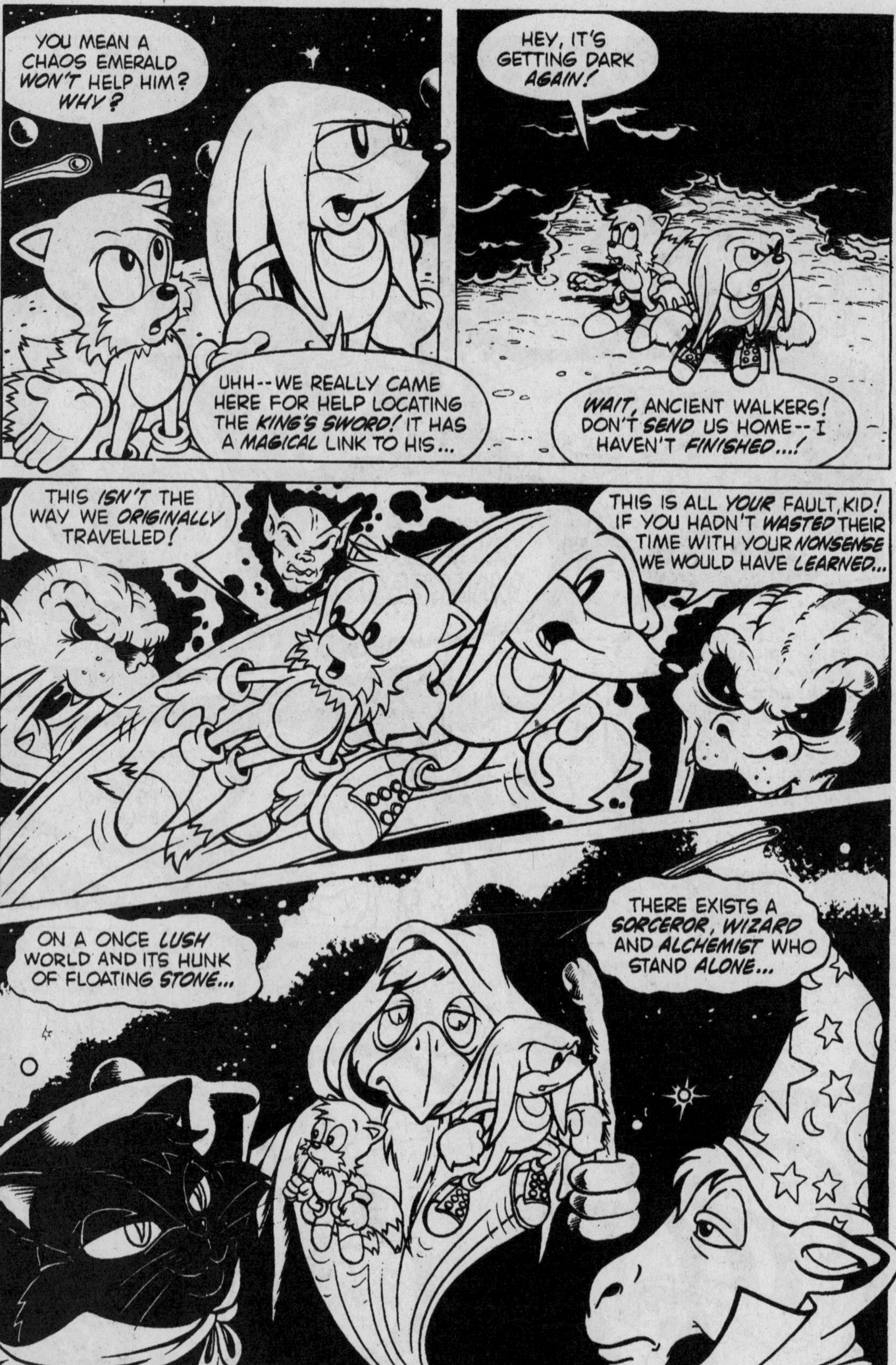
YOU MEAN A CHAOS EMERALD WON'T HELP HIM? WHY?
UHH--WE REALLY CAME HERE FOR HELP LOCATING THE KING'S SWORD! IT HAS A MAGICAL LINK TO HIS...
HEY, IT'S GETTING DARK AGAIN!
WAIT, ANCIENT WALKERS! DON'T SEND US HOME--I HAVEN'T FINISHED...!
THIS ISN'T THE WAY WE ORIGINALLY TRAVELLED!
THIS IS ALL YOUR FAULT, KID! IF YOU HADN'T WASTED THEIR TIME WITH YOUR NONSENSE WE WOULD HAVE LEARNED...
ON A ONCE LUSH WORLD AND ITS HUNK OF FLOATING STONE...
THERE EXISTS A SORCEROR, WIZARD AND ALCHEMIST WHO STAND ALONE...
7

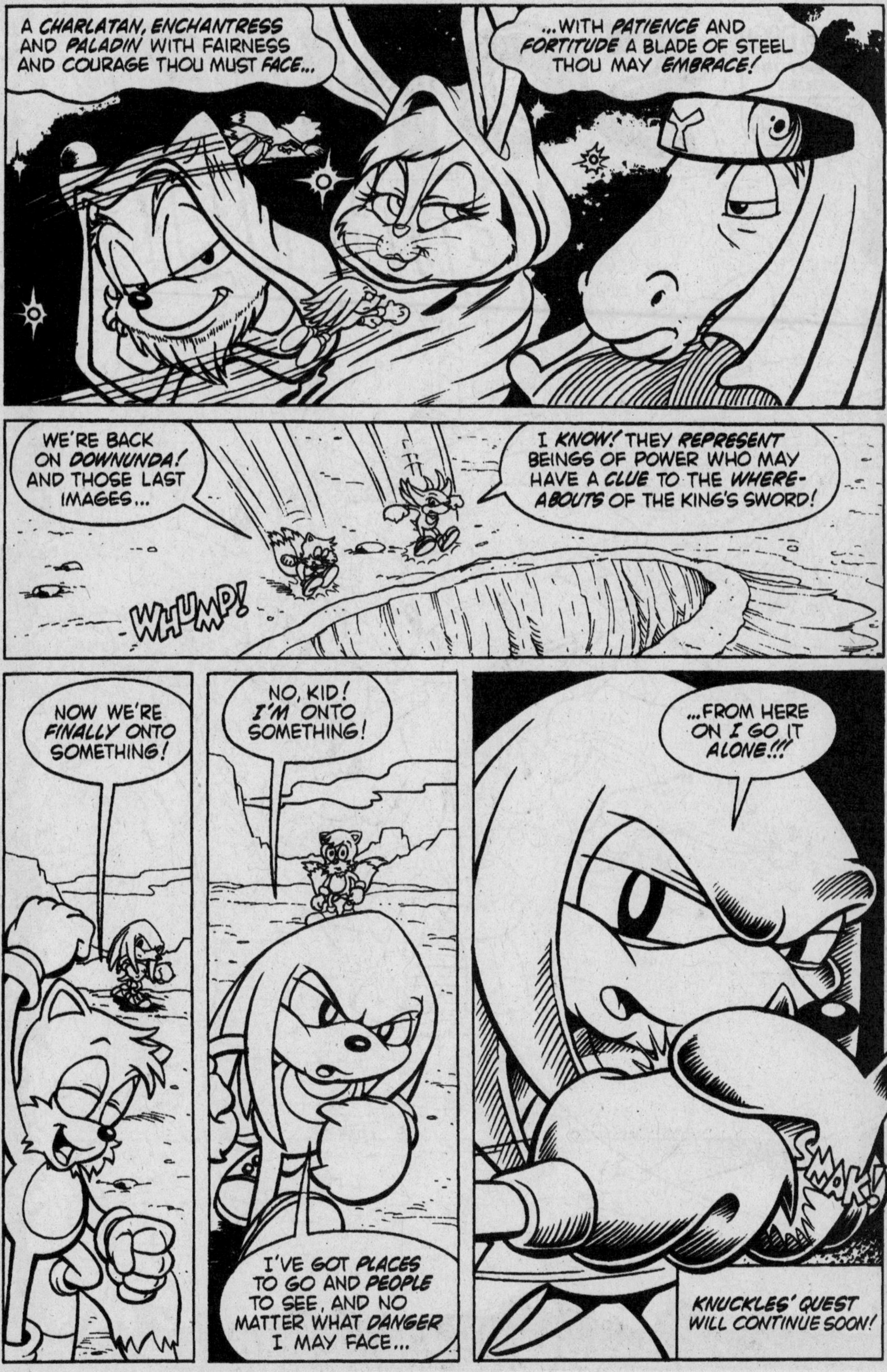
A CHARLATAN, ENCHANTRESS AND PALADIN WITH FAIRNESS AND COURAGE THOU MUST FACE...
...WITH PATIENCE AND FORTITUDE A BLADE OF STEEL THOU MAY EMBRACE!
WE'RE BACK ON DOWNUNDA! AND THOSE LAST IMAGES...
I KNOW! THEY REPRESENT BEINGS OF POWER WHO MAY HAVE A CLUE TO THE WHEREABOUTS OF THE KING'S SWORD!
WHUMP!
NOW WE'RE FINALLY ONTO SOMETHING!
NO, KID! I'M ONTO SOMETHING!
I'VE GOT PLACES TO GO AND PEOPLE TO SEE, AND NO MATTER WHAT DANGER I MAY FACE...
...FROM HERE ON I GO IT ALONE!!!
SMAK!
KNUCKLES' QUEST WILL CONTINUE SOON!

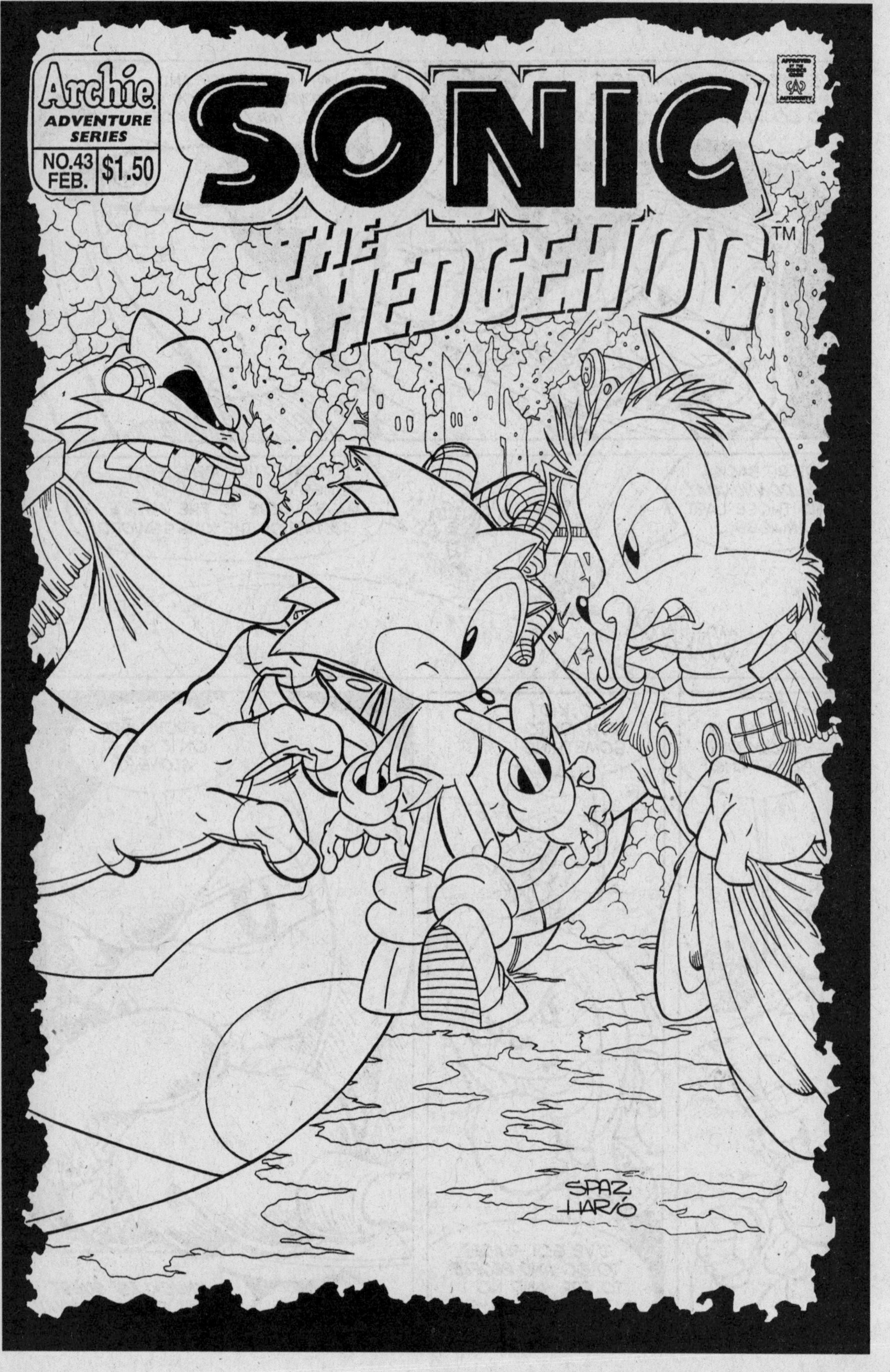
Archie
ADVENTURE SERIES
NO.43 FEB.
$1.50
SONIC THE HEDGEHOG™
SPAZ
HARIO

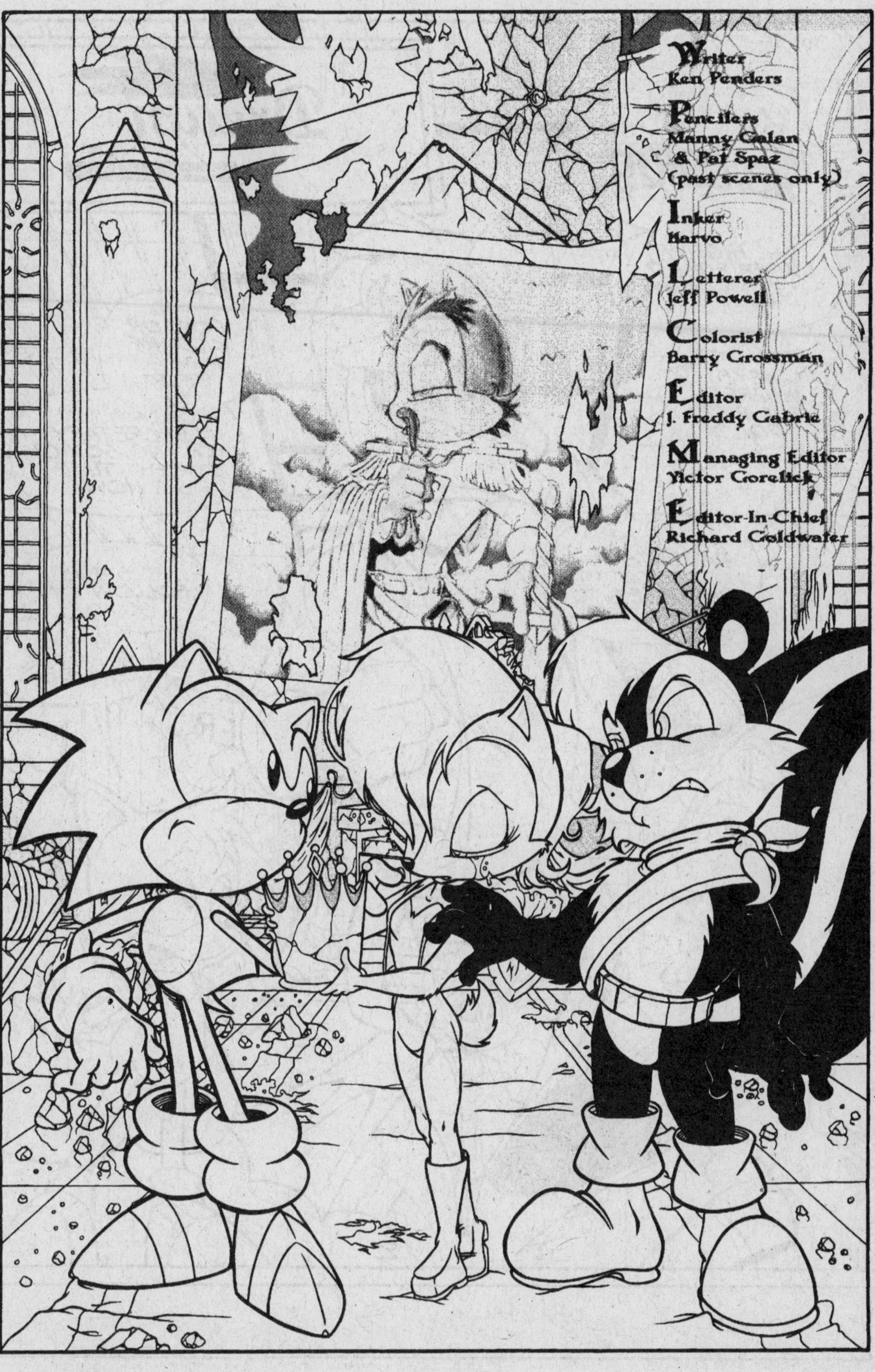
Writer
Ken Penders
Pencilers
Manny Galan
& Pat Spaz
(past scenes only)
Inker
Harvo
Letterer
Jeff Powell
Colorist
Barry Grossman
Editor
J. Freddy Gabrie
Managing Editor
Victor Gorelick
Editor-In-Chief
Richard Goldwater

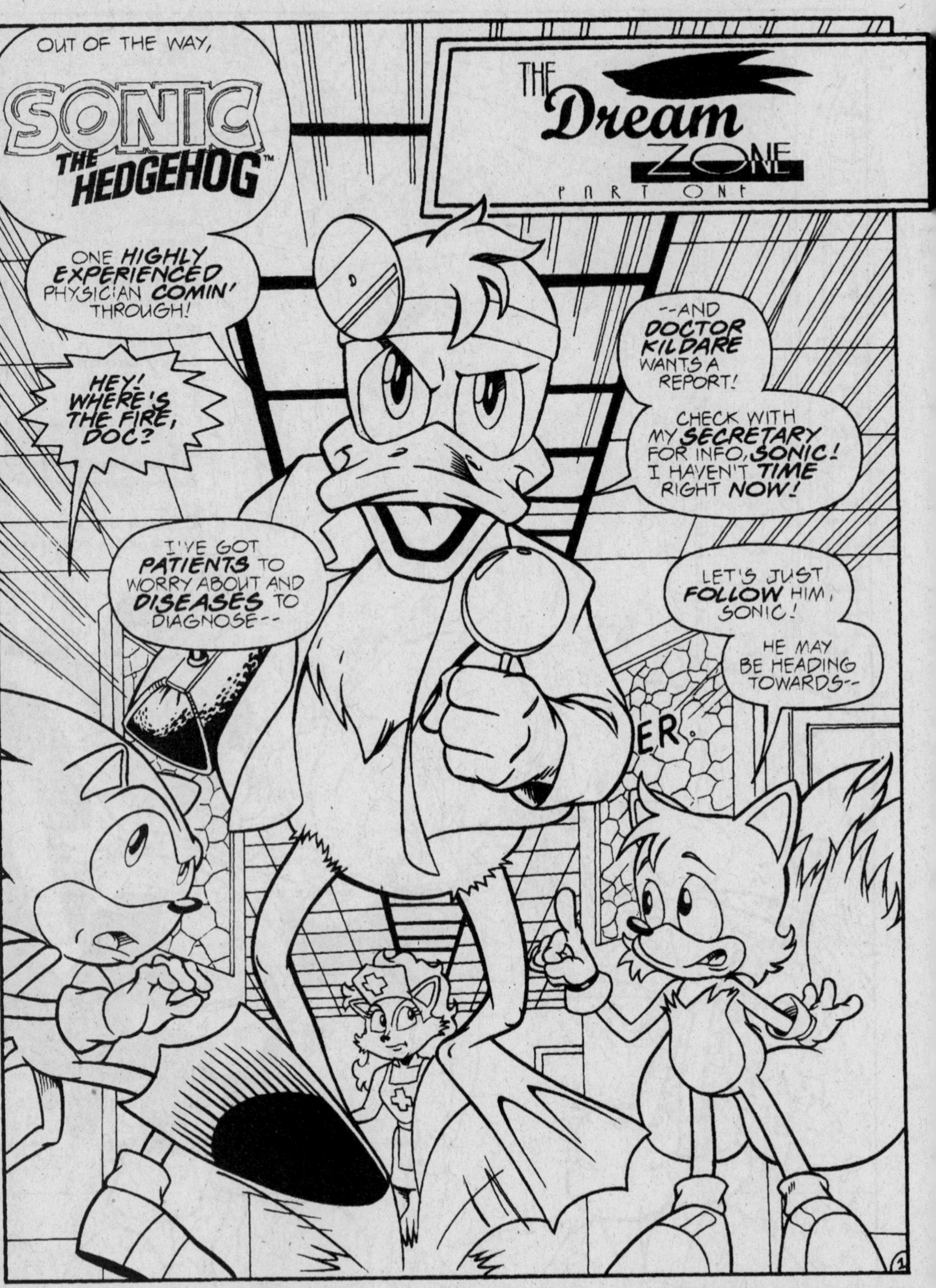
OUT OF THE WAY,
SONIC THE HEDGEHOG™
THE Dream ZONE PART ONE
ONE HIGHLY EXPERIENCED PHYSICIAN COMIN' THROUGH!
HEY! WHERE'S THE FIRE, DOC?
--AND DOCTOR KILDARE WANTS A REPORT!
CHECK WITH MY SECRETARY FOR INFO, SONIC! I HAVEN'T TIME RIGHT NOW!
I'VE GOT PATIENTS TO WORRY ABOUT AND DISEASES TO DIAGNOSE--
LET'S JUST FOLLOW HIM, SONIC!
HE MAY BE HEADING TOWARDS--
ER.
1

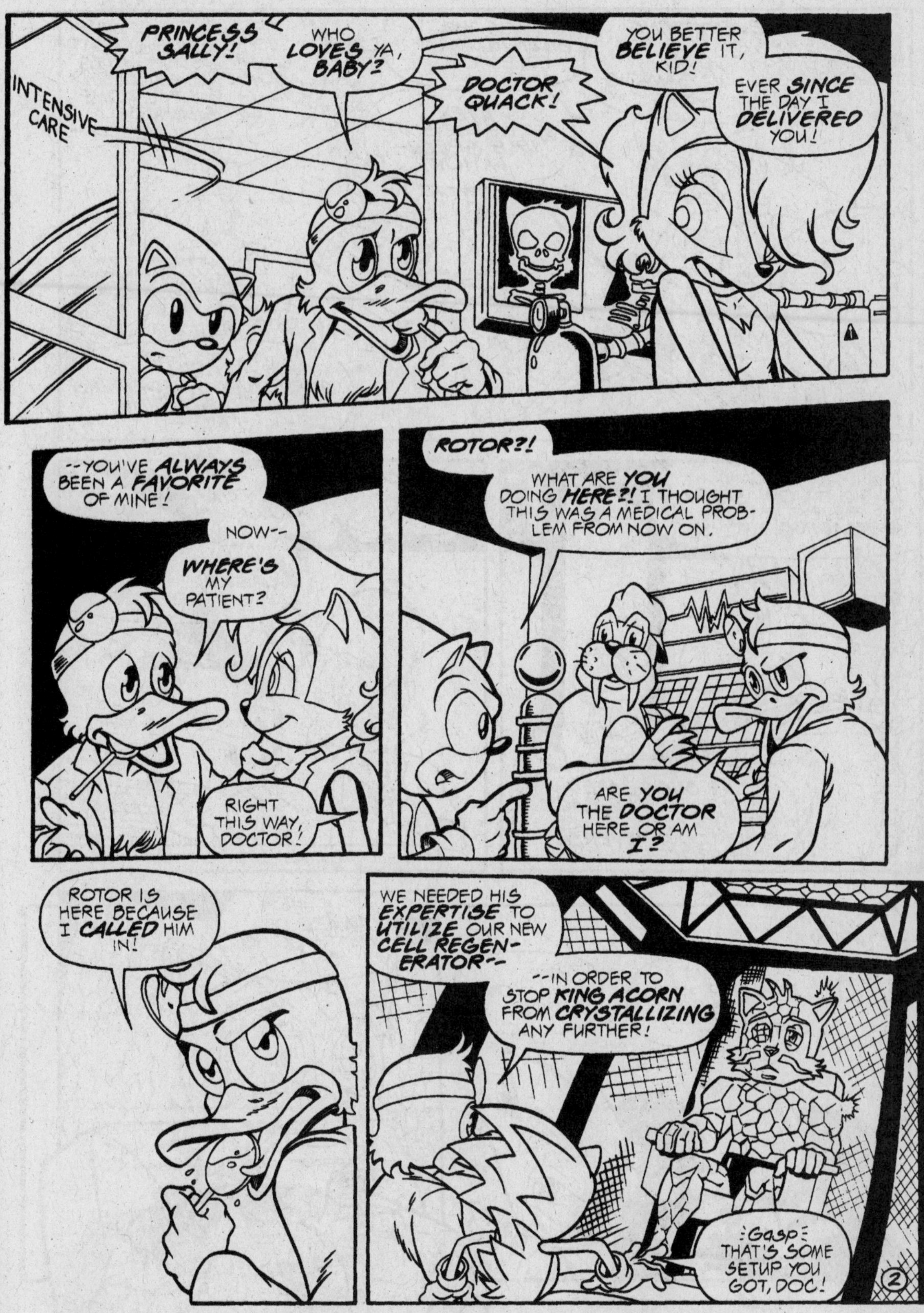
INTENSIVE CARE
PRINCESS SALLY!
WHO LOVES YA, BABY?
DOCTOR QUACK!
YOU BETTER BELIEVE IT, KID!
EVER SINCE THE DAY I DELIVERED YOU!
--YOU'VE ALWAYS BEEN A FAVORITE OF MINE!
NOW--
WHERE'S MY PATIENT?
RIGHT THIS WAY, DOCTOR!
ROTOR?!
WHAT ARE YOU DOING HERE?! I THOUGHT THIS WAS A MEDICAL PROB-LEM FROM NOW ON.
ARE YOU THE DOCTOR HERE OR AM I?
ROTOR IS HERE BECAUSE I CALLED HIM IN!
WE NEEDED HIS EXPERTISE TO UTILIZE OUR NEW CELL REGEN-ERATOR--
--IN ORDER TO STOP KING ACORN FROM CRYSTALLIZING ANY FURTHER!
Gasp
THAT'S SOME SETUP YOU GOT, DOC!
2

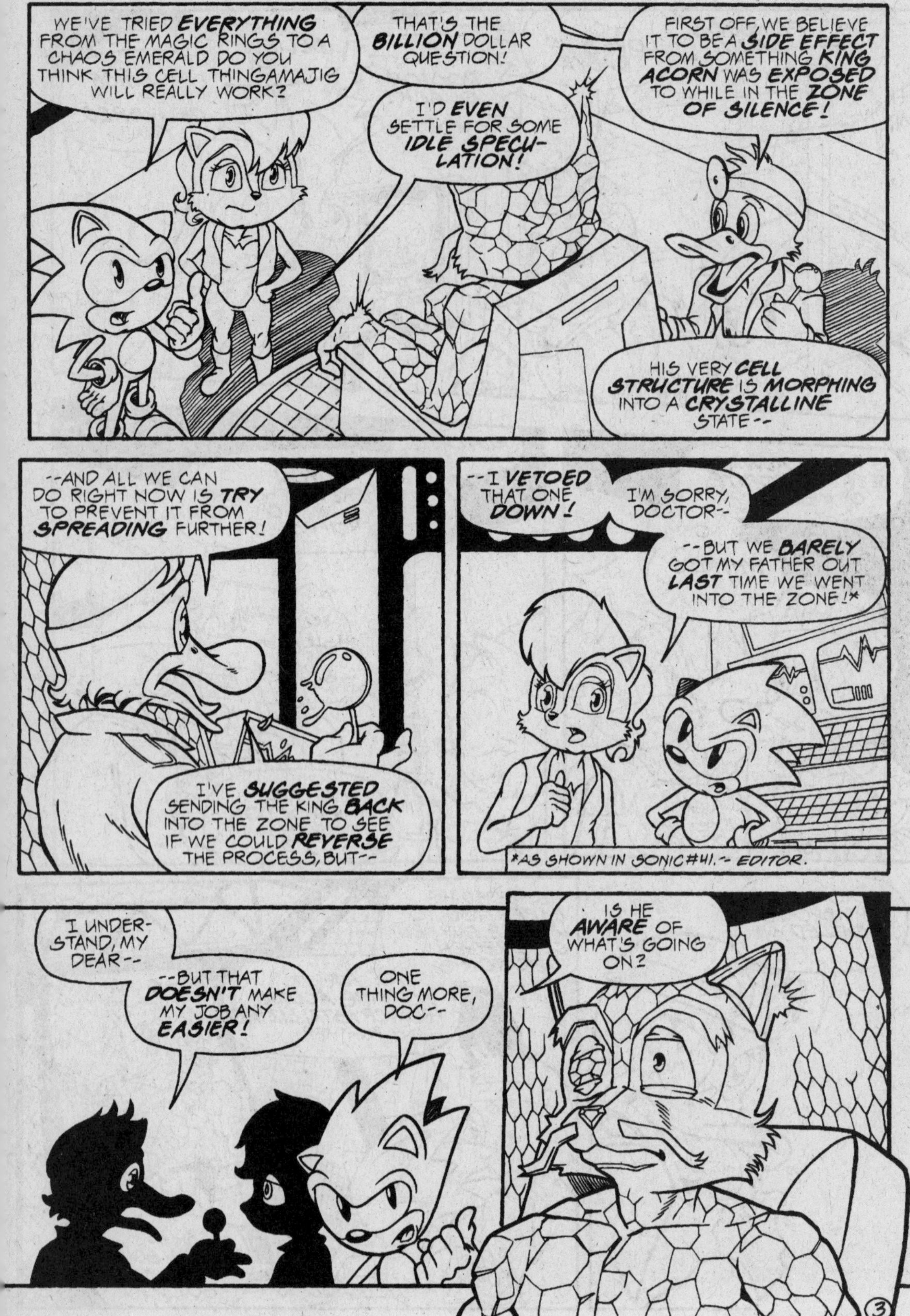
WE'VE TRIED EVERYTHING FROM THE MAGIC RINGS TO A CHAOS EMERALD DO YOU THINK THIS CELL THINGAMAJIG WILL REALLY WORK?
THAT'S THE BILLION DOLLAR QUESTION!
I'D EVEN SETTLE FOR SOME IDLE SPECU-LATION!
FIRST OFF, WE BELIEVE IT TO BE A SIDE EFFECT FROM SOMETHING KING ACORN WAS EXPOSED TO WHILE IN THE ZONE OF SILENCE!
HIS VERY CELL STRUCTURE IS MORPHING INTO A CRYSTALLINE STATE--
--AND ALL WE CAN DO RIGHT NOW IS TRY TO PREVENT IT FROM SPREADING FURTHER!
I'VE SUGGESTED SENDING THE KING BACK INTO THE ZONE TO SEE IF WE COULD REVERSE THE PROCESS, BUT--
--I VETOED THAT ONE DOWN!
I'M SORRY, DOCTOR--
--BUT WE BARELY GOT MY FATHER OUT LAST TIME WE WENT INTO THE ZONE!*
*AS SHOWN IN SONIC #41.- EDITOR.
I UNDER-STAND, MY DEAR--
--BUT THAT DOESN'T MAKE MY JOB ANY EASIER!
ONE THING MORE, DOC--
IS HE AWARE OF WHAT'S GOING ON?
3

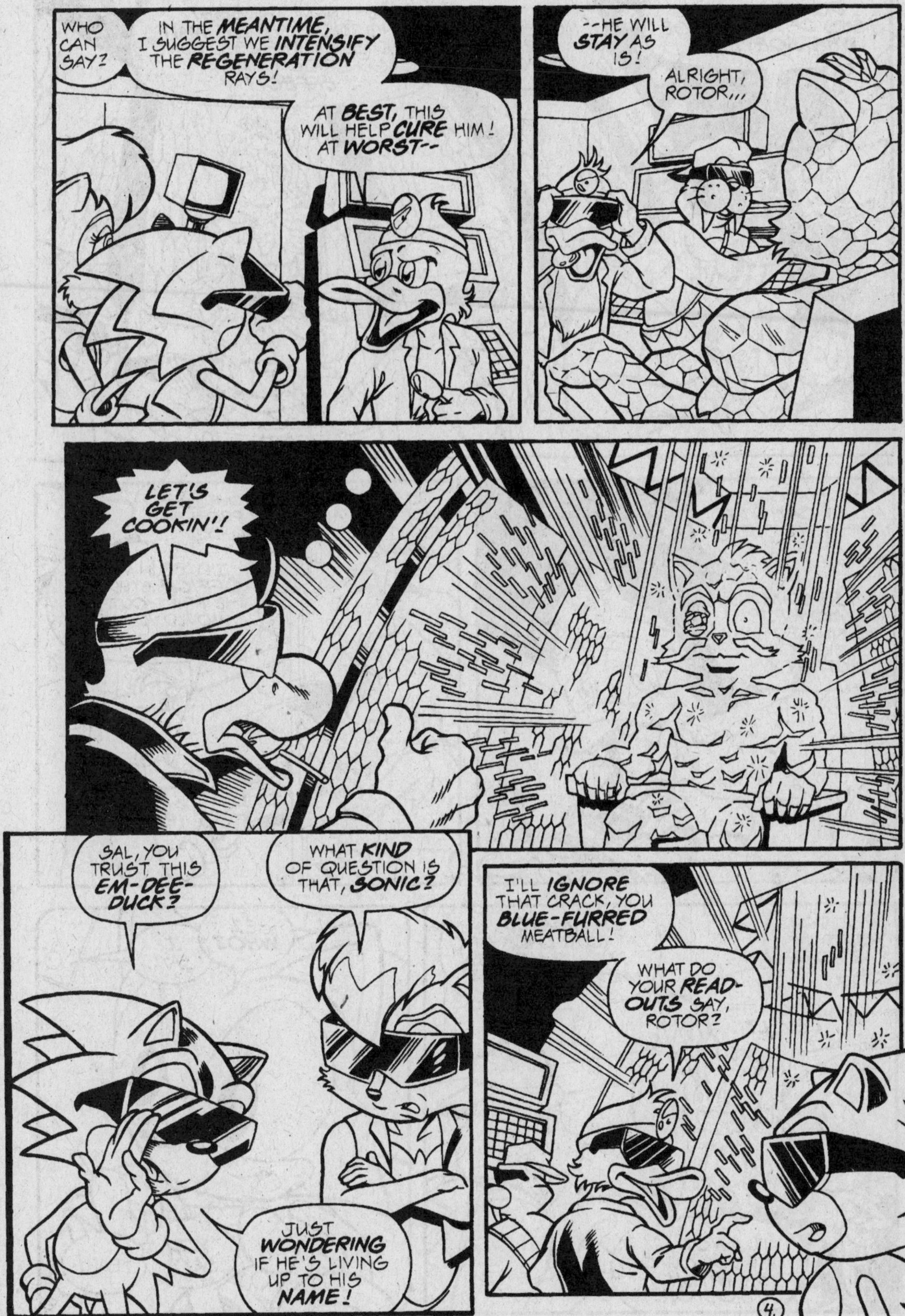
WHO CAN SAY?
IN THE MEANTIME, I SUGGEST WE INTENSIFY THE REGENERATION RAYS!
AT BEST, THIS WILL HELP CURE HIM! AT WORST--
--HE WILL STAY AS IS!
ALRIGHT, ROTOR...
LET'S GET COOKIN'!
SAL, YOU TRUST THIS EM-DEE-DUCK?
WHAT KIND OF QUESTION IS THAT, SONIC?
JUST WONDERING IF HE'S LIVING UP TO HIS NAME!
I'LL IGNORE THAT CRACK, YOU BLUE-FURRED MEATBALL!
WHAT DO YOUR READ-OUTS SAY, ROTOR?
4.

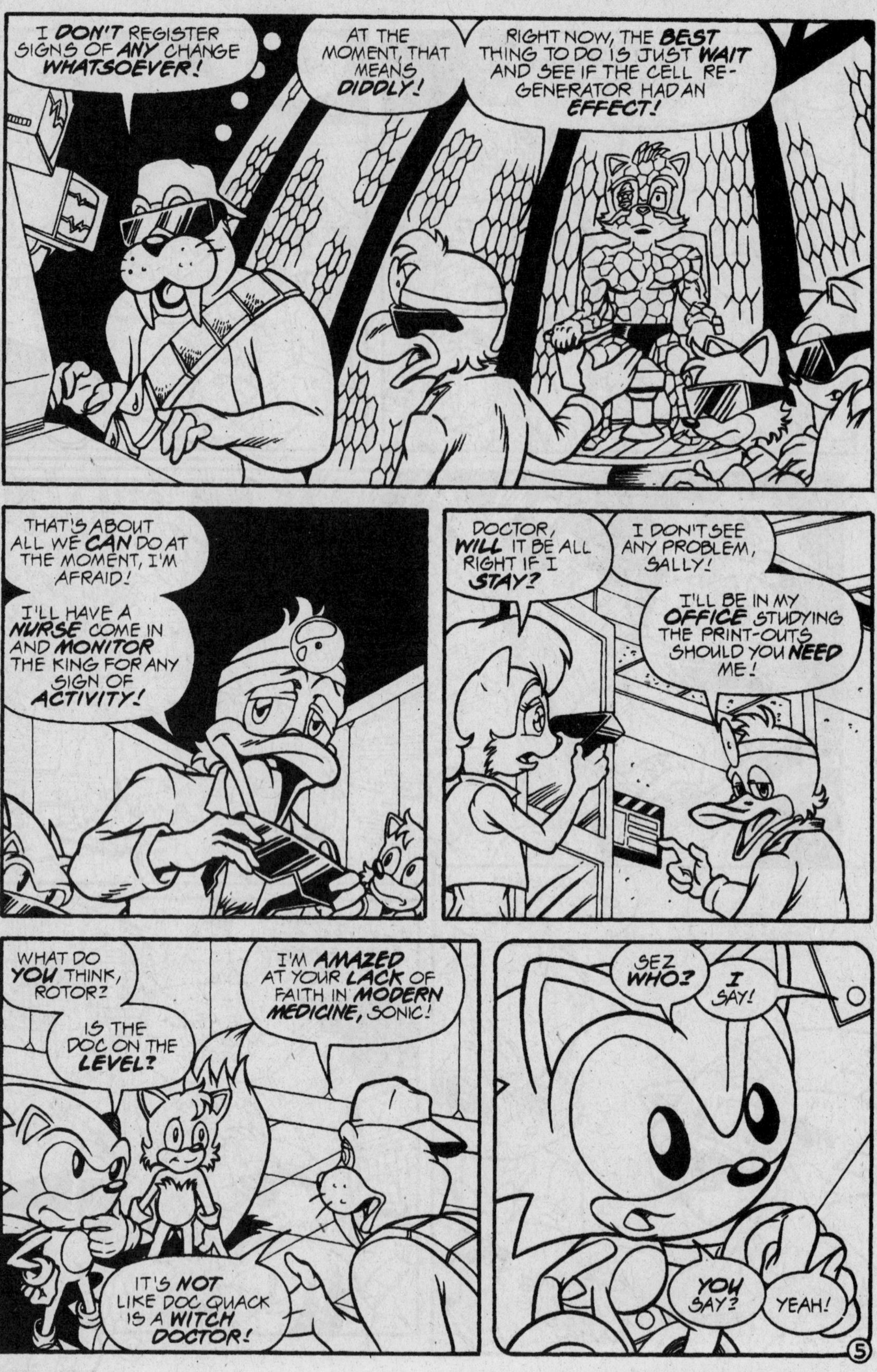
I DON'T REGISTER SIGNS OF ANY CHANGE WHATSOEVER!
AT THE MOMENT, THAT MEANS DIDDLY!
RIGHT NOW, THE BEST THING TO DO IS JUST WAIT AND SEE IF THE CELL RE-GENERATOR HAD AN EFFECT!
THAT'S ABOUT ALL WE CAN DO AT THE MOMENT, I'M AFRAID!
I'LL HAVE A NURSE COME IN AND MONITOR THE KING FOR ANY SIGN OF ACTIVITY!
DOCTOR, WILL IT BE ALL RIGHT IF I STAY?
I DON'T SEE ANY PROBLEM, SALLY!
I'LL BE IN MY OFFICE STUDYING THE PRINT-OUTS SHOULD YOU NEED ME!
WHAT DO YOU THINK, ROTOR?
IS THE DOC ON THE LEVEL?
I'M AMAZED AT YOUR LACK OF FAITH IN MODERN MEDICINE, SONIC!
IT'S NOT LIKE DOC QUACK IS A WITCH DOCTOR!
SEZ WHO?
I SAY!
YOU SAY?
YEAH!
5

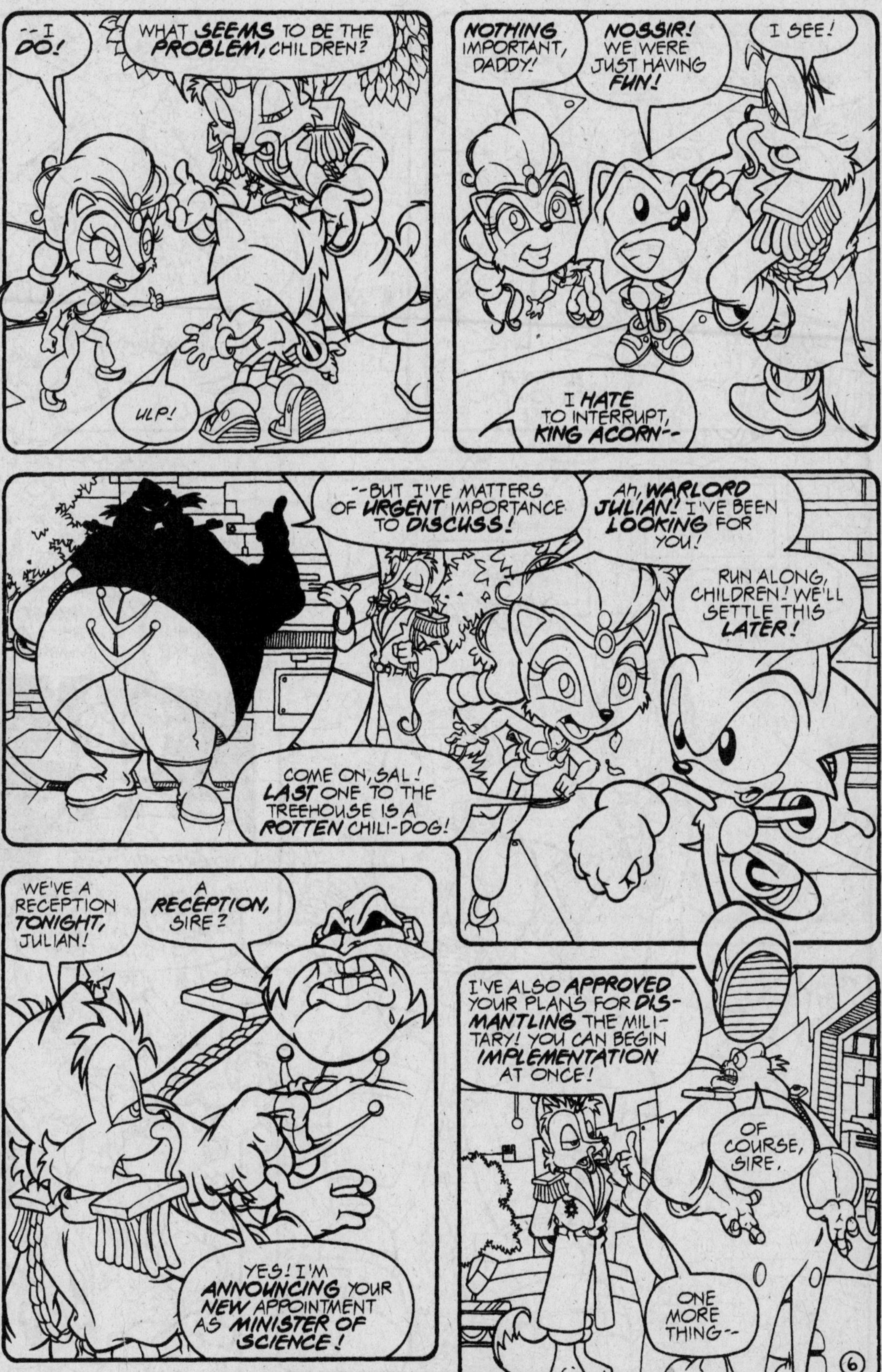
--I DO!
WHAT SEEMS TO BE THE PROBLEM, CHILDREN?
ULP!
NOTHING IMPORTANT, DADDY!
NOSSIR! WE WERE JUST HAVING FUN!
I SEE!
I HATE TO INTERRUPT, KING ACORN--
--BUT I'VE MATTERS OF URGENT IMPORTANCE TO DISCUSS!
Ah, WARLORD JULIAN! I'VE BEEN LOOKING FOR YOU!
RUN ALONG, CHILDREN! WE'LL SETTLE THIS LATER!
COME ON, SAL! LAST ONE TO THE TREEHOUSE IS A ROTTEN CHILI-DOG!
WE'VE A RECEPTION TONIGHT, JULIAN!
A RECEPTION, SIRE?
YES! I'M ANNOUNCING YOUR NEW APPOINTMENT AS MINISTER OF SCIENCE!
I'VE ALSO APPROVED YOUR PLANS FOR DISMANTLING THE MILITARY! YOU CAN BEGIN IMPLEMENTATION AT ONCE!
OF COURSE, SIRE.
ONE MORE THING--
6

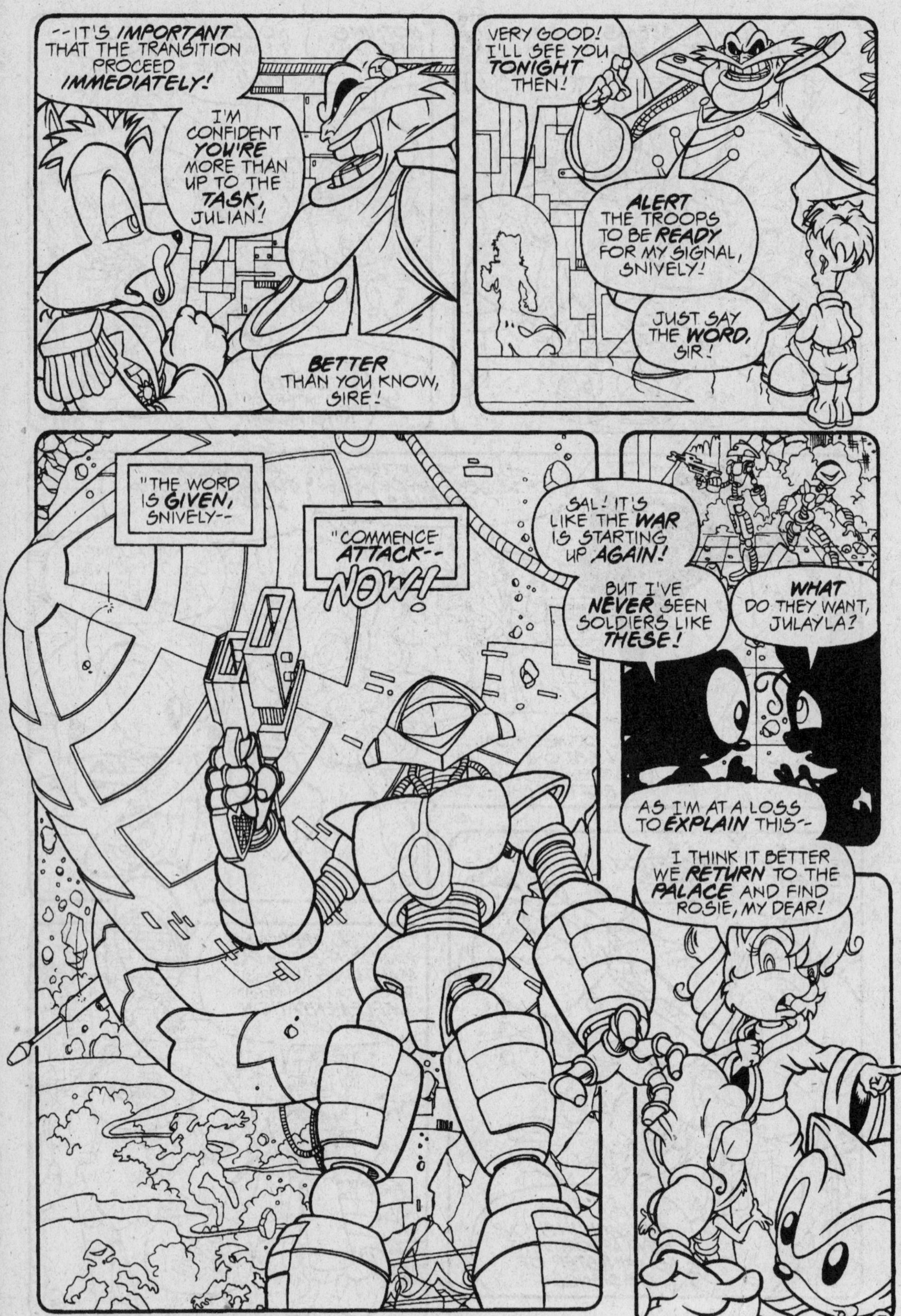
--IT'S IMPORTANT THAT THE TRANSITION PROCEED IMMEDIATELY!
I'M CONFIDENT YOU'RE MORE THAN UP TO THE TASK, JULIAN!
BETTER THAN YOU KNOW, SIRE!
VERY GOOD! I'LL SEE YOU TONIGHT THEN!
ALERT THE TROOPS TO BE READY FOR MY SIGNAL, SNIVELY!
JUST SAY THE WORD, SIR!
"THE WORD IS GIVEN, SNIVELY--
"COMMENCE ATTACK-- NOW!"
SAL! IT'S LIKE THE WAR IS STARTING UP AGAIN!
BUT I'VE NEVER SEEN SOLDIERS LIKE THESE!
WHAT DO THEY WANT, JULAYLA?
AS I'M AT A LOSS TO EXPLAIN THIS--
I THINK IT BETTER WE RETURN TO THE PALACE AND FIND ROSIE, MY DEAR!
7

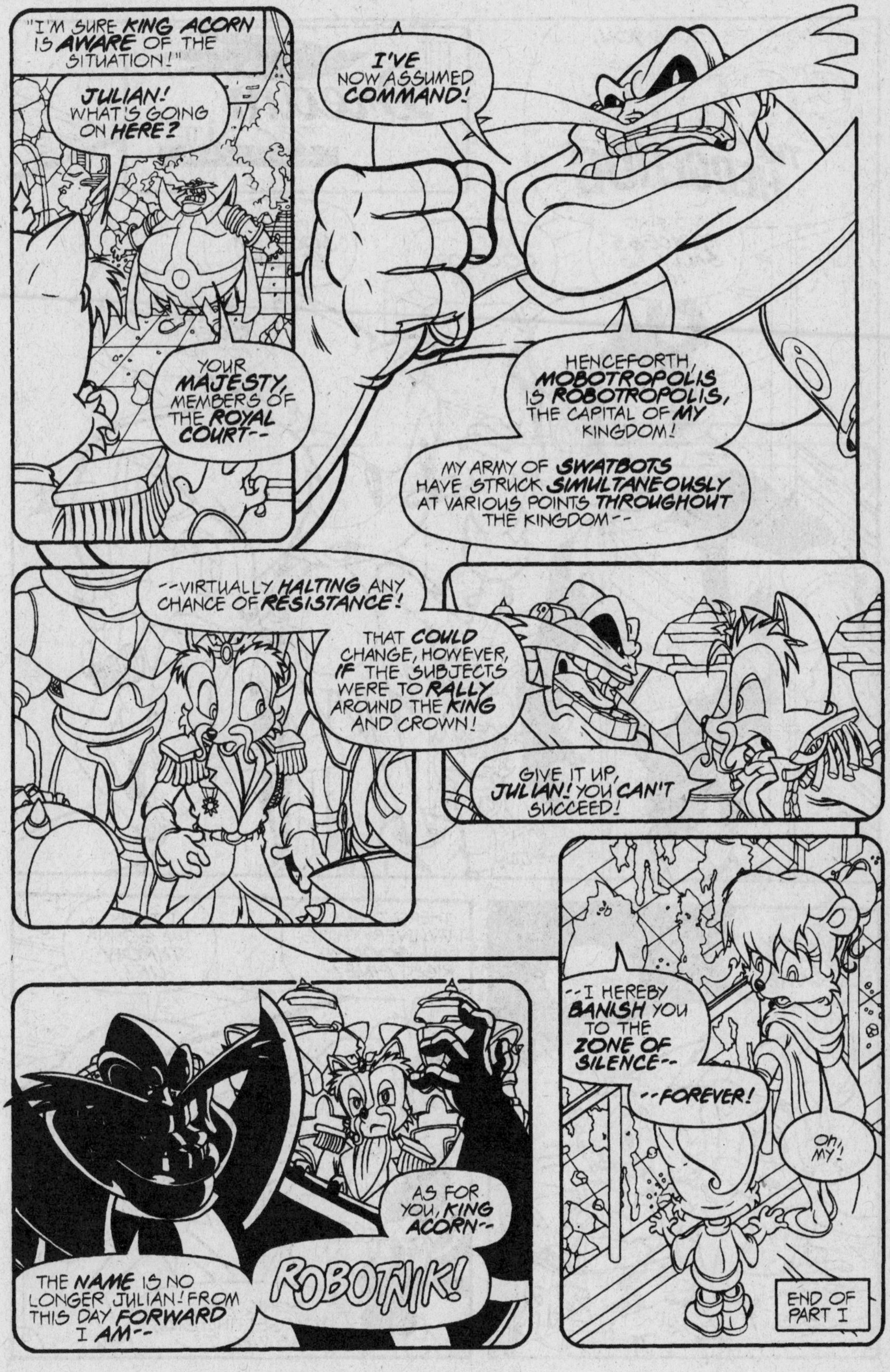
"I'M SURE KING ACORN IS AWARE OF THE SITUATION!"
JULIAN! WHAT'S GOING ON HERE?
YOUR MAJESTY, MEMBERS OF THE ROYAL COURT--
I'VE NOW ASSUMED COMMAND!
HENCEFORTH, MOBOTROPOLIS IS ROBOTROPOLIS, THE CAPITAL OF MY KINGDOM!
MY ARMY OF SWATBOTS HAVE STRUCK SIMULTANEOUSLY AT VARIOUS POINTS THROUGHOUT THE KINGDOM--
--VIRTUALLY HALTING ANY CHANCE OF RESISTANCE!
THAT COULD CHANGE, HOWEVER, IF THE SUBJECTS WERE TO RALLY AROUND THE KING AND CROWN!
GIVE IT UP, JULIAN! YOU CAN'T SUCCEED!
AS FOR YOU, KING ACORN--
THE NAME IS NO LONGER JULIAN! FROM THIS DAY FORWARD I AM--
ROBOTNIK!
--I HEREBY BANISH YOU TO THE ZONE OF SILENCE--
--FOREVER!
OH, MY!
END OF PART I

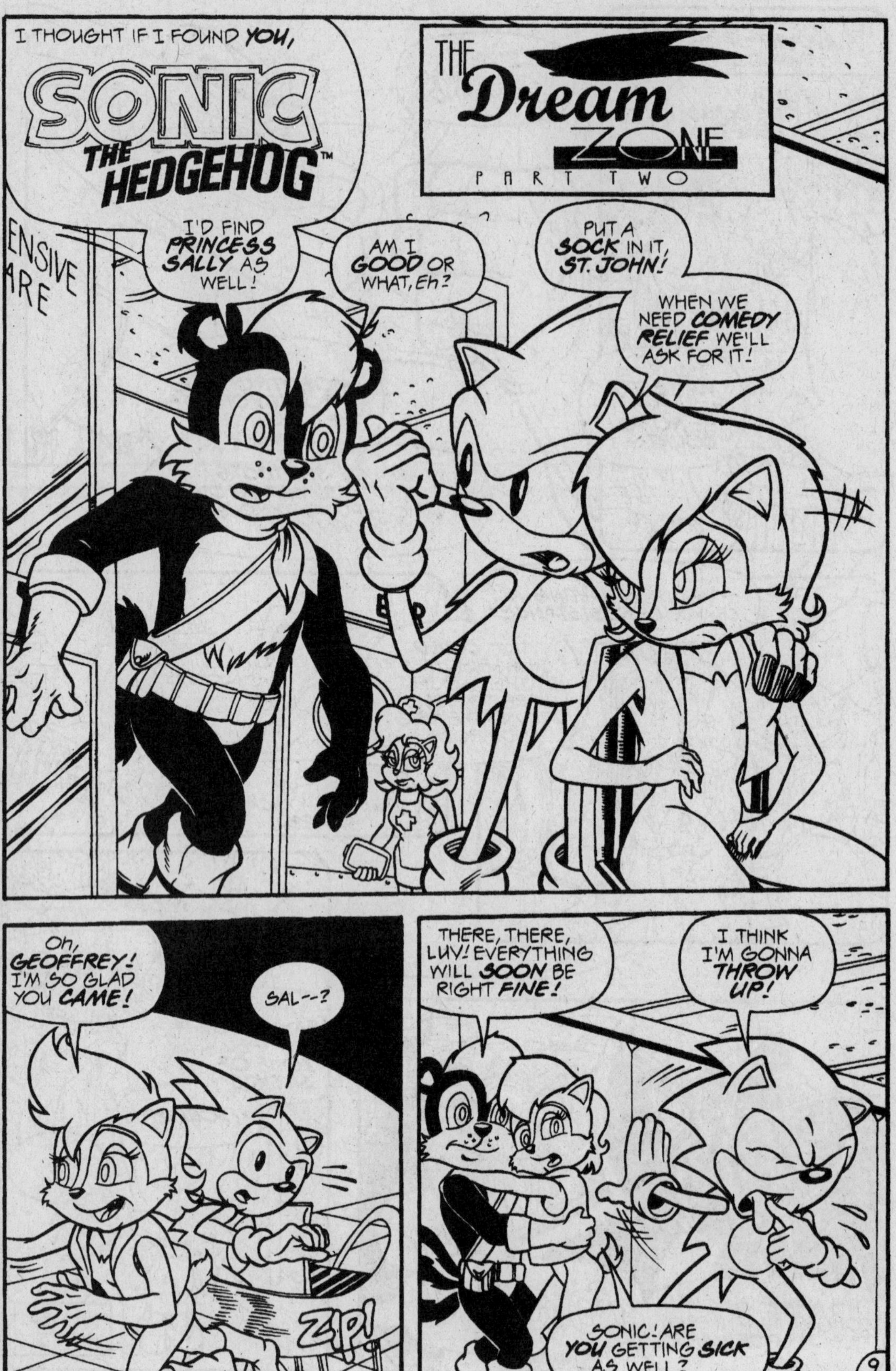
I THOUGHT IF I FOUND YOU,
SONIC THE HEDGEHOG™
THE Dream ZONE
PART TWO
I'D FIND PRINCESS SALLY AS WELL!
AM I GOOD OR WHAT, Eh?
PUT A SOCK IN IT, ST. JOHN!
WHEN WE NEED COMEDY RELIEF WE'LL ASK FOR IT!
Oh, GEOFFREY! I'M SO GLAD YOU CAME!
SAL--?
ZIP!
THERE, THERE, LUV! EVERYTHING WILL SOON BE RIGHT FINE!
I THINK I'M GONNA THROW UP!
SONIC! ARE YOU GETTING SICK AS WELL?
9.

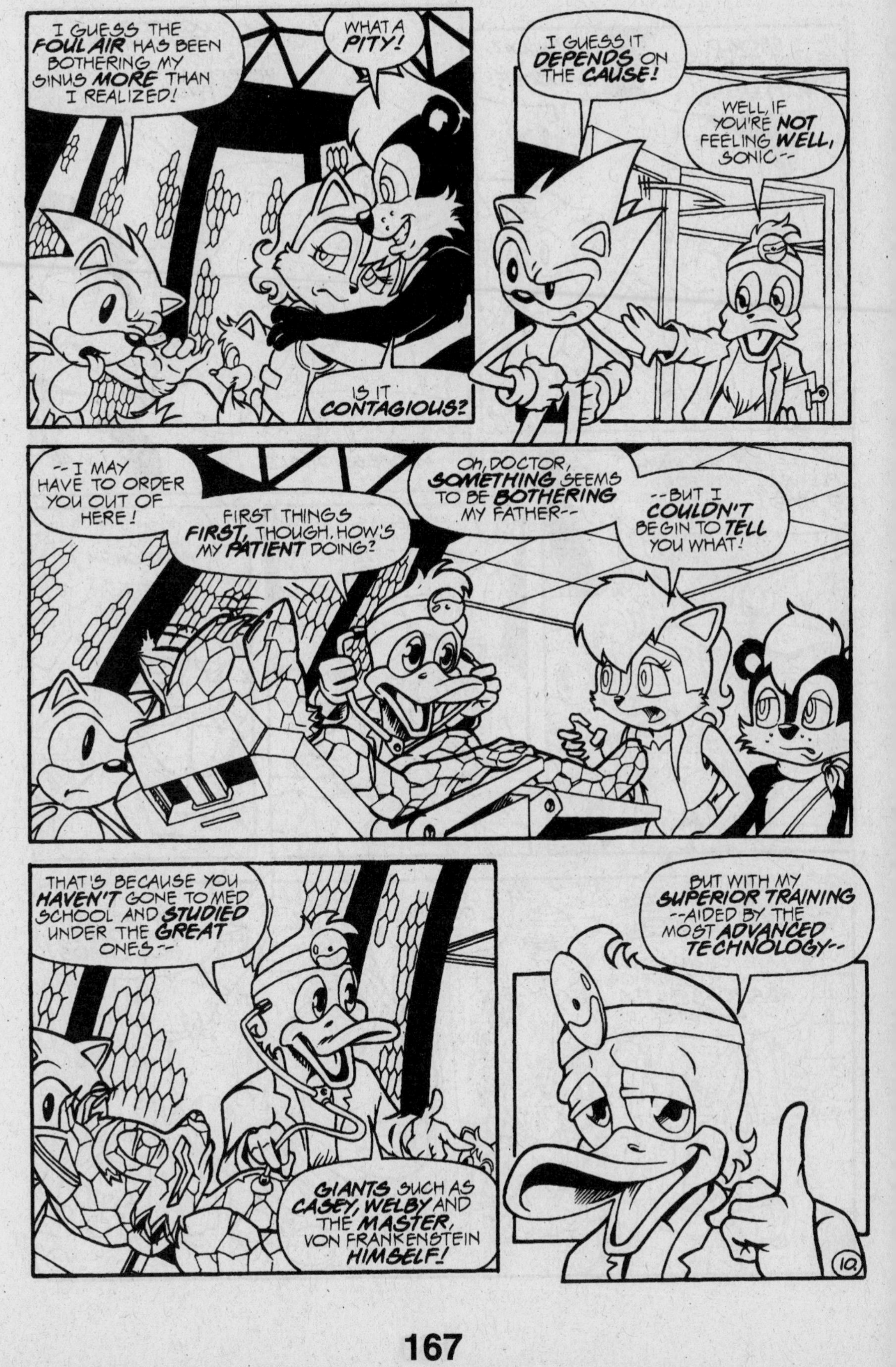
I GUESS THE FOUL AIR HAS BEEN BOTHERING MY SINUS MORE THAN I REALIZED!
WHAT A PITY!
IS IT CONTAGIOUS?
I GUESS IT DEPENDS ON THE CAUSE!
WELL, IF YOU'RE NOT FEELING WELL, SONIC--
--I MAY HAVE TO ORDER YOU OUT OF HERE!
FIRST THINGS FIRST, THOUGH. HOW'S MY PATIENT DOING?
Oh, DOCTOR, SOMETHING SEEMS TO BE BOTHERING MY FATHER--
--BUT I COULDN'T BEGIN TO TELL YOU WHAT!
THAT'S BECAUSE YOU HAVEN'T GONE TO MED SCHOOL AND STUDIED UNDER THE GREAT ONES--
GIANTS SUCH AS CASEY, WELBY AND THE MASTER, VON FRANKENSTEIN HIMSELF!
BUT WITH MY SUPERIOR TRAINING --AIDED BY THE MOST ADVANCED TECHNOLOGY--
10.

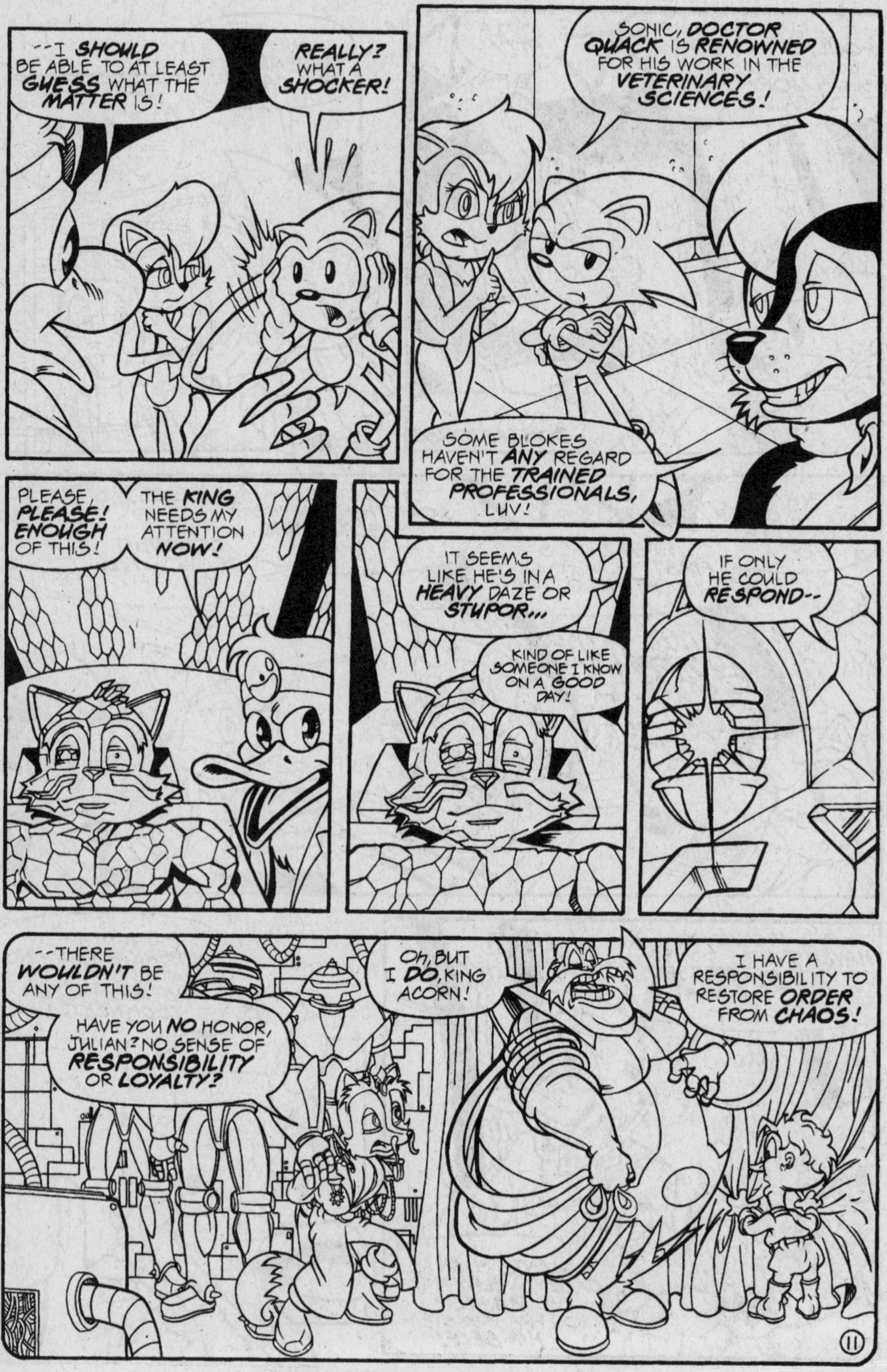
--I SHOULD BE ABLE TO AT LEAST GUESS WHAT THE MATTER IS!
REALLY? WHAT A SHOCKER!
SONIC, DOCTOR QUACK IS RENOWNED FOR HIS WORK IN THE VETERINARY SCIENCES!
SOME BLOKES HAVEN'T ANY REGARD FOR THE TRAINED PROFESSIONALS, LUV!
PLEASE, PLEASE! ENOUGH OF THIS!
THE KING NEEDS MY ATTENTION NOW!
IT SEEMS LIKE HE'S IN A HEAVY DAZE OR STUPOR...
KIND OF LIKE SOMEONE I KNOW ON A GOOD DAY!
IF ONLY HE COULD RESPOND--
--THERE WOULDN'T BE ANY OF THIS!
HAVE YOU NO HONOR, JULIAN? NO SENSE OF RESPONSIBILITY OR LOYALTY?
Oh, BUT I DO, KING ACORN!
I HAVE A RESPONSIBILITY TO RESTORE ORDER FROM CHAOS!
11

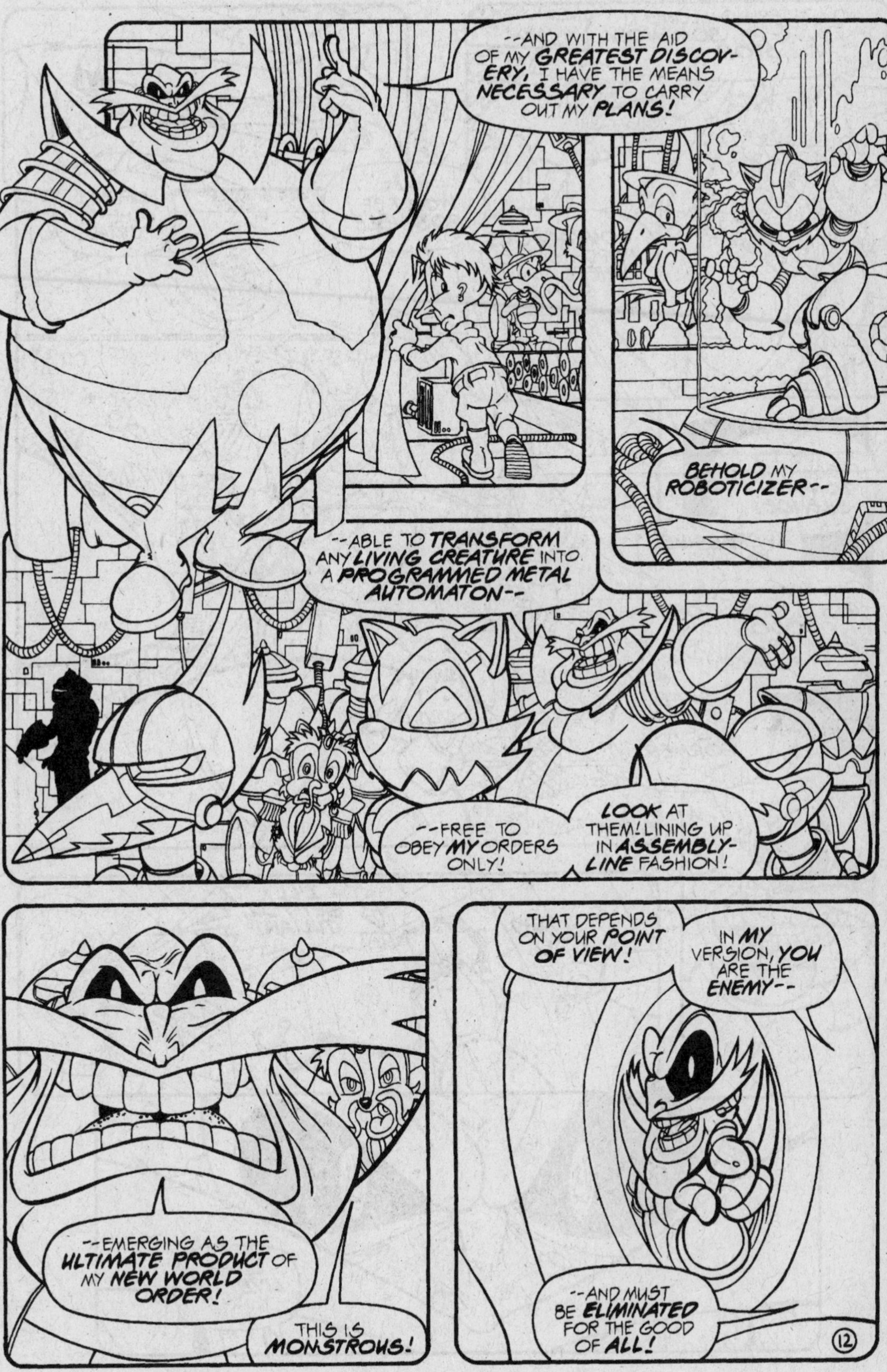
--AND WITH THE AID OF MY GREATEST DISCOVERY, I HAVE THE MEANS NECESSARY TO CARRY OUT MY PLANS!
BEHOLD MY ROBOTICIZER--
--ABLE TO TRANSFORM ANY LIVING CREATURE INTO A PROGRAMMED METAL AUTOMATON--
--FREE TO OBEY MY ORDERS ONLY!
LOOK AT THEM! LINING UP IN ASSEMBLY-LINE FASHION!
--EMERGING AS THE ULTIMATE PRODUCT OF MY NEW WORLD ORDER!
THIS IS MONSTROUS!
THAT DEPENDS ON YOUR POINT OF VIEW!
IN MY VERSION, YOU ARE THE ENEMY--
--AND MUST BE ELIMINATED FOR THE GOOD OF ALL!
12

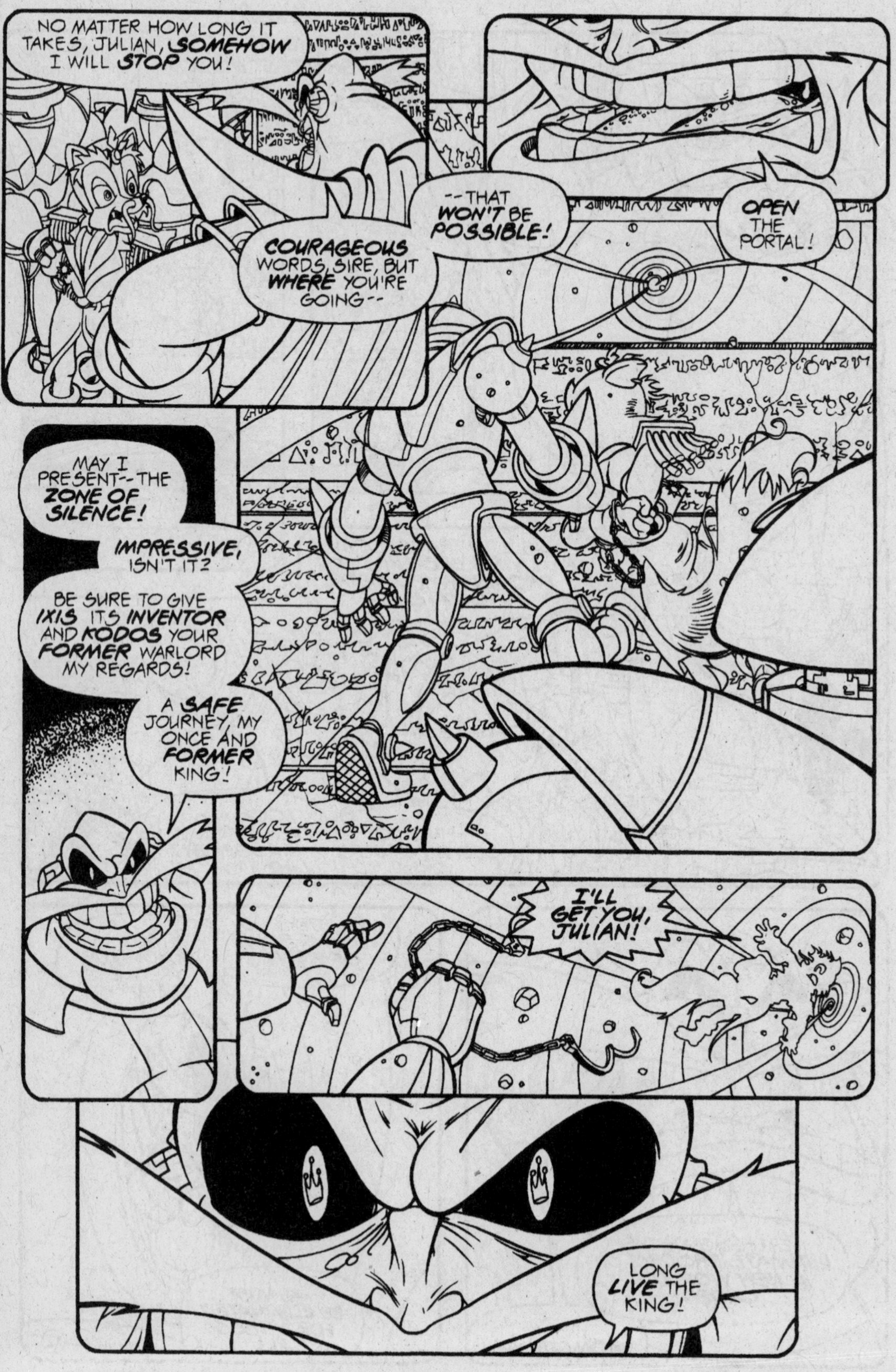
NO MATTER HOW LONG IT TAKES, JULIAN, SOMEHOW I WILL STOP YOU!
COURAGEOUS WORDS, SIRE, BUT WHERE YOU'RE GOING--
--THAT WON'T BE POSSIBLE!
OPEN THE PORTAL!
MAY I PRESENT--THE ZONE OF SILENCE!
IMPRESSIVE, ISN'T IT?
BE SURE TO GIVE IXIS ITS INVENTOR AND KODOS YOUR FORMER WARLORD MY REGARDS!
A SAFE JOURNEY, MY ONCE AND FORMER KING!
I'LL GET YOU, JULIAN!
LONG LIVE THE KING!

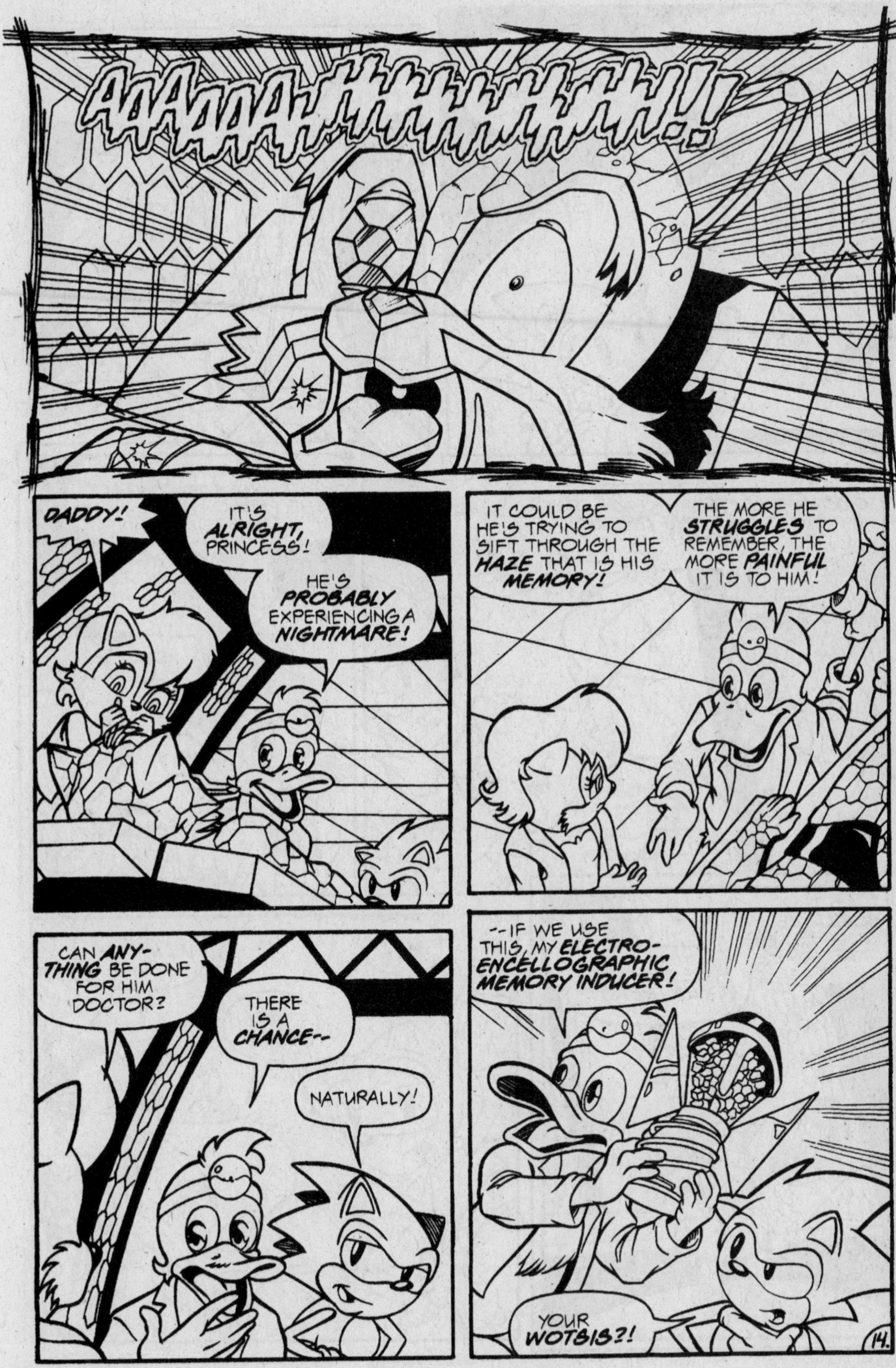
AAAAAHHHHHHHHH!!
DADDY!
IT'S ALRIGHT, PRINCESS!
HE'S PROBABLY EXPERIENCING A NIGHTMARE!
IT COULD BE HE'S TRYING TO SIFT THROUGH THE HAZE THAT IS HIS MEMORY!
THE MORE HE STRUGGLES TO REMEMBER, THE MORE PAINFUL IT IS TO HIM!
CAN ANYTHING BE DONE FOR HIM DOCTOR?
THERE IS A CHANCE--
NATURALLY!
--IF WE USE THIS, MY ELECTRO-ENCELLOGRAPHIC MEMORY INDUCER!
YOUR WOTSIS?!
14.

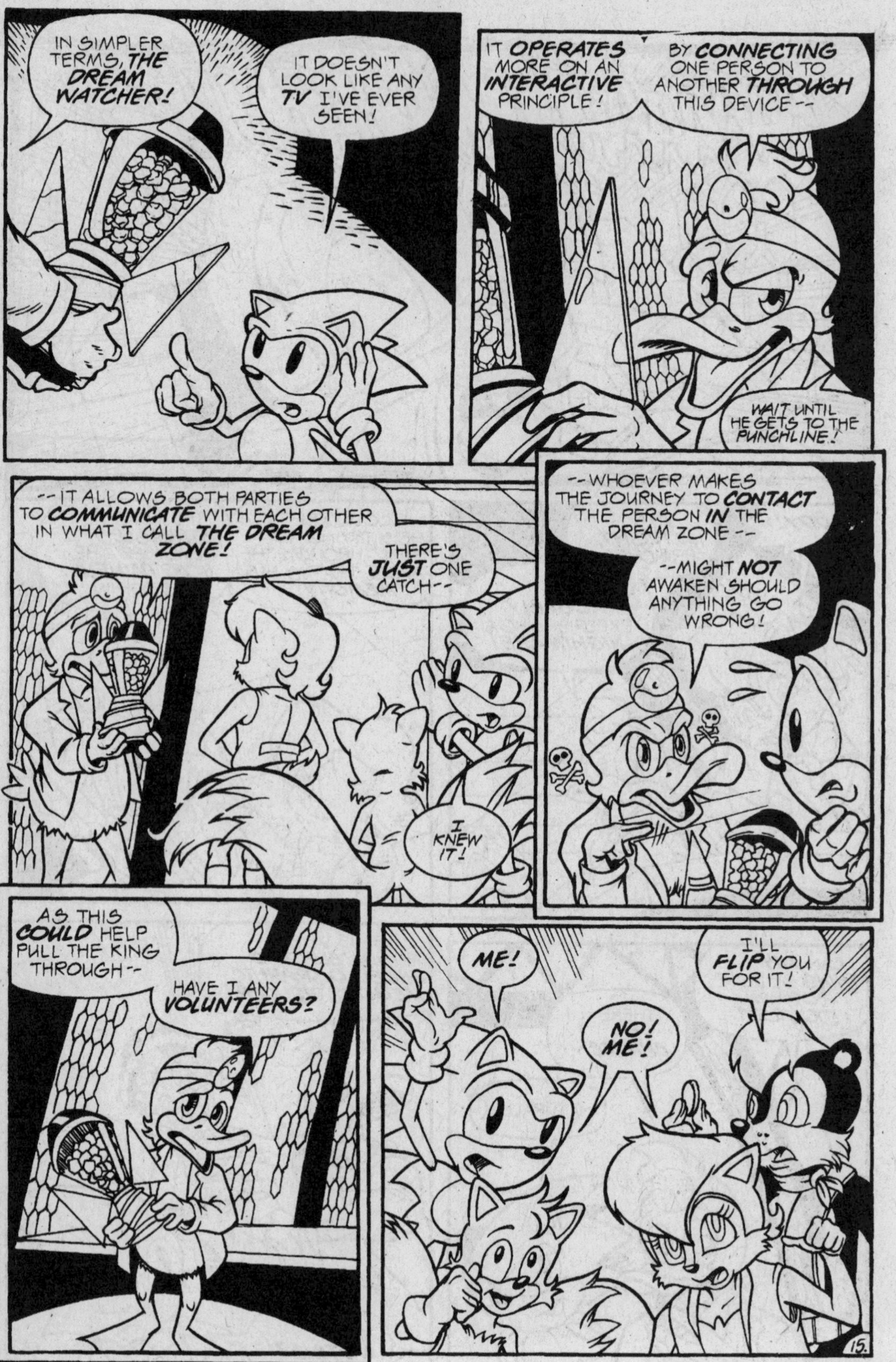
IN SIMPLER TERMS, THE DREAM WATCHER!
IT DOESN'T LOOK LIKE ANY TV I'VE EVER SEEN!
IT OPERATES MORE ON AN INTERACTIVE PRINCIPLE!
BY CONNECTING ONE PERSON TO ANOTHER THROUGH THIS DEVICE --
WAIT UNTIL HE GETS TO THE PUNCHLINE!
-- IT ALLOWS BOTH PARTIES TO COMMUNICATE WITH EACH OTHER IN WHAT I CALL THE DREAM ZONE!
THERE'S JUST ONE CATCH --
I KNEW IT!
-- WHOEVER MAKES THE JOURNEY TO CONTACT THE PERSON IN THE DREAM ZONE --
-- MIGHT NOT AWAKEN SHOULD ANYTHING GO WRONG!
AS THIS COULD HELP PULL THE KING THROUGH --
HAVE I ANY VOLUNTEERS?
ME!
NO! ME!
I'LL FLIP YOU FOR IT!
15.

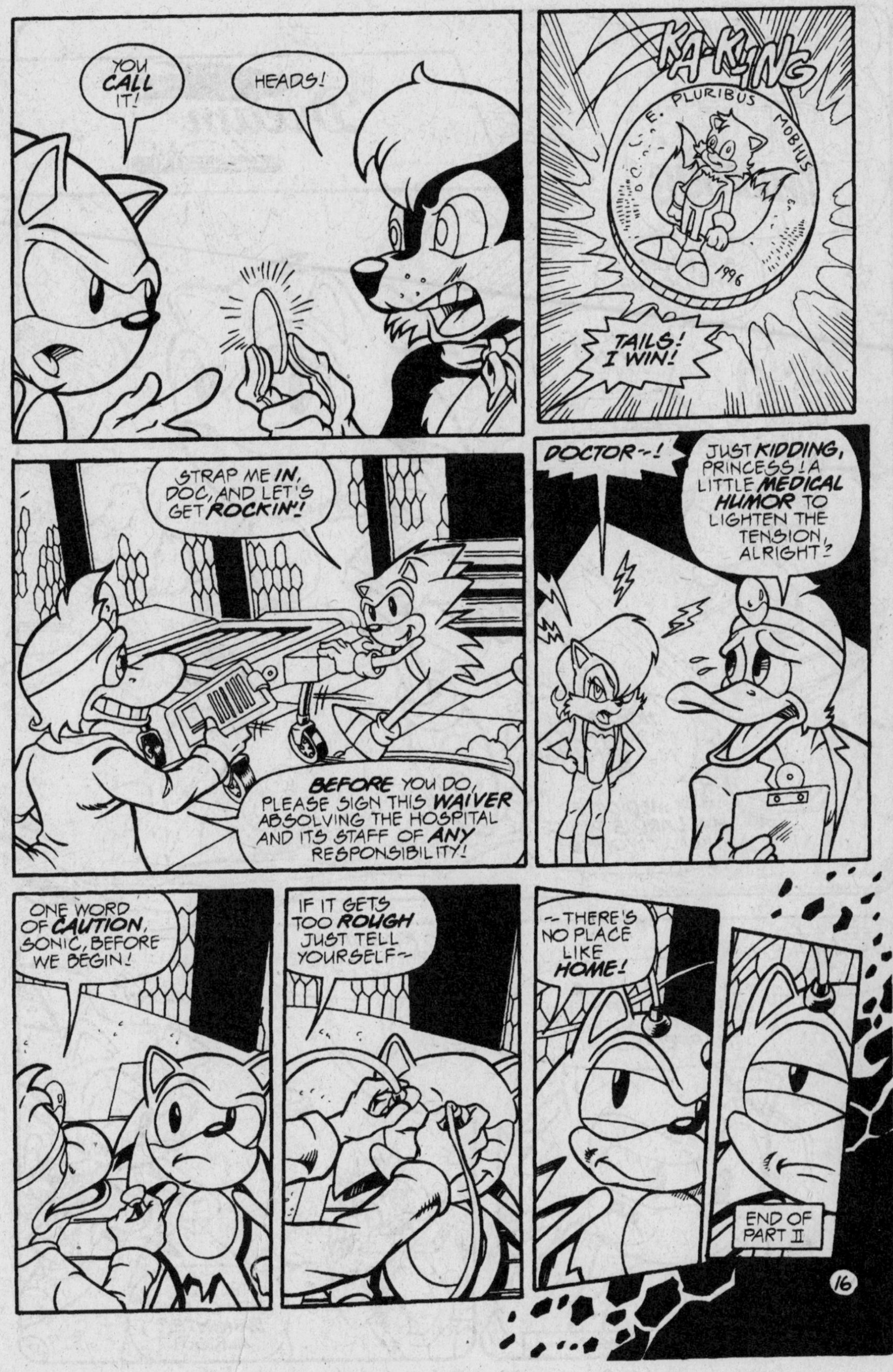
YOU CALL IT!
HEADS!
KA-KLING
E. PLURIBUS MOBIUS
1996
TAILS! I WIN!
STRAP ME IN, DOC, AND LET'S GET ROCKIN'!
BEFORE YOU DO, PLEASE SIGN THIS WAIVER ABSOLVING THE HOSPITAL AND ITS STAFF OF ANY RESPONSIBILITY!
DOCTOR--!
JUST KIDDING, PRINCESS! A LITTLE MEDICAL HUMOR TO LIGHTEN THE TENSION, ALRIGHT?
ONE WORD OF CAUTION, SONIC, BEFORE WE BEGIN!
IF IT GETS TOO ROUGH JUST TELL YOURSELF--
--THERE'S NO PLACE LIKE HOME!
END OF PART II
16

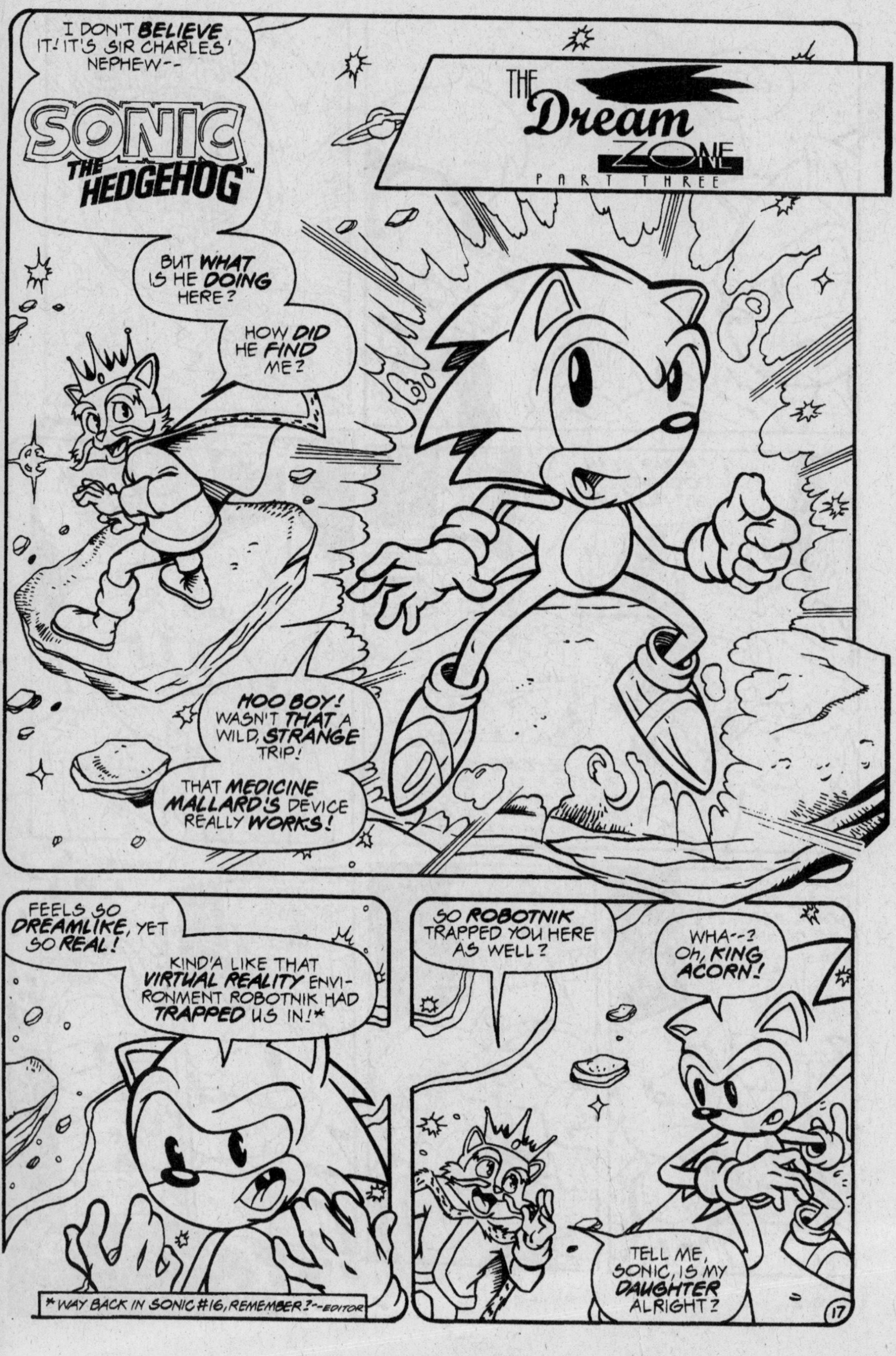
I DON'T BELIEVE IT! IT'S SIR CHARLES' NEPHEW--
SONIC THE HEDGEHOG™
THE Dream ZONE PART THREE
BUT WHAT IS HE DOING HERE?
HOW DID HE FIND ME?
HOO BOY! WASN'T THAT A WILD, STRANGE TRIP!
THAT MEDICINE MALLARD'S DEVICE REALLY WORKS!
FEELS SO DREAMLIKE, YET SO REAL!
KIND'A LIKE THAT VIRTUAL REALITY ENVI-RONMENT ROBOTNIK HAD TRAPPED US IN!*
* WAY BACK IN SONIC #16, REMEMBER?--EDITOR
SO ROBOTNIK TRAPPED YOU HERE AS WELL?
WHA--? Oh, KING ACORN!
TELL ME, SONIC, IS MY DAUGHTER ALRIGHT?
17

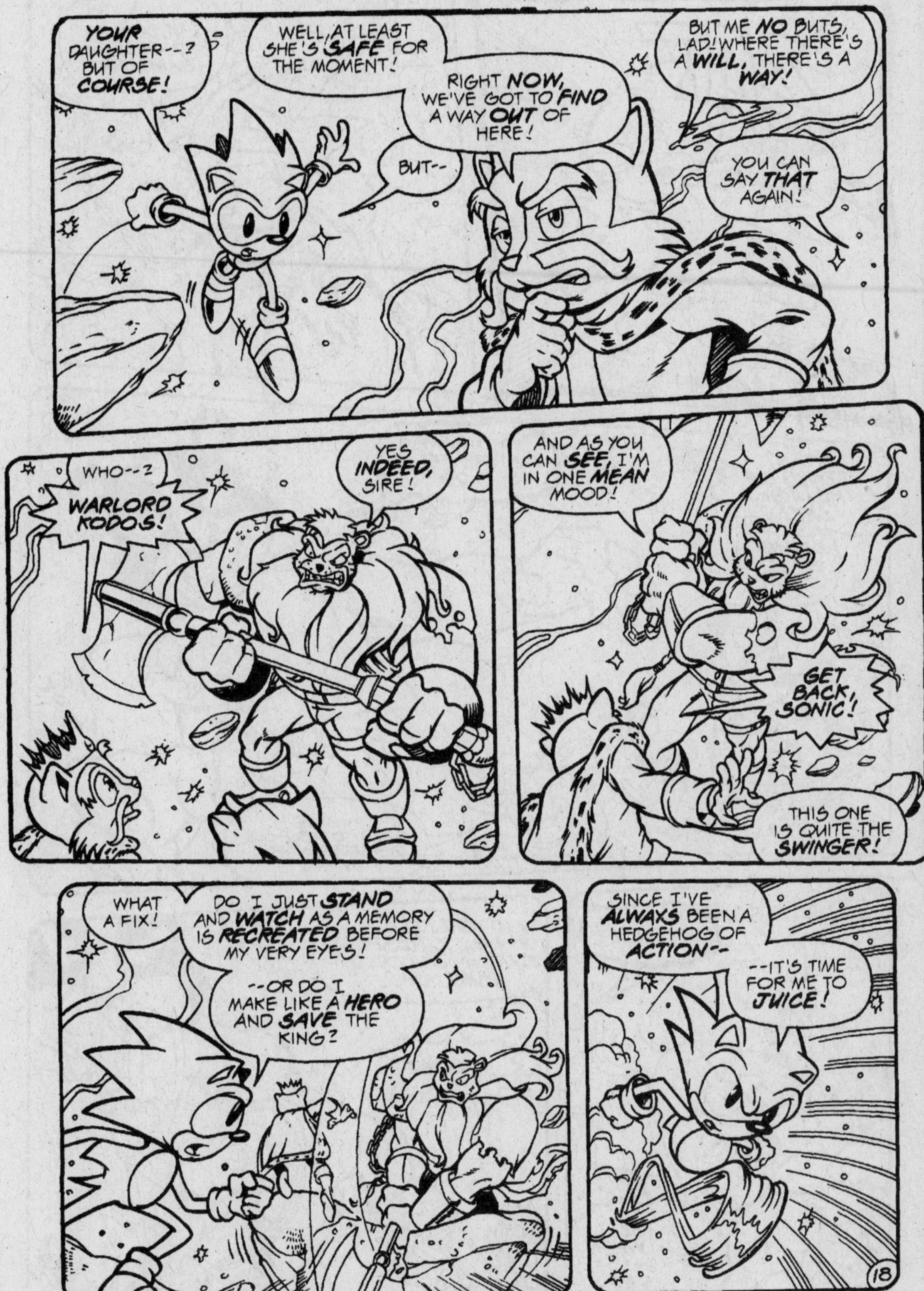
YOUR DAUGHTER--? BUT OF COURSE!
WELL, AT LEAST SHE'S SAFE FOR THE MOMENT!
RIGHT NOW, WE'VE GOT TO FIND A WAY OUT OF HERE!
BUT--
BUT ME NO BUTS, LAD! WHERE THERE'S A WILL, THERE'S A WAY!
YOU CAN SAY THAT AGAIN!
WHO--?
WARLORD KODOS!
YES INDEED, SIRE!
AND AS YOU CAN SEE, I'M IN ONE MEAN MOOD!
GET BACK, SONIC!
THIS ONE IS QUITE THE SWINGER!
WHAT A FIX!
DO I JUST STAND AND WATCH AS A MEMORY IS RECREATED BEFORE MY VERY EYES!
--OR DO I MAKE LIKE A HERO AND SAVE THE KING?
SINCE I'VE ALWAYS BEEN A HEDGEHOG OF ACTION--
--IT'S TIME FOR ME TO JUICE!
18

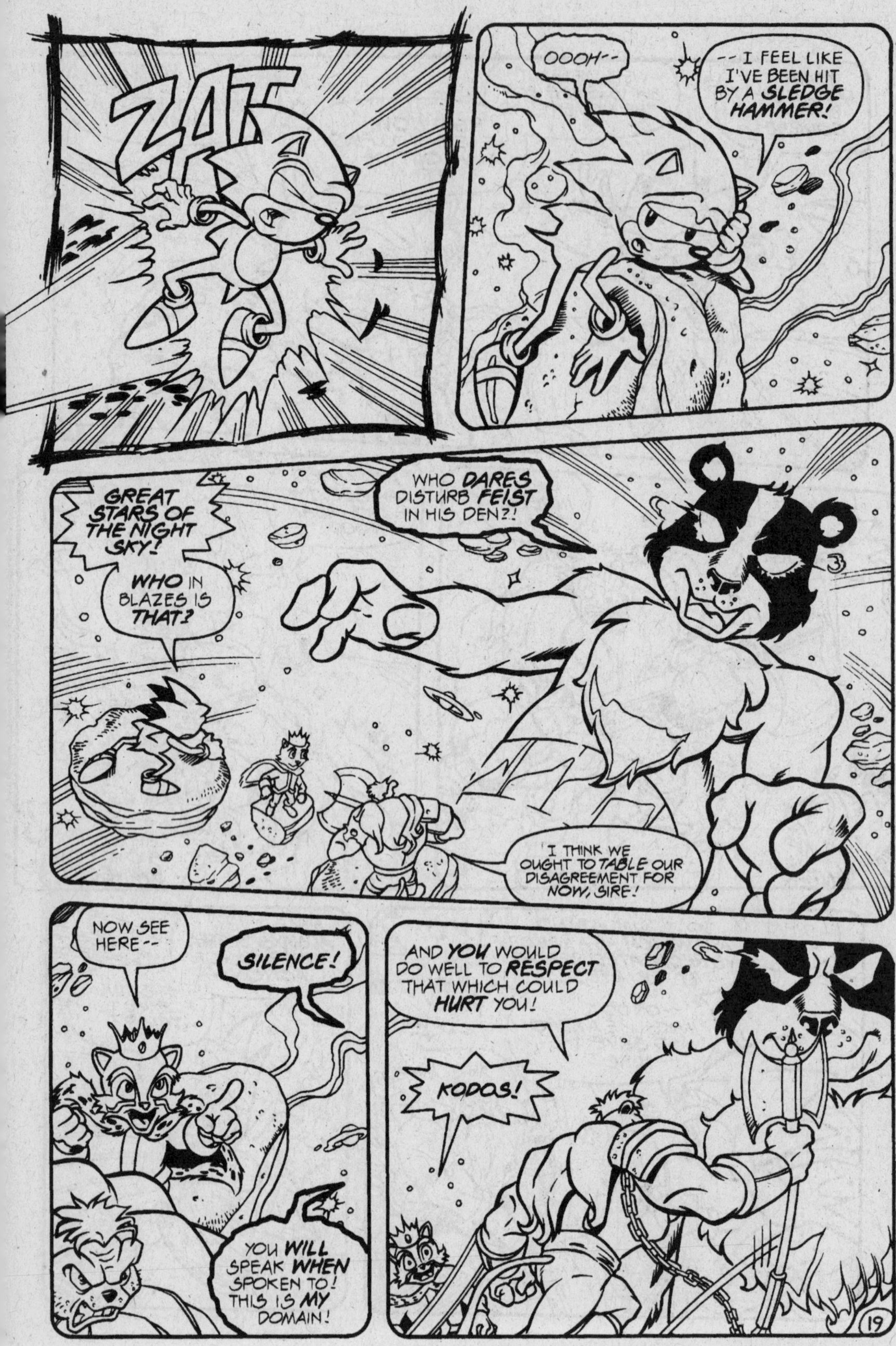
ZAT
OOOH--
--I FEEL LIKE I'VE BEEN HIT BY A SLEDGE HAMMER!
GREAT STARS OF THE NIGHT SKY!
WHO IN BLAZES IS THAT?
WHO DARES DISTURB FEIST IN HIS DEN?!
I THINK WE OUGHT TO TABLE OUR DISAGREEMENT FOR NOW, SIRE!
NOW SEE HERE--
SILENCE!
YOU WILL SPEAK WHEN SPOKEN TO! THIS IS MY DOMAIN!
AND YOU WOULD DO WELL TO RESPECT THAT WHICH COULD HURT YOU!
KODOS!
19

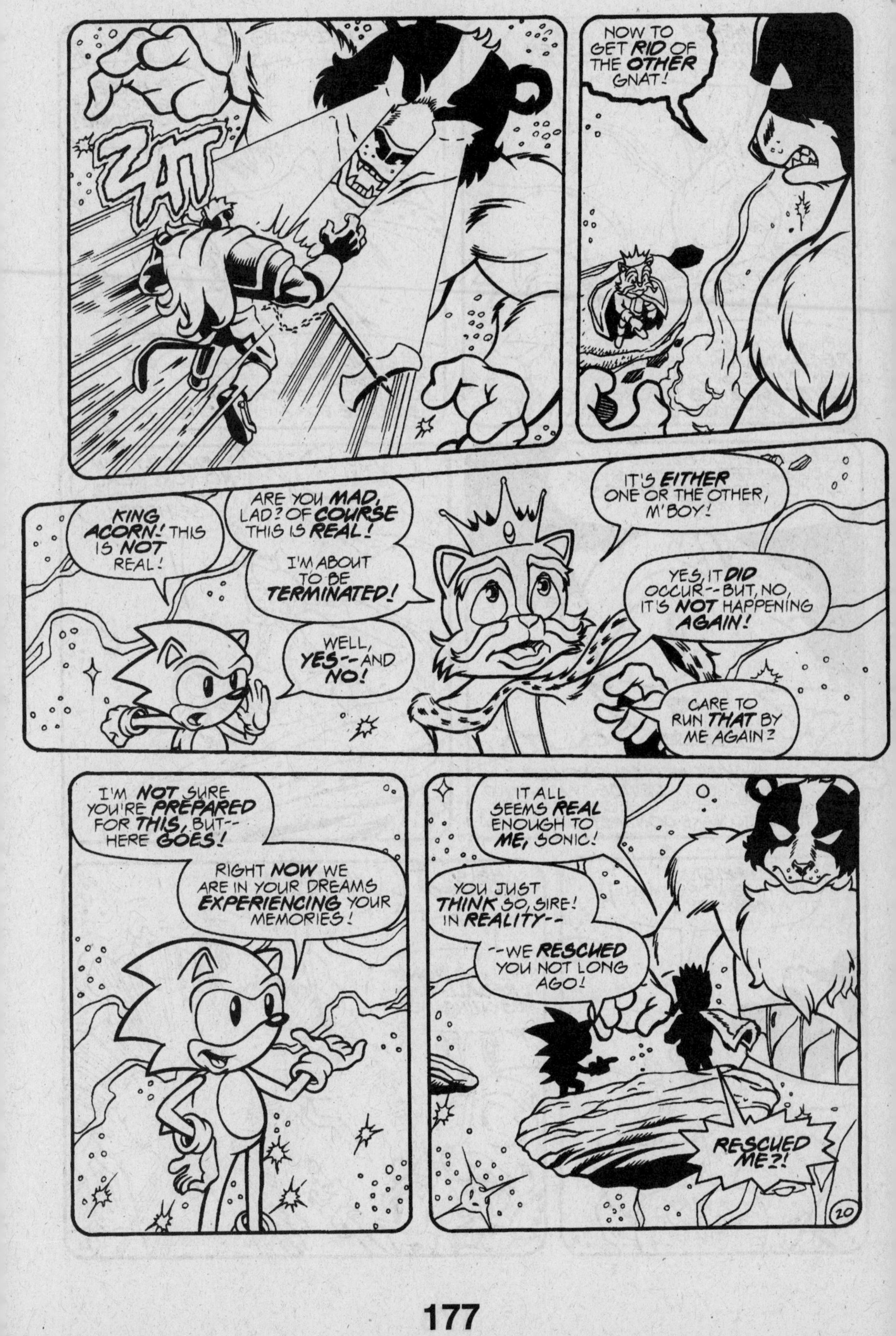
ZAT
NOW TO GET RID OF THE OTHER GNAT!
KING ACORN! THIS IS NOT REAL!
ARE YOU MAD, LAD? OF COURSE THIS IS REAL!
I'M ABOUT TO BE TERMINATED!
WELL, YES--AND NO!
IT'S EITHER ONE OR THE OTHER, M'BOY!
YES, IT DID OCCUR--BUT, NO, IT'S NOT HAPPENING AGAIN!
CARE TO RUN THAT BY ME AGAIN?
I'M NOT SURE YOU'RE PREPARED FOR THIS, BUT--HERE GOES!
RIGHT NOW WE ARE IN YOUR DREAMS EXPERIENCING YOUR MEMORIES!
IT ALL SEEMS REAL ENOUGH TO ME, SONIC!
YOU JUST THINK SO, SIRE! IN REALITY--
--WE RESCUED YOU NOT LONG AGO!
RESCUED ME?!
20

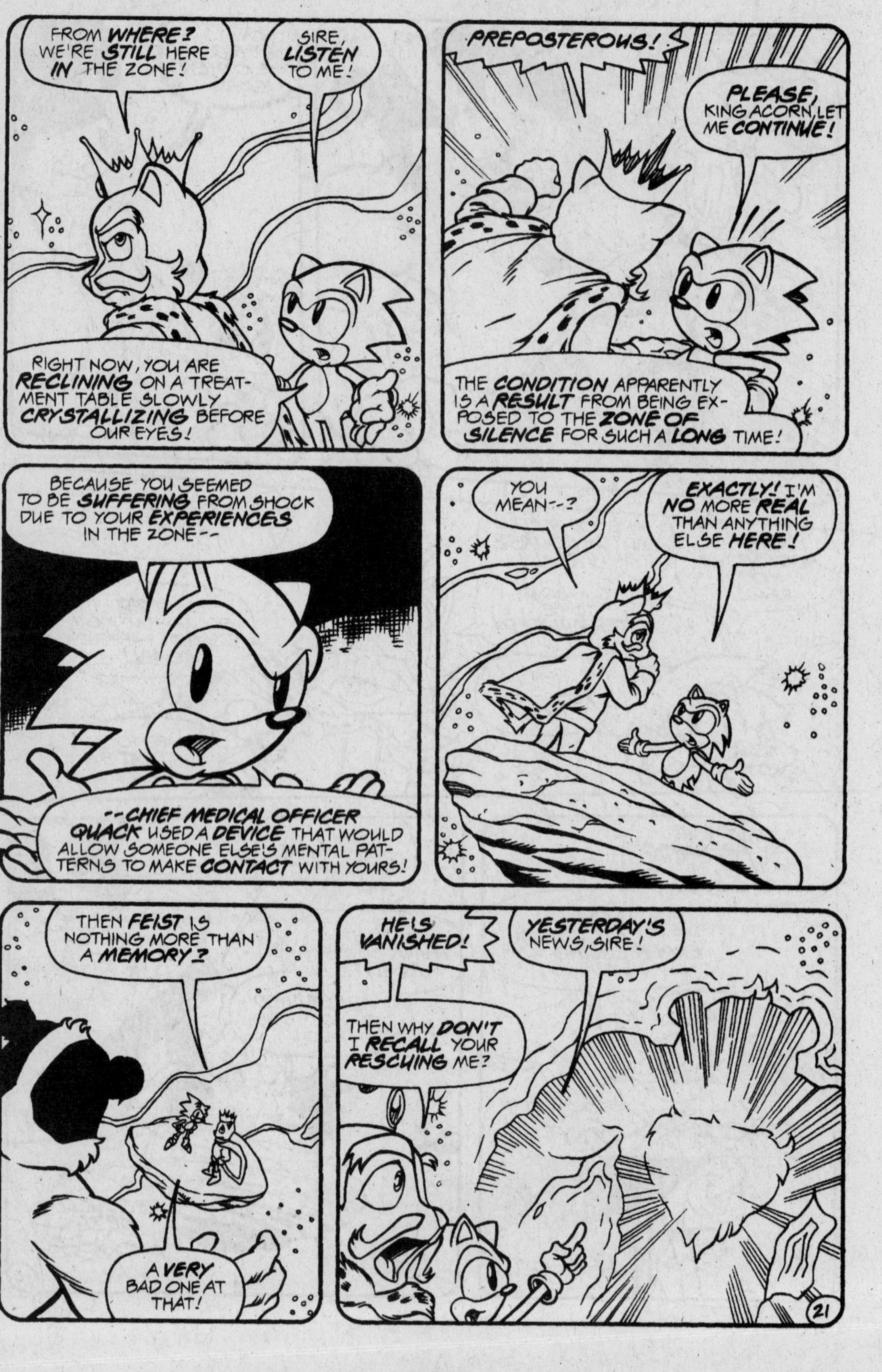
FROM WHERE? WE'RE STILL HERE IN THE ZONE!
SIRE, LISTEN TO ME!
RIGHT NOW, YOU ARE RECLINING ON A TREATMENT TABLE SLOWLY CRYSTALLIZING BEFORE OUR EYES!
PREPOSTEROUS!
PLEASE, KING ACORN, LET ME CONTINUE!
THE CONDITION APPARENTLY IS A RESULT FROM BEING EXPOSED TO THE ZONE OF SILENCE FOR SUCH A LONG TIME!
BECAUSE YOU SEEMED TO BE SUFFERING FROM SHOCK DUE TO YOUR EXPERIENCES IN THE ZONE--
--CHIEF MEDICAL OFFICER QUACK USED A DEVICE THAT WOULD ALLOW SOMEONE ELSE'S MENTAL PATTERNS TO MAKE CONTACT WITH YOURS!
YOU MEAN--?
EXACTLY! I'M NO MORE REAL THAN ANYTHING ELSE HERE!
THEN FEIST IS NOTHING MORE THAN A MEMORY?
A VERY BAD ONE AT THAT!
HE'S VANISHED!
YESTERDAY'S NEWS, SIRE!
THEN WHY DON'T I RECALL YOUR RESCUING ME?
21

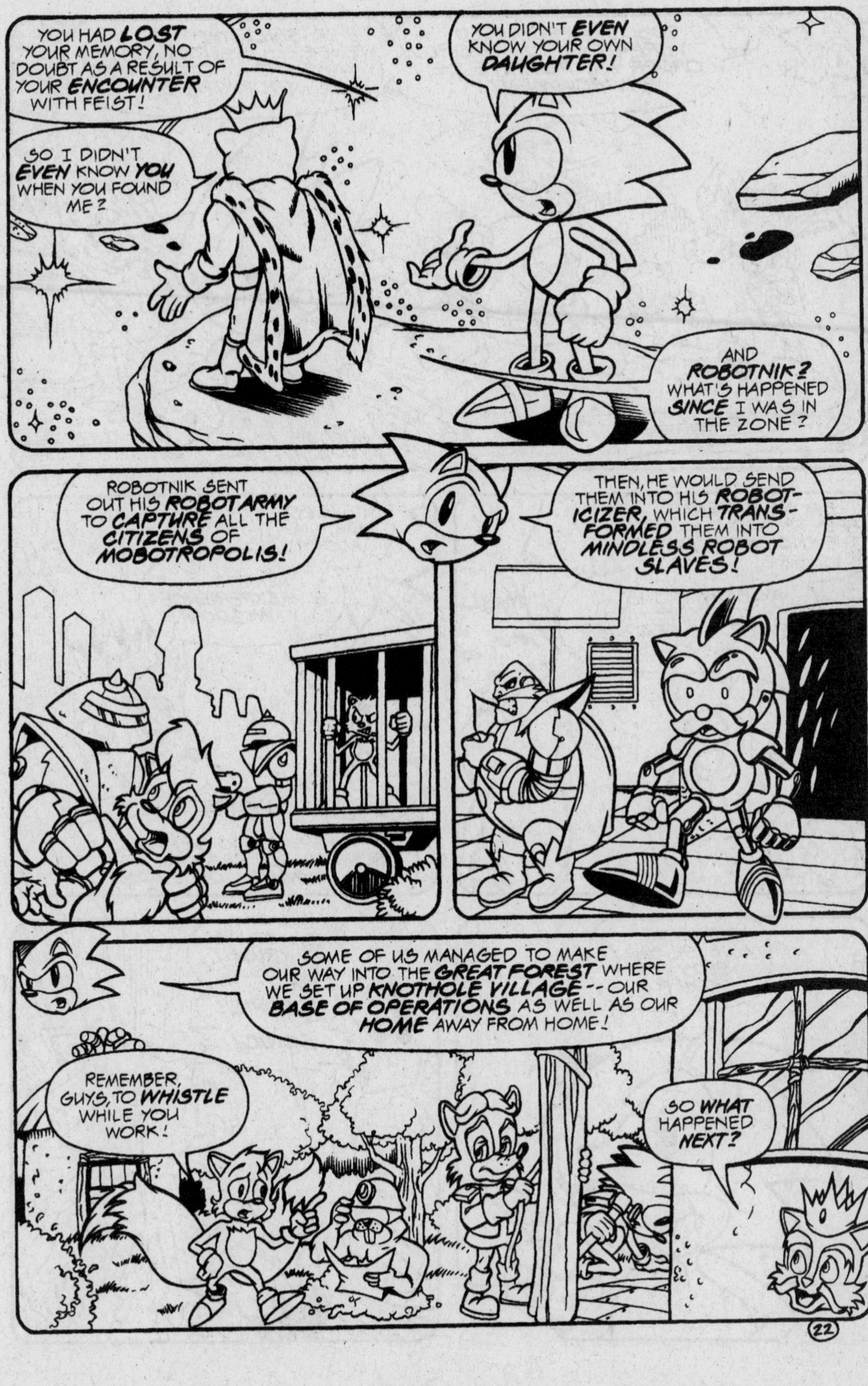
YOU HAD LOST YOUR MEMORY, NO DOUBT AS A RESULT OF YOUR ENCOUNTER WITH FEIST!
SO I DIDN'T EVEN KNOW YOU WHEN YOU FOUND ME?
YOU DIDN'T EVEN KNOW YOUR OWN DAUGHTER!
AND ROBOTNIK? WHAT'S HAPPENED SINCE I WAS IN THE ZONE?
ROBOTNIK SENT OUT HIS ROBOT ARMY TO CAPTURE ALL THE CITIZENS OF MOBOTROPOLIS!
THEN, HE WOULD SEND THEM INTO HIS ROBOTICIZER, WHICH TRANSFORMED THEM INTO MINDLESS ROBOT SLAVES!
SOME OF US MANAGED TO MAKE OUR WAY INTO THE GREAT FOREST WHERE WE SET UP KNOTHOLE VILLAGE -- OUR BASE OF OPERATIONS AS WELL AS OUR HOME AWAY FROM HOME!
REMEMBER, GUYS, TO WHISTLE WHILE YOU WORK!
SO WHAT HAPPENED NEXT?
22

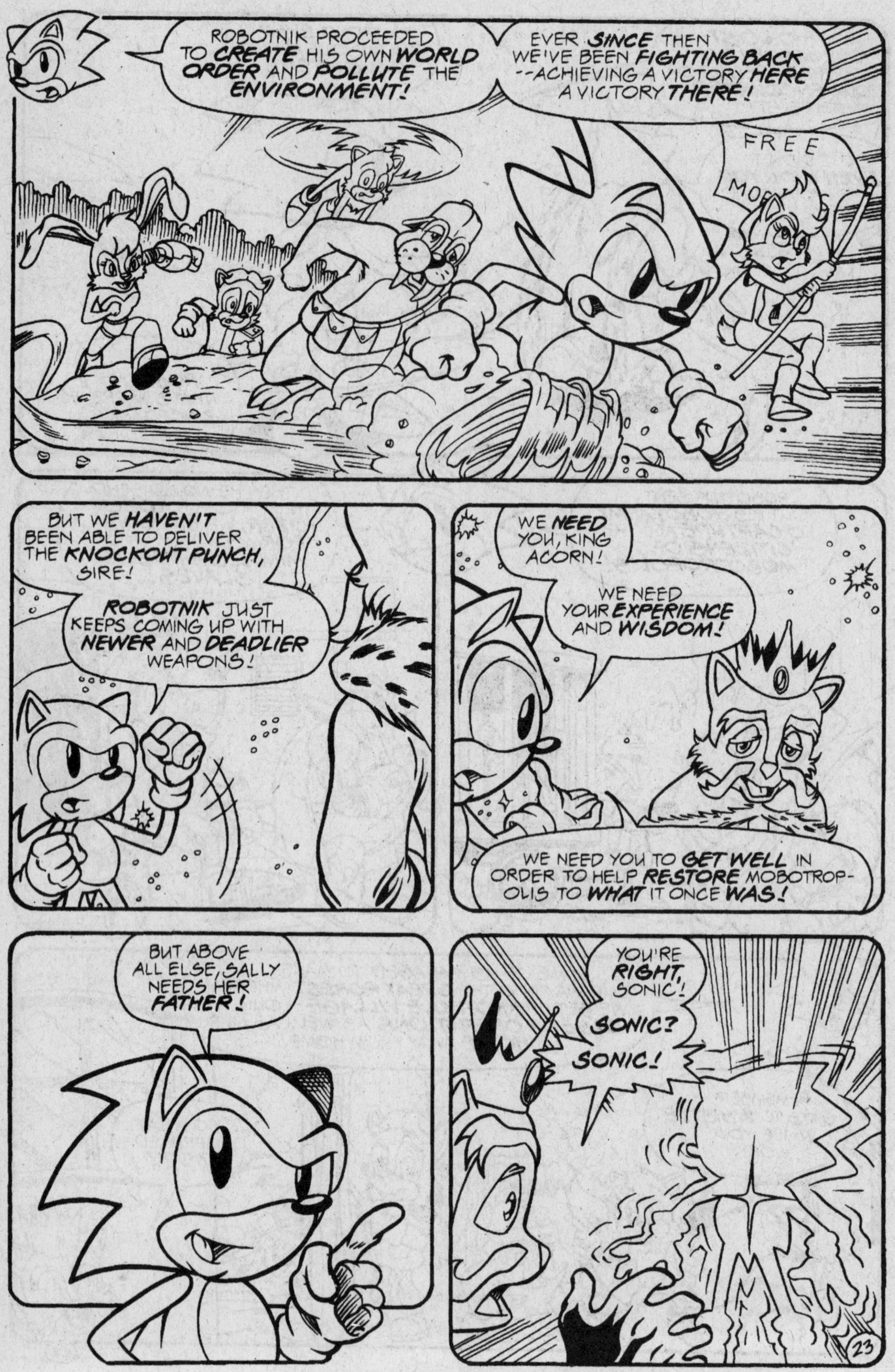
ROBOTNIK PROCEEDED TO CREATE HIS OWN WORLD ORDER AND POLLUTE THE ENVIRONMENT!
EVER SINCE THEN WE'VE BEEN FIGHTING BACK --ACHIEVING A VICTORY HERE A VICTORY THERE!
FREE
BUT WE HAVEN'T BEEN ABLE TO DELIVER THE KNOCKOUT PUNCH, SIRE!
ROBOTNIK JUST KEEPS COMING UP WITH NEWER AND DEADLIER WEAPONS!
WE NEED YOU, KING ACORN!
WE NEED YOUR EXPERIENCE AND WISDOM!
WE NEED YOU TO GET WELL IN ORDER TO HELP RESTORE MOBOTROP-OLIS TO WHAT IT ONCE WAS!
BUT ABOVE ALL ELSE, SALLY NEEDS HER FATHER!
YOU'RE RIGHT, SONIC!
SONIC?
SONIC!
23

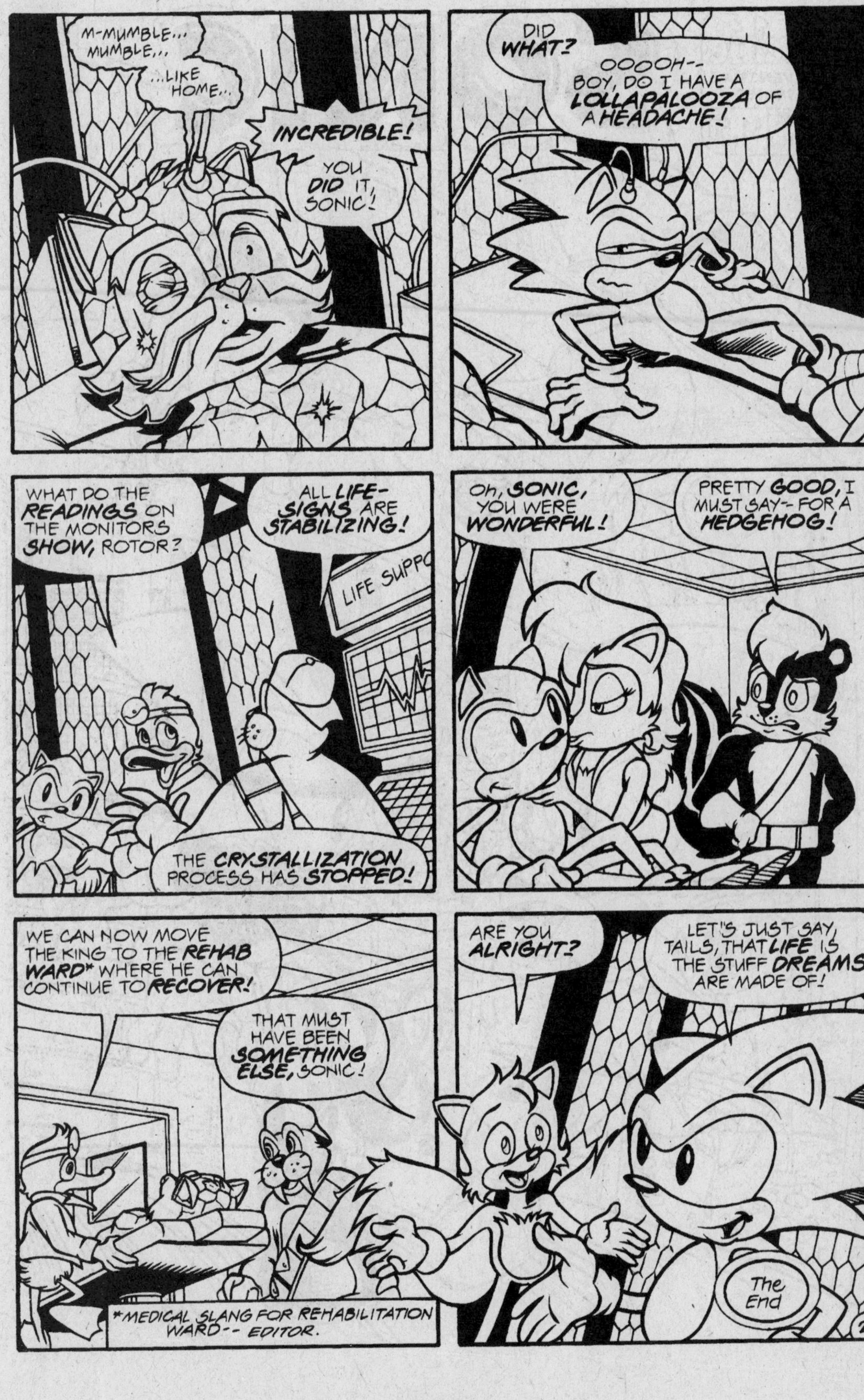
M-MUMBLE... MUMBLE...
...LIKE HOME...
INCREDIBLE!
YOU DID IT, SONIC!
DID WHAT?
OOOOOH-- BOY, DO I HAVE A LOLLAPALOOZA OF A HEADACHE!
WHAT DO THE READINGS ON THE MONITORS SHOW, ROTOR?
ALL LIFE-SIGNS ARE STABILIZING!
LIFE SUPPO
THE CRYSTALLIZATION PROCESS HAS STOPPED!
Oh, SONIC, YOU WERE WONDERFUL!
PRETTY GOOD, I MUST SAY-- FOR A HEDGEHOG!
WE CAN NOW MOVE THE KING TO THE REHAB WARD* WHERE HE CAN CONTINUE TO RECOVER!
THAT MUST HAVE BEEN SOMETHING ELSE, SONIC!
*MEDICAL SLANG FOR REHABILITATION WARD-- EDITOR.
ARE YOU ALRIGHT?
LET'S JUST SAY, TAILS, THAT LIFE IS THE STUFF DREAMS ARE MADE OF!
The End
24

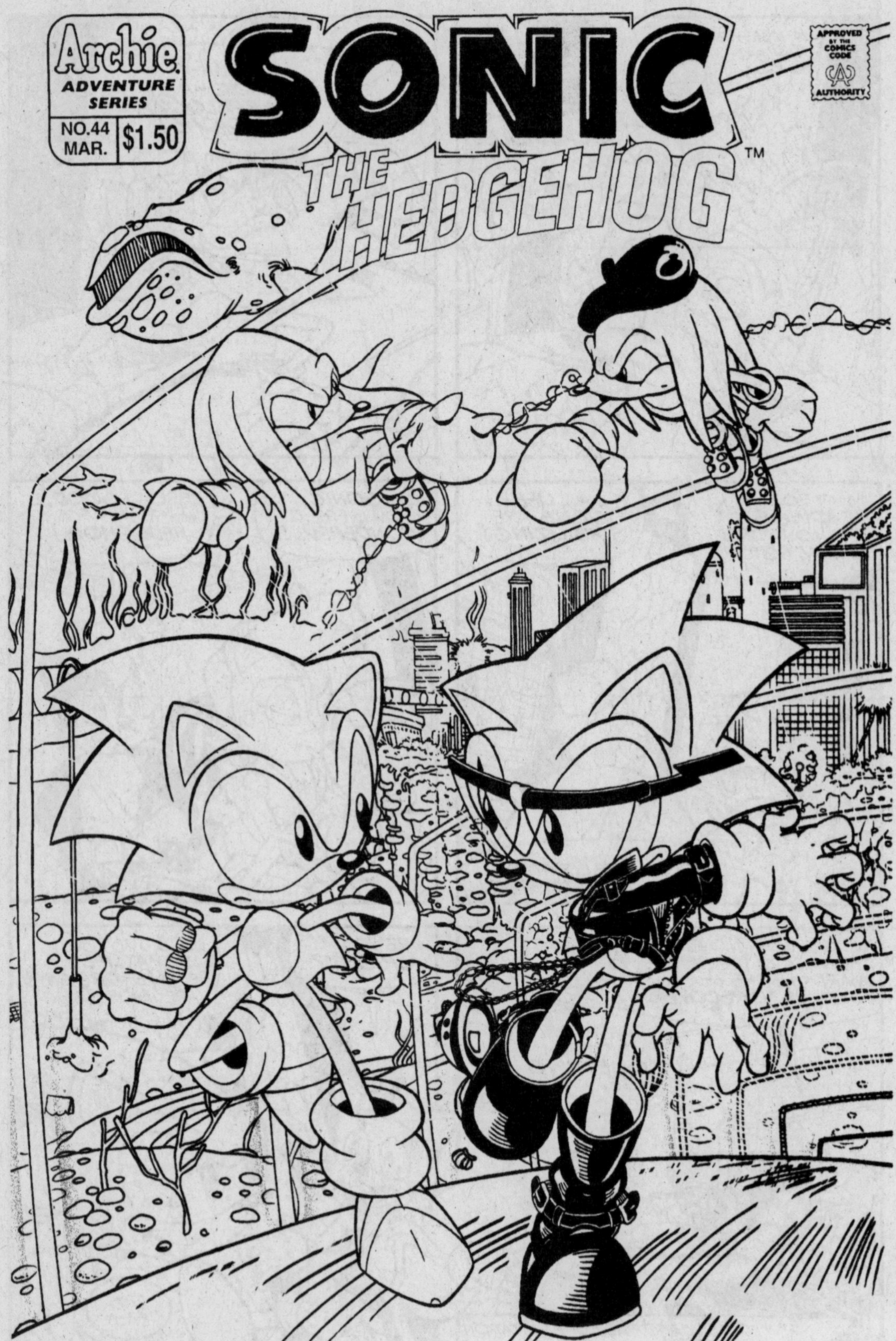
Archie
ADVENTURE SERIES
NO.44
MAR.
$1.50
SONIC
THE HEDGEHOG
™
APPROVED BY THE COMICS CODE AUTHORITY

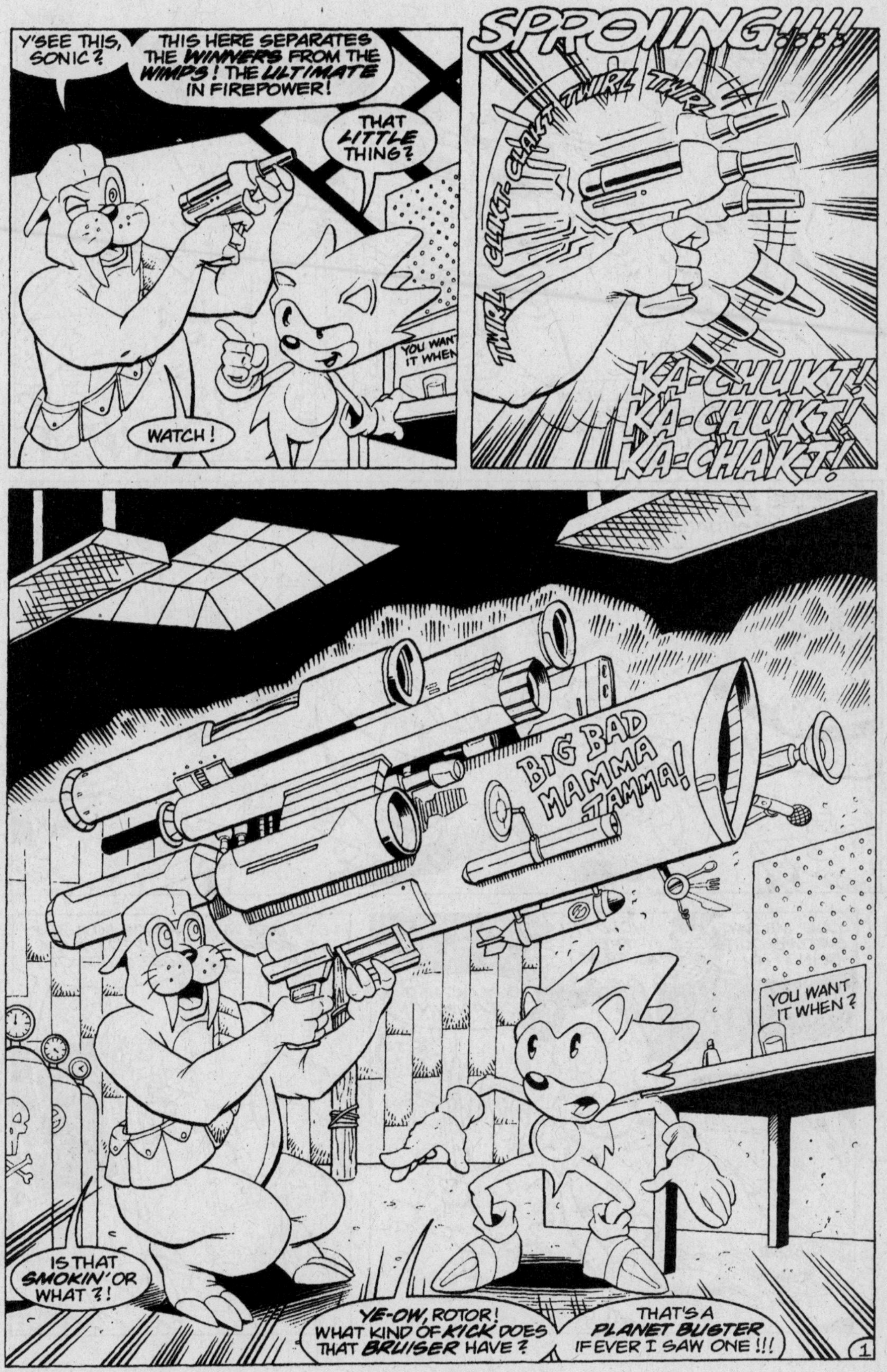
Y'SEE THIS, SONIC?
THIS HERE SEPARATES THE WINNERS FROM THE WIMPS! THE ULTIMATE IN FIREPOWER!
THAT LITTLE THING?
YOU WANT IT WHEN
WATCH!
SPPROIING!!!...
TWIRL TWIRL THIR
TWIRL CLIKT-CLAKT
KA-CHUKT! KA-CHUKT! KA-CHAKT!
BIG BAD MAMMA JAMMA!
YOU WANT IT WHEN?
IS THAT SMOKIN' OR WHAT?!
YE-OW, ROTOR! WHAT KIND OF KICK DOES THAT BRUISER HAVE?
THAT'S A PLANET BUSTER IF EVER I SAW ONE!!!
1

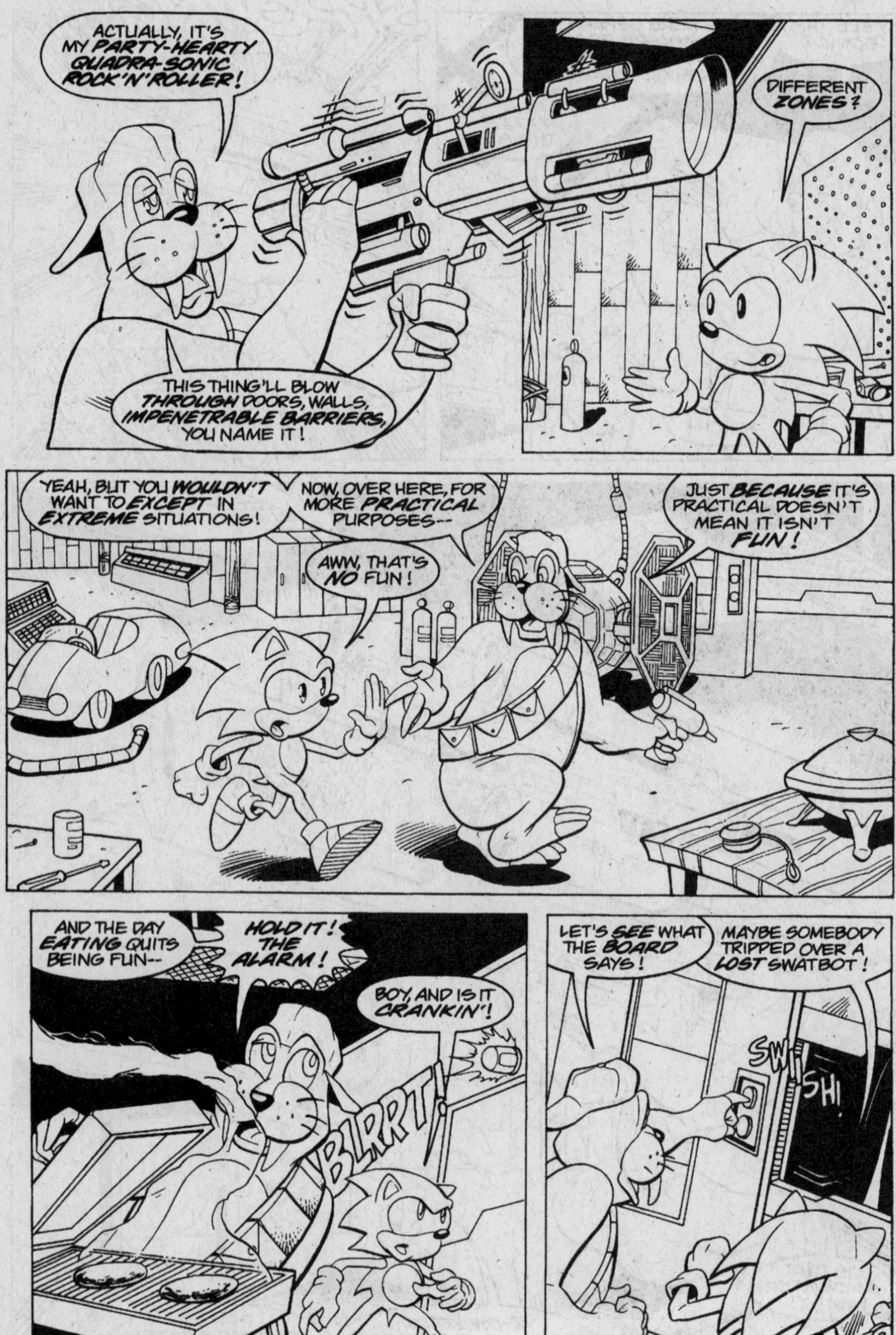
ACTUALLY, IT'S MY PARTY-HEARTY QUADRA-SONIC ROCK'N'ROLLER!
THIS THING'LL BLOW THROUGH DOORS, WALLS, IMPENETRABLE BARRIERS, YOU NAME IT!
DIFFERENT ZONES?
YEAH, BUT YOU WOULDN'T WANT TO EXCEPT IN EXTREME SITUATIONS!
NOW, OVER HERE, FOR MORE PRACTICAL PURPOSES--
AWW, THAT'S NO FUN!
JUST BECAUSE IT'S PRACTICAL DOESN'T MEAN IT ISN'T FUN!
AND THE DAY EATING QUITS BEING FUN--
HOLD IT! THE ALARM!
BOY, AND IS IT CRANKIN'!
BLRRT!
LET'S SEE WHAT THE BOARD SAYS!
MAYBE SOMEBODY TRIPPED OVER A LOST SWATBOT!
SWISH!
2

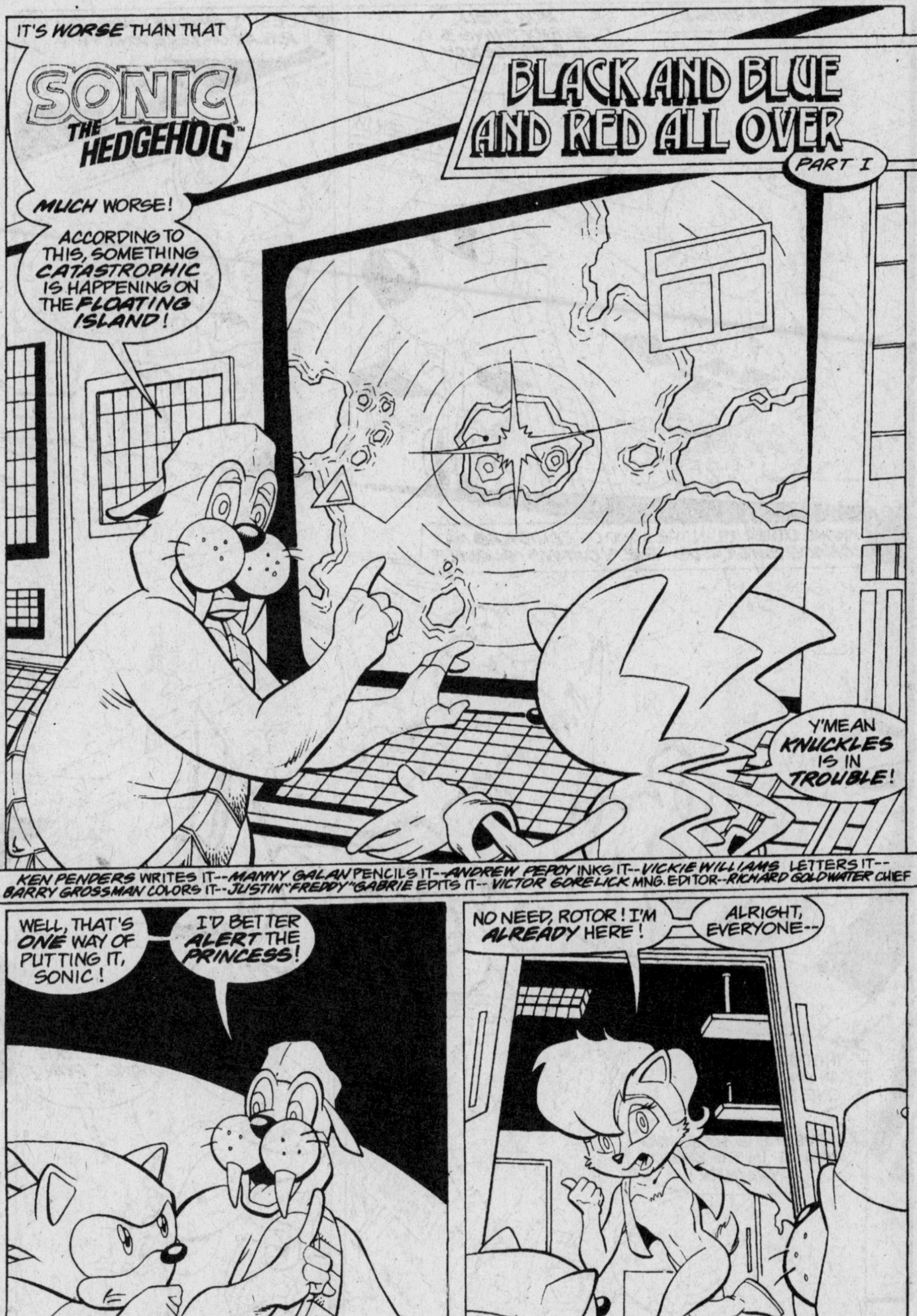
IT'S WORSE THAN THAT
SONIC THE HEDGEHOG™
BLACK AND BLUE AND RED ALL OVER
PART I
MUCH WORSE!
ACCORDING TO THIS, SOMETHING CATASTROPHIC IS HAPPENING ON THE FLOATING ISLAND!
Y'MEAN KNUCKLES IS IN TROUBLE!
KEN PENDERS WRITES IT--MANNY GALAN PENCILS IT--ANDREW PEPOY INKS IT--VICKIE WILLIAMS LETTERS IT--
BARRY GROSSMAN COLORS IT--JUSTIN"FREDDY"GABRIE EDITS IT-- VICTOR GORELICK MNG. EDITOR--RICHARD GOLDWATER CHIEF
WELL, THAT'S ONE WAY OF PUTTING IT, SONIC!
I'D BETTER ALERT THE PRINCESS!
NO NEED, ROTOR! I'M ALREADY HERE!
ALRIGHT, EVERYONE--
3

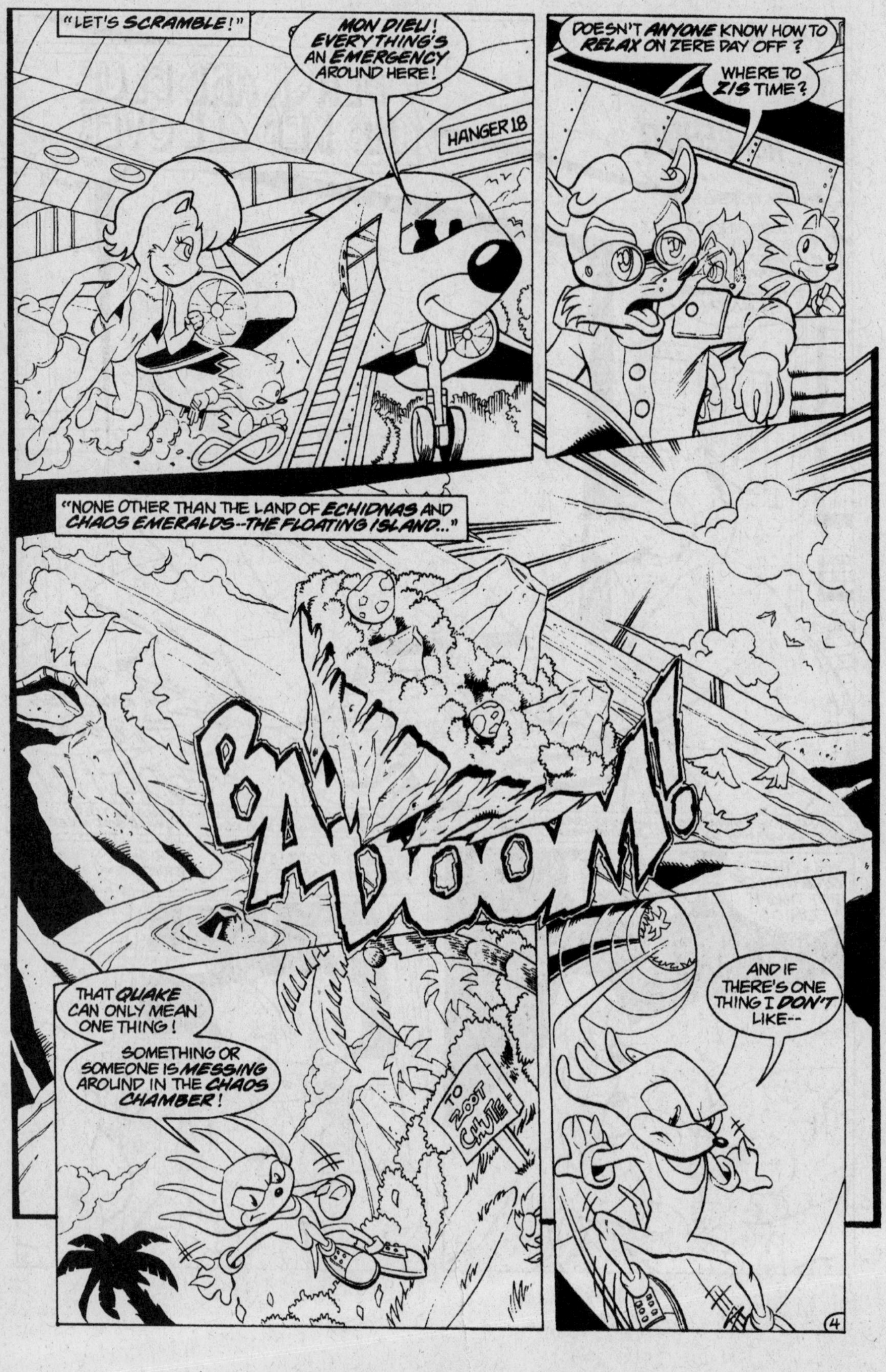
"LET'S SCRAMBLE!"
MON DIEU! EVERYTHING'S AN EMERGENCY AROUND HERE!
HANGER 18
DOESN'T ANYONE KNOW HOW TO RELAX ON ZERE DAY OFF?
WHERE TO ZIS TIME?
"NONE OTHER THAN THE LAND OF ECHIDNAS AND CHAOS EMERALDS--THE FLOATING ISLAND..."
BADOOM!
THAT QUAKE CAN ONLY MEAN ONE THING!
SOMETHING OR SOMEONE IS MESSING AROUND IN THE CHAOS CHAMBER!
TO ZOOT CHUTE
AND IF THERE'S ONE THING I DON'T LIKE--
4

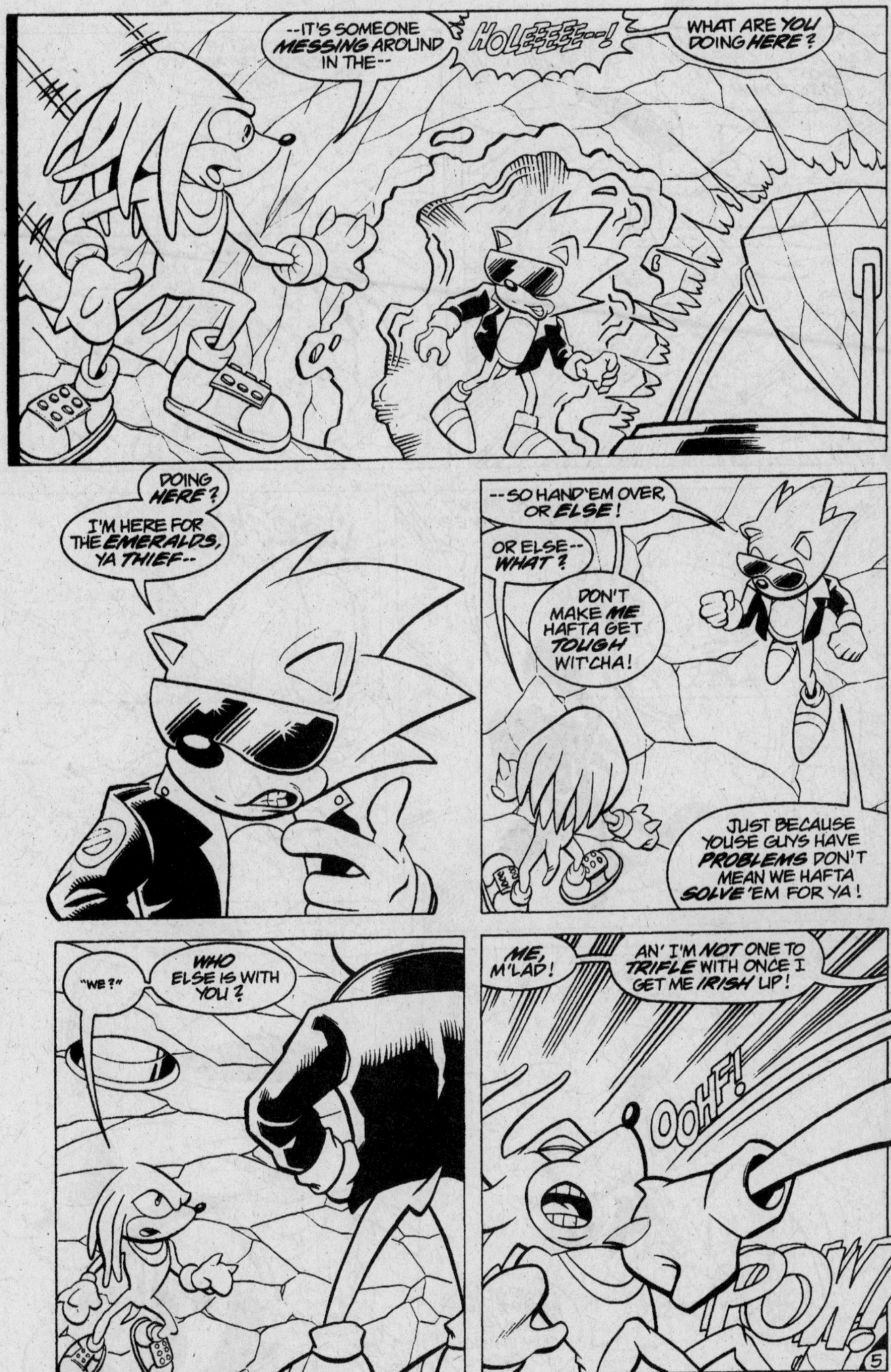
--IT'S SOMEONE MESSING AROUND IN THE--
HOLEEEEE--!
WHAT ARE YOU DOING HERE?
DOING HERE? I'M HERE FOR THE EMERALDS, YA THIEF--
--SO HAND 'EM OVER, OR ELSE!
OR ELSE-- WHAT?
DON'T MAKE ME HAFTA GET TOUGH WIT'CHA!
JUST BECAUSE YOUSE GUYS HAVE PROBLEMS DON'T MEAN WE HAFTA SOLVE 'EM FOR YA!
"WE?"
WHO ELSE IS WITH YOU?
ME, M'LAD!
AN' I'M NOT ONE TO TRIFLE WITH ONCE I GET ME IRISH UP!
OOHF!
POW!
5

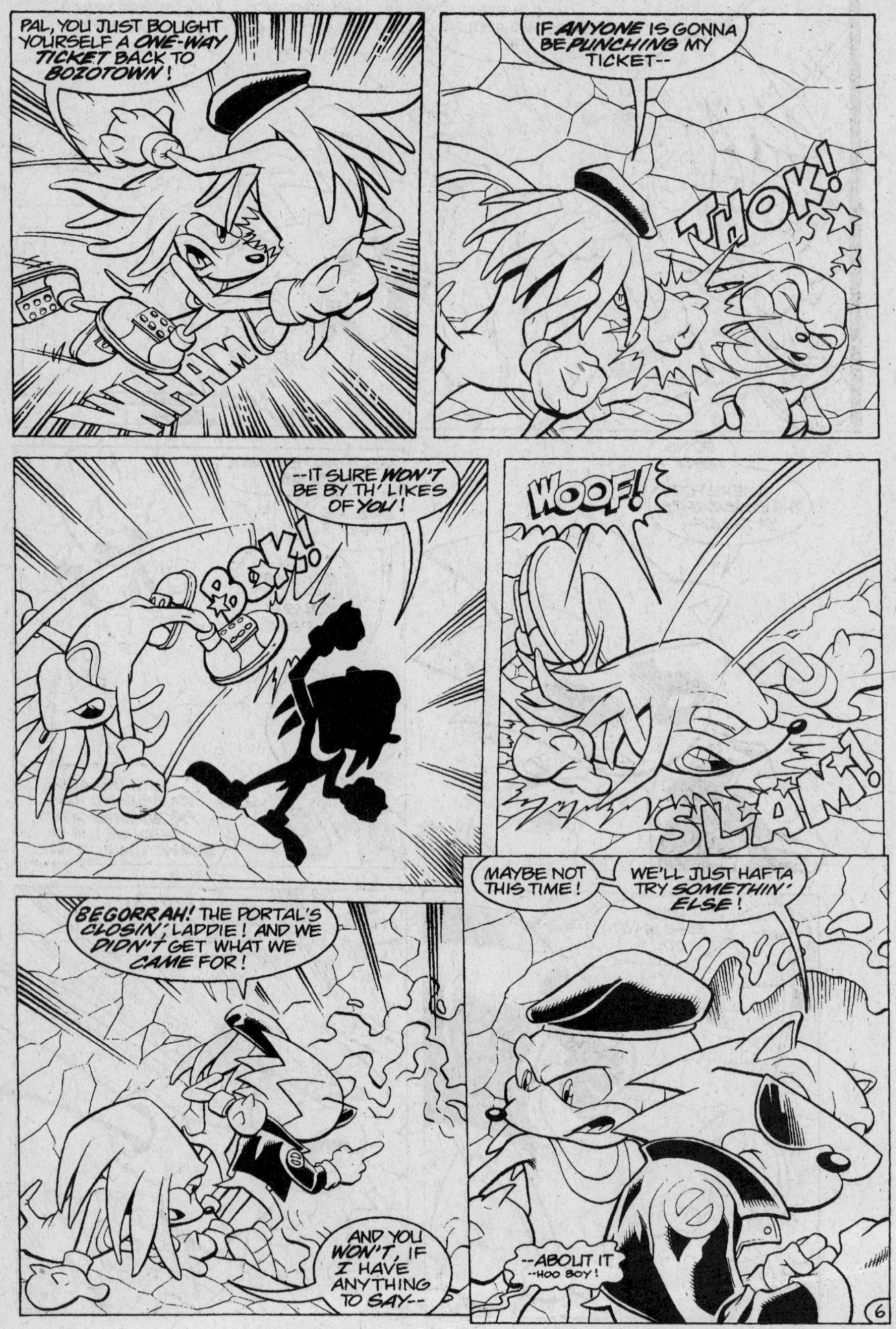
PAL, YOU JUST BOUGHT YOURSELF A ONE-WAY TICKET BACK TO BOZOTOWN!
WHAM
IF ANYONE IS GONNA BE PUNCHING MY TICKET--
THOK!
--IT SURE WON'T BE BY TH' LIKES OF YOU!
BOK!
WOOF!
SLAM!
BEGORRAH! THE PORTAL'S CLOSIN', LADDIE! AND WE DIDN'T GET WHAT WE CAME FOR!
AND YOU WON'T, IF I HAVE ANYTHING TO SAY--
MAYBE NOT THIS TIME!
WE'LL JUST HAFTA TRY SOMETHIN' ELSE!
--ABOUT IT --HOO BOY!
6

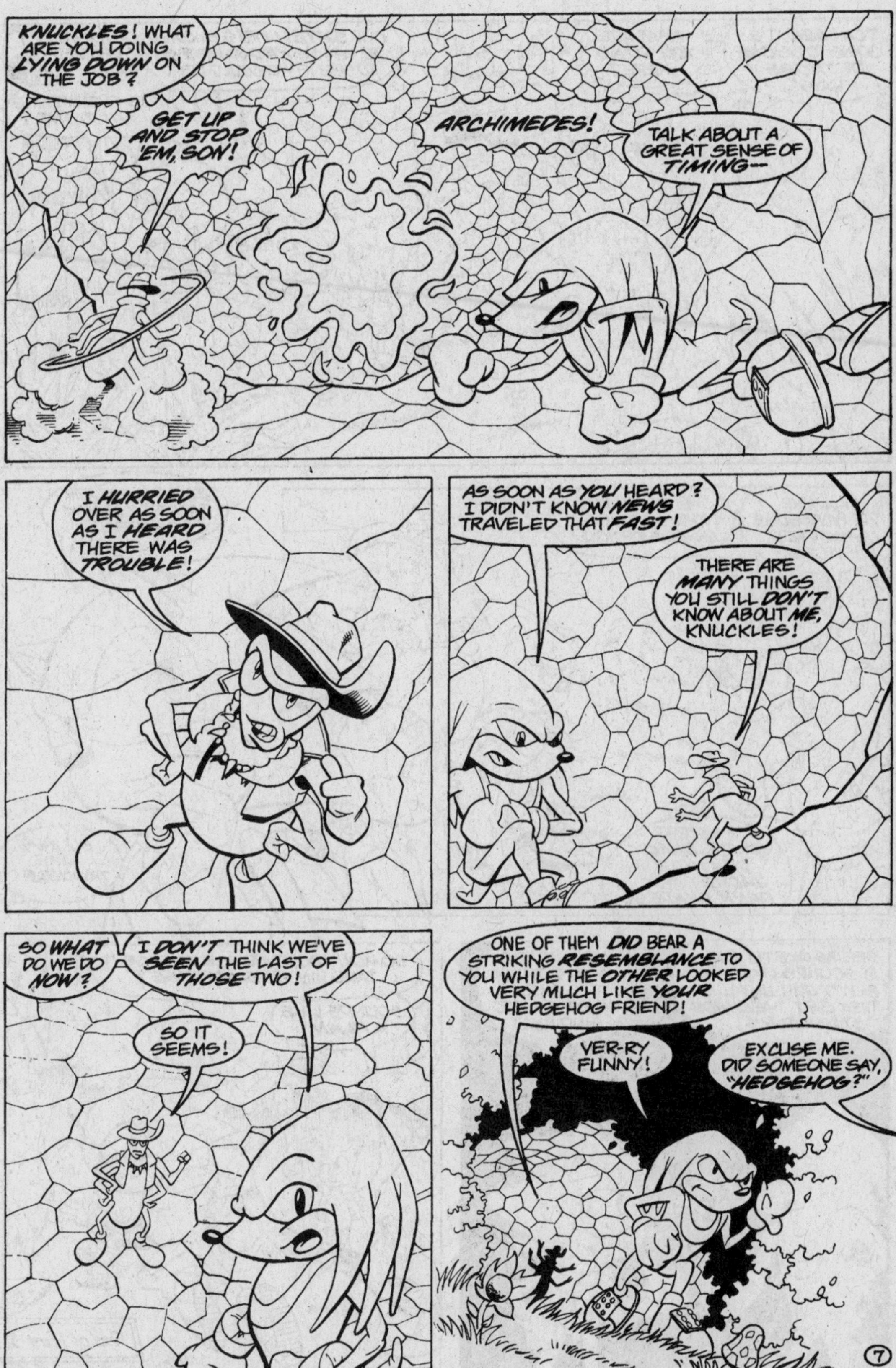
KNUCKLES! WHAT ARE YOU DOING LYING DOWN ON THE JOB?
GET UP AND STOP 'EM, SON!
ARCHIMEDES!
TALK ABOUT A GREAT SENSE OF TIMING--
I HURRIED OVER AS SOON AS I HEARD THERE WAS TROUBLE!
AS SOON AS YOU HEARD? I DIDN'T KNOW NEWS TRAVELED THAT FAST!
THERE ARE MANY THINGS YOU STILL DON'T KNOW ABOUT ME, KNUCKLES!
SO WHAT DO WE DO NOW?
I DON'T THINK WE'VE SEEN THE LAST OF THOSE TWO!
SO IT SEEMS!
ONE OF THEM DID BEAR A STRIKING RESEMBLANCE TO YOU WHILE THE OTHER LOOKED VERY MUCH LIKE YOUR HEDGEHOG FRIEND!
VER-RY FUNNY!
EXCUSE ME. DID SOMEONE SAY, "HEDGEHOG?"
7

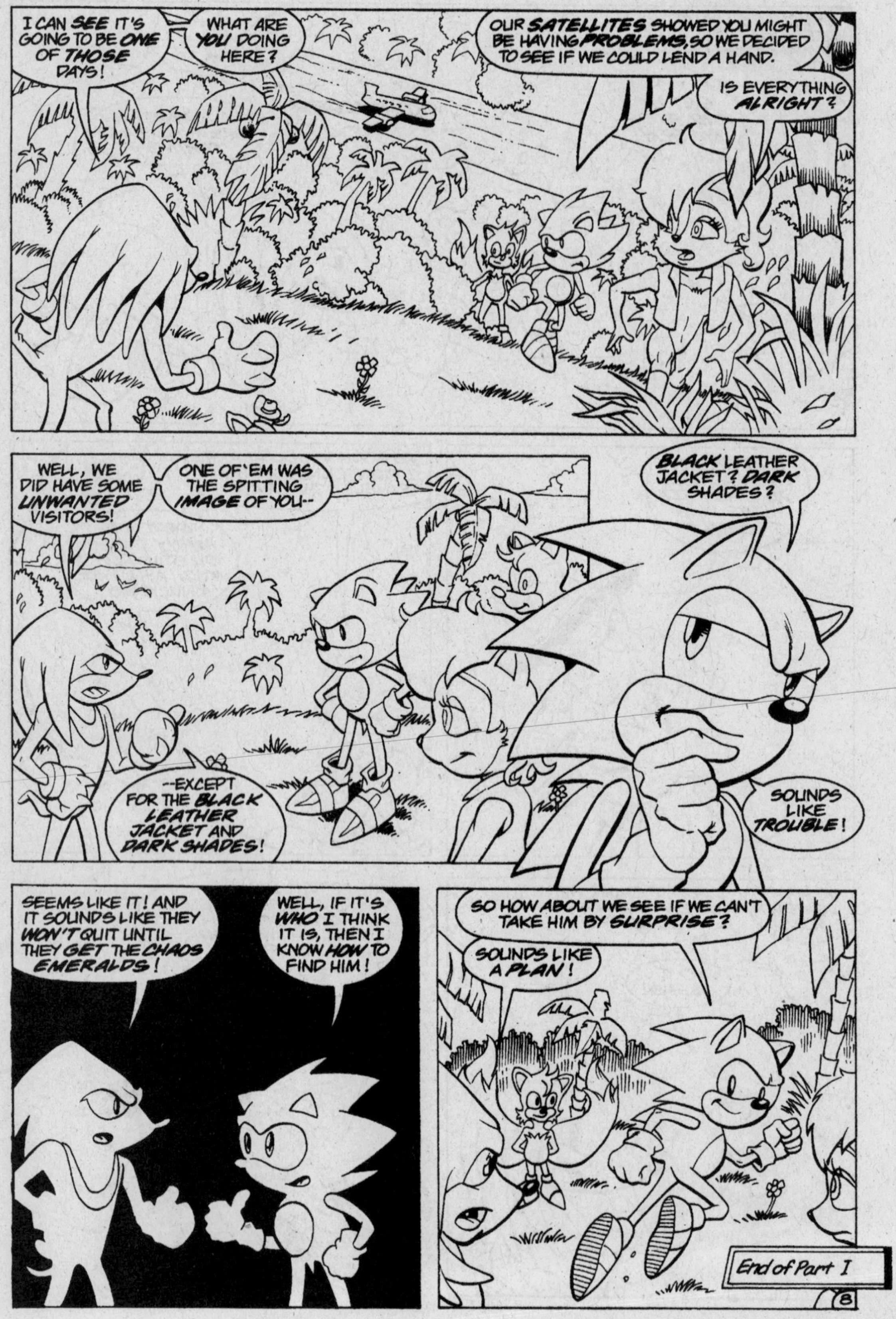

I CAN SEE IT'S GOING TO BE ONE OF THOSE DAYS!
WHAT ARE YOU DOING HERE?
OUR SATELLITES SHOWED YOU MIGHT BE HAVING PROBLEMS, SO WE DECIDED TO SEE IF WE COULD LEND A HAND.
IS EVERYTHING ALRIGHT?
WELL, WE DID HAVE SOME UNWANTED VISITORS!
ONE OF 'EM WAS THE SPITTING IMAGE OF YOU--
--EXCEPT FOR THE BLACK LEATHER JACKET AND DARK SHADES!
BLACK LEATHER JACKET? DARK SHADES?
SOUNDS LIKE TROUBLE!
SEEMS LIKE IT! AND IT SOUNDS LIKE THEY WON'T QUIT UNTIL THEY GET THE CHAOS EMERALDS!
WELL, IF IT'S WHO I THINK IT IS, THEN I KNOW HOW TO FIND HIM!
SO HOW ABOUT WE SEE IF WE CAN'T TAKE HIM BY SURPRISE?
SOUNDS LIKE A PLAN!
End of Part I
8

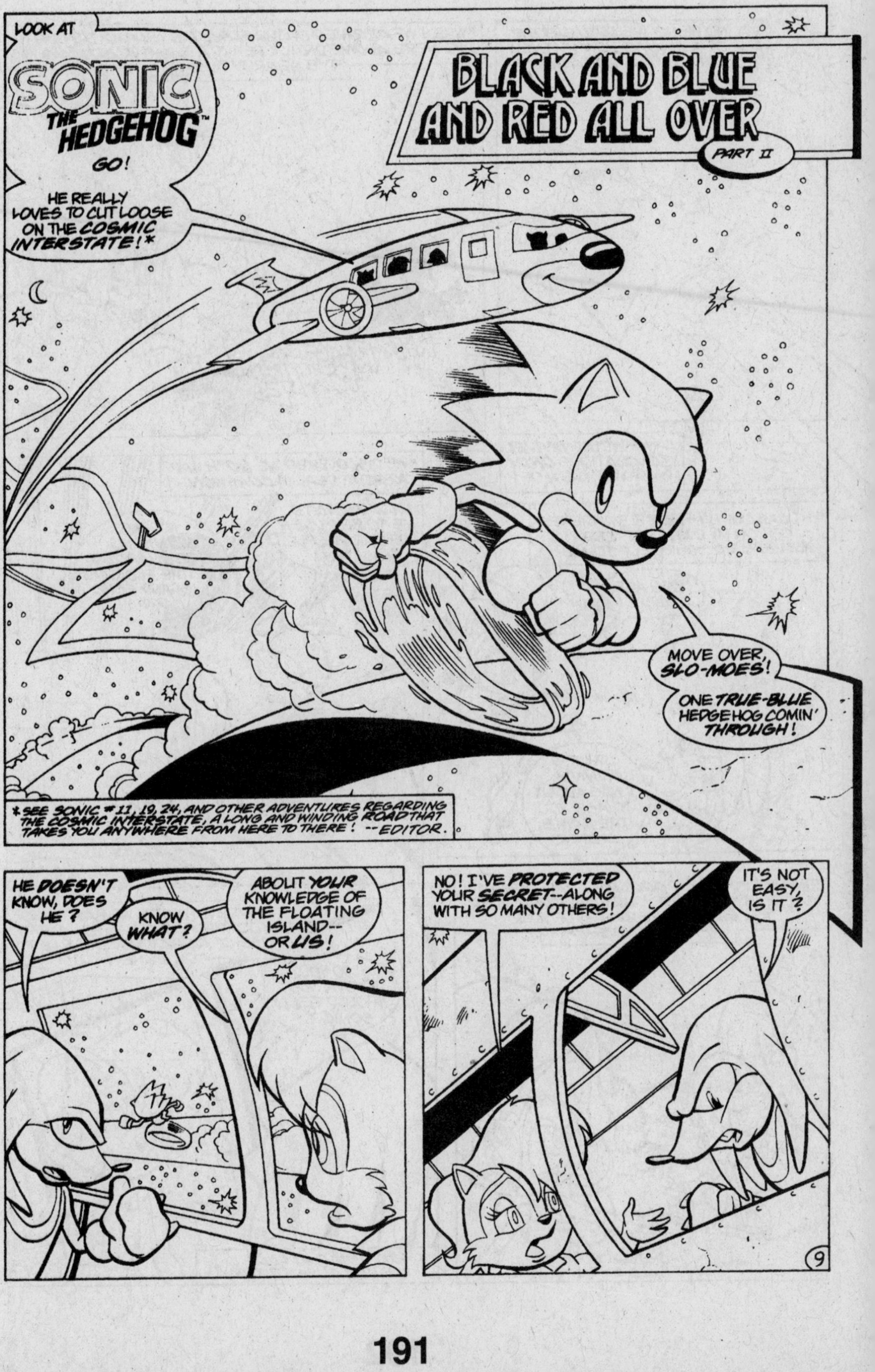
LOOK AT SONIC THE HEDGEHOG GO!
BLACK AND BLUE AND RED ALL OVER
PART II
HE REALLY LOVES TO CUT LOOSE ON THE COSMIC INTERSTATE!*
MOVE OVER, SLO-MOES!
ONE TRUE-BLUE HEDGEHOG COMIN' THROUGH!
*SEE SONIC #11, 19, 24, AND OTHER ADVENTURES REGARDING THE COSMIC INTERSTATE, A LONG AND WINDING ROAD THAT TAKES YOU ANYWHERE FROM HERE TO THERE! --EDITOR.
HE DOESN'T KNOW, DOES HE?
KNOW WHAT?
ABOUT YOUR KNOWLEDGE OF THE FLOATING ISLAND-- OR US!
NO! I'VE PROTECTED YOUR SECRET--ALONG WITH SO MANY OTHERS!
IT'S NOT EASY, IS IT?
9

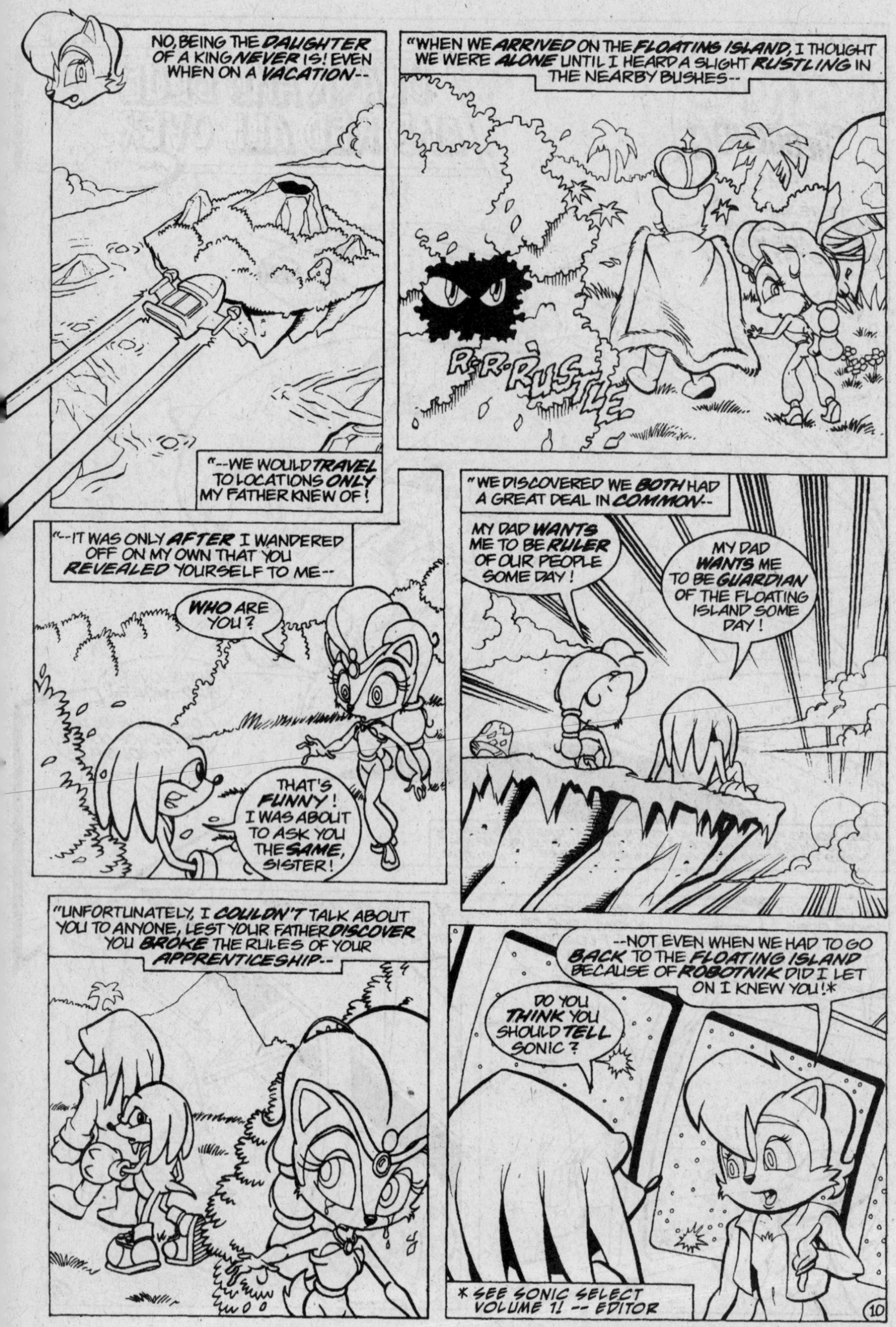
NO, BEING THE DAUGHTER OF A KING NEVER IS! EVEN WHEN ON A VACATION--
"--WE WOULD TRAVEL TO LOCATIONS ONLY MY FATHER KNEW OF!
"WHEN WE ARRIVED ON THE FLOATING ISLAND, I THOUGHT WE WERE ALONE UNTIL I HEARD A SLIGHT RUSTLING IN THE NEARBY BUSHES--
R-R-RUSTLE
"--IT WAS ONLY AFTER I WANDERED OFF ON MY OWN THAT YOU REVEALED YOURSELF TO ME--
WHO ARE YOU?
THAT'S FUNNY! I WAS ABOUT TO ASK YOU THE SAME, SISTER!
"WE DISCOVERED WE BOTH HAD A GREAT DEAL IN COMMON--
MY DAD WANTS ME TO BE RULER OF OUR PEOPLE SOME DAY!
MY DAD WANTS ME TO BE GUARDIAN OF THE FLOATING ISLAND SOME DAY!
"UNFORTUNATELY, I COULDN'T TALK ABOUT YOU TO ANYONE, LEST YOUR FATHER DISCOVER YOU BROKE THE RULES OF YOUR APPRENTICESHIP--
--NOT EVEN WHEN WE HAD TO GO BACK TO THE FLOATING ISLAND BECAUSE OF ROBOTNIK DID I LET ON I KNEW YOU!*
DO YOU THINK YOU SHOULD TELL SONIC?
* SEE SONIC SELECT VOLUME 1! -- EDITOR
10

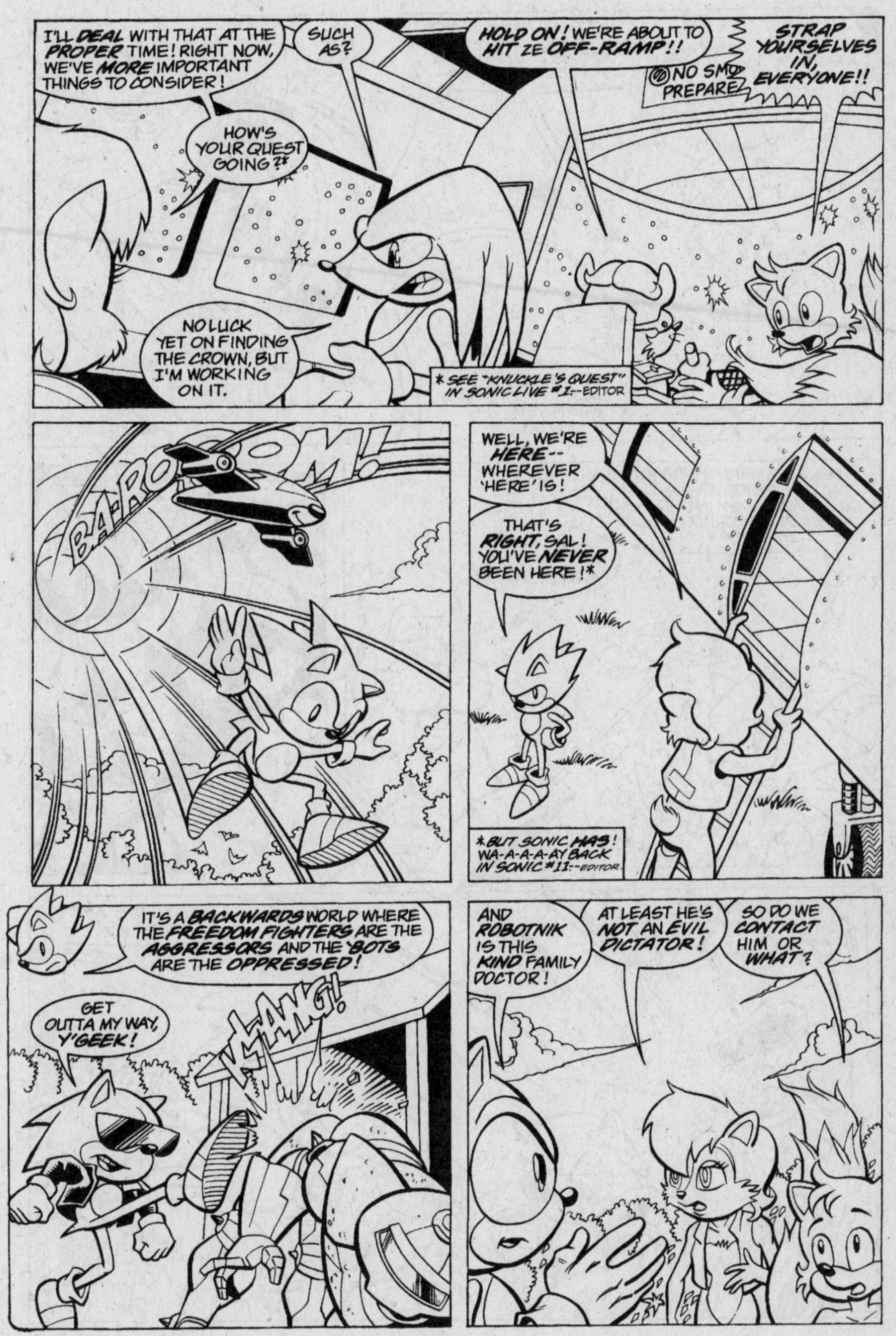
I'LL DEAL WITH THAT AT THE PROPER TIME! RIGHT NOW, WE'VE MORE IMPORTANT THINGS TO CONSIDER!
SUCH AS?
HOW'S YOUR QUEST GOING?*
NO LUCK YET ON FINDING THE CROWN, BUT I'M WORKING ON IT.
*SEE "KNUCKLE'S QUEST" IN SONIC LIVE #1.--EDITOR
HOLD ON! WE'RE ABOUT TO HIT ZE OFF-RAMP!!
STRAP YOURSELVES IN, EVERYONE!!
BA-ROOOM!
WELL, WE'RE HERE-- WHEREVER 'HERE' IS!
THAT'S RIGHT, SAL! YOU'VE NEVER BEEN HERE!*
*BUT SONIC HAS! WA-A-A-AY BACK IN SONIC #11.--EDITOR
IT'S A BACKWARDS WORLD WHERE THE FREEDOM FIGHTERS ARE THE AGGRESSORS AND THE 'BOTS ARE THE OPPRESSED!
GET OUTTA MY WAY, Y'GEEK!
KLANG!
AND ROBOTNIK IS THIS KIND FAMILY DOCTOR!
AT LEAST HE'S NOT AN EVIL DICTATOR!
SO DO WE CONTACT HIM OR WHAT?

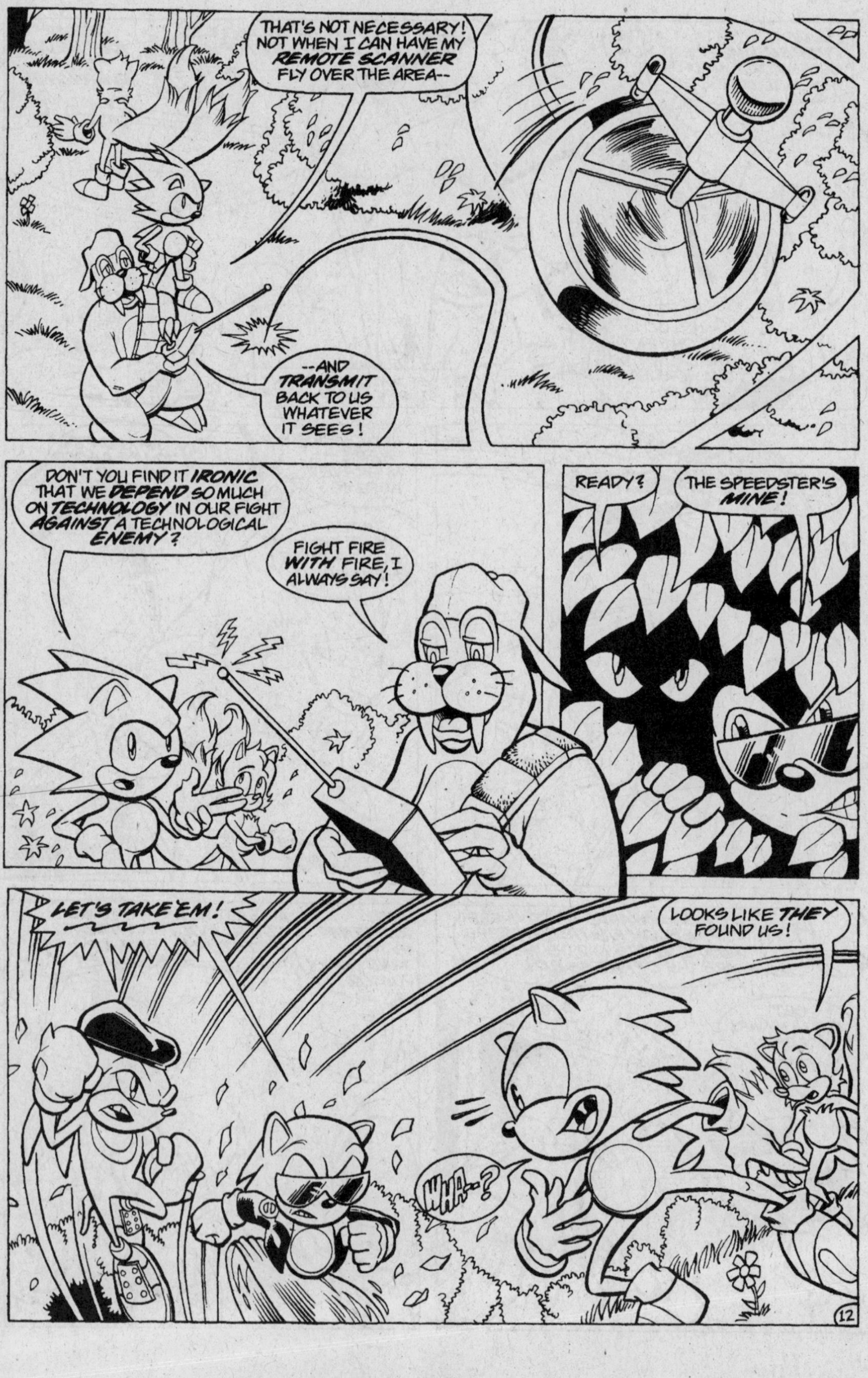
THAT'S NOT NECESSARY! NOT WHEN I CAN HAVE MY REMOTE SCANNER FLY OVER THE AREA--
--AND TRANSMIT BACK TO US WHATEVER IT SEES!
DON'T YOU FIND IT IRONIC THAT WE DEPEND SO MUCH ON TECHNOLOGY IN OUR FIGHT AGAINST A TECHNOLOGICAL ENEMY?
FIGHT FIRE WITH FIRE, I ALWAYS SAY!
READY?
THE SPEEDSTER'S MINE!
LET'S TAKE 'EM!
LOOKS LIKE THEY FOUND US!
WHA-?
12

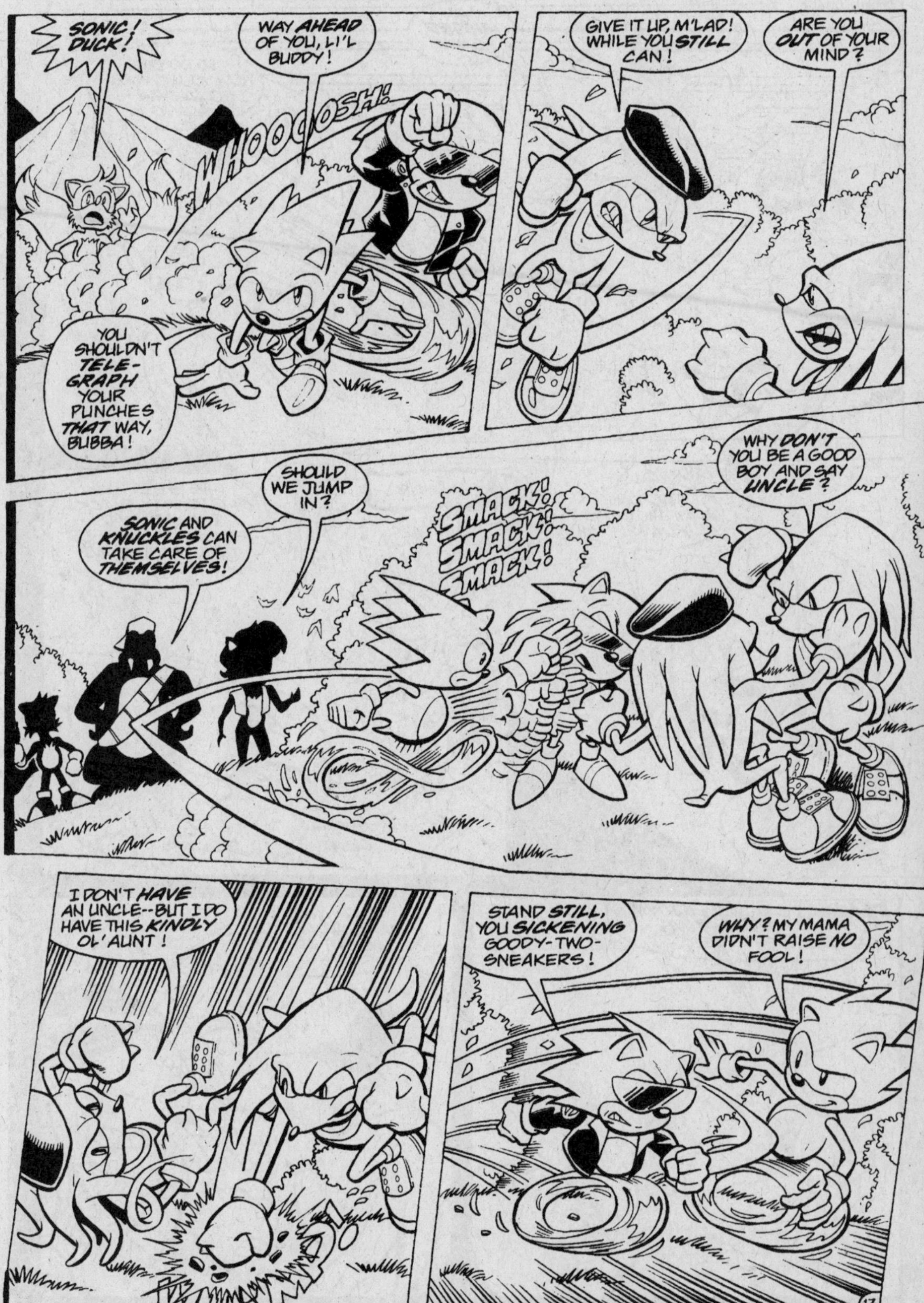
SONIC! DUCK!
WAY AHEAD OF YOU, LI'L BUDDY!
WHOOOOSH!
YOU SHOULDN'T TELE-GRAPH YOUR PUNCHES THAT WAY, BUBBA!
GIVE IT UP, M'LAD! WHILE YOU STILL CAN!
ARE YOU OUT OF YOUR MIND?
SONIC AND KNUCKLES CAN TAKE CARE OF THEMSELVES!
SHOULD WE JUMP IN?
SMACK! SMACK! SMACK!
WHY DON'T YOU BE A GOOD BOY AND SAY UNCLE?
I DON'T HAVE AN UNCLE--BUT I DO HAVE THIS KINDLY OL' AUNT!
WHAMM!
STAND STILL, YOU SICKENING GOODY-TWO-SNEAKERS!
WHY? MY MAMA DIDN'T RAISE NO FOOL!
13

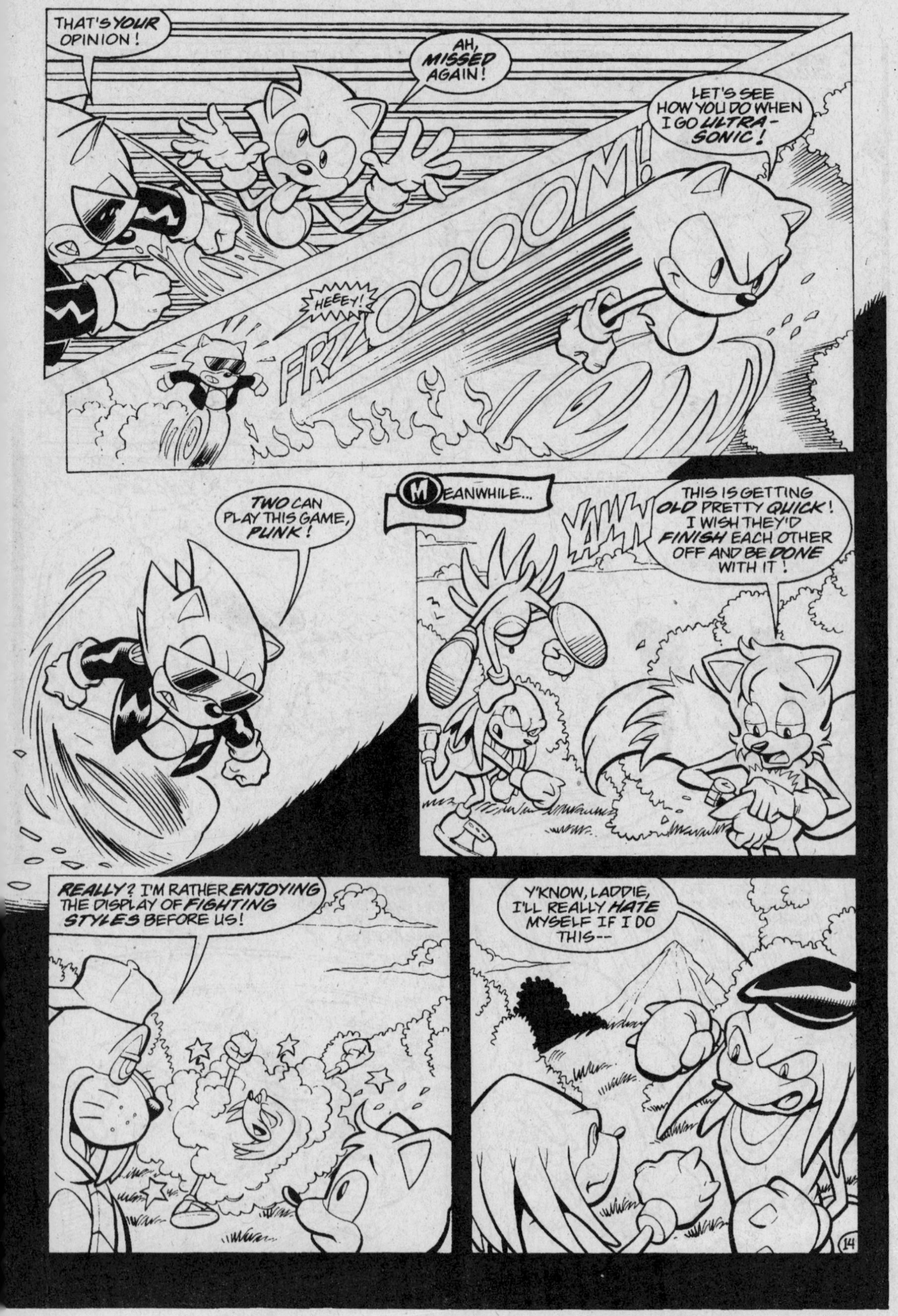
THAT'S YOUR OPINION!
AH, MISSED AGAIN!
LET'S SEE HOW YOU DO WHEN I GO ULTRA-SONIC!
FRZOOOOOM!
HEEEY!
TWO CAN PLAY THIS GAME, PUNK!
MEANWHILE...
YAWN
THIS IS GETTING OLD PRETTY QUICK! I WISH THEY'D FINISH EACH OTHER OFF AND BE DONE WITH IT!
REALLY? I'M RATHER ENJOYING THE DISPLAY OF FIGHTING STYLES BEFORE US!
Y'KNOW, LADDIE, I'LL REALLY HATE MYSELF IF I DO THIS--
14

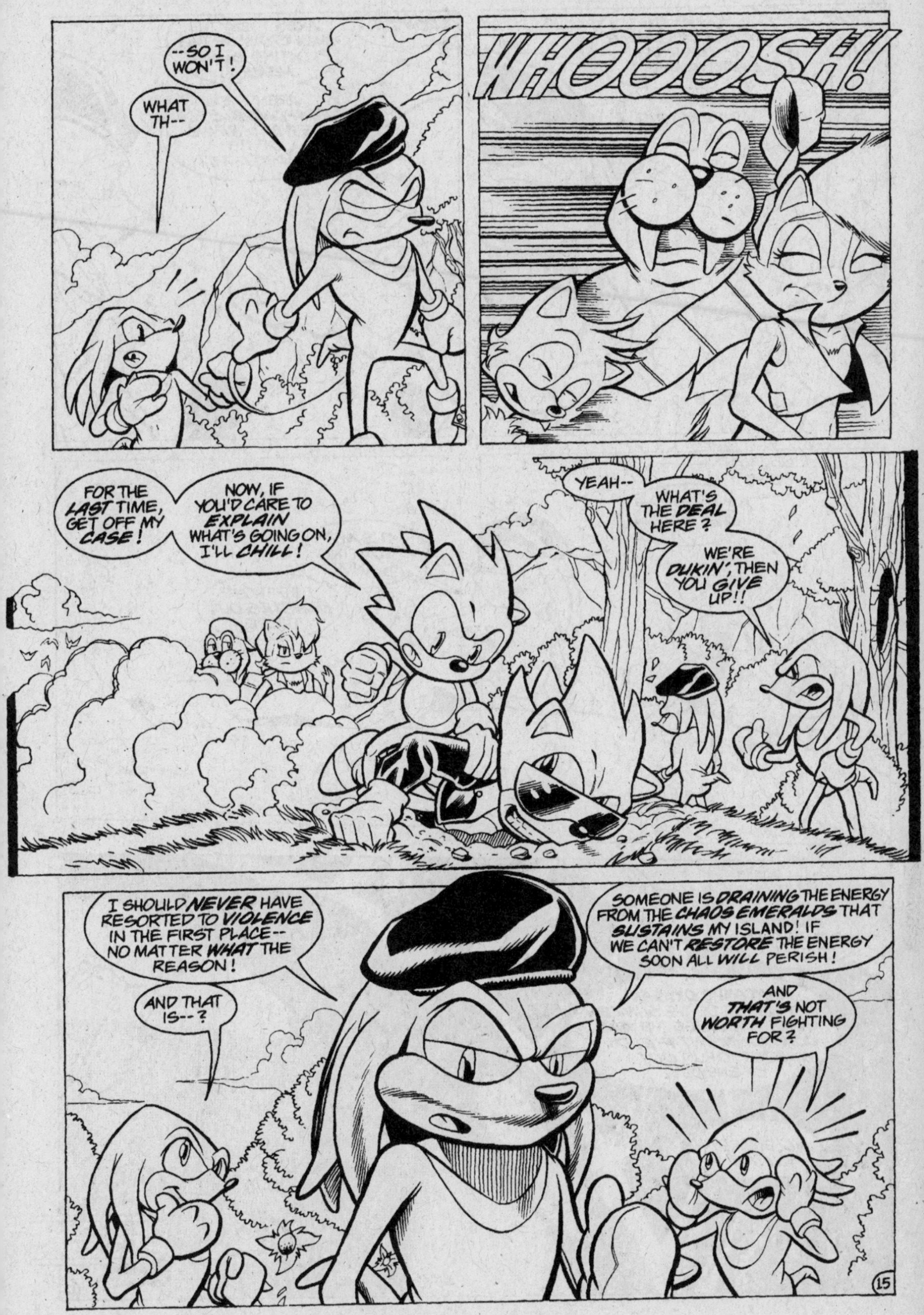
--SO I WON'T!
WHAT TH--
WHOOOOSH!
FOR THE LAST TIME, GET OFF MY CASE!
NOW, IF YOU'D CARE TO EXPLAIN WHAT'S GOING ON, I'LL CHILL!
YEAH--
WHAT'S THE DEAL HERE?
WE'RE DUKIN', THEN YOU GIVE UP!!
I SHOULD NEVER HAVE RESORTED TO VIOLENCE IN THE FIRST PLACE-- NO MATTER WHAT THE REASON!
AND THAT IS--?
SOMEONE IS DRAINING THE ENERGY FROM THE CHAOS EMERALDS THAT SUSTAINS MY ISLAND! IF WE CAN'T RESTORE THE ENERGY SOON ALL WILL PERISH!
AND THAT'S NOT WORTH FIGHTING FOR?
15

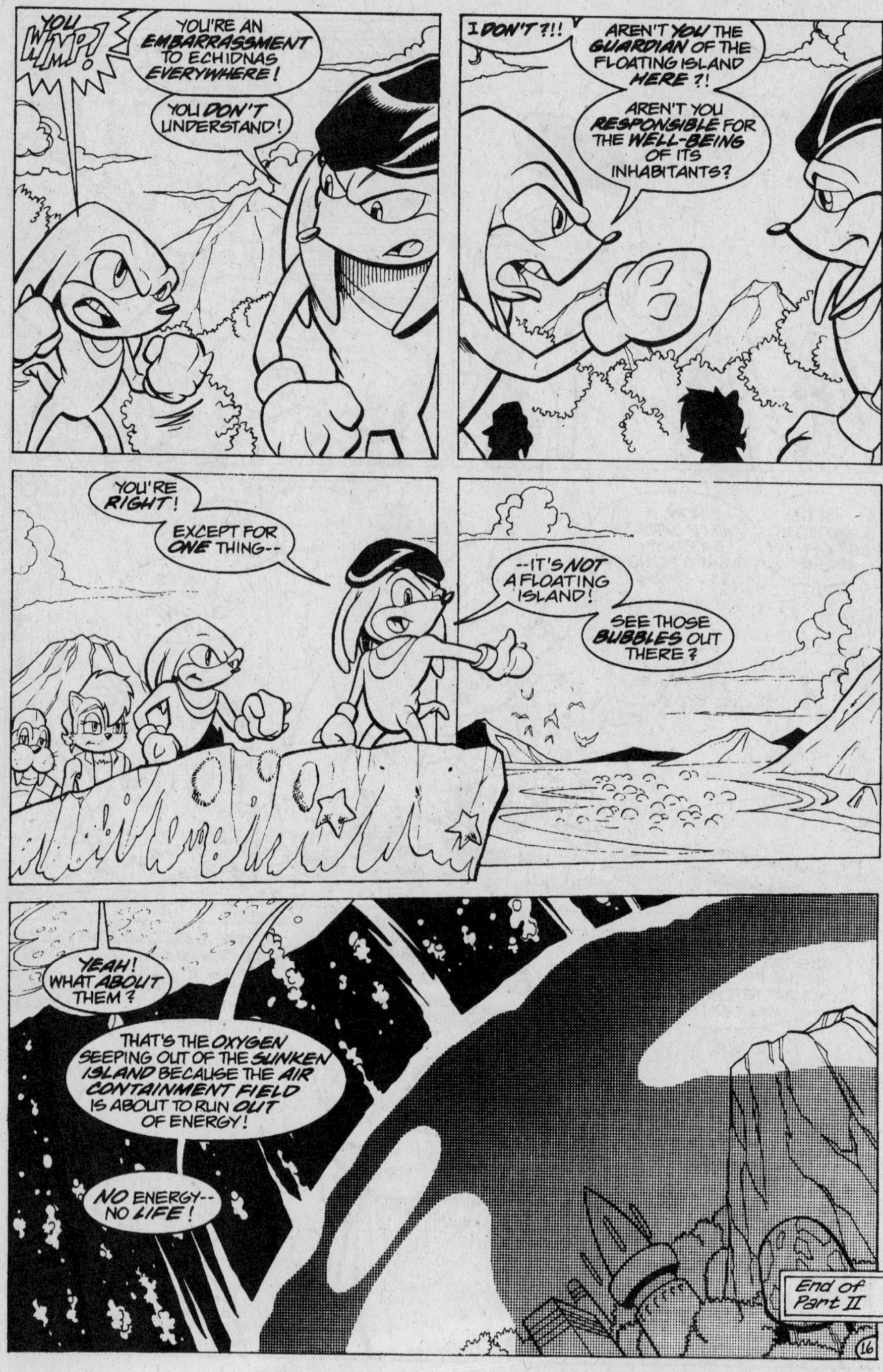
YOU WIMP!
YOU'RE AN EMBARRASSMENT TO ECHIDNAS EVERYWHERE!
YOU DON'T UNDERSTAND!
I DON'T?!!
AREN'T YOU THE GUARDIAN OF THE FLOATING ISLAND HERE?!
AREN'T YOU RESPONSIBLE FOR THE WELL-BEING OF ITS INHABITANTS?
YOU'RE RIGHT!
EXCEPT FOR ONE THING--
--IT'S NOT A FLOATING ISLAND!
SEE THOSE BUBBLES OUT THERE?
YEAH! WHAT ABOUT THEM?
THAT'S THE OXYGEN SEEPING OUT OF THE SUNKEN ISLAND BECAUSE THE AIR CONTAINMENT FIELD IS ABOUT TO RUN OUT OF ENERGY!
NO ENERGY-- NO LIFE!
End of Part II
16

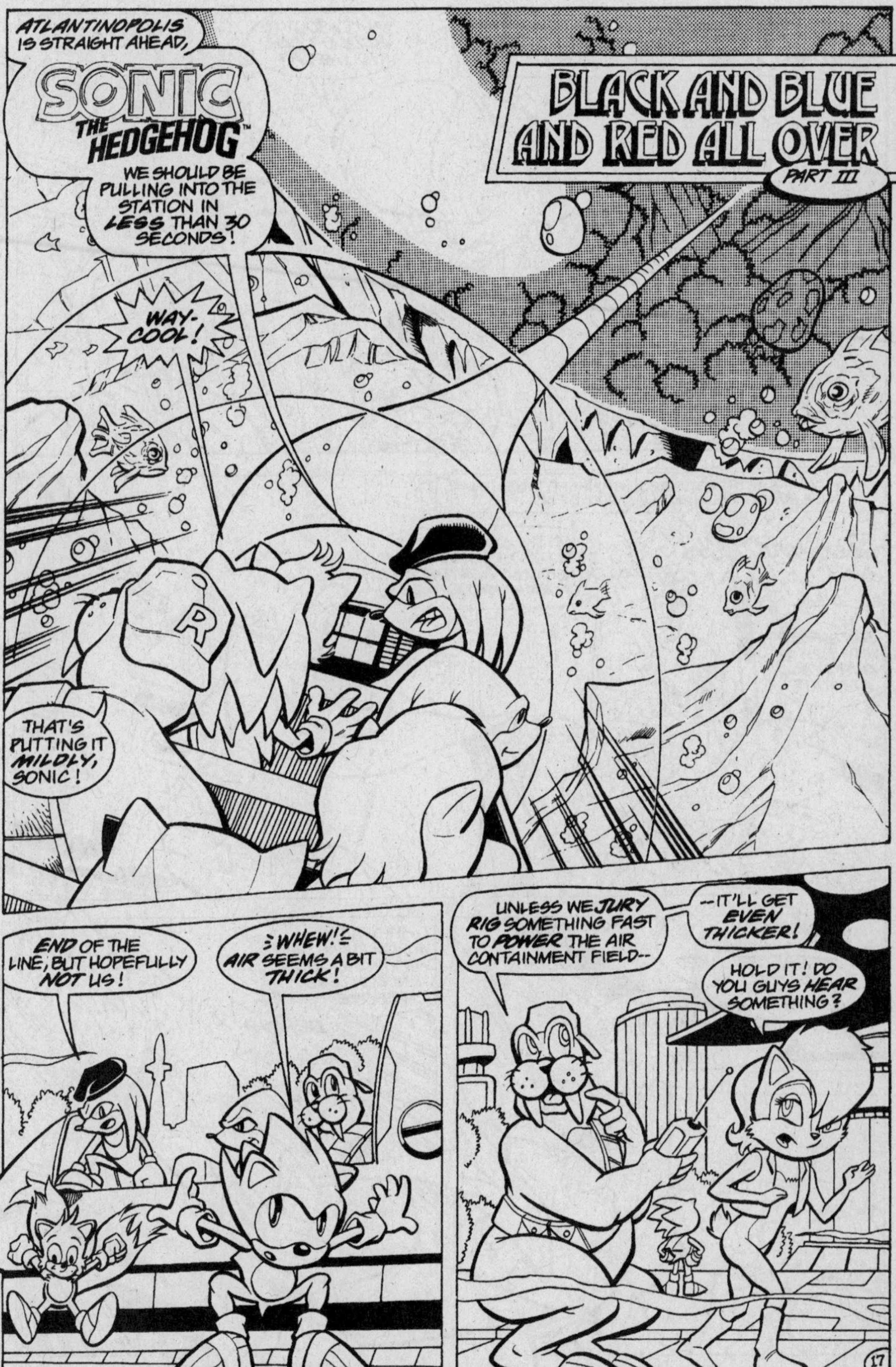
ATLANTINOPOLIS IS STRAIGHT AHEAD,
SONIC THE HEDGEHOG™
BLACK AND BLUE AND RED ALL OVER
PART III
WE SHOULD BE PULLING INTO THE STATION IN LESS THAN 30 SECONDS!
WAY-COOL!
THAT'S PUTTING IT MILDLY, SONIC!
END OF THE LINE, BUT HOPEFULLY NOT US!
WHEW! AIR SEEMS A BIT THICK!
UNLESS WE JURY RIG SOMETHING FAST TO POWER THE AIR CONTAINMENT FIELD--
--IT'LL GET EVEN THICKER!
HOLD IT! DO YOU GUYS HEAR SOMETHING?
17

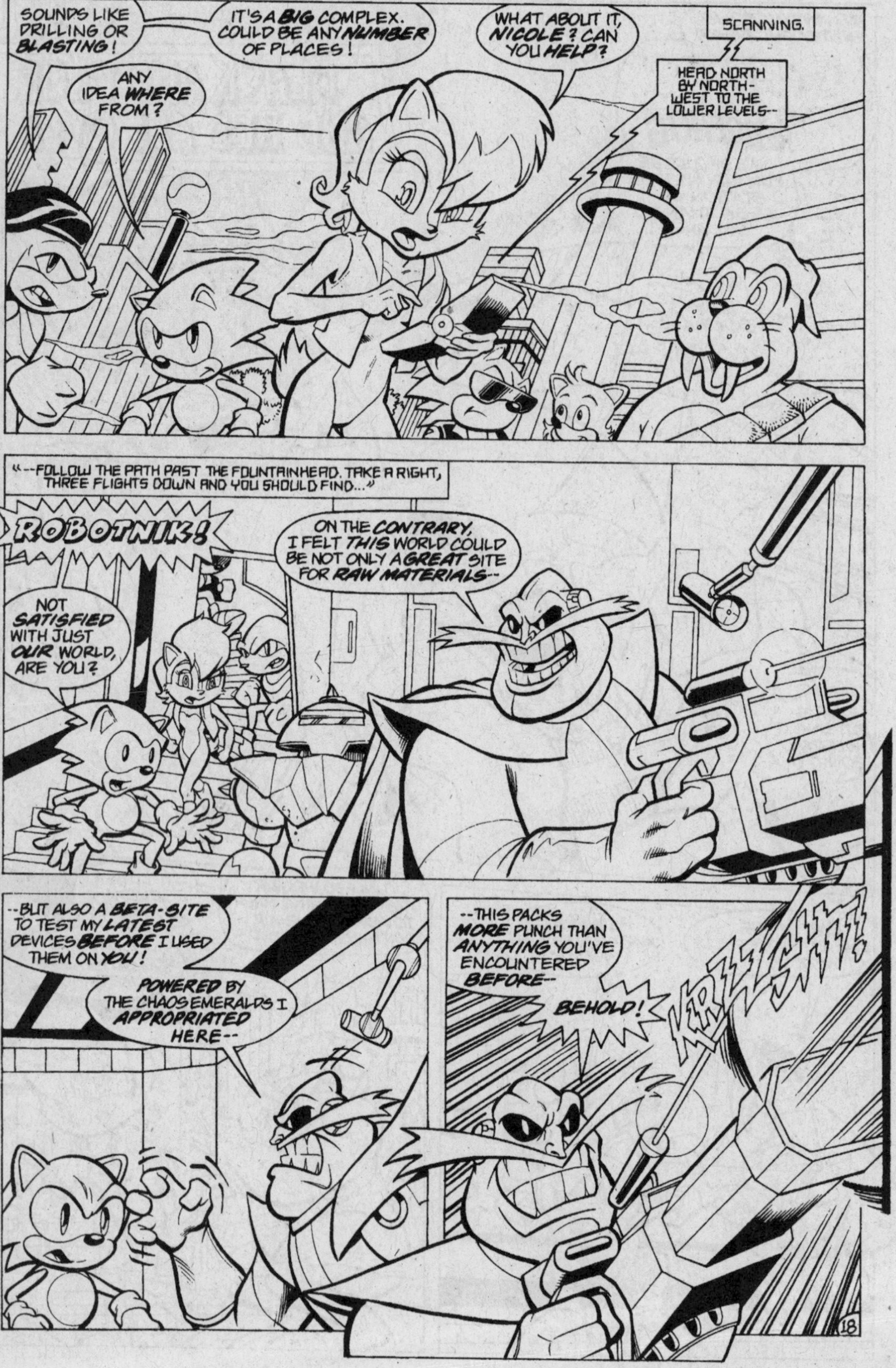
SOUNDS LIKE DRILLING OR BLASTING!
ANY IDEA WHERE FROM?
IT'S A BIG COMPLEX. COULD BE ANY NUMBER OF PLACES!
WHAT ABOUT IT, NICOLE? CAN YOU HELP?
SCANNING.
HEAD NORTH BY NORTH-WEST TO THE LOWER LEVELS--
"--FOLLOW THE PATH PAST THE FOUNTAINHEAD. TAKE A RIGHT, THREE FLIGHTS DOWN AND YOU SHOULD FIND..."
ROBOTNIK!
NOT SATISFIED WITH JUST OUR WORLD, ARE YOU?
ON THE CONTRARY, I FELT THIS WORLD COULD BE NOT ONLY A GREAT SITE FOR RAW MATERIALS--
--BUT ALSO A BETA-SITE TO TEST MY LATEST DEVICES BEFORE I USED THEM ON YOU!
POWERED BY THE CHAOS EMERALDS I APPROPRIATED HERE--
--THIS PACKS MORE PUNCH THAN ANYTHING YOU'VE ENCOUNTERED BEFORE--
BEHOLD!
KRZZSHH!
18

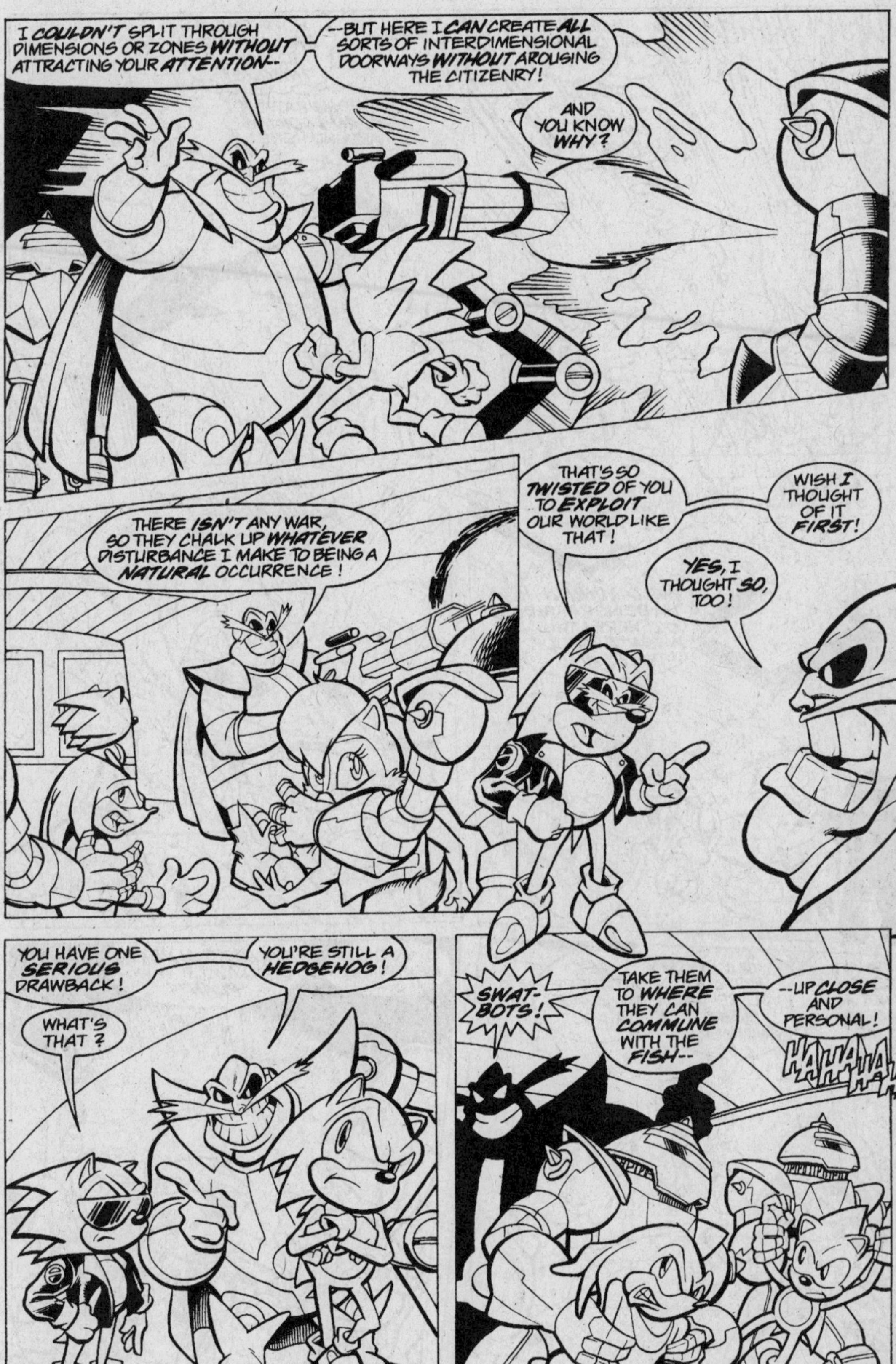
I COULDN'T SPLIT THROUGH DIMENSIONS OR ZONES WITHOUT ATTRACTING YOUR ATTENTION--
--BUT HERE I CAN CREATE ALL SORTS OF INTERDIMENSIONAL DOORWAYS WITHOUT AROUSING THE CITIZENRY!
AND YOU KNOW WHY?
THERE ISN'T ANY WAR, SO THEY CHALK UP WHATEVER DISTURBANCE I MAKE TO BEING A NATURAL OCCURRENCE!
THAT'S SO TWISTED OF YOU TO EXPLOIT OUR WORLD LIKE THAT!
WISH I THOUGHT OF IT FIRST!
YES, I THOUGHT SO, TOO!
YOU HAVE ONE SERIOUS DRAWBACK!
WHAT'S THAT?
YOU'RE STILL A HEDGEHOG!
SWAT-BOTS!
TAKE THEM TO WHERE THEY CAN COMMUNE WITH THE FISH--
--UP CLOSE AND PERSONAL!
HAHAHAHAHA
19

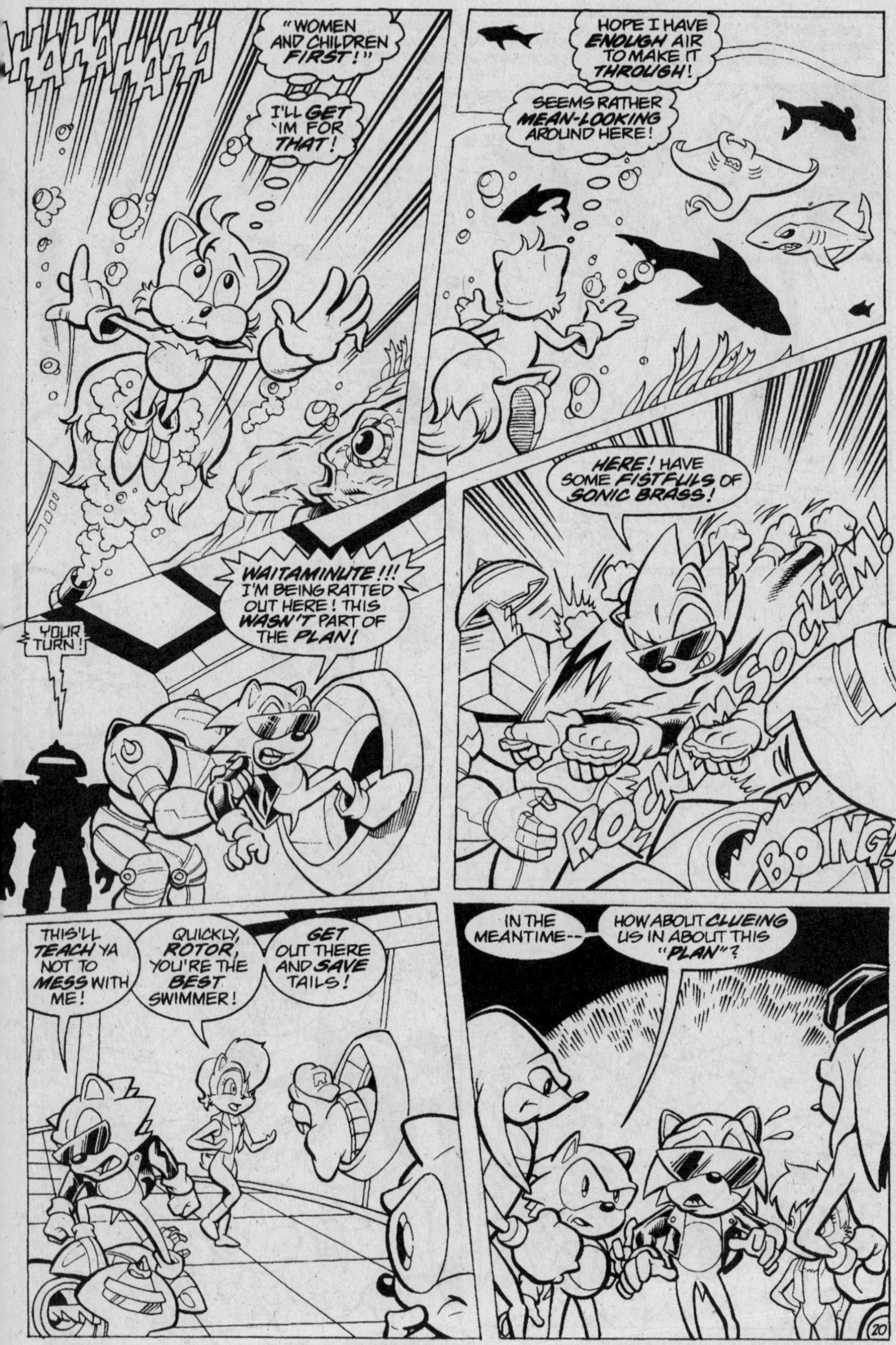

HAHAHAHA
"WOMEN AND CHILDREN FIRST!"
I'LL GET 'IM FOR THAT!
HOPE I HAVE ENOUGH AIR TO MAKE IT THROUGH!
SEEMS RATHER MEAN-LOOKING AROUND HERE!
WAITAMINUTE!!! I'M BEING RATTED OUT HERE! THIS WASN'T PART OF THE PLAN!
YOUR TURN!
HERE! HAVE SOME FISTFULS OF SONIC BRASS!
SOCKEM!
ROCK
BOING!
THIS'LL TEACH YA NOT TO MESS WITH ME!
QUICKLY, ROTOR, YOU'RE THE BEST SWIMMER!
GET OUT THERE AND SAVE TAILS!
IN THE MEANTIME--
HOW ABOUT CLUEING US IN ABOUT THIS "PLAN"?
20

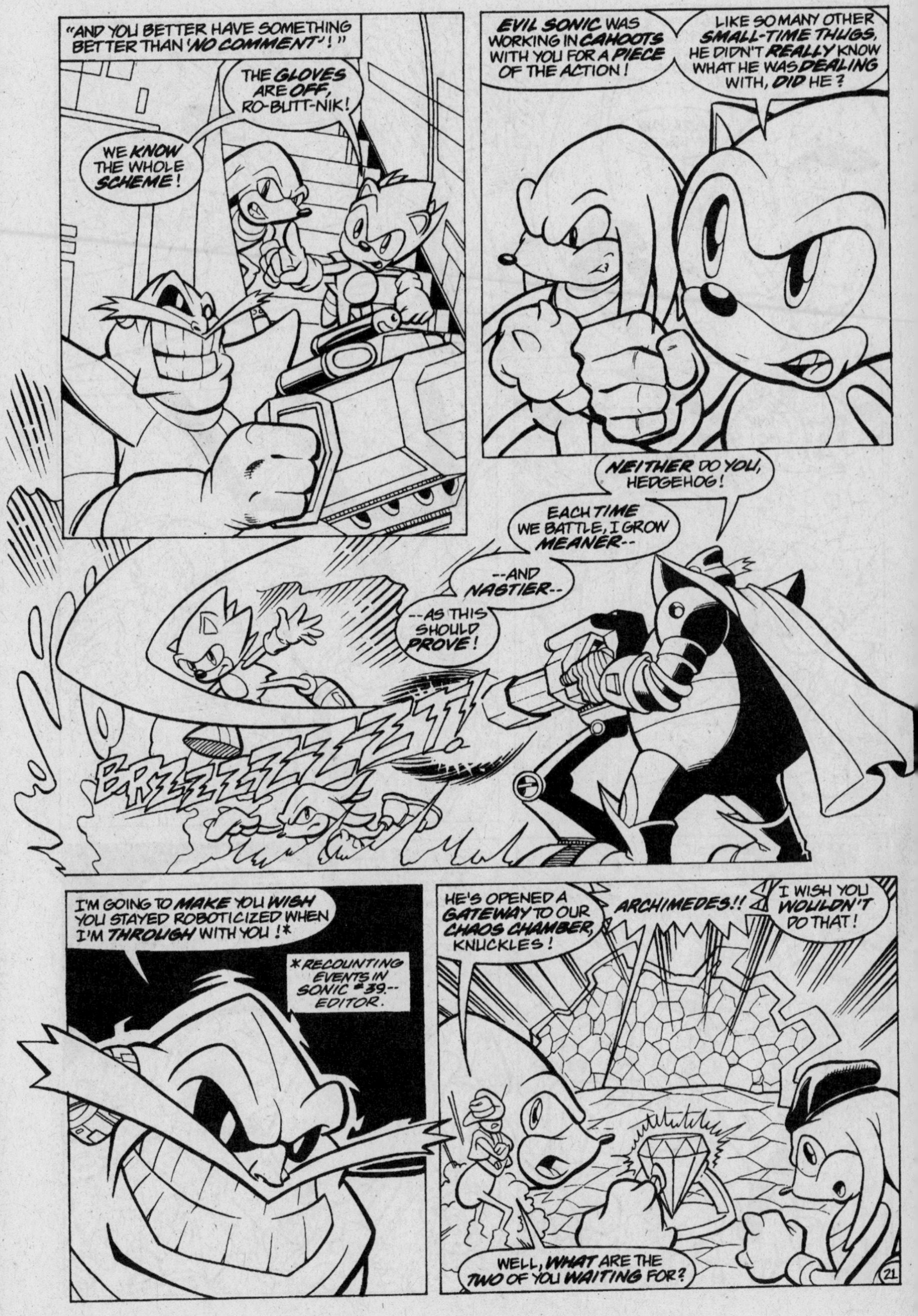

"AND YOU BETTER HAVE SOMETHING BETTER THAN 'NO COMMENT'!"
THE GLOVES ARE OFF, RO-BUTT-NIK!
WE KNOW THE WHOLE SCHEME!
EVIL SONIC WAS WORKING IN CAHOOTS WITH YOU FOR A PIECE OF THE ACTION!
LIKE SO MANY OTHER SMALL-TIME THUGS, HE DIDN'T REALLY KNOW WHAT HE WAS DEALING WITH, DID HE?
NEITHER DO YOU, HEDGEHOG!
EACH TIME WE BATTLE, I GROW MEANER--
--AND NASTIER--
--AS THIS SHOULD PROVE!
BRZZZZZZZZZT!
I'M GOING TO MAKE YOU WISH YOU STAYED ROBOTICIZED WHEN I'M THROUGH WITH YOU!*
*RECOUNTING EVENTS IN SONIC #39.-- EDITOR.
HE'S OPENED A GATEWAY TO OUR CHAOS CHAMBER, KNUCKLES!
ARCHIMEDES!!
I WISH YOU WOULDN'T DO THAT!
WELL, WHAT ARE THE TWO OF YOU WAITING FOR?
21

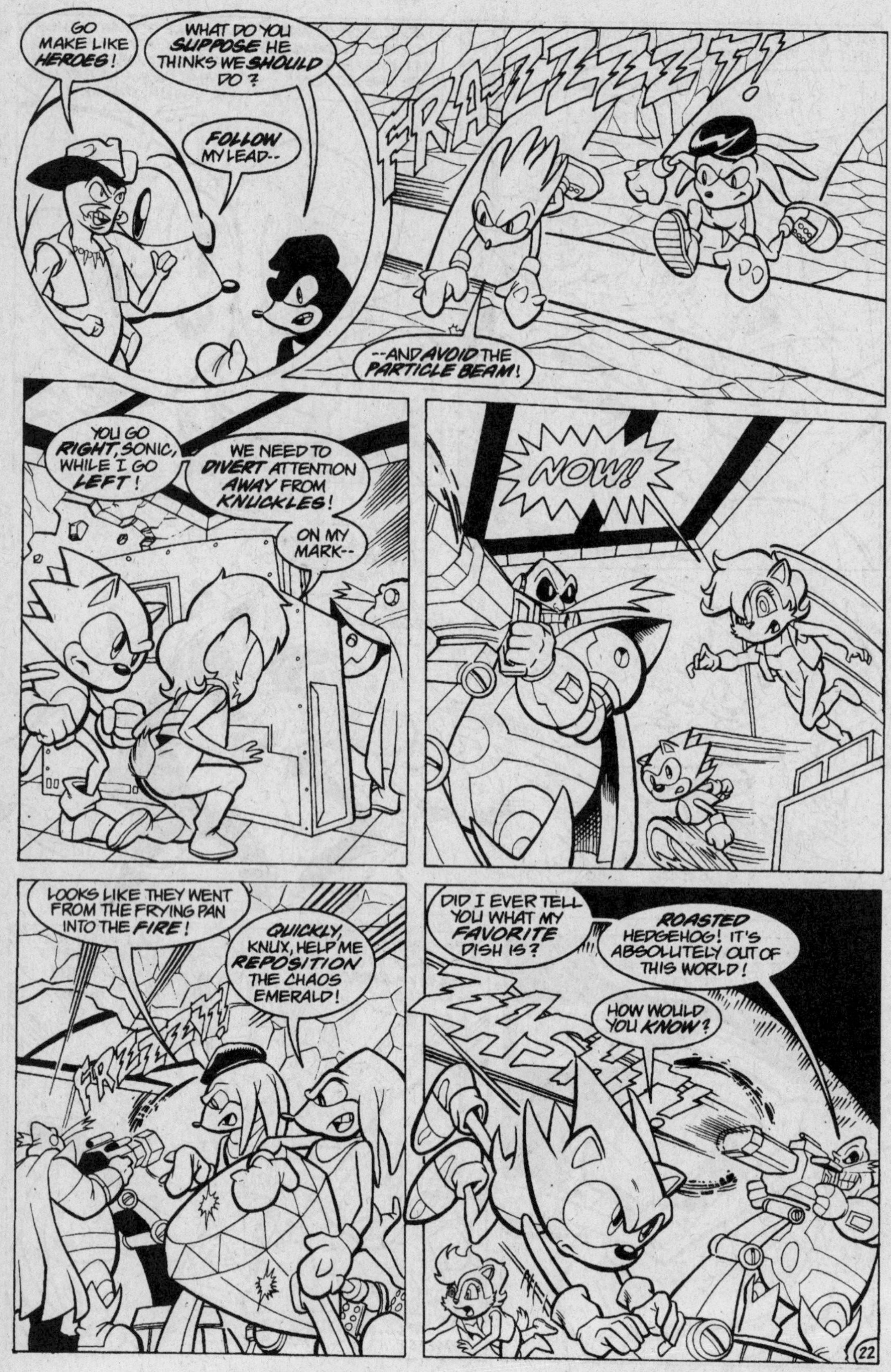

GO MAKE LIKE HEROES!
WHAT DO YOU SUPPOSE HE THINKS WE SHOULD DO?
FOLLOW MY LEAD--
FRA-ZZZZZT!
--AND AVOID THE PARTICLE BEAM!
YOU GO RIGHT, SONIC, WHILE I GO LEFT!
WE NEED TO DIVERT ATTENTION AWAY FROM KNUCKLES!
ON MY MARK--
NOW!
LOOKS LIKE THEY WENT FROM THE FRYING PAN INTO THE FIRE!
QUICKLY, KNUX, HELP ME REPOSITION THE CHAOS EMERALD!
DID I EVER TELL YOU WHAT MY FAVORITE DISH IS?
ROASTED HEDGEHOG! IT'S ABSOLUTELY OUT OF THIS WORLD!
HOW WOULD YOU KNOW?
22

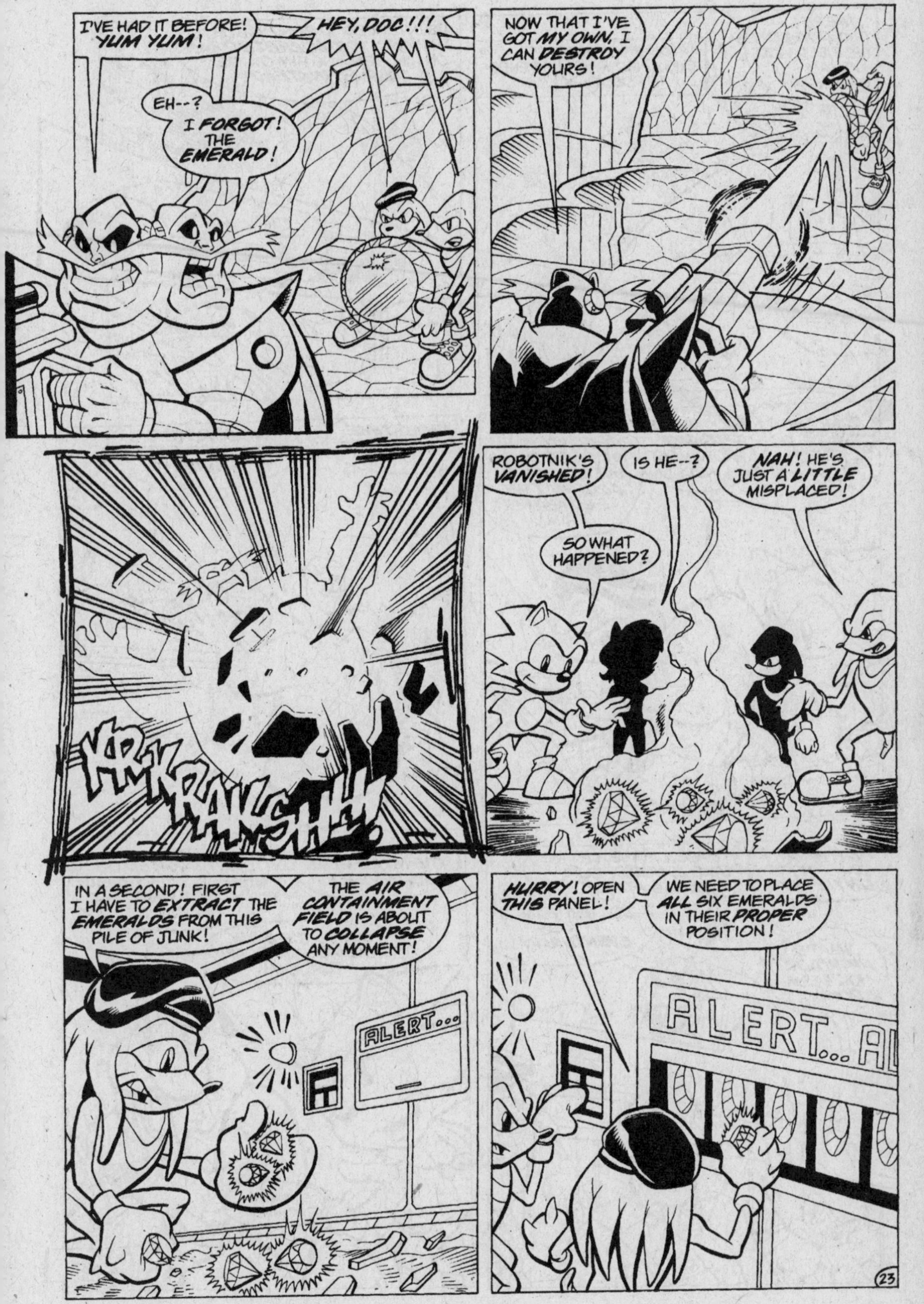

I'VE HAD IT BEFORE! YUM YUM!
HEY, DOC!!!
EH--? I FORGOT! THE EMERALD!
NOW THAT I'VE GOT MY OWN, I CAN DESTROY YOURS!
ROBOTNIK'S VANISHED!
SO WHAT HAPPENED?
IS HE--?
NAH! HE'S JUST A LITTLE MISPLACED!
IN A SECOND! FIRST I HAVE TO EXTRACT THE EMERALDS FROM THIS PILE OF JUNK!
THE AIR CONTAINMENT FIELD IS ABOUT TO COLLAPSE ANY MOMENT!
ALERT...
HURRY! OPEN THIS PANEL!
WE NEED TO PLACE ALL SIX EMERALDS IN THEIR PROPER POSITION!
23

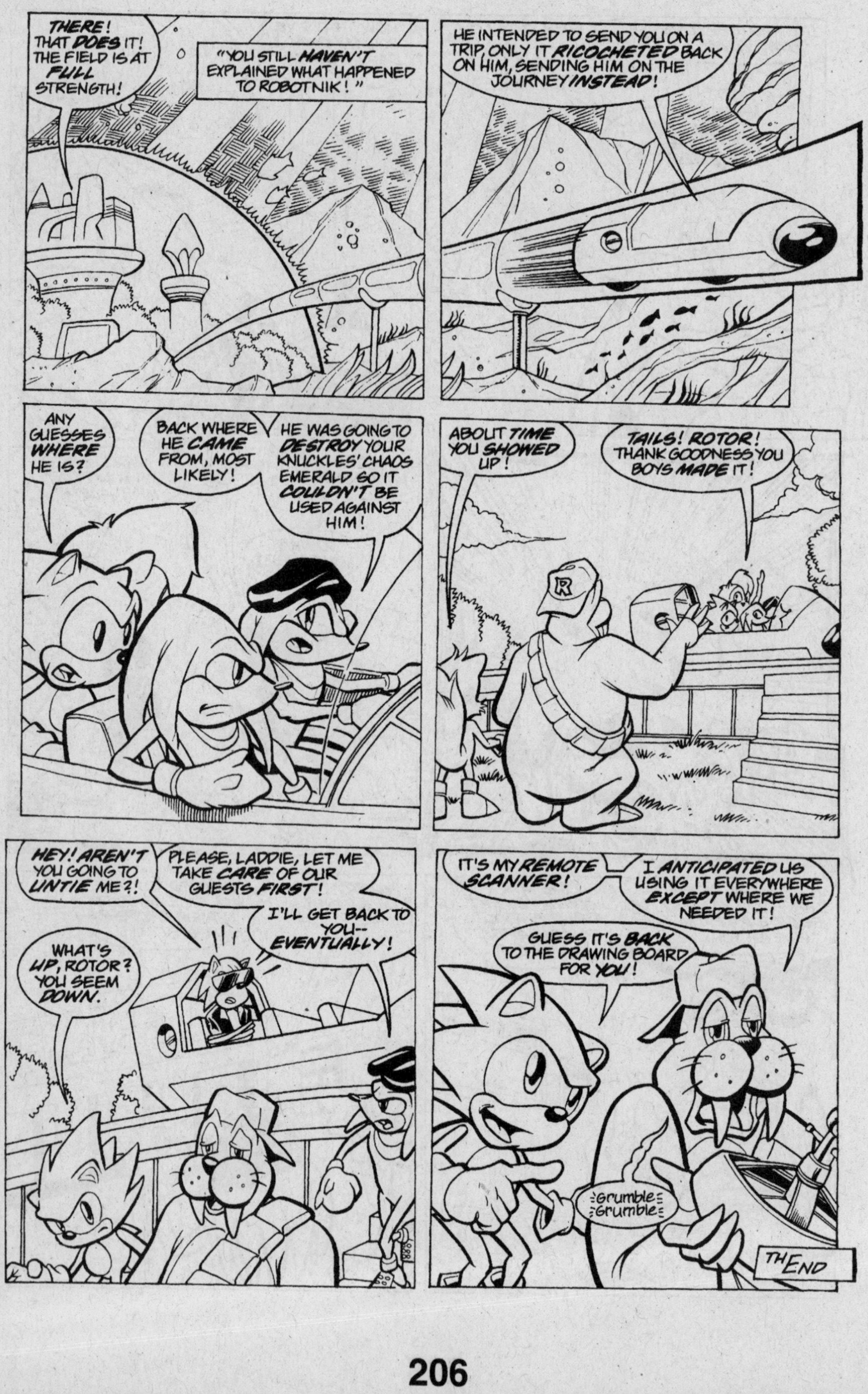
THERE! THAT DOES IT! THE FIELD IS AT FULL STRENGTH!
"YOU STILL HAVEN'T EXPLAINED WHAT HAPPENED TO ROBOTNIK!"
HE INTENDED TO SEND YOU ON A TRIP, ONLY IT RICOCHETED BACK ON HIM, SENDING HIM ON THE JOURNEY INSTEAD!
ANY GUESSES WHERE HE IS?
BACK WHERE HE CAME FROM, MOST LIKELY!
HE WAS GOING TO DESTROY YOUR KNUCKLES' CHAOS EMERALD SO IT COULDN'T BE USED AGAINST HIM!
ABOUT TIME YOU SHOWED UP!
TAILS! ROTOR! THANK GOODNESS YOU BOYS MADE IT!
HEY! AREN'T YOU GOING TO UNTIE ME?!
PLEASE, LADDIE, LET ME TAKE CARE OF OUR GUESTS FIRST!
I'LL GET BACK TO YOU-- EVENTUALLY!
WHAT'S UP, ROTOR? YOU SEEM DOWN.
IT'S MY REMOTE SCANNER!
I ANTICIPATED US USING IT EVERYWHERE EXCEPT WHERE WE NEEDED IT!
GUESS IT'S BACK TO THE DRAWING BOARD FOR YOU!
Grumble Grumble
THE END

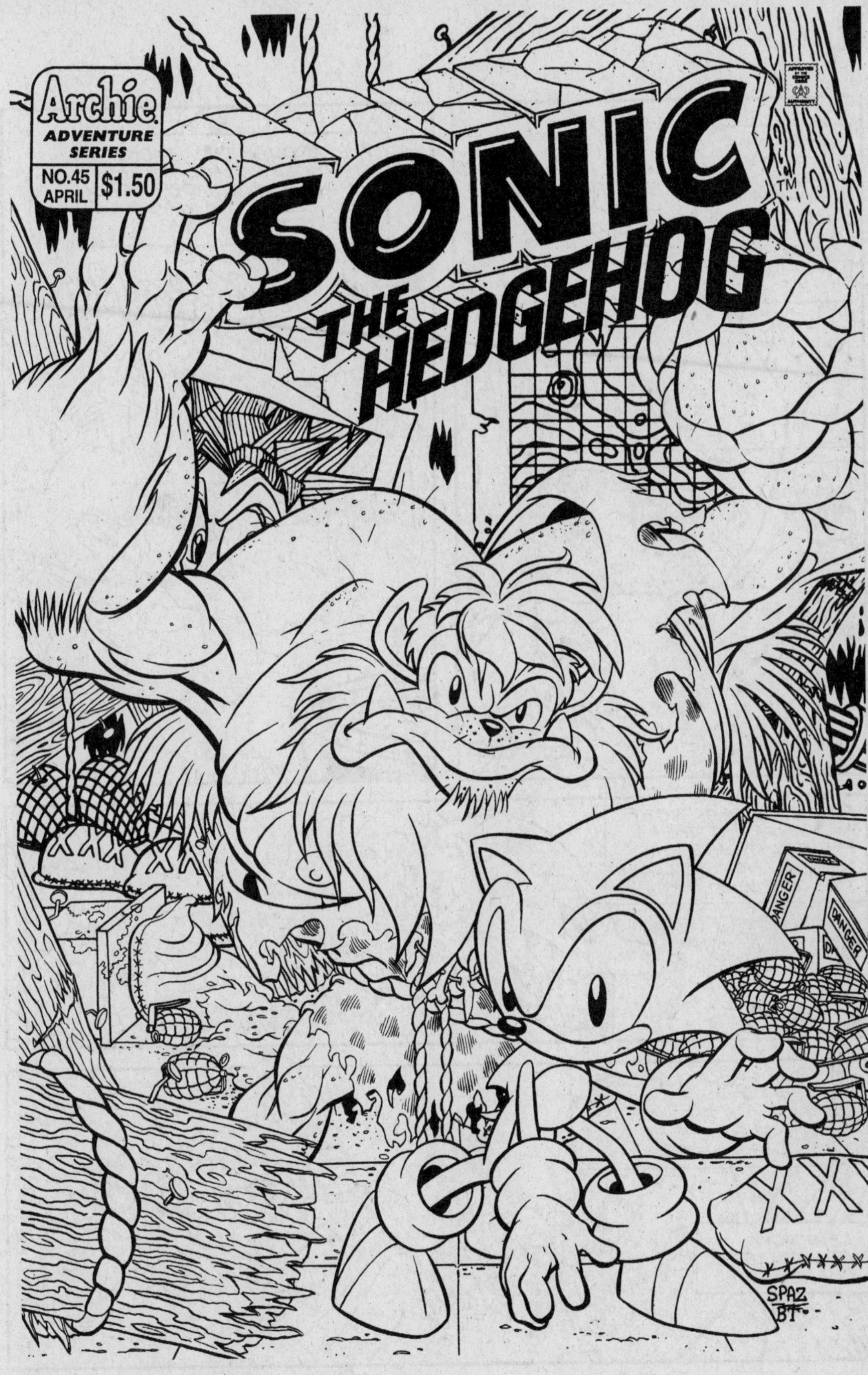
Archie
ADVENTURE SERIES
NO.45 APRIL
$1.50
SONIC THE HEDGEHOG
TM
DANGER
DANGER
SPAZ BT

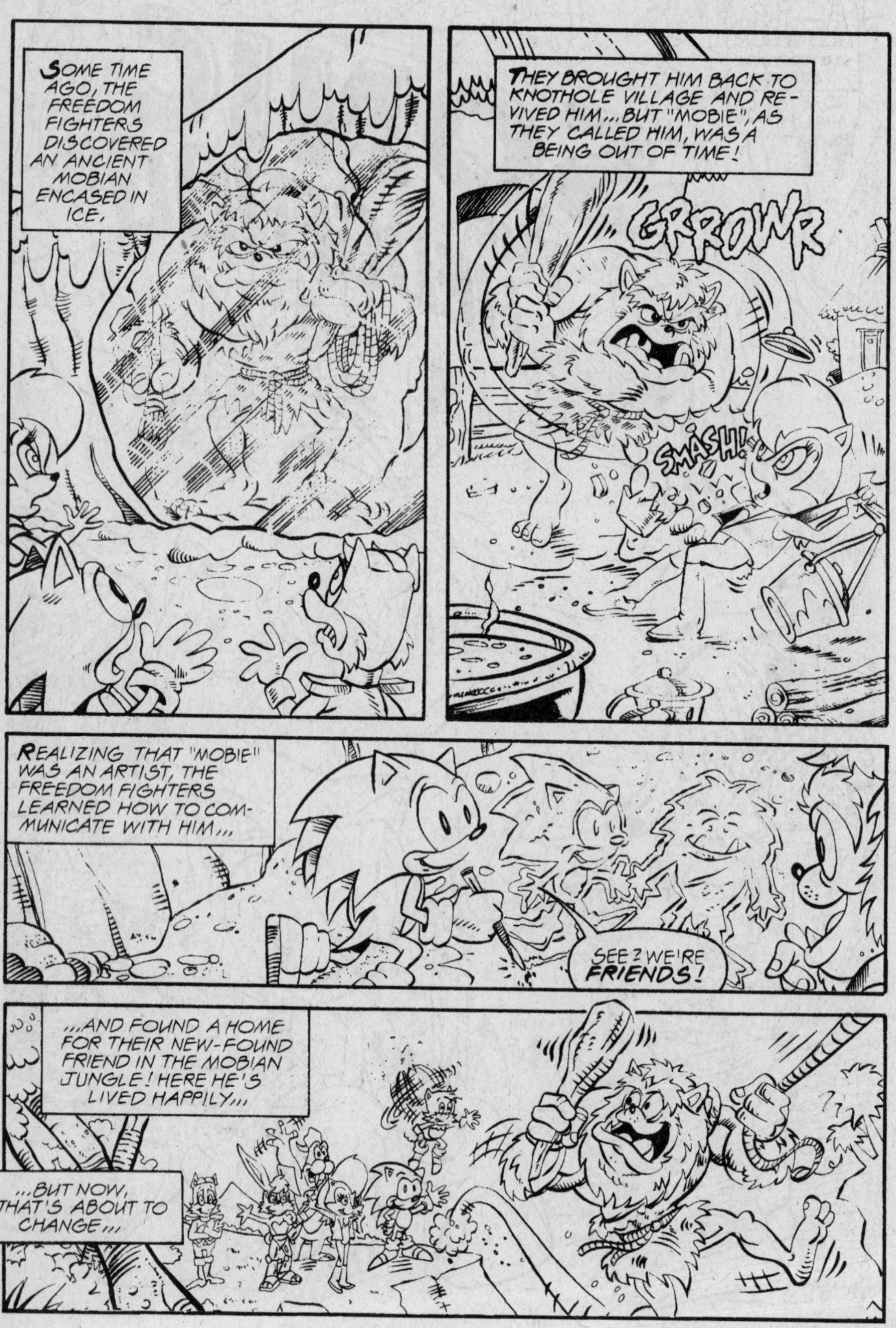
SOME TIME AGO, THE FREEDOM FIGHTERS DISCOVERED AN ANCIENT MOBIAN ENCASED IN ICE.
THEY BROUGHT HIM BACK TO KNOTHOLE VILLAGE AND RE-VIVED HIM... BUT "MOBIE", AS THEY CALLED HIM, WAS A BEING OUT OF TIME!
GRROWR
SMASH!
REALIZING THAT "MOBIE" WAS AN ARTIST, THE FREEDOM FIGHTERS LEARNED HOW TO COM-MUNICATE WITH HIM...
SEE? WE'RE FRIENDS!
...AND FOUND A HOME FOR THEIR NEW-FOUND FRIEND IN THE MOBIAN JUNGLE! HERE HE'S LIVED HAPPILY...
...BUT NOW, THAT'S ABOUT TO CHANGE...

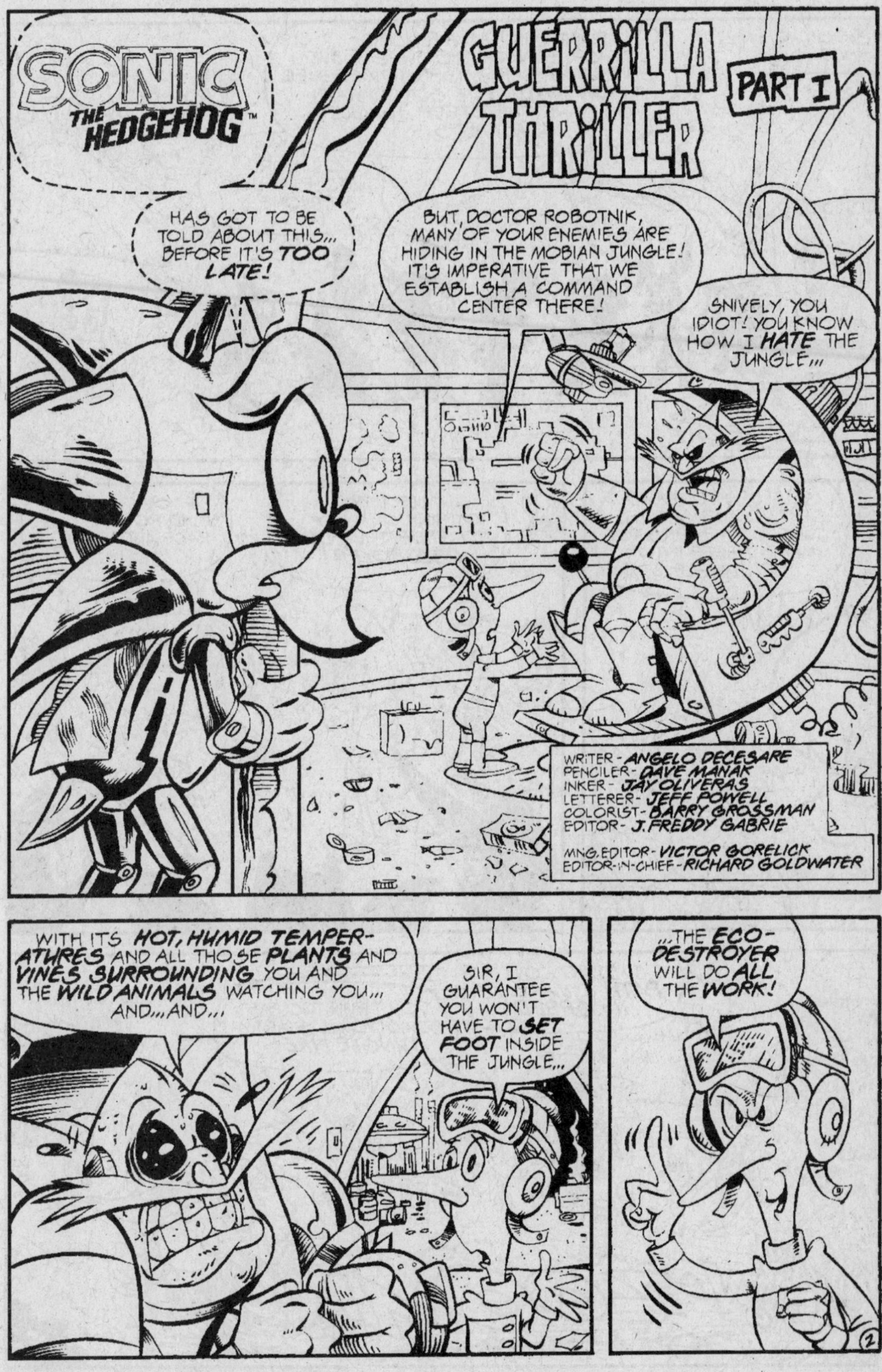
SONIC THE HEDGEHOG™
GUERRILLA THRILLER
PART I
HAS GOT TO BE TOLD ABOUT THIS... BEFORE IT'S TOO LATE!
BUT, DOCTOR ROBOTNIK, MANY OF YOUR ENEMIES ARE HIDING IN THE MOBIAN JUNGLE! IT'S IMPERATIVE THAT WE ESTABLISH A COMMAND CENTER THERE!
SNIVELY, YOU IDIOT! YOU KNOW HOW I HATE THE JUNGLE...
WRITER - ANGELO DECESARE
PENCILER - DAVE MANAK
INKER - JAY OLIVERAS
LETTERER - JEFF POWELL
COLORIST - BARRY GROSSMAN
EDITOR - J. FREDDY GABRIE
MNG. EDITOR - VICTOR GORELICK
EDITOR-IN-CHIEF - RICHARD GOLDWATER
WITH ITS HOT, HUMID TEMPERATURES AND ALL THOSE PLANTS AND VINES SURROUNDING YOU AND THE WILD ANIMALS WATCHING YOU... AND... AND...
SIR, I GUARANTEE YOU WON'T HAVE TO SET FOOT INSIDE THE JUNGLE...
...THE ECO-DESTROYER WILL DO ALL THE WORK!
2

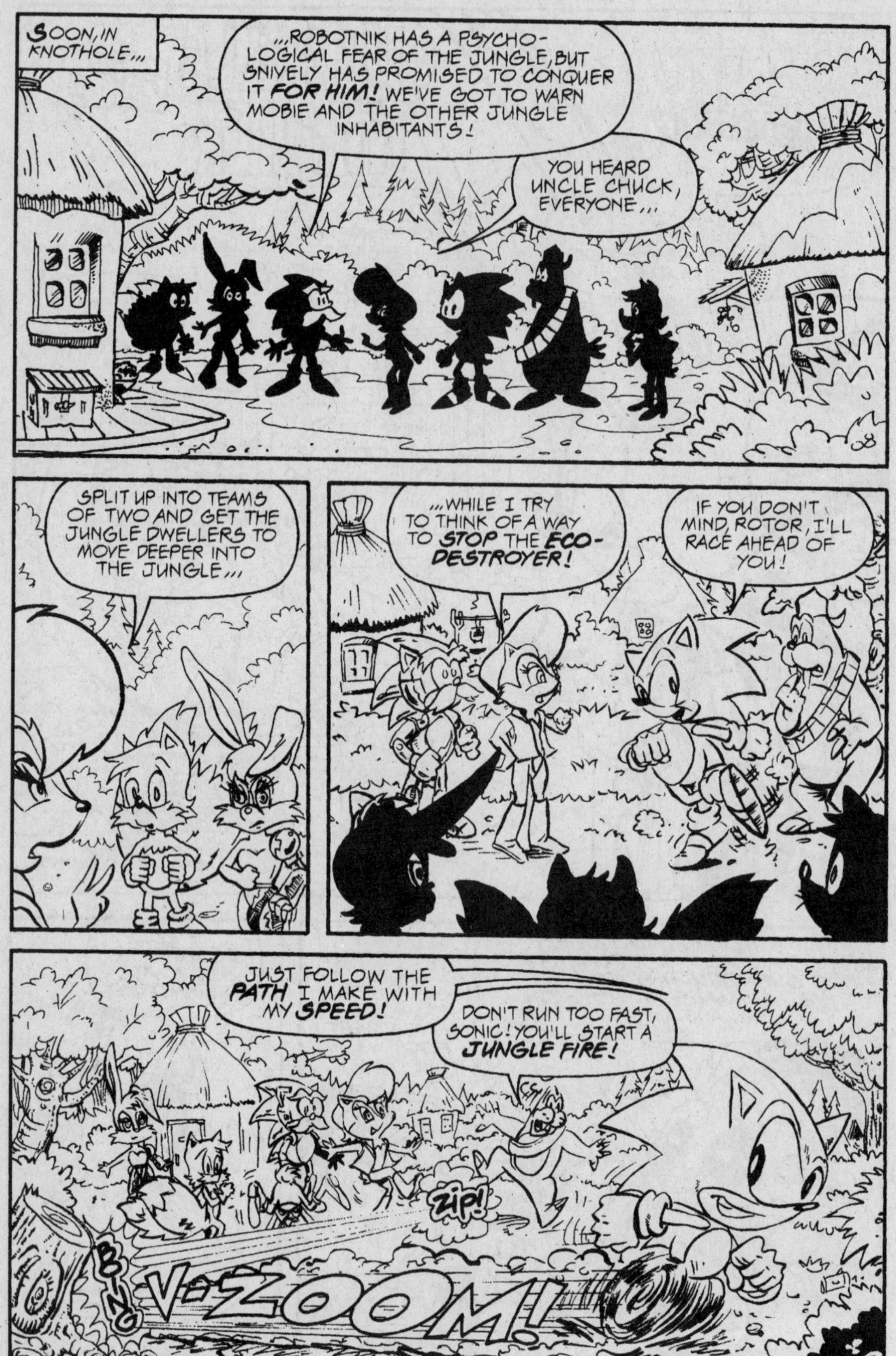
SOON, IN KNOTHOLE...
...ROBOTNIK HAS A PSYCHOLOGICAL FEAR OF THE JUNGLE, BUT SNIVELY HAS PROMISED TO CONQUER IT FOR HIM! WE'VE GOT TO WARN MOBIE AND THE OTHER JUNGLE INHABITANTS!
YOU HEARD UNCLE CHUCK, EVERYONE...
SPLIT UP INTO TEAMS OF TWO AND GET THE JUNGLE DWELLERS TO MOVE DEEPER INTO THE JUNGLE...
...WHILE I TRY TO THINK OF A WAY TO STOP THE ECO-DESTROYER!
IF YOU DON'T MIND, ROTOR, I'LL RACE AHEAD OF YOU!
JUST FOLLOW THE PATH I MAKE WITH MY SPEED!
DON'T RUN TOO FAST, SONIC! YOU'LL START A JUNGLE FIRE!
ZIP!
BOING
V-ZOOM!
3

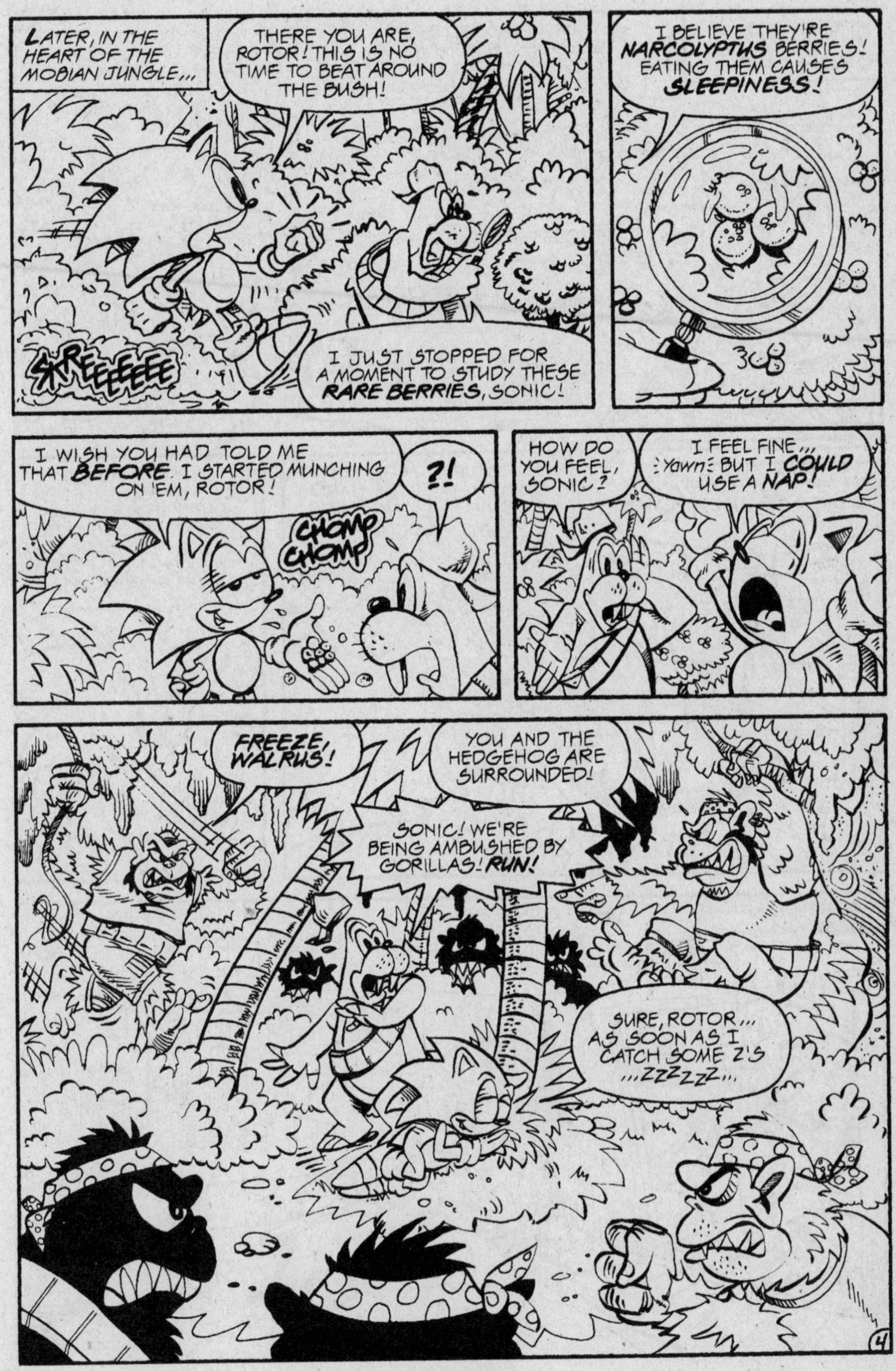
LATER, IN THE HEART OF THE MOBIAN JUNGLE,,,
THERE YOU ARE, ROTOR! THIS IS NO TIME TO BEAT AROUND THE BUSH!
SKREEEEEEEE
I JUST STOPPED FOR A MOMENT TO STUDY THESE RARE BERRIES, SONIC!
I BELIEVE THEY'RE NARCOLYPTUS BERRIES! EATING THEM CAUSES SLEEPINESS!
I WISH YOU HAD TOLD ME THAT BEFORE I STARTED MUNCHING ON 'EM, ROTOR!
?!
CHOMP CHOMP
HOW DO YOU FEEL, SONIC?
I FEEL FINE,,, Yawn BUT I COULD USE A NAP!
FREEZE, WALRUS!
YOU AND THE HEDGEHOG ARE SURROUNDED!
SONIC! WE'RE BEING AMBUSHED BY GORILLAS! RUN!
SURE, ROTOR,,, AS SOON AS I CATCH SOME Z'S ,,,ZZZZZZ,,,
4

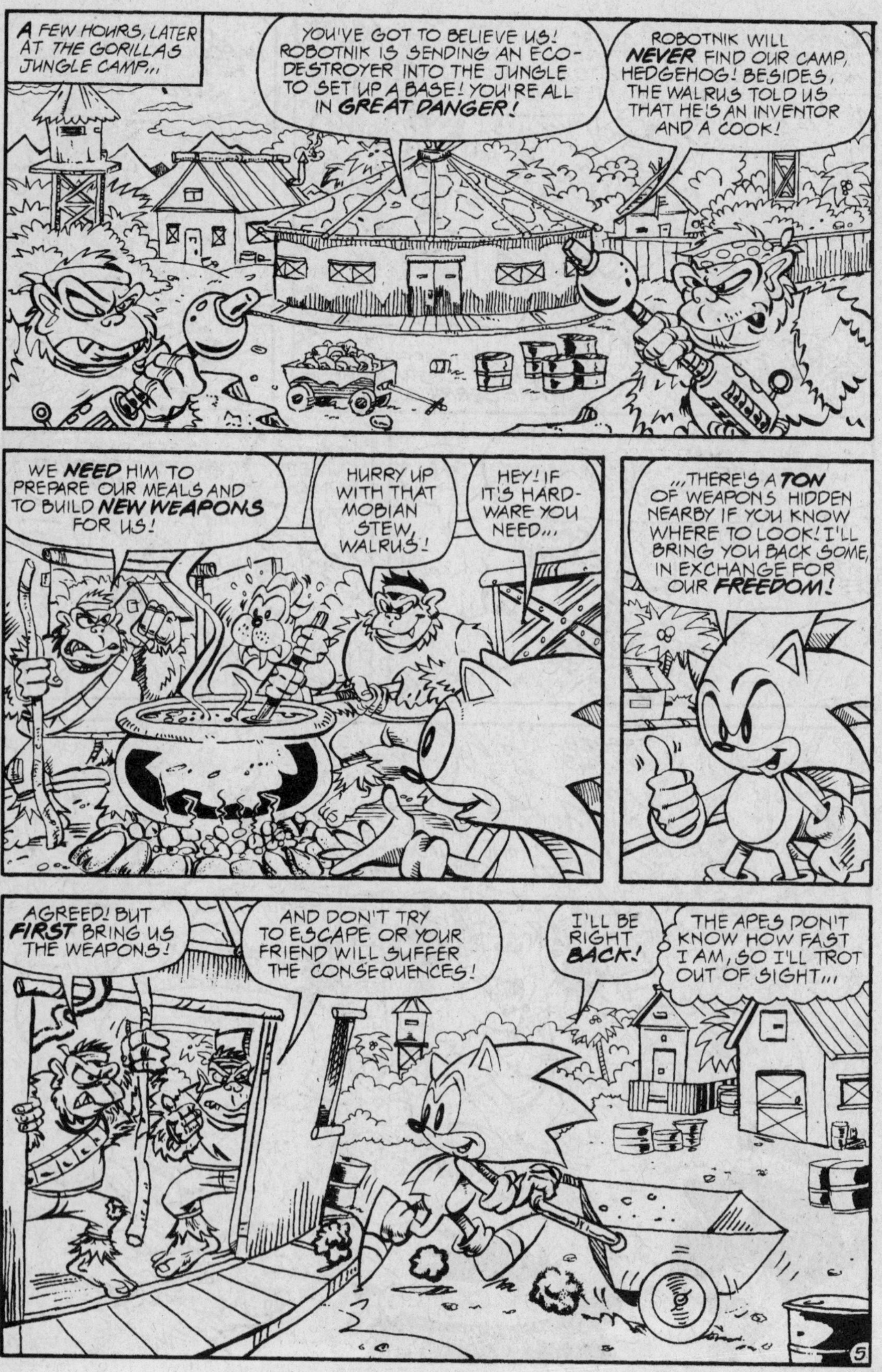
A FEW HOURS, LATER AT THE GORILLAS JUNGLE CAMP...
YOU'VE GOT TO BELIEVE US! ROBOTNIK IS SENDING AN ECO-DESTROYER INTO THE JUNGLE TO SET UP A BASE! YOU'RE ALL IN GREAT DANGER!
ROBOTNIK WILL NEVER FIND OUR CAMP, HEDGEHOG! BESIDES, THE WALRUS TOLD US THAT HE'S AN INVENTOR AND A COOK!
WE NEED HIM TO PREPARE OUR MEALS AND TO BUILD NEW WEAPONS FOR US!
HURRY UP WITH THAT MOBIAN STEW, WALRUS!
HEY! IF IT'S HARD-WARE YOU NEED...
...THERE'S A TON OF WEAPONS HIDDEN NEARBY IF YOU KNOW WHERE TO LOOK! I'LL BRING YOU BACK SOME, IN EXCHANGE FOR OUR FREEDOM!
AGREED! BUT FIRST BRING US THE WEAPONS!
AND DON'T TRY TO ESCAPE OR YOUR FRIEND WILL SUFFER THE CONSEQUENCES!
I'LL BE RIGHT BACK!
THE APES DON'T KNOW HOW FAST I AM, SO I'LL TROT OUT OF SIGHT...
5

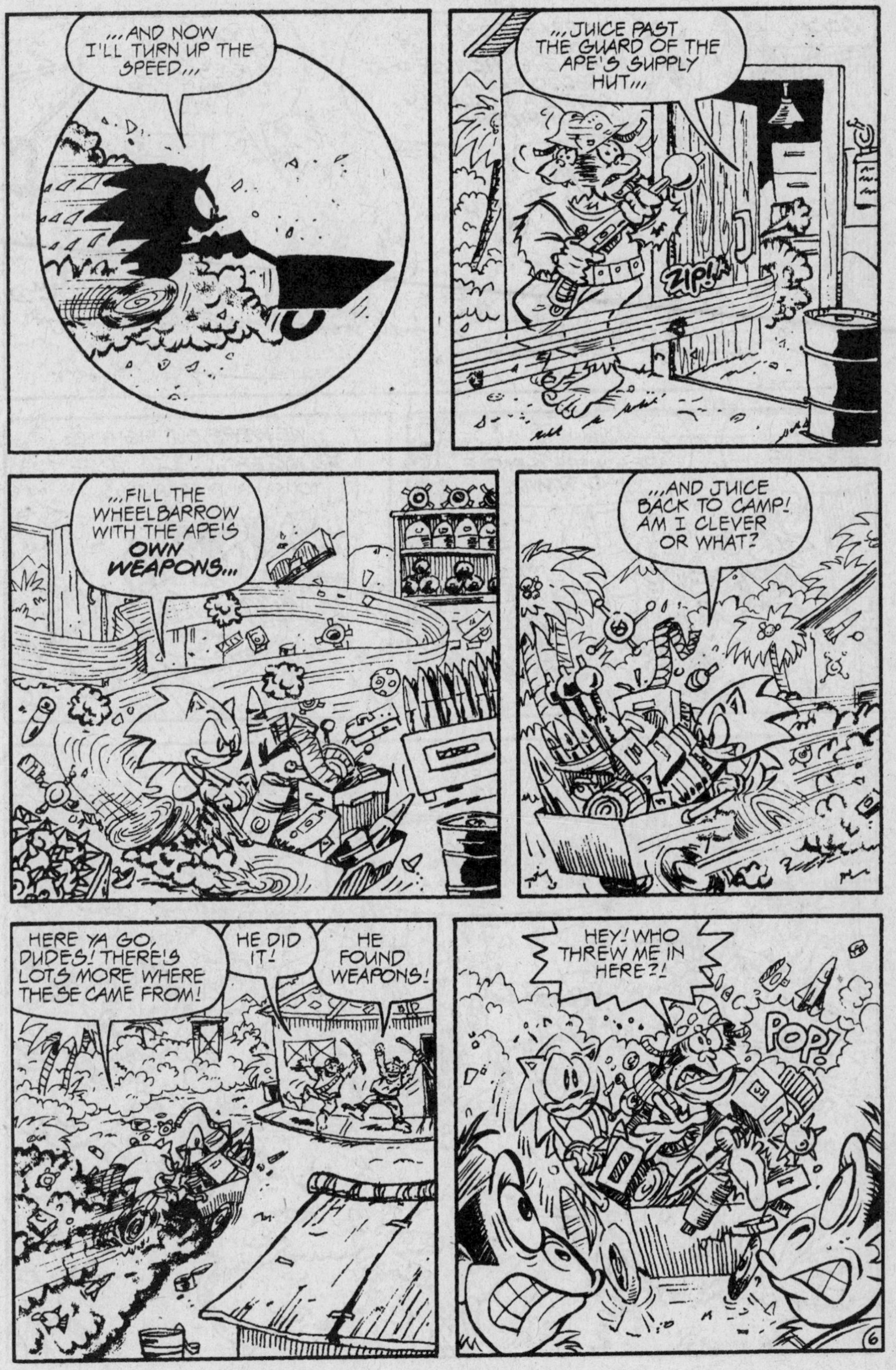
...AND NOW I'LL TURN UP THE SPEED...
...JUICE PAST THE GUARD OF THE APE'S SUPPLY HUT...
ZIP!
...FILL THE WHEELBARROW WITH THE APE'S OWN WEAPONS...
...AND JUICE BACK TO CAMP! AM I CLEVER OR WHAT?
HERE YA GO, DUDES! THERE'S LOTS MORE WHERE THESE CAME FROM!
HE DID IT!
HE FOUND WEAPONS!
HEY! WHO THREW ME IN HERE?!
POP!
6

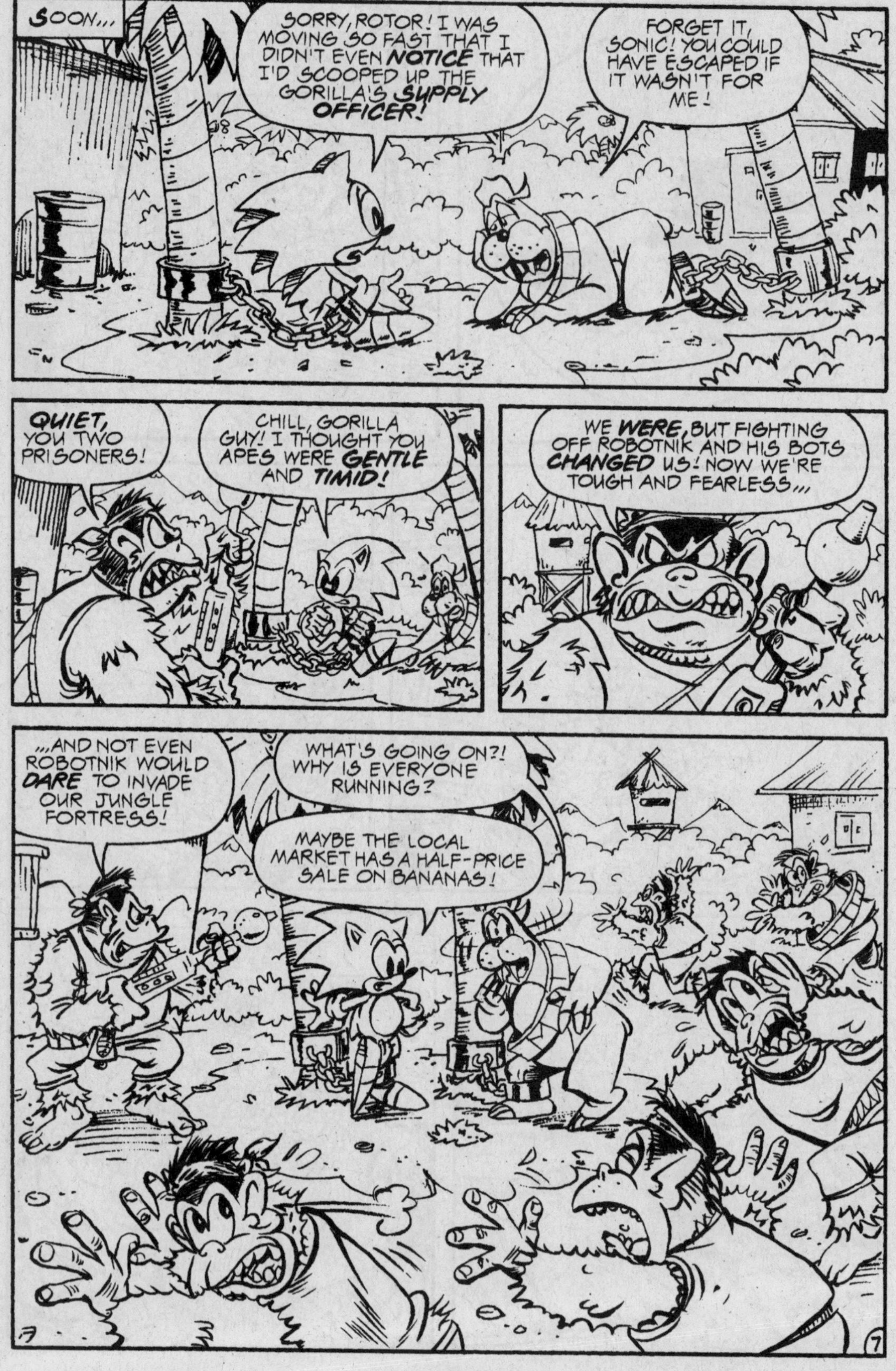
SOON...
SORRY, ROTOR! I WAS MOVING SO FAST THAT I DIDN'T EVEN NOTICE THAT I'D SCOOPED UP THE GORILLA'S SUPPLY OFFICER!
FORGET IT, SONIC! YOU COULD HAVE ESCAPED IF IT WASN'T FOR ME!
QUIET, YOU TWO PRISONERS!
CHILL, GORILLA GUY! I THOUGHT YOU APES WERE GENTLE AND TIMID!
WE WERE, BUT FIGHTING OFF ROBOTNIK AND HIS BOTS CHANGED US! NOW WE'RE TOUGH AND FEARLESS...
...AND NOT EVEN ROBOTNIK WOULD DARE TO INVADE OUR JUNGLE FORTRESS!
WHAT'S GOING ON?! WHY IS EVERYONE RUNNING?
MAYBE THE LOCAL MARKET HAS A HALF-PRICE SALE ON BANANAS!
7

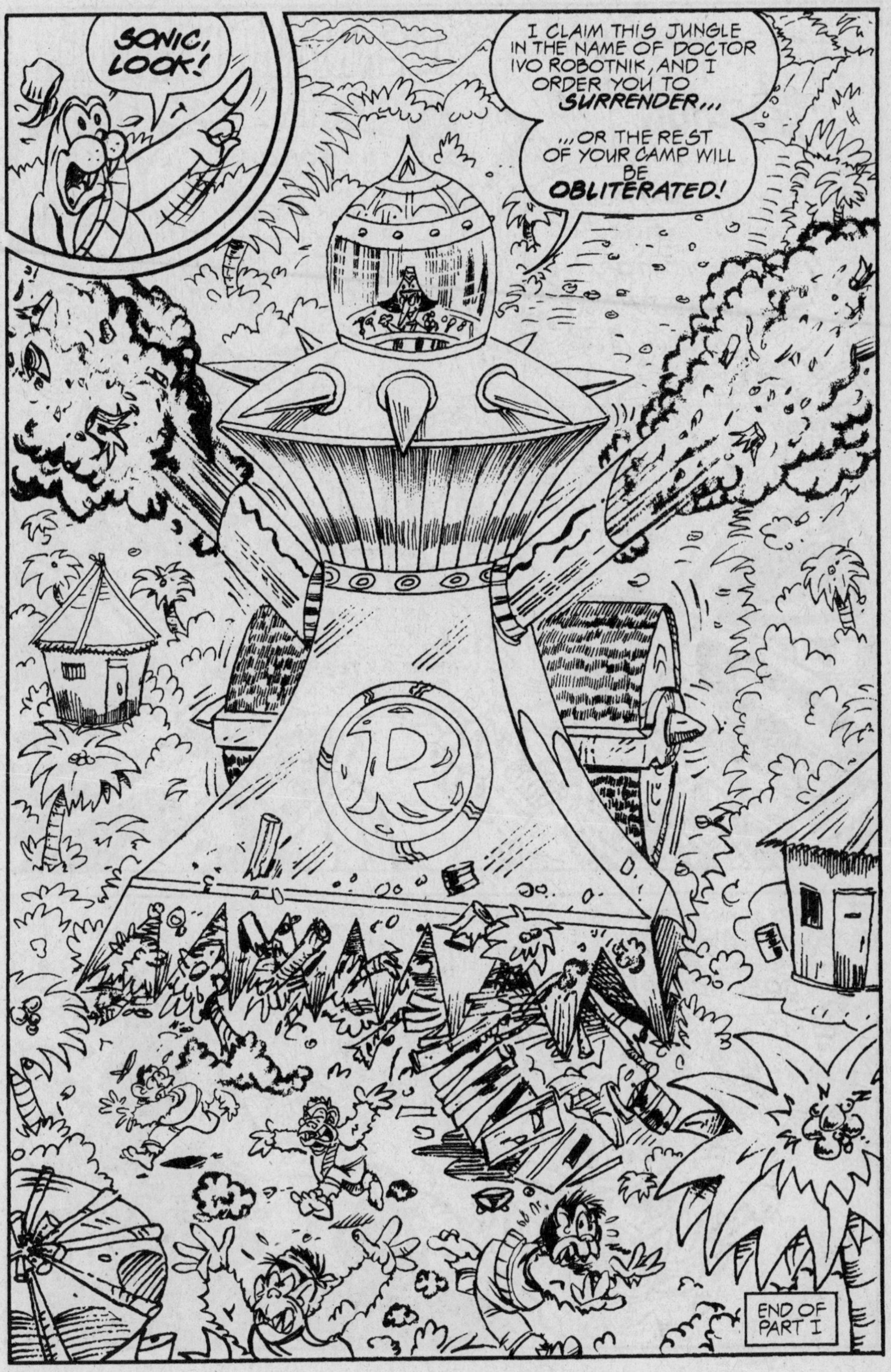
SONIC, LOOK!
I CLAIM THIS JUNGLE IN THE NAME OF DOCTOR IVO ROBOTNIK, AND I ORDER YOU TO SURRENDER...
...OR THE REST OF YOUR CAMP WILL BE OBLITERATED!
END OF PART I

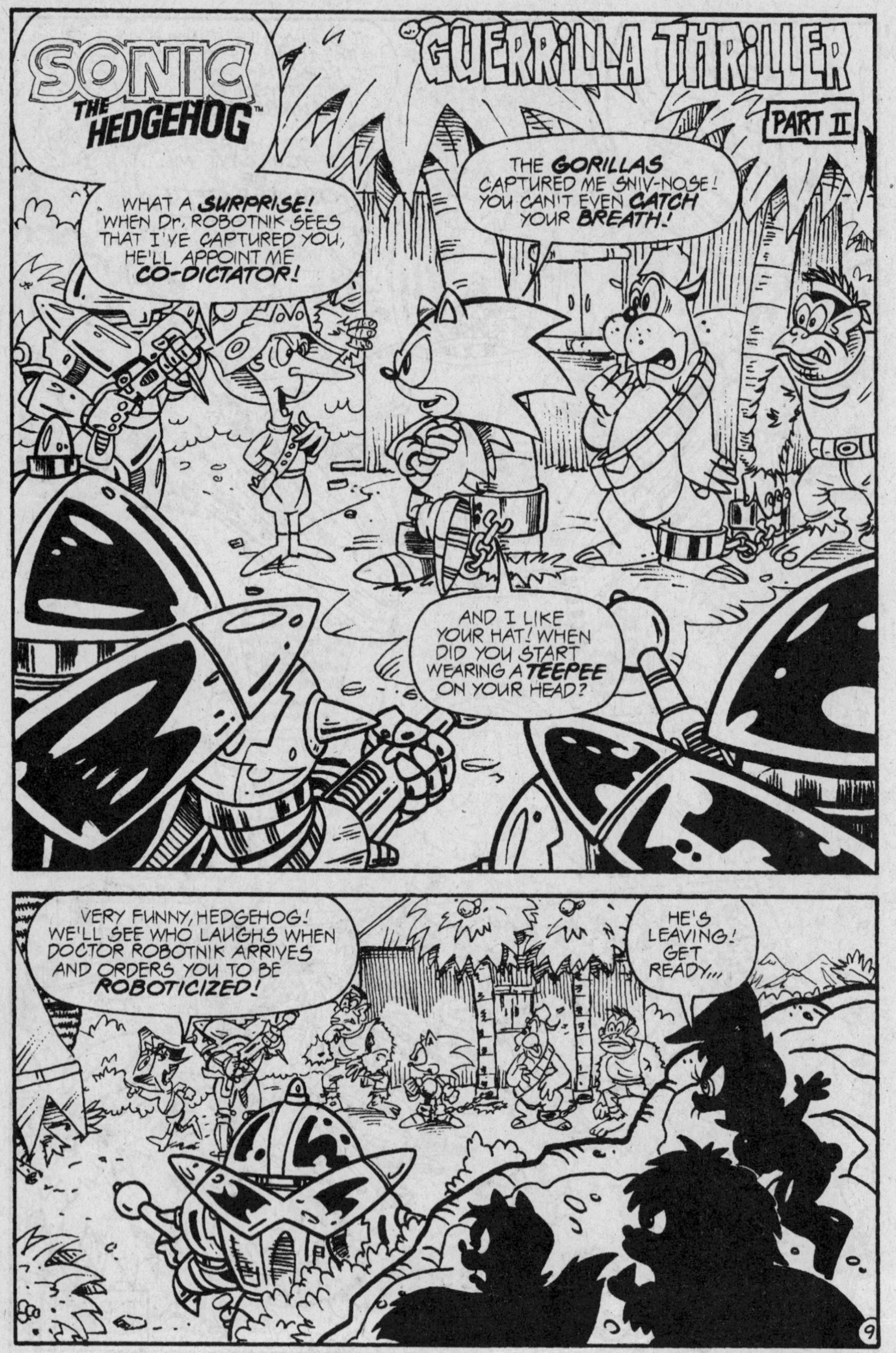
SONIC THE HEDGEHOG™
GUERRILLA THRILLER
PART II
WHAT A SURPRISE! WHEN Dr. ROBOTNIK SEES THAT I'VE CAPTURED YOU, HE'LL APPOINT ME CO-DICTATOR!
THE GORILLAS CAPTURED ME SNIV-NOSE! YOU CAN'T EVEN CATCH YOUR BREATH!
AND I LIKE YOUR HAT! WHEN DID YOU START WEARING A TEEPEE ON YOUR HEAD?
VERY FUNNY, HEDGEHOG! WE'LL SEE WHO LAUGHS WHEN DOCTOR ROBOTNIK ARRIVES AND ORDERS YOU TO BE ROBOTICIZED!
HE'S LEAVING! GET READY...
9

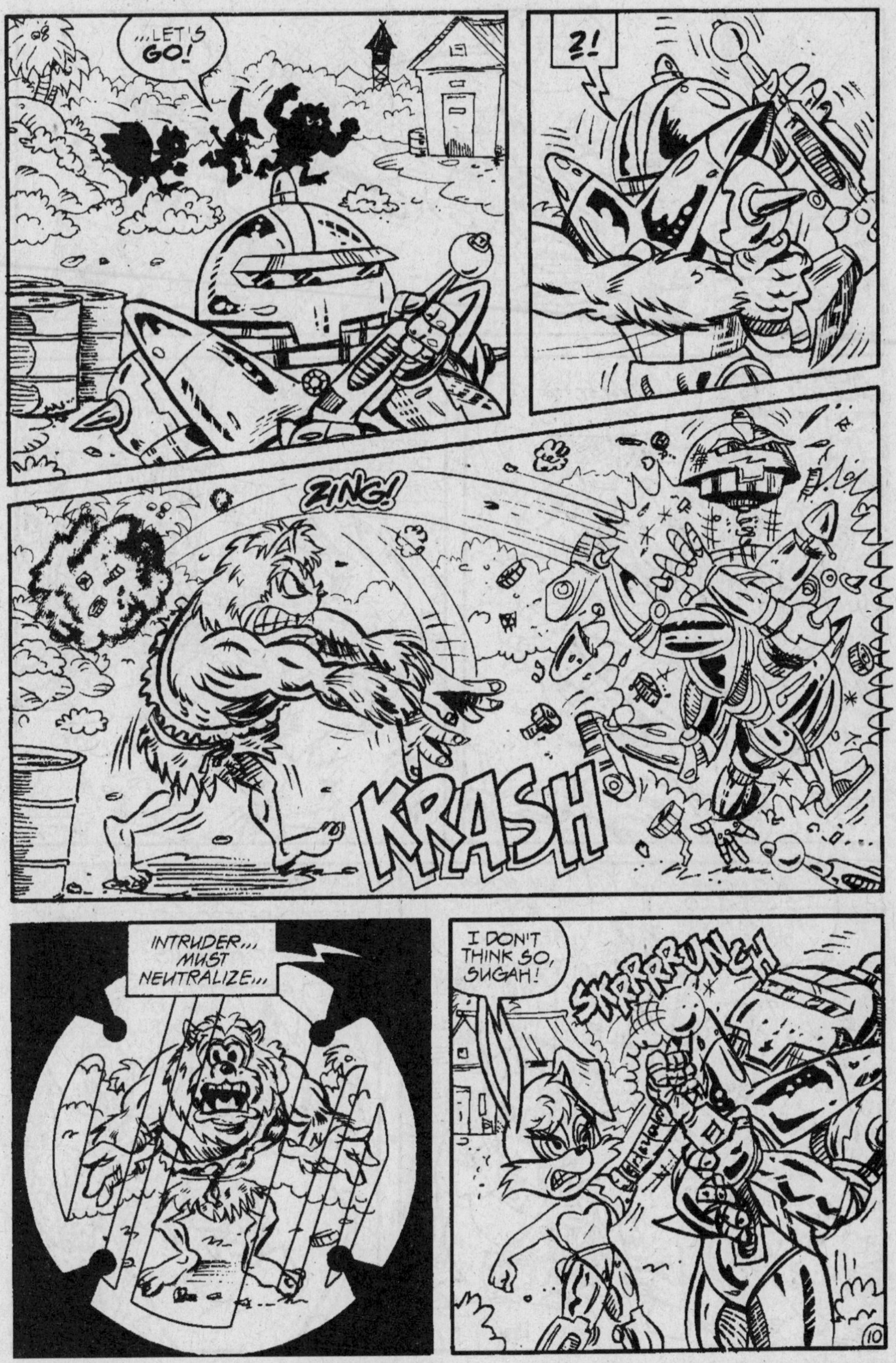
...LET'S GO!
?!
ZING!
KRASH
INTRUDER... MUST NEUTRALIZE...
I DON'T THINK SO, SUGAH!
SKRRRUNCH
10

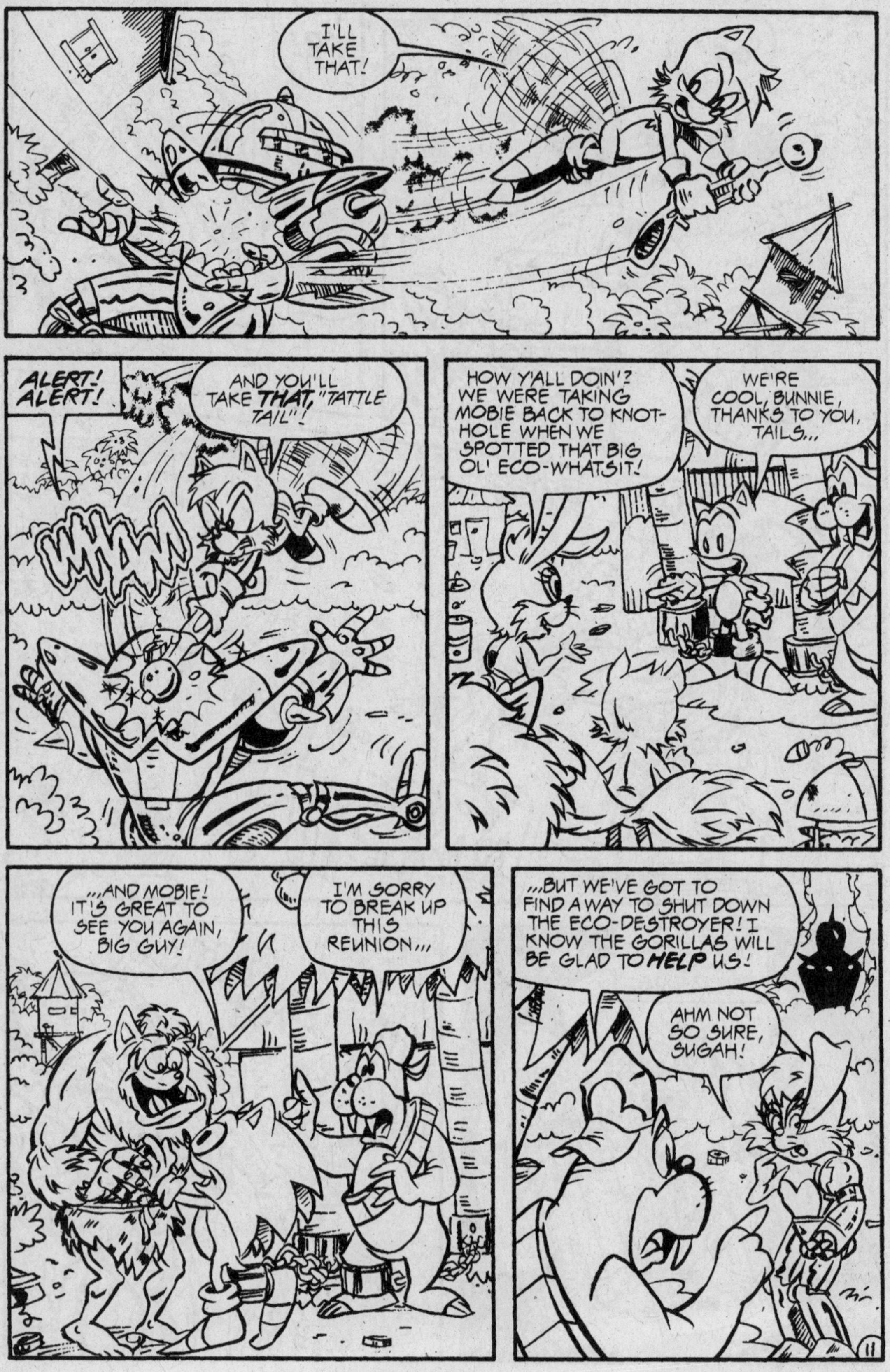
I'LL TAKE THAT!
ALERT! ALERT!
AND YOU'LL TAKE THAT, "TATTLE TAIL"!
WHAM
HOW Y'ALL DOIN'? WE WERE TAKING MOBIE BACK TO KNOT-HOLE WHEN WE SPOTTED THAT BIG OL' ECO-WHATSIT!
WE'RE COOL, BUNNIE, THANKS TO YOU, TAILS...
...AND MOBIE! IT'S GREAT TO SEE YOU AGAIN, BIG GUY!
I'M SORRY TO BREAK UP THIS REUNION...
...BUT WE'VE GOT TO FIND A WAY TO SHUT DOWN THE ECO-DESTROYER! I KNOW THE GORILLAS WILL BE GLAD TO HELP US!
AHM NOT SO SURE, SUGAH!

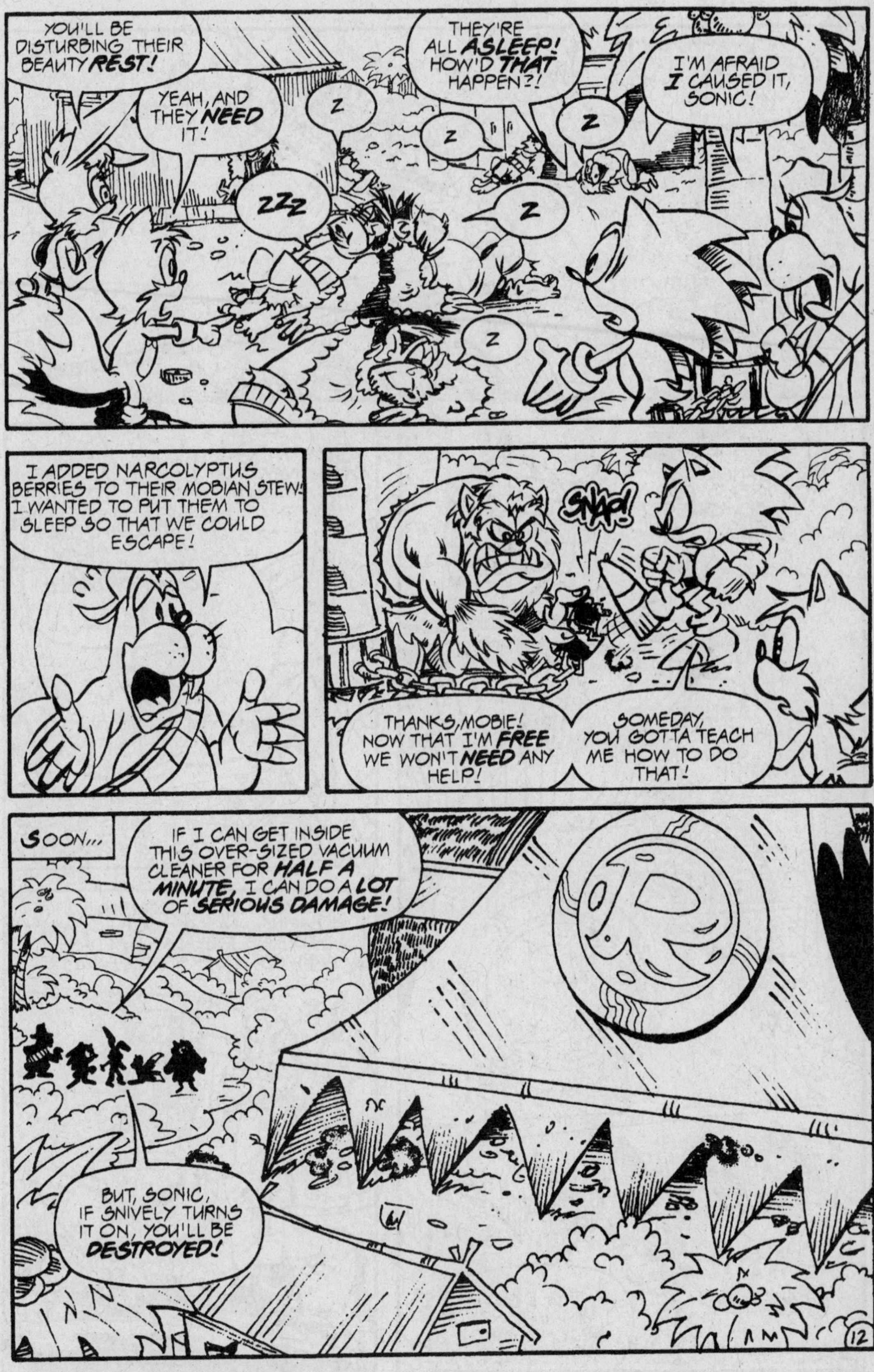
YOU'LL BE DISTURBING THEIR BEAUTY REST!
YEAH, AND THEY NEED IT!
Z
ZZZ
THEY'RE ALL ASLEEP! HOW'D THAT HAPPEN?!
Z
Z
Z
I'M AFRAID I CAUSED IT, SONIC!
Z
I ADDED NARCOLYPTUS BERRIES TO THEIR MOBIAN STEW! I WANTED TO PUT THEM TO SLEEP SO THAT WE COULD ESCAPE!
SNAP!
THANKS, MOBIE! NOW THAT I'M FREE WE WON'T NEED ANY HELP!
SOMEDAY, YOU GOTTA TEACH ME HOW TO DO THAT!
SOON...
IF I CAN GET INSIDE THIS OVER-SIZED VACUUM CLEANER FOR HALF A MINUTE, I CAN DO A LOT OF SERIOUS DAMAGE!
BUT, SONIC, IF SNIVELY TURNS IT ON, YOU'LL BE DESTROYED!
12

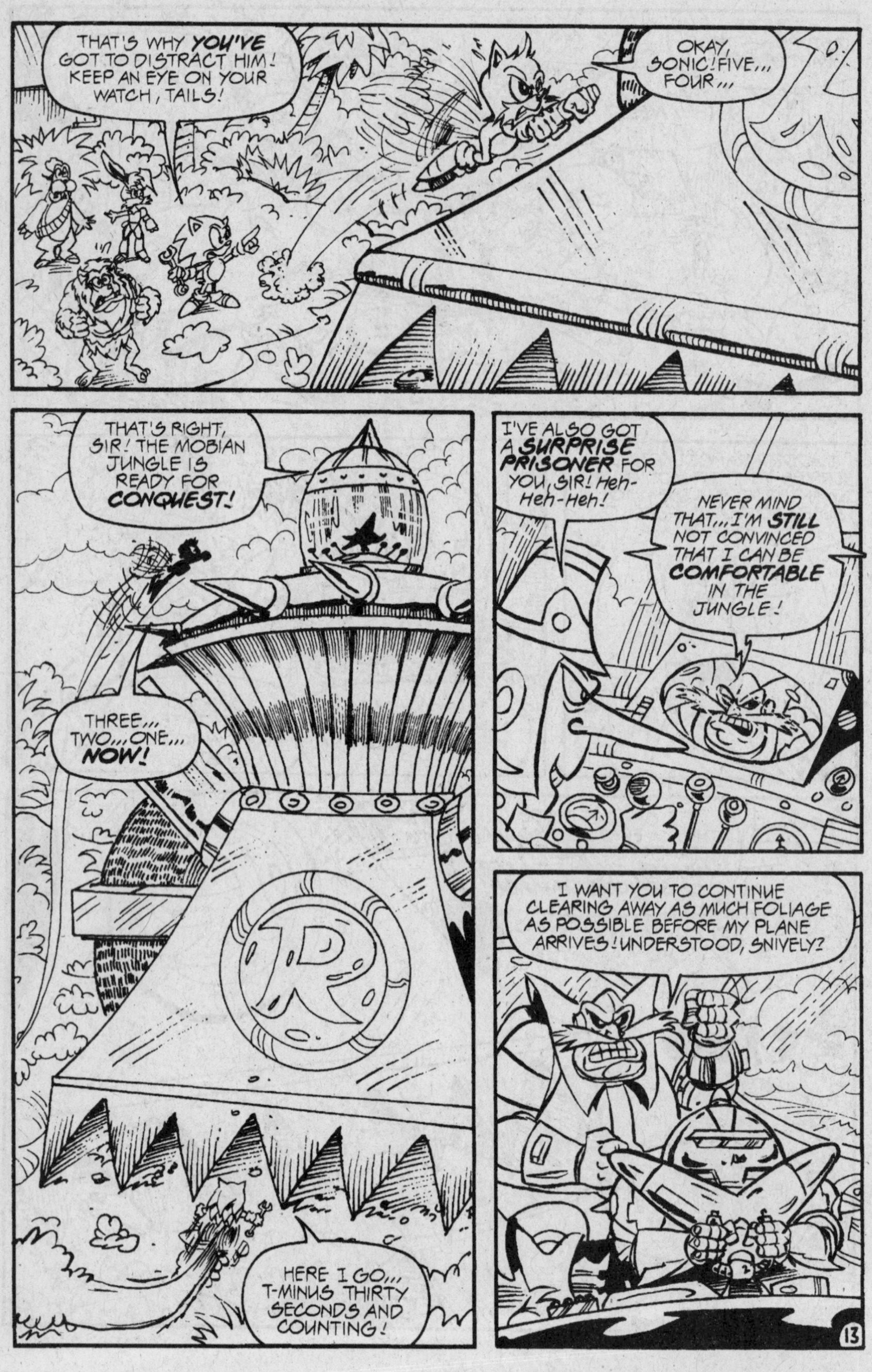
THAT'S WHY YOU'VE GOT TO DISTRACT HIM! KEEP AN EYE ON YOUR WATCH, TAILS!
OKAY, SONIC! FIVE... FOUR...
THAT'S RIGHT, SIR! THE MOBIAN JUNGLE IS READY FOR CONQUEST!
THREE... TWO... ONE... NOW!
HERE I GO... T-MINUS THIRTY SECONDS AND COUNTING!
I'VE ALSO GOT A SURPRISE PRISONER FOR YOU, SIR! Heh-Heh-Heh!
NEVER MIND THAT... I'M STILL NOT CONVINCED THAT I CAN BE COMFORTABLE IN THE JUNGLE!
I WANT YOU TO CONTINUE CLEARING AWAY AS MUCH FOLIAGE AS POSSIBLE BEFORE MY PLANE ARRIVES! UNDERSTOOD, SNIVELY?
13

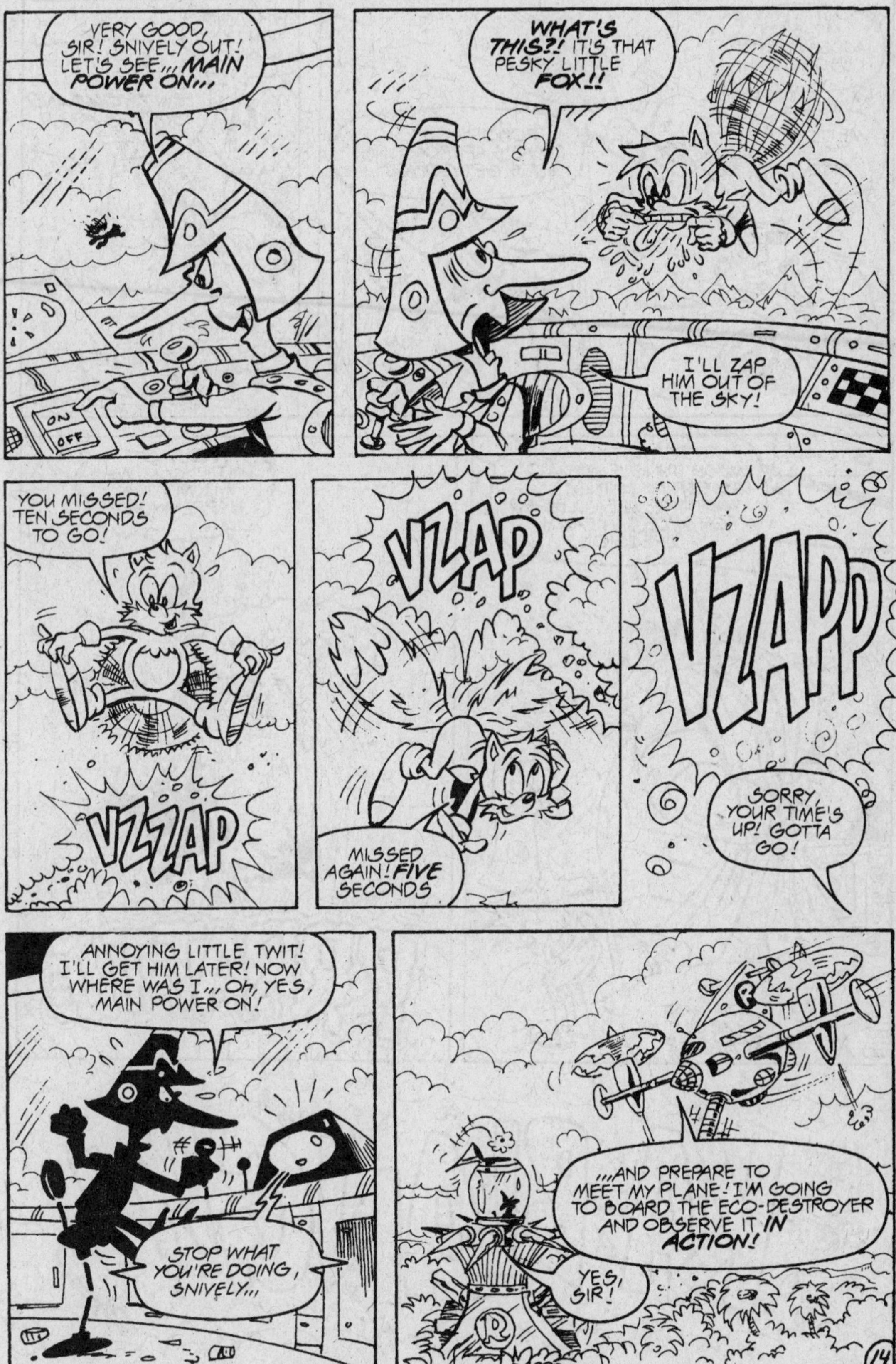
VERY GOOD, SIR! SNIVELY OUT! LET'S SEE... MAIN POWER ON...
ON
OFF
WHAT'S THIS?! IT'S THAT PESKY LITTLE FOX!!
I'LL ZAP HIM OUT OF THE SKY!
YOU MISSED! TEN SECONDS TO GO!
VZZAP
VZAP
MISSED AGAIN! FIVE SECONDS
VZAPP
SORRY, YOUR TIME'S UP! GOTTA GO!
ANNOYING LITTLE TWIT! I'LL GET HIM LATER! NOW WHERE WAS I... OH, YES, MAIN POWER ON!
STOP WHAT YOU'RE DOING, SNIVELY...
...AND PREPARE TO MEET MY PLANE! I'M GOING TO BOARD THE ECO-DESTROYER AND OBSERVE IT IN ACTION!
YES, SIR!
14

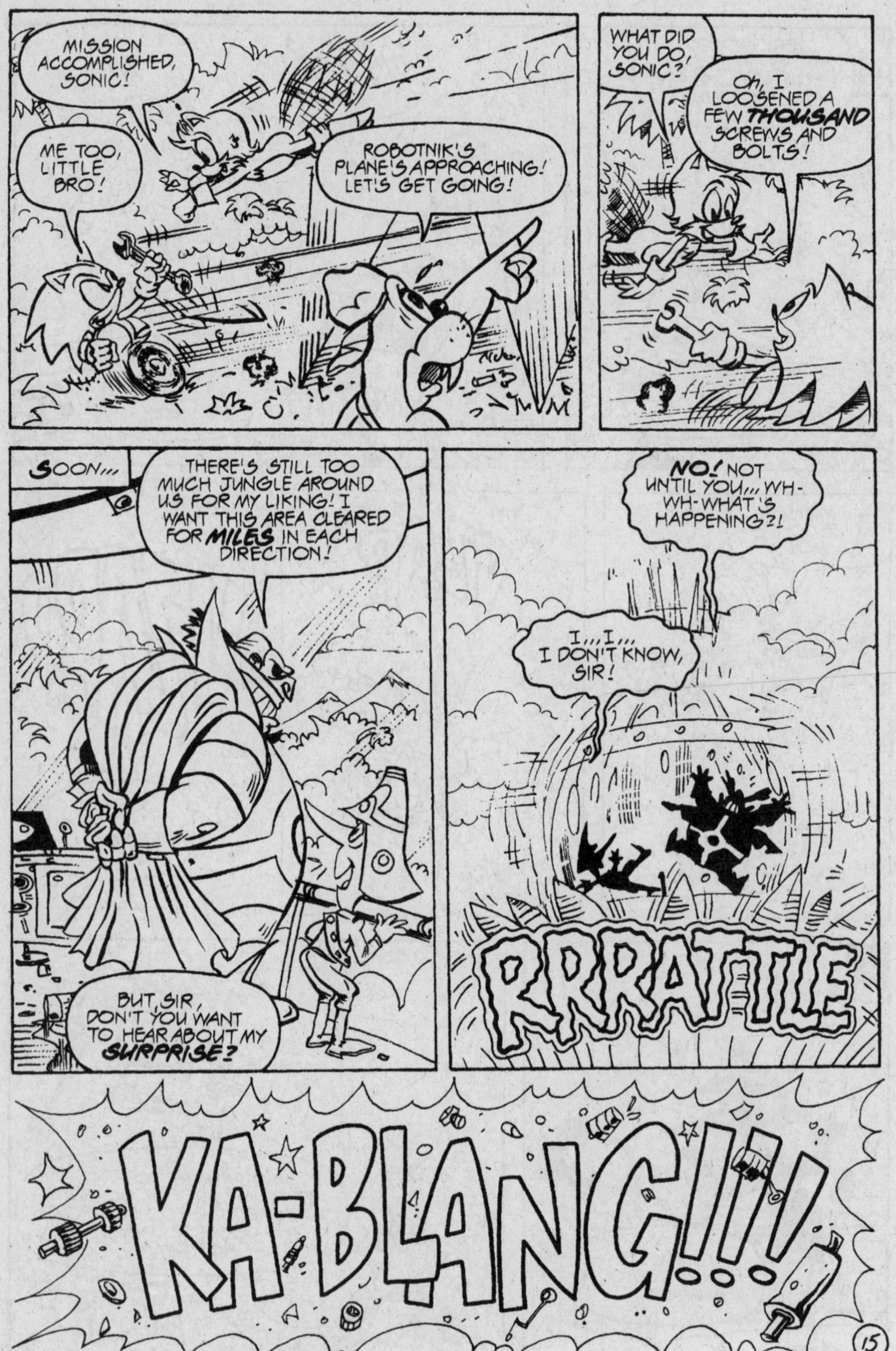
MISSION ACCOMPLISHED, SONIC!
ME TOO, LITTLE BRO!
ROBOTNIK'S PLANE'S APPROACHING! LET'S GET GOING!
WHAT DID YOU DO, SONIC?
OH, I LOOSENED A FEW THOUSAND SCREWS AND BOLTS!
SOON...
THERE'S STILL TOO MUCH JUNGLE AROUND US FOR MY LIKING! I WANT THIS AREA CLEARED FOR MILES IN EACH DIRECTION!
BUT, SIR, DON'T YOU WANT TO HEAR ABOUT MY SURPRISE?
NO! NOT UNTIL YOU... WH- WH-WHAT'S HAPPENING?!
I... I... I DON'T KNOW, SIR!
RRRATTLE
KA-BLANG!!!
15

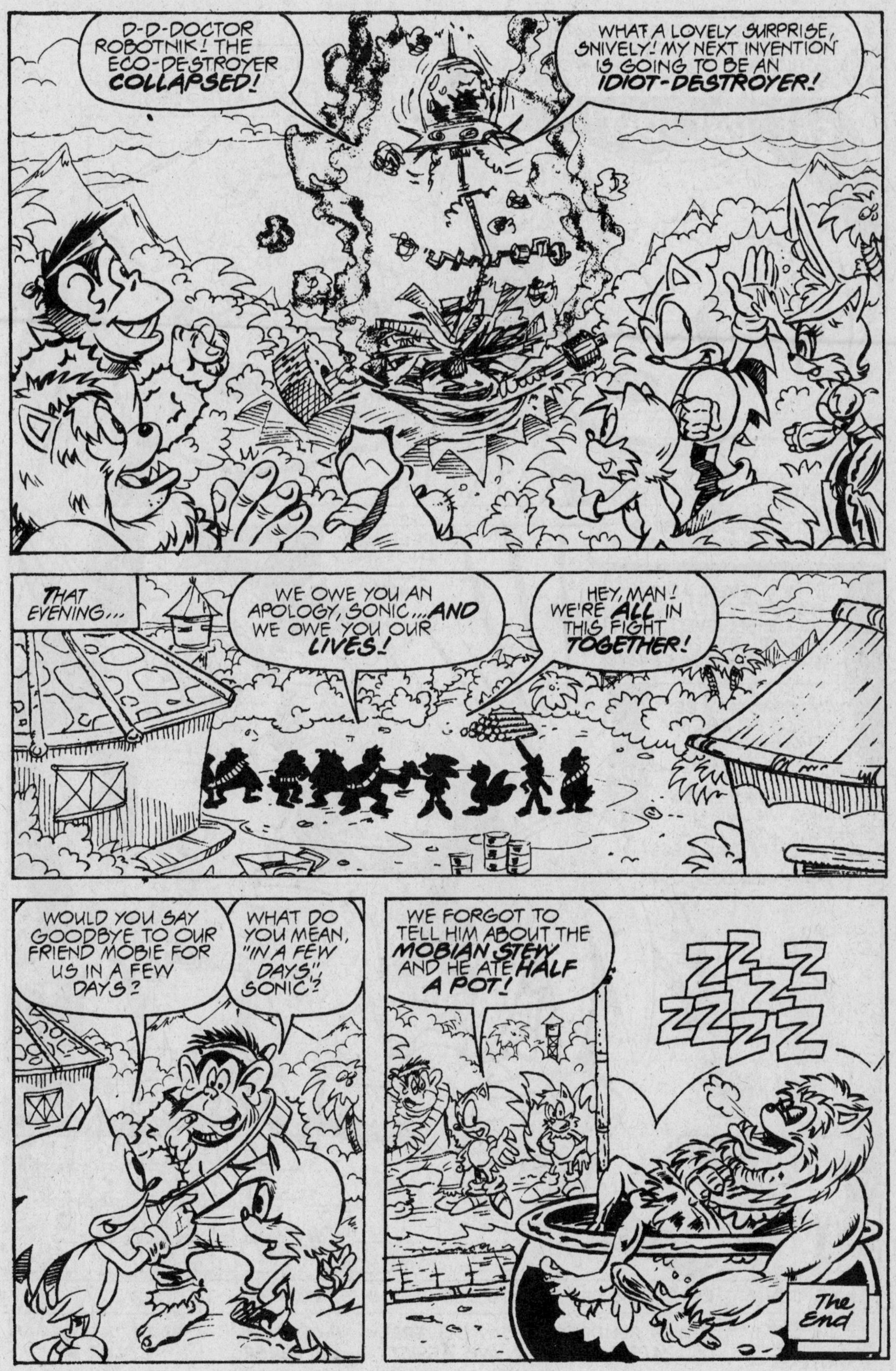
D-D-DOCTOR ROBOTNIK! THE ECO-DESTROYER COLLAPSED!
WHAT A LOVELY SURPRISE, SNIVELY! MY NEXT INVENTION IS GOING TO BE AN IDIOT-DESTROYER!
THAT EVENING...
WE OWE YOU AN APOLOGY, SONIC... AND WE OWE YOU OUR LIVES!
HEY, MAN! WE'RE ALL IN THIS FIGHT TOGETHER!
WOULD YOU SAY GOODBYE TO OUR FRIEND MOBIE FOR US IN A FEW DAYS?
WHAT DO YOU MEAN, "IN A FEW DAYS", SONIC?
WE FORGOT TO TELL HIM ABOUT THE MOBIAN STEW AND HE ATE HALF A POT!
ZZZZZZZZZ
The End

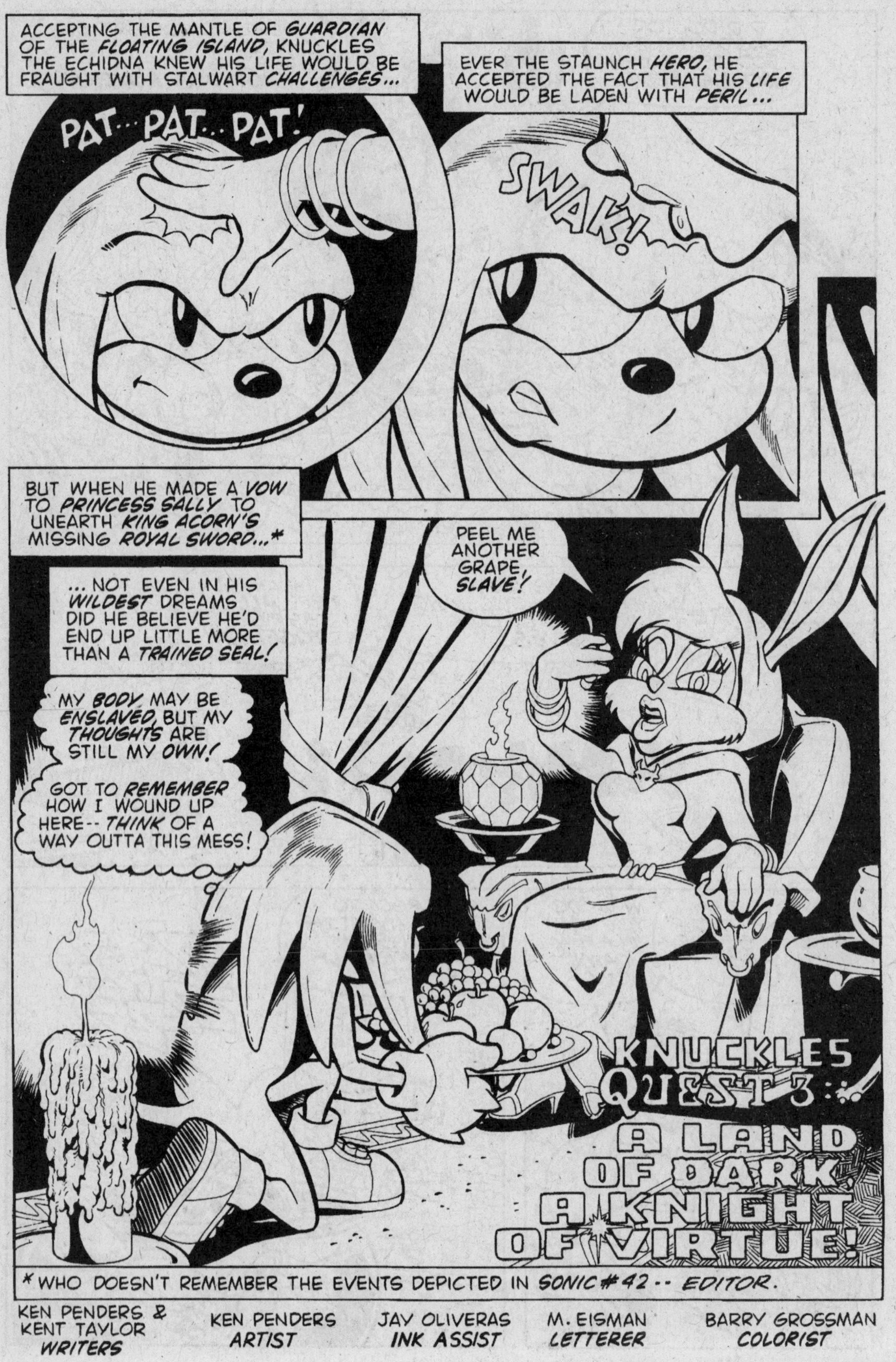

ACCEPTING THE MANTLE OF GUARDIAN OF THE FLOATING ISLAND, KNUCKLES THE ECHIDNA KNEW HIS LIFE WOULD BE FRAUGHT WITH STALWART CHALLENGES...
PAT... PAT... PAT!
EVER THE STAUNCH HERO, HE ACCEPTED THE FACT THAT HIS LIFE WOULD BE LADEN WITH PERIL...
SWAK!
BUT WHEN HE MADE A VOW TO PRINCESS SALLY TO UNEARTH KING ACORN'S MISSING ROYAL SWORD...*
...NOT EVEN IN HIS WILDEST DREAMS DID HE BELIEVE HE'D END UP LITTLE MORE THAN A TRAINED SEAL!
PEEL ME ANOTHER GRAPE, SLAVE!
MY BODY MAY BE ENSLAVED, BUT MY THOUGHTS ARE STILL MY OWN!
GOT TO REMEMBER HOW I WOUND UP HERE-- THINK OF A WAY OUTTA THIS MESS!
KNUCKLES QUEST 3:
A LAND OF DARK, A KNIGHT OF VIRTUE!

*WHO DOESN'T REMEMBER THE EVENTS DEPICTED IN *SONIC* #42 -- EDITOR.

KEN PENDERS & KENT TAYLOR *WRITERS* | KEN PENDERS *ARTIST* | JAY OLIVERAS *INK ASSIST* | M. EISMAN *LETTERER* | BARRY GROSSMAN *COLORIST*

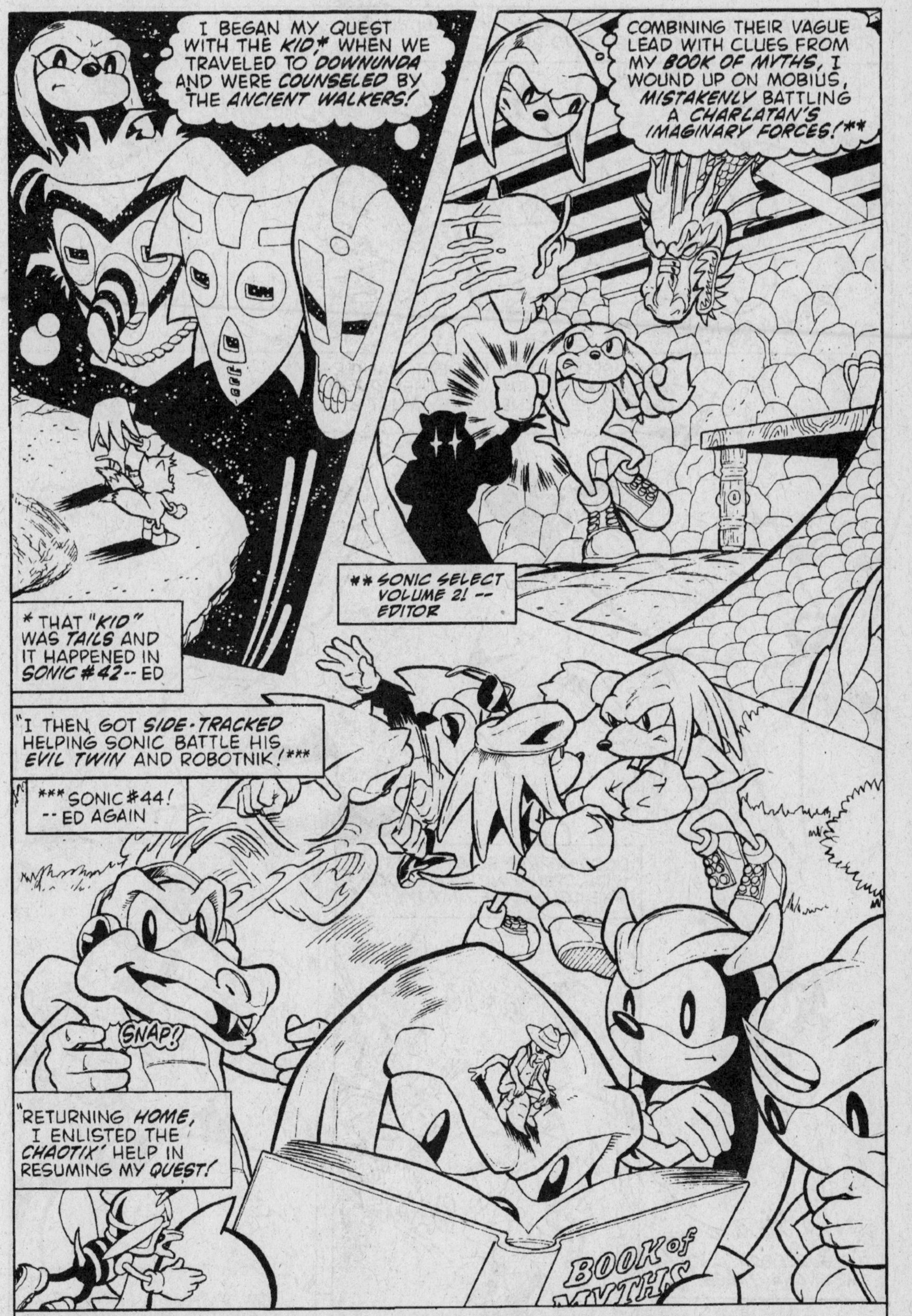

I BEGAN MY QUEST WITH THE KID,* WHEN WE TRAVELED TO DOWNUNDA AND WERE COUNSELED BY THE ANCIENT WALKERS!
* THAT "KID" WAS TAILS AND IT HAPPENED IN SONIC #42 -- ED
COMBINING THEIR VAGUE LEAD WITH CLUES FROM MY BOOK OF MYTHS, I WOUND UP ON MOBIUS, MISTAKENLY BATTLING A CHARLATAN'S IMAGINARY FORCES!**
** SONIC SELECT VOLUME 2! -- EDITOR
"I THEN GOT SIDE-TRACKED HELPING SONIC BATTLE HIS EVIL TWIN AND ROBOTNIK!***
*** SONIC #44! -- ED AGAIN
SNAP!
"RETURNING HOME, I ENLISTED THE CHAOTIX' HELP IN RESUMING MY QUEST!
BOOK of MYTHS
"BELIEVING THE CHARLATAN'S CLUE OF THE LAND OF DARK TO BE AN OLD NAME FOR THE OUTSKIRTS OF THE ISLAND'S FORBIDDEN ZONE, I VENTURED FORTH...
2

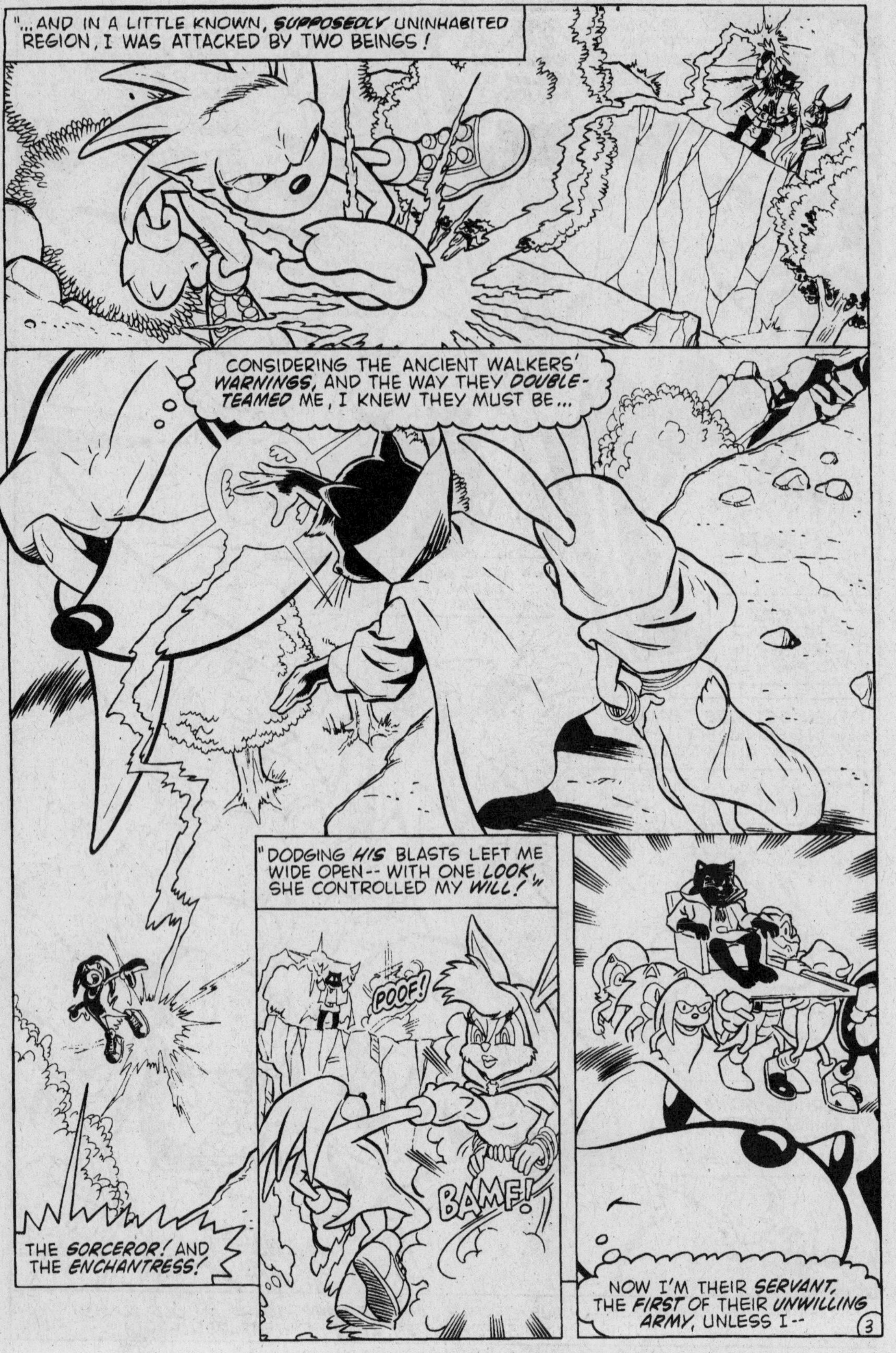
"...AND IN A LITTLE KNOWN, SUPPOSEDLY UNINHABITED REGION, I WAS ATTACKED BY TWO BEINGS!
CONSIDERING THE ANCIENT WALKERS' WARNINGS, AND THE WAY THEY DOUBLE-TEAMED ME, I KNEW THEY MUST BE...
THE SORCEROR! AND THE ENCHANTRESS!
"DODGING HIS BLASTS LEFT ME WIDE OPEN-- WITH ONE LOOK, SHE CONTROLLED MY WILL!"
POOF!
BAMF!
NOW I'M THEIR SERVANT, THE FIRST OF THEIR UNWILLING ARMY, UNLESS I--
3

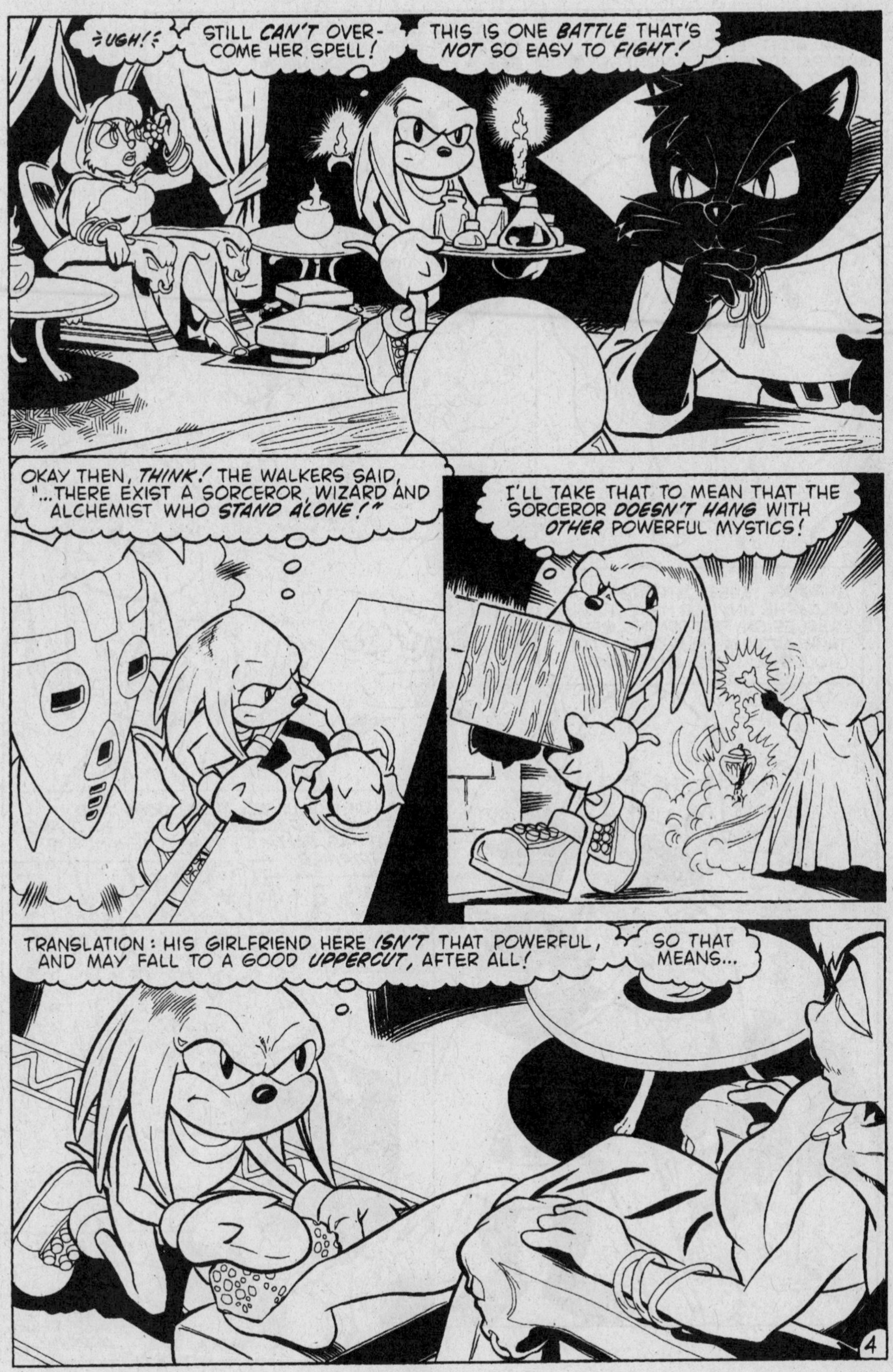

UGH!
STILL CAN'T OVERCOME HER SPELL!
THIS IS ONE BATTLE THAT'S NOT SO EASY TO FIGHT!
OKAY THEN, THINK! THE WALKERS SAID, "...THERE EXIST A SORCEROR, WIZARD AND ALCHEMIST WHO STAND ALONE!"
I'LL TAKE THAT TO MEAN THAT THE SORCEROR DOESN'T HANG WITH OTHER POWERFUL MYSTICS!
TRANSLATION: HIS GIRLFRIEND HERE ISN'T THAT POWERFUL, AND MAY FALL TO A GOOD UPPERCUT, AFTER ALL!
SO THAT MEANS...
4

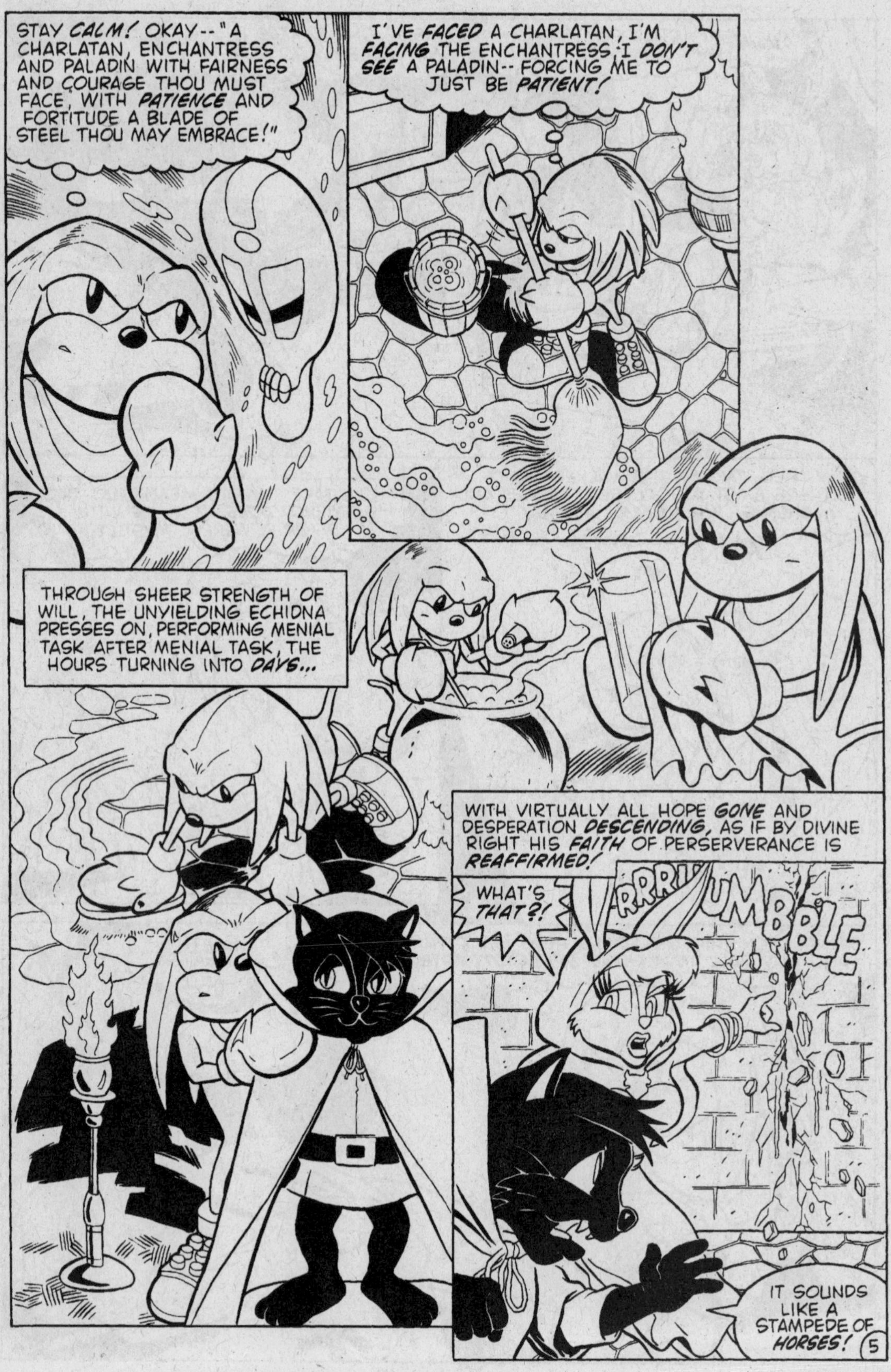
STAY *CALM!* OKAY-- "A CHARLATAN, ENCHANTRESS AND PALADIN WITH FAIRNESS AND COURAGE THOU MUST FACE, WITH *PATIENCE* AND FORTITUDE A BLADE OF STEEL THOU MAY EMBRACE!"
I'VE *FACED* A CHARLATAN, I'M *FACING* THE ENCHANTRESS; I *DON'T SEE* A PALADIN-- FORCING ME TO JUST BE *PATIENT!*
THROUGH SHEER STRENGTH OF WILL, THE UNYIELDING ECHIDNA PRESSES ON, PERFORMING MENIAL TASK AFTER MENIAL TASK, THE HOURS TURNING INTO *DAYS...*
WITH VIRTUALLY ALL HOPE *GONE* AND DESPERATION *DESCENDING,* AS IF BY DIVINE RIGHT HIS *FAITH* OF PERSERVERANCE IS *REAFFIRMED!*
WHAT'S *THAT?!*
RRRUMBBLE
IT SOUNDS LIKE A STAMPEDE OF *HORSES!*
5

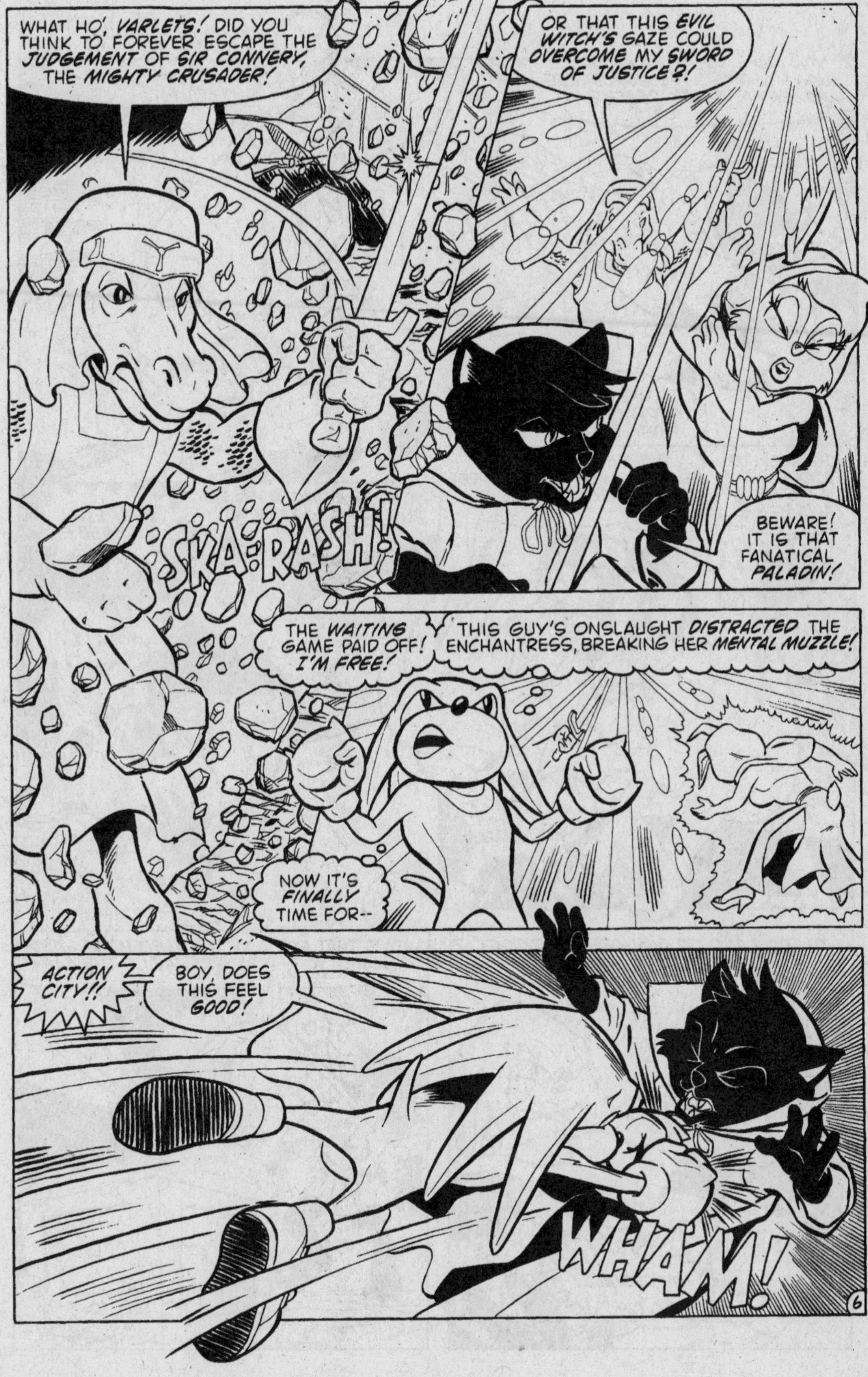
WHAT HO', VARLETS! DID YOU THINK TO FOREVER ESCAPE THE JUDGEMENT OF SIR CONNERY, THE MIGHTY CRUSADER!
OR THAT THIS EVIL WITCH'S GAZE COULD OVERCOME MY SWORD OF JUSTICE?!
SKA-RASH!
BEWARE! IT IS THAT FANATICAL PALADIN!
THE WAITING GAME PAID OFF! I'M FREE!
THIS GUY'S ONSLAUGHT DISTRACTED THE ENCHANTRESS, BREAKING HER MENTAL MUZZLE!
NOW IT'S FINALLY TIME FOR--
ACTION CITY!!
BOY, DOES THIS FEEL GOOD!
WHAM!
6

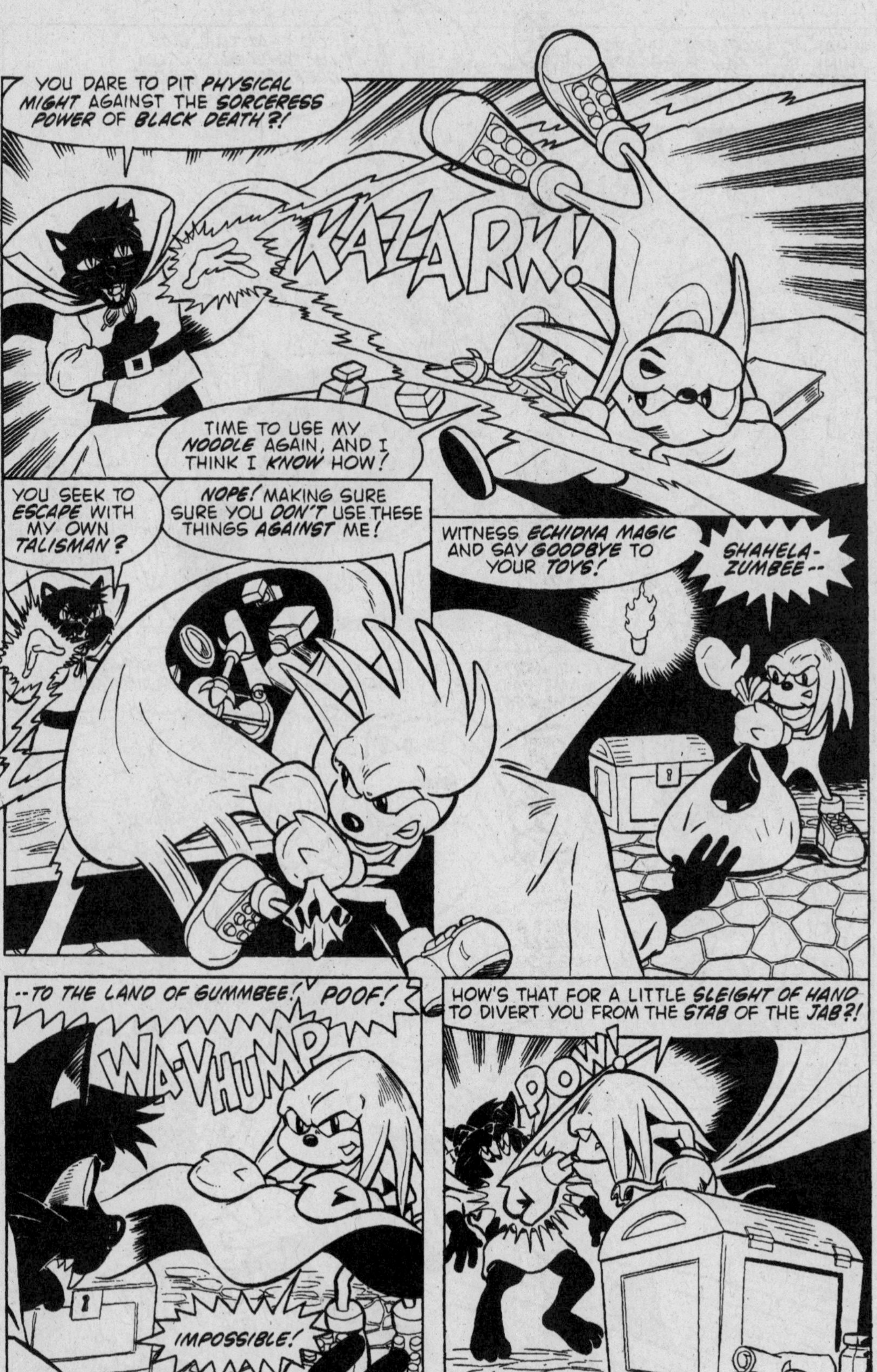
YOU DARE TO PIT PHYSICAL MIGHT AGAINST THE SORCERESS POWER OF BLACK DEATH?!
KAZARK!
TIME TO USE MY NOODLE AGAIN, AND I THINK I KNOW HOW!
YOU SEEK TO ESCAPE WITH MY OWN TALISMAN?
NOPE! MAKING SURE SURE YOU DON'T USE THESE THINGS AGAINST ME!
WITNESS ECHIDNA MAGIC AND SAY GOODBYE TO YOUR TOYS!
SHAHELA-ZUMBEE--
--TO THE LAND OF GUMMBEE!
POOF!
WA-VHUMP
IMPOSSIBLE!
HOW'S THAT FOR A LITTLE SLEIGHT OF HAND TO DIVERT YOU FROM THE STAB OF THE JAB?!
POW!
7

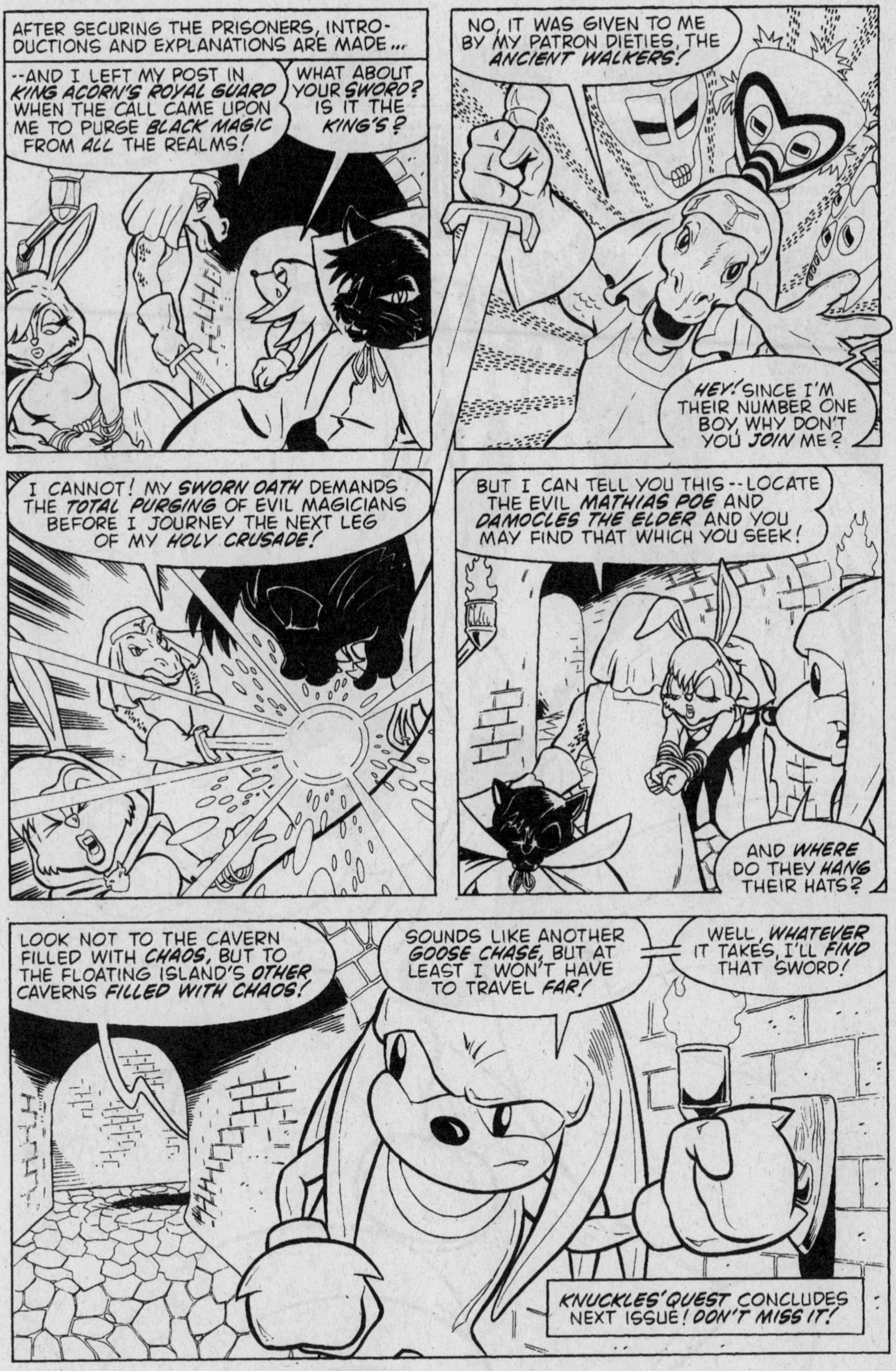
AFTER SECURING THE PRISONERS, INTRO-DUCTIONS AND EXPLANATIONS ARE MADE...
--AND I LEFT MY POST IN KING ACORN'S ROYAL GUARD WHEN THE CALL CAME UPON ME TO PURGE BLACK MAGIC FROM ALL THE REALMS!
WHAT ABOUT YOUR SWORD? IS IT THE KING'S?
NO, IT WAS GIVEN TO ME BY MY PATRON DIETIES, THE ANCIENT WALKERS!
HEY! SINCE I'M THEIR NUMBER ONE BOY, WHY DON'T YOU JOIN ME?
I CANNOT! MY SWORN OATH DEMANDS THE TOTAL PURGING OF EVIL MAGICIANS BEFORE I JOURNEY THE NEXT LEG OF MY HOLY CRUSADE!
BUT I CAN TELL YOU THIS--LOCATE THE EVIL MATHIAS POE AND DAMOCLES THE ELDER AND YOU MAY FIND THAT WHICH YOU SEEK!
AND WHERE DO THEY HANG THEIR HATS?
LOOK NOT TO THE CAVERN FILLED WITH CHAOS, BUT TO THE FLOATING ISLAND'S OTHER CAVERNS FILLED WITH CHAOS!
SOUNDS LIKE ANOTHER GOOSE CHASE, BUT AT LEAST I WON'T HAVE TO TRAVEL FAR!
WELL, WHATEVER IT TAKES, I'LL FIND THAT SWORD!
KNUCKLES' QUEST CONCLUDES NEXT ISSUE! DON'T MISS IT!

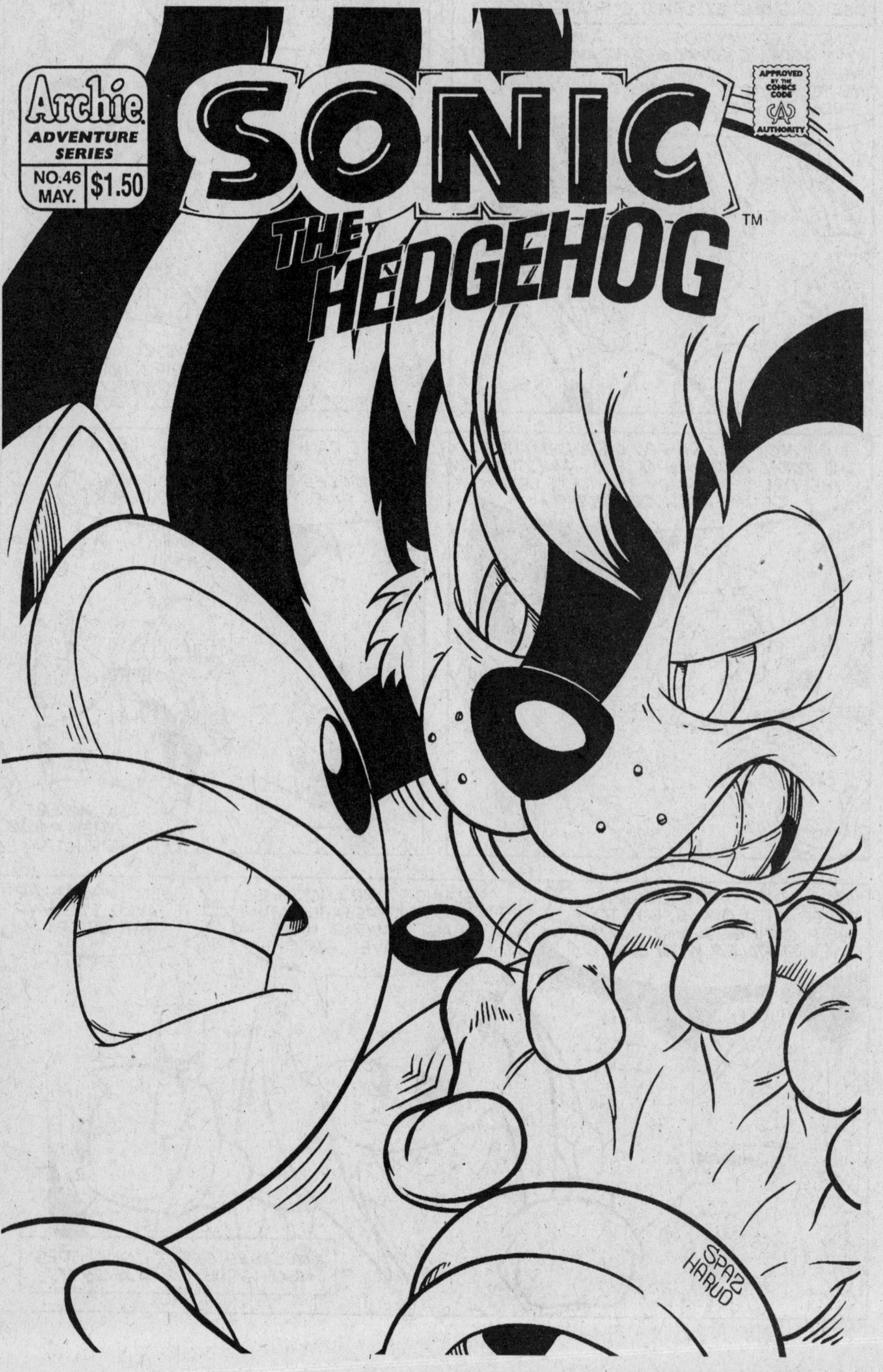
Archie
ADVENTURE SERIES
NO.46 MAY.
$1.50
SONIC THE HEDGEHOG™
APPROVED BY THE COMICS CODE AUTHORITY
SPAZ HARUO

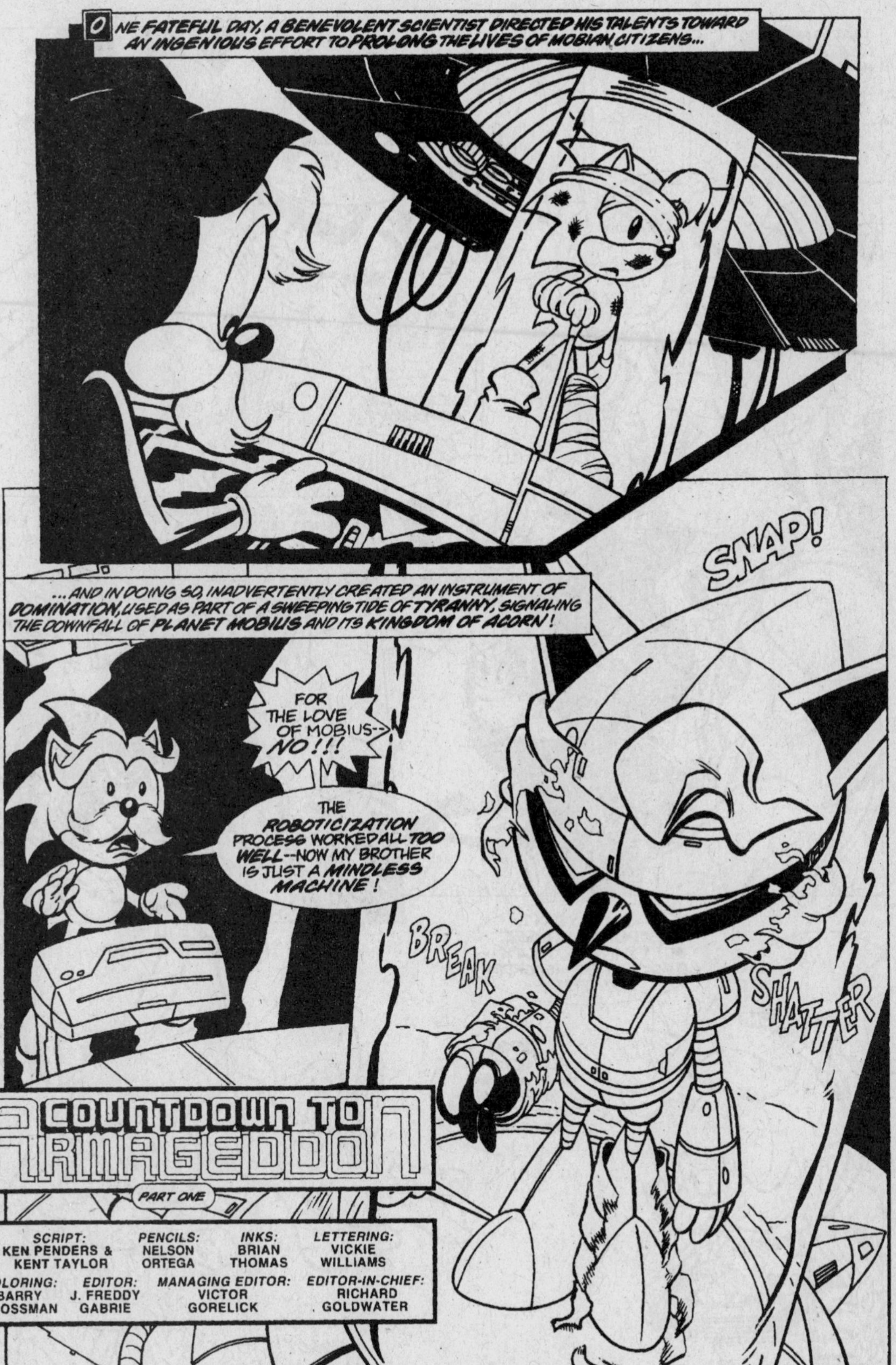
ONE FATEFUL DAY, A BENEVOLENT SCIENTIST DIRECTED HIS TALENTS TOWARD AN INGENIOUS EFFORT TO PROLONG THE LIVES OF MOBIAN CITIZENS...
...AND IN DOING SO, INADVERTENTLY CREATED AN INSTRUMENT OF DOMINATION, USED AS PART OF A SWEEPING TIDE OF TYRANNY, SIGNALING THE DOWNFALL OF PLANET MOBIUS AND ITS KINGDOM OF ACORN!
SNAP!
FOR THE LOVE OF MOBIUS--NO!!!
THE ROBOTICIZATION PROCESS WORKED ALL TOO WELL--NOW MY BROTHER IS JUST A MINDLESS MACHINE!
BREAK
SHATTER
A COUNTDOWN TO ARMAGEDDON
PART ONE
SCRIPT: KEN PENDERS & KENT TAYLOR
PENCILS: NELSON ORTEGA
INKS: BRIAN THOMAS
LETTERING: VICKIE WILLIAMS
COLORING: BARRY GROSSMAN
EDITOR: J. FREDDY GABRIE
MANAGING EDITOR: VICTOR GORELICK
EDITOR-IN-CHIEF: RICHARD GOLDWATER

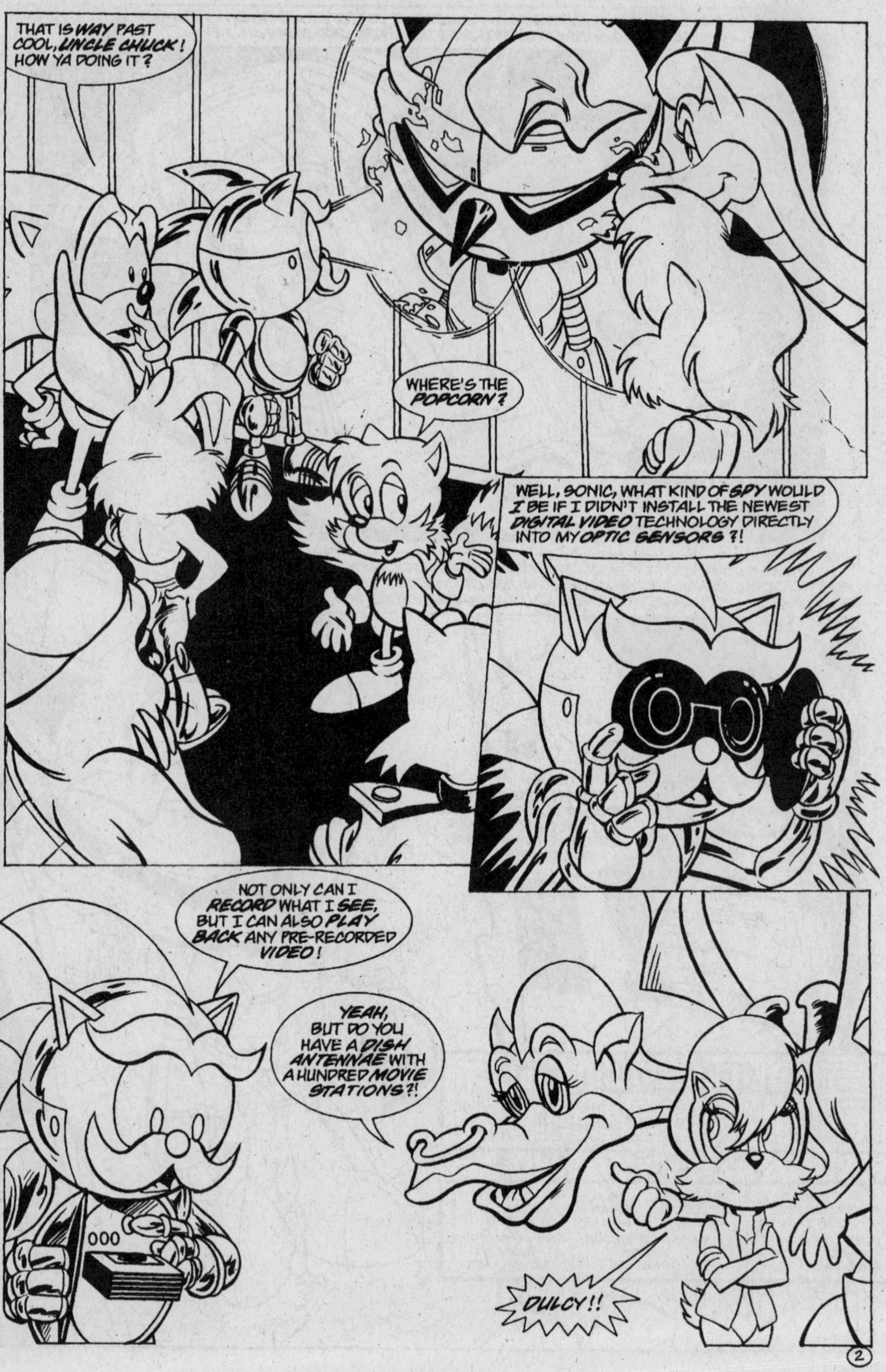

THAT IS WAY PAST COOL, UNCLE CHUCK! HOW YA DOING IT?
WHERE'S THE POPCORN?
WELL, SONIC, WHAT KIND OF SPY WOULD I BE IF I DIDN'T INSTALL THE NEWEST DIGITAL VIDEO TECHNOLOGY DIRECTLY INTO MY OPTIC SENSORS?!
NOT ONLY CAN I RECORD WHAT I SEE, BUT I CAN ALSO PLAY BACK ANY PRE-RECORDED VIDEO!
YEAH, BUT DO YOU HAVE A DISH ANTENNAE WITH A HUNDRED MOVIE STATIONS?!
DULCY!!
2

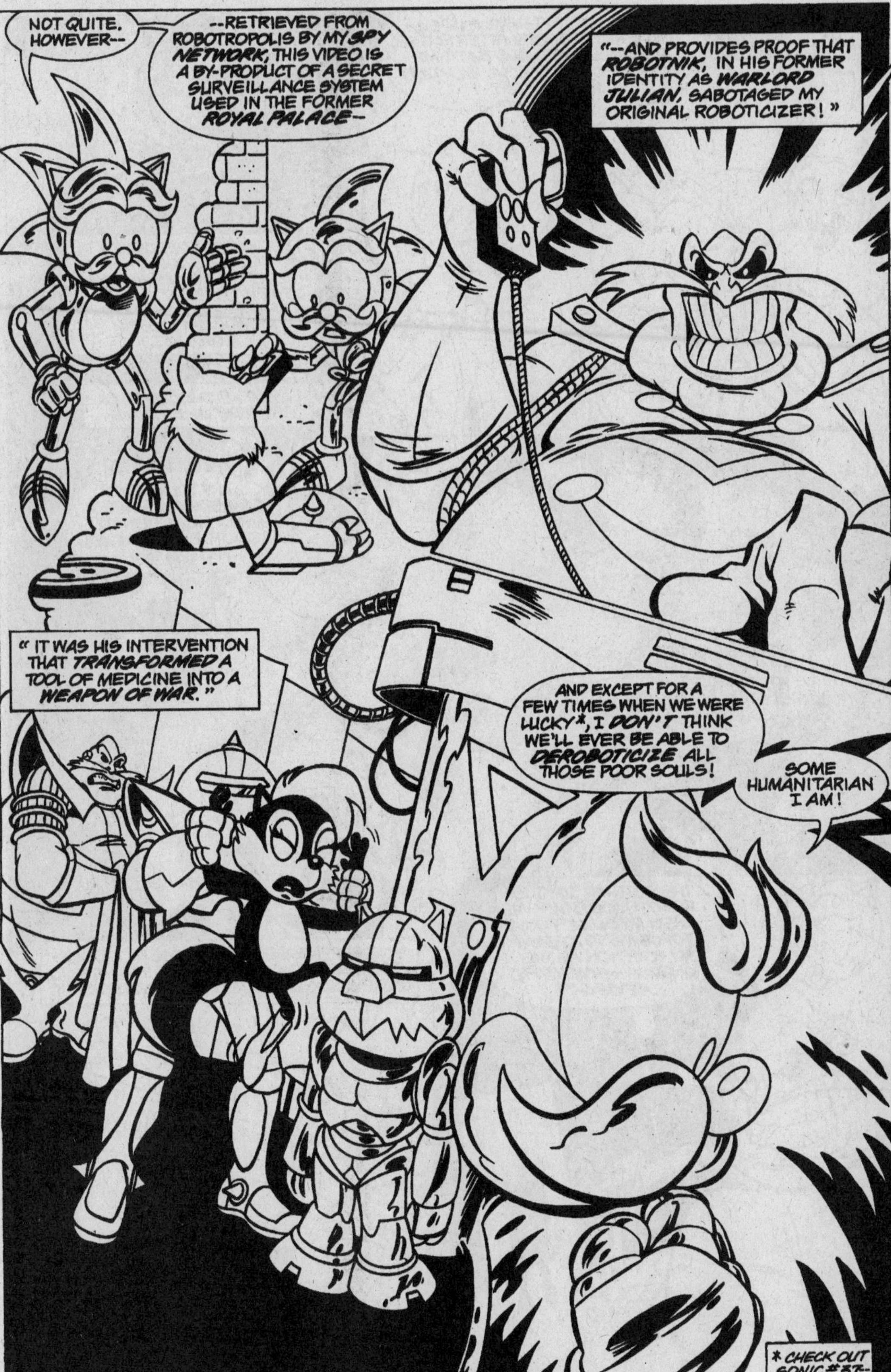
NOT QUITE. HOWEVER--
--RETRIEVED FROM ROBOTROPOLIS BY MY SPY NETWORK, THIS VIDEO IS A BY-PRODUCT OF A SECRET SURVEILLANCE SYSTEM USED IN THE FORMER ROYAL PALACE--
"--AND PROVIDES PROOF THAT ROBOTNIK, IN HIS FORMER IDENTITY AS WARLORD JULIAN, SABOTAGED MY ORIGINAL ROBOTICIZER!"
" IT WAS HIS INTERVENTION THAT TRANSFORMED A TOOL OF MEDICINE INTO A WEAPON OF WAR."
AND EXCEPT FOR A FEW TIMES WHEN WE WERE LUCKY*, I DON'T THINK WE'LL EVER BE ABLE TO DEROBOTICIZE ALL THOSE POOR SOULS!
SOME HUMANITARIAN I AM!
* CHECK OUT SONIC #37-- EDITOR.
3

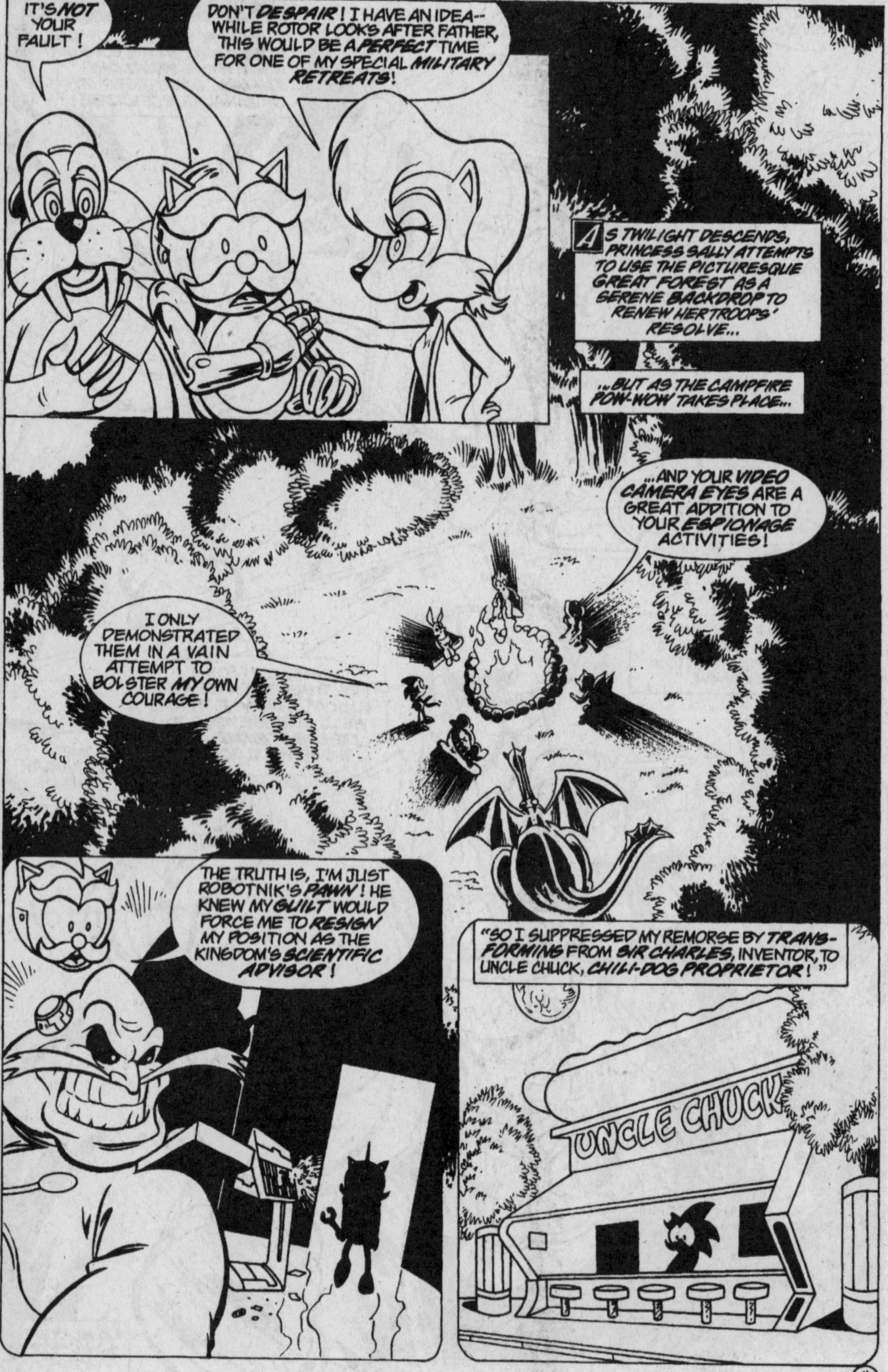
IT'S NOT YOUR FAULT!
DON'T DESPAIR! I HAVE AN IDEA-- WHILE ROTOR LOOKS AFTER FATHER, THIS WOULD BE A PERFECT TIME FOR ONE OF MY SPECIAL MILITARY RETREATS!
AS TWILIGHT DESCENDS, PRINCESS SALLY ATTEMPTS TO USE THE PICTURESQUE GREAT FOREST AS A SERENE BACKDROP TO RENEW HER TROOPS' RESOLVE...
...BUT AS THE CAMPFIRE POW-WOW TAKES PLACE...
...AND YOUR VIDEO CAMERA EYES ARE A GREAT ADDITION TO YOUR ESPIONAGE ACTIVITIES!
I ONLY DEMONSTRATED THEM IN A VAIN ATTEMPT TO BOLSTER MY OWN COURAGE!
THE TRUTH IS, I'M JUST ROBOTNIK'S PAWN! HE KNEW MY GUILT WOULD FORCE ME TO RESIGN MY POSITION AS THE KINGDOM'S SCIENTIFIC ADVISOR!
"SO I SUPPRESSED MY REMORSE BY TRANSFORMING FROM SIR CHARLES, INVENTOR, TO UNCLE CHUCK, CHILI-DOG PROPRIETOR!"
UNCLE CHUCK
4

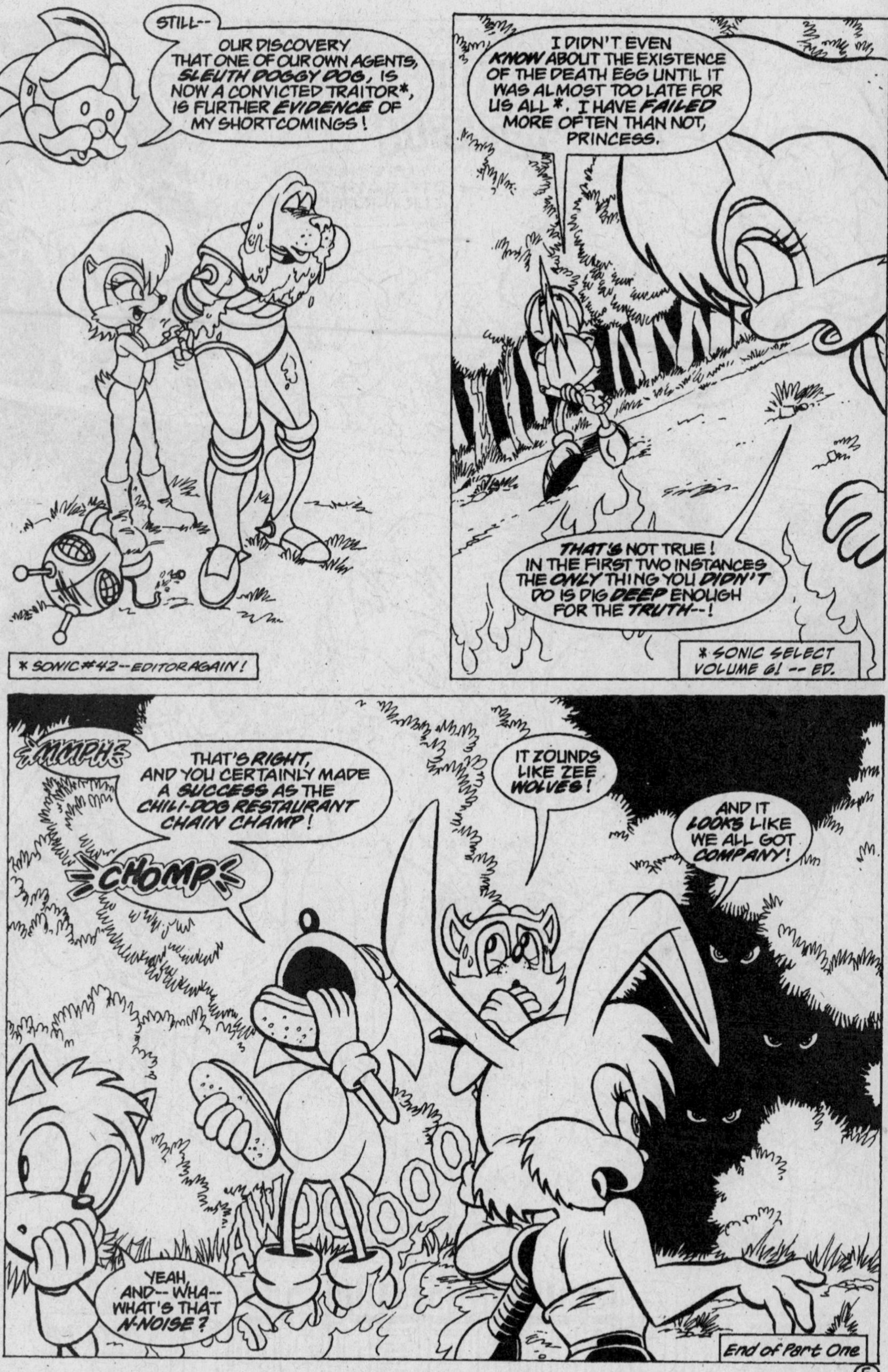
STILL--
OUR DISCOVERY THAT ONE OF OUR OWN AGENTS, SLEUTH DOGGY DOG, IS NOW A CONVICTED TRAITOR*, IS FURTHER EVIDENCE OF MY SHORTCOMINGS!
* SONIC #42--EDITOR AGAIN!
I DIDN'T EVEN KNOW ABOUT THE EXISTENCE OF THE DEATH EGG UNTIL IT WAS ALMOST TOO LATE FOR US ALL*. I HAVE FAILED MORE OFTEN THAN NOT, PRINCESS.
THAT'S NOT TRUE! IN THE FIRST TWO INSTANCES THE ONLY THING YOU DIDN'T DO IS DIG DEEP ENOUGH FOR THE TRUTH--!
* SONIC SELECT VOLUME 6! -- ED.
MMPH
THAT'S RIGHT, AND YOU CERTAINLY MADE A SUCCESS AS THE CHILI-DOG RESTAURANT CHAIN CHAMP!
CHOMP
IT ZOUNDS LIKE ZEE WOLVES!
AND IT LOOKS LIKE WE ALL GOT COMPANY!
AWOOOOOO
YEAH, AND-- WHA-- WHAT'S THAT N-NOISE?
End of Part One
5

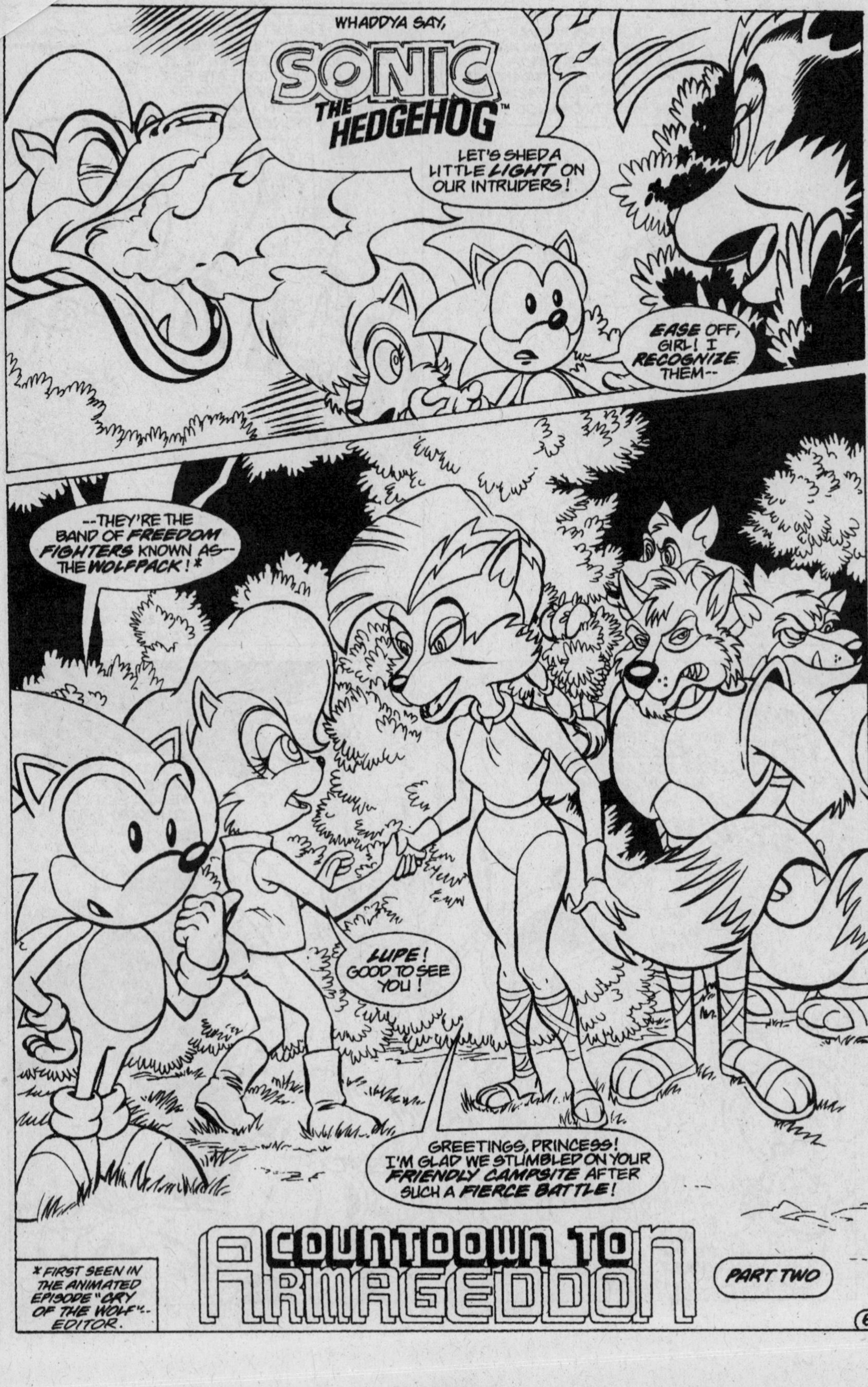
WHADDYA SAY,
SONIC THE HEDGEHOG™
LET'S SHED A LITTLE LIGHT ON OUR INTRUDERS!
EASE OFF, GIRL! I RECOGNIZE THEM--
--THEY'RE THE BAND OF FREEDOM FIGHTERS KNOWN AS-- THE WOLFPACK!*
LUPE! GOOD TO SEE YOU!
GREETINGS, PRINCESS! I'M GLAD WE STUMBLED ON YOUR FRIENDLY CAMPSITE AFTER SUCH A FIERCE BATTLE!
COUNTDOWN TO ARMAGEDDON
PART TWO
* FIRST SEEN IN THE ANIMATED EPISODE "CRY OF THE WOLF".-- EDITOR.
6

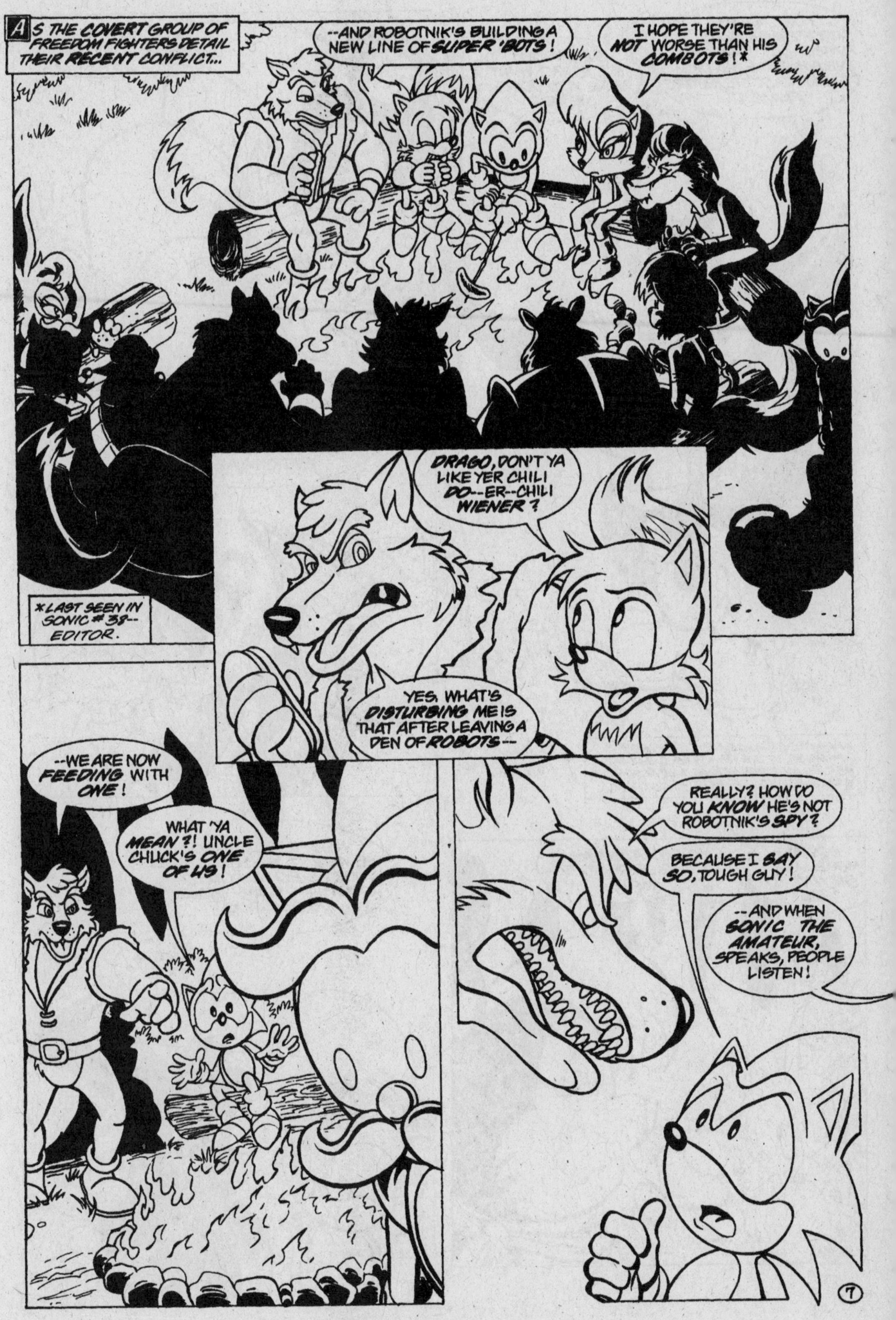
AS THE COVERT GROUP OF FREEDOM FIGHTERS DETAIL THEIR RECENT CONFLICT...
--AND ROBOTNIK'S BUILDING A NEW LINE OF SUPER 'BOTS!
I HOPE THEY'RE NOT WORSE THAN HIS COMBOTS!*
*LAST SEEN IN SONIC #38-- EDITOR.
DRAGO, DON'T YA LIKE YER CHILI DO--ER--CHILI WIENER?
YES. WHAT'S DISTURBING ME IS THAT AFTER LEAVING A DEN OF ROBOTS--
--WE ARE NOW FEEDING WITH ONE!
WHAT 'YA MEAN?! UNCLE CHUCK'S ONE OF US!
REALLY? HOW DO YOU KNOW HE'S NOT ROBOTNIK'S SPY?
BECAUSE I SAY SO, TOUGH GUY!
--AND WHEN SONIC THE AMATEUR, SPEAKS, PEOPLE LISTEN!
7

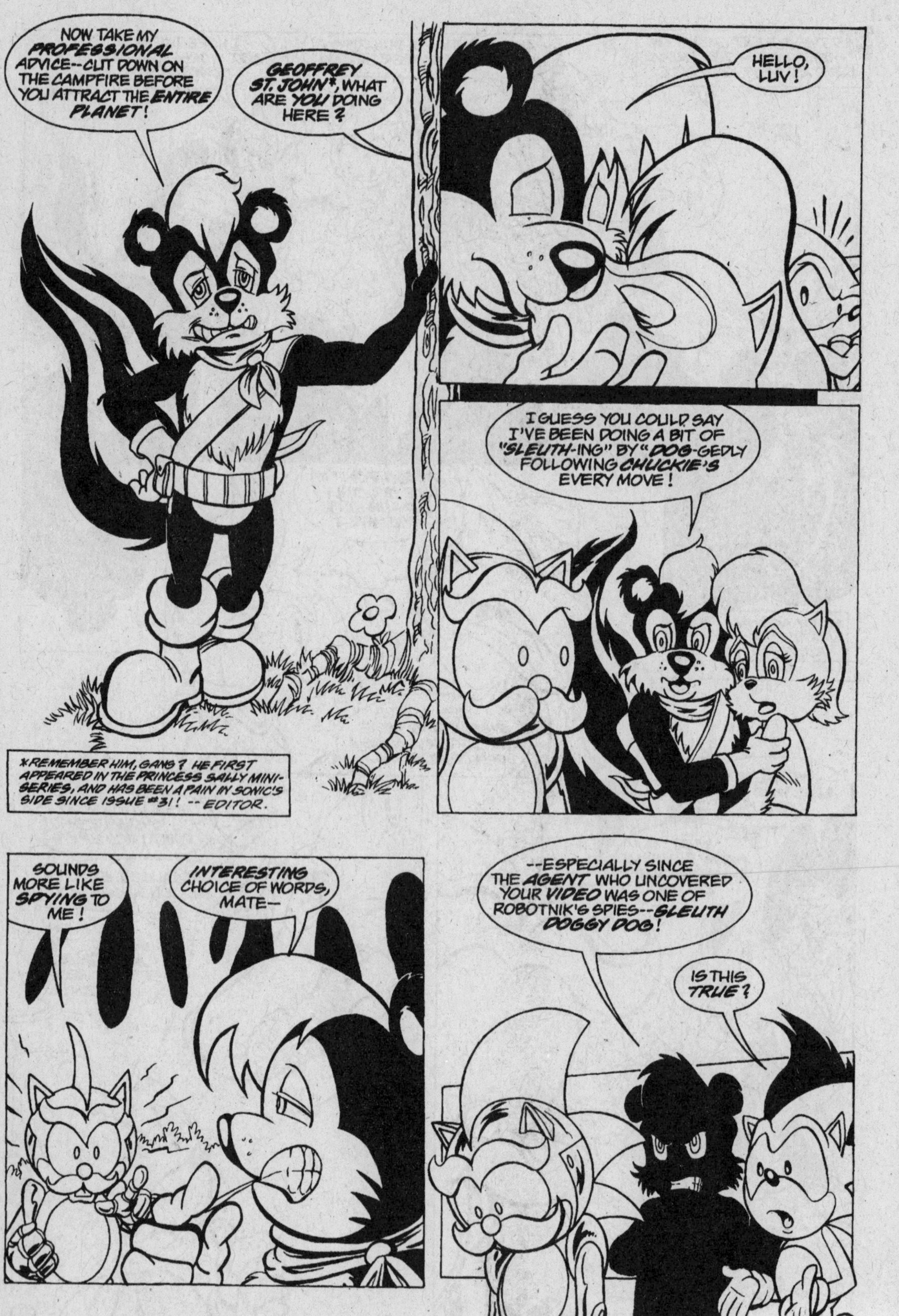
NOW TAKE MY PROFESSIONAL ADVICE--CUT DOWN ON THE CAMPFIRE BEFORE YOU ATTRACT THE ENTIRE PLANET!
GEOFFREY ST. JOHN*, WHAT ARE YOU DOING HERE?
HELLO, LUV!
I GUESS YOU COULD SAY I'VE BEEN DOING A BIT OF "SLEUTH-ING" BY "DOG-GEDLY FOLLOWING CHUCKIE'S EVERY MOVE!
*REMEMBER HIM, GANG? HE FIRST APPEARED IN THE PRINCESS SALLY MINI-SERIES, AND HAS BEEN A PAIN IN SONIC'S SIDE SINCE ISSUE #31! -- EDITOR.
SOUNDS MORE LIKE SPYING TO ME!
INTERESTING CHOICE OF WORDS, MATE--
--ESPECIALLY SINCE THE AGENT WHO UNCOVERED YOUR VIDEO WAS ONE OF ROBOTNIK'S SPIES--SLEUTH DOGGY DOG!
IS THIS TRUE?
8

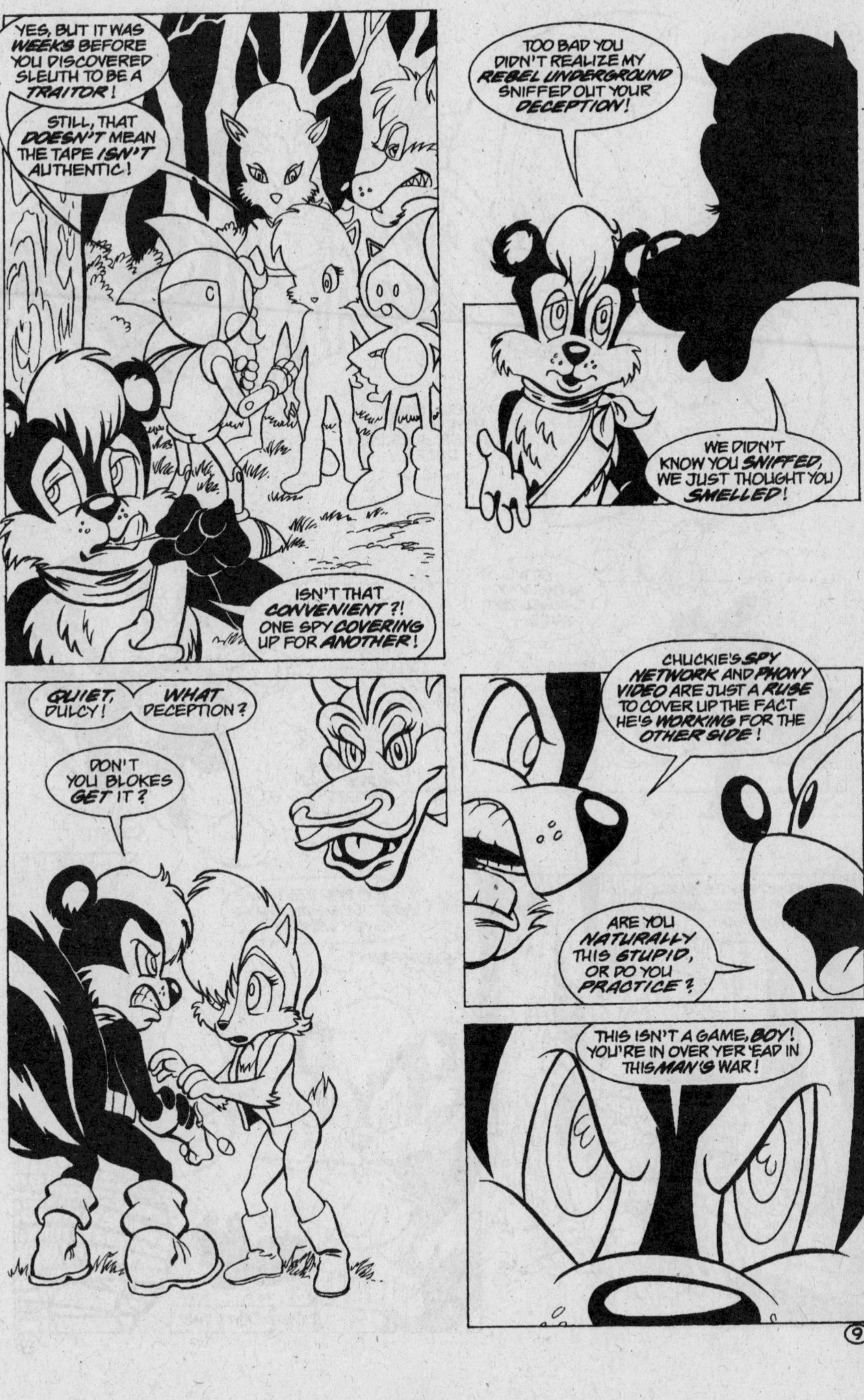
YES, BUT IT WAS WEEKS BEFORE YOU DISCOVERED SLEUTH TO BE A TRAITOR!
STILL, THAT DOESN'T MEAN THE TAPE ISN'T AUTHENTIC!
ISN'T THAT CONVENIENT?! ONE SPY COVERING UP FOR ANOTHER!
TOO BAD YOU DIDN'T REALIZE MY REBEL UNDERGROUND SNIFFED OUT YOUR DECEPTION!
WE DIDN'T KNOW YOU SNIFFED, WE JUST THOUGHT YOU SMELLED!
QUIET, DULCY!
WHAT DECEPTION?
DON'T YOU BLOKES GET IT?
CHUCKIE'S SPY NETWORK AND PHONY VIDEO ARE JUST A RUSE TO COVER UP THE FACT HE'S WORKING FOR THE OTHER SIDE!
ARE YOU NATURALLY THIS STUPID, OR DO YOU PRACTICE?
THIS ISN'T A GAME, BOY! YOU'RE IN OVER YER 'EAD IN THIS MAN'S WAR!
9

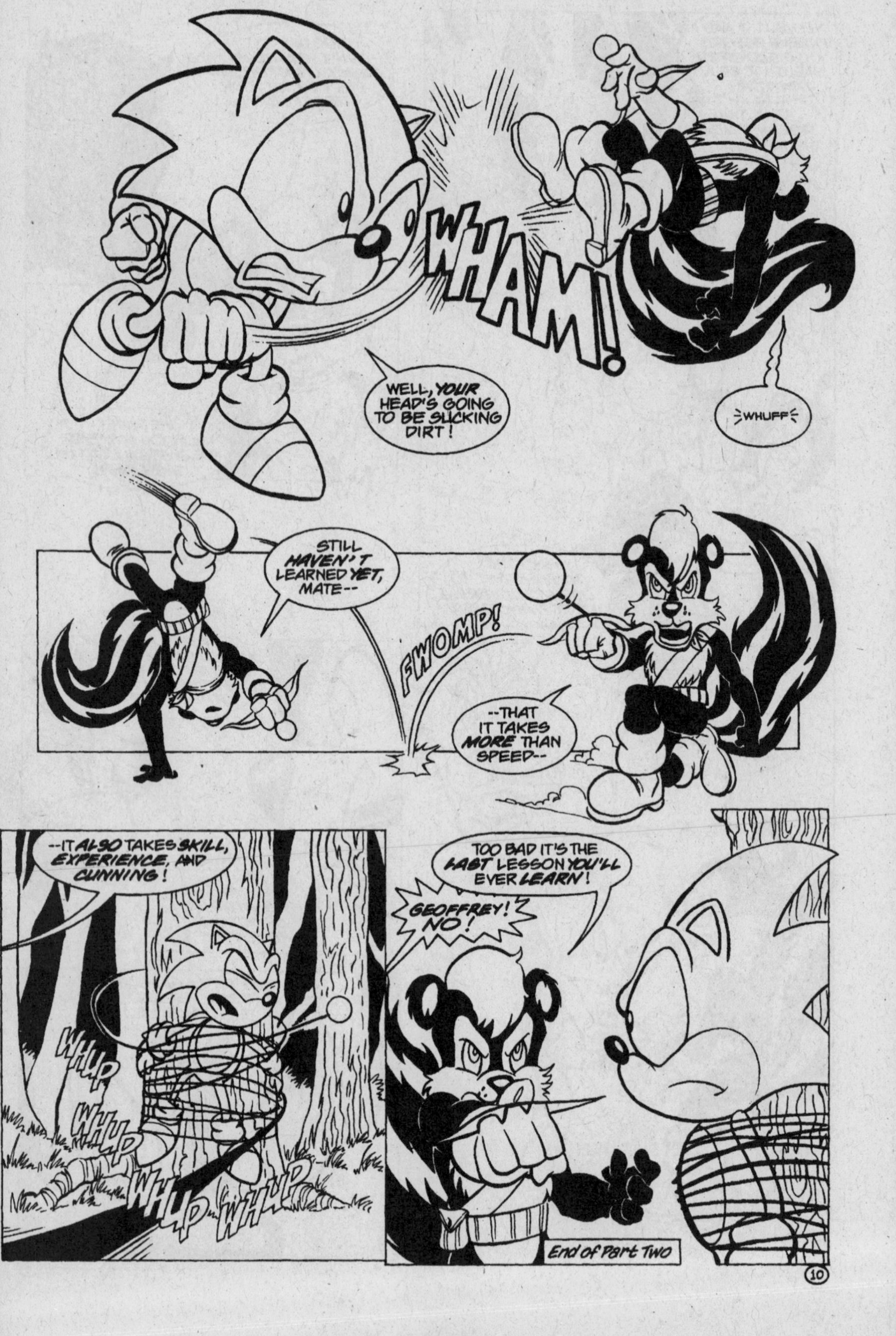
WHAM!
WELL, YOUR HEAD'S GOING TO BE SUCKING DIRT!
WHUFF
STILL HAVEN'T LEARNED YET, MATE--
FWOMP!
--THAT IT TAKES MORE THAN SPEED--
--IT ALSO TAKES SKILL, EXPERIENCE, AND CUNNING!
WHUP
WHUP
WHUP
WHUP
WHUP
TOO BAD IT'S THE LAST LESSON YOU'LL EVER LEARN!
GEOFFREY! NO!
End of Part Two
10

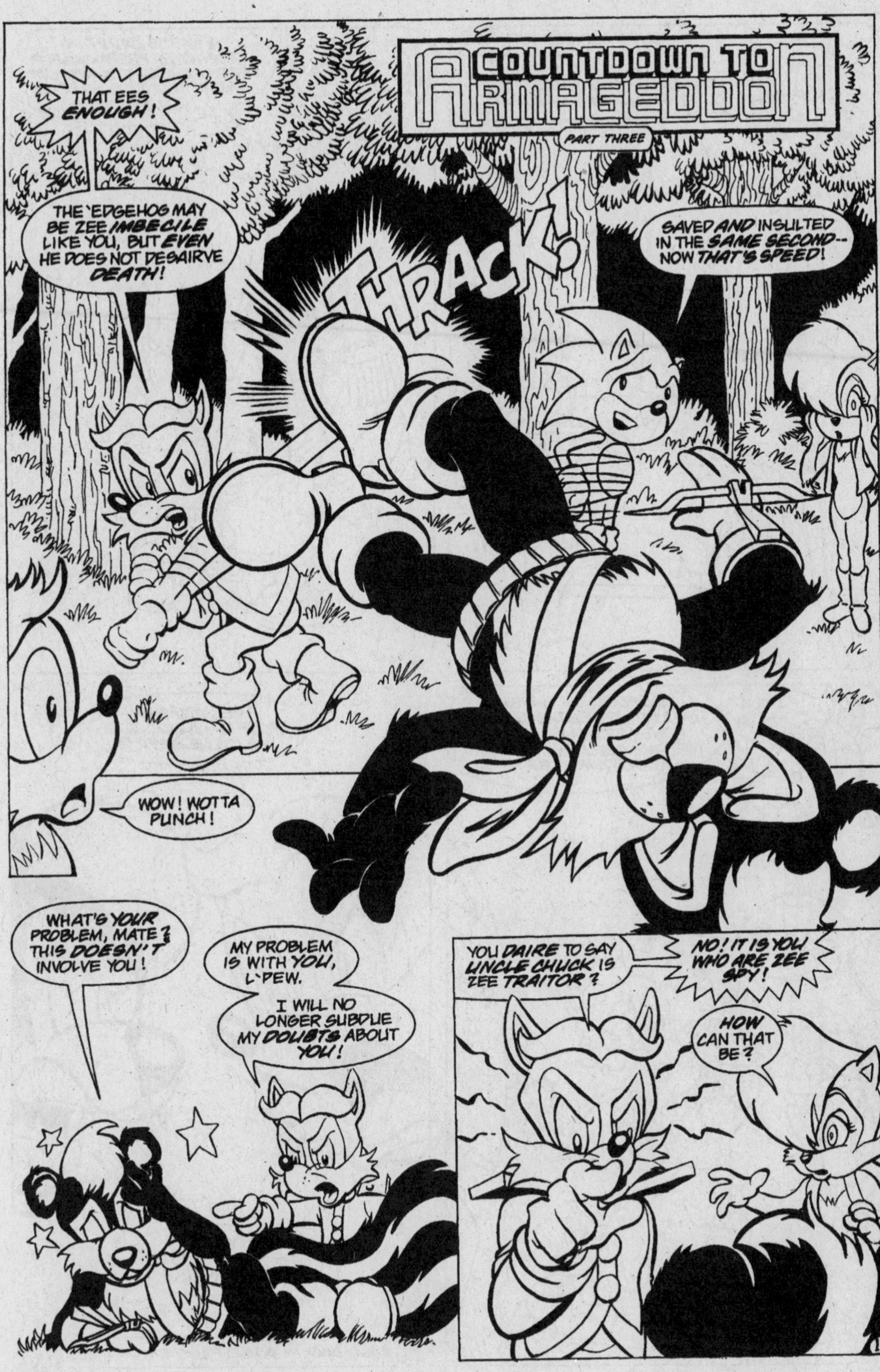
COUNTDOWN TO ARMAGEDDON
PART THREE
THAT EES ENOUGH!
THE 'EDGEHOG MAY BE ZEE IMBECILE LIKE YOU, BUT EVEN HE DOES NOT DESAIRVE DEATH!
THRACK!
SAVED AND INSULTED IN THE SAME SECOND-- NOW THAT'S SPEED!
WOW! WOTTA PUNCH!
WHAT'S YOUR PROBLEM, MATE? THIS DOESN'T INVOLVE YOU!
MY PROBLEM IS WITH YOU, L'PEW.
I WILL NO LONGER SUBDUE MY DOUBTS ABOUT YOU!
YOU DAIRE TO SAY UNCLE CHUCK IS ZEE TRAITOR?
NO! IT IS YOU WHO ARE ZEE SPY!
HOW CAN THAT BE?
11

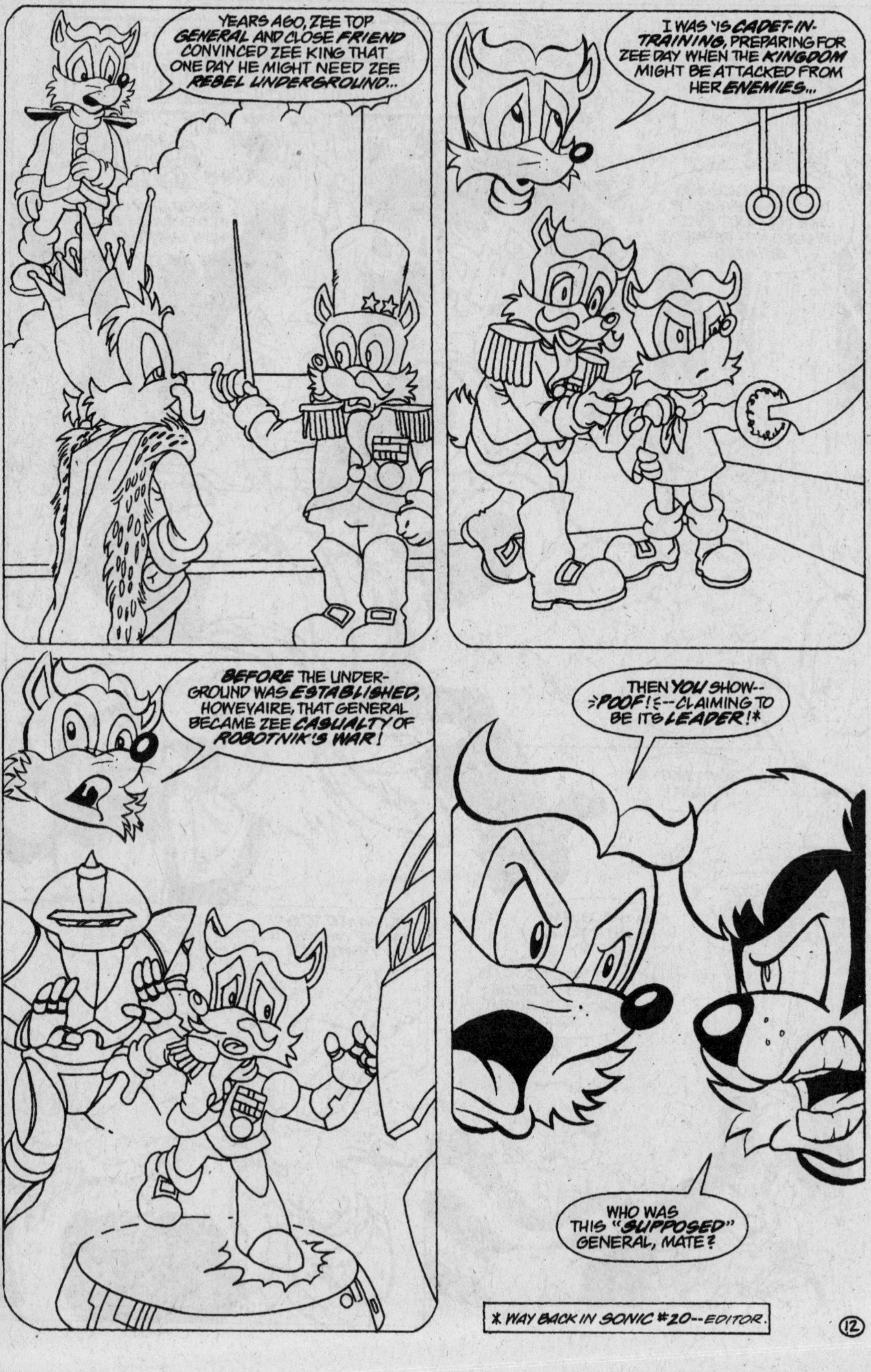
YEARS AGO, ZEE TOP GENERAL AND CLOSE FRIEND CONVINCED ZEE KING THAT ONE DAY HE MIGHT NEED ZEE REBEL UNDERGROUND...
I WAS 'IS CADET-IN-TRAINING, PREPARING FOR ZEE DAY WHEN THE KINGDOM MIGHT BE ATTACKED FROM HER ENEMIES...
BEFORE THE UNDERGROUND WAS ESTABLISHED, HOWEVAIRE, THAT GENERAL BECAME ZEE CASUALTY OF ROBOTNIK'S WAR!
THEN YOU SHOW-- POOF! --CLAIMING TO BE ITS LEADER!*
WHO WAS THIS "SUPPOSED" GENERAL, MATE?
* WAY BACK IN SONIC #20--EDITOR.
12

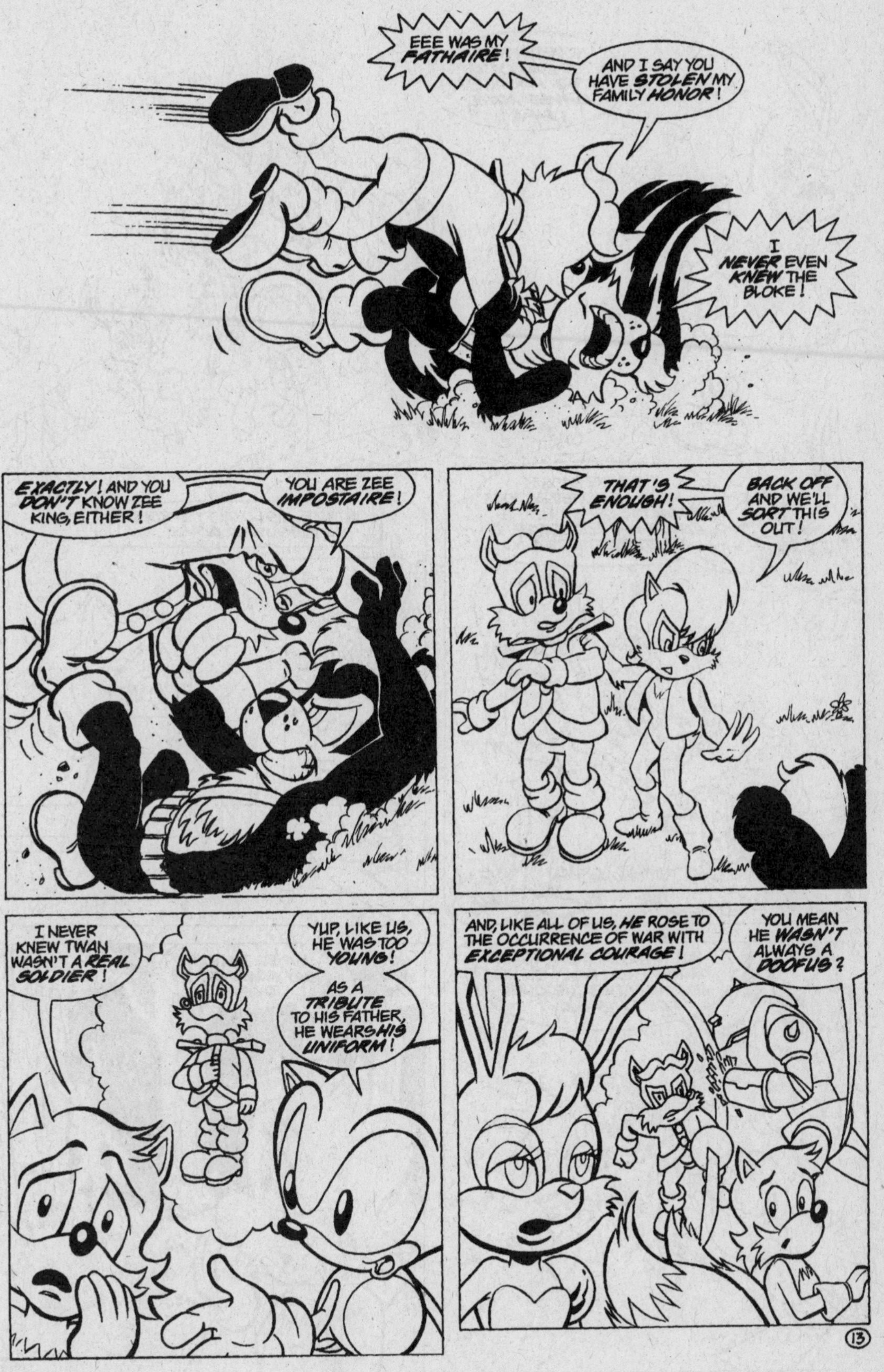

EEE WAS MY FATHAIRE!
AND I SAY YOU HAVE STOLEN MY FAMILY HONOR!
I NEVER EVEN KNEW THE BLOKE!
EXACTLY! AND YOU DON'T KNOW ZEE KING, EITHER!
YOU ARE ZEE IMPOSTAIRE!
THAT'S ENOUGH!
BACK OFF AND WE'LL SORT THIS OUT!
I NEVER KNEW TWAN WASN'T A REAL SOLDIER!
YUP, LIKE US, HE WAS TOO YOUNG!
AS A TRIBUTE TO HIS FATHER, HE WEARS HIS UNIFORM!
AND, LIKE ALL OF US, HE ROSE TO THE OCCURRENCE OF WAR WITH EXCEPTIONAL COURAGE!
YOU MEAN HE WASN'T ALWAYS A DOOFUS?
13

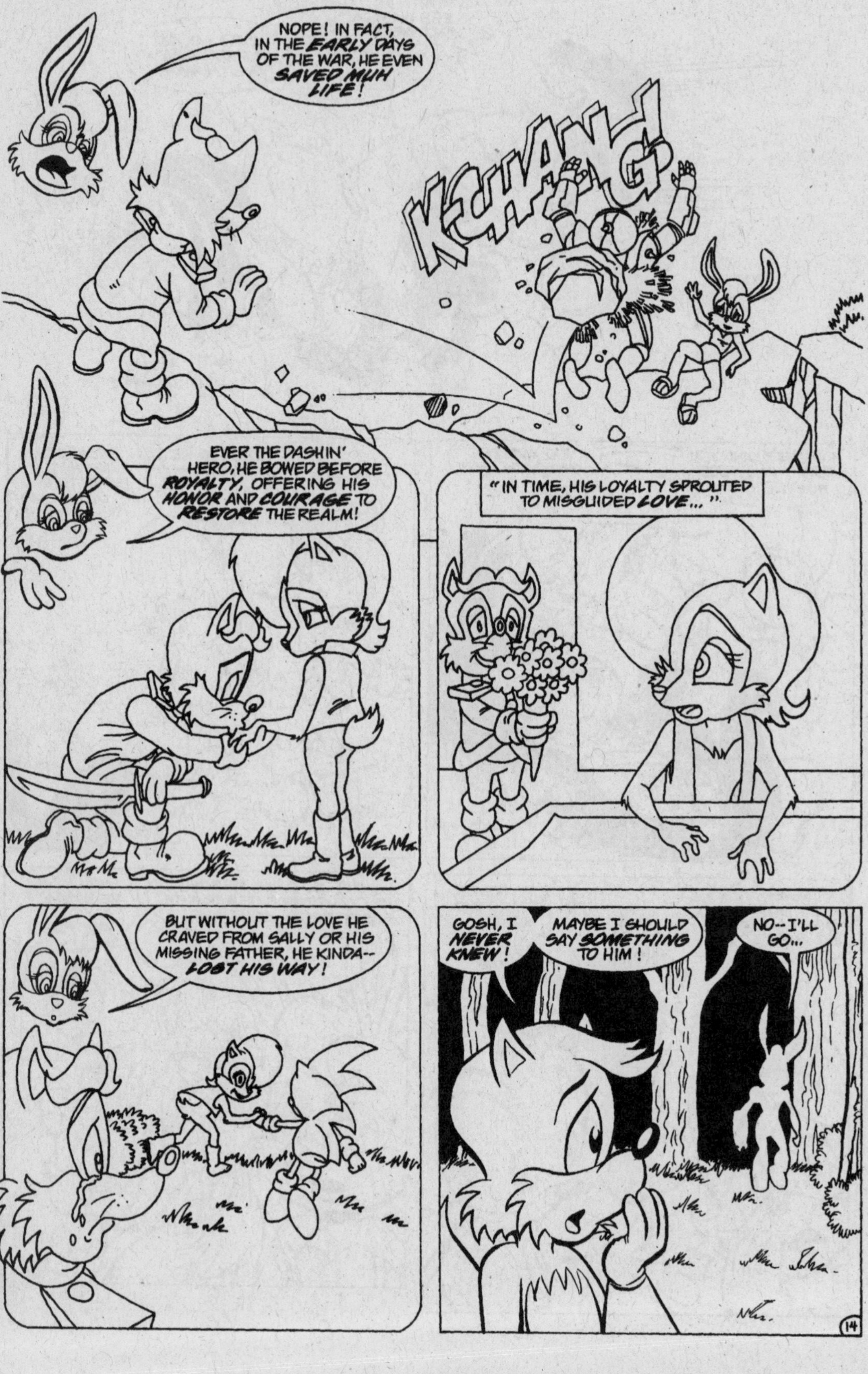
NOPE! IN FACT, IN THE EARLY DAYS OF THE WAR, HE EVEN SAVED MUH LIFE!
K-CHANG!
EVER THE DASHIN' HERO, HE BOWED BEFORE ROYALTY, OFFERING HIS HONOR AND COURAGE TO RESTORE THE REALM!
"IN TIME, HIS LOYALTY SPROUTED TO MISGUIDED LOVE..."
BUT WITHOUT THE LOVE HE CRAVED FROM SALLY OR HIS MISSING FATHER, HE KINDA-- LOST HIS WAY!
GOSH, I NEVER KNEW!
MAYBE I SHOULD SAY SOMETHING TO HIM!
NO-- I'LL GO...
14

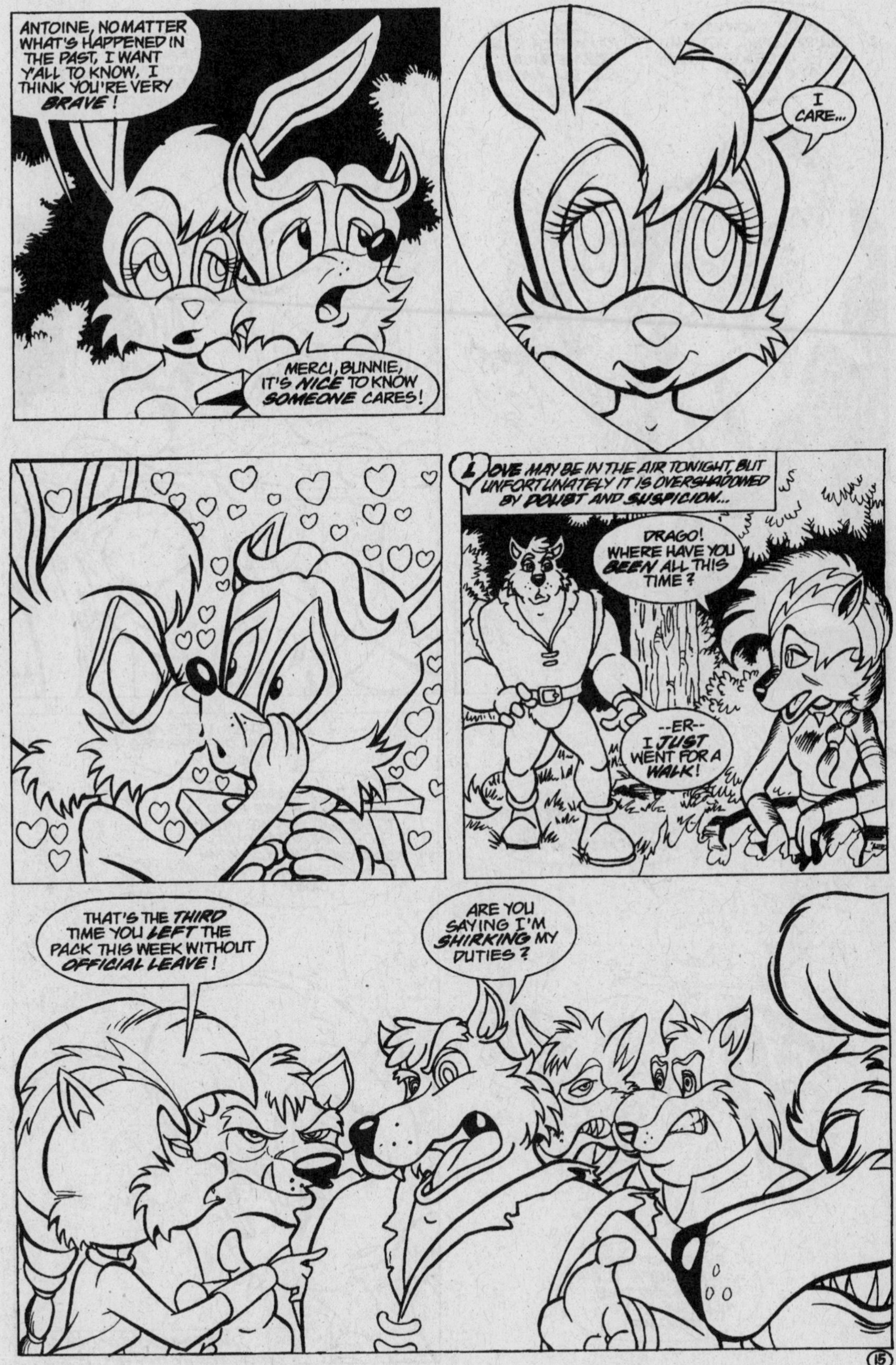

ANTOINE, NO MATTER WHAT'S HAPPENED IN THE PAST, I WANT Y'ALL TO KNOW, I THINK YOU'RE VERY BRAVE!
MERCI, BUNNIE, IT'S NICE TO KNOW SOMEONE CARES!
I CARE...
LOVE MAY BE IN THE AIR TONIGHT, BUT UNFORTUNATELY IT IS OVERSHADOWED BY DOUBT AND SUSPICION...
DRAGO! WHERE HAVE YOU BEEN ALL THIS TIME?
--ER-- I JUST WENT FOR A WALK!
THAT'S THE THIRD TIME YOU LEFT THE PACK THIS WEEK WITHOUT OFFICIAL LEAVE!
ARE YOU SAYING I'M SHIRKING MY DUTIES?
15

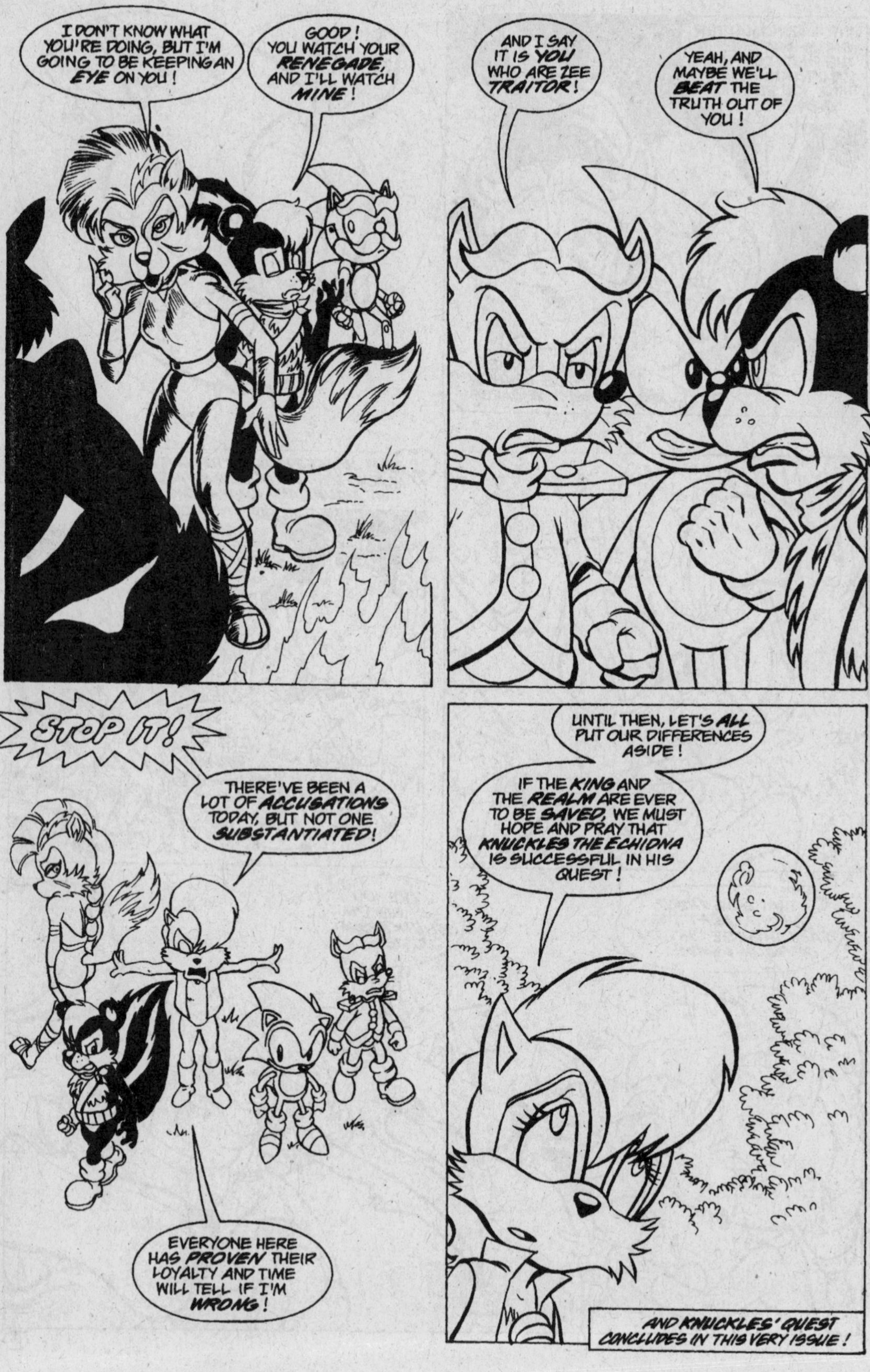
I DON'T KNOW WHAT YOU'RE DOING, BUT I'M GOING TO BE KEEPING AN EYE ON YOU!
GOOD! YOU WATCH YOUR RENEGADE, AND I'LL WATCH MINE!
AND I SAY IT IS YOU WHO ARE ZEE TRAITOR!
YEAH, AND MAYBE WE'LL BEAT THE TRUTH OUT OF YOU!
STOP IT!
THERE'VE BEEN A LOT OF ACCUSATIONS TODAY, BUT NOT ONE SUBSTANTIATED!
EVERYONE HERE HAS PROVEN THEIR LOYALTY AND TIME WILL TELL IF I'M WRONG!
UNTIL THEN, LET'S ALL PUT OUR DIFFERENCES ASIDE!
IF THE KING AND THE REALM ARE EVER TO BE SAVED, WE MUST HOPE AND PRAY THAT KNUCKLES THE ECHIDNA IS SUCCESSFUL IN HIS QUEST!
AND KNUCKLES' QUEST CONCLUDES IN THIS VERY ISSUE!

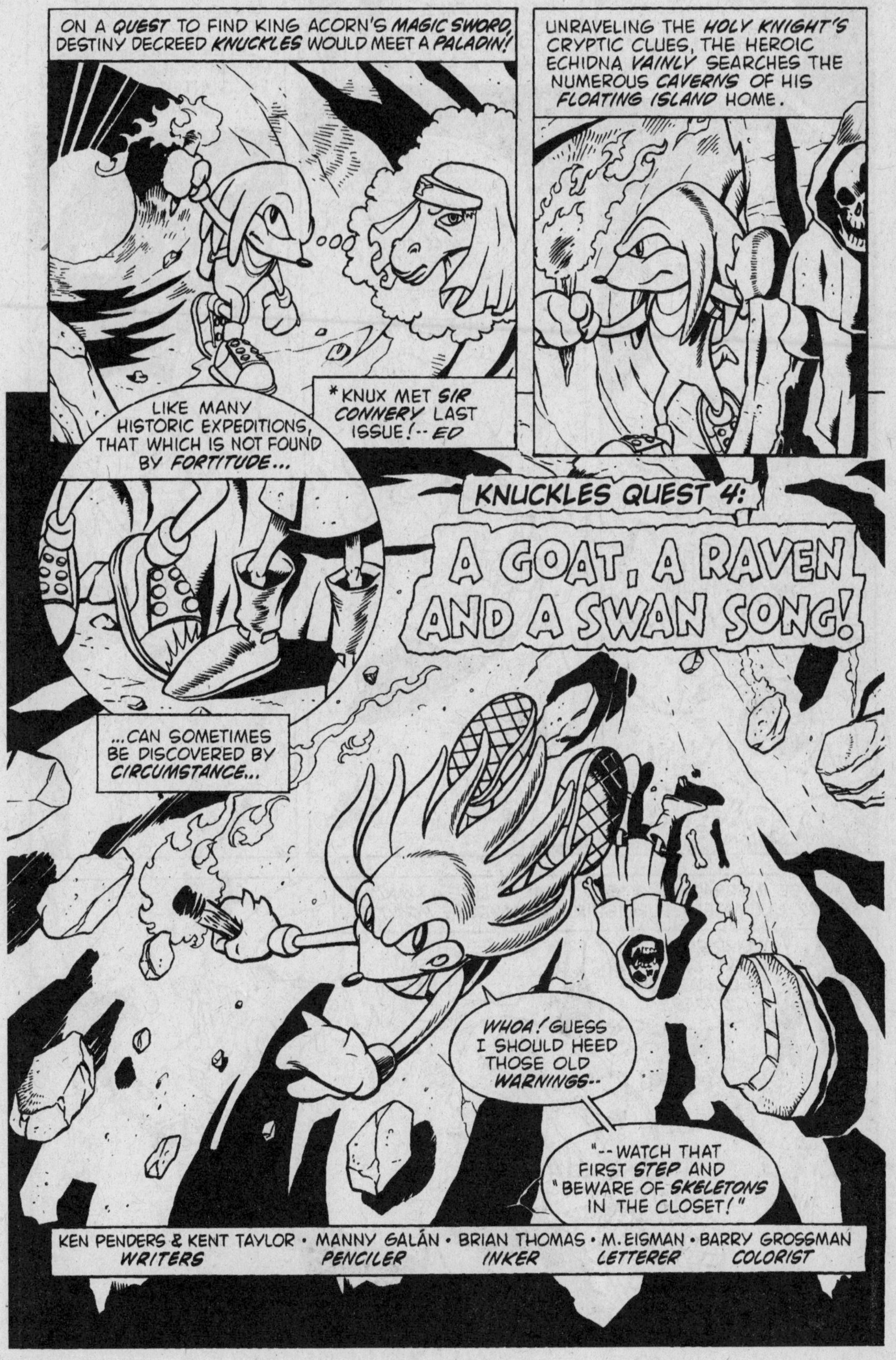
ON A QUEST TO FIND KING ACORN'S MAGIC SWORD, DESTINY DECREED KNUCKLES WOULD MEET A PALADIN!
*KNUX MET SIR CONNERY LAST ISSUE! --ED
UNRAVELING THE HOLY KNIGHT'S CRYPTIC CLUES, THE HEROIC ECHIDNA VAINLY SEARCHES THE NUMEROUS CAVERNS OF HIS FLOATING ISLAND HOME.
LIKE MANY HISTORIC EXPEDITIONS, THAT WHICH IS NOT FOUND BY FORTITUDE...
KNUCKLES QUEST 4:
A GOAT, A RAVEN AND A SWAN SONG!
...CAN SOMETIMES BE DISCOVERED BY CIRCUMSTANCE...
WHOA! GUESS I SHOULD HEED THOSE OLD WARNINGS--
"--WATCH THAT FIRST STEP AND "BEWARE OF SKELETONS IN THE CLOSET!"
KEN PENDERS & KENT TAYLOR • MANNY GALÁN • BRIAN THOMAS • M. EISMAN • BARRY GROSSMAN
WRITERS PENCILER INKER LETTERER COLORIST

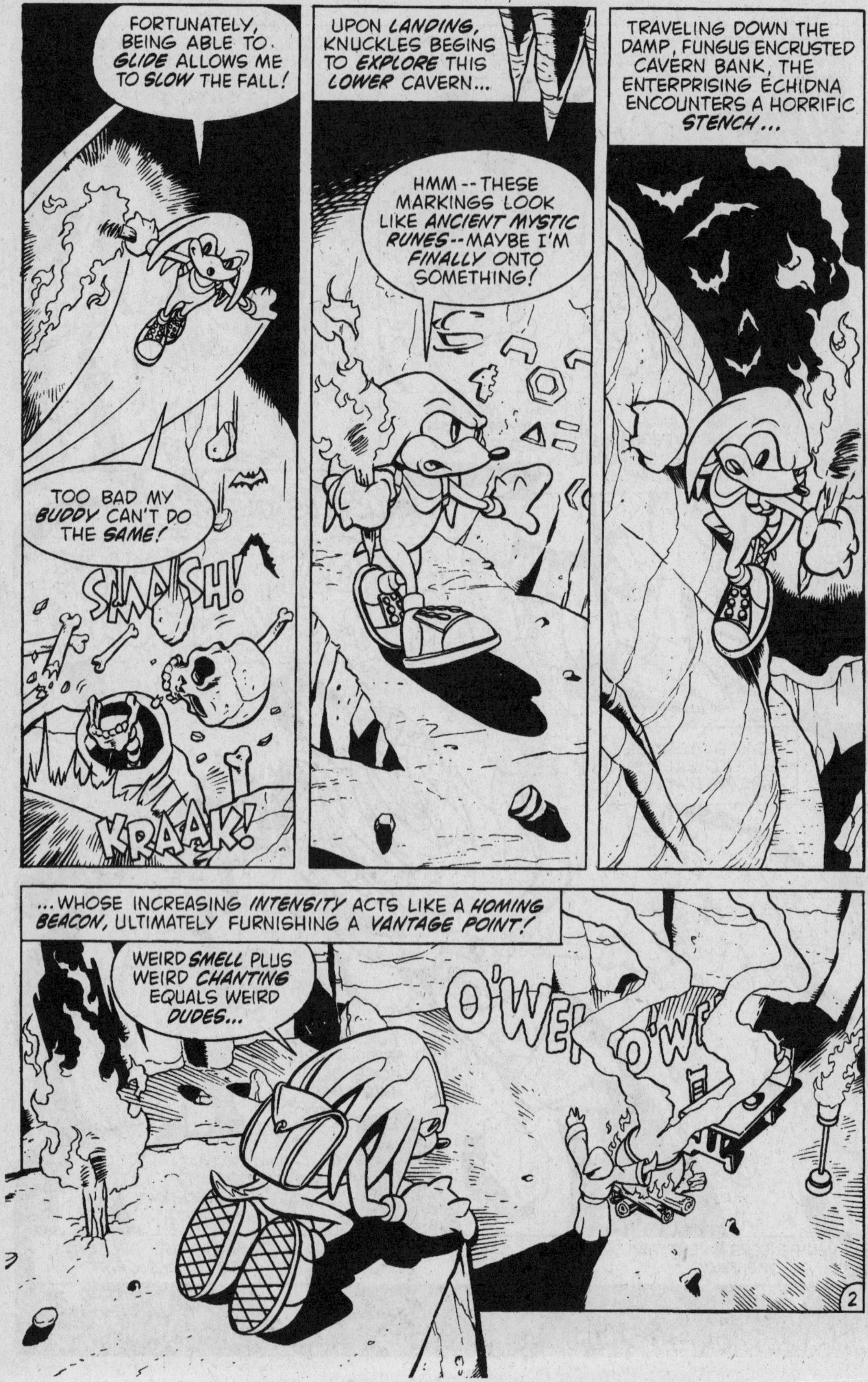
FORTUNATELY, BEING ABLE TO GLIDE ALLOWS ME TO SLOW THE FALL!
TOO BAD MY BUDDY CAN'T DO THE SAME!
SMASH!
KRAAK!
UPON LANDING, KNUCKLES BEGINS TO EXPLORE THIS LOWER CAVERN...
HMM -- THESE MARKINGS LOOK LIKE ANCIENT MYSTIC RUNES -- MAYBE I'M FINALLY ONTO SOMETHING!
TRAVELING DOWN THE DAMP, FUNGUS ENCRUSTED CAVERN BANK, THE ENTERPRISING ECHIDNA ENCOUNTERS A HORRIFIC STENCH...
...WHOSE INCREASING INTENSITY ACTS LIKE A HOMING BEACON, ULTIMATELY FURNISHING A VANTAGE POINT!
WEIRD SMELL PLUS WEIRD CHANTING EQUALS WEIRD DUDES...
O'WE
O'WE
2

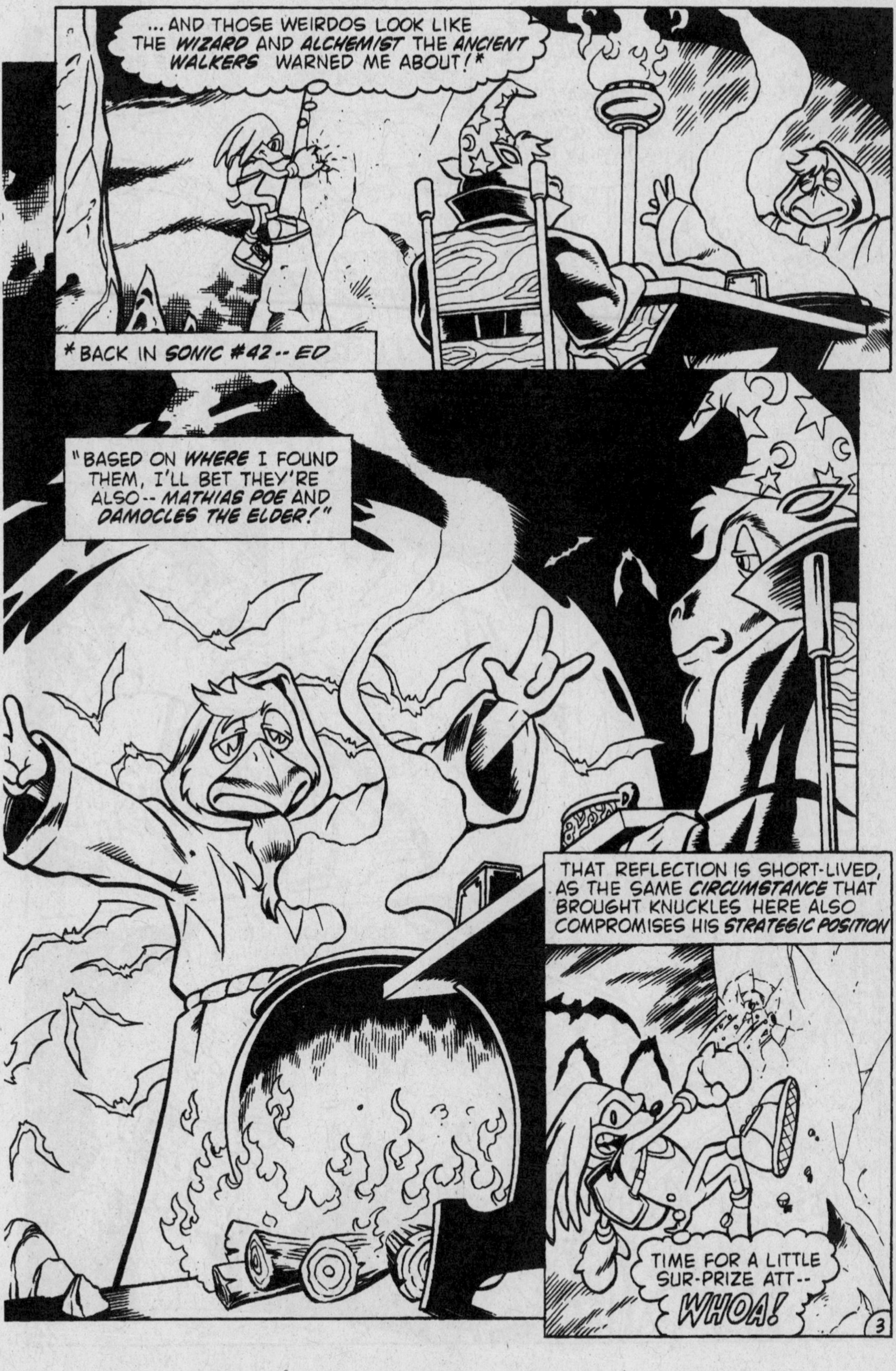
...AND THOSE WEIRDOS LOOK LIKE THE WIZARD AND ALCHEMIST THE ANCIENT WALKERS WARNED ME ABOUT!*
*BACK IN SONIC #42 -- ED
"BASED ON WHERE I FOUND THEM, I'LL BET THEY'RE ALSO -- MATHIAS POE AND DAMOCLES THE ELDER!"
THAT REFLECTION IS SHORT-LIVED, AS THE SAME CIRCUMSTANCE THAT BROUGHT KNUCKLES HERE ALSO COMPROMISES HIS STRATEGIC POSITION
TIME FOR A LITTLE SUR-PRIZE ATT--
WHOA!
3

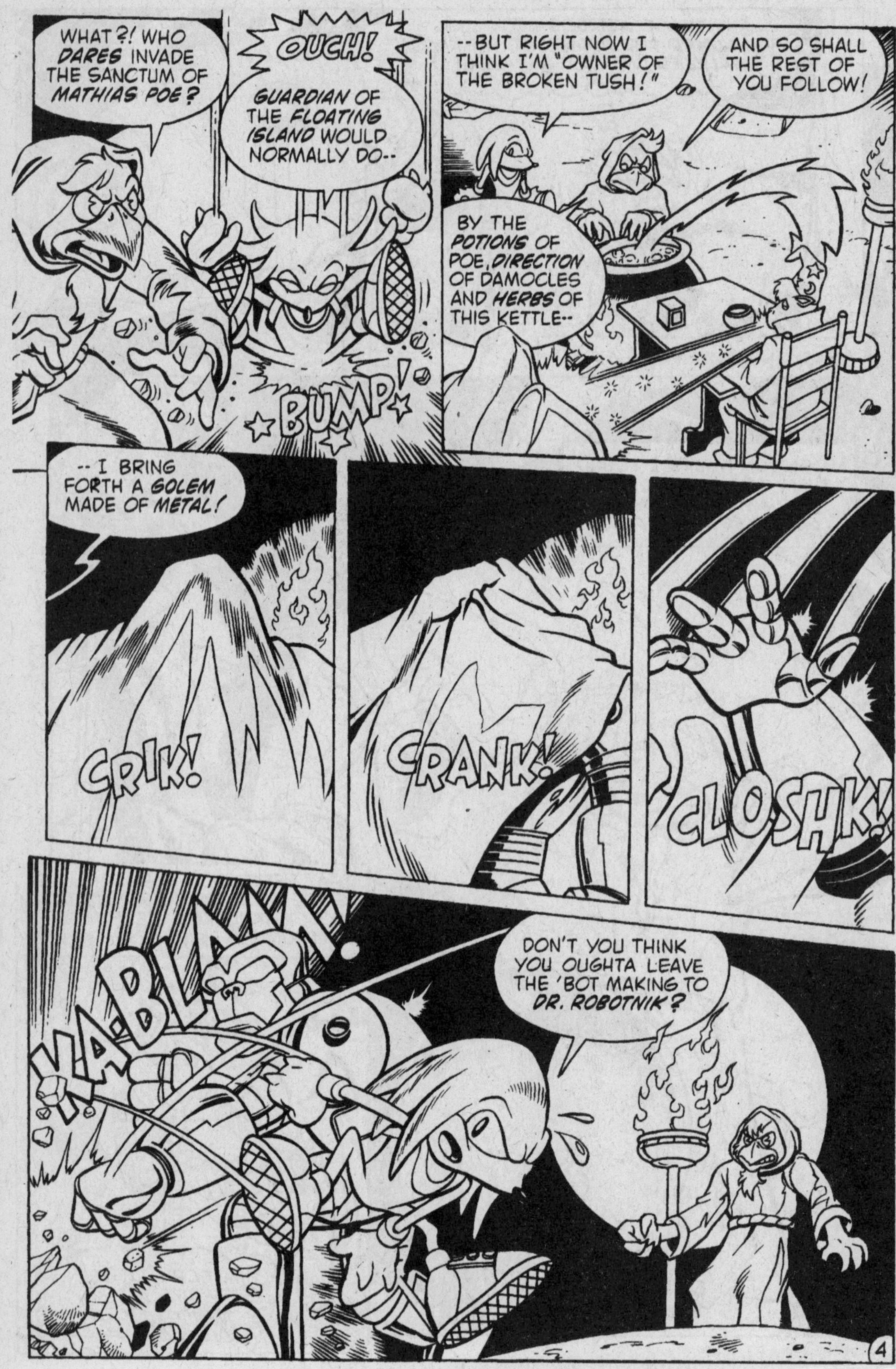
WHAT?! WHO DARES INVADE THE SANCTUM OF MATHIAS POE?
OUCH!
GUARDIAN OF THE FLOATING ISLAND WOULD NORMALLY DO--
BUMP!
--BUT RIGHT NOW I THINK I'M "OWNER OF THE BROKEN TUSH!"
AND SO SHALL THE REST OF YOU FOLLOW!
BY THE POTIONS OF POE, DIRECTION OF DAMOCLES AND HERBS OF THIS KETTLE--
-- I BRING FORTH A GOLEM MADE OF METAL!
CRIK!
CRANK!
CLOSHK!
KABLAM!
DON'T YOU THINK YOU OUGHTA LEAVE THE 'BOT MAKING TO DR. ROBOTNIK?
4

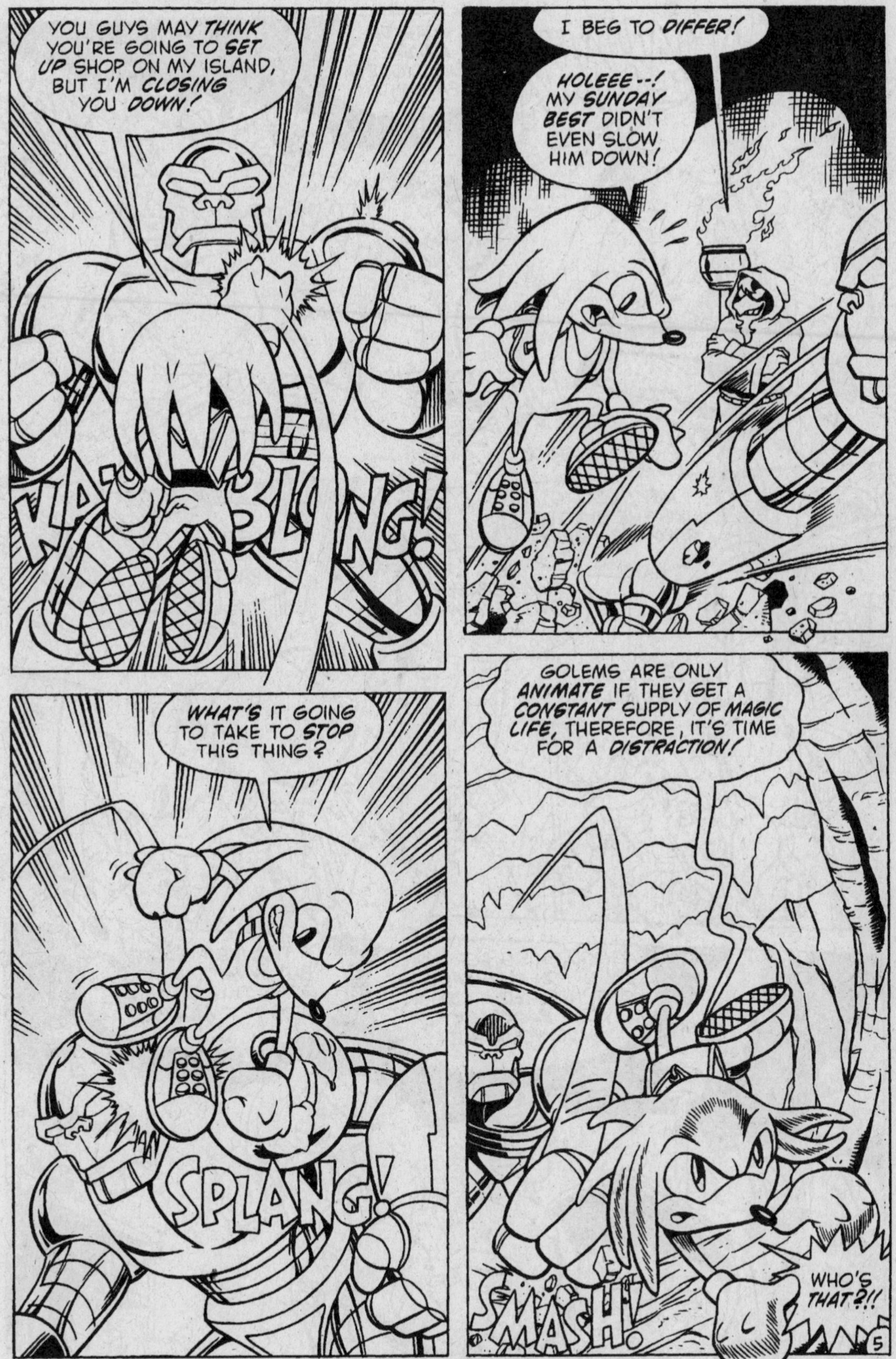
YOU GUYS MAY THINK YOU'RE GOING TO SET UP SHOP ON MY ISLAND, BUT I'M CLOSING YOU DOWN!
KA-BLONG!
I BEG TO DIFFER!
HOLEEE--! MY SUNDAY BEST DIDN'T EVEN SLOW HIM DOWN!
WHAT'S IT GOING TO TAKE TO STOP THIS THING?
SPLANG!
GOLEMS ARE ONLY ANIMATE IF THEY GET A CONSTANT SUPPLY OF MAGIC LIFE, THEREFORE, IT'S TIME FOR A DISTRACTION!
SMASH!
WHO'S THAT?!!
5

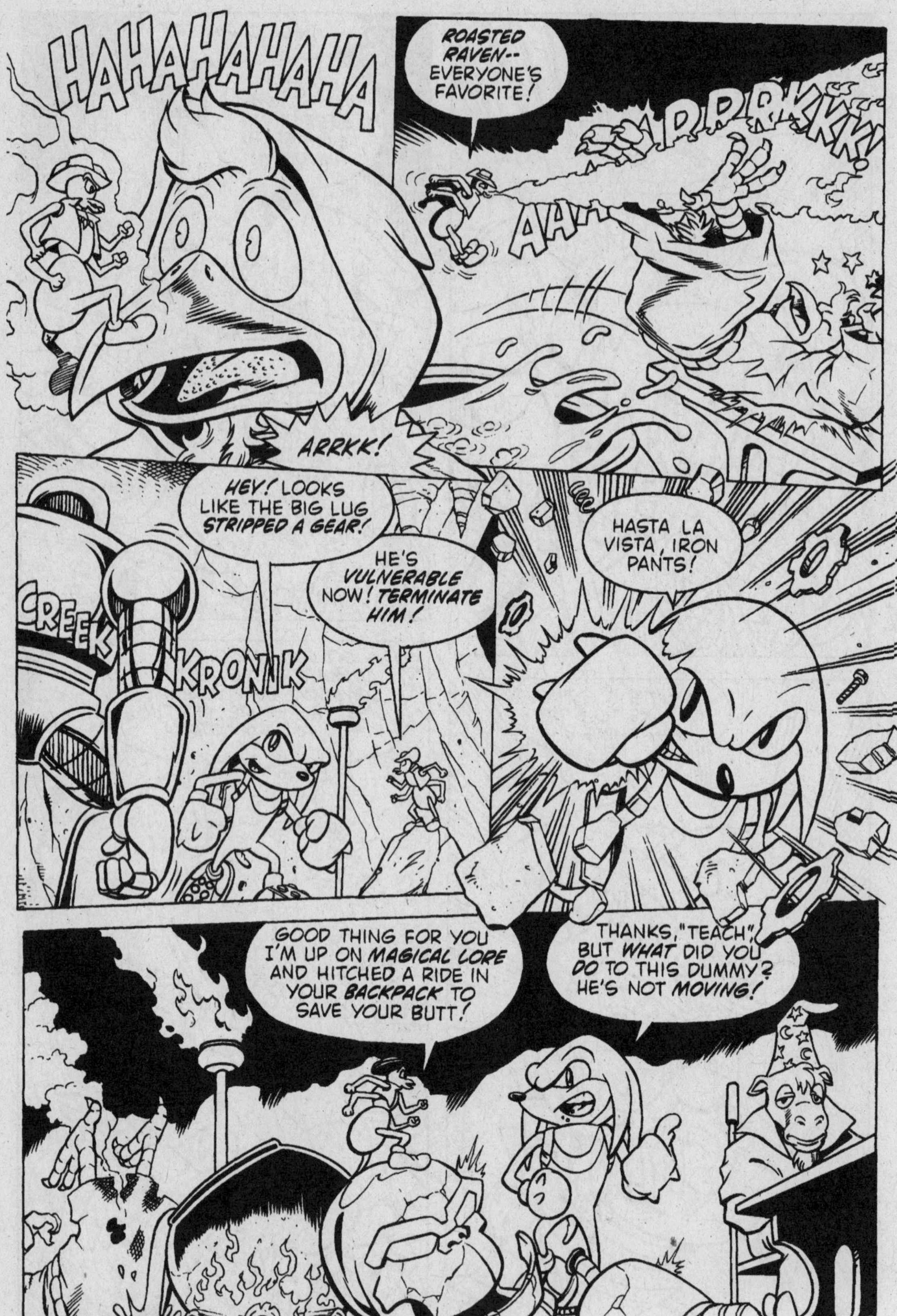
HAHAHAHAHAHA
ROASTED RAVEN-- EVERYONE'S FAVORITE!
DRRRKKK!
AAH
ARRKK!
HEY! LOOKS LIKE THE BIG LUG STRIPPED A GEAR!
CREEEK
KRONIK
HE'S VULNERABLE NOW! TERMINATE HIM!
HASTA LA VISTA, IRON PANTS!
GOOD THING FOR YOU I'M UP ON MAGICAL LORE AND HITCHED A RIDE IN YOUR BACKPACK TO SAVE YOUR BUTT!
THANKS, "TEACH", BUT WHAT DID YOU DO TO THIS DUMMY? HE'S NOT MOVING!
6

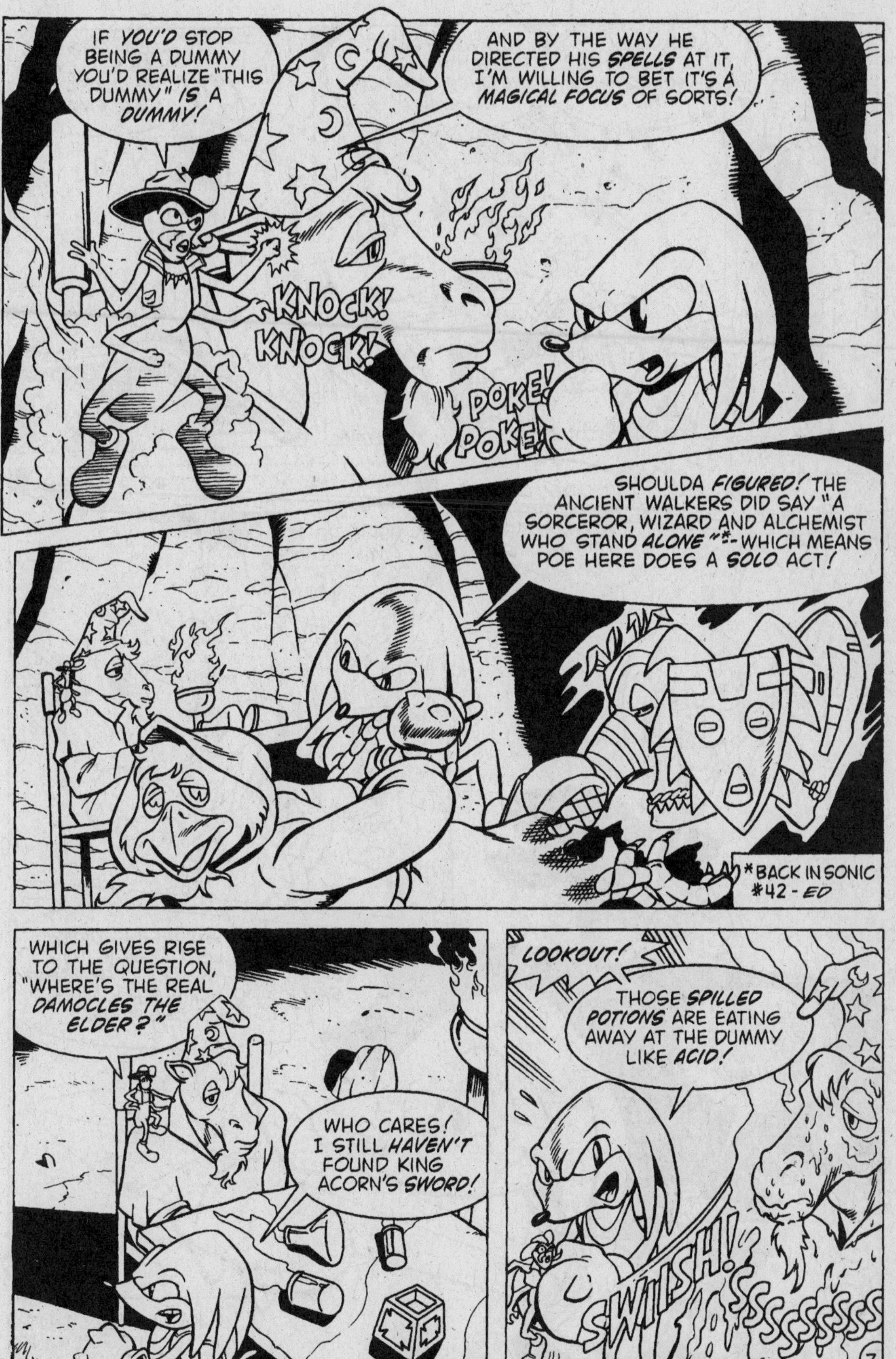

IF YOU'D STOP BEING A DUMMY YOU'D REALIZE "THIS DUMMY" IS A DUMMY!
AND BY THE WAY HE DIRECTED HIS SPELLS AT IT, I'M WILLING TO BET IT'S A MAGICAL FOCUS OF SORTS!
KNOCK! KNOCK!
POKE! POKE!
SHOULDA FIGURED! THE ANCIENT WALKERS DID SAY "A SORCEROR, WIZARD AND ALCHEMIST WHO STAND ALONE"*-WHICH MEANS POE HERE DOES A SOLO ACT!
*BACK IN SONIC #42 - ED
WHICH GIVES RISE TO THE QUESTION, "WHERE'S THE REAL DAMOCLES THE ELDER?"
WHO CARES! I STILL HAVEN'T FOUND KING ACORN'S SWORD!
LOOKOUT!
THOSE SPILLED POTIONS ARE EATING AWAY AT THE DUMMY LIKE ACID!
SWISH!
SSSSSSS
7

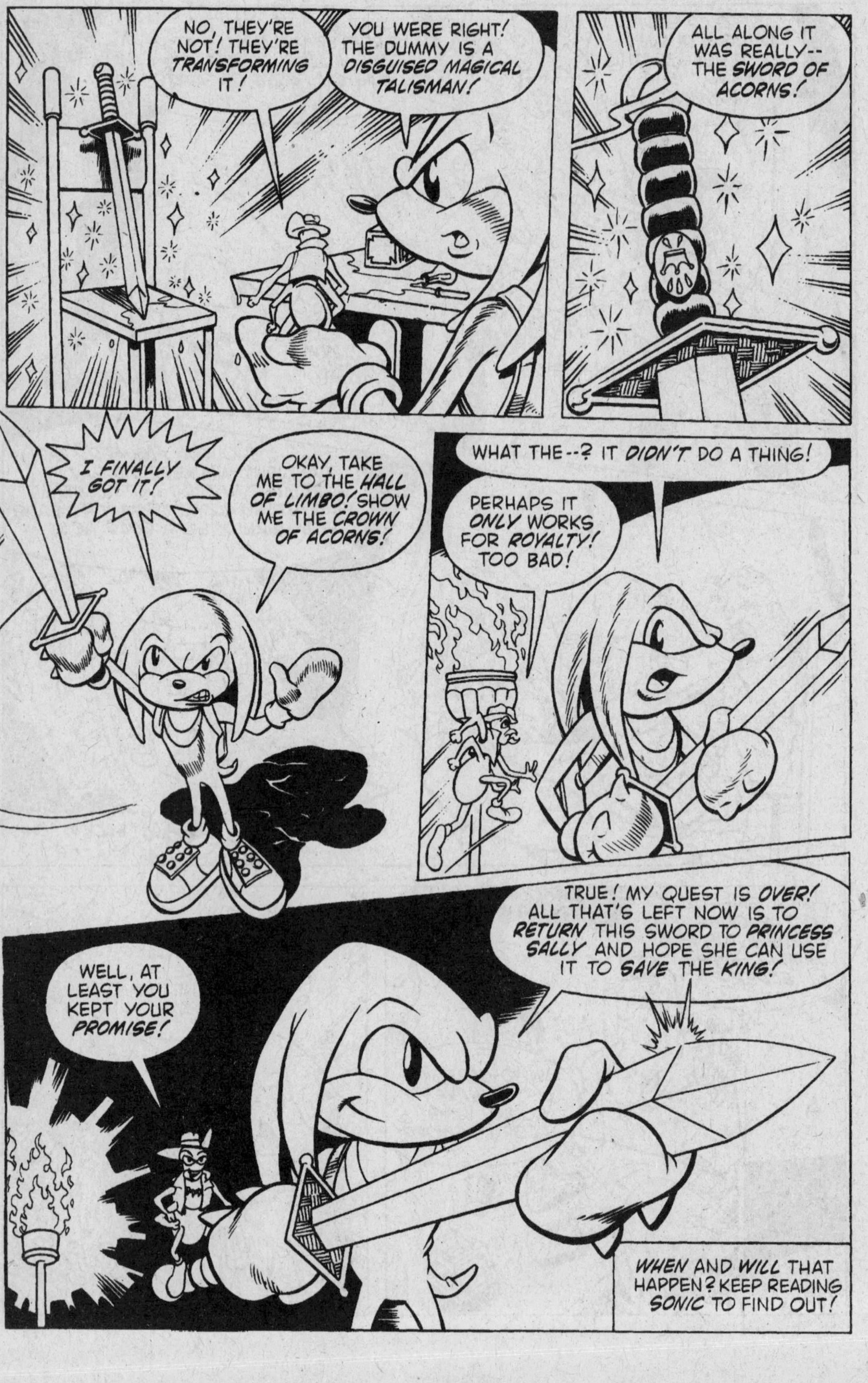
NO, THEY'RE NOT! THEY'RE *TRANSFORMING* IT!
YOU WERE RIGHT! THE DUMMY IS A *DISGUISED MAGICAL TALISMAN!*
ALL ALONG IT WAS REALLY-- THE *SWORD OF ACORNS!*
I FINALLY GOT IT!
OKAY, TAKE ME TO THE *HALL OF LIMBO!* SHOW ME THE *CROWN OF ACORNS!*
WHAT THE--? IT *DIDN'T* DO A THING!
PERHAPS IT *ONLY* WORKS FOR *ROYALTY!* TOO BAD!
WELL, AT LEAST YOU KEPT YOUR *PROMISE!*
TRUE! MY QUEST IS *OVER!* ALL THAT'S LEFT NOW IS TO *RETURN* THIS SWORD TO *PRINCESS SALLY* AND HOPE SHE CAN USE IT TO *SAVE* THE *KING!*
WHEN AND *WILL* THAT HAPPEN? KEEP READING *SONIC* TO FIND OUT!

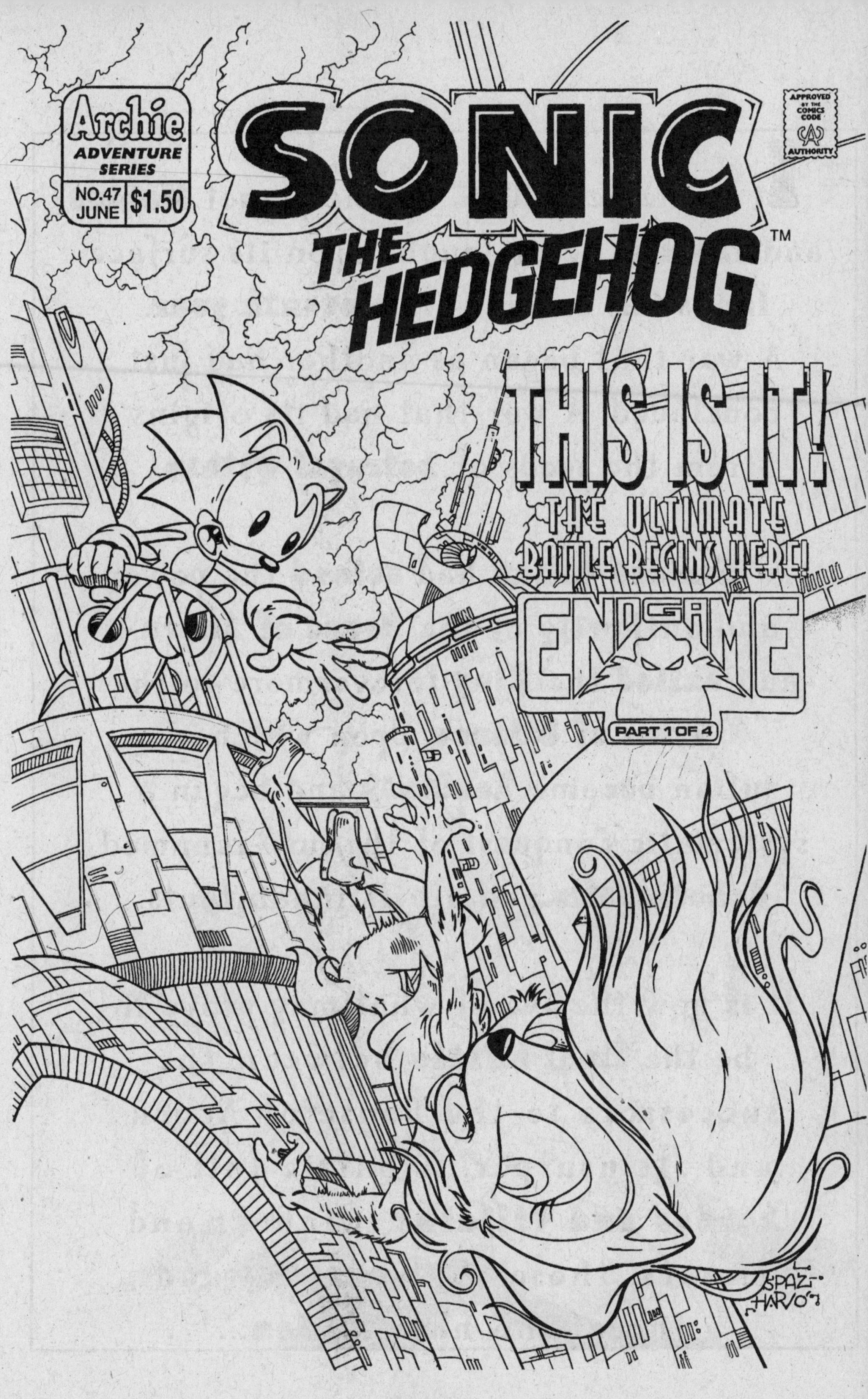
Archie
ADVENTURE SERIES
NO.47 JUNE
$1.50
SONIC THE HEDGEHOG™
APPROVED BY THE COMICS CODE AUTHORITY
THIS IS IT!
THE ULTIMATE BATTLE BEGINS HERE!
ENDGAME
PART 1 OF 4

It is the year 3235 on the planet Mobius and the war being fought upon its surface lands has entered its eleventh year. A war that began as another had just concluded. A war that had its origins from the seeds of betrayal within.

Warlord Julian had seized the power and authority of the House of Acorn, and exiled the King forevermore to the Zone of Silence. Upon which, Julian became Robotnik and began a systematic conquest of the now-renamed Robotropolis and all its inhabitants.

It is now the eve of what may prove to be the final battle between the successors to the House of Acorn and its usurper. A battle full of heroes and villains, winners and losers, those that survive and those who have fallen...

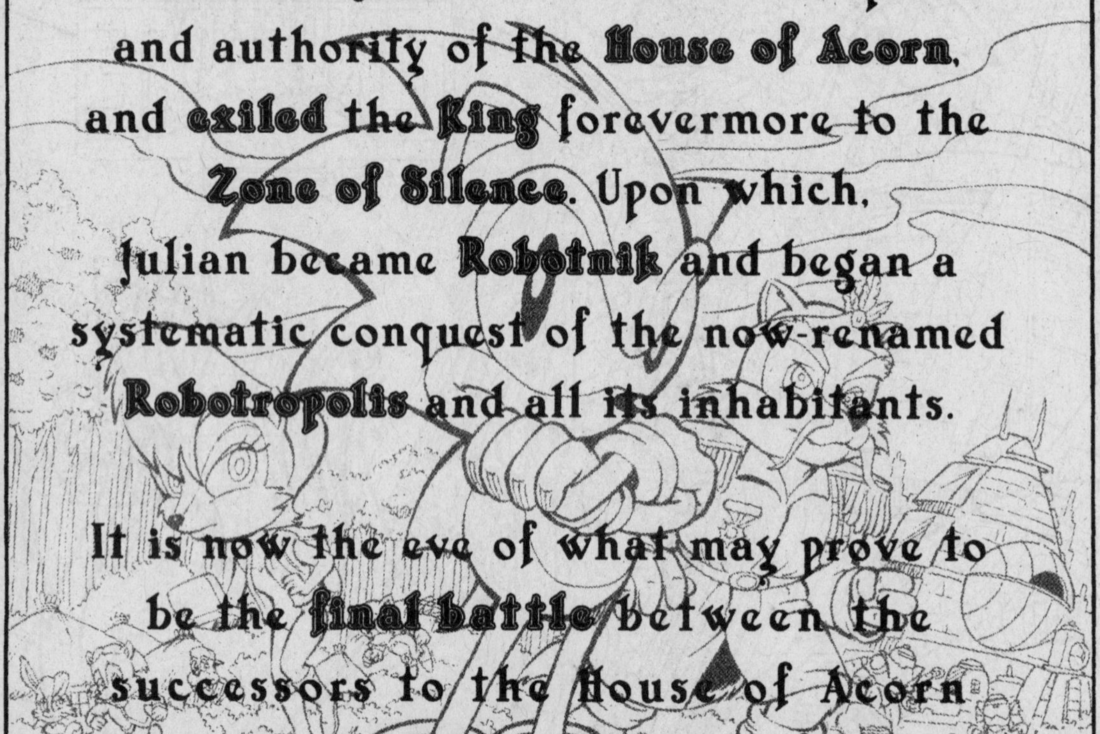

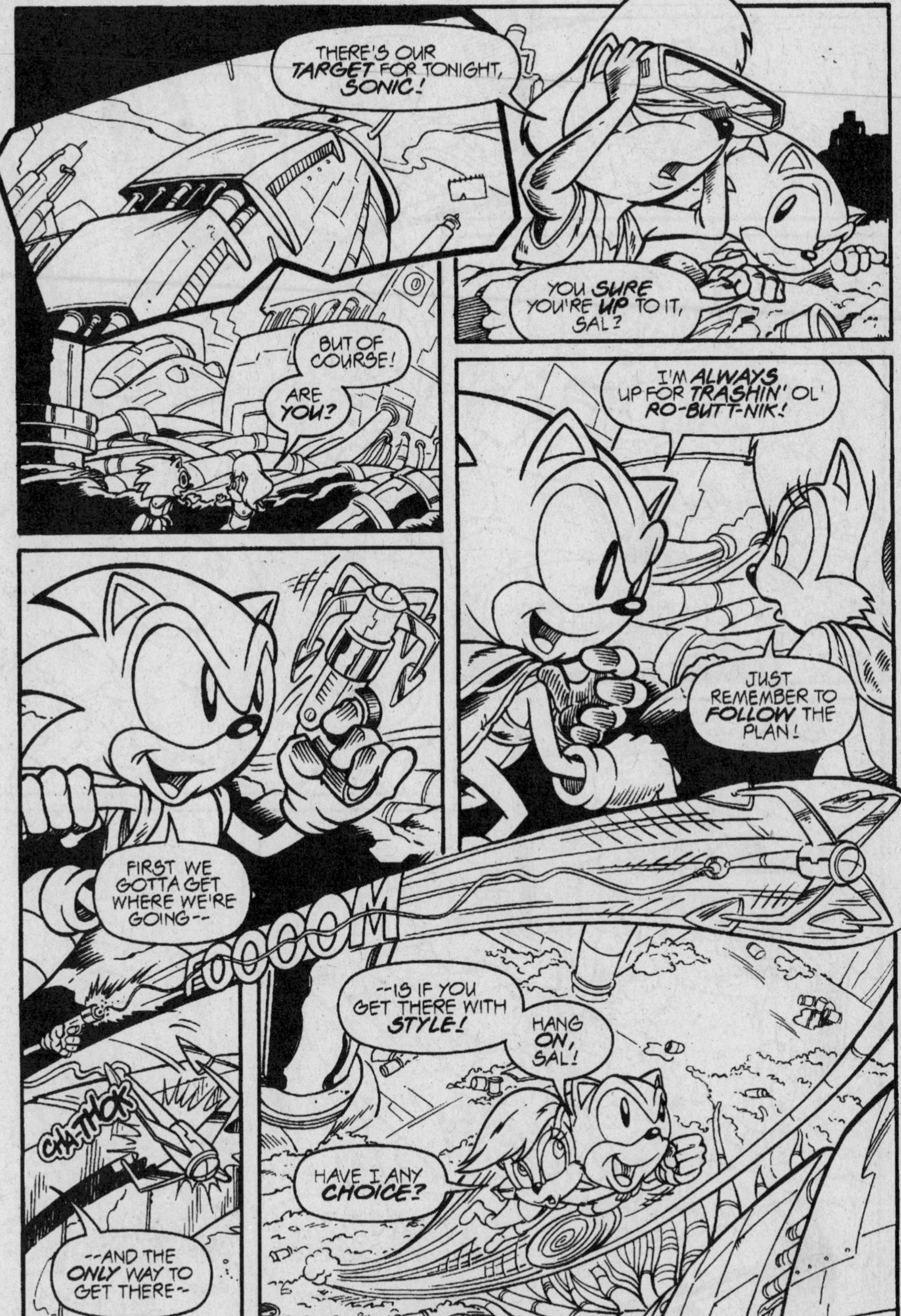
THERE'S OUR TARGET FOR TONIGHT, SONIC!
YOU SURE YOU'RE UP TO IT, SAL?
BUT OF COURSE!
ARE YOU?
I'M ALWAYS UP FOR TRASHIN' OL' RO-BUTT-NIK!
JUST REMEMBER TO FOLLOW THE PLAN!
FIRST WE GOTTA GET WHERE WE'RE GOING--
FOOOOOM
CHA-THOK
--AND THE ONLY WAY TO GET THERE--
--IS IF YOU GET THERE WITH STYLE!
HANG ON, SAL!
HAVE I ANY CHOICE?
1

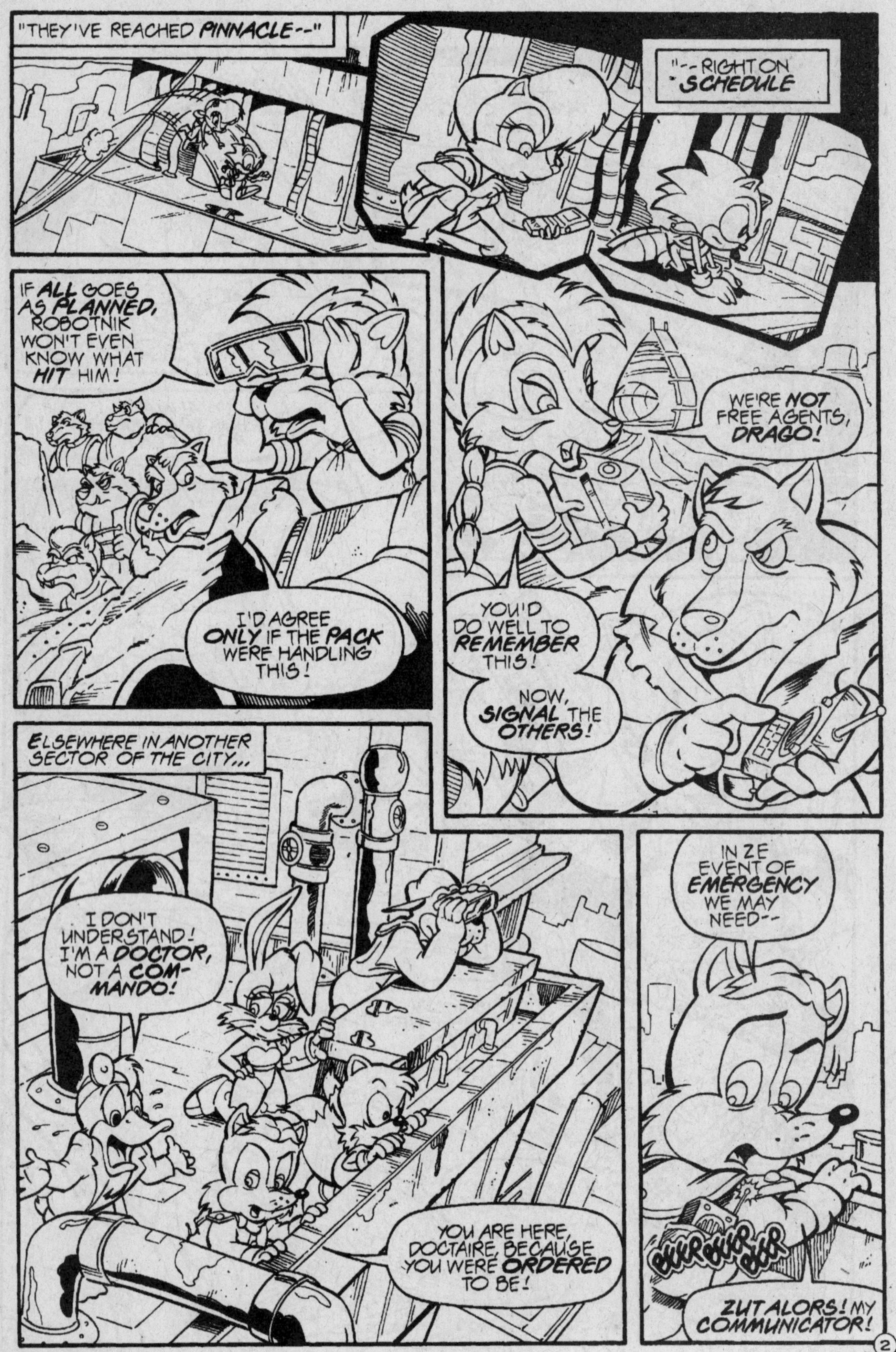
"THEY'VE REACHED PINNACLE--"
"--RIGHT ON SCHEDULE
IF ALL GOES AS PLANNED, ROBOTNIK WON'T EVEN KNOW WHAT HIT HIM!
I'D AGREE ONLY IF THE PACK WERE HANDLING THIS!
WE'RE NOT FREE AGENTS, DRAGO!
YOU'D DO WELL TO REMEMBER THIS!
NOW, SIGNAL THE OTHERS!
ELSEWHERE IN ANOTHER SECTOR OF THE CITY...
I DON'T UNDERSTAND! I'M A DOCTOR, NOT A COM-MANDO!
YOU ARE HERE, DOCTAIRE, BECAUSE YOU WERE ORDERED TO BE!
IN ZE EVENT OF EMERGENCY WE MAY NEED--
ZUT ALORS! MY COMMUNICATOR!
2

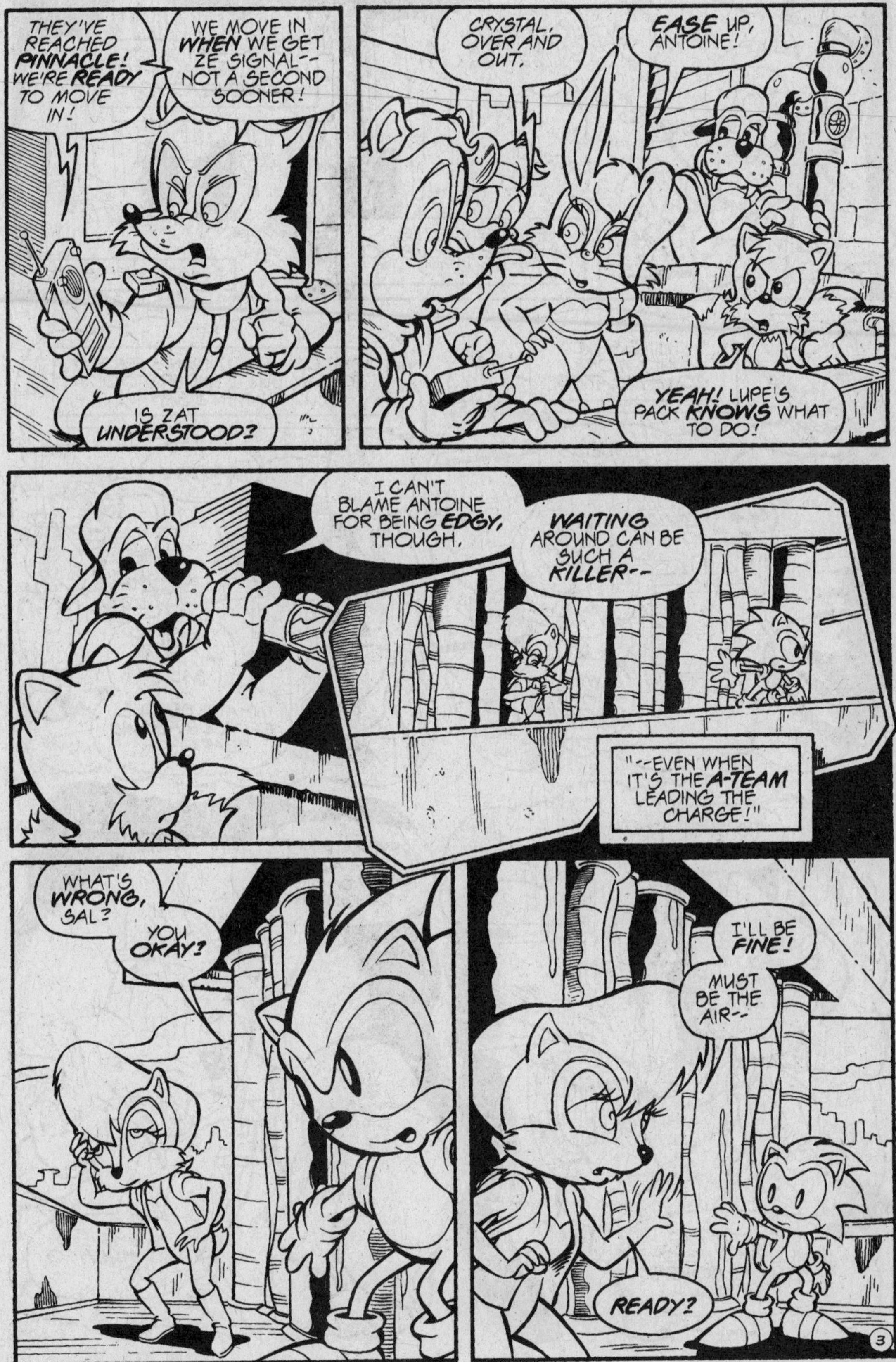
THEY'VE REACHED PINNACLE! WE'RE READY TO MOVE IN!
WE MOVE IN WHEN WE GET ZE SIGNAL-- NOT A SECOND SOONER!
IS ZAT UNDERSTOOD?
CRYSTAL, OVER AND OUT.
EASE UP, ANTOINE!
YEAH! LUPE'S PACK KNOWS WHAT TO DO!
I CAN'T BLAME ANTOINE FOR BEING EDGY, THOUGH.
WAITING AROUND CAN BE SUCH A KILLER--
"--EVEN WHEN IT'S THE A-TEAM LEADING THE CHARGE!"
WHAT'S WRONG, SAL?
YOU OKAY?
I'LL BE FINE!
MUST BE THE AIR--
READY?
3

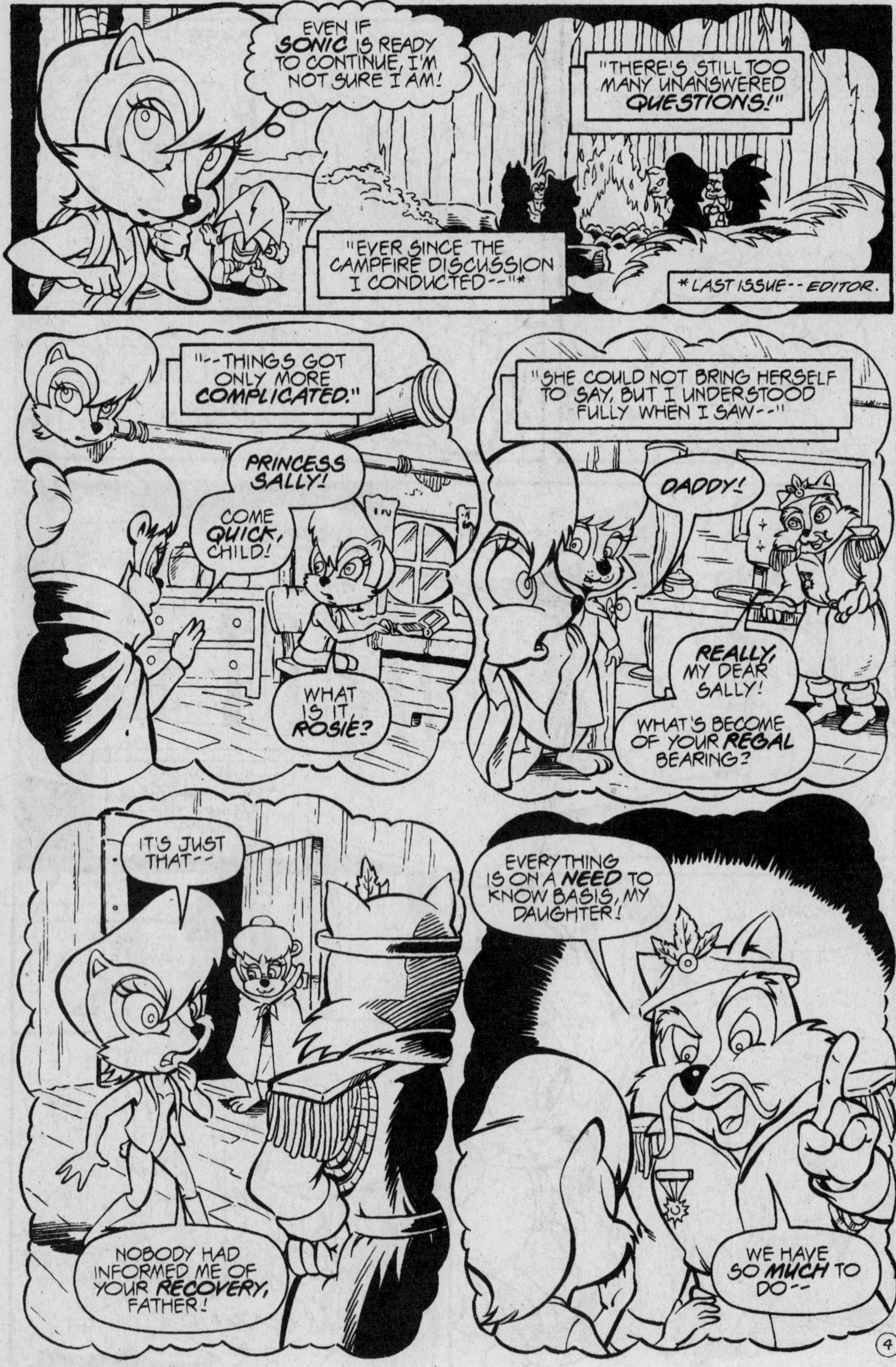

EVEN IF SONIC IS READY TO CONTINUE, I'M NOT SURE I AM!
"EVER SINCE THE CAMPFIRE DISCUSSION I CONDUCTED--"*
"THERE'S STILL TOO MANY UNANSWERED QUESTIONS!"
* LAST ISSUE--EDITOR.
"--THINGS GOT ONLY MORE COMPLICATED."
PRINCESS SALLY!
COME QUICK, CHILD!
WHAT IS IT, ROSIE?
"SHE COULD NOT BRING HERSELF TO SAY, BUT I UNDERSTOOD FULLY WHEN I SAW--"
DADDY!
REALLY, MY DEAR SALLY!
WHAT'S BECOME OF YOUR REGAL BEARING?
IT'S JUST THAT--
NOBODY HAD INFORMED ME OF YOUR RECOVERY, FATHER!
EVERYTHING IS ON A NEED TO KNOW BASIS, MY DAUGHTER!
WE HAVE SO MUCH TO DO--
4

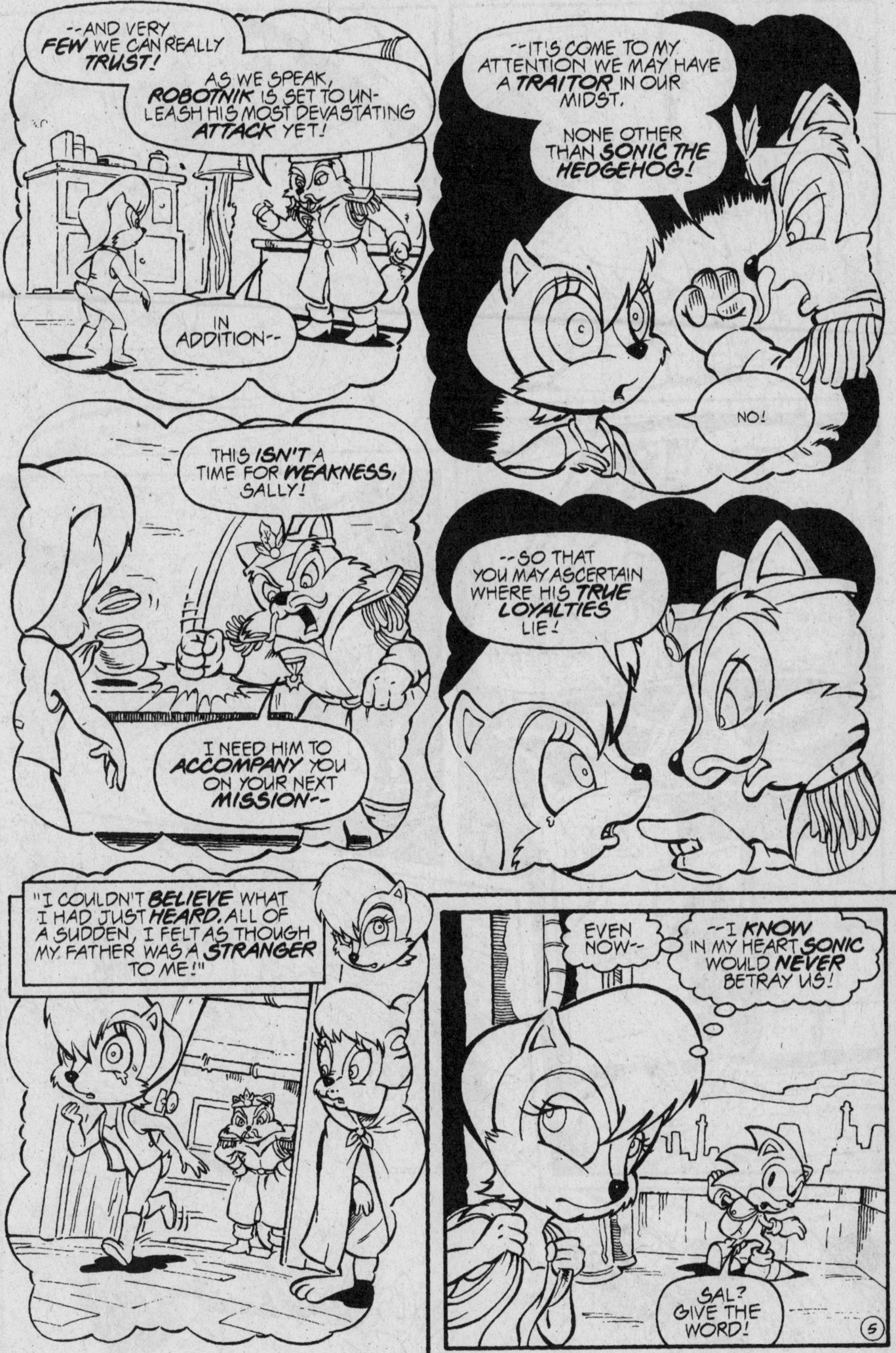
--AND VERY FEW WE CAN REALLY TRUST!
AS WE SPEAK, ROBOTNIK IS SET TO UN-LEASH HIS MOST DEVASTATING ATTACK YET!
IN ADDITION--
--IT'S COME TO MY ATTENTION WE MAY HAVE A TRAITOR IN OUR MIDST.
NONE OTHER THAN SONIC THE HEDGEHOG!
NO!
THIS ISN'T A TIME FOR WEAKNESS, SALLY!
I NEED HIM TO ACCOMPANY YOU ON YOUR NEXT MISSION--
--SO THAT YOU MAY ASCERTAIN WHERE HIS TRUE LOYALTIES LIE!
"I COULDN'T BELIEVE WHAT I HAD JUST HEARD. ALL OF A SUDDEN, I FELT AS THOUGH MY FATHER WAS A STRANGER TO ME!"
EVEN NOW--
--I KNOW IN MY HEART SONIC WOULD NEVER BETRAY US!
SAL? GIVE THE WORD!
5

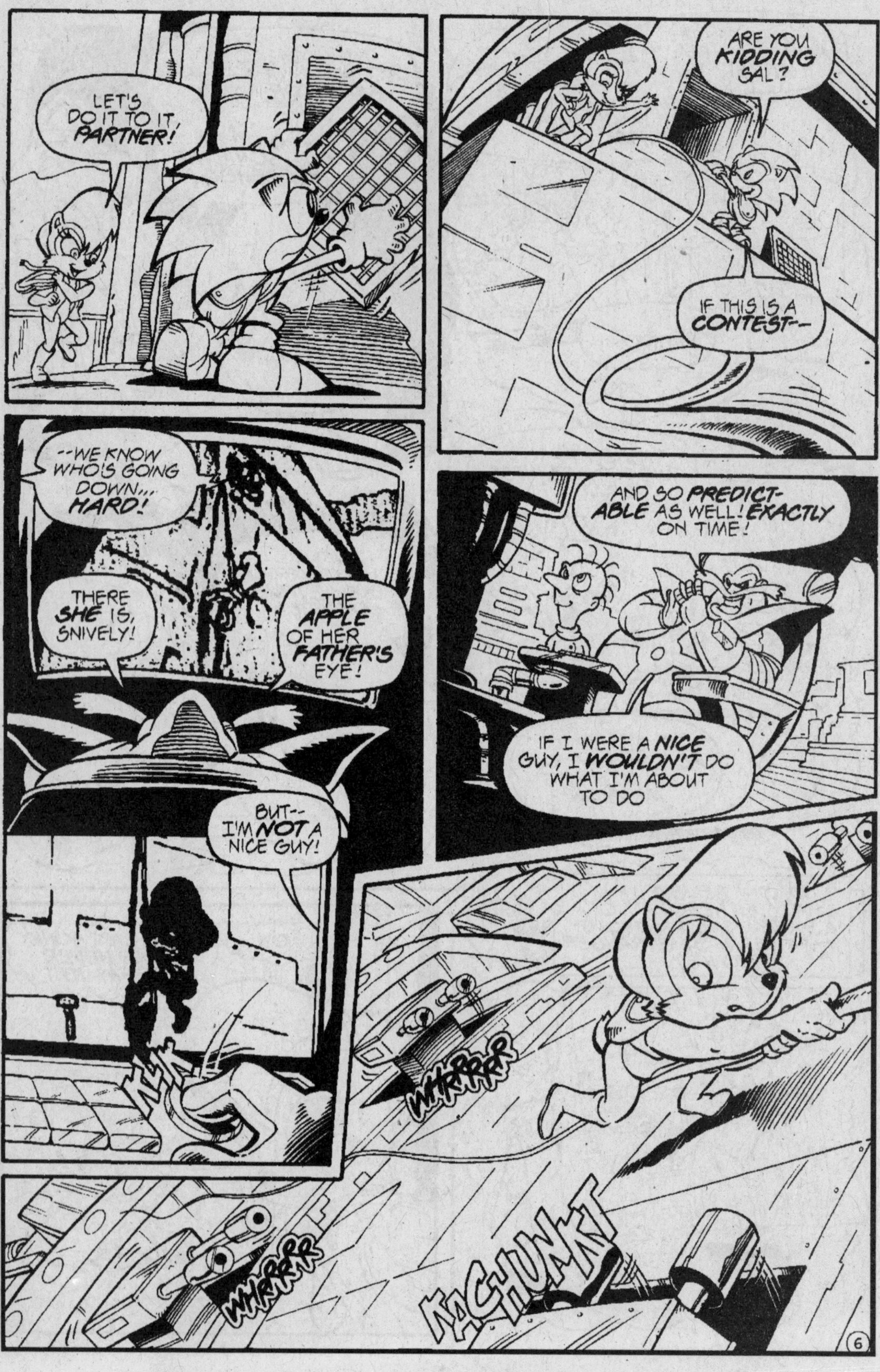
LET'S DO IT TO IT, PARTNER!
ARE YOU KIDDING SAL?
IF THIS IS A CONTEST--
--WE KNOW WHO'S GOING DOWN... HARD!
AND SO PREDICT-ABLE AS WELL! EXACTLY ON TIME!
THERE SHE IS, SNIVELY!
THE APPLE OF HER FATHER'S EYE!
IF I WERE A NICE GUY, I WOULDN'T DO WHAT I'M ABOUT TO DO
BUT-- I'M NOT A NICE GUY!
WHRRRRR
WHRRRR
KACHUNKT
6

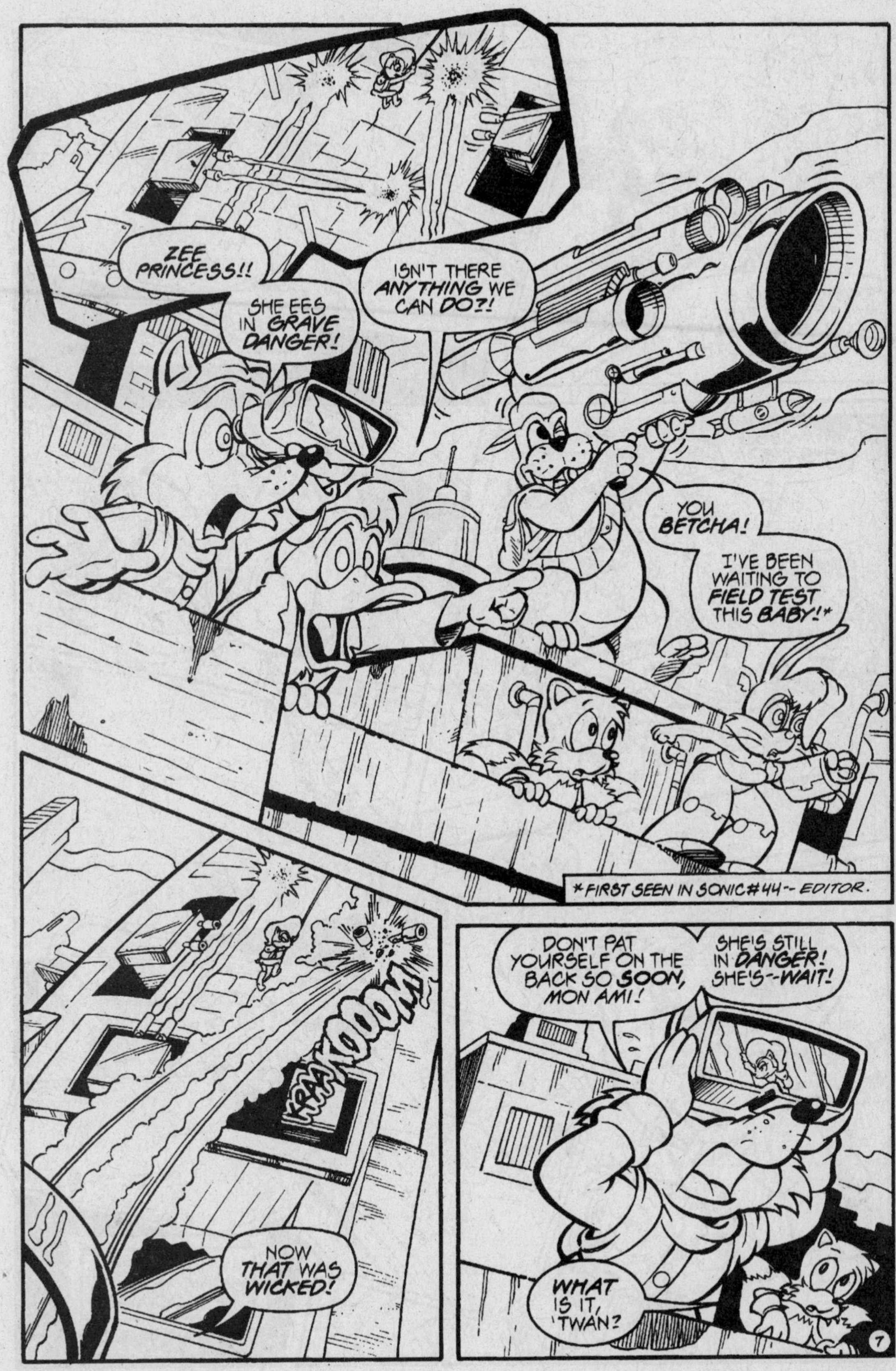
ZEE PRINCESS!!
SHE EES IN GRAVE DANGER!
ISN'T THERE ANYTHING WE CAN DO?!
YOU BETCHA!
I'VE BEEN WAITING TO FIELD TEST THIS BABY!*
*FIRST SEEN IN SONIC #44 -- EDITOR.
KRAAKOOOM!
NOW THAT WAS WICKED!
DON'T PAT YOURSELF ON THE BACK SO SOON, MON AMI!
SHE'S STILL IN DANGER! SHE'S--WAIT!
WHAT IS IT, 'TWAN?
7

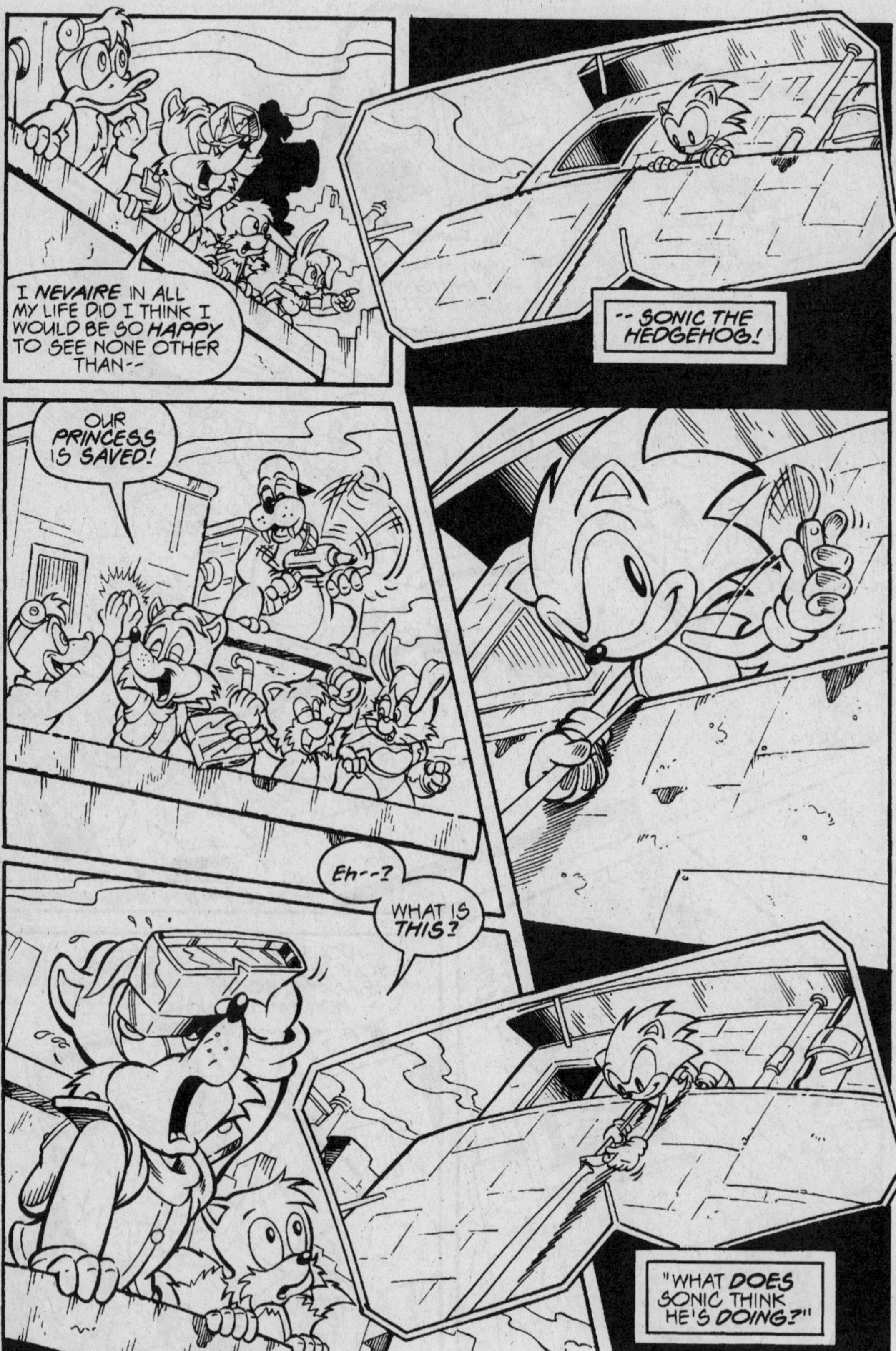
I NEVAIRE IN ALL MY LIFE DID I THINK I WOULD BE SO HAPPY TO SEE NONE OTHER THAN--
--SONIC THE HEDGEHOG!
OUR PRINCESS IS SAVED!
Eh--?
WHAT IS THIS?
"WHAT DOES SONIC THINK HE'S DOING?"
8

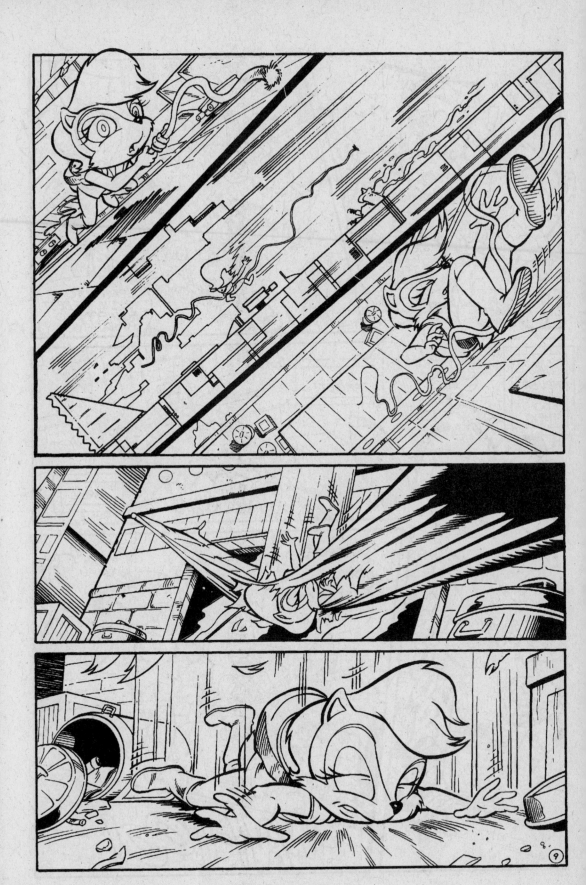

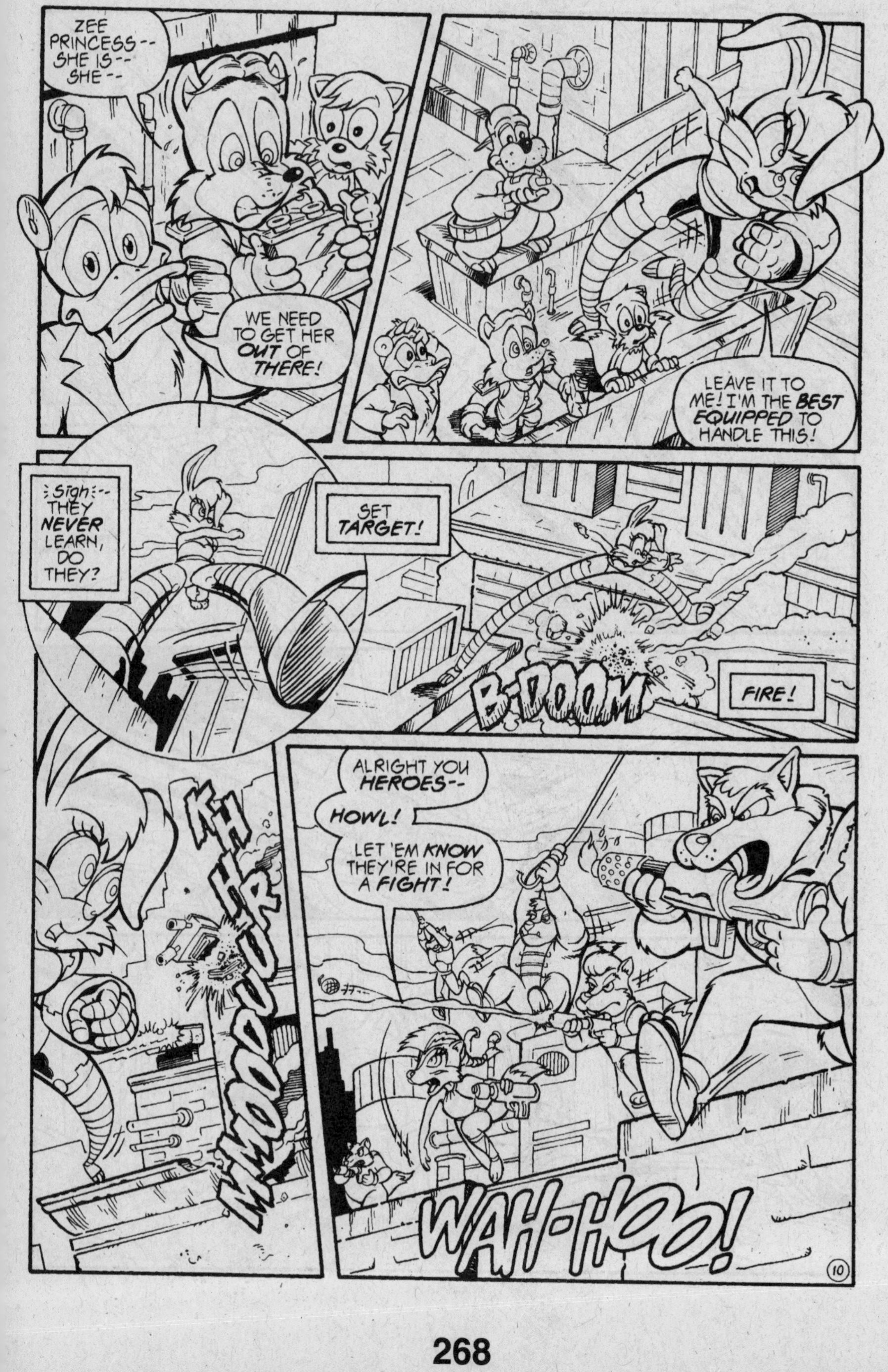
ZEE PRINCESS-- SHE IS-- SHE--
WE NEED TO GET HER OUT OF THERE!
LEAVE IT TO ME! I'M THE BEST EQUIPPED TO HANDLE THIS!
Sigh-- THEY NEVER LEARN, DO THEY?
SET TARGET!
B-DOOM
FIRE!
KH
HR
MMOODDOOR
ALRIGHT YOU HEROES--
HOWL!
LET 'EM KNOW THEY'RE IN FOR A FIGHT!
WAH-HOO!
10

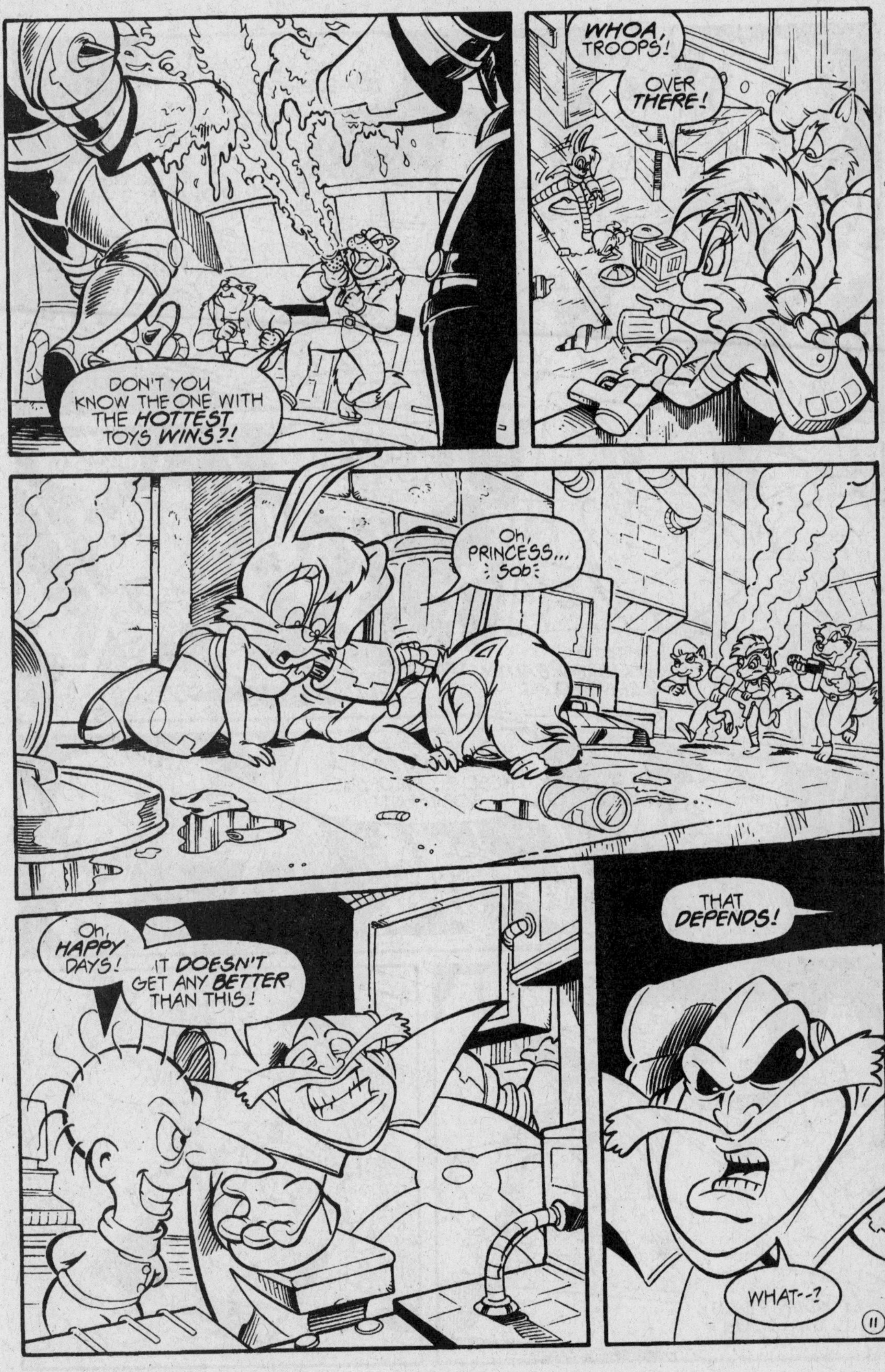
DON'T YOU KNOW THE ONE WITH THE HOTTEST TOYS WINS?!
WHOA, TROOPS!
OVER THERE!
Oh, PRINCESS... Sob
Oh, HAPPY DAYS!
IT DOESN'T GET ANY BETTER THAN THIS!
THAT DEPENDS!
WHAT--?
11

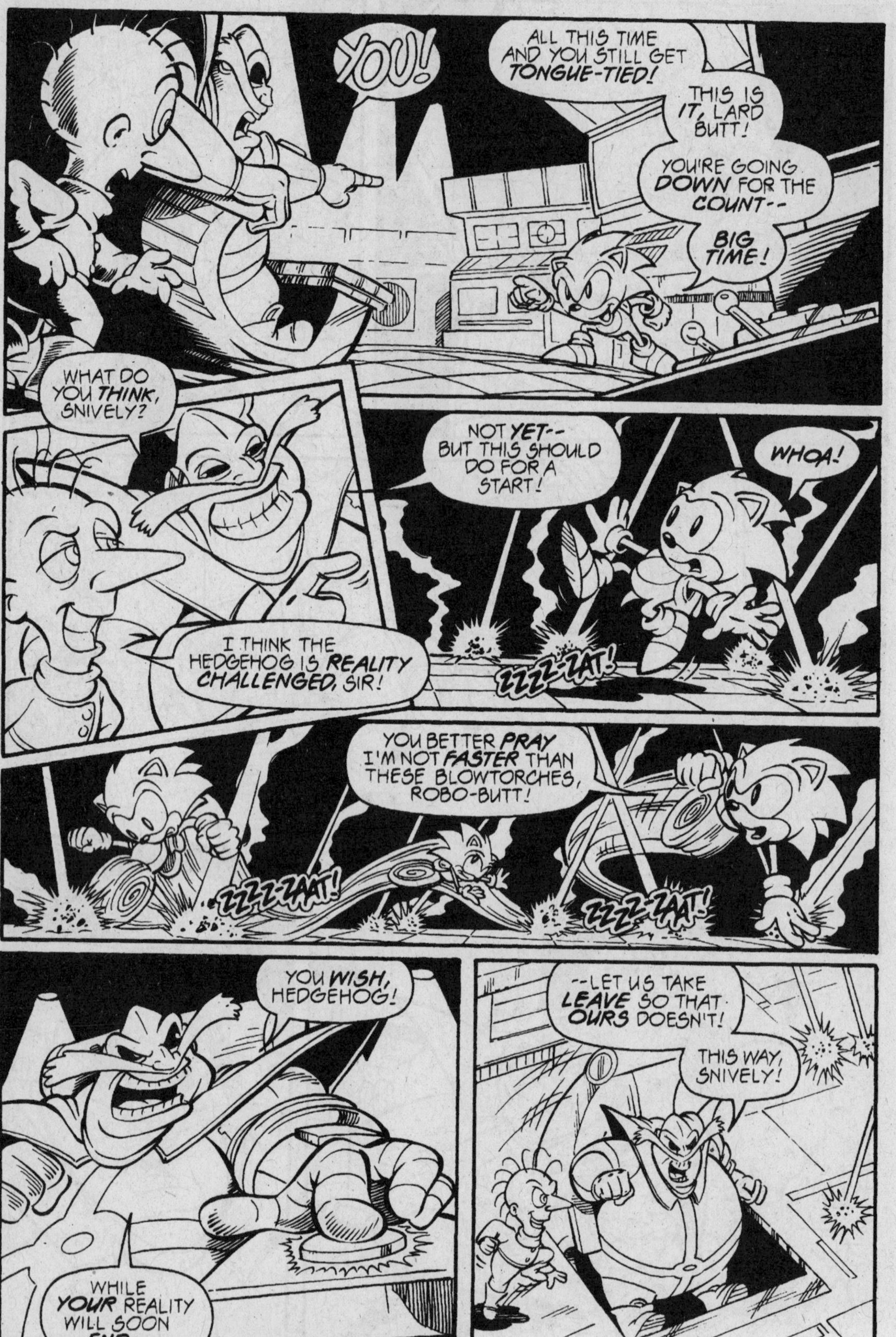
YOU!
ALL THIS TIME AND YOU STILL GET TONGUE-TIED!
THIS IS IT, LARD BUTT!
YOU'RE GOING DOWN FOR THE COUNT--
BIG TIME!
WHAT DO YOU THINK, SNIVELY?
I THINK THE HEDGEHOG IS REALITY CHALLENGED, SIR!
NOT YET-- BUT THIS SHOULD DO FOR A START!
WHOA!
ZZZZ-ZAT!
YOU BETTER PRAY I'M NOT FASTER THAN THESE BLOWTORCHES, ROBO-BUTT!
ZZZZ-ZAAT!
ZZZZ-ZAAT!
YOU WISH, HEDGEHOG!
WHILE YOUR REALITY WILL SOON END--
--LET US TAKE LEAVE SO THAT OURS DOESN'T!
THIS WAY, SNIVELY!
12

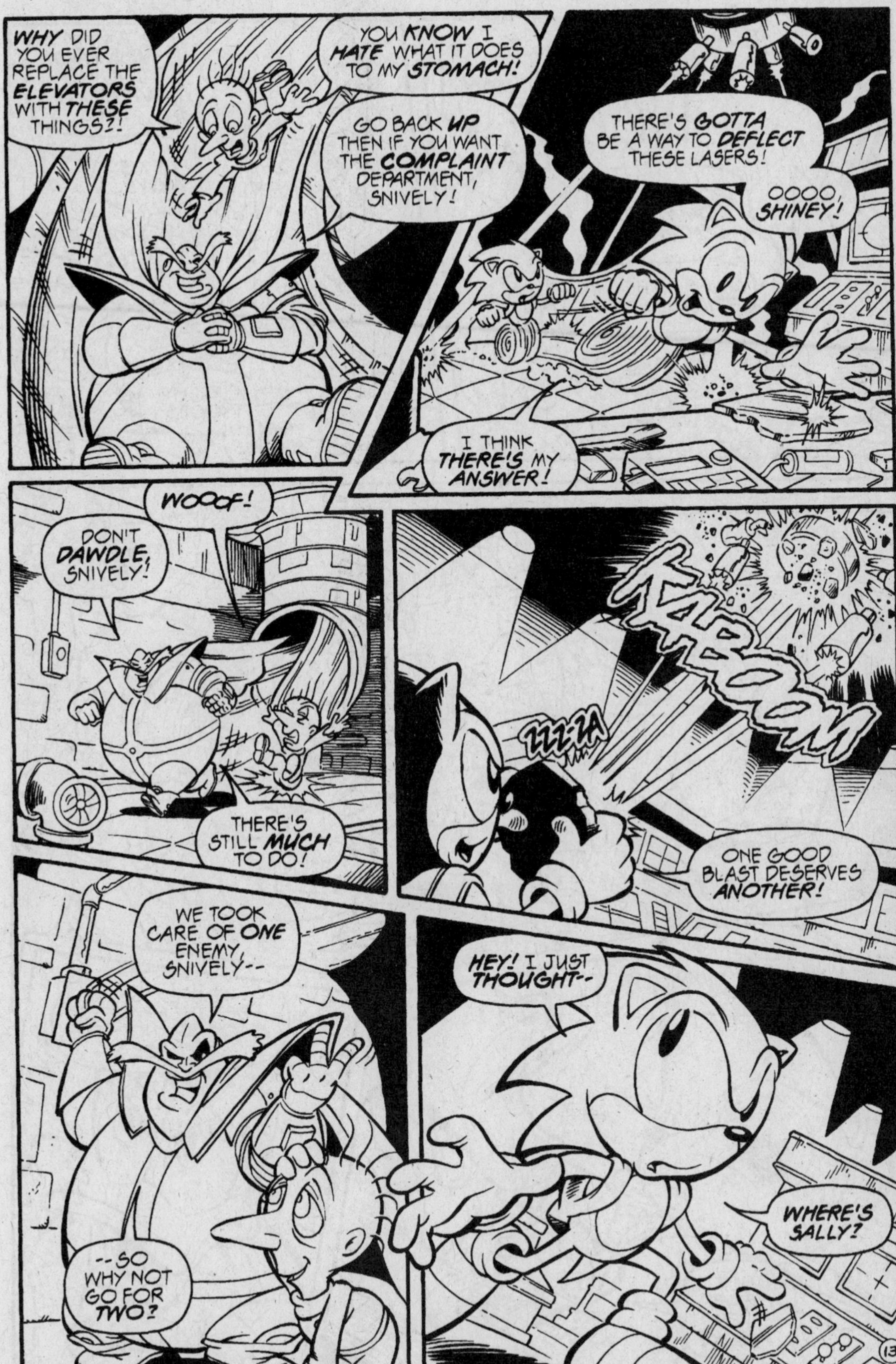

WHY DID YOU EVER REPLACE THE ELEVATORS WITH THESE THINGS?!
YOU KNOW I HATE WHAT IT DOES TO MY STOMACH!
GO BACK UP THEN IF YOU WANT THE COMPLAINT DEPARTMENT, SNIVELY!
THERE'S GOTTA BE A WAY TO DEFLECT THESE LASERS!
OOOO, SHINEY!
I THINK THERE'S MY ANSWER!
WOOOF!
DON'T DAWDLE, SNIVELY!
THERE'S STILL MUCH TO DO!
KABOOM
ZZZ-ZA
ONE GOOD BLAST DESERVES ANOTHER!
WE TOOK CARE OF ONE ENEMY, SNIVELY--
--SO WHY NOT GO FOR TWO?
HEY! I JUST THOUGHT--
WHERE'S SALLY?
13

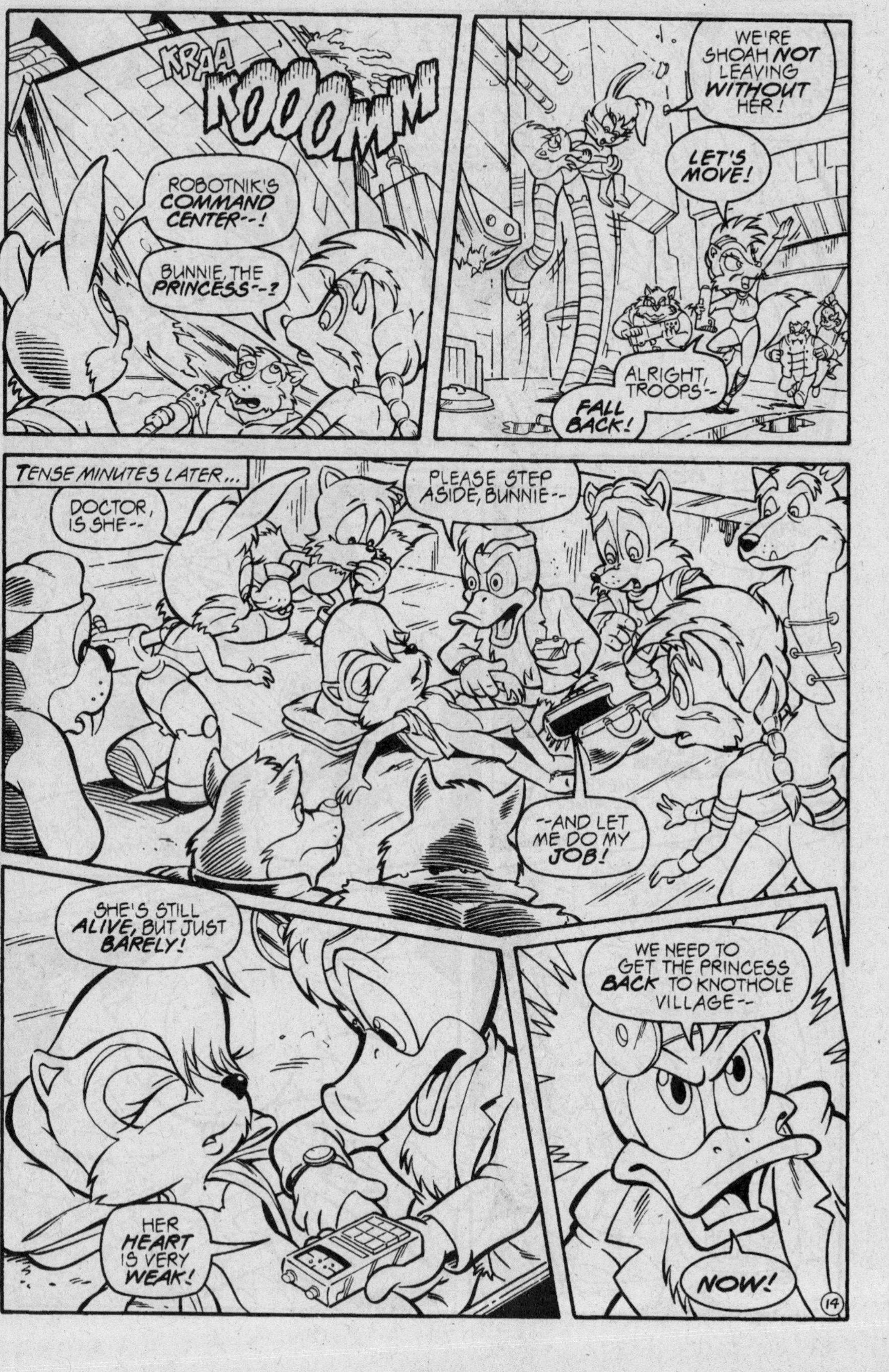
KRAA
KOOOMM
ROBOTNIK'S COMMAND CENTER--!
BUNNIE, THE PRINCESS--?
WE'RE SHOAH NOT LEAVING WITHOUT HER!
LET'S MOVE!
ALRIGHT, TROOPS--
FALL BACK!
TENSE MINUTES LATER...
DOCTOR, IS SHE--
PLEASE STEP ASIDE, BUNNIE--
--AND LET ME DO MY JOB!
SHE'S STILL ALIVE, BUT JUST BARELY!
HER HEART IS VERY WEAK!
WE NEED TO GET THE PRINCESS BACK TO KNOTHOLE VILLAGE--
NOW!
14

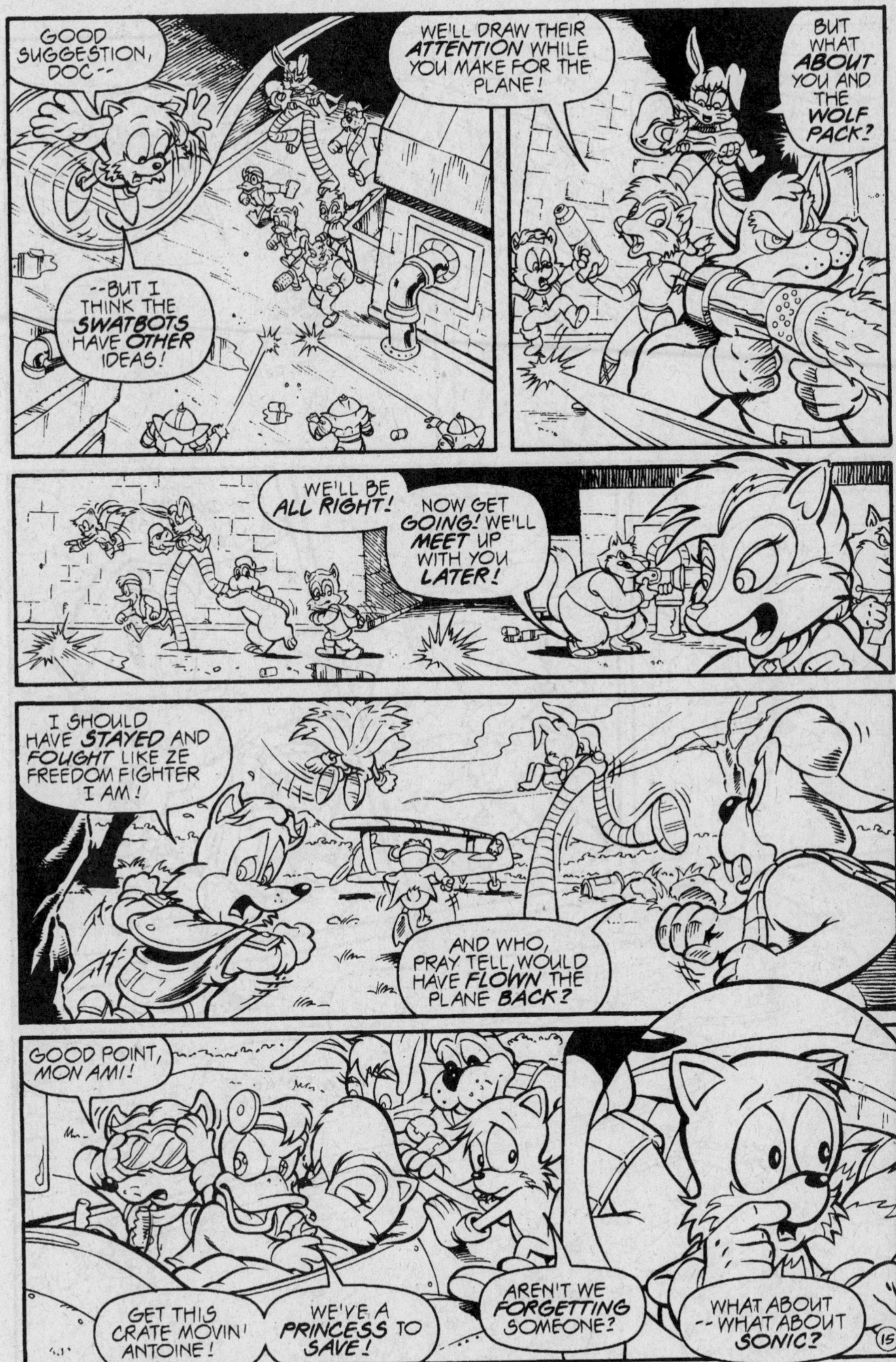
GOOD SUGGESTION, DOC--
--BUT I THINK THE SWATBOTS HAVE OTHER IDEAS!
WE'LL DRAW THEIR ATTENTION WHILE YOU MAKE FOR THE PLANE!
BUT WHAT ABOUT YOU AND THE WOLF PACK?
WE'LL BE ALL RIGHT!
NOW GET GOING! WE'LL MEET UP WITH YOU LATER!
I SHOULD HAVE STAYED AND FOUGHT LIKE ZE FREEDOM FIGHTER I AM!
AND WHO, PRAY TELL, WOULD HAVE FLOWN THE PLANE BACK?
GOOD POINT, MON AMI!
GET THIS CRATE MOVIN' ANTOINE!
WE'VE A PRINCESS TO SAVE!
AREN'T WE FORGETTING SOMEONE?
WHAT ABOUT --WHAT ABOUT SONIC?
15

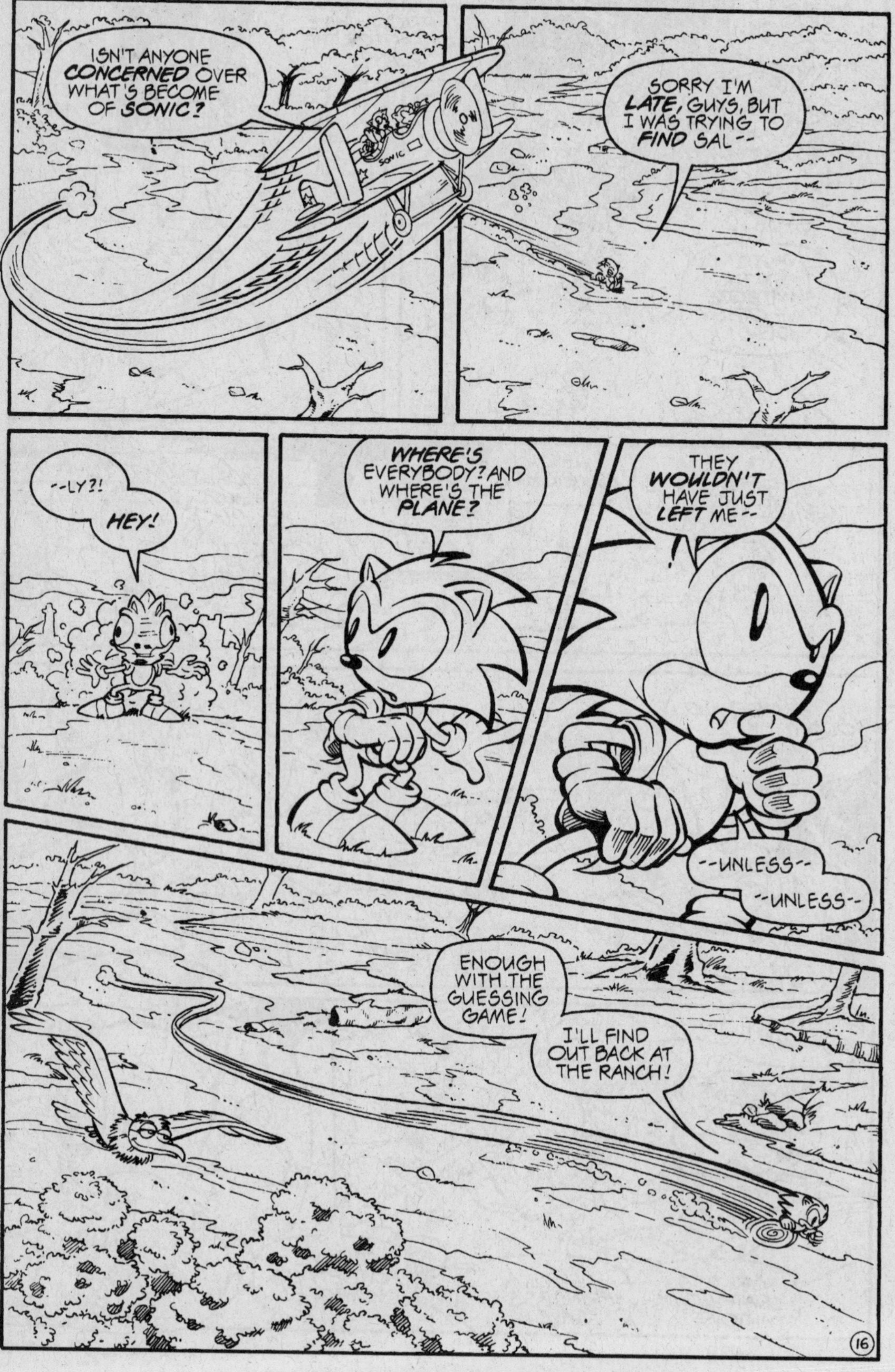
ISN'T ANYONE CONCERNED OVER WHAT'S BECOME OF SONIC?
SONIC
SORRY I'M LATE, GUYS, BUT I WAS TRYING TO FIND SAL--
--LY?!
HEY!
WHERE'S EVERYBODY? AND WHERE'S THE PLANE?
THEY WOULDN'T HAVE JUST LEFT ME--
--UNLESS--
--UNLESS--
ENOUGH WITH THE GUESSING GAME!
I'LL FIND OUT BACK AT THE RANCH!
16

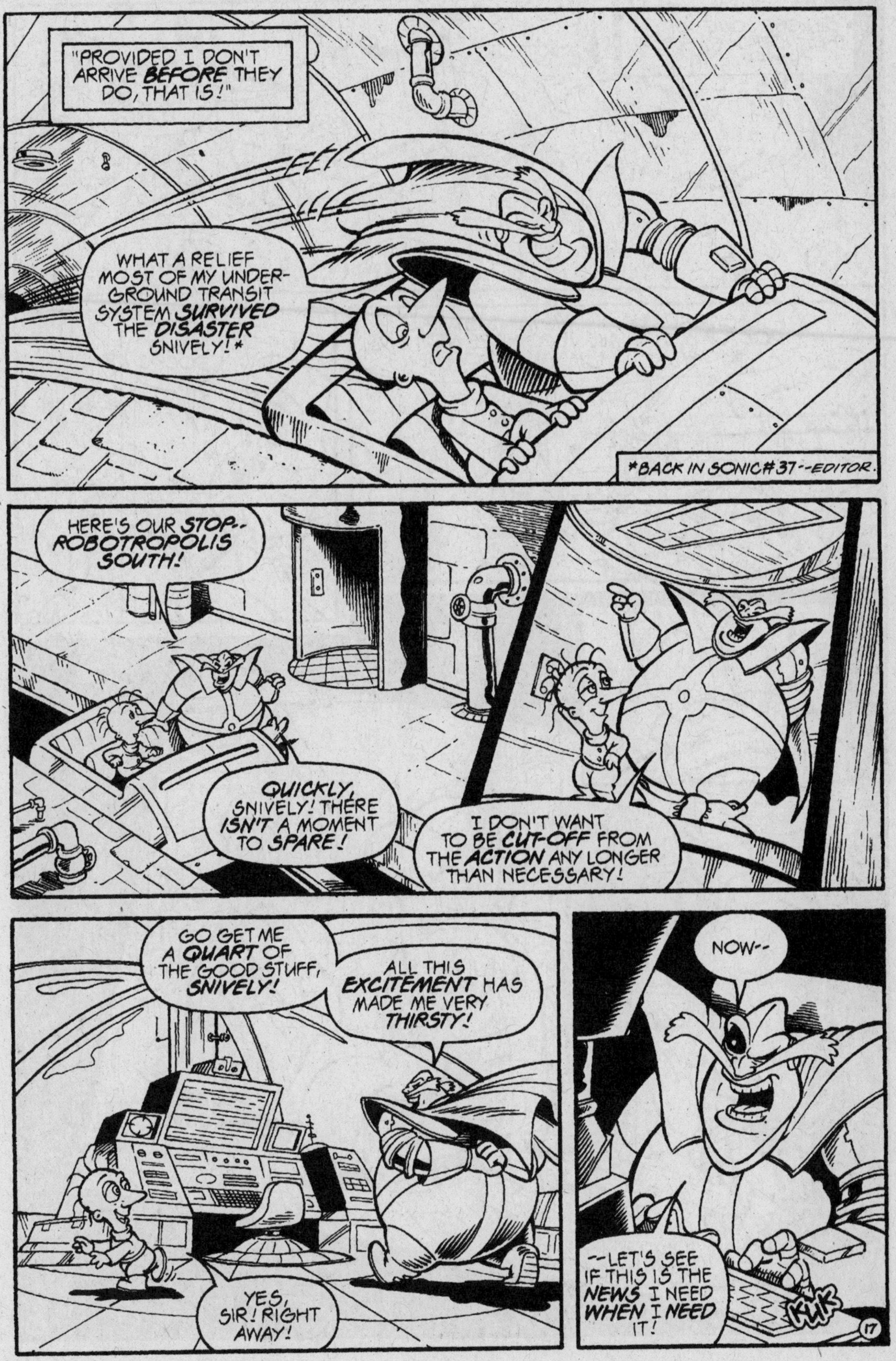
"PROVIDED I DON'T ARRIVE BEFORE THEY DO, THAT IS!"
WHAT A RELIEF MOST OF MY UNDER-GROUND TRANSIT SYSTEM SURVIVED THE DISASTER SNIVELY!*
*BACK IN SONIC #37--EDITOR.
HERE'S OUR STOP-- ROBOTROPOLIS SOUTH!
QUICKLY, SNIVELY! THERE ISN'T A MOMENT TO SPARE!
I DON'T WANT TO BE CUT-OFF FROM THE ACTION ANY LONGER THAN NECESSARY!
GO GET ME A QUART OF THE GOOD STUFF, SNIVELY!
ALL THIS EXCITEMENT HAS MADE ME VERY THIRSTY!
YES, SIR! RIGHT AWAY!
NOW--
--LET'S SEE IF THIS IS THE NEWS I NEED WHEN I NEED IT!
KLIK
17

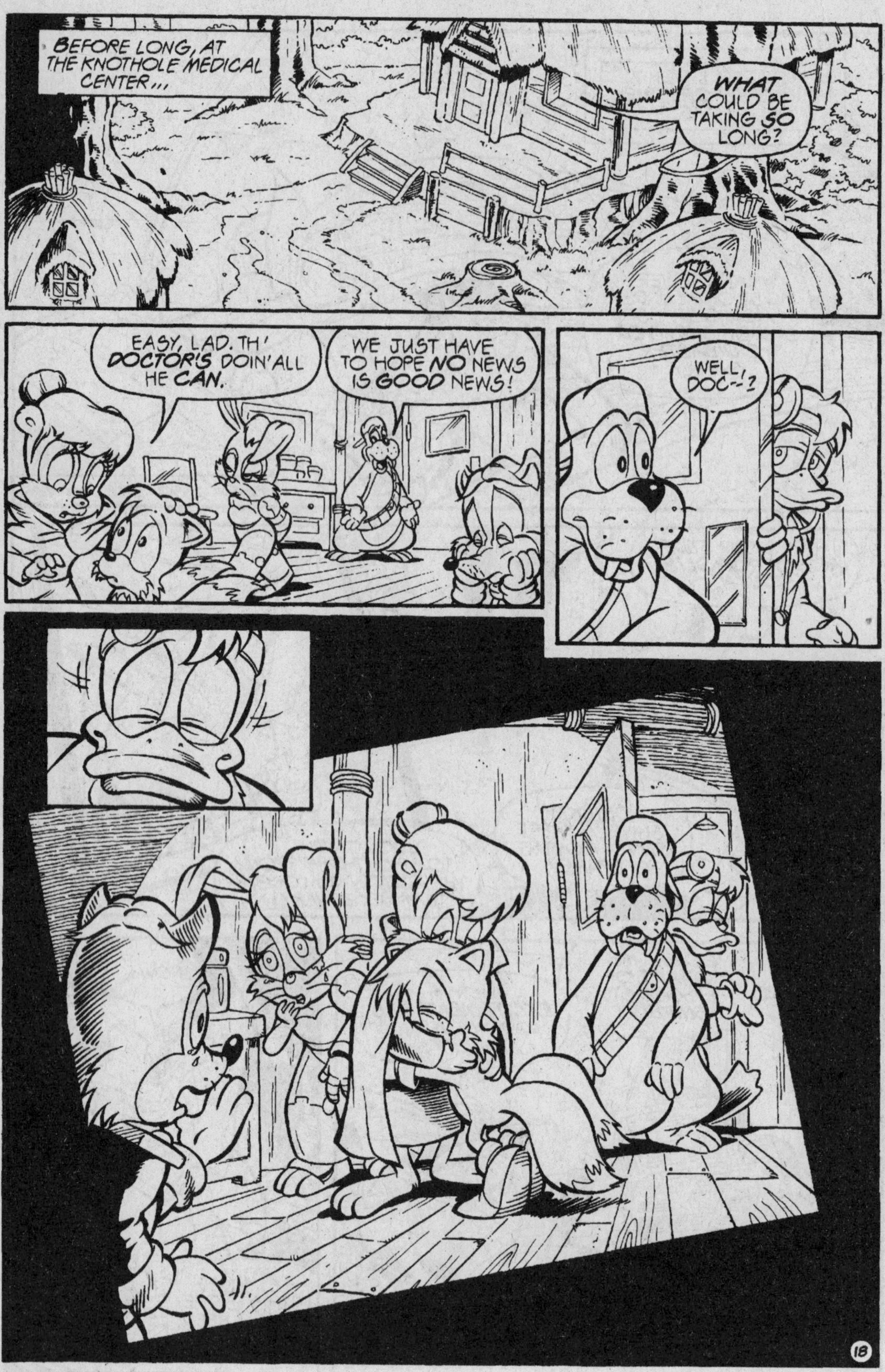
BEFORE LONG, AT THE KNOTHOLE MEDICAL CENTER...
WHAT COULD BE TAKING SO LONG?
EASY, LAD. TH' DOCTOR'S DOIN' ALL HE CAN.
WE JUST HAVE TO HOPE NO NEWS IS GOOD NEWS!
WELL, DOC--!?
18

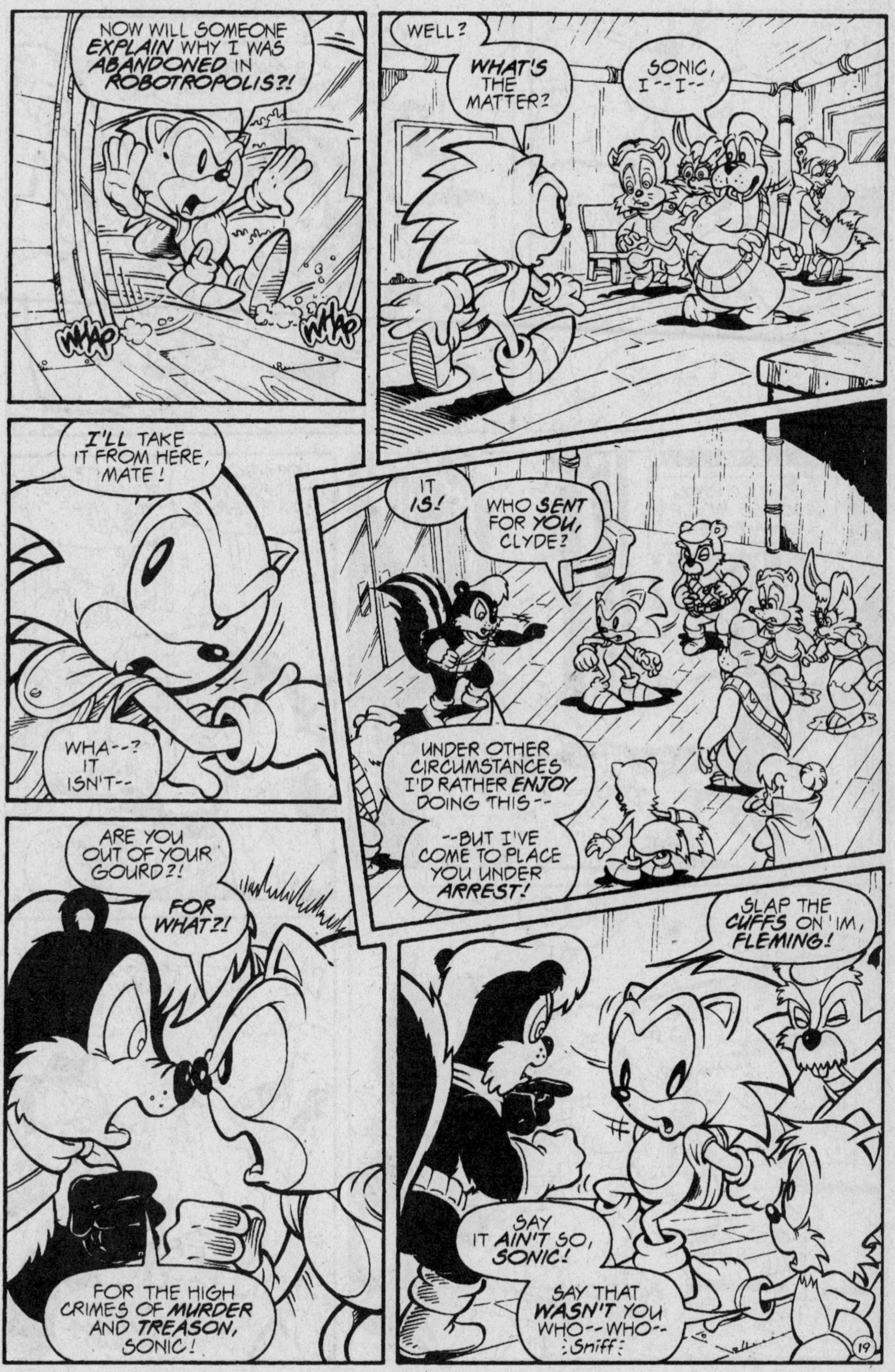

NOW WILL SOMEONE EXPLAIN WHY I WAS ABANDONED IN ROBOTROPOLIS?!
WHAP
WHAP
WELL?
WHAT'S THE MATTER?
SONIC, I--I--
I'LL TAKE IT FROM HERE, MATE!
WHA--? IT ISN'T--
IT IS!
WHO SENT FOR YOU, CLYDE?
UNDER OTHER CIRCUMSTANCES I'D RATHER ENJOY DOING THIS--
--BUT I'VE COME TO PLACE YOU UNDER ARREST!
ARE YOU OUT OF YOUR GOURD?!
FOR WHAT?!
FOR THE HIGH CRIMES OF MURDER AND TREASON, SONIC!
SLAP THE CUFFS ON 'IM, FLEMING!
SAY IT AIN'T SO, SONIC!
SAY THAT WASN'T YOU WHO--WHO-- :Sniff:
19

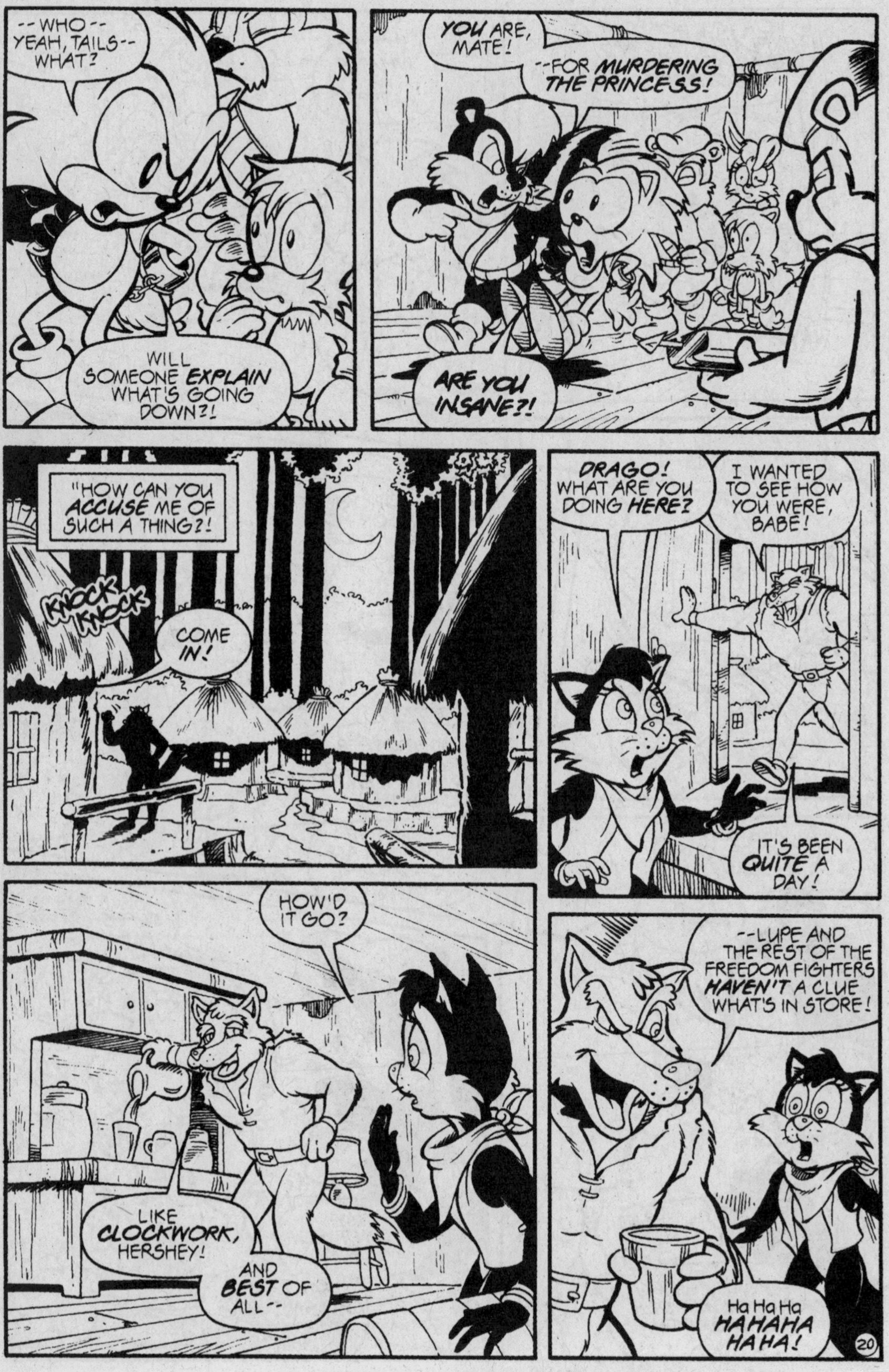
--WHO--
YEAH, TAILS--
WHAT?
WILL SOMEONE EXPLAIN WHAT'S GOING DOWN?!
YOU ARE, MATE!
--FOR MURDERING THE PRINCESS!
ARE YOU INSANE?!
"HOW CAN YOU ACCUSE ME OF SUCH A THING?!
KNOCK KNOCK
COME IN!
DRAGO! WHAT ARE YOU DOING HERE?
I WANTED TO SEE HOW YOU WERE, BABE!
IT'S BEEN QUITE A DAY!
HOW'D IT GO?
LIKE CLOCKWORK, HERSHEY!
AND BEST OF ALL--
--LUPE AND THE REST OF THE FREEDOM FIGHTERS HAVEN'T A CLUE WHAT'S IN STORE!
Ha Ha Ha HAHAHA HAHA!
20

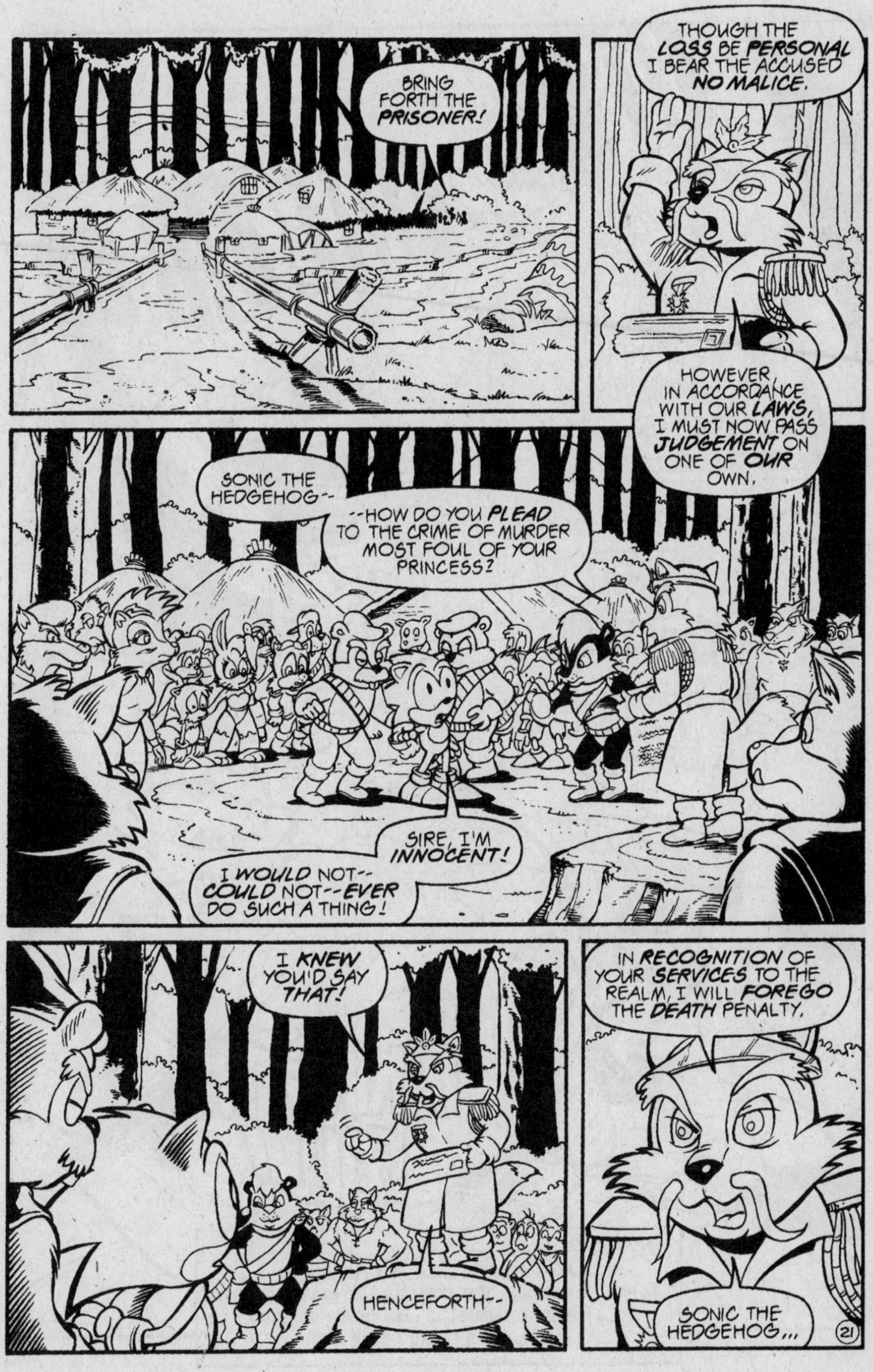
BRING FORTH THE PRISONER!
THOUGH THE LOSS BE PERSONAL I BEAR THE ACCUSED NO MALICE.
HOWEVER, IN ACCORDANCE WITH OUR LAWS, I MUST NOW PASS JUDGEMENT ON ONE OF OUR OWN.
SONIC THE HEDGEHOG--
--HOW DO YOU PLEAD TO THE CRIME OF MURDER MOST FOUL OF YOUR PRINCESS?
SIRE, I'M INNOCENT!
I WOULD NOT--COULD NOT--EVER DO SUCH A THING!
I KNEW YOU'D SAY THAT!
HENCEFORTH--
IN RECOGNITION OF YOUR SERVICES TO THE REALM, I WILL FOREGO THE DEATH PENALTY.
SONIC THE HEDGEHOG...
21

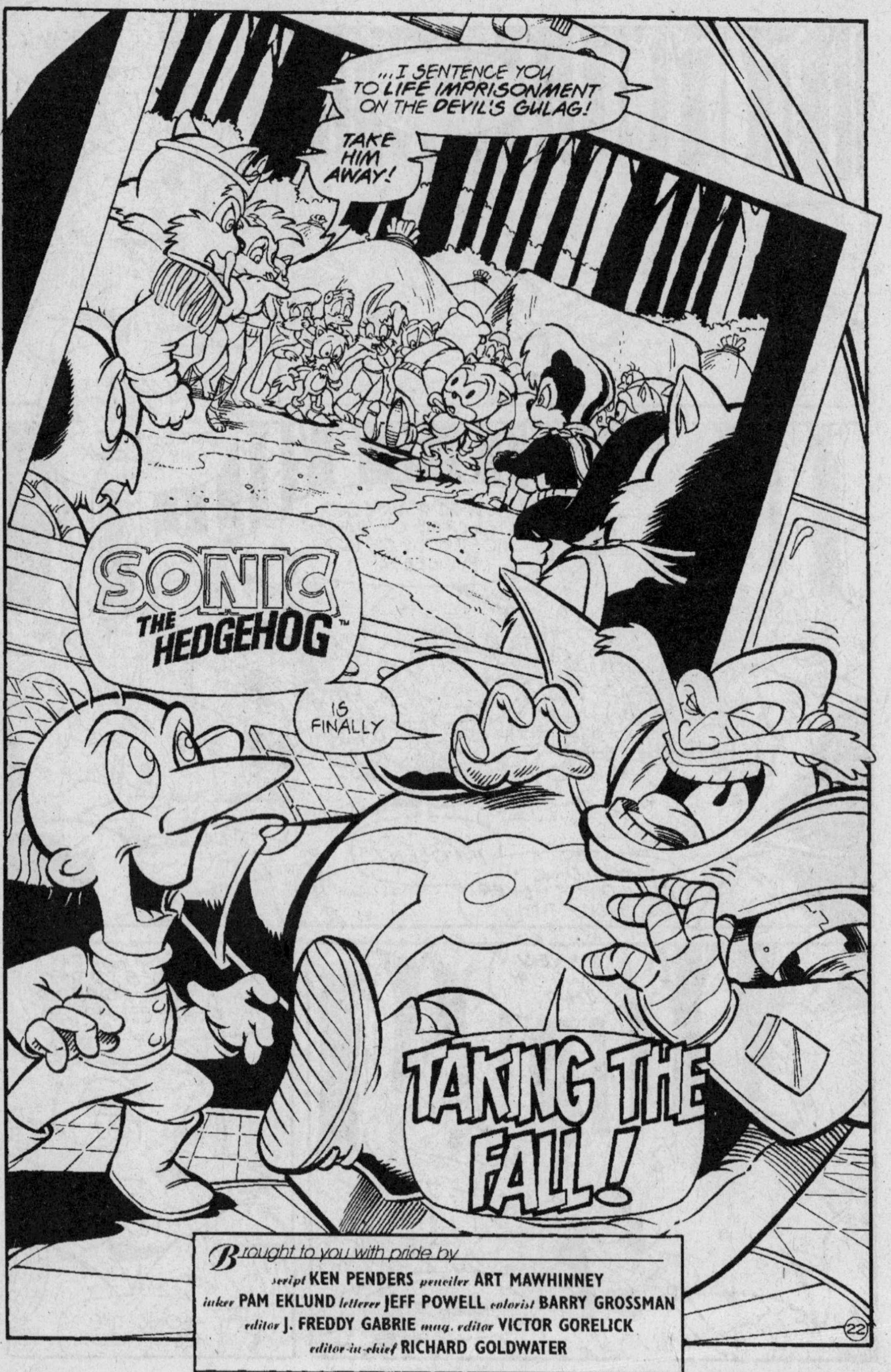

...I SENTENCE YOU TO LIFE IMPRISONMENT ON THE DEVIL'S GULAG!
TAKE HIM AWAY!
SONIC THE HEDGEHOG™
IS FINALLY
TAKING THE FALL!
Brought to you with pride by
script KEN PENDERS penciler ART MAWHINNEY
inker PAM EKLUND letterer JEFF POWELL colorist BARRY GROSSMAN
editor J. FREDDY GABRIE mag. editor VICTOR GORELICK
editor-in-chief RICHARD GOLDWATER
22

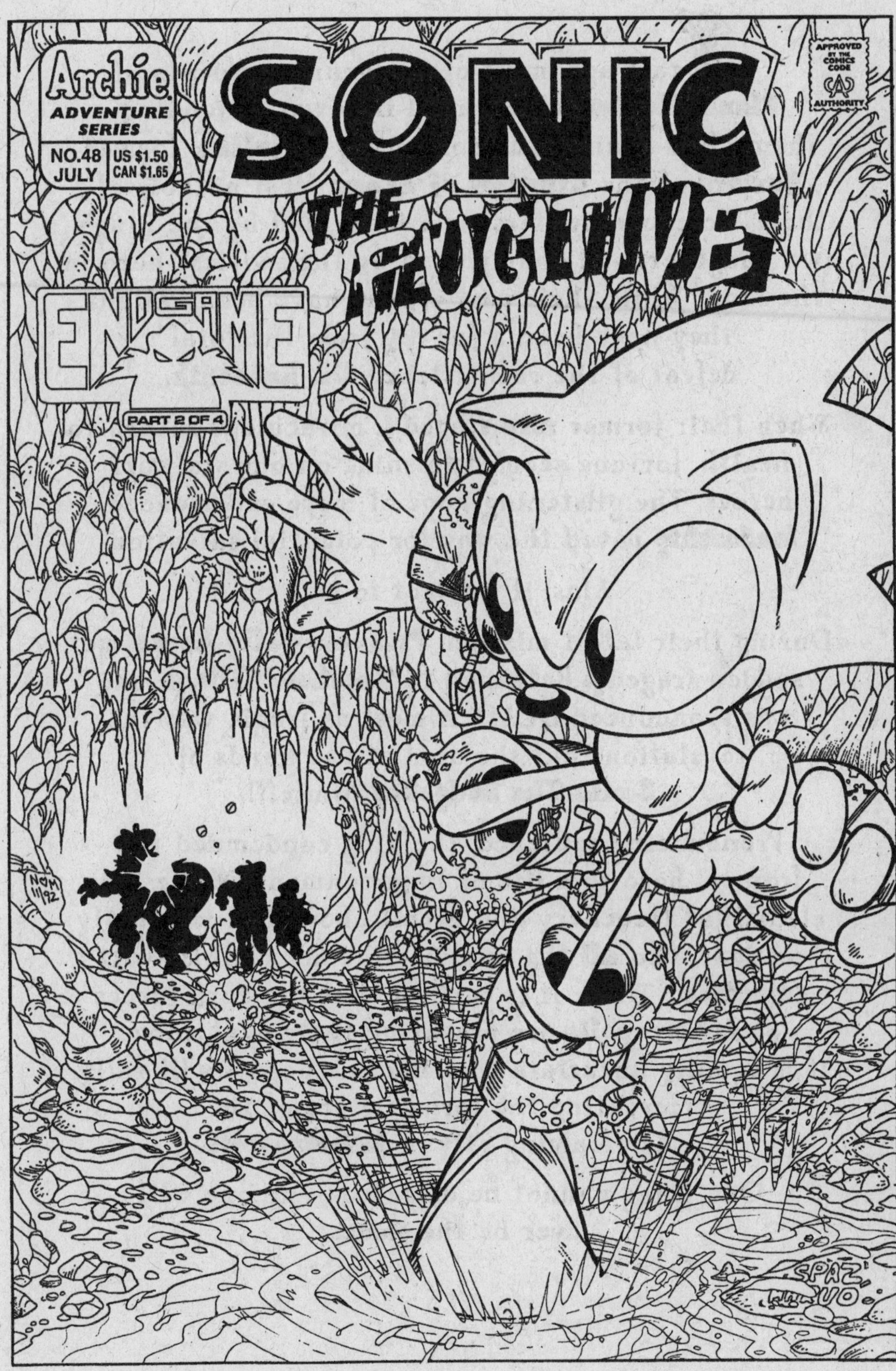

Archie
ADVENTURE SERIES
NO.48 JULY
US $1.50 CAN $1.65
APPROVED BY THE COMICS CODE AUTHORITY
SONIC
THE FUGITIVE
ENDGAME
PART 2 OF 4

Years ago, most of the young residents of **Planet Mobius** were forced into war, defending themselves against the conspiracy of **Julian**, former **Warlord** of the **Kingdom of Acorn**. Most notable of these "freedom fighters" is a team lead by the King's own daughter, and championed by the swiftest hero in the land. While their past efforts have been valiant, they have been a far cry from the total defeat of the rechristened **Dr. Robotnik**.

When their former **sire** staged a miraculous return to health, fortune seemed to shine on our stalwart heroes. The glistening hope of more experienced **leadership** paved the way for potential salvation.

Alas, it was not to be...

During their latest mission, **Princess Sally Acorn** met sudden tragedy. Returned to **Knothole Village**, she was pronounced DEAD. Almost as tragic was the revelation that she died at the hands of... **Sonic The Hedgehog** himself!

Pronouncing sentence, the king condemned the "former" hero to a life of imprisonment. While it is clear that treachery and deceit abound, it is equally unclear who **all** the conspirators are of this swift **injustice**. While it is certain that the dark forces of **Robotropolis** are preparing their next move, it is equally uncertain whether our heroes will rally, recreating the former glory of the once-gleaming city of **Mobotropolis**.

One thing cannot be disputed — no one will ever be the same...

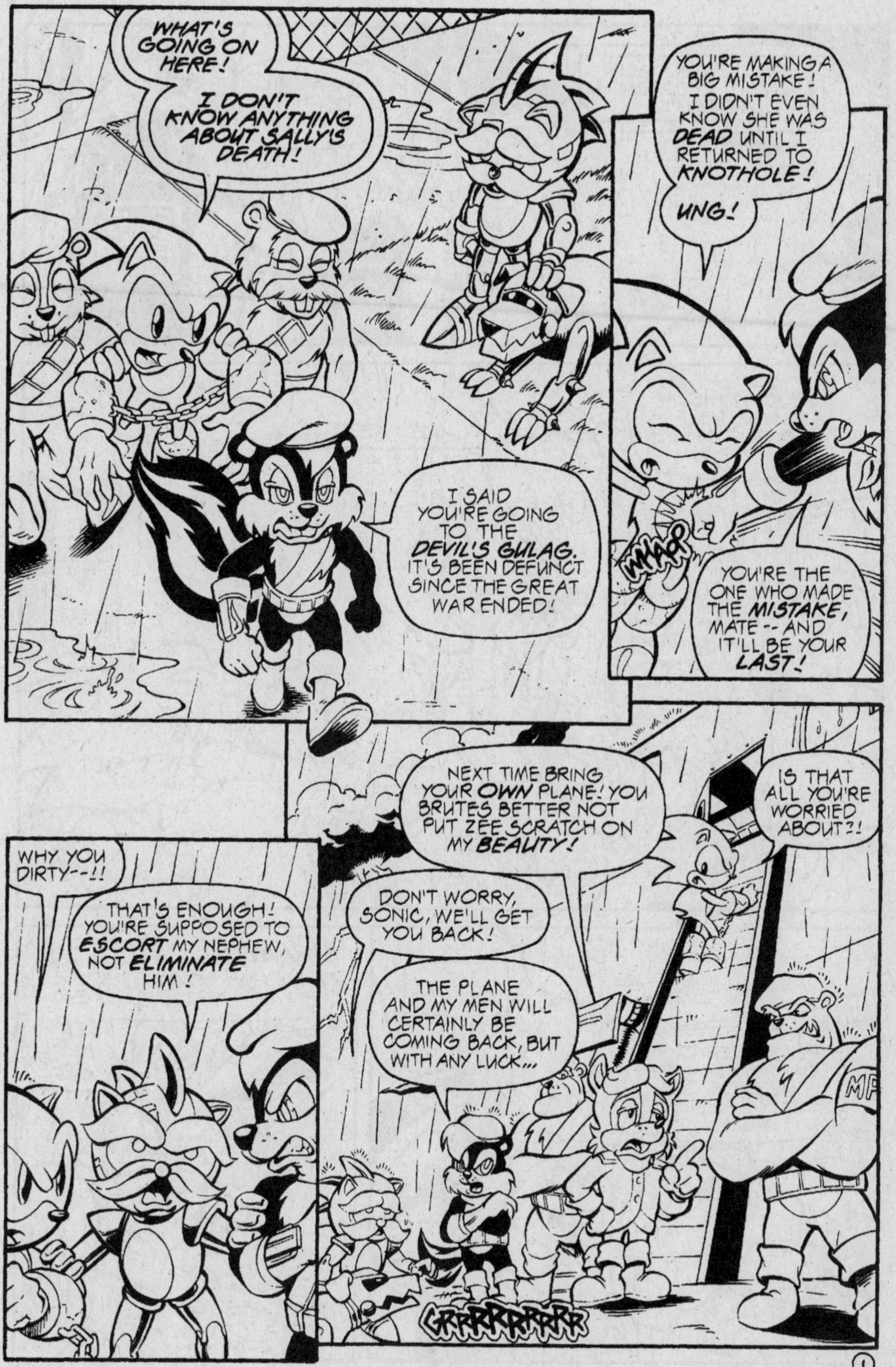
WHAT'S GOING ON HERE!
I DON'T KNOW ANYTHING ABOUT SALLY'S DEATH!
I SAID YOU'RE GOING TO THE DEVIL'S GULAG. IT'S BEEN DEFUNCT SINCE THE GREAT WAR ENDED!
YOU'RE MAKING A BIG MISTAKE! I DIDN'T EVEN KNOW SHE WAS DEAD UNTIL I RETURNED TO KNOTHOLE!
UNG!
WHAP
YOU'RE THE ONE WHO MADE THE MISTAKE, MATE -- AND IT'LL BE YOUR LAST!
WHY YOU DIRTY--!!
THAT'S ENOUGH! YOU'RE SUPPOSED TO ESCORT MY NEPHEW, NOT ELIMINATE HIM!
NEXT TIME BRING YOUR OWN PLANE! YOU BRUTES BETTER NOT PUT ZEE SCRATCH ON MY BEAUTY!
IS THAT ALL YOU'RE WORRIED ABOUT?!
DON'T WORRY, SONIC, WE'LL GET YOU BACK!
THE PLANE AND MY MEN WILL CERTAINLY BE COMING BACK, BUT WITH ANY LUCK...
GRRRRRRRRRR
1

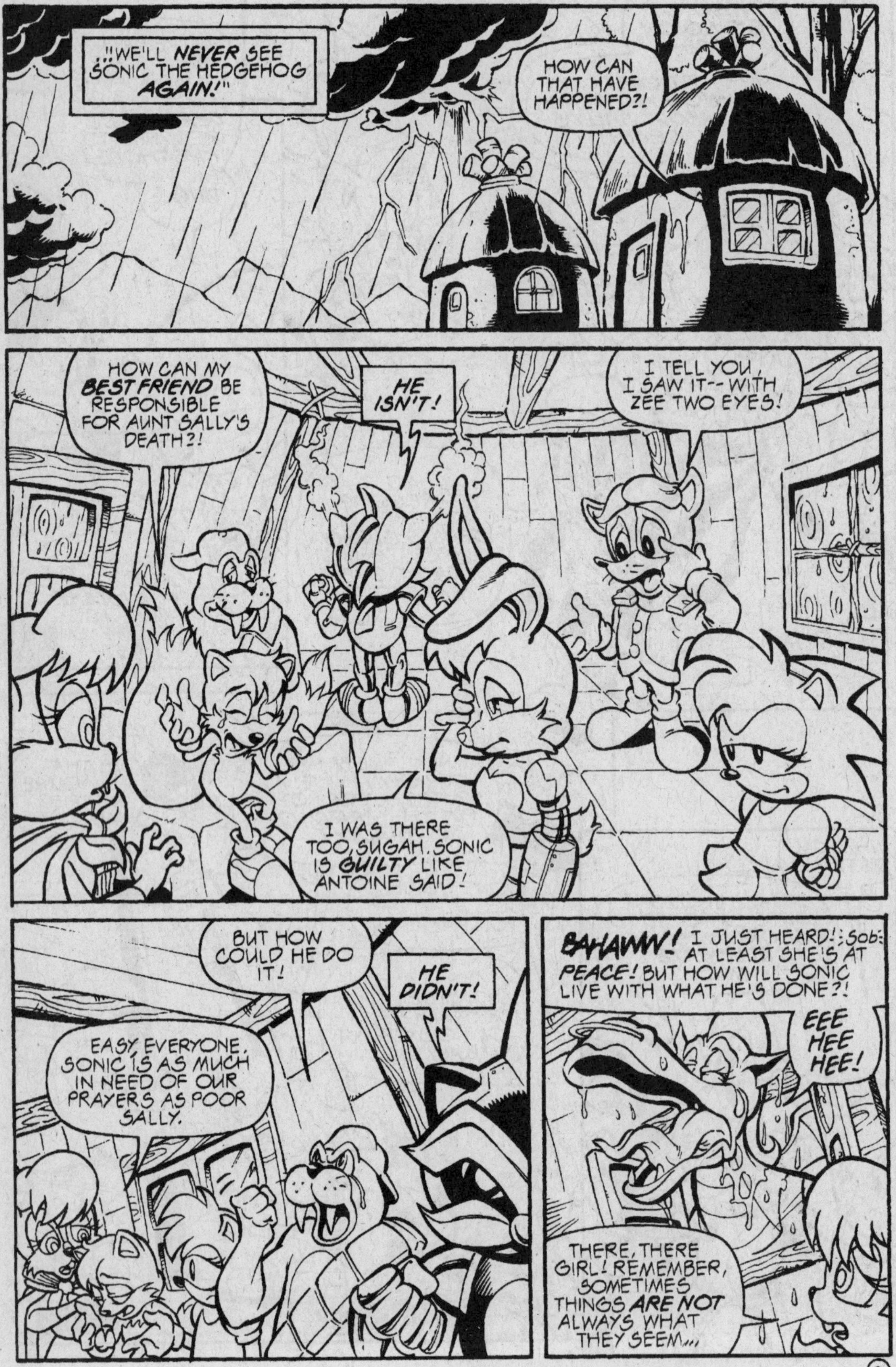
"...WE'LL NEVER SEE SONIC THE HEDGEHOG AGAIN!"
HOW CAN THAT HAVE HAPPENED?!
HOW CAN MY BEST FRIEND BE RESPONSIBLE FOR AUNT SALLY'S DEATH?!
HE ISN'T!
I TELL YOU, I SAW IT-- WITH ZEE TWO EYES!
I WAS THERE TOO, SUGAH. SONIC IS GUILTY LIKE ANTOINE SAID!
BUT HOW COULD HE DO IT!
HE DIDN'T!
EASY, EVERYONE. SONIC IS AS MUCH IN NEED OF OUR PRAYERS AS POOR SALLY.
BAHAWW! I JUST HEARD! :Sob: AT LEAST SHE'S AT PEACE! BUT HOW WILL SONIC LIVE WITH WHAT HE'S DONE?!
EEE HEE HEE!
THERE, THERE GIRL! REMEMBER, SOMETIMES THINGS ARE NOT ALWAYS WHAT THEY SEEM...
2

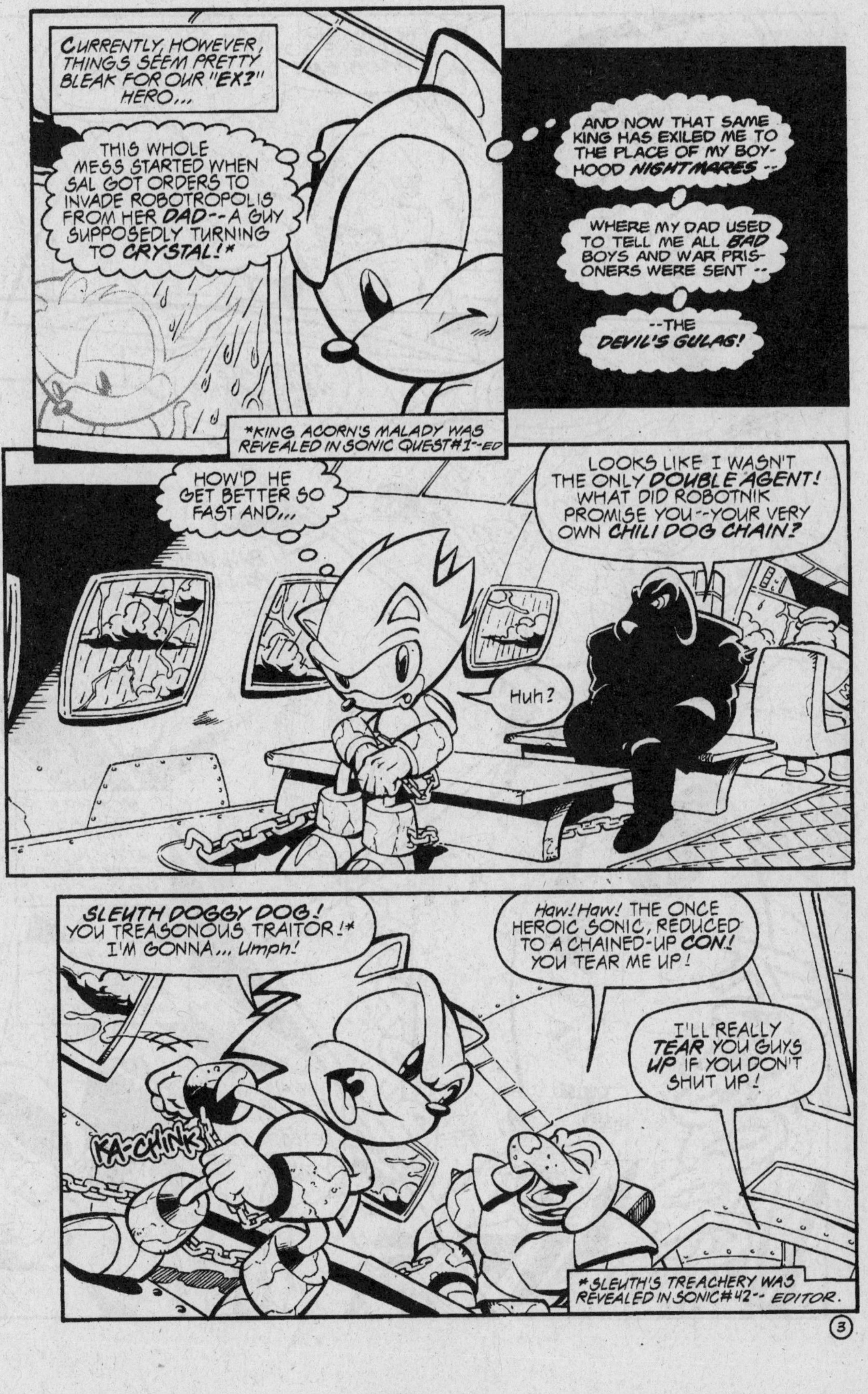

CURRENTLY, HOWEVER, THINGS SEEM PRETTY BLEAK FOR OUR "EX?" HERO...
THIS WHOLE MESS STARTED WHEN SAL GOT ORDERS TO INVADE ROBOTROPOLIS FROM HER DAD--A GUY SUPPOSEDLY TURNING TO CRYSTAL!*
AND NOW THAT SAME KING HAS EXILED ME TO THE PLACE OF MY BOY-HOOD NIGHTMARES--
WHERE MY DAD USED TO TELL ME ALL BAD BOYS AND WAR PRIS-ONERS WERE SENT--
--THE DEVIL'S GULAG!
*KING ACORN'S MALADY WAS REVEALED IN SONIC QUEST #1--ED
HOW'D HE GET BETTER SO FAST AND...
LOOKS LIKE I WASN'T THE ONLY DOUBLE AGENT! WHAT DID ROBOTNIK PROMISE YOU--YOUR VERY OWN CHILI DOG CHAIN?
Huh?
SLEUTH DOGGY DOG! YOU TREASONOUS TRAITOR!* I'M GONNA... Umph!
Haw! Haw! THE ONCE HEROIC SONIC, REDUCED TO A CHAINED-UP CON! YOU TEAR ME UP!
I'LL REALLY TEAR YOU GUYS UP IF YOU DON'T SHUT UP!
KA-CHINK
*SLEUTH'S TREACHERY WAS REVEALED IN SONIC #42-- EDITOR.
3

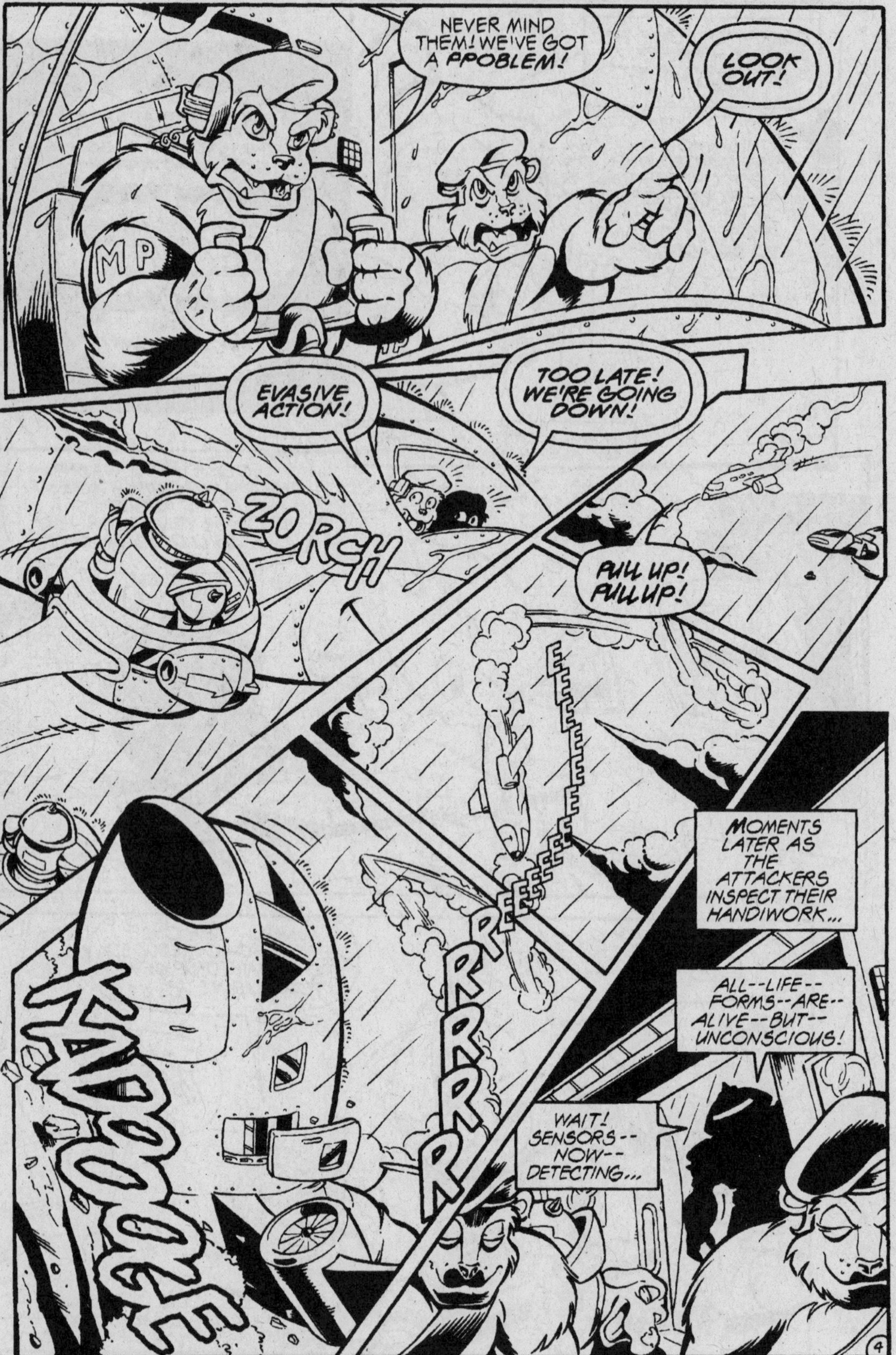
NEVER MIND THEM! WE'VE GOT A PROBLEM!
LOOK OUT!
EVASIVE ACTION!
TOO LATE! WE'RE GOING DOWN!
ZORCH
PULL UP! PULL UP!
EEEEEEEEEEEEE
RRRRRR
KAROOOM
MOMENTS LATER AS THE ATTACKERS INSPECT THEIR HANDIWORK...
ALL--LIFE--FORMS--ARE--ALIVE--BUT--UNCONSCIOUS!
WAIT! SENSORS--NOW--DETECTING...
4

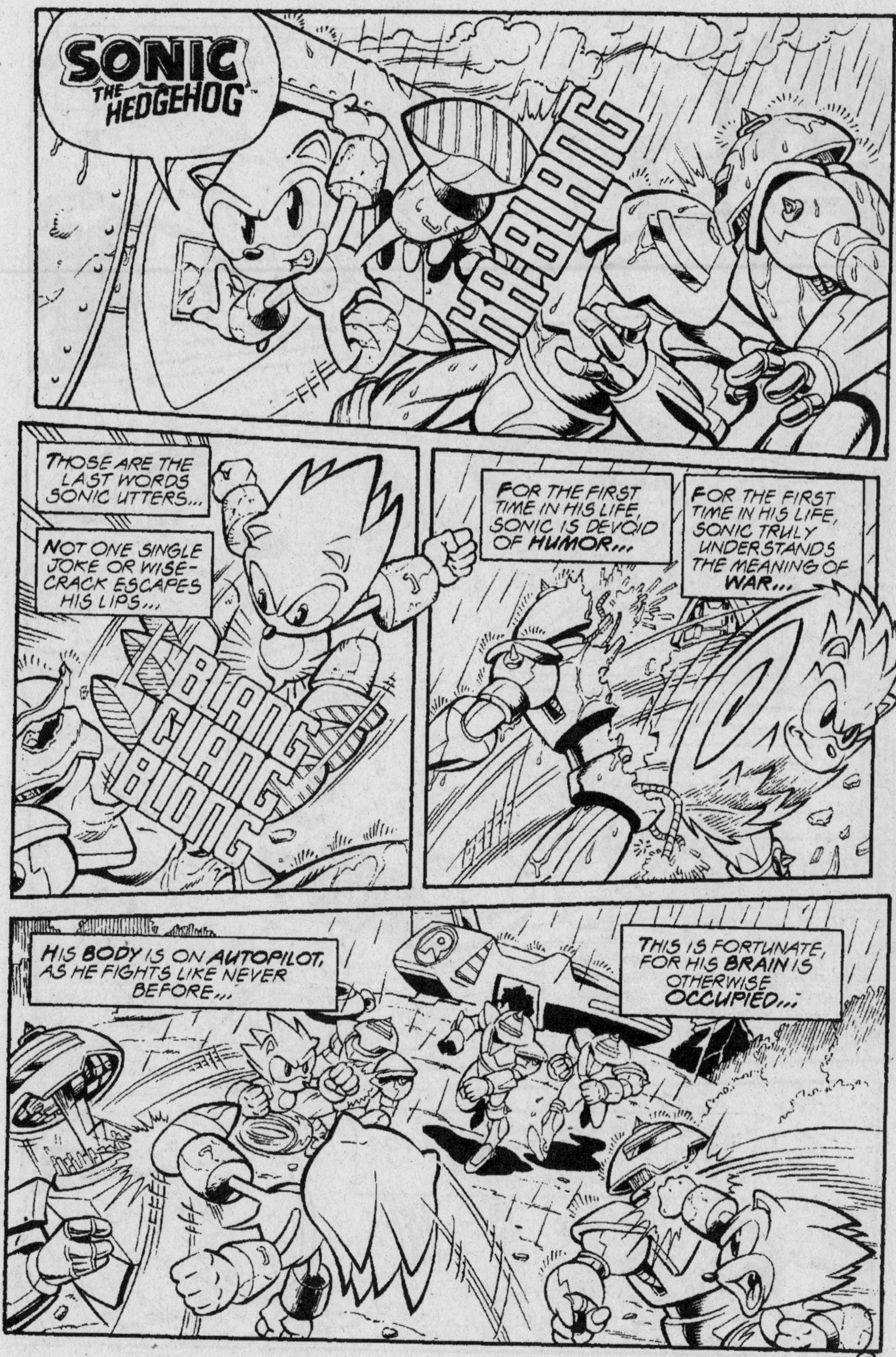
SONIC THE HEDGEHOG™
KA-BLONG
THOSE ARE THE LAST WORDS SONIC UTTERS...
NOT ONE SINGLE JOKE OR WISE-CRACK ESCAPES HIS LIPS...
BLANG CLANG BLONG
FOR THE FIRST TIME IN HIS LIFE, SONIC IS DEVOID OF **HUMOR**...
FOR THE FIRST TIME IN HIS LIFE, SONIC TRULY UNDERSTANDS THE MEANING OF **WAR**...
HIS **BODY** IS ON **AUTOPILOT**, AS HE FIGHTS LIKE NEVER BEFORE...
THIS IS FORTUNATE, FOR HIS **BRAIN** IS OTHERWISE **OCCUPIED**...
(5)

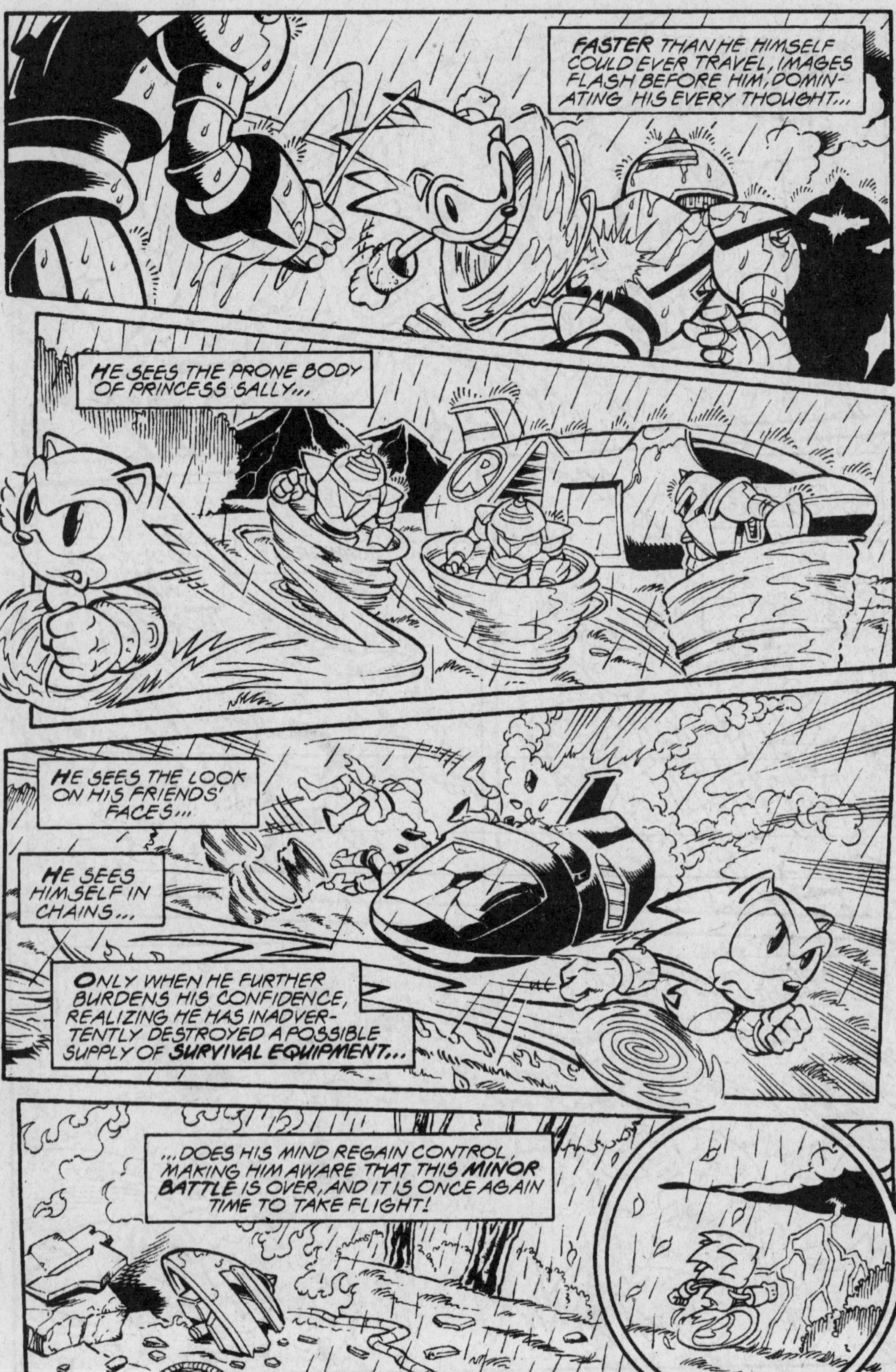
FASTER THAN HE HIMSELF COULD EVER TRAVEL, IMAGES FLASH BEFORE HIM, DOMINATING HIS EVERY THOUGHT...
HE SEES THE PRONE BODY OF PRINCESS SALLY...
HE SEES THE LOOK ON HIS FRIENDS' FACES...
HE SEES HIMSELF IN CHAINS...
ONLY WHEN HE FURTHER BURDENS HIS CONFIDENCE, REALIZING HE HAS INADVERTENTLY DESTROYED A POSSIBLE SUPPLY OF SURVIVAL EQUIPMENT...
...DOES HIS MIND REGAIN CONTROL, MAKING HIM AWARE THAT THIS MINOR BATTLE IS OVER, AND IT IS ONCE AGAIN TIME TO TAKE FLIGHT!
6

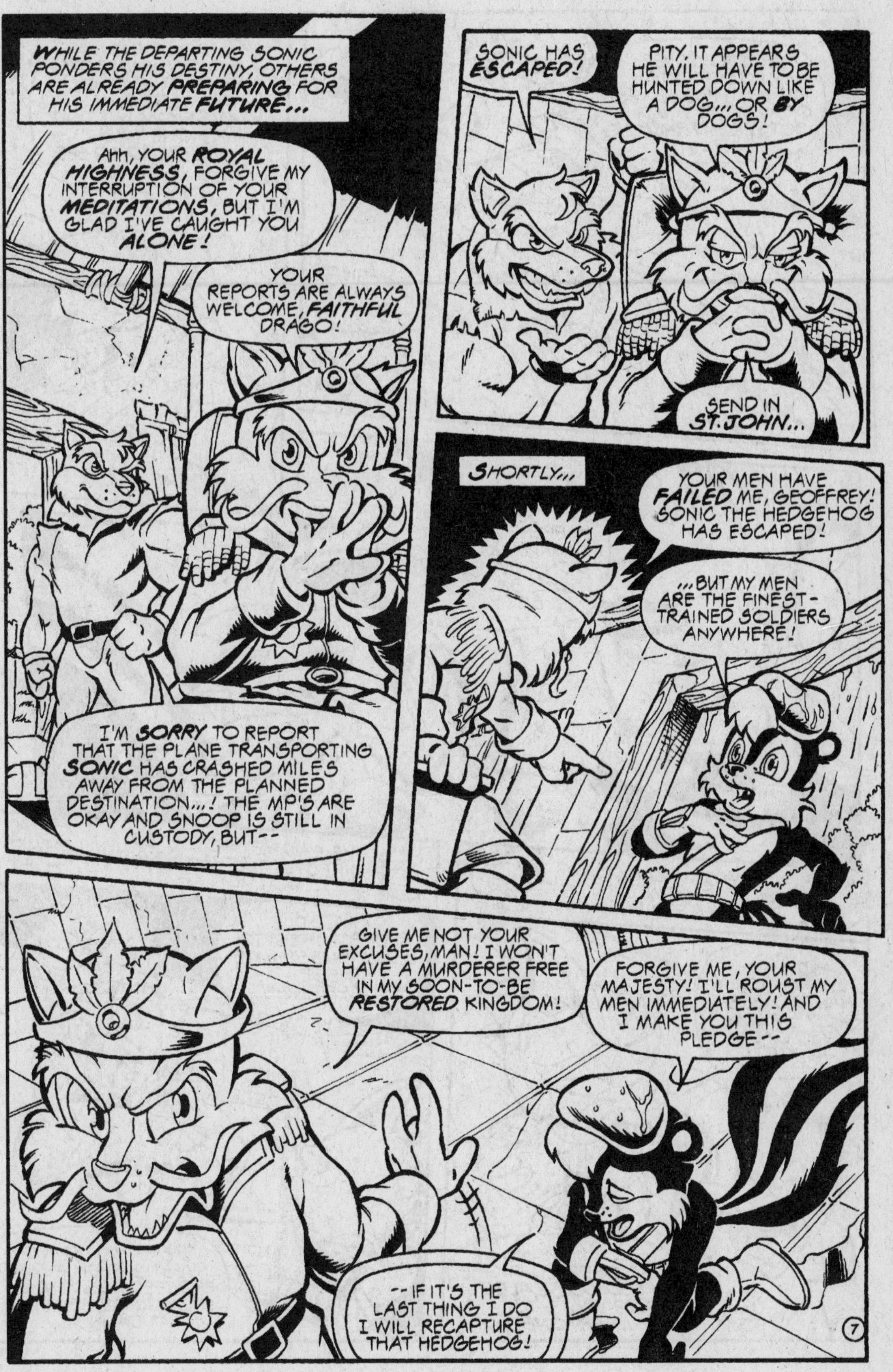
WHILE THE DEPARTING SONIC PONDERS HIS DESTINY, OTHERS ARE ALREADY PREPARING FOR HIS IMMEDIATE FUTURE...
Ahh, YOUR ROYAL HIGHNESS, FORGIVE MY INTERRUPTION OF YOUR MEDITATIONS, BUT I'M GLAD I'VE CAUGHT YOU ALONE!
YOUR REPORTS ARE ALWAYS WELCOME, FAITHFUL DRAGO!
I'M SORRY TO REPORT THAT THE PLANE TRANSPORTING SONIC HAS CRASHED MILES AWAY FROM THE PLANNED DESTINATION...! THE MP'S ARE OKAY AND SNOOP IS STILL IN CUSTODY, BUT--
SONIC HAS ESCAPED!
PITY. IT APPEARS HE WILL HAVE TO BE HUNTED DOWN LIKE A DOG... OR BY DOGS!
SEND IN ST. JOHN...
SHORTLY...
YOUR MEN HAVE FAILED ME, GEOFFREY! SONIC THE HEDGEHOG HAS ESCAPED!
...BUT MY MEN ARE THE FINEST-TRAINED SOLDIERS ANYWHERE!
GIVE ME NOT YOUR EXCUSES, MAN! I WON'T HAVE A MURDERER FREE IN MY SOON-TO-BE RESTORED KINGDOM!
FORGIVE ME, YOUR MAJESTY! I'LL ROUST MY MEN IMMEDIATELY! AND I MAKE YOU THIS PLEDGE--
--IF IT'S THE LAST THING I DO I WILL RECAPTURE THAT HEDGEHOG!
7

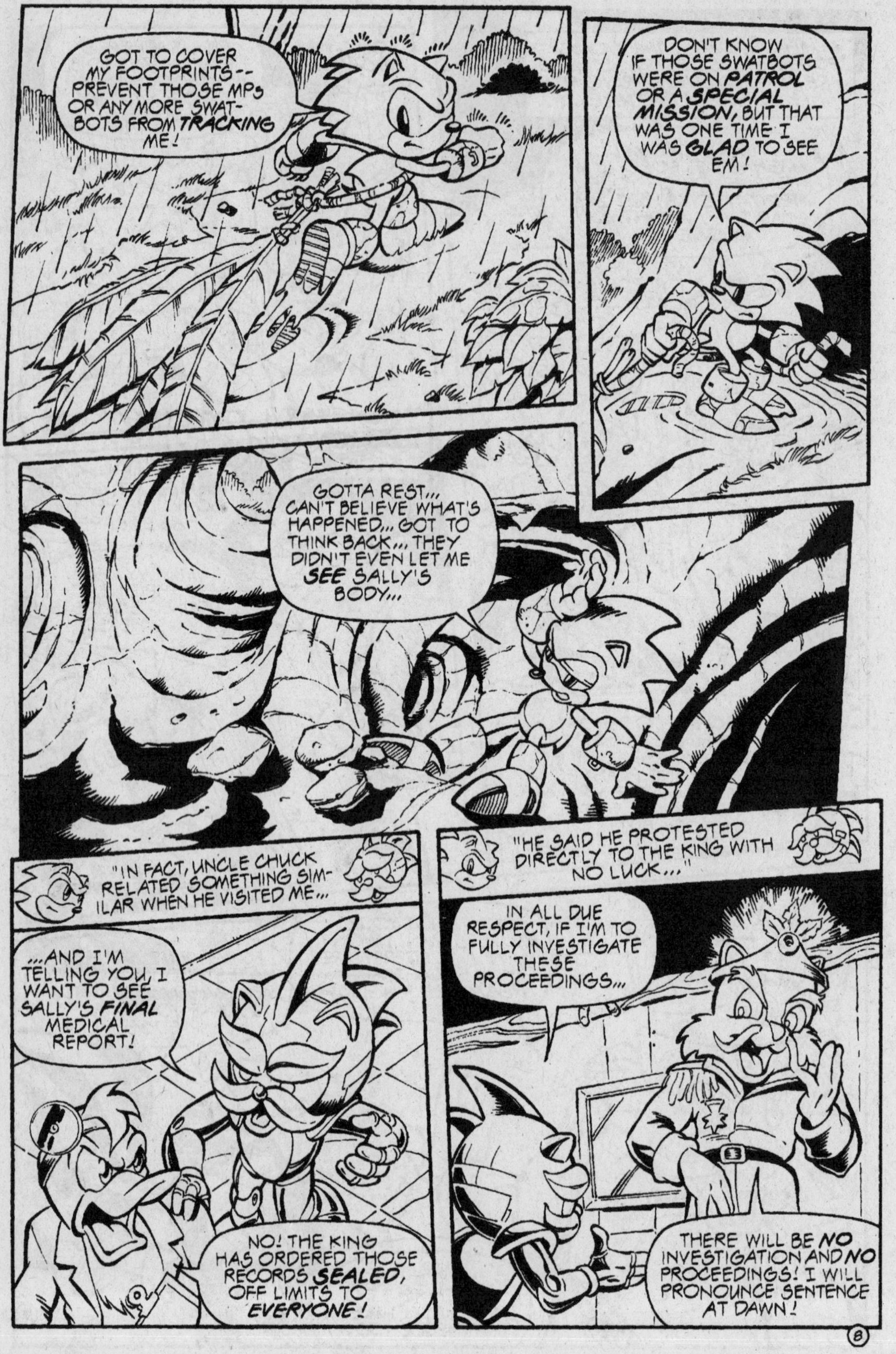
GOT TO COVER MY FOOTPRINTS-- PREVENT THOSE MPs OR ANY MORE SWAT-BOTS FROM TRACKING ME!
DON'T KNOW IF THOSE SWATBOTS WERE ON PATROL OR A SPECIAL MISSION, BUT THAT WAS ONE TIME I WAS GLAD TO SEE 'EM!
GOTTA REST... CAN'T BELIEVE WHAT'S HAPPENED... GOT TO THINK BACK... THEY DIDN'T EVEN LET ME SEE SALLY'S BODY...
"IN FACT, UNCLE CHUCK RELATED SOMETHING SIM-ILAR WHEN HE VISITED ME...
...AND I'M TELLING YOU, I WANT TO SEE SALLY'S FINAL MEDICAL REPORT!
NO! THE KING HAS ORDERED THOSE RECORDS SEALED, OFF LIMITS TO EVERYONE!
"HE SAID HE PROTESTED DIRECTLY TO THE KING WITH NO LUCK..."
IN ALL DUE RESPECT, IF I'M TO FULLY INVESTIGATE THESE PROCEEDINGS...
THERE WILL BE NO INVESTIGATION AND NO PROCEEDINGS! I WILL PRONOUNCE SENTENCE AT DAWN!
8

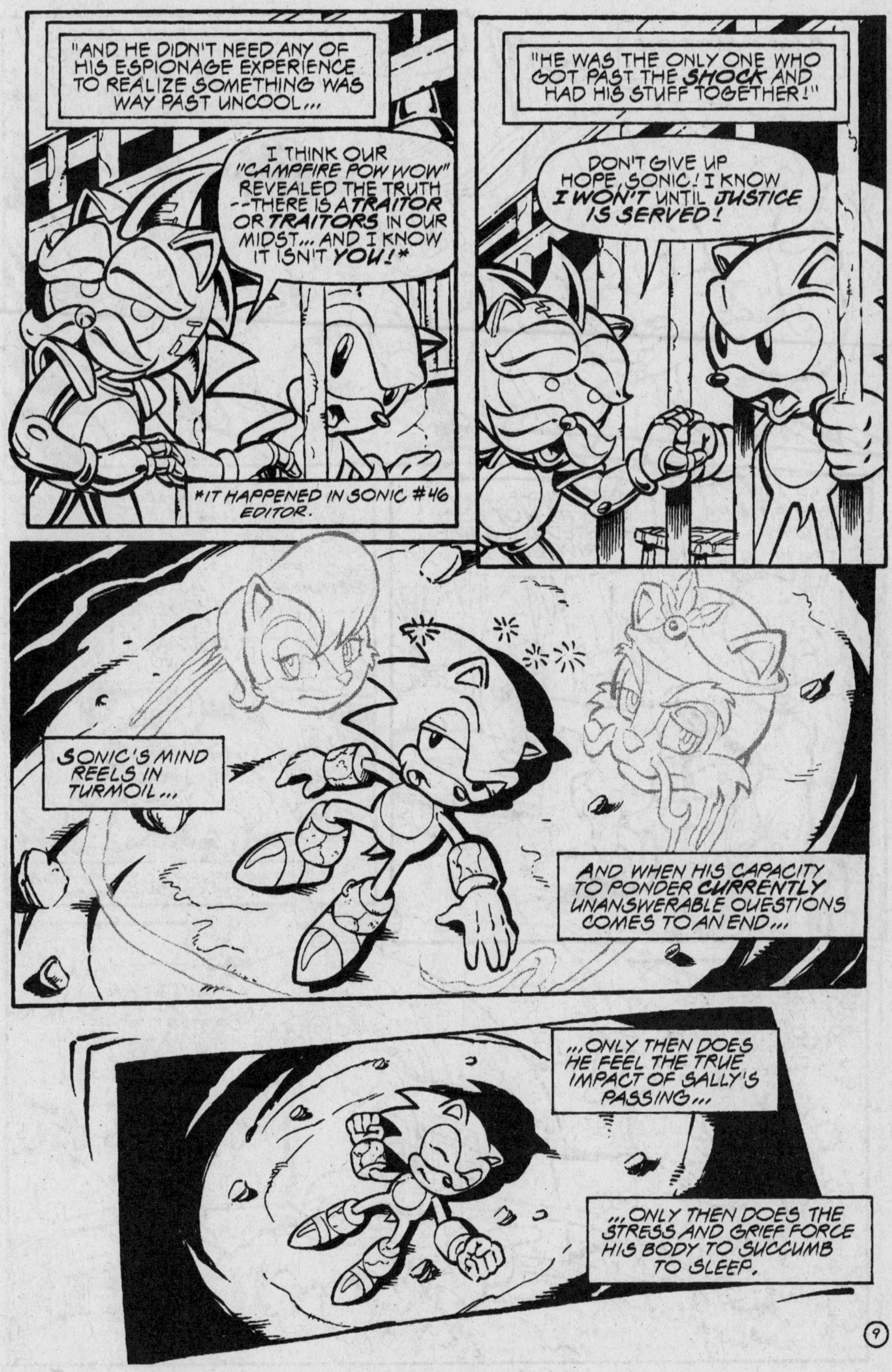
"AND HE DIDN'T NEED ANY OF HIS ESPIONAGE EXPERIENCE TO REALIZE SOMETHING WAS WAY PAST UNCOOL...
I THINK OUR "CAMPFIRE POW WOW" REVEALED THE TRUTH --THERE IS A TRAITOR OR TRAITORS IN OUR MIDST... AND I KNOW IT ISN'T YOU!*
*IT HAPPENED IN SONIC #46 EDITOR.
"HE WAS THE ONLY ONE WHO GOT PAST THE SHOCK AND HAD HIS STUFF TOGETHER!"
DON'T GIVE UP HOPE, SONIC! I KNOW I WON'T UNTIL JUSTICE IS SERVED!
SONIC'S MIND REELS IN TURMOIL...
AND WHEN HIS CAPACITY TO PONDER CURRENTLY UNANSWERABLE QUESTIONS COMES TO AN END...
...ONLY THEN DOES HE FEEL THE TRUE IMPACT OF SALLY'S PASSING...
...ONLY THEN DOES THE STRESS AND GRIEF FORCE HIS BODY TO SUCCUMB TO SLEEP.
9

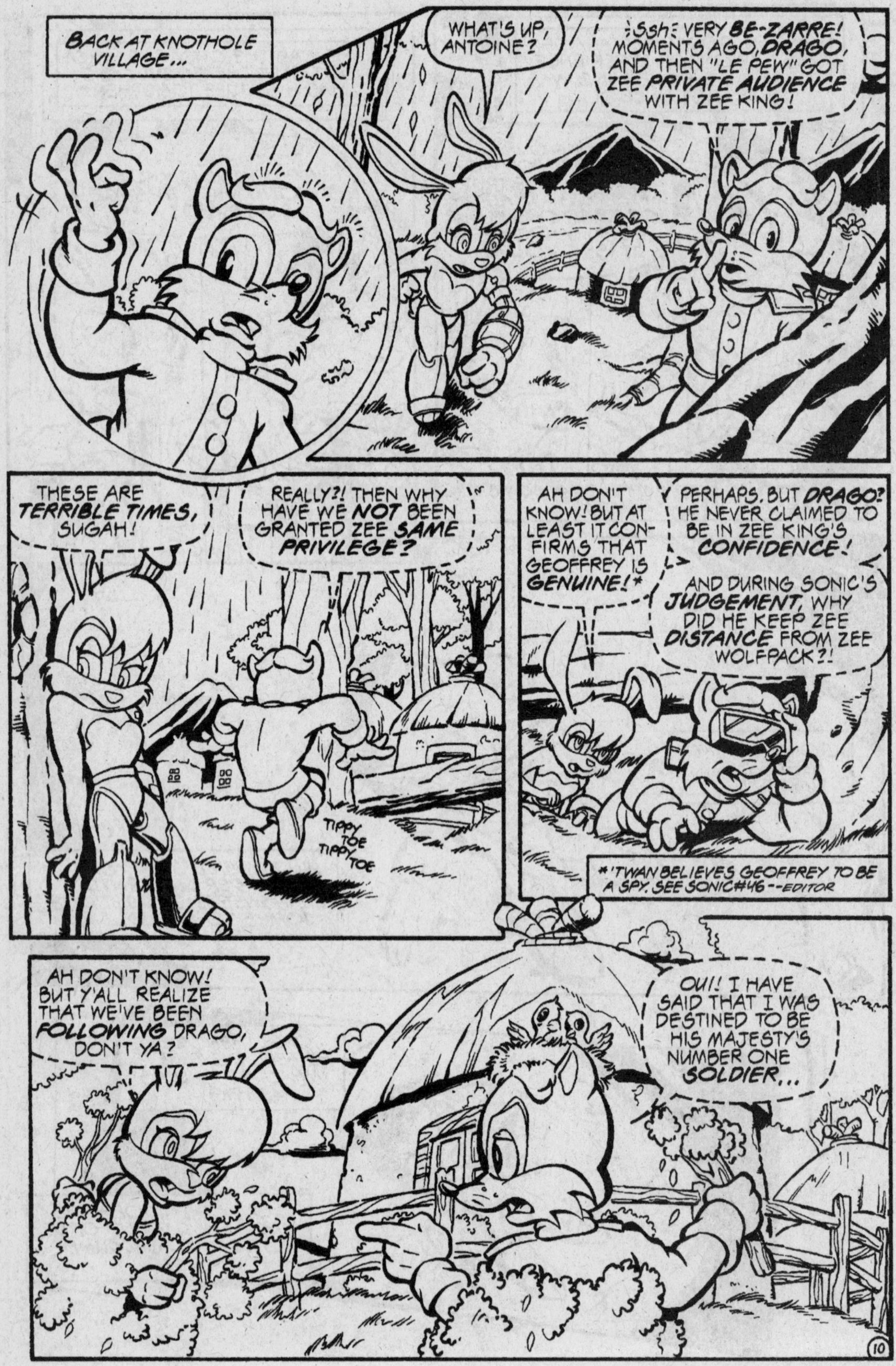
BACK AT KNOTHOLE VILLAGE...
WHAT'S UP, ANTOINE?
Ssh! VERY BE-ZARRE! MOMENTS AGO, DRAGO, AND THEN "LE PEW" GOT ZEE PRIVATE AUDIENCE WITH ZEE KING!
THESE ARE TERRIBLE TIMES, SUGAH!
REALLY?! THEN WHY HAVE WE NOT BEEN GRANTED ZEE SAME PRIVILEGE?
TIPPY TOE TIPPY TOE
AH DON'T KNOW! BUT AT LEAST IT CONFIRMS THAT GEOFFREY IS GENUINE!*
PERHAPS. BUT DRAGO? HE NEVER CLAIMED TO BE IN ZEE KING'S CONFIDENCE!
AND DURING SONIC'S JUDGEMENT, WHY DID HE KEEP ZEE DISTANCE FROM ZEE WOLFPACK?!
*'TWAN BELIEVES GEOFFREY TO BE A SPY. SEE SONIC #46 --EDITOR
AH DON'T KNOW! BUT Y'ALL REALIZE THAT WE'VE BEEN FOLLOWING DRAGO, DON'T YA?
OUI! I HAVE SAID THAT I WAS DESTINED TO BE HIS MAJESTY'S NUMBER ONE SOLDIER...
10

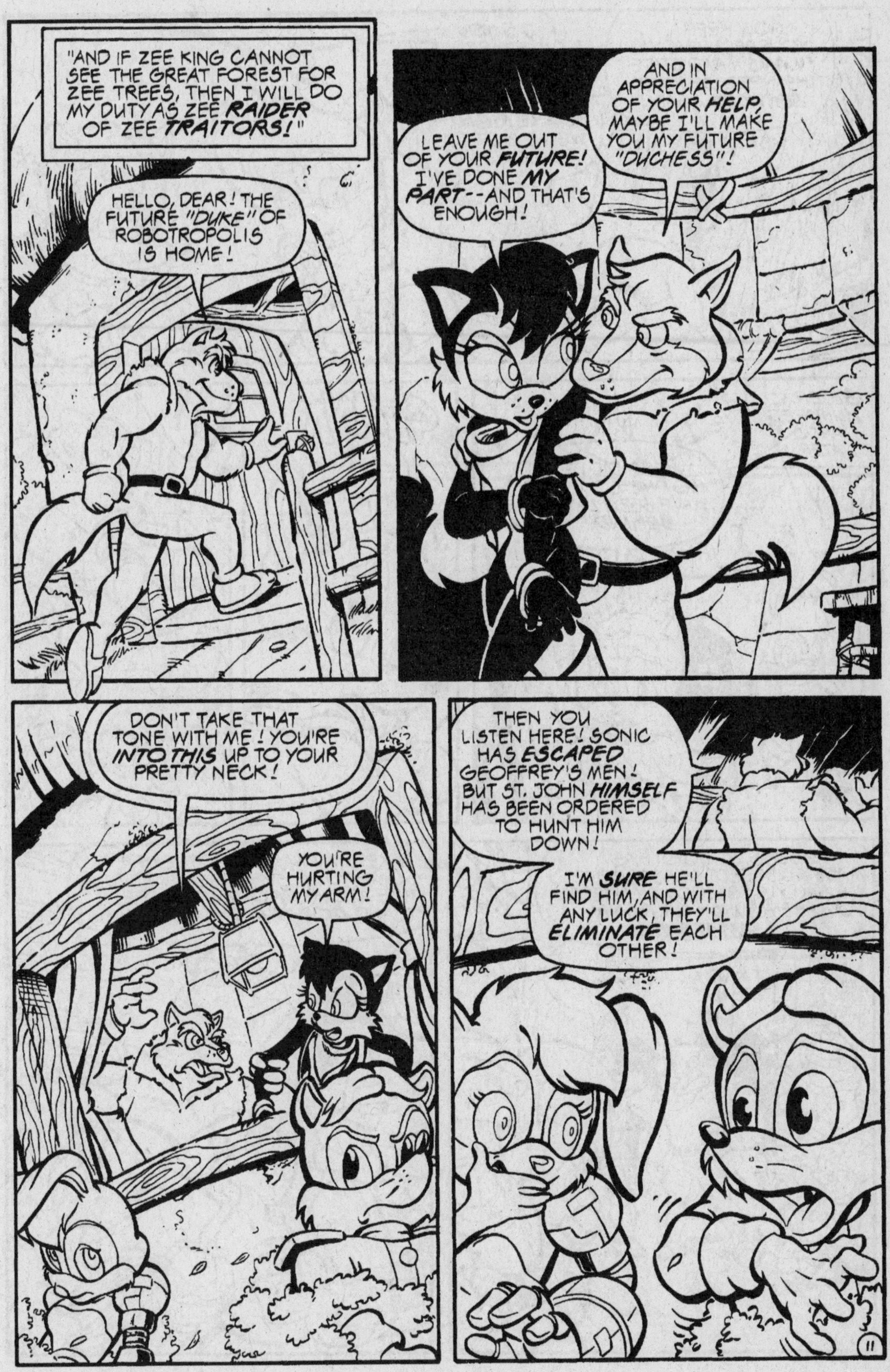
"AND IF ZEE KING CANNOT SEE THE GREAT FOREST FOR ZEE TREES, THEN I WILL DO MY DUTY AS ZEE RAIDER OF ZEE TRAITORS!"
HELLO, DEAR! THE FUTURE "DUKE" OF ROBOTROPOLIS IS HOME!
AND IN APPRECIATION OF YOUR HELP, MAYBE I'LL MAKE YOU MY FUTURE "DUCHESS"!
LEAVE ME OUT OF YOUR FUTURE! I'VE DONE MY PART--AND THAT'S ENOUGH!
DON'T TAKE THAT TONE WITH ME! YOU'RE INTO THIS UP TO YOUR PRETTY NECK!
YOU'RE HURTING MY ARM!
THEN YOU LISTEN HERE! SONIC HAS ESCAPED GEOFFREY'S MEN! BUT ST. JOHN HIMSELF HAS BEEN ORDERED TO HUNT HIM DOWN!
I'M SURE HE'LL FIND HIM, AND WITH ANY LUCK, THEY'LL ELIMINATE EACH OTHER!
11

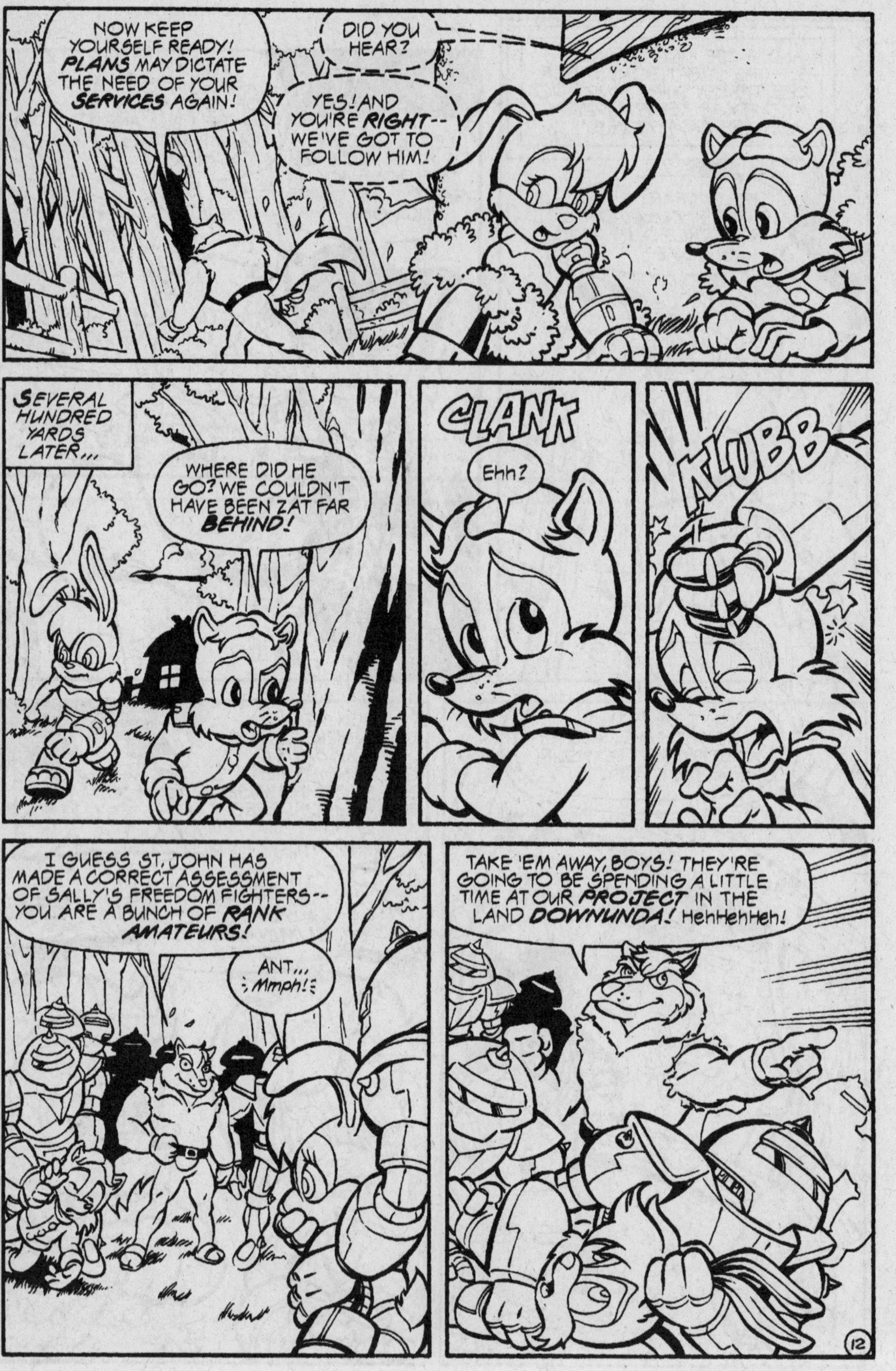
NOW KEEP YOURSELF READY! PLANS MAY DICTATE THE NEED OF YOUR SERVICES AGAIN!
DID YOU HEAR?
YES! AND YOU'RE RIGHT-- WE'VE GOT TO FOLLOW HIM!
SEVERAL HUNDRED YARDS LATER...
WHERE DID HE GO? WE COULDN'T HAVE BEEN ZAT FAR BEHIND!
CLANK
Ehh?
KLUBB
I GUESS ST. JOHN HAS MADE A CORRECT ASSESSMENT OF SALLY'S FREEDOM FIGHTERS-- YOU ARE A BUNCH OF RANK AMATEURS!
ANT... Mmph!
TAKE 'EM AWAY, BOYS! THEY'RE GOING TO BE SPENDING A LITTLE TIME AT OUR PROJECT IN THE LAND DOWNUNDA! HehHehHeh!
12

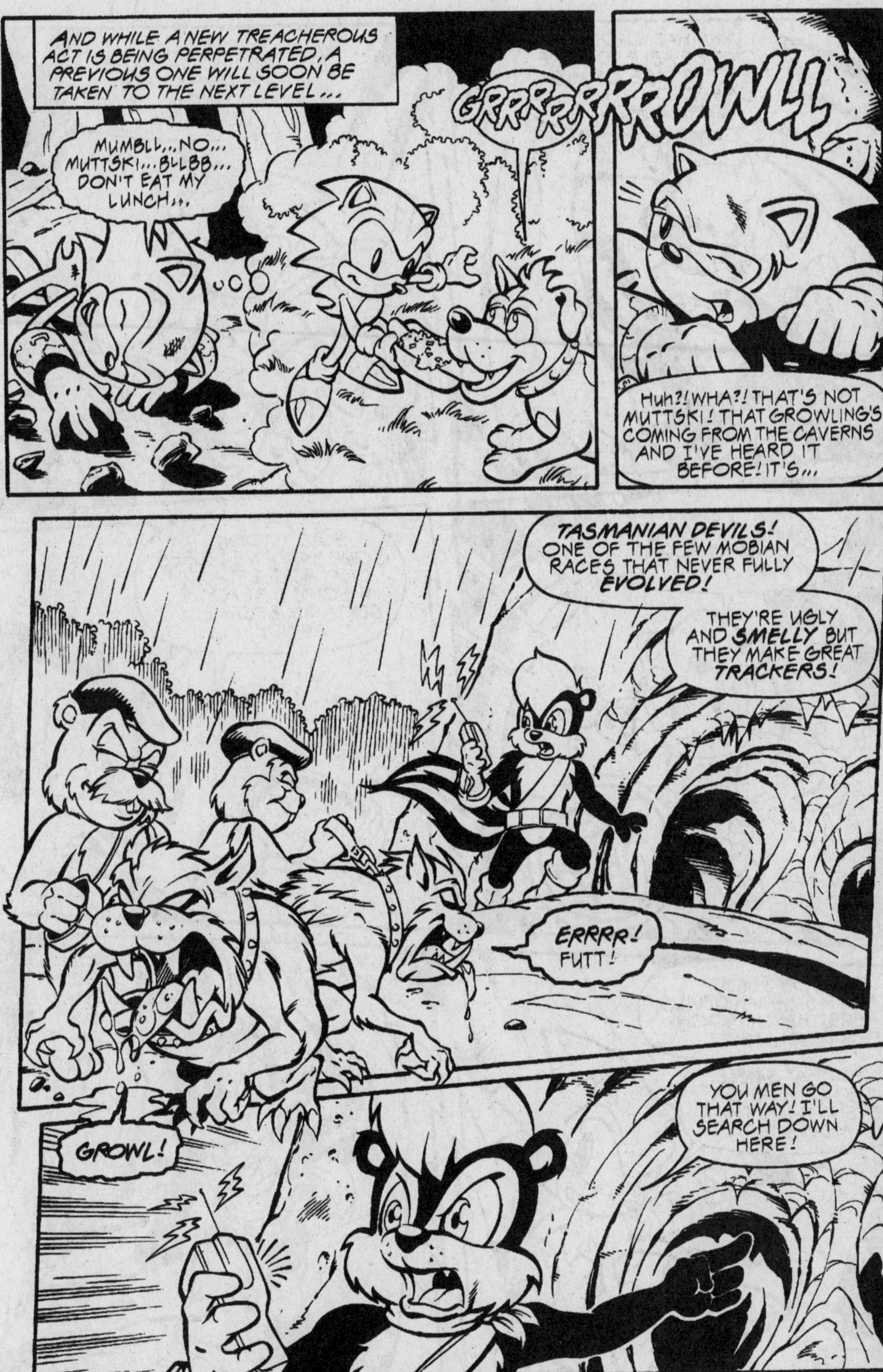
AND WHILE A NEW TREACHEROUS ACT IS BEING PERPETRATED, A PREVIOUS ONE WILL SOON BE TAKEN TO THE NEXT LEVEL...
MUMBLL...NO... MUTTSKI...BLLBB... DON'T EAT MY LUNCH...
GRRRRRRROWLL
Huh?! WHA?! THAT'S NOT MUTTSKI! THAT GROWLING'S COMING FROM THE CAVERNS AND I'VE HEARD IT BEFORE! IT'S...
TASMANIAN DEVILS! ONE OF THE FEW MOBIAN RACES THAT NEVER FULLY EVOLVED!
THEY'RE UGLY AND SMELLY BUT THEY MAKE GREAT TRACKERS!
ERRRR! FUTT!
GROWL!
YOU MEN GO THAT WAY! I'LL SEARCH DOWN HERE!
13

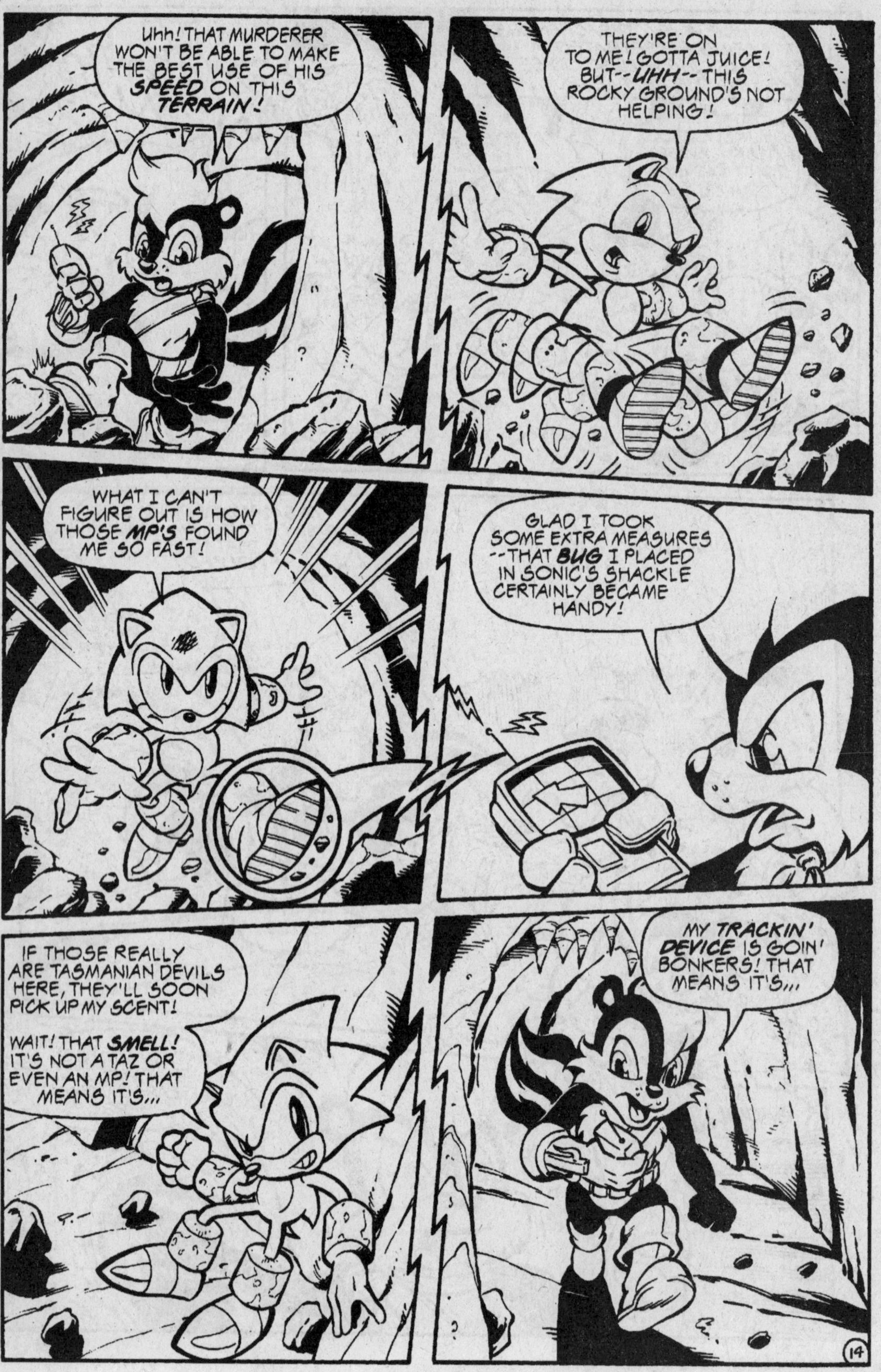
UHH! THAT MURDERER WON'T BE ABLE TO MAKE THE BEST USE OF HIS SPEED ON THIS TERRAIN!
THEY'RE ON TO ME! GOTTA JUICE! BUT--UHH--THIS ROCKY GROUND'S NOT HELPING!
WHAT I CAN'T FIGURE OUT IS HOW THOSE MP'S FOUND ME SO FAST!
GLAD I TOOK SOME EXTRA MEASURES --THAT BUG I PLACED IN SONIC'S SHACKLE CERTAINLY BECAME HANDY!
IF THOSE REALLY ARE TASMANIAN DEVILS HERE, THEY'LL SOON PICK UP MY SCENT!
WAIT! THAT SMELL! IT'S NOT A TAZ OR EVEN AN MP! THAT MEANS IT'S...
MY TRACKIN' DEVICE IS GOIN' BONKERS! THAT MEANS IT'S...
14

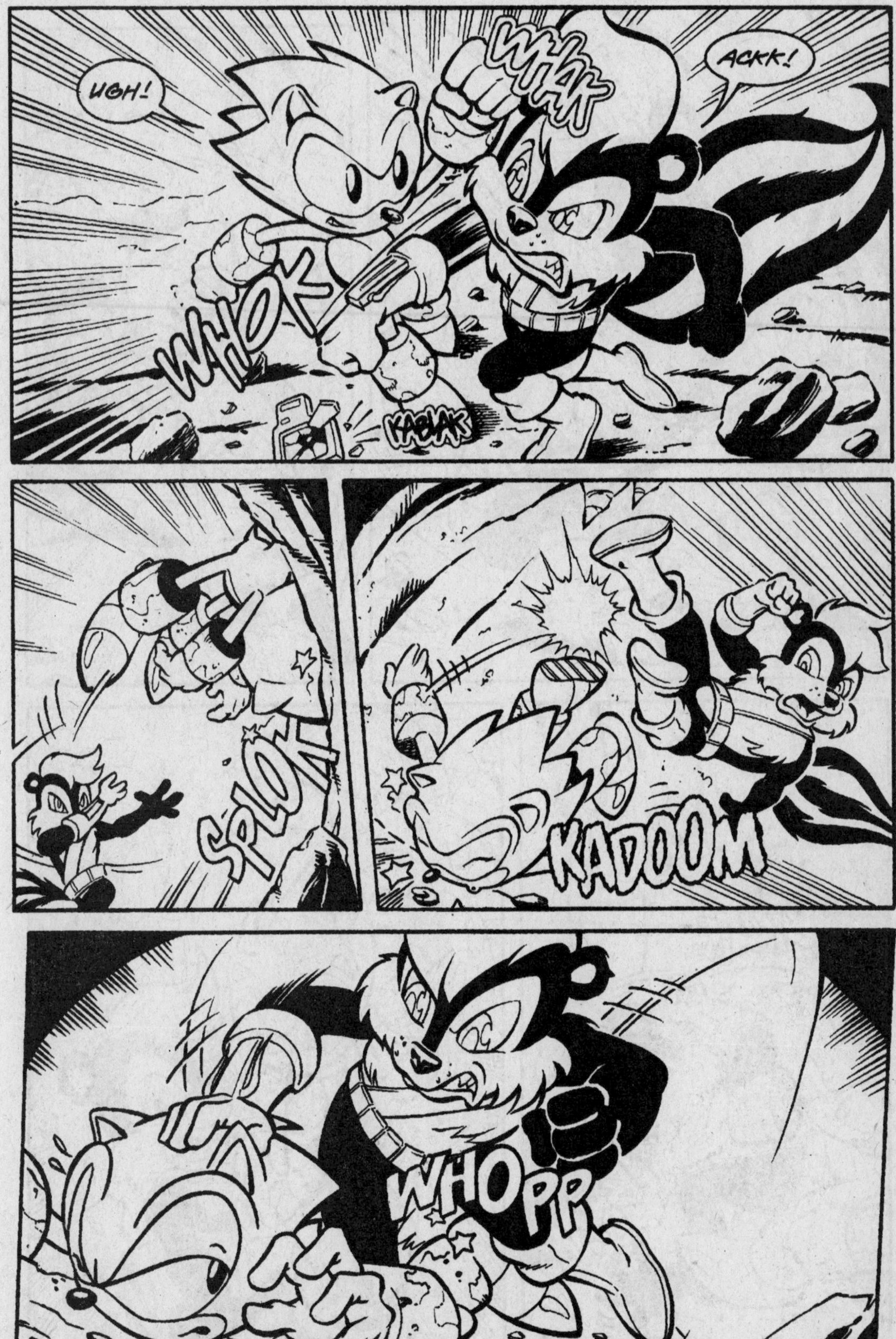
UGH!
WHAK
ACKK!
WHOK
KABLAK
SPLOK
KADOOM
WHOPP
15

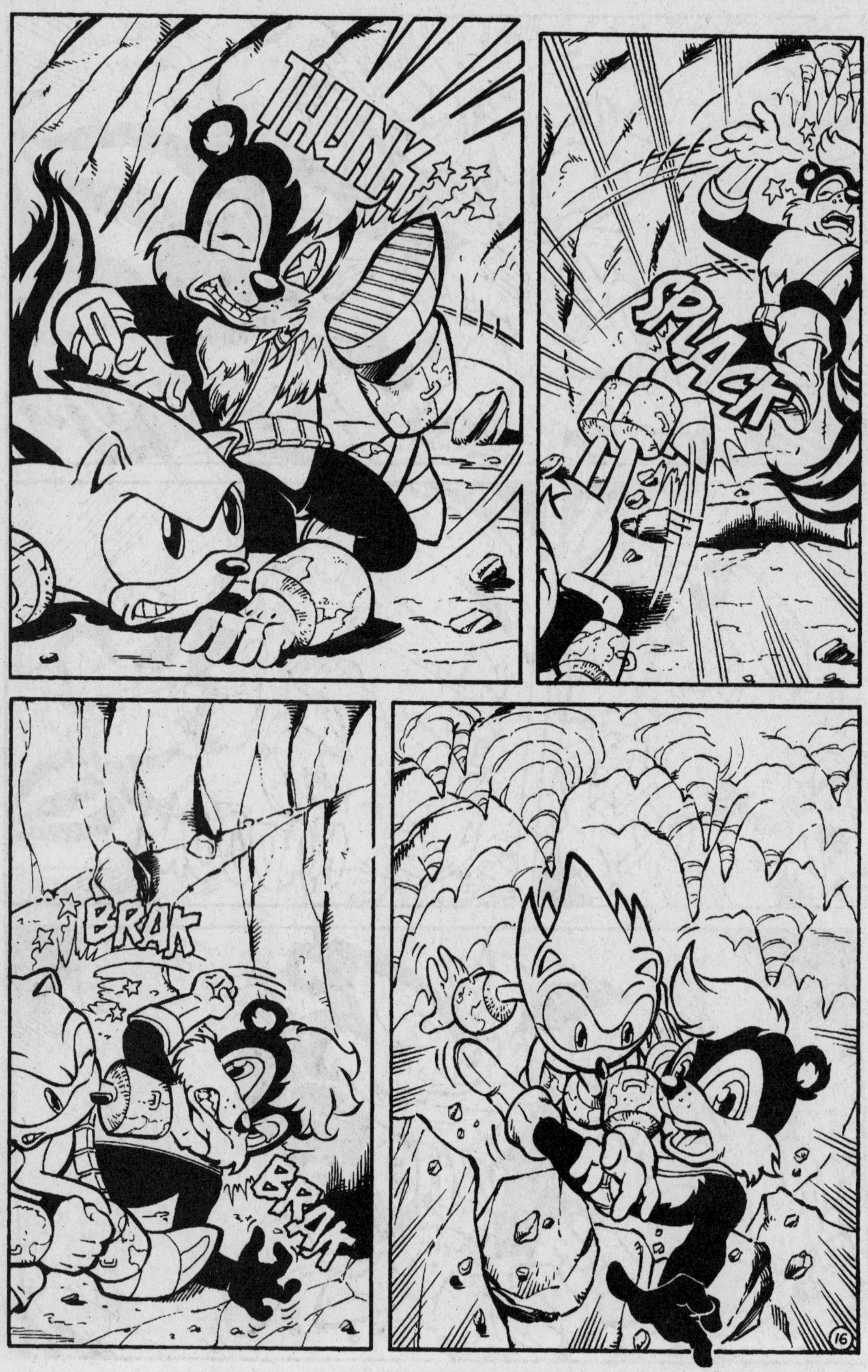

THUNK
SPLACK
BRAK
BRAK
16

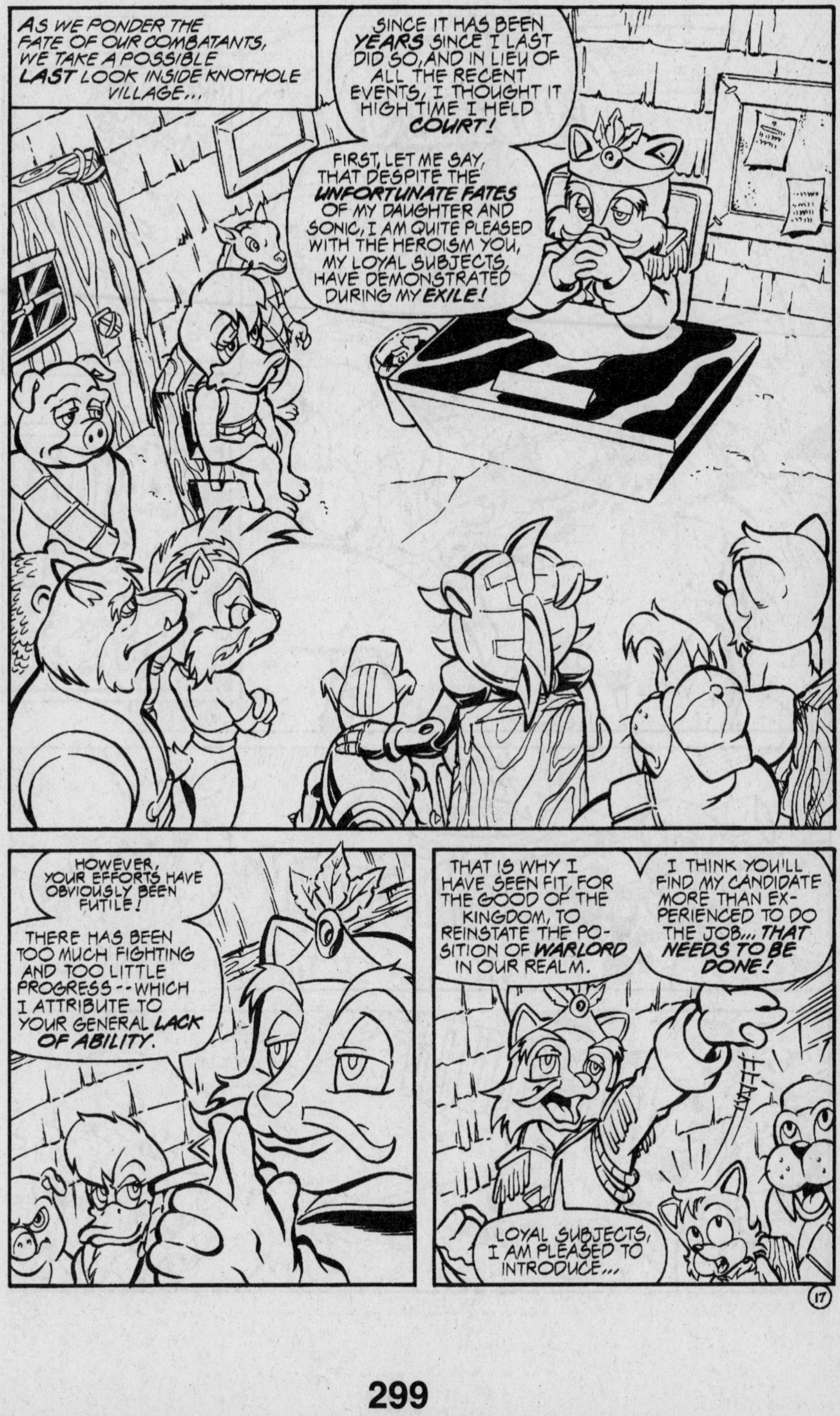
AS WE PONDER THE FATE OF OUR COMBATANTS, WE TAKE A POSSIBLE LAST LOOK INSIDE KNOTHOLE VILLAGE...
SINCE IT HAS BEEN YEARS SINCE I LAST DID SO, AND IN LIEU OF ALL THE RECENT EVENTS, I THOUGHT IT HIGH TIME I HELD COURT!
FIRST, LET ME SAY, THAT DESPITE THE UNFORTUNATE FATES OF MY DAUGHTER AND SONIC, I AM QUITE PLEASED WITH THE HEROISM YOU, MY LOYAL SUBJECTS, HAVE DEMONSTRATED DURING MY EXILE!
HOWEVER, YOUR EFFORTS HAVE OBVIOUSLY BEEN FUTILE!
THERE HAS BEEN TOO MUCH FIGHTING AND TOO LITTLE PROGRESS -- WHICH I ATTRIBUTE TO YOUR GENERAL LACK OF ABILITY.
THAT IS WHY I HAVE SEEN FIT, FOR THE GOOD OF THE KINGDOM, TO REINSTATE THE POSITION OF WARLORD IN OUR REALM.
I THINK YOU'LL FIND MY CANDIDATE MORE THAN EXPERIENCED TO DO THE JOB... THAT NEEDS TO BE DONE!
LOYAL SUBJECTS, I AM PLEASED TO INTRODUCE...

17

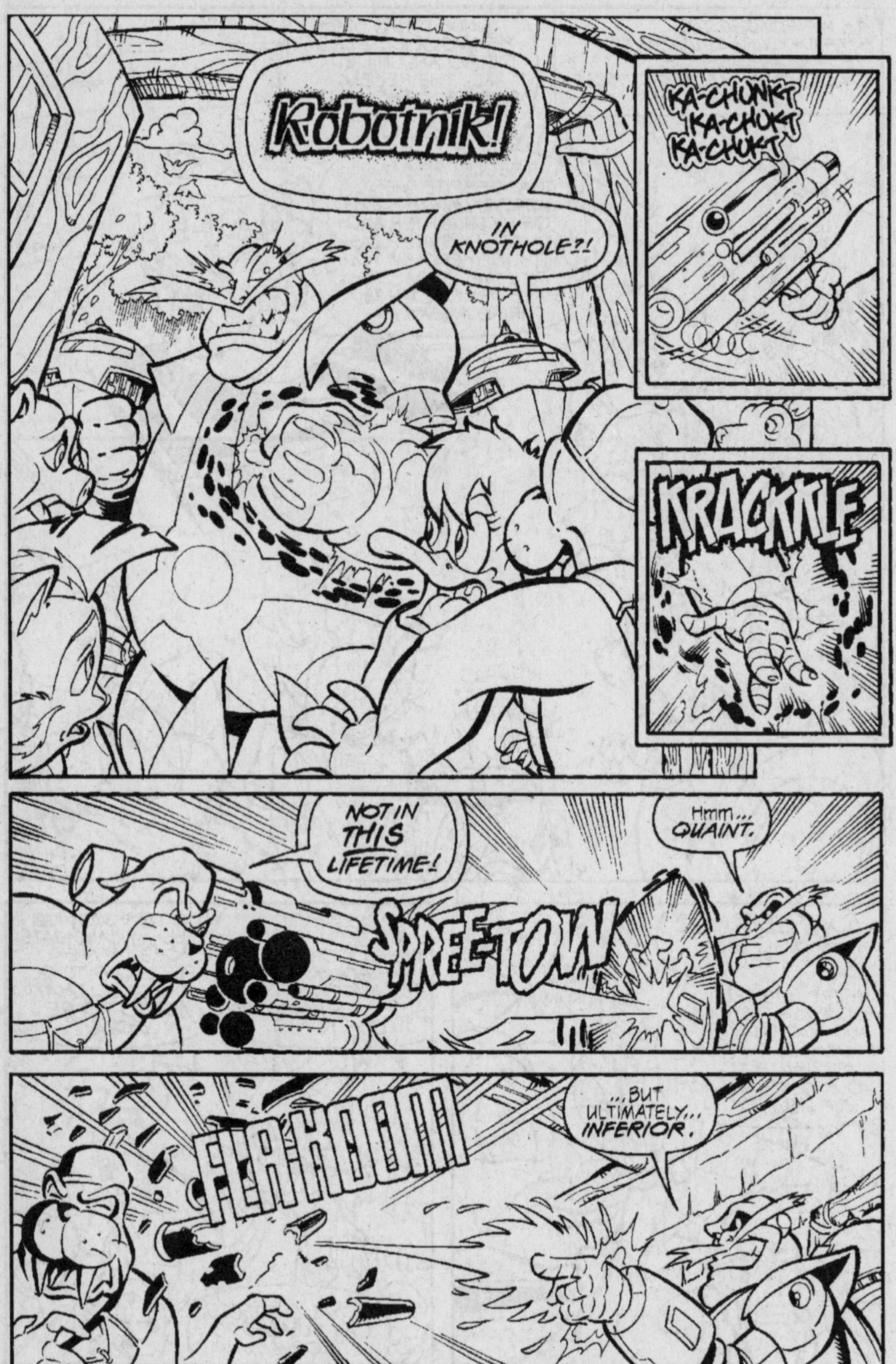
Robotnik!
IN KNOTHOLE?!
KA-CHUNK! KA-CHUK! KA-CHUK!
KRACKKLE
NOT IN THIS LIFETIME!
SPREE-TOW
Hmm... QUAINT.
FLAKOOM
...BUT ULTIMATELY... INFERIOR.
18

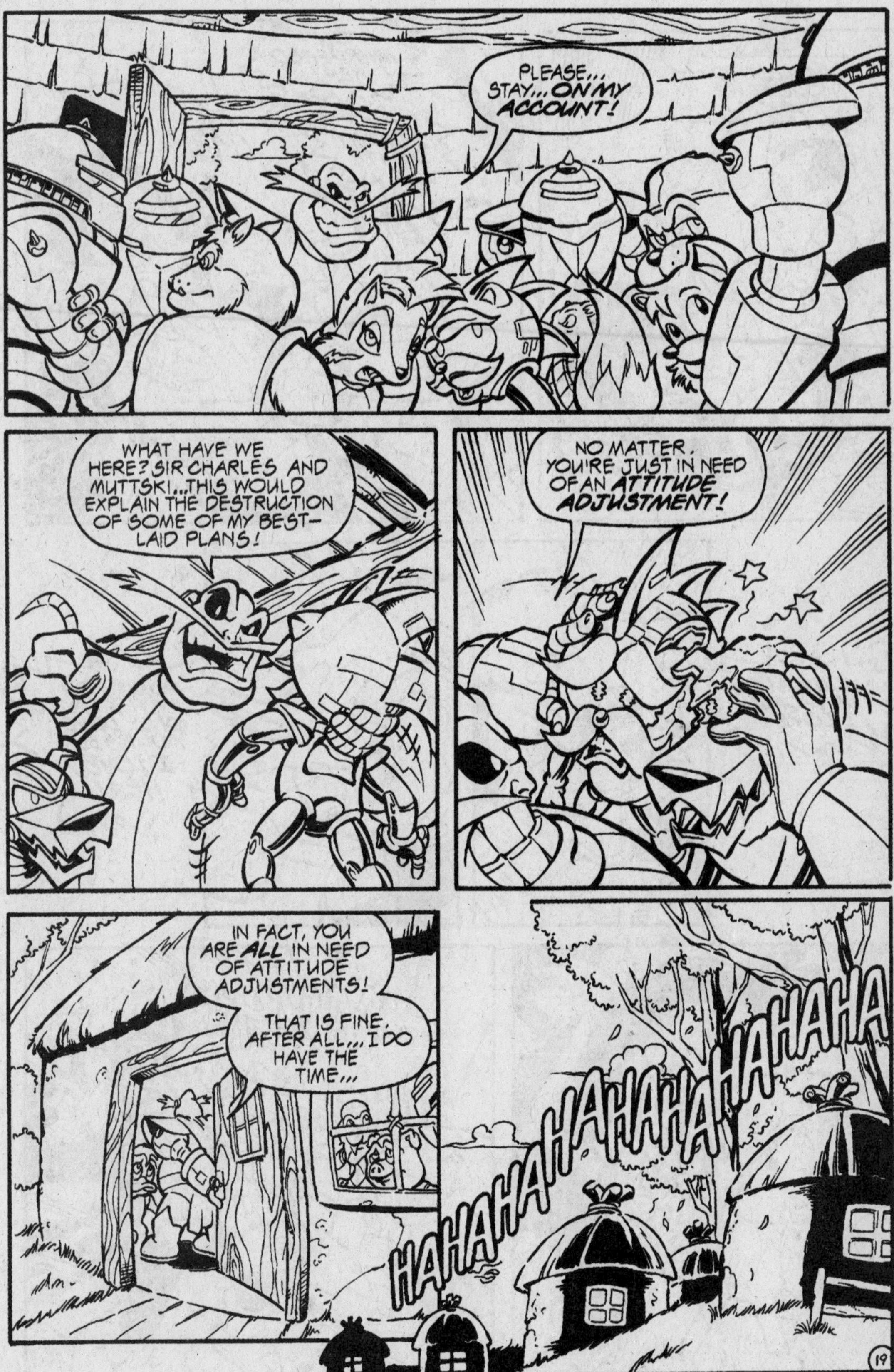
PLEASE... STAY... ON MY ACCOUNT!
WHAT HAVE WE HERE? SIR CHARLES AND MUTTSKI...THIS WOULD EXPLAIN THE DESTRUCTION OF SOME OF MY BEST-LAID PLANS!
NO MATTER. YOU'RE JUST IN NEED OF AN ATTITUDE ADJUSTMENT!
IN FACT, YOU ARE ALL IN NEED OF ATTITUDE ADJUSTMENTS!
THAT IS FINE. AFTER ALL... I DO HAVE THE TIME...
HAHAHAHAHAHAHAHAHAHAHAHA
19

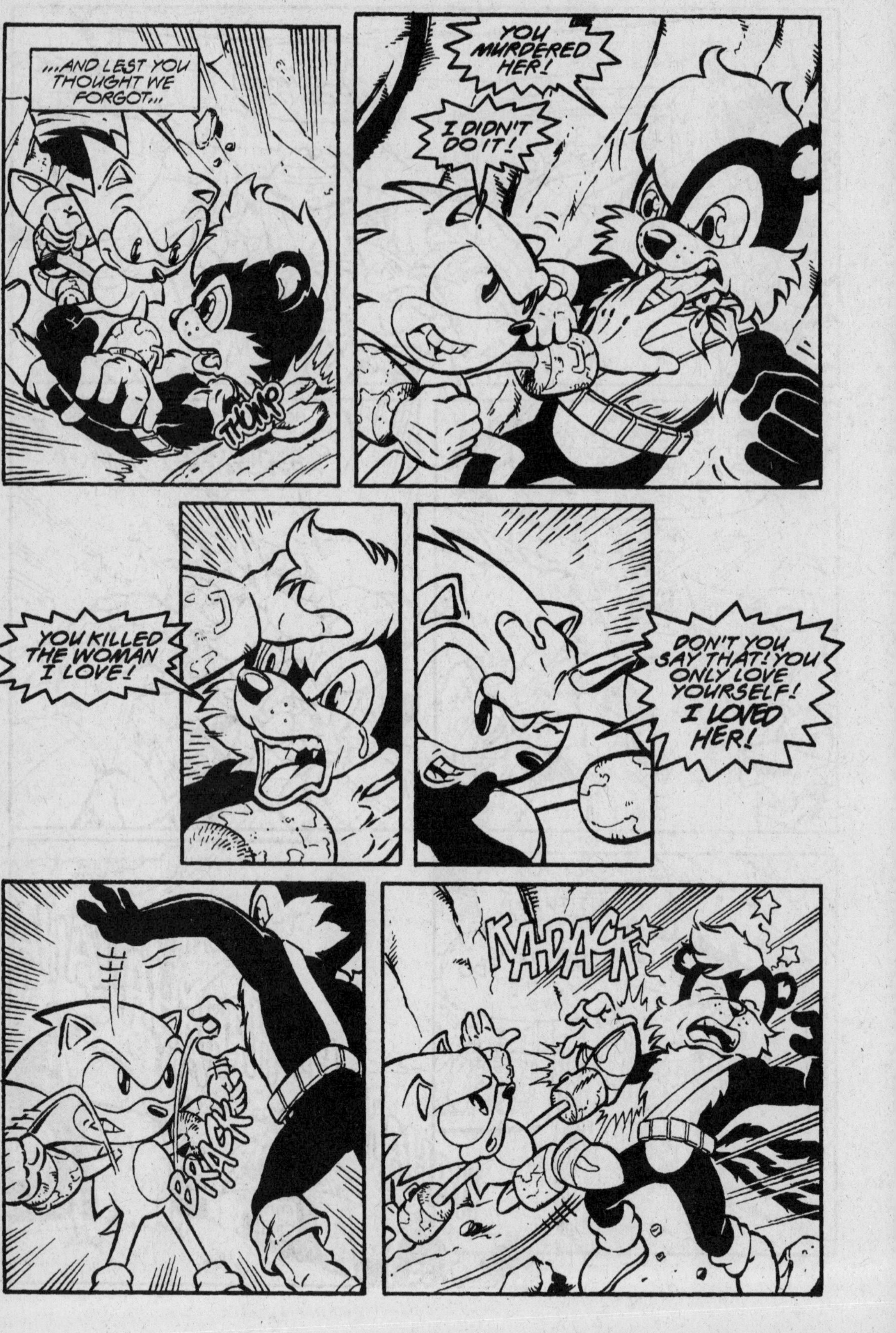

...AND LEST YOU THOUGHT WE FORGOT...
THUMP
YOU MURDERED HER!
I DIDN'T DO IT!
YOU KILLED THE WOMAN I LOVE!
DON'T YOU SAY THAT! YOU ONLY LOVE YOURSELF! I LOVED HER!
BLAAACK
KADACK

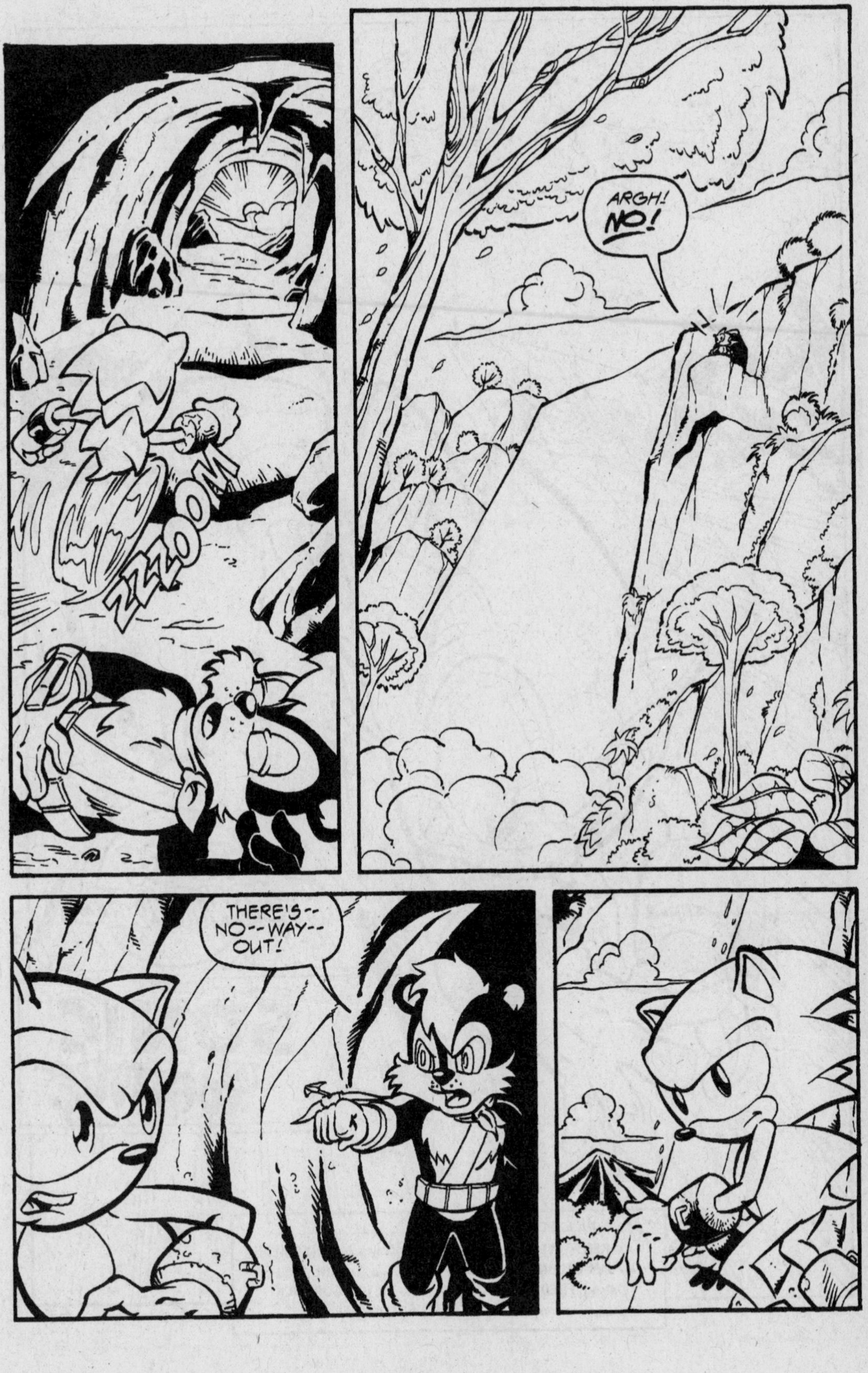
ZZZOOM
ARGH! NO!
THERE'S-- NO--WAY-- OUT!

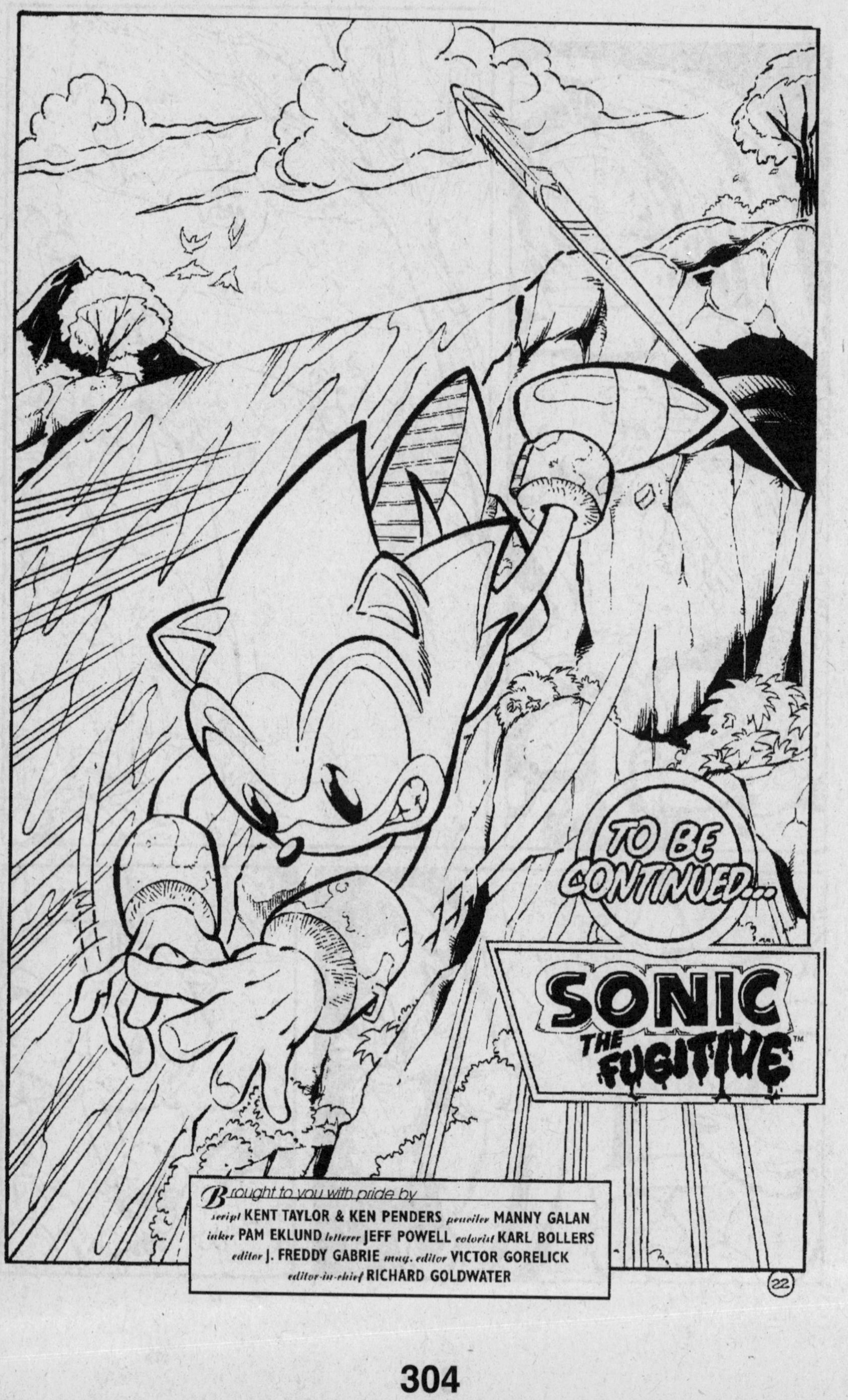
TO BE CONTINUED...
SONIC THE FUGITIVE™
Brought to you with pride by
script KENT TAYLOR & KEN PENDERS penciler MANNY GALAN
inker PAM EKLUND letterer JEFF POWELL colorist KARL BOLLERS
editor J. FREDDY GABRIE mng. editor VICTOR GORELICK
editor-in-chief RICHARD GOLDWATER
22

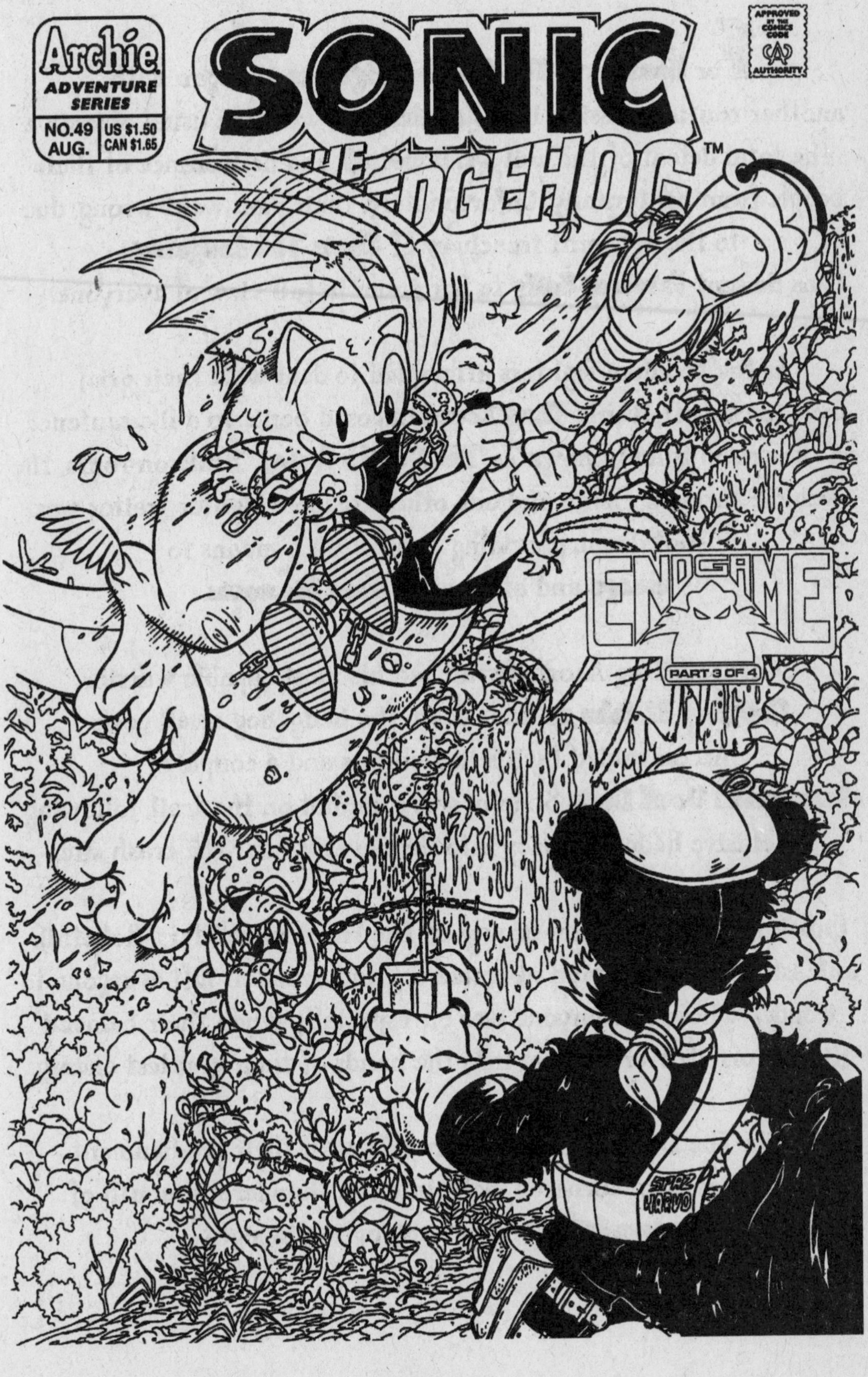

Archie
ADVENTURE SERIES
NO.49 AUG.
US $1.50 CAN $1.65
SONIC
APPROVED BY THE COMICS CODE AUTHORITY
ENDGAME
PART 3 OF 4

For **Sonic** and **The Freedom Fighters**, it began with another routine mission into **Robotropolis** with the usual objective: the total defeat of the evil **Dr. Robotnik** and deliverance of their people from his tyranny. Unfortunately, their plan went wrong, due to the apparent treachery of **Sonic The Hedgehog**, as he sent **Princess Sally** to her doom in full view of everyone.

As the Freedom Fighters attempted to deal with their grief over these past events, **King Acorn** imposed Sonic to a life sentence on the prison island known as **The Devil's Gulag**. While on route, the vehicle carrying Sonic and one other Freedom Fighter traitor was shot down, providing Sonic with a means to **escape** and attempt to **clear his name**.

Outraged, King Acorn dispatched his most capable warrior, **Geoffrey St. John**, to hunt down the hedgehog at all costs. Accompanied by his lieutenants and a couple of **Tasmanian Devil Dogs**, St. John was soon hot on the trail, following the elusive hedgehog deep into the caverns near the crash site.

Unbeknownst to St. John or any of The Freedom Fighters, Robotnik unleashed a massive plan of treachery and deceit. It left everyone to wonder whose side anyone was on, especially when their beloved King Acorn delivered them into the hands of their greatest enemy.

While The Freedom Fighters struggle with their predicament, Sonic has been cornered right into the thunderous mouth of **Angora Falls**, without any option in sight ...

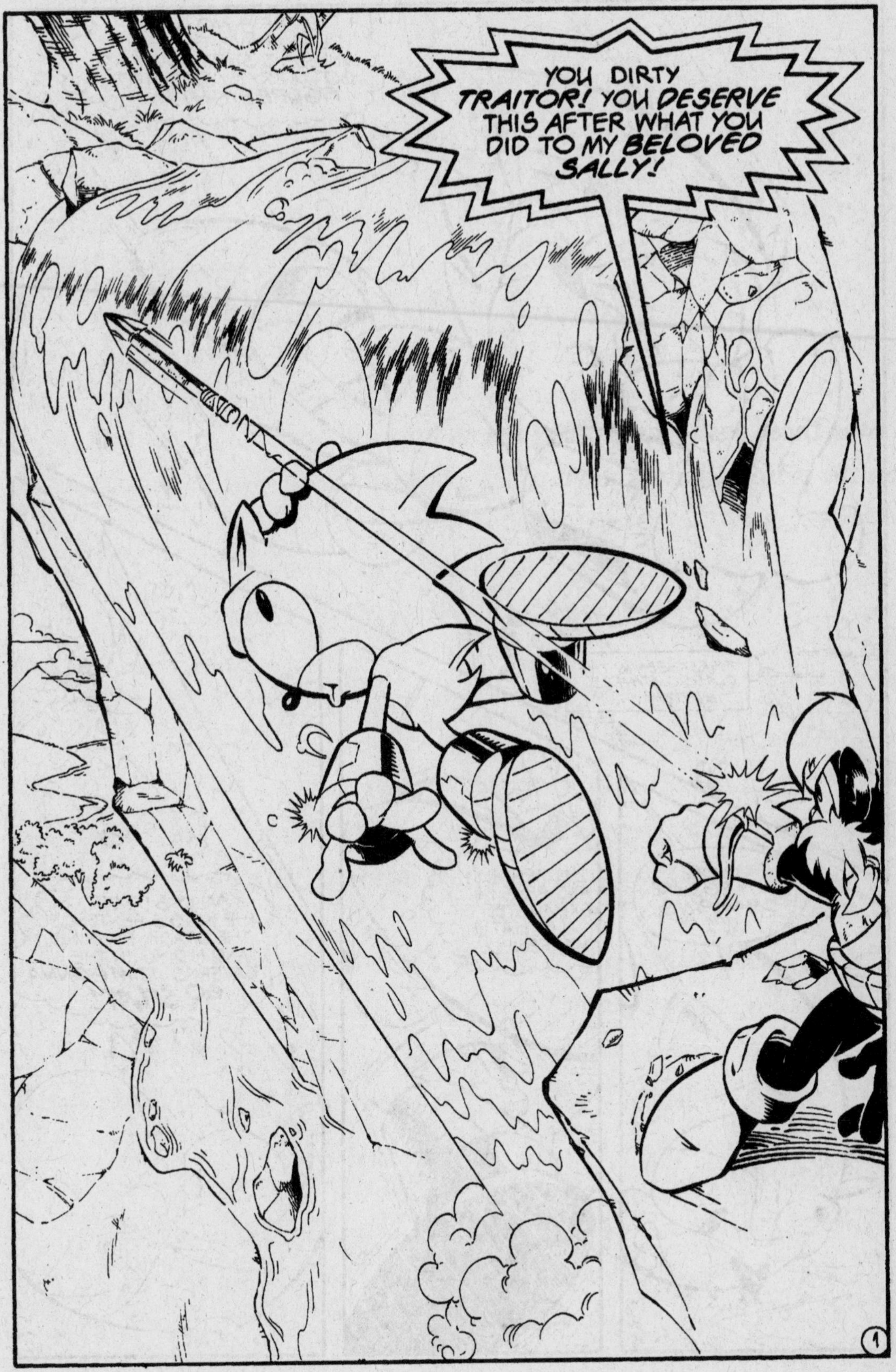
YOU DIRTY TRAITOR! YOU DESERVE THIS AFTER WHAT YOU DID TO MY BELOVED SALLY!
1

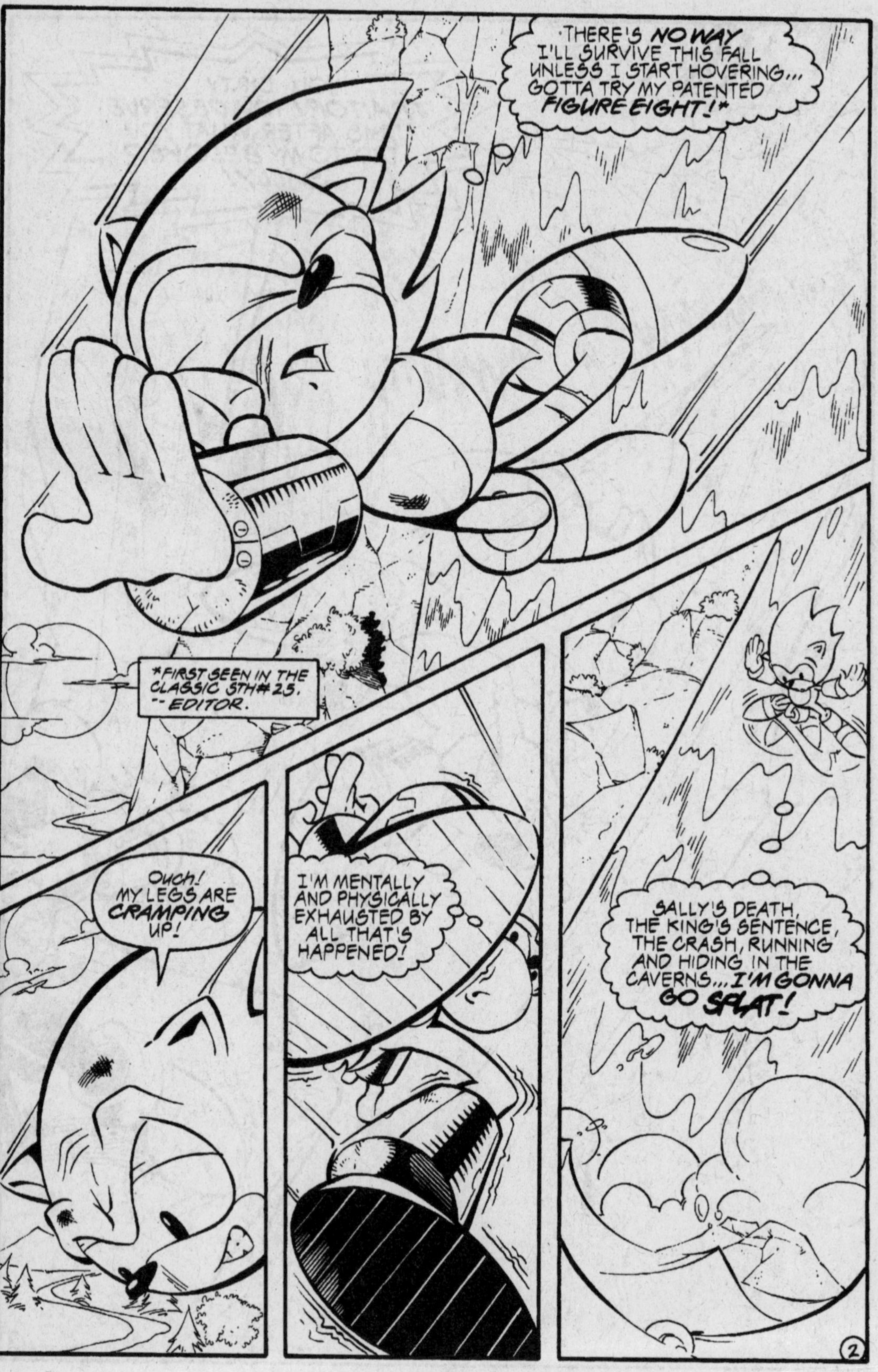

THERE'S NO WAY I'LL SURVIVE THIS FALL UNLESS I START HOVERING... GOTTA TRY MY PATENTED FIGURE EIGHT!*
*FIRST SEEN IN THE CLASSIC STH#25. --EDITOR.
Ouch! MY LEGS ARE CRAMPING UP!
I'M MENTALLY AND PHYSICALLY EXHAUSTED BY ALL THAT'S HAPPENED!
SALLY'S DEATH, THE KING'S SENTENCE, THE CRASH, RUNNING AND HIDING IN THE CAVERNS... I'M GONNA GO SPLAT!
2

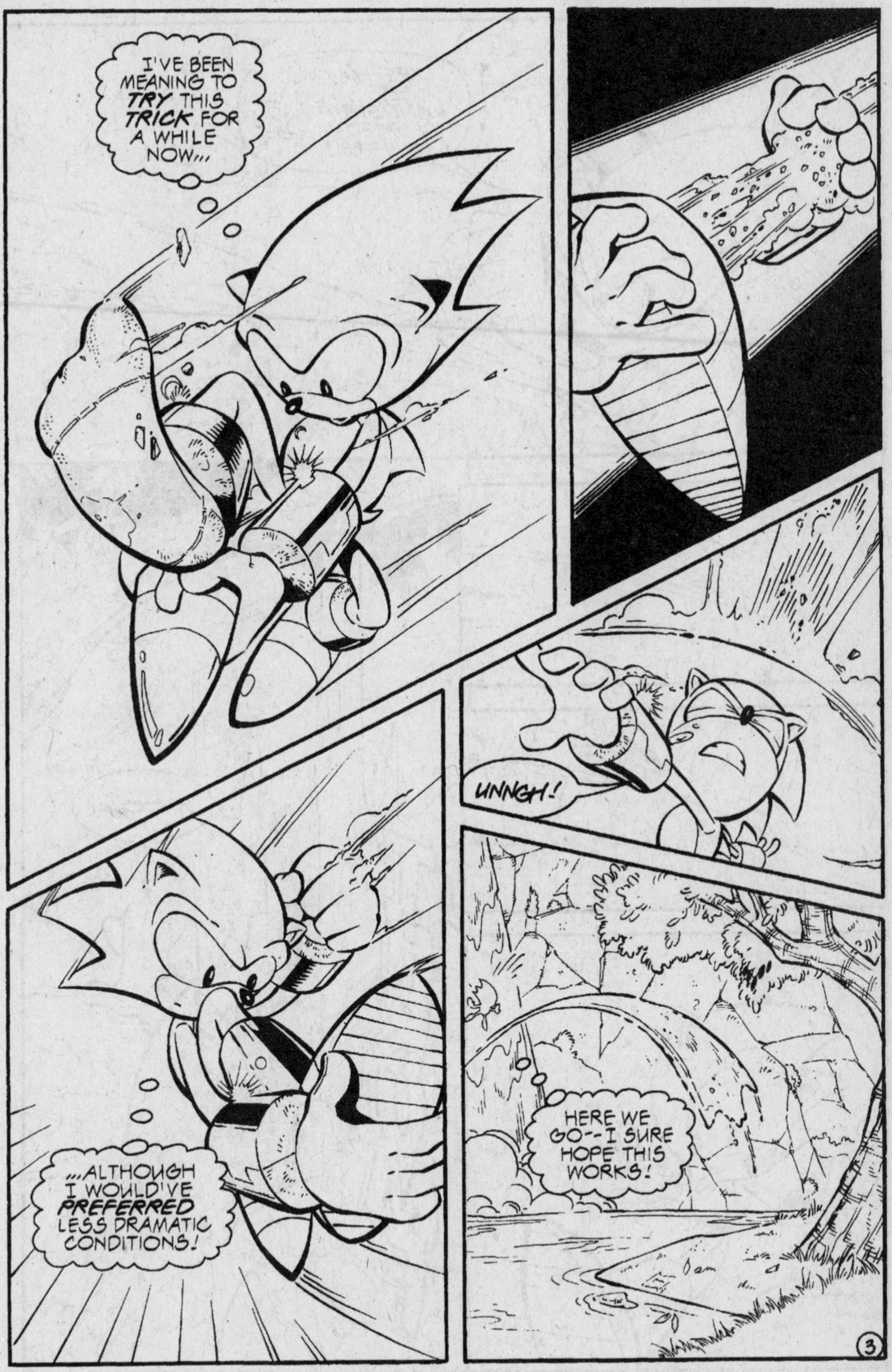
I'VE BEEN MEANING TO TRY THIS TRICK FOR A WHILE NOW...
UNNGH!
...ALTHOUGH I WOULD'VE PREFERRED LESS DRAMATIC CONDITIONS!
HERE WE GO--I SURE HOPE THIS WORKS!
3

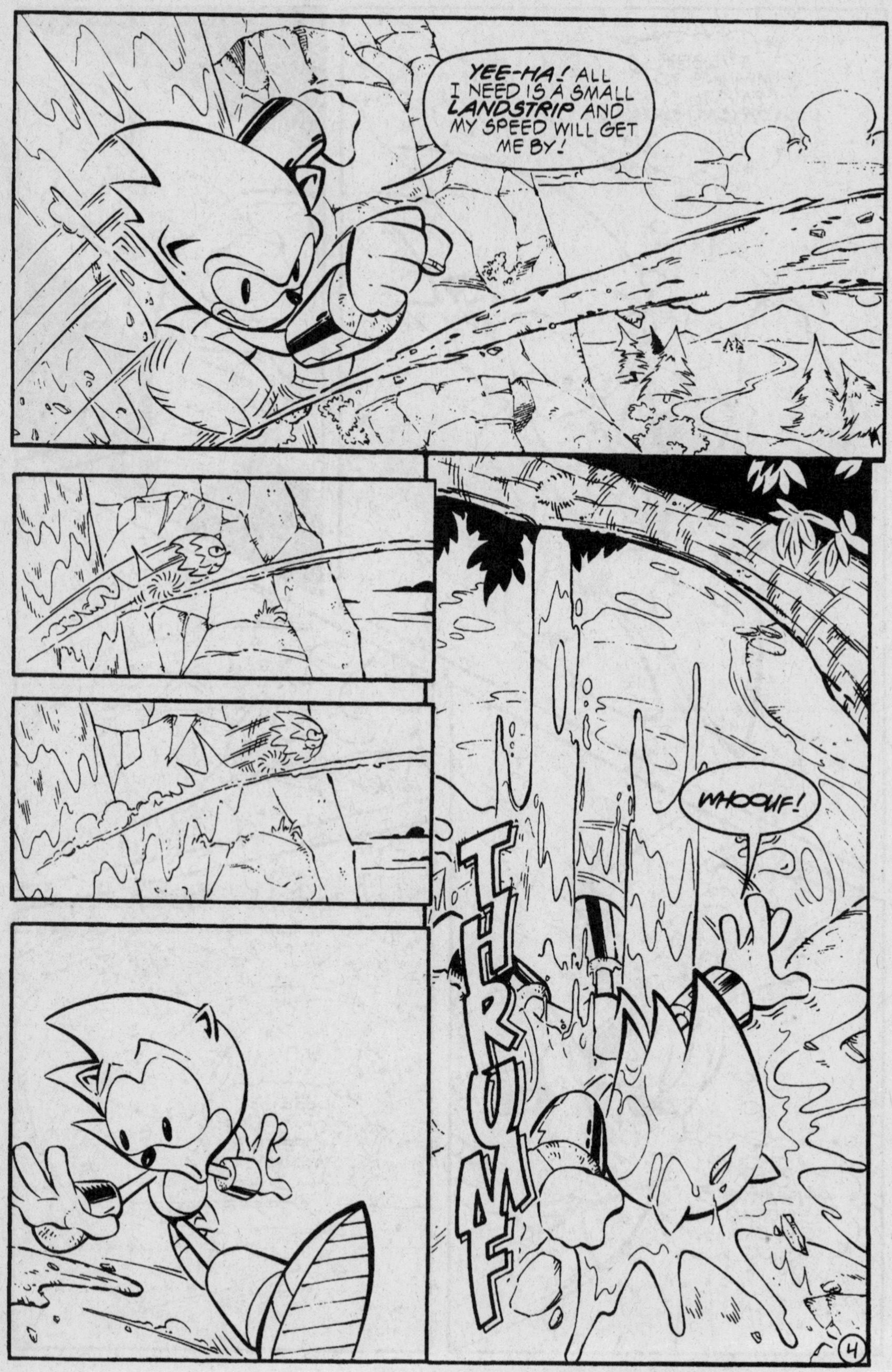
YEE-HA! ALL I NEED IS A SMALL LANDSTRIP AND MY SPEED WILL GET ME BY!
WHOOUF!
THRUMF
4

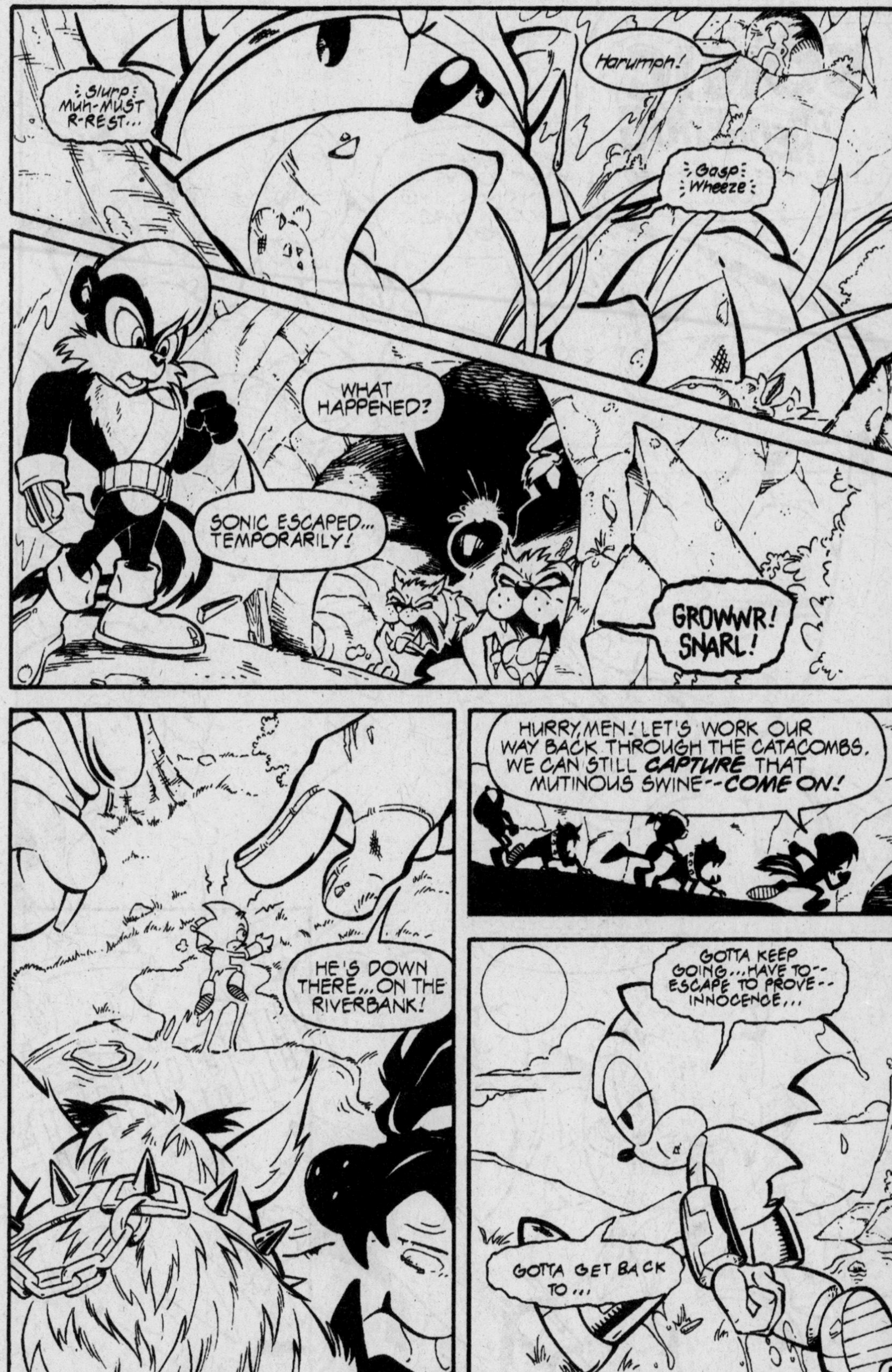

:Slurp: Muh-MUST R-REST...
Harumph!
:Gasp: :Wheeze:
WHAT HAPPENED?
SONIC ESCAPED... TEMPORARILY!
GROWWR! SNARL!
HURRY, MEN! LET'S WORK OUR WAY BACK THROUGH THE CATACOMBS. WE CAN STILL CAPTURE THAT MUTINOUS SWINE--COME ON!
HE'S DOWN THERE... ON THE RIVERBANK!
GOTTA KEEP GOING... HAVE TO-- ESCAPE TO PROVE-- INNOCENCE...
GOTTA GET BACK TO...
5

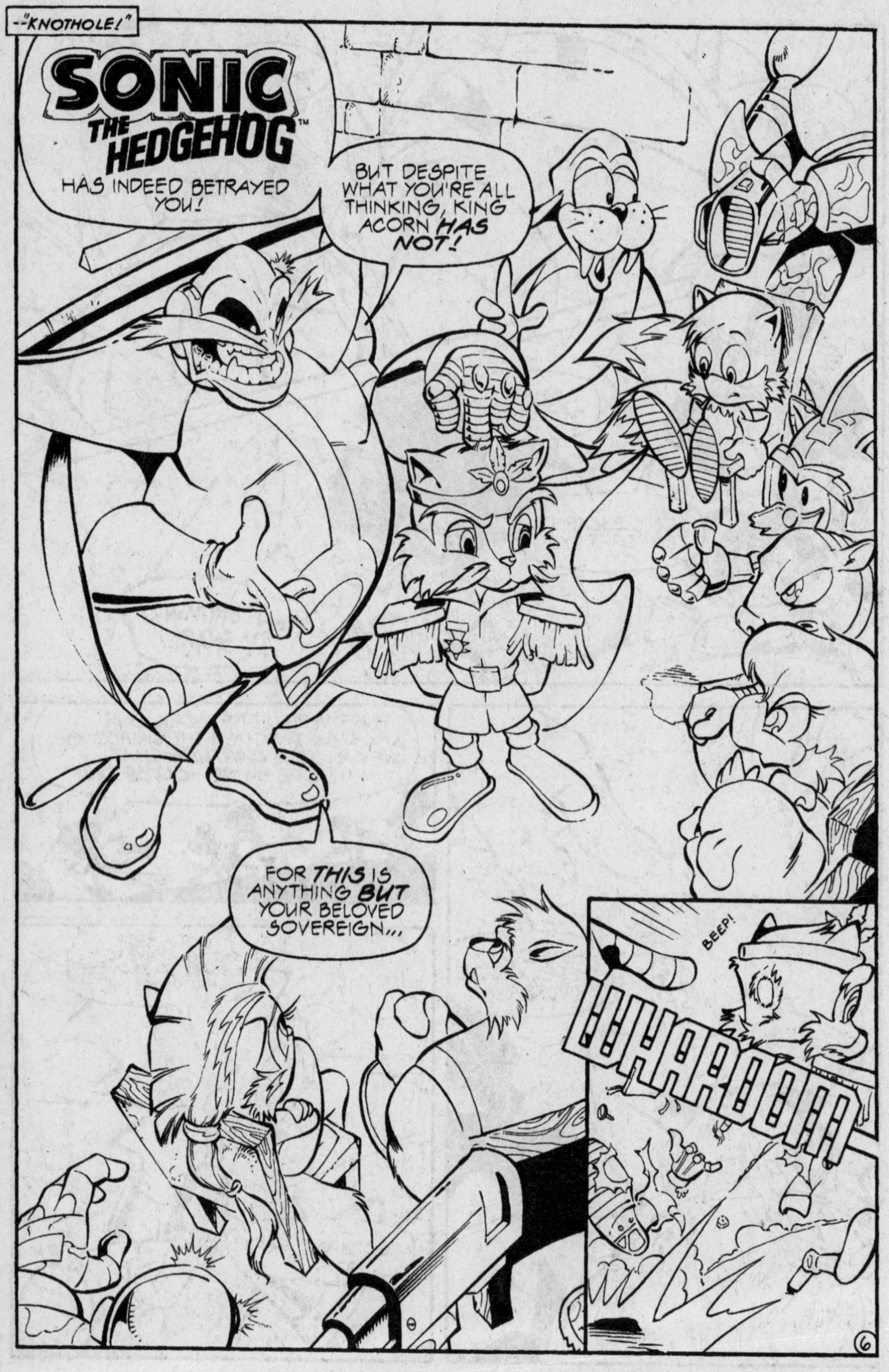
--"KNOTHOLE!"
SONIC THE HEDGEHOG™ HAS INDEED BETRAYED YOU!
BUT DESPITE WHAT YOU'RE ALL THINKING, KING ACORN HAS NOT!
FOR THIS IS ANYTHING BUT YOUR BELOVED SOVEREIGN...
BEEP!
WHAROOM!
6

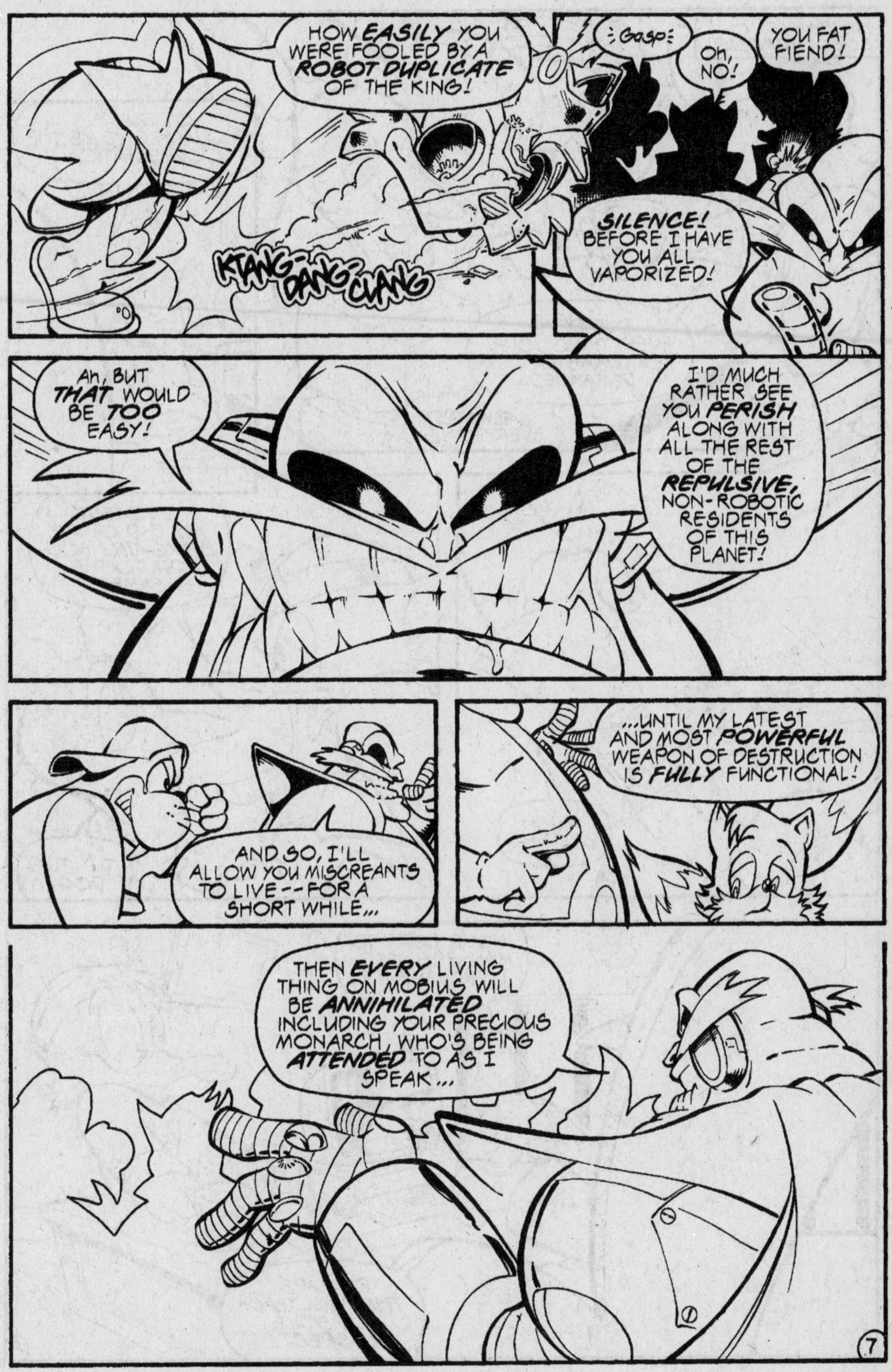
HOW EASILY YOU WERE FOOLED BY A ROBOT DUPLICATE OF THE KING!
KLANG-DANG-CLANG
:Gasp:
Oh, NO!
YOU FAT FIEND!
SILENCE! BEFORE I HAVE YOU ALL VAPORIZED!
Ah, BUT THAT WOULD BE TOO EASY!
I'D MUCH RATHER SEE YOU PERISH ALONG WITH ALL THE REST OF THE REPULSIVE, NON-ROBOTIC RESIDENTS OF THIS PLANET!
AND SO, I'LL ALLOW YOU MISCREANTS TO LIVE--FOR A SHORT WHILE...
...UNTIL MY LATEST AND MOST POWERFUL WEAPON OF DESTRUCTION IS FULLY FUNCTIONAL!
THEN EVERY LIVING THING ON MOBIUS WILL BE ANNIHILATED INCLUDING YOUR PRECIOUS MONARCH, WHO'S BEING ATTENDED TO AS I SPEAK...
7

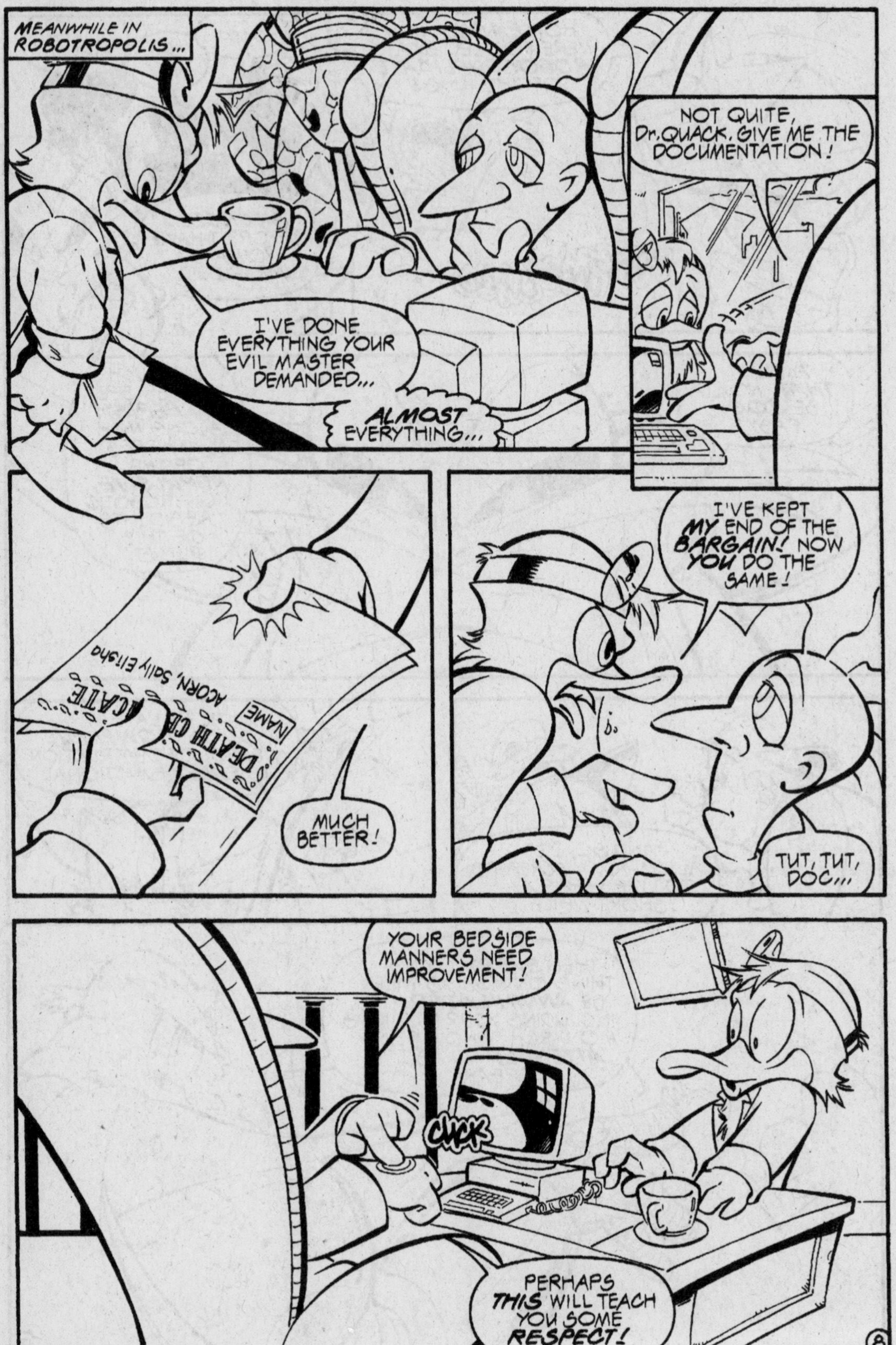
MEANWHILE IN ROBOTROPOLIS...
I'VE DONE EVERYTHING YOUR EVIL MASTER DEMANDED...
ALMOST EVERYTHING...
NOT QUITE, Dr. QUACK. GIVE ME THE DOCUMENTATION!
NAME
ACORN, Sally Elisha
MUCH BETTER!
I'VE KEPT MY END OF THE BARGAIN! NOW YOU DO THE SAME!
TUT, TUT, DOC...
YOUR BEDSIDE MANNERS NEED IMPROVEMENT!
CLICK
PERHAPS THIS WILL TEACH YOU SOME RESPECT!
8

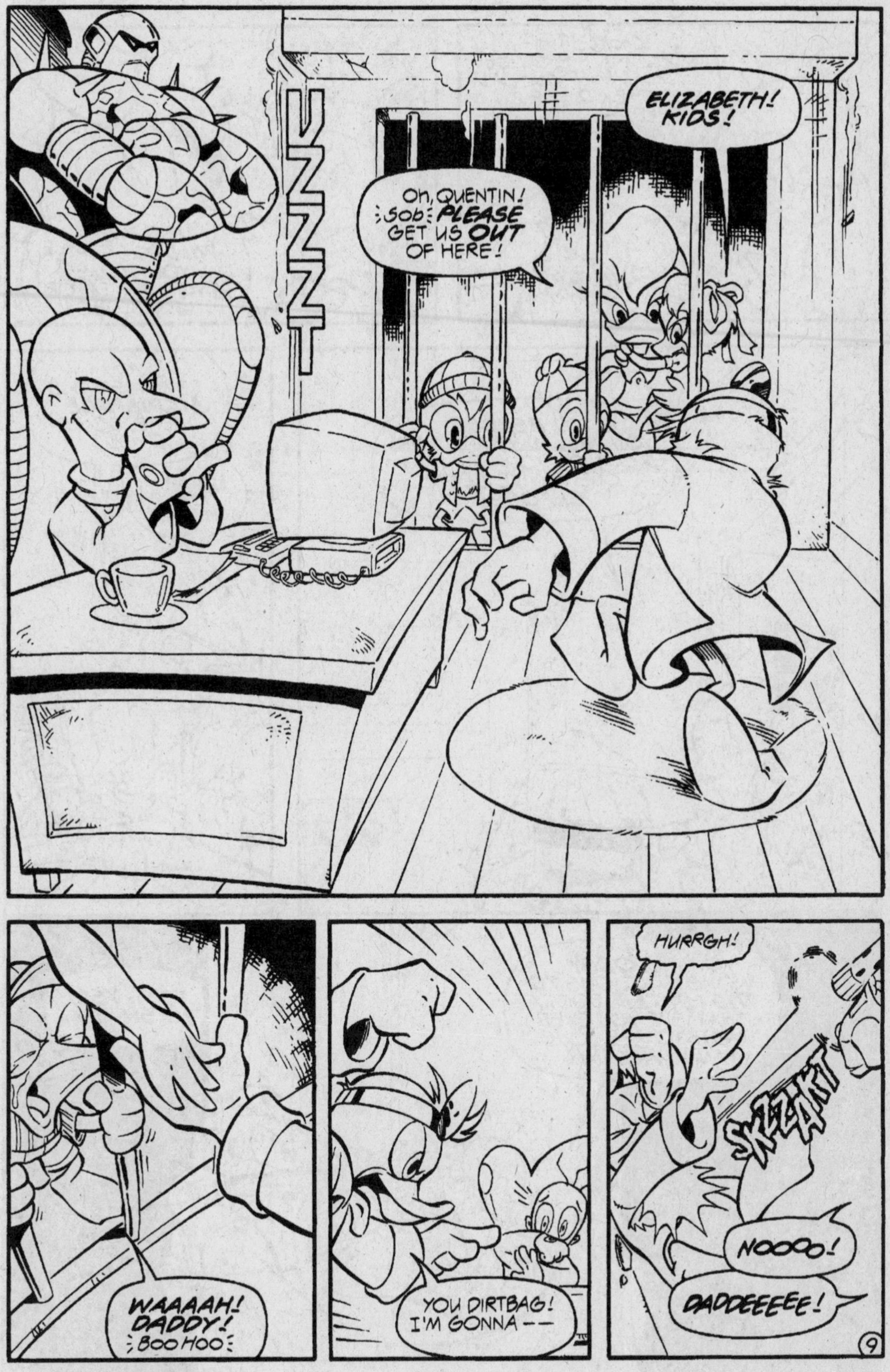

ZZZZT
Oh, QUENTIN! sob PLEASE GET US OUT OF HERE!
ELIZABETH! KIDS!
WAAAAH! DADDY! BOO HOO
YOU DIRTBAG! I'M GONNA --
HURRGH!
SKZZAKT
NOOOO!
DADDEEEEEE!
9

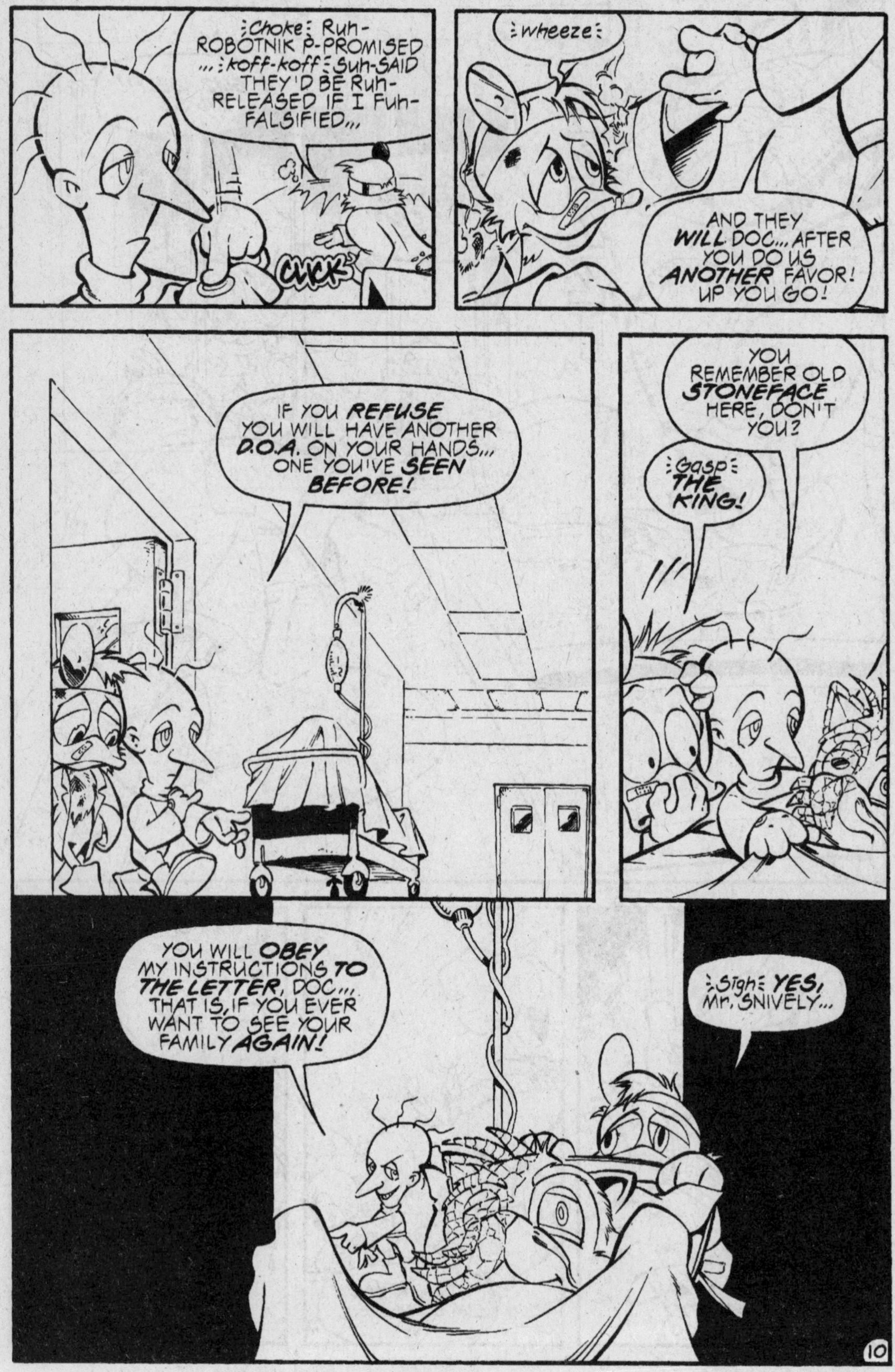

:Choke: Ruh-ROBOTNIK P-PROMISED ... :koff-koff: Suh-SAID THEY'D BE Ruh-RELEASED IF I Fuh-FALSIFIED...
CLICK
:wheeze:
AND THEY WILL DOC... AFTER YOU DO US ANOTHER FAVOR! UP YOU GO!
IF YOU REFUSE YOU WILL HAVE ANOTHER D.O.A. ON YOUR HANDS... ONE YOU'VE SEEN BEFORE!
YOU REMEMBER OLD STONEFACE HERE, DON'T YOU?
:Gasp: THE KING!
YOU WILL OBEY MY INSTRUCTIONS TO THE LETTER, DOC... THAT IS, IF YOU EVER WANT TO SEE YOUR FAMILY AGAIN!
:Sigh: YES, Mr. SNIVELY...
10

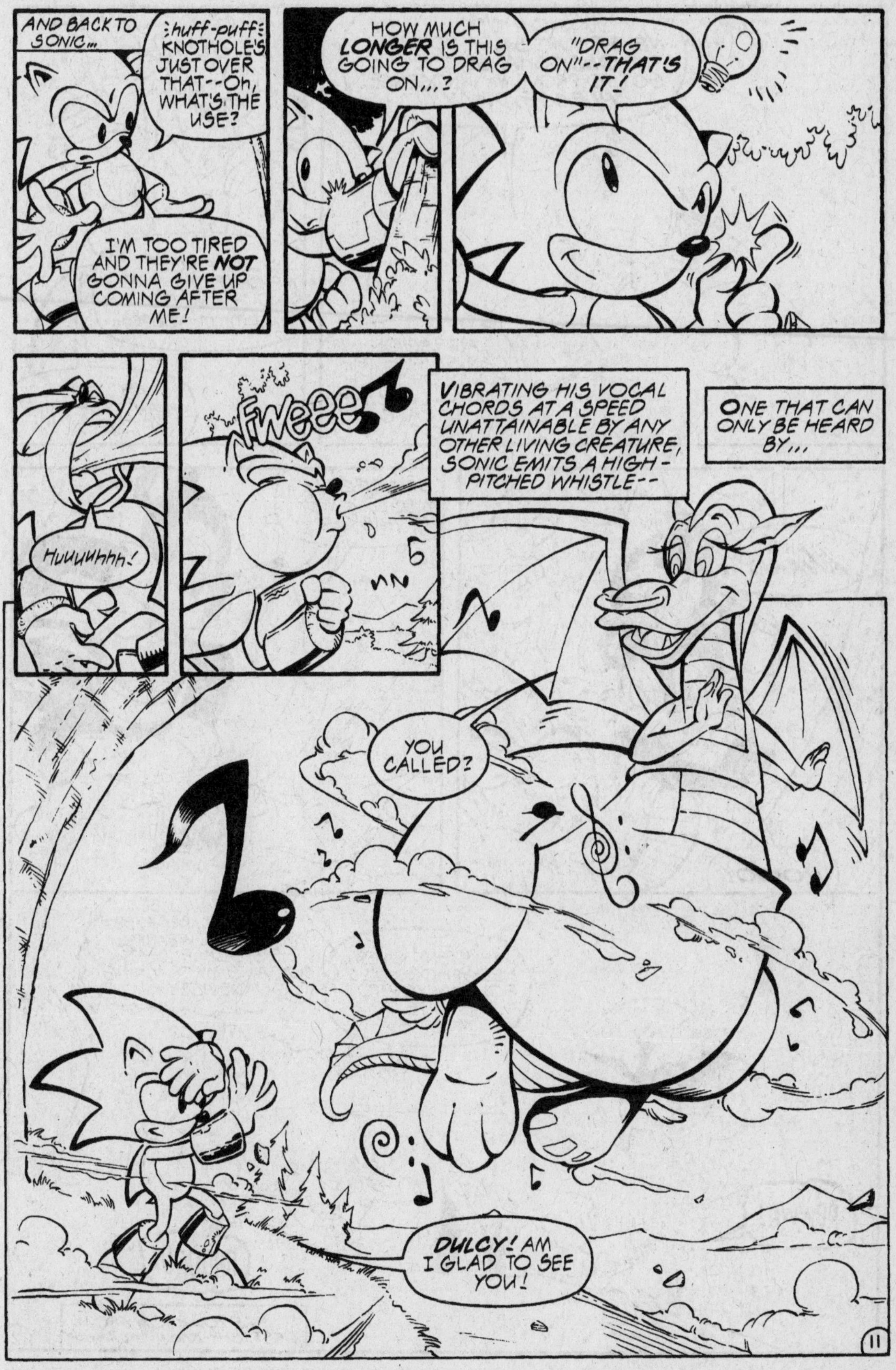
AND BACK TO SONIC...
huff-puff KNOTHOLE'S JUST OVER THAT--Oh, WHAT'S THE USE?
I'M TOO TIRED AND THEY'RE NOT GONNA GIVE UP COMING AFTER ME!
HOW MUCH LONGER IS THIS GOING TO DRAG ON...?
"DRAG ON"--THAT'S IT!
Huuuhhh!
Fweee
VIBRATING HIS VOCAL CHORDS AT A SPEED UNATTAINABLE BY ANY OTHER LIVING CREATURE, SONIC EMITS A HIGH-PITCHED WHISTLE--
ONE THAT CAN ONLY BE HEARD BY...
YOU CALLED?
DULCY! AM I GLAD TO SEE YOU!
11

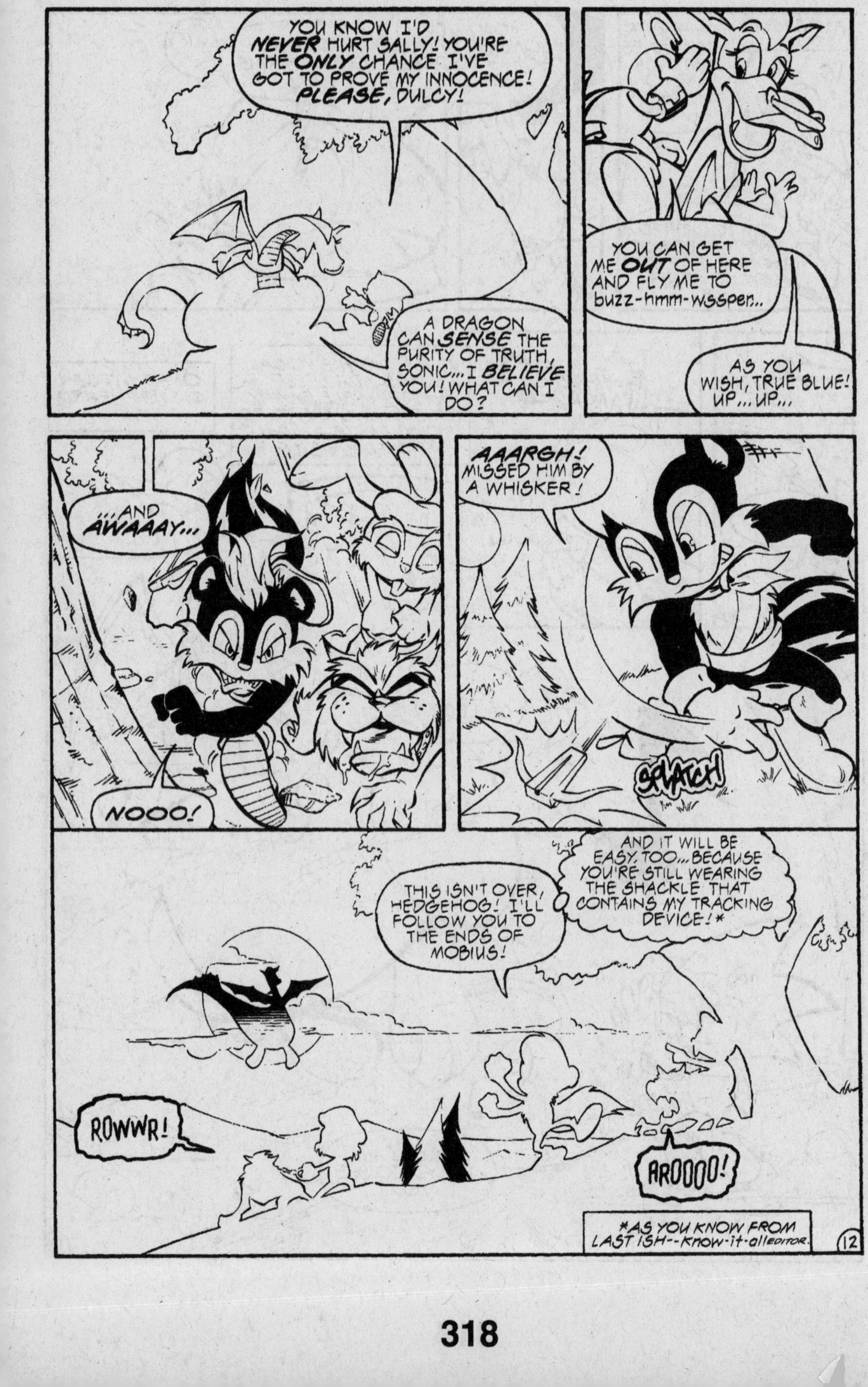
YOU KNOW I'D NEVER HURT SALLY! YOU'RE THE ONLY CHANCE I'VE GOT TO PROVE MY INNOCENCE! PLEASE, DULCY!
A DRAGON CAN SENSE THE PURITY OF TRUTH, SONIC... I BELIEVE YOU! WHAT CAN I DO?
YOU CAN GET ME OUT OF HERE AND FLY ME TO buzz-hmm-wssper...
AS YOU WISH, TRUE BLUE! UP... UP...
...AND AWAAAY...
NOOO!
AAARGH! MISSED HIM BY A WHISKER!
SPLATCH
THIS ISN'T OVER, HEDGEHOG! I'LL FOLLOW YOU TO THE ENDS OF MOBIUS!
AND IT WILL BE EASY, TOO... BECAUSE YOU'RE STILL WEARING THE SHACKLE THAT CONTAINS MY TRACKING DEVICE!*
ROWWR!
AROOOO!
*AS YOU KNOW FROM LAST ISH--know-it-all EDITOR.
12

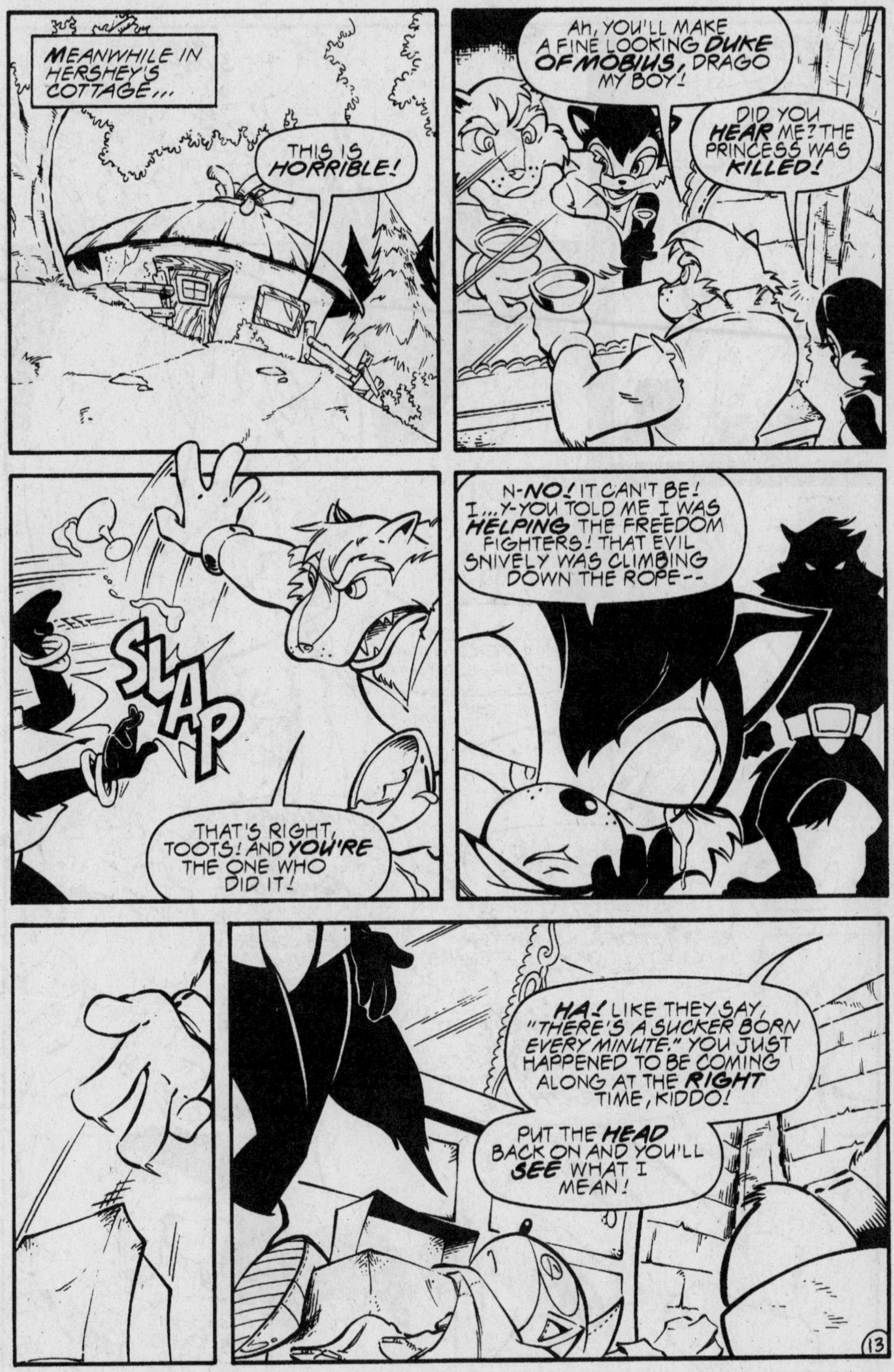
MEANWHILE IN HERSHEY'S COTTAGE...
THIS IS HORRIBLE!
AH, YOU'LL MAKE A FINE LOOKING DUKE OF MOBIUS, DRAGO MY BOY!
DID YOU HEAR ME? THE PRINCESS WAS KILLED!
SLAP
THAT'S RIGHT, TOOTS! AND YOU'RE THE ONE WHO DID IT!
N-NO! IT CAN'T BE! I...Y-YOU TOLD ME I WAS HELPING THE FREEDOM FIGHTERS! THAT EVIL SNIVELY WAS CLIMBING DOWN THE ROPE--
HA! LIKE THEY SAY, "THERE'S A SUCKER BORN EVERY MINUTE." YOU JUST HAPPENED TO BE COMING ALONG AT THE RIGHT TIME, KIDDO!
PUT THE HEAD BACK ON AND YOU'LL SEE WHAT I MEAN!
13

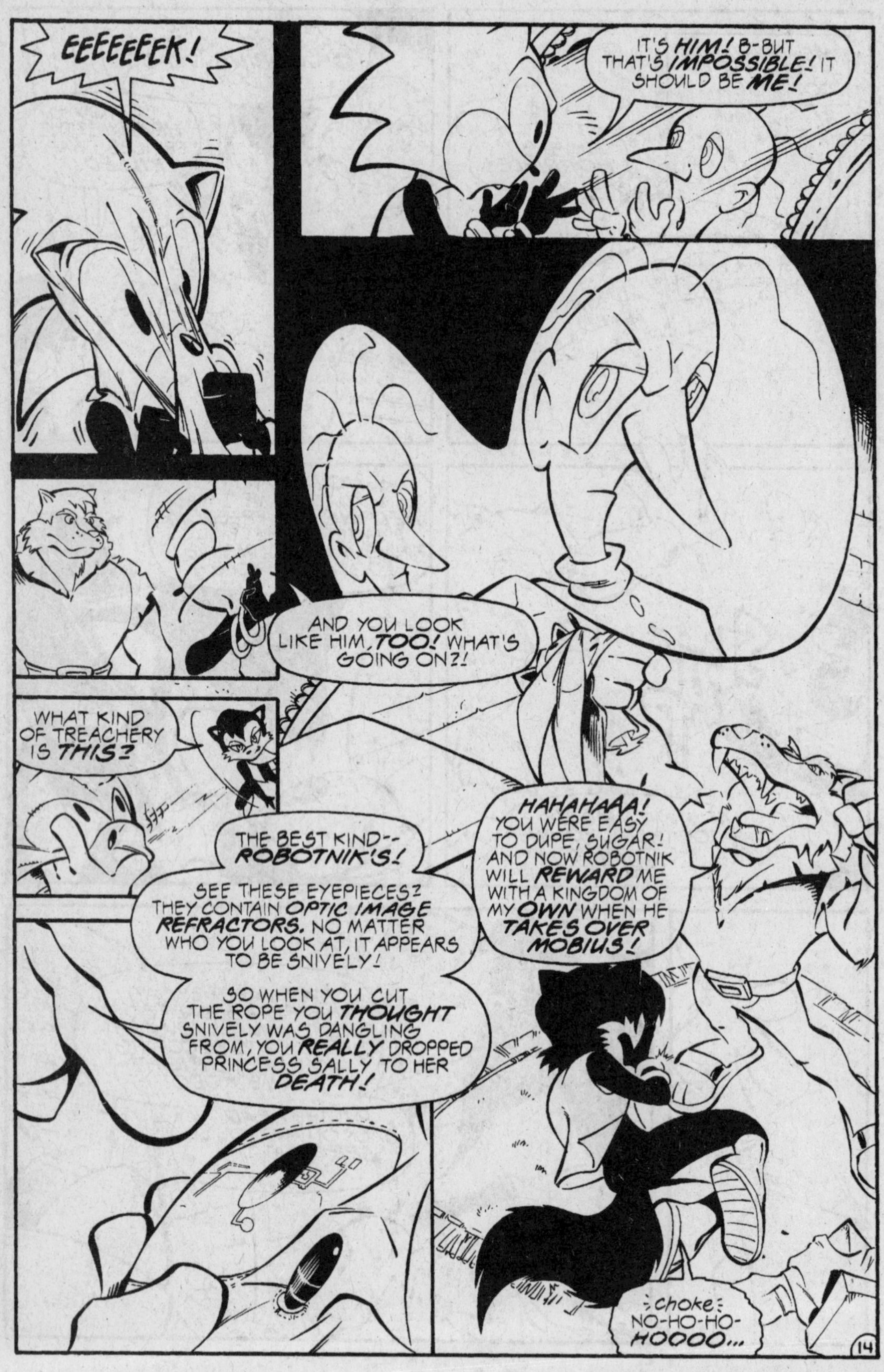
EEEEEEEK!
IT'S HIM! B-BUT THAT'S IMPOSSIBLE! IT SHOULD BE ME!
AND YOU LOOK LIKE HIM, TOO! WHAT'S GOING ON?!
WHAT KIND OF TREACHERY IS THIS?
THE BEST KIND-- ROBOTNIK'S!
SEE THESE EYEPIECES? THEY CONTAIN OPTIC IMAGE REFRACTORS. NO MATTER WHO YOU LOOK AT, IT APPEARS TO BE SNIVELY!
SO WHEN YOU CUT THE ROPE YOU THOUGHT SNIVELY WAS DANGLING FROM, YOU REALLY DROPPED PRINCESS SALLY TO HER DEATH!
HAHAHAAA! YOU WERE EASY TO DUPE, SUGAR! AND NOW ROBOTNIK WILL REWARD ME WITH A KINGDOM OF MY OWN WHEN HE TAKES OVER MOBIUS!
choke
NO-HO-HO-HOOOO...
14

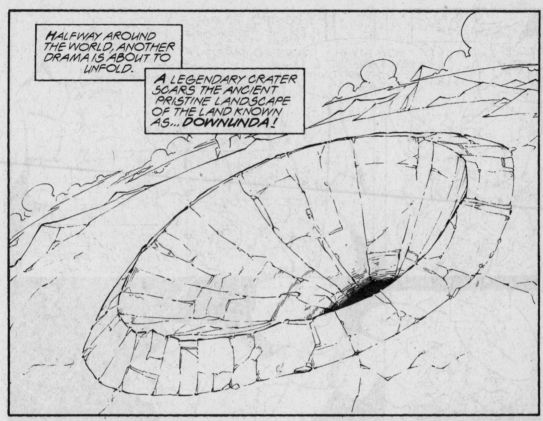

HALFWAY AROUND THE WORLD, ANOTHER DRAMA IS ABOUT TO UNFOLD.

A LEGENDARY CRATER SCARS THE ANCIENT PRISTINE LANDSCAPE OF THE LAND KNOWN AS... *DOWNUNDA!*

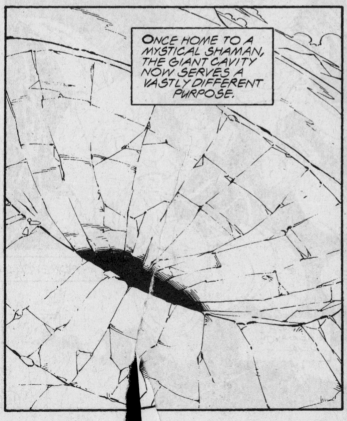

ONCE HOME TO A MYSTICAL SHAMAN, THE GIANT CAVITY NOW SERVES A VASTLY DIFFERENT PURPOSE.

ONE THAT REEKS OF SUFFERING, DESPAIR AND PALPABLE MALEVOLENCE!

MOVE-- QUICKLY!

15

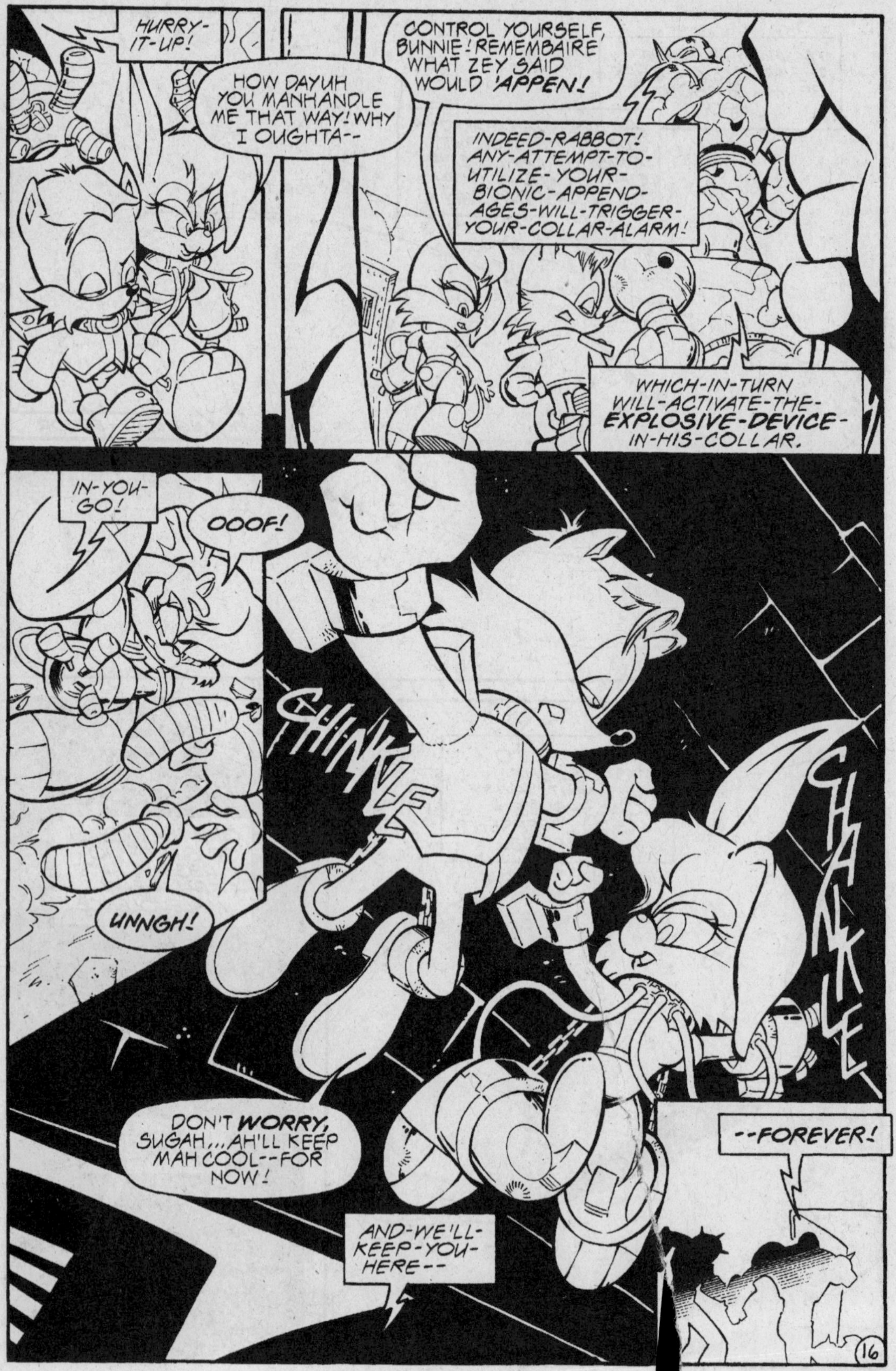
HURRY-IT-UP!
HOW DAYUH YOU MANHANDLE ME THAT WAY! WHY I OUGHTA--
CONTROL YOURSELF, BUNNIE! REMEMBAIRE WHAT ZEY SAID WOULD 'APPEN!
INDEED-RABBOT! ANY-ATTEMPT-TO-UTILIZE-YOUR-BIONIC-APPENDAGES-WILL-TRIGGER-YOUR-COLLAR-ALARM!
WHICH-IN-TURN WILL-ACTIVATE-THE-EXPLOSIVE-DEVICE-IN-HIS-COLLAR.
IN-YOU-GO!
OOOF!
UNNGH!
CHINKLE
CHAKLE
DON'T WORRY, SUGAH... AH'LL KEEP MAH COOL--FOR NOW!
AND-WE'LL-KEEP-YOU-HERE--
--FOREVER!
16

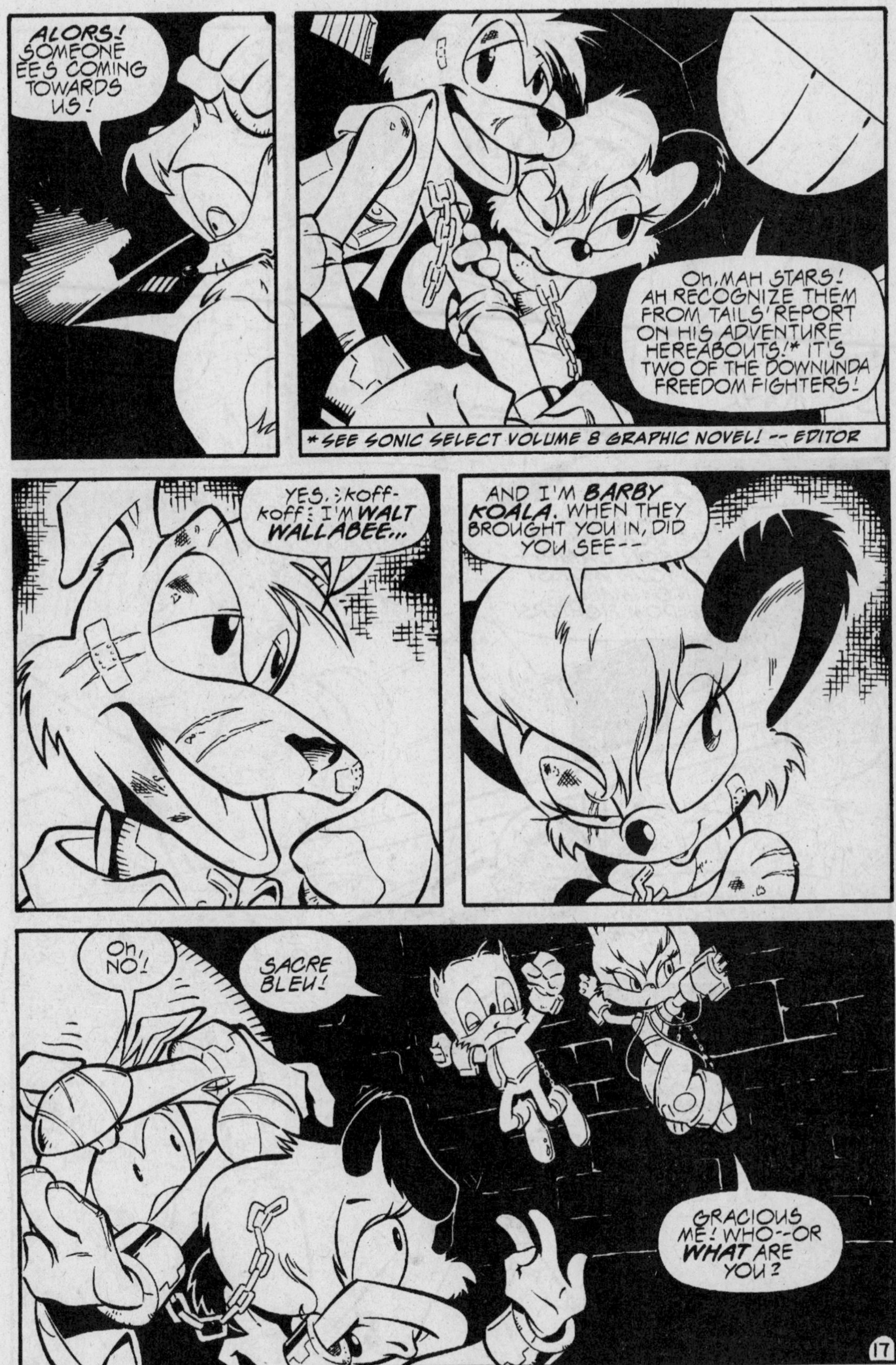
ALORS! SOMEONE EES COMING TOWARDS US!
OH, MAH STARS! AH RECOGNIZE THEM FROM TAILS' REPORT ON HIS ADVENTURE HEREABOUTS!* IT'S TWO OF THE DOWNUNDA FREEDOM FIGHTERS!
* SEE SONIC SELECT VOLUME 8 GRAPHIC NOVEL! -- EDITOR
YES. :koff-koff: I'M WALT WALLABEE...
AND I'M BARBY KOALA. WHEN THEY BROUGHT YOU IN, DID YOU SEE--
OH, NO!
SACRE BLEU!
GRACIOUS ME! WHO--OR WHAT ARE YOU?
17

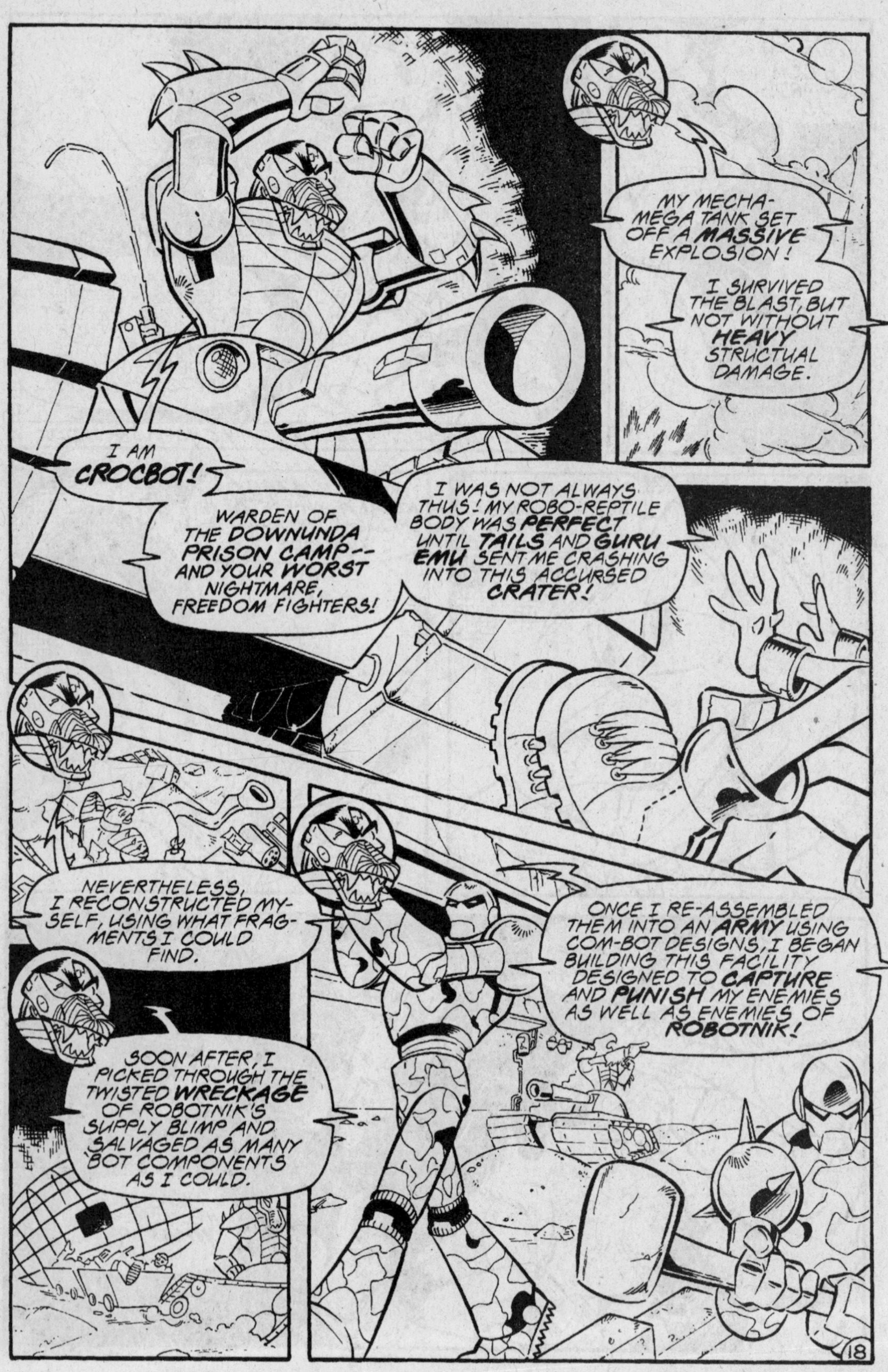
I AM CROCBOT!
WARDEN OF THE DOWNUNDA PRISON CAMP-- AND YOUR WORST NIGHTMARE, FREEDOM FIGHTERS!
MY MECHA-MEGA TANK SET OFF A MASSIVE EXPLOSION!
I SURVIVED THE BLAST, BUT NOT WITHOUT HEAVY STRUCTUAL DAMAGE.
I WAS NOT ALWAYS THUS! MY ROBO-REPTILE BODY WAS PERFECT UNTIL TAILS AND GURU EMU SENT ME CRASHING INTO THIS ACCURSED CRATER!
NEVERTHELESS, I RECONSTRUCTED MY-SELF, USING WHAT FRAG-MENTS I COULD FIND.
SOON AFTER, I PICKED THROUGH THE TWISTED WRECKAGE OF ROBOTNIK'S SUPPLY BLIMP AND SALVAGED AS MANY BOT COMPONENTS AS I COULD.
ONCE I RE-ASSEMBLED THEM INTO AN ARMY USING COM-BOT DESIGNS, I BEGAN BUILDING THIS FACILITY DESIGNED TO CAPTURE AND PUNISH MY ENEMIES AS WELL AS ENEMIES OF ROBOTNIK!
18

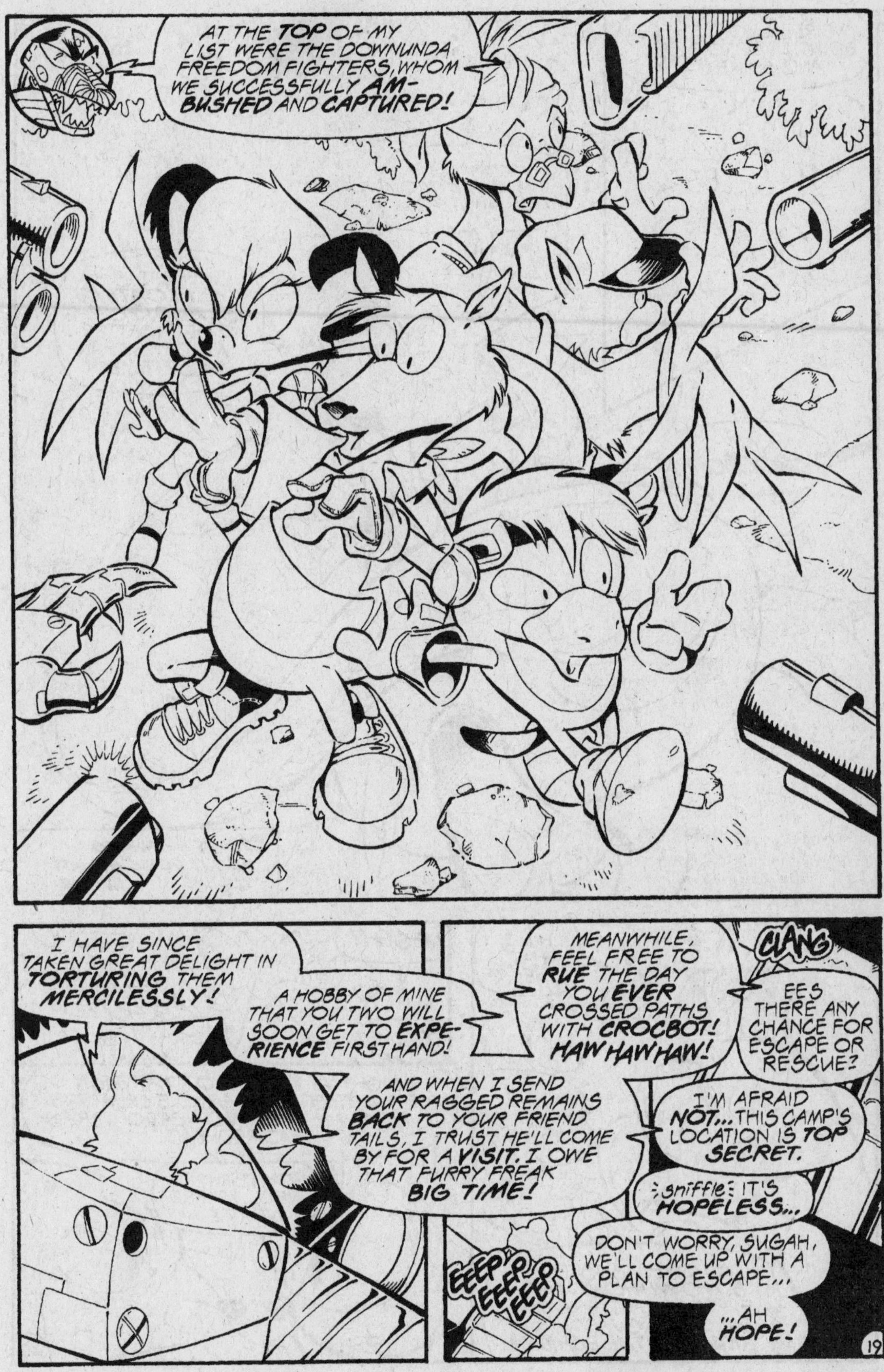
AT THE TOP OF MY LIST WERE THE DOWNUNDA FREEDOM FIGHTERS, WHOM WE SUCCESSFULLY AMBUSHED AND CAPTURED!
I HAVE SINCE TAKEN GREAT DELIGHT IN TORTURING THEM MERCILESSLY!
A HOBBY OF MINE THAT YOU TWO WILL SOON GET TO EXPERIENCE FIRST HAND!
AND WHEN I SEND YOUR RAGGED REMAINS BACK TO YOUR FRIEND TAILS, I TRUST HE'LL COME BY FOR A VISIT. I OWE THAT FURRY FREAK BIG TIME!
MEANWHILE, FEEL FREE TO RUE THE DAY YOU EVER CROSSED PATHS WITH CROCBOT! HAW HAW HAW!
CLANG
EES THERE ANY CHANCE FOR ESCAPE OR RESCUE?
I'M AFRAID NOT... THIS CAMP'S LOCATION IS TOP SECRET.
:sniffle: IT'S HOPELESS...
DON'T WORRY, SUGAH, WE'LL COME UP WITH A PLAN TO ESCAPE...
...AH HOPE!
EEEP EEEP EEEP
19

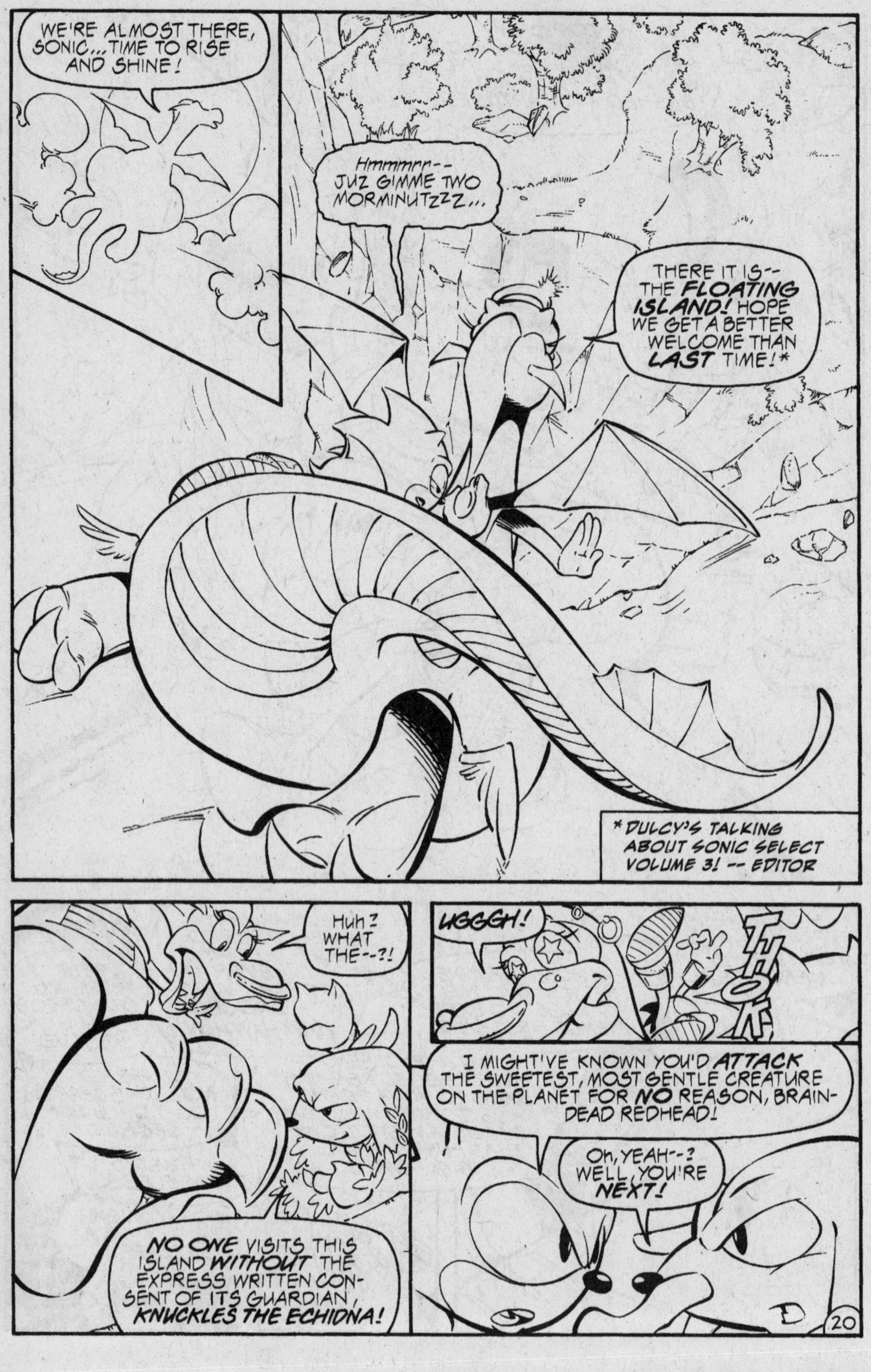
WE'RE ALMOST THERE, SONIC... TIME TO RISE AND SHINE!
Hmmmrrr-- JUZ GIMME TWO MORMINUTZZZ...
THERE IT IS-- THE FLOATING ISLAND! HOPE WE GET A BETTER WELCOME THAN LAST TIME!*
* DULCY'S TALKING ABOUT SONIC SELECT VOLUME 3! -- EDITOR
Huh? WHAT THE--?!
NO ONE VISITS THIS ISLAND WITHOUT THE EXPRESS WRITTEN CONSENT OF ITS GUARDIAN, KNUCKLES THE ECHIDNA!
UGGGH!
THOK
I MIGHT'VE KNOWN YOU'D ATTACK THE SWEETEST, MOST GENTLE CREATURE ON THE PLANET FOR NO REASON, BRAIN-DEAD REDHEAD!
Oh, YEAH--? WELL, YOU'RE NEXT!
20

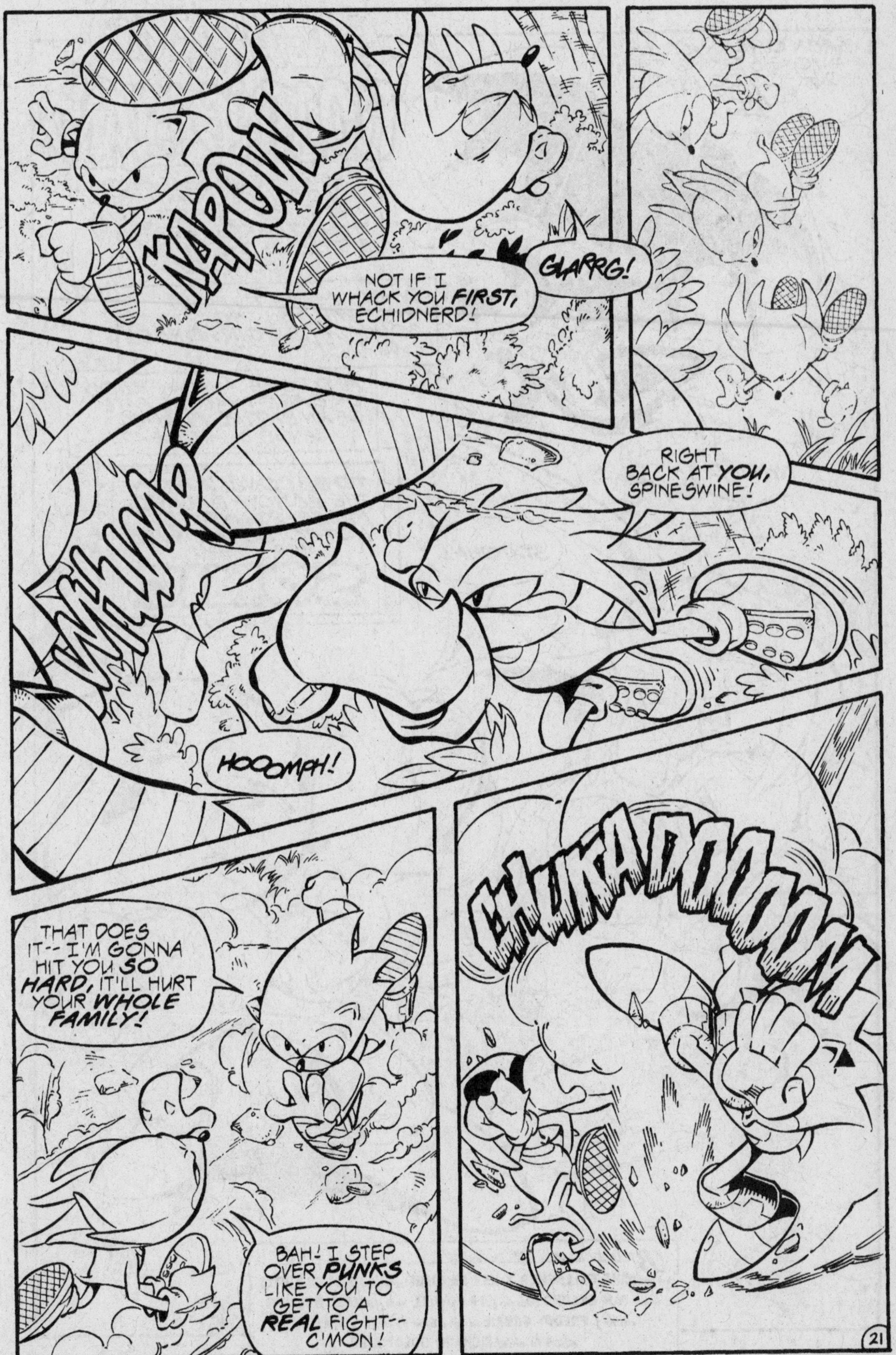
KAPOW
NOT IF I WHACK YOU FIRST, ECHIDNERD!
GLARRG!
RIGHT BACK AT YOU, SPINESWINE!
WHUMP
HOOOMPH!
THAT DOES IT-- I'M GONNA HIT YOU SO HARD, IT'LL HURT YOUR WHOLE FAMILY!
BAH! I STEP OVER PUNKS LIKE YOU TO GET TO A REAL FIGHT-- C'MON!
CHUKADOOOOM
21

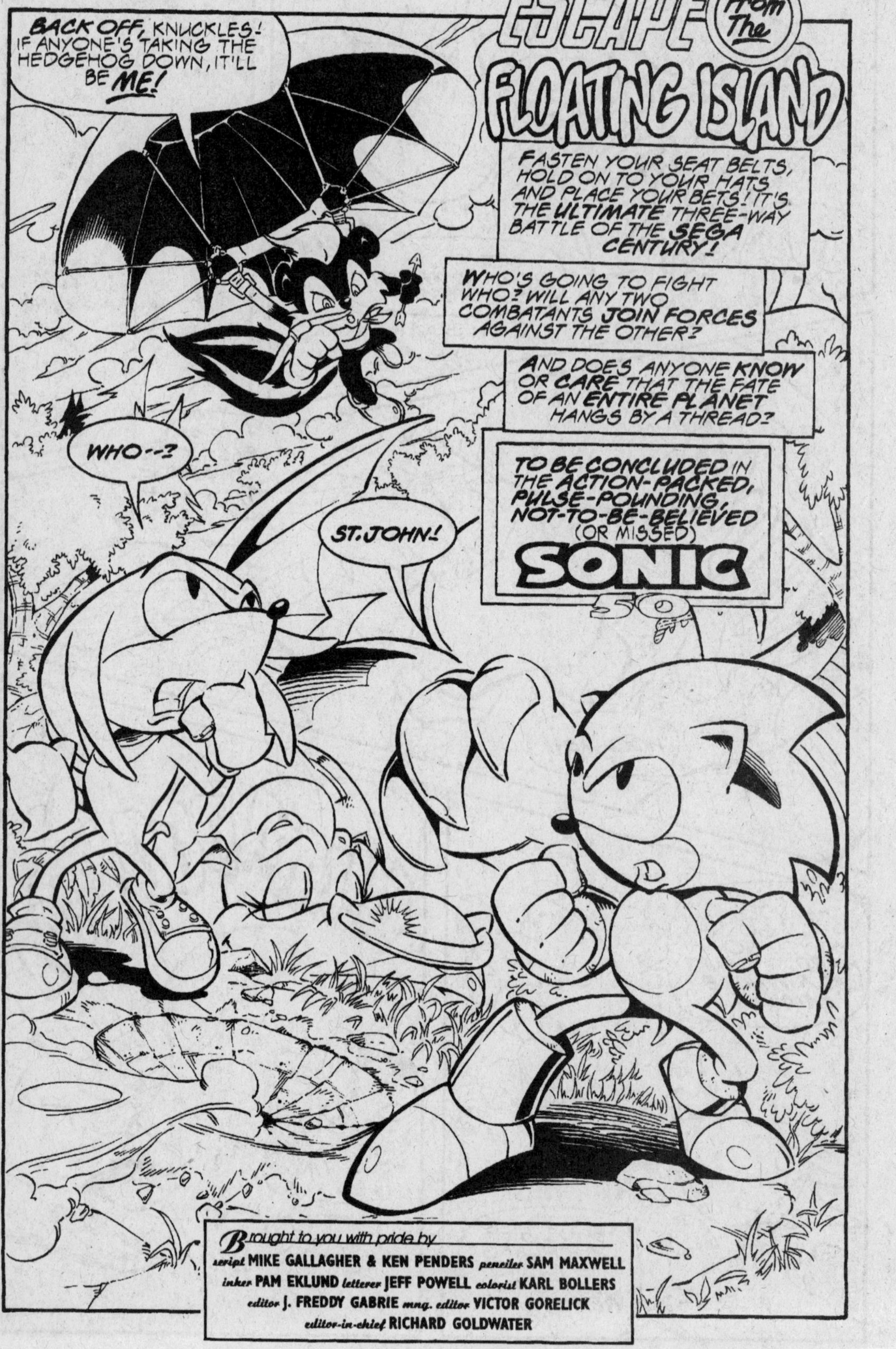
ESCAPE From The FLOATING ISLAND
BACK OFF, KNUCKLES! IF ANYONE'S TAKING THE HEDGEHOG DOWN, IT'LL BE ME!
FASTEN YOUR SEAT BELTS, HOLD ON TO YOUR HATS AND PLACE YOUR BETS! IT'S THE ULTIMATE THREE-WAY BATTLE OF THE SEGA CENTURY!
WHO'S GOING TO FIGHT WHO? WILL ANY TWO COMBATANTS JOIN FORCES AGAINST THE OTHER?
AND DOES ANYONE KNOW OR CARE THAT THE FATE OF AN ENTIRE PLANET HANGS BY A THREAD?
TO BE CONCLUDED IN THE ACTION-PACKED, PULSE-POUNDING, NOT-TO-BE-BELIEVED (OR MISSED) SONIC 50
WHO--?
ST. JOHN!
Brought to you with pride by
script MIKE GALLAGHER & KEN PENDERS penciler SAM MAXWELL
inker PAM EKLUND letterer JEFF POWELL colorist KARL BOLLERS
editor J. FREDDY GABRIE mng. editor VICTOR GORELICK
editor-in-chief RICHARD GOLDWATER

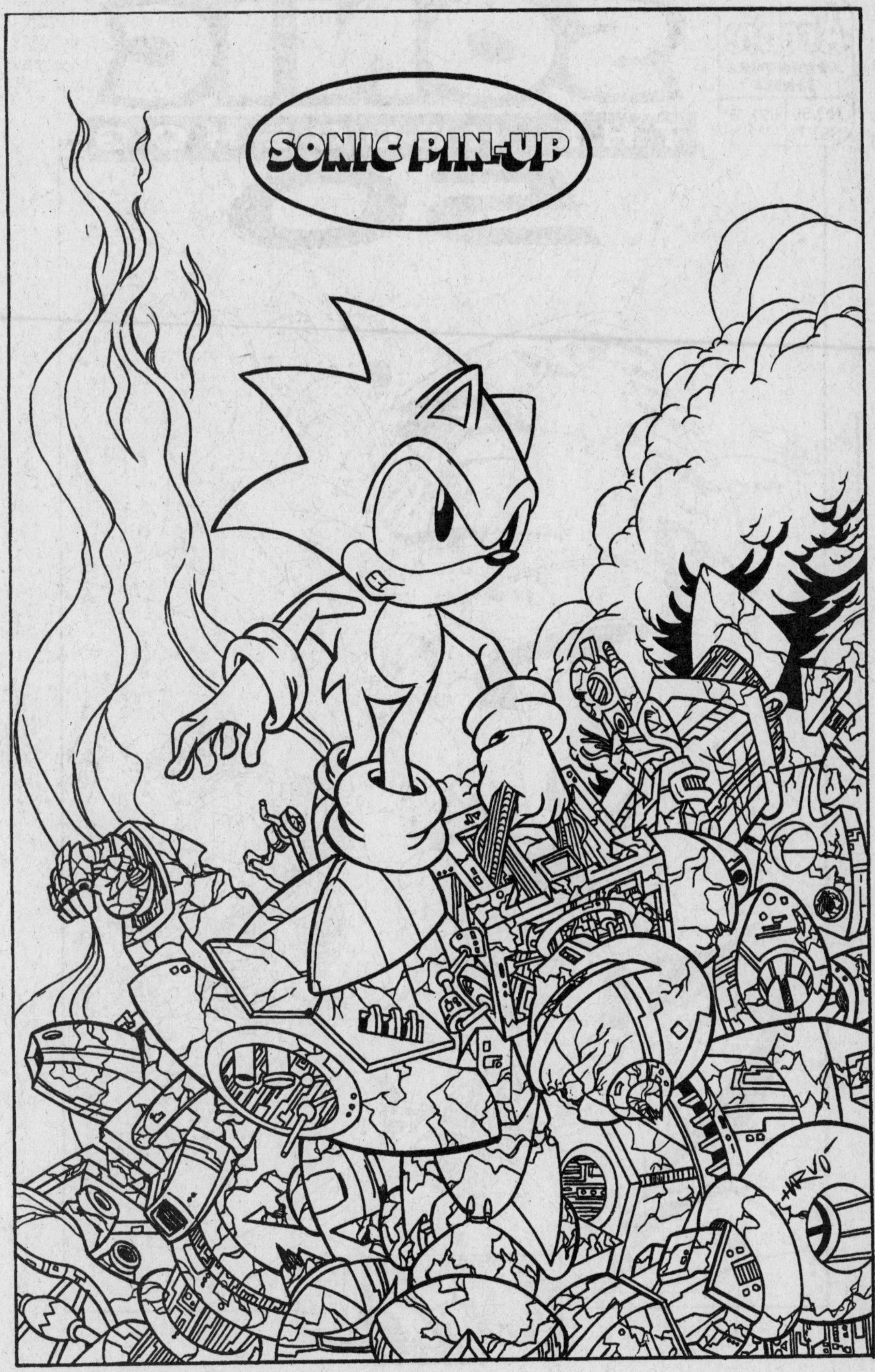
SONIC PIN-UP

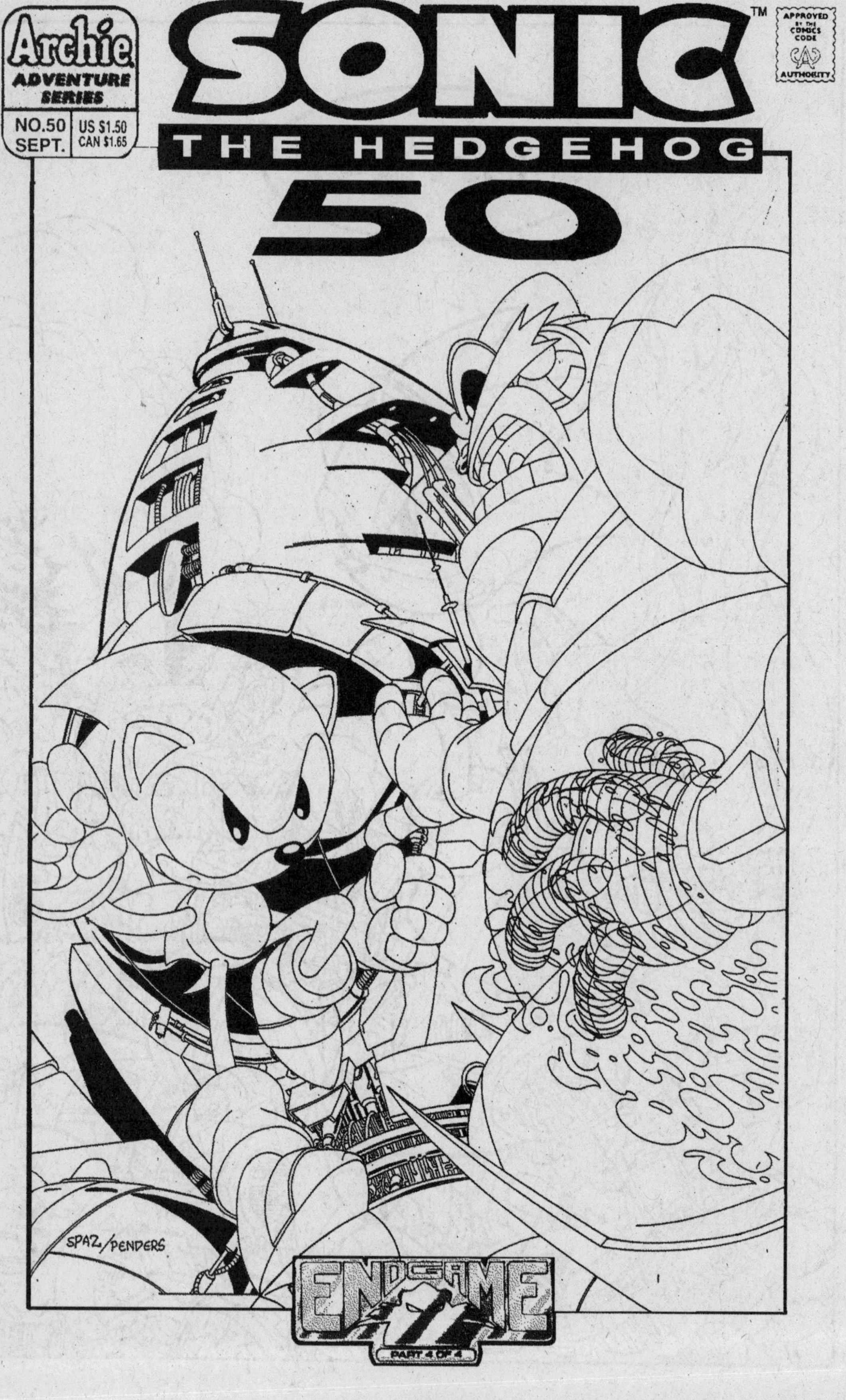
Archie
ADVENTURE SERIES
NO.50
SEPT.
US $1.50
CAN $1.65
SONIC™
THE HEDGEHOG
50
APPROVED BY THE COMICS CODE AUTHORITY
SPAZ/PENDERS
ENDGAME
PART 4 OF 4

In the year 3235, the ambitions of one being have affected the lives of **Sonic The Hedgehog**, his friends and all who dwell upon the planet **Mobius**. Up until now, the battle had been fought by a code of honor adhered to by the many, despite the treachery of the one.

But that was then. This is now.

Having lost his beloved by means most foul and framed for her apparent murder, Sonic now finds himself fighting for redemption against friend and foe alike, attempting to prove his innocence and ferret out the real villains in the process.

After surviving a crash landing on his way to the **Devil's Gulag**, a relentless pursuit by **Geoffrey St. John** and his crack troops, eventually making his way to **The Floating Island** with the assistance of the gentle dragon **Dulcy**, Sonic has come seeking the help of its guardian, **Knuckles The Echidna**.

Now, as the players assemble for the final act, they will all discover there is nothing more dangerous than a **hedgehog with a cause...**

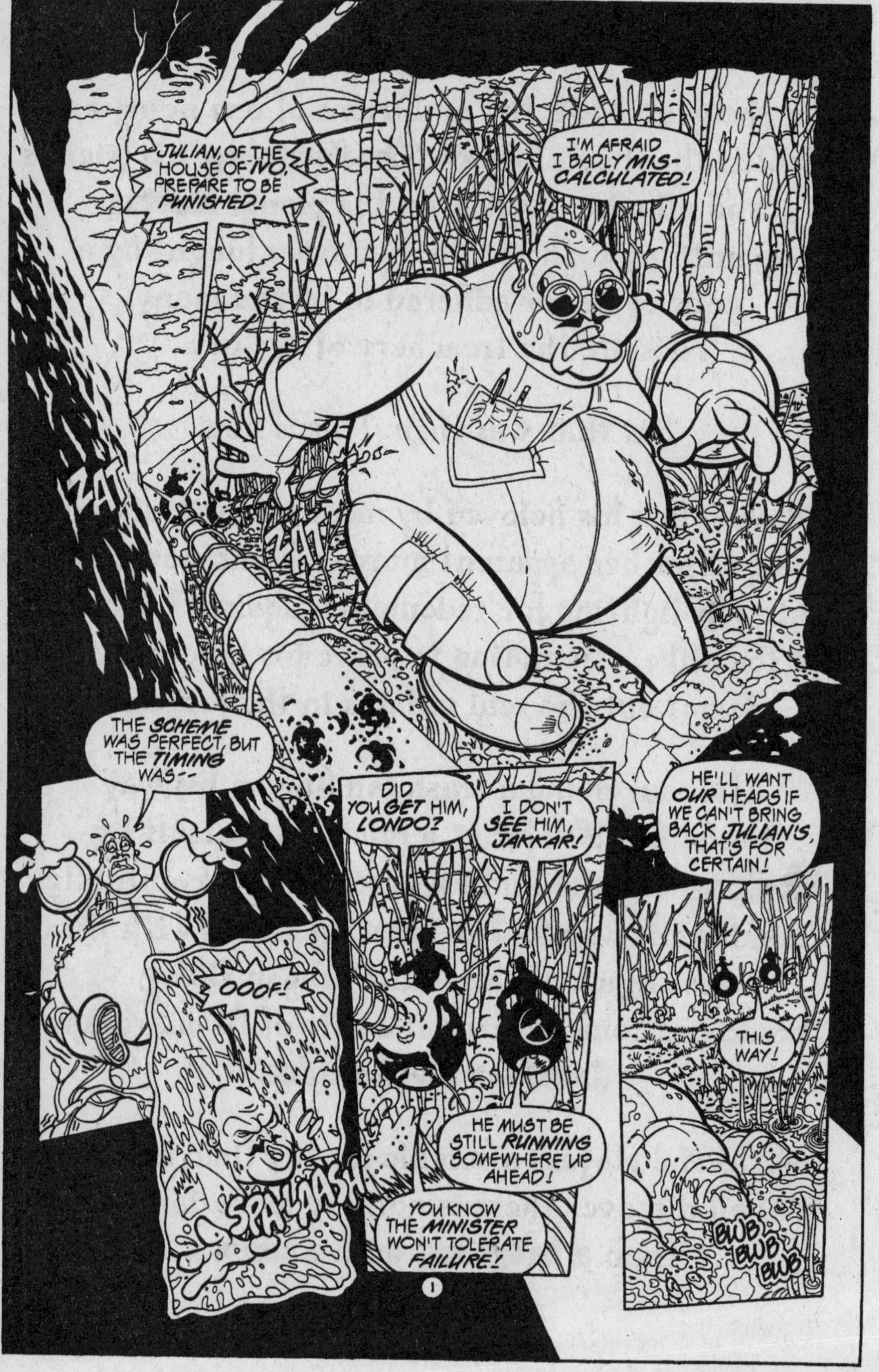
JULIAN, OF THE HOUSE OF IVO, PREPARE TO BE PUNISHED!
I'M AFRAID I BADLY MIS-CALCULATED!
ZAT
ZAT
THE SCHEME WAS PERFECT, BUT THE TIMING WAS--
OOOF!
SPA-LAASH
DID YOU GET HIM, LONDO?
I DON'T SEE HIM, JAKKAR!
HE MUST BE STILL RUNNING SOMEWHERE UP AHEAD!
YOU KNOW THE MINISTER WON'T TOLERATE FAILURE!
HE'LL WANT OUR HEADS IF WE CAN'T BRING BACK JULIAN'S, THAT'S FOR CERTAIN!
THIS WAY!
BWB BWB BWB
1

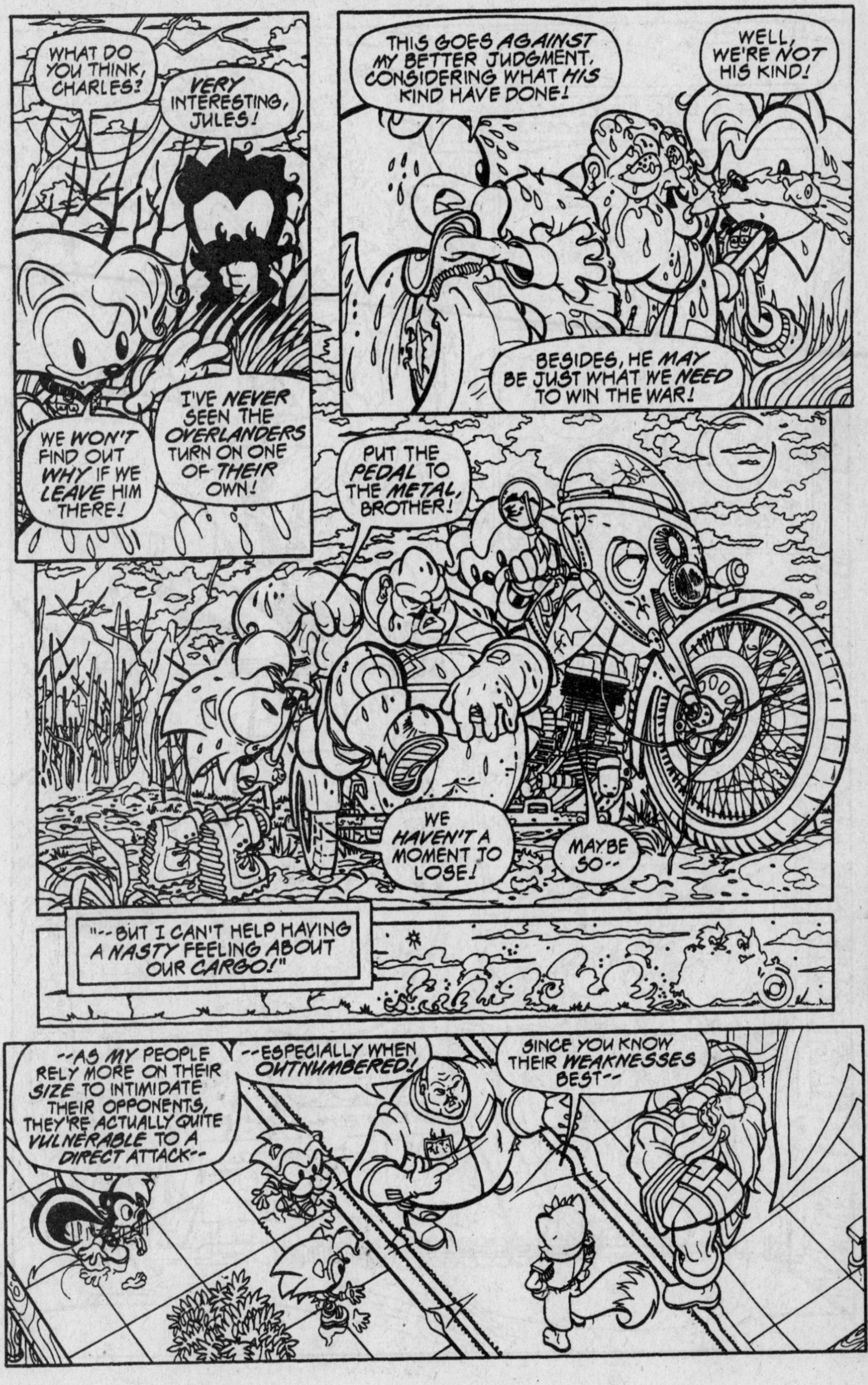
WHAT DO YOU THINK, CHARLES?
VERY INTERESTING, JULES!
I'VE NEVER SEEN THE OVERLANDERS TURN ON ONE OF THEIR OWN!
WE WON'T FIND OUT WHY IF WE LEAVE HIM THERE!
THIS GOES AGAINST MY BETTER JUDGMENT, CONSIDERING WHAT HIS KIND HAVE DONE!
WELL, WE'RE NOT HIS KIND!
BESIDES, HE MAY BE JUST WHAT WE NEED TO WIN THE WAR!
PUT THE PEDAL TO THE METAL, BROTHER!
WE HAVEN'T A MOMENT TO LOSE!
MAYBE SO--
"--BUT I CAN'T HELP HAVING A NASTY FEELING ABOUT OUR CARGO!"
--AS MY PEOPLE RELY MORE ON THEIR SIZE TO INTIMIDATE THEIR OPPONENTS, THEY'RE ACTUALLY QUITE VULNERABLE TO A DIRECT ATTACK--
--ESPECIALLY WHEN OUTNUMBERED!
SINCE YOU KNOW THEIR WEAKNESSES BEST--

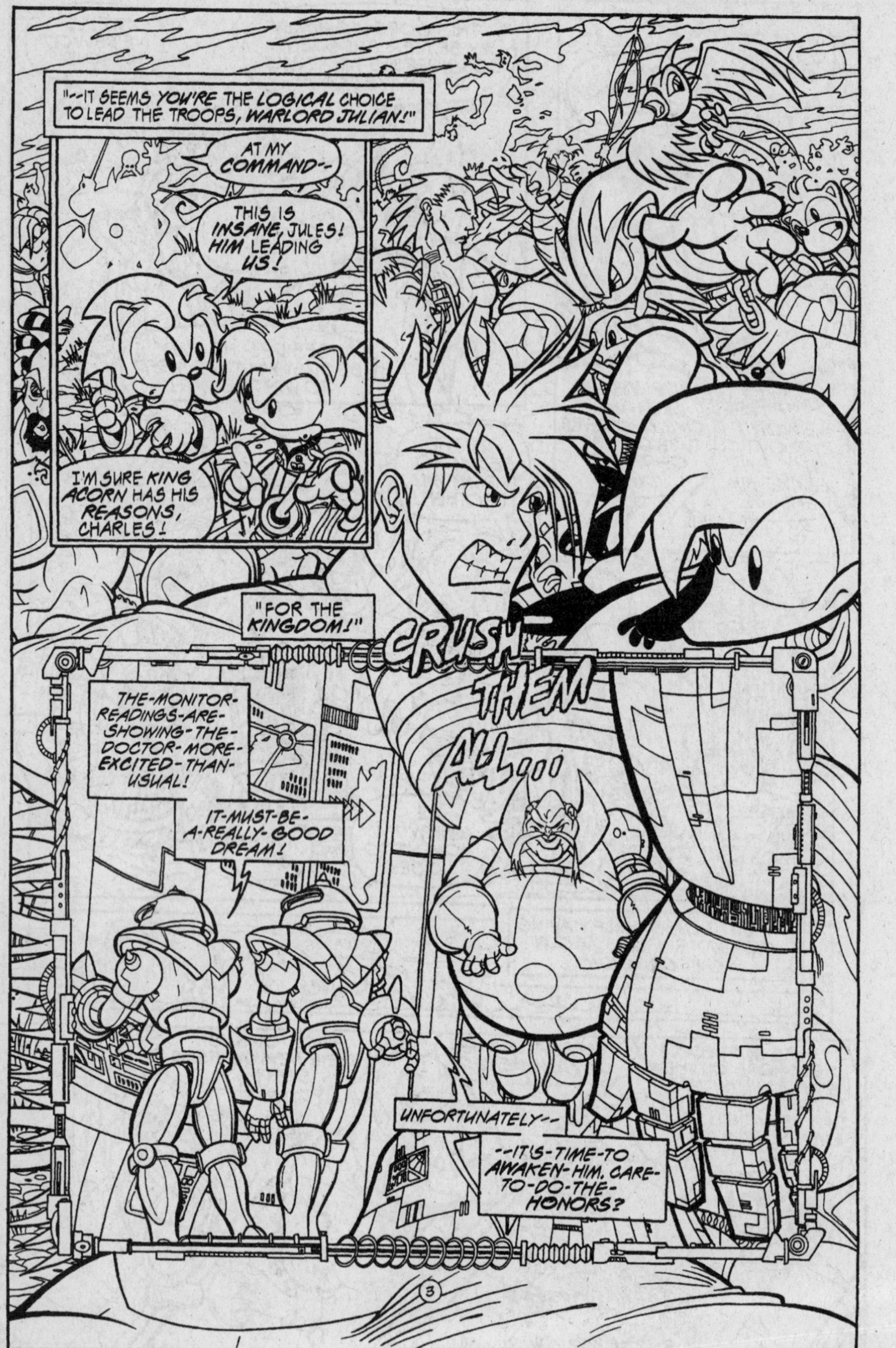
"--IT SEEMS YOU'RE THE LOGICAL CHOICE TO LEAD THE TROOPS, WARLORD JULIAN!"
AT MY COMMAND--
THIS IS INSANE, JULES! HIM LEADING US!
I'M SURE KING ACORN HAS HIS REASONS, CHARLES!
"FOR THE KINGDOM!"
CRUSH THEM ALL...
THE-MONITOR-READINGS-ARE-SHOWING-THE-DOCTOR-MORE-EXCITED-THAN-USUAL!
IT-MUST-BE-A-REALLY-GOOD DREAM!
UNFORTUNATELY--
--IT'S-TIME-TO AWAKEN-HIM. CARE-TO-DO-THE-HONORS?
3

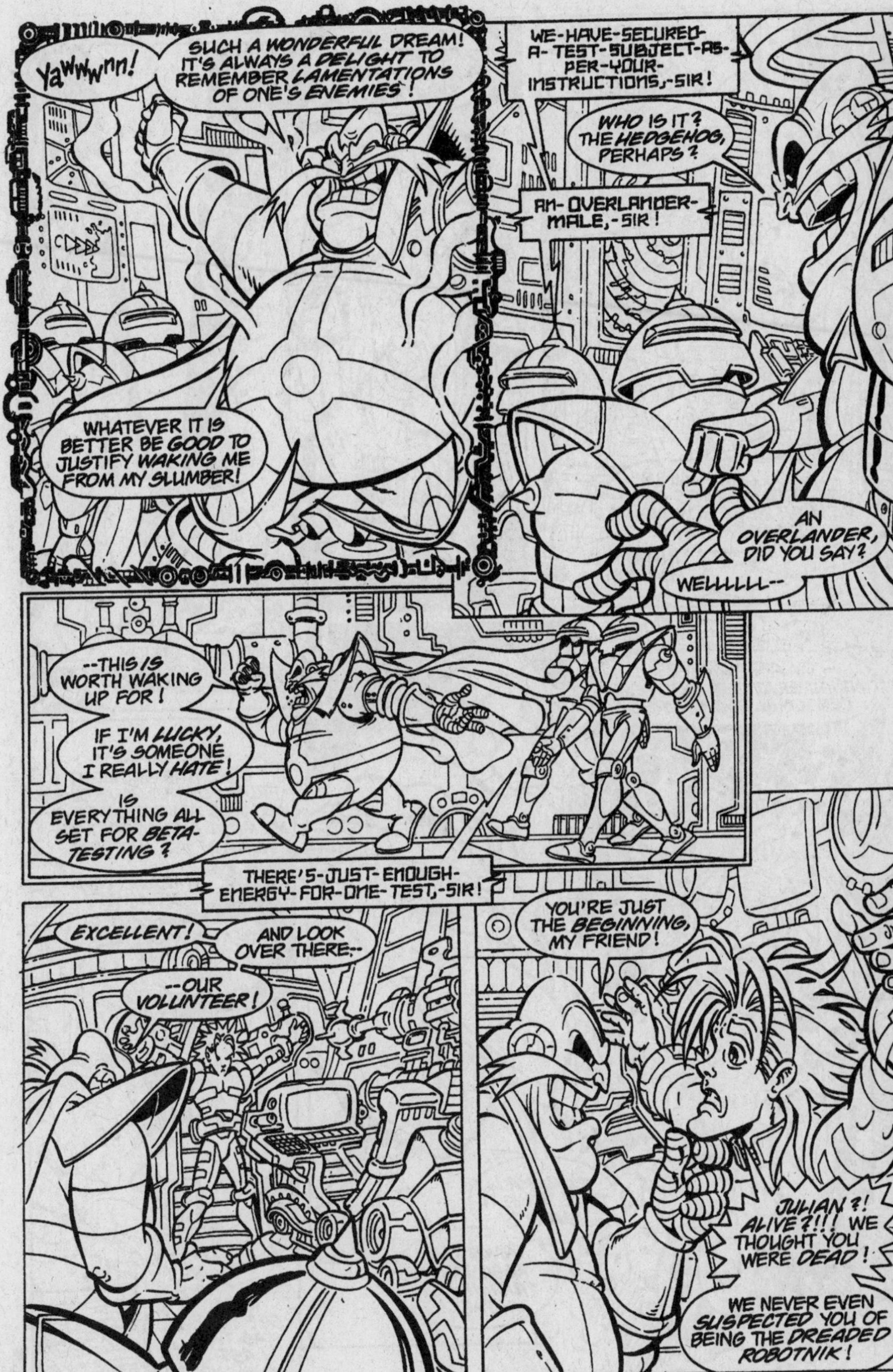
Yawwwwnn!
SUCH A WONDERFUL DREAM! IT'S ALWAYS A DELIGHT TO REMEMBER LAMENTATIONS OF ONE'S ENEMIES!
WHATEVER IT IS BETTER BE GOOD TO JUSTIFY WAKING ME FROM MY SLUMBER!
WE-HAVE-SECURED-A-TEST-SUBJECT-AS-PER-YOUR-INSTRUCTIONS,-SIR!
WHO IS IT? THE HEDGEHOG, PERHAPS?
AN-OVERLANDER-MALE,-SIR!
AN OVERLANDER, DID YOU SAY?
WELLLLLL--
--THIS IS WORTH WAKING UP FOR!
IF I'M LUCKY, IT'S SOMEONE I REALLY HATE!
IS EVERYTHING ALL SET FOR BETA-TESTING?
THERE'S-JUST-ENOUGH-ENERGY-FOR-ONE-TEST,-SIR!
EXCELLENT!
AND LOOK OVER THERE--
--OUR VOLUNTEER!
YOU'RE JUST THE BEGINNING, MY FRIEND!
JULIAN?! ALIVE?!!! WE THOUGHT YOU WERE DEAD!
WE NEVER EVEN SUSPECTED YOU OF BEING THE DREADED ROBOTNIK!

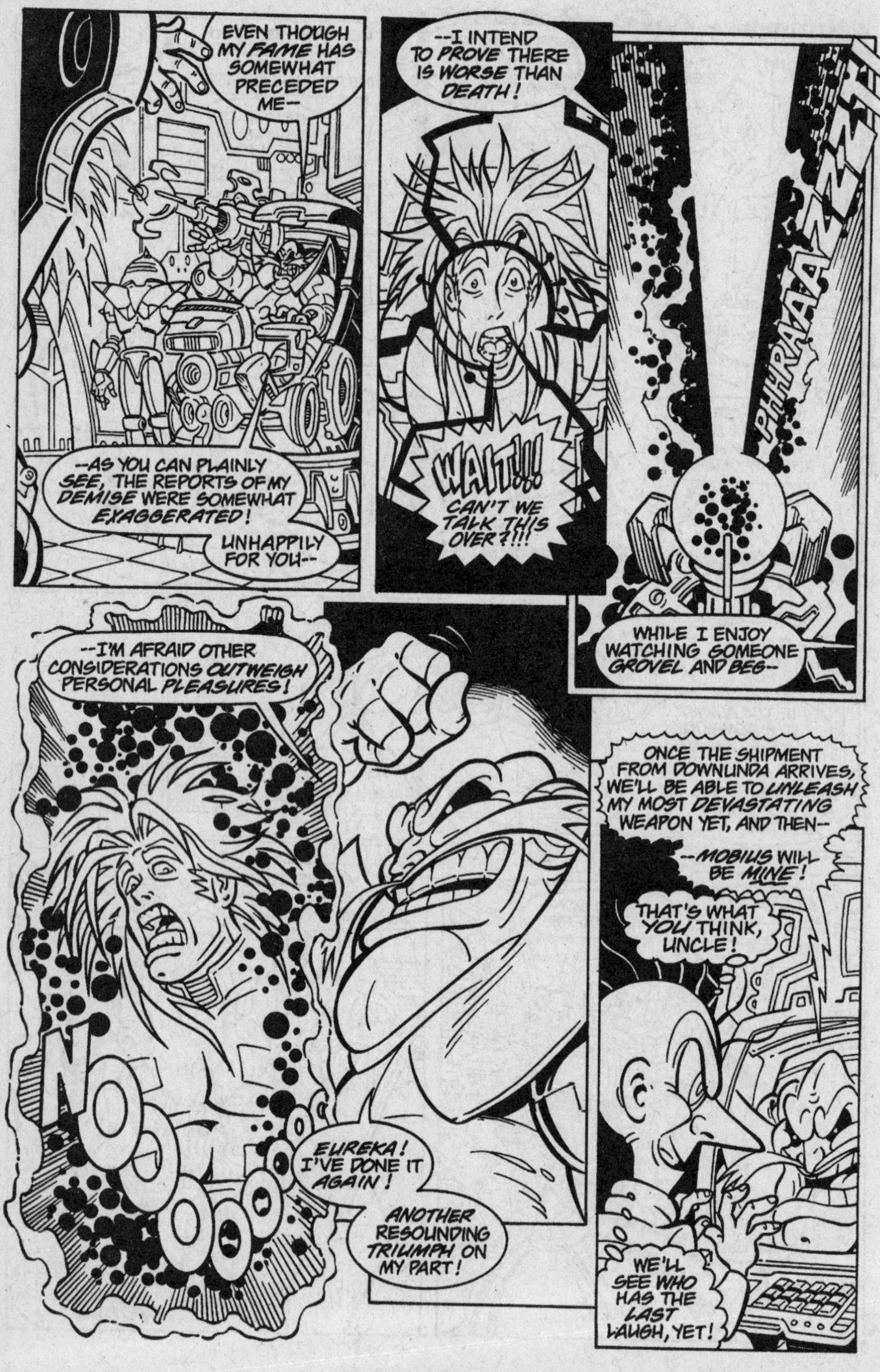
EVEN THOUGH MY FAME HAS SOMEWHAT PRECEDED ME--
--AS YOU CAN PLAINLY SEE, THE REPORTS OF MY DEMISE WERE SOMEWHAT EXAGGERATED!
UNHAPPILY FOR YOU--
--I INTEND TO PROVE THERE IS WORSE THAN DEATH!
WAIT!!! CAN'T WE TALK THIS OVER?!!!
PHRAAAAZZZT!!
WHILE I ENJOY WATCHING SOMEONE GROVEL AND BEG--
--I'M AFRAID OTHER CONSIDERATIONS OUTWEIGH PERSONAL PLEASURES!
NOOOOOOO
EUREKA! I'VE DONE IT AGAIN!
ANOTHER RESOUNDING TRIUMPH ON MY PART!
ONCE THE SHIPMENT FROM DOWNUNDA ARRIVES, WE'LL BE ABLE TO UNLEASH MY MOST DEVASTATING WEAPON YET, AND THEN--
--MOBIUS WILL BE MINE!
THAT'S WHAT YOU THINK, UNCLE!
WE'LL SEE WHO HAS THE LAST LAUGH, YET!

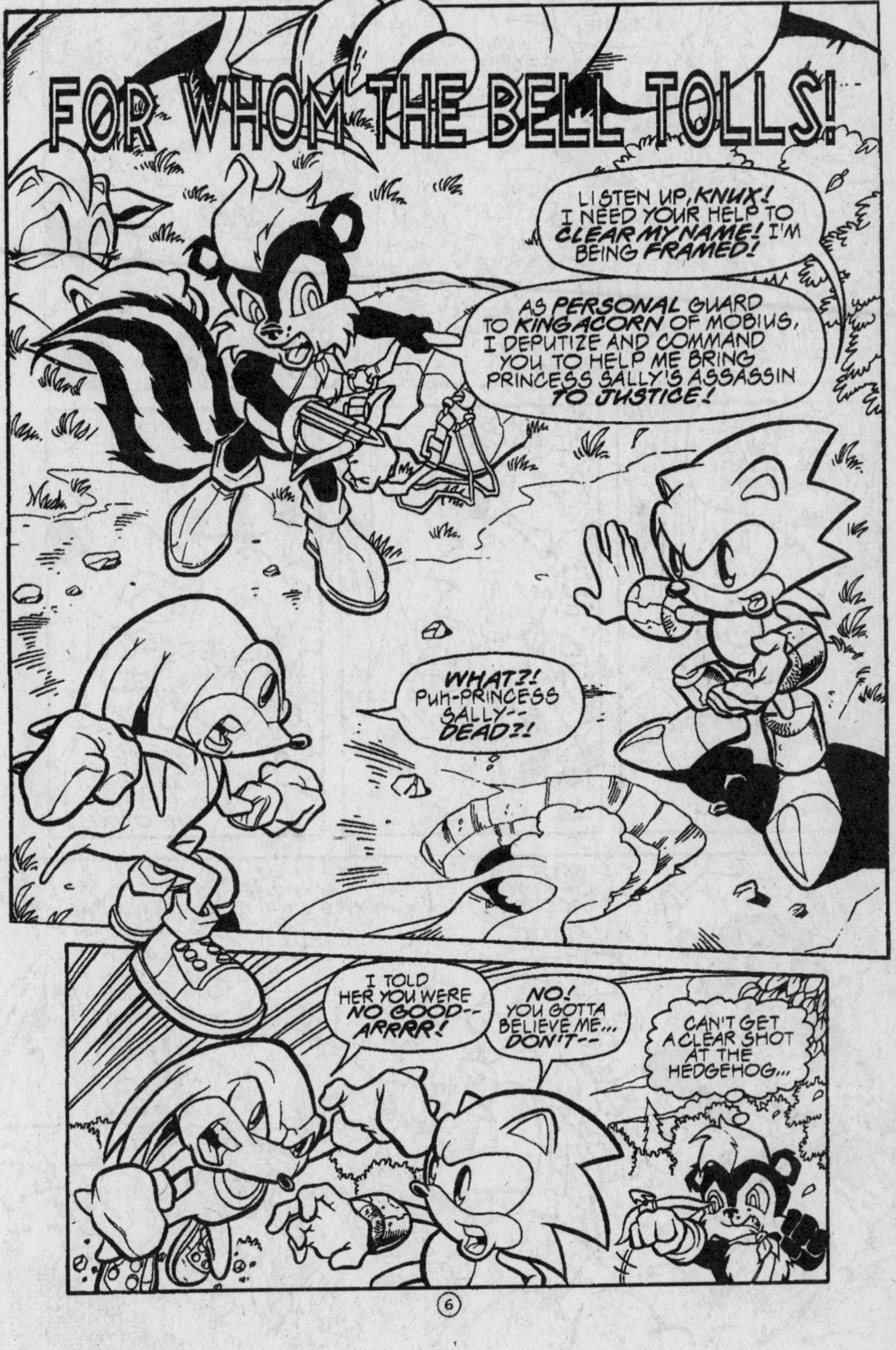
FOR WHOM THE BELL TOLLS!
LISTEN UP, KNUX! I NEED YOUR HELP TO CLEAR MY NAME! I'M BEING FRAMED!
AS PERSONAL GUARD TO KING ACORN OF MOBIUS, I DEPUTIZE AND COMMAND YOU TO HELP ME BRING PRINCESS SALLY'S ASSASSIN TO JUSTICE!
WHAT?! PUH-PRINCESS SALLY-- DEAD?!
I TOLD HER YOU WERE NO GOOD-- ARRRR!
NO! YOU GOTTA BELIEVE ME... DON'T--
CAN'T GET A CLEAR SHOT AT THE HEDGEHOG...
6

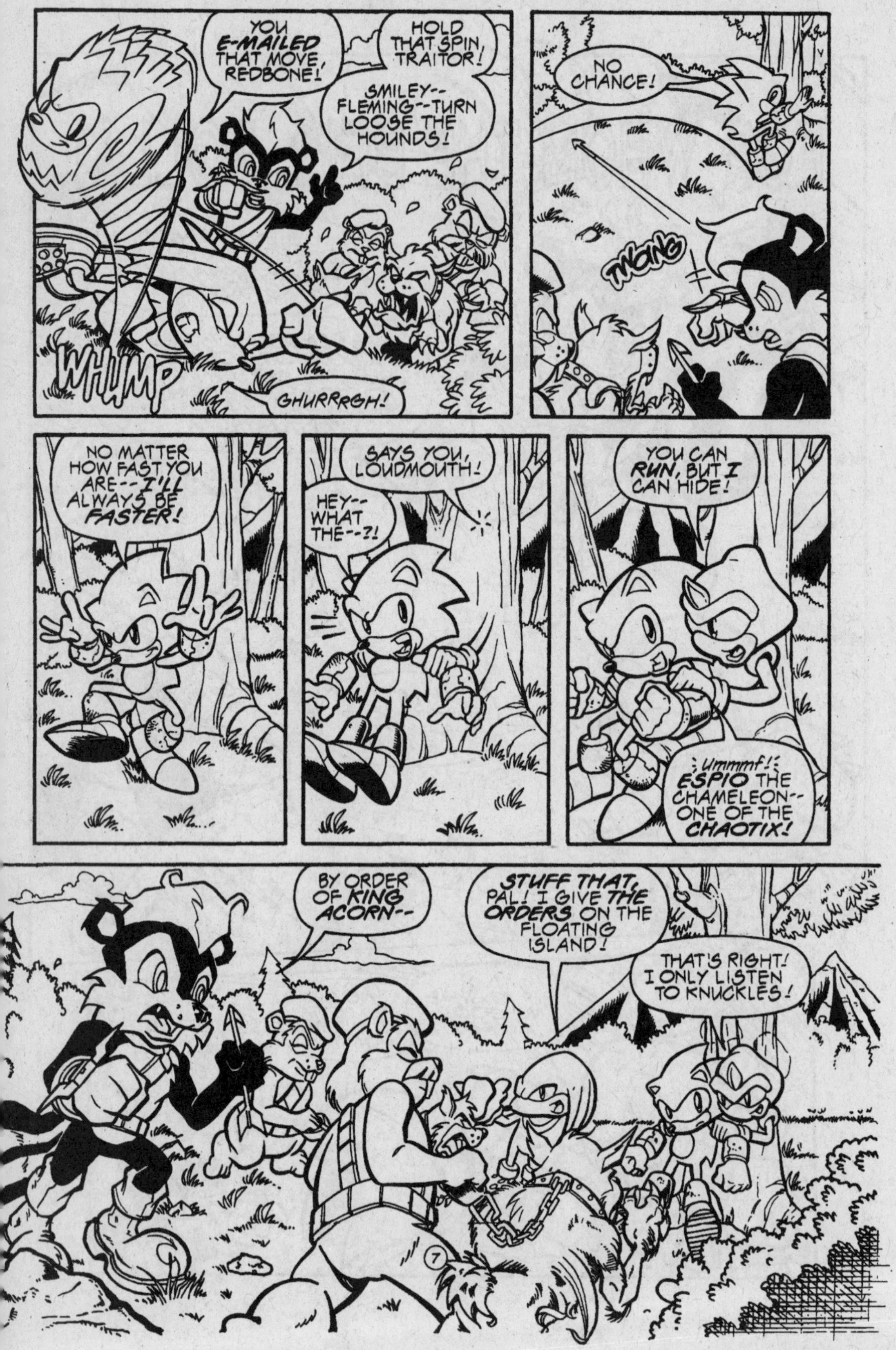
YOU E-MAILED THAT MOVE, REDBONE!
HOLD THAT SPIN, TRAITOR!
SMILEY--FLEMING--TURN LOOSE THE HOUNDS!
WHUMP
GHURRRGH!
NO CHANCE!
TWANG
NO MATTER HOW FAST YOU ARE--I'LL ALWAYS BE FASTER!
SAYS YOU, LOUDMOUTH!
HEY--WHAT THE--?!
YOU CAN RUN, BUT I CAN HIDE!
:UMMMF!: ESPIO THE CHAMELEON--ONE OF THE CHAOTIX!
BY ORDER OF KING ACORN--
STUFF THAT, PAL! I GIVE THE ORDERS ON THE FLOATING ISLAND!
THAT'S RIGHT! I ONLY LISTEN TO KNUCKLES!
7

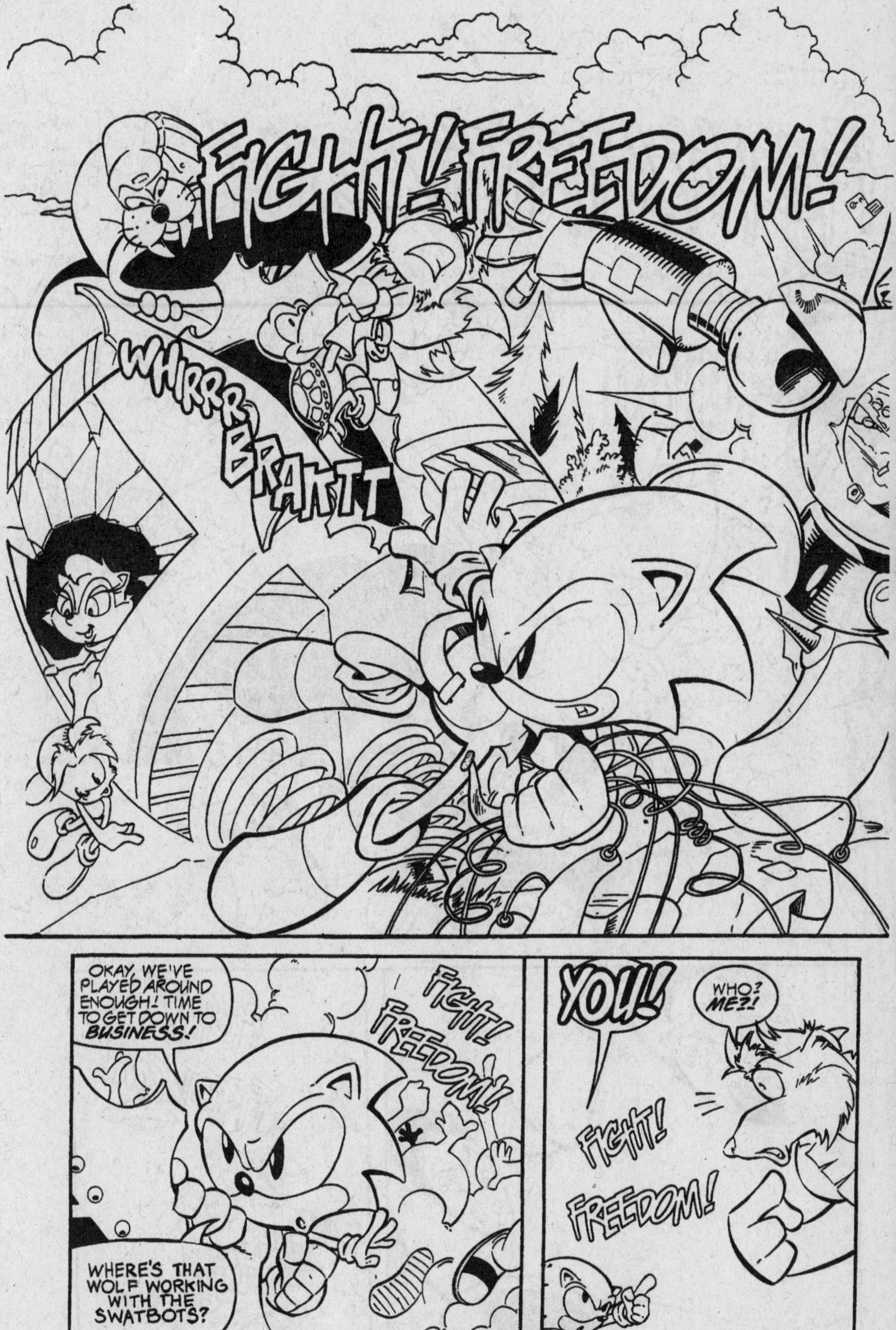
FIGHT! FREEDOM!
WHIRRR
BRATTT
OKAY, WE'VE PLAYED AROUND ENOUGH! TIME TO GET DOWN TO BUSINESS!
FIGHT! FREEDOM!
WHERE'S THAT WOLF WORKING WITH THE SWATBOTS?
YOU!
WHO? ME?!
FIGHT!
FREEDOM!

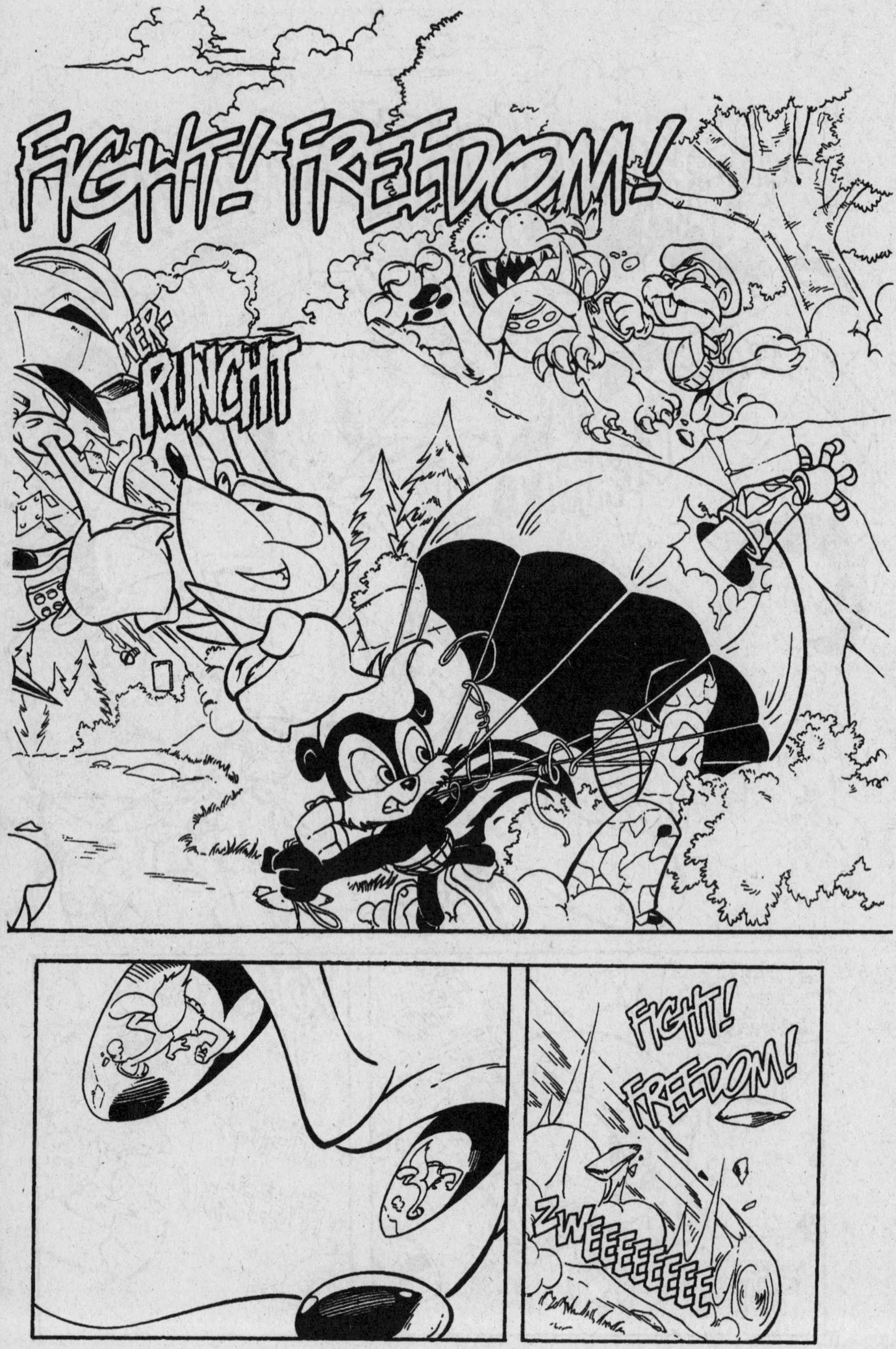
FIGHT! FREEDOM!
KER-RUNCHT
FIGHT! FREEDOM!
ZWEEEEEEEEE

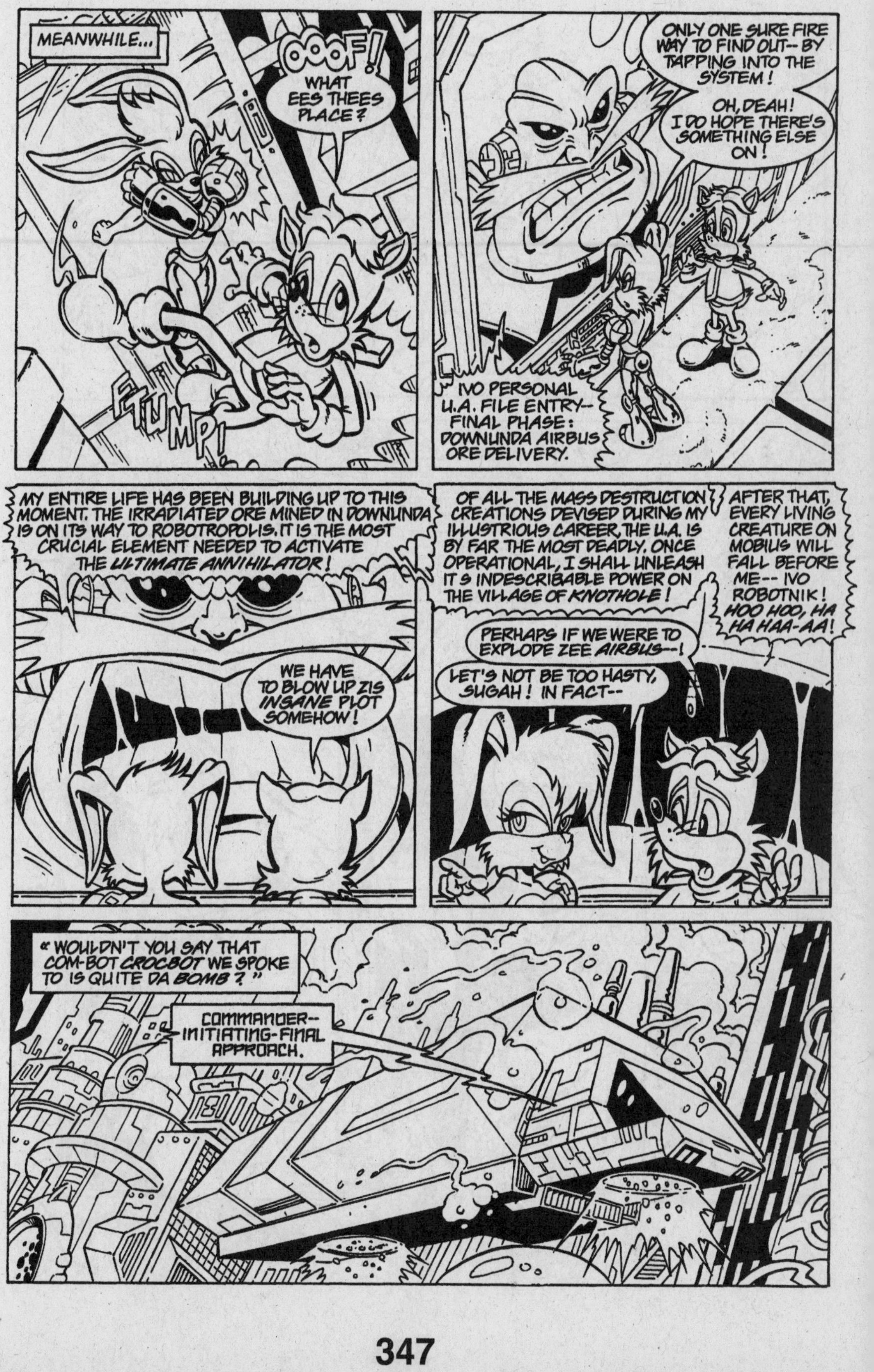
MEANWHILE...
OOOF!
WHAT EES THEES PLACE?
FTUMP!
ONLY ONE SURE FIRE WAY TO FIND OUT-- BY TAPPING INTO THE SYSTEM!
OH, DEAH! I DO HOPE THERE'S SOMETHING ELSE ON!
IVO PERSONAL U.A. FILE ENTRY-- FINAL PHASE: DOWNUNDA AIRBUS ORE DELIVERY.
MY ENTIRE LIFE HAS BEEN BUILDING UP TO THIS MOMENT. THE IRRADIATED ORE MINED IN DOWNUNDA IS ON ITS WAY TO ROBOTROPOLIS. IT IS THE MOST CRUCIAL ELEMENT NEEDED TO ACTIVATE THE ULTIMATE ANNIHILATOR!
WE HAVE TO BLOW UP ZIS INSANE PLOT SOMEHOW!
OF ALL THE MASS DESTRUCTION CREATIONS DEVISED DURING MY ILLUSTRIOUS CAREER, THE U.A. IS BY FAR THE MOST DEADLY. ONCE OPERATIONAL, I SHALL UNLEASH ITS INDESCRIBABLE POWER ON THE VILLAGE OF KNOTHOLE!
AFTER THAT, EVERY LIVING CREATURE ON MOBIUS WILL FALL BEFORE ME-- IVO ROBOTNIK! HOO HOO, HA HA HAA-AA!
PERHAPS IF WE WERE TO EXPLODE ZEE AIRBUS--!
LET'S NOT BE TOO HASTY, SUGAH! IN FACT--
« WOULDN'T YOU SAY THAT COM-BOT CROCBOT WE SPOKE TO IS QUITE DA BOMB? »
COMMANDER-- INITIATING-FINAL APPROACH.

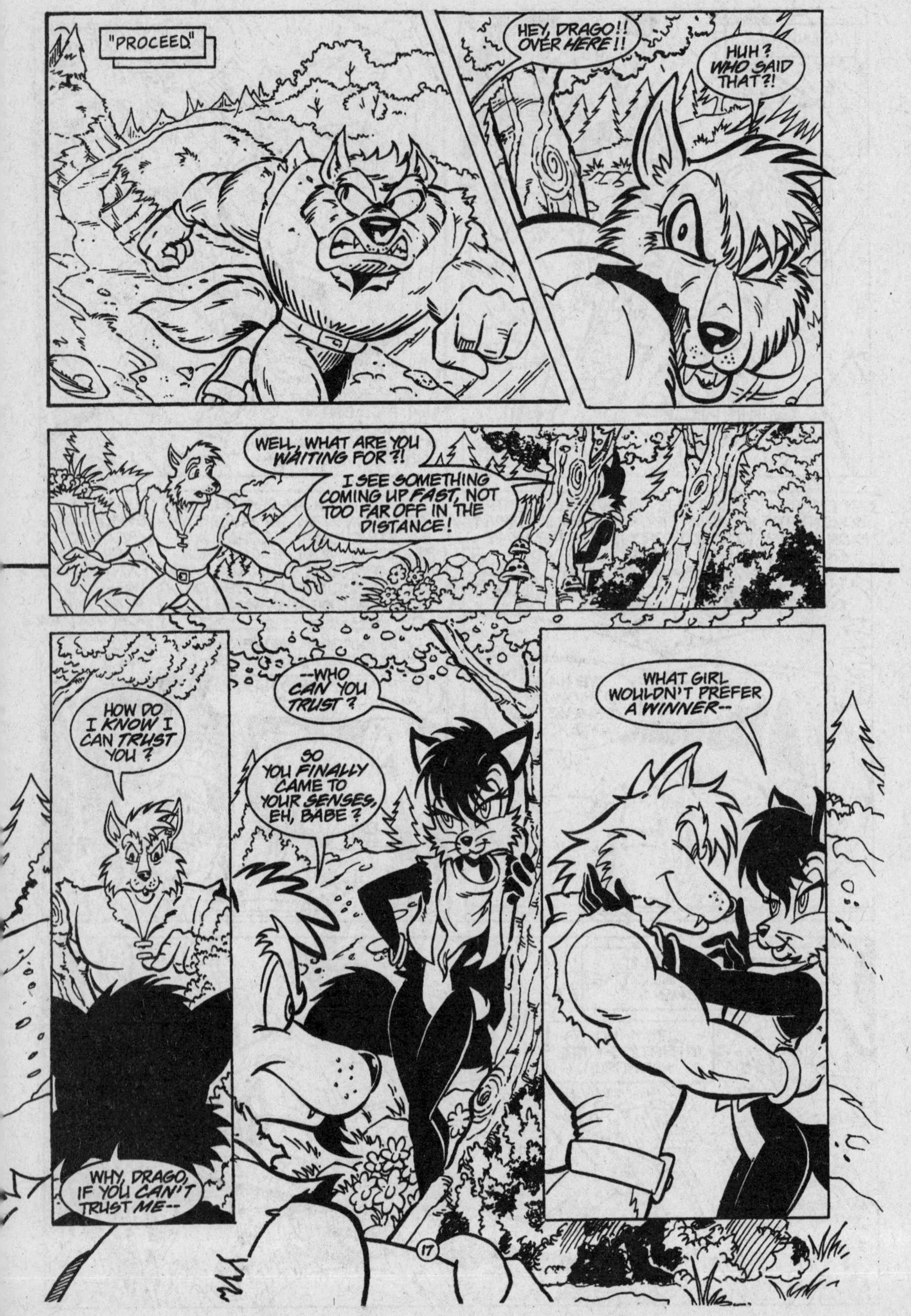
"PROCEED."
HEY, DRAGO!! OVER HERE!!
HUH? WHO SAID THAT?!
WELL, WHAT ARE YOU WAITING FOR?!
I SEE SOMETHING COMING UP FAST, NOT TOO FAR OFF IN THE DISTANCE!
HOW DO I KNOW I CAN TRUST YOU?
WHY, DRAGO, IF YOU CAN'T TRUST ME--
--WHO CAN YOU TRUST?
SO YOU FINALLY CAME TO YOUR SENSES, EH, BABE?
WHAT GIRL WOULDN'T PREFER A WINNER--
17

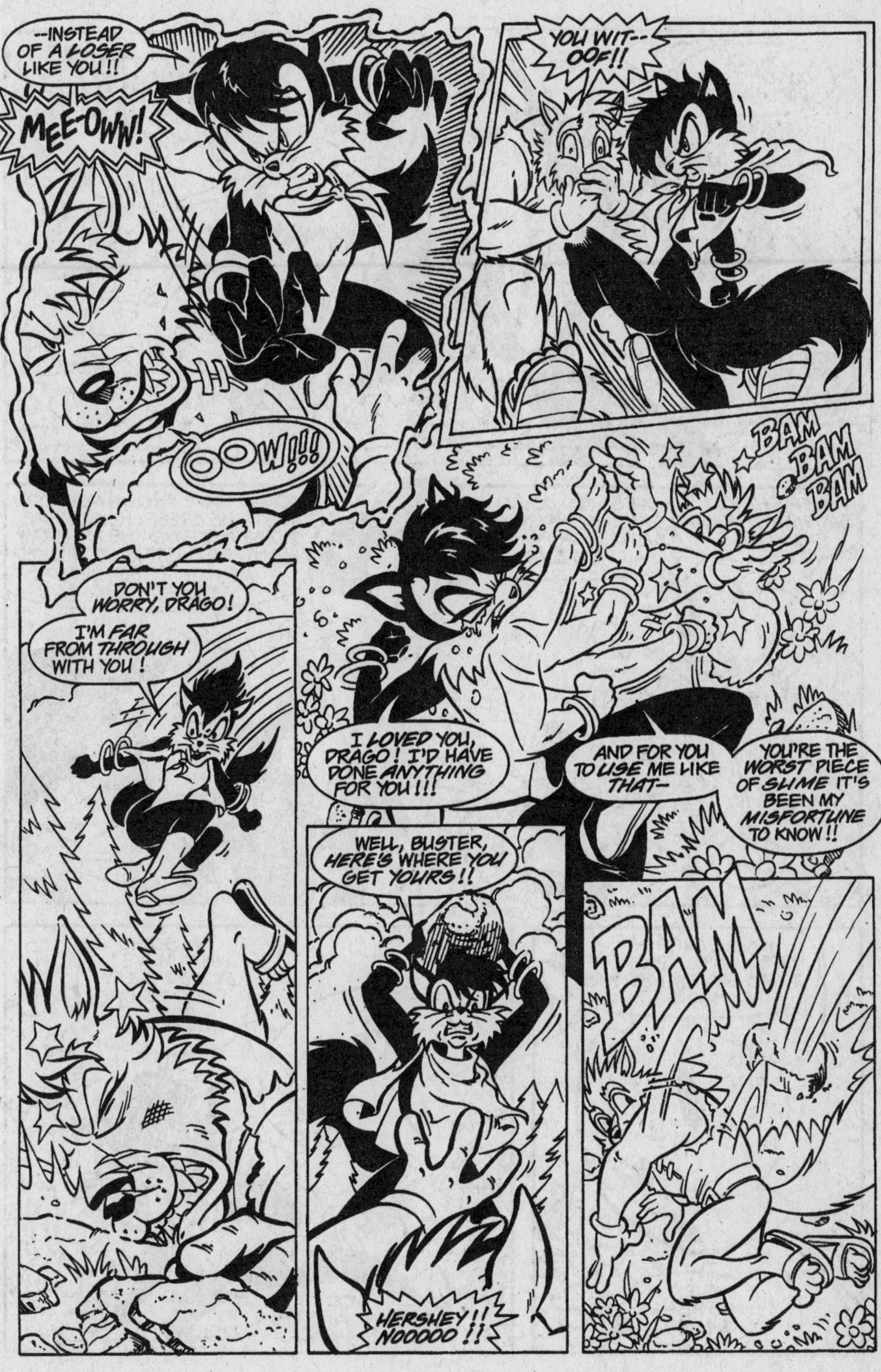
--INSTEAD OF A LOSER LIKE YOU!!
MEE-OWW!
OOW!!!
YOU WIT-- OOF!!
BAM BAM BAM
I LOVED YOU, DRAGO! I'D HAVE DONE ANYTHING FOR YOU!!!
AND FOR YOU TO USE ME LIKE THAT-
YOU'RE THE WORST PIECE OF SLIME IT'S BEEN MY MISFORTUNE TO KNOW!!
DON'T YOU WORRY, DRAGO!
I'M FAR FROM THROUGH WITH YOU!
WELL, BUSTER, HERE'S WHERE YOU GET YOURS!!
HERSHEY!! NOOOOO!!
BAM

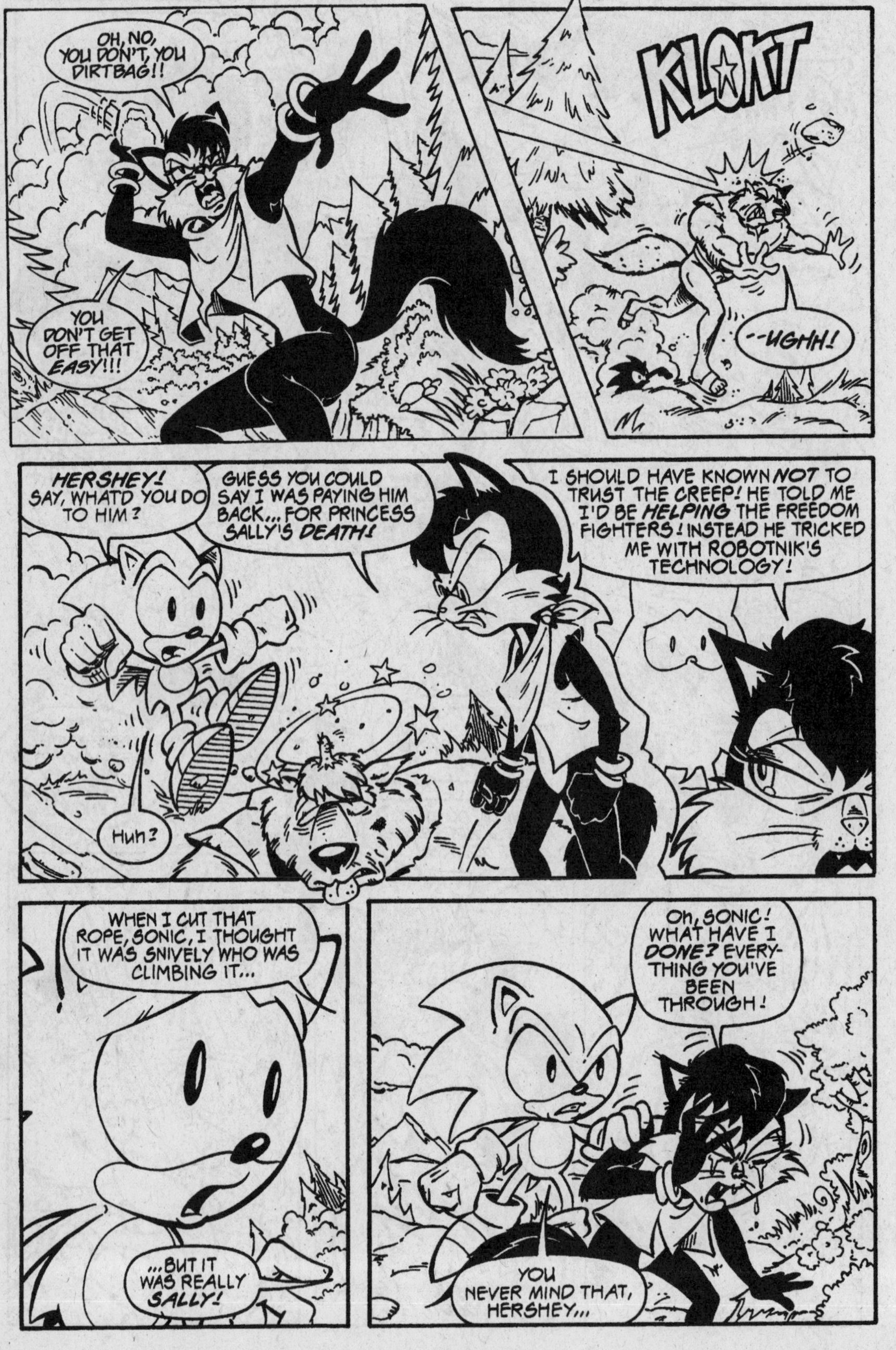
OH, NO, YOU DON'T, YOU DIRTBAG!!
YOU DON'T GET OFF THAT EASY!!!
KLOKT
--UGHH!
HERSHEY! SAY, WHAT'D YOU DO TO HIM?
GUESS YOU COULD SAY I WAS PAYING HIM BACK... FOR PRINCESS SALLY'S DEATH!
Huh?
I SHOULD HAVE KNOWN NOT TO TRUST THE CREEP! HE TOLD ME I'D BE HELPING THE FREEDOM FIGHTERS! INSTEAD HE TRICKED ME WITH ROBOTNIK'S TECHNOLOGY!
WHEN I CUT THAT ROPE, SONIC, I THOUGHT IT WAS SNIVELY WHO WAS CLIMBING IT...
...BUT IT WAS REALLY SALLY!
Oh, SONIC! WHAT HAVE I DONE? EVERYTHING YOU'VE BEEN THROUGH!
YOU NEVER MIND THAT, HERSHEY...

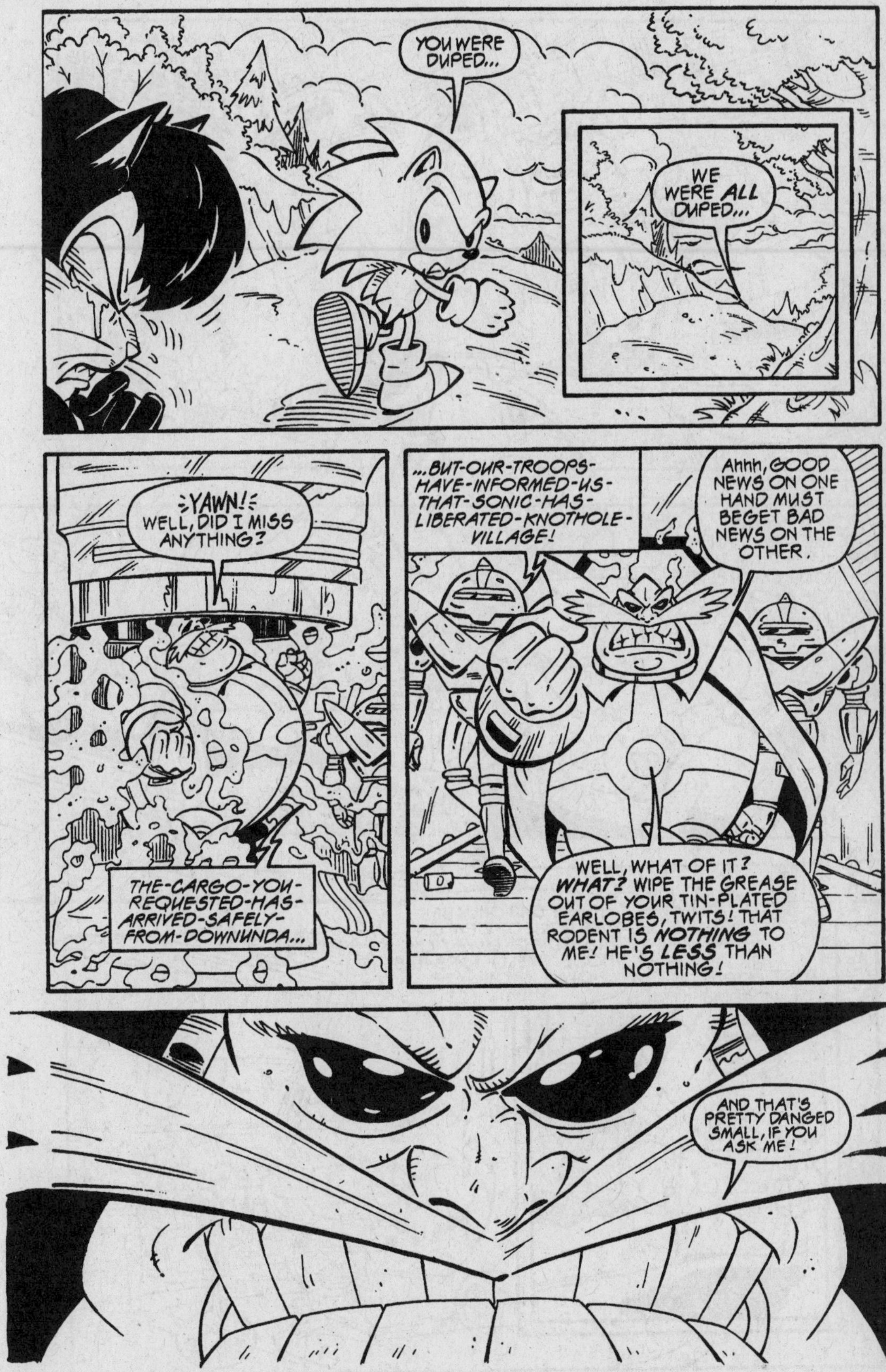
YOU WERE DUPED...
WE WERE ALL DUPED...
:YAWN!: WELL, DID I MISS ANYTHING?
THE-CARGO-YOU-REQUESTED-HAS-ARRIVED-SAFELY-FROM-DOWNUNDA...
...BUT-OUR-TROOPS-HAVE-INFORMED-US-THAT-SONIC-HAS-LIBERATED-KNOTHOLE-VILLAGE!
Ahhh, GOOD NEWS ON ONE HAND MUST BEGET BAD NEWS ON THE OTHER.
WELL, WHAT OF IT? WHAT? WIPE THE GREASE OUT OF YOUR TIN-PLATED EARLOBES, TWITS! THAT RODENT IS NOTHING TO ME! HE'S LESS THAN NOTHING!
AND THAT'S PRETTY DANGED SMALL, IF YOU ASK ME!

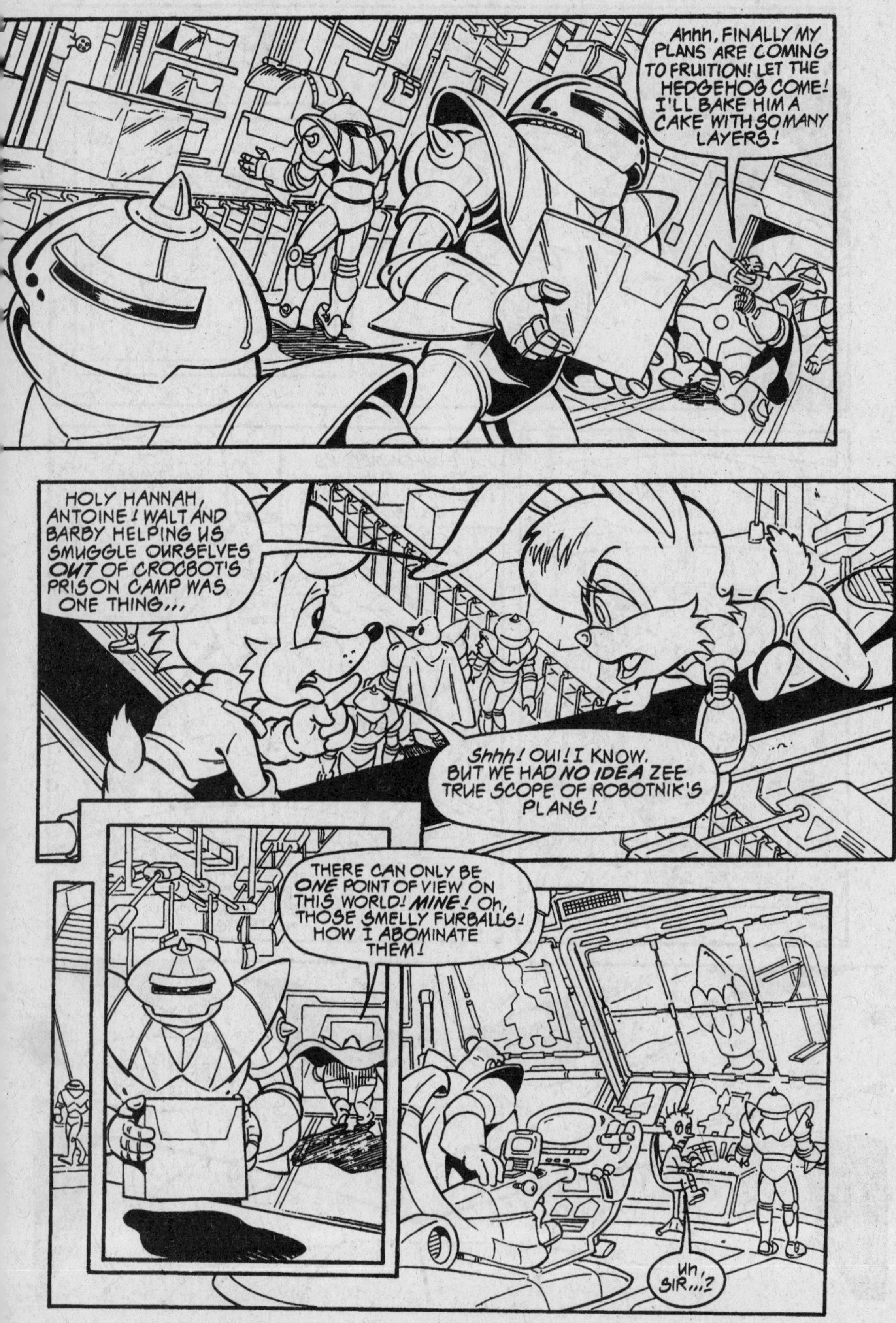

Ahhh, FINALLY MY PLANS ARE COMING TO FRUITION! LET THE HEDGEHOG COME! I'LL BAKE HIM A CAKE WITH SO MANY LAYERS!
HOLY HANNAH, ANTOINE! WALT AND BARBY HELPING US SMUGGLE OURSELVES OUT OF CROCBOT'S PRISON CAMP WAS ONE THING...
Shhh! OUI! I KNOW. BUT WE HAD NO IDEA ZEE TRUE SCOPE OF ROBOTNIK'S PLANS!
THERE CAN ONLY BE ONE POINT OF VIEW ON THIS WORLD! MINE! Oh, THOSE SMELLY FURBALLS! HOW I ABOMINATE THEM!
Uh, SIR...?

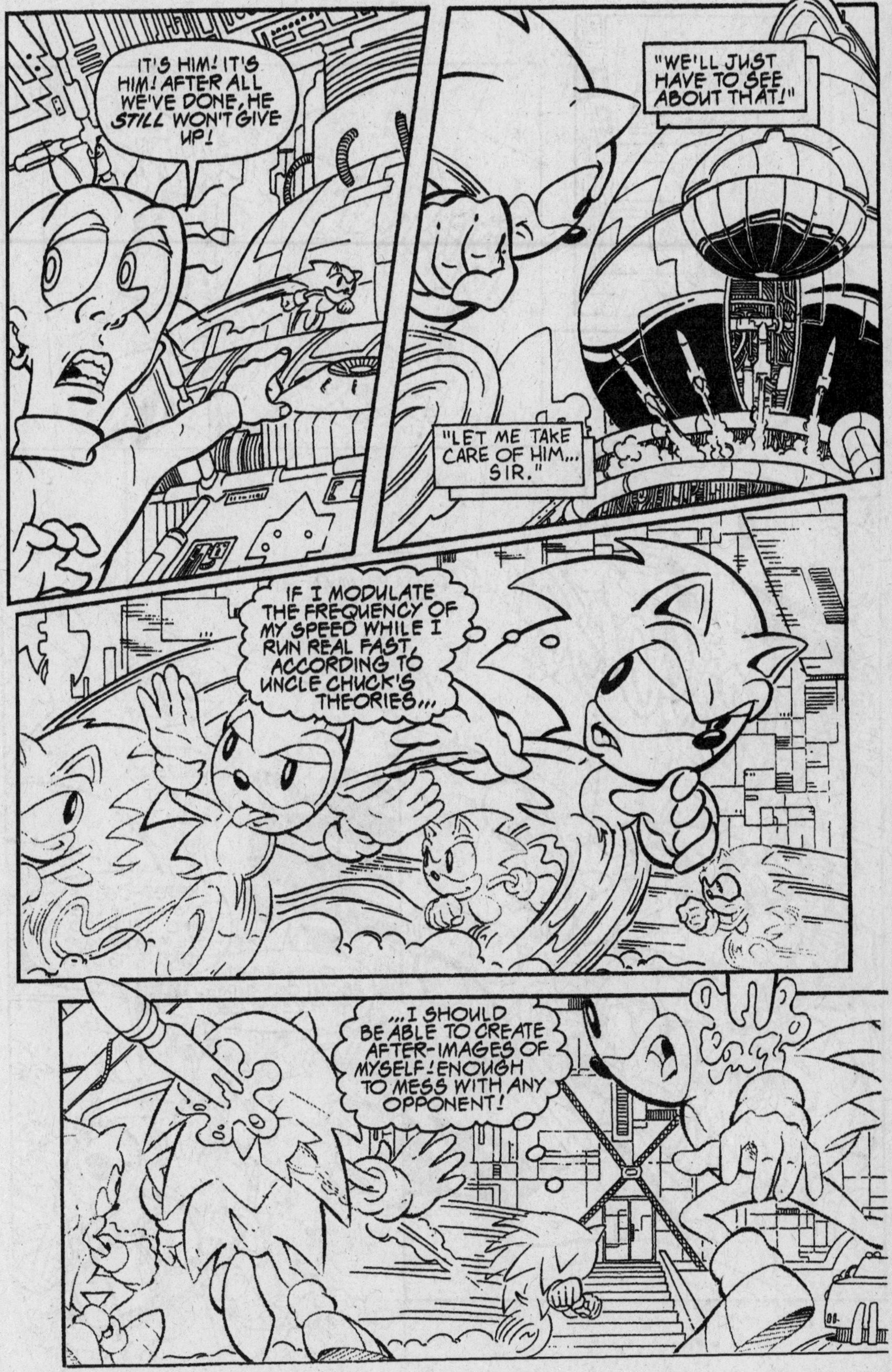
IT'S HIM! IT'S HIM! AFTER ALL WE'VE DONE, HE *STILL* WON'T GIVE UP!
"WE'LL JUST HAVE TO SEE ABOUT THAT!"
"LET ME TAKE CARE OF HIM... SIR."
IF I MODULATE THE FREQUENCY OF MY SPEED WHILE I RUN REAL FAST, ACCORDING TO UNCLE CHUCK'S THEORIES...
...I SHOULD BE ABLE TO CREATE AFTER-IMAGES OF MYSELF! ENOUGH TO MESS WITH ANY OPPONENT!

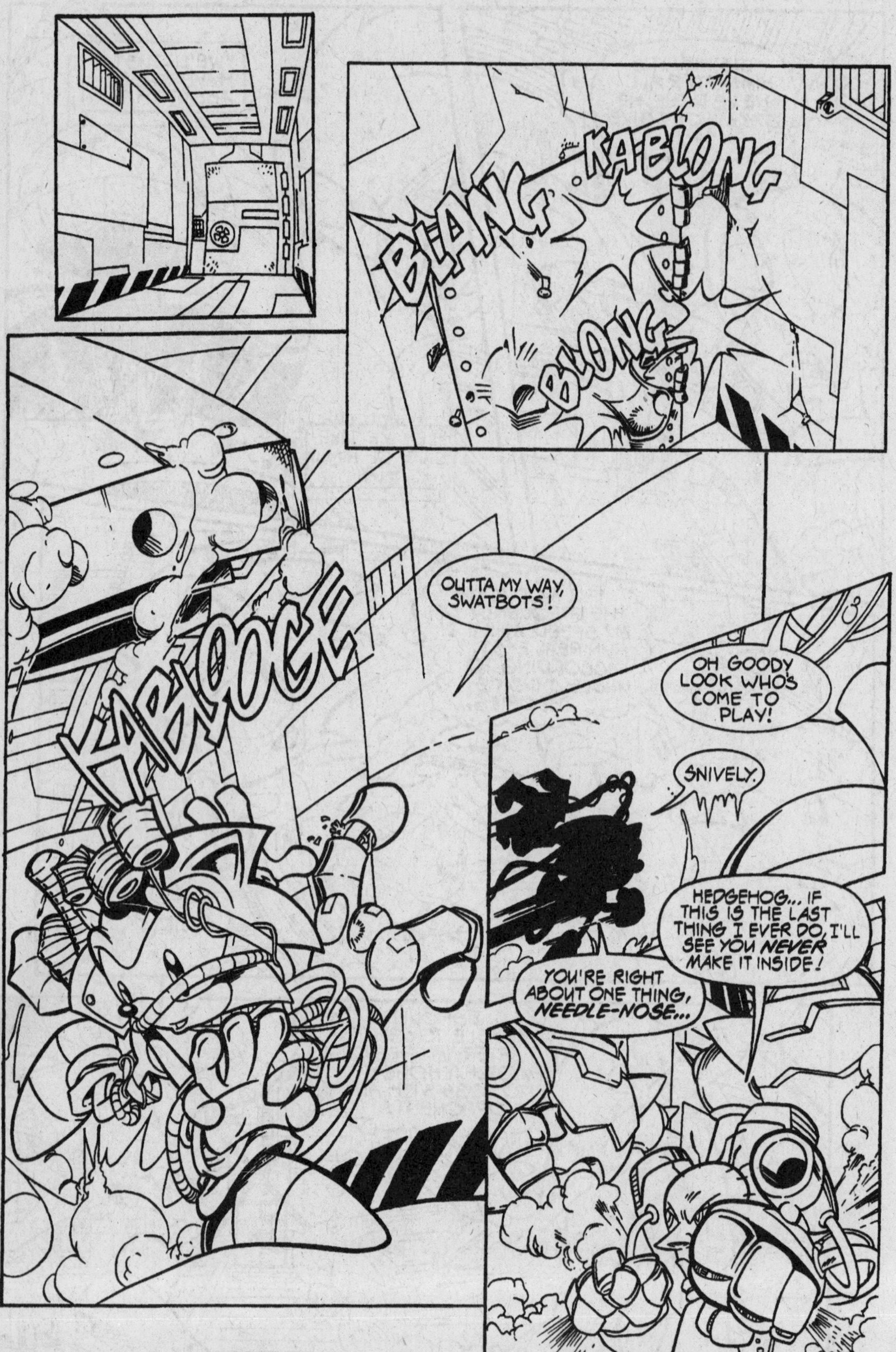
BLANG
KABLONG
BLONG
KABLOOCE
OUTTA MY WAY, SWATBOTS!
OH GOODY LOOK WHO'S COME TO PLAY!
SNIVELY.
HEDGEHOG... IF THIS IS THE LAST THING I EVER DO, I'LL SEE YOU *NEVER* MAKE IT INSIDE!
YOU'RE RIGHT ABOUT ONE THING, *NEEDLE-NOSE*...

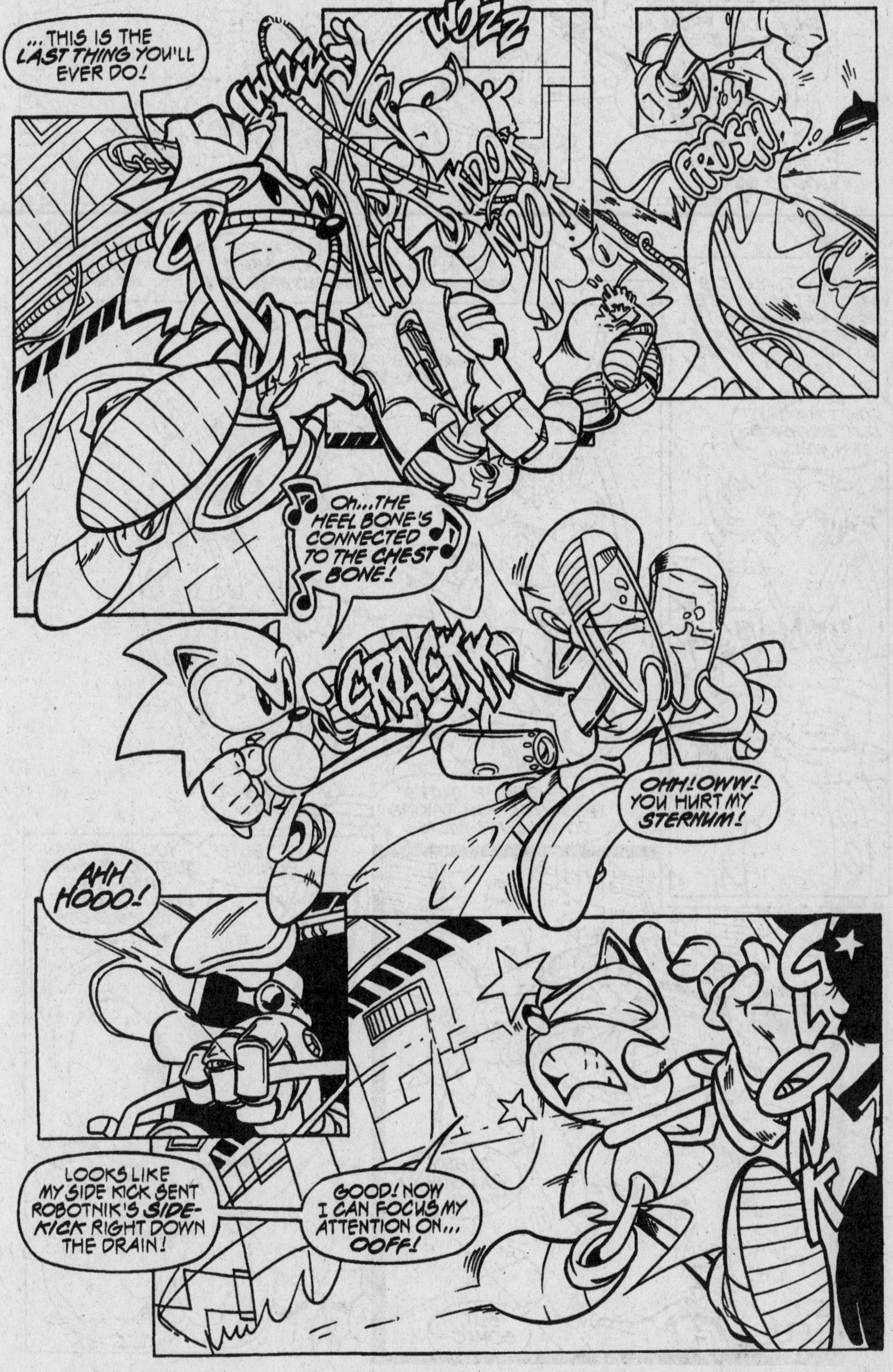

...THIS IS THE LAST THING YOU'LL EVER DO!
WIZZ
WOZZ
DOI DOI
FROSH!
Oh...THE HEEL BONE'S CONNECTED TO THE CHEST BONE!
CRACK
OHH! OWW! YOU HURT MY STERNUM!
AHH HOOO!
LOOKS LIKE MY SIDE KICK SENT ROBOTNIK'S SIDE-KICK RIGHT DOWN THE DRAIN!
GOOD! NOW I CAN FOCUS MY ATTENTION ON... OOFF!

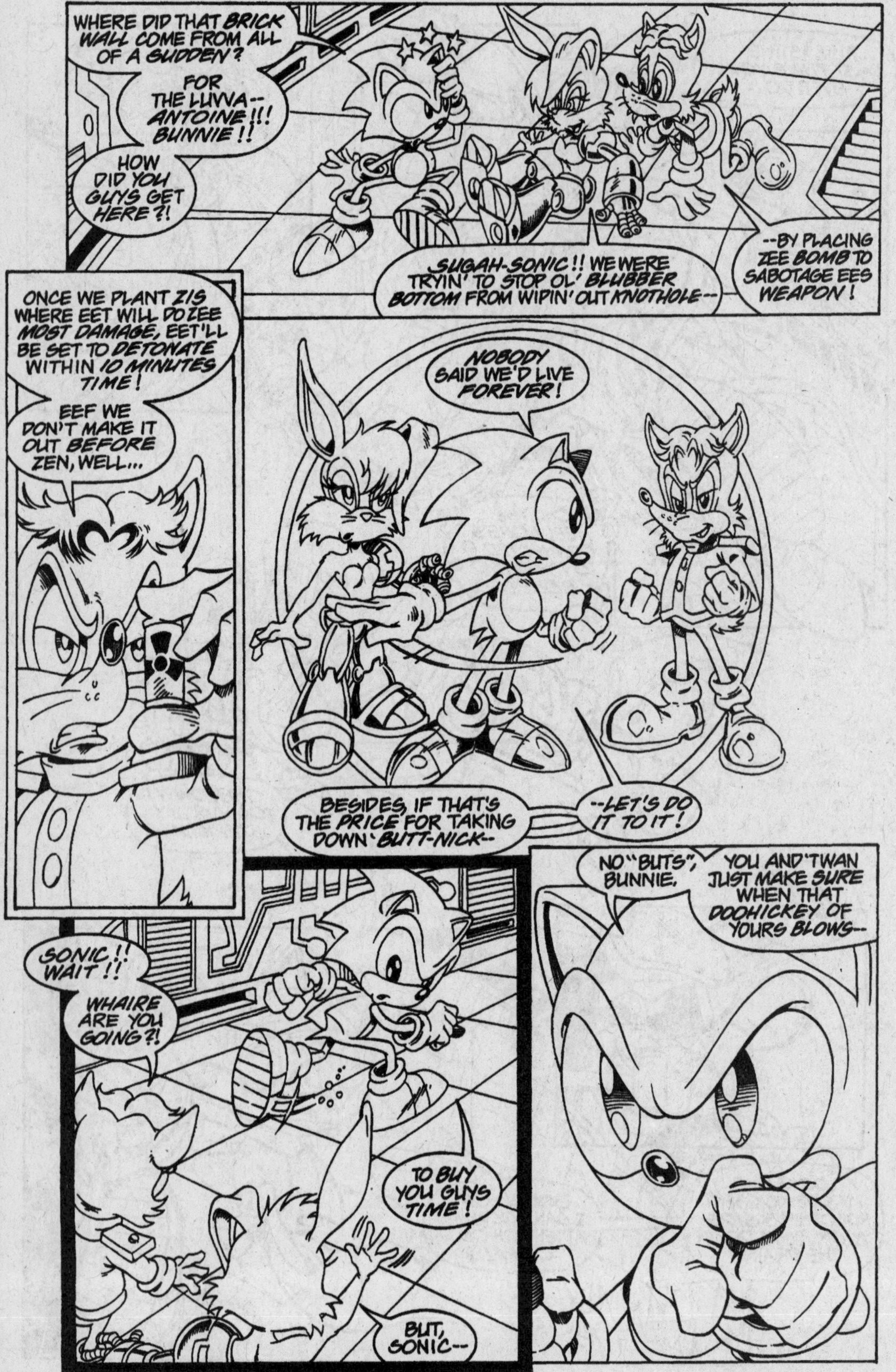
WHERE DID THAT BRICK WALL COME FROM ALL OF A SUDDEN?
FOR THE LUVVA-- ANTOINE!!! BUNNIE!!
HOW DID YOU GUYS GET HERE?!
SUGAH-SONIC!! WE WERE TRYIN' TO STOP OL' BLUBBER BOTTOM FROM WIPIN' OUT KNOTHOLE--
--BY PLACING ZEE BOMB TO SABOTAGE EES WEAPON!
ONCE WE PLANT ZIS WHERE EET WILL DO ZEE MOST DAMAGE, EET'LL BE SET TO DETONATE WITHIN 10 MINUTES TIME!
EEF WE DON'T MAKE IT OUT BEFORE ZEN, WELL...
NOBODY SAID WE'D LIVE FOREVER!
BESIDES, IF THAT'S THE PRICE FOR TAKING DOWN 'BUTT-NICK--
--LET'S DO IT TO IT!
SONIC!! WAIT!!
WHAIRE ARE YOU GOING?!
TO BUY YOU GUYS TIME!
BUT, SONIC--
NO "BUTS", BUNNIE.
YOU AND 'TWAN JUST MAKE SURE WHEN THAT DOOHICKEY OF YOURS BLOWS--

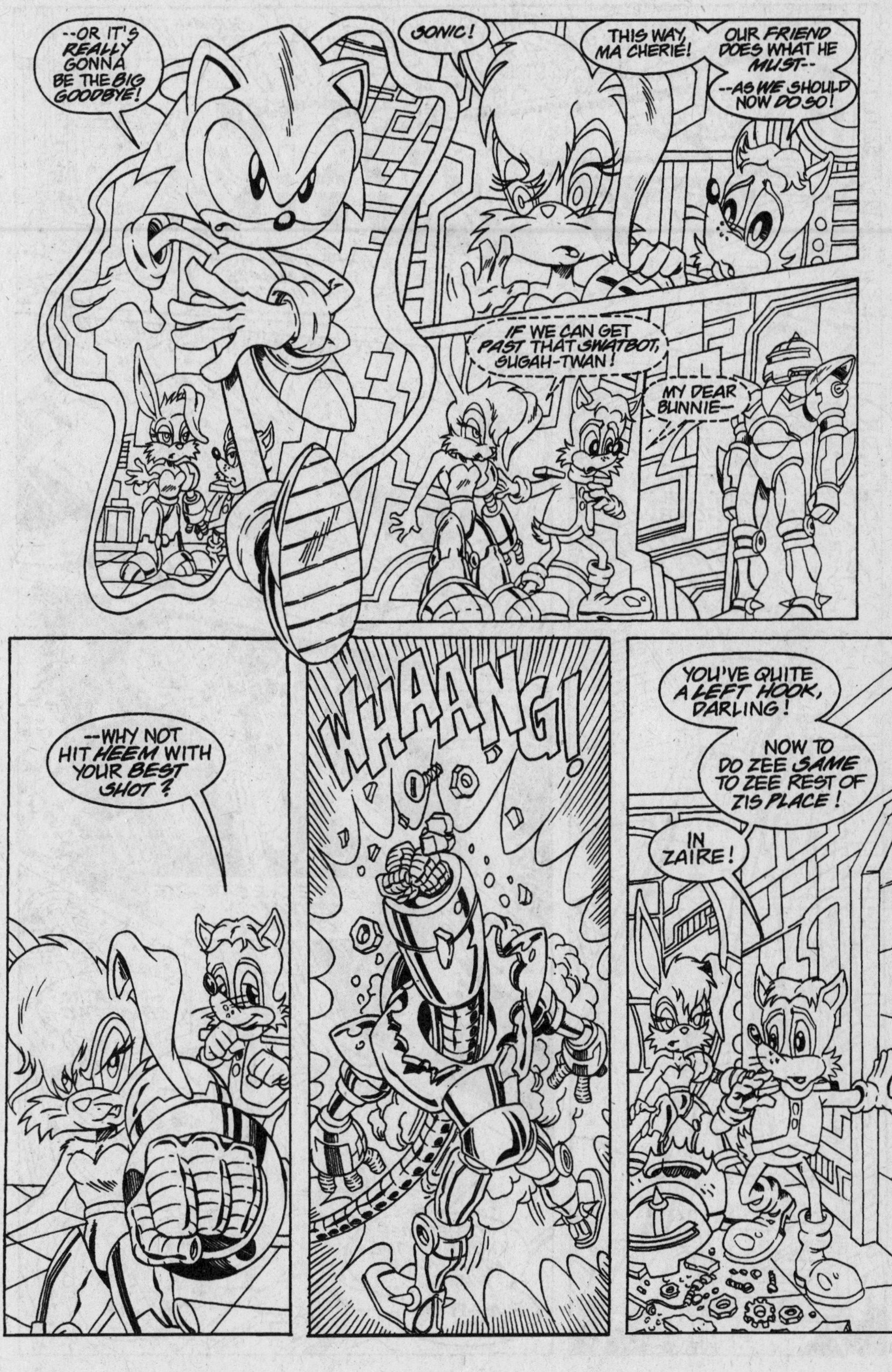
--OR IT'S REALLY GONNA BE THE BIG GOODBYE!
SONIC!
THIS WAY, MA CHERIE!
OUR FRIEND DOES WHAT HE MUST--
--AS WE SHOULD NOW DO SO!
IF WE CAN GET PAST THAT SWATBOT, SUGAH-TWAN!
MY DEAR BUNNIE--
--WHY NOT HIT HEEM WITH YOUR BEST SHOT?
WHAANG!
YOU'VE QUITE A LEFT HOOK, DARLING!
NOW TO DO ZEE SAME TO ZEE REST OF ZIS PLACE!
IN ZAIRE!

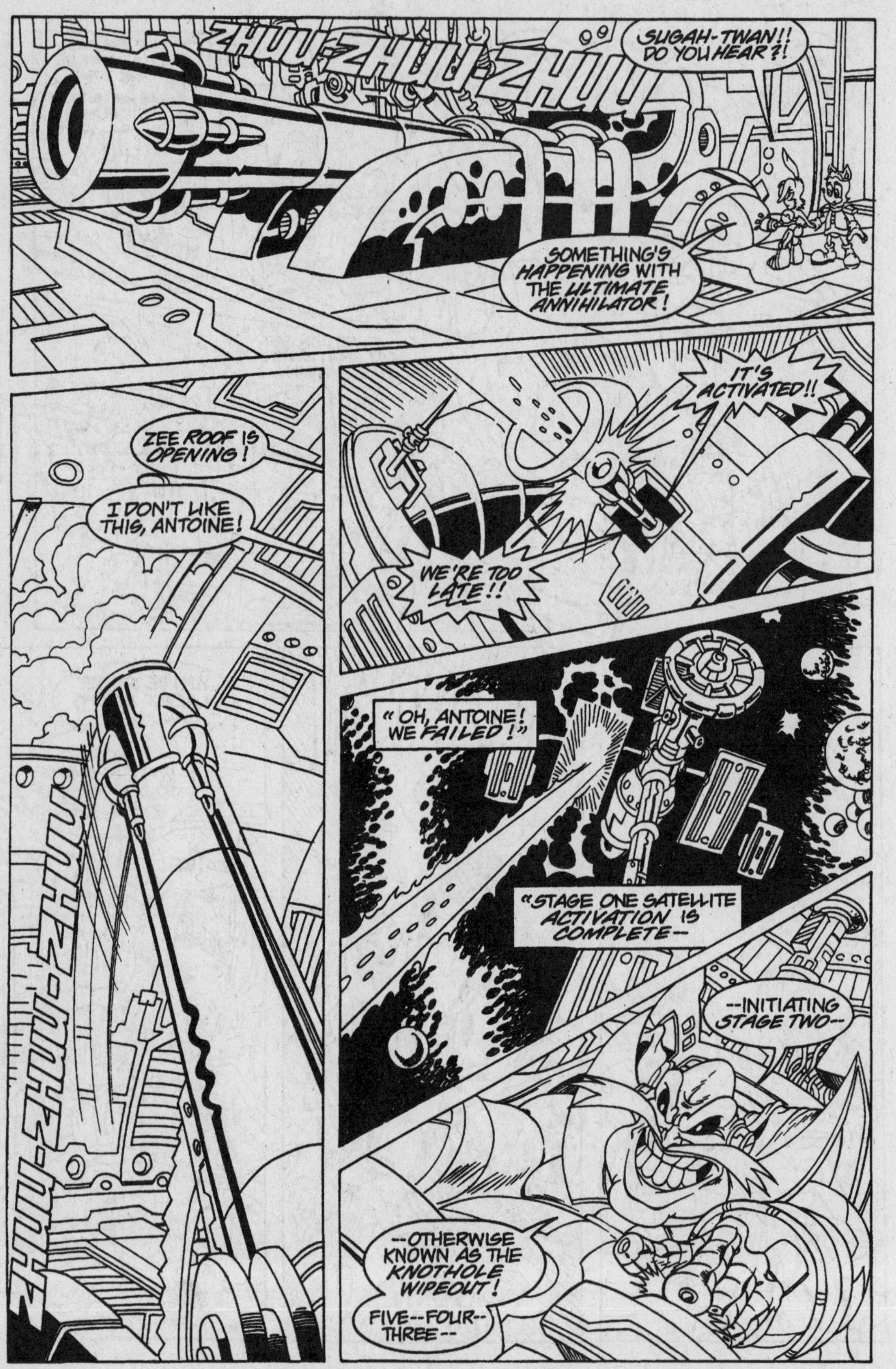
ZHUU-ZHUU-ZHUU-ZHUU
SUGAH-TWAN!! DO YOU HEAR?!
SOMETHING'S HAPPENING WITH THE ULTIMATE ANNIHILATOR!
ZEE ROOF IS OPENING!
I DON'T LIKE THIS, ANTOINE!
ZHUU-ZHUU-ZHUU-ZHUU
IT'S ACTIVATED!!
WE'RE TOO LATE!!
"OH, ANTOINE! WE FAILED!"
"STAGE ONE SATELLITE ACTIVATION IS COMPLETE--
--INITIATING STAGE TWO--
--OTHERWISE KNOWN AS THE KNOTHOLE WIPEOUT!
FIVE--FOUR--THREE--

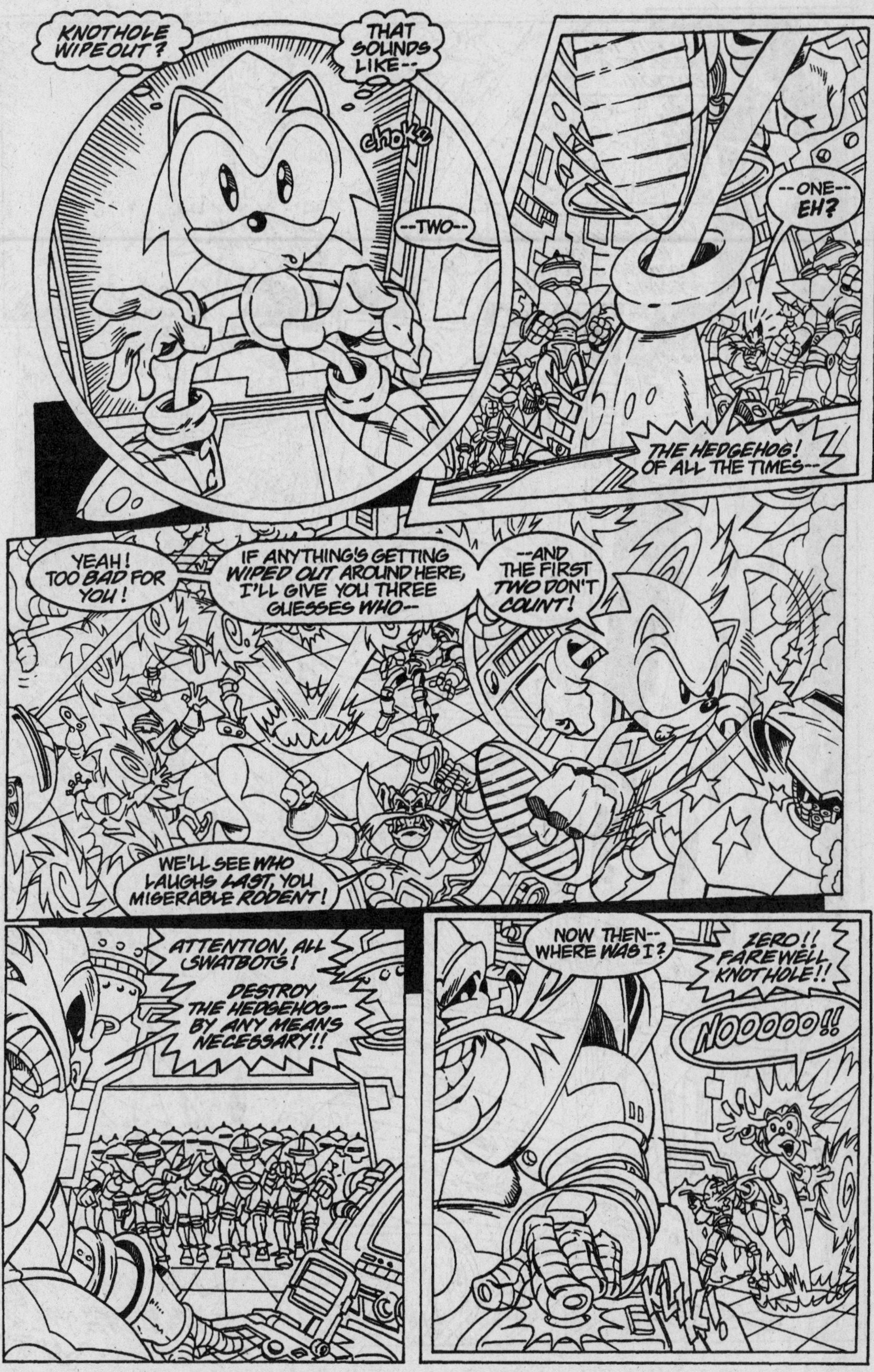

KNOTHOLE WIPE OUT?
THAT SOUNDS LIKE--
choke
--TWO--
--ONE-- EH?
THE HEDGEHOG! OF ALL THE TIMES--
YEAH! TOO BAD FOR YOU!
IF ANYTHING'S GETTING WIPED OUT AROUND HERE, I'LL GIVE YOU THREE GUESSES WHO--
--AND THE FIRST TWO DON'T COUNT!
WE'LL SEE WHO LAUGHS LAST, YOU MISERABLE RODENT!
ATTENTION, ALL SWATBOTS!
DESTROY THE HEDGEHOG-- BY ANY MEANS NECESSARY!!
NOW THEN-- WHERE WAS I?
ZERO!! FAREWELL KNOTHOLE!!
NOOOOO!!

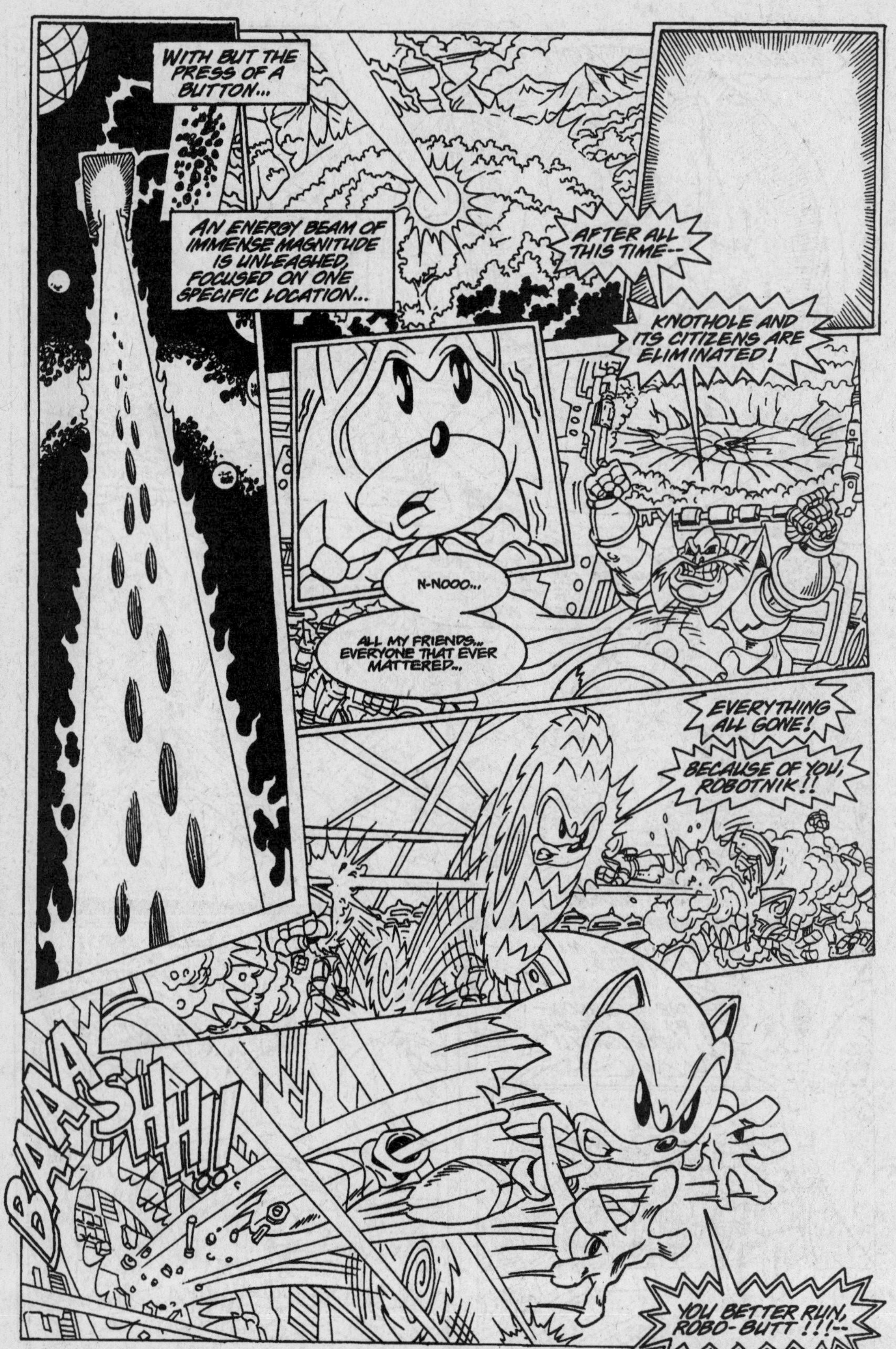
WITH BUT THE PRESS OF A BUTTON...
AN ENERGY BEAM OF IMMENSE MAGNITUDE IS UNLEASHED, FOCUSED ON ONE SPECIFIC LOCATION...
AFTER ALL THIS TIME--
KNOTHOLE AND ITS CITIZENS ARE ELIMINATED!
N-NOOO...
ALL MY FRIENDS... EVERYONE THAT EVER MATTERED...
EVERYTHING ALL GONE!
BECAUSE OF YOU, ROBOTNIK!!
BAASHH!
YOU BETTER RUN, ROBO-BUTT!!!--

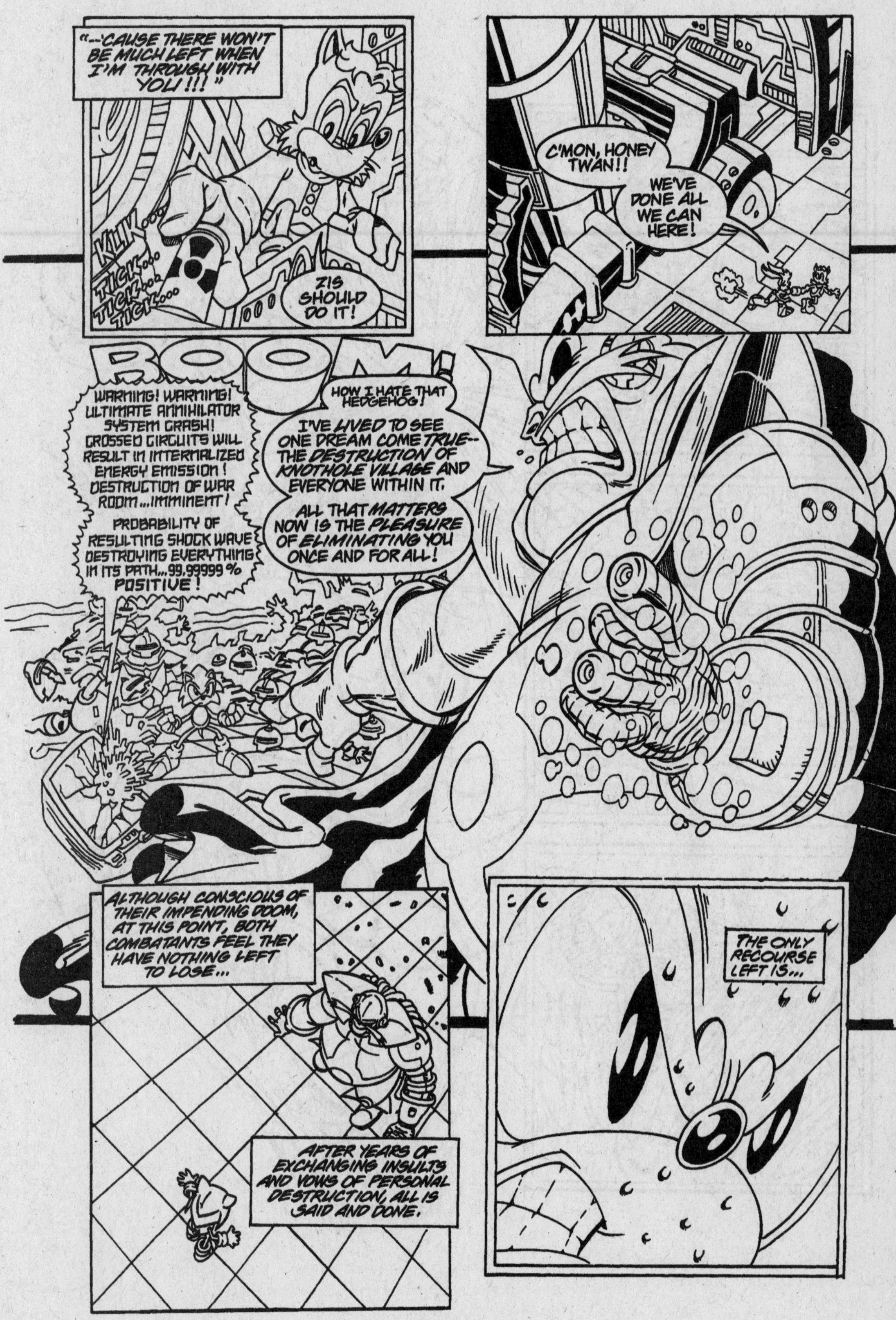
"—'CAUSE THERE WON'T BE MUCH LEFT WHEN I'M THROUGH WITH YOU!!!"
KLIK...
TICK...
TICK...
TICK...
ZIS SHOULD DO IT!
C'MON, HONEY TWAN!!
WE'VE DONE ALL WE CAN HERE!
BOOM!
WARNING! WARNING! ULTIMATE ANNIHILATOR SYSTEM CRASH! CROSSED CIRCUITS WILL RESULT IN INTERNALIZED ENERGY EMISSION! DESTRUCTION OF WAR ROOM...IMMINENT!
PROBABILITY OF RESULTING SHOCK WAVE DESTROYING EVERYTHING IN ITS PATH...99.99999 % POSITIVE!
HOW I HATE THAT HEDGEHOG!
I'VE LIVED TO SEE ONE DREAM COME TRUE-- THE DESTRUCTION OF KNOTHOLE VILLAGE AND EVERYONE WITHIN IT.
ALL THAT MATTERS NOW IS THE PLEASURE OF ELIMINATING YOU ONCE AND FOR ALL!
ALTHOUGH CONSCIOUS OF THEIR IMPENDING DOOM, AT THIS POINT, BOTH COMBATANTS FEEL THEY HAVE NOTHING LEFT TO LOSE...
AFTER YEARS OF EXCHANGING INSULTS AND VOWS OF PERSONAL DESTRUCTION, ALL IS SAID AND DONE.
THE ONLY RECOURSE LEFT IS...

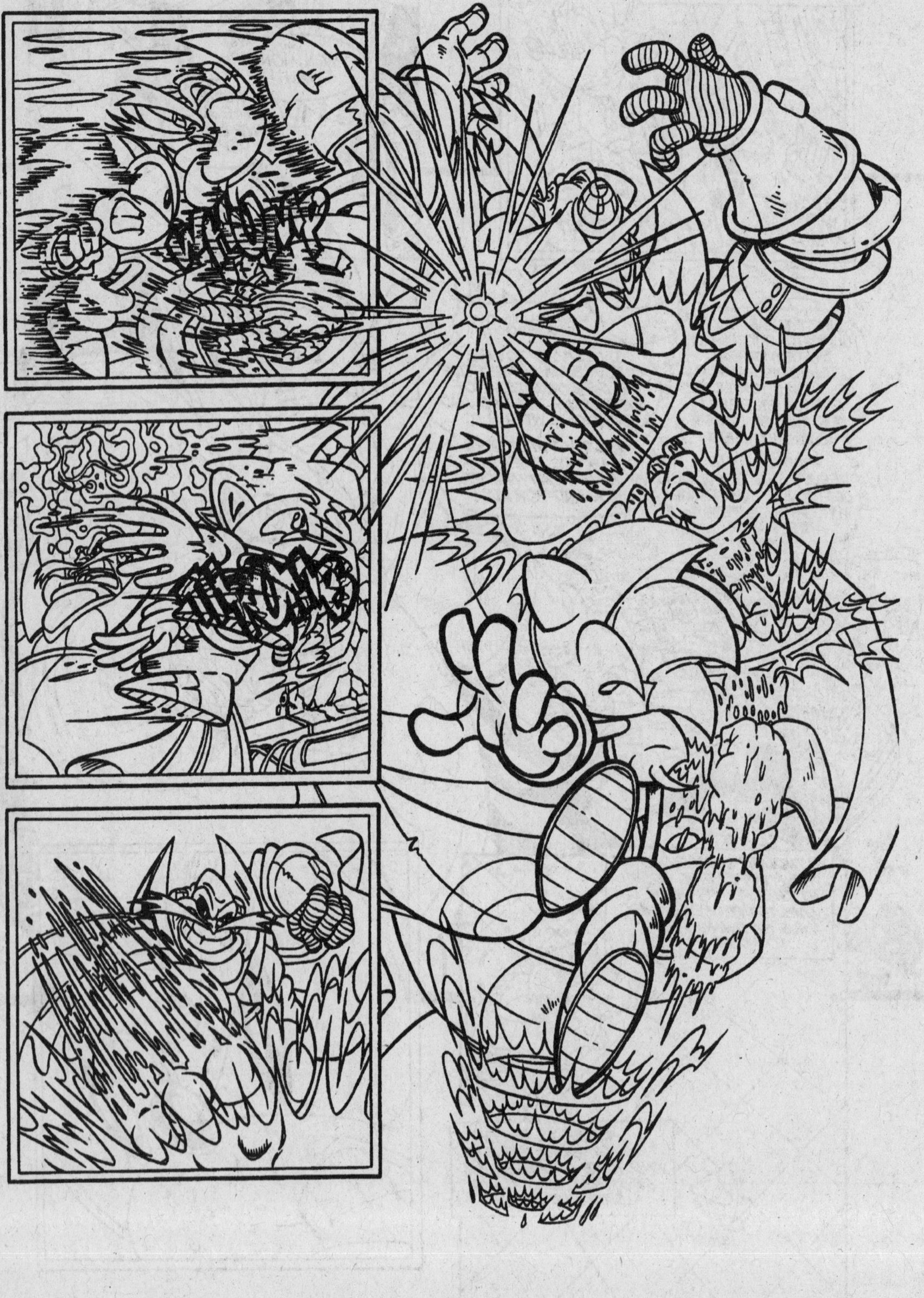

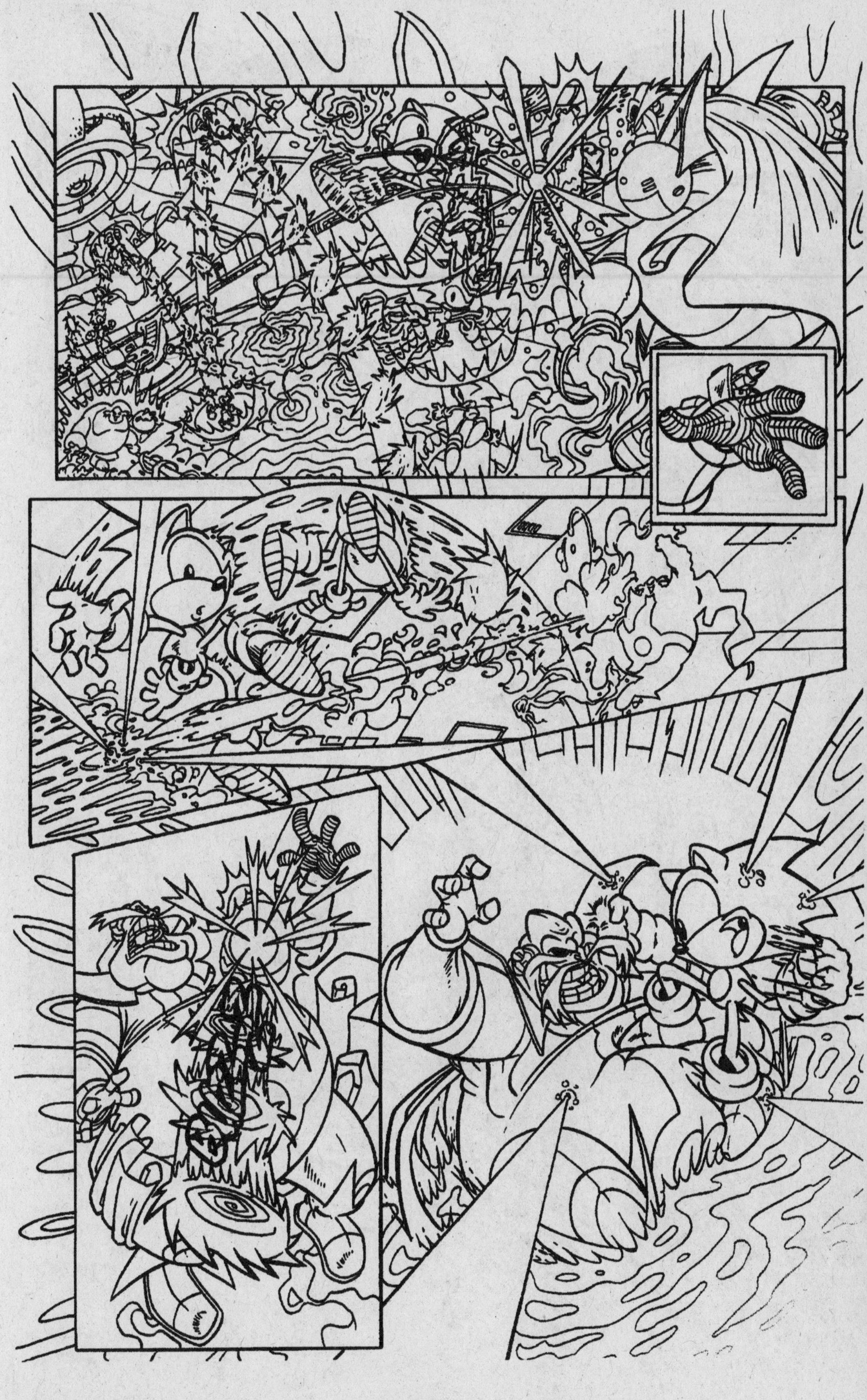

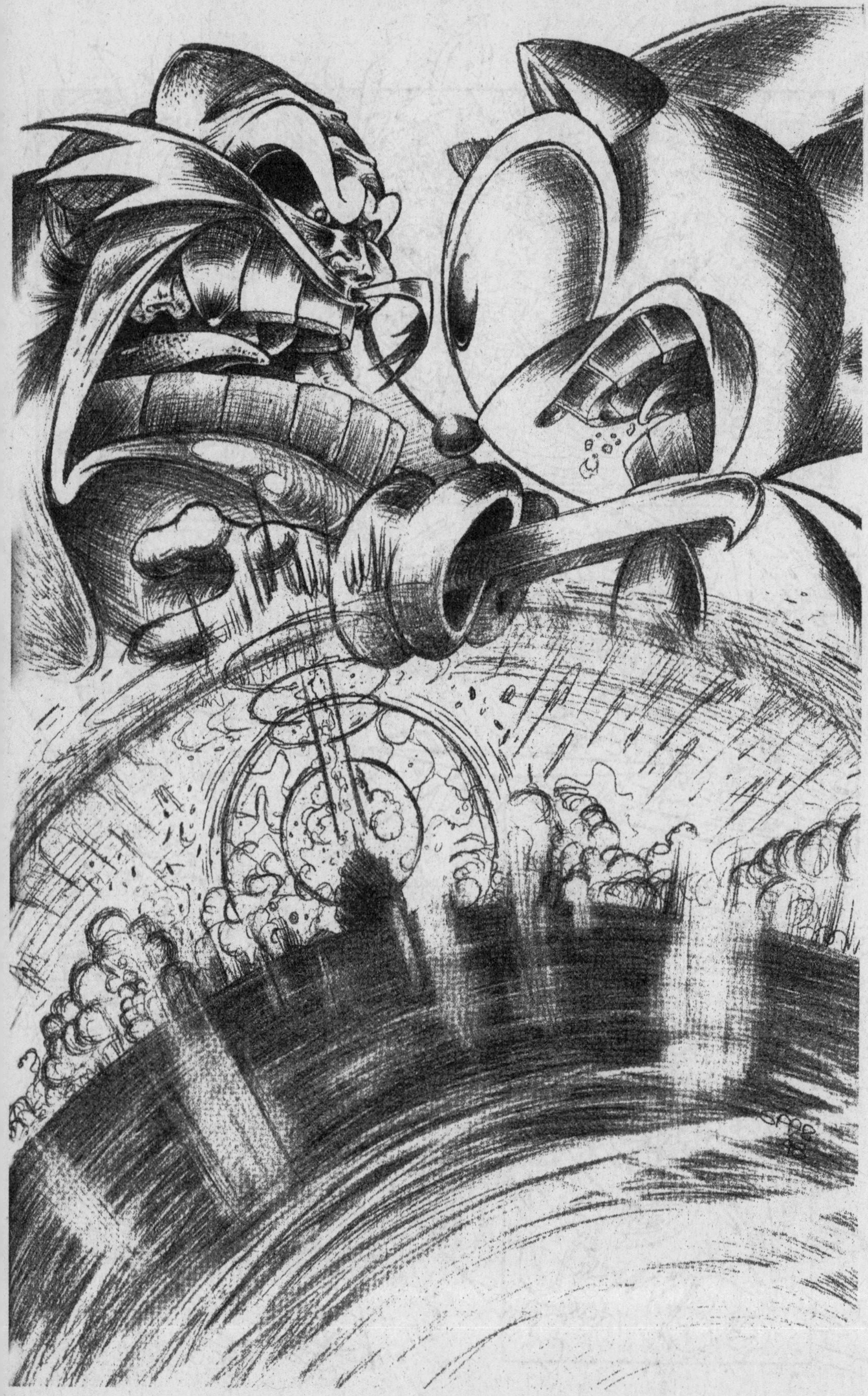

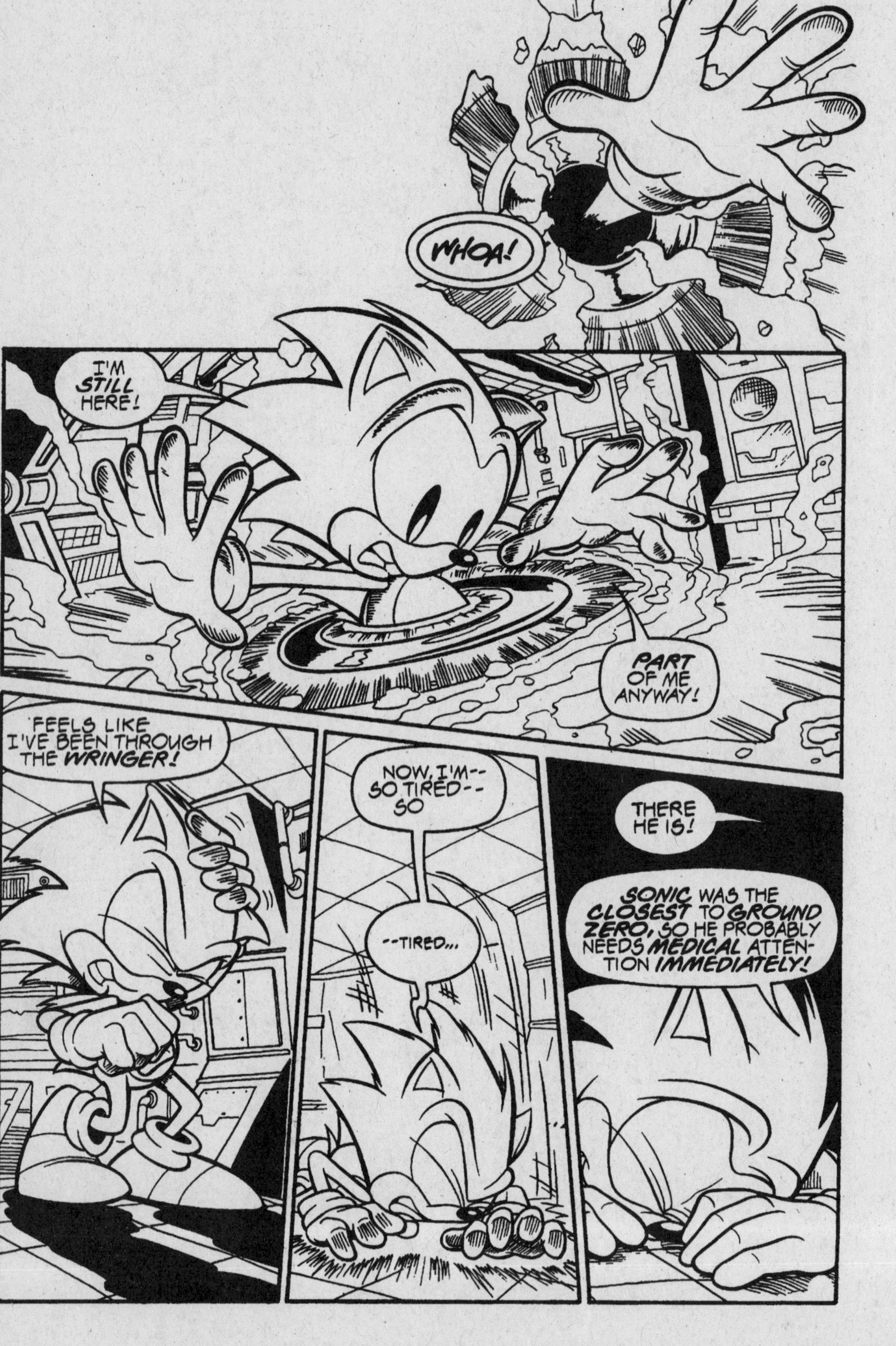
WHOA!
I'M STILL HERE!
PART OF ME ANYWAY!
'FEELS LIKE I'VE BEEN THROUGH THE WRINGER!
NOW, I'M-- SO TIRED-- SO
--TIRED...
THERE HE IS!
SONIC WAS THE CLOSEST TO GROUND ZERO, SO HE PROBABLY NEEDS MEDICAL ATTEN-TION IMMEDIATELY!

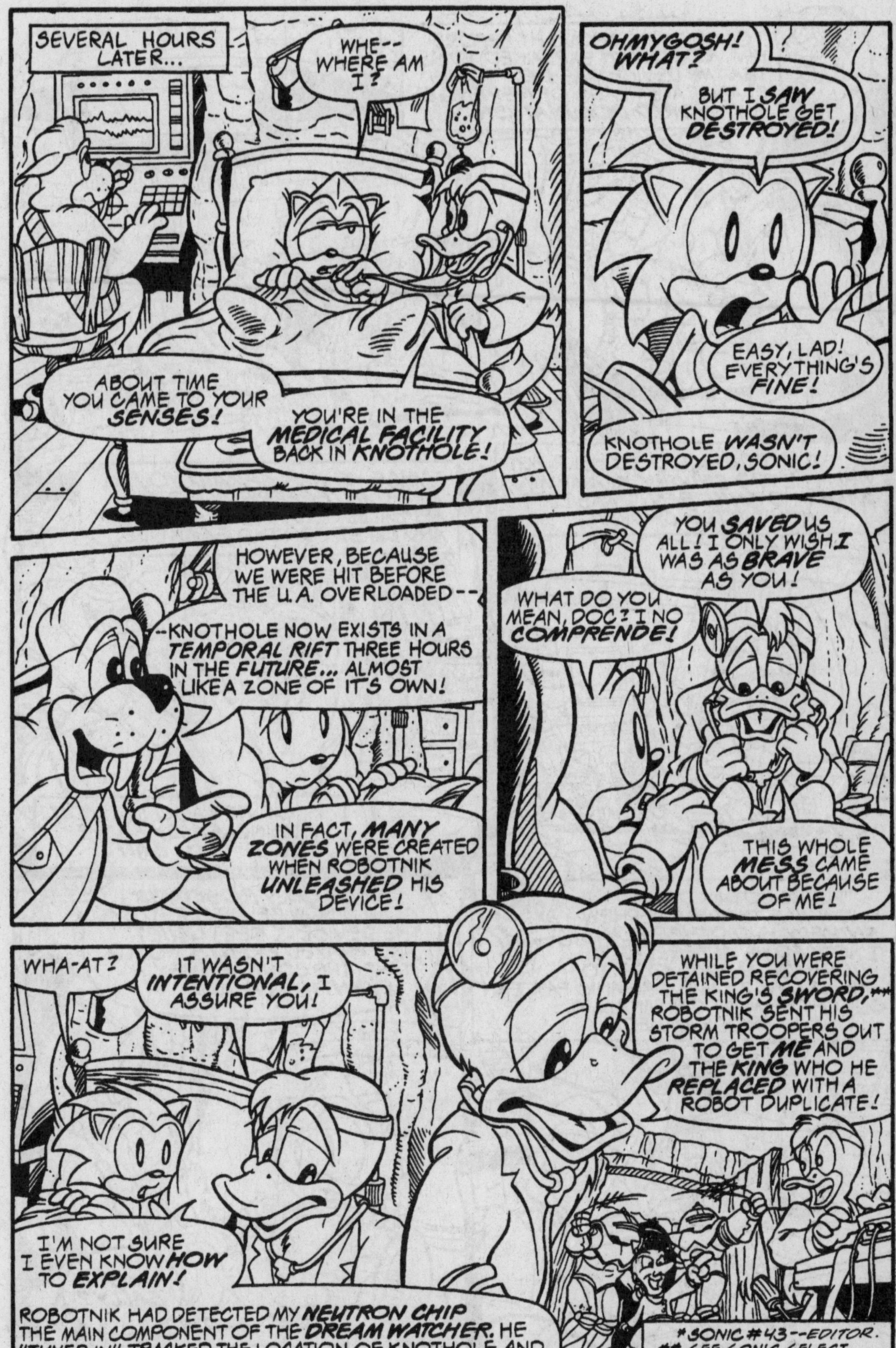
SEVERAL HOURS LATER...
WHE-- WHERE AM I?
ABOUT TIME YOU CAME TO YOUR SENSES!
YOU'RE IN THE MEDICAL FACILITY BACK IN KNOTHOLE!
OHMYGOSH! WHAT?
BUT I SAW KNOTHOLE GET DESTROYED!
EASY, LAD! EVERYTHING'S FINE!
KNOTHOLE WASN'T DESTROYED, SONIC!
HOWEVER, BECAUSE WE WERE HIT BEFORE THE U.A. OVERLOADED--
--KNOTHOLE NOW EXISTS IN A TEMPORAL RIFT THREE HOURS IN THE FUTURE... ALMOST LIKE A ZONE OF ITS OWN!
IN FACT, MANY ZONES WERE CREATED WHEN ROBOTNIK UNLEASHED HIS DEVICE!
WHAT DO YOU MEAN, DOC? I NO COMPRENDE!
YOU SAVED US ALL! I ONLY WISH I WAS AS BRAVE AS YOU!
THIS WHOLE MESS CAME ABOUT BECAUSE OF ME!
WHA-AT?
IT WASN'T INTENTIONAL, I ASSURE YOU!
I'M NOT SURE I EVEN KNOW HOW TO EXPLAIN!
WHILE YOU WERE DETAINED RECOVERING THE KING'S SWORD,** ROBOTNIK SENT HIS STORM TROOPERS OUT TO GET ME AND THE KING WHO HE REPLACED WITH A ROBOT DUPLICATE!
ROBOTNIK HAD DETECTED MY NEUTRON CHIP THE MAIN COMPONENT OF THE DREAM WATCHER. HE "TUNED IN", TRACKED THE LOCATION OF KNOTHOLE AND LEARNED OF KING ACORN'S RETURN FROM EXILE.*
*SONIC #43--EDITOR.
** SEE SONIC SELECT VOLUME 3! -- EDITOR

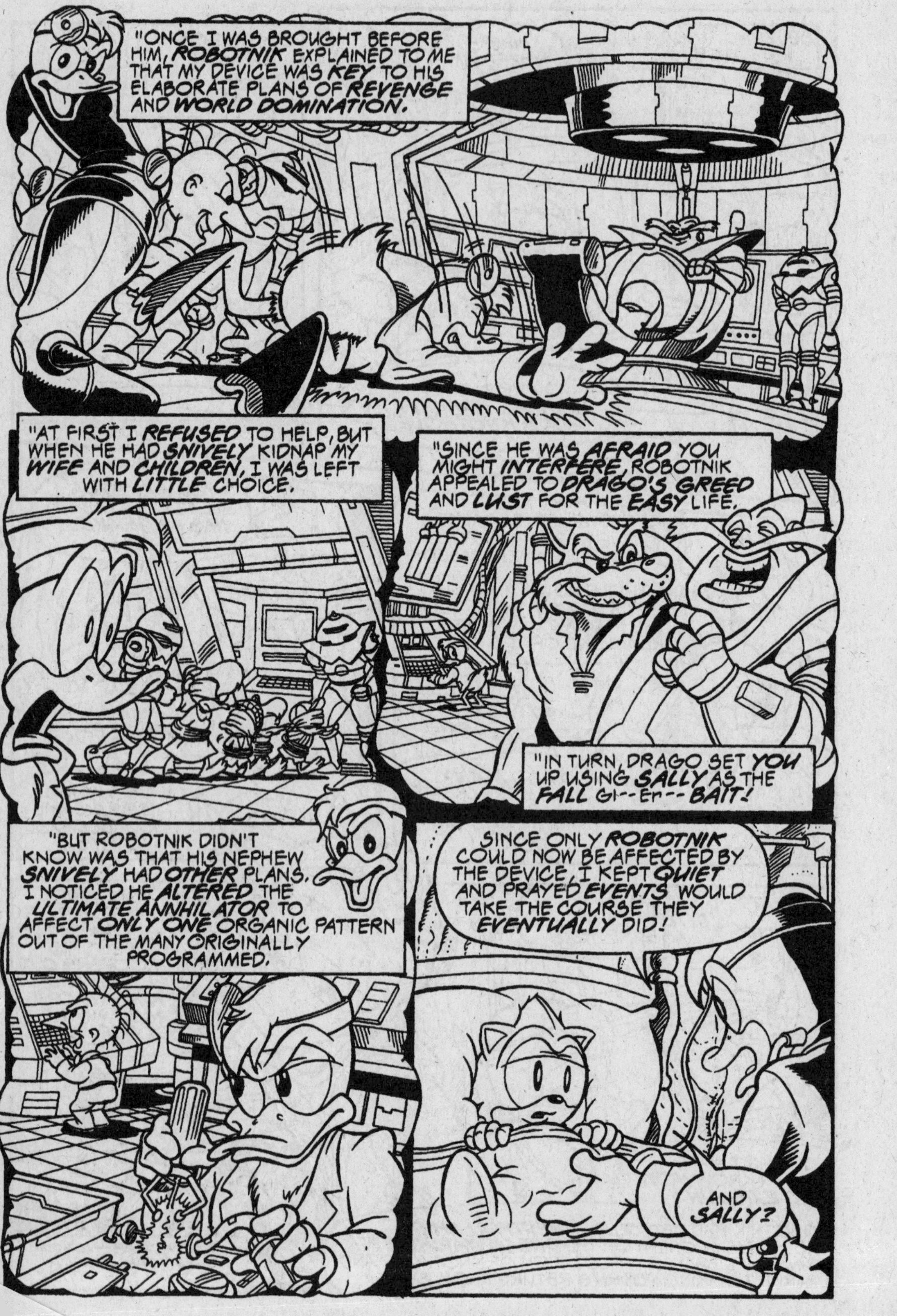
"ONCE I WAS BROUGHT BEFORE HIM, ROBOTNIK EXPLAINED TO ME THAT MY DEVICE WAS KEY TO HIS ELABORATE PLANS OF REVENGE AND WORLD DOMINATION.
"AT FIRST I REFUSED TO HELP, BUT WHEN HE HAD SNIVELY KIDNAP MY WIFE AND CHILDREN, I WAS LEFT WITH LITTLE CHOICE.
"SINCE HE WAS AFRAID YOU MIGHT INTERFERE, ROBOTNIK APPEALED TO DRAGO'S GREED AND LUST FOR THE EASY LIFE.
"IN TURN, DRAGO SET YOU UP USING SALLY AS THE FALL GI-- ER-- BAIT!
"BUT ROBOTNIK DIDN'T KNOW WAS THAT HIS NEPHEW SNIVELY HAD OTHER PLANS. I NOTICED HE ALTERED THE ULTIMATE ANNHILATOR TO AFFECT ONLY ONE ORGANIC PATTERN OUT OF THE MANY ORIGINALLY PROGRAMMED.
SINCE ONLY ROBOTNIK COULD NOW BE AFFECTED BY THE DEVICE, I KEPT QUIET AND PRAYED EVENTS WOULD TAKE THE COURSE THEY EVENTUALLY DID!
AND SALLY?

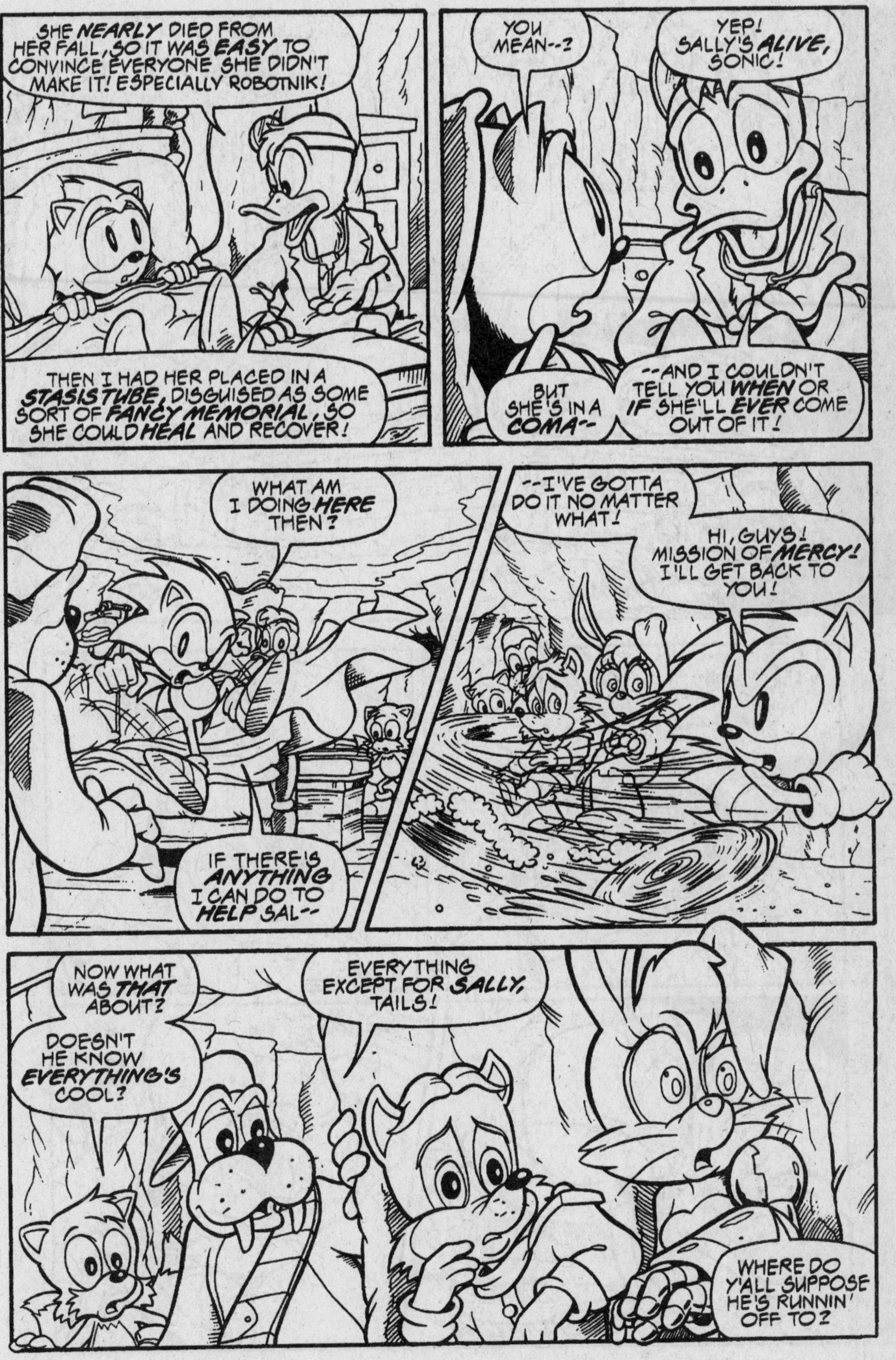
SHE NEARLY DIED FROM HER FALL, SO IT WAS EASY TO CONVINCE EVERYONE SHE DIDN'T MAKE IT! ESPECIALLY ROBOTNIK!
THEN I HAD HER PLACED IN A STASIS TUBE, DISGUISED AS SOME SORT OF FANCY MEMORIAL, SO SHE COULD HEAL AND RECOVER!
YOU MEAN--?
YEP! SALLY'S ALIVE, SONIC!
BUT SHE'S IN A COMA--
--AND I COULDN'T TELL YOU WHEN OR IF SHE'LL EVER COME OUT OF IT!
WHAT AM I DOING HERE THEN?
IF THERE'S ANYTHING I CAN DO TO HELP SAL--
--I'VE GOTTA DO IT NO MATTER WHAT!
HI, GUYS! MISSION OF MERCY! I'LL GET BACK TO YOU!
NOW WHAT WAS THAT ABOUT?
DOESN'T HE KNOW EVERYTHING'S COOL?
EVERYTHING EXCEPT FOR SALLY, TAILS!
WHERE DO Y'ALL SUPPOSE HE'S RUNNIN' OFF TO?

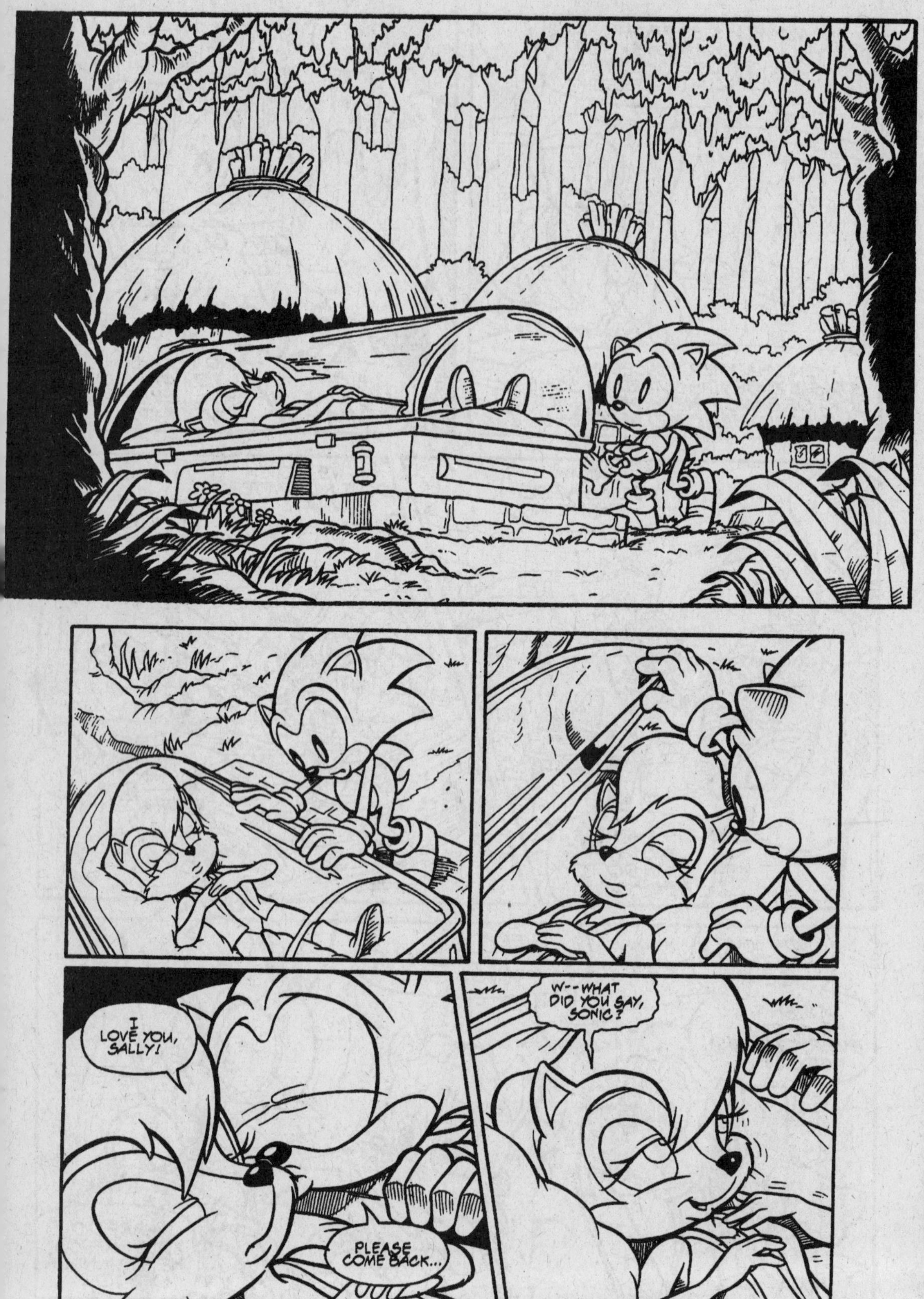
I LOVE YOU, SALLY!
PLEASE COME BACK...
W--WHAT DID YOU SAY, SONIC?

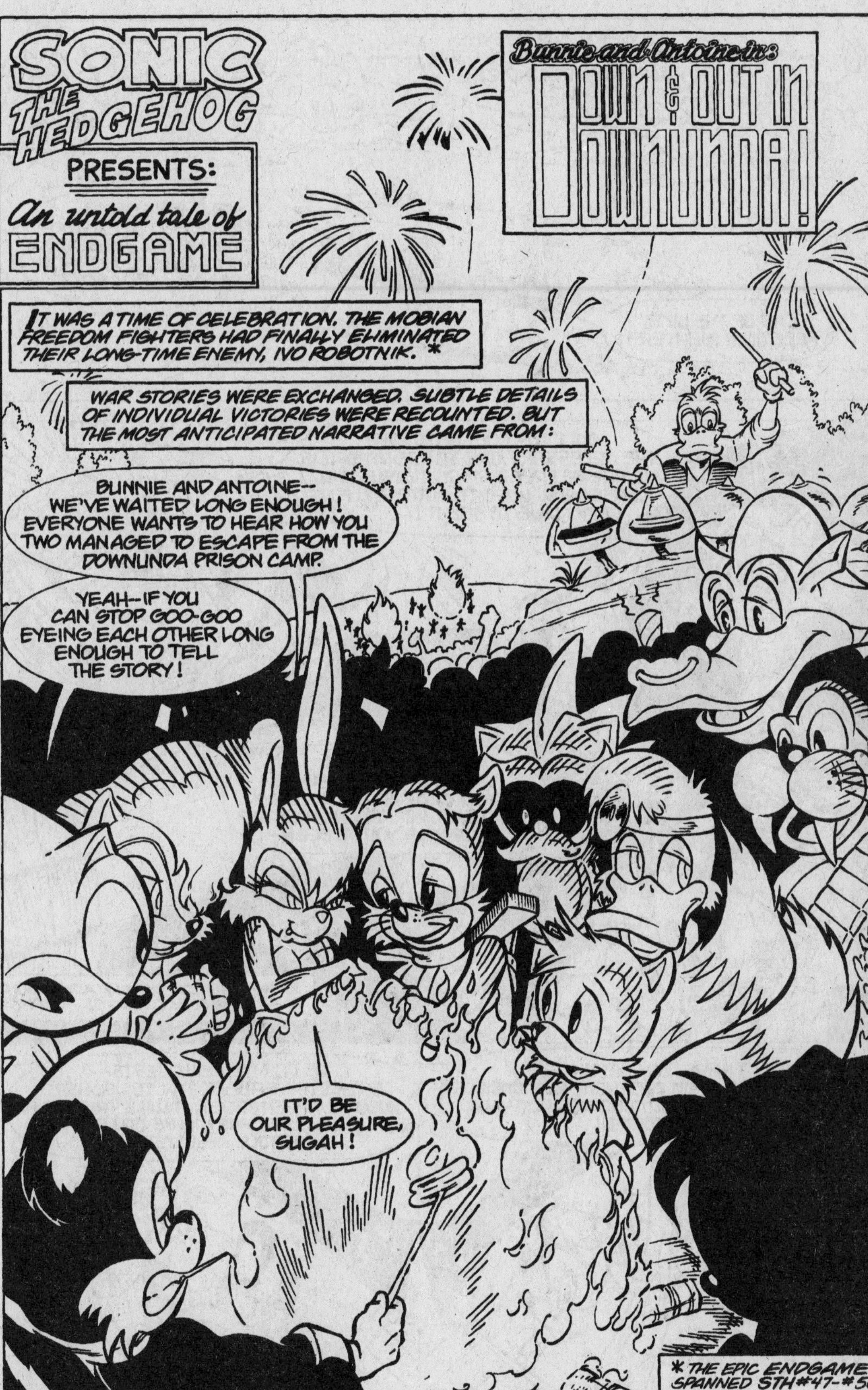
SONIC THE HEDGEHOG
PRESENTS:
An untold tale of
ENDGAME
Bunnie and Antoine in:
DOWN & OUT IN DOWNUNDA!
IT WAS A TIME OF CELEBRATION. THE MOBIAN FREEDOM FIGHTERS HAD FINALLY ELIMINATED THEIR LONG-TIME ENEMY, IVO ROBOTNIK. *
WAR STORIES WERE EXCHANGED. SUBTLE DETAILS OF INDIVIDUAL VICTORIES WERE RECOUNTED. BUT THE MOST ANTICIPATED NARRATIVE CAME FROM:
BUNNIE AND ANTOINE-- WE'VE WAITED LONG ENOUGH! EVERYONE WANTS TO HEAR HOW YOU TWO MANAGED TO ESCAPE FROM THE DOWNUNDA PRISON CAMP.
YEAH--IF YOU CAN STOP GOO-GOO EYEING EACH OTHER LONG ENOUGH TO TELL THE STORY!
IT'D BE OUR PLEASURE, SUGAH!
* THE EPIC ENDGAME SPANNED STH #47-#50-- EDITOR

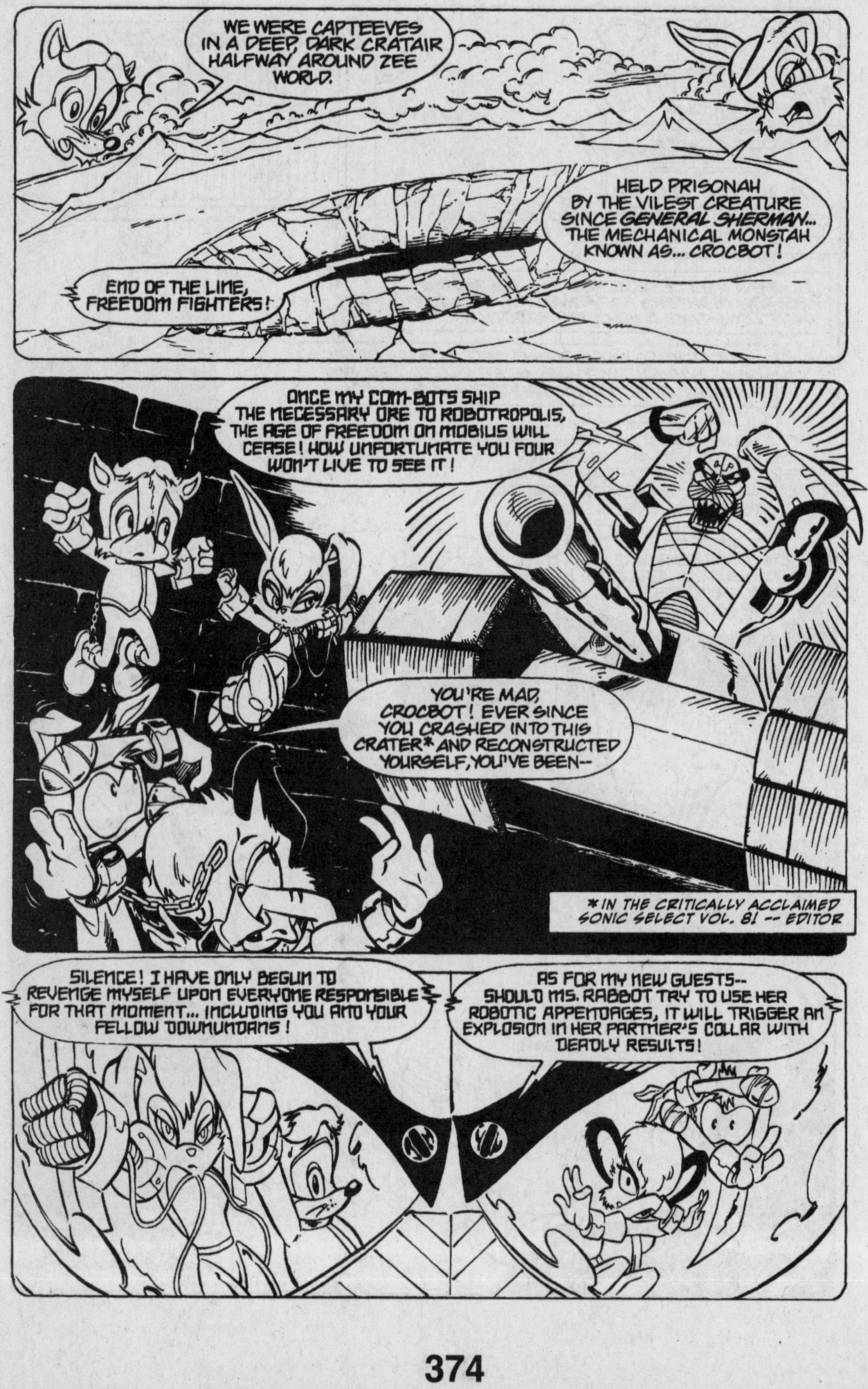
WE WERE CAPTEEVES IN A DEEP, DARK CRATAIR HALFWAY AROUND ZEE WORLD.
HELD PRISONAH BY THE VILEST CREATURE SINCE GENERAL SHERMAN... THE MECHANICAL MONSTAH KNOWN AS... CROCBOT!
END OF THE LINE, FREEDOM FIGHTERS!
ONCE MY COM-BOTS SHIP THE NECESSARY ORE TO ROBOTROPOLIS, THE AGE OF FREEDOM ON MOBIUS WILL CEASE! HOW UNFORTUNATE YOU FOUR WON'T LIVE TO SEE IT!
YOU'RE MAD, CROCBOT! EVER SINCE YOU CRASHED INTO THIS CRATER* AND RECONSTRUCTED YOURSELF, YOU'VE BEEN--
*IN THE CRITICALLY ACCLAIMED SONIC SELECT VOL. 8! -- EDITOR
SILENCE! I HAVE ONLY BEGUN TO REVENGE MYSELF UPON EVERYONE RESPONSIBLE FOR THAT MOMENT... INCLUDING YOU AND YOUR FELLOW DOWNUNDANS!
AS FOR MY NEW GUESTS-- SHOULD MS. RABBOT TRY TO USE HER ROBOTIC APPENDAGES, IT WILL TRIGGER AN EXPLOSION IN HER PARTNER'S COLLAR WITH DEADLY RESULTS!

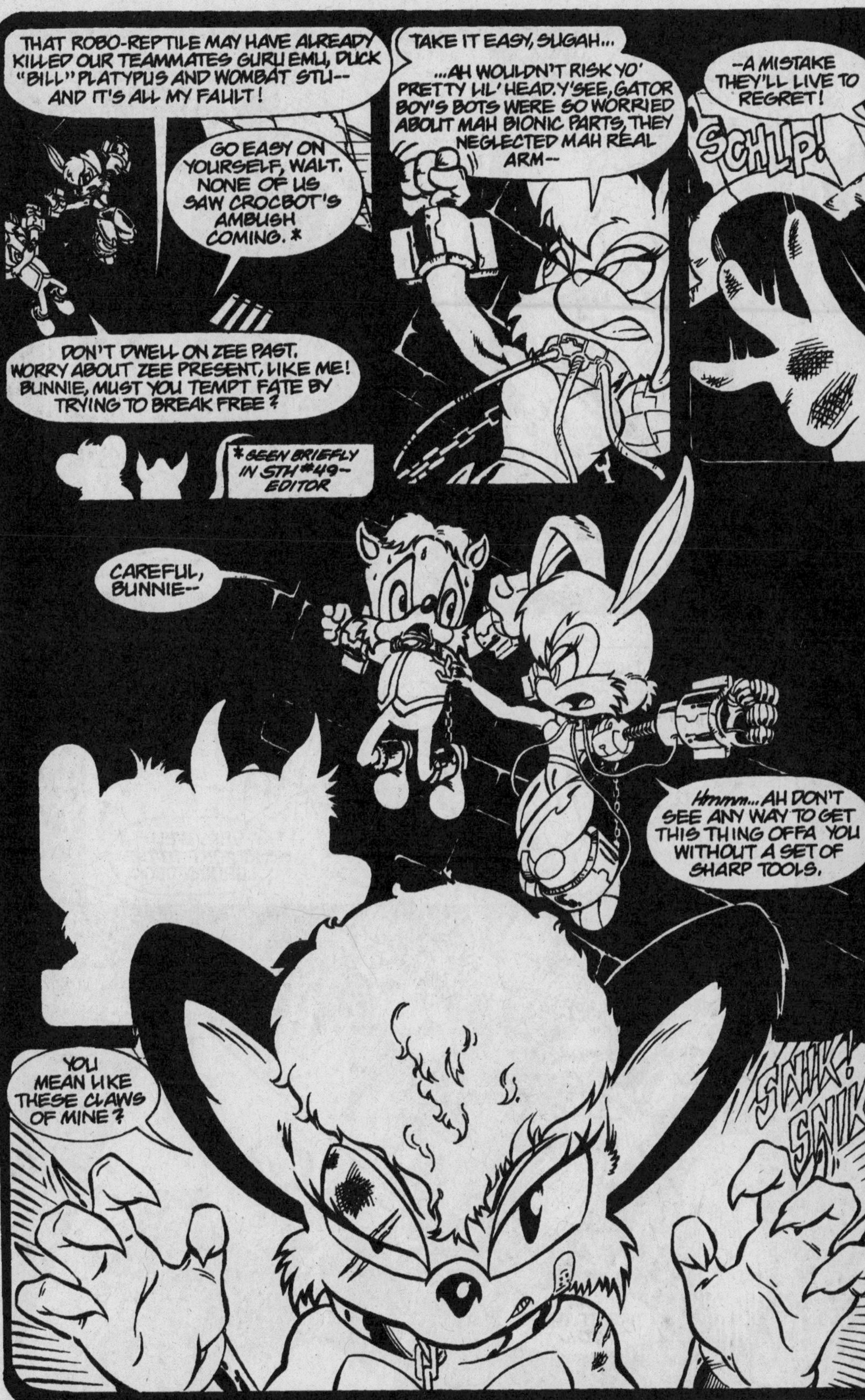
THAT ROBO-REPTILE MAY HAVE ALREADY KILLED OUR TEAMMATES GURU EMU, DUCK "BILL" PLATYPUS AND WOMBAT STU-- AND IT'S ALL MY FAULT!
GO EASY ON YOURSELF, WALT. NONE OF US SAW CROCBOT'S AMBUSH COMING. *
DON'T DWELL ON ZEE PAST. WORRY ABOUT ZEE PRESENT, LIKE ME! BUNNIE, MUST YOU TEMPT FATE BY TRYING TO BREAK FREE?
* SEEN BRIEFLY IN STH #49-- EDITOR
TAKE IT EASY, SUGAH...
...AH WOULDN'T RISK YO' PRETTY LIL' HEAD. Y'SEE, GATOR BOY'S BOTS WERE SO WORRIED ABOUT MAH BIONIC PARTS, THEY NEGLECTED MAH REAL ARM--
-A MISTAKE THEY'LL LIVE TO REGRET!
SCHLIP!
CAREFUL, BUNNIE--
Hmmm... AH DON'T SEE ANY WAY TO GET THIS THING OFFA YOU WITHOUT A SET OF SHARP TOOLS.
YOU MEAN LIKE THESE CLAWS OF MINE?
SNIK! SNIK!

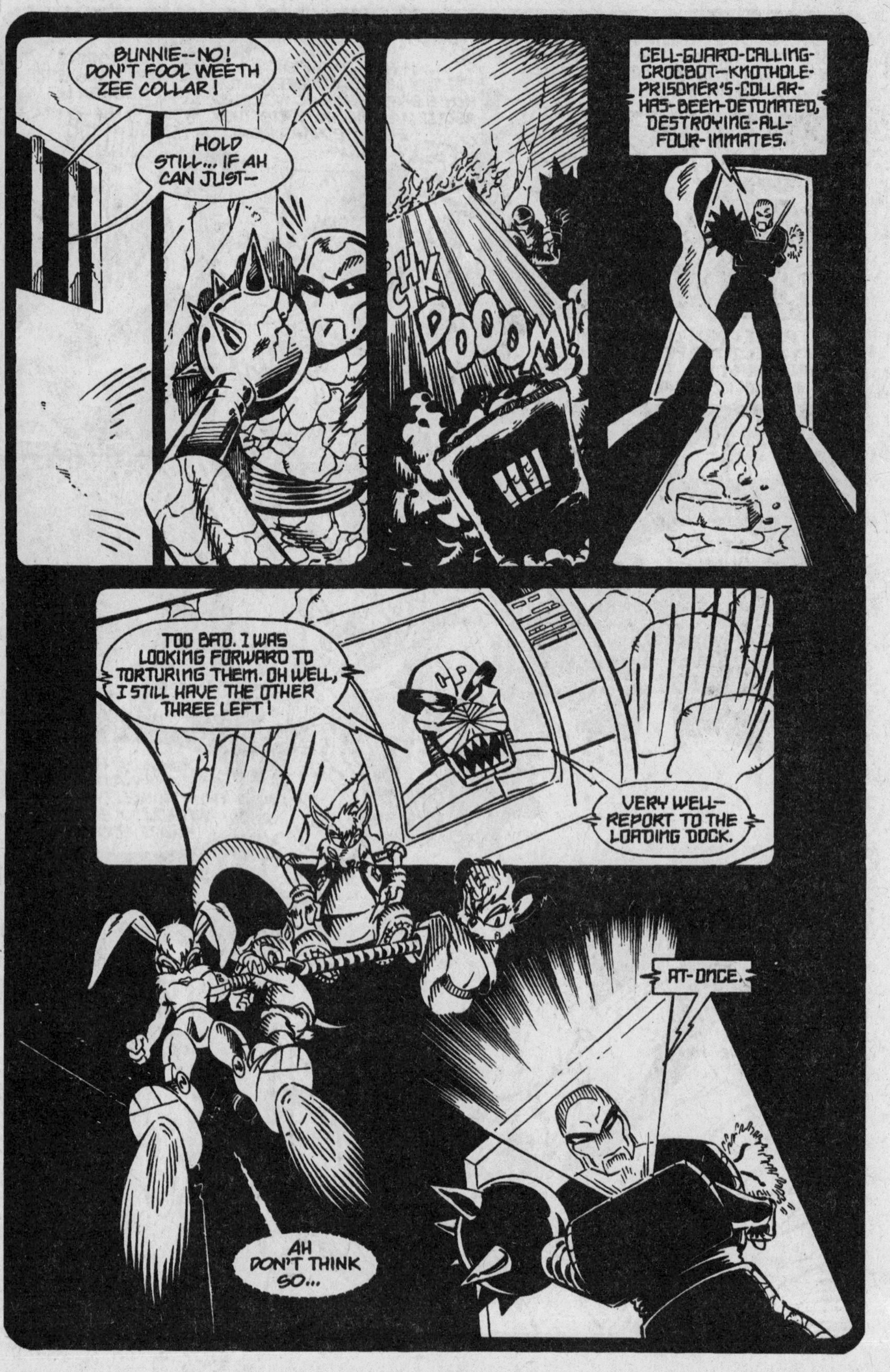
BUNNIE--NO! DON'T FOOL WEETH ZEE COLLAR!
HOLD STILL... IF AH CAN JUST--
CHK
DOOOM!
CELL-GUARD-CALLING-CROCBOT--KNOTHOLE-PRISONER'S-COLLAR-HAS-BEEN-DETONATED, DESTROYING-ALL-FOUR-INMATES.
TOO BAD. I WAS LOOKING FORWARD TO TORTURING THEM. OH WELL, I STILL HAVE THE OTHER THREE LEFT!
VERY WELL--REPORT TO THE LOADING DOCK.
AT-ONCE.
AH DON'T THINK SO...

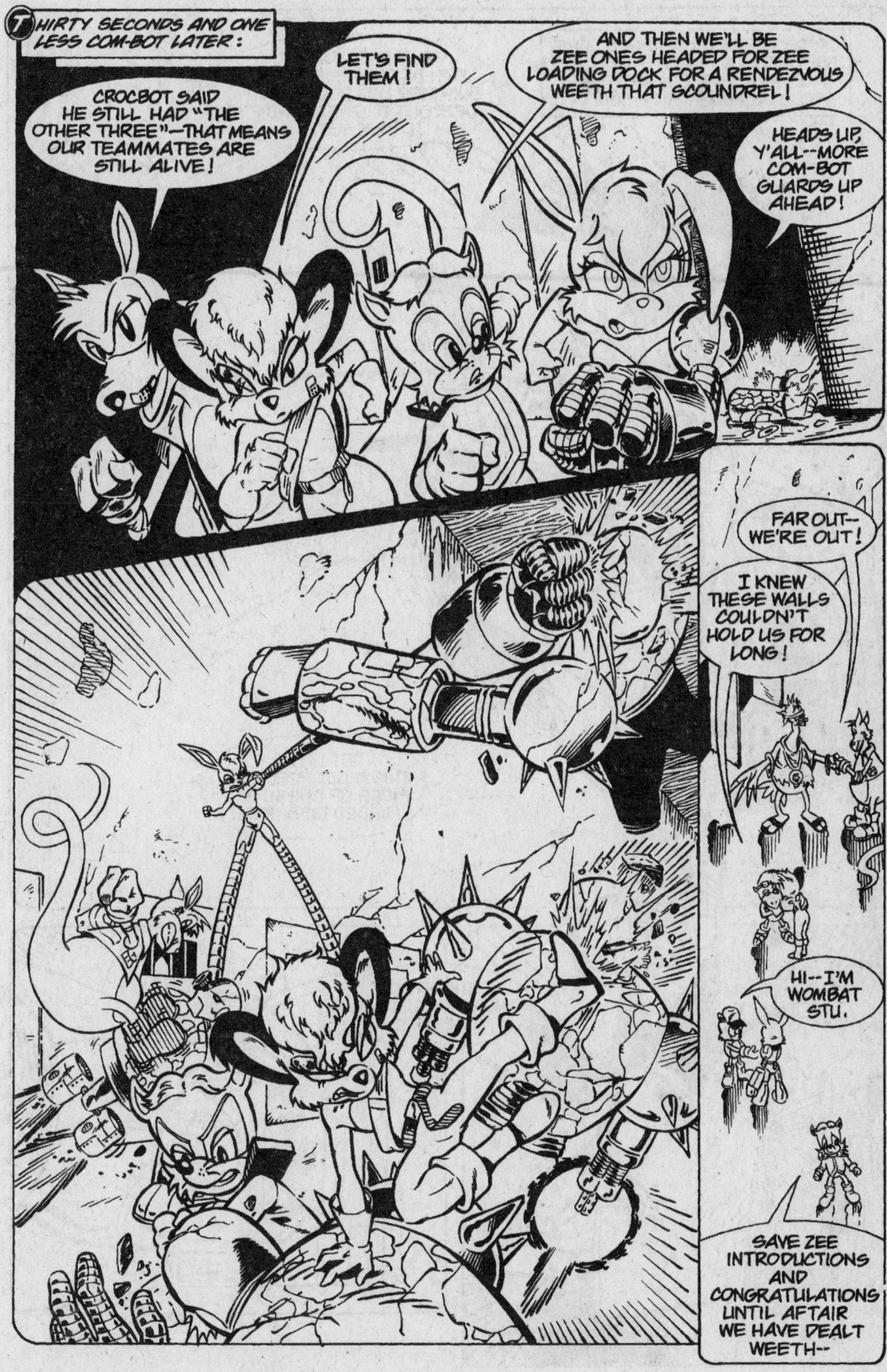
THIRTY SECONDS AND ONE LESS COM-BOT LATER:
CROCBOT SAID HE STILL HAD "THE OTHER THREE"—THAT MEANS OUR TEAMMATES ARE STILL ALIVE!
LET'S FIND THEM!
AND THEN WE'LL BE ZEE ONES HEADED FOR ZEE LOADING DOCK FOR A RENDEZVOUS WEETH THAT SCOUNDREL!
HEADS UP, Y'ALL--MORE COM-BOT GUARDS UP AHEAD!
FAR OUT-- WE'RE OUT!
I KNEW THESE WALLS COULDN'T HOLD US FOR LONG!
HI--I'M WOMBAT STU.
SAVE ZEE INTRODUCTIONS AND CONGRATULATIONS UNTIL AFTAIR WE HAVE DEALT WEETH--

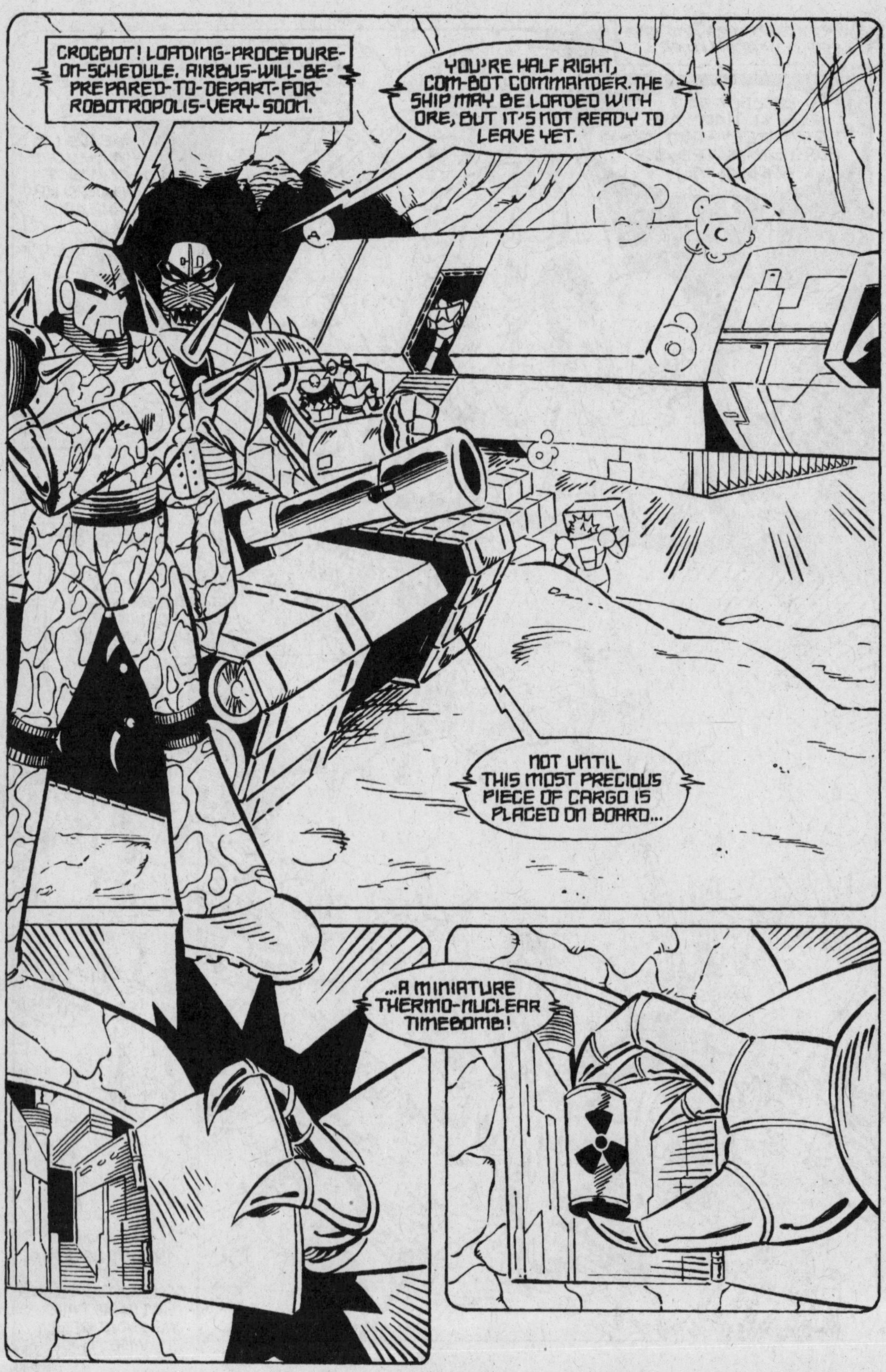
CROCBOT! LOADING-PROCEDURE-ON-SCHEDULE. AIRBUS-WILL-BE-PREPARED-TO-DEPART-FOR-ROBOTROPOLIS-VERY-SOON.
YOU'RE HALF RIGHT, COM-BOT COMMANDER. THE SHIP MAY BE LOADED WITH ORE, BUT IT'S NOT READY TO LEAVE YET.
NOT UNTIL THIS MOST PRECIOUS PIECE OF CARGO IS PLACED ON BOARD...
...A MINIATURE THERMO-NUCLEAR TIMEBOMB!

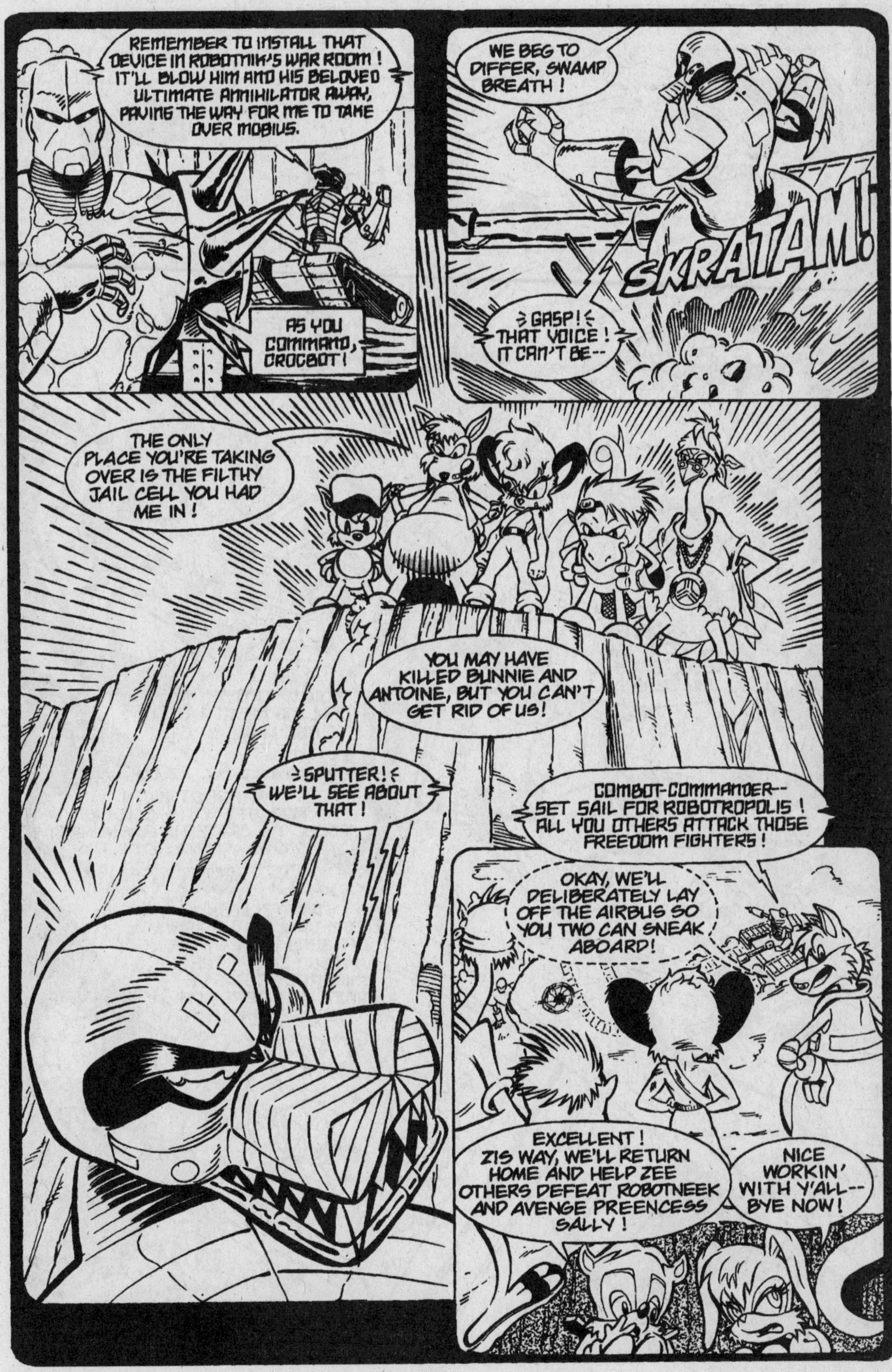
REMEMBER TO INSTALL THAT DEVICE IN ROBOTNIK'S WAR ROOM! IT'LL BLOW HIM AND HIS BELOVED ULTIMATE ANNIHILATOR AWAY, PAVING THE WAY FOR ME TO TAKE OVER MOBIUS.
AS YOU COMMAND, CROCBOT!
WE BEG TO DIFFER, SWAMP BREATH!
SKRATAM!
GASP! THAT VOICE! IT CAN'T BE--
THE ONLY PLACE YOU'RE TAKING OVER IS THE FILTHY JAIL CELL YOU HAD ME IN!
YOU MAY HAVE KILLED BUNNIE AND ANTOINE, BUT YOU CAN'T GET RID OF US!
SPUTTER! WE'LL SEE ABOUT THAT!
COMBOT-COMMANDER-- SET SAIL FOR ROBOTROPOLIS! ALL YOU OTHERS ATTACK THOSE FREEDOM FIGHTERS!
OKAY, WE'LL DELIBERATELY LAY OFF THE AIRBUS SO YOU TWO CAN SNEAK ABOARD!
EXCELLENT! ZIS WAY, WE'LL RETURN HOME AND HELP ZEE OTHERS DEFEAT ROBOTNEEK AND AVENGE PREENCESS SALLY!
NICE WORKIN' WITH Y'ALL-- BYE NOW!

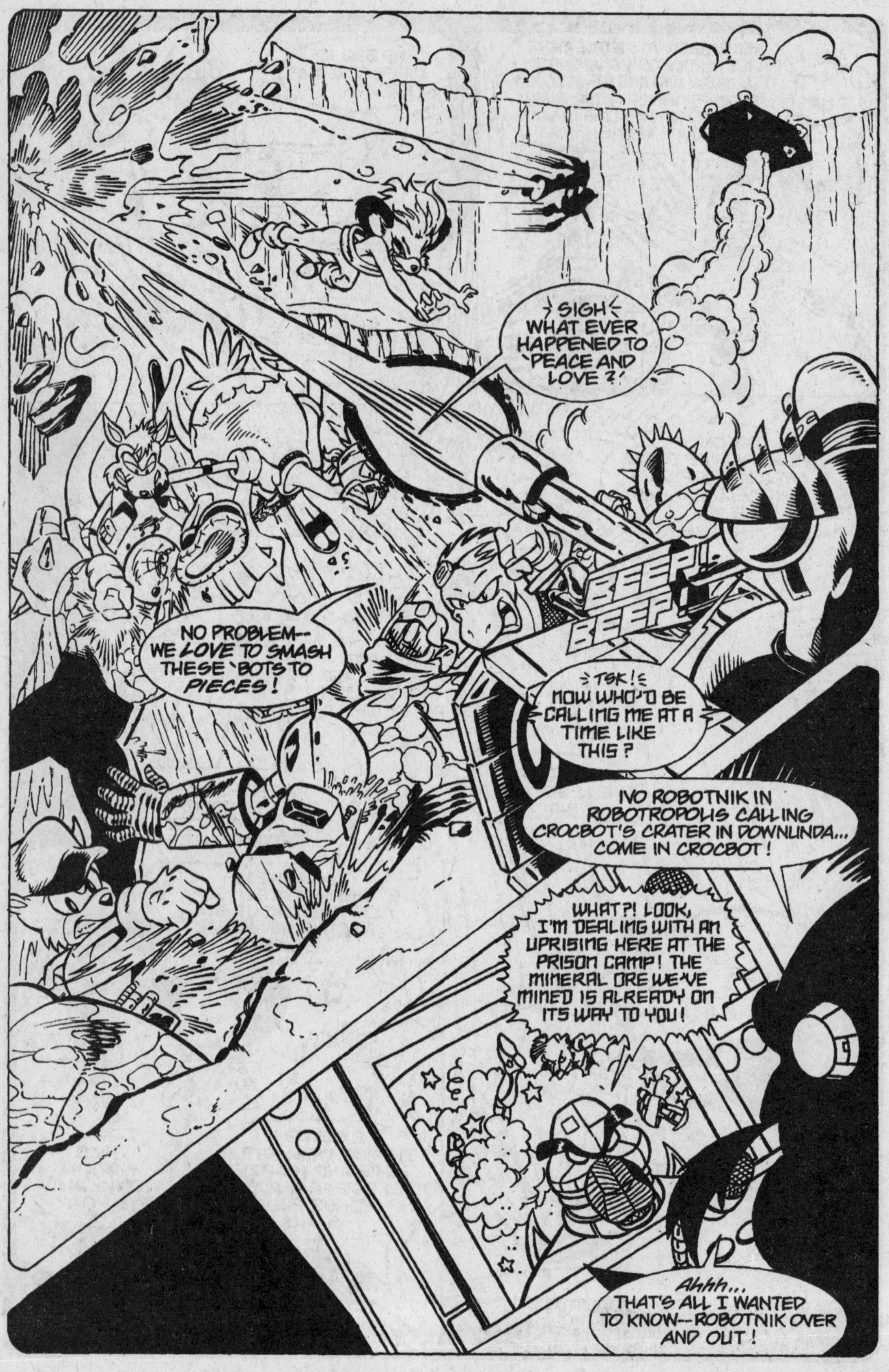
SIGH
WHAT EVER HAPPENED TO 'PEACE AND LOVE'?
NO PROBLEM-- WE LOVE TO SMASH THESE 'BOTS TO PIECES!
BEEP! BEEP!
TSK!
NOW WHO'D BE CALLING ME AT A TIME LIKE THIS?
IVO ROBOTNIK IN ROBOTROPOLIS CALLING CROCBOT'S CRATER IN DOWNUNDA... COME IN CROCBOT!
WHAT?! LOOK, I'M DEALING WITH AN UPRISING HERE AT THE PRISON CAMP! THE MINERAL ORE WE'VE MINED IS ALREADY ON ITS WAY TO YOU!
Ahhh... THAT'S ALL I WANTED TO KNOW-- ROBOTNIK OVER AND OUT!

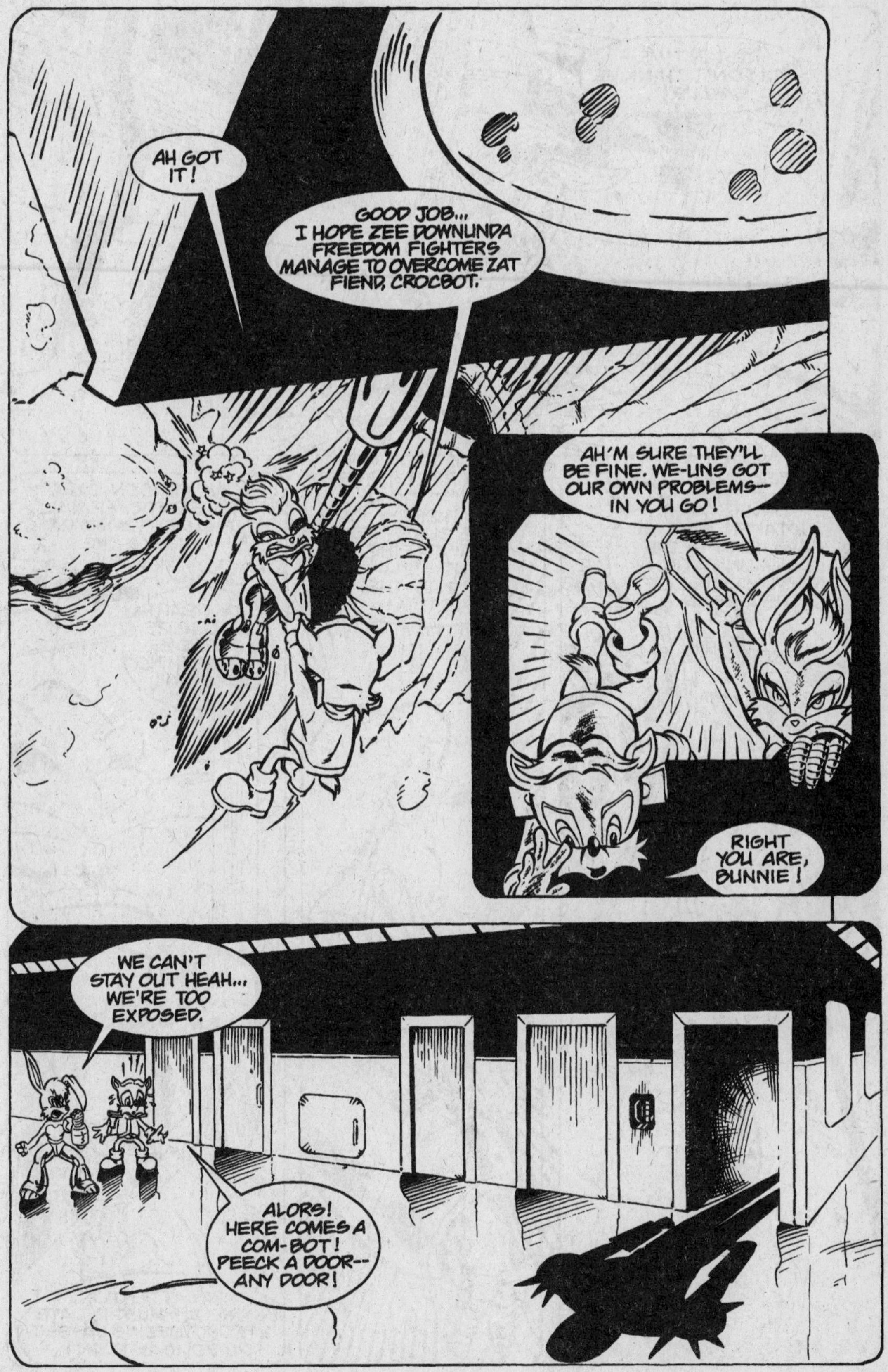
AH GOT IT!
GOOD JOB... I HOPE ZEE DOWNUNDA FREEDOM FIGHTERS MANAGE TO OVERCOME ZAT FIEND, CROCBOT.
AH'M SURE THEY'LL BE FINE. WE-UNS GOT OUR OWN PROBLEMS-- IN YOU GO!
RIGHT YOU ARE, BUNNIE!
WE CAN'T STAY OUT HEAH... WE'RE TOO EXPOSED.
ALORS! HERE COMES A COM-BOT! PEECK A DOOR-- ANY DOOR!

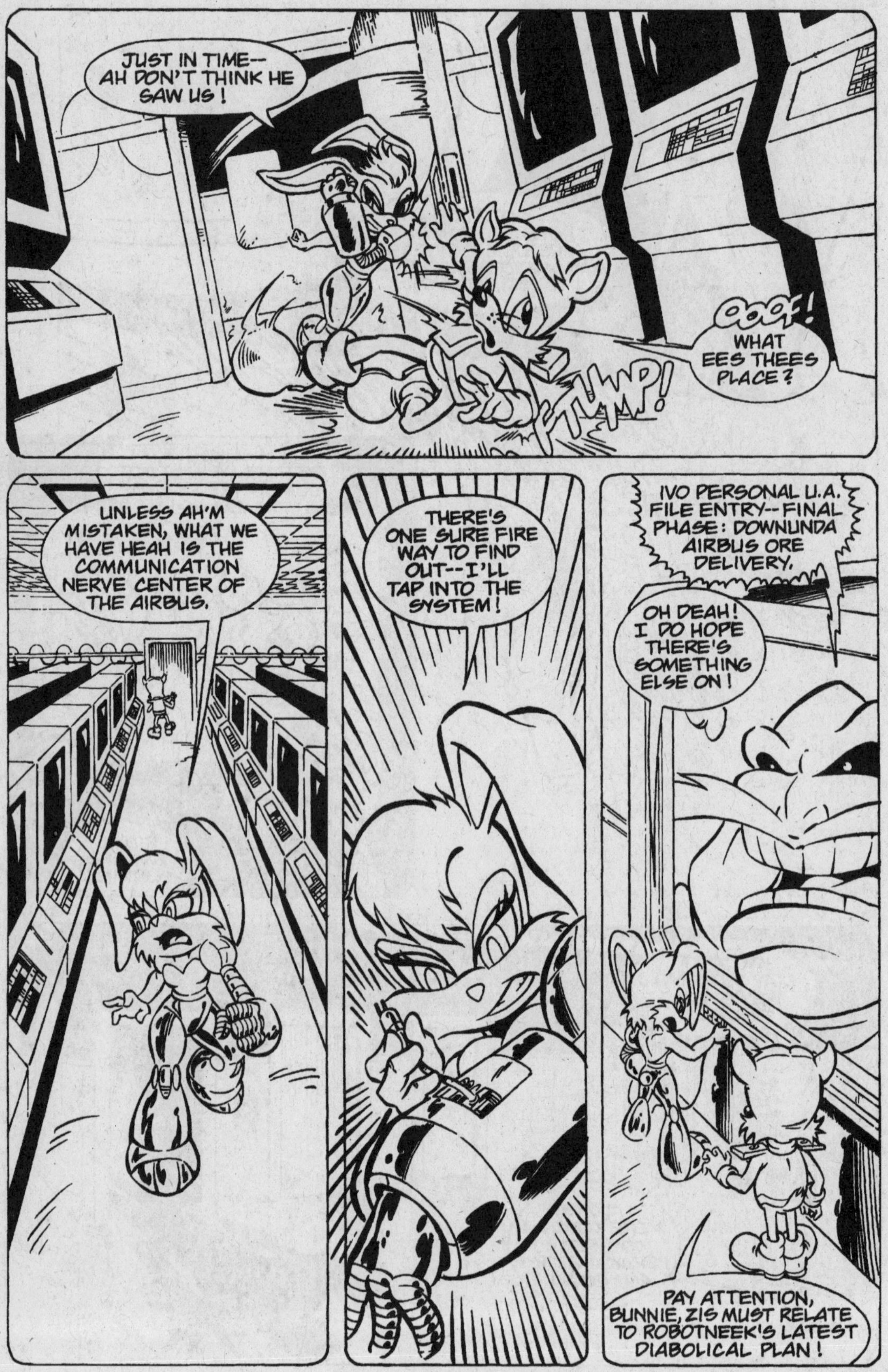
JUST IN TIME-- AH DON'T THINK HE SAW US!
OOOF! WHAT EES THEES PLACE?
FTUMP!
UNLESS AH'M MISTAKEN, WHAT WE HAVE HEAH IS THE COMMUNICATION NERVE CENTER OF THE AIRBUS.
THERE'S ONE SURE FIRE WAY TO FIND OUT--I'LL TAP INTO THE SYSTEM!
IVO PERSONAL U.A. FILE ENTRY--FINAL PHASE: DOWNUNDA AIRBUS ORE DELIVERY.
OH DEAH! I DO HOPE THERE'S SOMETHING ELSE ON!
PAY ATTENTION, BUNNIE, ZIS MUST RELATE TO ROBOTNEEK'S LATEST DIABOLICAL PLAN!

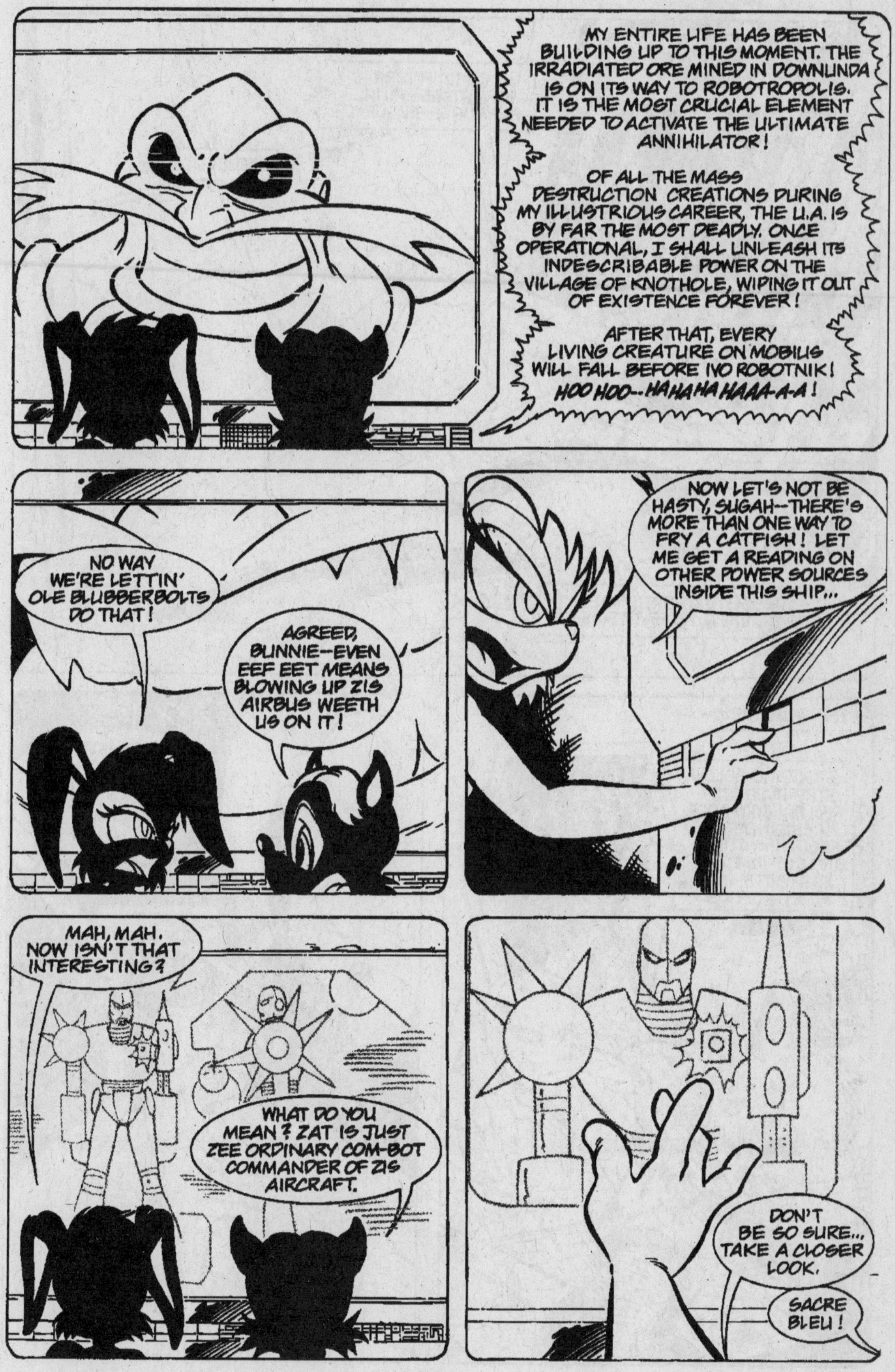
MY ENTIRE LIFE HAS BEEN BUILDING UP TO THIS MOMENT. THE IRRADIATED ORE MINED IN DOWNUNDA IS ON ITS WAY TO ROBOTROPOLIS. IT IS THE MOST CRUCIAL ELEMENT NEEDED TO ACTIVATE THE ULTIMATE ANNIHILATOR!
OF ALL THE MASS DESTRUCTION CREATIONS DURING MY ILLUSTRIOUS CAREER, THE U.A. IS BY FAR THE MOST DEADLY. ONCE OPERATIONAL, I SHALL UNLEASH ITS INDESCRIBABLE POWER ON THE VILLAGE OF KNOTHOLE, WIPING IT OUT OF EXISTENCE FOREVER!
AFTER THAT, EVERY LIVING CREATURE ON MOBIUS WILL FALL BEFORE IVO ROBOTNIK! HOO HOO--HAHAHA HAAA-A-A!
NO WAY WE'RE LETTIN' OLE BLUBBERBOLTS DO THAT!
AGREED, BUNNIE--EVEN EEF EET MEANS BLOWING UP ZIS AIRBUS WEETH US ON IT!
NOW LET'S NOT BE HASTY, SUGAH--THERE'S MORE THAN ONE WAY TO FRY A CATFISH! LET ME GET A READING ON OTHER POWER SOURCES INSIDE THIS SHIP...
MAH, MAH. NOW ISN'T THAT INTERESTING?
WHAT DO YOU MEAN? ZAT IS JUST ZEE ORDINARY COM-BOT COMMANDER OF ZIS AIRCRAFT.
DON'T BE SO SURE... TAKE A CLOSER LOOK.
SACRE BLEU!

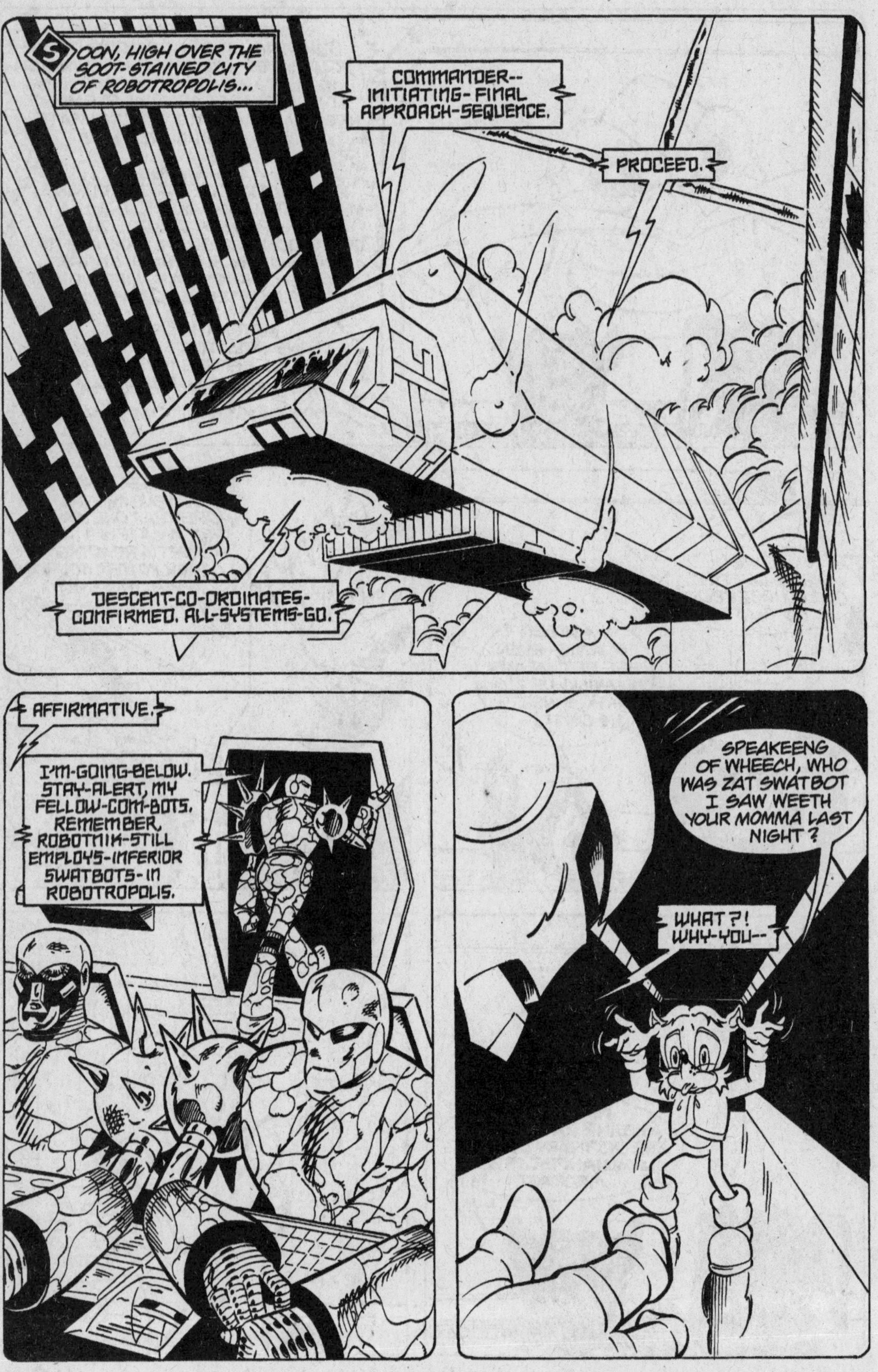
SOON, HIGH OVER THE SOOT-STAINED CITY OF ROBOTROPOLIS...
COMMANDER-- INITIATING-FINAL APPROACH-SEQUENCE.
PROCEED.
DESCENT-CO-ORDINATES-CONFIRMED. ALL-SYSTEMS-GO.
AFFIRMATIVE.
I'M-GOING-BELOW. STAY-ALERT, MY FELLOW-COM-BOTS. REMEMBER, ROBOTNIK-STILL EMPLOYS-INFERIOR SWATBOTS-IN ROBOTROPOLIS.
SPEAKEENG OF WHEECH, WHO WAS ZAT SWATBOT I SAW WEETH YOUR MOMMA LAST NIGHT?
WHAT?! WHY-YOU--

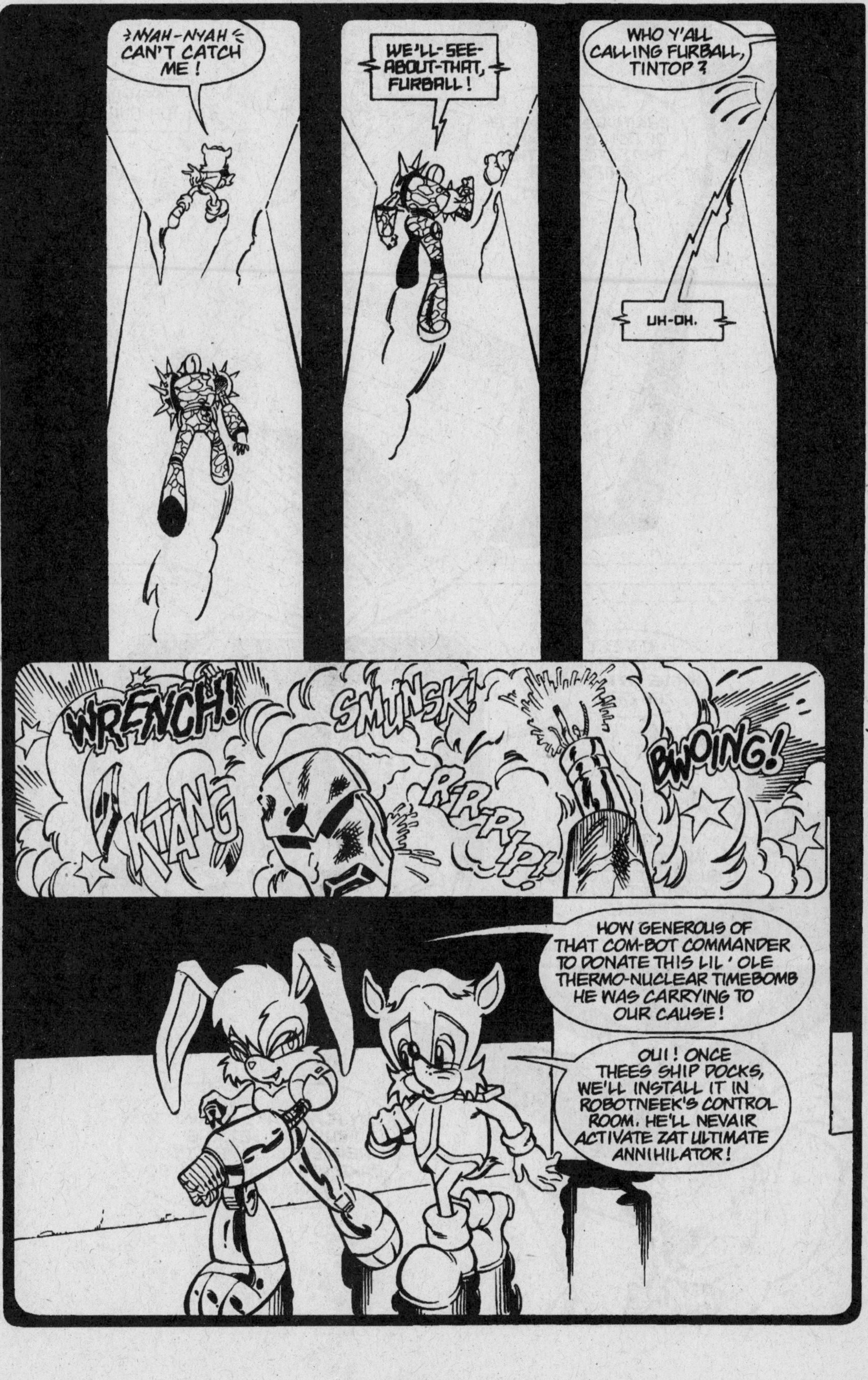
NYAH-NYAH CAN'T CATCH ME!
WE'LL-SEE-ABOUT-THAT, FURBALL!
WHO Y'ALL CALLING FURBALL, TINTOP?
UH-OH.
WRENCH!
SMUNSK!
KTANG
R-R-R-RIP!
BWOING!
HOW GENEROUS OF THAT COM-BOT COMMANDER TO DONATE THIS LIL' OLE THERMO-NUCLEAR TIMEBOMB HE WAS CARRYING TO OUR CAUSE!
OUI! ONCE THEES SHIP DOCKS, WE'LL INSTALL IT IN ROBOTNEEK'S CONTROL ROOM. HE'LL NEVAIR ACTIVATE ZAT ULTIMATE ANNIHILATOR!

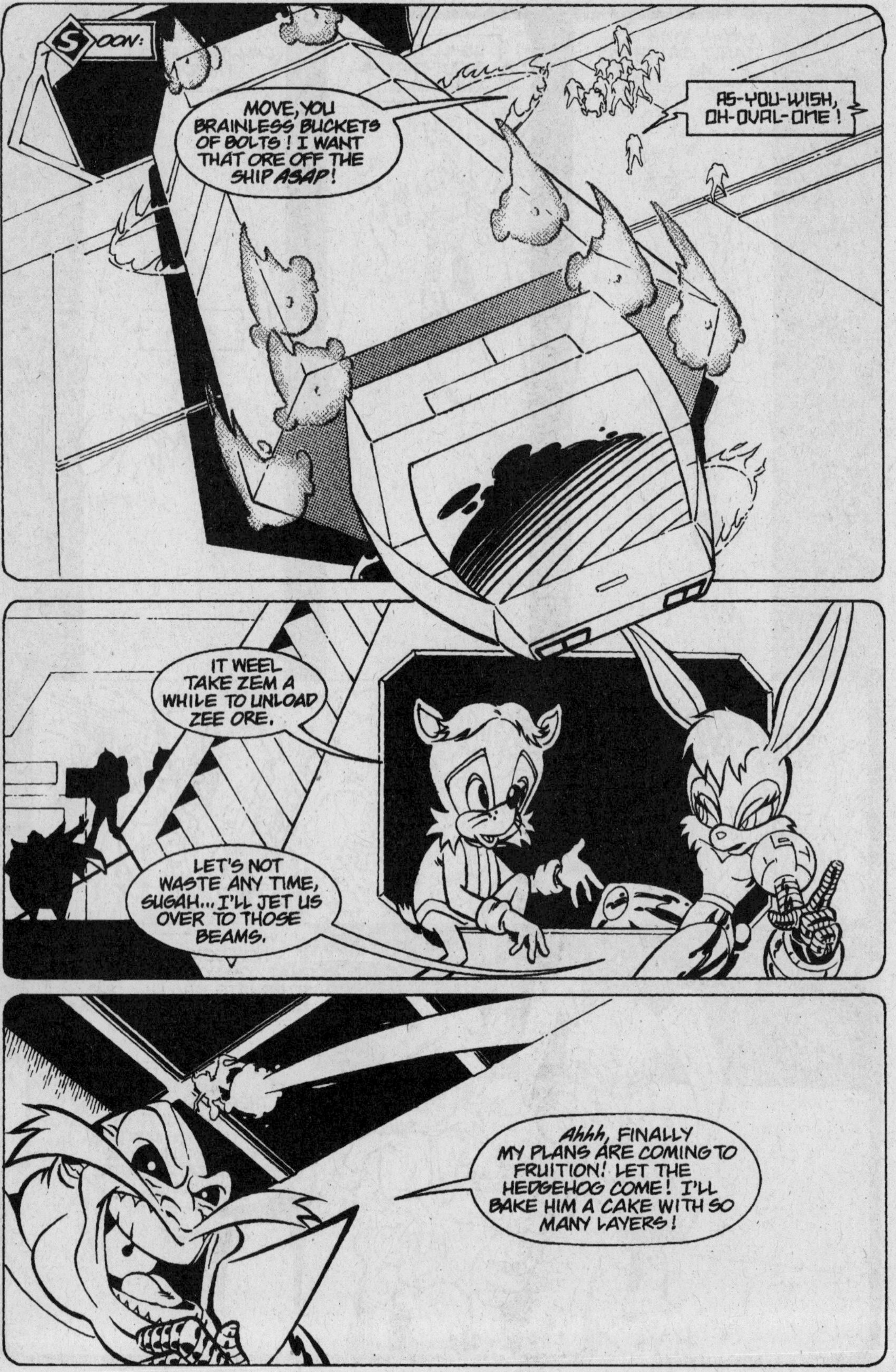
SOON:
MOVE, YOU BRAINLESS BUCKETS OF BOLTS! I WANT THAT ORE OFF THE SHIP ASAP!
AS-YOU-WISH, OH-OVAL-ONE!
IT WEEL TAKE ZEM A WHILE TO UNLOAD ZEE ORE.
LET'S NOT WASTE ANY TIME, SUGAH... I'LL JET US OVER TO THOSE BEAMS.
Ahhh, FINALLY MY PLANS ARE COMING TO FRUITION! LET THE HEDGEHOG COME! I'LL BAKE HIM A CAKE WITH SO MANY LAYERS!

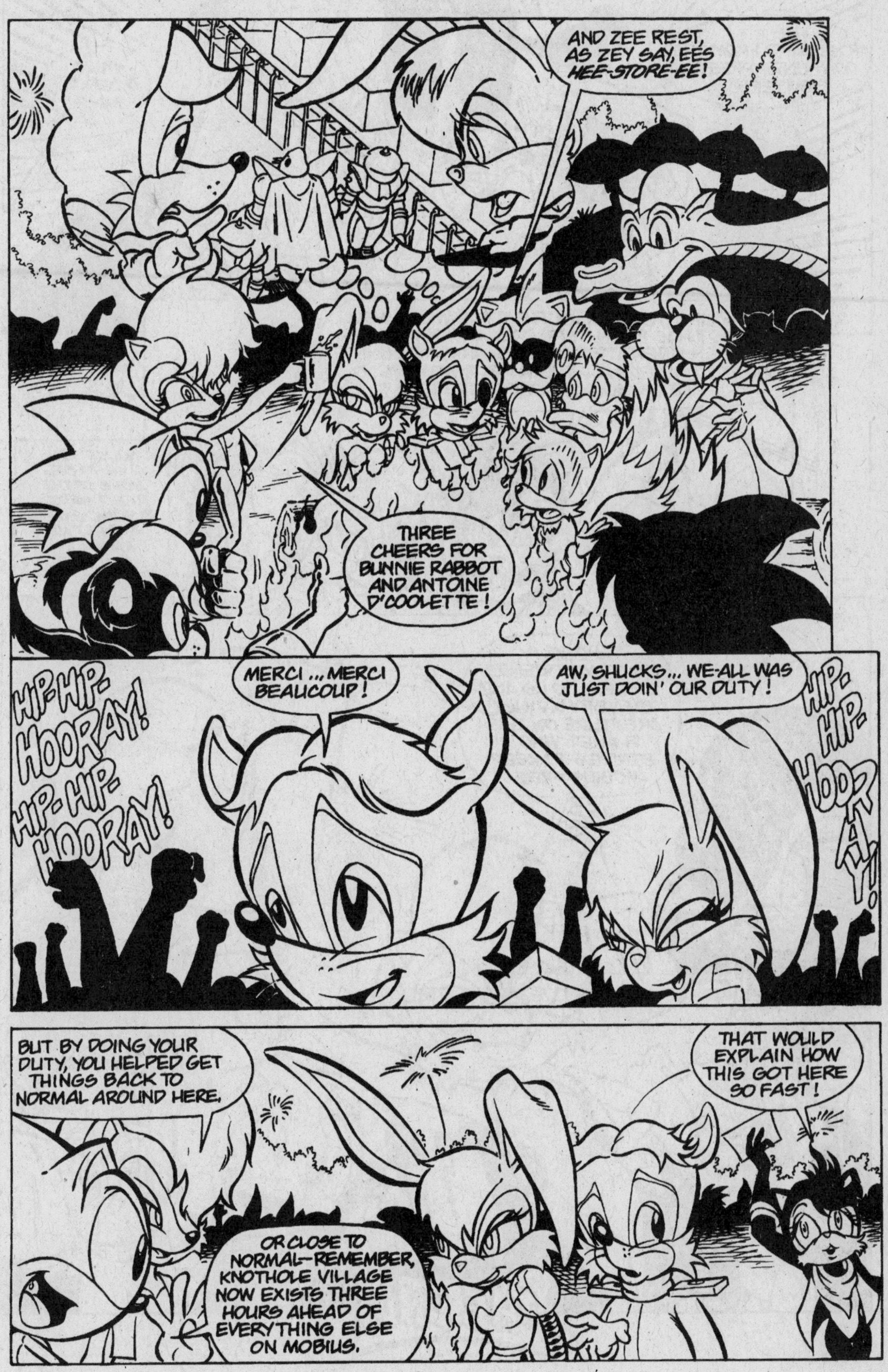
AND ZEE REST, AS ZEY SAY, EES HEE-STORE-EE!
THREE CHEERS FOR BUNNIE RABBOT AND ANTOINE D'COOLETTE!
HIP-HIP-HOORAY! HIP-HIP-HOORAY!
MERCI ... MERCI BEAUCOUP!
AW, SHUCKS... WE-ALL WAS JUST DOIN' OUR DUTY!
HIP-HIP-HOORAY!
BUT BY DOING YOUR DUTY, YOU HELPED GET THINGS BACK TO NORMAL AROUND HERE.
OR CLOSE TO NORMAL—REMEMBER, KNOTHOLE VILLAGE NOW EXISTS THREE HOURS AHEAD OF EVERYTHING ELSE ON MOBIUS.
THAT WOULD EXPLAIN HOW THIS GOT HERE SO FAST!

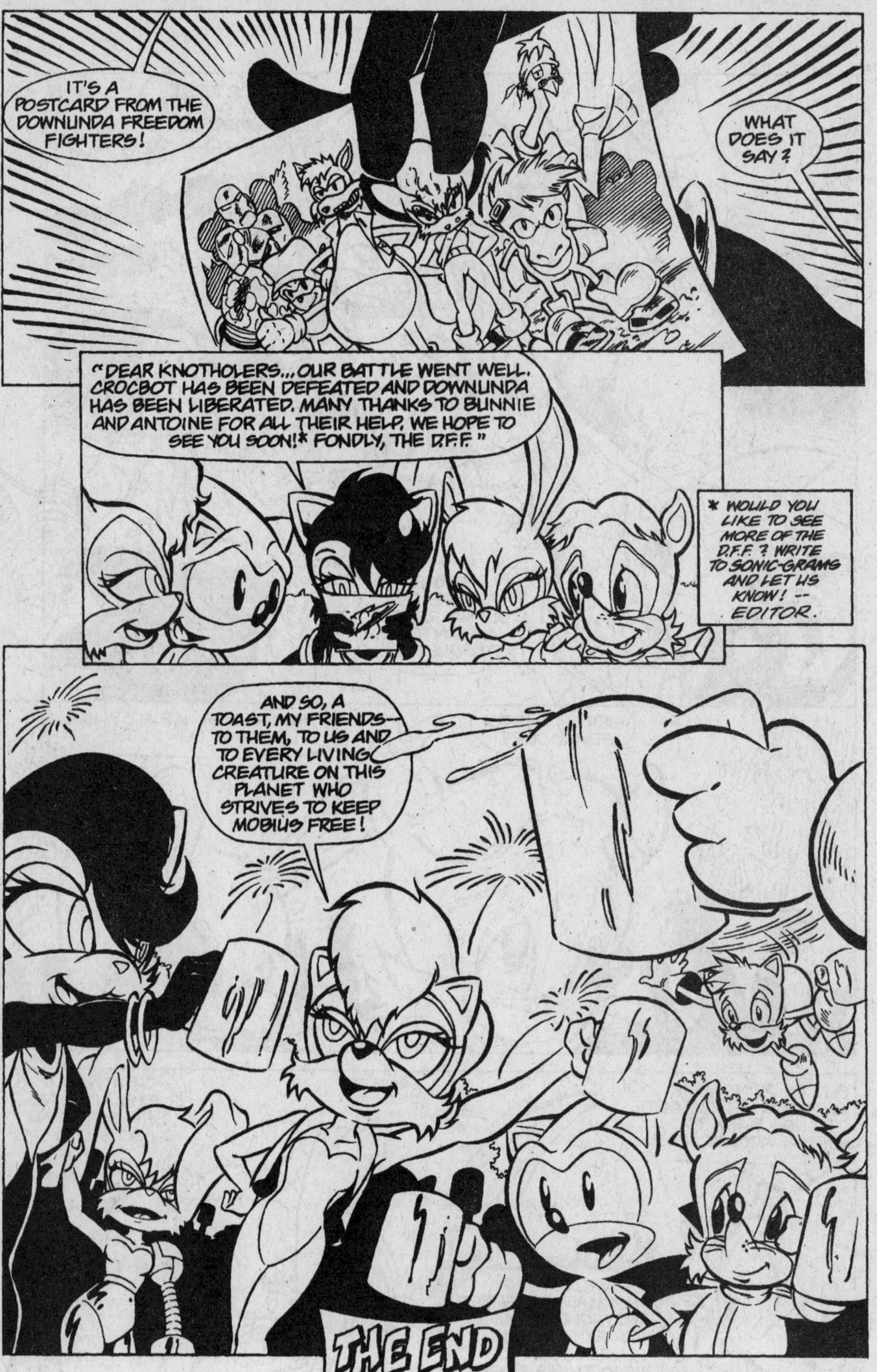
IT'S A POSTCARD FROM THE DOWNUNDA FREEDOM FIGHTERS!
WHAT DOES IT SAY?
"DEAR KNOTHOLERS... OUR BATTLE WENT WELL. CROCBOT HAS BEEN DEFEATED AND DOWNUNDA HAS BEEN LIBERATED. MANY THANKS TO BUNNIE AND ANTOINE FOR ALL THEIR HELP. WE HOPE TO SEE YOU SOON!* FONDLY, THE D.F.F."
* WOULD YOU LIKE TO SEE MORE OF THE D.F.F.? WRITE TO SONIC-GRAMS AND LET US KNOW! -- EDITOR.
AND SO, A TOAST, MY FRIENDS-- TO THEM, TO US AND TO EVERY LIVING CREATURE ON THIS PLANET WHO STRIVES TO KEEP MOBIUS FREE!
THE END

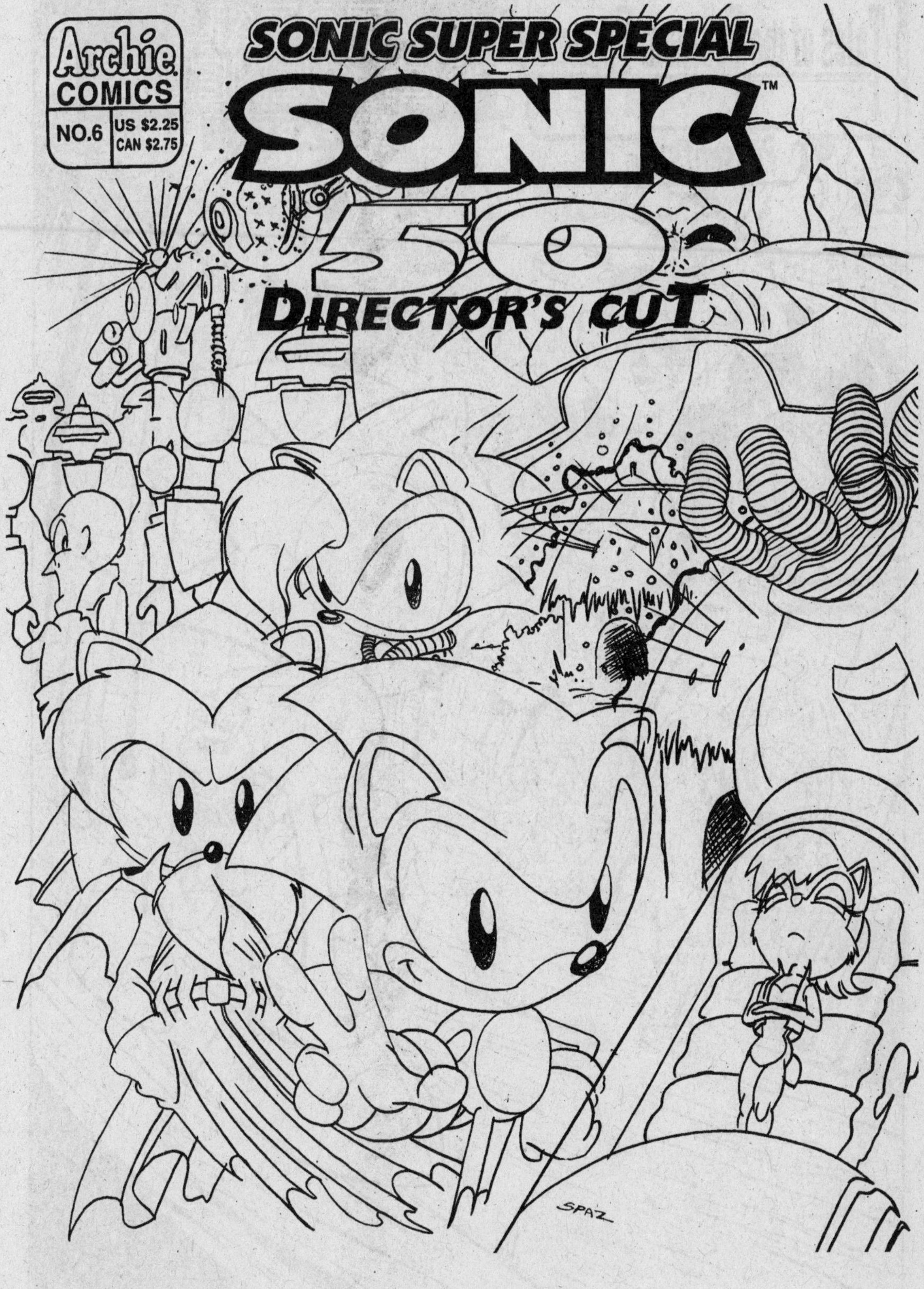
Archie COMICS
NO.6
US $2.25
CAN $2.75
SONIC SUPER SPECIAL
SONIC™
50
DIRECTOR'S CUT
SPAZ

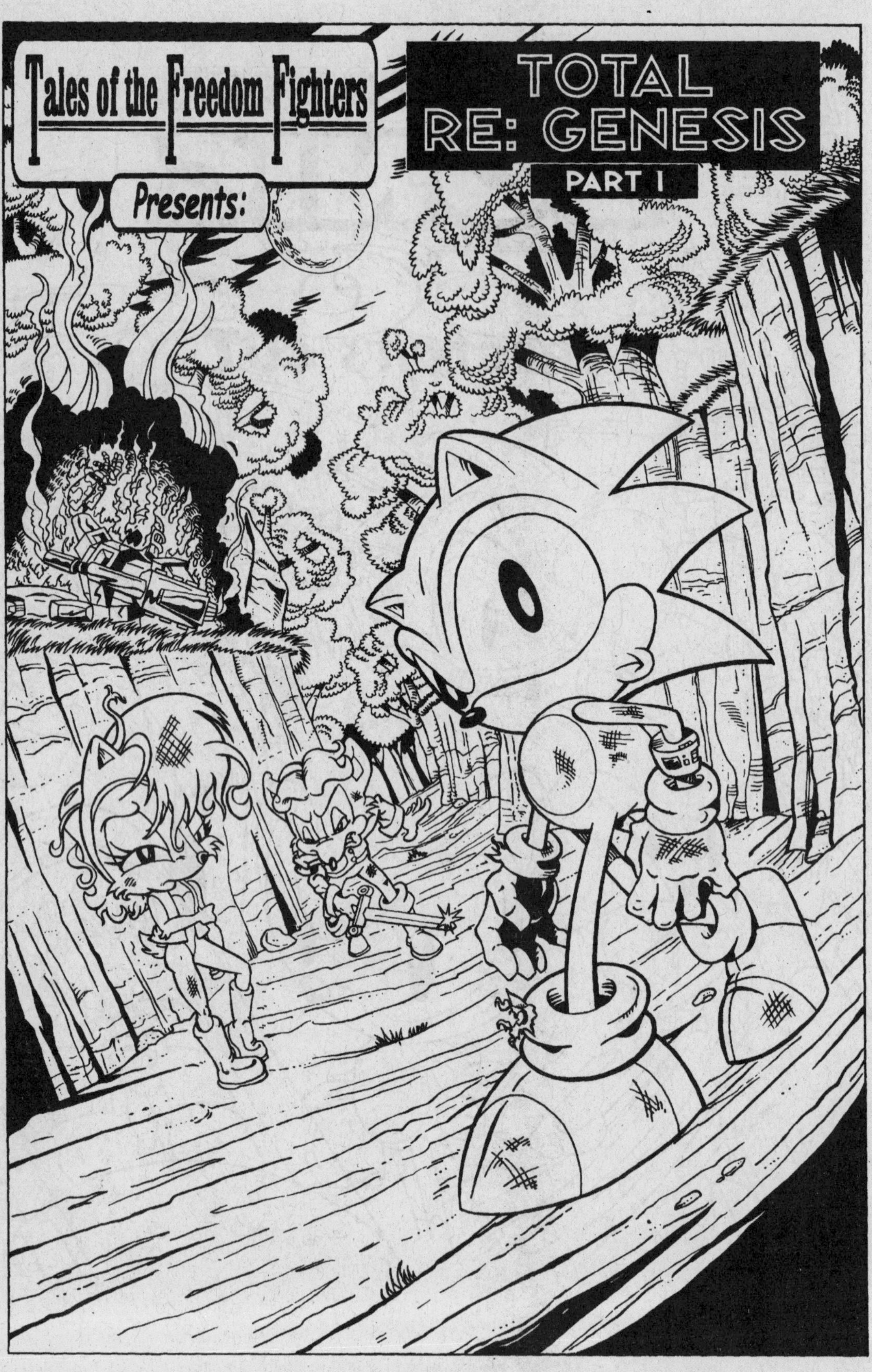
Tales of the Freedom Fighters
Presents:
TOTAL RE: GENESIS
PART 1

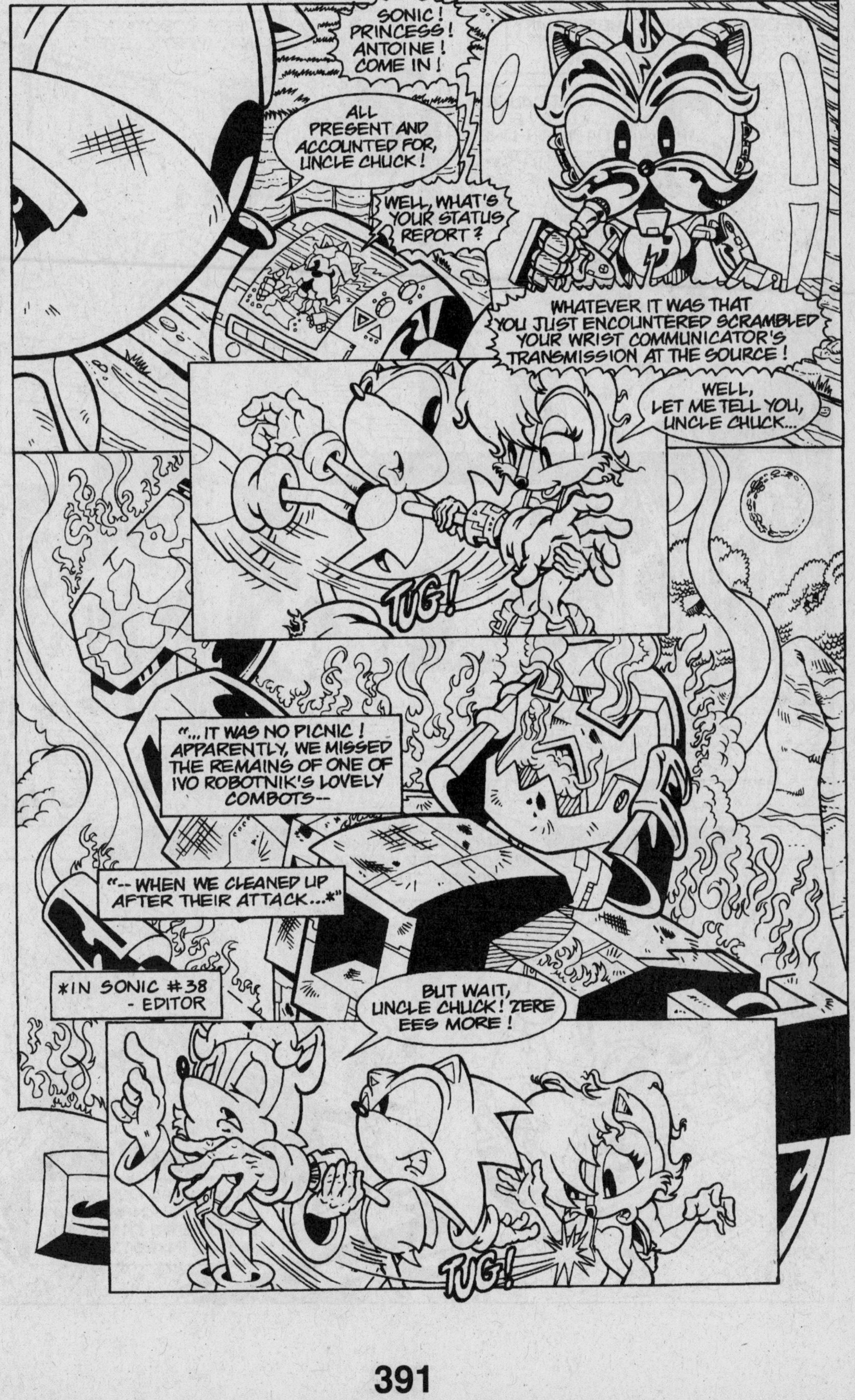
SONIC! PRINCESS! ANTOINE! COME IN!
ALL PRESENT AND ACCOUNTED FOR, UNCLE CHUCK!
WELL, WHAT'S YOUR STATUS REPORT?
WHATEVER IT WAS THAT YOU JUST ENCOUNTERED SCRAMBLED YOUR WRIST COMMUNICATOR'S TRANSMISSION AT THE SOURCE!
WELL, LET ME TELL YOU, UNCLE CHUCK...
TUG!
"...IT WAS NO PICNIC! APPARENTLY, WE MISSED THE REMAINS OF ONE OF IVO ROBOTNIK'S LOVELY COMBOTS--
"--WHEN WE CLEANED UP AFTER THEIR ATTACK...*"
*IN SONIC #38 - EDITOR
BUT WAIT, UNCLE CHUCK! ZERE EES MORE!
TUG!

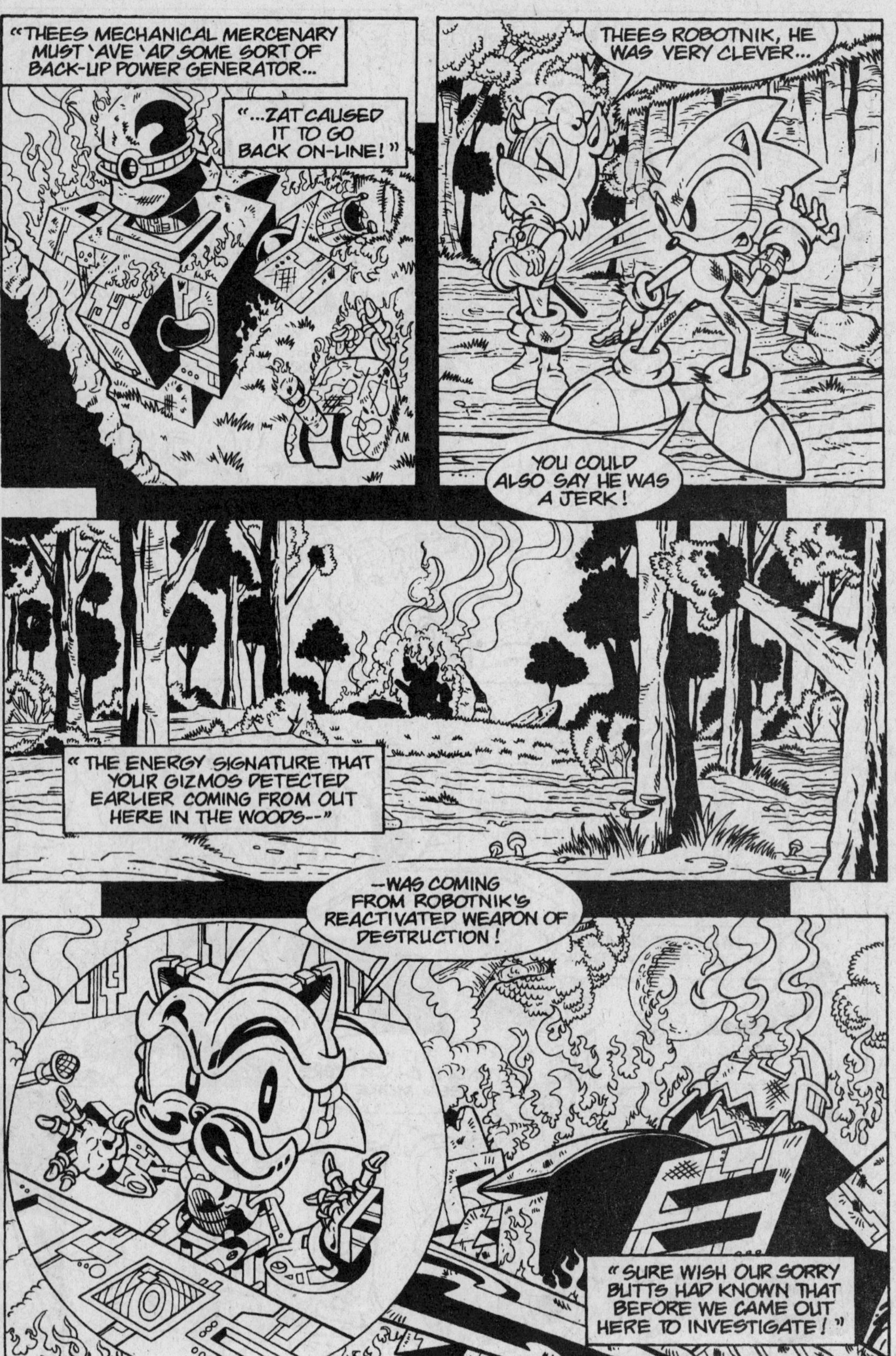

"THEES MECHANICAL MERCENARY MUST 'AVE 'AD SOME SORT OF BACK-UP POWER GENERATOR...
"...ZAT CAUSED IT TO GO BACK ON-LINE!"
THEES ROBOTNIK, HE WAS VERY CLEVER...
YOU COULD ALSO SAY HE WAS A JERK!
"THE ENERGY SIGNATURE THAT YOUR GIZMOS DETECTED EARLIER COMING FROM OUT HERE IN THE WOODS--"
--WAS COMING FROM ROBOTNIK'S REACTIVATED WEAPON OF DESTRUCTION!
"SURE WISH OUR SORRY BUTTS HAD KNOWN THAT BEFORE WE CAME OUT HERE TO INVESTIGATE!"

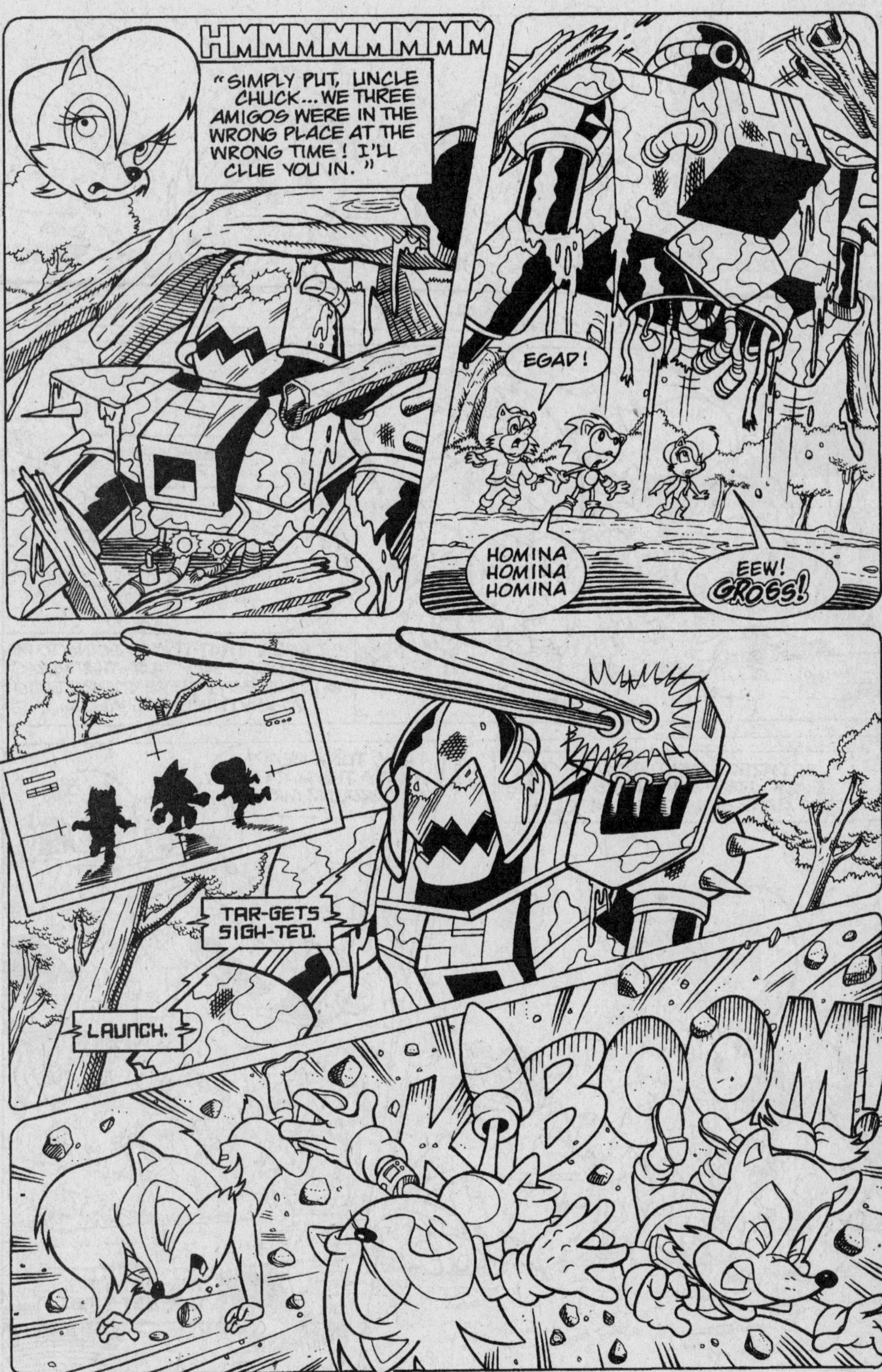
HMMMMMMMMM
"SIMPLY PUT, UNCLE CHUCK... WE THREE AMIGOS WERE IN THE WRONG PLACE AT THE WRONG TIME! I'LL CLUE YOU IN."
EGAD!
HOMINA HOMINA HOMINA
EEW! GROSS!
TAR-GETS SIGH-TED.
LAUNCH.
KA-BOOM!

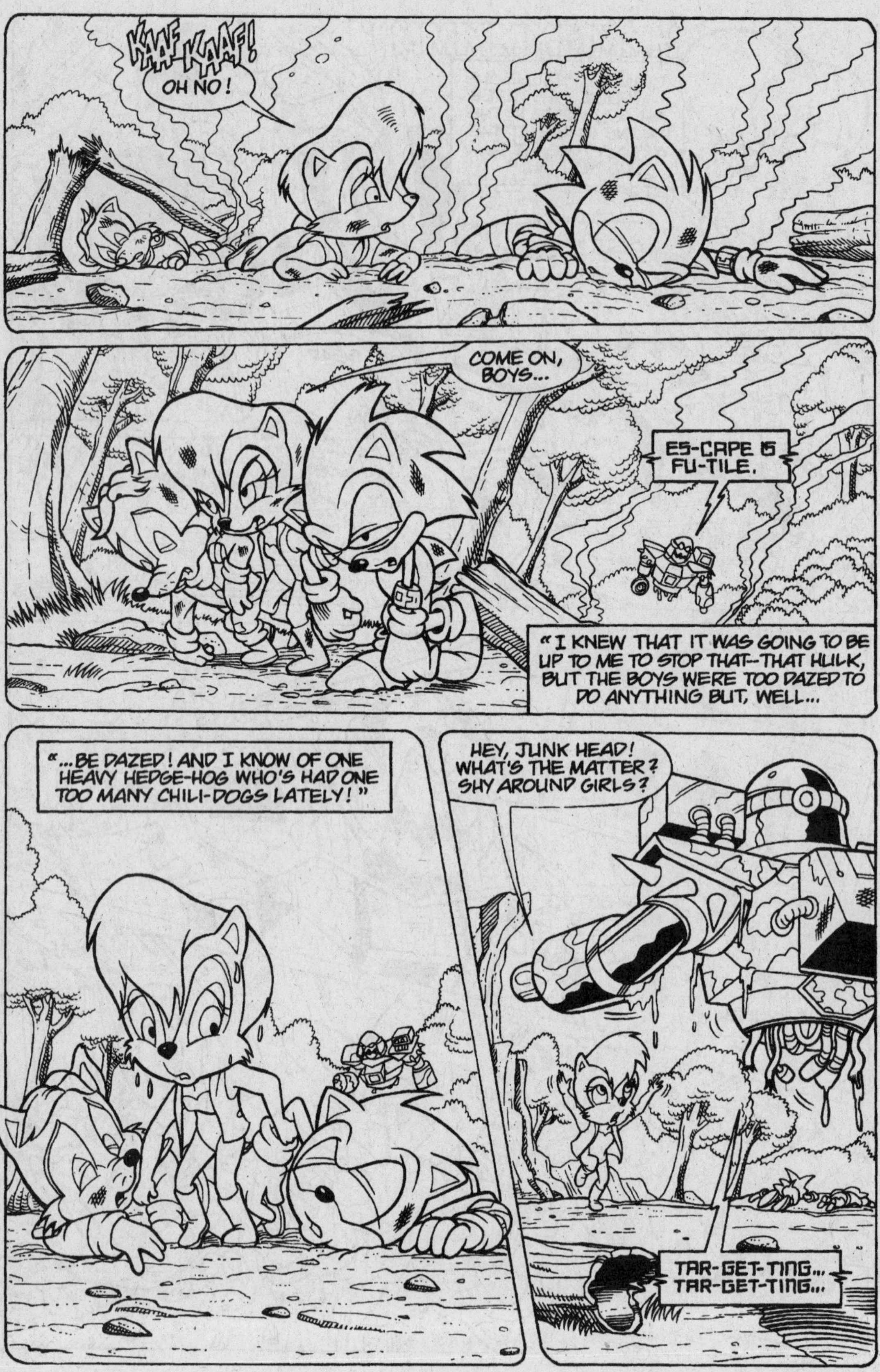
KAAF KAAF!
OH NO!
COME ON, BOYS...
ES-CAPE IS FU-TILE.
"I KNEW THAT IT WAS GOING TO BE UP TO ME TO STOP THAT--THAT HULK, BUT THE BOYS WERE TOO DAZED TO DO ANYTHING BUT, WELL...
"...BE DAZED! AND I KNOW OF ONE HEAVY HEDGE-HOG WHO'S HAD ONE TOO MANY CHILI-DOGS LATELY!"
HEY, JUNK HEAD! WHAT'S THE MATTER? SHY AROUND GIRLS?
TAR-GET-TING... TAR-GET-TING...

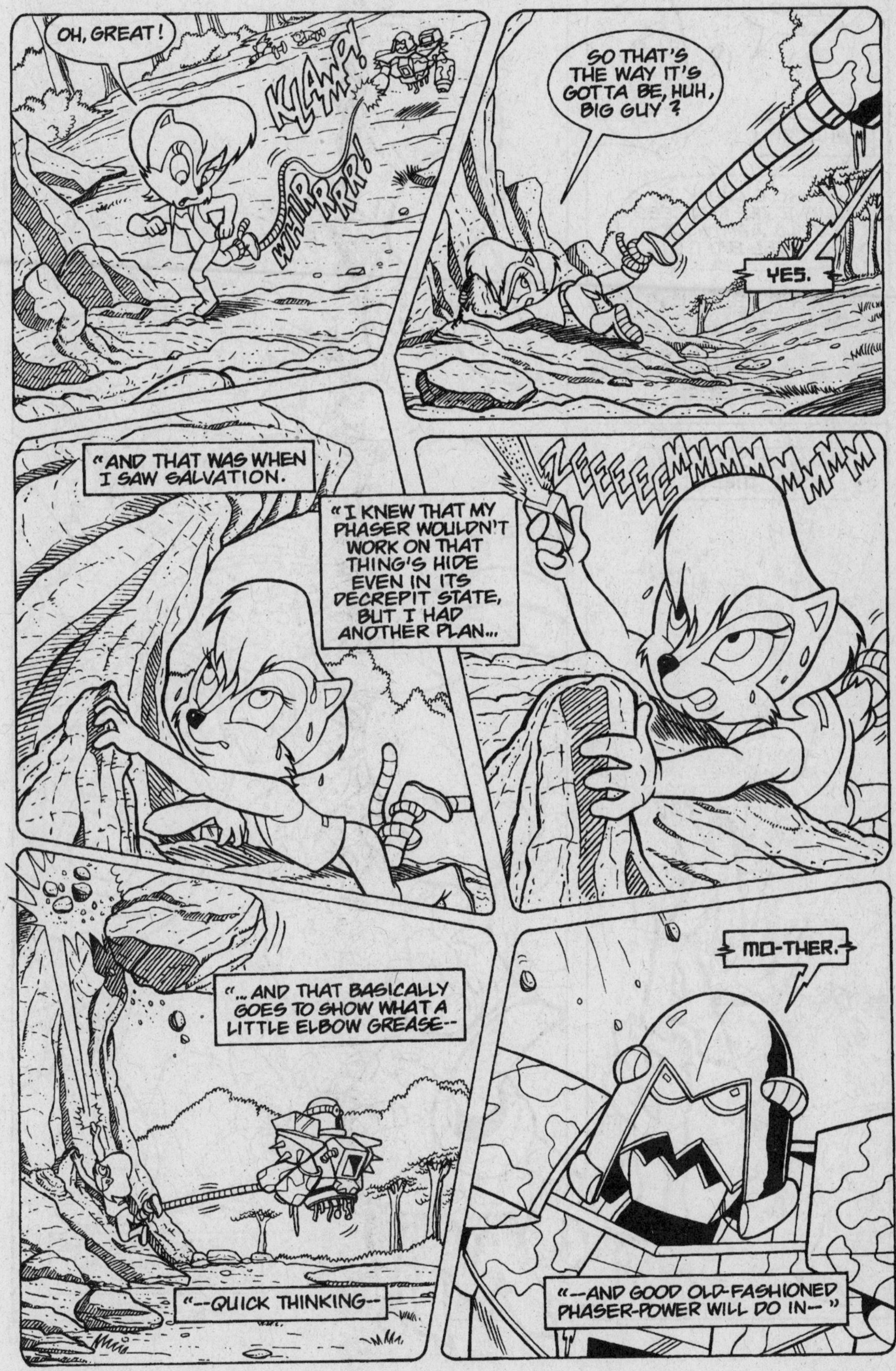
OH, GREAT!
KLAMP!
WHIRRRR!
SO THAT'S THE WAY IT'S GOTTA BE, HUH, BIG GUY?
YES.
"AND THAT WAS WHEN I SAW SALVATION.
"I KNEW THAT MY PHASER WOULDN'T WORK ON THAT THING'S HIDE EVEN IN ITS DECREPIT STATE, BUT I HAD ANOTHER PLAN...
ZEEEEEMMMMMMMMM
"...AND THAT BASICALLY GOES TO SHOW WHAT A LITTLE ELBOW GREASE--
"--QUICK THINKING--
MO-THER.
"--AND GOOD OLD-FASHIONED PHASER-POWER WILL DO IN--"

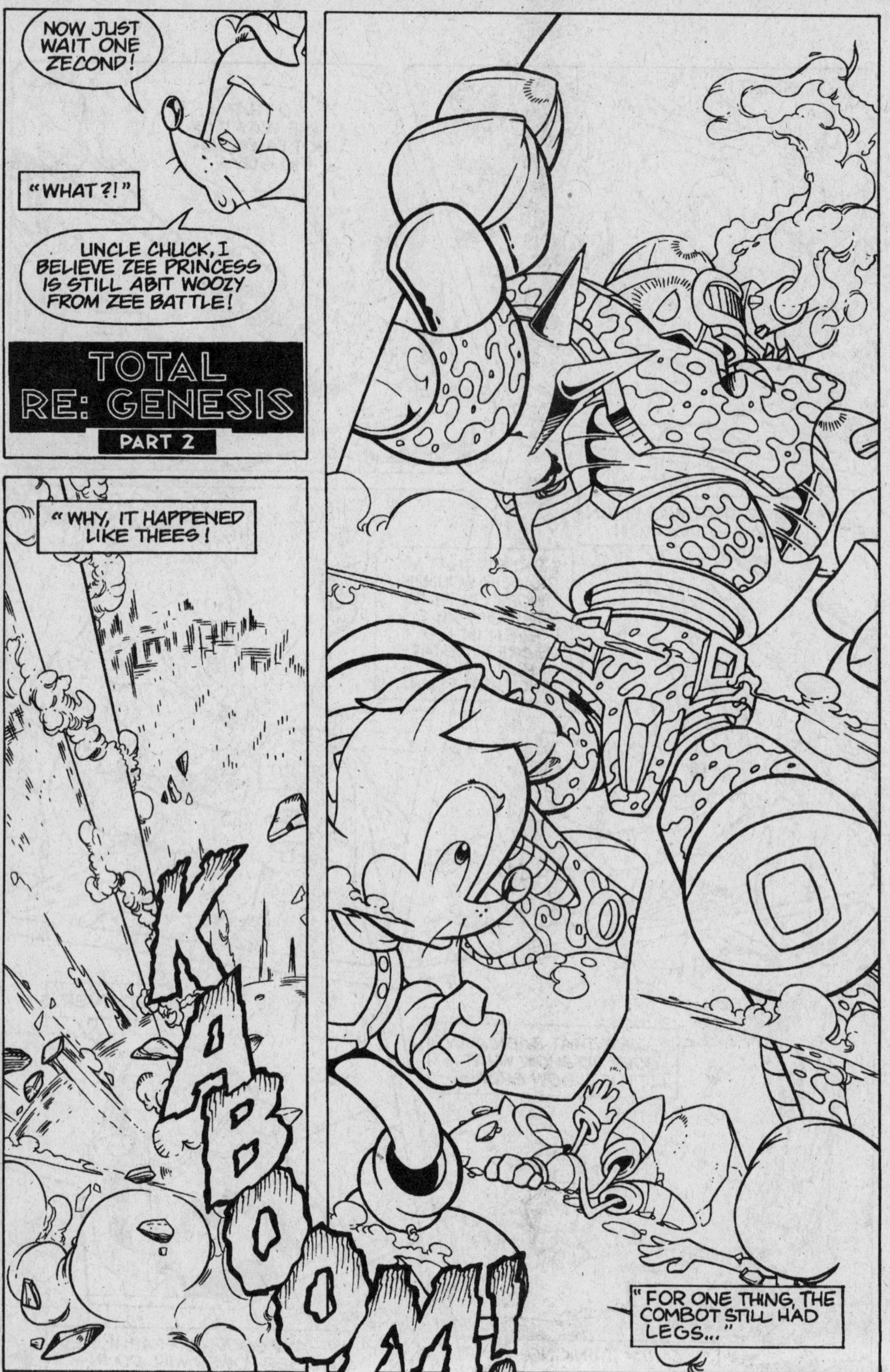
NOW JUST WAIT ONE ZECOND!
"WHAT?!"
UNCLE CHUCK, I BELIEVE ZEE PRINCESS IS STILL ABIT WOOZY FROM ZEE BATTLE!
TOTAL RE: GENESIS
PART 2
"WHY, IT HAPPENED LIKE THEES!
KABOOM!
"FOR ONE THING, THE COMBOT STILL HAD LEGS..."

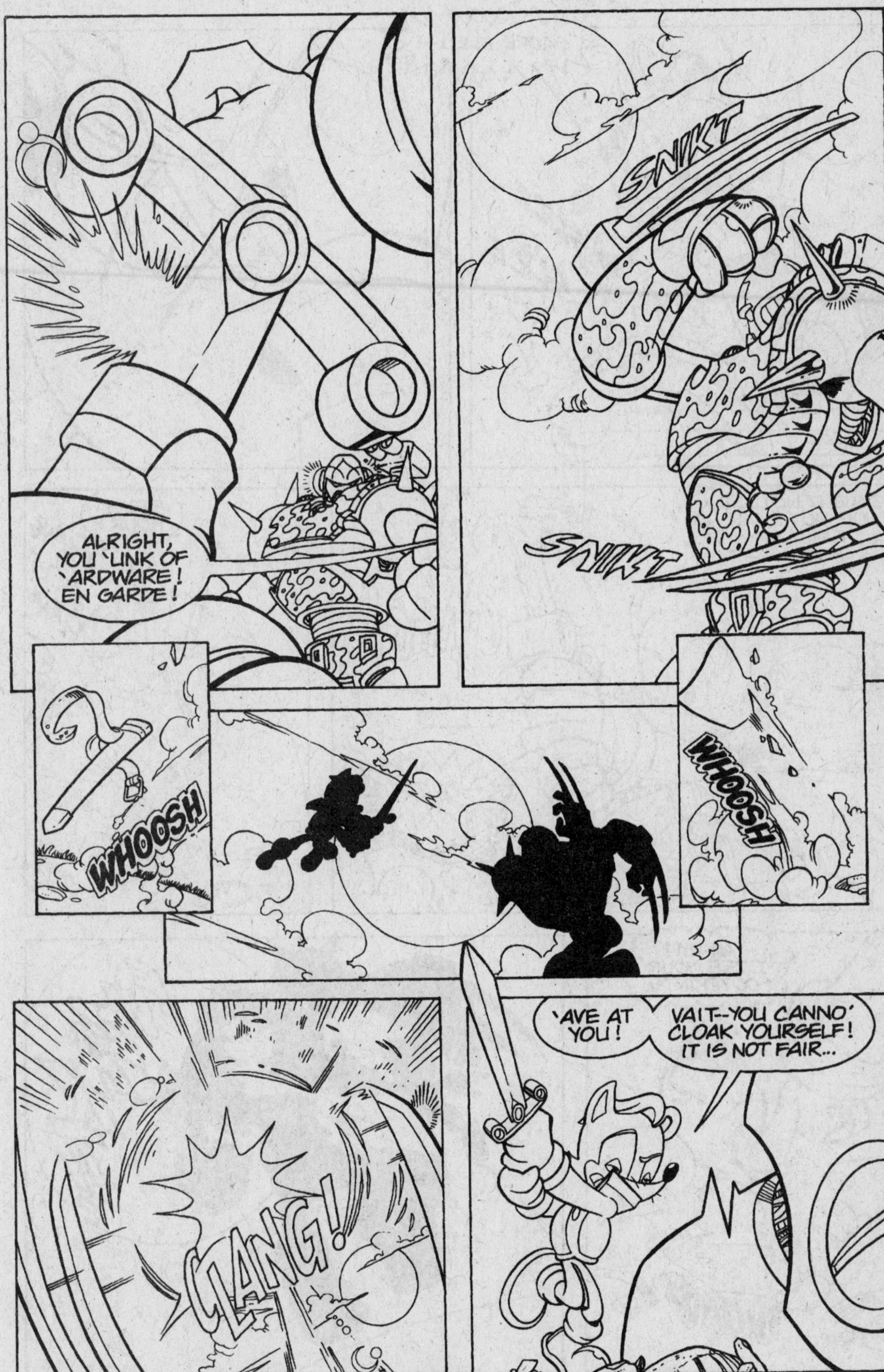
ALRIGHT, YOU `LINK OF `ARDWARE! EN GARDE!
SNIKT
SNIKT
WHOOSH
WHOOSH
CLANG!
`AVE AT YOU!
VAIT--YOU CANNO' CLOAK YOURSELF! IT IS NOT FAIR...

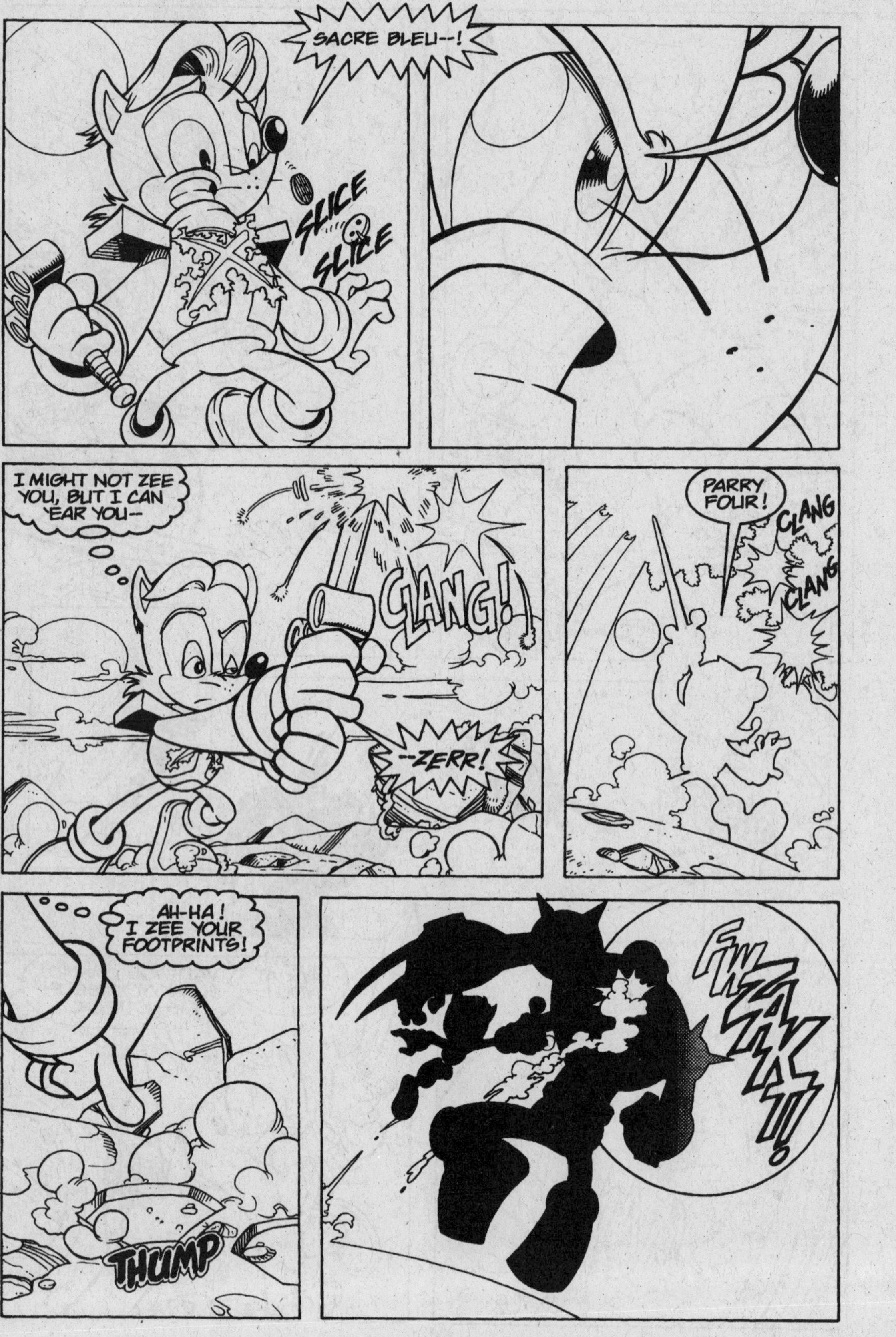
SACRE BLEU--!
SLICE
SLICE
I MIGHT NOT ZEE YOU, BUT I CAN 'EAR YOU--
CLANG!
--ZERR!
PARRY FOUR!
CLANG
CLANG
AH-HA! I ZEE YOUR FOOTPRINTS!
THUMP
FWZAKT!!

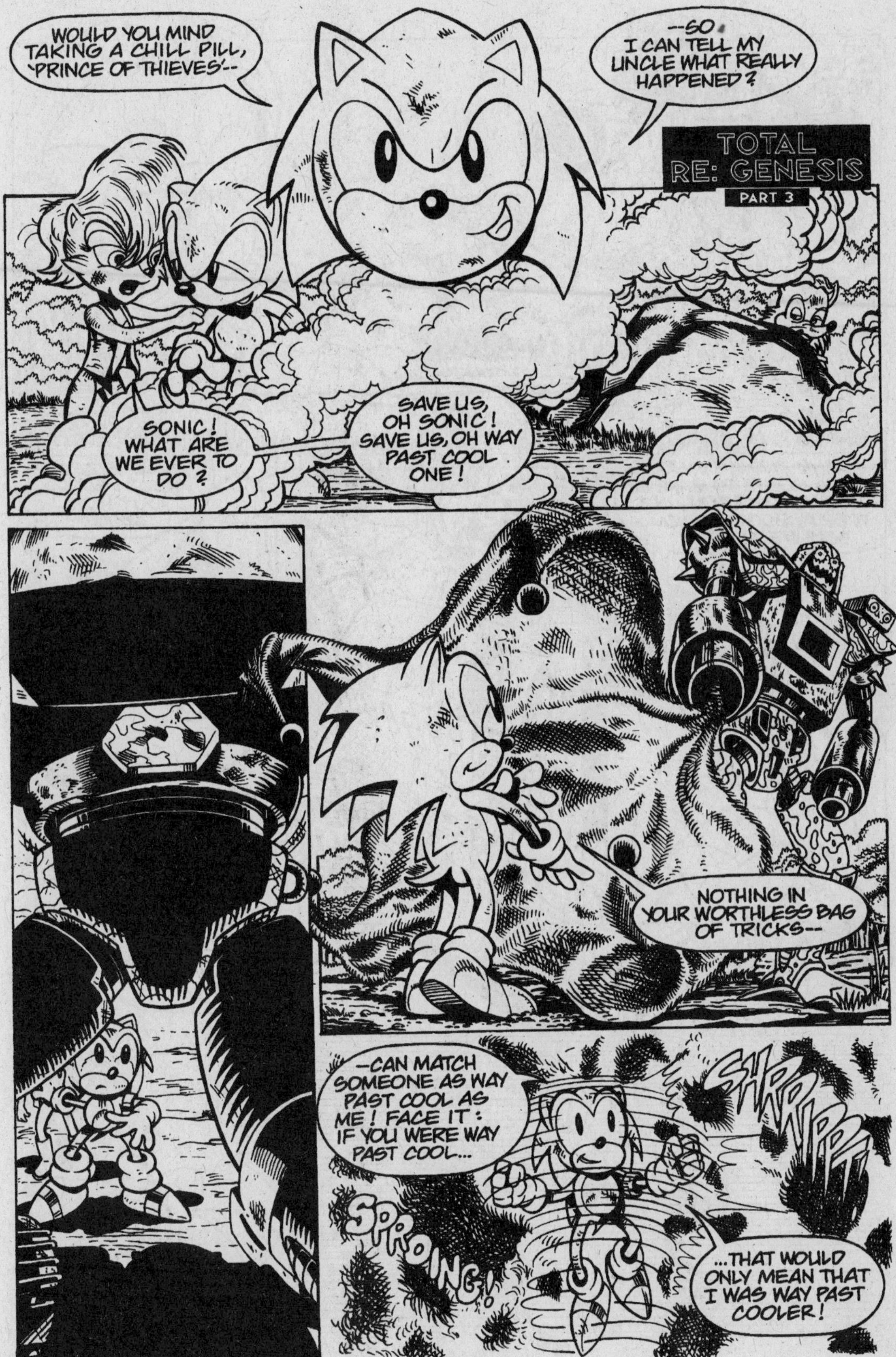
WOULD YOU MIND TAKING A CHILL PILL, 'PRINCE OF THIEVES'--
--SO I CAN TELL MY UNCLE WHAT REALLY HAPPENED?
TOTAL RE: GENESIS
PART 3
SONIC! WHAT ARE WE EVER TO DO?
SAVE US, OH SONIC! SAVE US, OH WAY PAST COOL ONE!
NOTHING IN YOUR WORTHLESS BAG OF TRICKS--
-CAN MATCH SOMEONE AS WAY PAST COOL AS ME! FACE IT: IF YOU WERE WAY PAST COOL...
SHRRIPPT
SPROING!
...THAT WOULD ONLY MEAN THAT I WAS WAY PAST COOLER!

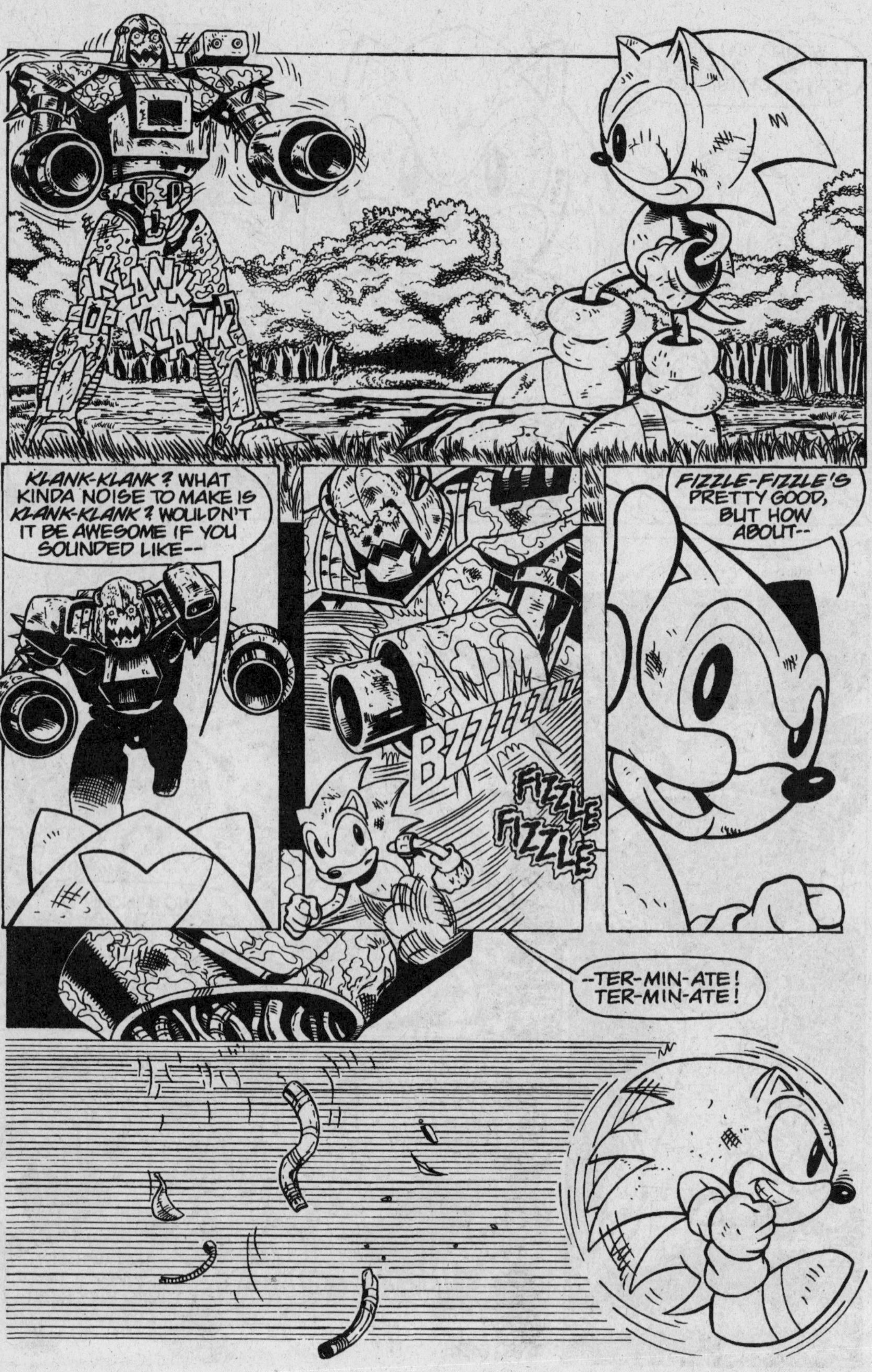
KLANK-O-KLANK
KLANK-KLANK? WHAT KINDA NOISE TO MAKE IS KLANK-KLANK? WOULDN'T IT BE AWESOME IF YOU SOUNDED LIKE--
BZZZZZZZ
FIZZLE FIZZLE
FIZZLE-FIZZLE'S PRETTY GOOD, BUT HOW ABOUT--
--TER-MIN-ATE! TER-MIN-ATE!

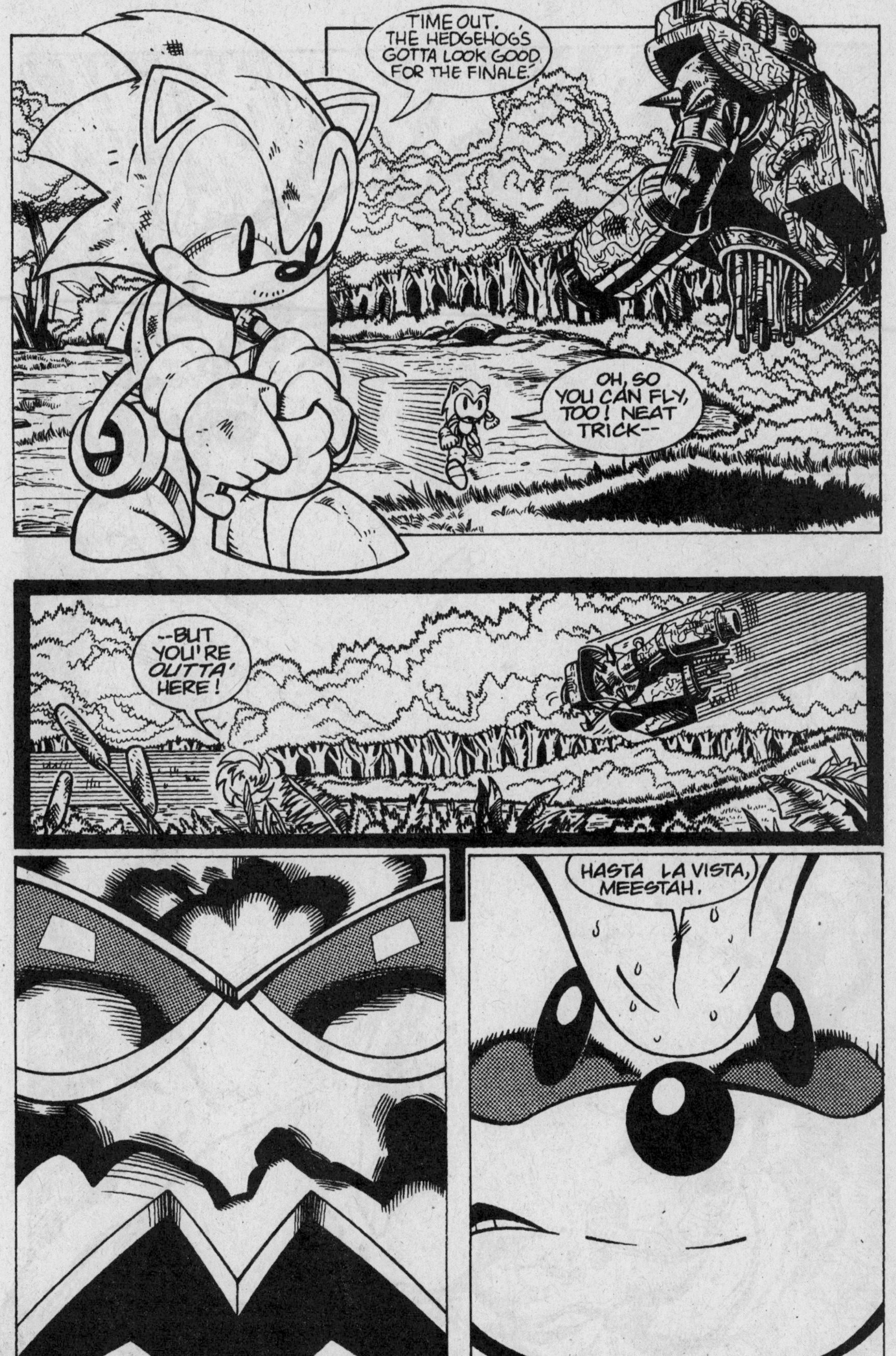
TIME OUT. THE HEDGEHOG'S GOTTA LOOK GOOD FOR THE FINALE.
OH, SO YOU CAN FLY, TOO! NEAT TRICK--
--BUT YOU'RE OUTTA' HERE!
HASTA LA VISTA, MEESTAH.

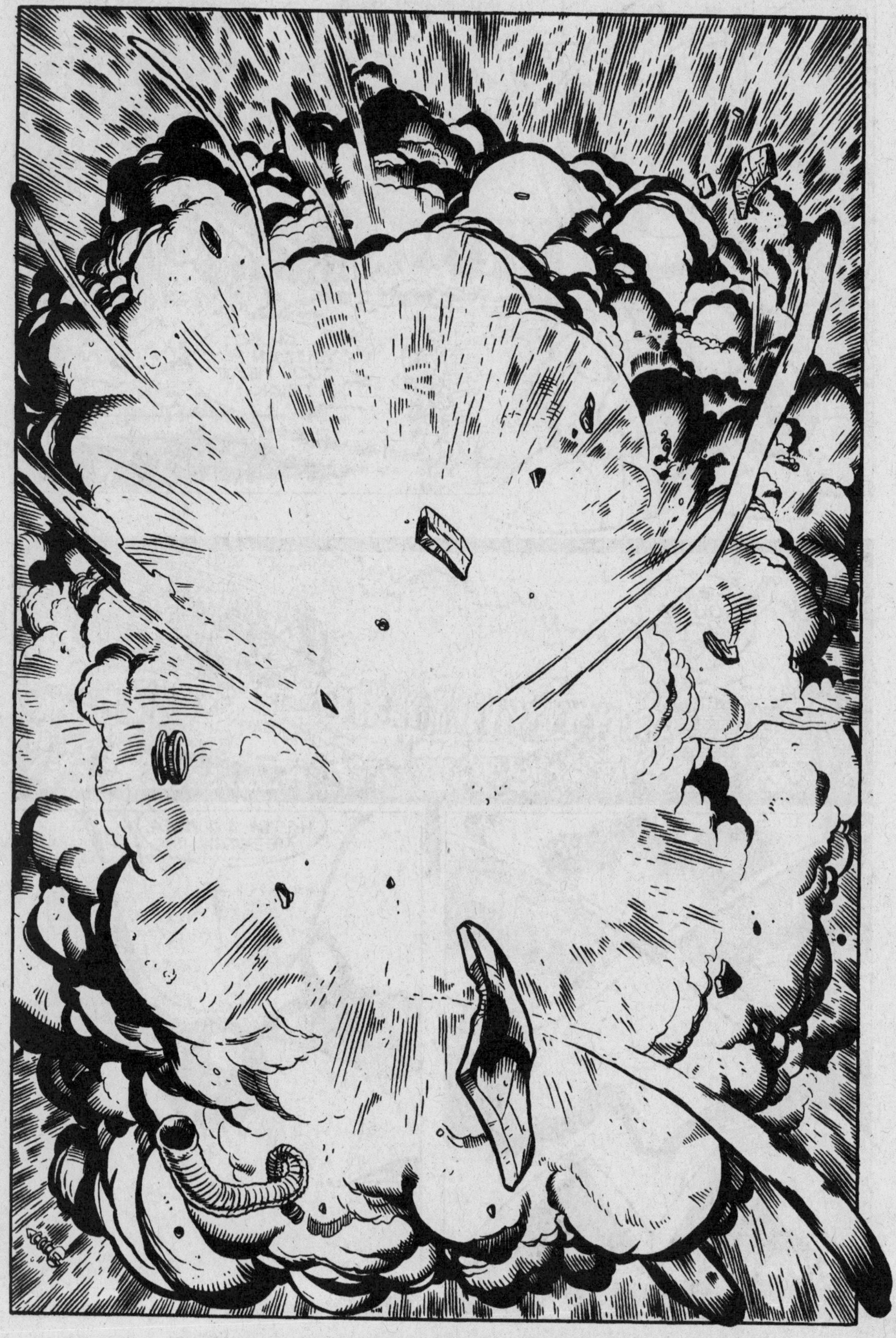

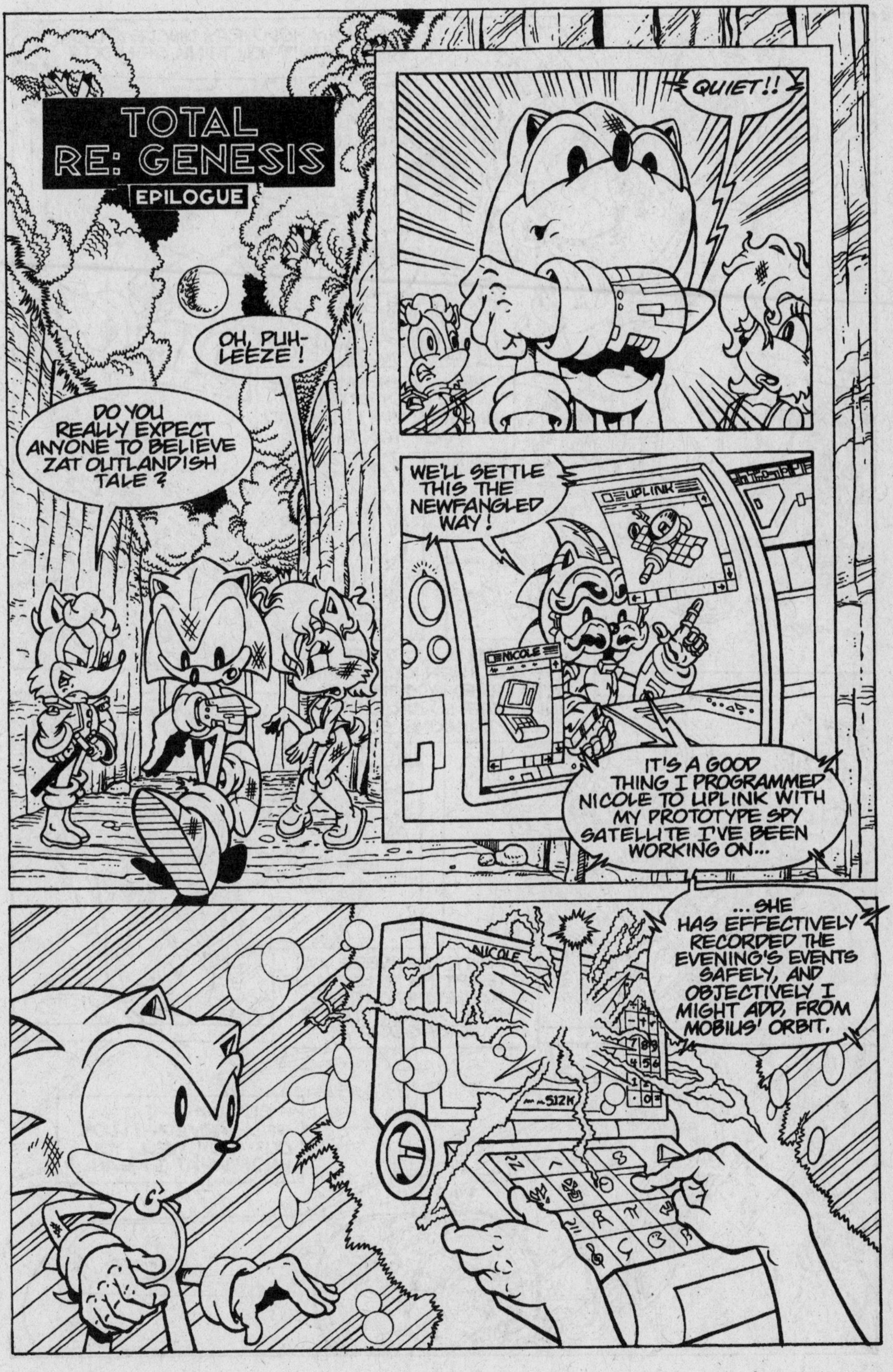

TOTAL RE: GENESIS
EPILOGUE
DO YOU REALLY EXPECT ANYONE TO BELIEVE ZAT OUTLANDISH TALE ?
OH, PUH-LEEZE !
QUIET!!
WE'LL SETTLE THIS THE NEWFANGLED WAY !
UPLINK
NICOLE
IT'S A GOOD THING I PROGRAMMED NICOLE TO UPLINK WITH MY PROTOTYPE SPY SATELLITE I'VE BEEN WORKING ON...
... SHE HAS EFFECTIVELY RECORDED THE EVENING'S EVENTS SAFELY, AND OBJECTIVELY I MIGHT ADD, FROM MOBIUS' ORBIT.
NICOLE

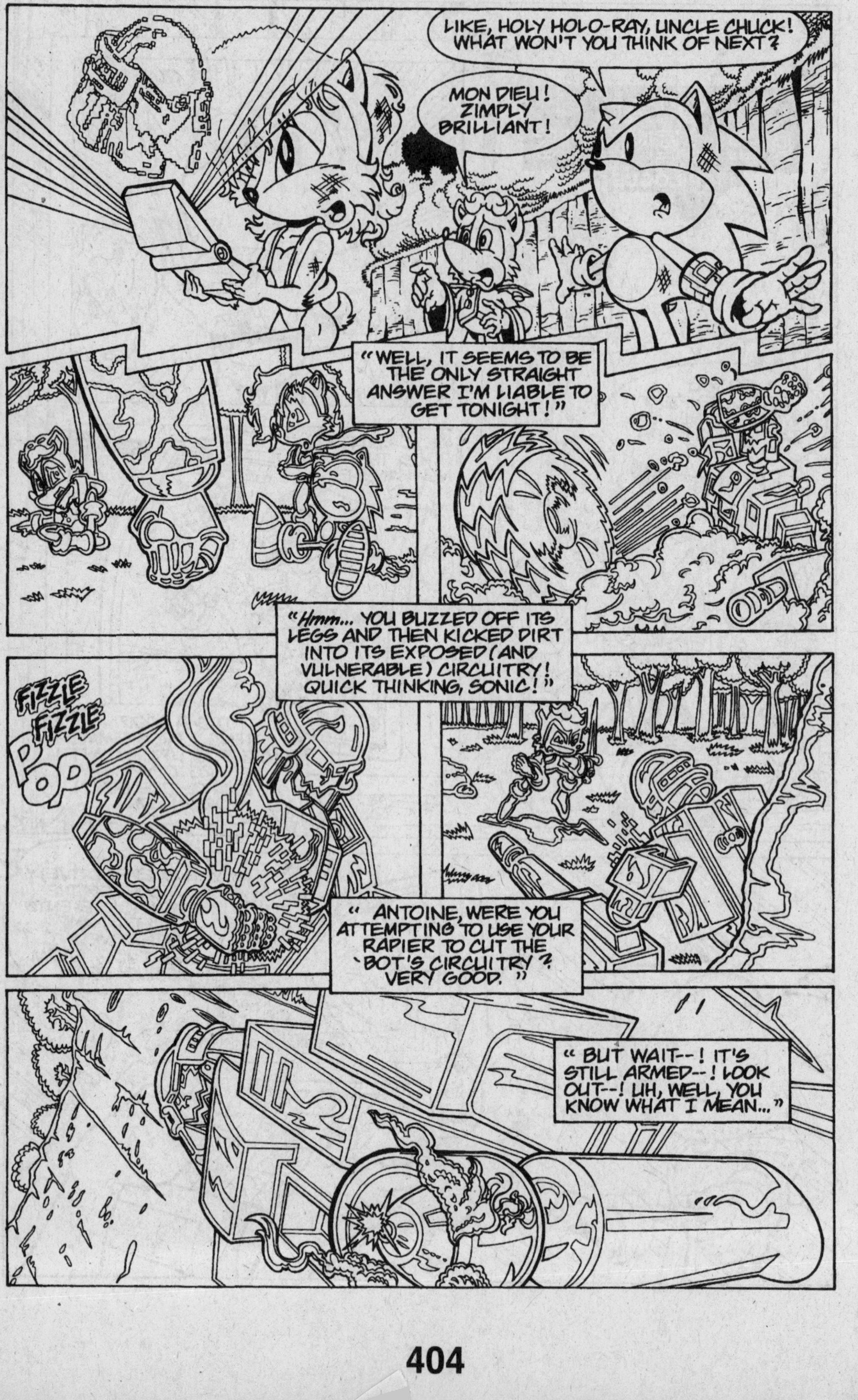

LIKE, HOLY HOLO-RAY, UNCLE CHUCK! WHAT WON'T YOU THINK OF NEXT?
MON DIEU! ZIMPLY BRILLIANT!
"WELL, IT SEEMS TO BE THE ONLY STRAIGHT ANSWER I'M LIABLE TO GET TONIGHT!"
"Hmm... YOU BUZZED OFF ITS LEGS AND THEN KICKED DIRT INTO ITS EXPOSED (AND VULNERABLE) CIRCUITRY! QUICK THINKING, SONIC!"
FIZZLE FIZZLE
POP
"ANTOINE, WERE YOU ATTEMPTING TO USE YOUR RAPIER TO CUT THE 'BOT'S CIRCUITRY? VERY GOOD."
"BUT WAIT--! IT'S STILL ARMED--! LOOK OUT--! UH, WELL, YOU KNOW WHAT I MEAN..."

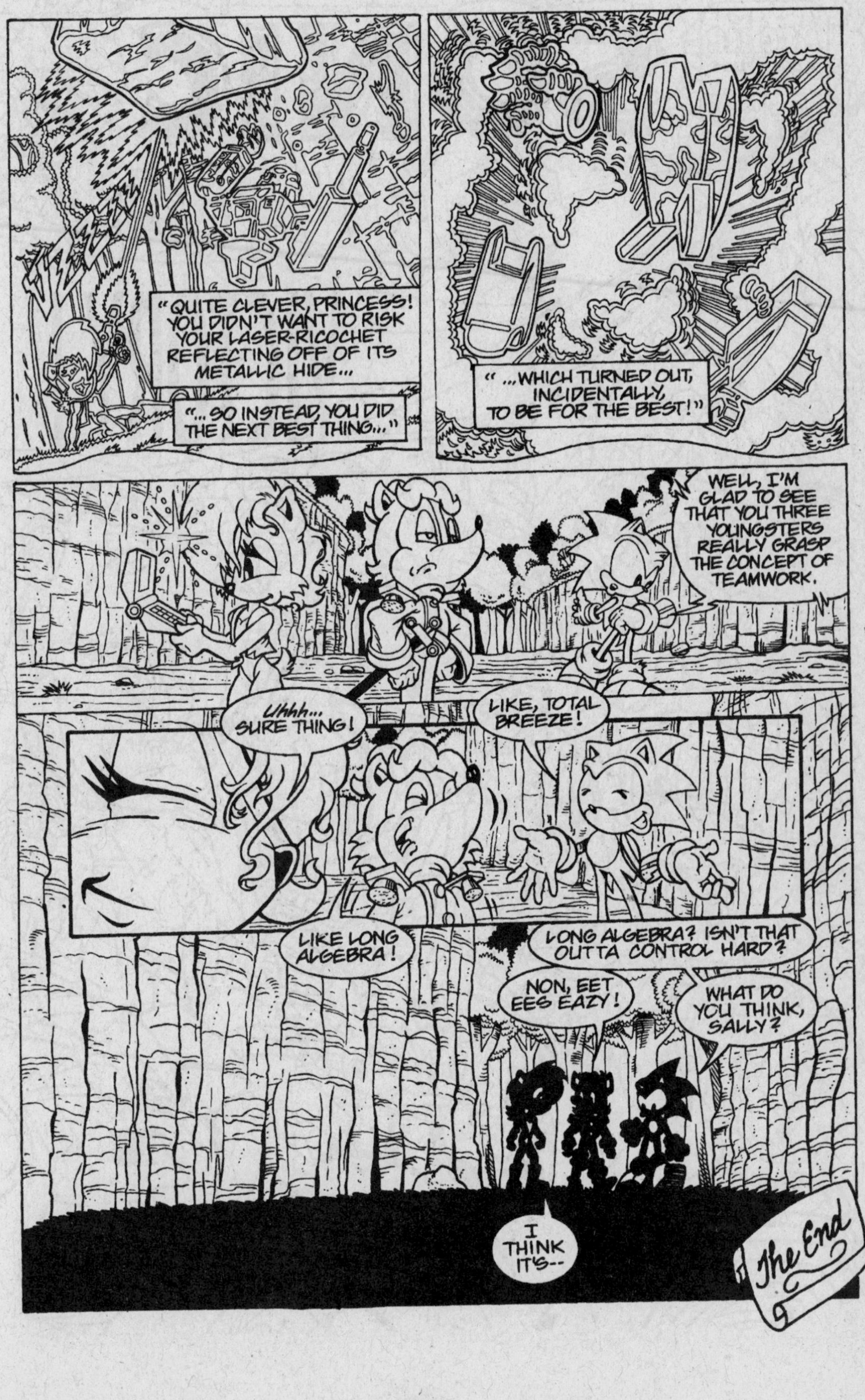
"QUITE CLEVER, PRINCESS! YOU DIDN'T WANT TO RISK YOUR LASER-RICOCHET REFLECTING OFF OF ITS METALLIC HIDE...
"...SO INSTEAD, YOU DID THE NEXT BEST THING..."
"...WHICH TURNED OUT, INCIDENTALLY, TO BE FOR THE BEST!"
WELL, I'M GLAD TO SEE THAT YOU THREE YOUNGSTERS REALLY GRASP THE CONCEPT OF TEAMWORK.
Uhhh... SURE THING!
LIKE, TOTAL BREEZE!
LIKE LONG ALGEBRA!
LONG ALGEBRA? ISN'T THAT OUTTA CONTROL HARD?
NON, EET EES EAZY!
WHAT DO YOU THINK, SALLY?
I THINK IT'S--
The End

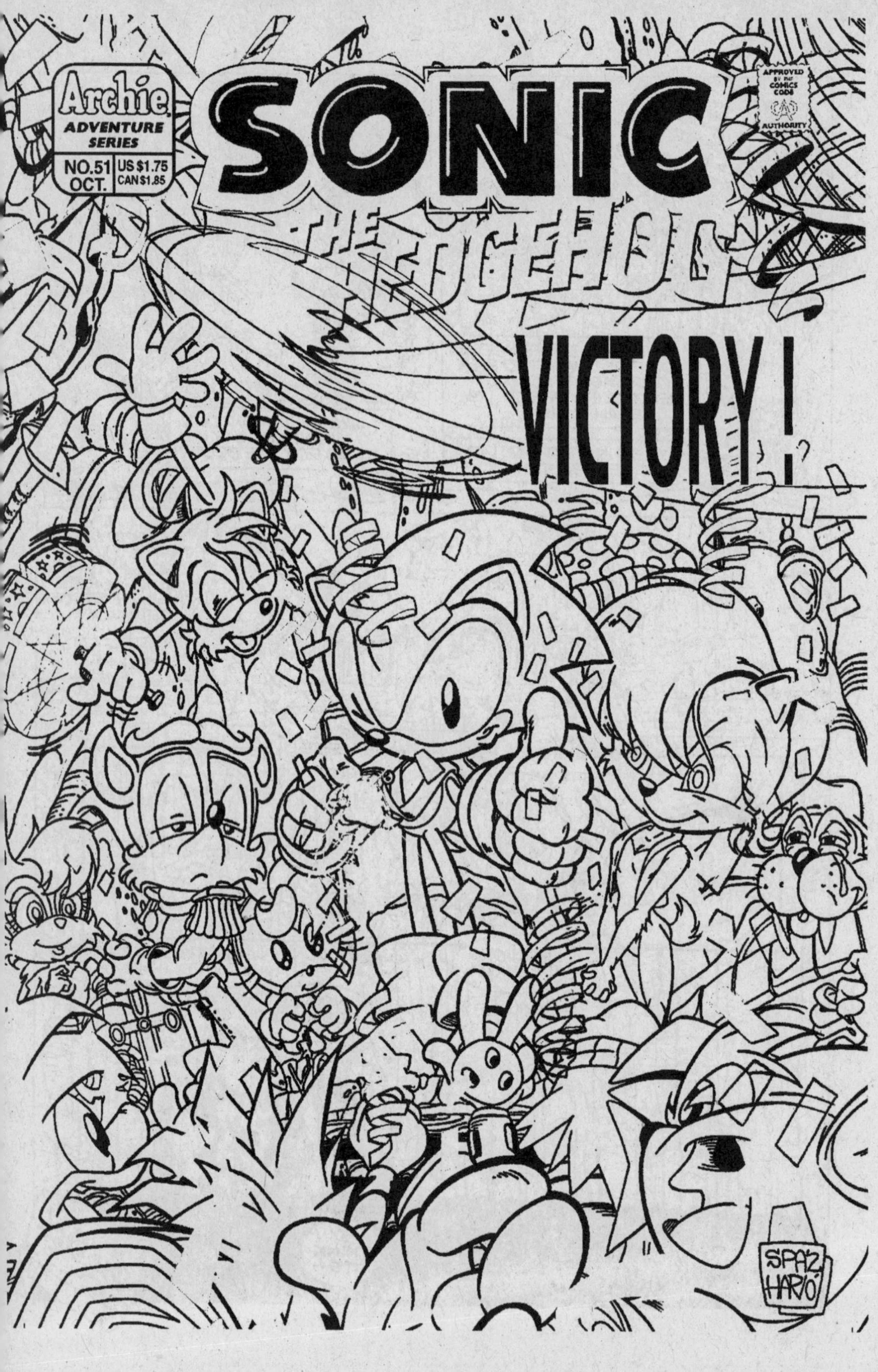
Archie
ADVENTURE SERIES
NO.51 OCT.
US $1.75
CAN $1.85
SONIC THE HEDGEHOG
APPROVED BY THE COMICS CODE AUTHORITY
VICTORY!
SPAZ HARVO

The planet Mobius was like a paradise... until the evil Doctor Robotnik and his mechanical legions conquered the land and its people, using his knowledge of technology and pollution. But many young, courageous citizens banded together as a brave group of "Freedom Fighters!" They struggle to overthrow the dictator and, one day, regain what was once theirs. Among them, the greatest of the Freedom Fighters is the fastest and way-coolest dude on two feet... SONIC The HEDGEHOG!

But now, with Robotnik's seeming demise, the freedom-fighting band of 'bot-kicking rebels who brought an end to his tyrannical reign of techno-terror can finally enjoy a long-awaited peace... or can they? Read closely, speed freaks, 'cause only Sonic The Hedgehog can answer that question for you!

The celebration is already underway! Let's join the Freedom Fighters as they corner Sonic away from the other villagers...

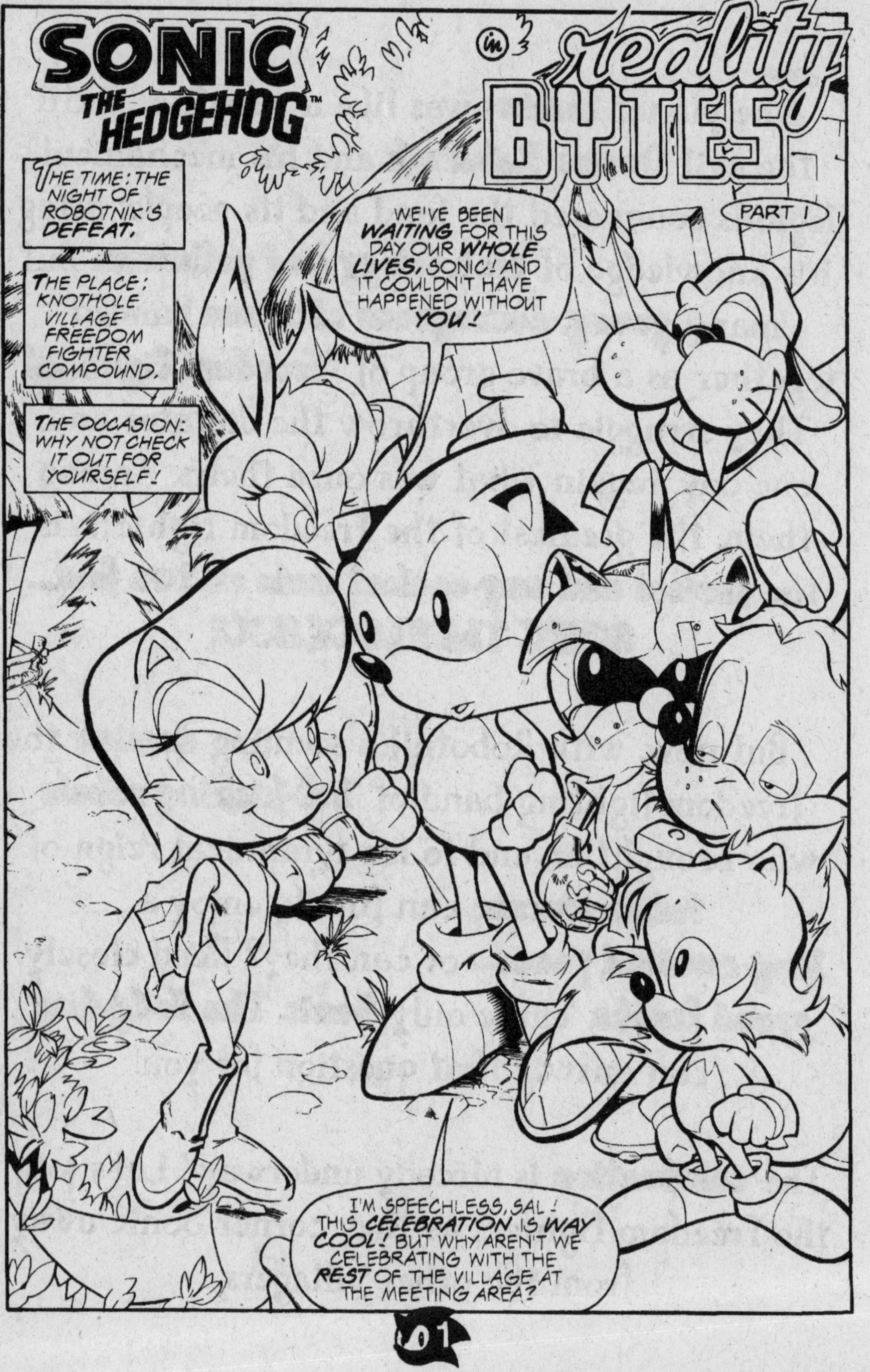
SONIC THE HEDGEHOG™
in
reality BYTES
PART 1
THE TIME: THE NIGHT OF ROBOTNIK'S DEFEAT.
THE PLACE: KNOTHOLE VILLAGE FREEDOM FIGHTER COMPOUND.
THE OCCASION: WHY NOT CHECK IT OUT FOR YOURSELF!
WE'VE BEEN WAITING FOR THIS DAY OUR WHOLE LIVES, SONIC! AND IT COULDN'T HAVE HAPPENED WITHOUT YOU!
I'M SPEECHLESS, SAL! THIS CELEBRATION IS WAY COOL! BUT WHY AREN'T WE CELEBRATING WITH THE REST OF THE VILLAGE AT THE MEETING AREA?
01

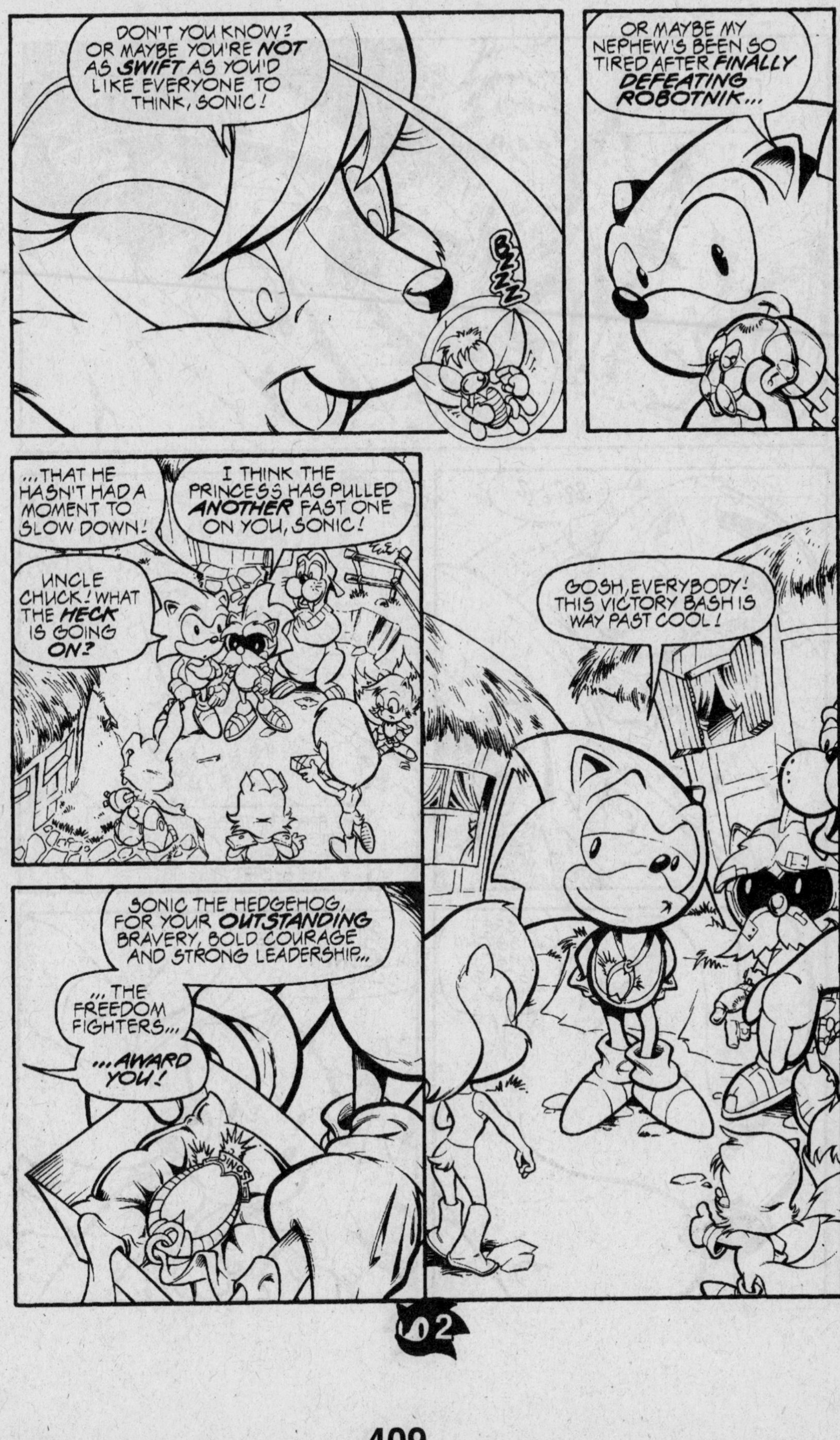
DON'T YOU KNOW? OR MAYBE YOU'RE NOT AS SWIFT AS YOU'D LIKE EVERYONE TO THINK, SONIC!
BZZZ
OR MAYBE MY NEPHEW'S BEEN SO TIRED AFTER FINALLY DEFEATING ROBOTNIK...
...THAT HE HASN'T HAD A MOMENT TO SLOW DOWN!
I THINK THE PRINCESS HAS PULLED ANOTHER FAST ONE ON YOU, SONIC!
UNCLE CHUCK! WHAT THE HECK IS GOING ON?
GOSH, EVERYBODY! THIS VICTORY BASH IS WAY PAST COOL!
SONIC THE HEDGEHOG, FOR YOUR OUTSTANDING BRAVERY, BOLD COURAGE AND STRONG LEADERSHIP...
...THE FREEDOM FIGHTERS...
...AWARD YOU!
SONIC
02

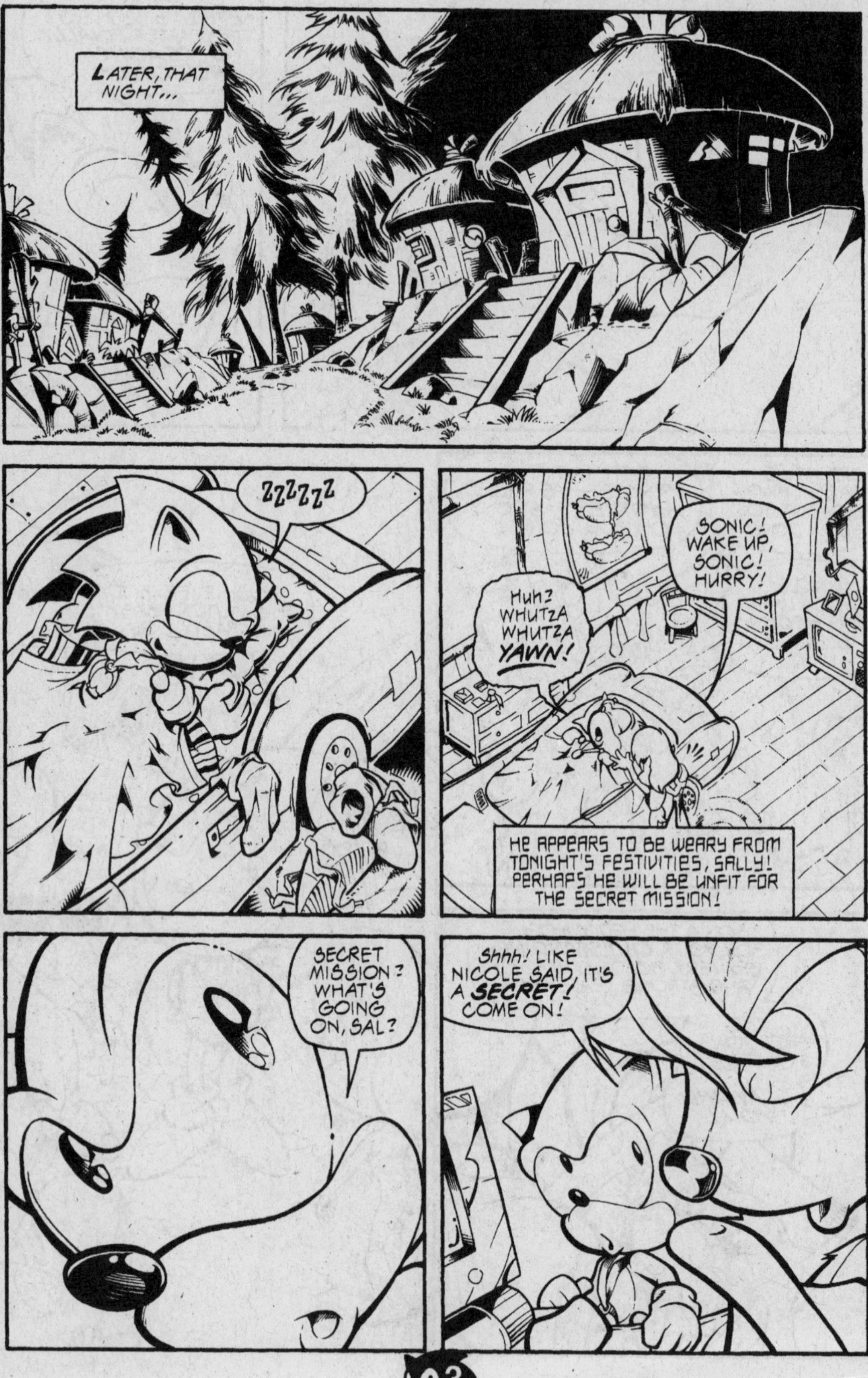
LATER, THAT NIGHT...
ZZZZZZ
SONIC! WAKE UP, SONIC! HURRY!
Huh? WHUTZA WHUTZA YAWN!
HE APPEARS TO BE WEARY FROM TONIGHT'S FESTIVITIES, SALLY! PERHAPS HE WILL BE UNFIT FOR THE SECRET MISSION!
...
SECRET MISSION? WHAT'S GOING ON, SAL?
Shhh! LIKE NICOLE SAID, IT'S A SECRET! COME ON!
03

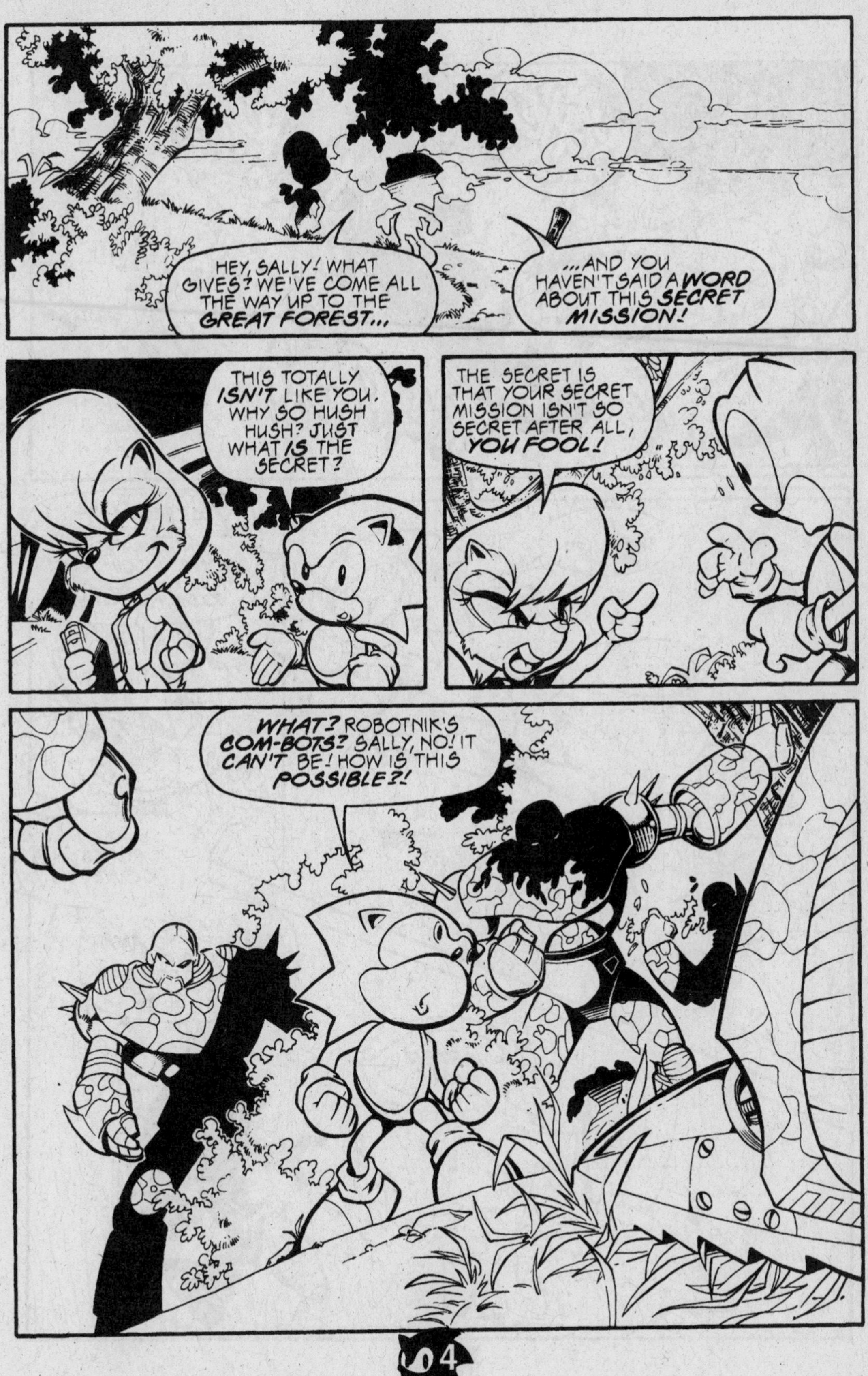
HEY, SALLY! WHAT GIVES? WE'VE COME ALL THE WAY UP TO THE GREAT FOREST...
...AND YOU HAVEN'T SAID A WORD ABOUT THIS SECRET MISSION!
THIS TOTALLY ISN'T LIKE YOU. WHY SO HUSH HUSH? JUST WHAT IS THE SECRET?
THE SECRET IS THAT YOUR SECRET MISSION ISN'T SO SECRET AFTER ALL, YOU FOOL!
WHAT? ROBOTNIK'S COM-BOTS? SALLY, NO! IT CAN'T BE! HOW IS THIS POSSIBLE?!
4

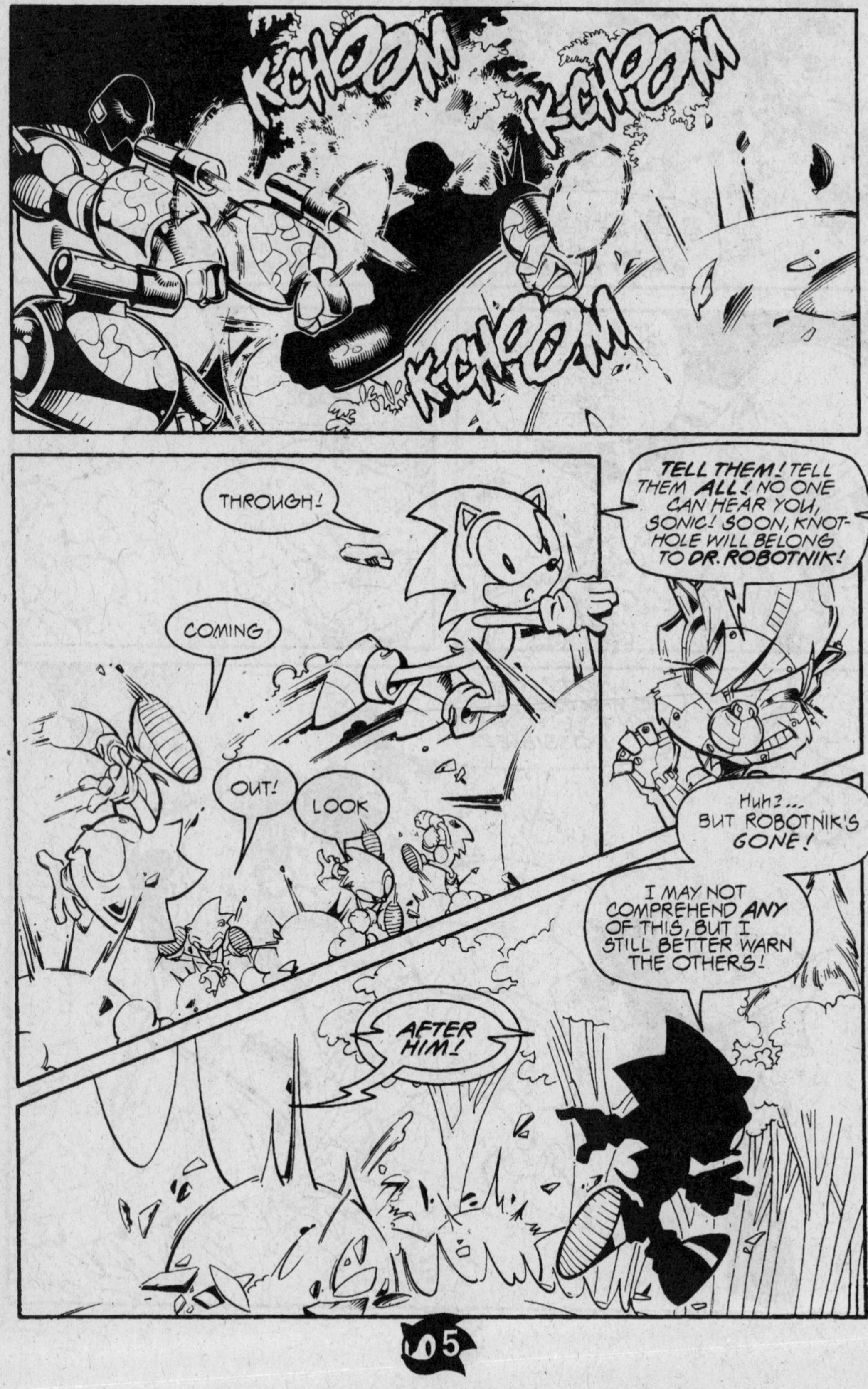

K-CHOOM
K-CHOOM
K-CHOOM
THROUGH!
COMING
OUT!
LOOK
TELL THEM! TELL THEM ALL! NO ONE CAN HEAR YOU, SONIC! SOON, KNOTHOLE WILL BELONG TO DR. ROBOTNIK!
Huh?... BUT ROBOTNIK'S GONE!
I MAY NOT COMPREHEND ANY OF THIS, BUT I STILL BETTER WARN THE OTHERS!
AFTER HIM!
5

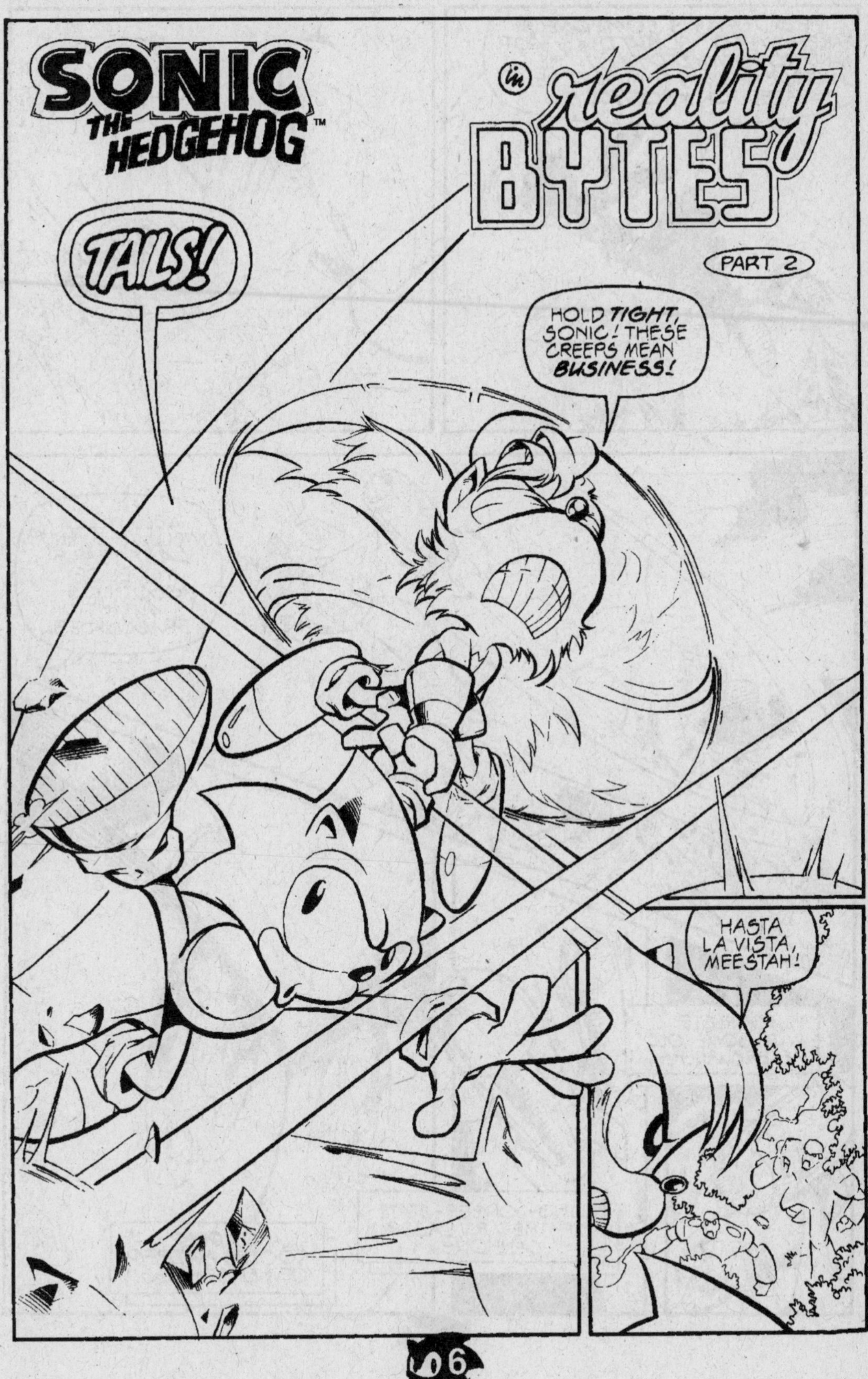
SONIC THE HEDGEHOG™
in reality BYTES
PART 2
TAILS!
HOLD TIGHT, SONIC! THESE CREEPS MEAN BUSINESS!
HASTA LA VISTA, MEESTAH!
06

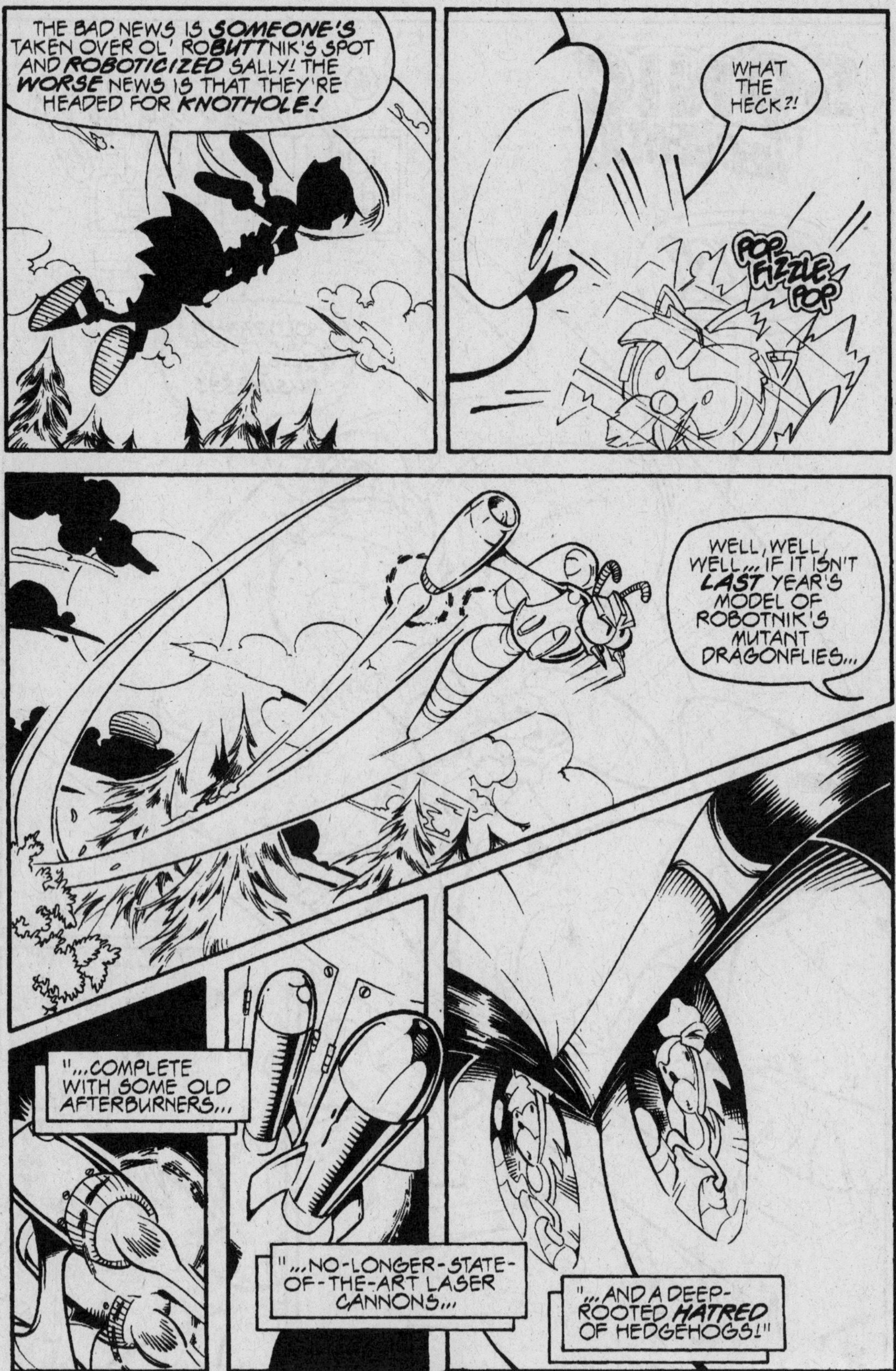
THE BAD NEWS IS SOMEONE'S TAKEN OVER OL' ROBUTTNIK'S SPOT AND ROBOTICIZED SALLY! THE WORSE NEWS IS THAT THEY'RE HEADED FOR KNOTHOLE!
WHAT THE HECK?!
POP FIZZLE POP
WELL, WELL, WELL... IF IT ISN'T LAST YEAR'S MODEL OF ROBOTNIK'S MUTANT DRAGONFLIES...
"...COMPLETE WITH SOME OLD AFTERBURNERS...
"...NO-LONGER-STATE-OF-THE-ART LASER CANNONS...
"...AND A DEEP-ROOTED HATRED OF HEDGEHOGS!"
107

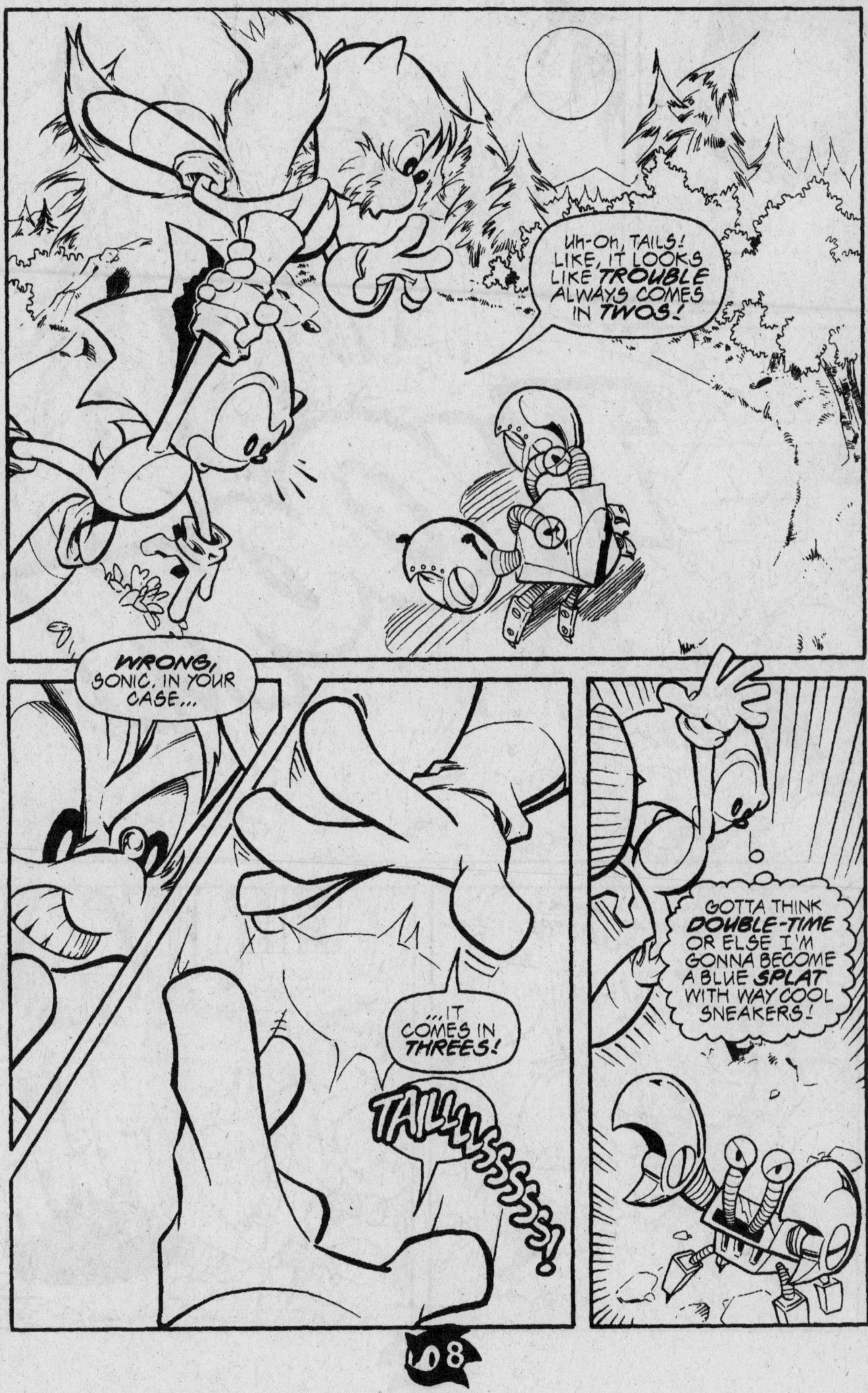
UH-OH, TAILS! LIKE, IT LOOKS LIKE TROUBLE ALWAYS COMES IN TWOS!
WRONG, SONIC, IN YOUR CASE...
...IT COMES IN THREES!
TAILLLSSSSSS!
GOTTA THINK DOUBLE-TIME OR ELSE I'M GONNA BECOME A BLUE SPLAT WITH WAY COOL SNEAKERS!
108

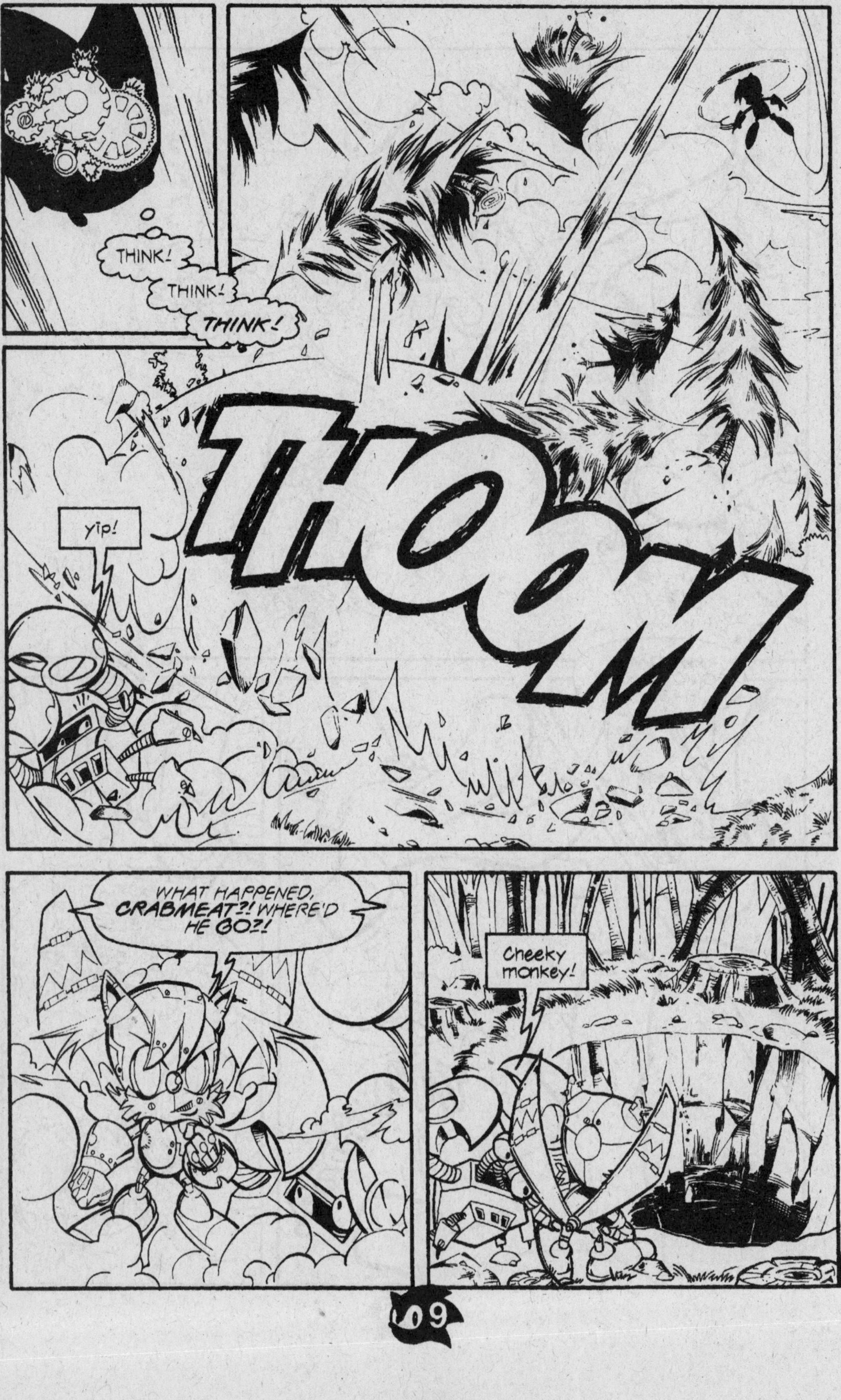
THINK!
THINK!
THINK!
THOOM
yip!
WHAT HAPPENED, CRABMEAT?! WHERE'D HE GO?!
Cheeky monkey!
09

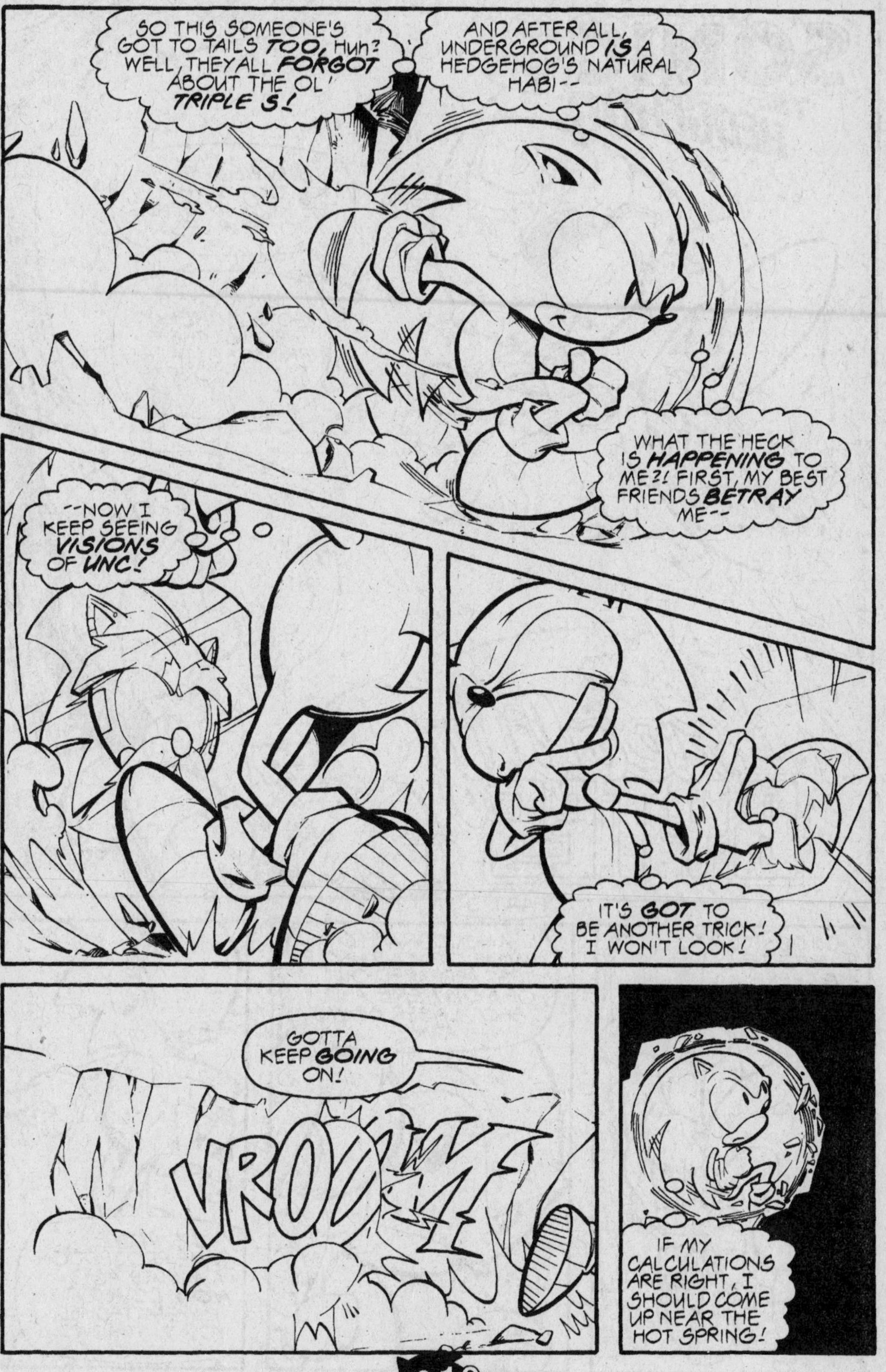
SO THIS SOMEONE'S GOT TO TAILS TOO, Huh? WELL, THEY ALL FORGOT ABOUT THE OL' TRIPLE S!
AND AFTER ALL, UNDERGROUND IS A HEDGEHOG'S NATURAL HABI--
WHAT THE HECK IS HAPPENING TO ME?! FIRST, MY BEST FRIENDS BETRAY ME--
--NOW I KEEP SEEING VISIONS OF UNC!
IT'S GOT TO BE ANOTHER TRICK! I WON'T LOOK!
GOTTA KEEP GOING ON!
VROOOM
IF MY CALCULATIONS ARE RIGHT, I SHOULD COME UP NEAR THE HOT SPRING!
10

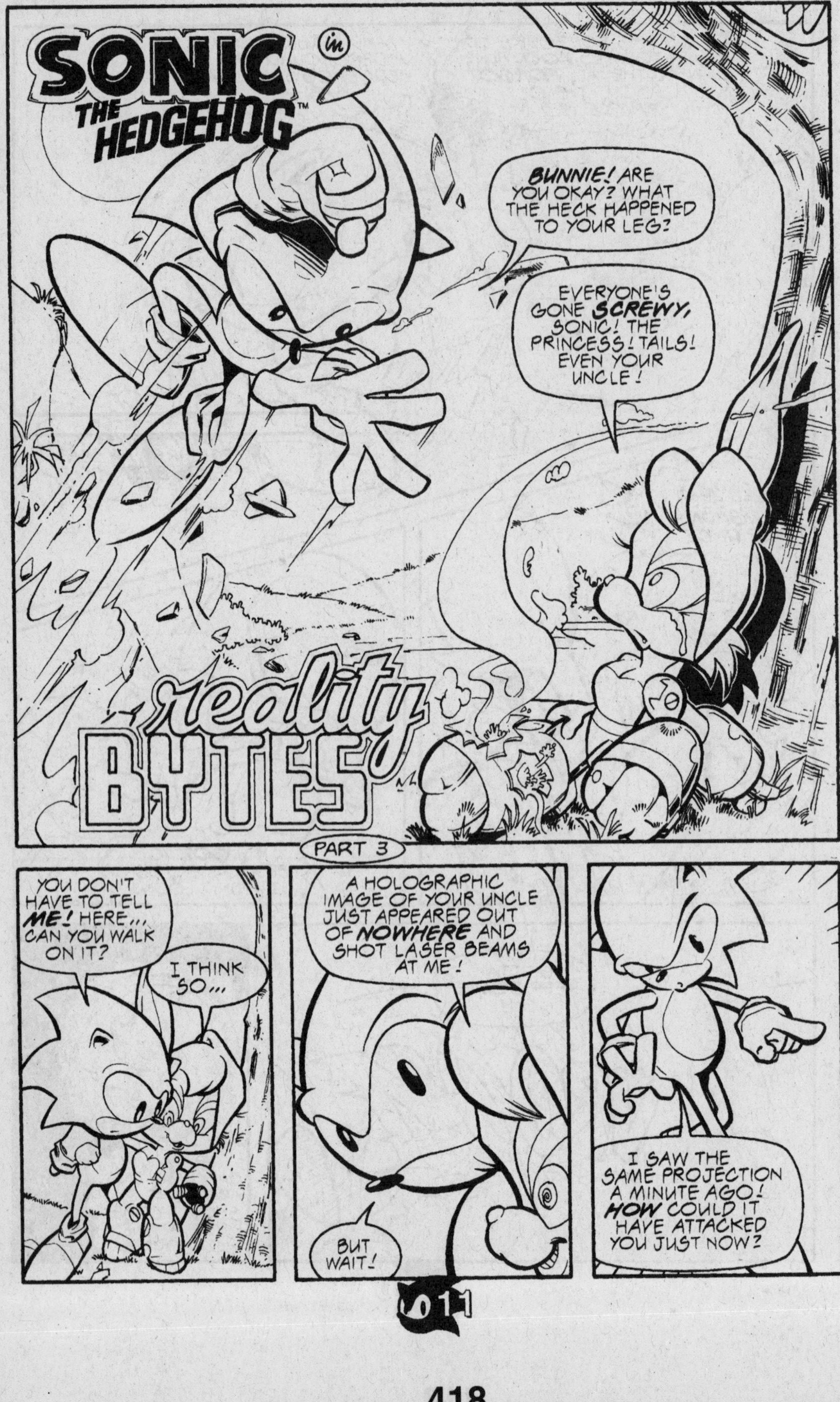
SONIC in THE HEDGEHOG
BUNNIE! ARE YOU OKAY? WHAT THE HECK HAPPENED TO YOUR LEG?
EVERYONE'S GONE SCREWY, SONIC! THE PRINCESS! TAILS! EVEN YOUR UNCLE!
reality BYTES
PART 3
YOU DON'T HAVE TO TELL ME! HERE... CAN YOU WALK ON IT?
I THINK SO...
A HOLOGRAPHIC IMAGE OF YOUR UNCLE JUST APPEARED OUT OF NOWHERE AND SHOT LASER BEAMS AT ME!
BUT WAIT!
I SAW THE SAME PROJECTION A MINUTE AGO! HOW COULD IT HAVE ATTACKED YOU JUST NOW?
011

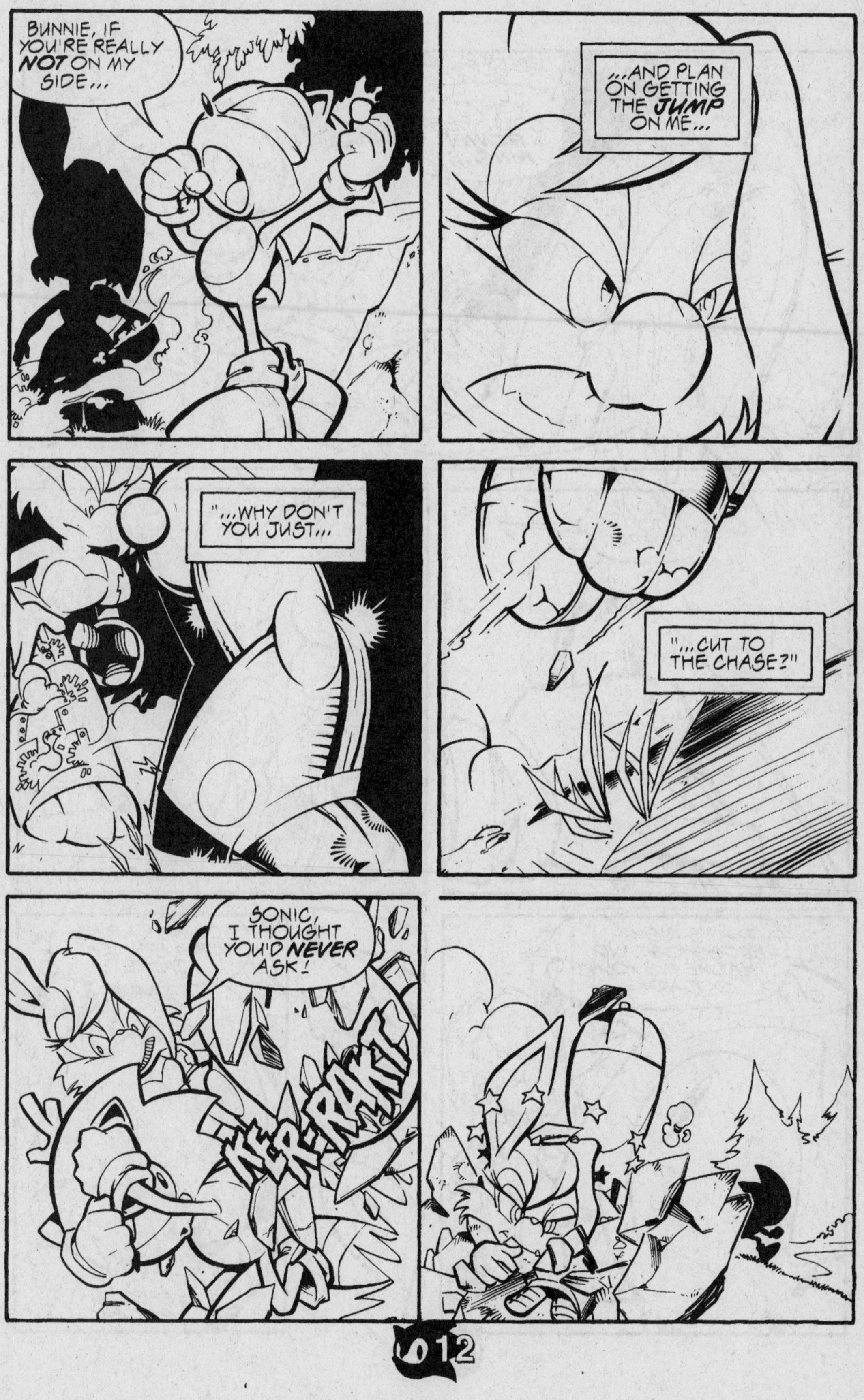
BUNNIE, IF YOU'RE REALLY **NOT** ON MY SIDE...
...AND PLAN ON GETTING THE **JUMP** ON ME...
"...WHY DON'T YOU JUST...
"...CUT TO THE CHASE?"
SONIC, I THOUGHT YOU'D **NEVER** ASK!
KER-RAKK!
12

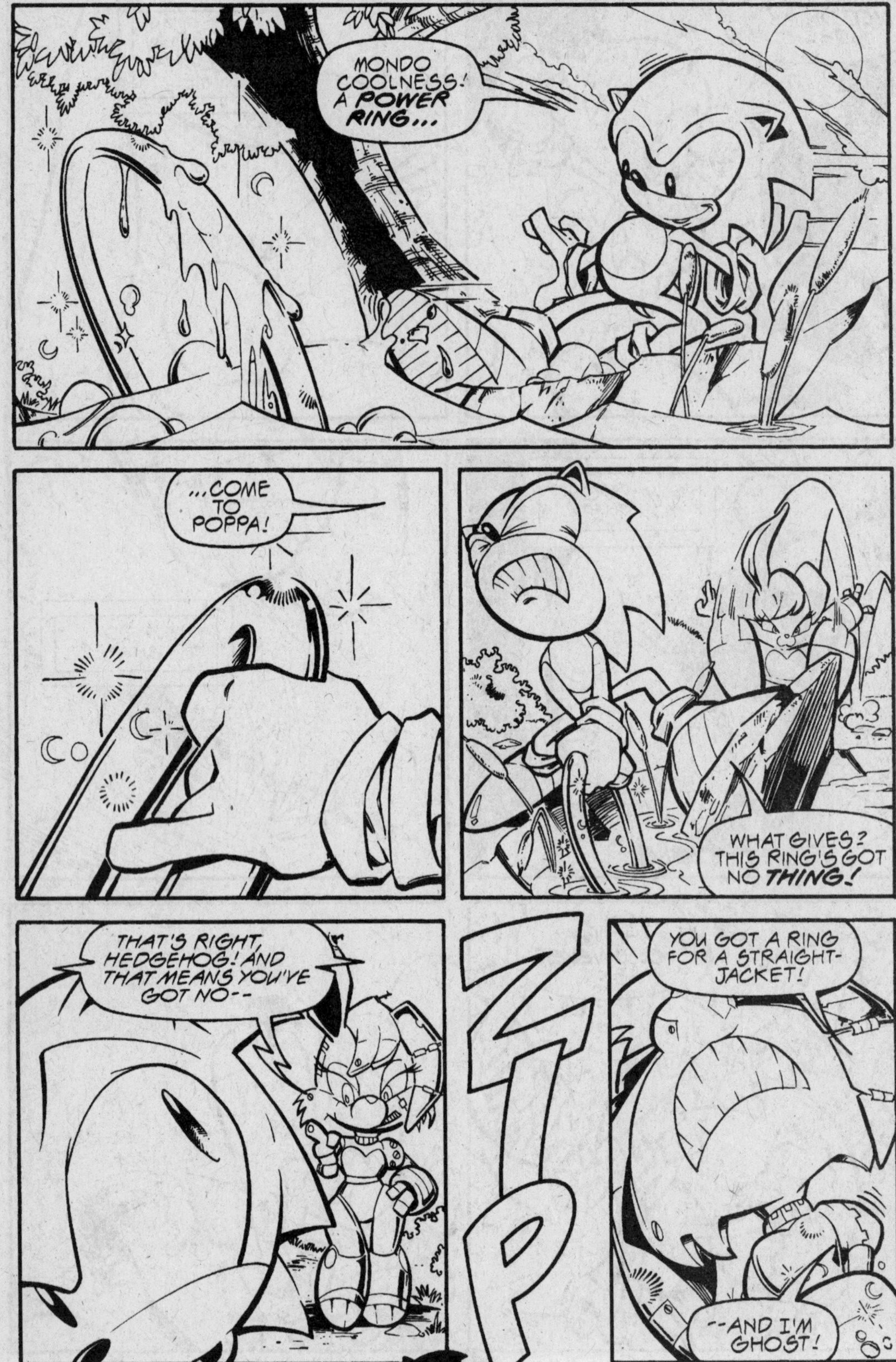
MONDO COOLNESS! A POWER RING...
...COME TO POPPA!
WHAT GIVES? THIS RING'S GOT NO THING!
THAT'S RIGHT, HEDGEHOG! AND THAT MEANS YOU'VE GOT NO--
ZIP
YOU GOT A RING FOR A STRAIGHT-JACKET!
--AND I'M GHOST!
13

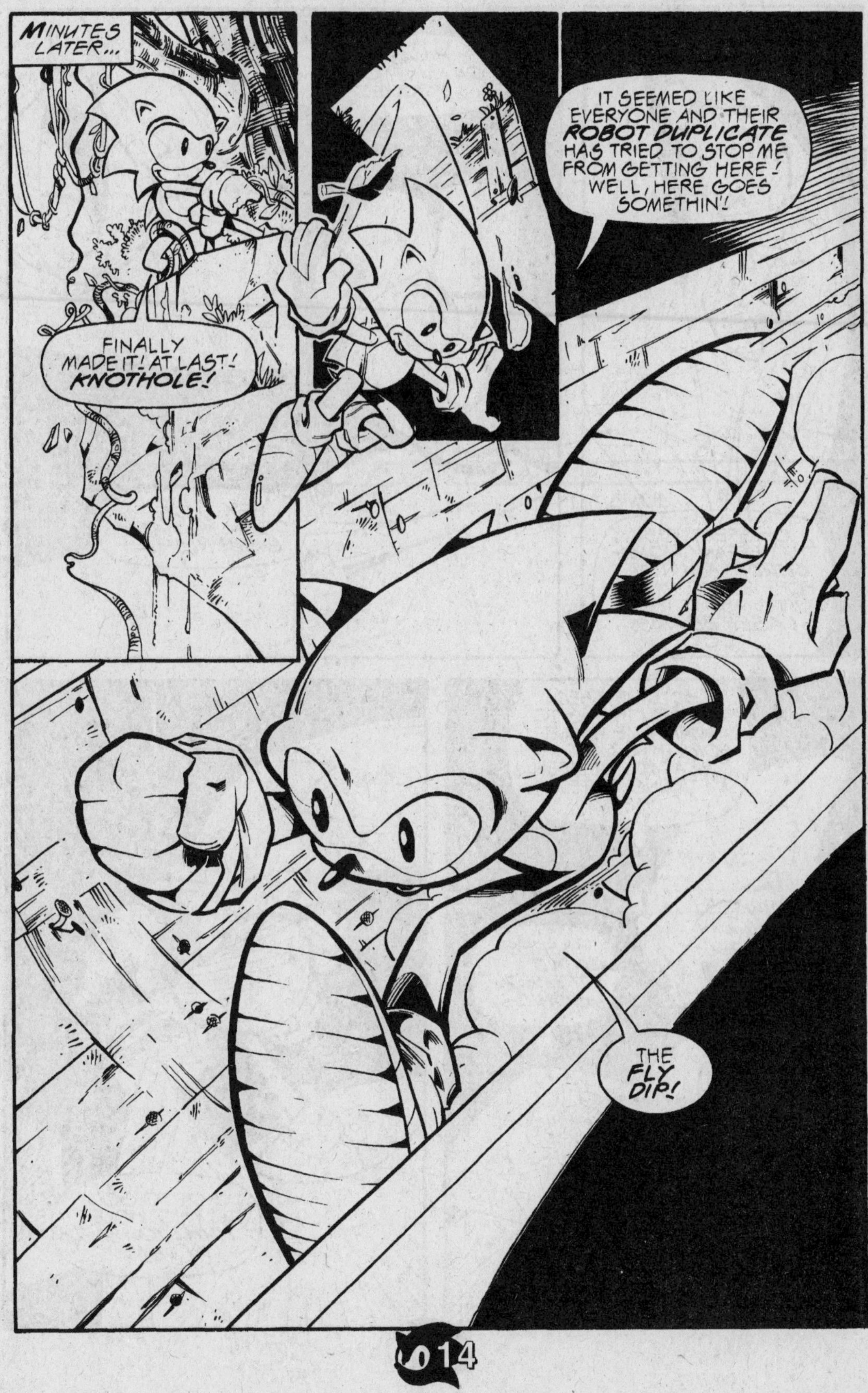
MINUTES LATER...
FINALLY MADE IT! AT LAST! KNOTHOLE!
IT SEEMED LIKE EVERYONE AND THEIR ROBOT DUPLICATE HAS TRIED TO STOP ME FROM GETTING HERE! WELL, HERE GOES SOMETHIN'!
THE FLY DIP!

14

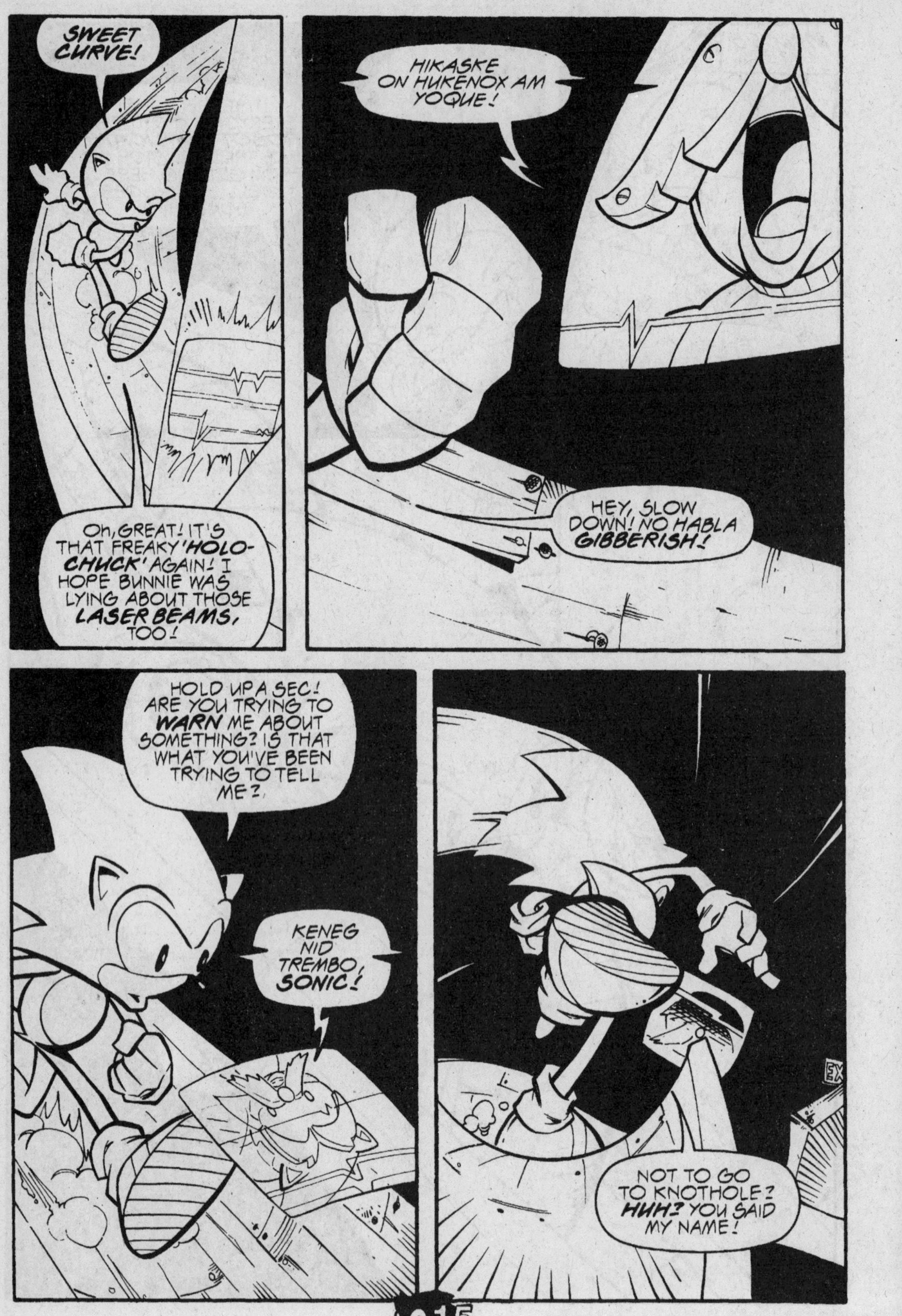
SWEET CURVE!
Oh, GREAT! IT'S THAT FREAKY 'HOLO-CHUCK' AGAIN! I HOPE BUNNIE WAS LYING ABOUT THOSE LASER BEAMS, TOO!
HIKASKE ON HUKENOX AM YOQUE!
HEY, SLOW DOWN! NO HABLA GIBBERISH!
HOLD UP A SEC! ARE YOU TRYING TO WARN ME ABOUT SOMETHING? IS THAT WHAT YOU'VE BEEN TRYING TO TELL ME?
KENEG NID TREMBO, SONIC!
NOT TO GO TO KNOTHOLE? HUH? YOU SAID MY NAME!

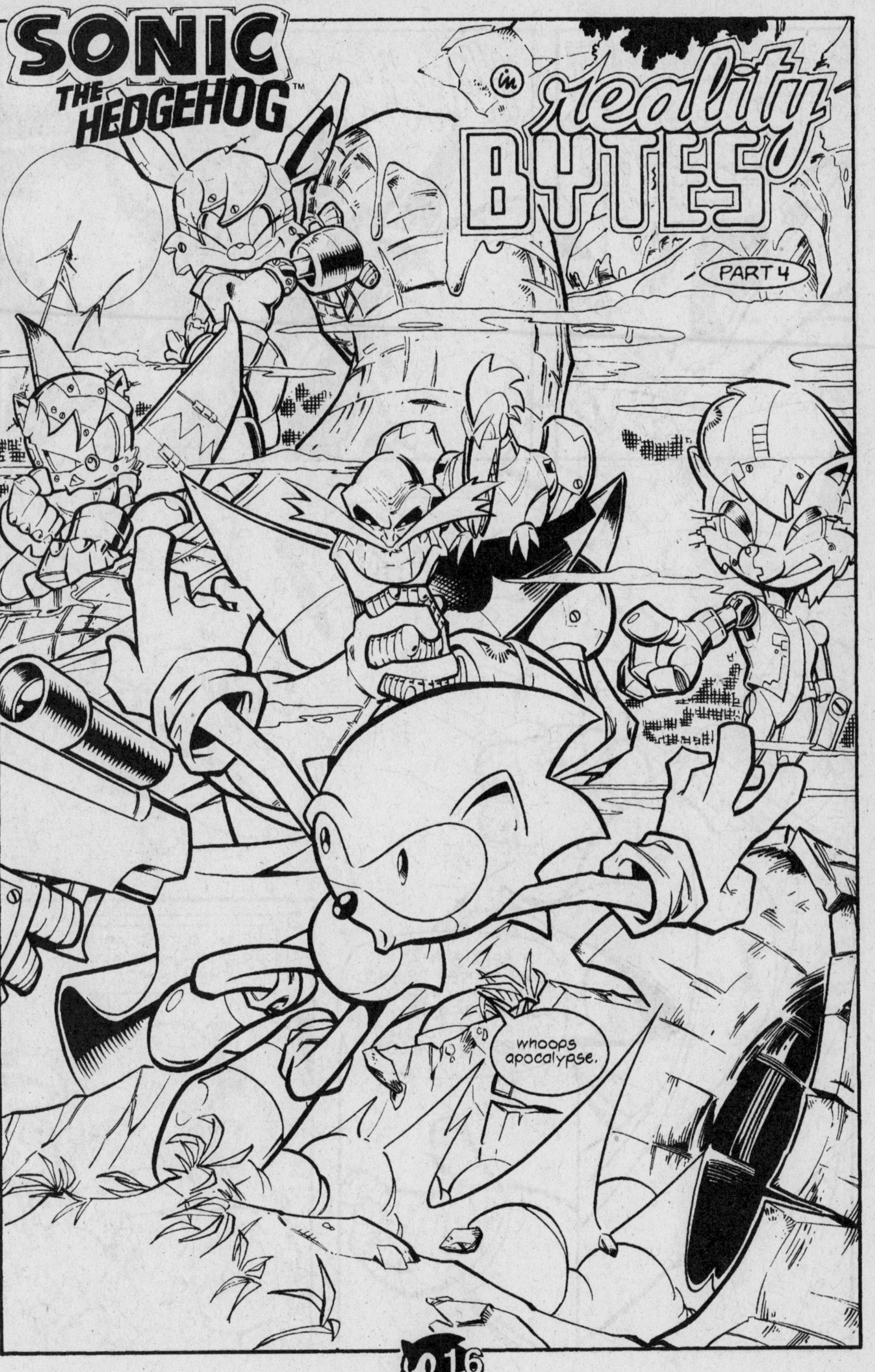
SONIC THE HEDGEHOG™
in
reality BYTES
PART 4
whoops apocalypse.
16

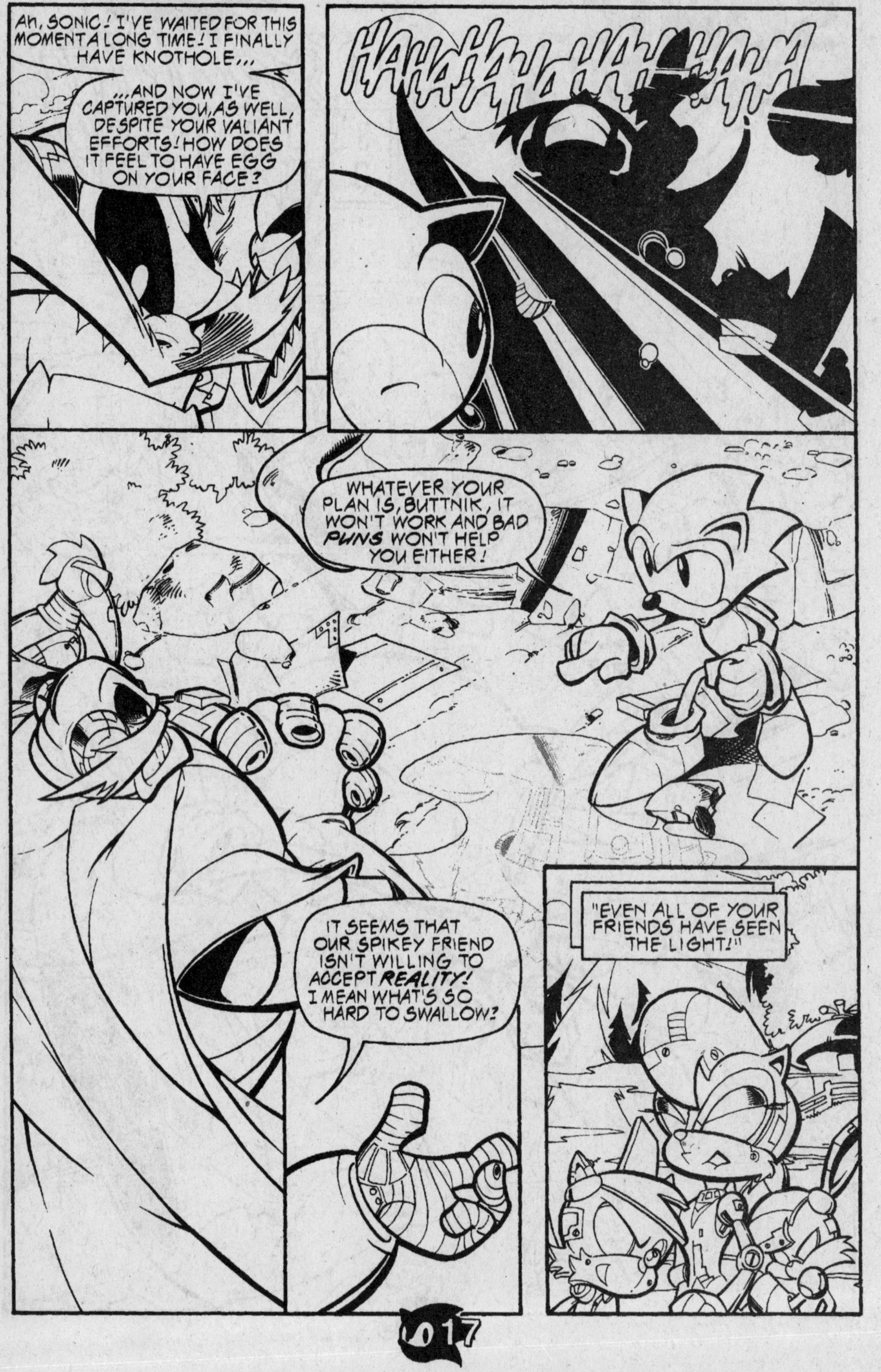

Ah, SONIC! I'VE WAITED FOR THIS MOMENT A LONG TIME! I FINALLY HAVE KNOTHOLE...
...AND NOW I'VE CAPTURED YOU, AS WELL, DESPITE YOUR VALIANT EFFORTS! HOW DOES IT FEEL TO HAVE EGG ON YOUR FACE?
HAHAHAHAHAHAHAA
WHATEVER YOUR PLAN IS, BUTTNIK, IT WON'T WORK AND BAD **PUNS** WON'T HELP YOU EITHER!
IT SEEMS THAT OUR SPIKEY FRIEND ISN'T WILLING TO ACCEPT **REALITY**! I MEAN WHAT'S SO HARD TO SWALLOW?
"EVEN ALL OF YOUR FRIENDS HAVE SEEN THE LIGHT!"
017

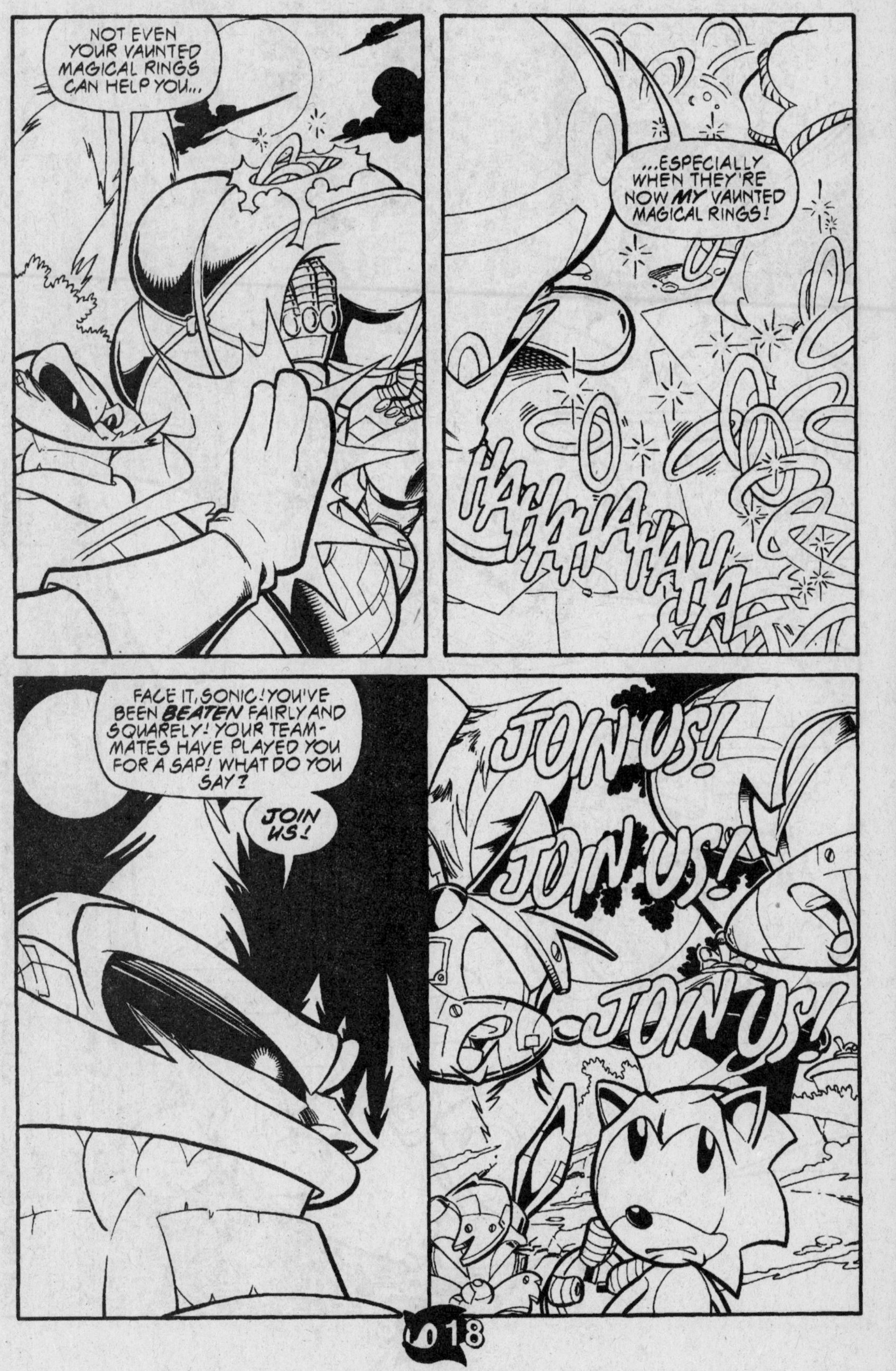
NOT EVEN YOUR VAUNTED MAGICAL RINGS CAN HELP YOU...
...ESPECIALLY WHEN THEY'RE NOW MY VAUNTED MAGICAL RINGS!
HA HA HA HA HA HA
FACE IT, SONIC! YOU'VE BEEN BEATEN FAIRLY AND SQUARELY! YOUR TEAM-MATES HAVE PLAYED YOU FOR A SAP! WHAT DO YOU SAY?
JOIN US!
JOIN US!
JOIN US!
JOIN US!

018

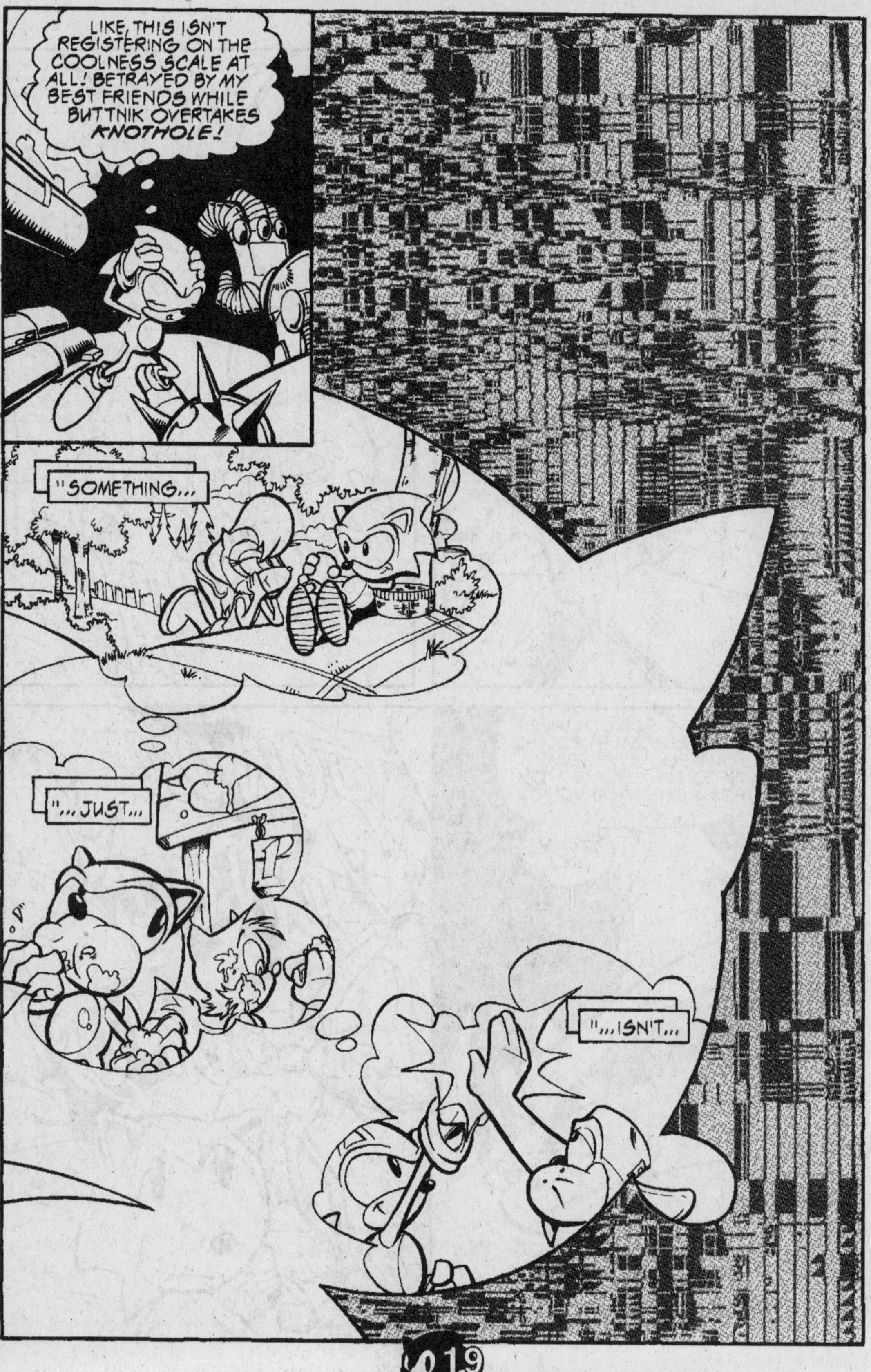
LIKE, THIS ISN'T REGISTERING ON THE COOLNESS SCALE AT ALL! BETRAYED BY MY BEST FRIENDS WHILE BUTTNIK OVERTAKES KNOTHOLE!
"SOMETHING...
"...JUST...
"...ISN'T...
019

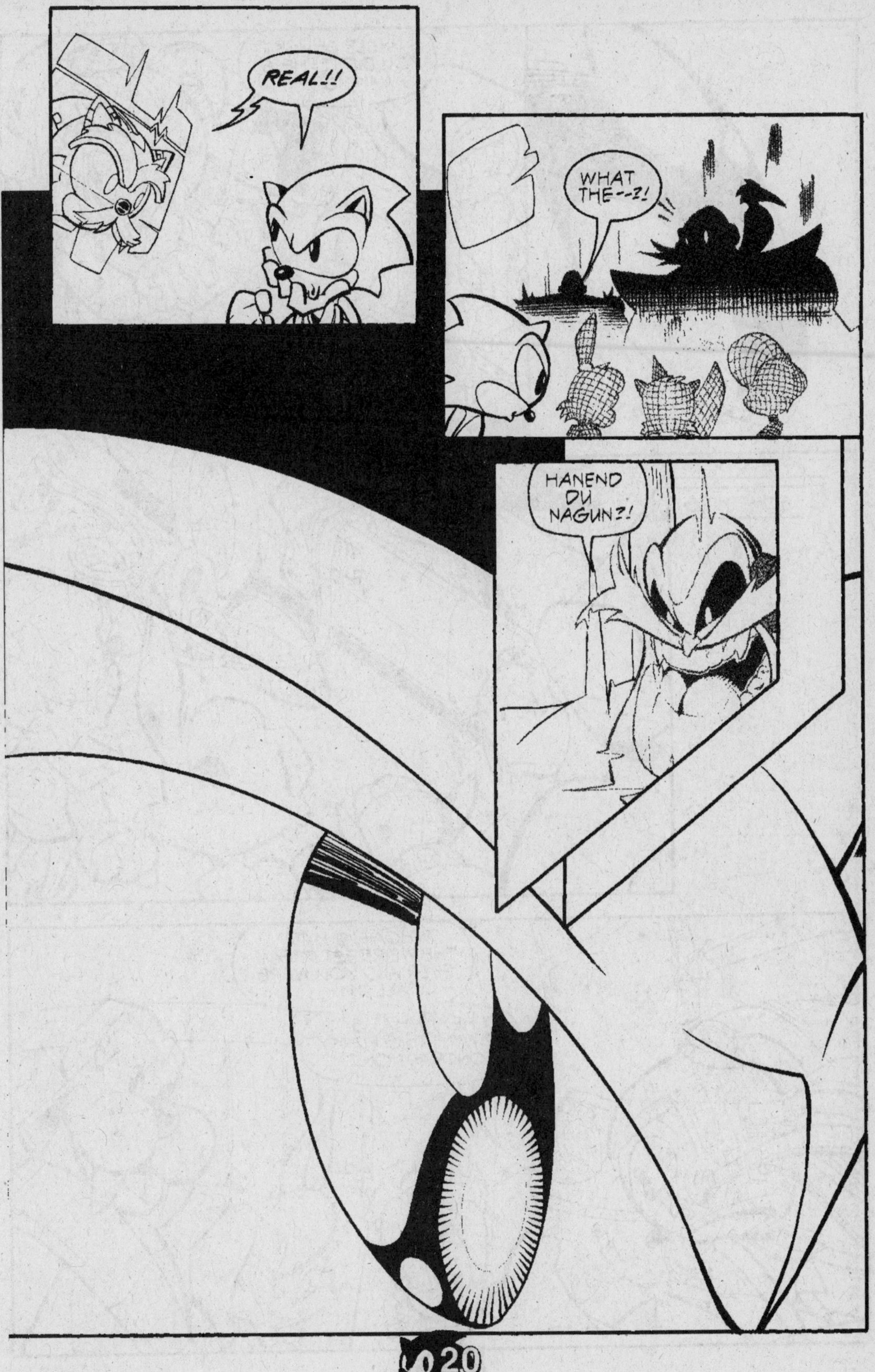
REAL!!
WHAT THE--?!
HANEND DU NAGUN?!

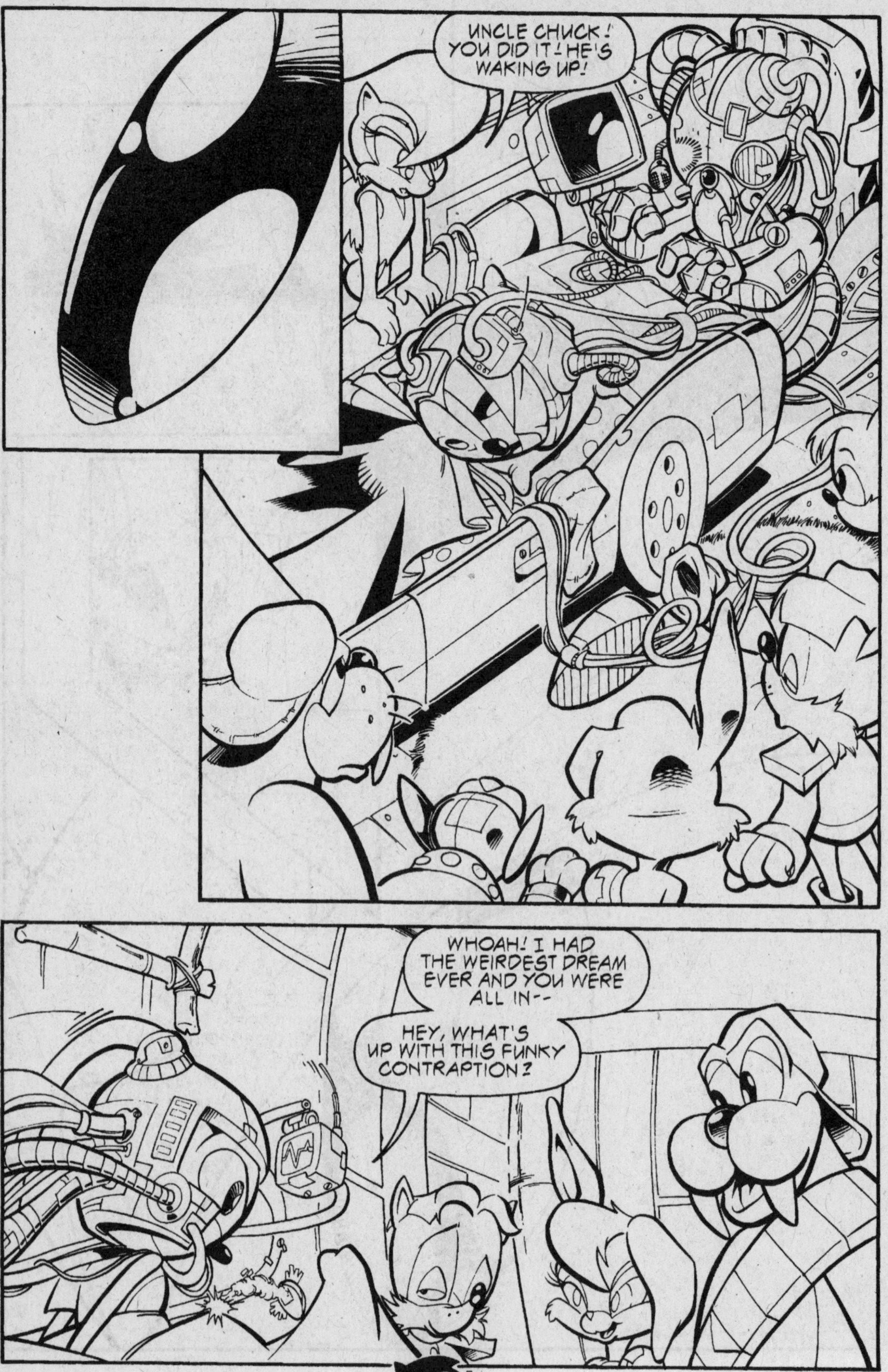
UNCLE CHUCK! YOU DID IT! HE'S WAKING UP!
WHOAH! I HAD THE WEIRDEST DREAM EVER AND YOU WERE ALL IN--
HEY, WHAT'S UP WITH THIS FUNKY CONTRAPTION?
21

WELL, LET ME TELL YOU...

...IF YOU HAD SAID "NIGHTMARE" YOU'D HAVE BEEN CLOSER TO THE TRUTH, SONIC!

IT SEEMS THAT YOUR AWARD WAS BOOBY-TRAPPED WITH AN ARTIFICIAL VIRUS THAT THREW INTO A VIRTUAL-REALITY NIGHTMARE WHILE YOU SLEPT!

Huh?

IT'S TRUE! AND FURTHERMORE, HAD YOU GIVEN INTO ROBOTNIK'S WISHES YOU WOULD HAVE BEEN TRAPPED IN VR FOREVER!

THE HOLOGRAPHIC IMAGE THAT YOU SAW WAS ME TRYING TO WARN YOU VIA THIS DEVICE I HASTILY WHIPPED UP!

IT'S GREAT TO HAVE YOU BACK, SONIC!

WE WERE VAIRY WORRIED ABOUT YOU!

022

429

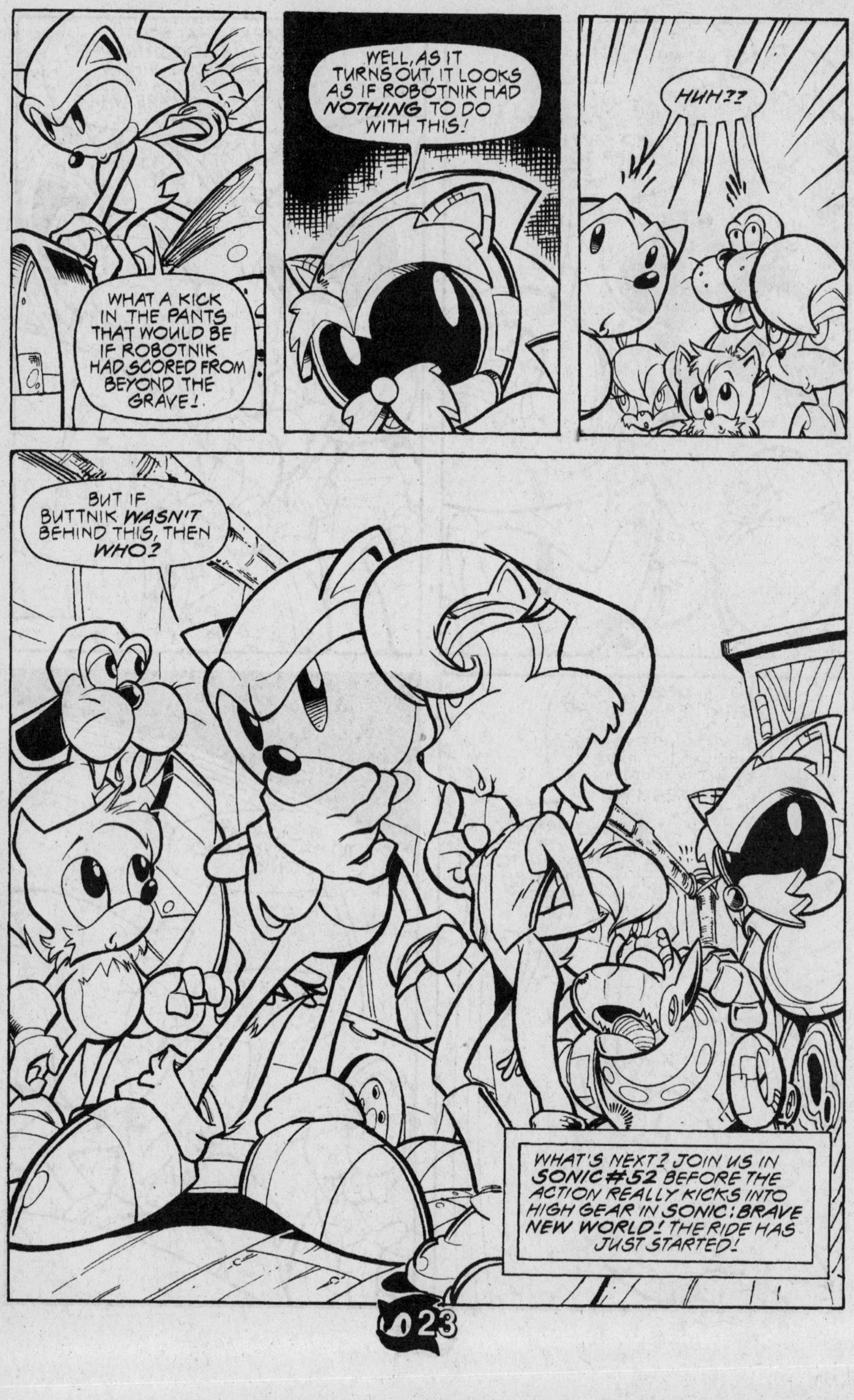
WHAT A KICK IN THE PANTS THAT WOULD BE IF ROBOTNIK HAD SCORED FROM BEYOND THE GRAVE!
WELL, AS IT TURNS OUT, IT LOOKS AS IF ROBOTNIK HAD NOTHING TO DO WITH THIS!
HUH??
BUT IF BUTTNIK WASN'T BEHIND THIS, THEN WHO?
WHAT'S NEXT? JOIN US IN SONIC #52 BEFORE THE ACTION REALLY KICKS INTO HIGH GEAR IN SONIC: BRAVE NEW WORLD! THE RIDE HAS JUST STARTED!
023

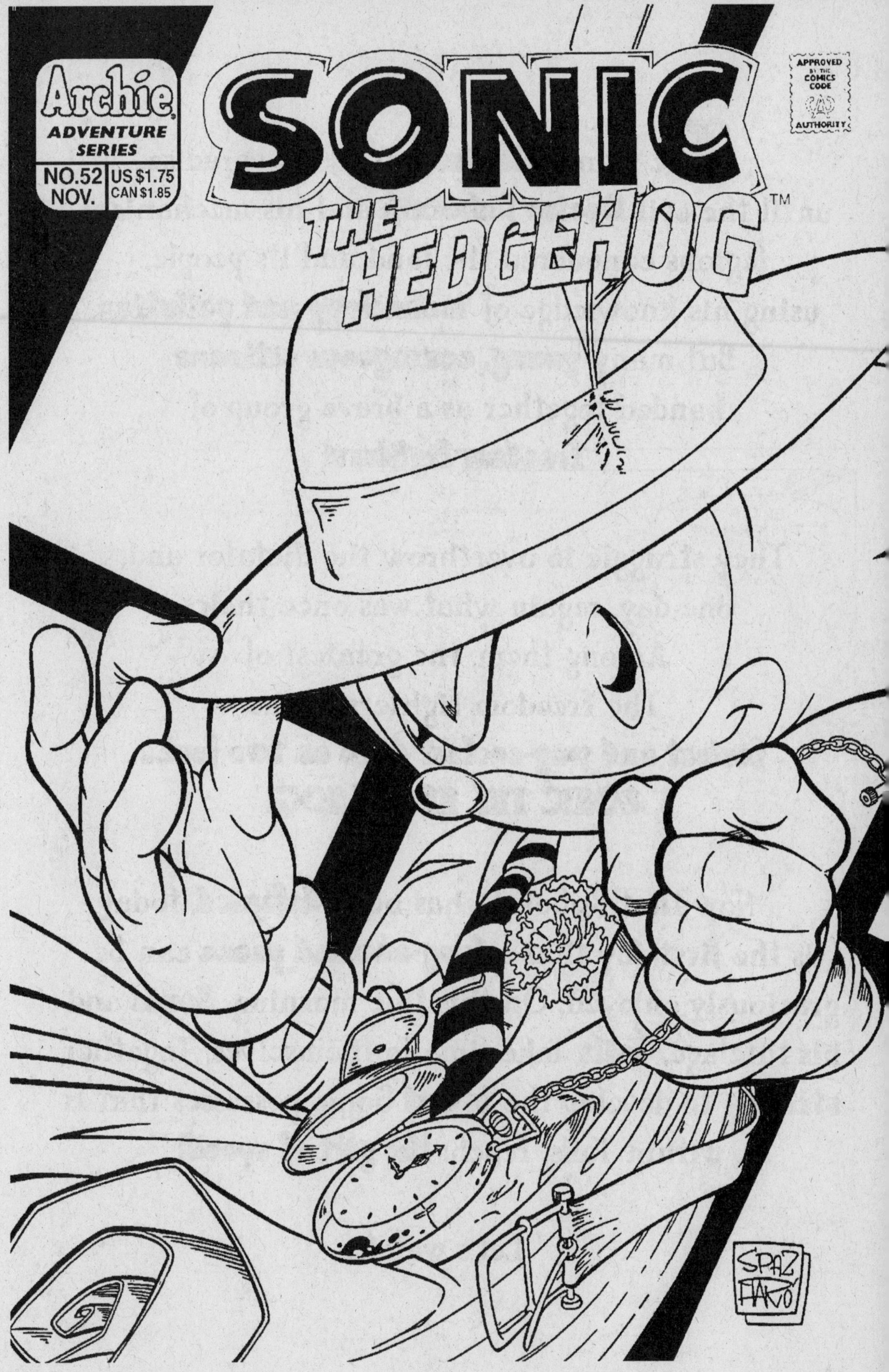
Archie
ADVENTURE SERIES
NO.52
NOV.
US $1.75
CAN $1.85
SONIC
THE HEDGEHOG
TM
APPROVED BY THE COMICS CODE AUTHORITY
SPAZ
FIARO

The planet Mobius was like a paradise...
until the evil Doctor Robotnik and his mechanical
legions conquered the land and its people,
using his knowledge of technology and pollution
But many young, courageous citizens
banded together as a brave group of
freedom fighters!

They struggle to overthrow the dictator and,
one day, regain what was once theirs.
Among them, the greatest of
The Freedom Fighters is the
fastest and way-coolest dude on two feet...
SONIC THE HEDGEHOG!

Now that Robotnik has been defeated, today
is the first day that a long-awaited peace can be
graciously enjoyed. On this fine morning, Sonic and
his tutelage, Tails, take time to themselves. Together
striving to develop the talent Sonic possesses that is
within Tails' reach: the gift of speed!

Let's watch...

432

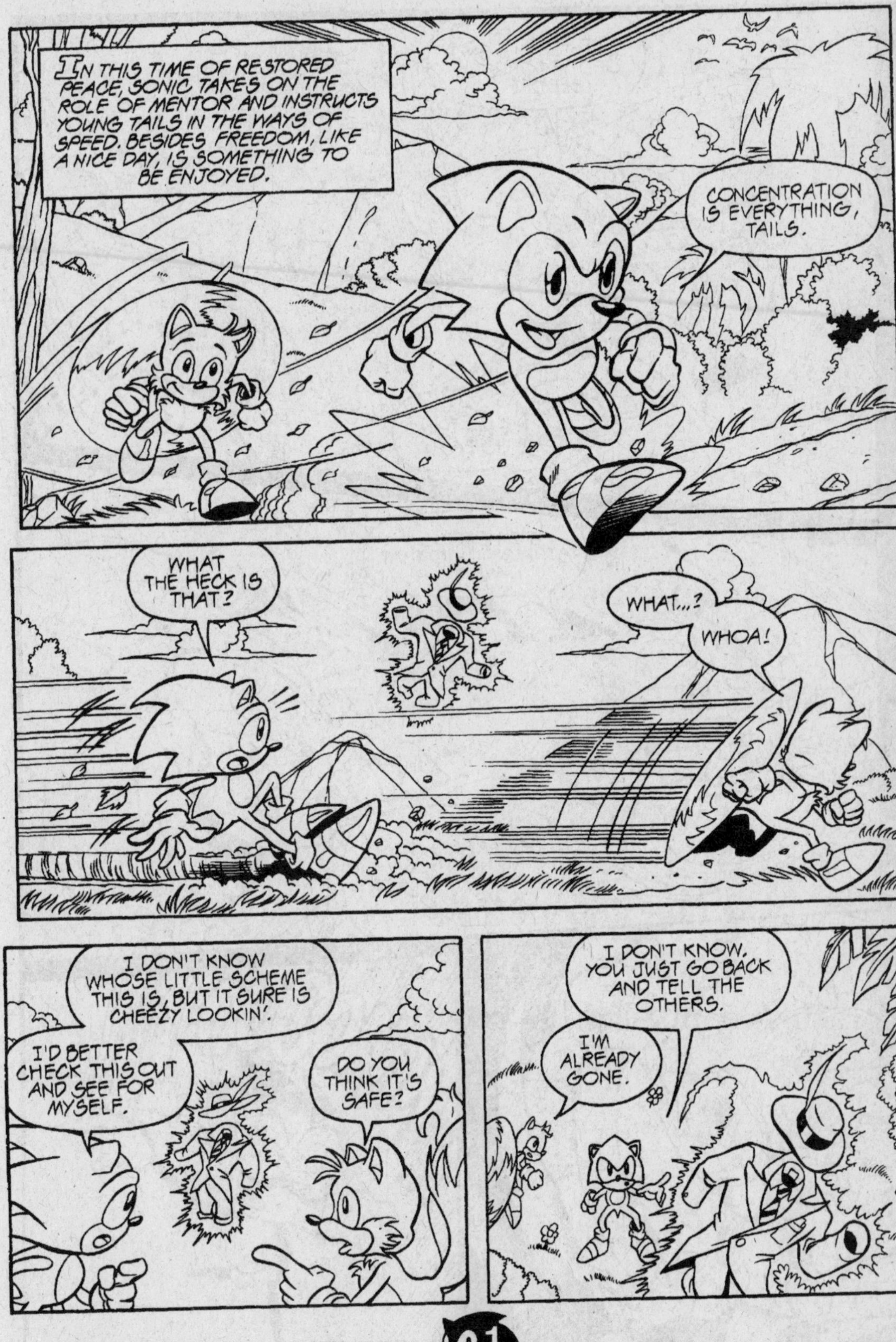
IN THIS TIME OF RESTORED PEACE, SONIC TAKES ON THE ROLE OF MENTOR AND INSTRUCTS YOUNG TAILS IN THE WAYS OF SPEED. BESIDES FREEDOM, LIKE A NICE DAY, IS SOMETHING TO BE ENJOYED.
CONCENTRATION IS EVERYTHING, TAILS.
WHAT THE HECK IS THAT?
WHAT...?
WHOA!
I DON'T KNOW WHOSE LITTLE SCHEME THIS IS, BUT IT SURE IS CHEEZY LOOKIN'.
I'D BETTER CHECK THIS OUT AND SEE FOR MYSELF.
DO YOU THINK IT'S SAFE?
I DON'T KNOW. YOU JUST GO BACK AND TELL THE OTHERS.
I'M ALREADY GONE.

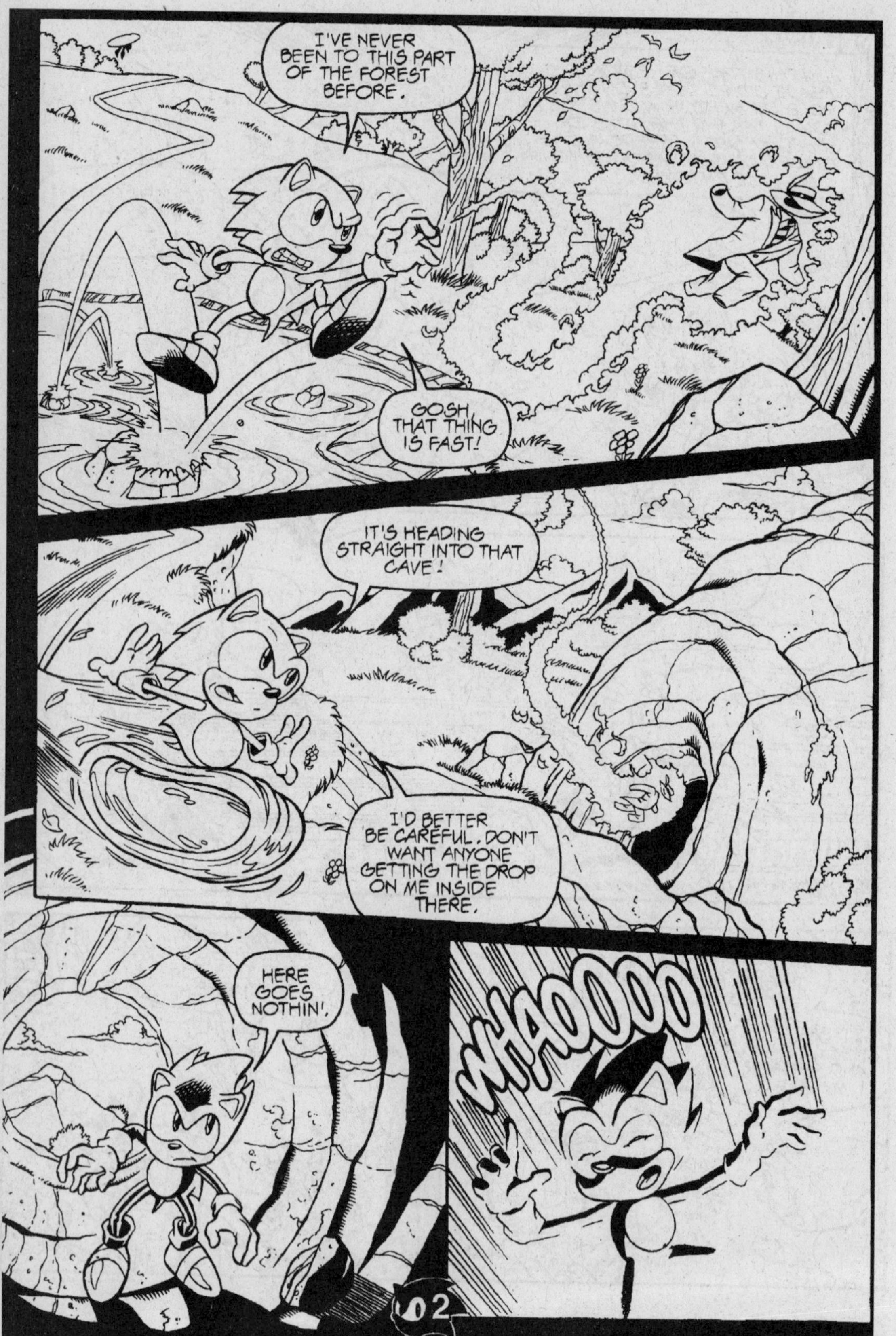
I'VE NEVER BEEN TO THIS PART OF THE FOREST BEFORE.
GOSH, THAT THING IS FAST!
IT'S HEADING STRAIGHT INTO THAT CAVE!
I'D BETTER BE CAREFUL. DON'T WANT ANYONE GETTING THE DROP ON ME INSIDE THERE.
HERE GOES NOTHIN'!
WHAOOOO
2

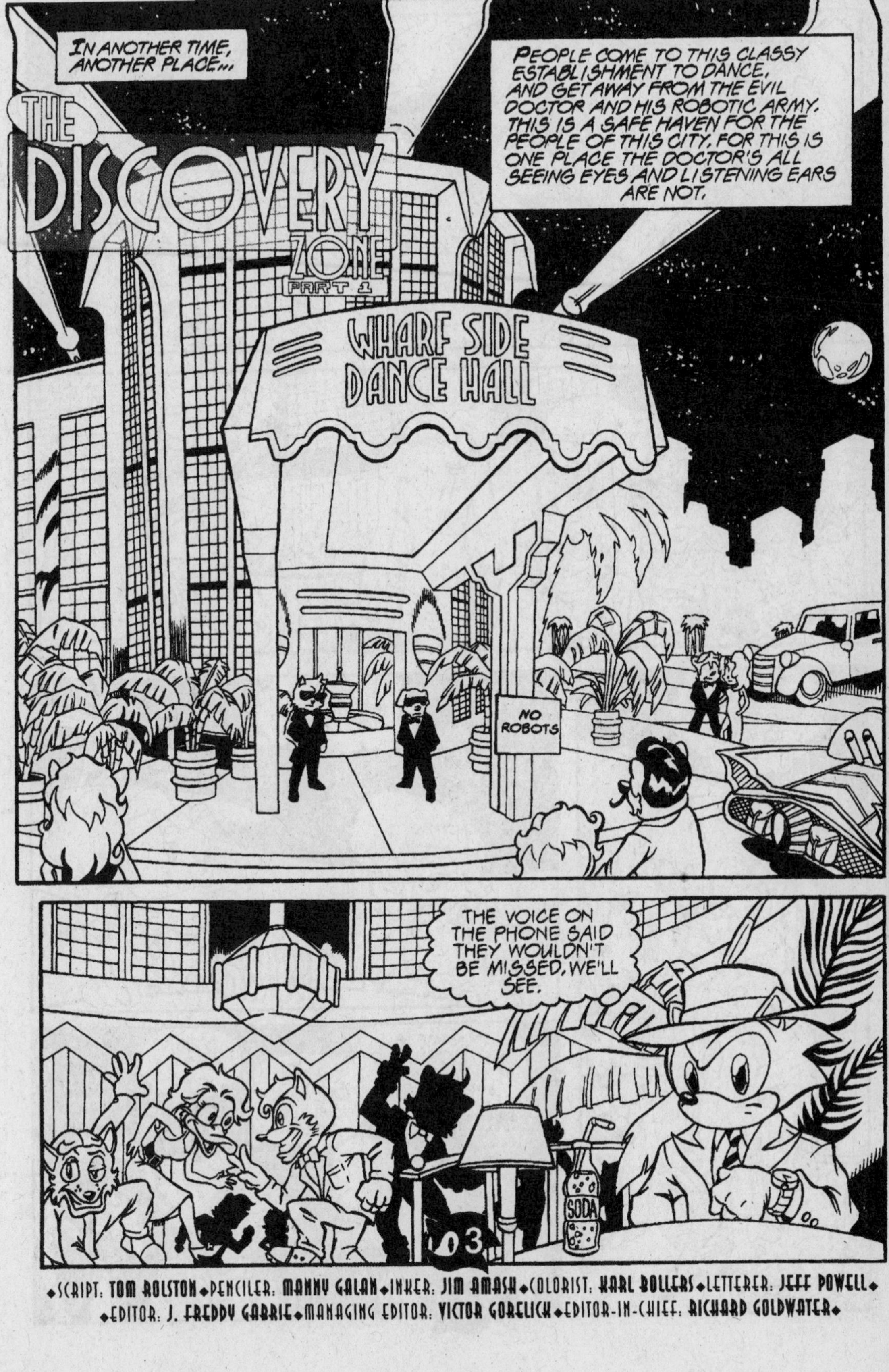

IN ANOTHER TIME, ANOTHER PLACE...
THE DISCOVERY ZONE PART 1
PEOPLE COME TO THIS CLASSY ESTABLISHMENT TO DANCE, AND GET AWAY FROM THE EVIL DOCTOR AND HIS ROBOTIC ARMY. THIS IS A SAFE HAVEN FOR THE PEOPLE OF THIS CITY. FOR THIS IS ONE PLACE THE DOCTOR'S ALL SEEING EYES AND LISTENING EARS ARE NOT.
WHARF SIDE DANCE HALL
NO ROBOTS
THE VOICE ON THE PHONE SAID THEY WOULDN'T BE MISSED. WE'LL SEE.
SODA
03

◆SCRIPT: TOM ROLSTON◆PENCILER: MANNY GALAN◆INKER: JIM AMASH◆COLORIST: KARL BOLLERS◆LETTERER: JEFF POWELL◆
◆EDITOR: J. FREDDY GABRIE◆MANAGING EDITOR: VICTOR GORELICK◆EDITOR-IN-CHIEF: RICHARD GOLDWATER◆

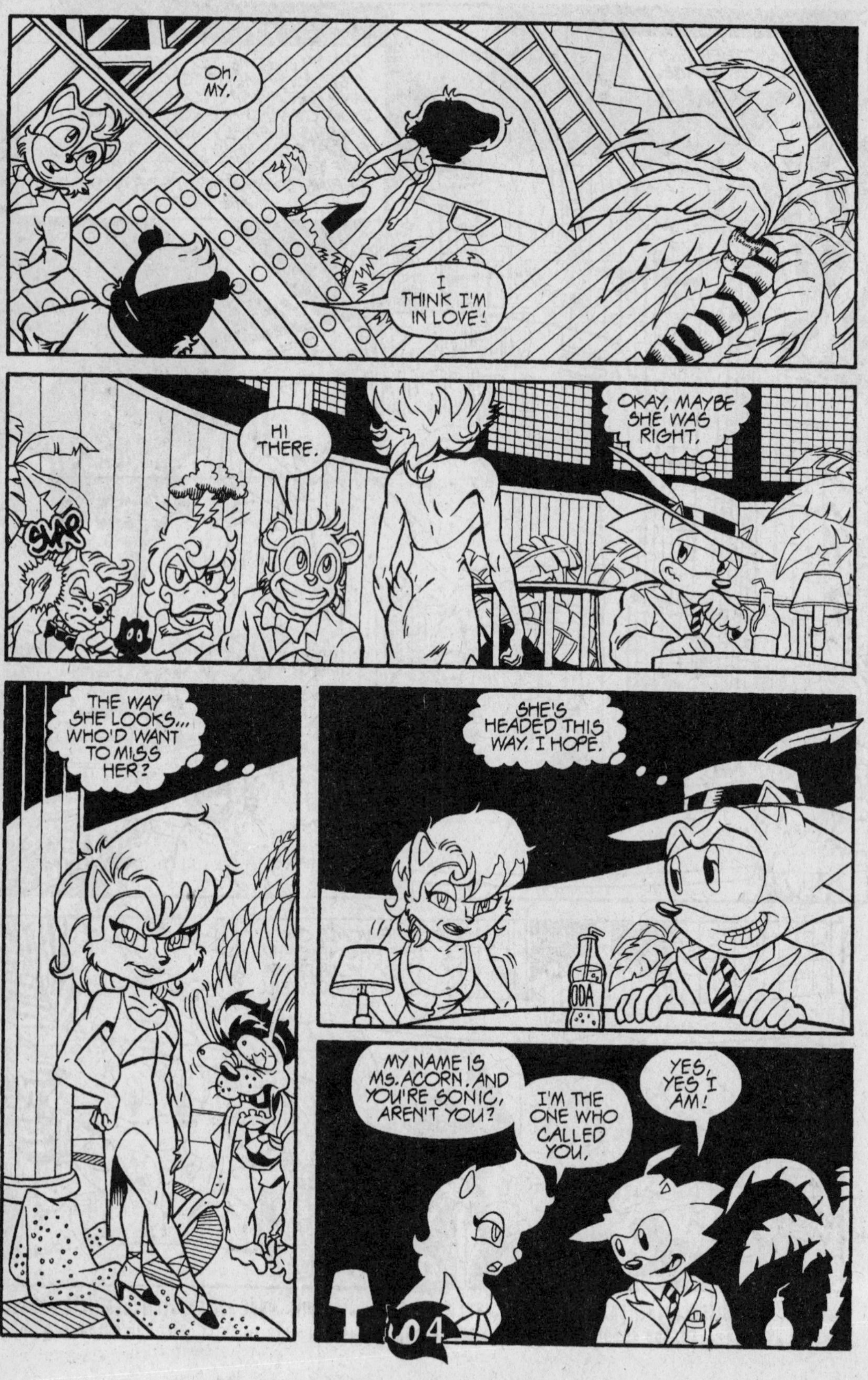

Oh, MY.
I THINK I'M IN LOVE!
SLAP
HI THERE.
OKAY, MAYBE SHE WAS RIGHT.
THE WAY SHE LOOKS... WHO'D WANT TO MISS HER?
SHE'S HEADED THIS WAY. I HOPE.
ODA
MY NAME IS MS. ACORN. AND YOU'RE SONIC, AREN'T YOU?
I'M THE ONE WHO CALLED YOU.
YES, YES I AM!
04

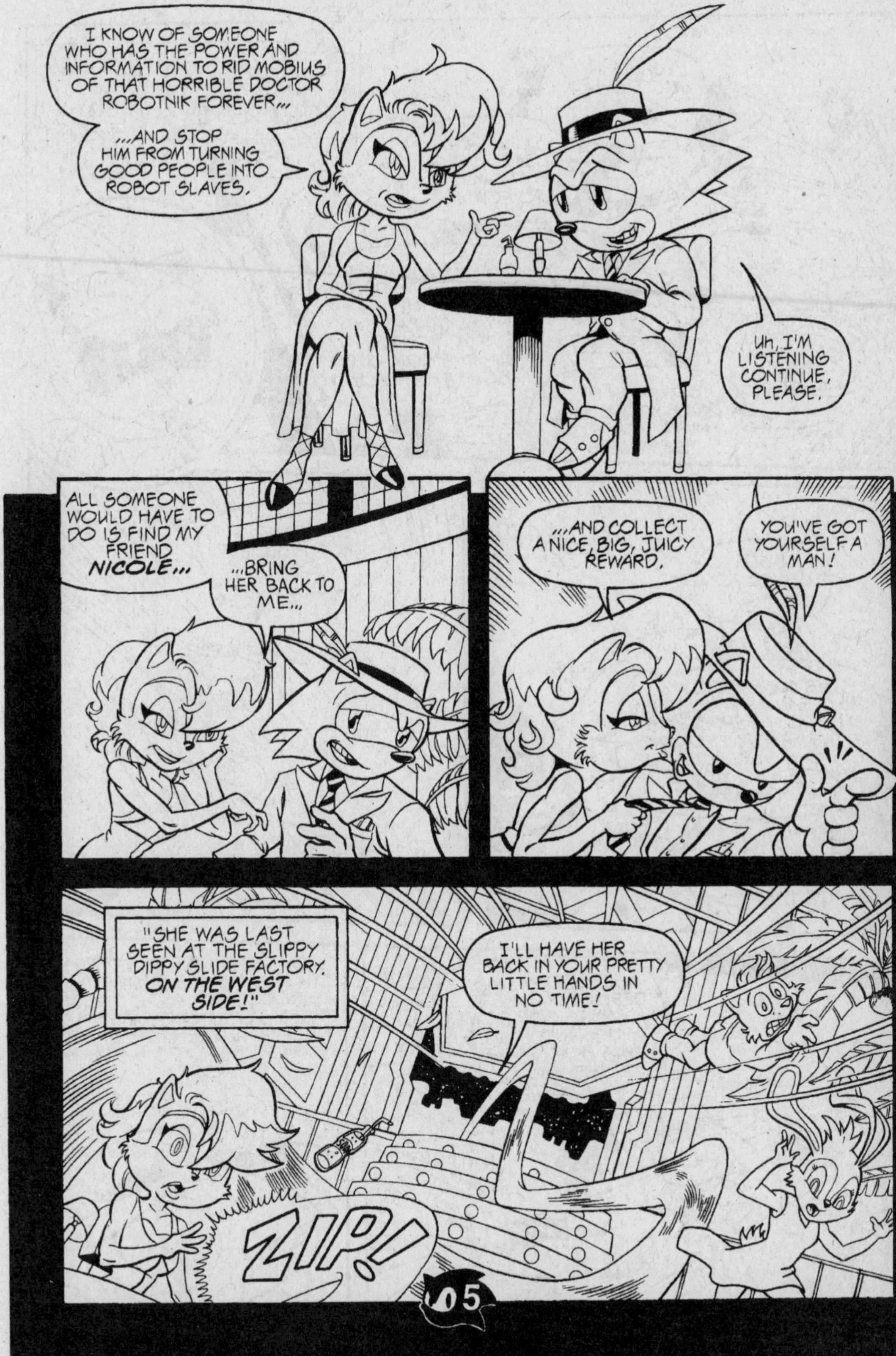
I KNOW OF SOMEONE WHO HAS THE POWER AND INFORMATION TO RID MOBIUS OF THAT HORRIBLE DOCTOR ROBOTNIK FOREVER...
...AND STOP HIM FROM TURNING GOOD PEOPLE INTO ROBOT SLAVES.
UH, I'M LISTENING CONTINUE, PLEASE.
ALL SOMEONE WOULD HAVE TO DO IS FIND MY FRIEND NICOLE...
...BRING HER BACK TO ME...
...AND COLLECT A NICE, BIG, JUICY REWARD.
YOU'VE GOT YOURSELF A MAN!
"SHE WAS LAST SEEN AT THE SLIPPY DIPPY SLIDE FACTORY. ON THE WEST SIDE!"
I'LL HAVE HER BACK IN YOUR PRETTY LITTLE HANDS IN NO TIME!
ZIP!
05

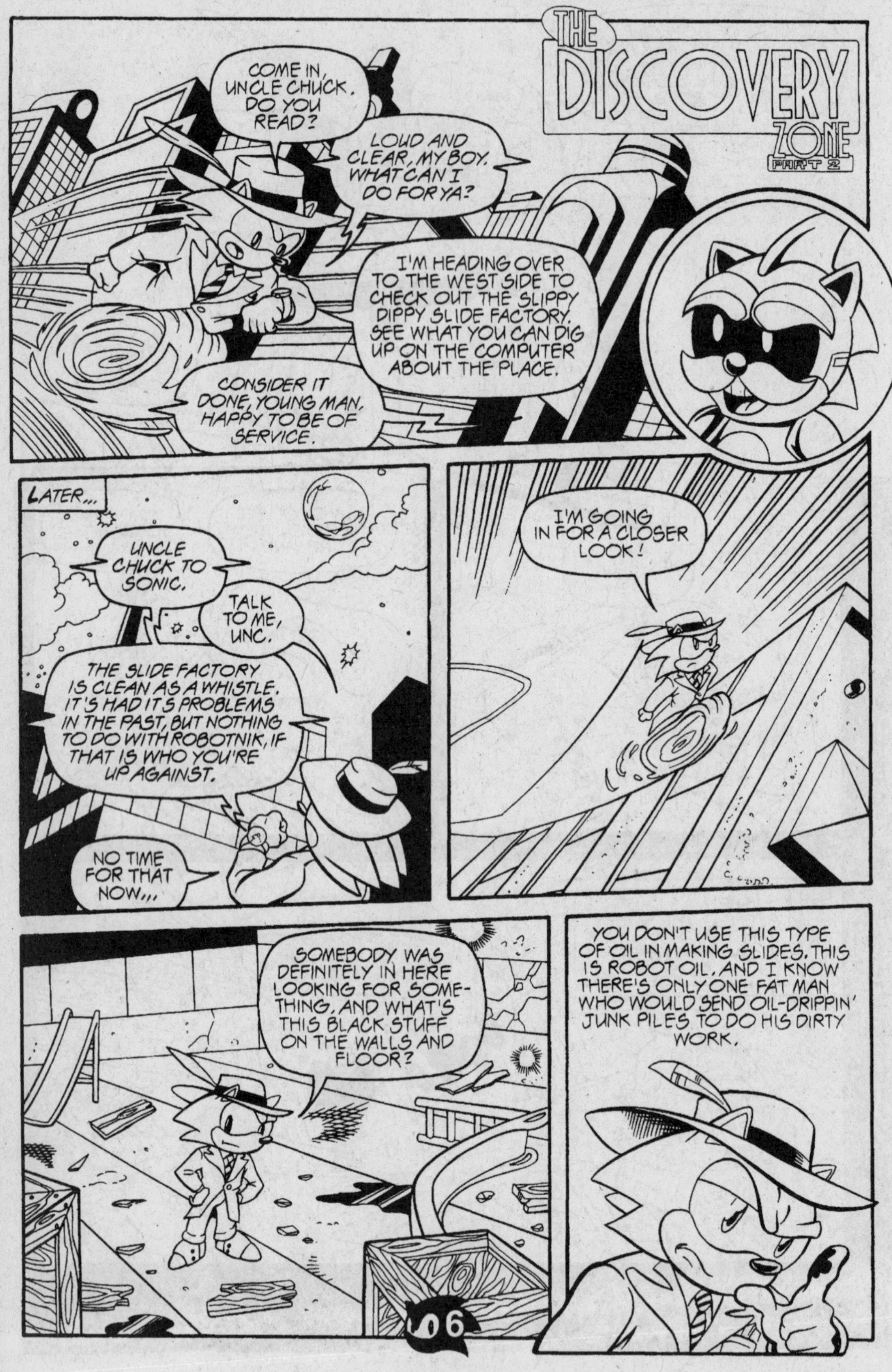

THE DISCOVERY ZONE
PART 2
COME IN, UNCLE CHUCK. DO YOU READ?
LOUD AND CLEAR, MY BOY. WHAT CAN I DO FOR YA?
I'M HEADING OVER TO THE WEST SIDE TO CHECK OUT THE SLIPPY DIPPY SLIDE FACTORY. SEE WHAT YOU CAN DIG UP ON THE COMPUTER ABOUT THE PLACE.
CONSIDER IT DONE, YOUNG MAN. HAPPY TO BE OF SERVICE.
LATER...
UNCLE CHUCK TO SONIC.
TALK TO ME, UNC.
THE SLIDE FACTORY IS CLEAN AS A WHISTLE. IT'S HAD ITS PROBLEMS IN THE PAST, BUT NOTHING TO DO WITH ROBOTNIK, IF THAT IS WHO YOU'RE UP AGAINST.
NO TIME FOR THAT NOW...
I'M GOING IN FOR A CLOSER LOOK!
SOMEBODY WAS DEFINITELY IN HERE LOOKING FOR SOMETHING. AND WHAT'S THIS BLACK STUFF ON THE WALLS AND FLOOR?
YOU DON'T USE THIS TYPE OF OIL IN MAKING SLIDES. THIS IS ROBOT OIL. AND I KNOW THERE'S ONLY ONE FAT MAN WHO WOULD SEND OIL-DRIPPIN' JUNK PILES TO DO HIS DIRTY WORK.
06

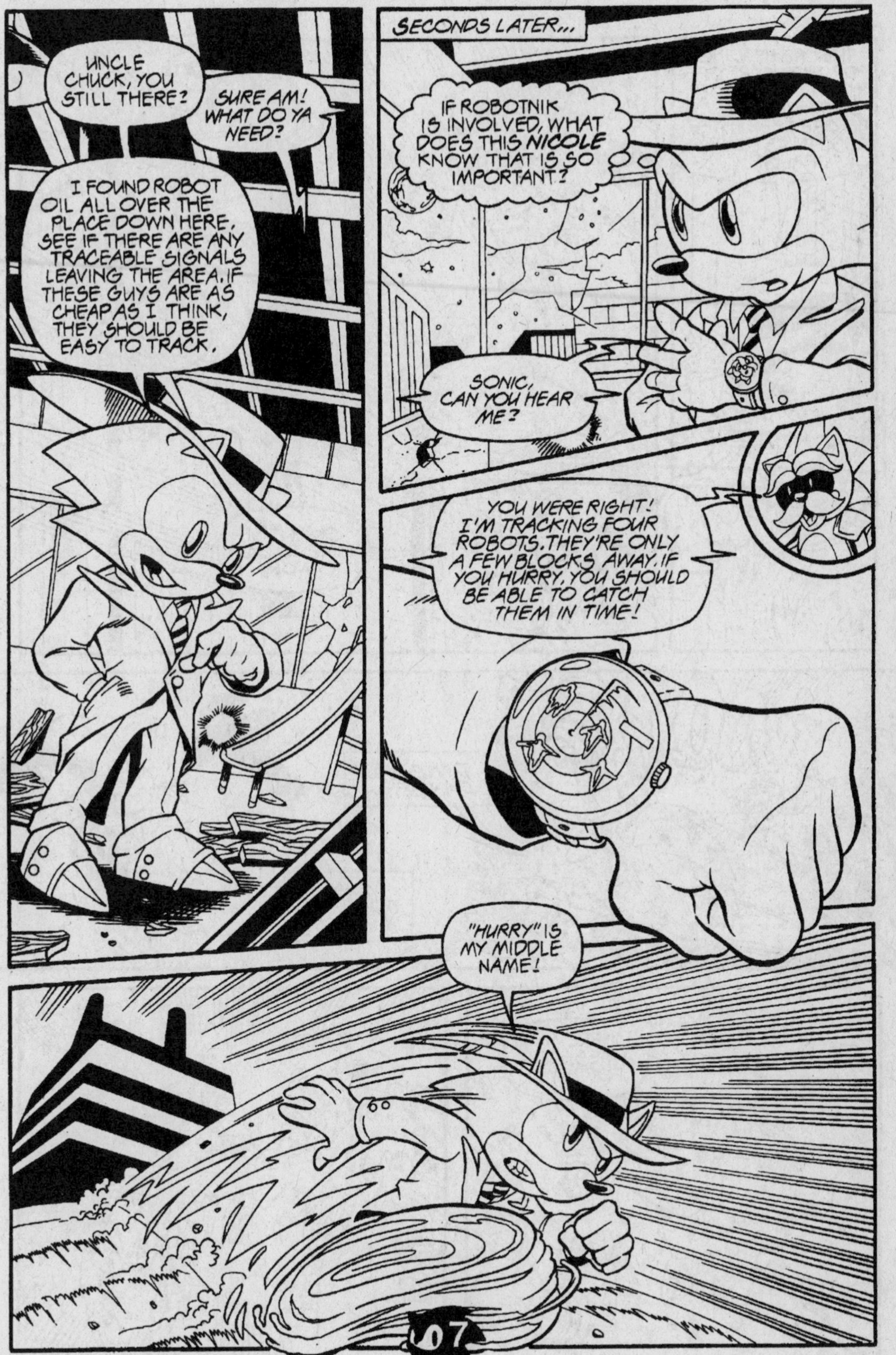
UNCLE CHUCK, YOU STILL THERE?
SURE AM! WHAT DO YA NEED?
I FOUND ROBOT OIL ALL OVER THE PLACE DOWN HERE. SEE IF THERE ARE ANY TRACEABLE SIGNALS LEAVING THE AREA. IF THESE GUYS ARE AS CHEAP AS I THINK, THEY SHOULD BE EASY TO TRACK.
SECONDS LATER...
IF ROBOTNIK IS INVOLVED, WHAT DOES THIS NICOLE KNOW THAT IS SO IMPORTANT?
SONIC, CAN YOU HEAR ME?
YOU WERE RIGHT! I'M TRACKING FOUR ROBOTS. THEY'RE ONLY A FEW BLOCKS AWAY. IF YOU HURRY, YOU SHOULD BE ABLE TO CATCH THEM IN TIME!
"HURRY" IS MY MIDDLE NAME!
07

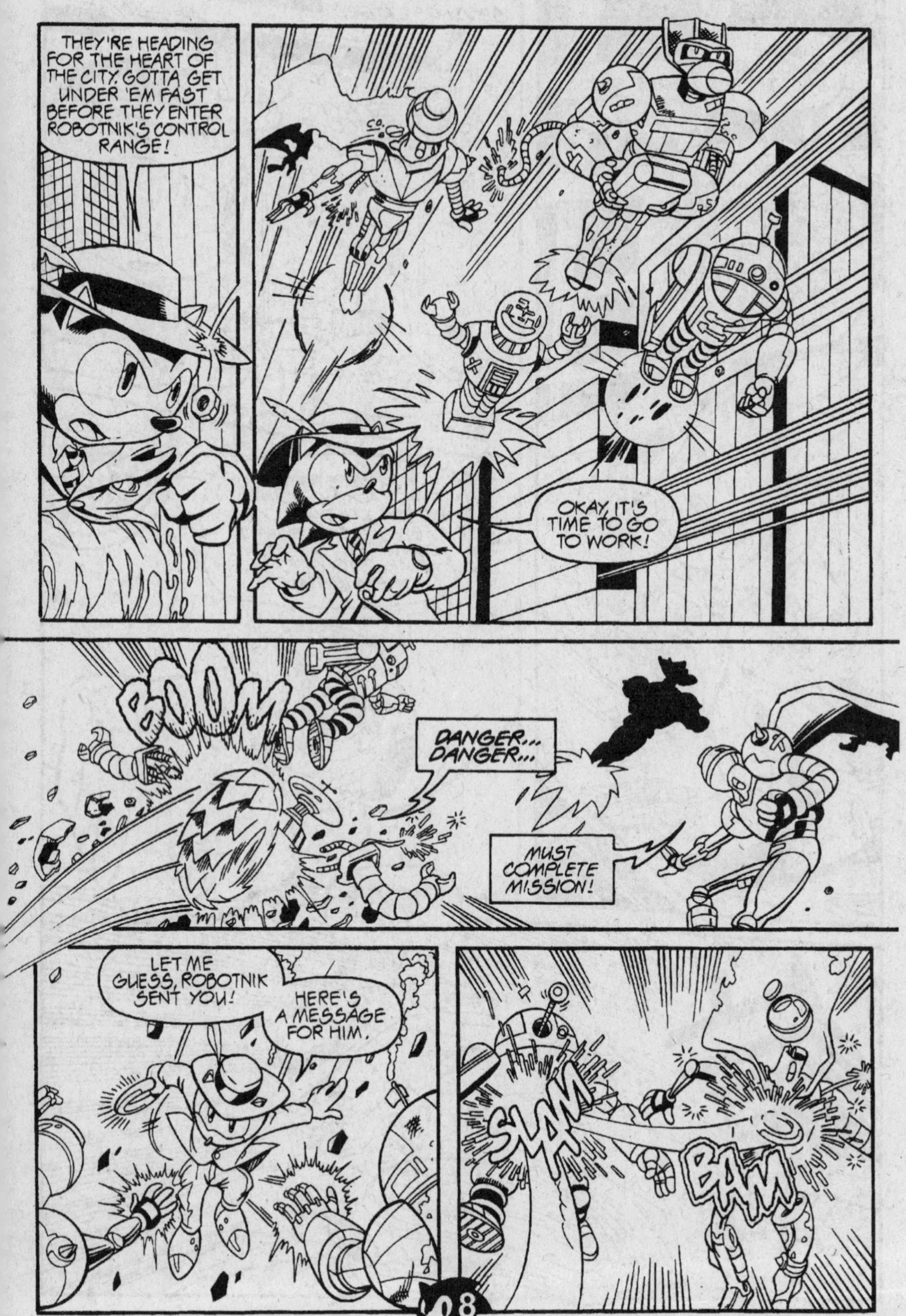
THEY'RE HEADING FOR THE HEART OF THE CITY. GOTTA GET UNDER 'EM FAST BEFORE THEY ENTER ROBOTNIK'S CONTROL RANGE!
OKAY, IT'S TIME TO GO TO WORK!
BOOM
DANGER... DANGER...
MUST COMPLETE MISSION!
LET ME GUESS, ROBOTNIK SENT YOU!
HERE'S A MESSAGE FOR HIM.
SLAM
BAM
08

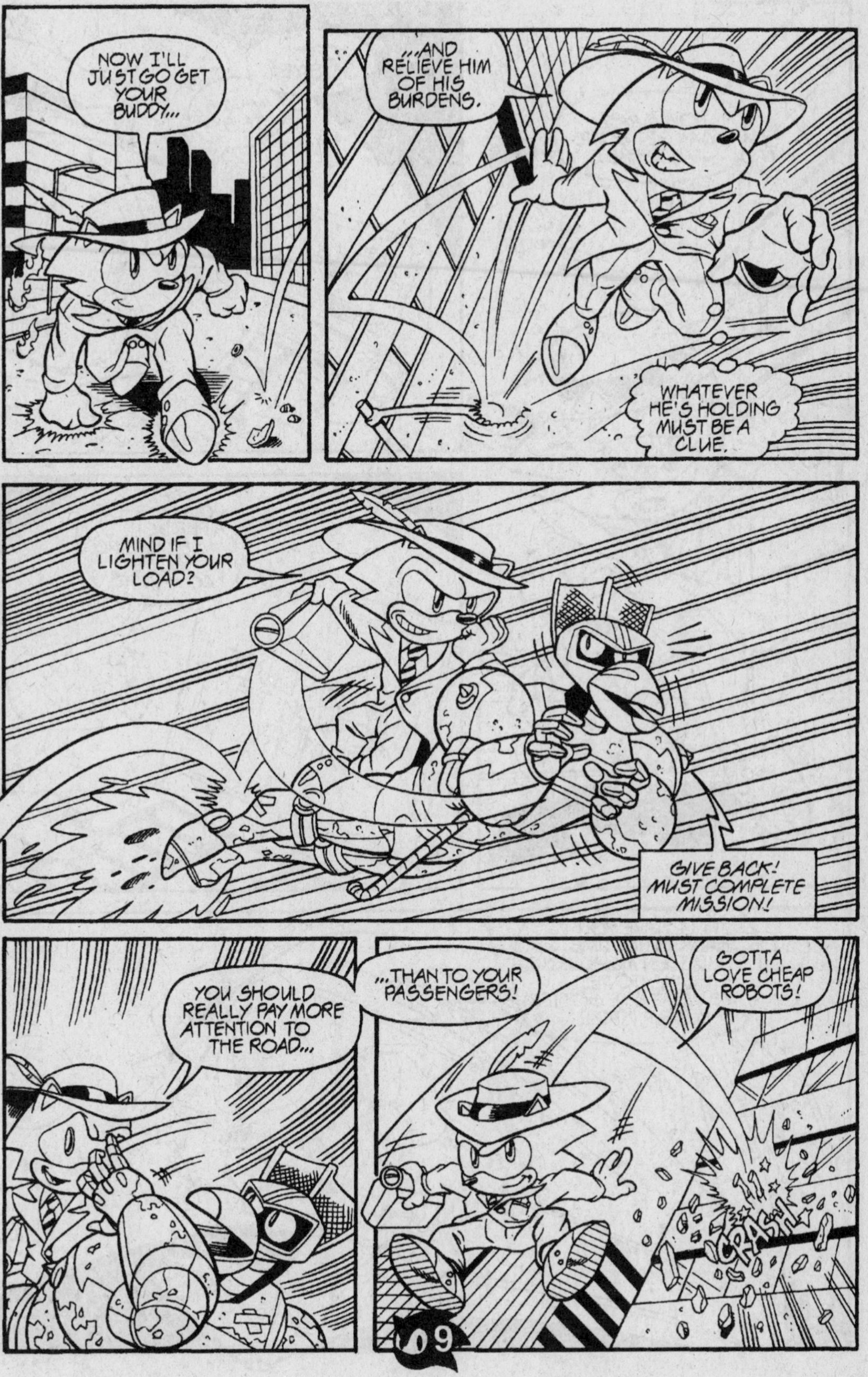
NOW I'LL JUST GO GET YOUR BUDDY...
...AND RELIEVE HIM OF HIS BURDENS.
WHATEVER HE'S HOLDING MUST BE A CLUE.
MIND IF I LIGHTEN YOUR LOAD?
GIVE BACK! MUST COMPLETE MISSION!
YOU SHOULD REALLY PAY MORE ATTENTION TO THE ROAD...
...THAN TO YOUR PASSENGERS!
GOTTA LOVE CHEAP ROBOTS!
CRASH!

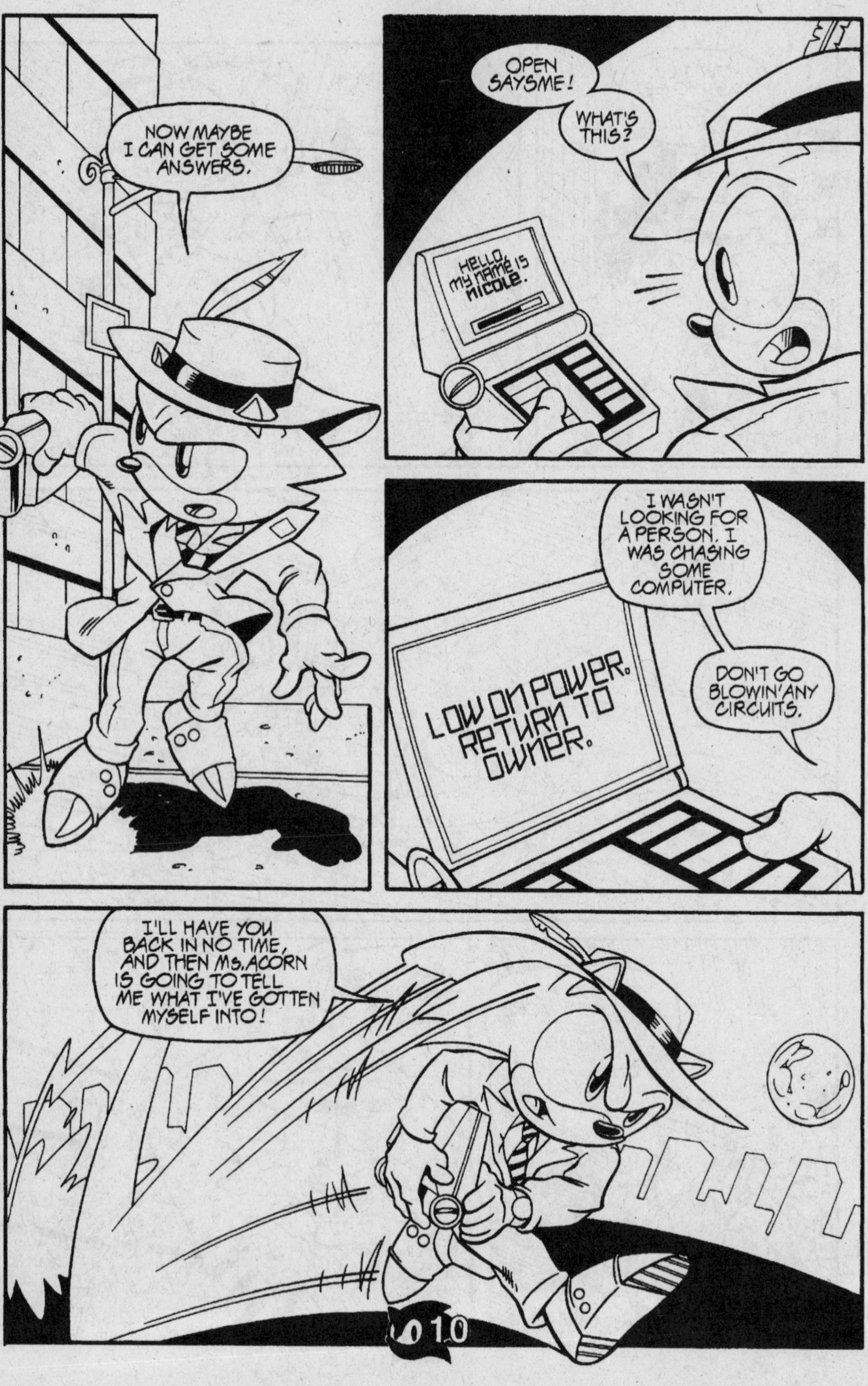
NOW MAYBE I CAN GET SOME ANSWERS.
OPEN SAYSME!
WHAT'S THIS?
HELLO, MY NAME IS NICOLE.
I WASN'T LOOKING FOR A PERSON. I WAS CHASING SOME COMPUTER.
LOW ON POWER. RETURN TO OWNER.
DON'T GO BLOWIN' ANY CIRCUITS.
I'LL HAVE YOU BACK IN NO TIME, AND THEN MS. ACORN IS GOING TO TELL ME WHAT I'VE GOTTEN MYSELF INTO!
10

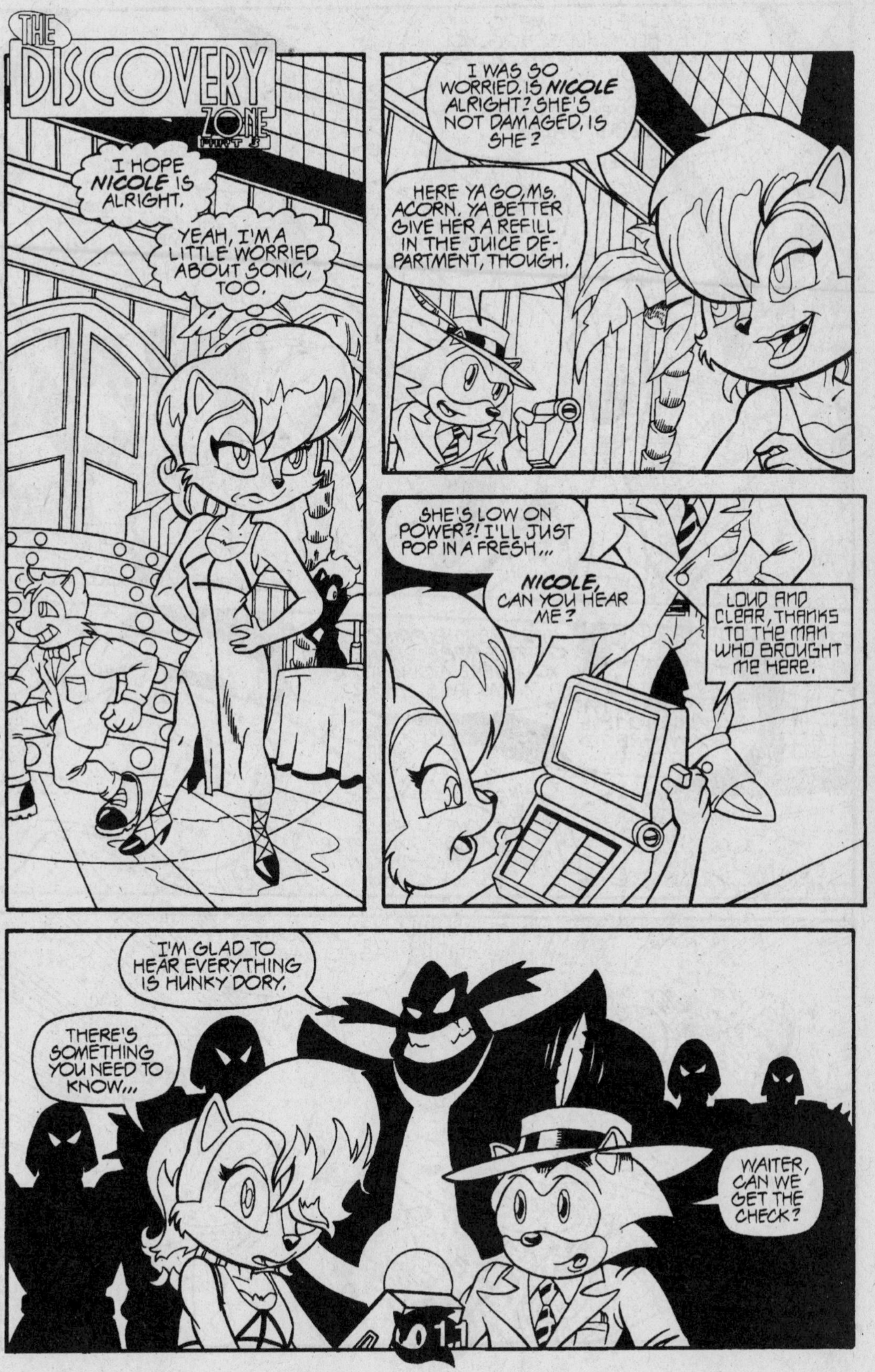
THE DISCOVERY ZONE PART 3
I HOPE NICOLE IS ALRIGHT.
YEAH, I'M A LITTLE WORRIED ABOUT SONIC, TOO.
I WAS SO WORRIED. IS NICOLE ALRIGHT? SHE'S NOT DAMAGED, IS SHE?
HERE YA GO, MS. ACORN. YA BETTER GIVE HER A REFILL IN THE JUICE DEPARTMENT, THOUGH.
SHE'S LOW ON POWER?! I'LL JUST POP IN A FRESH...
NICOLE, CAN YOU HEAR ME?
LOUD AND CLEAR, THANKS TO THE MAN WHO BROUGHT ME HERE.
I'M GLAD TO HEAR EVERYTHING IS HUNKY DORY.
THERE'S SOMETHING YOU NEED TO KNOW...
WAITER, CAN WE GET THE CHECK?

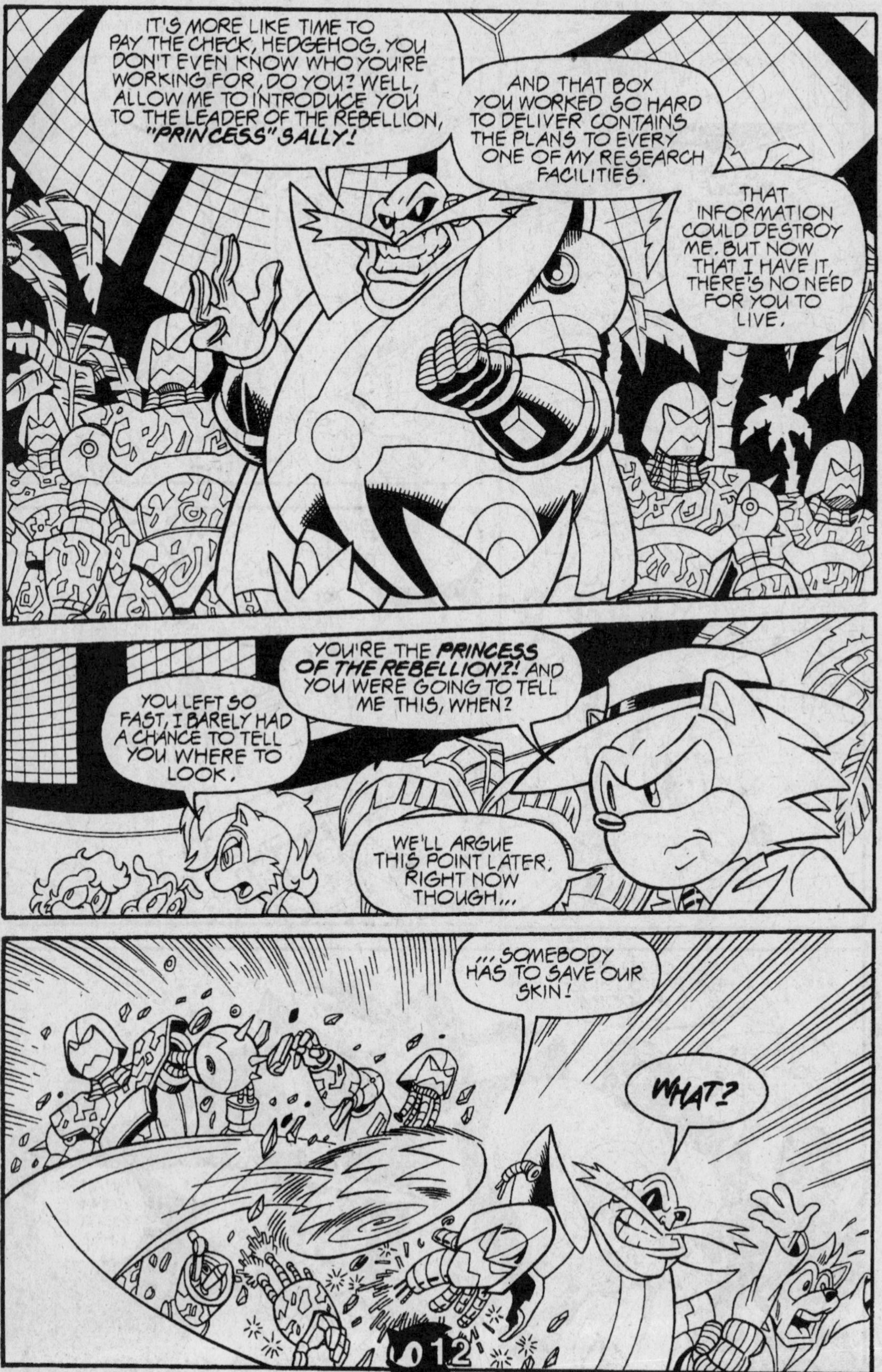
IT'S MORE LIKE TIME TO PAY THE CHECK, HEDGEHOG. YOU DON'T EVEN KNOW WHO YOU'RE WORKING FOR, DO YOU? WELL, ALLOW ME TO INTRODUCE YOU TO THE LEADER OF THE REBELLION, "PRINCESS" SALLY!
AND THAT BOX YOU WORKED SO HARD TO DELIVER CONTAINS THE PLANS TO EVERY ONE OF MY RESEARCH FACILITIES.
THAT INFORMATION COULD DESTROY ME. BUT NOW THAT I HAVE IT, THERE'S NO NEED FOR YOU TO LIVE.
YOU'RE THE PRINCESS OF THE REBELLION?! AND YOU WERE GOING TO TELL ME THIS, WHEN?
YOU LEFT SO FAST, I BARELY HAD A CHANCE TO TELL YOU WHERE TO LOOK.
WE'LL ARGUE THIS POINT LATER, RIGHT NOW THOUGH...
...SOMEBODY HAS TO SAVE OUR SKIN!
WHAT?
012

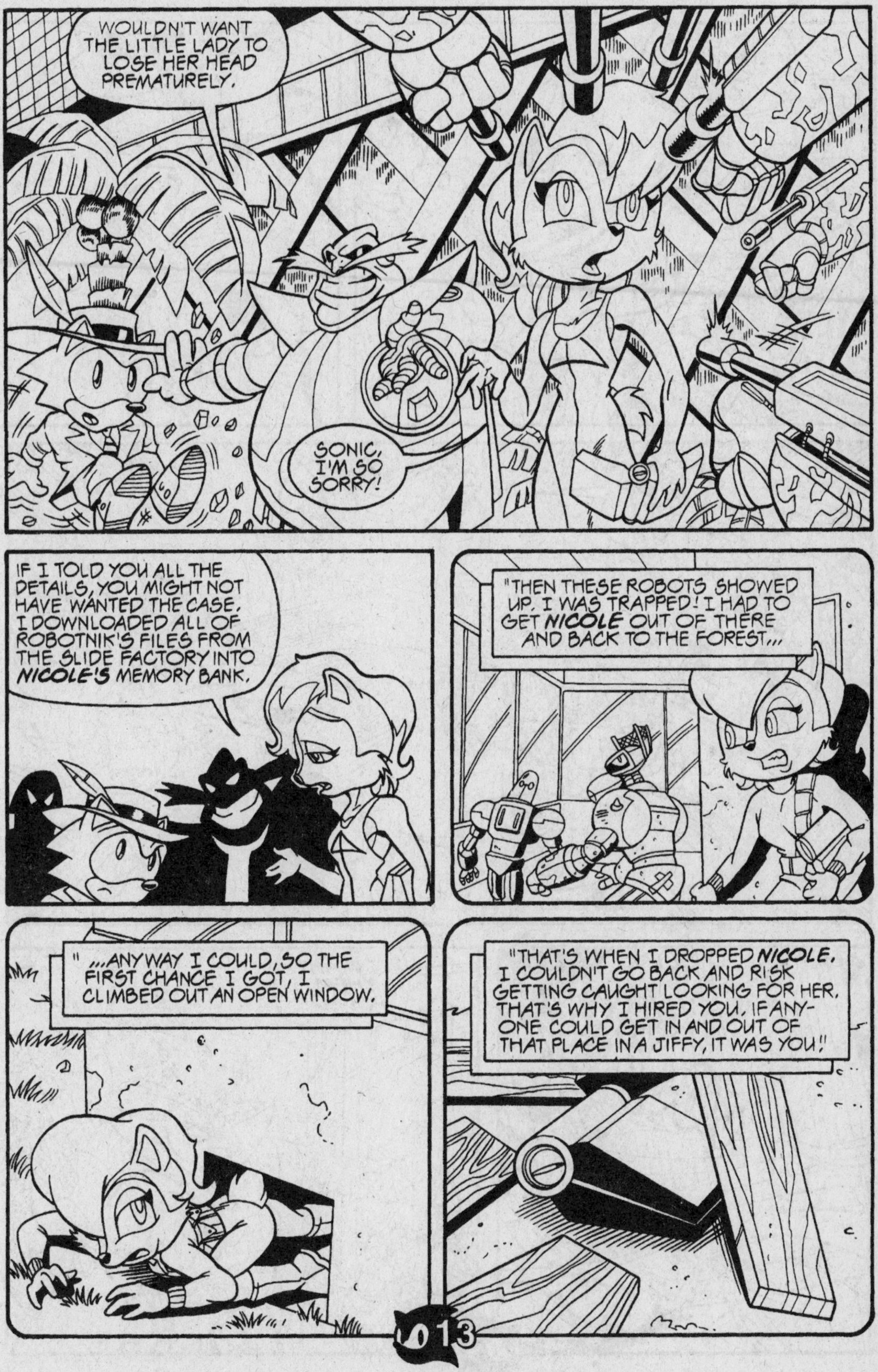
WOULDN'T WANT THE LITTLE LADY TO LOSE HER HEAD PREMATURELY.
SONIC, I'M SO SORRY!
IF I TOLD YOU ALL THE DETAILS, YOU MIGHT NOT HAVE WANTED THE CASE. I DOWNLOADED ALL OF ROBOTNIK'S FILES FROM THE SLIDE FACTORY INTO NICOLE'S MEMORY BANK.
"THEN THESE ROBOTS SHOWED UP. I WAS TRAPPED! I HAD TO GET NICOLE OUT OF THERE AND BACK TO THE FOREST...
"...ANYWAY I COULD, SO THE FIRST CHANCE I GOT, I CLIMBED OUT AN OPEN WINDOW.
"THAT'S WHEN I DROPPED NICOLE. I COULDN'T GO BACK AND RISK GETTING CAUGHT LOOKING FOR HER. THAT'S WHY I HIRED YOU. IF ANYONE COULD GET IN AND OUT OF THAT PLACE IN A JIFFY, IT WAS YOU!!
013

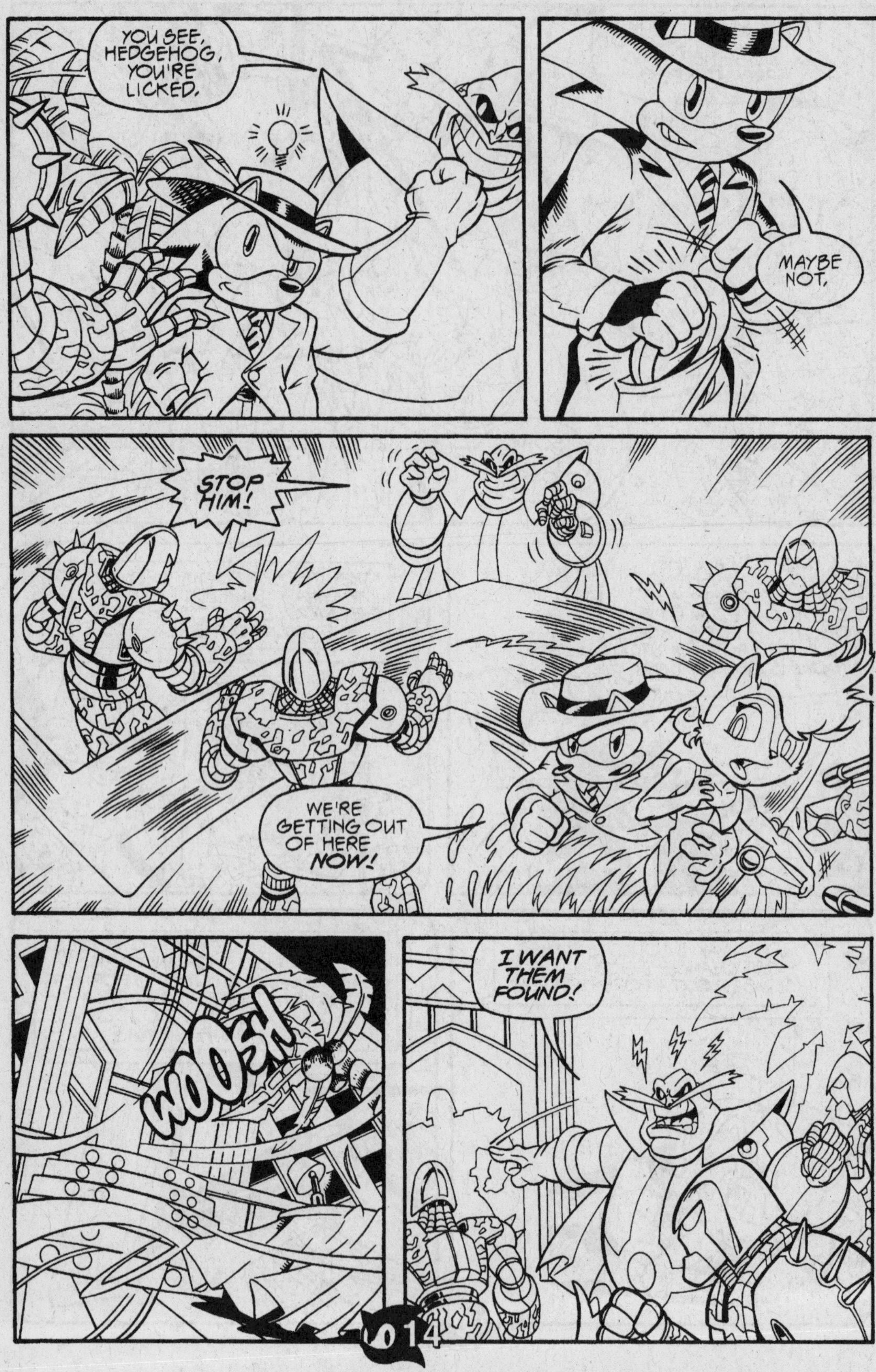
YOU SEE, HEDGEHOG, YOU'RE LICKED.
MAYBE NOT.
STOP HIM!
WE'RE GETTING OUT OF HERE NOW!
WOOSH
I WANT THEM FOUND!
014

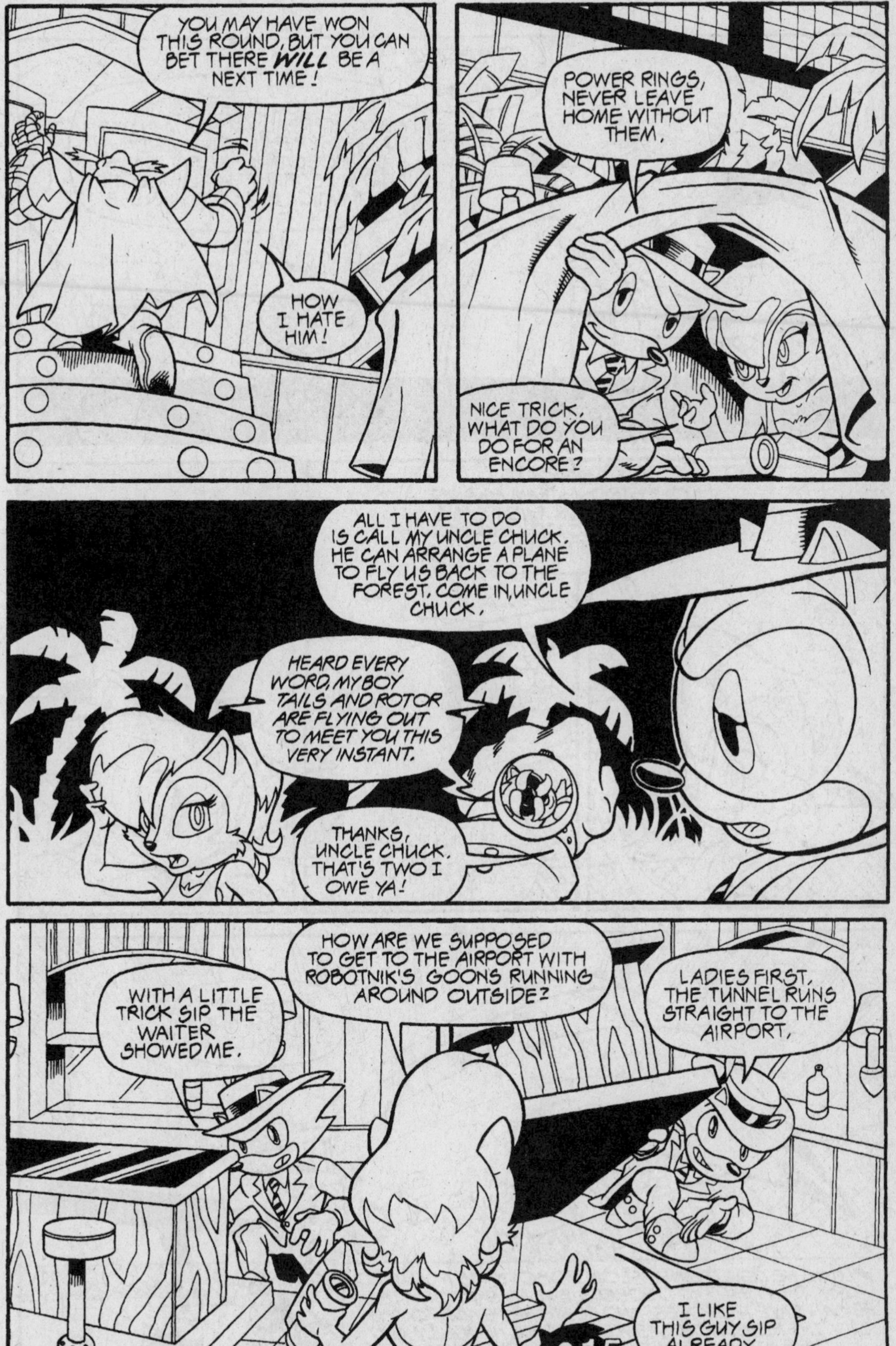
YOU MAY HAVE WON THIS ROUND, BUT YOU CAN BET THERE WILL BE A NEXT TIME!
HOW I HATE HIM!
POWER RINGS, NEVER LEAVE HOME WITHOUT THEM.
NICE TRICK. WHAT DO YOU DO FOR AN ENCORE?
ALL I HAVE TO DO IS CALL MY UNCLE CHUCK. HE CAN ARRANGE A PLANE TO FLY US BACK TO THE FOREST. COME IN, UNCLE CHUCK.
HEARD EVERY WORD, MY BOY. TAILS AND ROTOR ARE FLYING OUT TO MEET YOU THIS VERY INSTANT.
THANKS, UNCLE CHUCK. THAT'S TWO I OWE YA!
HOW ARE WE SUPPOSED TO GET TO THE AIRPORT WITH ROBOTNIK'S GOONS RUNNING AROUND OUTSIDE?
WITH A LITTLE TRICK SIP THE WAITER SHOWED ME.
LADIES FIRST. THE TUNNEL RUNS STRAIGHT TO THE AIRPORT.
I LIKE THIS GUY SIP ALREADY.
15

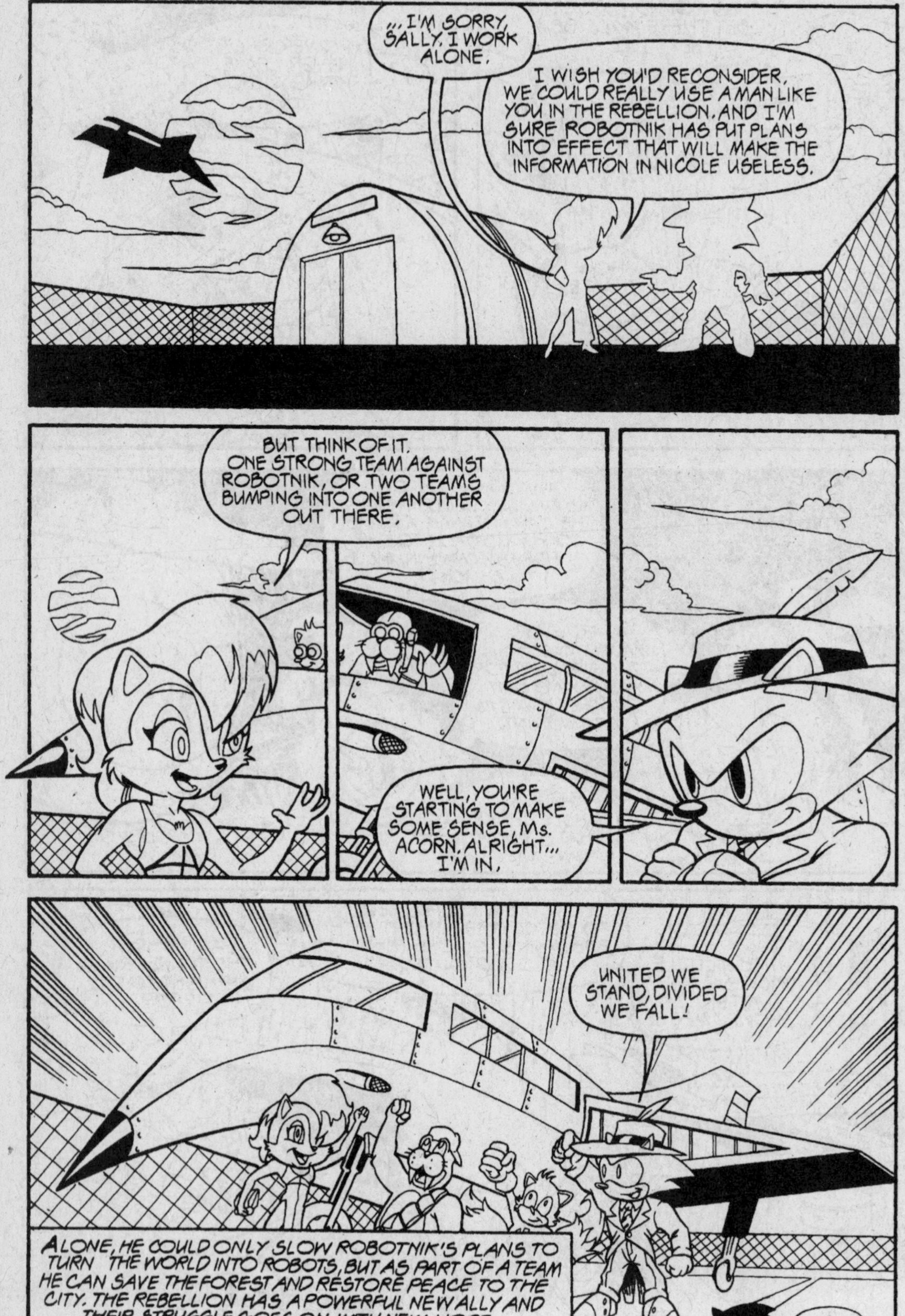
...I'M SORRY, SALLY. I WORK ALONE.
I WISH YOU'D RECONSIDER. WE COULD REALLY USE A MAN LIKE YOU IN THE REBELLION. AND I'M SURE ROBOTNIK HAS PUT PLANS INTO EFFECT THAT WILL MAKE THE INFORMATION IN NICOLE USELESS.
BUT THINK OF IT. ONE STRONG TEAM AGAINST ROBOTNIK, OR TWO TEAMS BUMPING INTO ONE ANOTHER OUT THERE.
WELL, YOU'RE STARTING TO MAKE SOME SENSE, Ms. ACORN. ALRIGHT... I'M IN.
UNITED WE STAND, DIVIDED WE FALL!
ALONE, HE COULD ONLY SLOW ROBOTNIK'S PLANS TO TURN THE WORLD INTO ROBOTS, BUT AS PART OF A TEAM HE CAN SAVE THE FOREST AND RESTORE PEACE TO THE CITY. THE REBELLION HAS A POWERFUL NEW ALLY AND THEIR STRUGGLE GOES ON, WITH NEW HOPE.
16

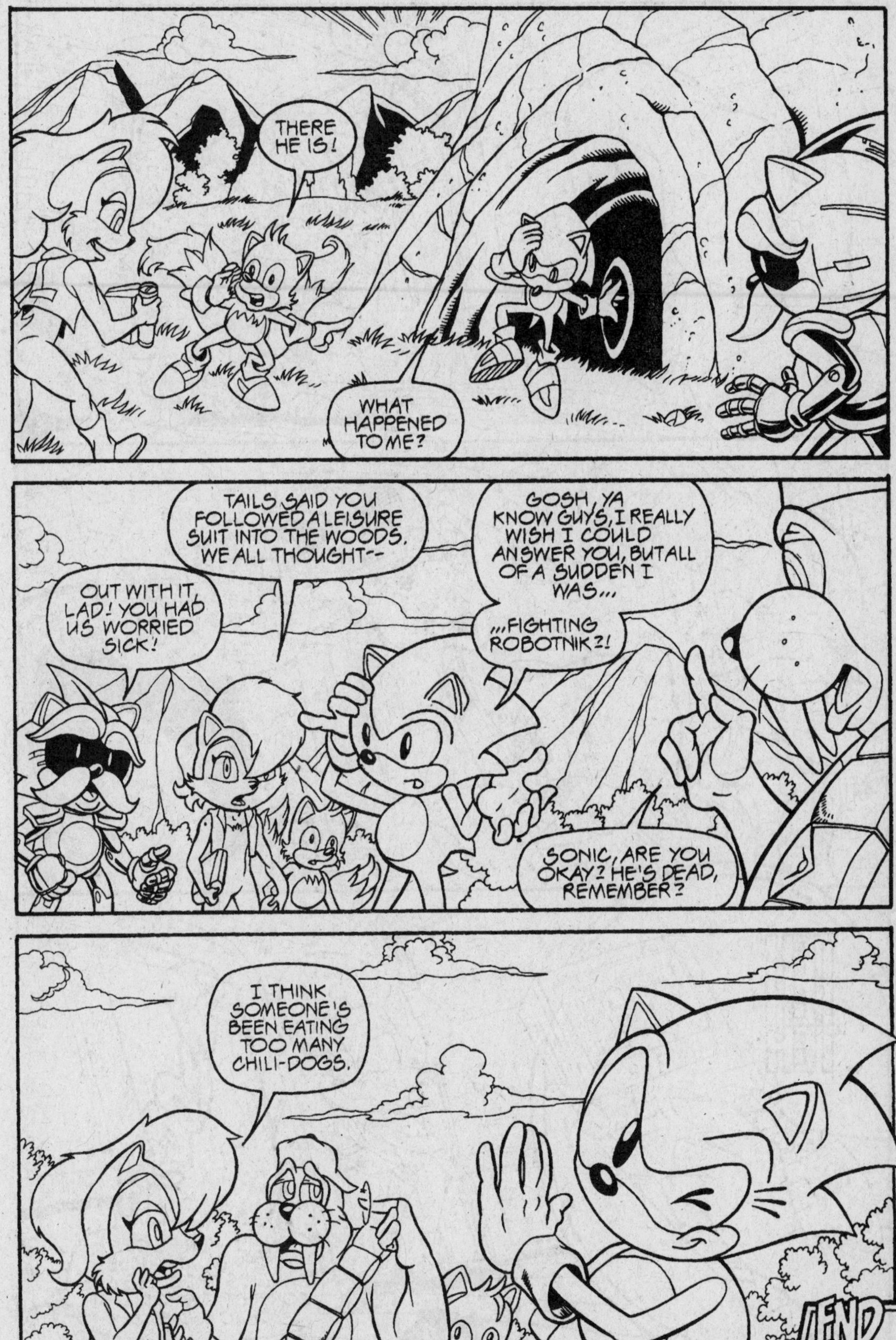
THERE HE IS!
WHAT HAPPENED TO ME?
OUT WITH IT, LAD! YOU HAD US WORRIED SICK!
TAILS SAID YOU FOLLOWED A LEISURE SUIT INTO THE WOODS. WE ALL THOUGHT--
GOSH, YA KNOW GUYS, I REALLY WISH I COULD ANSWER YOU, BUT ALL OF A SUDDEN I WAS...
...FIGHTING ROBOTNIK?!
SONIC, ARE YOU OKAY? HE'S DEAD, REMEMBER?
I THINK SOMEONE'S BEEN EATING TOO MANY CHILI-DOGS.
END

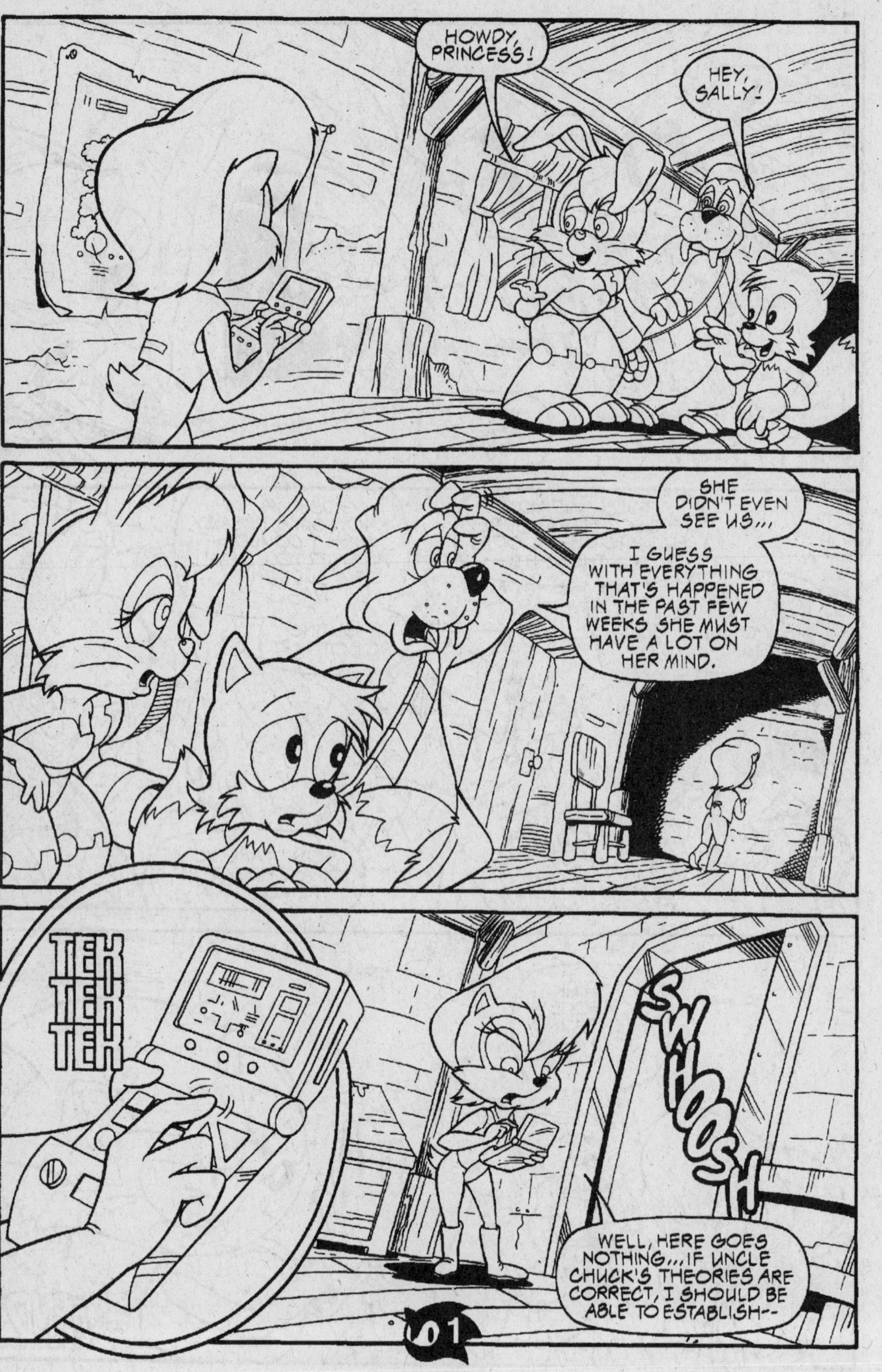
HOWDY, PRINCESS!
HEY, SALLY!
SHE DIDN'T EVEN SEE US...
I GUESS WITH EVERYTHING THAT'S HAPPENED IN THE PAST FEW WEEKS SHE MUST HAVE A LOT ON HER MIND.
TEK TEK TEK
SWHOOSH
WELL, HERE GOES NOTHING... IF UNCLE CHUCK'S THEORIES ARE CORRECT, I SHOULD BE ABLE TO ESTABLISH--

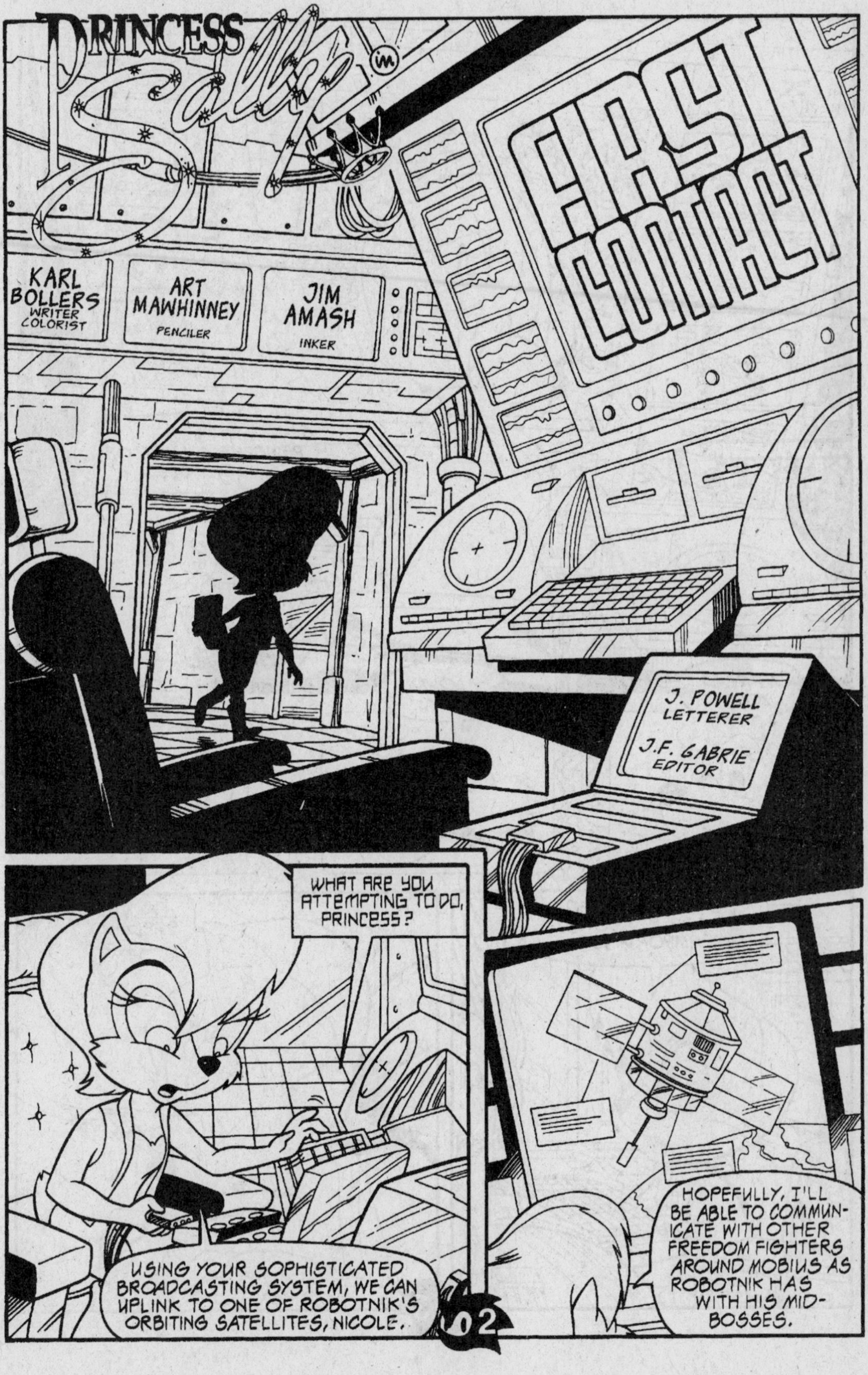

PRINCESS Sally in
FIRST CONTACT
KARL BOLLERS WRITER COLORIST
ART MAWHINNEY PENCILER
JIM AMASH INKER
J. POWELL LETTERER
J.F. GABRIE EDITOR
WHAT ARE YOU ATTEMPTING TO DO, PRINCESS?
USING YOUR SOPHISTICATED BROADCASTING SYSTEM, WE CAN UPLINK TO ONE OF ROBOTNIK'S ORBITING SATELLITES, NICOLE.
HOPEFULLY, I'LL BE ABLE TO COMMUNICATE WITH OTHER FREEDOM FIGHTERS AROUND MOBIUS AS ROBOTNIK HAS WITH HIS MID-BOSSES.

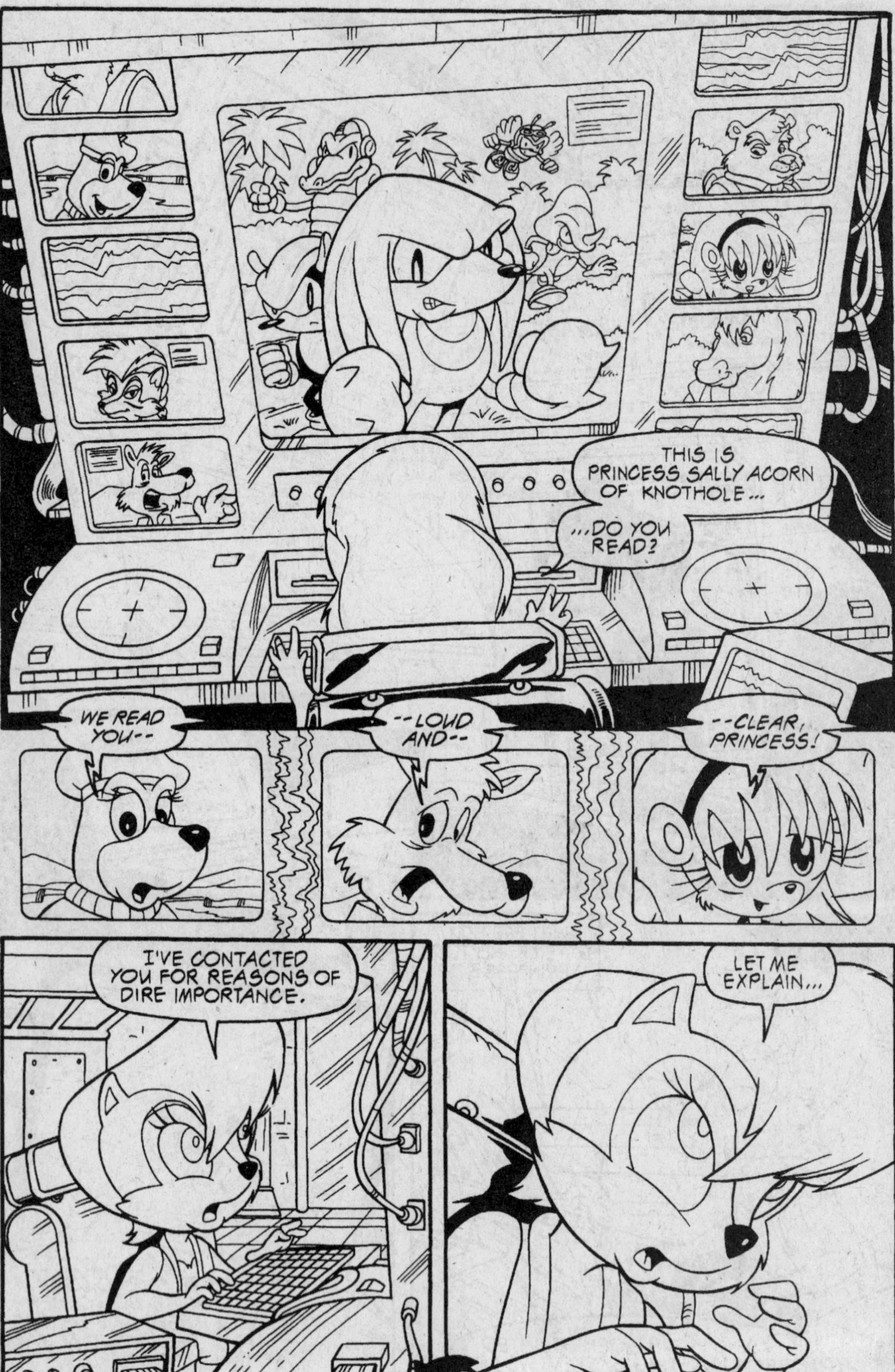
THIS IS PRINCESS SALLY ACORN OF KNOTHOLE...
...DO YOU READ?
WE READ YOU--
--LOUD AND--
--CLEAR, PRINCESS!
I'VE CONTACTED YOU FOR REASONS OF DIRE IMPORTANCE.
LET ME EXPLAIN...
3

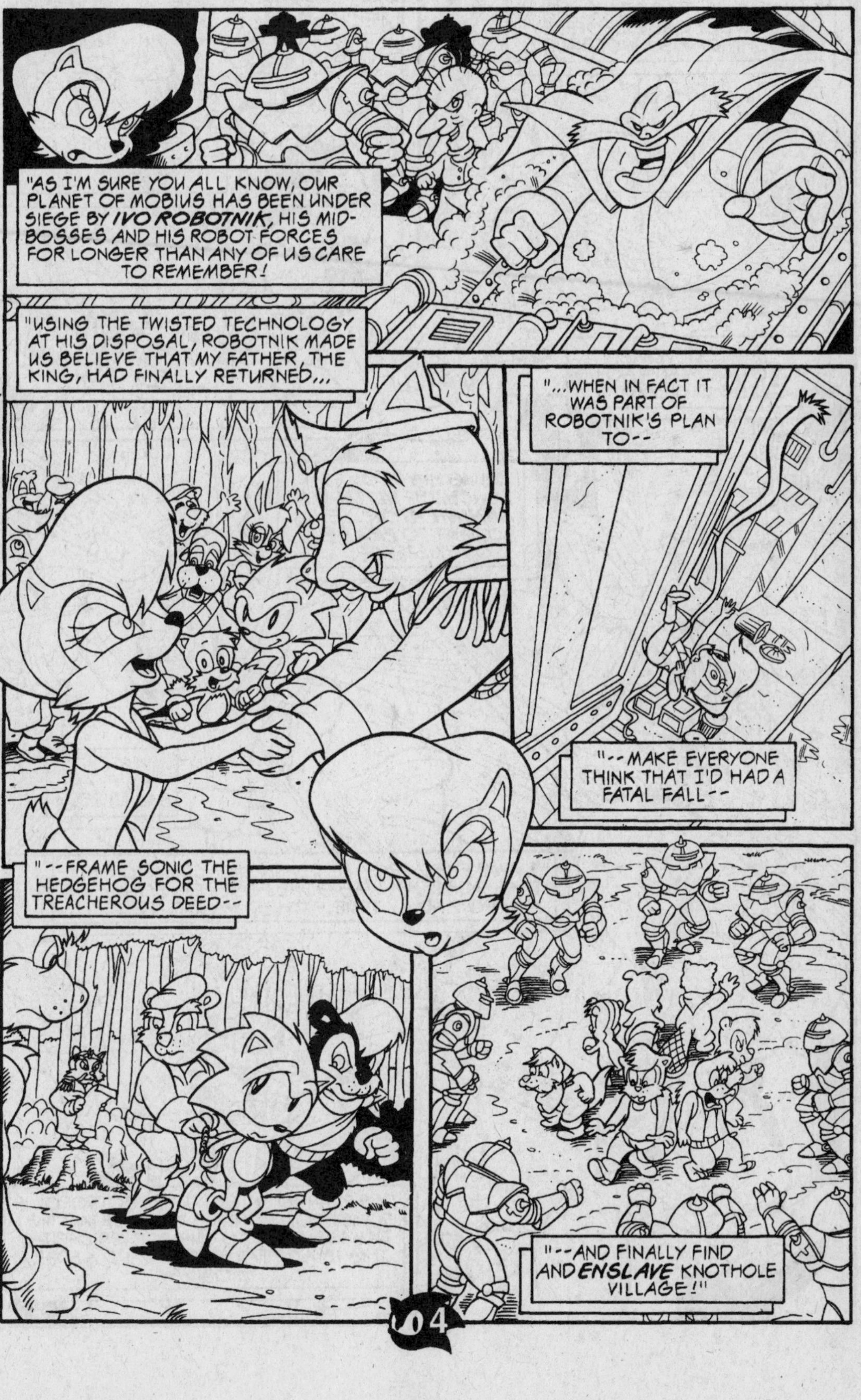
"AS I'M SURE YOU ALL KNOW, OUR PLANET OF MOBIUS HAS BEEN UNDER SIEGE BY IVO ROBOTNIK, HIS MID-BOSSES AND HIS ROBOT FORCES FOR LONGER THAN ANY OF US CARE TO REMEMBER!
"USING THE TWISTED TECHNOLOGY AT HIS DISPOSAL, ROBOTNIK MADE US BELIEVE THAT MY FATHER, THE KING, HAD FINALLY RETURNED...
"...WHEN IN FACT IT WAS PART OF ROBOTNIK'S PLAN TO--
"--MAKE EVERYONE THINK THAT I'D HAD A FATAL FALL--
"--FRAME SONIC THE HEDGEHOG FOR THE TREACHEROUS DEED--
"--AND FINALLY FIND AND ENSLAVE KNOTHOLE VILLAGE!"
04

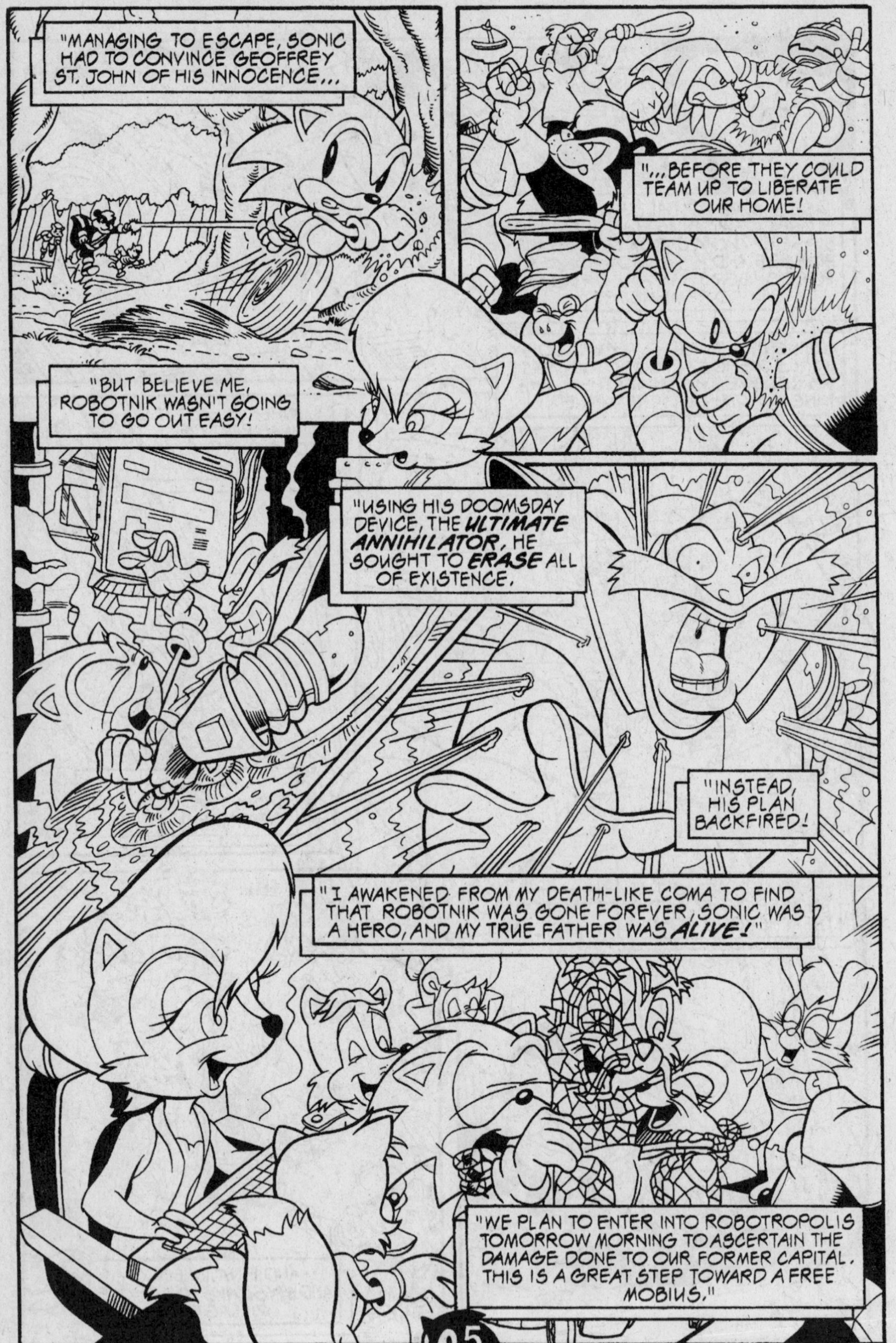
"MANAGING TO ESCAPE, SONIC HAD TO CONVINCE GEOFFREY ST. JOHN OF HIS INNOCENCE...
"...BEFORE THEY COULD TEAM UP TO LIBERATE OUR HOME!
"BUT BELIEVE ME, ROBOTNIK WASN'T GOING TO GO OUT EASY!
"USING HIS DOOMSDAY DEVICE, THE ULTIMATE ANNIHILATOR, HE SOUGHT TO ERASE ALL OF EXISTENCE.
"INSTEAD, HIS PLAN BACKFIRED!
"I AWAKENED FROM MY DEATH-LIKE COMA TO FIND THAT ROBOTNIK WAS GONE FOREVER, SONIC WAS A HERO, AND MY TRUE FATHER WAS ALIVE!"
"WE PLAN TO ENTER INTO ROBOTROPOLIS TOMORROW MORNING TO ASCERTAIN THE DAMAGE DONE TO OUR FORMER CAPITAL. THIS IS A GREAT STEP TOWARD A FREE MOBIUS."
05

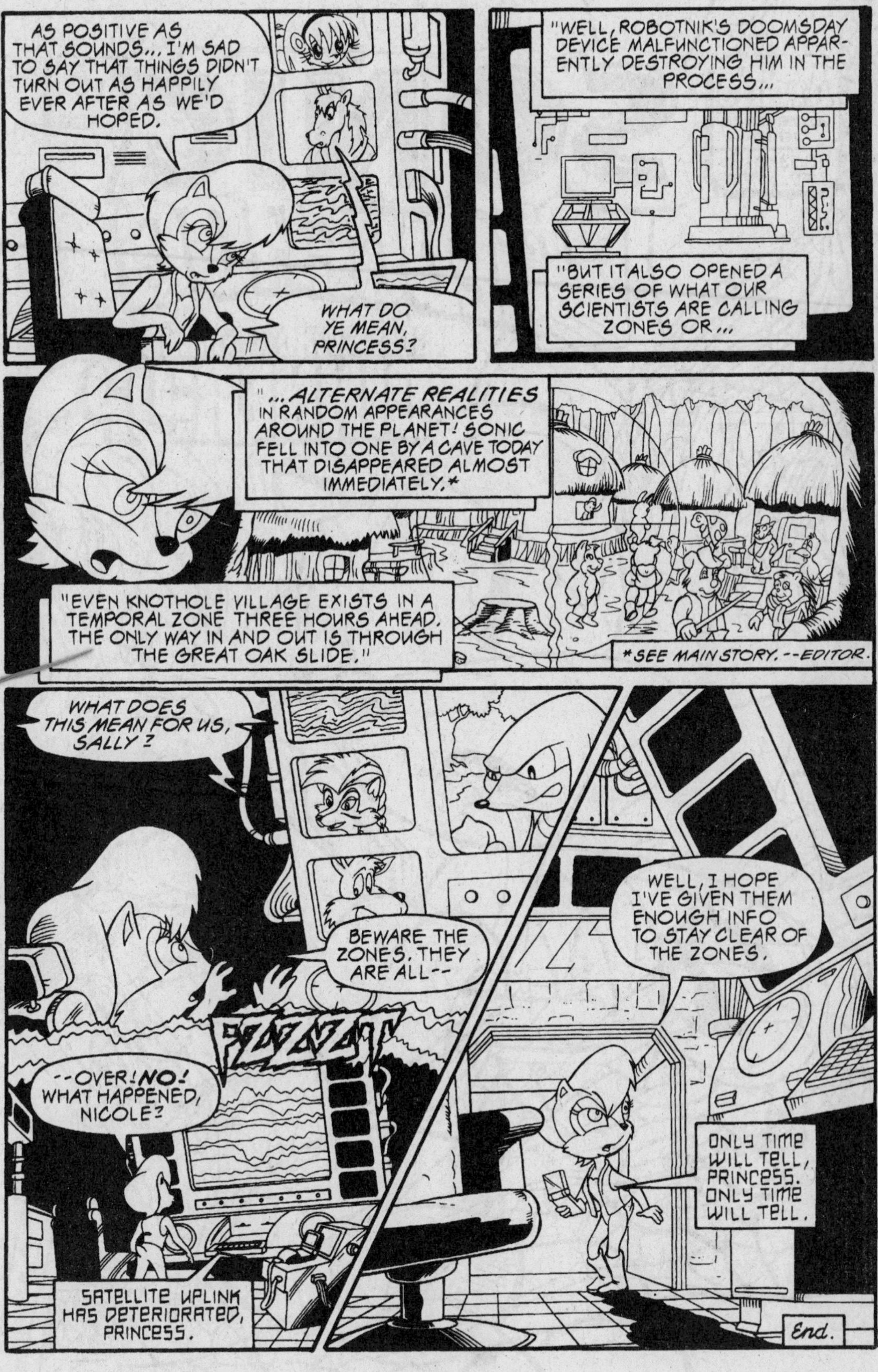
AS POSITIVE AS THAT SOUNDS... I'M SAD TO SAY THAT THINGS DIDN'T TURN OUT AS HAPPILY EVER AFTER AS WE'D HOPED.
WHAT DO YE MEAN, PRINCESS?
"WELL, ROBOTNIK'S DOOMSDAY DEVICE MALFUNCTIONED APPARENTLY DESTROYING HIM IN THE PROCESS...
"BUT IT ALSO OPENED A SERIES OF WHAT OUR SCIENTISTS ARE CALLING ZONES OR...
"...ALTERNATE REALITIES IN RANDOM APPEARANCES AROUND THE PLANET! SONIC FELL INTO ONE BY A CAVE TODAY THAT DISAPPEARED ALMOST IMMEDIATELY.*
"EVEN KNOTHOLE VILLAGE EXISTS IN A TEMPORAL ZONE THREE HOURS AHEAD. THE ONLY WAY IN AND OUT IS THROUGH THE GREAT OAK SLIDE."
*SEE MAIN STORY. --EDITOR.
WHAT DOES THIS MEAN FOR US, SALLY?
BEWARE THE ZONES. THEY ARE ALL--
FZZZZT
--OVER! NO! WHAT HAPPENED, NICOLE?
SATELLITE UPLINK HAS DETERIORATED, PRINCESS.
WELL, I HOPE I'VE GIVEN THEM ENOUGH INFO TO STAY CLEAR OF THE ZONES.
ONLY TIME WILL TELL, PRINCESS. ONLY TIME WILL TELL.
End.

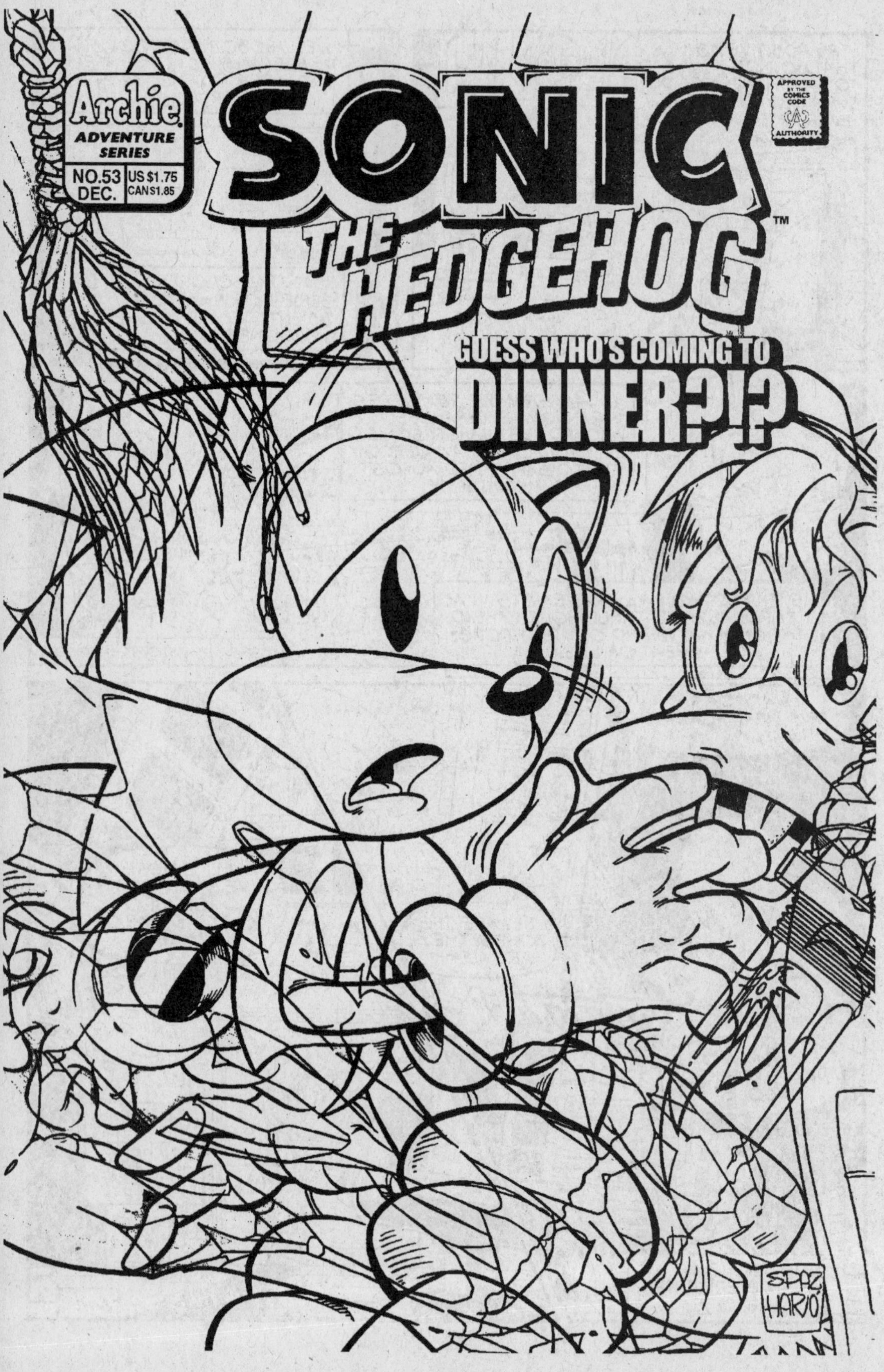
Archie
ADVENTURE SERIES
NO.53 DEC.
US $1.75 CAN $1.85
APPROVED BY THE COMICS CODE AUTHORITY
SONIC THE HEDGEHOG™
GUESS WHO'S COMING TO DINNER?!?
SPAZ HARVO

Once a virtual paradise, the planet
Mobius was enslaved when conquered by
the techno-evil of Doctor Robotnik.
In the aftermath, a
courageous group of "Freedom Fighters"
has risen to restore the order and
beauty that was once theirs.
The greatest among them is the
fastest and way-coolest
dude on two feet...
SONIC THE HEDGEHOG!

Now war-time has at long last ended
and a brave new world has started to emerge.
Its emergence, however, isn't easy.
Especially in the city of Mobotropolis.
Before the Knothole Villagers can transport
themselves here, The freedom fighters begin their
awesome task of dismantling the fiendish
devices left by Robotnik as a safety precaution.
Little do they know of the
secrets they will unleash.
Secrets of a past best left forgotten!

Especially for one King Acorn...

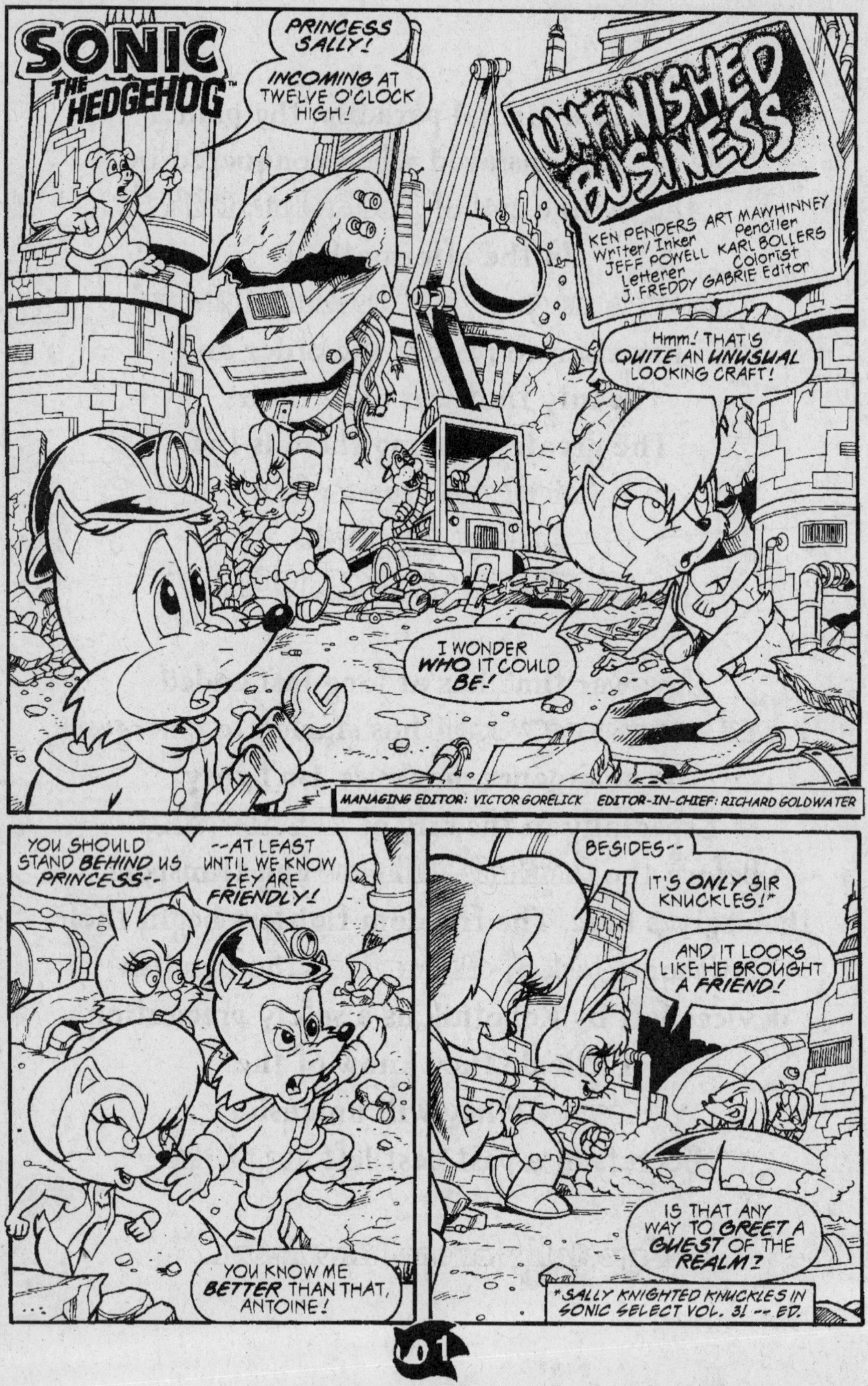
SONIC THE HEDGEHOG
PRINCESS SALLY!
INCOMING AT TWELVE O'CLOCK HIGH!
UNFINISHED BUSINESS
KEN PENDERS Writer/Inker ART MAWHINNEY Penciller JEFF POWELL Letterer KARL BOLLERS Colorist J. FREDDY GABRIE Editor
Hmm! THAT'S QUITE AN UNUSUAL LOOKING CRAFT!
I WONDER WHO IT COULD BE!
MANAGING EDITOR: VICTOR GORELICK EDITOR-IN-CHIEF: RICHARD GOLDWATER
YOU SHOULD STAND BEHIND US PRINCESS--
--AT LEAST UNTIL WE KNOW ZEY ARE FRIENDLY!
YOU KNOW ME BETTER THAN THAT, ANTOINE!
BESIDES--
IT'S ONLY SIR KNUCKLES!*
AND IT LOOKS LIKE HE BROUGHT A FRIEND!
IS THAT ANY WAY TO GREET A GUEST OF THE REALM?
*SALLY KNIGHTED KNUCKLES IN SONIC SELECT VOL. 3! -- ED.
01

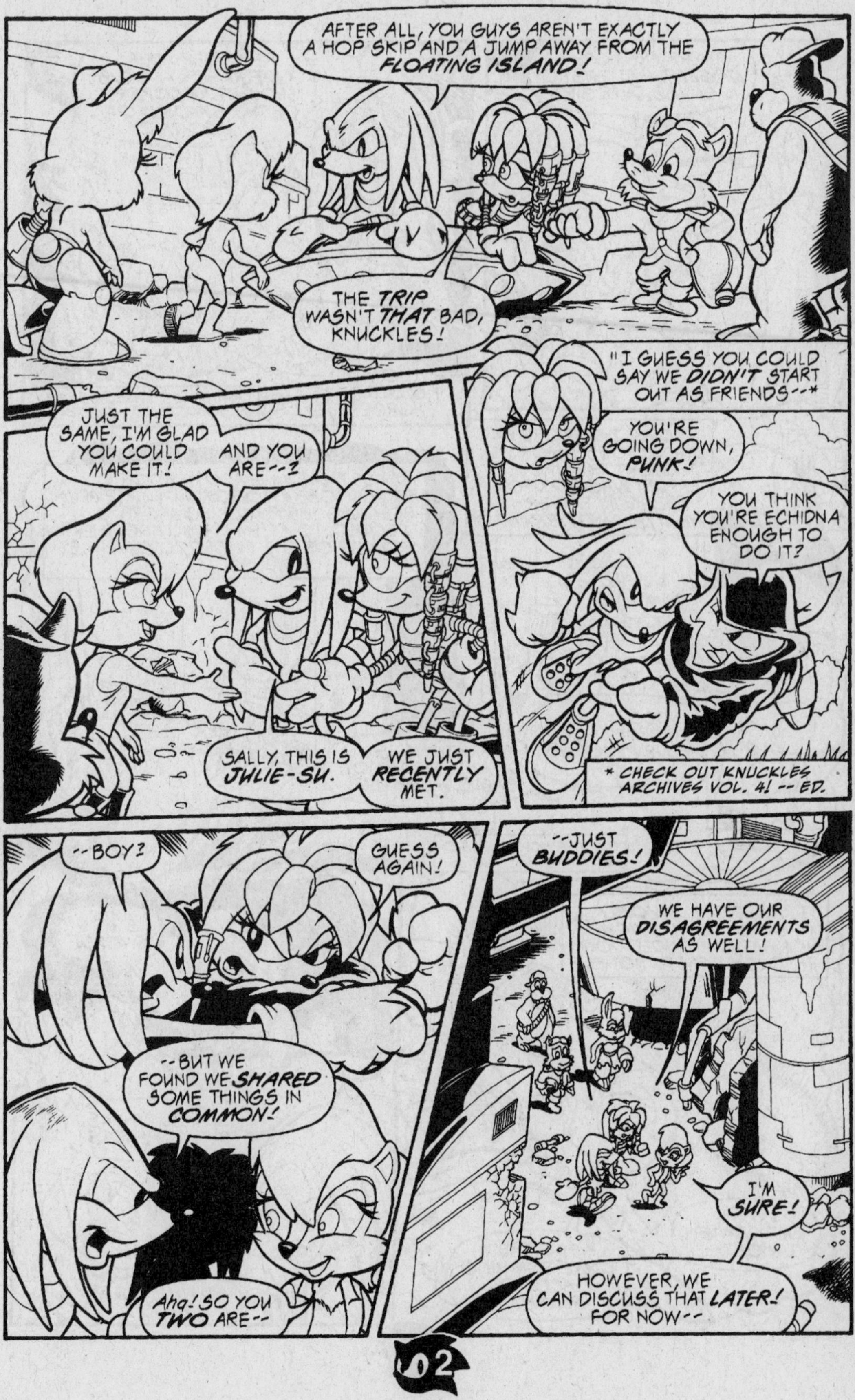
AFTER ALL, YOU GUYS AREN'T EXACTLY A HOP SKIP AND A JUMP AWAY FROM THE FLOATING ISLAND!
THE TRIP WASN'T THAT BAD, KNUCKLES!
JUST THE SAME, I'M GLAD YOU COULD MAKE IT!
AND YOU ARE--?
SALLY, THIS IS JULIE-SU.
WE JUST RECENTLY MET.
"I GUESS YOU COULD SAY WE DIDN'T START OUT AS FRIENDS--*
YOU'RE GOING DOWN, PUNK!
YOU THINK YOU'RE ECHIDNA ENOUGH TO DO IT?
* CHECK OUT KNUCKLES ARCHIVES VOL. 4! -- ED.
--BOY?
GUESS AGAIN!
--BUT WE FOUND WE SHARED SOME THINGS IN COMMON!
Aha! SO YOU TWO ARE--
--JUST BUDDIES!
WE HAVE OUR DISAGREEMENTS AS WELL!
I'M SURE!
HOWEVER, WE CAN DISCUSS THAT LATER! FOR NOW--
2

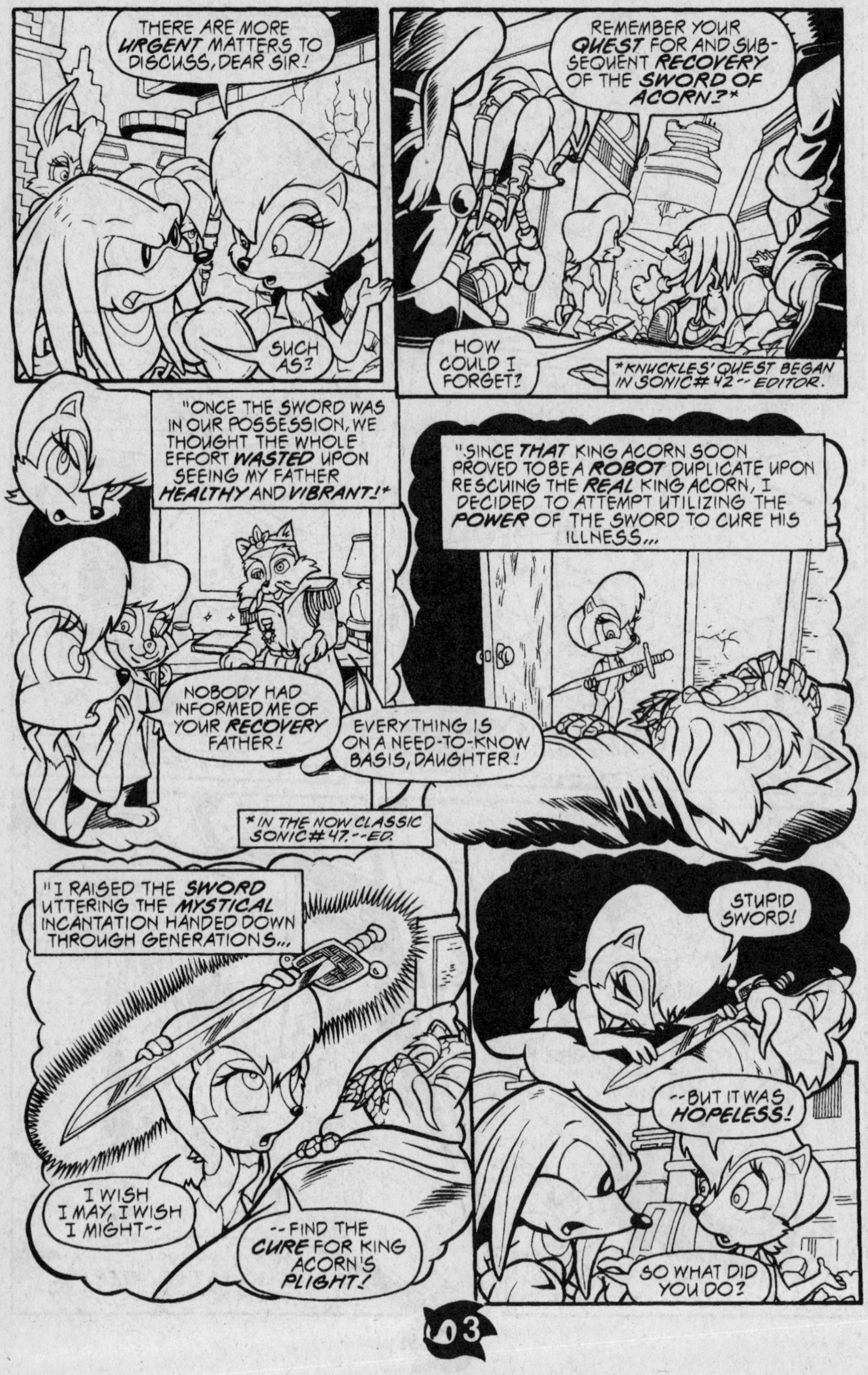
THERE ARE MORE URGENT MATTERS TO DISCUSS, DEAR SIR!
SUCH AS?
REMEMBER YOUR QUEST FOR AND SUB-SEQUENT RECOVERY OF THE SWORD OF ACORN?*
HOW COULD I FORGET?
*KNUCKLES' QUEST BEGAN IN SONIC #42 -- EDITOR.
"ONCE THE SWORD WAS IN OUR POSSESSION, WE THOUGHT THE WHOLE EFFORT WASTED UPON SEEING MY FATHER HEALTHY AND VIBRANT!*
NOBODY HAD INFORMED ME OF YOUR RECOVERY FATHER!
EVERYTHING IS ON A NEED-TO-KNOW BASIS, DAUGHTER!
*IN THE NOW CLASSIC SONIC #47.--ED.
"SINCE THAT KING ACORN SOON PROVED TO BE A ROBOT DUPLICATE UPON RESCUING THE REAL KING ACORN, I DECIDED TO ATTEMPT UTILIZING THE POWER OF THE SWORD TO CURE HIS ILLNESS...
"I RAISED THE SWORD UTTERING THE MYSTICAL INCANTATION HANDED DOWN THROUGH GENERATIONS...
I WISH I MAY, I WISH I MIGHT--
--FIND THE CURE FOR KING ACORN'S PLIGHT!
STUPID SWORD!
--BUT IT WAS HOPELESS!
SO WHAT DID YOU DO?
3

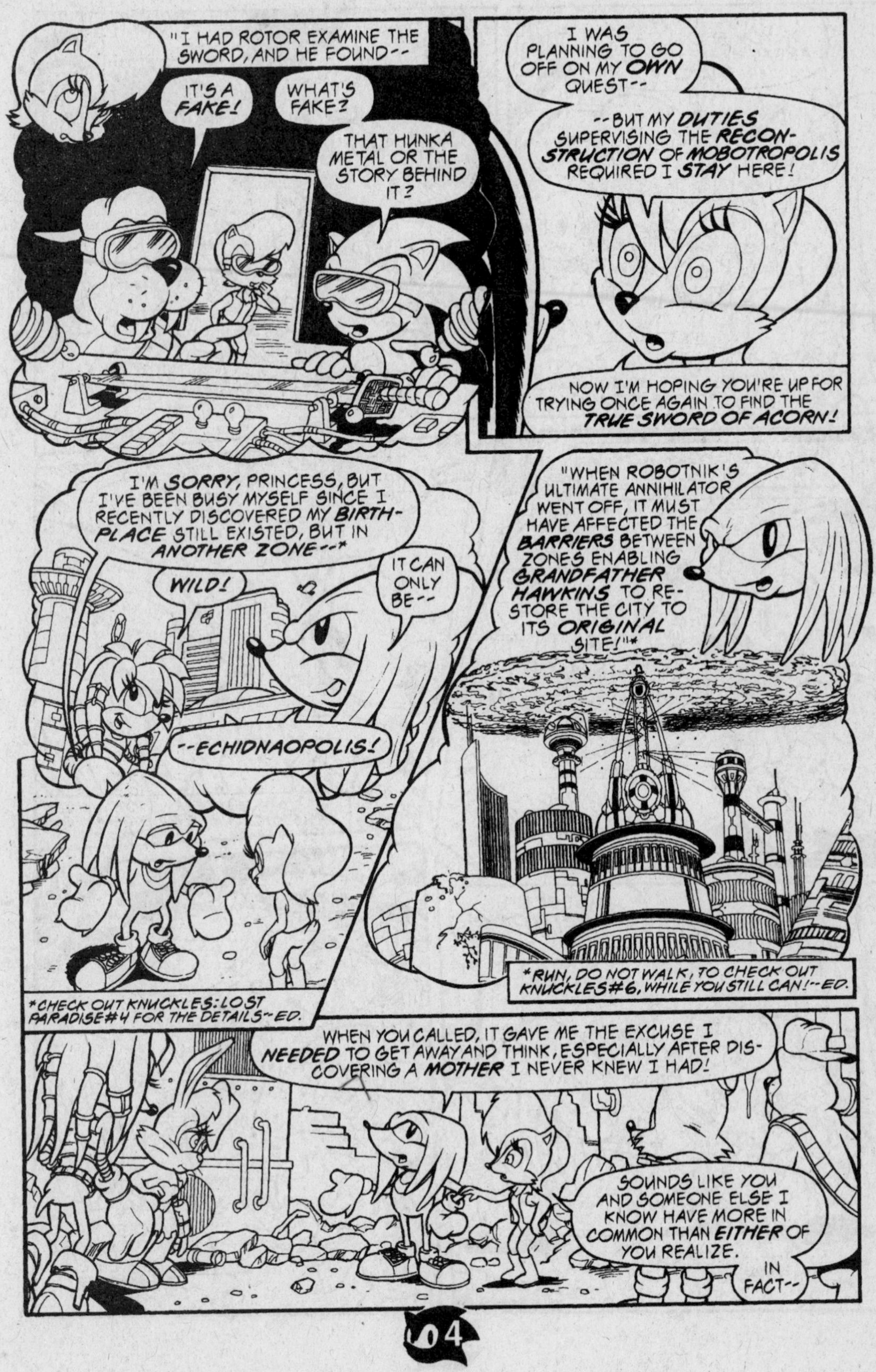
"I HAD ROTOR EXAMINE THE SWORD, AND HE FOUND--
IT'S A FAKE!
WHAT'S FAKE?
THAT HUNKA METAL OR THE STORY BEHIND IT?
I WAS PLANNING TO GO OFF ON MY OWN QUEST--
--BUT MY DUTIES SUPERVISING THE RECON-STRUCTION OF MOBOTROPOLIS REQUIRED I STAY HERE!
NOW I'M HOPING YOU'RE UP FOR TRYING ONCE AGAIN TO FIND THE TRUE SWORD OF ACORN!
I'M SORRY, PRINCESS, BUT I'VE BEEN BUSY MYSELF SINCE I RECENTLY DISCOVERED MY BIRTH-PLACE STILL EXISTED, BUT IN ANOTHER ZONE--*
WILD!
IT CAN ONLY BE--
--ECHIDNAOPOLIS!
*CHECK OUT KNUCKLES: LOST PARADISE #4 FOR THE DETAILS--ED.
"WHEN ROBOTNIK'S ULTIMATE ANNIHILATOR WENT OFF, IT MUST HAVE AFFECTED THE BARRIERS BETWEEN ZONES ENABLING GRANDFATHER HAWKINS TO RE-STORE THE CITY TO ITS ORIGINAL SITE!"*
*RUN, DO NOT WALK, TO CHECK OUT KNUCKLES #6, WHILE YOU STILL CAN!--ED.
WHEN YOU CALLED, IT GAVE ME THE EXCUSE I NEEDED TO GET AWAY AND THINK, ESPECIALLY AFTER DIS-COVERING A MOTHER I NEVER KNEW I HAD!
SOUNDS LIKE YOU AND SOMEONE ELSE I KNOW HAVE MORE IN COMMON THAN EITHER OF YOU REALIZE.
IN FACT--
4

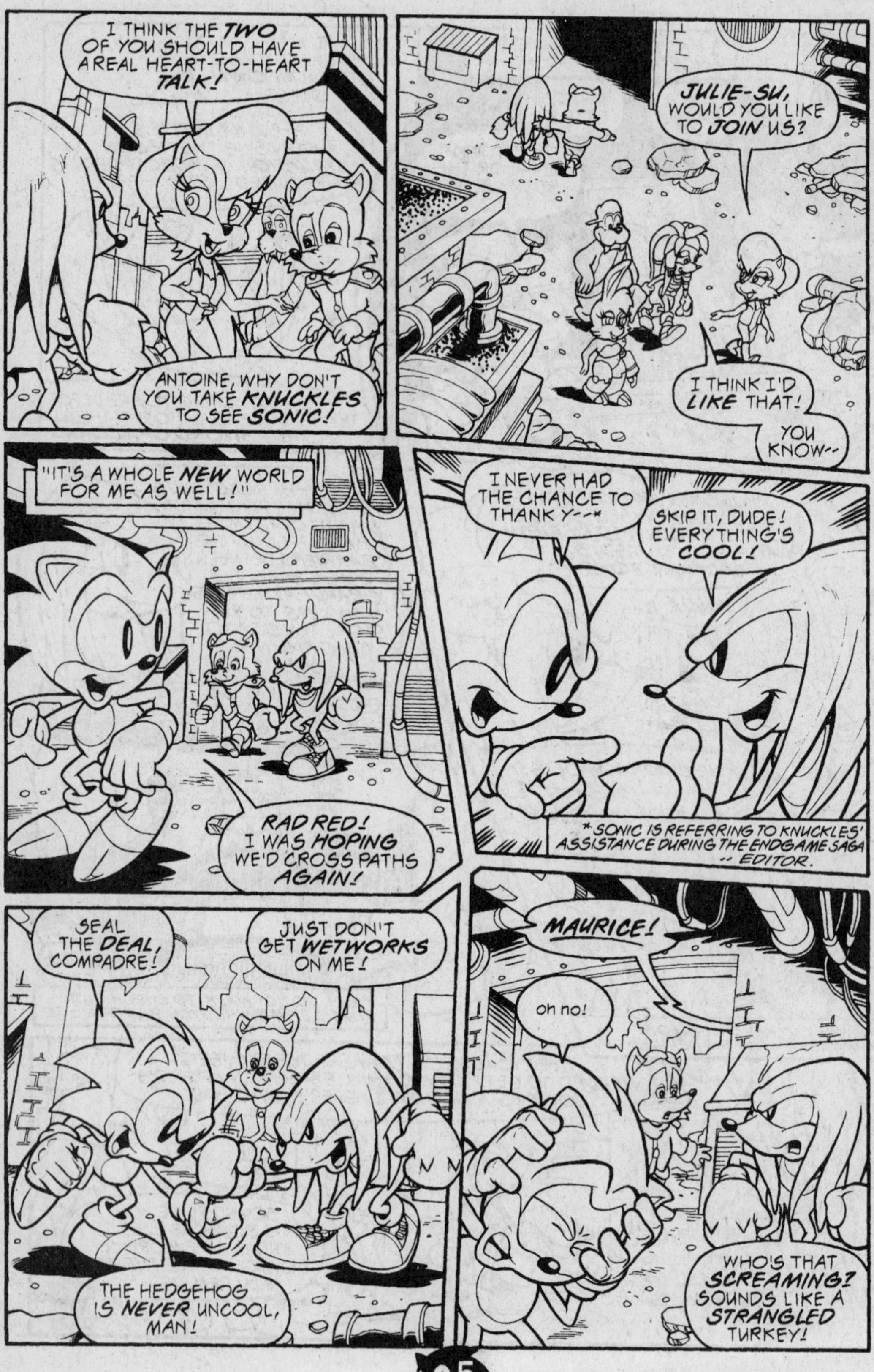
I THINK THE TWO OF YOU SHOULD HAVE A REAL HEART-TO-HEART TALK!
ANTOINE, WHY DON'T YOU TAKE KNUCKLES TO SEE SONIC!
JULIE-SU, WOULD YOU LIKE TO JOIN US?
I THINK I'D LIKE THAT!
YOU KNOW--
"IT'S A WHOLE NEW WORLD FOR ME AS WELL!"
RAD RED! I WAS HOPING WE'D CROSS PATHS AGAIN!
I NEVER HAD THE CHANCE TO THANK Y--*
SKIP IT, DUDE! EVERYTHING'S COOL!
*SONIC IS REFERRING TO KNUCKLES' ASSISTANCE DURING THE ENDGAME SAGA -- EDITOR.
SEAL THE DEAL, COMPADRE!
JUST DON'T GET WETWORKS ON ME!
THE HEDGEHOG IS NEVER UNCOOL, MAN!
MAURICE!
oh no!
WHO'S THAT SCREAMING! SOUNDS LIKE A STRANGLED TURKEY!
5

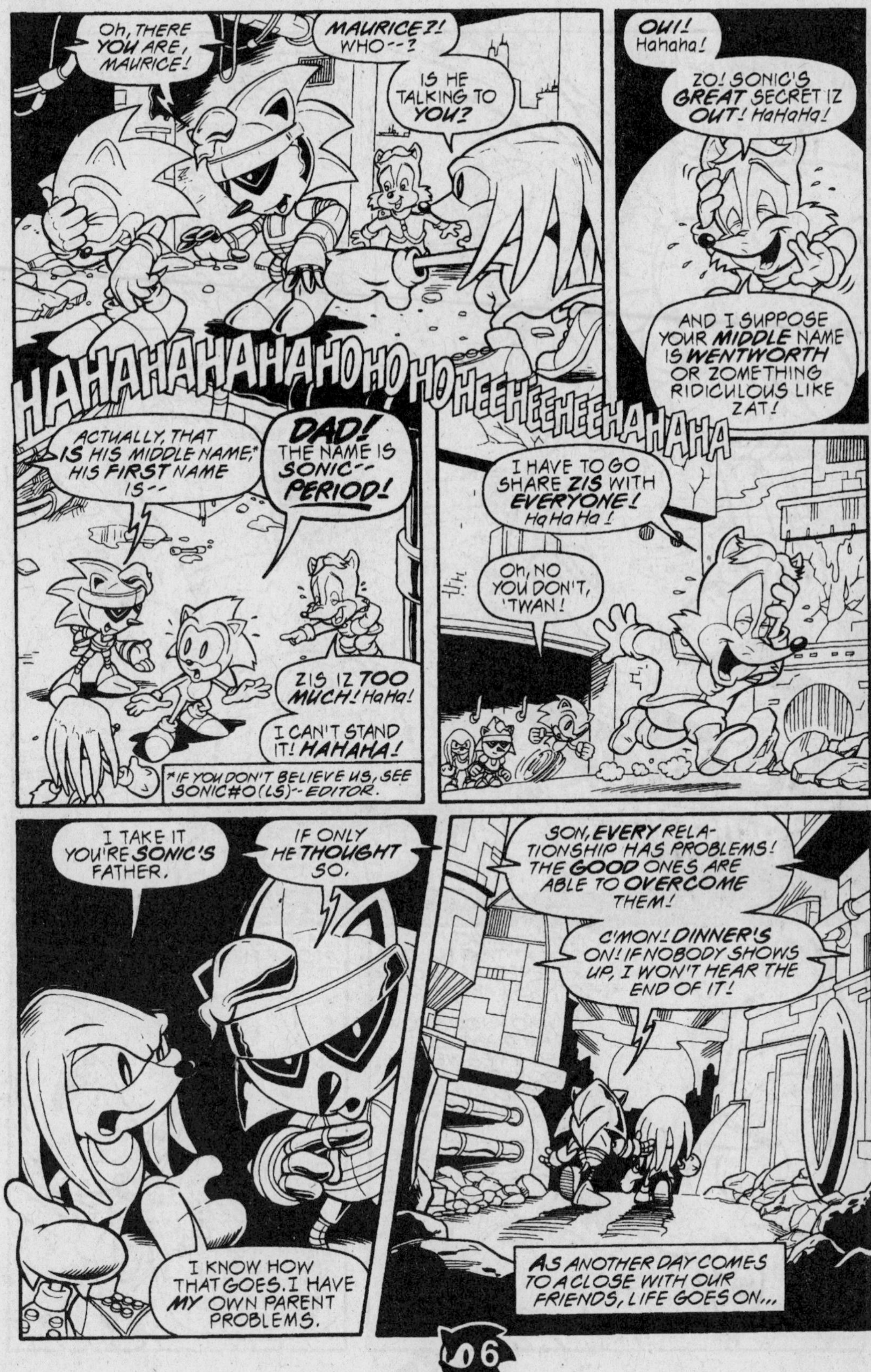

Oh, THERE YOU ARE, MAURICE!
MAURICE?! WHO--?
IS HE TALKING TO YOU?
OUI! Hahaha!
ZO! SONIC'S GREAT SECRET IZ OUT! HaHaHa!
AND I SUPPOSE YOUR MIDDLE NAME IS WENTWORTH OR ZOMETHING RIDICULOUS LIKE ZAT!
HAHAHAHAHAHOHOHOHEEHEEHEEHAHAHA
ACTUALLY, THAT IS HIS MIDDLE NAME!* HIS FIRST NAME IS--
DAD! THE NAME IS SONIC--PERIOD!
ZIS IZ TOO MUCH! HaHa!
I CAN'T STAND IT! HAHAHA!
*IF YOU DON'T BELIEVE US, SEE SONIC#0(LS)--EDITOR.
I HAVE TO GO SHARE ZIS WITH EVERYONE! HaHaHa!
Oh, NO YOU DON'T, 'TWAN!
I TAKE IT YOU'RE SONIC'S FATHER.
IF ONLY HE THOUGHT SO.
I KNOW HOW THAT GOES. I HAVE MY OWN PARENT PROBLEMS.
SON, EVERY RELATIONSHIP HAS PROBLEMS! THE GOOD ONES ARE ABLE TO OVERCOME THEM!
C'MON! DINNER'S ON! IF NOBODY SHOWS UP, I WON'T HEAR THE END OF IT!
AS ANOTHER DAY COMES TO A CLOSE WITH OUR FRIENDS, LIFE GOES ON...
6

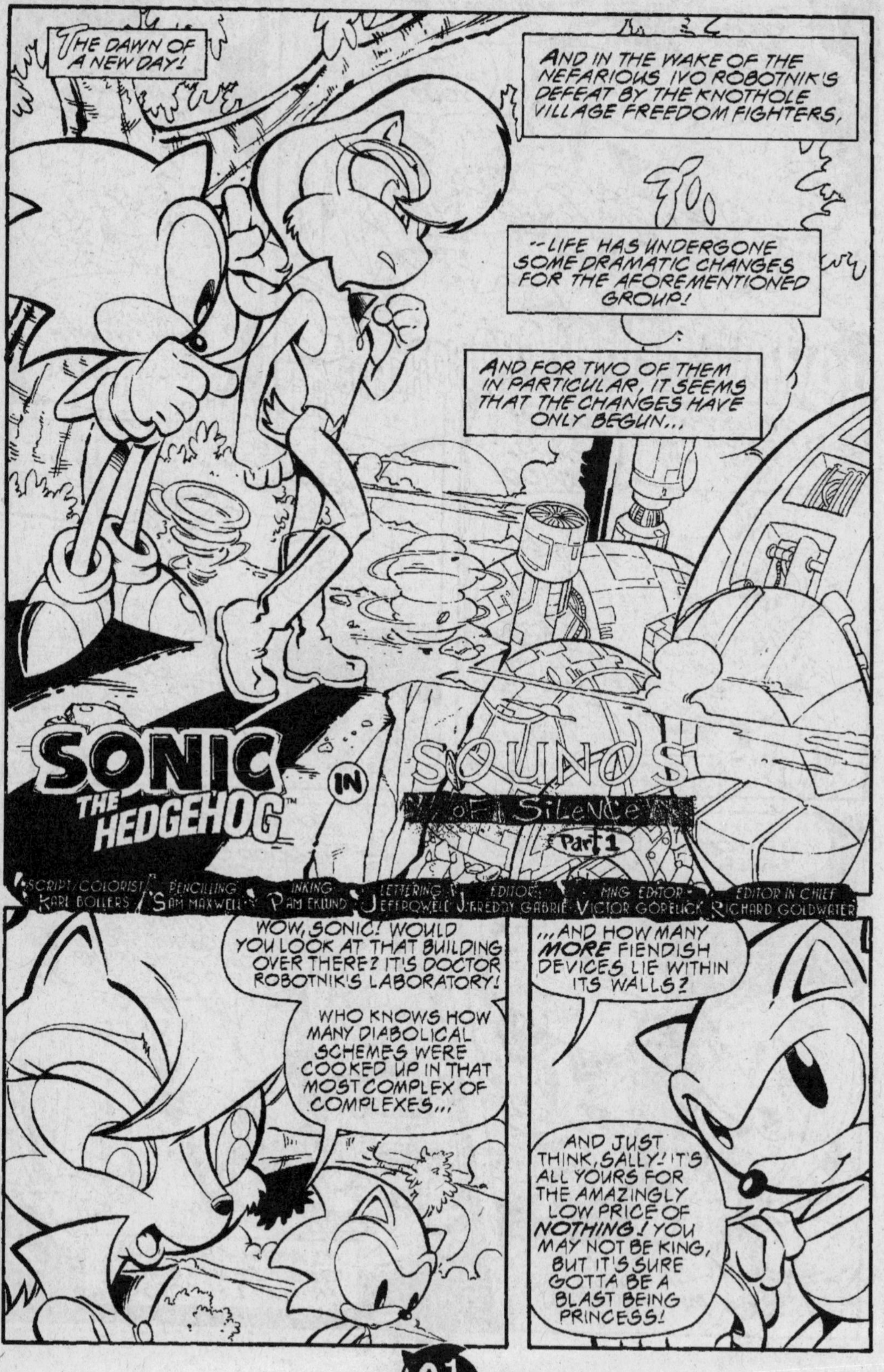
THE DAWN OF A NEW DAY!
AND IN THE WAKE OF THE NEFARIOUS IVO ROBOTNIK'S DEFEAT BY THE KNOTHOLE VILLAGE FREEDOM FIGHTERS,
--LIFE HAS UNDERGONE SOME DRAMATIC CHANGES FOR THE AFOREMENTIONED GROUP!
AND FOR TWO OF THEM IN PARTICULAR, IT SEEMS THAT THE CHANGES HAVE ONLY BEGUN...
SONIC THE HEDGEHOG™ IN
SOUNDS OF SILENCE
PART 1
SCRIPT/COLORIST KARL BOLLERS
PENCILLING SAM MAXWELL
INKING PAM EKLUND
LETTERING JEFF POWELL
EDITOR J. FREDDY GABRIE
MNG EDITOR VICTOR GORELICK
EDITOR IN CHIEF RICHARD GOLDWATER
WOW, SONIC! WOULD YOU LOOK AT THAT BUILDING OVER THERE? IT'S DOCTOR ROBOTNIK'S LABORATORY!
WHO KNOWS HOW MANY DIABOLICAL SCHEMES WERE COOKED UP IN THAT MOST COMPLEX OF COMPLEXES...
...AND HOW MANY MORE FIENDISH DEVICES LIE WITHIN ITS WALLS?
AND JUST THINK, SALLY! IT'S ALL YOURS FOR THE AMAZINGLY LOW PRICE OF NOTHING! YOU MAY NOT BE KING, BUT IT'S SURE GOTTA BE A BLAST BEING PRINCESS!
01

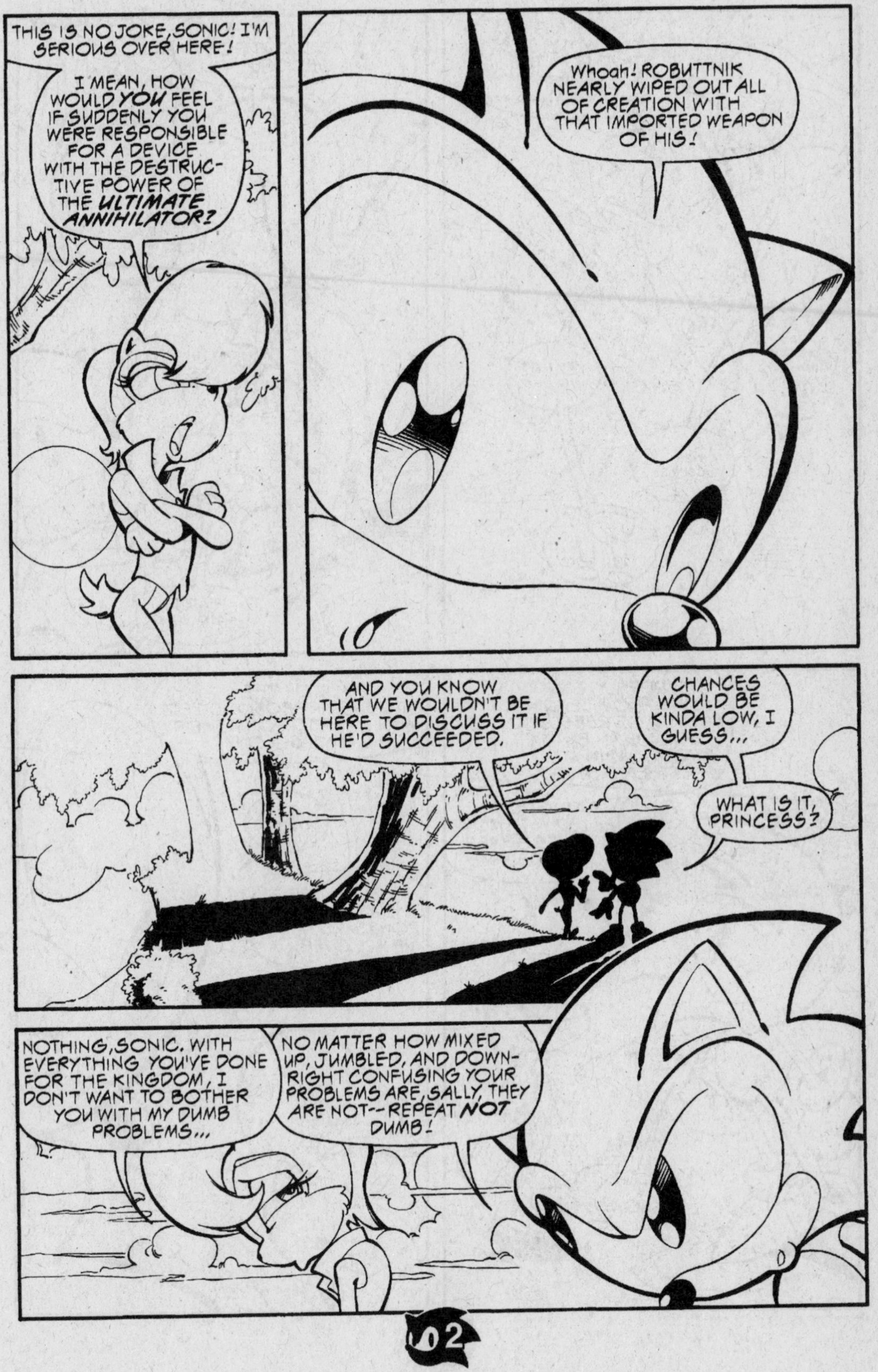
THIS IS NO JOKE, SONIC! I'M SERIOUS OVER HERE!
I MEAN, HOW WOULD YOU FEEL IF SUDDENLY YOU WERE RESPONSIBLE FOR A DEVICE WITH THE DESTRUCTIVE POWER OF THE ULTIMATE ANNIHILATOR?
Whoah! ROBUTTNIK NEARLY WIPED OUT ALL OF CREATION WITH THAT IMPORTED WEAPON OF HIS!
AND YOU KNOW THAT WE WOULDN'T BE HERE TO DISCUSS IT IF HE'D SUCCEEDED.
CHANCES WOULD BE KINDA LOW, I GUESS...
WHAT IS IT, PRINCESS?
NOTHING, SONIC. WITH EVERYTHING YOU'VE DONE FOR THE KINGDOM, I DON'T WANT TO BOTHER YOU WITH MY DUMB PROBLEMS...
NO MATTER HOW MIXED UP, JUMBLED, AND DOWNRIGHT CONFUSING YOUR PROBLEMS ARE, SALLY, THEY ARE NOT--REPEAT NOT DUMB!
2

YOU'RE RIGHT, I KNOW. IT'S JUST THAT FOR THE FIRST TIME IN MY LIFE, I'M...

YOU'RE WHAT?

Well... scared.

?!?!

WELL, THINK ABOUT IT FOR A SECOND--

DONE.

HARDY HAR HAR.

SUDDENLY, I'VE GONE FROM LEADING A BAND OF REBELS TO RULING AN ENTIRE KINGDOM IN MY FATHER'S STEAD.

I KNOW.

A KINGDOM FILLED WITH MORE THAN ITS SHARE OF PROBLEMS.

I KNOW.

HALF OF THE CITIZENS ARE ROBOTICIZED AND WANT TO FORM THEIR OWN COLONY.

I KNOW.

THEN THERE'S THE MYSTERIOUS ZONES POPPING UP ALL OVER...

I KNOW.

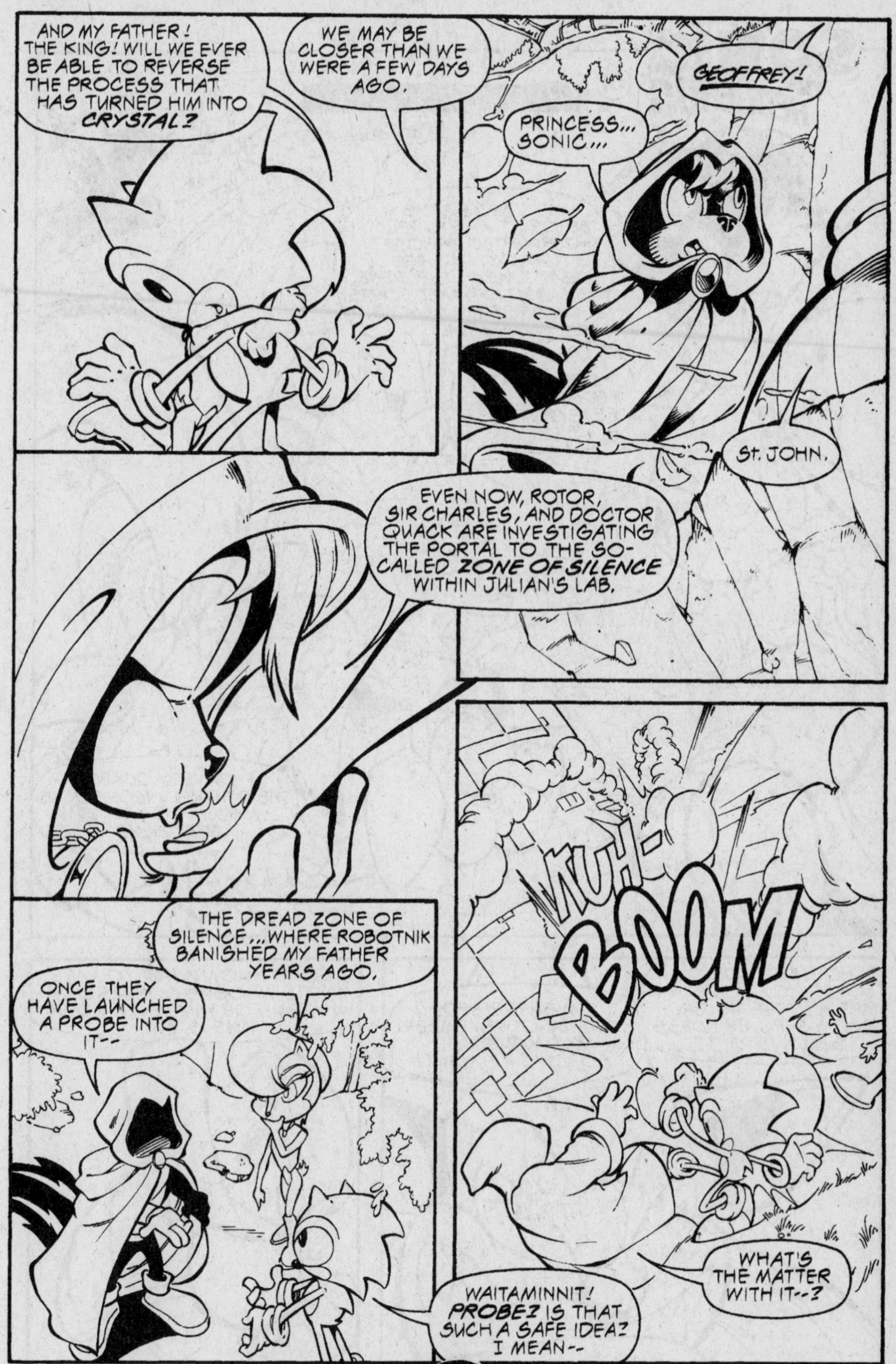

AND MY FATHER! THE KING! WILL WE EVER BE ABLE TO REVERSE THE PROCESS THAT HAS TURNED HIM INTO CRYSTAL?
WE MAY BE CLOSER THAN WE WERE A FEW DAYS AGO.
GEOFFREY!
PRINCESS... SONIC...
St. JOHN.
EVEN NOW, ROTOR, SIR CHARLES, AND DOCTOR QUACK ARE INVESTIGATING THE PORTAL TO THE SO-CALLED ZONE OF SILENCE WITHIN JULIAN'S LAB.
THE DREAD ZONE OF SILENCE... WHERE ROBOTNIK BANISHED MY FATHER YEARS AGO.
ONCE THEY HAVE LAUNCHED A PROBE INTO IT--
WAITAMINNIT! PROBE? IS THAT SUCH A SAFE IDEA? I MEAN--
KUH-BOOM
WHAT'S THE MATTER WITH IT--?

104

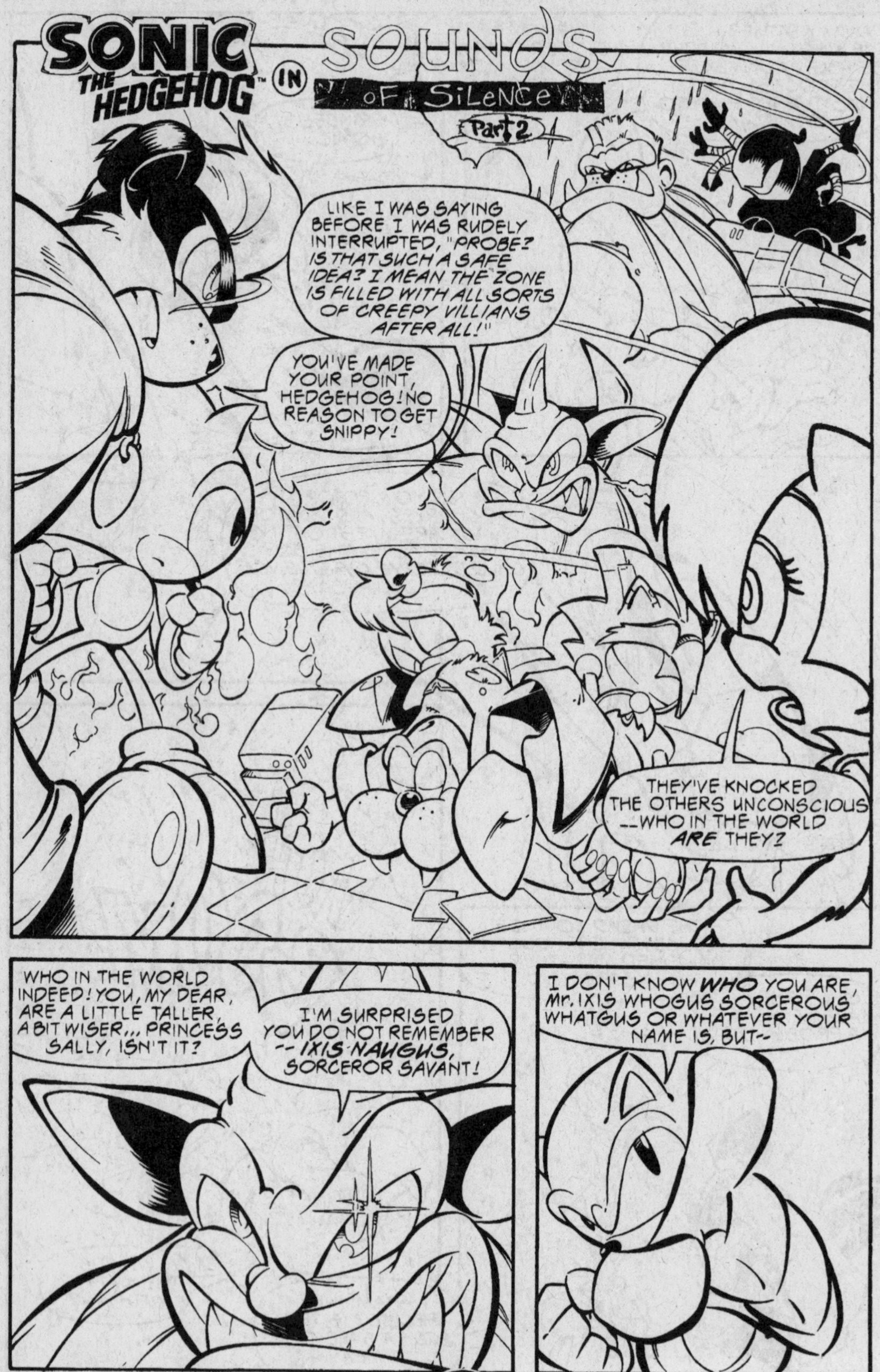
SONIC THE HEDGEHOG™ IN
SOUNDS OF SILENCE
Part 2
LIKE I WAS SAYING BEFORE I WAS RUDELY INTERRUPTED, "PROBE? IS THAT SUCH A SAFE IDEA? I MEAN THE ZONE IS FILLED WITH ALL SORTS OF CREEPY VILLIANS AFTER ALL!"
YOU'VE MADE YOUR POINT, HEDGEHOG! NO REASON TO GET SNIPPY!
THEY'VE KNOCKED THE OTHERS UNCONSCIOUS --WHO IN THE WORLD ARE THEY?
WHO IN THE WORLD INDEED! YOU, MY DEAR, ARE A LITTLE TALLER, A BIT WISER,,, PRINCESS SALLY, ISN'T IT?
I'M SURPRISED YOU DO NOT REMEMBER -- IXIS NAUGUS, SORCEROR SAVANT!
I DON'T KNOW WHO YOU ARE, Mr. IXIS WHOGUS SORCEROUS WHATGUS OR WHATEVER YOUR NAME IS, BUT--
05

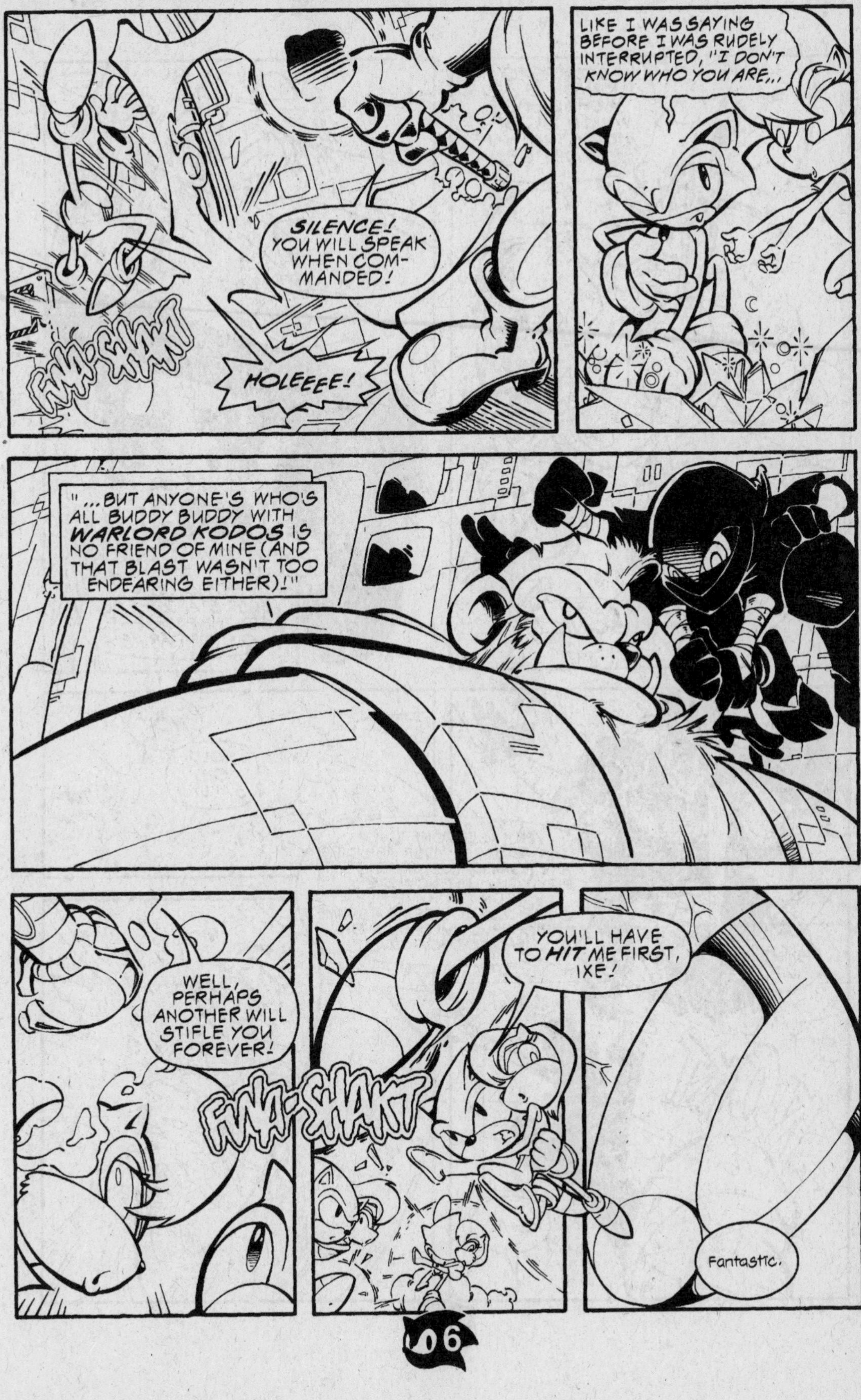
SILENCE! YOU WILL SPEAK WHEN COMMANDED!
FWA-SHAKT
HOLEEEE!
LIKE I WAS SAYING BEFORE I WAS RUDELY INTERRUPTED, "I DON'T KNOW WHO YOU ARE...
"...BUT ANYONE'S WHO'S ALL BUDDY BUDDY WITH WARLORD KODOS IS NO FRIEND OF MINE (AND THAT BLAST WASN'T TOO ENDEARING EITHER)!"
WELL, PERHAPS ANOTHER WILL STIFLE YOU FOREVER!
FWA-SHAKT
YOU'LL HAVE TO HIT ME FIRST, IXE!
Fantastic.
06

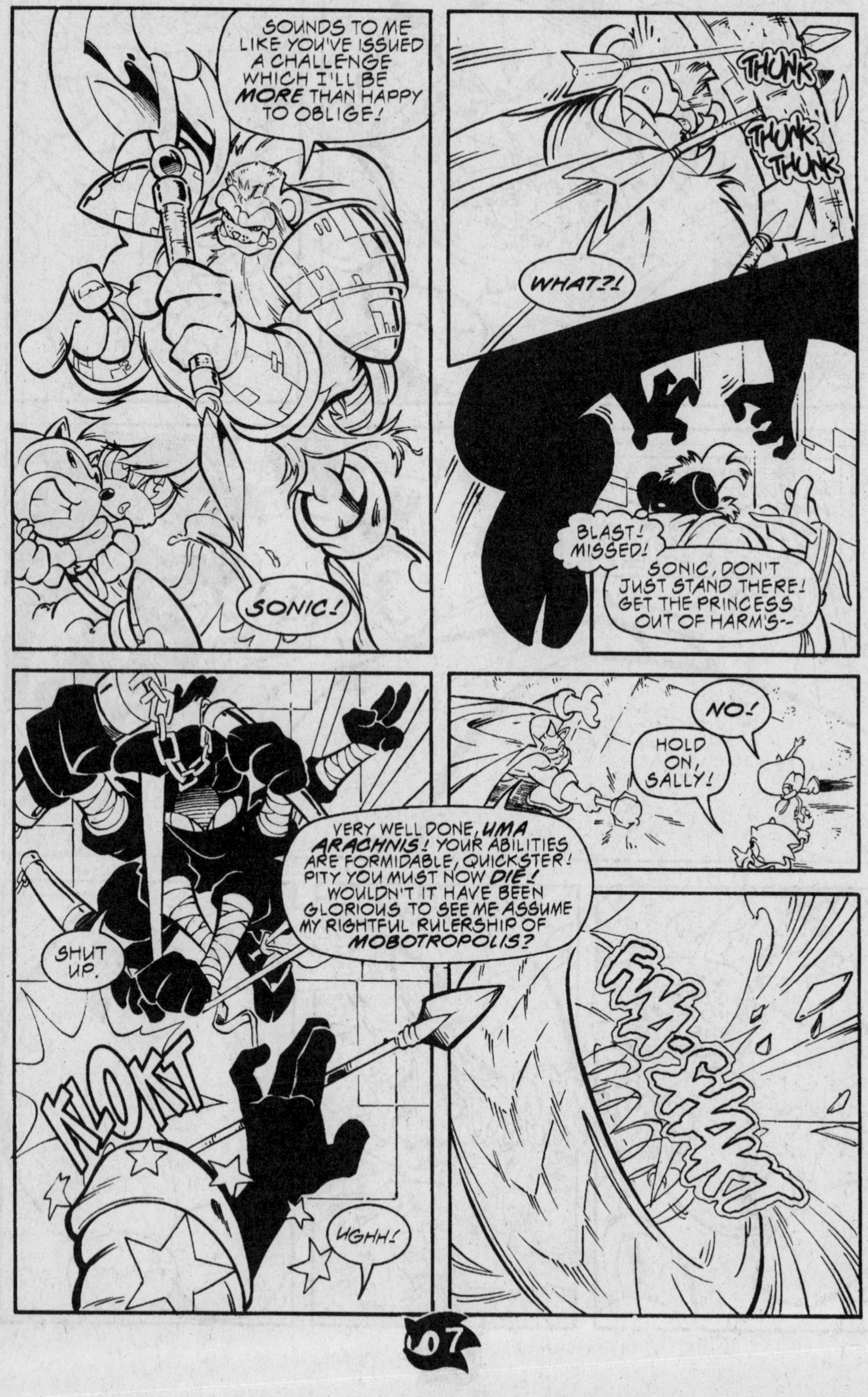
SOUNDS TO ME LIKE YOU'VE ISSUED A CHALLENGE WHICH I'LL BE **MORE** THAN HAPPY TO OBLIGE!
SONIC!
THUNK
THUNK THUNK
WHAT?!
BLAST! MISSED!
SONIC, DON'T JUST STAND THERE! GET THE PRINCESS OUT OF HARM'S-
VERY WELL DONE, **UMA ARACHNIS**! YOUR ABILITIES ARE FORMIDABLE, QUICKSTER! PITY YOU MUST NOW **DIE**! WOULDN'T IT HAVE BEEN GLORIOUS TO SEE ME ASSUME MY RIGHTFUL RULERSHIP OF **MOBOTROPOLIS**?
SHUT UP.
KLOKT
UGHH!
NO!
HOLD ON, SALLY!
FWA-SHAM

07

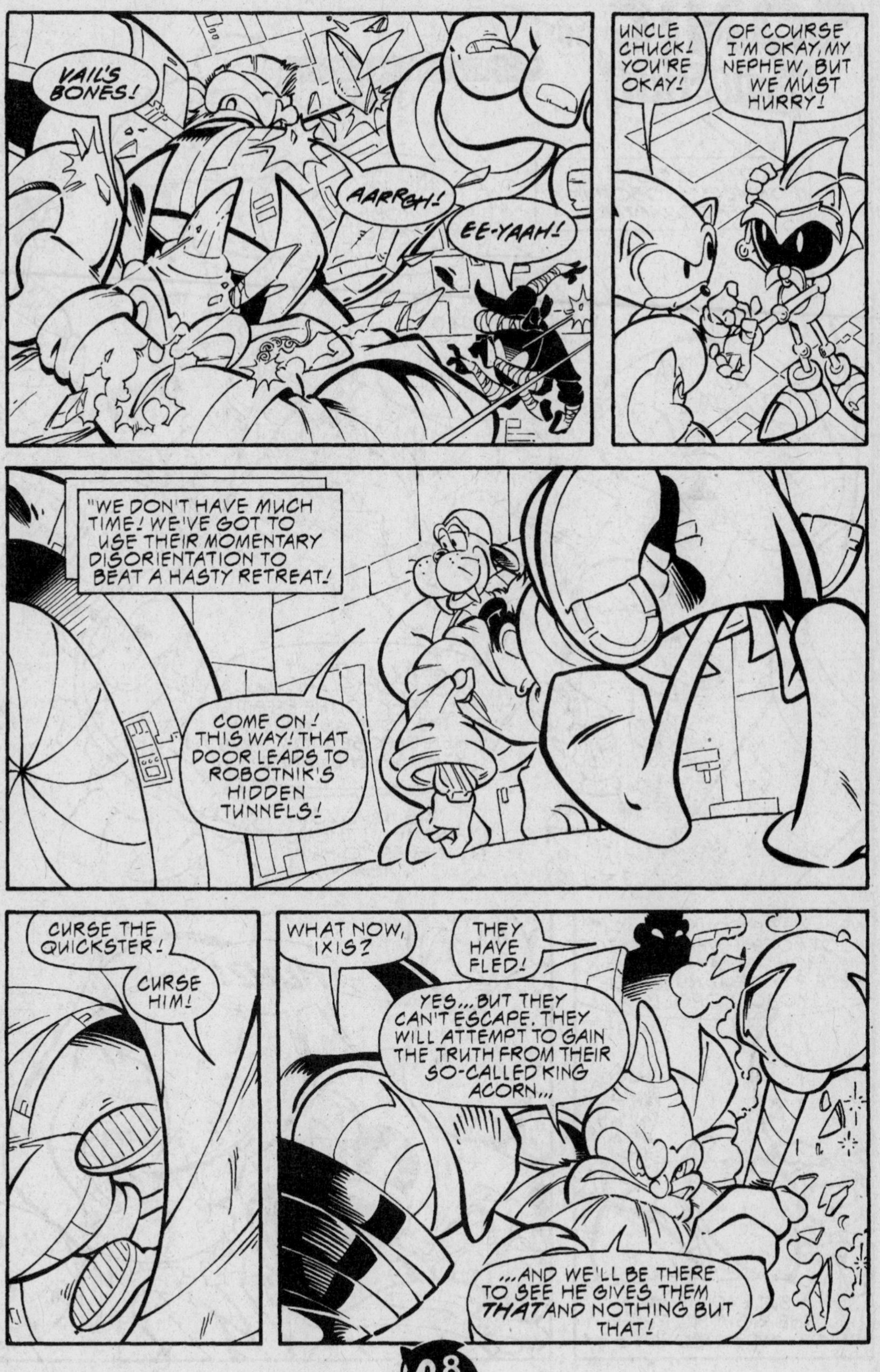
VAIL'S BONES!
AARRGH!
EE-YAAH!
UNCLE CHUCK! YOU'RE OKAY!
OF COURSE I'M OKAY, MY NEPHEW, BUT WE MUST HURRY!
"WE DON'T HAVE MUCH TIME! WE'VE GOT TO USE THEIR MOMENTARY DISORIENTATION TO BEAT A HASTY RETREAT!
COME ON! THIS WAY! THAT DOOR LEADS TO ROBOTNIK'S HIDDEN TUNNELS!
CURSE THE QUICKSTER!
CURSE HIM!
WHAT NOW, IXIS?
THEY HAVE FLED!
YES... BUT THEY CAN'T ESCAPE. THEY WILL ATTEMPT TO GAIN THE TRUTH FROM THEIR SO-CALLED KING ACORN...
...AND WE'LL BE THERE TO SEE HE GIVES THEM *THAT* AND NOTHING BUT THAT!
8

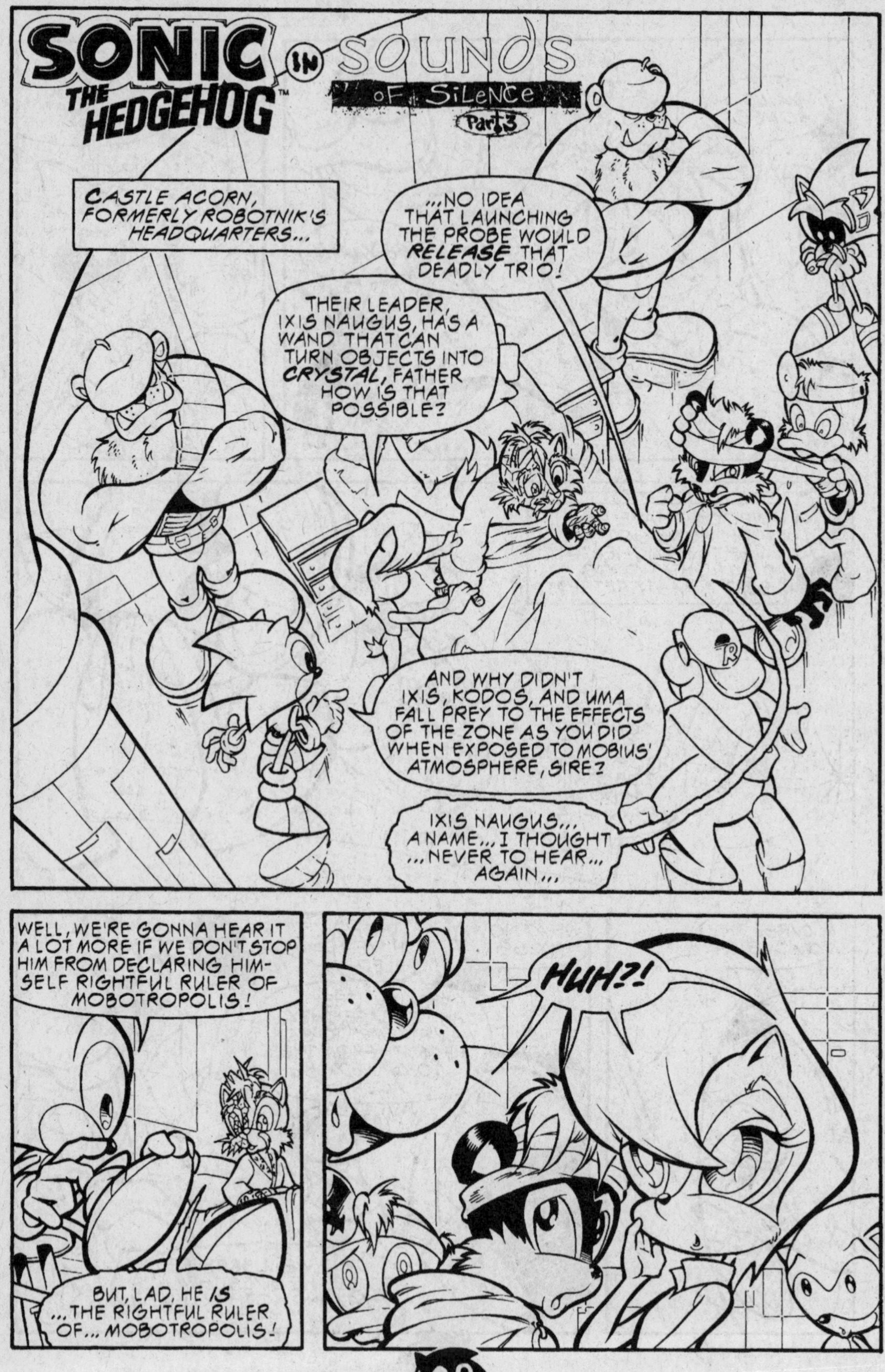

SONIC THE HEDGEHOG™ IN SOUNDS OF SILENCE Part 3
CASTLE ACORN, FORMERLY ROBOTNIK'S HEADQUARTERS...
...NO IDEA THAT LAUNCHING THE PROBE WOULD RELEASE THAT DEADLY TRIO!
THEIR LEADER, IXIS NAUGUS, HAS A WAND THAT CAN TURN OBJECTS INTO CRYSTAL, FATHER HOW IS THAT POSSIBLE?
AND WHY DIDN'T IXIS, KODOS, AND UMA FALL PREY TO THE EFFECTS OF THE ZONE AS YOU DID WHEN EXPOSED TO MOBIUS' ATMOSPHERE, SIRE?
IXIS NAUGUS... A NAME... I THOUGHT ...NEVER TO HEAR... AGAIN...
WELL, WE'RE GONNA HEAR IT A LOT MORE IF WE DON'T STOP HIM FROM DECLARING HIM-SELF RIGHTFUL RULER OF MOBOTROPOLIS!
BUT, LAD, HE IS ...THE RIGHTFUL RULER OF... MOBOTROPOLIS!
HUH?!
9

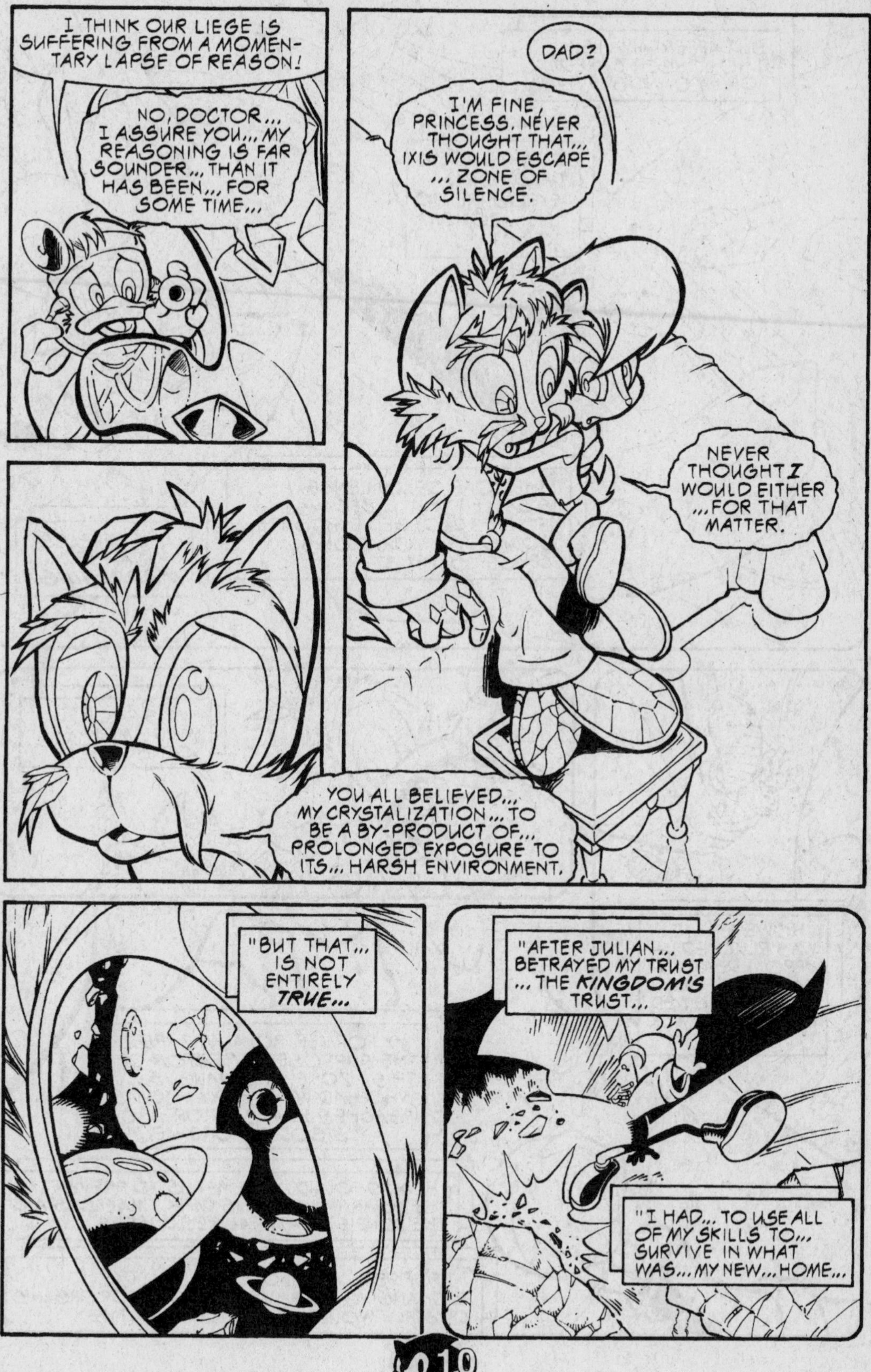
I THINK OUR LIEGE IS SUFFERING FROM A MOMENTARY LAPSE OF REASON!
NO, DOCTOR... I ASSURE YOU... MY REASONING IS FAR SOUNDER... THAN IT HAS BEEN... FOR SOME TIME...
DAD?
I'M FINE, PRINCESS. NEVER THOUGHT THAT... IXIS WOULD ESCAPE ... ZONE OF SILENCE.
NEVER THOUGHT I WOULD EITHER ...FOR THAT MATTER.
YOU ALL BELIEVED... MY CRYSTALIZATION... TO BE A BY-PRODUCT OF... PROLONGED EXPOSURE TO ITS... HARSH ENVIRONMENT.
"BUT THAT... IS NOT ENTIRELY TRUE...
"AFTER JULIAN... BETRAYED MY TRUST ... THE KINGDOM'S TRUST...
"I HAD... TO USE ALL OF MY SKILLS TO... SURVIVE IN WHAT WAS... MY NEW... HOME...
10

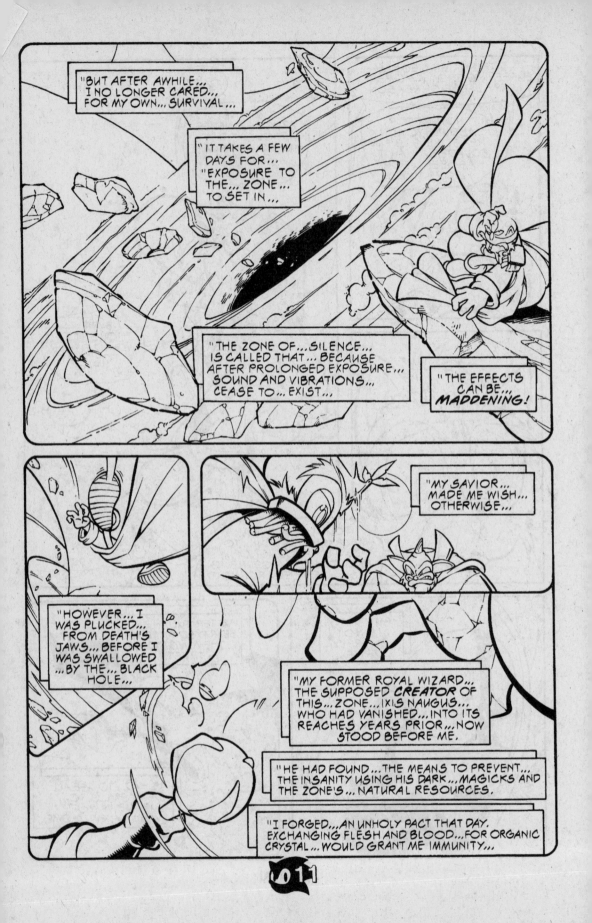

"BUT AFTER AWHILE... I NO LONGER CARED... FOR MY OWN... SURVIVAL...

"IT TAKES A FEW DAYS FOR... "EXPOSURE TO THE... ZONE... TO SET IN...

"THE ZONE OF... SILENCE... IS CALLED THAT... BECAUSE AFTER PROLONGED EXPOSURE... SOUND AND VIBRATIONS... CEASE TO... EXIST...

"THE EFFECTS CAN BE... MADDENING!

"MY SAVIOR... MADE ME WISH... OTHERWISE...

"HOWEVER... I WAS PLUCKED... FROM DEATH'S JAWS... BEFORE I WAS SWALLOWED ...BY THE... BLACK HOLE...

"MY FORMER ROYAL WIZARD... THE SUPPOSED CREATOR OF THIS... ZONE... IXIS NAUGUS... WHO HAD VANISHED... INTO ITS REACHES YEARS PRIOR... NOW STOOD BEFORE ME.

"HE HAD FOUND... THE MEANS TO PREVENT... THE INSANITY USING HIS DARK... MAGICKS AND THE ZONE'S... NATURAL RESOURCES.

"I FORGED... AN UNHOLY PACT THAT DAY. EXCHANGING FLESH AND BLOOD... FOR ORGANIC CRYSTAL... WOULD GRANT ME IMMUNITY...

011

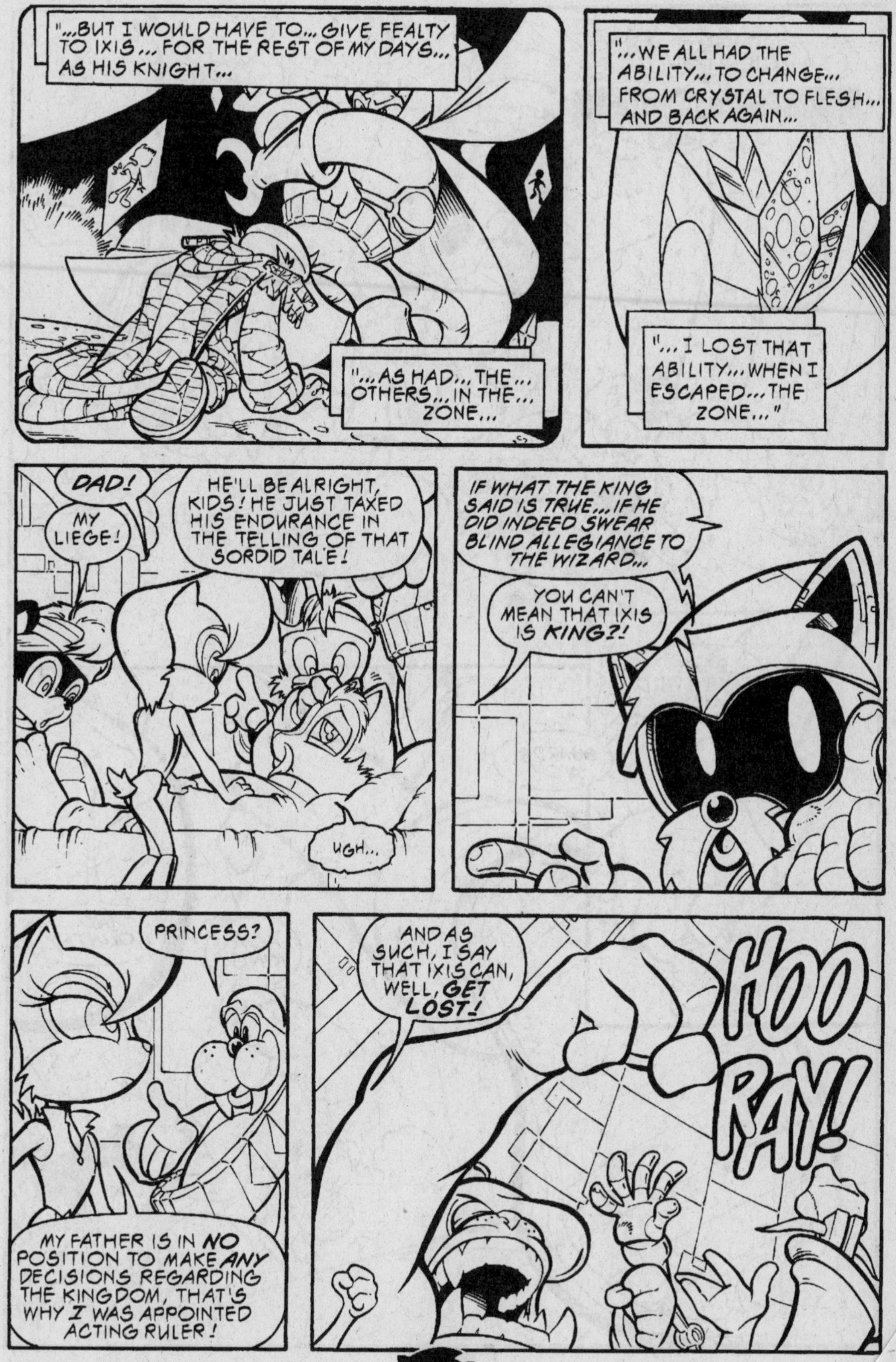
"...BUT I WOULD HAVE TO... GIVE FEALTY TO IXIS... FOR THE REST OF MY DAYS... AS HIS KNIGHT...
"...AS HAD... THE... OTHERS... IN THE... ZONE...
"...WE ALL HAD THE ABILITY... TO CHANGE... FROM CRYSTAL TO FLESH... AND BACK AGAIN...
"... I LOST THAT ABILITY... WHEN I ESCAPED... THE ZONE..."
DAD!
MY LIEGE!
HE'LL BE ALRIGHT, KIDS! HE JUST TAXED HIS ENDURANCE IN THE TELLING OF THAT SORDID TALE!
UGH...
IF WHAT THE KING SAID IS TRUE... IF HE DID INDEED SWEAR BLIND ALLEGIANCE TO THE WIZARD...
YOU CAN'T MEAN THAT IXIS IS KING?!
PRINCESS?
MY FATHER IS IN NO POSITION TO MAKE ANY DECISIONS REGARDING THE KINGDOM, THAT'S WHY I WAS APPOINTED ACTING RULER!
AND AS SUCH, I SAY THAT IXIS CAN, WELL, GET LOST!
HOO RAY!
012

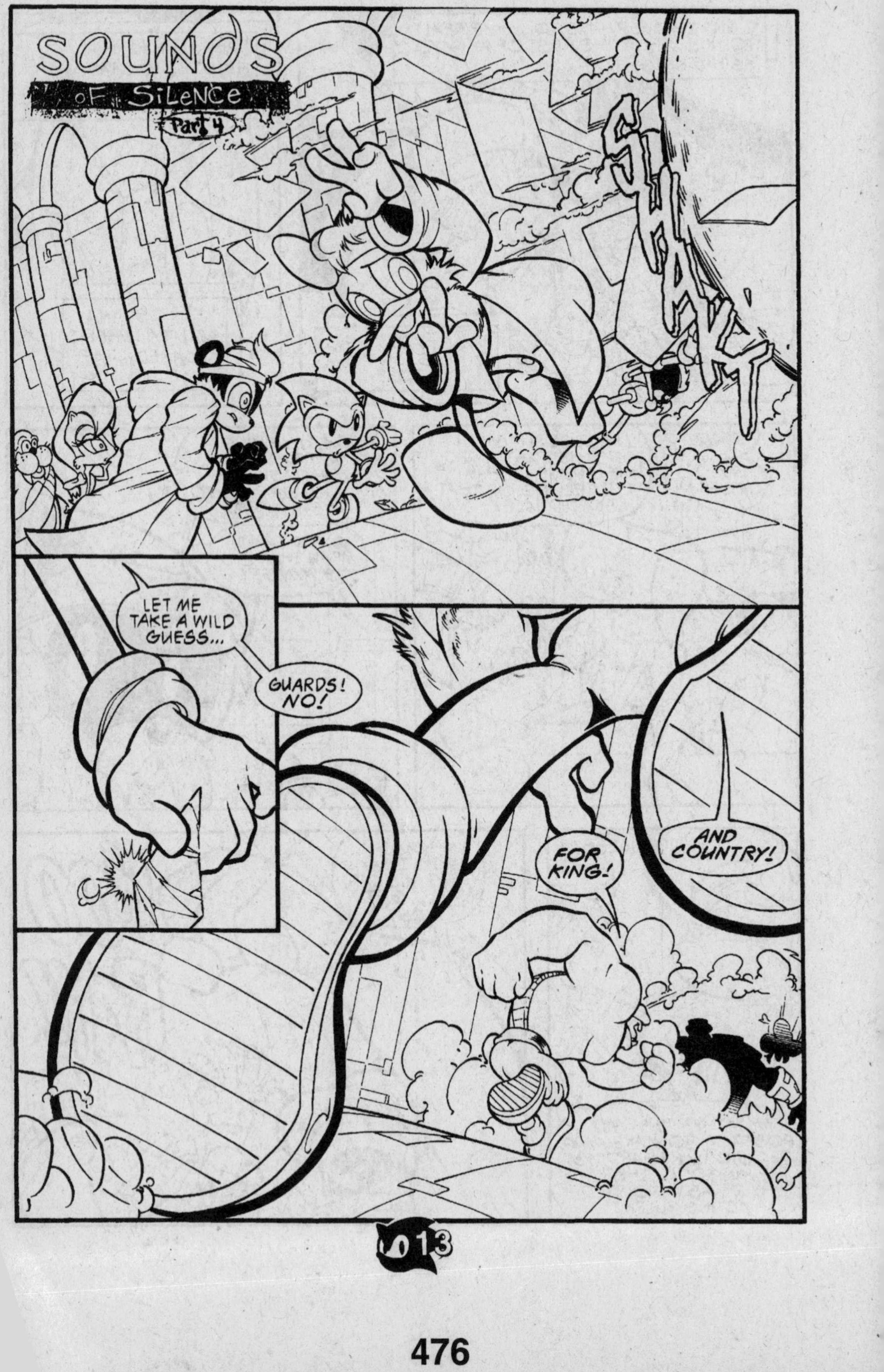
SOUNDS
OF SILENCE
Part 4
SHAKA
LET ME TAKE A WILD GUESS...
GUARDS! NO!
FOR KING!
AND COUNTRY!

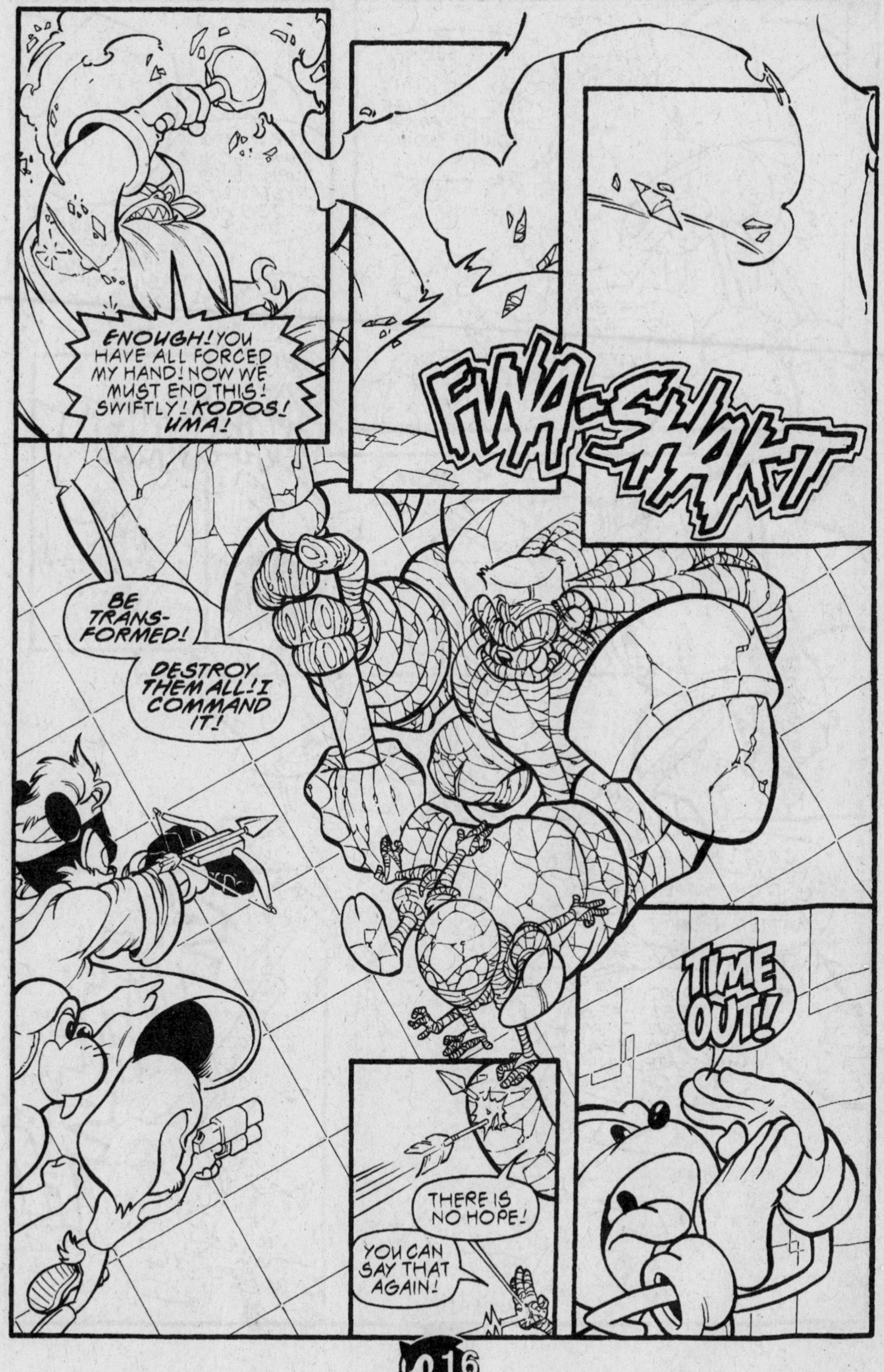
ENOUGH! YOU HAVE ALL FORCED MY HAND! NOW WE MUST END THIS! SWIFTLY! KODOS! UMA!
FWA-SHAKT
BE TRANS-FORMED!
DESTROY THEM ALL! I COMMAND IT!
TIME OUT!
THERE IS NO HOPE!
YOU CAN SAY THAT AGAIN!
16

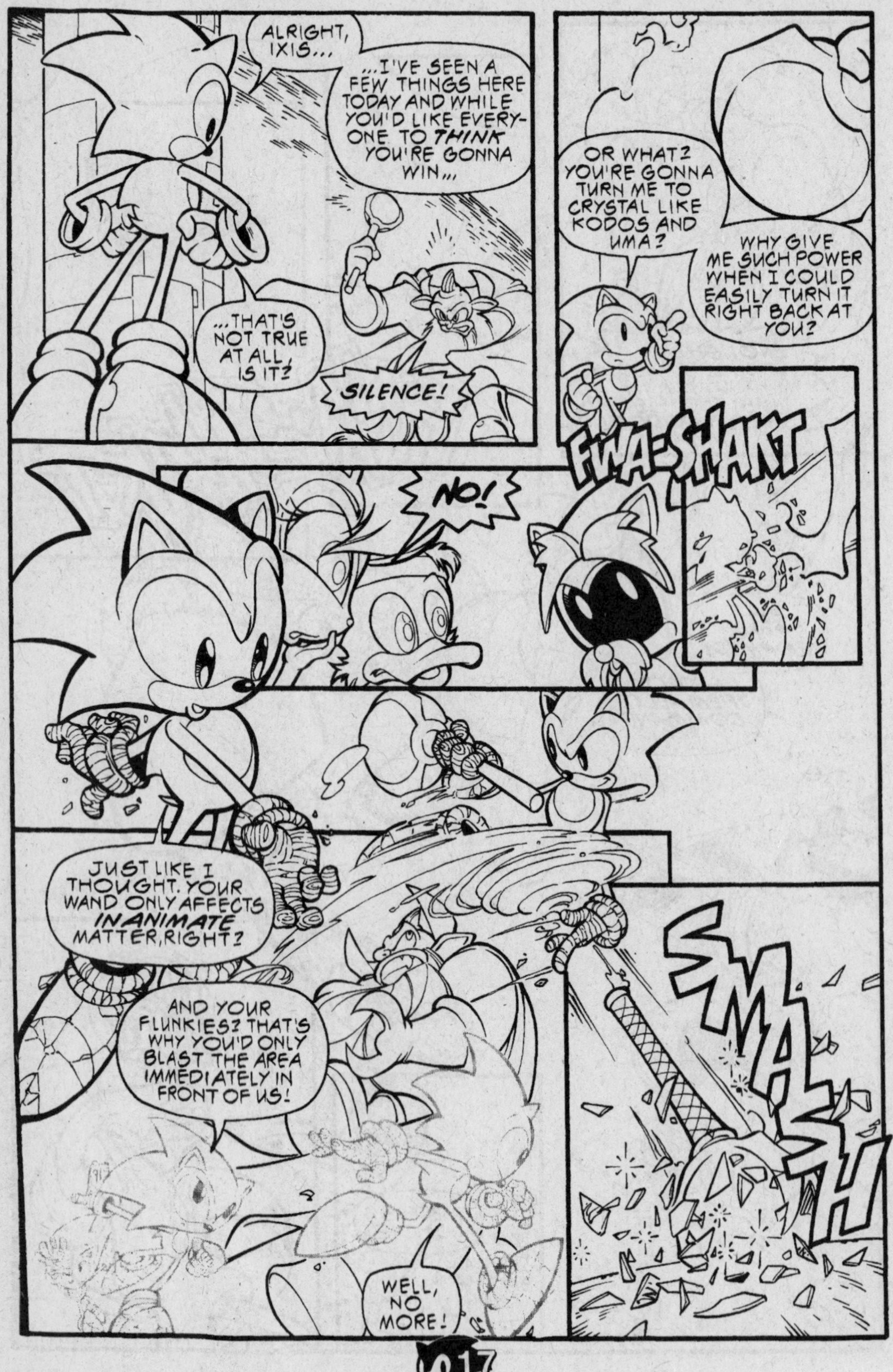
ALRIGHT, IXIS...
...I'VE SEEN A FEW THINGS HERE TODAY AND WHILE YOU'D LIKE EVERY-ONE TO THINK YOU'RE GONNA WIN...
...THAT'S NOT TRUE AT ALL, IS IT?
SILENCE!
OR WHAT? YOU'RE GONNA TURN ME TO CRYSTAL LIKE KODOS AND UMA?
WHY GIVE ME SUCH POWER WHEN I COULD EASILY TURN IT RIGHT BACK AT YOU?
FWA-SHAKT
NO!
JUST LIKE I THOUGHT. YOUR WAND ONLY AFFECTS INANIMATE MATTER, RIGHT?
AND YOUR FLUNKIES? THAT'S WHY YOU'D ONLY BLAST THE AREA IMMEDIATELY IN FRONT OF US!
WELL, NO MORE!
SMASH
17

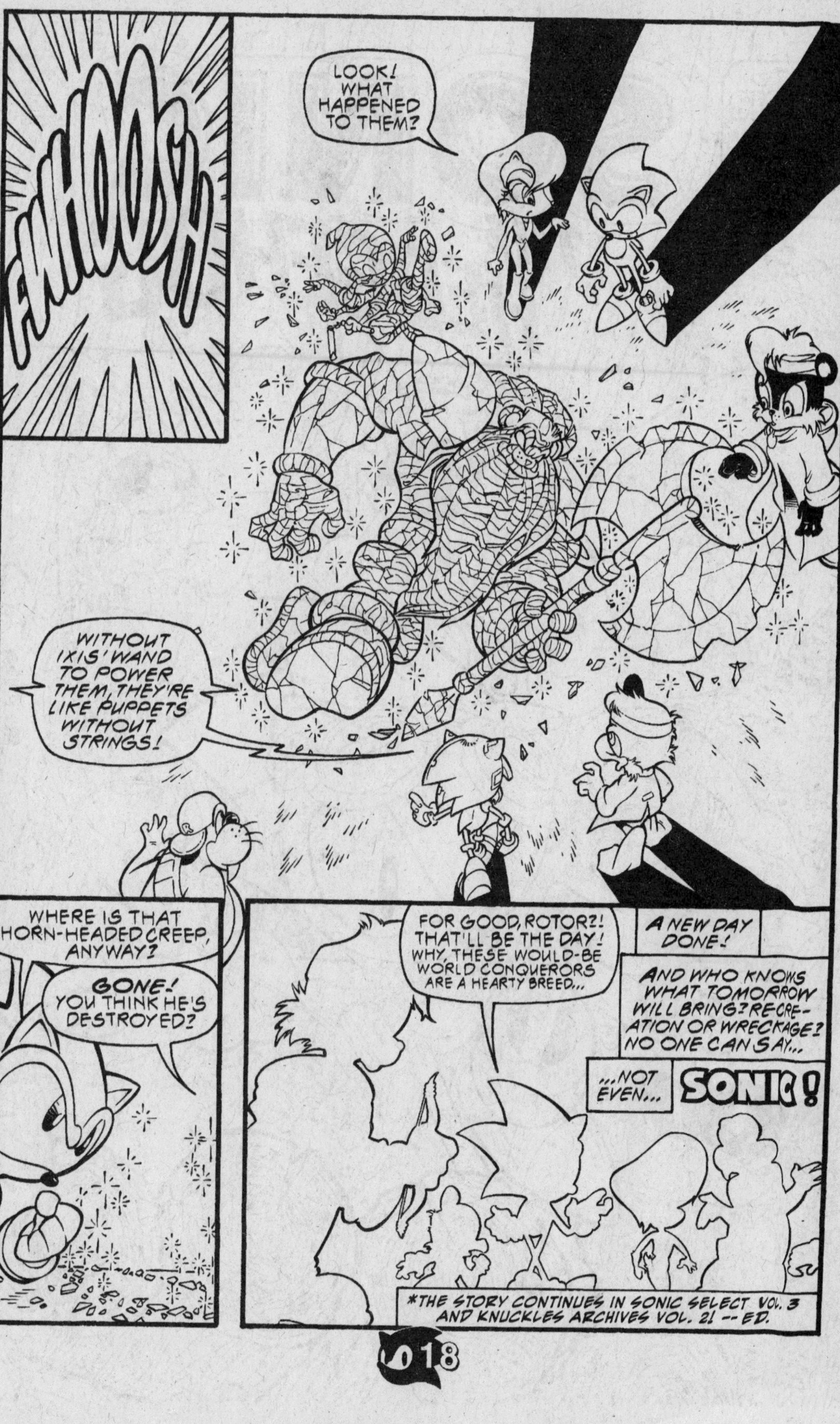
FWHOOSH
LOOK! WHAT HAPPENED TO THEM?
WITHOUT IXIS' WAND TO POWER THEM, THEY'RE LIKE PUPPETS WITHOUT STRINGS!
WHERE IS THAT HORN-HEADED CREEP, ANYWAY?
GONE! YOU THINK HE'S DESTROYED?
FOR GOOD, ROTOR?! THAT'LL BE THE DAY! WHY, THESE WOULD-BE WORLD CONQUERORS ARE A HEARTY BREED...
A NEW DAY DONE!
AND WHO KNOWS WHAT TOMORROW WILL BRING? RE-CREATION OR WRECKAGE? NO ONE CAN SAY...
...NOT EVEN...
SONIC!
*THE STORY CONTINUES IN SONIC SELECT VOL. 3 AND KNUCKLES ARCHIVES VOL. 2! -- ED.
018

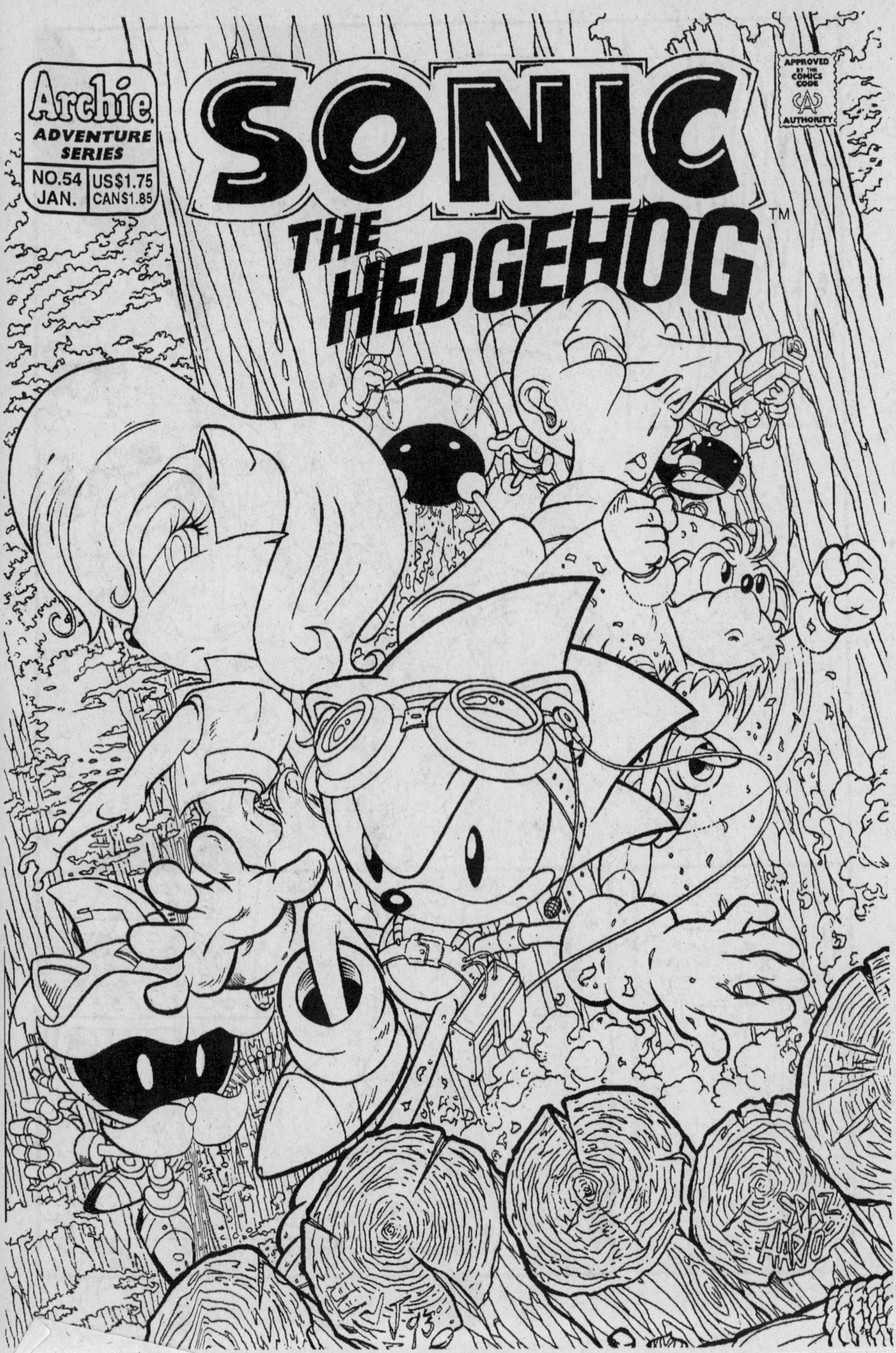
Archie
ADVENTURE SERIES
NO.54 JAN.
US$1.75 CAN$1.85
SONIC THE HEDGEHOG™
APPROVED BY THE COMICS CODE AUTHORITY

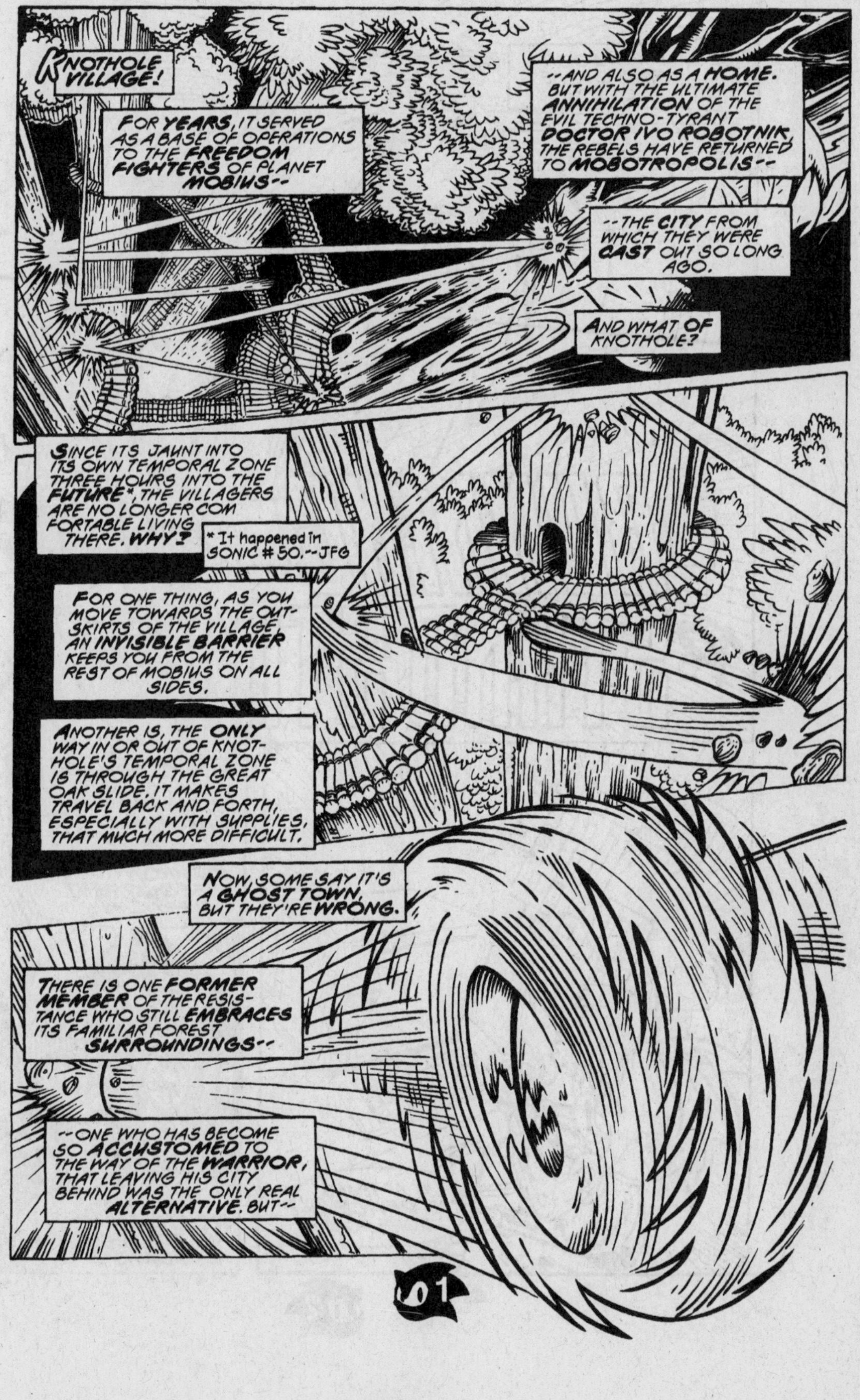
KNOTHOLE VILLAGE!
FOR YEARS, IT SERVED AS A BASE OF OPERATIONS TO THE FREEDOM FIGHTERS OF PLANET MOBIUS--
--AND ALSO AS A HOME. BUT WITH THE ULTIMATE ANNIHILATION OF THE EVIL TECHNO-TYRANT DOCTOR IVO ROBOTNIK, THE REBELS HAVE RETURNED TO MOBOTROPOLIS--
--THE CITY FROM WHICH THEY WERE CAST OUT SO LONG AGO.
AND WHAT OF KNOTHOLE?
SINCE ITS JAUNT INTO ITS OWN TEMPORAL ZONE THREE HOURS INTO THE FUTURE*, THE VILLAGERS ARE NO LONGER COM FORTABLE LIVING THERE. WHY?
* It happened in SONIC #50.--JFG
FOR ONE THING, AS YOU MOVE TOWARDS THE OUT-SKIRTS OF THE VILLAGE, AN INVISIBLE BARRIER KEEPS YOU FROM THE REST OF MOBIUS ON ALL SIDES.
ANOTHER IS, THE ONLY WAY IN OR OUT OF KNOT-HOLE'S TEMPORAL ZONE IS THROUGH THE GREAT OAK SLIDE. IT MAKES TRAVEL BACK AND FORTH, ESPECIALLY WITH SUPPLIES, THAT MUCH MORE DIFFICULT.
NOW, SOME SAY IT'S A GHOST TOWN, BUT THEY'RE WRONG.
THERE IS ONE FORMER MEMBER OF THE RESIS-TANCE WHO STILL EMBRACES ITS FAMILIAR FOREST SURROUNDINGS--
--ONE WHO HAS BECOME SO ACCUSTOMED TO THE WAY OF THE WARRIOR, THAT LEAVING HIS CITY BEHIND WAS THE ONLY REAL ALTERNATIVE. BUT--
1

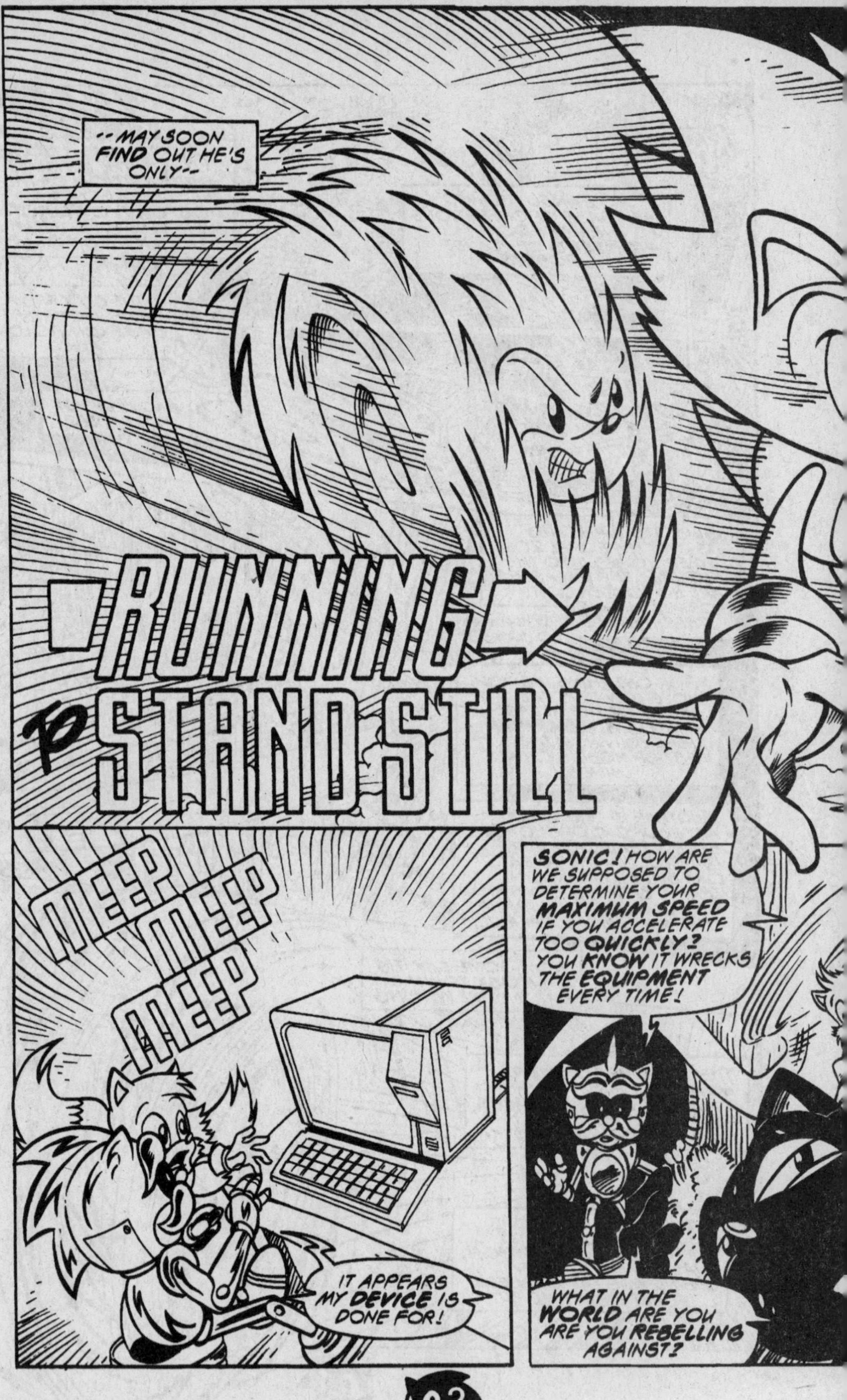
-- MAY SOON FIND OUT HE'S ONLY--
RUNNING TO STAND STILL
MEEP MEEP MEEP
IT APPEARS MY DEVICE IS DONE FOR!
SONIC! HOW ARE WE SUPPOSED TO DETERMINE YOUR MAXIMUM SPEED IF YOU ACCELERATE TOO QUICKLY? YOU KNOW IT WRECKS THE EQUIPMENT EVERY TIME!
WHAT IN THE WORLD ARE YOU ARE YOU REBELLING AGAINST?
2

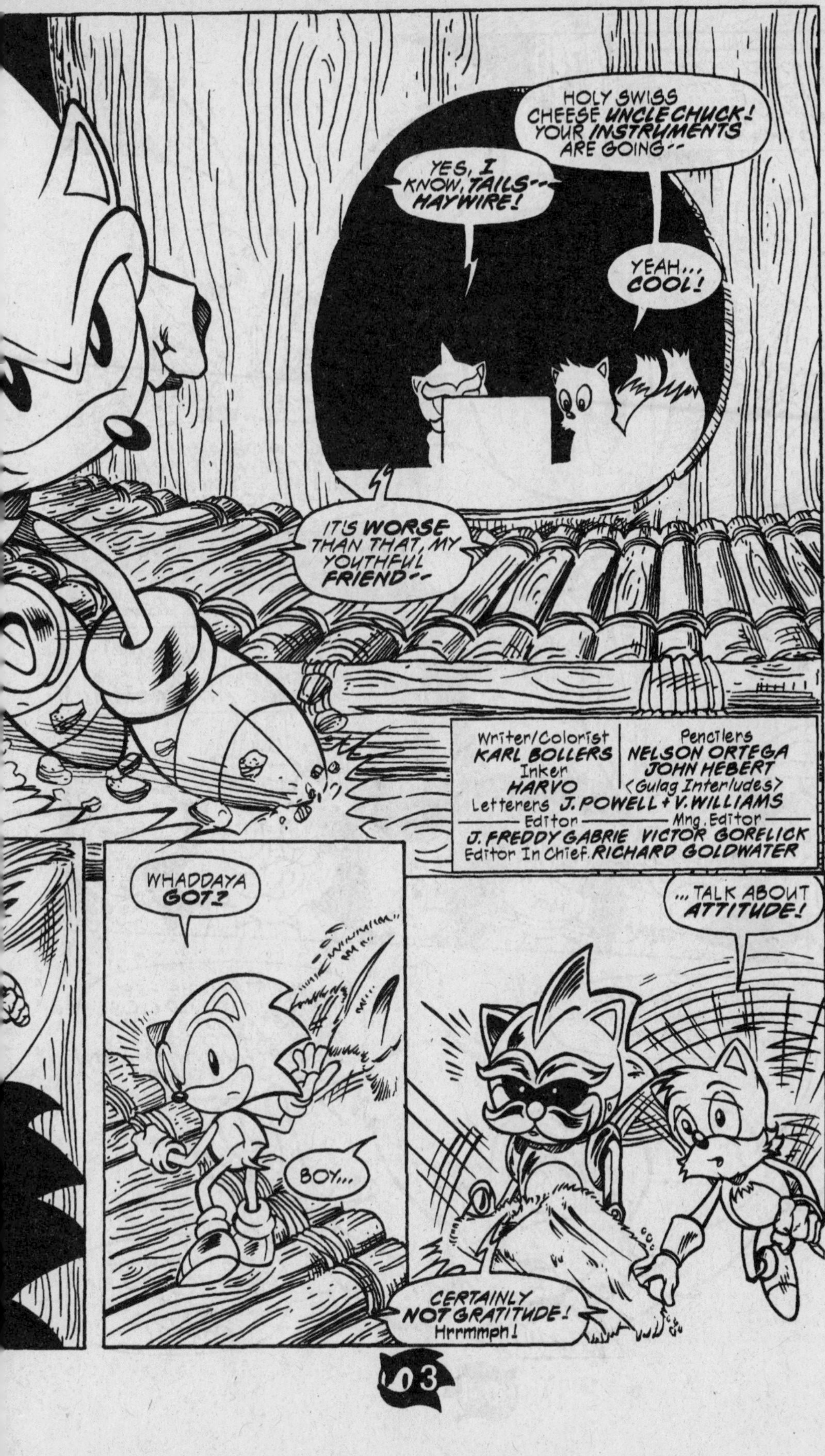
HOLY SWISS CHEESE UNCLE CHUCK! YOUR INSTRUMENTS ARE GOING--
YES, I KNOW, TAILS-- HAYWIRE!
YEAH... COOL!
IT'S WORSE THAN THAT, MY YOUTHFUL FRIEND--
Writer/Colorist KARL BOLLERS
Pencilers NELSON ORTEGA JOHN HEBERT <Gulag Interludes>
Inker HARVO
Letterers J. POWELL + V. WILLIAMS
Editor J. FREDDY GABRIE
Mng. Editor VICTOR GORELICK
Editor In Chief RICHARD GOLDWATER
WHADDAYA GOT?
BOY...
...TALK ABOUT ATTITUDE!
CERTAINLY NOT GRATITUDE! Hrrmmph!
03

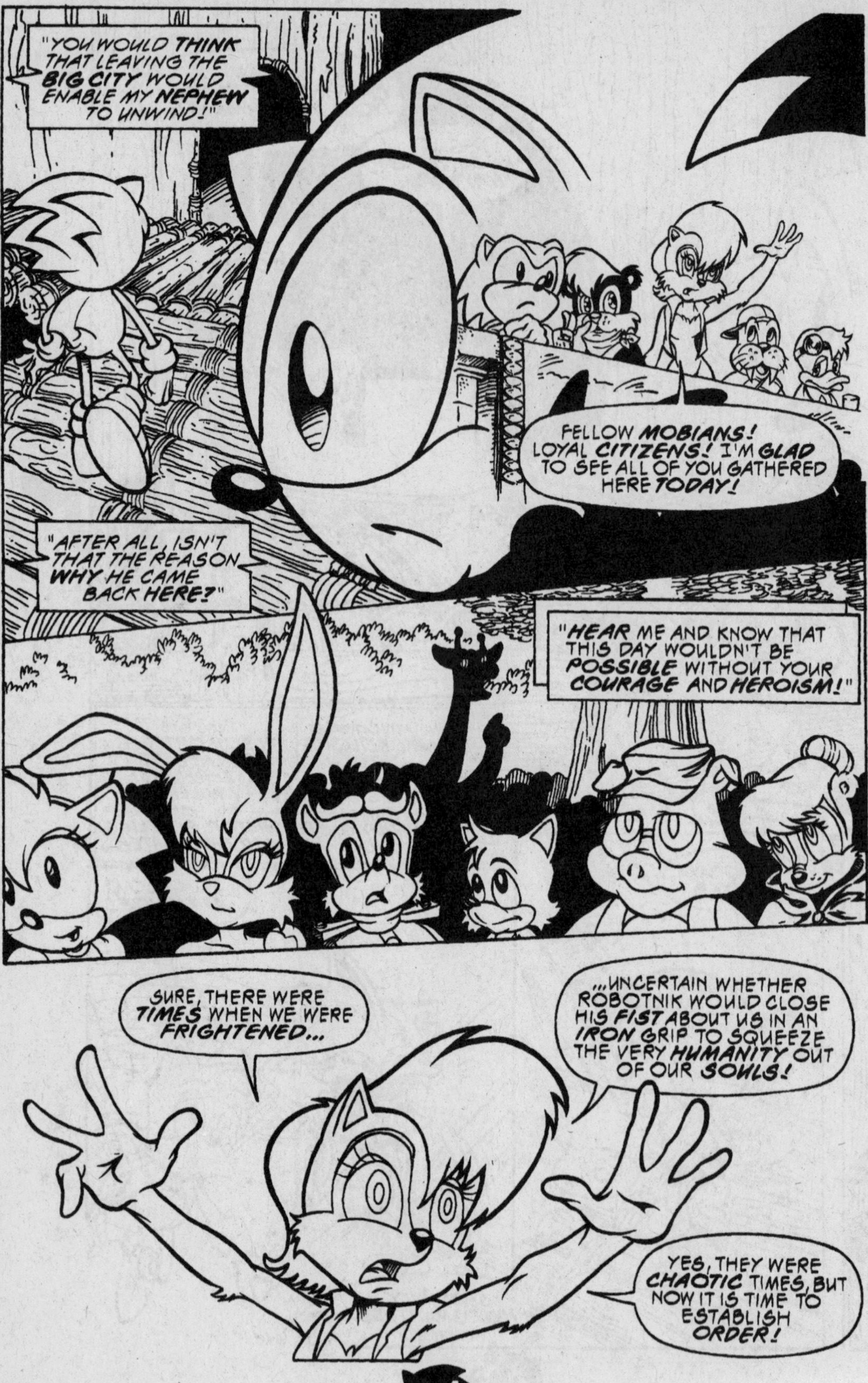
"YOU WOULD THINK THAT LEAVING THE BIG CITY WOULD ENABLE MY NEPHEW TO UNWIND!"
FELLOW MOBIANS! LOYAL CITIZENS! I'M GLAD TO SEE ALL OF YOU GATHERED HERE TODAY!
"AFTER ALL, ISN'T THAT THE REASON WHY HE CAME BACK HERE?"
"HEAR ME AND KNOW THAT THIS DAY WOULDN'T BE POSSIBLE WITHOUT YOUR COURAGE AND HEROISM!"
SURE, THERE WERE TIMES WHEN WE WERE FRIGHTENED...
...UNCERTAIN WHETHER ROBOTNIK WOULD CLOSE HIS FIST ABOUT US IN AN IRON GRIP TO SQUEEZE THE VERY HUMANITY OUT OF OUR SOULS!
YES, THEY WERE CHAOTIC TIMES, BUT NOW IT IS TIME TO ESTABLISH ORDER!
04

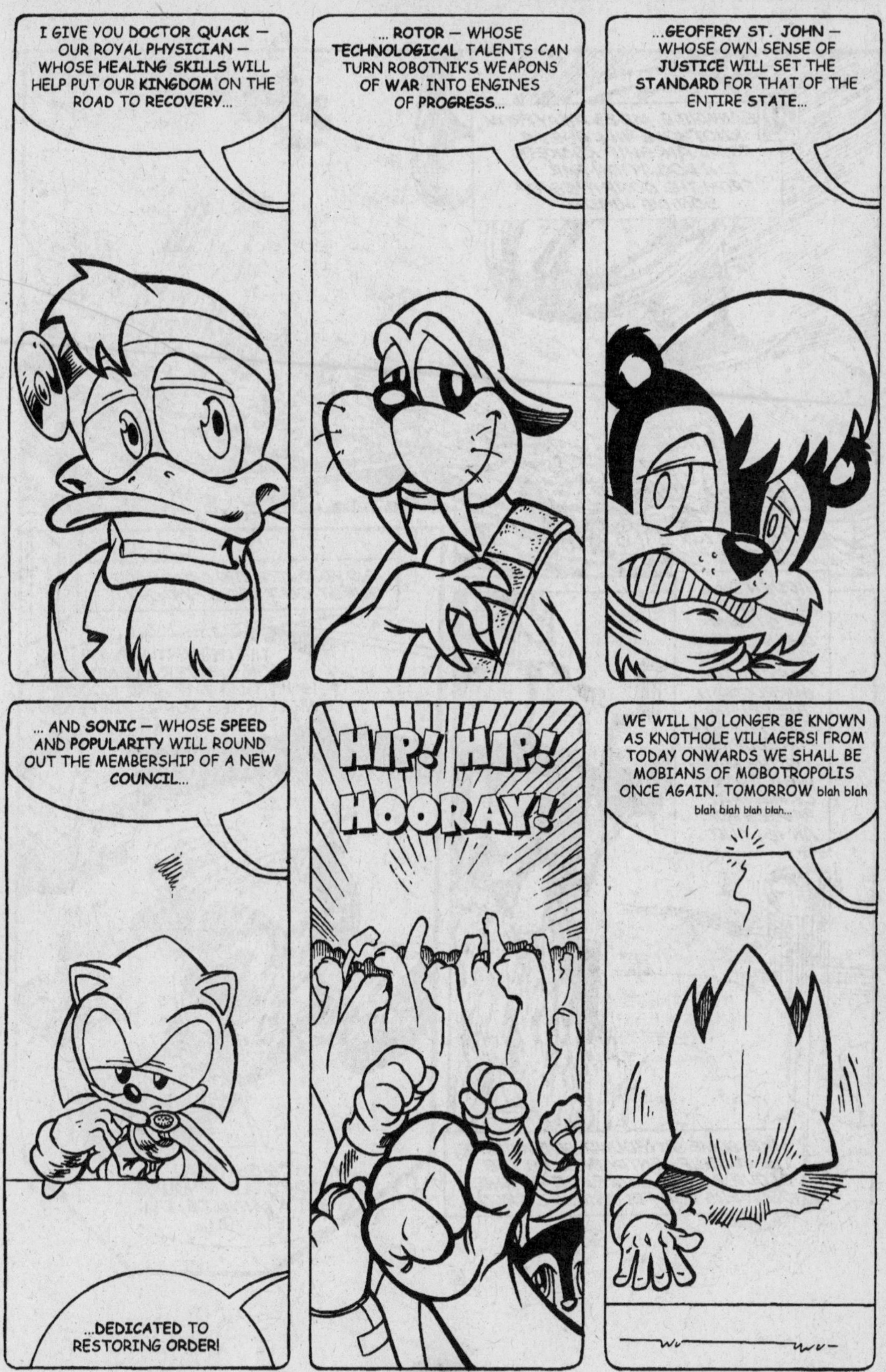
I GIVE YOU DOCTOR QUACK — OUR ROYAL PHYSICIAN — WHOSE HEALING SKILLS WILL HELP PUT OUR KINGDOM ON THE ROAD TO RECOVERY...
... ROTOR — WHOSE TECHNOLOGICAL TALENTS CAN TURN ROBOTNIK'S WEAPONS OF WAR INTO ENGINES OF PROGRESS...
...GEOFFREY ST. JOHN — WHOSE OWN SENSE OF JUSTICE WILL SET THE STANDARD FOR THAT OF THE ENTIRE STATE...
... AND SONIC — WHOSE SPEED AND POPULARITY WILL ROUND OUT THE MEMBERSHIP OF A NEW COUNCIL...
...DEDICATED TO RESTORING ORDER!
HIP! HIP! HOORAY!
WE WILL NO LONGER BE KNOWN AS KNOTHOLE VILLAGERS! FROM TODAY ONWARDS WE SHALL BE MOBIANS OF MOBOTROPOLIS ONCE AGAIN. TOMORROW blah blah blah blah blah blah...

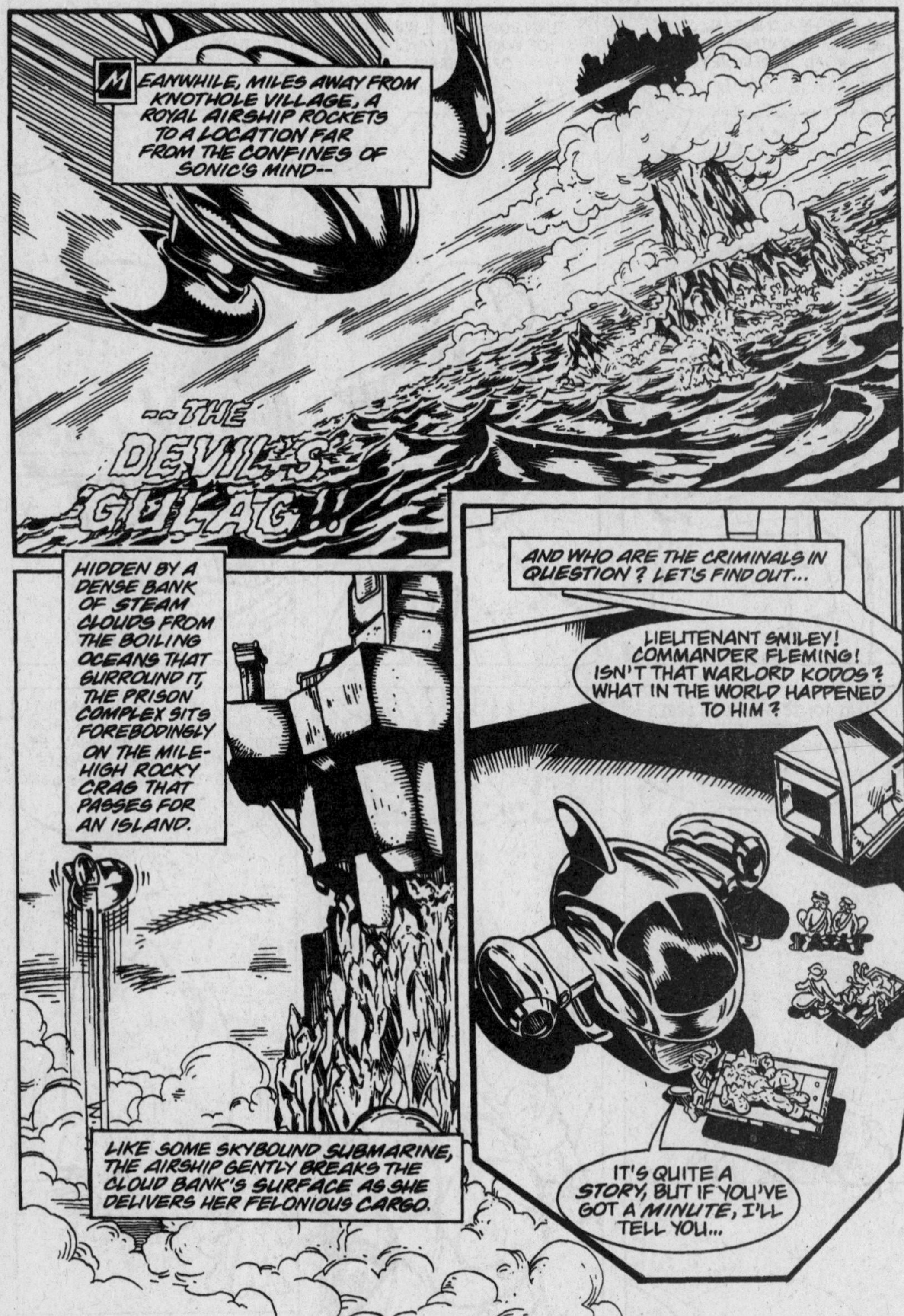
MEANWHILE, MILES AWAY FROM KNOTHOLE VILLAGE, A ROYAL AIRSHIP ROCKETS TO A LOCATION FAR FROM THE CONFINES OF SONIC'S MIND--
--THE DEVIL'S GULAG!!
HIDDEN BY A DENSE BANK OF STEAM CLOUDS FROM THE BOILING OCEANS THAT SURROUND IT, THE PRISON COMPLEX SITS FOREBODINGLY ON THE MILE-HIGH ROCKY CRAG THAT PASSES FOR AN ISLAND.
LIKE SOME SKYBOUND SUBMARINE, THE AIRSHIP GENTLY BREAKS THE CLOUD BANK'S SURFACE AS SHE DELIVERS HER FELONIOUS CARGO.
AND WHO ARE THE CRIMINALS IN QUESTION? LET'S FIND OUT...
LIEUTENANT SMILEY! COMMANDER FLEMING! ISN'T THAT WARLORD KODOS? WHAT IN THE WORLD HAPPENED TO HIM?
IT'S QUITE A STORY, BUT IF YOU'VE GOT A MINUTE, I'LL TELL YOU...
06

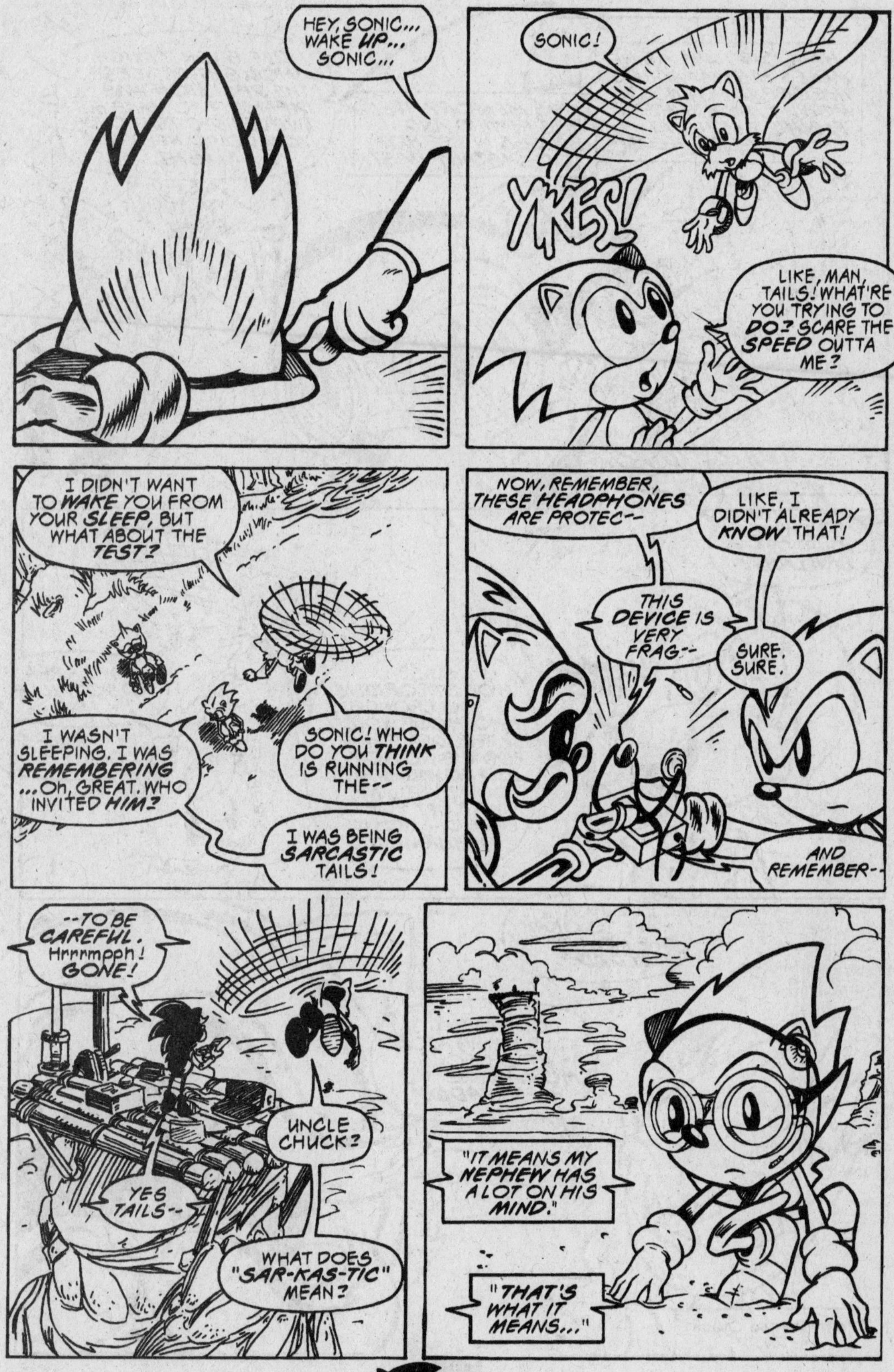
HEY, SONIC... WAKE UP... SONIC...
SONIC!
YKES!
LIKE, MAN, TAILS! WHAT'RE YOU TRYING TO DO? SCARE THE SPEED OUTTA ME?
I DIDN'T WANT TO WAKE YOU FROM YOUR SLEEP, BUT WHAT ABOUT THE TEST?
I WASN'T SLEEPING. I WAS REMEMBERING ...Oh, GREAT. WHO INVITED HIM?
SONIC! WHO DO YOU THINK IS RUNNING THE--
I WAS BEING SARCASTIC TAILS!
NOW, REMEMBER, THESE HEADPHONES ARE PROTEC--
LIKE, I DIDN'T ALREADY KNOW THAT!
THIS DEVICE IS VERY FRAG--
SURE, SURE.
AND REMEMBER--
--TO BE CAREFUL. Hrrrmmph! GONE!
UNCLE CHUCK?
YES TAILS--
WHAT DOES "SAR-KAS-TIC" MEAN?
"IT MEANS MY NEPHEW HAS A LOT ON HIS MIND."
"THAT'S WHAT IT MEANS..."
07

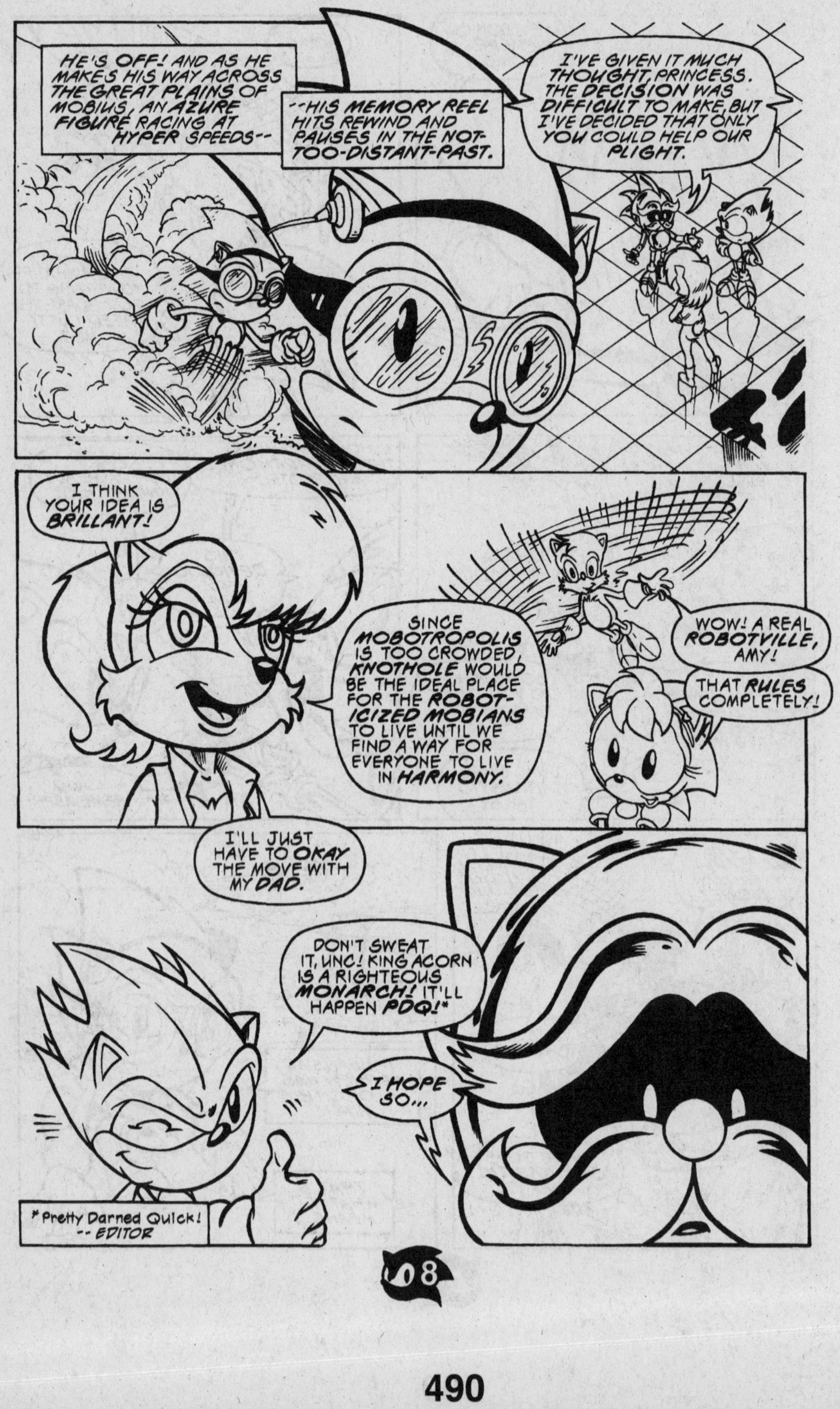
HE'S OFF! AND AS HE MAKES HIS WAY ACROSS THE GREAT PLAINS OF MOBIUS, AN AZURE FIGURE RACING AT HYPER SPEEDS--
--HIS MEMORY REEL HITS REWIND AND PAUSES IN THE NOT-TOO-DISTANT-PAST.
I'VE GIVEN IT MUCH THOUGHT, PRINCESS. THE DECISION WAS DIFFICULT TO MAKE, BUT I'VE DECIDED THAT ONLY YOU COULD HELP OUR PLIGHT.
I THINK YOUR IDEA IS BRILLANT!
SINCE MOBOTROPOLIS IS TOO CROWDED, KNOTHOLE WOULD BE THE IDEAL PLACE FOR THE ROBOTICIZED MOBIANS TO LIVE UNTIL WE FIND A WAY FOR EVERYONE TO LIVE IN HARMONY.
WOW! A REAL ROBOTVILLE, AMY!
THAT RULES COMPLETELY!
I'LL JUST HAVE TO OKAY THE MOVE WITH MY DAD.
DON'T SWEAT IT, UNC! KING ACORN IS A RIGHTEOUS MONARCH! IT'LL HAPPEN PDQ!*
I HOPE SO...
* Pretty Darned Quick! -- EDITOR
8

SCANT MINUTES LATER...

SAY, WHERE'D *EVERYBODY* TAKE OFF TO?

BOTH *SALLY* AND YOUR UNCLE LEFT FOR *CASTLE ACORN*--

--TO *PETITION* THE KING

Oh, GREAT! *JUST* GREAT! CAN'T A HEDGEHOG EVEN PUT ON A FRESH PAIR OF *RUNNING SHOES* WITHOUT EVERYONE GOING OUT AND TRYING TO *CHANGE* THE WORLD WITHOUT HIM?

HUH?

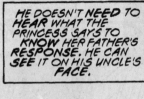

HE'S *EXAGGERATING!*

PERHAPS HE *IS.*

FOR STOPPING SOME *SEVERAL YARDS* AWAY FROM THE KING'S *CASTLE,* SONIC WIT-NESSES A SIGHT THAT SINKS EVEN *HIS,* THE *SWIFTEST* OF SPIRITS.

HE DOESN'T *NEED* TO *HEAR* WHAT THE PRINCESS SAYS TO *KNOW* HER FATHER'S RESPONSE. HE CAN *SEE* IT ON HIS UNCLE'S *FACE.*

YES, THE WORLD IS *CHANGING...*

...BUT IS IT FOR THE BETTER?

109

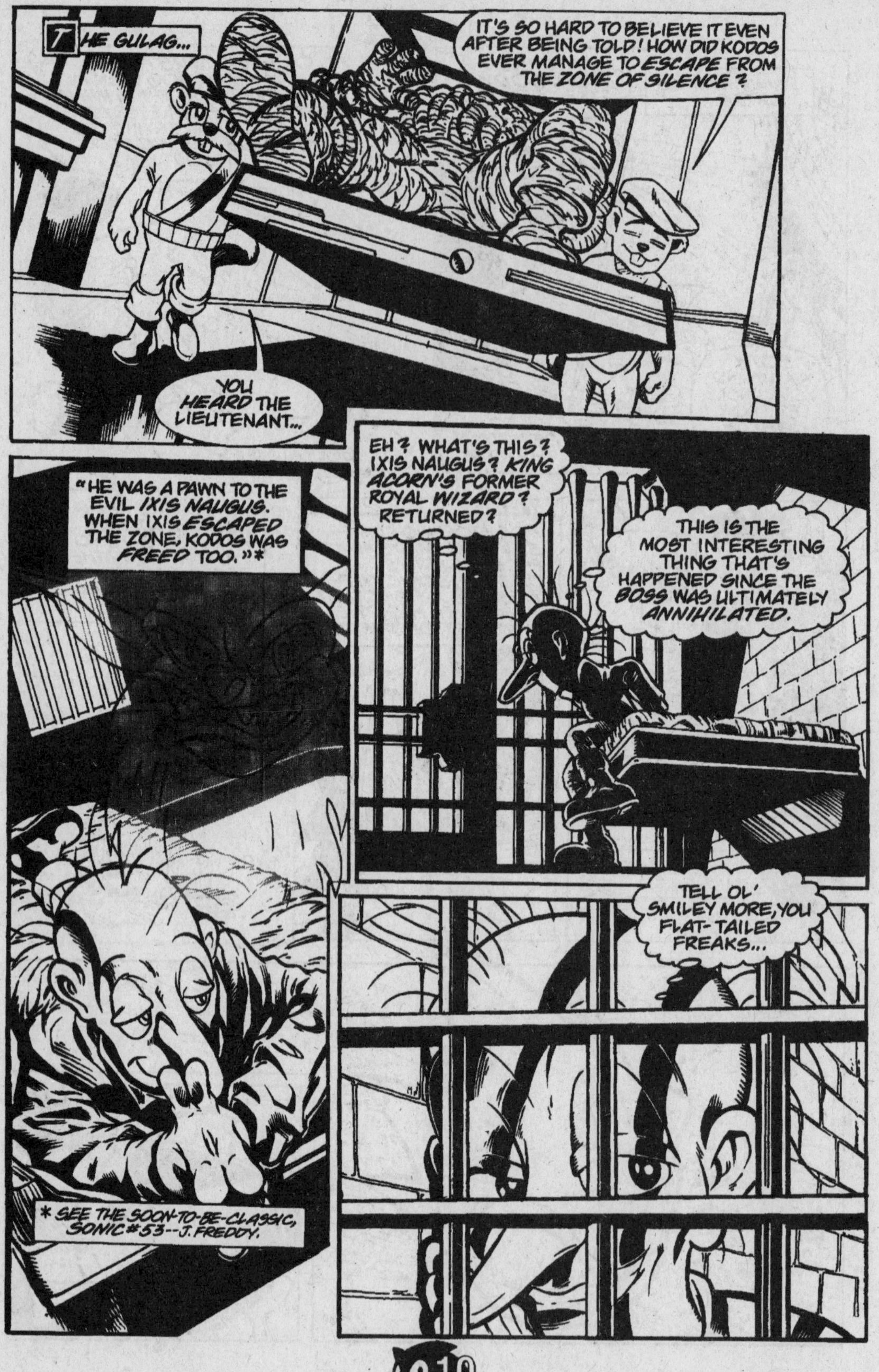
THE GULAG...
IT'S SO HARD TO BELIEVE IT EVEN AFTER BEING TOLD! HOW DID KODOS EVER MANAGE TO ESCAPE FROM THE ZONE OF SILENCE?
YOU HEARD THE LIEUTENANT...
"HE WAS A PAWN TO THE EVIL IXIS NAUGUS. WHEN IXIS ESCAPED THE ZONE, KODOS WAS FREED TOO."*
EH? WHAT'S THIS? IXIS NAUGUS? KING ACORN'S FORMER ROYAL WIZARD? RETURNED?
THIS IS THE MOST INTERESTING THING THAT'S HAPPENED SINCE THE BOSS WAS ULTIMATELY ANNIHILATED.
TELL OL' SMILEY MORE, YOU FLAT-TAILED FREAKS...
* SEE THE SOON-TO-BE-CLASSIC, SONIC #53--J. FREDDY.
10

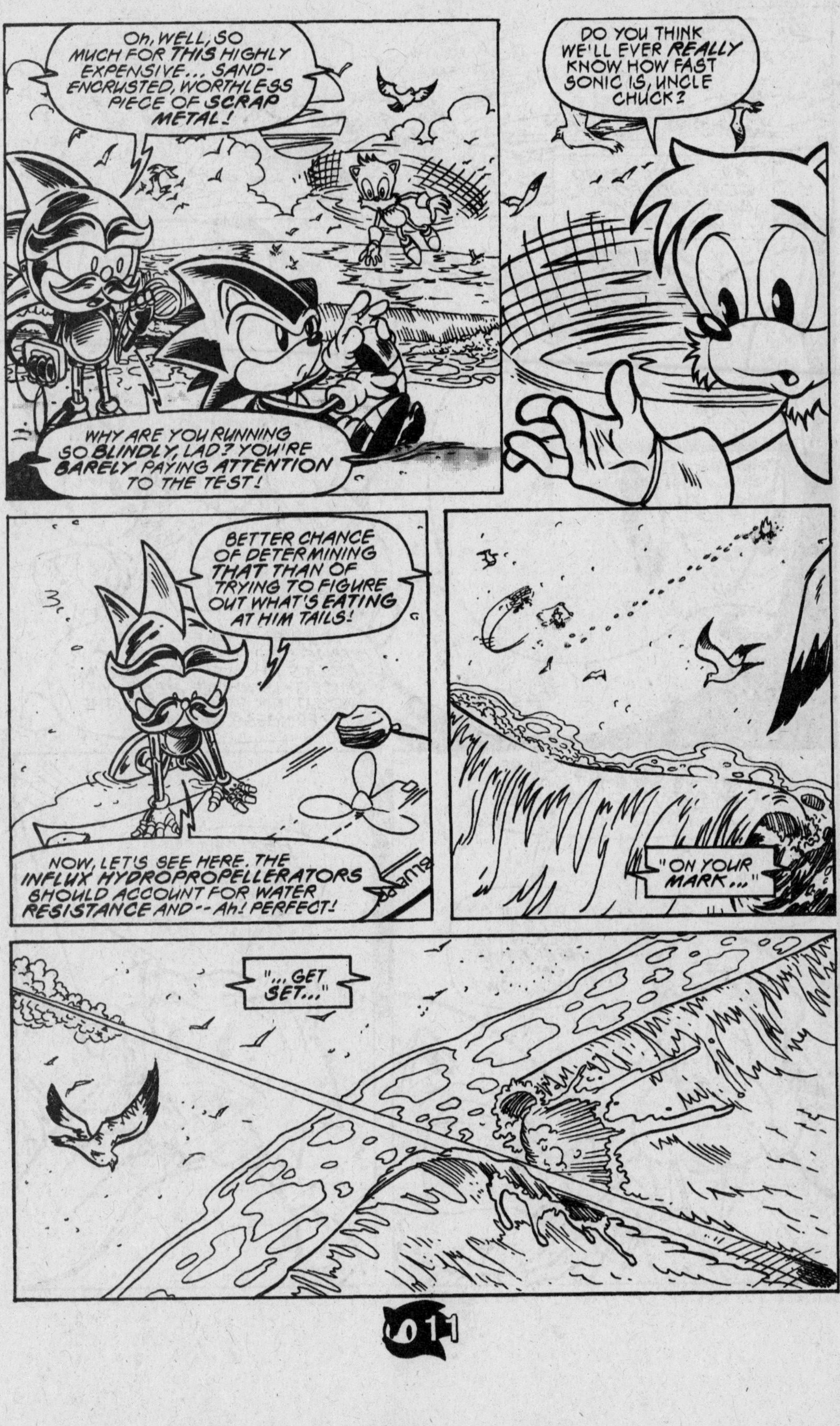
Oh, WELL, SO MUCH FOR THIS HIGHLY EXPENSIVE... SAND-ENCRUSTED, WORTHLESS PIECE OF SCRAP METAL!
WHY ARE YOU RUNNING SO BLINDLY, LAD? YOU'RE BARELY PAYING ATTENTION TO THE TEST!
DO YOU THINK WE'LL EVER REALLY KNOW HOW FAST SONIC IS, UNCLE CHUCK?
BETTER CHANCE OF DETERMINING THAT THAN OF TRYING TO FIGURE OUT WHAT'S EATING AT HIM TAILS!
NOW, LET'S SEE HERE. THE INFLUX HYDROPROPELLERATORS SHOULD ACCOUNT FOR WATER RESISTANCE AND--Ah! PERFECT!
"ON YOUR MARK..."
"...GET SET..."
11

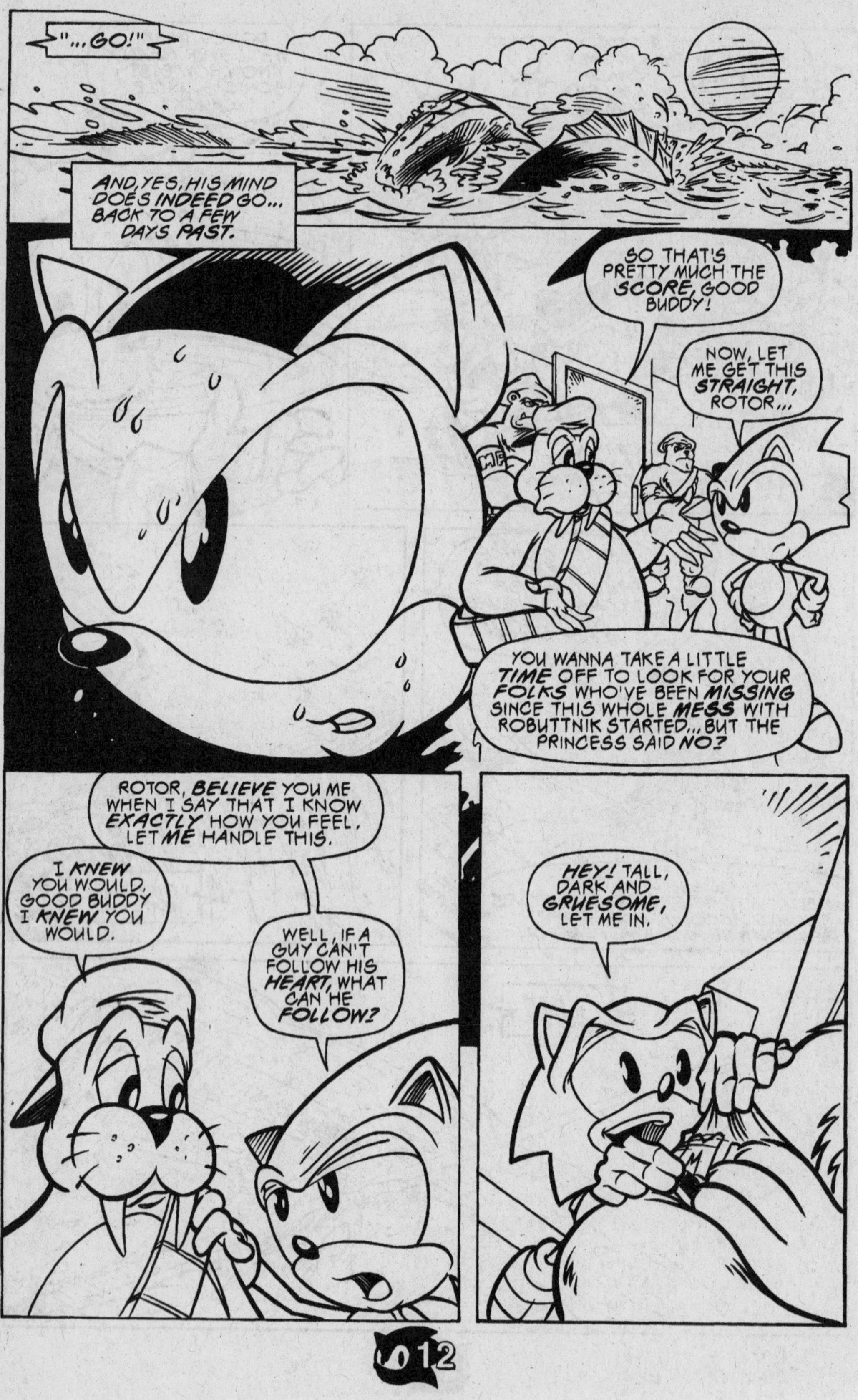
"...GO!"
AND, YES, HIS MIND DOES INDEED GO... BACK TO A FEW DAYS PAST.
SO THAT'S PRETTY MUCH THE SCORE, GOOD BUDDY!
NOW, LET ME GET THIS STRAIGHT, ROTOR...
YOU WANNA TAKE A LITTLE TIME OFF TO LOOK FOR YOUR FOLKS WHO'VE BEEN MISSING SINCE THIS WHOLE MESS WITH ROBUTTNIK STARTED... BUT THE PRINCESS SAID NO?
ROTOR, BELIEVE YOU ME WHEN I SAY THAT I KNOW EXACTLY HOW YOU FEEL. LET ME HANDLE THIS.
I KNEW YOU WOULD, GOOD BUDDY I KNEW YOU WOULD.
WELL, IF A GUY CAN'T FOLLOW HIS HEART, WHAT CAN HE FOLLOW?
HEY! TALL, DARK AND GRUESOME, LET ME IN.
12

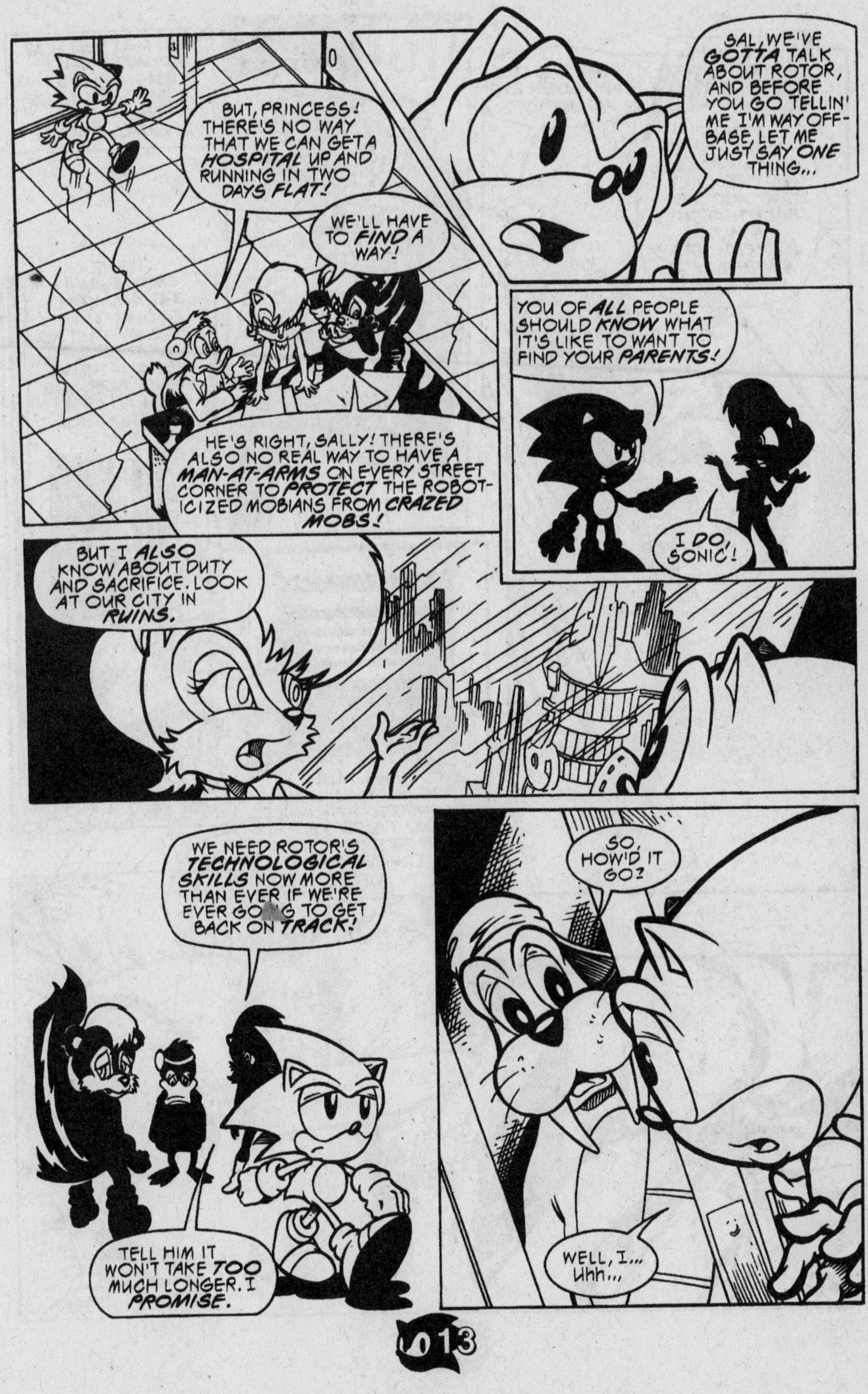
BUT, PRINCESS! THERE'S NO WAY THAT WE CAN GET A HOSPITAL UP AND RUNNING IN TWO DAYS FLAT!
WE'LL HAVE TO FIND A WAY!
HE'S RIGHT, SALLY! THERE'S ALSO NO REAL WAY TO HAVE A MAN-AT-ARMS ON EVERY STREET CORNER TO PROTECT THE ROBOTICIZED MOBIANS FROM CRAZED MOBS!
SAL, WE'VE GOTTA TALK ABOUT ROTOR, AND BEFORE YOU GO TELLIN' ME I'M WAY OFF-BASE, LET ME JUST SAY ONE THING...
YOU OF ALL PEOPLE SHOULD KNOW WHAT IT'S LIKE TO WANT TO FIND YOUR PARENTS!
I DO, SONIC!
BUT I ALSO KNOW ABOUT DUTY AND SACRIFICE. LOOK AT OUR CITY IN RUINS.
WE NEED ROTOR'S TECHNOLOGICAL SKILLS NOW MORE THAN EVER IF WE'RE EVER GOING TO GET BACK ON TRACK!
TELL HIM IT WON'T TAKE TOO MUCH LONGER. I PROMISE.
SO, HOW'D IT GO?
WELL, I... Uhh...

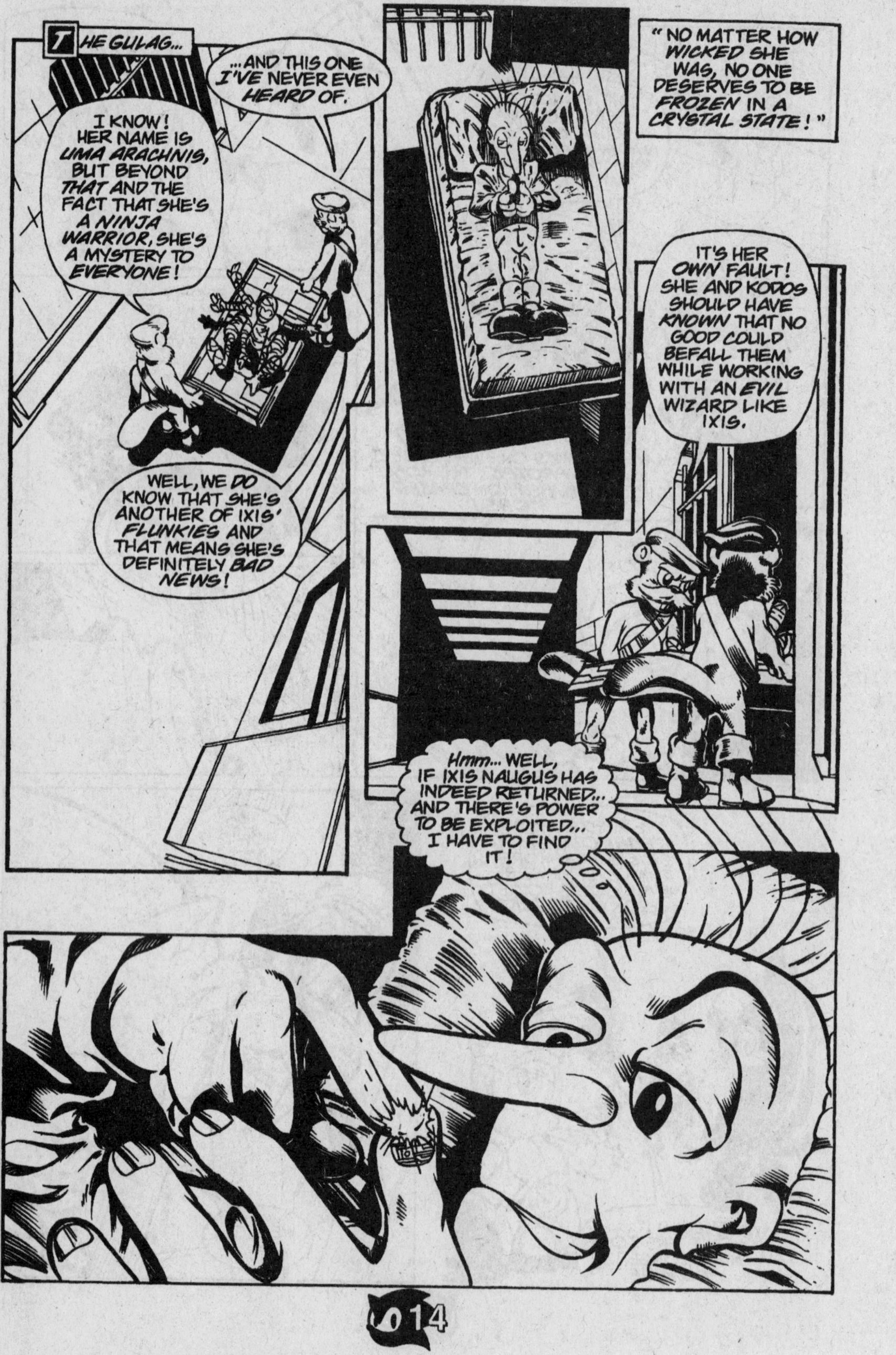
THE GULAG...
...AND THIS ONE I'VE NEVER EVEN HEARD OF.
I KNOW! HER NAME IS UMA ARACHNIS, BUT BEYOND THAT AND THE FACT THAT SHE'S A NINJA WARRIOR, SHE'S A MYSTERY TO EVERYONE!
WELL, WE DO KNOW THAT SHE'S ANOTHER OF IXIS' FLUNKIES AND THAT MEANS SHE'S DEFINITELY BAD NEWS!
" NO MATTER HOW WICKED SHE WAS, NO ONE DESERVES TO BE FROZEN IN A CRYSTAL STATE! "
IT'S HER OWN FAULT! SHE AND KODOS SHOULD HAVE KNOWN THAT NO GOOD COULD BEFALL THEM WHILE WORKING WITH AN EVIL WIZARD LIKE IXIS.
Hmm... WELL, IF IXIS NAUGUS HAS INDEED RETURNED... AND THERE'S POWER TO BE EXPLOITED... I HAVE TO FIND IT!
14

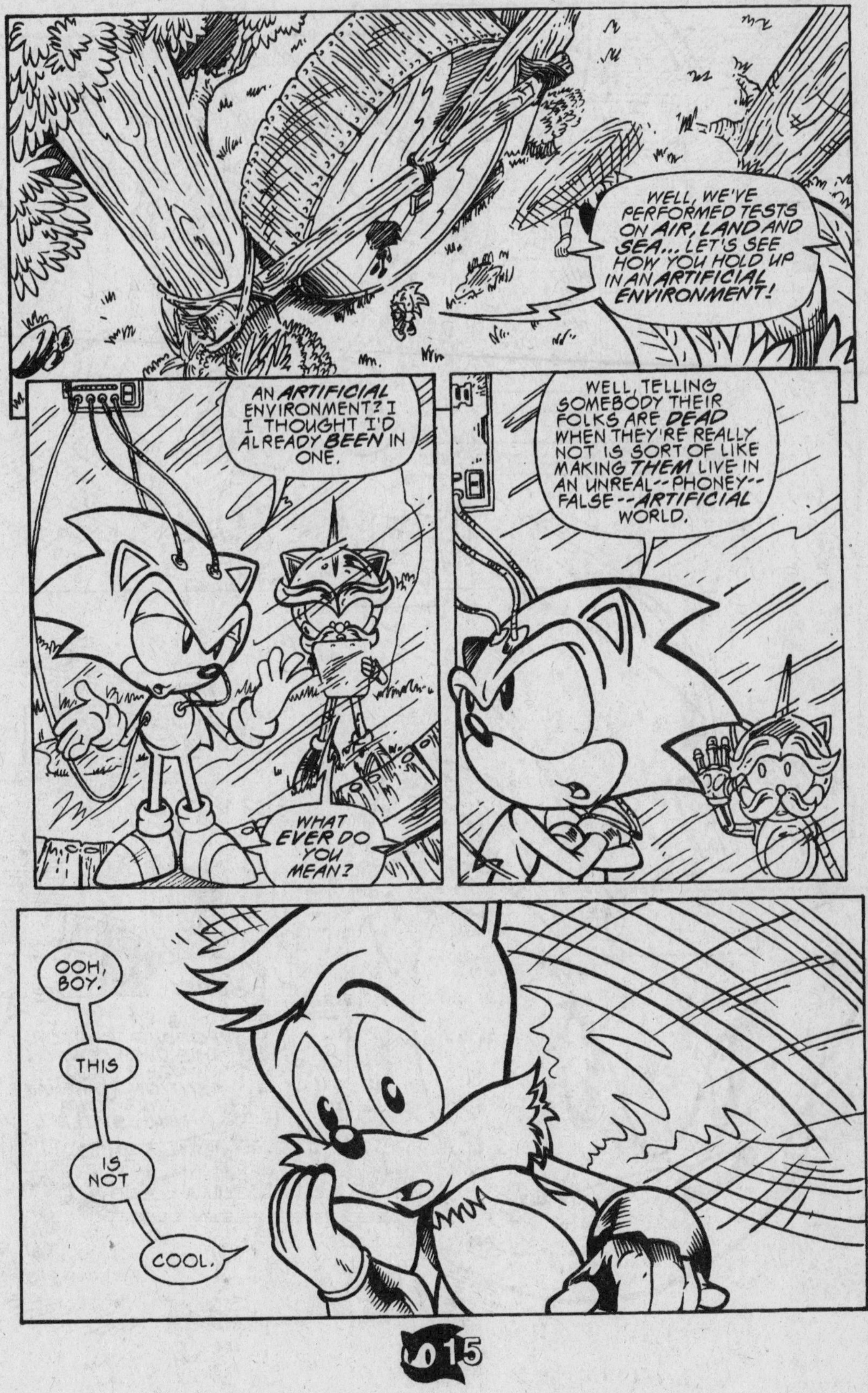
WELL, WE'VE PERFORMED TESTS ON AIR, LAND AND SEA... LET'S SEE HOW YOU HOLD UP IN AN ARTIFICIAL ENVIRONMENT!
AN ARTIFICIAL ENVIRONMENT? I I THOUGHT I'D ALREADY BEEN IN ONE.
WHAT EVER DO YOU MEAN?
WELL, TELLING SOMEBODY THEIR FOLKS ARE DEAD WHEN THEY'RE REALLY NOT IS SORT OF LIKE MAKING THEM LIVE IN AN UNREAL--PHONEY--FALSE--ARTIFICIAL WORLD.
OOH, BOY.
THIS
IS NOT
COOL.
15

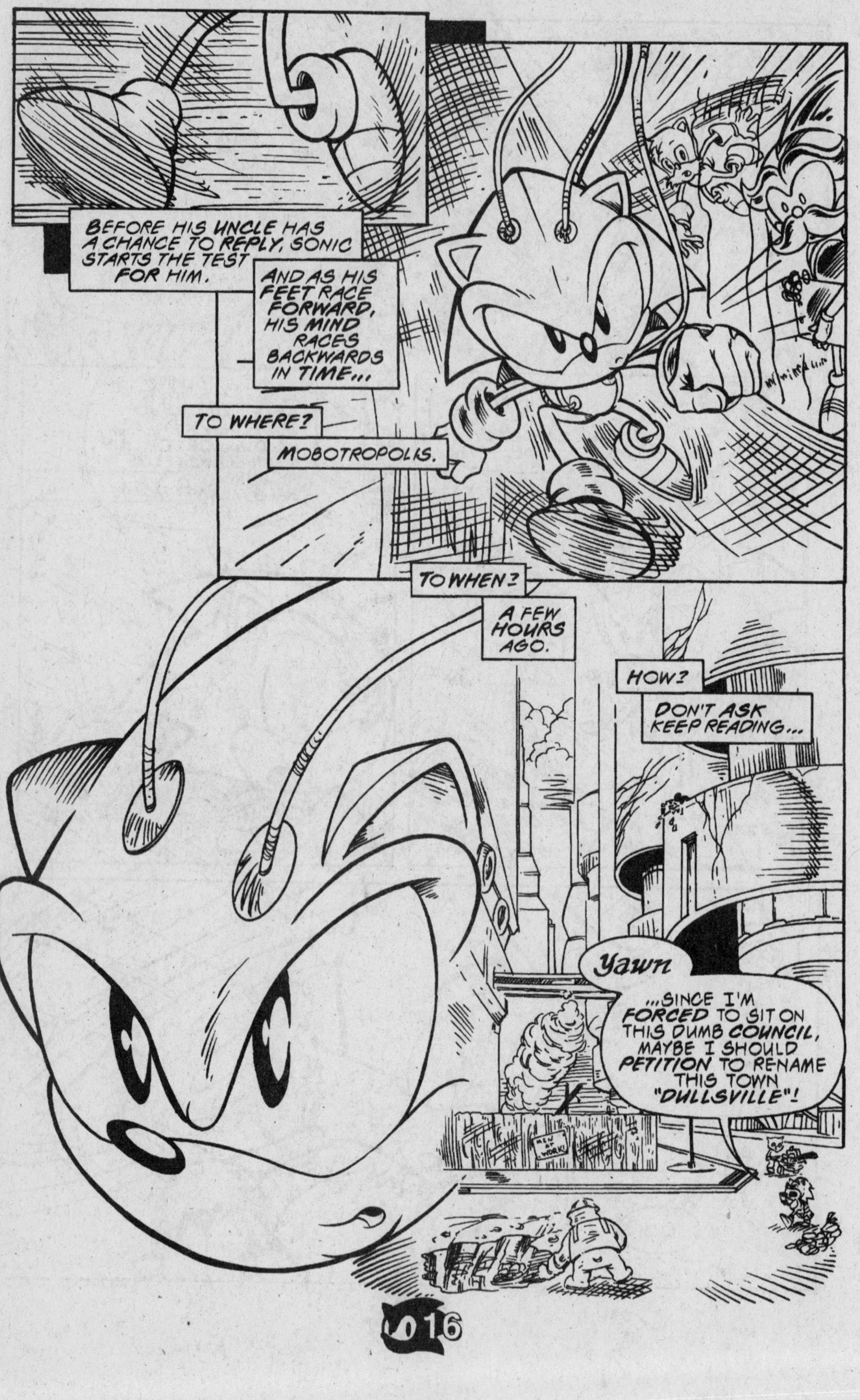
BEFORE HIS UNCLE HAS A CHANCE TO REPLY, SONIC STARTS THE TEST FOR HIM.
AND AS HIS FEET RACE FORWARD, HIS MIND RACES BACKWARDS IN TIME...
TO WHERE?
MOBOTROPOLIS.
TO WHEN?
A FEW HOURS AGO.
HOW?
DON'T ASK KEEP READING...
Yawn
...SINCE I'M FORCED TO SIT ON THIS DUMB COUNCIL, MAYBE I SHOULD PETITION TO RENAME THIS TOWN "DULLSVILLE"!
16

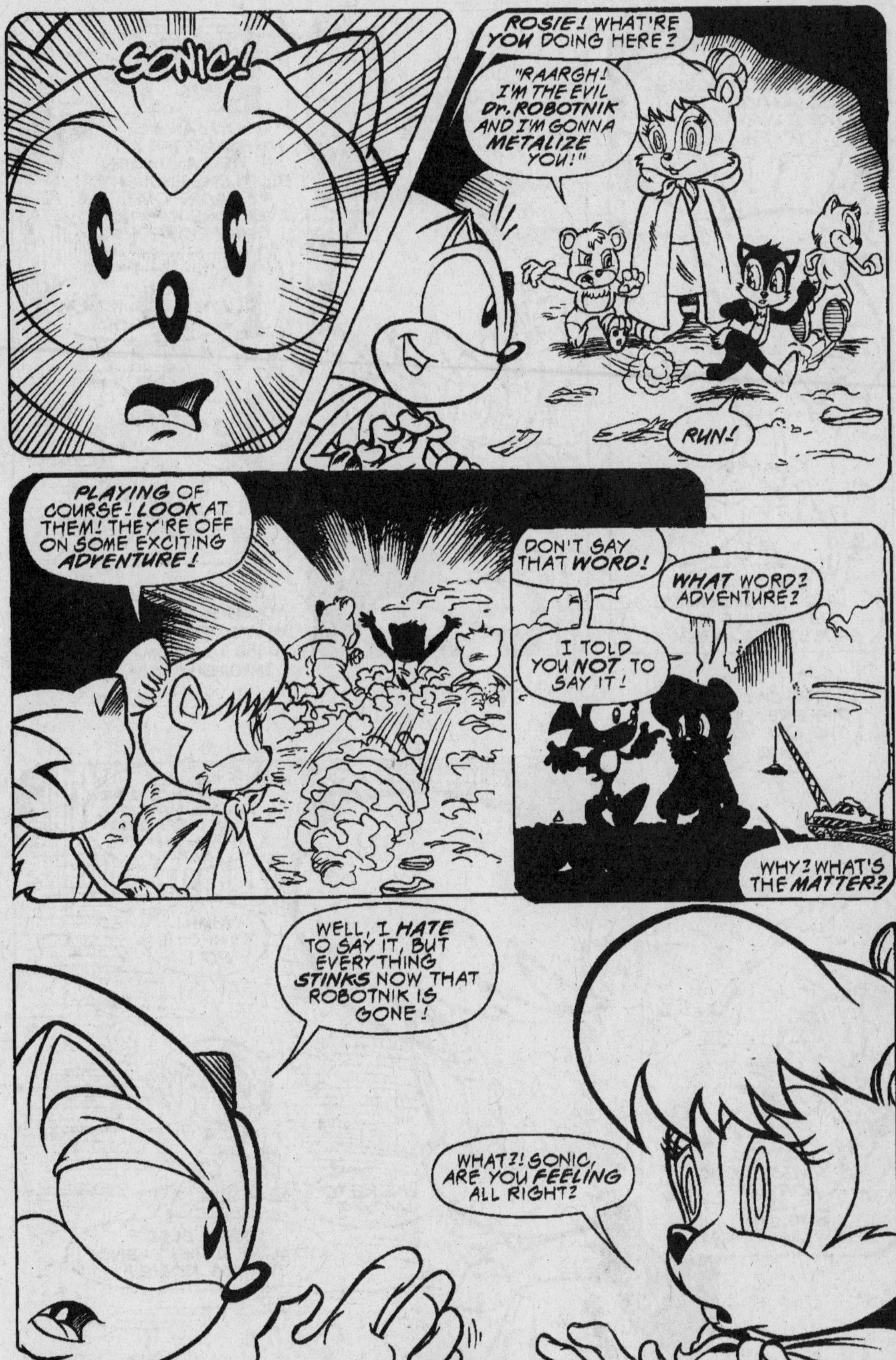
SONIC!
ROSIE! WHAT'RE YOU DOING HERE?
"RAARGH! I'M THE EVIL Dr. ROBOTNIK AND I'M GONNA METALIZE YOU!"
RUN!
PLAYING OF COURSE! LOOK AT THEM! THEY'RE OFF ON SOME EXCITING ADVENTURE!
DON'T SAY THAT WORD!
WHAT WORD? ADVENTURE?
I TOLD YOU NOT TO SAY IT!
WHY? WHAT'S THE MATTER?
WELL, I HATE TO SAY IT, BUT EVERYTHING STINKS NOW THAT ROBOTNIK IS GONE!
WHAT?! SONIC, ARE YOU FEELING ALL RIGHT?
017

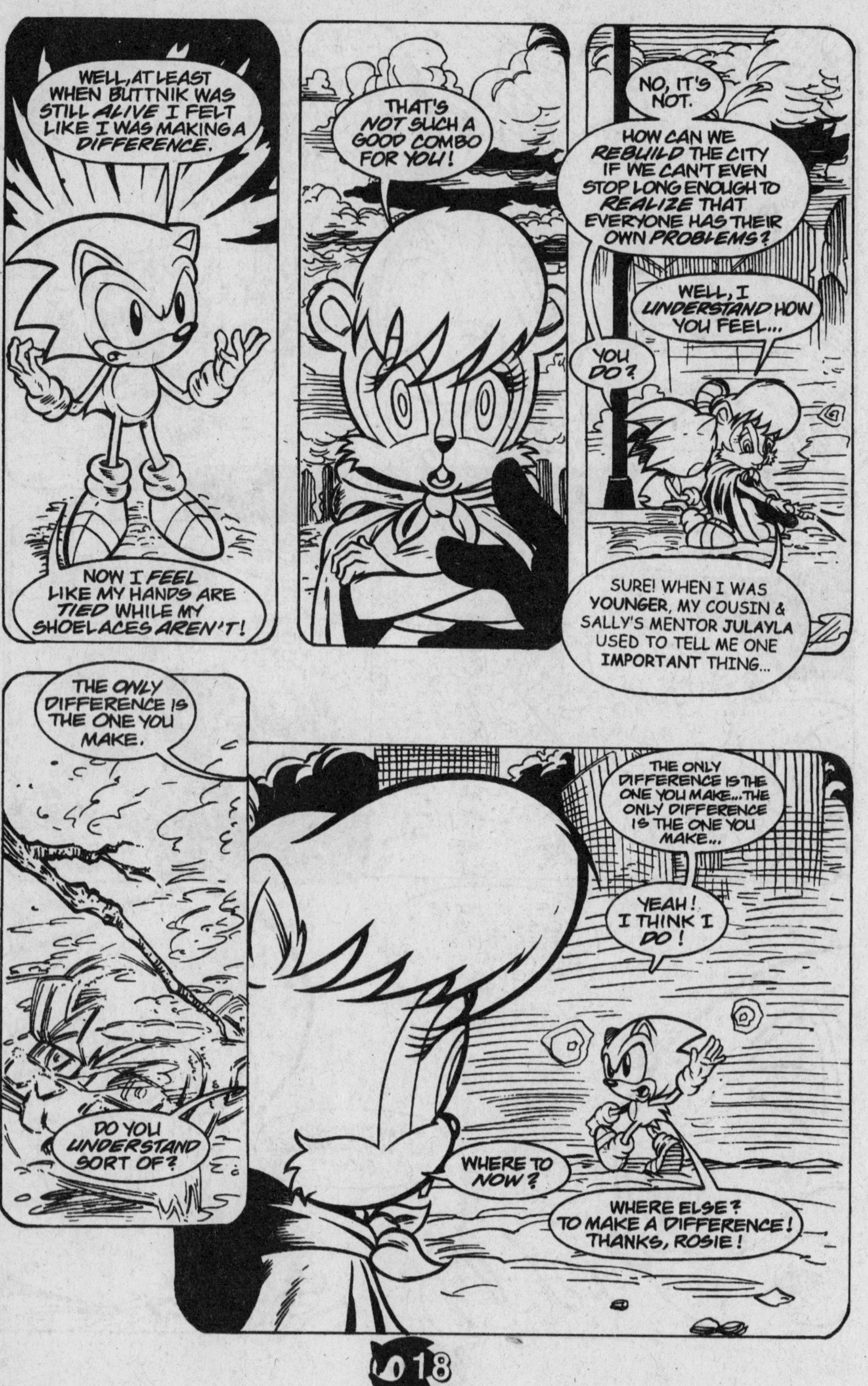
WELL, AT LEAST WHEN BUTTNIK WAS STILL ALIVE I FELT LIKE I WAS MAKING A DIFFERENCE.
NOW I FEEL LIKE MY HANDS ARE TIED WHILE MY SHOELACES AREN'T!
THAT'S NOT SUCH A GOOD COMBO FOR YOU!
NO, IT'S NOT.
HOW CAN WE REBUILD THE CITY IF WE CAN'T EVEN STOP LONG ENOUGH TO REALIZE THAT EVERYONE HAS THEIR OWN PROBLEMS?
WELL, I UNDERSTAND HOW YOU FEEL...
YOU DO?
SURE! WHEN I WAS YOUNGER, MY COUSIN & SALLY'S MENTOR JULAYLA USED TO TELL ME ONE IMPORTANT THING...
THE ONLY DIFFERENCE IS THE ONE YOU MAKE.
DO YOU UNDERSTAND SORT OF?
THE ONLY DIFFERENCE IS THE ONE YOU MAKE... THE ONLY DIFFERENCE IS THE ONE YOU MAKE...
YEAH! I THINK I DO!
WHERE TO NOW?
WHERE ELSE? TO MAKE A DIFFERENCE! THANKS, ROSIE!
18

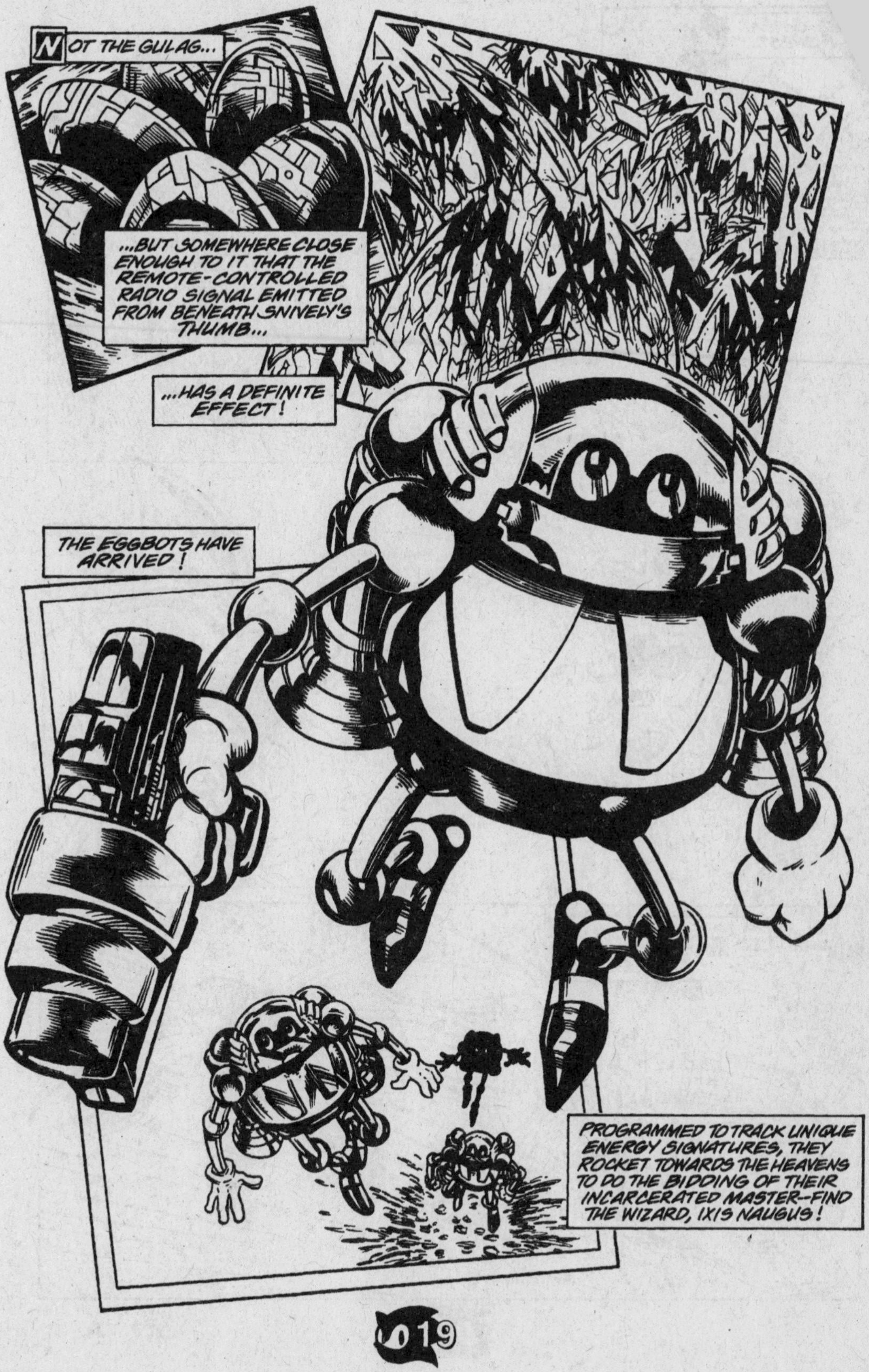
NOT THE GULAG...
...BUT SOMEWHERE CLOSE ENOUGH TO IT THAT THE REMOTE-CONTROLLED RADIO SIGNAL EMITTED FROM BENEATH SNIVELY'S THUMB...
...HAS A DEFINITE EFFECT!
THE EGGBOTS HAVE ARRIVED!
PROGRAMMED TO TRACK UNIQUE ENERGY SIGNATURES, THEY ROCKET TOWARDS THE HEAVENS TO DO THE BIDDING OF THEIR INCARCERATED MASTER--FIND THE WIZARD, IXIS NAUGUS!
19

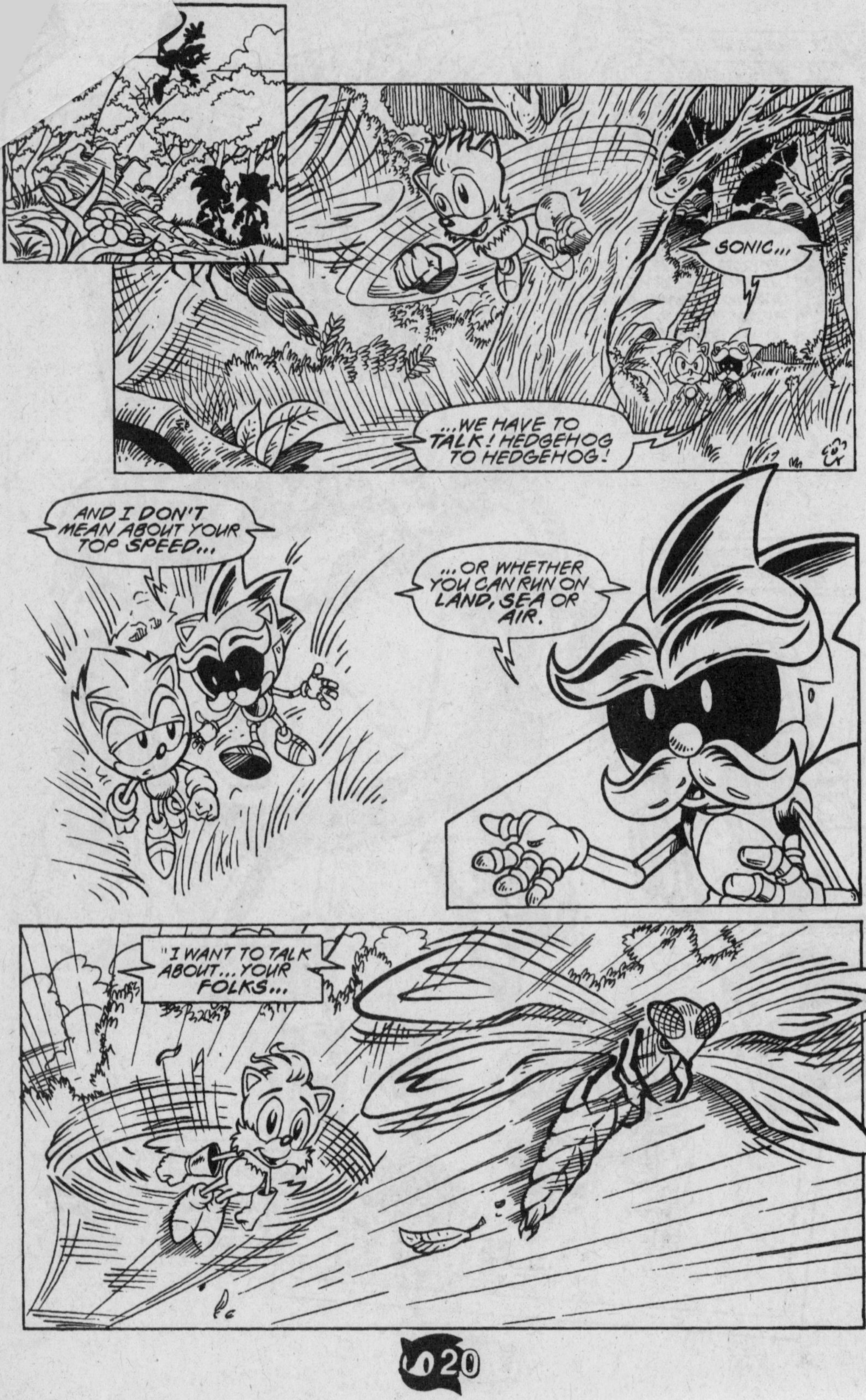
SONIC...
...WE HAVE TO TALK! HEDGEHOG TO HEDGEHOG!
AND I DON'T MEAN ABOUT YOUR TOP SPEED...
...OR WHETHER YOU CAN RUN ON LAND, SEA OR AIR.
"I WANT TO TALK ABOUT... YOUR FOLKS...
20

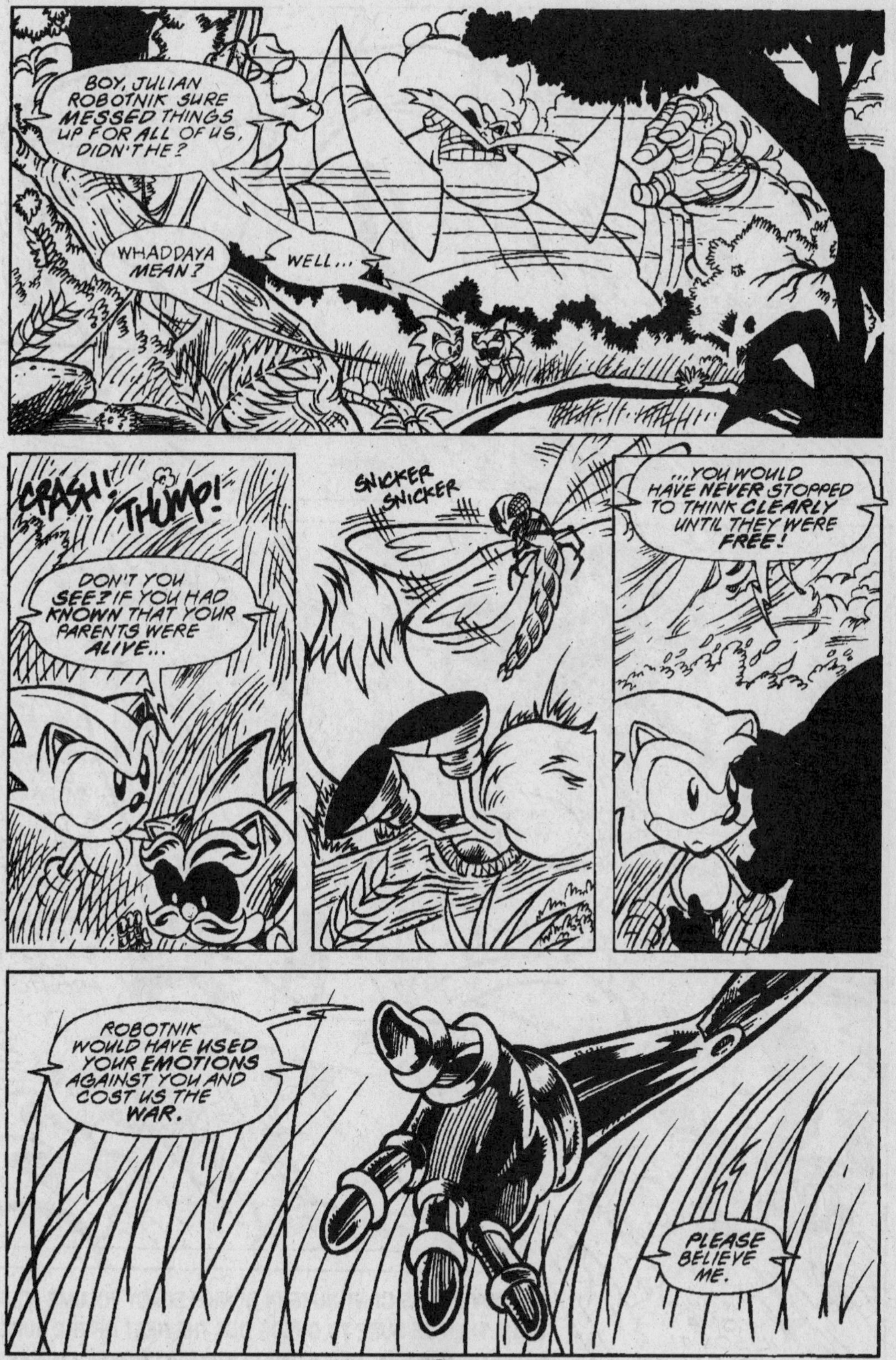
BOY, JULIAN ROBOTNIK SURE MESSED THINGS UP FOR ALL OF US, DIDN'T HE?
WHADDAYA MEAN?
WELL...
CRASH! THUMP!
DON'T YOU SEE? IF YOU HAD KNOWN THAT YOUR PARENTS WERE ALIVE...
SNICKER SNICKER
...YOU WOULD HAVE NEVER STOPPED TO THINK CLEARLY UNTIL THEY WERE FREE!
ROBOTNIK WOULD HAVE USED YOUR EMOTIONS AGAINST YOU AND COST US THE WAR.
PLEASE BELIEVE ME.

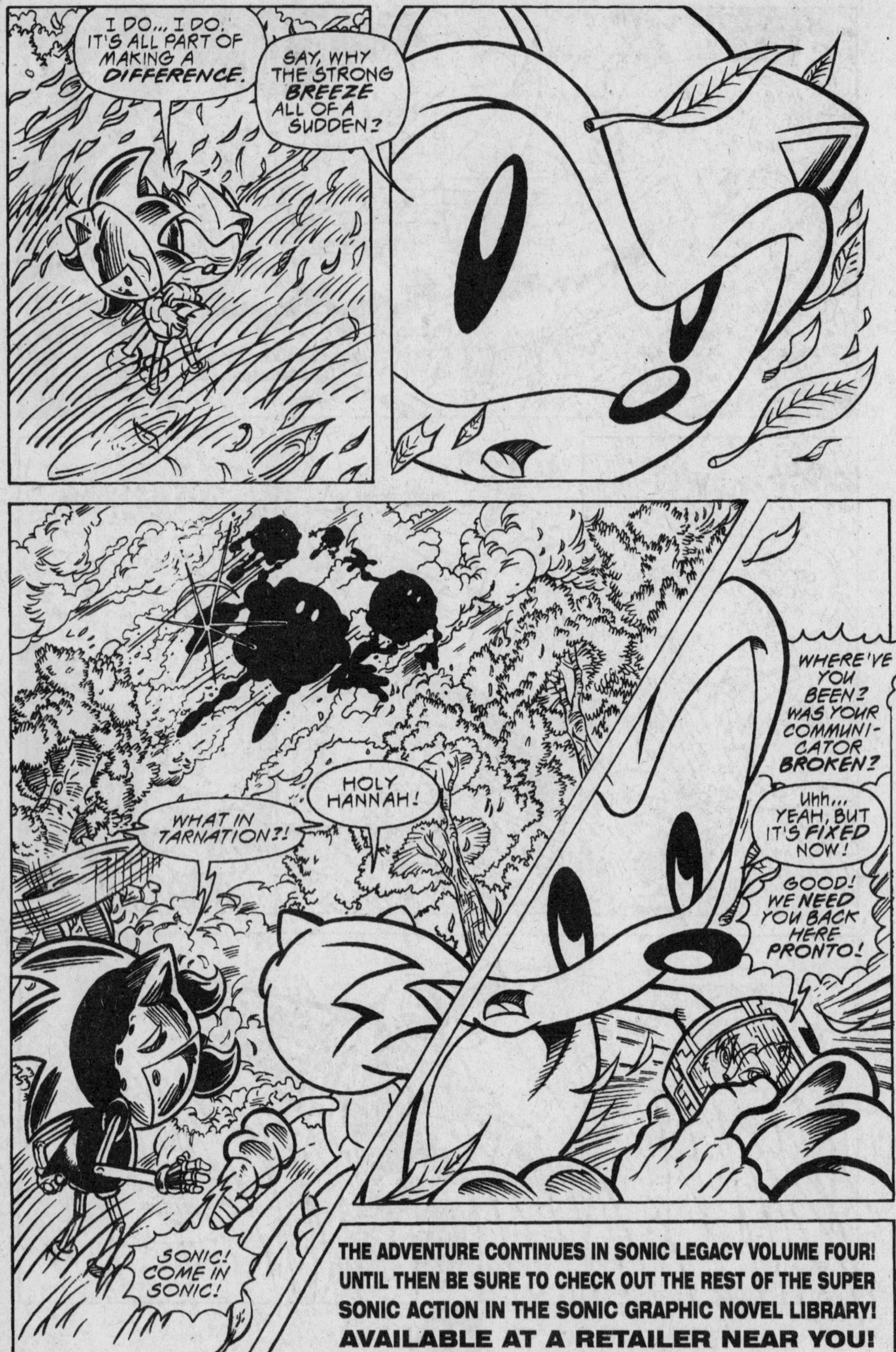
I DO... I DO. IT'S ALL PART OF MAKING A DIFFERENCE.
SAY, WHY THE STRONG BREEZE ALL OF A SUDDEN?
WHAT IN TARNATION?!
HOLY HANNAH!
SONIC! COME IN SONIC!
WHERE'VE YOU BEEN? WAS YOUR COMMUNI-CATOR BROKEN?
Uhh... YEAH, BUT IT'S FIXED NOW!
GOOD! WE NEED YOU BACK HERE PRONTO!
THE ADVENTURE CONTINUES IN SONIC LEGACY VOLUME FOUR! UNTIL THEN BE SURE TO CHECK OUT THE REST OF THE SUPER SONIC ACTION IN THE SONIC GRAPHIC NOVEL LIBRARY!
AVAILABLE AT A RETAILER NEAR YOU!

SPECIAL FEATURES

This section is filled with awesome extras and artwork from the production of the stories collected in this graphic novel!

SONIC ARCHIVES COVER GALLERY

COVERS BY PATRICK SPAZIANTE

COLLECTING SONIC THE HEDGEHOG #'S 37-54 IN FULL COLOR, AVAILABLE NOW!

SONIC
THE HEDGEHOG
ARCHIVES VOLUME 10

SONIC
THE HEDGEHOG
ARCHIVES VOLUME 11

SONIC
THE HEDGEHOG
ARCHIVES VOLUME 12

SONIC
THE HEDGEHOG
ARCHIVES VOLUME 13

SONIC
THE HEDGEHOG
ARCHIVES VOLUME 14

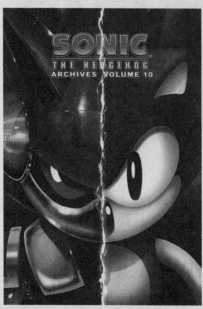

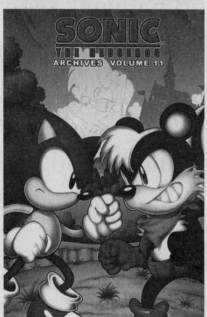

SONIC THE HEDGEHOG 47 FRONTIS

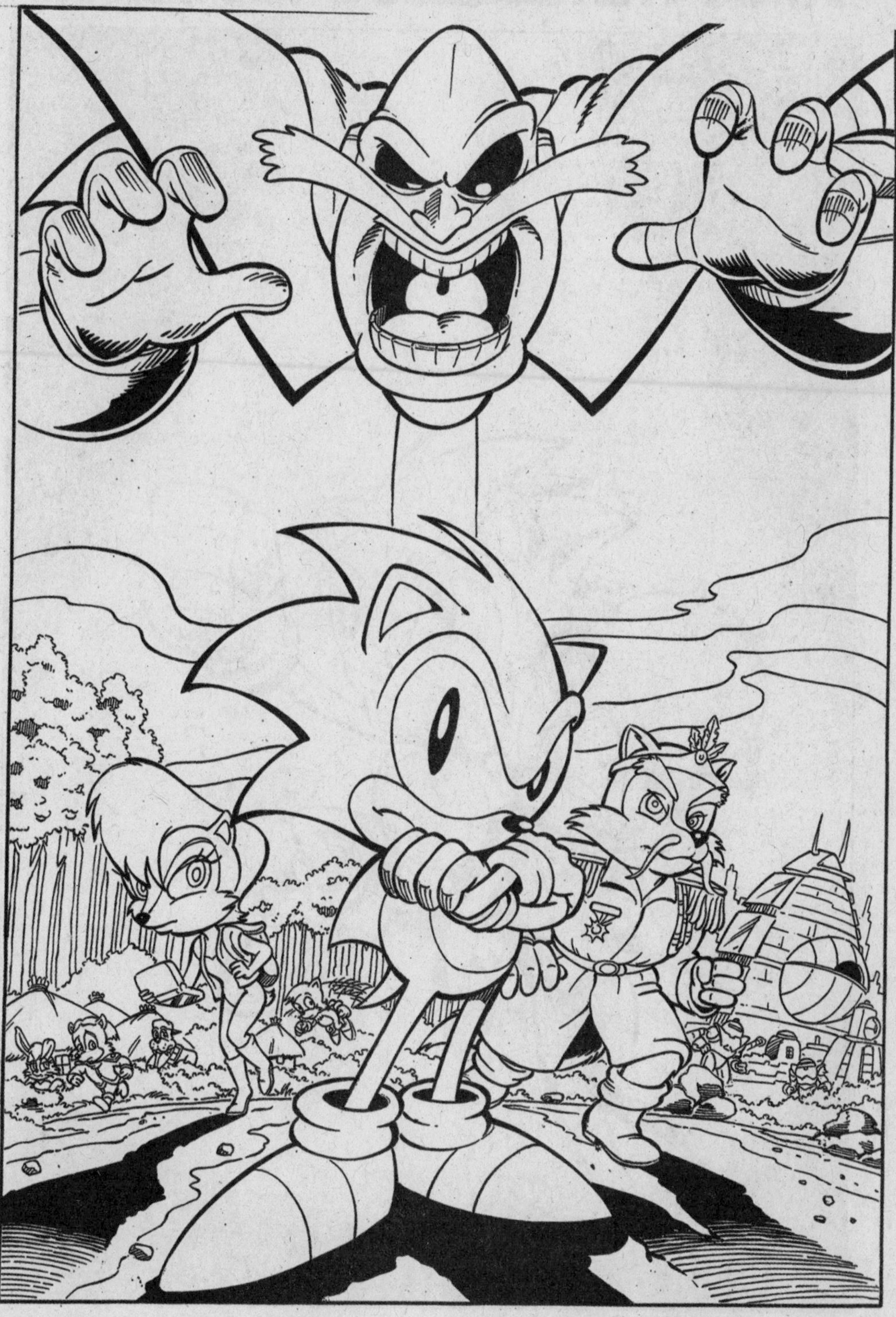

BY KEN PENDERS, ART MAWHINNEY, PAM EKLUND AND BARRY GROSSMAN

SONIC THE HEDGEHOG 48 FRONTIS

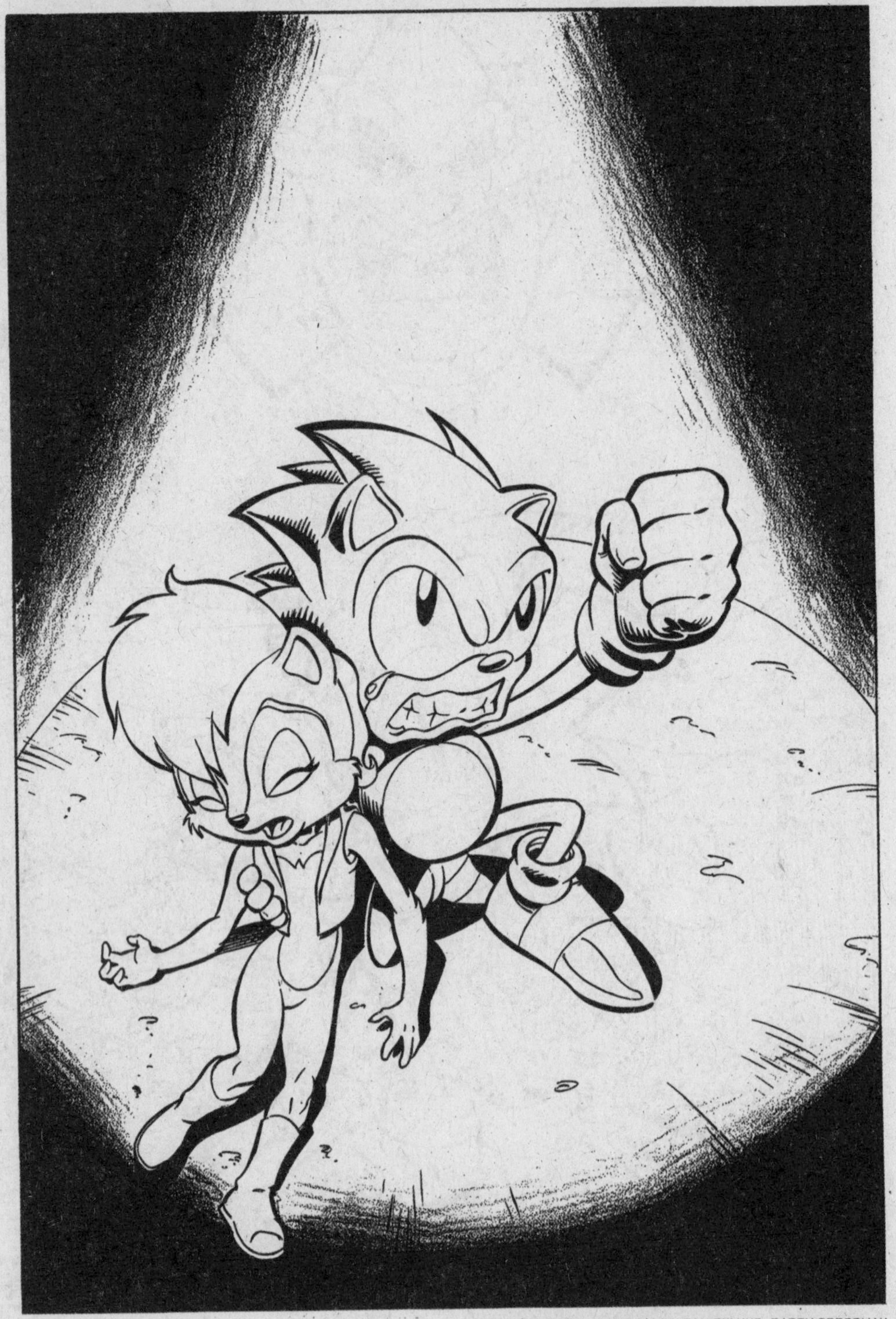

BY KEN PENDERS, MANNY GALAN, PAM EKLUND, BARRY GROSSMAN

SONIC THE HEDGEHOG 49 FRONTIS

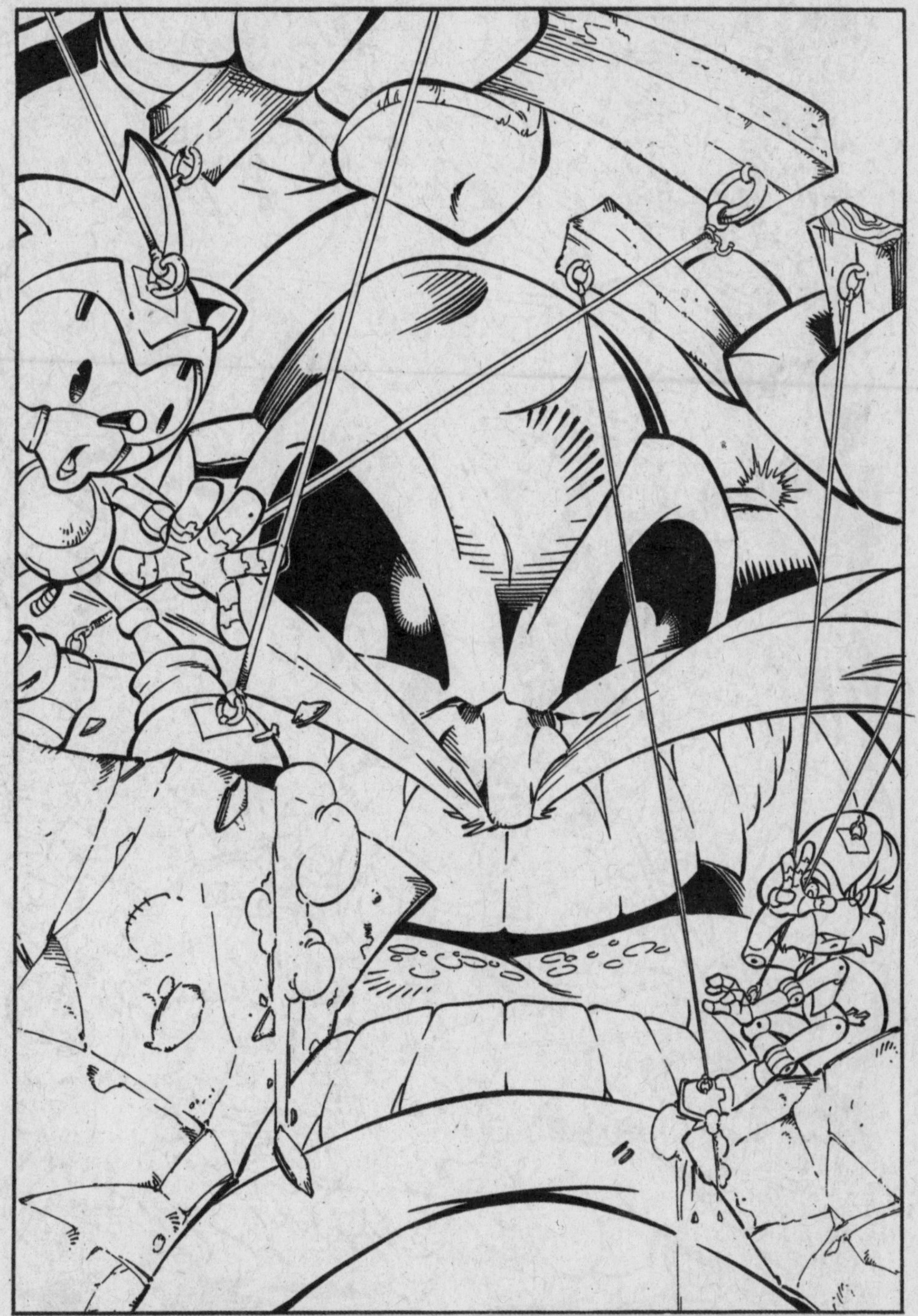

BY KEN PENDERS, MICHAEL GALLAGHER, SAM MAXWELL, PAM EKLUND AND KARL BOLLERS

SONIC THE HEDGEHOG 50 FRONTIS

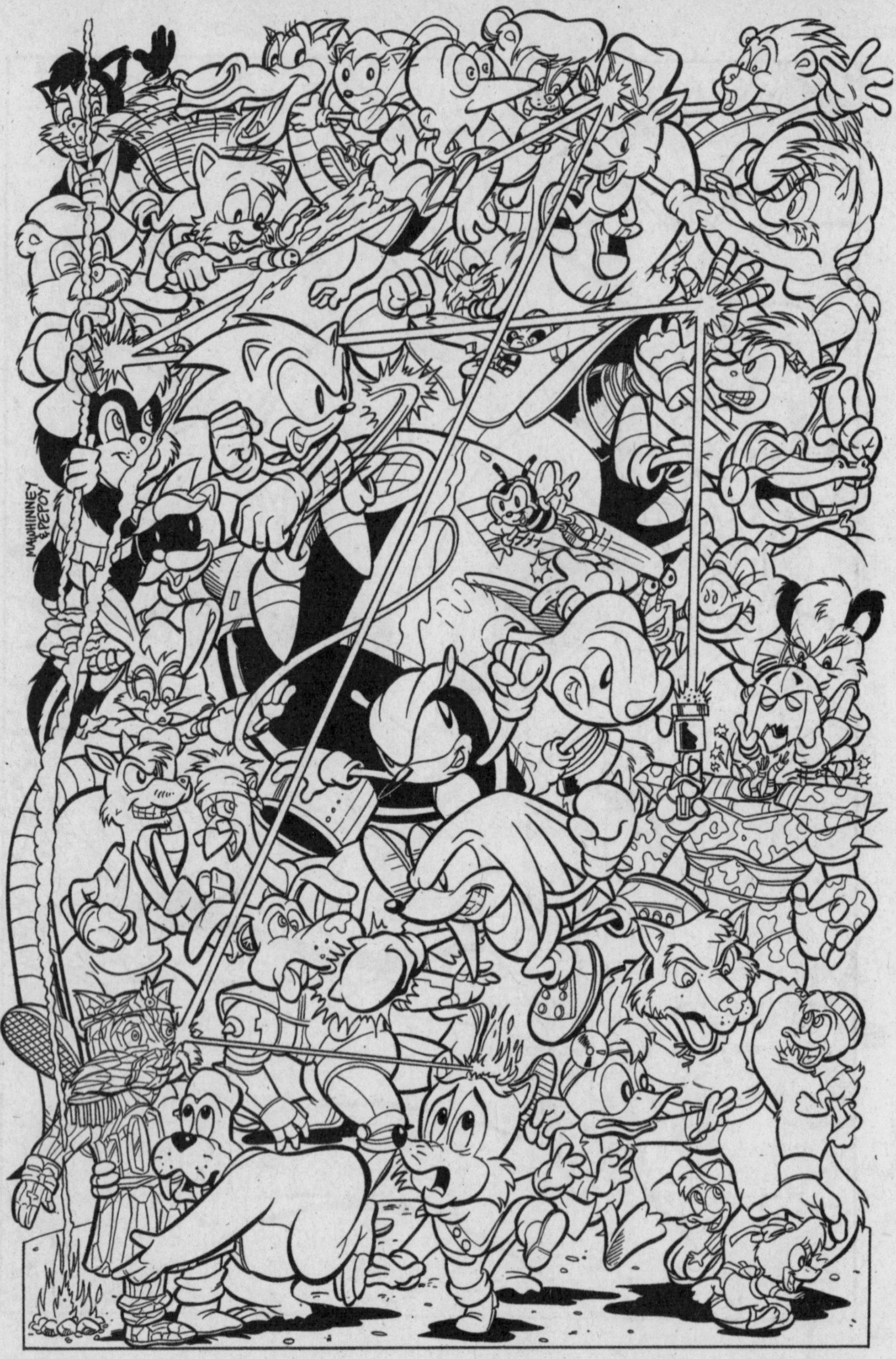
MAWHINNEY & PEPOY

BY KEN PENDERS, ART MAWHINNEY, ANDREW PEPOY AND KARL BOLLERS

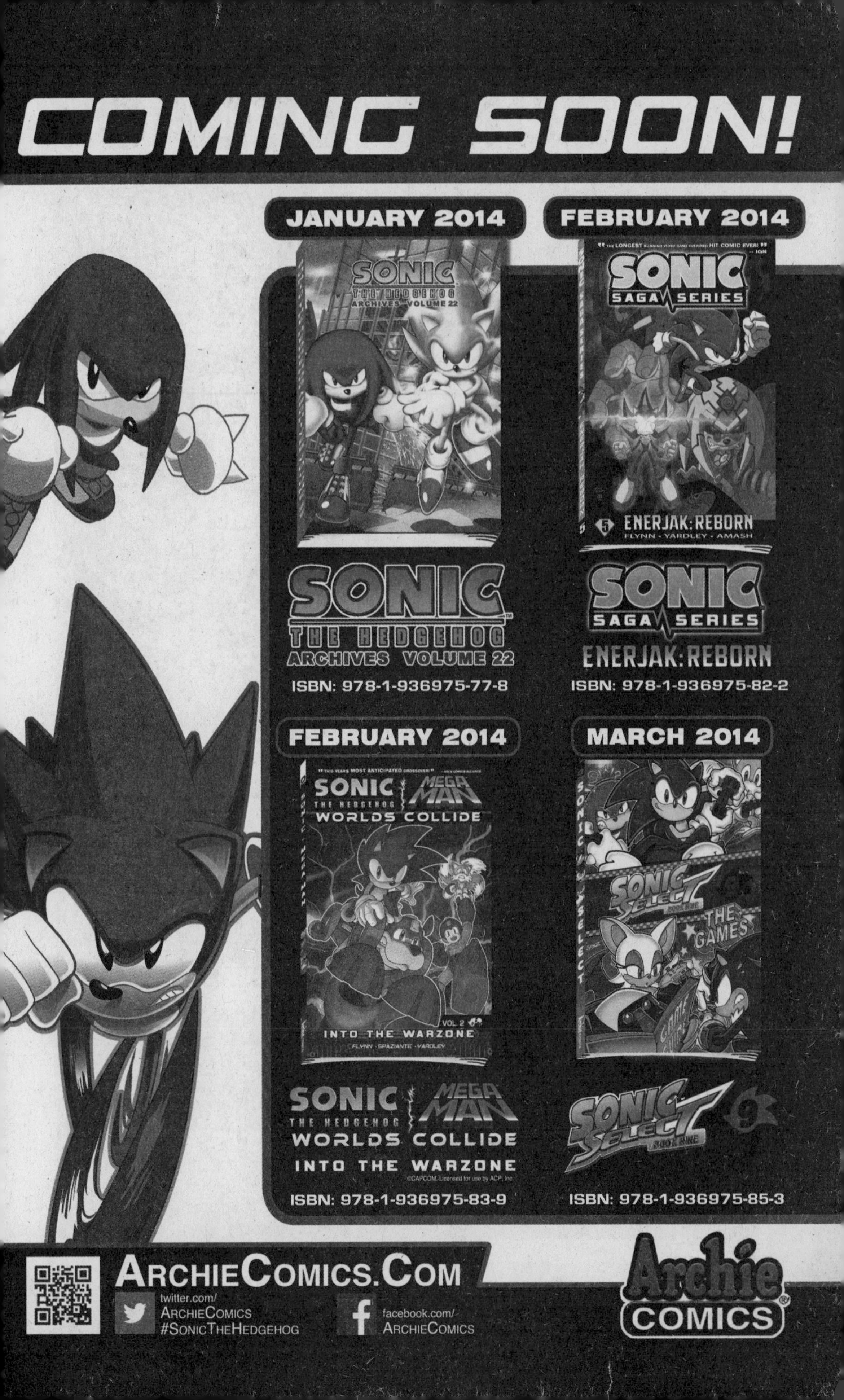

COMING SOON!
JANUARY 2014
SONIC THE HEDGEHOG ARCHIVES VOLUME 22
ISBN: 978-1-936975-77-8
FEBRUARY 2014
SONIC SAGA SERIES
ENERJAK: REBORN
FLYNN · YARDLEY · AMASH
ISBN: 978-1-936975-82-2
FEBRUARY 2014
SONIC THE HEDGEHOG MEGA MAN WORLDS COLLIDE
INTO THE WARZONE
VOL. 2
FLYNN · SPAZIANTE · YARDLEY
©CAPCOM. Licensed for use by ACP, Inc.
ISBN: 978-1-936975-83-9
MARCH 2014
SONIC SELECT BOOK NINE
THE GAMES
ISBN: 978-1-936975-85-3
ARCHIECOMICS.COM
twitter.com/ ARCHIECOMICS #SONICTHEHEDGEHOG
facebook.com/ ARCHIECOMICS
Archie COMICS

NEXT TIME IN
SONIC LEGACY

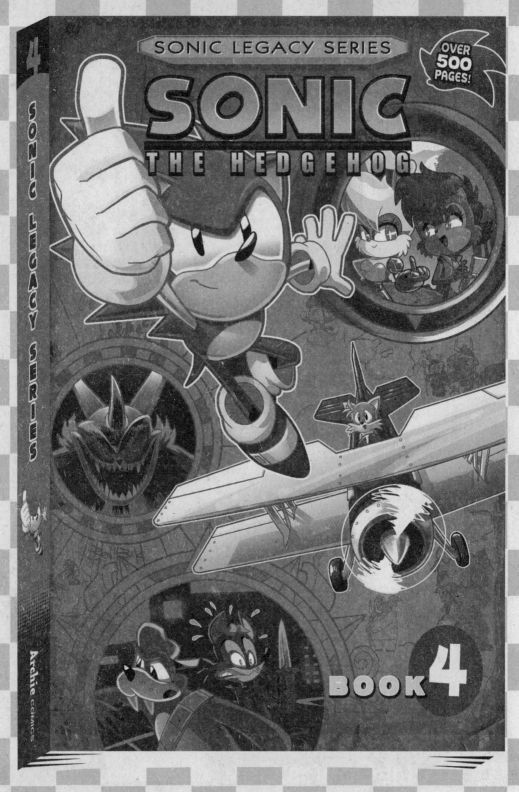

ON SALE DECEMBER 2014